STAR WARS BOOKS BY TIMOTHY ZAHN

THE LAST COMMAND

STAR WARS

THE
LAST COMMAND

TIMOTHY ZAHN

NEW YORK

2021 Del Rey Trade Paperback Edition

Copyright © 1993 by Lucasfilm Ltd. & ® or ™ where indicated.
All rights reserved.
Excerpt from *Star Wars: The High Republic: Light of the Jedi*
by Charles Soule copyright © 2021 by Lucasfilm Ltd. & ® or ™
where indicated. All rights reserved.

Published in the United States by Del Rey,
an imprint of Random House, a division of
Penguin Random House LLC, New York.

DEL REY is a registered trademark and the CIRCLE colophon is a trademark of
Penguin Random House LLC.

Originally published in paperback in the United States
by Bantam Spectra, an imprint of Random House, a division of
Penguin Random House, in 1993.

ISBN 978-0-593-49703-6
Ebook ISBN 978-0-307-79620-2

Printed in the United States of America on acid-free paper

randomhousebooks.com

6 8 9 7

Book design by Edwin Vazquez

For all those who helped make
these books possible, especially
Anna Zahn
Betsy Mitchell
Lucy Autrey Wilson
and, of course,
the man whose vision started it all,
George Lucas

THE ESSENTIAL
LEGENDS COLLECTION

For more than forty years, novels set in a galaxy far, far away have enriched the *Star Wars* experience for fans seeking to continue the adventure beyond the screen. When he created *Star Wars*, George Lucas built a universe that sparked the imagination and inspired others to create. He opened up that universe to be a creative space for other people to tell their own tales. This became known as the Expanded Universe, or EU, of novels, comics, videogames, and more.

To this day, the EU remains an inspiration for *Star Wars* creators and is published under the label Legends. Ideas, characters, story elements, and more from new *Star Wars* entertainment trace their origins back to material from the Expanded Universe. This Essential Legends Collection curates some of the most treasured stories from that expansive legacy.

THE LAST COMMAND

CHAPTER 1

GLIDING THROUGH THE BLACKNESS of deep space, the Imperial Star Destroyer *Chimaera* pointed its mighty arrowhead shape toward the dim star of its target system, three thousandths of a light-year away. And prepared itself for war.

"All systems show battle ready, Admiral," the comm officer reported from the portside crew pit. "The task force is beginning to check in."

"Very good, Lieutenant," Grand Admiral Thrawn nodded. "Inform me when all have done so. Captain Pellaeon?"

"Sir?" Pellaeon said, searching his superior's face for the stress the Grand Admiral must be feeling. The stress he himself was certainly feeling. This was not just another tactical strike against the Rebellion, after all—not a minor shipping raid or even a complex but straightforward hit-and-fade against some insignificant planetary base. After nearly a month of frenzied preparations, Thrawn's master campaign for the Empire's final victory was about to be launched.

But if the Grand Admiral was feeling any tension, he was keeping it to himself. "Begin the countdown," he told Pellaeon, his voice as calm as if he were ordering dinner.

"Yes, sir," Pellaeon said, turning back to the group of one-quarter-size holographic figures standing before him in the

Chimaera's aft bridge hologram pod. "Gentlemen: launch marks. *Bellicose:* three minutes."

"Acknowledged, *Chimaera*," Captain Aban nodded, his proper military demeanor not quite masking his eagerness to take this war back to the Rebellion. "Good hunting."

The holo image sputtered and vanished as the *Bellicose* raised its deflector shields, cutting off long-range communications. Pellaeon shifted his attention to the next image in line. "*Relentless:* four point five minutes."

"Acknowledged," Captain Dorja said, cupping his right fist in his left in an ancient Mirshaf gesture of victory as he, too, vanished from the hologram pod.

Pellaeon glanced at his data pad. "*Judicator:* six minutes."

"We're ready, *Chimaera*," Captain Brandei said, his voice soft. Soft, and just a little bit wrong. . . .

Pellaeon frowned at him. Quarter-sized holos didn't show a lot of detail, but even so the expression on Brandei's face was easy to read. It was the expression of a man out for blood.

"This is war, Captain Brandei," Thrawn said, coming up silently to Pellaeon's side. "Not an opportunity for personal revenge."

"I understand my duty, Admiral," Brandei said stiffly.

Thrawn's blue-black eyebrows lifted slightly. "Do you, Captain? Do you indeed?"

Slowly, reluctantly, some of the fire faded from Brandei's face. "Yes, sir," he muttered. "My duty is to the Empire, and to you, and to the ships and crews under my command."

"Very good," Thrawn said. "To the living, in other words. Not to the dead."

Brandei was still glowering, but he gave a dutiful nod. "Yes, sir."

"Never forget that, Captain," Thrawn warned him. "The fortunes of war rise and fall, and you may be assured that the Rebellion will be repaid in full for their destruction of the *Peremptory* at the *Katana* fleet skirmish. But that repayment will occur in the context of our overall strategy. Not as an act of private vengeance." His glowing red eyes narrowed slightly. "Certainly not by any Fleet captain under my command. I trust I make myself clear."

Brandei's cheek twitched. Pellaeon had never thought of the man as brilliant, but he was smart enough to recognize a threat when he heard one. "Very clear, Admiral."

"Good." Thrawn eyed him a moment longer, then nodded. "I believe you've been given your launch mark?"

"Yes, sir. *Judicator* out."

Thrawn looked at Pellaeon. "Continue, Captain," he said, and turned away.

"Yes, sir." Pellaeon looked at his data pad. "*Nemesis* . . ."

He finished the list without further incident. By the time the last holo image disappeared, the final check-in from their own task force was complete.

"The timetable appears to be running smoothly," Thrawn said as Pellaeon returned to his command station. "The *Stormhawk* reports that the guide freighters launched on time with tow cables functioning properly. And we've just intercepted a general emergency call from the Ando system."

The *Bellicose* and its task force, right on schedule. "Any response, sir?" Pellaeon asked.

"The Rebel base at Ord Pardron acknowledged," Thrawn said. "It should be interesting to see how much help they send."

Pellaeon nodded. The Rebels had seen enough of Thrawn's tactics by now to expect Ando to be a feint, and to respond accordingly. But on the other hand, an attack force consisting of an Imperial Star Destroyer and eight *Katana* fleet Dreadnaughts was hardly something they could afford to dismiss out of hand, either.

Not that it really mattered. They would send a few ships to Ando to fight the *Bellicose*, and a few more to Filve to fight the *Judicator*, and a few more to Crondre to fight the *Nemesis*, and so on and so on. By the time the *Death's Head* hit the base itself, Ord Pardron would be down to a skeleton defense and screaming itself for all the reinforcements the Rebellion could scramble.

And that was where those reinforcements would go. Leaving the Empire's true target ripe for the picking.

Pellaeon looked out the forward viewport at the star of the Ukio system dead ahead, his throat tightening as he contemplated again the enormous conceit of this whole plan. With planetary shields able to hold off all but the most massive turbolaser and proton torpedo bombardment, conventional wisdom held that the only way to subdue a modern world was to put a fast-moving ground force down at the edges and send them overland to destroy the shield generators. Between the fire laid down by the ground force and the subsequent orbital assault, the target world was always badly damaged by the time it was finally taken. The alternative, landing hundreds of thousands of troops in a major ground campaign that could stretch into months or years, was no better. To capture a planet relatively undamaged but with shield generators still intact was considered an impossibility.

That bit of military wisdom would fall today. Along with Ukio itself.

"Intercepted distress signal from Filve, Admiral," the comm officer reported. "Ord Pardron again responding."

"Good." Thrawn consulted his chrono. "Seven minutes, I think, and we'll be able to move." His lips compressed, just noticeably. "I suppose we'd better confirm that our exalted Jedi Master is ready to do his part."

Pellaeon hid a grimace. Joruus C'baoth, insane clone of the long-dead Jedi Master Jorus C'baoth, who a month ago had proclaimed himself the true heir to the Empire. He didn't like talking to the man any more than Thrawn did; but he might as well volunteer. If he didn't, it would simply become an order. "I'll go, sir," he said, standing up.

"Thank you, Captain," Thrawn said. As if Pellaeon would have had a choice.

He felt the mental summons the moment he stepped beyond the Force-protection of the ysalamiri scattered about the bridge on their nutrient frames. Master C'baoth, clearly, was impatient for the operation to begin. Preparing himself as best he could, fighting against C'baoth's casual mental pressure to hurry, Pellaeon made his way down to Thrawn's command room.

The chamber was brightly lit, in marked contrast to the subdued lighting the Grand Admiral usually preferred. "Captain Pellaeon," C'baoth called, beckoning to him from the double display ring in the center of the room. "Come in. I've been waiting for you."

"The rest of the operation has taken my full attention," Pellaeon told him stiffly, trying to hide his distaste for the man. Knowing full well how futile such attempts were.

"Of course," C'baoth smiled, a smile that showed more effectively than any words his amusement with Pellaeon's discomfort. "No matter. I take it Grand Admiral Thrawn is finally ready?"

"Almost," Pellaeon said. "We want to clear out Ord Pardron as much as possible before we move."

C'baoth snorted. "You continue to assume the New Republic will dance to the Grand Admiral's tune."

"They will," Pellaeon said. "The Grand Admiral has studied the enemy thoroughly."

"He's studied their artwork," C'baoth countered with another snort. "That will be useful if the time ever comes when the New Republic has nothing but artists left to throw against us."

A signal from the display ring saved Pellaeon from the need to reply. "We're moving," he told C'baoth, starting a mental countdown of the seventy-six seconds it would take to reach the Ukio system from their position and trying not to let C'baoth's words get under his skin. He didn't understand himself how Thrawn could so accurately learn the innermost secrets of a species from its artwork. But he'd seen that knowledge proved often enough to trust the Grand Admiral's instincts on such things. C'baoth hadn't.

But then, C'baoth wasn't really interested in an honest debate on the subject. For the past month, ever since declaring himself to be the true heir to the Emperor, C'baoth had been pressing this quiet war against Thrawn's credibility, implying that true insight came only through the Force. And, therefore, only through him.

Pellaeon himself didn't buy that argument. The Emperor had been deep into this Force thing, too, and he hadn't even been able to predict his own death at Endor. But the seeds of uncertainty C'baoth was trying to sow were nevertheless starting to take hold, particularly among the less experienced of Thrawn's officers.

Which was, for Pellaeon, just one more reason why this attack had to succeed. The outcome hinged as much on Thrawn's reading of the Ukian cultural ethos as it did on straight military tactics. On Thrawn's conviction that, at a basic psychological level, the Ukians were terrified of the impossible.

"He will not always be right," C'baoth said into Pellaeon's musings.

Pellaeon bit down hard on the inside of his cheek, the skin of his back crawling at having had his thoughts so casually invaded. "You don't have any concept of privacy, do you?" he growled.

"I am the Empire, Captain Pellaeon," C'baoth said, his eyes glowing with a dark, fanatical fire. "Your thoughts are a part of your service to me."

"My service is to Grand Admiral Thrawn," Pellaeon said stiffly.

C'baoth smiled. "You may believe that if you wish. But to business—true Imperial business. When the battle here is over, Captain Pellaeon, I want a message sent to Wayland."

"Announcing your imminent return, no doubt," Pellaeon said sourly. C'baoth had been insisting for nearly a month now that he would soon be going back to his former home on Wayland, where he would take command of the cloning facility in the Emperor's old storehouse inside Mount Tantiss. So far, he'd been too busy trying to subvert Thrawn's position to do anything more than talk about it.

"Do not worry, Captain Pellaeon," C'baoth said, all amused again. "When the time is right, I will indeed return to Wayland. Which is why you will contact Wayland after this battle is over and order them to create a clone for me. A very special clone."

Grand Admiral Thrawn will have to authorize that, were the words that came to mind. "What kind do you want?" were the ones that inexplicably came out. Pellaeon blinked, running the memory over in his mind again. Yes, that was what he'd said, all right.

C'baoth smiled again at his silent confusion. "I merely wish a servant," he said. "Someone who will be waiting there for me when I return. Formed from one of the Emperor's prize souvenirs—sample B-2332-54, I believe it was. You will, of course, impress upon the garrison commander there that this must be done in total secrecy."

I will do nothing of the sort. "Yes," Pellaeon heard himself say instead. The sound of the word shocked him; but certainly he didn't mean it. On the contrary, as soon as the battle was over he'd be reporting this little incident directly to Thrawn.

"You will also keep this conversation a private matter between ourselves," C'baoth said lazily. "Once you have obeyed, you will forget it even happened."

"Of course," Pellaeon nodded, just to shut him up. Yes, he'd report this to Thrawn, all right. The Grand Admiral would know what to do.

The countdown reached zero, and on the main wall display the planet Ukio appeared. "We should put up a tactical display, Master C'baoth," he said.

C'baoth waved a hand. "As you wish."

Pellaeon reached over the double display ring and touched the proper key, and in the center of the room the holographic tactical display appeared. The *Chimaera* was driving toward high orbit above the sunside equator; the ten *Katana* fleet Dreadnaughts of its task force were splitting up into outer and inner defense positions; and the *Stormhawk* was coming in as backstop from the night side. Other ships, mostly freighters and other commercial types, could be seen dropping through the brief gaps Ground Control was opening for them in Ukio's energy shield, a hazy blue shell surrounding the planet about fifty kilometers above the surface. Two of the blips flashed red: the guide freighters from the *Stormhawk*, looking as innocent as all the rest of the ships scurrying madly for cover. The freighters, and the four invisible companions they towed.

"Invisible only to those without eyes to see them," C'baoth murmured.

"So now you can see the ships themselves, can you?" Pellaeon growled. "How Jedi skills grow."

He'd been hoping to irritate C'baoth a little—not much, just a little. But it was a futile effort. "I can see the men inside your precious cloaking shields," the Jedi Master said placidly. "I can see their thoughts and guide their wills. What does the metal itself matter?"

Pellaeon felt his lip twist. "I suppose there's a lot that doesn't matter to you," he said.

From the corner of his eye he saw C'baoth smile. "What doesn't matter to a Jedi Master does not matter to the universe."

The freighters and cloaked cruisers were nearly to the shield now. "They'll be dropping the tow cables as soon as they're inside the shield," Pellaeon reminded C'baoth. "Are you ready?"

The Jedi Master straightened up in his seat and closed his eyes to slits. "I await the Grand Admiral's command," he said sardonically.

For another second Pellaeon looked at the other's composed expression, a shiver running up through him. He could remember vividly the first time C'baoth had tried this kind of direct long-distance control. Could remember the pain that had been on C'baoth's face; the pinched look of concentration and agony as he struggled to hold the mental contacts.

Barely two months ago, Thrawn had confidently said that C'baoth would never be a threat to the Empire because he lacked the ability to focus and concentrate his Jedi power on a long-term basis. Somehow, between that time and now, C'baoth had obviously succeeded in learning the necessary control.

Which left C'baoth as a threat to the Empire. A very dangerous threat indeed.

The intercom beeped. "Captain Pellaeon?"

Pellaeon reached over the display ring and touched the key, pushing away his fears about C'baoth as best he could. For the moment, at least, the Fleet needed C'baoth. Fortunately, perhaps, C'baoth also needed the Fleet. "We're ready, Admiral," he said.

"Stand by," Thrawn said. "Tow cables detaching now."

"They are free," C'baoth said. "They are under power . . . moving now to their appointed positions."

"Confirm that they're beneath the planetary shield," Thrawn ordered.

For the first time a hint of the old strain crossed C'baoth's face. Hardly surprising; with the cloaking shield preventing the *Chimaera* from seeing the cruisers and at the same time blinding the cruisers' own sensors, the only way to know exactly where they were was for C'baoth to do a precise location check on the minds he was touching. "All four ships are beneath the shield," he said.

"Be absolutely certain, Jedi Master. If you're wrong—"

"I am not wrong, Grand Admiral Thrawn," C'baoth cut him off harshly. "I will do my part in this battle. Concern yourself with yours."

For a moment the intercom was silent. Pellaeon winced, visualizing the Grand Admiral's expression. "Very well, Jedi Master," Thrawn said calmly. "Prepare to do your part."

There was the double click of an opening comm channel. "This is the Imperial Star Destroyer *Chimaera*, calling the Overliege of Ukio," Thrawn said. "In the name of the Empire, I declare the Ukian system to be once again under the mandate of Imperial law and the protection of Imperial forces. You will lower your shields, recall all military units to their bases, and prepare for an orderly transfer of command."

There was no response. "I know you're receiving this message," Thrawn continued. "If you fail to respond, I will have to assume that you mean to resist the Empire's offer. In that event, I would have no choice but to open hostilities."

Again, silence. "They're sending another transmission," Pellaeon heard the comm officer say. "Sounds a little more panicked than the first one was."

"I'm certain their third will be even more so," Thrawn told him. "Prepare for firing sequence one. Master C'baoth?"

"The cruisers are ready, Grand Admiral Thrawn," C'baoth said. "As am I."

"Be sure that you are," Thrawn said, quietly threatening. "Unless the timing is absolutely perfect, this entire show will be worse than useless. Turbolaser battery three: stand by firing sequence one on my mark. Three . . . two . . . one . . . fire."

On the tactical hologram a double lance of green fire angled out from the *Chimaera*'s turbolaser batteries toward the planet below. The blasts struck the hazy blue of the planetary shield, splashed slightly as their energy was defocused and reflected back into space—

And with the desired perfect timing the two cloaked cruisers hovering on repulsorlifts beneath the shield at those two points fired in turn, their turbolaser blasts sizzling through the atmosphere into two of Ukio's major air defense bases.

That was what Pellaeon saw. The Ukians, with no way of knowing about the cloaked cruisers, would have seen the *Chimaera* fire two devastating shots cleanly through an impenetrable planetary shield.

"Third transmission cut off right in the middle, sir," the

comm officer reported with a touch of dark humor. "I think we surprised them."

"Let's convince them it wasn't a fluke," Thrawn said. "Prepare firing sequence two. Master C'baoth?"

"The cruisers are ready."

"Turbolaser battery two: stand by firing sequence two on my mark. Three . . . two . . . one . . . fire."

Again the green fire lanced out, and again, with perfect timing, the cloaked cruisers created their illusion. "Well done," Thrawn said. "Master C'baoth, move the cruisers into position for sequences three and four."

"As you command, Grand Admiral Thrawn."

Unconsciously, Pellaeon braced himself. Sequence four had two of the Ukians' thirty overlapping shield generators as its targets. Launching such an attack would mean that Thrawn had given up on his stated goal of taking Ukio with its planetary defenses intact.

"Imperial Star Destroyer *Chimaera*, this is Tol dosLla of the Ukian Overliege," a slightly quavering voice came from the intercom speaker. "We would ask you to cease your bombardment of Ukio while we discuss terms for surrender."

"My terms are quite simple," Thrawn said. "You will begin by lowering your planetary shield and allowing my forces to land. They will be given control of the shield generators themselves and of all ground-to-space weaponry. All fighting vehicles larger than command speeders will be moved to designated military bases and turned over to Imperial control. Though you will, of course, be ultimately answerable to the Empire, your political and social systems will remain under your control. Provided your people behave themselves, of course."

"And once these changes have been implemented?"

"Then you will be part of the Empire, with all the rights and duties that implies."

"There will be no war-level tax levies?" dosLla asked suspiciously. "No forced conscription of our young people?"

Pellaeon could imagine Thrawn's grim smile. No, the Empire would never need to bother with forced conscription again. Not with the Emperor's collection of Spaarti cloning cylinders in their hands.

"No, to your second question; a qualified no to your first," Thrawn told the Ukian. "As you are obviously aware, most Imperial worlds are currently under war-status taxation levels. However, there are exceptions, and it is likely that your share of the war effort will come directly from your extensive food production and processing facilities."

There was a long pause from the other end. DosLla was no fool, Pellaeon realized—the Ukian knew full well what Thrawn had in mind for his world. First it would be direct Imperial control of the ground/space defenses, then direct control of the food distribution system, the processing facilities, and the vast farming and livestock grazing regions themselves; and in a very short time the entire planet would have become nothing more than a supply depot for the Imperial war machine.

But the alternative was for him to stand silently by and watch as his world was utterly and impossibly demolished before his eyes. And he knew that, too.

"We will lower the planetary shields, *Chimaera*, as a gesture of good faith," dosLla said at last, his tone defiant but with a hint of defeat to it. "But before the generators and ground/space weaponry can be turned over to Imperial forces we shall require certain guarantees regarding the safety of the Ukian people and our land."

"Certainly," Thrawn said, without any trace of the gloating that most Imperial commanders would have indulged in at this point. A small act of courtesy that, Pellaeon knew, was as precisely calculated as the rest of the attack had been. Permitting the Ukian leaders to surrender with their dignity intact would slow down the inevitable resistance to Imperial rule until it was too late. "A representative will be on his way shortly to discuss the particulars with your government," Thrawn continued. "Meanwhile, I presume you have no objection to our forces taking up preliminary defense positions?"

A sigh, more felt than really heard. "We have no objections, *Chimaera*," dosLla said reluctantly. "We are lowering the shield now."

On the tactical display, the blue haze surrounding the planet faded away. "Master C'baoth, have the cruisers move to polar positions," Thrawn ordered. "We don't want any of the drop ships blundering into them. General Covell, you may begin transporting your forces to the surface. Standard defensive positions around all targets."

"Acknowledged, Admiral," Covell's voice said, a little too dryly, and Pellaeon felt a tight smile twitch at his lip. It had only been two weeks since the top Fleet and army commanders had been let in on the secret of the Mount Tantiss cloning project, and Covell was one of those who still hadn't adjusted completely to the idea.

Though the fact that three of the companies he was about to lead down to the surface were composed entirely of clones might have had something to do with his skepticism.

On the tactical hologram the first waves of drop ships and TIE fighter escorts had exited the *Chimaera* and *Stormhawk*, fanning out toward their assigned targets. Clones in drop ships, about to carry out Imperial orders. As the clone crews in the cloaked cruisers had already done so well.

Pellaeon frowned, an odd and uncomfortable thought suddenly striking him. Had C'baoth been able to guide the cruisers so well because each of their thousand-man crews were composed of variants on just twenty or so different minds? Or—even more disturbing—could part of the Jedi Master's split-second control have been due to the fact that C'baoth was himself a clone?

And either way, did that mean that the Mount Tantiss project was playing directly into C'baoth's hands in his bid for power? Perhaps. One more question he would have to bring to Thrawn's attention.

Pellaeon looked down at C'baoth, belatedly remembering that in the Jedi Master's presence such thoughts were not his private property. But C'baoth wasn't looking at him, knowingly or otherwise. He was staring straight ahead, his eyes unfocused, the skin of his face taut. A faint smile just beginning to crease his lips. "Master C'baoth?"

"They're there," C'baoth whispered, his voice deep and husky. "They're there," he repeated, louder this time.

Pellaeon frowned back at the tactical hologram. "Who's where?" he asked.

"They're at Filve," C'baoth said. Abruptly, he looked up at Pellaeon, his eyes bright and insane. "My Jedi are at Filve."

"Master C'baoth, confirm that the cruisers have moved to polar positions," Thrawn's voice came sharply. "Then report on the feint battles—"

"My Jedi are at Filve," C'baoth cut him off. "What do I care about your battles?"

"C'baoth—"

With a wave of his hand, C'baoth shut off the intercom. "Now, Leia Organa Solo," he murmured softly, "you are mine."

THE MILLENNIUM FALCON twisted hard to starboard as a TIE fighter shot past overhead, lasers blazing away madly as it tried unsuccessfully to track the freighter's maneuver. Clenching her teeth firmly against the movement, Leia Organa Solo watched as one of their escort X-wings blew the Imperial starfighter into a cloud of flaming dust. The sky spun around the Falcon's canopy as the ship rolled back toward its original heading—

"Look out!" Threepio wailed from the seat behind Leia as another TIE fighter roared in toward them from the side. The warning was unnecessary; with deceptive ungainliness the Falcon was already corkscrewing back the other direction to bring its ventral quad laser battery to bear. Faintly audible even through the cockpit door, Leia heard the sound of a Wookiee battle roar, and the TIE fighter went the way of its late partner.

"Good shot, Chewie," Han Solo called into the intercom as he got the *Falcon* leveled again. "Wedge?"

"Still with you, *Falcon*," Wedge Antilles' voice came promptly. "We're clear for now, but there's another wave of TIE fighters on the way."

"Yeah." Han glanced at Leia. "It's your call, sweetheart. You still want to try to reach ground?"

Threepio gave a little electronic gasp. "Surely, Captain Solo, you aren't suggesting—"

"Put a choke valve on it, Goldenrod," Han cut him off. "Leia?"

Leia looked out the cockpit canopy at the Imperial Star Destroyer and eight Dreadnaughts arrayed against the beleaguered planet ahead. Clustering around it like mynocks around an unshielded power generator. It was to have been her last diplomatic mission before settling in to await the birth of her twins: a quick trip to calm a nervous Filvian government and demonstrate the New Republic's determination to protect the systems in this sector.

Some demonstration.

"There's no way we can make it through all that," she told Han reluctantly. "Even if we could, I doubt the Filvians would risk opening the shield to let us in. We'd better make a run for it."

"Sounds good to me," Han grunted. "Wedge? We're pulling out. Stay with us."

"Copy, *Falcon*" Wedge said. "You'll have to give us a few minutes to calculate the jump back."

"Don't bother," Han said, swiveling around in his seat to key in the nav computer. "We'll feed you the numbers from here."

"Copy. Rogue Squadron: screen formation."

"You know, I'm starting to get tired of this," Han told Leia, swiveling back to face front. "I thought you said your Noghri pals were going to leave you alone."

"This has nothing to do with the Noghri." Leia shook her

head, an odd half-felt tension stretching at her forehead. Was it her imagination, or were the Imperial ships surrounding Filve starting to break formation? "This is Grand Admiral Thrawn playing with his new Dark Force Dreadnaughts."

"Yeah," Han agreed quietly, and Leia winced at the momentary flash of bitterness in his sense. Despite everyone's best efforts to persuade him otherwise, Han still considered it his own personal fault that Thrawn had gotten to the derelict *Katana* fleet ships—the so-called Dark Force—ahead of the New Republic. "I wouldn't have thought he could get them reconditioned this fast," Han added as he twisted the *Falcon*'s nose away from Filve and back toward deep space.

Leia swallowed. The strange tension was still there, like a distant malevolence pressing against the edges of her mind. "Maybe he has enough Spaarti cylinders to clone some engineers and techs as well as soldiers."

"That's sure a fun thought," Han said; and through her tension Leia could sense his sudden change in mood as he tapped the comm switch. "Wedge, take a look back at Filve and tell me if I'm seeing things."

Over the comm, Leia could hear Wedge's thoughtful intake of air. "You mean like the whole Imperial force breaking off their attack and coming after us?"

"Yeah. That."

"Looks real enough to me," Wedge said. "Could be a good time to get out of here."

"Yeah," Han said slowly. "Maybe."

Leia frowned at her husband. There'd been something in his voice. . . . "Han?"

"The Filvians would've called for help before they put up their shield, right?" Han asked her, forehead furrowed with thought.

"Right," Leia agreed cautiously.

"And the nearest New Republic base is Ord Pardron, right?"

"Right."

"Okay. Rogue Squadron, we're changing course to starboard. Stay with me."

He keyed his board, and the Falcon started a sharp curve to the right. "Watch it, *Falcon*—this is taking us back toward that TIE fighter group," Wedge warned.

"We're not going that far," Han assured him. "Here's our vector."

He straightened out the ship onto their new course heading and threw a look at the rear display. "Good—they're still chasing us."

Behind him, the nav computer beeped its notification that the jump coordinates were ready. "Wedge, we've got your coordinates," Leia said, reaching for the data transmission key.

"Hold it, *Falcon*," Wedge cut her off. "We've got company to starboard."

Leia looked that direction, her throat tightening as she saw what Wedge meant. The approaching TIE fighters were coming up fast, and already were close enough to eavesdrop on any transmission the *Falcon* tried to make to its escort. Sending Wedge the jump coordinates now would be an open invitation for the Imperials to have a reception committee waiting at the other end.

"Perhaps I can be of assistance, Your Highness," Threepio offered brightly. "As you know, I am fluent in over six million forms of communication. I could transmit the coordinates to Commander Antilles in Boordist or Vaathkree trade language, for example—"

"And then you'd send them the translation?" Han put in dryly.

"Of course—" The droid broke off. "Oh, dear," he said, sounding embarrassed.

"Yeah, well, don't worry about it," Han said. "Wedge, you were at Xyquine two years ago, weren't you?"

"Yes. Ah. A Cracken Twist?"

"Right. On two: one, two."

Outside the canopy, Leia caught a glimpse of the X-wings swinging into a complicated new escort formation around the *Falcon*. "What does this buy us?" she asked.

"Our way out," Han told her, checking the rear display again. "Pull the coordinates, add a two to the second number of each one, and then send the whole package to the X-wings."

"I see," Leia nodded her understanding as she got to work. Altering the second digit wouldn't change the appearance of their exit vector enough for the Imperials to catch on to the trick, but it would be more than enough to put any chase force a couple of light-years off target. "Clever. And that little flight maneuver they did just now was just window dressing?"

"Right. Makes anyone watching think that's all there is to it. A little something Pash Cracken came up with at that fiasco off Xyquine." Han glanced at the rear display again. "I think we've got enough lead to outrun them," he said. "Let's try."

"We're not jumping to lightspeed?" Leia frowned, an old and rather painful memory floating up from the back of her mind. That mad scramble away from Hoth, with Darth Vader's whole fleet breathing down their necks and a hyperdrive that turned out to be broken . . .

Han threw her a sideways look. "Don't worry, sweetheart. The hyperdrive's working fine today."

"Let's hope so," Leia murmured.

"See, as long as they're chasing us they can't bother Filve," Han went on. "And the further we draw them away, the longer the backup force'll have to get here from Ord Pardron."

The brilliant green flash of a near miss cut off Leia's intended response. "I think we've given them all the time we can," she told Han. Within her, she could sense the turmoil coming from her unborn twins. "Can we please get out of here?"

A second bolt spattered off the *Falcon*'s upper deflector shield. "Yeah, I think you're right," Han agreed. "Wedge? You ready to leave this party?"

"Whenever you are, *Falcon*," Wedge said. "Go ahead—we'll follow when you're clear."

"Right." Reaching over, Han gripped the hyperdrive levers and pulled them gently back. Through the cockpit canopy the stars stretched themselves into starlines, and they were safe.

Leia took a deep breath, let it out slowly. Within her, she could still sense the twins' anxiety, and for a moment she turned her mind to the job of calming them down. It was a strange sensation, she'd often thought, touching minds that dealt in emotion and pure sensation instead of pictures and words. So different from the minds of Han and Luke and her other friends.

So different, too, from the distant mind that had been orchestrating that Imperial attack force.

Behind her, the door slid open and Chewbacca came into the cockpit. "Good shooting, Chewie," Han told the Wookiee as he heaved his massive bulk into the portside passenger seat beside Threepio. "You have any more trouble with the horizontal control arm?"

Chewbacca rumbled a negative. His dark eyes studying Leia's face, he growled her a question. "I'm all right," Leia assured him, blinking back sudden and inexplicable tears. "Really."

She looked at Han, to find him frowning at her, too.

"You weren't worried, were you?" he asked. "It was just an Imperial task force. Nothing to get excited about."

She shook her head. "It wasn't that, Han. There was something else back there. A kind of . . ." She shook her head again. "I don't know."

"Perhaps it was similar to your indisposition at Endor," Threepio offered helpfully. "You remember—when you collapsed while Chewbacca and I were repairing the—?"

Chewbacca rumbled a warning, and the droid abruptly shut up. But far too late. "No—let him talk," Han said, his sense going all protectively suspicious as he looked at Leia. "What indisposition was this?"

"There wasn't anything to it, Han," Leia assured him, reaching over to take his hand. "On our first orbit around Endor we passed through the spot where the Death Star blew up. For a few seconds I could feel something like the Emperor's presence around me. That's all."

"Oh, that's all," Han said sarcastically, throwing a brief glare back at Chewbacca. "A dead Emperor tries to make a grab for you, and you don't think it's worth mentioning?"

"Now you're being silly," Leia chided. "There was nothing to worry about—it was over quickly, and there weren't any aftereffects. Really. Anyway, what I felt back at Filve was completely different."

"Glad to hear it," Han said, not yet ready to let it go. "Did you have any of the med people check you over or anything after you got back?"

"Well, there really wasn't any time before—"

"Fine. You do it as soon as we're back."

Leia nodded with a quiet sigh. She knew that tone; and it wasn't something she could wholeheartedly argue against, anyway. "All right. If I can find time."

"You'll *make* time," Han countered. "Or I'll have Luke lock you in the med center when he gets back. I mean it, sweetheart."

Leia squeezed his hand, feeling a similar squeeze on her heart as she did so. Luke, off alone in Imperial territory . . . but he was all right. He had to be. "All right," she told Han. "I'll get checked out. I promise."

"Good," he said, his eyes searching her face. "So what was it you felt back at Filve?"

"I don't know." She hesitated. "Maybe it was the same thing Luke felt on the *Katana*. You know—when the Imperials put that landing party of clones aboard."

"Yeah," Han agreed doubtfully. "Maybe. Those Dreadnaughts were awfully far away."

"There were probably a lot more clones, though, too."

"Yeah. Maybe," Han said again. "Well . . . I suppose Chewie

and me'd better get to work on that ion flux stabilizer before it quits on us completely. Can you handle things up here okay, sweetheart?"

"I'm fine," Leia assured him, just as glad to be leaving this line of conversation. "You two go ahead."

Because the other possibility was one she'd just as soon not think about right now. The Emperor, it had long been rumored, had had the ability to use the Force to exercise direct control over his military forces. If the Jedi Master Luke had confronted on Jomark had that same ability . . .

Reaching down, she caressed her belly and focused on the pair of tiny minds within her. No, it was indeed not something she wanted to think about.

"I PRESUME," THRAWN said in that deadly calm voice of his, "that you have some sort of explanation."

Slowly, deliberately, C'baoth lifted his head from the command room's double display circle to look at the Grand Admiral. At the Grand Admiral and, with undisguised contempt, at the ysalamir on its nutrient frame slung across Thrawn's shoulders. "Do you likewise have an explanation, Grand Admiral Thrawn?" he demanded.

"You broke off the diversionary attack on Filve," Thrawn said, ignoring C'baoth's question. "You then proceeded to send the entire task force on a dead-end chase."

"And you, Grand Admiral Thrawn, have failed to bring my Jedi to me," C'baoth countered. His voice, Pellaeon noticed uneasily, was slowly rising in both pitch and volume. "You, your tame Noghri, your entire Empire—all of you have failed."

Thrawn's glowing red eyes narrowed. "Indeed? And was it also our failure that you were unable to hold on to Luke Skywalker after we delivered him to you on Jomark?"

"You did not deliver him to me, Grand Admiral Thrawn," C'baoth insisted. "I summoned him there through the Force—"

"It was Imperial Intelligence who planted the rumor that

Jorus C'baoth had returned and been seen on Jomark," Thrawn cut him off coldly. "It was Imperial Transport who brought you there, Imperial Supply who arranged and provisioned that house for you, and Imperial Engineering who built the camouflaged island landing site for your use. The Empire did its part to get Skywalker into your hands. It was you who failed to keep him there."

"No!" C'baoth snapped. "Skywalker left Jomark because Mara Jade escaped from you and twisted his mind against me. And she will pay for that. You hear me? She shall pay."

For a long moment Thrawn was silent. "You threw the entire Filve task force against the *Millennium Falcon*," he said at last, his voice under control again. "Did you succeed in capturing Leia Organa Solo?"

"No," C'baoth growled. "But not because she didn't want to come to me. She does. Just as Skywalker does."

Thrawn threw a glance at Pellaeon. "She wants to come to you?" he asked.

C'baoth smiled. "Very much," he said, his voice unexpectedly losing all its anger. Becoming almost dreamy . . . "She wants me to teach her children," he continued, his eyes drifting around the command room. "To instruct them in the ways of the Jedi. To create them in my own image. Because I am the master. The only one there is."

He looked back at Thrawn. "You must bring her to me, Grand Admiral Thrawn," he said, his manner somewhere halfway between solemn and pleading, "We must free her from her entrapment among those who fear her powers. They'll destroy her if we don't."

"Of course we must," Thrawn said soothingly. "But you must leave that task to me. All I need is a little more time."

C'baoth frowned with thought, his hand slipping up beneath his beard to finger the medallion hanging on its neck chain, and Pellaeon felt a shiver run up his back. No matter how many times he saw it happen, he would never get used to these sudden dips into the slippery twilight of clone madness.

It had, he knew, been a universal problem with the early cloning experiments: a permanent mental and emotional instability, inversely scaled to the length of the duplicate's growth cycle. Few of the scientific papers on the subject had survived the Clone Wars era, but Pellaeon had come across one that had suggested that no clone grown to maturity in less than a year would be stable enough to survive outside of a totally controlled environment.

Given the destruction they'd unleashed on the galaxy, Pellaeon had always assumed that the clonemasters had eventually found at least a partial solution to the problem. Whether they had recognized the underlying cause of the madness was another question entirely.

It could very well be that Thrawn was the first to truly understand it.

"Very well, Grand Admiral Thrawn," C'baoth said abruptly. "You may have one final chance. But I warn you: it will be your last. After that, I will take the matter into my own hands." Beneath the bushy eyebrows his eyes flashed. "And I warn you further: if you cannot accomplish even so small a task, perhaps I will deem you unworthy to lead the military forces of my Empire."

Thrawn's eyes glittered, but he merely inclined his head slightly. "I accept your challenge, Master C'baoth."

"Good." Deliberately, C'baoth resettled himself into his seat and closed his eyes. "You may leave me now, Grand Admiral Thrawn. I wish to meditate, and to plan for the future of my Jedi."

For a moment Thrawn stood silently, his glowing red eyes gazing unblinkingly at C'baoth. Then he shifted his gaze to Pellaeon. "You'll accompany me to the bridge, Captain," he said. "I want you to oversee the defense arrangements for the Ukio system."

"Yes, sir," Pellaeon said, glad of any excuse to get away from C'baoth.

For a moment he paused, feeling a frown cross his face as he

looked down at C'baoth. Had there been something he had
wanted to bring to Thrawn's attention? He was almost certain
there was. Something having to do with C'baoth, and clones,
and the Mount Tantiss project . . .

But the thought wouldn't come, and with a mental shrug,
he pushed the question aside. It would surely come to him in
time.

Stepping around the display ring, he followed his commander from the room.

CHAPTER 2

I T WAS CALLED the Calius saj Leeloo, the City of Glowing Crystal of Berchest, and it had been one of the most spectacular wonders of the galaxy since the earliest days of the Old Republic. The entire city was nothing more or less than a single gigantic crystal, created over the eons by saltile spray from the dark red-orange waters of the Leefari Sea that roiled up against the low bluff upon which it rested. The original city had been painstakingly sculpted from the crystal over decades by local Berchestian artisans, whose descendants continued to guide and nurture its slow growth.

At the height of the Old Republic Calius had been a major tourist attraction, its populace making a comfortable living from the millions of beings who flocked to the stunning beauty of the city and its surroundings. But the chaos of the Clone Wars and the subsequent rise of the Empire had taken a severe toll on such idle amusements, and Calius had been forced to turn to other means for its support.

Fortunately, the tourist trade had left a legacy of well-established trade routes between Berchest and most of the galaxy's major systems. The obvious solution was for the Berchestians to promote Calius as a trade center; and while the city was hardly to the level yet of Svivren or Ketaris, they had achieved a modest degree of success.

The only problem was that it was a trade center on the Imperial side of the line.

A squad of stormtroopers strode down the crowded street, their white armor taking on a colored tinge from the angular red-orange buildings around them. Taking a long step out of their way, Luke Skywalker pulled his hood a bit closer around his face. He could sense no particular alertness from the squad, but this deep into Imperial space there was no reason to take chances. The stormtroopers strode past without so much as a glance in his direction, and with a quiet sigh of relief Luke returned his attention to his contemplation of the city. Between the stormtroopers, the Imperial fleet crewers on layover between flights, and the smugglers poking around hoping to pick up jobs, the darkly businesslike sense of the city was in strange and pointed contrast to its serene beauty.

And somewhere in all that serene beauty was something far more dangerous than mere Imperial stormtroopers.

A group of clones.

Or so New Republic Intelligence thought. Painstakingly sifting through thousands of intercepted Imperial communiqués, they'd tentatively pinpointed Calius and the Berchest system as one of the transfer points in the new flood of human duplicates beginning to man the ships and troop carriers of Grand Admiral Thrawn's war machine.

That flood had to be stopped, and quickly. Which meant finding the location of the cloning tanks and destroying them. Which first meant backtracking the traffic pattern from a known transfer point. Which first meant confirming that clones were indeed coming through Calius.

A group of men dressed in the dulbands and robes of Svivreni traders came around a corner two blocks ahead, and as he had so many times in the past two days, Luke reached out toward them with the Force. One quick check was all it took: the traders did not have the strange aura he'd detected in the boarding party of clones that had attacked them aboard the *Katana*.

But even as he withdrew his consciousness, something else caught Luke's attention. Something he had almost missed amid the torrent of human and alien thoughts and sensations that swirled together around him like bits of colored glass in a sandstorm. A coolly calculating mind, one which Luke felt certain he'd encountered before but couldn't quite identify through the haze of mental noise between them.

And the owner of that mind was, in turn, fully aware of Luke's presence in Calius. And was watching him.

Luke grimaced. Alone in enemy territory, with his transport two kilometers away at the Calius landing field and his only weapon a lightsaber that would identify him the minute he drew it from his tunic, he was not exactly holding the high ground here.

But he had the Force . . . and he knew his follower was there. All in all, it gave him fair odds.

A couple of meters to his left was the entrance to the long arched tunnel of a pedestrian bridgeway. Turning down it, Luke stepped up his pace, trying to remember from his study of the city maps exactly where this particular bridge went. Across the city's icy river, he decided, and up toward the taller and higher-class regions overlooking the sea itself. Behind him, he sensed his pursuer follow him into the bridgeway; and as Luke put distance between himself and the mental din of the crowded market regions behind him, he was finally able to identify the man.

It was not as bad as he'd feared. But potentially at least, it was bad enough. With a sigh, Luke stopped and waited. The bridgeway, with its gentle curve hiding both ends from view, was as good a place as any for a confrontation.

His pursuer came to the last part of the curve. Then, as if anticipating that his quarry would be waiting there, he stopped just out of sight. Luke extended his senses, caught the sound of a blaster being drawn—"It's all right," he called softly. "We're alone. Come on out."

There was a brief hesitation, and Luke caught the momentary flicker of surprise; and then, Talon Karrde stepped into sight.

"I see the universe hasn't run out of ways to surprise me," the smuggler commented, inclining his head to Luke in an abbreviated bow as he slid his blaster back into its holster. "From the way you were acting I thought you were probably a spy from the New Republic. But I have to admit you're the last person I would have expected them to send."

Luke eyed him, trying hard to read the sense of the man. The last time he'd seen Karrde, just after the battle for the *Katana*, the other had emphasized that he and his smuggling group intended to remain neutral in this war. "And what were you going to do after you knew for sure?"

"I hadn't planned on turning you in, if that's what you mean," Karrde said, throwing a glance behind him down the bridgeway. "If it's all the same to you, I'd like to move on. Berchestians don't normally hold extended conversations in bridgeways. And the tunnel can carry voices a surprising distance."

And if there were an ambush waiting for them at the other end of the bridgeway? But if there were, Luke would know before they reached it. "Fine with me," he said, stepping to the side and gesturing Karrde forward.

The other favored him with a sardonic smile. "You don't trust me, do you?" he said, brushing past Luke and heading down the bridgeway.

"Must be Han's influence," Luke said apologetically, falling into step beside him. "His, or yours. Or maybe Mara's."

He caught the shift in Karrde's sense: a quick flash of concern that was as quickly buried again. "Speaking of Mara, how is she?"

"Nearly recovered," Luke assured him. "The medics tell me that repairing that kind of light neural damage isn't difficult, just time-consuming."

Karrde nodded, his eyes on the tunnel ahead. "I appreciate

you taking care of her," he said, almost grudgingly. "Our own medical facilities wouldn't have been up to the task."

Luke waved the thanks away. "It was the least we could do after the help you gave us at the *Katana*."

"Perhaps."

They reached the end of the bridgeway and stepped out into a street considerably less crowded than the one they'd left. Above and ahead of them, the three intricately carved government headquarter towers that faced the sea could be seen above the nearby buildings. Reaching out with the Force, Luke did a quick reading of the people passing by. Nothing. "You heading anywhere in particular?" he asked Karrde.

The other shook his head. "Wandering the city," he said casually. "You?"

"The same," Luke said, trying to match the other's tone.

"And hoping to see a familiar face or two? Or three, or four, or five?"

So Karrde knew, or had guessed, why he was here. Somehow, that didn't really surprise him. "If they're here to be seen, I'll find them," he said. "I don't suppose you have any information I could use?"

"I might," Karrde said. "Do you have enough money to pay for it?"

"Knowing your prices, probably not," Luke said. "But I could set you up a credit line when I get back."

"*If* you get back," Karrde countered. "Considering how many Imperial troops there are between you and safe territory, you're not what I would call a good investment risk at the moment."

Luke cocked an eyebrow at him. "As opposed to a smuggler at the top of the Empire's locate-and-detain list?" he asked pointedly.

Karrde smiled. "As it happens, Calius is one of the few places in Imperial space where I'm perfectly safe. The Berchestian governor and I have known each other for several years.

More to the point, there are certain items important to him which only I can supply."

"Military items?"

"I'm not part of your war, Skywalker," Karrde reminded him coolly. "I'm neutral, and I intend to stay that way. I thought I'd made that clear to you and your sister when we last parted company."

"Oh, it was clear enough," Luke agreed. "I just thought that events of the past month might have changed your mind."

Karrde's expression didn't change, but Luke could detect the almost unwilling shift in his sense. "I don't particularly like the idea of Grand Admiral Thrawn having access to a cloning facility," he conceded. "It has the long-term potential for shifting the balance of power in his favor, and that's something neither of us wants to see happen. But I think your side is rather overreacting to the situation."

"I don't know how you can call it overreacting," Luke said. "The Empire has most of the two hundred Dreadnaughts of the *Katana* fleet, and now they've got an unlimited supply of clones to crew them with."

"'Unlimited' is hardly the word I would use," Karrde said. "Clones can only be grown so quickly if you want them mentally stable enough to trust with your warships. One year minimum per clone, as I recall the old rule of thumb."

A group of five Vaathkree passed by in front of them along a cross street. So far the Empire had been only cloning humans, but Luke checked them out anyway. Again, nothing. "A year per clone, you say?"

"At the absolute minimum," Karrde said. "The pre–Clone Wars documents I've seen suggest three to five years would be a more appropriate period. Quicker than the standard human growth cycle, certainly, but hardly any reason for panic."

Luke looked up at the carved towers, their sunlit red-orange in sharp contrast to the billowing white clouds rolling in from the sea behind them. "What would you say if I told you the clones who attacked us on the *Katana* were grown in less than a year?"

Karrde shrugged. "That depends on how much less."

"The full cycle was fifteen to twenty days."

Karrde stopped short. "What?" he demanded, turning to stare at Luke.

"Fifteen to twenty days," Luke repeated, stopping beside him.

For a long moment Karrde locked eyes with him. Then, slowly, he turned away and began walking again. "That's impossible," he said. "There must be an error."

"I can get you a copy of the studies."

Karrde nodded thoughtfully, his eyes focused on nothing in particular. "At least that explains Ukio."

"Ukio?" Luke frowned.

Karrde glanced at him. "That's right—you've probably been out of touch for a while. Two days ago the Imperials launched a multiple attack on targets in the Abrion and Dufilvian sectors. They severely damaged the military base at Ord Pardron and captured the Ukio system."

Luke felt a hollow sensation in his stomach. Ukio was one of the top five producers of foodstuffs in the entire New Republic. The repercussions for Abrion sector alone—"How badly was Ukio damaged?"

"Apparently not at all," Karrde said. "My sources tell me it was taken with its shields and ground/space weaponry intact."

The hollow feeling got a little bigger. "I thought that was impossible to do."

"A knack for doing the impossible was one of the things Grand Admirals were selected for," Karrde said dryly. "Details of the attack are still sketchy; it'll be interesting to see how he pulled it off."

So Thrawn had the *Katana* Dreadnaughts; and he had clones to man them with; and now he had the ability to provide food for those clones. "This isn't just the setup to another series of raids," Luke said slowly. "The Empire's getting ready to launch a major offensive."

"It does begin to look that way," Karrde agreed. "Offhand, I'd say you have your work cut out for you."

Luke studied him. Karrde's voice and face were as calm as ever, but the sense behind them wasn't nearly so certain anymore. "And none of this changes your mind?" he prompted the other.

"I'm not joining the New Republic, Skywalker," Karrde said, shaking his head. "For many reasons. Not the least being that I don't entirely trust certain elements in your government."

"I think Fey'lya's been pretty well discredited—"

"I wasn't referring only to Fey'lya," Karrde cut him off. "You know as well as I do how fond the Mon Calamari have always been of smugglers. Now that Admiral Ackbar's been reinstated to his Council and Supreme Commander positions, all of us in the trade are going to have to start watching over our shoulders again."

"Oh, come on," Luke snorted. "You don't think Ackbar's going to have time to worry about smugglers, do you?"

Karrde smiled wryly. "Not really. But I'm not willing to risk my life on it, either."

Stalemate. "All right, then," Luke said. "Let's put it on a strictly business level. We need to know the Empire's movements and intentions, which is something you probably keep track of anyway. Can we buy that information from you?"

Karrde considered. "That might be possible," he said cautiously. "But only if I have the final say on what I pass on to you. I won't have you turning my group into an unofficial arm of New Republic Intelligence."

"Agreed," Luke said. It was less than he might have hoped for, but it was better than nothing. "I'll set up a credit line for you as soon as I get back."

"Perhaps we should start with a straight information

trade," Karrde said, looking around at the crystalline buildings. "Tell me what started your people looking at Calius."

"I'll do better than that," Luke said. The distant touch on his mind was faint but unmistakable. "How about if I confirm the clones are here?"

"Where?" Karrde asked sharply.

"Somewhere that way," Luke said, pointing ahead and slightly to the right. "Half a kilometer away, maybe—it's hard to tell."

"Inside one of the Towers," Karrde decided. "Nice and secure and well hidden from prying eyes. I wonder if there's any way to get inside for a look."

"Wait a minute—they're moving," Luke said, frowning as he tried to hang on to the contact. "Heading . . . almost toward us, but not quite."

"Probably being taken to the landing field," Karrde said. He glanced around, pointed to their right. "They'll probably use Mavrille Street—two blocks that direction."

Balancing speed with the need to remain inconspicuous, they covered the distance in three minutes. "They'll probably use a cargo carrier or light transport," Karrde said as they found a spot where they could watch the street without being run over by the pedestrian traffic along the edges of the vehicle way. "Anything obviously military would attract attention."

Luke nodded. Mavrille, he remembered from the maps, was one of the handful of streets in Calius that had been carved large enough for vehicles to use, with the result that the traffic was running pretty much fore to aft. "I wish I had some macrobinoculars with me," he commented.

"Trust me—you're conspicuous enough as it is," Karrde countered as he craned his neck over the passing crowds. "Any sign of them?"

"They're definitely coming this way," Luke told him. He reached out with the Force, trying to sort out the clone sense

from the sandstorm of other thoughts and minds surrounding
him. "I'd guess twenty to thirty of them."

"A cargo carrier, then," Karrde decided. "There's one coming now—just behind that Trast speeder truck."

"I see it." Luke took a deep breath, calling on every bit of
his Jedi skill. "That's them," he murmured, a shiver running
up his back.

"All right," Karrde said, his voice grim. "Watch closely; they
might have left one or more of the ventilation panels open."

The cargo carrier made its way toward them on its repulsorlifts, coming abruptly to a halt a short block away as the
driver of the speeder truck in front of it suddenly woke up to
the fact that he'd reached his turn. Gingerly, the truck eased
around the corner, blocking the whole traffic flow behind it.

"Wait here," Karrde said, and dived into the stream of pedestrians heading that direction. Luke kept his eyes sweeping
the area, alert for any sense that he or Karrde had been seen
and recognized. If this whole setup was some kind of elaborate trap for offworld spies, now would be the obvious time to
spring it.

The truck finally finished its turn, and the cargo carrier
lumbered on. It passed Luke and continued down the street,
disappearing within a few seconds around one of the red-
orange buildings. Stepping back into the side street behind
him, Luke waited; and a minute later Karrde had returned.
"Two of the vents were open, but I couldn't see enough to be
sure," he told Luke, breathing heavily. "You?"

Luke shook his head. "I couldn't see anything, either. But it
was them. I'm sure of it."

For a moment Karrde studied his face. Then, he gave a curt
nod. "All right. What now?"

"I'm going to see if I can get my ship offplanet ahead of
them," Luke said. "If I can track their hyperspace vector,
maybe we can figure out where they go from here." He lifted
his eyebrows. "Though two ships working together could do a
better track."

Karrde smiled slightly. "You'll forgive me if I decline the offer," he said. "Flying in tandem with a New Republic agent is not exactly what I would call maintaining neutrality." He glanced over Luke's shoulder at the street behind him. "At any rate, I think I'd prefer to try backtracking them from here. See if I can identify their point of origin."

"Sounds good," Luke nodded. "I'd better get over to the landing field and get my ship prepped."

"I'll be in touch," Karrde promised. "Make sure that credit line is a generous one."

STANDING AT THE UPPERMOST window of Central Government Tower Number One, Governor Staffa lowered his macrobinoculars with a satisfied snort. "That was him, all right, Fingal," he said to the little man hovering at his side. "No doubt about it. Luke Skywalker himself."

"Do you suppose he saw the special transport?" Fingal asked, fingering his own macrobinoculars nervously.

"Well, of course he saw it," Staffa growled. "You think he was hanging around Mavrille Street for his health?"

"I only thought—"

"Don't think, Fingal," Staffa cut him off. "You aren't properly equipped for it."

He sauntered to his desk, dropped the macrobinoculars into a drawer, and pulled up Grand Admiral Thrawn's directive on his data pad. It was a rather bizarre directive, in his private and strictly confidential opinion, more peculiar even than these mysterious troop transfers the Imperial High Command had been running through Calius of late. But one had no choice under the circumstances but to assume Thrawn knew what he was doing.

At any rate, it was on his own head—not Staffa's—if he didn't, and that was the important thing. "I want you to send a message to the Imperial Star Destroyer *Chimaera*," he told Fingal, lowering his bulk carefully into his chair and pushing the data pad across the desk. "Coded as per the instructions here. Inform Grand Admiral Thrawn that Skywalker has been on Calius and that I have personally observed him near the special transport. Also as per the Grand Admiral's directive, he has been allowed to leave Berchest unhindered."

"Yes, Governor," Fingal said, making notes on his own data pad. If the little man saw anything unusual about letting a Rebel spy walk freely through Imperial territory, he wasn't showing it. "What about the other man, Governor? The one who was with Skywalker down there?"

Staffa pursed his lips. The price on Talon Karrde's head was up to nearly fifty thousand now—a great deal of money, even for a man with a planetary governor's salary and perks. He had always known that someday it would be in his best interests to terminate the quiet business relationship he had with Karrde. Perhaps that time had finally come.

No. No, not while war still raged through the galaxy. Later, perhaps, when victory was near and private supply lines could be made more reliable. But not now. "The other man is of no importance," he told Fingal. "A special agent I sent to help smoke the Rebel spy into the open. Forget him. Go on—get that message coded and sent."

"Yes, sir," Fingal nodded, stepping toward the door.

The panel slid open . . . and for just a second, as Fingal stepped through, Staffa thought he saw an odd glint in the little man's eye. Some strange trick of the outer office light, of course. Next to his unbending loyalty for his governor, Fingal's most prominent and endearing attribute was his equally unbending lack of imagination.

Taking a deep breath, putting Fingal and Rebel spies and even Grand Admirals out of his mind, Staffa leaned back in his chair and began to consider how he would use the shipment that Karrde's people were even now unloading at the landing field.

CHAPTER 3

Slowly, as if climbing a long dark staircase, Mara Jade pulled herself out of a deep sleep. She opened her eyes, looked around the softly lit room, and wondered where in the galaxy she was.

It was a medical area—that much was obvious from the biomonitors, the folded room dividers, and the other multiposition beds scattered around the one she was lying in. But it wasn't one of Karrde's facilities, at least not one she was familiar with.

But the layout itself was all too familiar. It was a standard Imperial recovery room.

For the moment she seemed to be alone, but she knew that wouldn't last. Silently, she rolled out of bed into a crouching position on the floor, taking a quick inventory of her physical condition as she did so. No aches or pains; no dizziness or obvious injuries. Slipping into the robe and bedshoes at the end of the bed, she padded silently to the door, preparing herself mentally to silence or disable whatever was out there. She waved at the door release, and as the panel slid open she leaped through into the recovery anteroom—

And came to a sudden, slightly disoriented halt.

"Oh, hi, Mara," Ghent said distractedly, glancing up from

the computer terminal he was hunched over before returning his attention to it. "How're you feeling?"

"Not too bad," Mara said, staring at the kid and sifting furiously through a set of hazy memories. Ghent—one of Karrde's employees and possibly the best slicer in the galaxy. And the fact that he was sitting at a terminal meant they weren't prisoners, unless their captor was so abysmally stupid that he didn't know better than to let a slicer get within spitting distance of a computer.

But hadn't she sent Ghent to the New Republic headquarters on Coruscant? Yes, she had. On Karrde's instructions, just before collecting some of his group together and leading them into that melee at the *Katana* fleet.

Where she'd run her Z-95 up against an Imperial Star Destroyer . . . and had had to eject . . . and had brilliantly arranged to fly her ejector seat straight through an ion cannon beam. Which had fried her survival equipment and set her drifting, lost forever, in interstellar space.

She looked around her. Apparently, forever hadn't lasted as long as she'd expected it to. "Where are we?" she asked, though she had a pretty good idea now what the answer would be.

She was right. "The old Imperial Palace on Coruscant," Ghent told her, frowning a little. "Medical wing. They had to do some reconstruction of your neural pathways. Don't you remember?"

"It's a little vague," Mara admitted. But as the last cobwebs cleared from her brain, the rest of it was beginning to fall into place. Her ejector seat's ruined life-support system; and a strange, light-headed vagueness as she drifted off to sleep in the darkness. She'd probably suffered oxygen deprivation before they'd been able to locate her and get her to a ship.

No. Not *they: him*. There was only one person who could possibly have found a single crippled ejector seat in all the emptiness and battle debris out there. Luke Skywalker, the last of the Jedi Knights.

The man she was going to kill.

YOU WILL KILL LUKE SKYWALKER.

She took a step back to lean against the doorjamb, knees suddenly feeling weak as the Emperor's words echoed through her mind. She'd been here, on this world and in this building, when he'd died over Endor. Had watched through his mind as Luke Skywalker cut him down and brought her life crashing in ruins around her head.

"I see you're awake," a new voice said.

Mara opened her eyes. The newcomer, a middle-aged woman in a duty medic's tunic, was marching briskly across the room toward her from a far door, an Emdee droid trailing in her wake. "How are you feeling?"

"I'm fine," Mara said, feeling a sudden urge to lash out at the other woman. These people—these enemies of the Empire—had no right to be here in the Emperor's palace. . . .

She took a careful breath, fighting back the flash of emotion. The medic had stopped short, a professional frown on her face; Ghent, his cherished computers momentarily forgotten, had a puzzled look on his. "Sorry," she muttered. "I guess I'm still a little disoriented."

"Understandable," the medic nodded. "You've been lying in that bed for a month, after all."

Mara stared at her. "A *month?*"

"Well, most of a month," the medic corrected herself. "You also spent some time in a bacta tank. Don't worry—short-term memory problems are common during neural reconstructions, but they nearly always clear up after the treatment."

"I understand," Mara said mechanically. A month. She'd lost a whole month here. And in that time—

"We have a guest suite arranged for you upstairs whenever you feel ready to leave here," the medic continued. "Would you like me to see if it's ready?"

Mara focused on her. "That would be fine," she said.

The medic pulled out a comlink and thumbed it on; and as she began talking, Mara stepped past her to Ghent's side.

"What's been happening with the war during the last month?" she asked him.

"Oh, the Empire's been making the usual trouble," Ghent said, waving toward the sky. "They've got the folks here pretty stirred up, anyway. Ackbar and Madine and the rest have been running around like crazy. Trying to push em back or cut 'em off—something like that."

And that was, Mara knew, about all she would get out of him on the subject of current events. Aside from a fascination with smuggler folklore, the only thing that really mattered to Ghent was slicing at computers.

She frowned, belatedly remembering why Karrde had ordered Ghent here in the first place. "Wait a minute," she said. "Ackbar's back in command? You mean you've cleared him already?"

"Sure," Ghent said. "That suspicious bank deposit thing Councilor Fey'lya made such a fuss over was a complete fraud—the guys who did that electronic break-in at the bank planted it in his account at the same time. Probably Imperial Intelligence—it had their noseprints all over the programming. Oh, sure; I proved that two days after I got here."

"I imagine they were pleased. So why are you still here?"

"Well . . ." For a moment Ghent seemed taken aback. "No one's come back to get me, for one thing." His face brightened. "Besides, there's this really neat encrypt code someone nearby is using to send information to the Empire. General Bel Iblis says the Imperials call it Delta Source, and that it's sending them stuff right out of the Palace."

"And he asked you to slice it for them," Mara nodded, feeling her lip twist. "I don't suppose he offered to pay you or anything?"

"Well . . ." Ghent shrugged. "Probably they did. I don't remember, really."

The medic replaced her comlink in her belt. "Your guide will be here momentarily," she told Mara.

"Thank you," Mara said, resisting the urge to tell the other that she probably knew the Imperial Palace better in her sleep than any guide they had could do in broad daylight. Cooperation and politeness—those were the keys to talking them out of a ship and getting her and Ghent out of this place and out of their war.

Behind the medic the door slid open, and a tall woman with pure white hair glided into the room. "Hello, Mara," she said, smiling gravely. "My name is Winter, personal aide to Princess Leia Organa Solo. I'm glad to see you on your feet again."

"I'm glad to be there," Mara said, trying to keep her voice polite. Someone else associated with Skywalker. Just what she needed. "I take it you're my guide?"

"Your guide, your assistant, and anything else you need for the next few days," Winter said. "Princess Leia asked me to look after you until she and Captain Solo return from Filve."

"I don't need an assistant, and I don't need looking after," Mara said. "All I really need is a ship."

"I've already started working on that," Winter said. "I'm hoping we'll be able to find something for you soon. In the meantime, may I show you to your suite?"

Mara hid a grimace. The usurpers of the New Republic, graciously offering her hospitality in what had once been her own home. "That's very kind of you," she said, trying not to sound sarcastic. "You coming, Ghent?"

"You go on ahead," Ghent said absently, gazing at the computer display. "I want to sit on this run for a while."

"He'll be all right here," Winter assured her. "This way, please."

They left the anteroom, and Winter led the way toward the rear of the Palace. "Ghent has a suite right next to yours," Winter commented as they walked, "but I don't think he's been there more than twice in the past month. He set up temporary shop out there in the recovery anteroom where he could keep an eye on you."

Mara had to smile at that. Ghent, who spent roughly 90 percent of his waking hours oblivious to the outside world, was not exactly what she would go looking for in either a nurse or a bodyguard. But it was the thought that counted. "I appreciate you people taking care of me," she told Winter.

"It's the least we could do to thank you for coming to our assistance at the *Katana* battle."

"It was Karrde's idea," Mara said shortly. "Thank him, not me."

"We did," Winter said. "But you risked your life, too, on our behalf. We won't forget that."

Mara threw a sideways look at the white-haired woman. She had read the Emperor's files on the Rebellion's leaders, including Leia Organa, and the name Winter wasn't ringing any bells at all. "How long have you been with Organa Solo?" she asked.

"I grew up with her in the royal court of Alderaan," Winter said, a bittersweet smile touching her lips. "We were friends in childhood, and when she began her first steps into galactic politics, her father assigned me to be her aide. I've been with her ever since."

"I don't recall hearing about you during the height of the Rebellion," Mara probed gently.

"I spent most of the war moving from planet to planet working with Supply and Procurement," Winter told her. "If my colleagues could get me into a warehouse or depot on some pretext, I could draw a map for them of where the items were that they wanted. It made the subsequent raids quicker and safer."

Mara nodded as understanding came. "So you were the one called Targeter. The one with the perfect memory."

Winter's forehead creased slightly. "Yes, that was one of my code names," she said. "I had many others over the years."

"I see," Mara said. She could remember a fair number of references in pre-Yavin Intelligence reports to the mysterious Rebel named Targeter, much of the politely heated discussion centering around his or her possible identity. She wondered if the data-pushers had ever even gotten close.

They'd reached the set of turbolifts at the rear of the Imperial Palace now, one of the major renovations the Emperor had made in the deliberately antiquated design of the building when he'd taken it over. The turbolifts saved a lot of walking up and down the sweeping staircases in the more public parts of the building . . . as well as masking certain other improvements the Emperor had made in the Palace. "So what's the problem with getting me a ship?" Mara asked as Winter tapped the call plate.

"The problem is the Empire," Winter said. "They've launched a massive attack against us, and it's tied up basically everything we have available, from light freighter on up."

Mara frowned. Massive attacks against superior forces didn't sound like Grand Admiral Thrawn at all. "It's that bad?"

"It's bad enough," Winter said. "I don't know if you knew it, but they beat us to the *Katana* fleet. They'd already moved nearly a hundred and eighty of the Dreadnaughts by the time we arrived. Combined with their new bottomless source of crewers and soldiers, the balance of power has been badly shifted."

Mara nodded, a sour taste in her mouth. Put that way, it *did* sound like Thrawn. "Which means I nearly got myself killed for nothing."

Winter smiled tightly. "If it helps, so did a lot of other people."

The turbolift car arrived. They stepped inside, and Winter keyed for the Palace's residential areas. "Ghent mentioned that the Empire was making trouble," Mara commented as the car began moving upward. "I should have realized that anything that could penetrate that fog he walks around in had to be serious."

" 'Serious' is an understatement," Winter said grimly. "In the past five days we've effectively lost control of four sectors, and thirteen more are on the edge. The biggest loss was the food production facilities at Ukio. Somehow, they managed to take it with its defenses intact."

Mara felt her lip twist. "Someone asleep at the board?"

"Not according to the preliminary reports." Winter hesitated. "There are rumors that the Imperials used a new superweapon that was able to fire straight through the Ukians' planetary shield. We're still trying to check that out."

Mara swallowed, visions of the old Death Star spec sheets floating up from her memory. A weapon like that in the hands of a strategist like Grand Admiral Thrawn . . .

She shook the thought away. This wasn't her war. Karrde had promised they would stay neutral in this thing. "I suppose I'd better get in touch with Karrde, then," she said. "See if he can send someone to pick us up."

"It would probably be faster than waiting for one of our ships to be free," Winter agreed. "He left a data card with the name of a contact you can send a message through. He said you'd know which encrypt code to use."

The turbolift let them out on the Presidents Guests floor, one of the few sections of the Palace that the Emperor had left strictly alone during his reign. With its old-fashioned hinge doors and hand-carved exotic wood furnishings, walking around the floor was like stepping a thousand years into the past. The Emperor had generally reserved the suites here for those emissaries who had fond feelings for such bygone days, or for those who could be impressed by his carefully manufactured continuity with that era. "Captain Karrde left some of your clothes and personal effects for you after the *Katana* battle," Winter said, unlocking one of the carved doors and pushing it open. "If he missed anything, let me know and I can probably supply it. Here's the data card I mentioned," she added, pulling it from her tunic.

"Thank you," Mara said, inhaling deeply as she took the card. This particular suite was done largely in Fijisi wood from Cardooine; and as the delicate scent rose around her, her thoughts flashed back to the glittering days of grand Imperial power and majesty. . . .

"Can I get you anything else?"

The memory faded. Winter was standing before her . . . and the glory days of the Empire were gone. "No, I'm fine," she said.

Winter nodded. "If you want anything, just call the duty officer," she said, gesturing to the desk. "I'll be available later; right now, there's a Council meeting I need to sit in on."

"Go ahead," Mara said. "And thank you."

Winter smiled and left. Mara took another deep breath of Fijisi wood, and with an effort pushed the last of the lingering memories away. She was here, and it was now; and as the Emperor's instructors had so often drummed into her, the first item of business was to fit into her surroundings. And that meant not looking like an escapee from the medical wing.

Karrde had left a good assortment of clothing for her: a semiformal gown, two outfits of a nondescript type that she could wear on the streets of a hundred worlds without looking out of place, and four of the no-nonsense tunic/jumpsuit outfits that she usually wore aboard ship. Choosing one of the latter, she got dressed, then began sorting through the other things Karrde had left. With any luck—and maybe a little foresight on Karrde's part—

There it was: the forearm holster for her tiny blaster. The blaster itself was missing, of course—the captain of the *Adamant* had taken it away from her, and the Imperials weren't likely to return it anytime soon. Looking for a duplicate in the New Republic's arsenals would probably be a waste of effort, as well, though she was tempted to ask Winter for one just to see the reaction.

Fortunately, there was another way.

Each residential floor of the Imperial Palace had an extensive library, and in each of those libraries was a multicard set entitled *The Complete History of Corvis Minor*. Given how unexceptional most of Corvis Minor's history had been, the odds of anyone actually pulling the set off the shelf were extremely slim. Which, given there were no actual data cards in the box, was just as well.

The blaster was a slightly different style from the one Mara had lost to the Imperials. But its power pack was still adequately charged, and it fit snugly into her forearm holster, and that was all that mattered. Now, whatever happened with either the war or New Republic infighting, she would at least have a fighting chance.

She paused, the false data card box in her hand, a stray question belatedly flicking through her mind. What had Winter meant by that reference to a bottomless source for crewers and soldiers? Had one or more of the New Republic's systems gone over to the Imperial side? Or could Thrawn have discovered a hitherto unknown colony world with a populace ripe for recruitment?

It was something she should probably ask about sometime. First, though, she needed to get a message encrypted and relayed out to Karrde's designated contact. The sooner she was out of this place, the better.

Replacing the empty data card set, the comforting weight of the blaster snugged up against her left arm, she headed back to her suite.

THRAWN RAISED HIS glowing red eyes from the putrid-looking alien artwork displayed on the double display ring surrounding his command chair. "No," he said. "Completely out of the question."

Slowly, deliberately, C'baoth turned back from the holographic Woostroid statue he'd been gazing at. "No?" he repeated, his voice rumbling like an approaching thunderstorm. "What do you mean, no?"

"The word is self-explanatory," Thrawn said icily. "The military logic should be, as well. We don't have the numbers for a frontal assault on Coruscant; neither have we the supply lines and bases necessary for a traditional siege. Any attack would be both useless and wasteful, and the Empire will therefore not launch one."

C'baoth's face darkened. "Have a care, Grand Admiral Thrawn," he warned. "I rule the Empire, not you."

"Do you really?" Thrawn countered, reaching up behind him to stroke the ysalamir arched over his shoulder on its nutrient frame.

C'baoth drew himself up to his full height, eyes blazing with sudden fire. "I rule the Empire!" he shouted, his voice echoing through the command room. "You will obey me, or you will die!"

Carefully, Pellaeon eased a little deeper into the Force-empty bubble that surrounded Thrawn's ysalamir. At those times when he was in control of himself, C'baoth appeared more confident and in control than he ever had before; but at the same time these violent bursts of clone madness were becoming more frequent and more vicious. Like a system in a positive feedback loop, swinging further from its core point with each oscillation until it ripped itself apart.

So far C'baoth hadn't killed anyone or destroyed anything. In Pellaeon's opinion it was just a matter of time before that changed.

Perhaps the same thought had occurred to Thrawn. "If you kill me, you'll lose the war," he reminded the Jedi Master. "And if you lose the war, Leia Organa Solo and her twins will never be yours."

C'baoth took a step toward Thrawn's command seat, eyes blazing even hotter—and then, abruptly, he seemed to shrink again to normal size. "You would never speak that way to the Emperor," he said, almost petulantly.

"On the contrary," Thrawn told him. "On no fewer than four occasions I told the Emperor that I would not waste his troops and ships attacking an enemy which I was not yet prepared to defeat."

C'baoth snorted. "Only fools spoke that way to the Emperor," he sneered. "Fools, or those tired of life."

"The Emperor also thought that way," Thrawn agreed. "The first time I refused he called me a traitor and gave my attack force to someone else." The Grand Admiral reached up again to stroke his ysalamir. "After its destruction, he knew better than to ignore my recommendations."

For a long minute C'baoth studied Thrawn's face, his own expression twitching back and forth as if the mind behind it was having trouble maintaining a grip on thought or emotion. "You could repeat the Ukian fraud," he suggested at last. "That trick with cloaked cruisers and timed turbolaser blasts. I would help you."

"That's most generous of you," Thrawn said. "Unfortunately, that, too, would be a waste of effort. The Rebel leaders on Coruscant wouldn't be as quick to surrender as Ukio's farmfolk were. No matter how accurate our timing, they'd eventually realize that the turbolaser blasts hitting the surface weren't the same as those fired by the *Chimaera*, and come to the proper conclusion."

He gestured to the holographic statues filling the room. "The people and leaders of Woostri, on the other hand, are a different matter entirely. Like the Ukians, they have a strong fear of the unknown and what they perceive to be the impossible. Equally important, they have a tendency to magnify rumors of menace far out of proportion. The cloaked cruiser stratagem should work quite well there."

C'baoth's face was starting to redden again. "Grand Admiral Thrawn—"

"But as to Organa Solo and her twins," Thrawn cut him off smoothly, "you can have them whenever you wish."

The embryonic tantrum evaporated. "What do you mean?" C'baoth demanded warily.

"I mean that attacking Coruscant and carrying off Organa Solo by brute force is impractical," Thrawn said. "Sending in a small group to kidnap her, on the other hand, is perfectly feasible. I've already ordered Intelligence to assemble a commando team for that purpose. It should be ready within the day."

"A commando team." C'baoth's lip twisted. "Need I remind you how your Noghri have continually failed you in this matter?"

"I agree," Thrawn said, an oddly grim note to his voice. "Which is why the Noghri will not be involved."

Pellaeon looked down at the Grand Admiral in surprise, then threw an involuntary glance at the door to the command room anteroom where Thrawn's bodyguard Rukh was waiting. Ever since the Lord Darth Vader had first duped the Noghri into their perpetual service to the Empire, the gullible gray-skinned aliens had insisted on putting their own personal honor on the line with each mission. Being pulled off an assignment, especially one this important, would be like a slap in the face to them. Or worse. "Admiral?" he murmured. "I'm not sure—"

"We'll discuss it later, Captain," Thrawn said. "For now, all I need to know is whether Master C'baoth is truly ready to receive his young Jedi." One blue-black eyebrow lifted. "Or whether he prefers simply discussing it."

C'baoth smiled thinly. "Am I to take that as a challenge, Grand Admiral Thrawn?"

"Take it any way you like," Thrawn said. "I merely point out that a wise tactician considers the cost of an operation before launching it. Organa Solo's twins are due to be born any day now, which means you would have two infants as well as Organa Solo herself to deal with. If you're not certain you can handle that, it would be best to postpone the operation."

Pellaeon braced himself for another explosion of clone madness. But to his surprise, it didn't come. "The only question, Grand Admiral Thrawn," C'baoth said softly, "is whether newborn infants will be too much for your Imperial commandos to handle."

"Very well," Thrawn nodded. "Our rendezvous with the rest of the fleet will be in thirty minutes; you'll transfer to the *Death's Head* at that time to assist in their attack on Woostri. By the time you return to the *Chimaera*"—again the eyebrow lifted—"we should have your Jedi for you."

"Very well, Grand Admiral Thrawn," C'baoth said. He drew himself up again, smoothing his long white beard away from his robe. "But I warn you: if you fail me this time, you will not be pleased with the consequences." Turning, he strode across the command room and through the door.

"It's always such a pleasure," Thrawn commented under his breath as the door slid shut.

Pellaeon worked moisture into his mouth. "Admiral, with all due respect—"

"You're worried about my having promised to get Organa Solo out of possibly the most secure place in Rebellion-held territory?" Thrawn said.

"Actually, sir, yes," Pellaeon said. "The Imperial Palace is supposed to be an impregnable fortress."

"Yes, indeed," Thrawn agreed. "But it was the Emperor who made it that way . . . and as in most things, the Emperor kept a few small secrets about the Palace to himself. And to certain of his favorites."

Pellaeon frowned down at him. Secrets . . . "Such as a private way in and out?" he hazarded.

Thrawn smiled up at him. "Precisely. And now that we can finally ensure that Organa Solo will be staying put in the Palace for a while, it becomes profitable to try sending in a commando team."

"But not a Noghri team."

Thrawn lowered his eyes to the collection of holographic sculptures surrounding them. "There's something wrong with the Noghri, Captain," he said quietly. "I don't yet know what it is, but I know it's there. I can sense it with every communication I have with the dynasts on Honoghr."

Pellaeon thought back to that awkward scene a month ago, when that painfully apologetic envoy from the Noghri dynasts had come aboard with the news that the suspected traitor Khabarakh had escaped from their custody. So far, despite their best efforts, they'd been unable to recapture him. "Perhaps they're still fidgeting over that Khabarakh thing," he suggested.

"And well they should be," Thrawn said coldly. "But it's more than that. And until I find out how much more, the Noghri will remain under suspicion."

He leaned forward, tapped two controls on his board. The holographic sculptures faded and were replaced by a tactical map of the current position of the major battle planes. "But at the moment we have two more pressing matters to consider," he continued, leaning back in his seat again. "First, we have to divert our increasingly arrogant Jedi Master from this mistaken notion that he has the right to rule my Empire. Organa Solo and her twins are that diversion."

Pellaeon thought about all the other attempts to capture Organa Solo. "And if the team fails?"

"There are contingencies," Thrawn assured him. "Despite his power and even his unpredictability, Master C'baoth can still be manipulated."

He gestured toward the tactical map. "What's even more important right now, though, is that we ensure the momentum of our battle plan. So far, the campaign is reasonably on schedule. The Rebellion has resisted more firmly than anticipated in the Farrfin and Dolomar sectors, but elsewhere the target systems have generally bowed to Imperial power."

"I wouldn't consider any of the gains all that solid yet," Pellaeon pointed out.

"Precisely," Thrawn nodded. "Each depends on our maintaining a strong and highly visible Imperial presence. And for that, it's vital that we maintain our supply of clones."

He paused. Pellaeon looked at the tactical map, his mind racing as he searched for the response Thrawn was obviously waiting for him to come up with. The Spaarti cloning cylinders, hidden away for decades in the Emperor's private storehouse on Wayland, were about as safe as anything in the galaxy could be. Buried beneath a mountain, protected by an Imperial garrison, and surrounded by hostile locals, its very existence was unknown to anyone except the top Imperial commanders.

He froze. Top Imperial commanders; and perhaps—"Mara Jade," he said. "She's convalescing on Coruscant. Would she have known about the storehouse?"

"That is indeed the question," Thrawn agreed. "There's a good chance she doesn't—I knew many of the Emperor's secrets, and it still took me a great deal of effort to find Wayland. But it's not a risk we can afford to take."

Pellaeon nodded, suppressing a shiver. He'd been wondering why the Grand Admiral had chosen an Intelligence squad for this mission. Unlike standard commando units, Intelligence units were trained in such nonmilitary methods as assassination. . . . "Will a single team be handling both missions, sir, or will you be sending in two?"

"One team should be adequate," Thrawn said. "The two objectives are well enough interlocked to make that reasonable. And neutralizing Jade does not necessarily mean killing her."

Pellaeon frowned. But before he could ask what Thrawn had meant by that, the Grand Admiral touched his board and the tactical holo was replaced by a map of Orus sector. "In the meantime, I think it's time to underline the importance of the Calius saj Leeloo for our enemies. Do we have a follow-up report yet from Governor Staffa?"

"Yes, sir," Pellaeon said, pulling it up on his data pad. "Skywalker left at the same time as the decoy shuttle, and is presumed to have followed its vector. If so, he'll reach the Poderis system in approximately thirty hours."

"Excellent," Thrawn said. "He'll undoubtedly report in to Coruscant before he reaches Poderis. His subsequent disappearance should go a long way toward convincing them that they've found the conduit for our clone traffic."

"Yes, sir," Pellaeon said, keeping to himself his doubts as to their chances of actually causing Skywalker to disappear.

Thrawn presumably knew what he was doing. "One other thing, sir. There was a second follow-up to Staffa's original report, one that came in under an Intelligence encrypt code."

"From his aide, Fingal," Thrawn nodded. "A man with Governor Staffa's casual loyalties practically begs us to assign him a quiet watchdog. Were there any discrepancies with the governor's report?"

"Just one, sir. The follow-up gave a complete description of Skywalker's contact, a man Staffa had indicated was one of his own agents. Fingal's description strongly suggests the man was, in fact, Talon Karrde."

Thrawn exhaled thoughtfully. "Indeed. Did Fingal suggest any explanation for Karrde's presence in Calius?"

"According to him, there are indications that Governor Staffa has had a private trade arrangement with Karrde for several years," Pellaeon said. "Fingal reports he was going to have the man picked up for questioning, but was unable to find a way to do so that wouldn't have alerted Skywalker."

"Yes," Thrawn murmured. "Well . . . what's done is done. And if smuggling was all that was involved, there's no harm. Still, we can't have random smugglers buzzing around our deceptions and perhaps accidentally poking holes in them. And Karrde has already proved he can be a great deal of trouble."

For a moment Thrawn gazed in silence at the Orus sector map. Then, he looked up at Pellaeon. "But for now we have other matters to deal with. Prepare a course for the Poderis system, Captain; I want the *Chimaera* there within forty hours." He smiled thinly. "And signal the garrison commander that I expect him to have a proper reception prepared by the time we arrive. Perhaps in two or three days' time we'll have an unexpected gift to present to our beloved Jedi Master."

"Yes, sir." Pellaeon hesitated. "Admiral . . . what happens if we get Organa Solo and her twins for C'baoth and he's able to turn them the way he thinks he can? We'd have four of them to deal with then instead of just one. Five, if we're able to capture Skywalker at Poderis."

"There's no need for concern," Thrawn said, shaking his head. "Turning either Organa Solo or Skywalker would take C'baoth a great deal of time and effort. It would be even longer before the infants are old enough to be of any danger to us, no matter what he does to them. Long before any of that occurs"—Thrawn's eyes glittered—"we'll have come to a suitable arrangement with our Jedi Master over the sharing of power in the Empire."

Pellaeon swallowed. "Understood, sir," he managed.

"Good. Then you're dismissed, Captain. Return to the bridge."

"Yes, sir." Pellaeon turned and headed across the room, the muscles in his throat feeling tight. Yes, he understood, all right. Thrawn would come to an arrangement with C'baoth . . . or he would have the Jedi Master killed.

If he could. It was not, Pellaeon decided, a confrontation he would like to place any bets on.

Or, for that matter, be anywhere near when it happened.

CHAPTER 4

PODERIS WAS ONE of that select group of worlds generally referred to in the listings as marginal: planets that had remained colonized not because of valuable resources or convenient location, but solely because of the stubborn spirit of its colonists. With a disorienting ten-hour rotational cycle, a lowland slough ecology that had effectively confined the colonists to a vast archipelago of tall mesas, and a nearly perpendicular axial tilt that created tremendous winds every spring and autumn, Poderis was not the sort of place wandering travelers generally bothered with. Its people were tough and independent, tolerant to visitors but with a long history of ignoring the politics of the outside galaxy.

All of which made it an ideal transfer point for the Empire's new clone traffic. And an ideal place for that same Empire to set a trap.

The man shadowing Luke was short and plain, the sort of person who would fade into the background almost anywhere he went. He was good at his job, too, with a skill that implied long experience in Imperial Intelligence. But that experience had naturally not extended to trailing Jedi Knights. Luke had sensed his presence almost as soon as the man had begun following him, and had been able to visually pick him out of the crowd a minute later.

Leaving only the problem of what to do about him.

"Artoo?" Luke called softly into the comlink he'd surreptitiously wedged into the neckband of his hooded robe. "We've got company. Probably Imperials."

There was a soft, worried trill from the comlink, followed by something that was obviously a question. "There's nothing you can do," Luke told him, taking a guess as to the content of the question and wishing Threepio was there to translate. He could generally pick up the gist of what Artoo was saying, but in a situation like this the gist might not be enough. "Is there anyone poking around the freighter? Or around the landing field in general?"

Artoo chirped a definite negative. "Well, they'll be there soon enough," Luke warned him, pausing to look in a shop window. The tail, he noted, moved forward a few more steps before finding an excuse of his own to stop. A professional, indeed. "Get as much of the preflight done as you can without attracting attention. We'll want to get off as soon as I get there."

The droid warbled acknowledgment. Reaching to his neck, Luke shut off the comlink and gave the area a quick scan. The first priority was to lose the tail before the Imperials made any more overt moves against him. And to do that, he needed some kind of distraction. . . .

Fifty meters ahead in the crowd was what looked to be his best opportunity: another man striding along the street in a robe of similar cut and color to Luke's. Cautiously picking up his pace, trying not to give the appearance of hurrying, Luke moved toward him.

The other robed figure continued to the T-junction ahead and turned the corner to his right. Luke picked up his pace a bit more, sensing as he did so his shadower's suspicion that he'd been spotted. Resisting the urge to break into a flat-out run, Luke strolled casually around the corner.

It was a street like most of the others he'd already seen in the city: wide, rock-paved, reasonably crowded, and lined on both sides with graystone buildings. Automatically, he reached out with the Force, scanning the area around him and as far ahead as he could sense—

And abruptly caught his breath. Directly ahead, still distant but clearly detectable, were small pockets of darkness where his Jedi senses could read absolutely nothing. As if the Force that carried the information to him had somehow ceased to exist . . . or was being blocked.

Which meant this was no ordinary ambush, for an ordinary New Republic spy. The Imperials knew he was here and had come to Poderis equipped with ysalamiri.

And unless he did something fast, they were going to take him.

He looked again at the buildings around him. Squat, two-story structures, for the most part, with textured facades and decorative roof parapets. Those to his immediate right were built in a single solid row; directly across the street to his left, the first building after the T-junction had a warped facade, leaving a narrow gap between it and its neighbor's. It wasn't much in the way of cover—and the distance itself was going to be a reach—but it was all he had. Hurrying across the street, half expecting the trap to be sprung before he got there, he slipped into the opening. Bending his knees, letting the Force flow into his muscles, he jumped.

He almost didn't make it. The parapet directly above him was angled and smooth, and for a second he seemed to hang in midair as his fingers scrabbled for a hold. Then, he found a grip, and with a surge of effort pulled himself up and over to lie flat along the rooftop.

Just in time. Even as he eased one eye over the edge of the parapet, he saw his tail come racing around the corner, all efforts at subtlety abandoned. Shoving aside those in his way, he said something inaudible into the comlink in his hand—

And from the cross street a block away, a row of white-armored stormtroopers stepped into view. Blaster rifles held high against their chests, the dark elongated shapes of ysalamiri slung on backpack nutrient frames across their shoulders, they cordoned off the end of the street.

It was a well-planned, well-executed net; and Luke had maybe three minutes to get across the roof and down before they realized their fish had slipped out of it. Easing back from the edge, he turned his head toward the other side of the roof.

The roof didn't have another side. Barely sixty centimeters from where he lay, the roof abruptly became a blank wall that angled steeply downward for perhaps a hundred meters, extending in both directions as far as Luke could see. Beyond its lower edge, there was nothing but the distant mists in the lowlands beneath the mesa.

He'd miscalculated, possibly fatally. Preoccupied with the man shadowing him, he'd completely missed the fact that his path had taken him to the outer edge of the mesa. The slanting wall beside him was one of the massive shield-barriers designed to deflect the planet's vicious seasonal winds harmlessly over the city.

Luke had escaped the Imperial net . . . only to discover that there was literally nowhere else for him to go.

"Great," he muttered under his breath, easing back to the parapet and looking down into the street. More stormtroopers had joined the first squad now and were beginning to sift through the stunned crowd of people caught in the trap; behind them, two squads from the other direction of the T-junction had moved in to seal off the rear of the street. Luke's erstwhile shadow, a blaster now gripped in his hand, was pushing his way through the crowd, making for the other robed figure Luke had noticed earlier.

The other robed figure . . .

Luke bit at his lip. It would be a rather unfriendly trick to play on a totally innocent bystander. But on the other hand, the Imperials obviously knew who they were looking for and just as obviously wanted him alive. Putting the man down there in deadly danger, he knew, would be unacceptable behavior for a Jedi. Luke could only hope that inconveniencing him wouldn't fall under the same heading.

Gritting his teeth, he reached out with the Force and plucked the blaster from the shadow's hand. Spinning it low over the heads of the crowd, he dropped it squarely into the other robed figure's hand.

The shadow shouted to the stormtroopers; but what had begun as a call of triumph quickly became a screech of warning. Focusing the Force with all the control he could manage, Luke turned the blaster back toward its former owner and fired.

Fired safely over the crowd, of course—there was no possible way for him to aim accurately enough to hit the Imperial, even if he'd wanted to. But even a clean miss was enough to jolt the stormtroopers into action. The Imperials who'd been checking faces and IDs abandoned their task to push through the crowd toward the man in the robe, while those guarding the ends of the street hurried forward into backup positions.

It was, not surprisingly, too much for the man in the robe. Shaking away the blaster that had inexplicably become attached to his hand, he slipped past the frozen onlookers beside him and disappeared into a narrow alleyway.

Luke didn't wait to see any more. The minute anyone got a good look at the fleeing man's face, the diversion would be over, and he had to be off this roof and on his way to the landing field before that happened. Sidling to the edge of his narrow ledge, he looked down.

It didn't look promising. Built to withstand two-hundred-kilometer winds, it was perfectly smooth, with no protuberances that could get caught in eddy currents. Nor were there any windows, service doors, or other openings visible. That, at least, shouldn't be a problem; he could cut himself a makeshift doorway with his lightsaber if it came to that. The real question was how to get out of range of the Imperials' trap before they started hunting him in earnest.

He glanced back. And he had to do it fast. From the direction of the official landing area at the far end of the city, the distant specks of airspeeders had begun to appear over the squat city buildings.

He couldn't drop back down on the street side without attracting unwelcome attention. He couldn't crawl along the narrow upper edge of the shield-barrier, at least not fast enough to get out of sight before the airspeeders got here. Which left him only one direction. Down.

But not necessarily *straight* down . . .

He squinted into the sky. Poderis's sun was nearly to the horizon, moving almost visibly through its ten-hour circuit. Right now its light was shining straight into the eyes of the approaching airspeeder pilots, but within five minutes it would be completely below the horizon. *Giving* the searchers a clear view again, and leaving behind a dusk where a lightsaber blade would be instantly visible.

It was now or never.

Pulling his lightsaber from beneath his robe, Luke ignited it, making sure to keep the glowing green blade out of sight of the approaching airspeeders. Using the tip, he carefully made a shallow cut to the right and a few degrees down across the slanting shield-barrier. His robe was made of relatively flimsy material, and it took only a second to tear off the left sleeve and wrap it around the fingertips of his left hand. The padded fingers slipped easily into the groove he'd just made, with enough room to slide freely along it. Getting a firm grip, he set the tip of his lightsaber blade into the end of the groove and rolled off the ledge. Supported by his fingertips, the lightsaber held outstretched in his right hand carving out his path for him as he went, he slid swiftly across and down the shield-barrier.

It was at the same time exhilarating and terrifying. Memories flooded back: the wind whipping past him as he fell through the center core of the Cloud City of Bespin; hanging literally by his fingertips barely minutes later beneath the city; lying exhausted on the floor in the second Death Star, sensing through his pain the enraged helplessness of the Emperor as Vader hurled him to his death. Beneath his chest and legs, the smooth surface of the shield-barrier slid past, marking his rapid approach to the edge and the empty space beyond. . . .

Lifting his head, blinking against the wind slapping into his face, he looked over his shoulder. The lethal edge was visible now, racing upward toward him at what felt like breakneck speed. Closer and closer it came . . . and then, at the last second, he changed the angle of his lightsaber. The downward path of his fingerguide shifted toward horizontal, and a few seconds later he slid smoothly to a halt.

For a moment he just hung there, dangling precariously by one hand as he caught his breath and got his heartbeat back under control. Above him, its edge catching the last rays of the setting sun, he could see the groove he'd just cut, angling up and to his left. Over a hundred meters to his left, he estimated. Hopefully, far enough to put him outside the Imperials' trap.

He'd find out soon enough.

Behind him, the sun dipped below the horizon, erasing the thin line of his passage. Moving carefully, trying not to dislodge his straining fingertips, he began to cut a hole through the shield-barrier.

"REPORT FROM THE STORMTROOPER commander, Admiral," Pellaeon called, grimacing as he read it off his comm display. "Skywalker does not appear to be within the cordon."

"I'm not surprised," Thrawn said darkly, glowering at his displays. "I've warned Intelligence repeatedly about underestimating the range of Skywalker's sensing abilities. Obviously, they didn't take me seriously."

Pellaeon swallowed hard. "Yes, sir. But we know he *was* there, and he couldn't have gotten very far. The stormtroopers have established a secondary cordon and begun a building-to-building search."

Thrawn took a deep breath, then let it out. "No," he said, his voice even again. "He didn't go into any of the buildings. Not Skywalker. That little diversion with the decoy and the blaster . . ." He looked at Pellaeon. "Up, Captain. He went up onto the rooftops."

"The spotters are already sweeping that direction," Pellaeon said. "If he's up there, they'll spot him."

"Good." Thrawn tapped a switch on his command console, calling up a holographic map of that section of the mesa. "What about the shield-barrier on the west edge of the cordon? Can it be climbed?"

"Our people here say no," Pellaeon shook his head. "Too smooth and too sharply angled, with no lip or other barrier at the bottom. If Skywalker went up that side of the street, he's still there. Or at the bottom of the mesa."

"Perhaps," Thrawn said. "Assign one of the spotters to search that area anyway. What about Skywalker's ship?"

"Intelligence is still trying to identify which one is his," Pellaeon admitted. "There's some problem with the records. We should have it in a few more minutes."

"Minutes which we no longer have, thanks to their shadower's carelessness," Thrawn bit out. "He's to be demoted one grade."

"Yes, sir," Pellaeon said, logging the order. A rather severe punishment, but it could have been far worse. The late Lord Vader would have summarily strangled the man. "The landing field itself is surrounded, of course."

Thrawn rubbed his chin thoughtfully. "A probable waste of time," he said slowly. "On the other hand . . ."

He turned his head to gaze out the viewport at the slowly rotating planet. "Pull them off, Captain," he ordered. "All except the clone troopers. Leave those on guard near the likeliest possibilities for Skywalker's ship."

Pellaeon blinked. "Sir?"

Thrawn turned back to face him, a fresh glint in those glowing red eyes. "The landing field cordon doesn't have nearly enough ysalamiri to stop a Jedi, Captain. So we won't bother trying. We'll let him get his ship into space, and take him with the *Chimaera*."

"Yes, sir," Pellaeon said, feeling his forehead furrow. "But then . . ."

"Why leave the clones?" Thrawn finished for him. "Because while Skywalker is valuable to us, the same is not true of his astromech droid." He smiled slightly. "Unless, of course, Skywalker's heroic efforts to escape Poderis convince it that this is indeed the main conduit for our clone traffic."

"Ah," Pellaeon said, finally understanding. "In which case, we find a way to allow the droid to escape back to the Rebellion?"

"Exactly," Thrawn gestured to Pellaeon's board. "Orders, Captain."

"Yes, sir." Pellaeon turned back to his board, feeling a cautious stirring of excitement as he began issuing the Grand Admiral's commands. Maybe this time Skywalker would finally be theirs.

ARTOO WAS JABBERING nervously when Luke finally charged through the door of their small freighter and slapped the seal behind him. "Everything ready to go?" he shouted over his shoulder to the droid as he hurried to the cockpit alcove.

Artoo trilled back an affirmative. Luke dropped into the pilot's seat, giving the instruments a quick once-over as he strapped himself in. "Okay," he called back. "Here we go."

Throwing power to the repulsorlifts, Luke kicked the freighter clear of the ground, wrenching it hard to starboard. A pair of Skipray blastboats rose with him, moving into tandem pursuit formation as he headed for the edge of the mesa. "Watch those Skiprays, Artoo," Luke called, splitting his own attention between the rapidly approaching city's edge and the airspace above them. The fight with those clone troopers guarding the landing field had been intense, but it had been far too brief to be realistic. Either the Empire had left someone totally incompetent in charge, or they'd let him get to his ship on purpose. Carefully herding him into the real trap . . .

The edge of the mesa shot past beneath him. Luke threw a quick glance at the rear display to confirm that he was clear of the city, then punched in the main sublight drive.

The freighter shot skyward like a scalded mynock, leaving the pursuing Skiprays flatfooted in its wake. The official-sounding orders to halt that had been blaring from the board turned into a surprised yelp as Luke reached over and shut the comm off. "Artoo? You all right back there?"

The droid chirped an affirmative, and a question scrolled across Luke's computer screen. "They were clones, all right," he confirmed grimly, an uncomfortable shiver running through him. The strange aura that seemed to surround the Empire's new duplicate humans was twice as eerie up close. "I'll tell you something else, too," he added to Artoo. "The Imperials knew it was me they were chasing. Those stormtroopers were carrying ysalamiri on their backs."

Artoo whistled thoughtfully, gave a questioning gurgle. "Right—that whole Delta Source thing," Luke agreed, reading the droid's comment. "Leia told me that if we couldn't get the leak closed fast, she was going to recommend we move operations out of the Imperial Palace. Maybe even off Coruscant entirely."

Though if Delta Source was a human or alien spy instead of some impossibly undetectable listening system in the Palace itself, moving anywhere would just be so much wasted effort. From Artoo's rather pointed silence, Luke guessed the droid was thinking that, too.

The distant horizon, barely visible as dark planet against dark but starlit sky, was starting to show a visible curvature now. "Better start calculating our jump to lightspeed, Artoo," he called over his shoulder. "We're probably going to have to get out of here in a hurry."

He got a confirming beep from the droid's position and turned his attention back to the horizon ahead. A whole fleet of Star Destroyers, he knew, could be lurking below that horizon, out of range of his instruments, waiting for him to get too far from any possible cover to launch their attack.

Out of range of his instruments, but perhaps not out of range of Jedi senses. Closing his eyes to slits, flooding his mind with calmness, he stretched out through the Force—

He got it an instant before Artoo's startled warning shrill shattered the air. An Imperial Star Destroyer all right; but not cutting across his path as Luke had expected. Instead, it was coming up from behind, in an atmosphere-top forced orbit that had allowed it to build up speed without sacrificing the advantages of planetary cover.

"Hang on!" Luke shouted, throwing emergency power to the drive. But it was a futile gesture, and both he and the Imperials knew it. The Star Destroyer was coming up fast, its tractor beams already activated and tracking him. Within a handful of seconds, they were going to get him.

Or at least, they were going to get the freighter . . .

Luke hit his strap release, opening a disguised panel as he did so and touching the three switches hidden there. The first switch keyed in the limited autopilot; the second unlocked the aft proton torpedo launcher and started it firing blindly back toward the Star Destroyer.

The third activated the freighter's self-destruct.

His X-wing was wedged nose forward in the cargo area behind the cockpit alcove, looking for all the world like some strange metallic animal peering out of its burrow. Luke leaped to the open canopy, coming within an ace of cracking his head on the freighter's low ceiling in the process. Artoo, already snugged into the X-wing's droid socket, was jabbering softly to himself as he ran the star-fighter's systems from standby to full ready. Even as Luke strapped in and pulled on his flight helmet, the droid signaled they were clear to fly.

"Okay," Luke told him, resting his left hand on the special switch that had been added to his control board. "If this is going to work, we're going to have to time it just right. Be ready."

Again he closed his eyes, letting the Force flow through his senses. Once before, on his first attempt to locate the Jedi Master C'baoth, he'd tangled like this with the Imperials—an X-wing against an Imperial Star Destroyer. That, too, had been a deliberate ambush, though he hadn't realized it until C'baoth's unholy alliance with the Empire had been laid bare. In that battle, skill and luck and the Force had saved him.

This time, if the specialists back at Coruscant had done their job right, the luck was already built in.

With his mind deeply into the Force, he sensed the locking of the tractor beam a half second before it actually occurred. His hand jabbed the switch; and even as the freighter jerked in the tractor beam's powerful grip, the front end blew apart into a cloud of metallic shards. An instant later, kicked forward by a deck-mounted blast-booster, the X-wing shot through the glittering debris. For a long, heart-stopping moment it seemed as though the tractor beam was going to be able to maintain its hold despite the obscuring particle fog. Then, all at once, the grip slackened and was gone.

"We're free!" Luke shouted back at Artoo, rolling the X-wing over and driving hard for deep space. "I'm going evasive—hang on."

He rolled the X-wing again, and as he did so a pair of brilliant green flashes shot past the transparisteel canopy. With their tractor beams outdistanced, the Imperials had apparently decided to settle for shooting him out of the sky. Another barrage of green flame scorched past, and there was a yelp from Artoo as something burned through the deflectors to slap against the X-wing's underside. Reaching out again to the Force, Luke let it guide his hands on the controls—

And then, almost without warning, it was time. Reaching to the hyperdrive lever, Luke pulled it back.

WITH A FLICKER of pseudomotion, the X-wing vanished into the safety of hyperspace, the *Chimaera*'s turbolaser batteries still firing uselessly for a second at where it had been. The batteries fell silent; and Pellaeon let out a long breath, afraid to look over at Thrawn's command station. It was the second time Skywalker had escaped from this kind of trap . . . and the last time he'd done so, a man had died for that failure.

The rest of the bridge crew hadn't forgotten that, either. In the brittle silence the faint rustling of cloth against seat material was clearly audible as Thrawn stood up. "Well," the Grand Admiral said, his voice strangely calm. "One must give the Rebels full credit for ingenuity. I've seen that trick worked before, but not nearly so effectively."

"Yes, sir," Pellaeon said, trying without success to hide the strain in his voice.

Out of the corner of his eye he could see Thrawn looking at him. "At ease, Captain," the Grand Admiral said soothingly. "Skywalker would have made an interesting package to present to Master C'baoth, but his escape is hardly cause for major concern. The primary objective of this exercise was to convince the Rebellion that they'd discovered the clone conduit. That objective has been achieved."

The tightness in Pellaeon's chest began to dissipate. If the Grand Admiral wasn't angry about it . . .

"That does not mean, however," Thrawn went on, "that the actions of the *Chimaera*'s crew should be ignored. Come with me, Captain."

Pellaeon got to his feet, the tightness returning. "Yes, sir."

Thrawn led the way to the aft stairway and descended to the starboard crew pit. He walked past the crewers at their consoles, past the officers standing stiffly behind them, and came to a halt at the control station for the starboard tractor beams. "Your name," he said quietly to the young man standing at rigid attention there.

"Ensign Mithel," the other said, his face pale but composed. The expression of a man facing his death.

"Tell me what happened, Ensign."

Mithel swallowed. "Sir, I had just established a positive lock on the freighter when it broke up into a cluster of trac-reflective particles. The targeting system tried to lock on all of them at once and went into a loop snarl."

"And what did you do?"

"I—sir, I knew that if I waited for the particles to dissipate normally, the target starfighter would be out of range. So I tried to dissipate them myself by shifting the tractor beam into sheer-plane mode."

"It didn't work."

A quiet sigh slipped through Mithel's lips. "No, sir. The target-lock system couldn't handle it. It froze up completely."

"Yes." Thrawn cocked his head slightly. "You've had a few moments now to consider your actions, Ensign. Can you think of anything you should have done instead?"

The young man's lip twitched. "No, sir. I'm sorry, but I can't. I don't remember anything in the manual that covers this kind of situation."

Thrawn nodded. "Correct," he agreed. "There isn't anything. Several methods have been suggested over the past few decades for counteracting the covert shroud gambit, none of which has ever been made practical. Yours was one of the more innovative attempts, particularly given how little time you had to come up with it. The fact that it failed does not in any way diminish that."

A look of cautious disbelief was starting to edge into Mithel's face. "Sir?"

"The Empire needs quick and creative minds, Ensign," Thrawn said. "You're hereby promoted to lieutenant . . . and your first assignment is to find a way to break a covert shroud. After their success here, the Rebellion may try the gambit again."

"Yes, sir," Mithel breathed, the color starting to come back into his face. "I—thank you, sir."

"Congratulations, Lieutenant Mithel." Thrawn nodded to him, then turned to Pellaeon. "The bridge is yours, Captain. Resume our scheduled flight. I'll be in my command room if you require me."

"Yes, sir," Pellaeon managed.

And stood there beside the newly minted lieutenant, feeling the stunned awe pervading the bridge as he watched Thrawn leave. Yesterday, the *Chimaera*'s crew had trusted and respected the Grand Admiral. After today, they would be ready to die for him.

And for the first time in five years, Pellaeon finally knew in the deepest level of his being that the old Empire was gone. The new Empire, with Grand Admiral Thrawn at its head, had been born.

THE X-WING HUNG suspended in the blackness of space, light-years away from any solid mass larger than a grain of dust. It was, Luke thought, almost like a replay of that other battle with a Star Destroyer, the one that had left him stranded in deep space and had ultimately led him to Talon Karrde and Mara Jade and the planet Myrkr.

Fortunately, appearance was the only thing they had in common. Mostly.

From the droid socket behind him came a nervous warble. "Come on, Artoo, relax," Luke soothed him. "It's not that bad. We couldn't have made it anywhere near Coruscant without refueling anyway. We'll just have to do it a little sooner, that's all."

The response was a sort of indignant grunt. "I *am* taking you seriously, Artoo," Luke said patiently, keying the listing on his nav display over to the droid. "Look—here are all the places we can get to with half our primary power cells blown out. See?"

For a moment the droid seemed to mull over the list, and Luke took the opportunity to give it another look himself. There were a lot of choices there, all right. The problem was that many of them wouldn't be especially healthy for a lone New Republic X-wing to show up at. Half were under direct Imperial control, and most of the others were either leaning that way or keeping their political options open.

Still, even on an Imperial-held world, there were sensor gaps a single starfighter could probably slip through. He could put down in some isolated place, make his way on foot to a spaceport, and buy some replacement fuel cells with the Imperial currency he still had left. Getting the cells back to the X-wing could be a bit of a problem, but nothing he and Artoo couldn't solve.

Artoo chirped a suggestion. "Kessel's a possibility," Luke agreed. "I don't know, though—last I heard Moruth Doole was still in charge there, and Han's never really trusted him. I think we'd do better with Fwillsving, or even—"

He broke off as one of the planets on the list caught his eye. A planet Leia had programmed into his onboard nav system, almost as an afterthought, before he left on this mission.

Honoghr.

"I've got a better idea, Artoo," Luke said slowly. "Let's go visit the Noghri."

There was a startled, disbelieving squawk from behind him. "Oh, come on," Luke admonished him. "Leia and Chewie went there and got back all right, didn't they? And Threepio, too," he added. "You don't want Threepio saying you were afraid to go somewhere *he* wasn't afraid of, would you?"

Artoo grunted again. "Doesn't matter whether or not he had a choice," Luke said firmly. "The point is that he went."

The droid gave a mournful and rather resigned gurgle. "That's the spirit," Luke encouraged him, keying the nav computer to start the calculation to Honoghr. "Leia's been wanting me to go visit them, anyway. This way we kill two dune lizards with one throw."

Artoo gave a single discomfited gurgle and fell silent . . . and even Luke, who fully trusted Leia's judgment of the Noghri, privately conceded that it was perhaps not the most comforting figure of speech he could have used.

CHAPTER 5

THE BATTLE DATA from the Woostri system scrolled to the bottom of the data pad and stopped. "I still don't believe it," Leia said, shaking her head as she laid the data pad back down on the table. "If the Empire had a superweapon that could shoot through planetary shields, they'd be using it in every system they attacked. It has to be a trick or illusion of some kind."

"I agree," Mon Mothma said quietly. "The question is, how do we convince the rest of the Council and the Assemblage of that? Not to mention the outer systems themselves?"

"We must solve the puzzle of what happened at Ukio and Woostri," Admiral Ackbar said, his voice even more gravelly than usual. "And we must solve it quickly."

Leia picked up her data pad again, throwing a quick look across the table at Ackbar as she did so. The Mon Calamari's huge eyes seemed unusually heavy-lidded, his normal salmon color noticeably faded. He was tired, desperately so . . . and with the Empire's grand offensive still rolling toward them across the galaxy, he wasn't likely to be getting much rest anytime soon.

Neither were any of the rest of them, for that matter. "We already know that Grand Admiral Thrawn has a talent for understanding the minds of his opponents," she reminded the others. "Could he have predicted how quick both the Ukians and the Woostroids would be to surrender?"

"As opposed to, say, the Filvians?" Mon Mothma nodded slowly. "Interesting point. That might indicate the illusion is one that can't be maintained for very long."

"Or that the power requirements are exceedingly high," Ackbar added. "If the Empire has learned a method for focusing nonvisible energy against a shield, it could conceivably weaken a section long enough to fire a turbolaser blast through the opening. But such a thing would take a tremendous power output."

"And should also show up as an energy stress on the shield," Mon Mothma pointed out. "None of our information suggests that was the case."

"Our information may be wrong," Ackbar retorted. He threw a brief glare at Councilor Borsk Fey'lya. "Or it may have been manipulated by the Empire," he added pointedly. "Such things have happened before."

Leia looked at Fey'lya, too, wondering if the thinly veiled insult to his people would finally drive the Bothan out of his self-imposed silence. But Fey'lya just sat there, his eyes on the table, his cream-colored fur motionless. Not speaking, not reacting, perhaps not even thinking.

Eventually, she supposed, he would regain his verbal courage and a measure of his old political strength. But for now, with his false denunciation of Ackbar still fresh in everyone's minds, he was in the middle of his species' version of penance.

Leia's stomach tightened in frustration. Once again, the Bothans' inflexible all-or-nothing approach to politics was running squarely counter to the New Republic's best interests. A few months earlier, Fey'lya's accusations against Ackbar had wasted valuable time and energy; now, when the Council needed every bit of insight and resourcefulness it could muster—including Fey'lya's—he was playing the silent martyr.

There were days—and long, dark nights—when Leia privately despaired of ever holding the New Republic together.

"You're right, of course, Admiral," Mon Mothma said with a sigh. "We need more information. And we need it quickly."

"Talon Karrde's organization is still our best chance," Leia said. "They've got the contacts, both here and on the Imperial side. And from what Luke said in his last message, Karrde sounded interested."

"We can't afford to wait on the convenience of a smuggler," Ackbar growled, his mouth tendrils stiffening with distaste. "What about General Bel Iblis? He was fighting alone against the Empire for several years."

"The General has already turned his intelligence contacts over to us," Mon Mothma said, a muscle in her cheek twitching. "So far, we're still integrating them into our own system."

"I wasn't referring to his contacts," Ackbar said. "I meant the General himself. Why isn't he here?"

Leia looked at Mon Mothma, her stomach tightening again. Garm Bel Iblis had been one of the early forces behind the consolidation of individual resistance units into the all-encompassing Rebel Alliance, and for years had formed a shadowy triad of leadership with Mon Mothma and Leia's own adoptive father, Bail Organa. But when Organa died with his people in the Death Star's attack on Alderaan—and as Mon Mothma began subsequently to draw more and more power to herself—Bel Iblis had left the Alliance and struck out on his own. Since then, he had continued his private war against the Empire . . . until, almost by accident, he had crossed paths with fellow Corellian Han Solo.

It was Han's urgent request that had brought Bel Iblis and his force of six Dreadnaughts to the New Republic's aid at the *Katana* battle. Mon Mothma, speaking words about burying past differences, had welcomed Bel Iblis back.

And had then turned around and sent him to bolster the

defenses in the outer sectors of the New Republic. As far from Coruscant as he could possibly have gone.

Leia was not yet ready to ascribe vindictiveness to Mon Mothma's decision. But there were others in the New Republic hierarchy who remembered Bel Iblis and his tactical genius . . . and not all of them were quite so willing to give Mon Mothma the benefit of the doubt.

"The General's expertise is needed at the battlefront," Mon Mothma said evenly.

"His expertise is also needed here," Ackbar retorted; but Leia could hear the resignation in his voice. Ackbar himself had just returned from a tour of the Farrfin and Dolomar defenses, and would be leaving in the morning for Dantooine. With the Imperial war machine on the move, the New Republic couldn't afford the luxury of burying their best line commanders away in ground-side offices.

"I understand your concerns," Mon Mothma said, more gently. "When we get the situation out there stabilized, I fully intend to bring General Bel Iblis back and put him in charge of tactical planning."

If we get the situation stabilized, Leia amended silently, again feeling her stomach tighten. So far, the offensive was going uniformly the Empire's way—

The thought broke off in midstride, a sudden belated awareness flooding in on her. No—it wasn't her *stomach* that was tightening. . . .

Ackbar was speaking again. "Excuse me," Leia cut him off, getting carefully to her feet. "I'm sorry to interrupt, but I need to get down to Medical."

Mon Mothma's eyes widened. "The twins?"

Leia nodded. "I think they're on their way."

THE WALLS AND CEILING of the birth room were a warm tan color, with a superimposed series of shifting lights that had been synchronized with Leia's own brain wave patterns. Theoretically, it was supposed to help her relax and concentrate. As a practical matter, Leia had already decided that after ten hours of looking at it, the technique had pretty well lost its effectiveness.

Another contraction came, the hardest one yet. Automatically, Leia reached out with the Force, using the methods Luke had taught her to hold off the pain coming from protesting muscles. If nothing else, this whole birth process was giving her the chance to practice her Jedi techniques.

And not just those having to do with pain control. *It's all right*, she thought soothingly toward the small minds within her. *It's all right Mother's here.*

It didn't really help. Caught in forces they couldn't comprehend, their tiny bodies being squeezed and pushed as they were driven slowly toward the unknown, their undeveloped minds were fluttering with fear.

Though to be perfectly fair, their father wasn't in much better shape.

"You all right?" Han asked for the umpteenth time since they'd come in here. He squeezed her hand a little more tightly, also for the umpteenth time, in sympathetic tension with her hunching shoulders.

"I'm still fine," Leia assured him. Her shoulders relaxed as the contraction ended, and she gave his hand a squeeze in return. "You don't look so good, though."

Han made a face at her. "It's past my bedtime," he said dryly.

"That must be it," Leia agreed. Han had been as nervous as a tauntaun on ball bearings ever since the labor started in earnest, but he was making a manly effort not to show it. More for her sake, Leia suspected, than for any damage such an admission might do to his image. "Sorry."

"Don't worry about it." Han threw a look to the side, where the medic and two Emdee droids were hovering around the business end of the birth bed. "Looks like we're getting close, sweetheart."

"Count on it," Leia agreed, the last word strangled off as another contraction took her attention. "Oh . . ."

Han's anxiety level jumped another notch. "You all right?"

Leia nodded, throat muscles momentarily too tight to speak through. "Hold me, Han," she breathed when she could talk again. "Just hold me."

"I'm right here," he said quietly, sliding his free hand into a comfortable grip under her shoulder.

She hardly heard him. Deep within her, the small lives that she and Han had created were starting to move . . . and abruptly their fluttering fear had become full-blown terror.

Don't be afraid, she thought at them. *Don't be afraid. It'll be all right. I'm here. Soon, you'll be with me.*

She wasn't really expecting a reaction—the twins' minds were far too undeveloped to understand anything as abstract as words or the concept of future events. But she continued anyway, wrapping them and their fear as best she could in her love and peace and comfort. There was another contraction—the inexorable movement toward the outside world continued—

And then, to Leia's everlasting joy, one of the tiny minds reached back to her, touching her in a way that neither twin had ever responded to her nonverbal caresses before. The rising fear slowed in its advance, and Leia had the sudden mental image of a baby's hand curled tightly around her finger. *Yes*, she told the infant. *I'm your mother, and I'm here.*

The tiny mind seemed to consider that. Leia continued her assurances, and the mind shifted a little away from her, as if the infant's attention had been drawn somewhere else. A good sign, she decided; if it was able to be distracted from what was happening to it—

And then, to her amazement, the second mind's panic also began to fade. The second mind, which to the best of her knowledge had not yet even noticed her presence . . .

Later, in retrospect, the whole thing would seem obvious, if not completely inevitable. But at that moment, the revelation was startling enough to send a shiver through the core of Leia's soul. The twins, growing together in the Force even as they'd grown together within her, had somehow become attuned to each other—attuned in a way and to a depth that Leia knew she herself would never entirely share.

It was, at the same time, one of the proudest and yet one of the most poignant moments of Leia's life. To get such a glimpse into the future—to see her children growing and strengthening themselves in the Force . . . and to know that there would be a part of their lives together that she would never share.

The contraction eased, the grand and bittersweet vision of the future fading into a small nugget of ache in a corner of her mind. An ache that was made all the worse by the private shame that, in all of that flood of selfish emotion, it hadn't even occurred to her that Han would be able to share even less of their lives than she would.

And suddenly, through the mental haze, a bright light seemed to explode in her eyes. Reflexively, she clutched harder at Han's hand. "What—?"

"It's coming," Han yelped, gripping back. "First one's halfway out."

Leia blinked, the half-imagined light vanishing as her mind fumbled free of her contact with her children. Her children, whose eyes had never had to deal with anything brighter than a dim, diffuse glow. "Turn that light down," she gasped. "It's too bright. The children's eyes—"

"It's all right," the medic assured her. "Their eyes will adjust. All right: one last push."

And then, seemingly without warning, the first part was suddenly over. "Got one," Han told her, his voice sounding strangely breathless. "It's—" He craned his neck. "It's our daughter." He looked back at Leia, the tension in his face plastered over with the lopsided grin she knew so well. "Jaina."

Leia nodded. "Jaina," she repeated. Somehow, the names they'd decided on had never sounded quite the same as they did right now. "What about Jacen?"

"Offhand, I'd say he's anxious to join his sister," the medic said dryly. "Get ready to push—he looks like he's trying to crawl out on his own. Okay . . . *push.*"

Leia took a deep breath. Finally. After ten hours of labor—after nine months of pregnancy—the end was finally in sight. No. Not the end. The beginning.

They laid the twins in her arms a few minutes later . . . and as she looked first at them and then up at Han, she felt a sense of utter peace settle over her. Out among the stars there might be a war going on; but for here, and for now, all was right with the universe.

"WATCH IT, ROGUE LEADER," the voice of Rogue Ten snapped in Wedge's ear. "You've picked up a tail."

"Got it," Wedge told him, cutting his X-wing hard over. The TIE interceptor shot past, spitting laser fire as he went, and attempted to match Wedge's maneuver. Blurring in barely half a second behind the Imperial, a pursuing X-wing blew him into a cloud of flaming dust.

"Thanks, Rogue Eight," Wedge said, blowing a drop of sweat from the tip of his nose and checking his scanners. Temporarily, at least, it looked like their little corner of the melee was in the clear. Putting his X-wing into a slow turn, he gave the overall battle scene a quick assessment.

It was worse than he'd feared. Worse, for that matter, than it had been even five minutes ago. Two more *Victory*-class Star Destroyers had appeared from hyperspace, dropping into mauling position at point-blank range from one of their three remaining Calamari Star Cruisers. And at the rate the Star Destroyers were pouring turbolaser fire into it—"Rogue Squadron: change course to twenty-two mark eight," he ordered, turning onto the intercept heading and wondering how in blazes the Imperials had managed this one. Making so precise a jump was difficult under ideal circumstances; to do so into the heat and confusion of a battle should have been well-nigh impossible. Just one more example of the Empire's incredible new talent for coordinating their forces.

There was a warning twitter from the astromech droid riding in the socket behind him: they were now registering too close to a large mass to jump to lightspeed. Wedge glanced around with a frown, finally spotted the Interdictor Cruiser hovering off in the distance, keeping well out of the main battle itself. Apparently, the Imperials didn't want any of the New Republic ships sneaking out of the party early.

Dead ahead, some of the Victory Star Destroyers' TIE fighters were sweeping up to meet them. "Porkins' Formation," Wedge ordered his team. "Watch out for flankers. Star Cruiser *Orthavan*, this is Rogue Squadron; we're coming in."

"Stay there, Rogue Leader," a gravelly Mon Calamari voice said. "We're too badly overmatched. You can't help us."

Wedge gritted his teeth. The Mon Cal was probably right. "We're going to try, anyway," he told the other. The advancing TIE fighters were almost in range now. "Hang on."

"Rogue Squadron, this is Bel Iblis," a new voice cut in. "Break off your attack. On my mark cut thirty degrees to portside."

With an effort, Wedge suppressed the urge to say something that would probably have earned him a court-martial. On his list, as long as a ship was in one piece, there was still hope of saving it. Apparently, the great General Bel Iblis had decided otherwise. "Copy, General," he sighed. "Rogue Squadron: stand by."

"Rogue Squadron . . . mark."

Obediently, reluctantly, Wedge swung his X-wing to the side. The TIE fighters shifted course to follow; seemed to suddenly get flustered—

And with a roar that carried clearly even through the tenuous gases of interplanetary space, an assault formation of A-wings shot through the space Rogue Squadron had just exited. The TIE fighters, already in motion to match the X-wings' maneuver, were caught flat-footed. Before they could get back into barricade position, the A-wings were past them, heading at full throttle for the embattled Star Cruiser. "Okay, Rogue Squadron," Bel Iblis said. "Your turn. Clear their backs for them."

Wedge grinned tightly. He should have known better of Bel Iblis. "Copy, General. Rogue Squadron, let's take them."

"And then," Bel Iblis added grimly, "prepare to retreat."

Wedge blinked, the grin fading. *Retreat?* Turning his X-wing toward the TIE fighters, he looked back at the main battle area.

A few minutes earlier, he'd realized the situation had looked bad. Now, it was on the edge of disaster. Bel Iblis's force was down to barely two-thirds of the fifteen capital ships he'd started with, with most of those huddled into a last-ditch bastion formation. Surrounding it, systematically battering at its defenses, were over twenty Star Destroyers and Dreadnaughts.

Wedge looked back at the approaching TIE fighters; and, beyond them, to the Interdictor Cruiser. The Interdictor Cruiser, whose gravity well projectors were keeping the beleaguered battle force from escaping to lightspeed . . .

And then they were on the TIE fighters, and there was no more time for thought. The battle was sharp, but short—the sudden appearance of the A-wings from Rogue Squadron's shadow had apparently thrown the TIE fighters just enough off stride. Three minutes, maybe four, and Rogue Squadron was again in the clear.

"What now, Rogue Leader?" Rogue Two asked as the squadron re-formed through the debris.

Mentally crossing his fingers, Wedge looked back at the *Orthavan*. If Bel Iblis's gamble hadn't worked . . .

It had. The A-wing slash had distracted the Victory Star Destroyers' attack just enough for the Star Cruiser to catch its breath and go back on the offensive. The *Orthavan* had both its extensive turbolaser and ion cannon batteries going, scrambling the Imperials' systems and pummeling away at their hulls. Even as Wedge watched, a geyser of superheated gas erupted from the midsection of the nearer Star Destroyer, sending the ship rotating ponderously away. Pulling under the derelict's hull, the Star Cruiser moved away from the battle and headed for the Interdictor Cruiser.

"Change course for the *Orthavan*," Wedge ordered. "They may need backup."

The words were barely out of his mouth when, shooting in from lightspeed, a pair of Dreadnaughts suddenly appeared at the *Orthavan*'s flank. Wedge held his breath, but the Star Cruiser was already moving too fast for the Dreadnaughts to get more than a wild shot at it. It passed them without pausing; and as they turned to follow it, the A-wing squadron reenacted their earlier slash maneuver. Once again, the distraction's effectiveness was vastly out of proportion to the actual damage inflicted. By the time the starfighters broke off, the *Orthavan* was beyond any chance the Dreadnaughts might have to catch up.

And the Imperials knew it. Behind Wedge, the astromech droid beeped: the pseudogravity field was fading away as the distant Interdictor Cruiser shut down its gravity well projectors in preparation for its own escape to lightspeed.

The Interdictor Cruiser . . .

And belatedly the explanation struck him. He'd been wrong—those Victory Star Destroyers hadn't needed to rely on any half-mystical coordination technique to jump in so close to the Star Cruiser. All they'd had to do was fly in along a hyperspace vector supplied to them by the Interdictor Cruiser and wait until the edge of the gravity well cone yanked them back into normal space.

Wedge felt his lip twist. Overestimating the enemy's abilities, he'd been taught a long time ago, could be just as dangerous as underestimating them. It was a lesson he would have to start remembering.

"Interdictor gravfield is down," Bel Iblis's voice came in his ear. "All units, acknowledge and prepare to retreat on your marks."

"Rogue Squadron: copy," Wedge said, grimacing as he turned onto their preplanned escape vector and looked back at what was left of the main battle group. There was no doubt about it: they'd been beaten, and beaten badly, and about all Bel Iblis's legendary tactical skill had been able to do had been to keep the defeat from turning into a rout.

And the price was likely to be yet another system lost to the Empire.

"Rogue Squadron: go."

"Copy," Wedge sighed, and pulled back the hyperspace lever . . . and as the stars flared into starlines, a sobering thought occurred to him.

For the foreseeable future, at least, underestimating the Empire was not likely to be all that much of a problem.

CHAPTER 6

THE STARLINES SHRANK back into stars, and the *Wild Karrde* was back in normal space. Straight ahead was the tiny white dwarf sun of the Chazwa system, not all that distinguishable from the bright background stars around it. Nearby and a little to one side, a mostly dark circle edged by a slender lighted crescent, was the planet Chazwa itself. Scattered around it in the darkness of space the exhaust glows of perhaps fifty ships could be seen, both incoming and outgoing. Most were freighters and bulk cruisers, taking advantage of Chazwa's central transshipment location. A few were clearly Imperial warships.

"Well, here we are," Aves said conversationally from the co-pilot station. "Incidentally, Karrde, I'd like to go on record as saying this is an insane idea."

"Perhaps," Karrde conceded, shifting course toward the planet and checking his displays. Good; the rest of the group had made it in all right. "But if the Empire's clone transport route does indeed run through the Orus sector, the Chazwa garrison should have records of the operation. Possibly even the origin point, if someone was careless."

"I wasn't referring to the details of the raid," Aves said. "I meant that it was crazy for us to be getting involved in the first place. It's the New Republic's war, not ours—let them chase it down."

"If I could trust them to do so, I would," Karrde said, peering out the starboard viewport. Another freighter seemed to be sidling slowly in the *Wild Karrde*'s general direction. "But I'm not sure they're up to the task."

Aves grunted. "I still don't buy Skywalker's numbers. Seems to me that if you could grow stable clones that fast, the old clonemasters would have done it."

"Perhaps they did," Karrde pointed out. "I don't think any information on the cloning techniques of that era has survived. Everything I've ever seen has come from the much earlier pre-war experiments."

"Yeah, well . . ." Aves shook his head. "I'd still rather sit the whole thing out."

"We may discover we don't have a choice in the matter." Karrde gestured to the freighter still moving up on them. "We seem to have a caller. Would you pull up an ID on him?"

"Sure." Aves threw a quick look at the freighter, then turned to his board. "Not registering as any ship I've ever heard of. Wait a minute . . . yeah. Yeah, they've altered their ID—simple transponder overlay, looks like. Let's see if Ghent's magic decoder package can untangle it."

Karrde nodded, the mention of Ghent's name sending his thoughts flicking briefly across the galaxy to Coruscant and the two associates he'd left there under New Republic care. If the timetable their medical people had given him was correct, Mara should be about recovered by now. She should be trying to get in touch with him soon, and he made a mental note to check in with the contact pipeline as soon as they were finished here.

"Got it," Aves said triumphantly. "Well, well—I do believe it's an old friend of yours, Karrde. The *Kern's Pride;* the slightly less-than-honorable Samuel Tomas Gillespee, proprietor."

"Is it, now," Karrde said, eyeing the ship pacing them a

hundred meters away. "I suppose we'd better see what he wants."

He keyed for a tight-beam transmission. "This is Talon Karrde calling the *Kern's Pride*," he said. "Don't just sit there, Gillespee—say hello."

"Hello, Karrde," a familiar voice came back. "You don't mind if I figure out who I'm talking to before I say hello, do you?"

"Not at all," Karrde assured him. "Nice little overlay on your ship ID, by the way."

"Obviously could have been nicer," Gillespee said dryly. "We weren't even close to slicing yours yet. What are you doing here?"

"I was about to ask you the same thing," Karrde said. "I was under the impression you'd been planning to retire."

"I did," Gillespee said grimly. "Out of the business for good, and thanks for everything. Bought myself a big chunk of land on a nice little out-of-the-way world where I could watch the trees grow and stay out of everything that smelled like trouble. Place called Ukio—ever hear of it?"

Beside Karrde, Aves shook his head and muttered something under his breath. "I seem to remember hearing that name recently, yes," Karrde conceded. "Were you there for the Imperial attack?"

"I was there for the attack, the surrender, and all the occupation I could stomach," Gillespee growled. "Matter of fact, I had about as good a front-row seat to the bombardment as you could get. It was pretty spectacular, I'll tell you that."

"It could be profitable as well," Karrde said, thinking hard. As far as he knew, the New Republic still didn't have a handle on what exactly the Empire had done at Ukio. Hard data on the attack could be invaluable to their tactical people. As well as commanding a hefty fee for both witness and finder. "I don't suppose you took any readings during the attack."

"I've got a little from the bombardment part of it," Gillespee said. "The data card from my macrobinoculars. Why?"

"There's a good chance I can find you a buyer for it," Karrde told him. "It might compensate somewhat for your lost property."

"I doubt your buyer's got that much to spend," Gillespee sniffed. "You wouldn't have believed it, Karrde—you really wouldn't. I mean, we're not talking Svivren here, but even Ukio should have taken them a little longer to overrun."

"The Empire's had a lot of practice overrunning worlds," Karrde reminded him. "You're lucky you made it out at all."

"You got that one right," Gillespee agreed. "Faughn and Rappapor popped me about half a jump ahead of the stormtroopers. And half a jump behind the workers they sent to turn my land into a crop farm. I'm telling you, that new clone system they've got going is really creepy."

Karrde threw a look at Aves. "How so?"

"What do you mean, how so?" Gillespee retorted. "I don't happen to think people ought to come off an assembly line, thanks. And if they did, I sure as mynocks wouldn't put the Empire in charge of the factory. You should have seen the guys they had manning the roadblocks—put a shiver right straight through you."

"I don't doubt it," Karrde said. "What are your plans after leaving Chazwa?"

"I don't hardly have any plans *before* I get there," Gillespee countered sourly. "I was hoping to get in touch with Brasck's old contact man here, see if they'd be interested in taking us on. Why, you got something better?"

"Possibly. We can start by sending that macrobinocular data card on to my buyer, drawing payment for you against a credit line I have set up with him. After that, I have another project in mind which you might find both interesting—"

"We got company," Aves cut him off. "Two Imperial ships, heading this way. Looks like Lancer-class Frigates."

"Uh-oh," Gillespee muttered. "Maybe we didn't get off Ukio as clean as I thought."

"I think it more likely that we're their target," Karrde said, feeling his lip twist as he keyed an evasion course into the helm. "It's been nice talking to you, Gillespee. If you want to continue the conversation, meet me in eight days at the Trogan system—you know the place."

"I can make it if you can," Gillespee countered. "If you can't, don't make it too easy for them."

Karrde broke the contact. "Hardly," he murmured. "All right; here we go. Nice and easy . . ."

He eased the *Wild Karrde* into a shallow portside drop, trying to make it look as if they were planning to cut past the planet itself and pick up a new hyperspace vector. "Do I alert the others?" Aves asked.

"Not yet," Karrde said, giving his displays a quick look and setting the nav computer to work calculating their jump to lightspeed. "I'd rather abort the mission and try again later than tangle with a pair of Lancers who were serious about fighting."

"Yeah," Aves said slowly. "Karrde . . . they're not changing course."

Karrde looked up. Aves was right: neither Lancer had so much as twitched. They were still heading on their original vector.

Straight for the *Kern's Pride*.

He looked at Aves, to find the other looking back at him. "What do we do?" Aves asked.

Karrde looked back at the Imperial ships. The *Wild Karrde* was a long way from being helpless in a fight, and his people were some of the best. But with weaponry that had been designed to take out enemy starfighters, two Lancers would be better than an even match for the group he'd brought to Chazwa.

As he watched, the *Kern's Pride* suddenly made its move. Rolling into a sort of mutated drop-kick Koiogran maneuver, it took off at high speed at a sharp angle from its original course. The Lancers, not fooled a bit by the ploy, were right behind it.

Which left the *Wild Karrde* completely in the clear. They could continue on to Chazwa, hit the garrison records, and be out before the Lancers could make it back. Fast, clean, and certainly preferable as far as the New Republic was concerned.

But Gillespee was an old acquaintance . . . and on Karrde's scale, a fellow smuggler placed higher than any interstellar government he didn't belong to. "Apparently, Gillespee didn't get off Ukio as cleanly as he thought," he commented, bringing the *Wild Karrde* around and keying for intercom. "Lachton, Chin, Corvis—fire up the turbo-lasers. We're going in."

"What about the other ships?" Aves asked as he activated the deflector shields and punched up a tactical display.

"Let's get the Lancers' attention first," Karrde said. The three men at the turbolasers signaled ready; taking a deep breath, he threw power to the drive.

The Lancers' commander wasn't anyone's fool. Even as the *Wild Karrde* drove toward them, one of the Imperial ships broke off its pursuit of the *Kern's Pride* and turned to confront this new threat. "I think we've got their attention," Aves said tightly. "Can I call the others into the party yet?"

"Go ahead," Karrde told him, keying his own comm for a tight beam to the *Kern's Pride*. "Gillespee, this is Karrde."

"Yeah, I see you," Gillespee came back. "What do you think you're doing?"

"Giving you a hand," Karrde said. Ahead, the Lancer's twenty quad laser batteries opened up, raining green flashes down on the *Wild Karrde*. The turbolasers fired back, their three groups of fire looking rather pathetic in comparison. "All right—we've got this one tied down. Better get out before that other one finds the range."

"*You've* got *him* tied down?" Gillespee retorted. "Look, Karrde—"

"I said get out," Karrde cut him off sharply. "We can't hold him forever. Don't worry about me—I'm not exactly alone out here."

"Here they come," Aves said, and Karrde took a moment to glance into the rear display. They were coming, all right: fifteen freighters strong, all zeroing in on the suddenly outgunned Lancer.

From the comm came an amazed whistle. "You weren't kidding, were you?" Gillespee commented.

"No, I wasn't," Karrde said. "Now get going, will you?"

Gillespee laughed out loud. "I'll let you in on a little secret, Karrde. I'm not alone, either."

And suddenly, barely visible through the haze of laser fire hammering at the *Wild Karrde*'s viewports, the exhaust glows of nearly twenty ships suddenly veered off their individual courses. Sweeping in like hungry Barabel, they converged on the second Lancer.

"So, Karrde," Gillespee continued conversationally. "At a guess, I'd say neither of us is going to get much business done at Chazwa this time around. What say we continue this conversation somewhere else? Say, in eight days?"

Karrde smiled. "I'll look forward to it."

He looked back at the Lancer, and his smile faded. Standard Lancer crew was 850; and from the capable way that one was holding off the rest of the ships, he would guess they were running with full complement. How many of them, he wondered, had been freshly created at Grand Admiral Thrawn's clone factory? "By the way, Gillespee," he added, "if you happen to run into any of our colleagues on the way, you might want to invite them along. I think they'd be interested in what I have to say."

"You got it, Karrde," Gillespee grunted. "See you in eight."

Karrde switched off the comm. So that was it. Gillespee would broadcast the word to the other major smuggling groups; and knowing Gillespee, the open invitation would quickly transmute into something just short of a command appearance. They'd be at Trogan—all of them, or near enough.

Now all he had to figure out was what exactly he was going to say to them.

———

GRAND ADMIRAL THRAWN leaned back in his command chair. "All right, gentlemen," he said, his gaze flicking in turn to each of the fourteen men standing in a loose semicircle around his console. "Are there any questions?"

The slightly rumpled-looking man at one end of the semicircle glanced at the others. "No questions, Admiral," he said, his precise military voice in sharp contrast to his civilian-sloppy appearance. "What's our timetable?"

"Your freighter is being prepped now," Thrawn told him. "You'll leave as soon as it's ready. How soon do you expect to penetrate the Imperial Palace?"

"No sooner than six days from now, sir," the rumpled man said. "I'd like to hit one or two other ports before taking the ship in to Coruscant—their security will be easier to breach if we have a legitimate data trail they can backtrack. Unless you want it done sooner, of course."

Thrawn's glowing eyes narrowed slightly, and Pellaeon could tell what he was thinking. Mara Jade, sitting there in the middle of Rebel headquarters. Perhaps at this very moment giving them the location of the Emperor's storehouse on Wayland . . . "Timing is critical in this operation," Thrawn told the commando leader. "But speed alone is useless if you're compromised before even entering the Palace. You will be the man on the scene, Major Himron. I leave it to your judgment."

The commando leader nodded. "Yes, sir. Thank you, Admiral. We won't fail you."

Thrawn smiled fractionally. "I know you won't, Major. Dismissed."

Silently, the fourteen men turned and filed out of the command room. "You seemed surprised, Captain, at some of my instructions," Thrawn commented as the door slid shut behind them.

"Yes, sir, I was," Pellaeon admitted. "It all made sense, of course," he added hastily. "I simply hadn't thought the operation out to that end point."

"All end points must be prepared for," Thrawn said, keying his board. The lights muted, and on the walls of the command room a sampling of holographic paintings and planics appeared. "Mriss artwork," he identified it for Pellaeon's benefit. "One of the most curious examples of omission to be found anywhere in the civilized galaxy. Until they were contacted by the Tenth Alderaanian Expedition, not a single one of the dozens of Mriss cultures had ever developed any form of three-dimensional artwork."

"Interesting," Pellaeon said dutifully. "Some flaw in their perceptual makeup?"

"Many of the experts still think so," Thrawn said. "It seems clear to me, though, that the oversight was actually a case of cultural blind spots combined with a very subtle but equally strong social harmonization. A combination of traits we'll be able to exploit."

Pellaeon looked at the artwork, his stomach tightening. "We're attacking Mrisst?"

"It's certainly ripe for the taking," Thrawn pointed out. "And a base there would give us the capability to launch attacks into the very heart of the Rebellion."

"Except that the Rebellion must know that," Pellaeon said carefully. If C'baoth's ongoing demands for an attack on Coruscant had finally gotten to the Grand Admiral . . . "They'd launch a massive counterattack, sir, if we so much as made a move toward Mrisst."

"Exactly," Thrawn said, smiling with grim satisfaction. "Which means that when we're finally ready to draw the Coruscant sector fleet into ambush, Mrisst will be the perfect lure to use. If they come out to meet us, we'll defeat them then and there. And if they somehow sense the trap and refuse to engage, we'll have our forward base. Either way, the Empire will triumph."

He reached to his board again, and the holographic art-work faded into a tactical star map. "But that battle is still in the future," he said. "For now, our prime goal is to build a force strong enough to ensure that ultimate victory. And to keep the Rebellion off balance while we do so."

Pellaeon nodded. "The assault on Ord Mantell should go a long way toward accomplishing that."

"It will certainly create a degree of fear in the surrounding systems," Thrawn agreed. "As well as drawing away some of the Rebel pressure on our shipyard supply lines."

"That would be helpful," Pellaeon said with a scowl. "The last report from Bilbringi said the shipyards there were run-ning critically low on Tibanna gas, as well as hfredium and kammris."

"I've already ordered the Bespin garrison to step up their Tibanna gas production," Thrawn said, tapping his control board. "As for the metals, Intelligence recently reported locat-ing a convenient stockpile."

The report came up, and Pellaeon leaned forward to read it. He got as far as the location listing—"*This* is Intelligence's idea of a convenient stockpile?"

"I take it you disagree?" Thrawn asked mildly.

Pellaeon looked at the report again, feeling a grimace set-tling in on his face. The Empire had hit Lando Calrissian's walking mining complex on the superhot plane Nkllon once before, back when they needed mole miners for Thrawn's as-sault on the Sluis Van shipyards. That other raid had cost the Empire over a million man-hours, first in preparing the Star Destroyer *Judicator* for the intense heat at Nkllon's close-orbit distance from its sun, and then for repairing the damage after-ward. "I suppose that depends, sir," he said, "on how long we'll be losing the use of whichever Star Destroyer is detailed to the raid."

"A valid question," Thrawn agreed. "Fortunately, there will be no need this time to tie up any Star Destroyers. Three of our

new Dreadnaughts should be more than adequate to neutralize Nkllon's security."

"But a Dreadnaught won't be able to—ah," Pellaeon interrupted himself as he suddenly understood. "It won't have to be
big enough to survive in open sunlight. If they can take over
one of the shieldships that fly freighters in and out of the inner
system, a Dreadnaught would be small enough to stay behind
its umbrella."

"Exactly," Thrawn nodded. "And capturing one should
pose no problem. For all their impressive size, shieldships are
little more than shielding, coolant systems, and a small container ship's worth of power and crew. Six fully loaded assault
shuttles should make quick work of it."

Pellaeon nodded, still skimming the report. "What happens
if Calrissian sells his stockpiles before the assault force gets
there?"

"He won't," Thrawn assured him. "The market price for
metals has just begun to rise again; and men like Calrissian
always wait for it to go just a little higher."

Unless Calrissian was suddenly overcome with a swell of
patriotic fervor toward his friends back in the New Republic
hierarchy and decided to sell his metals at a reduced price. "I'd
still recommend, sir, that the attack be carried out as soon as
possible."

"Recommendation noted, Captain," Thrawn said, smiling
slightly. "And, as it happens, already acted upon, The raid was
launched ten minutes ago."

Pellaeon smiled tightly. Some day, he decided, he'd learn not
to try to second-guess the Grand Admiral. "Yes, sir."

Thrawn leaned back in his chair. "Return to the bridge,
Captain, and prepare to make the jump to lightspeed. Ord
Mantell is waiting."

CHAPTER 7

THE BEEPING FROM his board prodded Luke out of his light doze. Blinking away the sleep, he gave the displays a quick scan. "Artoo?" he called, stretching as best he could in the tight confines of the cockpit. "We're just about there. Get ready."

A nervous-sounding warble came in acknowledgment. "Come on, Artoo, relax," Luke urged the droid, settling his fingertips around the X-wing's hyperspace lever and letting the Force flow through him. Almost time . . . *now.* He pulled the lever back, and the starlines appeared and collapsed back into stars.

And there, directly ahead, was the Noghri home world of Honoghr.

Artoo gave a soft whistle. "I know," Luke agreed, feeling a little sick himself. Leia had told him what to expect; but even with that warning the sight of the world lying in the X-wing's path was a shock. Beneath the sparse white clouds floating over the surface, the entire planetary landmass was a flat, uniform brown. Kholm-grass, Leia had called it: the local Honoghran plants the Empire had genetically modified to perpetuate their systematic destruction of the planet's ecology. That deceit, combined with first Vader's and later Thrawn's carefully limited aid, had bought the Empire four decades of Noghri service. Even now, squads of Noghri Death Comman-

dos were scattered around the galaxy, fighting and dying for
those whose coldblooded treachery and counterfeit compassion had turned them into slaves.

Artoo warbled something, and Luke broke his gaze away
from the silent monument to Imperial ruthlessness. "I don't
know," he admitted as the droid's question scrolled across his
computer display. "We'd have to get a team of environment
and ecology specialists out here before we could tell. Doesn't
look very hopeful, though, does it?"

The droid chirped—an electronic shrug that turned suddenly into a startled shrill. Luke's head jerked up, just as a
small fast-attack patrol ship shot past overhead. "I think
they've spotted us," he commented as casually as possible.
"Let's hope it's the Noghri and not an Imp—"

"Starfighter, identify yourself," a deep, catlike voice mewed
from the comm.

Luke keyed for transmission, reaching out with the Force
toward the patrol ship that was now curving back into attack
position. Even at this range he should have been able to sense
a human pilot, which meant that it was indeed a Noghri out
there. At least, he hoped so. "This is Luke Skywalker," he said.
"Son of the Lord Darth Vader, brother of Leia Organa Solo."

For a long moment the comm was silent. "Why have you
come?"

Normal prudence, Luke knew, would have suggested that
he not bring up the matter of his power cells until he had a
better idea of how matters stood politically with the Noghri
leaders. But Leia had mentioned several times how impressed
she'd been by the Noghri sense of honor and straightforward
honesty. "My ship's primary power cells have been damaged,"
he told the other. "I thought you might be able to help me."

There was a soft hiss from the comm. "You place us in great
danger, son of Vader," the Noghri said. "Imperial ships come
to Honoghr at random times. If you are sighted, all will suffer."

"I understand," Luke said, a small weight lifting from him.

If the Noghri were worried about him being spotted by Imperials, at least they hadn't completely rejected Leia's invitation to rebel against the Empire. "If you'd prefer, I'll leave."

He held his breath as, behind him, Artoo moaned softly. If the Noghri took him up on his offer, it was questionable as to whether they'd be able to get anywhere else on the power they had left.

Apparently, the Noghri pilot was thinking along the same lines. "The Lady Vader has already risked much on behalf of the Noghri," he said. "We cannot permit you to endanger your life. Follow me, son of Vader. I will bring you to what safety the Noghri can offer."

ACCORDING TO LEIA, there was only a single small area on Honoghr that had been made capable of supporting any plant life other than the Empire's bioengineered *kholm*-grass. Khabarakh and the maitrakh of the clan Kihm'bar had kept her, Chewbacca, and Threepio in one of the villages there, managing with skill and more than a little luck to hide her from prying Imperial eyes. Leia had included the location of the Clean Land along with the coordinates of the system itself . . . and as Luke followed the patrol ship down toward the surface of the planet, it quickly became apparent that they weren't going there.

"Where are we headed?" he asked the Noghri pilot as they dipped beneath a layer of clouds.

"To the future of our world," the alien said.

"Ah," Luke murmured under his breath. A double line of jagged cliffs could be seen ahead, looking a little like stylized dorsal ridges from a pair of Tatooine krayt dragons, "Is your future in those mountains?" he suggested.

There was another soft hiss from the comm. "As the Lady Vader, and the Lord Vader before her," the Noghri said. "You also read the souls of the Noghri."

Luke shrugged. It hadn't been much more than a lucky guess, actually. "Where do we go?"

"Others will show you," the pilot said. "For here I must leave you. Farewell, son of Vader. My family will long cherish the honor of this day." The patrol ship cut sharply upward, heading back toward space—

And in perfect synchronization, two combat-equipped cloudcars rose from seemingly nowhere to settle into flanking positions. "We greet you, son of Vader," a new voice said from the comm. "We are honored to guide you. Follow."

One of the cloudcars moved ahead to take the point, the other dropping back to rearguard position. Luke stayed with the formation, trying to see just where they might be headed. As far as he could tell, the cliffs were as barren as the rest of the planet.

Artoo chirped, and a message scrolled across Luke's display. "A river?" Luke asked, peering out his canopy. "Where—oh, there it is. Emptying out from between the two cliff lines, right?"

The droid beeped an affirmative. It looked to be a pretty fast-moving river, too, Luke decided as they flew closer and he could see the numerous lines of white water indicating submerged rocks. Probably explained why the gorge between the two cliff lines was so sharp and deep.

They reached the end of the cliff lines a few minutes later. The lead cloudcar turned to portside, lifting smoothly over a set of foothills and disappearing around the side of one of the higher crags. Luke followed, smiling tightly as an old memory came to mind. *You're required to maneuver straight down this trench. . . .* Guiding the X-wing around the foothills, he flew into the shadow of the cliffs themselves.

And into an entirely different world. Along the narrow banks of the river the ground was a solid mass of brilliant green.

Artoo whistled in startled amazement. "They're plants,"

Luke said, realizing only after the words were out of his mouth how ridiculous they sounded. Of course they were plants; but to find plants on Honoghr—

"It is the future of our world," one of his escort said, and there was no mistaking the grim pride in his voice. "The future which the Lady Vader gave us. Continue to follow, son of Vader. The landing area is still ahead."

The landing area turned out to be a large, flat-topped boulder jutting partway into the swift-moving river about two kilometers along the gorge. With a cautious eye on the racing water beneath him, Luke eased the X-wing down. Fortunately, it was larger than it had looked from fifty meters up. The cloudcars waited until he had touched down, then swung around and headed back down the gorge. Shutting the X-wings systems back to standby, Luke looked around.

The greenery, he saw now, was not as monochromatic as he'd first thought. There were at least four slightly different shades represented, intermingled in a pattern that was too consistent to be accidental. A pipe could be seen angling down into the river at one point, its other end disappearing up into the plant growth. Utilizing the pressure of the current, he decided, to bring water up over the bank for irrigation. A few meters downstream from the boulder, hidden from view by a rock overhang, he could see a small hutlike building. Two Noghri stood just outside its door: one with steely-gray skin, the other a much darker gray. Even as he watched, they started toward him.

"Looks like the reception committee," Luke commented to Artoo, hitting the switch to pop his canopy. "You stay put here. And I mean *stay put*. You fall in the water like you did that first trip to Dagobah and you'll be lucky if we can even find all the pieces."

There was no need to give the order twice. Artoo warbled a nervous acknowledgment, then an equally nervous question. "Yes, I'm sure they're friendly," Luke assured him, pulling off his flight helmet and getting to his feet. "Don't worry, I won't be going far." Vaulting over the X-wing's side, he headed toward his hosts.

The two Noghri were already at the edge of the landing boulder, standing silently watching him. Luke grimaced to himself as he walked toward them, stretching out with the Force and wishing he were skilled enough to get some reading—any reading—on this species. "In the name of the New Republic, I bring you greetings," he said when he was close enough to be heard over the roar of the river. "I'm Luke Skywalker. Son of the Lord Darth Vader, brother of Leia Organa Solo." He held out his left hand, palm upward, as Leia had instructed him to do.

The older Noghri stepped forward and touched his snout to Luke's palm. The nostrils flattened themselves against his skin, and Luke had to fight to keep from twitching away from the tickling sensation. "I greet you, son of Vader," the alien said, releasing Luke's hand. In unison, both Noghri dropped to their knees, hands splaying out to the sides in the deference gesture Leia had described. "I am Ovkhevam clan Bakh'tor. I serve the Noghri people here at the future of our world. You honor us with your presence."

"I am honored by your hospitality," Luke said as both aliens rose again to their feet. "And your companion is . . . ?"

"I am Khabarakh clan Kihm'bar," the younger Noghri said. "The clan of Vader has now doubly honored me."

"Khabarakh clan Kihm'bar," Luke repeated, eyeing the young alien with new appreciation. So this was the young Noghri commando who had risked everything, first in bringing Leia to his people, then in protecting her from Grand Admiral Thrawn. "For your service to my sister Leia I thank you. My family and I are in your debt."

"The debt is not yours, son of Vader," Ovkhevam said. "The debt rather belongs to the Noghri people. The actions of Khabarakh clan Kihm'bar were only the first line of repayment."

Luke nodded, not really sure of what to say to that. "You

called this place the future of your world?" he asked, hoping to change the subject.

"It is the future given to the Noghri people by the Lady Vader," Ovkhevam said, waving his hands in a circular gesture that took in the entire valley. "Here with her gift we cleansed the land of the Empire's poisoned plants. Here will someday be enough food to provide for all."

"It's impressive," Luke said, and meant it. Out in the open, all that greenery would have stood out against the background *kholm*-grass like a bantha at a Jawa family gathering. But here, with the twin cliff lines blocking the view from everywhere except more or less straight up, there was a good chance incoming Imperial ships would never even suspect its existence. The river supplied ample water, the lower latitude implied a slightly longer growing season than that at the Clean Land itself; and if worse came to worst, a number of properly placed explosives could dam the river or bring down part of the cliffs themselves, burying the evidence of their quiet rebellion against the Empire.

And the Noghri had had barely a month to plan, design, and build it all. No wonder Thrawn and Vader before him had found the Noghri to be such useful servants.

"It was the Lady Vader who made it possible," Ovkhevam said. "We have little to offer in the way of hospitality, son of Vader. But what we have is yours."

"Thank you," Luke nodded. "But as your patrol ship pilot pointed out, my presence on Honoghr is a danger to you. If you can provide my ship with replacement power cells, I'll be on my way as quickly as I can. I would pay, of course."

"We could accept no payment from the son of Vader," Ovkhevam said, looking shocked at the very idea. "It would be merely a single line of the debt owed by the Noghri people."

"I understand," Luke said, stifling a sigh. They meant well, certainly, but all this guilt about their service to the Empire was going to have to stop. Races and beings far more sophisticated than they were had been equally taken in by the Emperor's deceits. "I suppose the first step is to find out whether you have spares that'll fit my ship. How do we go about doing that?"

"It is already done," Khabarakh said. "The cloudcars will carry word of your need to the spaceport at Nystao. The power cells and technicians to install them will be here by nightfall."

"Meanwhile, we offer you our hospitality," Ovkhevam added, throwing a sideways look at Khabarakh. Perhaps feeling the younger Noghri should let his elder do the talking.

"I'd be honored," Luke said. "Lead the way."

The hut under the cliff overhang was as small as it had looked from the landing boulder. Most of the available space was taken up by two narrow cots, a low table, and what appeared to be the food storage/preparation module from a small spaceship. But at least it was quieter than outside.

"This will be your home while you are on Honoghr," Ovkhevam told him. "Khabarakh and I will stand guard outside. To protect you with our lives."

"That won't be necessary," Luke assured them, looking around the room. Clearly, it had been set up for long-term occupancy. "What do you two do here, if I may ask?"

"I am caretaker to this place," Ovkhevam said. "I walk the land, to see that the plants are growing properly. Khabarakh clan Kihm'bar—" He looked at the younger alien, and Luke got the distinct impression of a grim humor in the glance. "Khabarakh clan Kihm'bar is a fugitive from the Noghri people. Even now we have many ships searching for him."

"Of course," Luke said dryly. With Grand Admiral Thrawn threatening to subject Khabarakh to a complete Imperial interrogation, it had been vital that the young commando "escape" from custody and drop out of sight. It was equally vital that knowledge of the Empire's betrayal be passed on to the Noghri commando teams scattered around the galaxy. The two objectives dovetailed rather nicely.

"Do you require food?" Ovkhevam asked. "Or rest?"

"I'm fine, thank you," Luke said. "I think the best thing

would probably be for me to go back to my ship and start pulling those power cells out."

"May I assist?" Khabarakh asked.

"I'd appreciate that, yes," Luke said. He didn't need any help, but the sooner the Noghri worked out this supposed debt of theirs, the better. "Come on—tool kit's in the ship."

"THERE IS FURTHER word from Nystao," Khabarakh said, moving invisibly through the darkness to where Luke sat with his back against the X-wing's landing skid. "The captain of the Imperial ship has decided to complete minor repairs here. He expects the work to take two days." He hesitated. "To you, son of Vader, the dynasts express their apologies."

"No apology necessary," Luke assured him, looking up past the shadow of the starfighter's wing at the thin band of stars shining down amid the otherwise total blackness. So that was that. He was stuck here for two more days. "I knew when I came here that this might happen. I'm just sorry I have to impose further on you."

"Your presence is not an imposition."

"I appreciate the hospitality." Luke nodded toward the stars overhead. "I take it there's still no indication they might have spotted my ship?"

"Would the son of Vader not know if that happened?" Khabarakh countered.

Luke smiled in the darkness. "Even Jedi have limitations, Khabarakh. Distant danger is very hard to detect."

And yet, he reminded himself silently, the Force was obviously still with him. That Strike Cruiser up there could easily have turned up at a far more awkward time—say, while the Noghri tech team had been in transit to or from the valley, or even while Luke himself was heading out to space. An alert captain could have picked up on either, and brought the whole thing crashing down right there.

There was a whisper of movement, felt rather than heard

over the sound of the river, as Khabarakh sat down beside him. "It is not enough, is it?" the Noghri asked quietly. "This place. The dynasts call it our future. But it is not."

Luke shook his head. "No," he had to admit. "You've done a tremendous job with this place, and it'll certainly help you feed your people. But the future of Honoghr itself . . . I'm not an expert, Khabarakh. But from what I've seen here, I don't think Honoghr can be saved."

The Noghri hissed between his needle teeth, the sound barely audible over the racing water below. "You speak the thought of many of the Noghri people," he said. "Perhaps none really believe otherwise."

"We can help you find a new home," Luke promised. "There are many worlds in the galaxy. We'll find you a place where you can begin again."

Khabarakh hissed again. "But it will not be Honoghr."

Luke swallowed hard. "No."

For a minute neither spoke. Luke listened to the sounds of the river, his heart aching with sympathy for the Noghri. But what had been done to Honoghr was far beyond his power to change. The Jedi, indeed, had their limitations.

There was another ripple of air as Khabarakh climbed back to his feet. "Are you hungry?" he asked Luke. "If so, I can bring food."

"Yes, thank you," Luke said.

The Noghri left. Stifling a sigh, Luke shifted position against the landing skid. It was bad enough knowing there was a problem he was helpless to solve; to have to sit here for two days with the whole thing staring him accusingly in the face only made it worse.

He looked up at the thin trail of stars, wondering what Leia had thought of the whole situation. Had she, too, realized that Honoghr was too far gone to save? Or could she have had some idea of how to bring it back?

Or had she been too busy with the immediate concerns of survival to even think that far ahead?

He grimaced as another small pang of guilt tugged at him. Somewhere out there, on Coruscant, his sister was about to give birth to her twins. Might have already done so, for all he knew. Han was with her, of course, but he'd wanted to be there, too.

But if he couldn't be there in person . . .

Taking a deep breath, he allowed his body to relax. Once before, on Dagobah, he'd been able to reach out to the future. To see his friends, and the path they were on. Then, he'd had Yoda to guide him . . . but if he could find the proper pattern on his own, he might be able to catch a glimpse of his niece and nephew. Carefully, keeping his thoughts and will focused, he stretched out through the Force. . . .

Leia was crouching in the darkness, her blaster and lightsaber in her hands, her heart racing with fear and determination. Behind her was Winter, holding tightly to two small lives, helpless and fragile. A voice—Han's—filled with anger and the same determination. Chewbacca was somewhere nearby— somewhere overhead, he thought—and Lando was with him. Before them were shadowy figures, their minds filled with menace and a cold and deadly purpose. A blaster fired—and another—a door burst open—

"Leia!" Luke blurted, his body jerking violently as the trance broke like a bubble, one final image flickering and vanishing into the Honoghr night. A faceless person, moving toward his sister and her children from behind the shadowy evil. A person edged with the power of the Force . . .

"What is it?" a Noghri voice snapped beside him.

Luke opened his eyes to find Khabarakh and Ovkhevam crouching in front of him, a small glow rod bathing their nightmare faces in dim light. "I saw Leia," he told them, hearing the trembling of reaction in his voice. "She and her children were in danger." He took a shuddering breath, purging the adrenaline from his body. "I have to get back to Coruscant."

Ovkhevam and Khabarakh exchanged glances. "But if the danger is now . . . ?" Ovkhevam said.

"It wasn't now," Luke shook his head. "It was the future. I don't know how far ahead."

Khabarakh touched Ovkhevam's shoulder, and for a minute the Noghri conversed quietly in their own language. *All right*, Luke told himself, running through the Jedi calming techniques. *All right* Lando had been in the vision—he distinctly remembered seeing Lando there. But Lando, as far as he knew, was still out at his Nomad City mining operation on Nkllon. Which meant Luke still had time to get back to Coruscant before the attack on Leia could happen.

Or did it? Was the vision a true image of the future? Or could a change in events alter what he'd seen? *Difficult to see*, Master Yoda had said of Luke's vision on Dagobah. *Always in motion is the future.* And if someone of Yoda's depth of knowledge in the Force had been unable to sift through the uncertainties . . .

"If you wish it, son of Vader, the commandos will seize the Imperial ship," Ovkhevam said. "If its people were destroyed quickly, there would be no word from it that would point blame at the Noghri."

"I can't let you do that," Luke shook his head. "It's too dangerous. There's no way to guarantee they wouldn't get a message off."

Ovkhevam drew himself up. "If the Lady Vader is in danger, the Noghri people are willing to take that risk."

Luke looked up at them, an odd sensation rippling through him. Those nightmare Noghri faces hadn't changed; but in the space of a heartbeat, Luke's perception of them had. No longer were they just another abstract set of alien features. Suddenly, they had become the faces of friends.

"The last time I had a vision like this, I rushed off without thinking to try to help," he told them quietly. "Not only didn't I help them any, but I also nearly cost them their own chance at escape." He looked down at his artificial right hand. Feeling again the ghostly memory of Vader's lightsaber slicing through his wrist . . . "And lost other things, too."

He looked back up at them. "I won't make that same mistake again. Not with the lives of the Noghri people at stake. I'll wait until the Imperial ship is gone."

Khabarakh reached out to gently touch his shoulder. "Do not be concerned for their safety, son of Vader," he said. "The Lady Vader will not easily be defeated. Not with the Wookiee Chewbacca at her side."

Luke looked up at the stars overhead. No, with Han and Chewie and the whole of Palace security beside her, Leia should be able to handle any normal intruders.

But there was that final unformed image. The person who he'd sensed drawing on the Force . . .

On Jomark, the Jedi Master C'baoth had made it abundantly clear that he wanted Leia and her children. Could he want them badly enough to personally go to Coruscant for them?

"They will prevail," Khabarakh repeated.

With an effort, Luke nodded. "I know," he said, trying to sound like he meant it. There was no sense in all of them worrying.

THE LAST OF THE FIRES were out, the last of the microfractures sealed, the last of the injured taken to sick bay . . . and with an odd mixture of resignation and cold-blooded fury, Lando Calrissian gazed out his private command room window and knew that it was over. Cloud City on Bespin; and now Nomad City on Nkllon. For the second time, the Empire had taken something he'd worked to create—had worked and sweated and connived to build—and had turned it into ashes.

From his desk console came a beep. Stepping over to it, he leaned down and touched the comm switch. "Calrissian," he said, wiping his other hand across his forehead.

"Sir, this is Bagitt in Engine Central," a tired voice came. "The last drive motivator just went."

Lando grimaced; but after all the damage those TIE fighters had inflicted on his walking mining operation, it didn't exactly come as a surprise. "Any chance of fixing enough of them to get us moving again?" he asked.

"Not without a frigate's worth of spare parts," Bagitt said. "Sorry, sir, but there are just too many things broken or fused."

"Understood. In that case, you'd better have your people concentrate on keeping life support going."

"Yes, sir. Uh . . . sir, there's a rumor going around that we've lost all long-range communications."

"It's only temporary," Lando assured him. "We've got people working on it right now. And enough spare parts to build two new transmitters."

"Yes, sir," Bagitt said, sounding a shade less discouraged. "Well . . . I guess I'll get over to life support."

"Keep me informed," Lando told him.

Switching off the comm, he walked back to the window. Twenty days, they had; just twenty days before Nkllon's slow rotation took them from the center of the night side across into full sunlight. At which point it wouldn't much matter whether or not the drive motivators, communication gear, or even life support were working. When the sun began its slow crawl up the horizon over there, everyone still left in Nomad City would be on their way to a very fast and very warm death.

Twenty days.

Lando gazed out the viewport at the night sky, letting his eyes flick across the constellation patterns he'd dreamed up in his occasional idle moments. If they could get the long-range transmitter fixed in the next day or so, they should be able to call Coruscant for help. No matter what the Imperial attack force might have done to the shield-ships at the outer system depot, the New Republic's spaceship techs ought to be able to get one of them flying again, at least well enough for one last trip into the inner system. It would be tight, but with any luck at all—

Abruptly, his train of thought broke off. There, just shy of directly overhead, the brilliant star of an approaching shield-ship had appeared.

Reflexively, he took a step toward his desk to sound battle stations. If that was the Imperials again, come to finish the job . . .

He stopped. No. If it was the Imperials, then that was that. He had no more fighters left to send against them, and no defenses remaining on Nomad City itself. There was no point in stirring up the rest of his people for nothing.

And then, from the desk came the screeching static of a comm override signal. "Nomad City, this is General Bel Iblis," a well-remembered voice boomed out. "Can anyone hear me?"

Lando dived for the desk. "This is Lando Calrissian, General," he said, striving for as much nonchalance as he could muster. "Is that you out there?"

"That's us," Bel Iblis acknowledged. "We were out at Qat Chrystac when we picked up your distress signal. I'm sorry we couldn't get here in time."

"So am I," Lando said. "What's it look like at the shieldship depot?"

"Afraid it's something of a mess," Bel Iblis said. "These shieldships of yours are too big to easily destroy, but the Imperials took a crack at it just the same. At the moment this one seems to be the only one in any shape to fly."

"Well, it's all pretty academic, anyway," Lando said. "Nomad City is done for."

"No way to get it moving again?"

"Not in the twenty days we've got before the dawn line catches up with us," Lando told him. "We might be able to dig it underground deep enough to last out a trip around the day side, but we'd need heavy equipment that we haven't got."

"Maybe we can pull it off Nkllon entirely and take it to the outer system for repairs," Bel Iblis suggested. "An Assault Frigate and a couple of heavy lifters should do the trick if we can get another shieldship flying."

"And can convince Admiral Ackbar to divert an Assault Frigate from the battle planes," Lando reminded him.

"Point," Bel Iblis admitted. "I suppose I should hear the rest of the bad news. What all did the Empire get?"

Lando sighed. "Everything," he said. "All our stockpiles. Hfredium, kammris, dolovite—you name it. If we mined it, they got it."

"How much in all?"

"About four months' worth. A little over three million at current market prices."

For a moment Bel Iblis was silent. "I didn't realize this place was that productive. Makes it all the more imperative that we persuade Coruscant to help get you up and running again. How many people do you have down there?"

"Just under five thousand," Lando told him. "Some of them are in pretty bad shape, though."

"I've had plenty of experience moving injured people," Bel Iblis said grimly. "Don't worry, we'll get them aboard. I'd like you to detail a group to stay behind and get the shieldships operational. We'll transport everyone else to Qat Chrystac. Be as good a place as any for you to transmit a formal request for assistance to Coruscant."

"I didn't think there *were* any good places to transmit requests from," Lando growled.

"They've got a lot on their minds back there," Bel Iblis agreed. "For what it's worth, I'd say you've got a better-than-average chance that yours won't get lost in the shuffle."

Lando chewed at his lip. "So let's skip the shuffle entirely. Take me to Coruscant and let me talk to them in person."

"That'll cost you an extra five days in travel time," Bel Iblis pointed out. "Can you afford it?"

"Better five days spent that way than sitting around Qat Chrystac wondering if my transmission has even gotten out of the communications center yet," Lando countered. "Figure five days to Coruscant, another day or two to talk Leia into reassigning a ship and lifters, and then ten more to get them here and finish the job."

"Seventeen days. Cuts it pretty close."

"I don't have any better ideas. What do you say?"

Bel Iblis snorted gently. "Well, I'd been planning to head over to Coruscant soon anyway. Might as well be now."

"Thank you, General," Lando said.

"No problem. Better start getting your people ready—we'll be launching our shuttles as soon as we're in the planetary umbra."

"Right. See you soon."

Lando switched off the comm. It was a long shot, all right—he knew that much going in. But realistically, it was the only shot he had. And besides, even if they turned him down flat, a trip to Coruscant right now wouldn't be such a bad idea. He'd get to see Leia and Han and the brand-new twins, maybe even run into Luke or Wedge.

He glanced out the viewport, his lip twisting. And on Coruscant, at least he wouldn't have to worry about Imperial attacks.

Keying the intercom, he began issuing the evacuation orders.

CHAPTER 8

JACEN HAD FALLEN asleep midway through his dinner, but Jaina was still going at it. Lying on her side, Leia shifted position as much as she could on the bed without pulling out of her daughter's reach and picked up her data pad again. By her own slightly fuzzy count, she'd tried at least four times to get through this page. "Fifth time's the charm," she commented wryly to Jaina, stroking her daughter's head with her free hand.

Jaina, with more immediate things on her mind, didn't respond. For a moment Leia gazed down at her daughter, a fresh surge of wonder rippling upward through her weariness. Those tiny hands that flailed gently and randomly against her body; the skullcap of short black hairs covering her head; that small face with its wonderfully earnest expression of infant concentration as she worked at eating. A brand-new life, so fragile and yet so remarkably resilient.

And she and Han had created it. Had created both of them.

Across the room, the door from the living areas of their suite opened. "Hi, sweetheart," Han called quietly. "Everything all right?"

"Fine," she murmured back. "We're just having another dinner."

"They eat like starving Wookiees," Han said, crossing to

the bed and giving the situation a quick scan. "Jacen done already?"

"Just wanted a snack, I guess," Leia said, craning her neck to look at the sleeping baby lying on the bed behind her. "He'll probably want the second course in an hour or so."

"I wish they'd get together on scheduling," Han said, sitting carefully down on the side of the bed and easing the tip of his forefinger into Jacen's palm. The tiny hand curled reflexively around his finger, and Leia looked up at her husband in time to see his familiar lopsided grin. "He's going to be a strong one."

"You should feel the grip at this end," Leia told him, looking back at Jaina. "Is Lando still downstairs?"

"Yeah, he and Bel Iblis are still talking to Admiral Drayson," Han said, reaching over to rest his free hand on Leia's shoulder. The warmth felt good through her thin dressing gown. Almost as good as the warmth of his thoughts against her mind. "Still trying to convince him to divert a couple of ships to Nkllon."

"How does it look?"

Han wiggled his finger gently in Jacen's grip, clucking softly at his sleeping son. "Not too good," he admitted. "We're not going to get Nomad City off the ground without something the size of an Assault Frigate. Drayson isn't exactly eager to pull anything that big off the line."

"Did you point out how much we need the metals Lando's been mining there?"

"I mentioned it. He wasn't impressed."

"You have to know how to talk to Drayson." Leia looked down at Jaina. She was still going at it, but her eyes were beginning to drift closed. "Maybe when Jaina's asleep I can go downstairs and give Lando a hand."

"Right," Han said dryly. "No offense, sweetheart, but falling asleep on the table's not going to impress anyone."

Leia made a face at him. "I'm not *that* tired, thank you. And I'm certainly getting as much sleep as you are."

"Not even close," Han said, shifting his hand from Leia's shoulder to stroke Jaina's cheek. "I get to doze in the middle of those late-night feedings."

"You shouldn't be waking up for them at all," Leia said. "Winter or I could get the babies out of their crib just as well as you can."

"Nice," Han said in mock indignation. "You know, you thought I was pretty handy to have around before the kids showed up. Now you don't need me anymore, huh? Just go ahead and toss me aside."

"Of course I need you," Leia soothed him. "As long as most of the droids are out on defense duty and there are two babies who have to be changed, you'll always have a place here."

"Oh, great," Han growled. "I think I'd rather get tossed aside."

"It's way too late for that," Leia assured him, stroking his hand and turning serious again. "I know you want to help, Han, and I really do appreciate it. I just feel guilty."

"Well, don't," Han told her, taking her hand and squeezing it. "We old-time smugglers are used to strange hours, remember." He glanced over at the door to Winter's room. "Winter gone to bed already?"

"No, she hasn't come back up yet," Leia said, stretching her mind toward the room. As near as she could tell, it was indeed empty. "She's got some project of her own going downstairs— I don't know what."

"I do," Han said, his sense turning thoughtful. "She's been down in the library sifting through the old Alliance archives."

Leia craned her neck to study his face. "Trouble?"

"I don't know," Han said slowly. "Winter doesn't talk much about what she's thinking. Not to me, anyway. But she's worried about something."

Beyond the door, Leia caught the flicker of another presence. "She's back," she told Han. "I'll see if I can get her to tell me about it."

"Good luck," Han grunted, giving Leia's hand one last

squeeze and standing up. "I guess I'll go back downstairs. See if I can help Lando sweet-talk Drayson a little."

"The two of you ought to get him into a sabacc game," Leia suggested. "Play for ships, like you and Lando did with the *Falcon*. Maybe you can win an Assault Frigate."

"What, playing against Drayson?" Han said with a snort. "Thanks, hon, but Lando and I wouldn't know what to do with a fleet of our own. I'll see you later."

"Okay. I love you, Han."

He gave her another lopsided smile. "I know," he said, and left. With a sigh, Leia adjusted her shoulder against the pillow and half turned toward Winter's room. "Winter?" she called softly.

There was a short pause; then the door swung quietly open. "Yes, Your Highness?" Winter asked, stepping into the room.

"I'd like to talk to you for a minute, if it's convenient," Leia said.

"Of course," Winter said, gliding forward in that wonderfully graceful way of hers that Leia had always envied. "I think Jacen's asleep. Shall I put him in the crib?"

"Please," Leia nodded. "Han tells me you've been doing some research in the old Alliance archives."

Winter's face didn't change, but Leia could sense the subtle change in her sense and body language. "Yes."

"May I ask why?"

Carefully, Winter lifted Jacen from the bed and carried him toward the crib. "I think I may have discovered an Imperial agent in the Palace," she said. "I was trying to confirm that."

Leia felt the hairs on the back of her neck stand up. "Who is it?"

"I'd really rather not make any accusations before I have more information," Winter said. "I could easily be wrong."

"I appreciate your scruples," Leia said. "But if you have an idea about this Delta Source information leak, we need to know about it right away."

"This isn't connected with Delta Source," Winter said,

shaking her head. "At least, not directly. She hasn't been here long enough for that."

Leia frowned at her, trying to read her sense. There was a great deal of worry there, running squarely into an equally strong desire not to throw around hasty allegations. "Is it Mara Jade?" she asked.

Winter hesitated. "Yes. But again, I don't have any proof."

"What *do* you have?"

"Not very much," Winter said, tucking the blanket carefully around Jacen. "Really only a short conversation with her when I was escorting her up from the medical section. She asked me what I did during the height of the Rebellion, and I told her about my job with Supply and Procurement. She then identified me as Targeter."

Leia thought back. Winter had had so many code names during that time. "Was that incorrect?"

"No, I had that name for a short time," Winter said. "Which is the point, really. I was only known as Targeter for a few weeks on Averam. Before Imperial Intelligence broke the cell there."

"I see," Leia said slowly. "And Mara wasn't with the Averists?"

"I don't know," Winter said, shaking her head. "I never met more than a few of that group. That's why I've been searching the records. I thought there might be a complete listing somewhere."

"I doubt it," Leia said. "Local cells like that almost never kept personnel files. It would be a group death warrant if it fell into Imperial hands."

"I know." Winter looked across the crib at her. "Which rather leaves us at an impasse."

"Perhaps," Leia said, gazing past Winter and trying to pull together everything she knew about Mara. It wasn't all that much. As far as she knew, Mara had never claimed any past Alliance affiliation, which would tend to support Winter's suspicions. On the other hand, it had been less than two months since she'd enlisted Luke to help her free Karrde from a detention cell on Grand Admiral Thrawn's own flagship. That didn't make much sense if she was an Imperial agent herself. "I think," she told Winter slowly, "that whatever side Mara was once on, she's not there anymore. Any loyalty she has now is probably to Karrde and his people."

Winter smiled faintly. "Is that Jedi insight, Your Highness? Or just your trained diplomatic opinion?"

"Some of each," Leia said. "I don't think we have anything to fear from her."

"I hope you're right." Winter gestured. "Shall I put Jaina to bed now?"

Leia looked down. Jaina's eyes were closed tightly, her tiny mouth making soft sucking motions at the empty air. "Yes, thank you," she said, giving her daughter's cheek one final caress. "Is that reception for the Sarkan delegation still going on downstairs?" she asked as she rolled away from Jaina and stretched cramped muscles.

"It was when I passed by," Winter said, picking Jaina up and setting her in the crib next to Jacen. "Mon Mothma asked me to suggest you drop in for a few minutes if you had the chance."

"Yes, I'll bet she did," Leia said, getting off the bed and crossing to the wardrobe. One of the little side benefits of having twin infants on her hands was that she finally had an armor-plated excuse for getting out of these superficial government functions that always seemed to take up more time than they were worth. Now here was Mon Mothma, trying to chicane her back into that whole crazy runaround again. "And I'm sorry to have to disappoint her," she added. "But I'm afraid I have something more urgent to do right now. Will you watch the twins for me?"

"Certainly," Winter said. "May I ask where you'll be?"

From the wardrobe Leia selected something more suitable for public wear than her dressing gown and started to change.

"I'm going to see what I can find out about Mara Jade's past," she said.

She could sense Winter's frown all the way across the room. "May I ask how?"

Leia smiled tightly. "I'm going to ask her."

HE STOOD BEFORE HER, his face half hidden by the cowl of his robe, his yellow eyes piercingly bright as they gazed across the infinite distance between them. His lips moved, but his words were drowned out by the throaty hooting of alarms all around them, filling Mara with an urgency that was rapidly edging into panic. Between her and the Emperor two figures appeared: the dark, imposing image of Darth Vader, and the smaller black-clad figure of Luke Skywalker. They stood before the Emperor, facing each other, and ignited their lightsabers. The blades crossed, brilliant red-white against brilliant green-white, and they prepared for battle.

And then, without warning, the blades disengaged . . . and with twin roars of hatred audible even over the alarms, both turned and strode toward the Emperor.

Mara heard herself cry out as she struggled to rush to her master's aid. But the distance was too great, her body too sluggish. She screamed a challenge, trying to at least distract them. But neither Vader nor Skywalker seemed to hear her. They moved outward to flank the Emperor . . . and as they lifted their lightsabers high, she saw that the Emperor was gazing at her.

She looked back at him, wanting desperately to turn away from the coming disaster but unable to move. A thousand thoughts and emotions flooded in through that gaze, a glittering kaleidoscope of pain and fear and rage that spun far too fast for her to really absorb. The Emperor raised his hands, sending cascades of jagged blue-white lightning at his enemies. Both men staggered under the counterattack, and

Mara watched with the sudden agonized hope that this time it might end differently. But no. Vader and Skywalker straightened, and with another roar of rage, they lifted their lightsabers high.

And then, over the raised lightsabers came a roll of distant thunder—

And with a jerk that nearly threw her out of her chair Mara snapped out of the dream.

She took a deep, shuddering breath against the flood of post-dream emotion; against the turmoil of pain, anger, and loneliness. But this time she wasn't going to have the luxury of working her way through the tangle in solitude. From outside her room she could vaguely sense another presence; and even as she rolled out of the desk chair into a reflexive combat crouch, the roll of thunder from her dream—a quiet knock—was repeated.

For a long moment she considered keeping quiet and seeing if whoever it was would decide the room was empty and go away. But the light from her room, she knew, would be visible beneath the old-style hinged door. And if the person out there was who she suspected, he wouldn't be fooled by silence, anyway. "Come in," she called.

The door unlocked and swung open . . . but it wasn't Luke Skywalker who stood there. "Hello, Mara," Leia Organa Solo nodded to her. "Am I interrupting anything?"

"Not at all," Mara said politely, suppressing a grimace. The last thing she wanted right now was company, particularly company that was in any way associated with Skywalker. But as long as she and Ghent were still stuck here it wouldn't be smart to deliberately alienate someone of Organa Solo's influence. "I was just reading some of the news reports from the battle regions. Please come in."

"Thank you," Organa Solo said, stepping past her into the suite. "I was looking over those same reports a little while ago. Grand Admiral Thrawn is certainly justifying the late Emperor's confidence in his ability."

Mara threw her a sharp look, wondering what Skywalker had told her. But Organa Solo's eyes were turned toward the window and the lights of the Imperial City below. And what little Mara could discern of the other woman's sense didn't seem to be taunting. "Yes, Thrawn was one of the best," she said. "Brilliant and innovative, with an almost compulsive thirst for victory."

"Perhaps he needed to prove he was the equal of the other Grand Admirals," Organa Solo suggested. "Particularly given his mixed heritage and the Emperor's feelings toward non-humans."

"I'm sure that was part of it," Mara said.

Organa Solo took another step toward the window, her back still turned to Mara. "Did you know the Grand Admiral well?" she asked.

"Not really," Mara said cautiously. "He communicated with Karrde a few times when I was there and visited our Myrkr base once. He had a big business going in Myrkr ysalamiri for a while—Karrde once figured they'd hauled five or six thousand of them out of there—"

"I meant, did you know him during the war," Organa Solo said, turning finally to face her.

Mara returned her gaze steadily. If Skywalker had told her . . . but if he'd told her, why wasn't Mara in a detention cell somewhere? No; Organa Solo had to be on a fishing expedition. "Why should I have known Thrawn during the war?" she countered.

Organa Solo shrugged fractionally. "There's been a suggestion made that you might once have served with the Empire."

"And you wanted to make sure before you locked me up?"

"I wanted to see if you might have knowledge about the Grand Admiral we could use against him," Organa Solo corrected.

Mara snorted. "There isn't anything," she said. "Not with Thrawn. He has no patterns; no favorite strategies; no discernible weaknesses. He studies his enemies and tailors his attacks against psychological blind spots. He doesn't overcommit his forces, and he's not too proud to back off when it's clear he's losing. Which doesn't happen very often. As you're finding out." She cocked an eyebrow. "Any of that help you?" she added sarcastically.

"Actually, it does," Organa Solo said. "If we can identify the weaknesses he's planning to exploit, we might be able to anticipate the thrust of his attack."

"That's not going to be easy," Mara warned.

Organa Solo smiled faintly. "No, but it gives us a place to start. Thank you for your help."

"You're welcome," Mara said, the words coming out automatically. "Was there anything else?"

"No, I don't think so," Organa Solo said, stepping away from the window and heading for the door. "I need to get back and get some sleep before the twins wake up again. And you'll probably want to be going to bed soon, too."

"And I'm still free to move around the Palace?"

Organa Solo smiled again. "Of course. Whatever you did in the past, it's clear you're not serving with the Empire now. Good night." She turned to the door, reached for the handle—

"I'm going to kill your brother," Mara told her. "Did he tell you that?"

Organa Solo stiffened, just noticeably, and Mara could sense the ripple of shock run through that Jedi-trained calmness. Her hand, on the door handle, dropped back to her side. "No, he didn't," she said, her back still to Mara. "May I ask why?"

"He destroyed my life," Mara told her, feeling the old ache deep in her throat and wondering why she was even telling Organa Solo this. "You're wrong; I didn't just serve with the Empire. I was a personal agent of the Emperor himself. He brought me here to Coruscant and the Imperial Palace and trained me to be an extension of his will across the galaxy. I could hear his voice from anywhere in the Empire, and knew how to give his orders to anyone from a stormtrooper brigade all the way up to a Grand Moff. I had authority and power and a purpose in life. They knew me as the Emperor's Hand, and they respected me the same way they did him. Your brother took all that away from me."

Organa Solo turned back to face her. "I'm sorry," she said. "But there was no other choice. The lives and freedom of billions of beings——"

"I'm not going to debate the issue with you," Mara cut her off. "You couldn't possibly understand what I've been through."

A shadow of distant pain crossed Organa Solo's face. "You're wrong," she said quietly. "I understand very well."

Mara glared at her; but it was a glare without any real force of hatred behind it. Leia Organa Solo of Alderaan, who'd been forced to watch as the first Death Star obliterated her entire world . . . "At least you had a life to go to afterward," she growled at last. "You had the whole Rebellion—more friends and allies than you could even count. I had no one."

"It must have been hard."

"I survived it," Mara said briefly. "So *now* are you going to have me hauled off to detention?"

Those Alderaanian-cultured eyebrows lifted slightly. "You keep suggesting that I should have you locked up. Is that what you want?"

"I already told you what I want. I want to kill your brother."

"Do you?" Organa Solo asked. "Do you really?"

Mara smiled thinly. "Bring him here and I'll prove it."

Organa Solo studied her face, and Mara could feel the tenuous touch of her rudimentary Jedi senses as well. "From what Luke's told me, it sounds like you've already had several chances to kill him," Organa Solo pointed out. "You didn't take them."

"It wasn't from lack of intent," Mara said. But it was a thought that had been gnawing at her as well. "I just keep getting into situations where I need him alive. But that'll change."

"Perhaps," Organa Solo said, her eyes still moving across

Mara's face. "Or perhaps it's not really you who wants him dead."

Mara frowned. "What's *that* supposed to mean?"

Organa Solo's gaze drifted away from Mara to the window, and Mara could feel a tightening of the other woman's sense. "I was at Endor a couple of months ago," she said.

An icy sensation crawled up Mara's spine. She'd been at Endor, too, taken there to face Grand Admiral Thrawn . . . and she remembered what the space around the world of the Emperor's death had felt like. "And?" she prompted. Even to herself, her voice sounded strained.

Organa Solo heard it, too. "You know what I'm talking about, don't you?" she asked, her eyes still on the lights of the Imperial City. "There's some shadow of the Emperor's presence still there. Some of that final surge of hatred and anger. Like a—I don't know what."

"Like an emotional bloodstain," Mara said quietly, the image springing spontaneously and vividly into her mind. "Marking the spot where he died."

She looked at Organa Solo, to find the other woman's eyes on her. "Yes," Organa Solo said. "That's exactly what it was like."

Mara took a deep breath, forcing the black chill from her mind. "So what does that have to do with me?"

Organa Solo studied her. "I think you know."

YOU WILL KILL LUKE SKYWALKER. "No," Mara said, her mouth suddenly dry. "You're wrong."

"Am I?" Organa Solo asked softly. "You said you could hear the Emperor's voice from anywhere in the galaxy."

"I could hear his *voice*," Mara snapped. "Nothing more."

Organa Solo shrugged slightly. "You know best, of course. It might still be worth thinking about."

"I'll do that," Mara said stiffly. "If that's all, you can go."

Organa Solo nodded, her sense showing no irritation at being dismissed like some minor underling. "Thank you for your assistance," she said. "I'll talk with you later."

With a final smile, she pulled the door open and left. "Don't count on it," Mara muttered after her, turning back to the desk and dropping into the chair. This had gone far enough. If Karrde was too preoccupied with business to get in touch with his contact man, then the contact man himself was going to get her and Ghent out of here. Pulling up her code file, she keyed for long-range comm access.

The response was prompt, UNABLE TO ACCESS, the words scrolled across her display. LONG-RANGE COMMUNICATIONS SYSTEM TEMPORARILY DOWN.

"Terrific," she growled under her breath. "How soon till it's back up?"

UNABLE TO DETERMINE. REPEATING, LONG-RANGE COMMUNICATIONS SYSTEM TEMPORARILY DOWN.

With a curse, she shut the terminal off. The whole universe seemed to be against her tonight. She picked up the data pad she'd been reading earlier, put it down again, and stood back up. It was late, she'd already fallen asleep once at her desk, and if she had any sense she would just give it up and go to bed.

Stepping across to the window, she leaned against the carved wooden frame and gazed out at the city lights stretching halfway to infinity. And tried to think.

No. It was impossible. Impossible, absurd, and unthinkable. Organa Solo could waste as much breath as she wanted spinning these clever speculations of hers. After five years of living with this thing, Mara ought to know her own thoughts and feelings. Ought to know what was real, and what wasn't.

And yet . . .

The image of the dream rose up before her. The Emperor, gazing at her with bitter intensity as Vader and Skywalker closed in on him. The unspoken but tangible accusation in those yellow eyes: that it was her failure to take care of Skywalker at Jabba the Hutt's hideout that had caused this. That flood of powerless rage as the two lightsabers were lifted over him. That final cry, ringing forever through her head—

YOU WILL KILL LUKE SKYWALKER.

"Stop it!" she snarled, slapping the side of her head hard against the window jamb. The image and words exploded into a flash of pain and a shower of sparks and vanished.

For a long time she just stood there, listening to the rapid thudding of her heartbeat in her ears, the conflicting thoughts chasing each other around her mind. Certainly the Emperor would have wanted Skywalker dead . . . but Organa Solo was still wrong. She had to be. It was Mara herself who wanted to kill Luke Skywalker, not some ghost from the past.

Far across the city, a multicolored light rippled gently against the surrounding buildings and clouds overhead, jolting her out of her musings. The clock at the ancient Central Gathering Hall, marking the hour as it had for the past three centuries. The light changed texture and rippled again, then winked out.

Half an hour past midnight. Lost in her thoughts, Mara hadn't realized it had gotten that late. And all of this wasn't accomplishing anything, anyway. She might as well go to bed and try to put the whole thing out of her mind long enough to get some sleep. With a sigh, she pushed away from the window—

And froze. Deep in the back of her mind, the quiet alarm bell had just gone off.

Somewhere nearby, there was danger.

She slid her tiny blaster out of its forearm holster, listening hard. Nothing. Glancing back once at the window, wondering briefly if anyone was watching her through the privacy laminate, she moved silently to the door. Putting her ear against it, she listened again.

For a moment there was nothing. Then, almost inaudible through the thick wood, she heard the sound of approaching footsteps. Footsteps with the kind of quiet but purposeful stride that she had always associated with combat professionals. She tensed; but the footsteps passed her door without pausing, fading away toward the far end of the hallway.

She waited a count of ten to let them get a good lead on her. Then, carefully, she opened her door and looked outside.

There were four of them, dressed in the uniforms of Palace security, walking in a bent diamond formation. They reached the hallway and slowed as the point man eased a quick look around it. His hand curved slightly, and all four continued around the corner and disappeared. Heading toward the stairway that led down to the central sections of the palace below or up to the Tower and the permanent residential suites above.

Mara stared after them, her fatigue gone in a surge of adrenaline. The bent diamond formation, the obvious caution, the hand signal, and her own premonition of danger—they all pointed to the same conclusion.

Imperial Intelligence had penetrated the Palace.

She turned back toward her desk, stopped short with a quiet curse. One of the first tasks the team would have carried out would have been to get into the Palace's computer and comm systems. Any attempt to sound the alarm would probably be intercepted, and would certainly tip them off.

Which meant that if they were going to be stopped, she was going to have to do it herself. Gripping her blaster tightly, she slipped out of her room and headed after them.

She'd made it to the corner and was just easing forward for a careful look when she heard the quiet click of a blaster safety behind her. "All right, Jade," a voice murmured in her ear. "Nice and easy. Its all over."

CHAPTER 9

ADMIRAL DRAYSON LEANED back in his seat and shook his head. "I'm sorry, Calrissian, General Bel Iblis," he said for probably the tenth time since the session had begun. "We just can't risk it."

Lando took a deep breath, trying to scrape together a few last shards of patience. This was his sweat and work that Drayson was casually throwing away. "Admiral—"

"It's not that much of a risk, Admiral," Bel Iblis cut in smoothly and with far more courtesy than Lando had left at his disposal. "I've shown you at least eight places we could draw an Assault Frigate from which would have it out of service less than ten days."

Drayson snorted. "At the rate he's going, Grand Admiral Thrawn could take three more sectors in ten days. You want to give him a shot at four?"

"Admiral, we're talking a single Assault Frigate here," Lando said. "Not a dozen Star Cruisers or an orbital battle station. What could Thrawn possibly have up his sleeve where one Assault Frigate could make or break the attack?"

"What could he do against a heavily defended shipyard with a single rigged freighter?" Drayson retorted. "Face it, gentlemen: when you go up against someone like Thrawn, all the usual rules get tossed out the lock. He could spin a net out of this so transparent that we'd never even see it until it was too late. He's done it before."

Lando grimaced; but it was hardly a frame of mind he could really blame Drayson for. A couple of months back, when he and Han had first been brought to Bel Iblis's hidden military base, he'd been three-quarters convinced himself that the whole thing was some gigantic and convoluted scheme that Thrawn had created for their benefit. It had taken him until after the *Katana* battle to finally be convinced otherwise, and it had taught him a valuable lesson. "Admiral, we all agree that Thrawn is a brilliant tactician," he said, choosing his words carefully. "But we can't assume that everything that happens in the galaxy is part of some grand, all-encompassing scheme that he's dreamed up. He got my metal stockpiles and put Nomad City out of commission. Odds are that's all he wanted."

Drayson shook his head. "I'm afraid 'odds are' isn't good enough, Calrissian. You find me proof that the Empire won't take advantage of a missing Assault Frigate and I'll consider loaning you one."

"Oh, come on, Admiral—"

"And if I were you," Drayson added, starting to gather his data cards together, "I'd play down my connection with the whole Nkllon mining project. A lot of us still remember that it was your mole miners Thrawn used in his attack on the Sluis Van shipyards."

"And it was his knowledge of them that kept that attack from succeeding," Bel Iblis reminded the other quietly. "A number of us remember that, too."

"That assumes Thrawn actually intended to steal the ships," Drayson shot back as he stood up from the table. "Personally, I expect he was just as happy to have them put out of commission. Now if you'll excuse me, gentlemen, I have a war to run."

He left, and Lando let out a quiet sigh of defeat. "So much for that," he said, pulling his own data cards together.

"Don't let it worry you," Bel Iblis advised, getting up from his chair and stretching tiredly. "It's not you and Nomad City so much as it is me. Drayson was always one of those who considered disagreement with Mon Mothma to be one step down from Imperial collaboration. Obviously, he still does."

"I thought you and Mon Mothma had patched all that up," Lando said, getting to his feet.

"Oh, we have," Bel Iblis shrugged, circling the table and heading for the door. "More or less. She's invited me back into the New Republic, I've accepted her leadership, and officially all is well. But old memories fade slowly." His lip twisted slightly. "And I have to admit that my departure from the Alliance after Alderaan could have been handled more diplomatically. You up on the President's Guests floor?"

"Yes. You?"

"The same. Come on—I'll walk you up."

They left the conference room and headed down the arched hallway toward the turbolifts. "You think he might change his mind?" Lando asked.

"Drayson?" Bel Iblis shook his head. "Not a chance. Unless we can pry Mon Mothma out of the war room and get you a hearing, I think your only chance is to hope Ackbar gets back to Coruscant in the next couple of days. The importance of Nomad City aside, I imagine he still owes you a favor or two."

Lando thought about that rather awkward scene back when he'd first told Ackbar that he was resigning his general's commission. "Favors won't mean anything if he agrees that it might be a setup," he said instead. "Not after being burned once at Sluis Van."

"True," Bel Iblis conceded. He glanced down a cross corridor as they passed, and when he turned forward again Lando thought he could see a slight frown on his face. "All of which is unfortunately complicated by the presence of this Delta Source thing the Empire's got planted here in the Palace. Just because Thrawn doesn't have any current plans for Nkllon doesn't mean he won't think some up once he finds out what we're going to do."

"*If* he finds out," Lando corrected. "Delta Source isn't omniscient, you know. Han and Leia have managed to run some important missions past it."

"Proving once again the basic strength of small groups. Still, the sooner you identify this leak and put it out of commission, the better."

They passed another hallway, and again Bel Iblis glanced down it. And this time, there was no doubt about the frown. "Trouble?" Lando asked quietly.

"I'm not sure," Bel Iblis said. "Shouldn't there be occasional guards in this part of the Palace?"

Lando looked around. They *were* rather alone out here. "Could they all have been shifted down to the Sarkan reception for the evening?"

"They were here earlier," Bel Iblis said. "I saw at least two when I came down from my suite."

Lando looked back along the hallway, an unpleasant sensation starting to crawl along his backbone. "So what happened to them?"

"I don't know." Bel Iblis took a deep breath. "I don't suppose you're armed."

Lando shook his head. "Blaster's up in my room. I didn't think I'd need it here."

"You probably don't," Bel Iblis said, the fingertips of his right hand easing beneath his jacket as he looked around. "There's probably some simple, perfectly innocuous explanation."

"Sure," Lando said, pulling out his comlink. "Let's call in and find out what it is." He thumbed the device on—

And as quickly shut it off as a soft squeal of static erupted from the speaker. "I think the explanation just stopped being simple," he said grimly. Suddenly his hand was itching to have a blaster in it. "What now?"

"We find some way to alert Palace Security," Bel Iblis. said, looking around. "All right. The turbolifts up ahead won't help us—they only serve the residential areas. But there's a stairway at the far end that leads down to Palace Central. We'll try that way."

"Sounds good," Lando nodded. "Let's swing up to my suite first and pick up my blaster."

"Good idea," Bel Iblis agreed. "We'll pass on the turbolift—stairs are over this way. Nice and quiet."

The stairs were as deserted as the corridor behind them had been. But as Bel Iblis started out of the stairway door, he suddenly held up a warning hand. Moving to his side, Lando looked out onto the floor.

Ahead, moving cautiously down the hallway away from them, was a lone figure. A slender woman with red-gold hair, a small blaster gripped ready in her hand.

Mara Jade.

There was a soft whisper of metal on cloth as Bel Iblis drew his blaster. Motioning Lando to follow, he started silently down the hallway after her.

They had nearly caught up by the time she reached the far corner. There she paused, poised to look around it—

Bel Iblis leveled his blaster. "All right, Jade," he said quietly. "Nice and easy. It's all over."

For a second Lando was sure she was going to argue the point. She turned her head halfway, looking back over her shoulder as if targeting her opponents—"Calrissian!" she said, and there was no mistaking the relief in her voice. Or the underlying tension, either. "There are Imperials in the Palace, dressed as Security. I've just seen four of them."

"Interesting," Bel Iblis said, eyeing her closely. "Where were you going?"

"I thought it might be a good idea to find out what they were up to," she growled sarcastically. "You want to help, or not?"

Bel Iblis eased a look around the corner. "I don't see any-one. They've probably already headed down. Best guess is ei-ther the war room or the Sarkan reception."

And suddenly, the whole thing clicked together in Lando's mind. "No," he said. "They haven't gone down, they've gone *up*. They're after Leia's twins."

Mara swore under her breath. "You're right. Thrawn's promised them to that lunatic C'baoth. That has to be it."

"You could be right," Bel Iblis said. "Where's your room, Calrissian?"

"Two doors back," Lando told him, nodding over his shoul-der.

"Get your blaster," Bel Iblis ordered, peering again around the corner. "You and Jade head down the hallway over there and find the main stairway. See if anyone's up there yet; maybe try to warn Leia and Solo. I'll go downstairs and scare up some reinforcements."

"Be careful—they may have left a rear guard on the stair-way down," Mara warned.

"They'll certainly have one on the way up," Bel Iblis coun-tered. "Watch yourselves." With one final look around the cor-ner, he eased past and was gone.

"Wait here," Lando told Mara, starting back toward his room. "I'll be right back."

"Just hurry it up," she called after him.

"Right."

He ran to his room; and as he keyed the door open, he threw a quick look back at Mara. She was still standing there, turned halfway around the corner, an intense yet strangely empty expression on the part of her face he could see.

That face. That somehow, somewhere familiar face. Fitting into a time and place and background he could almost but not quite make out in his mind's eye.

He shook off the thought. Whoever she had been, now was definitely not the time to try to figure it out. Han, Leia, and their children were in deadly danger . . . and it was up to him and Mara to get them out of it.

Turning back to his room, he hurried inside.

LEIA ORGANA SOLO. Leia Organa Solo. Wake up. You're in danger. Wake up. Leia Organa Solo, wake up—

With a gasp, Leia snapped out of the dream, the last remnants of that insistent voice echoing through her mind as she came awake. For a handful of dream-fogged heartbeats she couldn't remember where she was, and her eyes and Jedi senses flicked tensely around the darkened room as she struggled for recognition. Then the last of the sleep evaporated, and she was back in her suite in the Imperial Palace. Beside her, Han grunted gently in his sleep as he rolled over; across the room, the twins were huddled together in their crib; in the next room over, Winter was also asleep, no doubt dreaming in the laser-sharp images of her perfect memory. And outside the suite—

She frowned. There was someone at the outer door. No— more than one. Five or six of them at least, standing grouped around it.

She slipped out of bed, hands automatically scooping up her blaster and lightsaber from the floor as she did so. It was probably nothing—most likely simply a group of Security guards taking a moment for idle conversation among themselves before continuing on their rounds. Though if so, they were breaking several fairly strict rules about on-duty personnel. She would have to find a diplomatic but firm way of reminding them.

Padding silently on the thick carpet, she left the bedroom and headed across the living areas toward the door, working through the Jedi sensory enhancement routine as she walked. If she could hear and identify the guards' voices from inside the suite, she could warn them individually and privately in the morning.

She never made it to the door. Halfway across the living

area, she stopped short as her enhanced hearing began to pick up a faint hum coming from ahead of her. She strained her ears, trying to ignore the sudden distraction of her own heartbeat as she listened. The sound was faint but very distinctive, and she knew she'd heard it somewhere before.

And then, abruptly, she had it: the hum of an electronic lock-breaker. Someone was trying to break into their suite.

And even as she stood there, frozen with shock, the lock clicked open.

There was no time to run and nowhere to run to . . . but the designers of the Tower hadn't been blind to this sort of danger. Lifting her blaster, hoping fervently the mechanism still worked, Leia fired two quick shots into the door.

The wood was one of the hardest and strongest known in the galaxy, and her shots probably didn't gouge their way more than a quarter of the way through. But it was enough. The embedded sensors had taken note of the attack; and even as the sound of the blasts thundered in Leia's enhanced hearing, the heavy metal security door slammed down along the wooden door's inside edge.

"Leia?" Han's voice demanded from behind her, sounding distant through the ringing in her ears.

"Someone's trying to break in," she said, turning and hurrying back to where he stood in the bedroom doorway, blaster ready in his hand. "I got the security door closed in time, but that won't hold them."

"Not for long," Han agreed, eyeing the door as Leia reached him. "Get in the bedroom and call Security—I'll see what I can do about slowing them down."

"All right. Be careful—they're serious about this."

The words were barely out of her mouth when the whole room seemed to shake. The intruders, abandoning subtlety, had set to work blowing the outer door to splinters.

"Yeah, I'd call that serious," Han seconded grimly. "Get Winter and Threepio and grab the twins. We got some fast planning to do."

———

THE FIRST SOUND that drifted down the delicate arch of the
Tower staircase might have been a distant blaster shot—Mara
couldn't tell for sure. The next one, a handful of seconds later,
left no doubt.

"Uh-oh," Calrissian muttered. "That's trouble."

Another shot echoed down the staircase. "Sounds like a
heavy blaster," Mara said, listening hard. "They must not have
been able to get the door open quietly."

"Or else they only want the twins," Calrissian countered
darkly, heaving himself away from the corner they'd paused at.
"Come on."

"Hold it," Mara said, grabbing his arm with her free hand
as she studied the territory in front of them. The wide arch of
the first flight of stairs ended at a presentation landing with an
elaborate wrought-stone balustrade. Just visible from where
they stood were the openings of two narrower stairways that
continued upward, double-helix fashion, from opposite ends
of the landing. "That landing would be a good spot for a rear
guard, and I don't feel like stopping a blaster bolt."

Calrissian muttered something impatient sounding under
his breath, but he stayed put. A moment later, he was probably
glad he had. "You're right—there's someone near the stairway
to the left," he murmured.

"Means there'll be one on the right, too," Mara said, her
eyes searching the contours and crevices of the balustrade's
stonework as another blaster shot echoed down. Intelligence
operatives liked lurking in shadows. . . . "And there's one on
each side of the main stairway," she added. "About two meters
out from the edges."

"I see them," Calrissian said. "This isn't going to be easy."
He looked back over his shoulder, to where the stairway picked
up again. "Come on, Bel Iblis, get up here."

"He'd better hurry," Mara seconded, peering cautiously at

the four Imperials and trying to remember the details of the Tower's layout. "Organa Solo's door isn't going to last long."

"Not nearly as long as that rear guard can hold us off," Calrissian agreed, hissing softly between his teeth. "Wait a minute. Stay here—I've got an idea."

"Where are you going?" Mara demanded as he moved away from the corner.

"Main hangar," Calrissian told her, heading for the stairway behind them. "Chewie was down there earlier working on the *Falcon*. If he's still there, we can go up the outside of the Tower and get them out."

"How?" Mara persisted. "Those are transparisteel windows up there—you'll never blast through them without killing everyone inside."

"I won't have to," Calrissian said with a tightly sly smile. "Leia's got a lightsaber. Keep these guys busy, okay?"

He sprinted to the stairway and vanished down it. "Right," Mara growled after him, turning her attention back to the Imperials up on the stairway. Had they spotted her and Calrissian skulking around down here? Probably. In which case, that guy at the leftmost stairway was probably standing too far out of cover just to bait her.

Well, she was willing to oblige. Switching her blaster to her left hand, she braced her wrist against the corner, took careful aim. . . .

The shot from the other stairway spattered off the wall above her blaster, scattering hot splinters of stone across her hand. "Blast!" she snarled, snatching her hand back and brushing the fragments off. So they wanted to play cute, did they? Fine—she could handle cute. Getting a fresh grip on her blaster, she eased back to the corner—

It was the sudden tingle of danger in the back of her mind that saved her life. She dropped to one knee; and as she did so, a pair of blaster shots from straight ahead flashed into the stonework where her head had been. Instantly, she threw herself backward to land on her side on the floor, eyes and blaster tracking toward where the shots had come from.

There were two of them, moving quietly toward her along the corridor on the opposite side of the stairway. She got off two quick shots as she rolled over onto her stomach, both of them missing. Shifting to a two-handed grip, trying to ignore the shots that were beginning to come uncomfortably close, she lined up her blaster on the rightmost of her assailants and fired twice.

He jerked and collapsed to the floor, his blaster still firing reflexively and uselessly into the ceiling. A shot sizzled past Mara's ear as she shifted aim toward the second assailant, another came even closer as his weapon tracked toward her—

And abruptly, the air over Mara's head was filled with a blazing storm of blaster fire. The Imperial across the way went down like a stuck bantha and lay still.

Mara twisted around. A half-dozen security guards were hurrying toward her from the lower staircase weapons at the ready. Behind them was Bel Iblis. "You all right?" he called to her.

"I'm fine," she grunted, rolling further back from the corner. Just in time; the Imperials on the landing, their little surprise attack having fizzled, opened fire in full force. Mara got to her feet, ducking away from the rain of stone chips. "Calrissian's gone down to the hangar," she told Bel Iblis, raising her voice over the din.

"Yes, we passed him on the way up," the other nodded as the security guards hurried forward. "What happened here?"

"Couple of latecomers to the party," Mara told him, jerking her head back toward the corridor. "Probably on their way back from the comm section. Their friends on the landing tried to keep my attention while they sneaked up on me. Just about worked, too."

"I'm glad it didn't," Bel Iblis said; shifting his attention over her shoulder. "Lieutenant?"

"Not going to be easy, sir," the guard commander called

over the noise. "We've got an E-Web repeating blaster on its way up from the armory—soon as it gets here, we can cut them right off that landing. Until then, about all we can do is keep them busy and hope they do something stupid."

Bel Iblis nodded slowly, his lips compressed into a tight line, a hint of strain around his eyes. It was a look Mara had seen only rarely, and then only on the faces of the best military commanders: the expression of a leader preparing to send men to their deaths. "We can't wait," he said. The strain was still there, but his voice was firm. "The group upstairs will have Solo's door open well before that. We'll have to take them now."

The guard commander took a deep breath. "Understood, sir. Right, men, you heard the General. Let's find ourselves some cover and get to it."

Mara took a step closer to Bel Iblis. "They'll never do it in time," she said quietly.

"I know that," the other said tightly. "But the more we can take out now, the fewer we'll have to deal with when the rest of them come downstairs."

His gaze shifted again over her shoulder. "When," he added softly, "they have hostages,"

THERE WAS ONE final stutter of heavy blaster fire, a vaguely metallic crash, and then silence. "Oh, dear," Threepio moaned from the corner where he was trying to make himself as inconspicuous as possible. "I believe the front security door has failed."

"Glad you're here to tell us these things," Han said irritably, his eyes roving restlessly around Winter's bedroom. It was so much useless exercise, Leia knew—everything they could possibly use in their defense had already been moved into position. Winter's bed and memento chest were against the two doors leading out of here, and the wardrobe had been moved near the window and tipped on its side to serve as a makeshift firing barricade. And that was it. Until the intruders broke through one or both of the doors, there was nothing to do but wait.

Leia took a deep breath, trying to calm her racing heart. Ever since the first of these kidnapping attempts on Bimmisaari, she'd been able to think of it as the Imperials gunning for her and her alone—not an especially pleasant thought, but one that she'd become more or less accustomed to after years of warfare.

This time it was different. This time, instead of being after her and her unborn twins, they were after her babies. Babies they could physically take from her arms and hide away where she might never see them again.

She squeezed her lightsaber tightly. No. It was not going to happen. She wouldn't let it.

There was a vaguely wooden-sounding crash from outside. "There goes the couch," Han muttered. Another crash—"And the chair. Didn't think they would slow 'em down any."

"It was worth a try," Leia said.

"Yeah." Han snorted under his breath. "You know, I've been telling you for months we needed more furniture in this place."

Leia smiled tightly and squeezed his hand. Trust Han to try to take the edge off a tense situation. "You have not," she told him. "You're never here anyway." She looked back at Winter, sitting on the floor beneath the transparisteel windows with one twin cradled in each arm. "How are they doing?"

"I think they're waking *up*," Winter murmured back.

"Yes, they are," Leia confirmed, giving each baby a quick mental caress with as much reassurance as she could manage.

"Try to keep them quiet," Han muttered. "Our pals out there don't need any help."

Leia nodded, feeling a fresh tension squeezing her heart. Both bedrooms—theirs and Winter's—opened out into the living area of the suite, giving the attackers a fifty-fifty chance at picking the door their targets were hiding behind. With the kind of weaponry they obviously had, a wrong choice wouldn't lose them more than a few minutes; but a few minutes could easily mean the difference between life and death.

The thud of a heavy blaster shot came through the wall from the direction of their room, and for a moment Leia began to breathe again. But only for a moment. A second later the sound was repeated, this time from the door in front of them. Faced with two doors, the Imperials had decided to break down both.

She turned to Han, to find him looking at her. "It'll still slow them down," he reminded her, the words more soothing than the sense behind them. "They have to split up their firepower. We've still got some time."

"Now if we just had something to do with it," Leia said, looking futilely around the room. Years of moving around the galaxy with the Rebellion's Supply and Procurement section had gotten Winter into the habit of traveling light, and there simply wasn't anything else in here that they could use.

Another volley of shots came from outside, followed by a faint splintering sound. The regular wooden bedroom doors would be down soon, leaving only the inner security doors. Leia looked around the room again, desperation starting to cloud her thoughts. The wardrobe, the bed, the memento chest; that was it. Nothing but the security doors, the transparisteel windows, and bare walls.

Bare walls . . .

She was suddenly and freshly aware of the lightsaber clutched in her hand. "Han—why don't we just get out of here?" she said, the first cautious wisp of hope flicking through her. "I can cut us through the wall to the next suite over with my lightsaber. And we wouldn't have to stop there—we could be halfway down the corridor before they get that door down."

"Yeah, I already thought of that," Han said tightly. "Problem is, they probably thought of it, too."

Leia swallowed. Yes—the Imperials would certainly be ready for them to try that. "How about going down, then?"

she persisted. "Or up? Do you think they'd be ready for us to go through the ceiling?"

"You've seen Thrawn in action," Han countered. "What do *you* think?"

Leia sighed, the brief glint of hope fading. He was right. If the Grand Admiral had planned this attack personally, they might as well open the security door and surrender right now. Everything they could possibly come up with would already have been anticipated in exquisite detail, with counters planned for each move.

She shook her head sharply. "No," she said aloud. "He's not infallible. We've outthought him before, and we can do it again." She turned around to look at Winter and the twins, still sleeping under the window.

The window . . .

"All right," she said slowly. "What if we go out the window?"

He stared at her. "Out the window to where?"

"Wherever we can get to," she said. The blasters outside were pounding at the security doors now. "Up, down, sideways—I don't care."

Han still had that astonished look on his face. "Sweetheart, in case you hadn't noticed, those walls are flat stone. Even Chewie couldn't climb it without mountain gear."

"That's why they won't expect us to go that way," Leia said, glancing at the window again. "Maybe I can carve out some hand- and footholds with the lightsaber—"

She stopped, giving the window a second look. It hadn't been a trick of the room's lighting: there were indeed a pair of headlights approaching. "Han . . ."

He swiveled to look. "Uh-oh," he muttered. "More company. Great."

"Could it be a rescue team?" Leia suggested hesitantly.

"Doubt it," Han shook his head, studying the approaching lights. "It's only been a few minutes since the shooting started. Wait a minute . . ."

Leia looked back. Outside, the headlights had begun to flicker. She watched the pattern, trying unsuccessfully to match it with any code she knew—

"Captain Solo!" Threepio spoke up, sounding excited. "As you know, I am fluent in over six million forms of communication—"

"It's Chewie," Han cut him off, scrambling to his feet and waving both hands in front of the window.

"—and this signal appears to be related to one of the codes used by professional sabacc players when dealing with—"

"We've got to get rid of this window," Han said, throwing a look back at the door. "Leia?"

"Right." Leia dropped her blaster and scrambled to her feet, lightsaber in hand.

"—cheating by third or fourth parties to the game—"

"Shut up, Goldenrod," Han snapped at Threepio, helping Winter and the twins out from under the window. The lights outside were getting rapidly closer, and now Leia could make out the faint shape of the *Falcon* in the backwash of light from the city lights below. A memory flickered back: the Noghri kidnapping attempt on Bpfassh had used a fake *Falcon* as a lure. But the Imperials wouldn't have thought to use a sabacc player's code . . . would they?

It almost didn't matter. She would rather face enemies aboard a ship than sit here waiting for them to walk in on her like this. And well before they got on board, she ought to be able to sense whether it was Chewbacca out there or not. Stepping to the window, she ignited her lightsaber and raised it high—

And behind her, with a final explosive crash, the security door blew in.

Leia spun around, catching a brief glimpse through the smoke and sparks of two men pushing aside the memento chest and diving to the floor as Han grabbed her arm and yanked her to the floor. A covering volley of blaster fire spattered against the wall and window as she shut down her lightsaber and

scooped up her blaster again. At her side Han was already returning fire, ignoring the danger as he crouched half protected
by the wardrobe. Four more Imperials were at the doorway
now, adding their contribution to the rapid splintering of the
wardrobe. Leia clenched her teeth, firing back as well as long
practice and the Force would let her, knowing full well how
futile it was. The longer this firefight went on, the greater the
chance that a stray shot would hit one of her babies—

And suddenly, unexpectedly, something touched her mind.
A mental pressure; half suggestion, half demand. And what it
told her . . .

She took a deep breath. "Stop!" she shouted over the din.
"Stop shooting. We surrender."

The firing hesitated, then came to a halt. Laying her blaster
on top of the shattered wardrobe, she raised her hands as the
two Imperials on the floor got cautiously to their feet and
started forward. And tried to ignore Han's stunned disbelief.

THE BALUSTRADE NEAR the rightmost stairway erupted in a
cloud of chips and stone dust as the concentrated fire of the
security guards finally broke through it. The answering fire
from the landing caught one of the guards as the balustrade
collapsed, sending him flopping backward to lie still. Mara
eased an inconspicuous eye around the corner, peering through
the debris and the blinding flashes of blaster bolts, wondering
if in all the mess they'd managed to take out the Imperial they
were trying for.

They had. Through the clearing smoke she could make out
the shape of a body, scorched and dust-covered. "They got
one," she reported, turning back to Bel Iblis. "Three to go."

"Plus however many there are upstairs," he reminded her,
his face grim. "Let's hope the legendary Solo luck extends to
Leia and the babies and anyone else up there they take hostage."

"That's the second time you've mentioned hostages," Mara said.

Bel Iblis shrugged. "A hostage screen is their only way out of here," he said. "And I'm sure they know it. Their only other option is to go up, and I've already told Calrissian to scramble some fighters to close off the airspace above the Palace. With the turbolift blocked, this stairway is it."

Mara stared at him, an icy shiver running abruptly through her. What with all the rush and commotion since this thing had started, she hadn't had time to pause and consider all the nuances of the situation. But now, Bel Iblis's words and her own distant memories had combined in a blinding flash of insight.

For a handful of heartbeats she stood there, thinking it through, wondering if it were real or a construct of her own imagination. But it held up. Logical, tactically brilliant, with Grand Admiral Thrawn's fingerprints all over it. It had to be the answer.

And it would have worked . . . except for a single flaw. Thrawn obviously didn't know she was here. Or didn't believe she'd really been the Emperor's Hand.

"I'll be back," she told Bel Iblis, stepping around him and hurrying back down the hallway. She rounded a corner into a cross corridor, eyes studying the carved frieze running along the top of the wall. Somewhere along here would be the subtle marking she was looking for.

There it was. She stopped in front of the otherwise ordinary-looking paneling, glancing both ways down the corridor as she did so. Skywalker and Organa Solo might accept her past associations without any qualms, but she doubted anyone else here would be quite so blasé about it. But the corridor was deserted. Stretching up to the frieze, she slid two fingers into the proper indentations, letting the warmth of her hand soak into the sensors there.

And with a faint click the panel unlocked.

She slipped inside, closing the panel behind her, and looked around. Built more or less parallel to the turbolift shafts, the Emperor's private passageways were by necessity narrow and cramped. But they were well lit, dust-free, and soundproof. And, more importantly, they would take her past the Imperials on the presentation landing.

Two minutes and three staircases later, she was at the exit that opened out onto Organa Solo's floor. Taking a couple of deep breaths, preparing herself for combat, she stepped through the panel and out into the hallway.

With the battle raging three staircases below, she would have expected to find a secondary rear guard stationed near their bolthole. She was right: two men in the by-now familiar Palace Security uniforms were crouched against the walls with their backs to her, keeping watch on the far end of the corridor. The noise of heavy blaster fire coming from the other direction was more than enough to cover her quiet footsteps, and it was likely neither of them had any idea she was even there as she shot them down. A quick check to make sure they were out of the fight, and she was heading down the corridor toward Organa Solo's suite.

She had reached it and was just starting to pick her way across the debris from the shattered outer door when the blaster fire from inside was suddenly punctuated by an explosive crash.

She clenched her teeth as the blasters of the defenders opened up, their noise mixing with that of the attackers. Rushing straight in without any attempt at stealth or cover would be a good way to get herself killed. But if she moved in more cautiously, someone in there was likely to be killed before she could get into firing position.

Unless . . .

Leia Organa Solo, she called silently, stretching out through the Force as she had earlier when Calrissian had gone for his blaster. No more certain now than she had been then that Organa Solo could even hear her. *It's Mara. I'm coming up be-*

hind them. Surrender. You hear me? Surrender. Surrender. Surrender.

And as she reached the outer door she heard Organa Solo's shout, barely audible over the blaster fire. "Stop! Stop shooting. We surrender."

Carefully, Mara eased an eye around the door. There they were: four Imperials standing or kneeling at the blackened edges of the doorway, blasters trained warily inside, with two more inside starting to get up from prone positions across the ruined security door. None of them giving the slightest bit of attention in her direction.

Smiling tightly to herself, Mara leveled her blaster and opened fire.

She had two of them down before the others even woke to the fact that she was there. A third fell as he spun around, trying in vain to bring his blaster to bear on her. The fourth was nearly to firing position when a shot from inside the room sent him spinning to the floor.

Five seconds later, it was all over.

THERE WAS ONE SURVIVOR. Barely.

"We think it's the group's leader," Bel Iblis told Han as the two of them strode down the corridor toward the medical wing. "Tentatively identified as a Major Himron. Though we won't know for certain until he's conscious again. If then."

Han nodded, throwing a quick glance at yet another pair of alert-looking guards as they passed. If nothing else, this little fiasco had sure gotten Security stirred up. About time, too. "Any idea how they got in?"

"That's going to be one of my first questions," Bel Iblis said. "He's in intensive care—this way."

Lando was waiting at the door with one of the medics when Han and Bel Iblis arrived. "Is everyone okay?" Lando asked, eyes flicking up and down his friend. "I sent Chewie up, but they told me I should stay here with the prisoner."

"Everyone's fine," Han assured him as Bel Iblis stepped past Lando and pulled the medic aside. "Chewie was up there before I left, and he's helping Leia and Winter set up in another suite. By the way, thanks for coming up after us."

"No charge," Lando grunted. "Especially since all we got to do was watch. What, you couldn't have held off your little fireworks display for two more minutes?"

"Don't look at me, pal," Han countered. "It was Mara's timing, not mine."

A shadow seemed to cross Lando's face. "Right. Mara."

Han frowned at him. "What's that supposed to mean?"

"I don't know," Lando said, shaking his head. "There's still something about her that bothers me. Remember back at Karrde's base on Myrkr, just before Thrawn dropped in and we had to go hide in the forest?"

"You said you thought you knew her from somewhere," Han said. It was a comment that had been stuck in the back of his mind all these months, too. "You ever figure out where?"

"Not yet," Lando growled. "But I'm getting close. I know it."

Han looked at Bel Iblis and the medic, thinking back to what Luke had said a couple of days later on their way off of Myrkr. That Mara had told Luke flat out that she wanted to kill him. "Wherever you saw her, she seems to be on our side now."

"Yeah," Lando said darkly. "Maybe."

Bel Iblis beckoned them over. "We're going to try to wake him up," he said. "Come on."

They went inside. Surrounding the ICU bed were half a dozen medics and Emdee droids, plus three of Ackbar's top security officers. At Bel Iblis's nod one of the medics did something to the treatment wrap around the Imperial's upper arm; and as Han and Lando found places at the side of the bed, he coughed suddenly and his eyes fluttered open. "Major Himron?" one of the security officers asked. "Can you hear me; Major?"

"Yes," the Imperial breathed, blinking a couple of times.

His eyes drifted between the people standing around him . . . and it seemed to Han that he suddenly became more alert. "Yes," he repeated, stronger this time.

"Your attack has failed," the officer told him. "Your men are all dead, and we're not sure yet whether you're going to live."

Himron sighed and closed his eyes. But that alertness was still in his face. "Fortunes of war," he said.

Bel Iblis leaned forward. "How did you get into the Palace, Major?"

"Guess it can't . . . hurt now," Himron murmured. His breathing was becoming labored. "Back door. Put in . . . same time . . . private passage system. Locked from inside. She let us in."

"Someone let you in?" Bel Iblis said. "Who?"

Himron opened his eyes. "Our contact here. Name . . . Jade."

Bel Iblis threw Han a startled glance. "Mara Jade?"

"Yes." Himron closed his eyes again, let out a deep breath. "Special agent of . . . Empire. Once called . . . Emperor's Hand."

He fell silent, and seemed to sink a little deeper into the bed. "That's all I can permit right now, General Bel Iblis," the chief medic said. "He needs rest, and we need to get him stabilized. In a day or two, perhaps, he'll be strong enough to answer more questions."

"That's all right," one of the security officers said, heading for the door. "He's given us enough to start with."

"Wait a minute," Han called, starting after him. "Where are you going?"

"Where do you think?" the officer retorted. "I'm going to have Mara Jade put under arrest."

"On what, the word of an Imperial officer?"

"He has no choice, Solo," Bel Iblis said quietly, laying a hand on Han's shoulder. "A precautionary detention is required after an accusation this serious. Don't worry—we'll get it straightened out."

"We'd better," Han warned. "Imperial agent, my eye—she took out at least three of them up there—"

He broke off at the look on Lando's face. "Lando?"

Slowly, the other focused on him. "That's it," he said quietly. "That's where I saw her before. She was one of the new dancers at Jabba the Hutt's place on Tatooine when we were setting up your rescue."

Han frowned. "At Jabba's?"

"Yes. And I'm not sure . . . but in all that confusion before we left for the Great Pit of Carkoon, I seem to remember hearing her asking Jabba to let her come along on the Sail Barge. No, not asking—begging was more like it."

Han looked down at the unconscious Major Himron. The Emperor's Hand? And Luke had said she wanted to kill him . . .

He shook off the thought. "I don't care where she was," he said. "She still shot those Imperials off our backs up there. Come on—let's go help Leia get the twins settled. And then figure out what's going on around here."

CHAPTER 10

THE WHISTLER'S WHIRLPOOL tapcafe on Trogan was one of the best examples Karrde had ever seen of a good idea ruined by the failure of its designers to think their whole plan through. Situated on the coast of Trogan's most densely populated continent, the Whirlpool had been built around a natural formation called the Drinking Cup, a bowl-shaped rock pit open to the sea at its base. Six times a day, Trogan's massive tidal shifts sent the water level inside the bowl either up or down, turning it into a violent white-water maelstrom in the process. With the tapcafe's tables arranged in concentric circles around the bowl, it made for a nice balance between luxury and spectacular natural drama—a perfect drawing card for the billions of humans and aliens enamored of that combination.

Or so the designers and their backers had thought. Unfortunately, they'd rather overlooked three points: first, that such a place was almost by definition a tourist attraction, dependent on the vagaries of that market; second, that once the charm of the Whirlpool itself wore off, the centralized design pretty well precluded remodeling the place for any other type of entertainment; and, third, that even if such remodeling had occurred, the racket from the miniature breakers in the Drinking Cup would probably have drowned it out anyway.

The people of the Calius saj Leeloo on Berchest had turned their fizzled tourist attraction into a trade center. The people of Trogan had simply abandoned the Whistler's Whirlpool.

"I keep expecting someone to buy this place and refurbish it," Karrde commented, looking around at the empty seats and tables as he and Aves walked down one of the aisles toward the Drinking Cup and the figure waiting there for them. The years of neglect showed, certainly, but the place wasn't nearly as bad as it could have been.

"I always liked it myself," Aves agreed. "Kind of noisy, but you get that almost everywhere you go these days."

"Certainly made eavesdropping between tables difficult," Karrde said. "That alone made the place worthwhile. Hello, Gillespee."

"Karrde." Gillespee nodded in greeting, getting up from his table and offering his hand. "I was starting to wonder if you were really going to show."

"The meeting's not for another two hours," Aves reminded him.

"Oh, come on," Gillespee said with a sly grin. "Since when does Talon Karrde ever arrive anywhere on time? Though you could have saved yourself the trouble—my people have already checked things out."

"I appreciate the effort," Karrde said. Which was not to say, of course, that he was going to pull his own people off that same job. With the Empire breathing down his neck and an Imperial garrison only twenty kilometers away, a little extra security wouldn't hurt. "You have the guest list?"

"Right here," Gillespee said, picking up a data pad and handing it over. "Afraid it's not as long as I'd hoped."

"That's all right," Karrde assured him, running his eyes down the list. Small, certainly, but highly select, with some of the biggest names in smuggling coming personally. Brasck, Par'tah, Ellor, Dravis—that would be Billey's group; Billey himself didn't get around too much anymore—Mazzic, Clyngunn the ZeHethbra, Ferrier—

He looked up sharply. "Ferrier?" he asked. "*Niles* Ferrier, the spaceship thief?"

"Yeah, that's him," Gillespee nodded, frowning. "He does smuggling, too."

"He also works for the Empire," Karrde countered.

"So do we," Gillespee shrugged. "Last I heard, so did you."

"I'm not talking about smuggling merchandise to or from Imperial worlds," Karrde said. "I'm talking about working directly for Grand Admiral Thrawn. Doing such minor jobs as snatching the man who located the *Katana* fleet for him."

Gillespee's face tightened, just noticeably. Remembering, perhaps, his mad scramble off Ukio one step ahead of the Imperial invasion force in those same *Katana*-fleet ships. "Ferrier did that?"

"And seemed to enjoy doing it," Karrde told him, pulling out his comlink and thumbing it on. "Lachton?"

"Right here," Lachton's voice came promptly from the comlink.

"How do things look at the garrison?"

"Like a morgue on its day off," Lachton said wryly. "There hasn't been any movement in or out of the place for at least three hours."

Karrde cocked an eyebrow. "Indeed. That's very interesting. How about flights in or out? Or activity within the garrison grounds themselves?"

"Nothing of either," Lachton said. "No kidding, Karrde, the place looks completely dead. Must have gotten some new training holos in or something."

Karrde smiled tightly. "Yes, I'm sure that's it. All right, keep on them. Let me know immediately if there's activity of any sort."

"You got it. Out."

Karrde thumbed off the comlink and returned it to his belt. "The Imperials aren't moving from their garrison," he told the others. "Apparently not at all."

"Isn't that the way we want it?" Gillespee asked. "They

can't drop a hammer on the party if they're snugged up there in their barracks."

"Agreed," Karrde nodded. "On the other hand, I've never yet heard of an Imperial garrison simply taking a day off."

"Point," Gillespee admitted. "Unless this big campaign of Thrawn's has all these third-rate garrisons undermanned."

"All the more reason for them to be running daily patrols as a visible show of force," Karrde said. "A man like Grand Admiral Thrawn counts on his opponents' perceptions to fill in the gaps in his actual strength."

"Maybe we should cancel the meeting," Aves suggested, looking uneasily back at the entrance. "Could be they're setting us up."

Karrde looked past Gillespee to the churning water sloshing up the walls of the Drinking Cup. In just under two hours, the water would be at its lowest and quietest level, which was why he'd arranged the meeting for then. If he called it off now—admitted to all these big-time smugglers that the Empire had Talon Karrde jumping at shadows . . . "No," he said slowly. "We'll stay. Our guests won't exactly be sitting here helpless, after all. And we should have adequate warning of any official moves against us." He smiled thinly. "Actually, it's almost worth the risk just to see what they have in mind."

Gillespee shrugged. "Maybe they're not planning anything at all. Maybe we chicaned Imperial Intelligence so good that they missed this completely."

"That hardly sounds like the Imperial Intelligence we all know and love," Karrde said, looking around. "Still, we have two hours before the meeting. Let's see what we can arrange, shall we?"

THEY SAT THERE in silence, each of the individuals and small groups sitting around its own table, while he made his pitch . . . and as he finished and looked around at them, Karrde knew they weren't convinced.

Brasck made it official. "You speak well, Karrde," the Brubb said, his thin tongue flicking out between his lips as he tasted the air. "One might say passionately, if such a word could ever be said to apply to you. But you do not persuade."

"Do I truly not persuade, Brasck?" Karrde countered. "Or do I merely fail to overcome your reluctance to stand up to the Empire?"

Brasck's expression didn't change, but the pitted gray-green skin of his face—about all of him that was visible outside his body armor—turned a little grayer. "The Empire pays well for smuggled goods," he said.

[And for slaves as well?] Par'tah demanded in the singsong Ho'Din language. Her snakelike head appendages bounced gently as she snapped her mouth in a Ho'Din gesture of contempt. [And for viyctiyms of kiydnap? You are no better than was the Hutt.]

One of Brasck's bodyguards shifted in his seat—a man, Karrde knew, who had escaped with Brasck from Jabba the Hutt's indentured servitude when Luke Skywalker and his allies had chopped off the head of that organization. "No one who knew the Hutt would say that," he growled, jabbing a stiff finger on the table beside him for emphasis.

"We're not here to argue," Karrde said before Par'tah or any of her entourage could respond.

"Why *are* we here?" Mazzic spoke up, lounging in his seat between a horn-headed Gotal and a decorative but vacant-faced woman with her hair done up in elaborate plaitlets around half a dozen large enameled needles. "You'll forgive me, Karrde, but this sounds very much like a New Republic recruitment speech."

"Yeah, and Han Solo's already pitched that one to us," Dravis agreed, propping his feet up on his table. "Billey's already said he wasn't interested in hauling the New Republic's cargo."

"Too dangerous," Clyngunn put in, shaking his shaggy black-and-white-striped mane. "Far too dangerous."

"Really?" Karrde said, feigning surprise. "Why is it dangerous?"

"You must be joking," the ZeHethbra rumbled, shaking his mane again. "With Imperial harassment of New Republic shipping as it is, you take your life in clawgrip every time you lift off."

"So what you're saying," Karrde suggested, "is that Imperial strength is becoming increasingly dangerous to our business activities?"

"Oh, no you don't, Karrde," Brasck said, waving a large finger toward him. "You're not going to persuade us into going along with this scheme by twisting our words."

"I haven't suggested any schemes, Brasck," Karrde said. "All I've suggested is that we provide the New Republic with any useful information we might happen to come across in the course of our activities."

"And you don't think the Empire would find this activity unacceptable?" Brasck asked.

[Siynce when do we care what the Empiyre thiynks?] Par'tah countered.

"Since Grand Admiral Thrawn took command," Brasck said bluntly. "I've heard stories of this warlord, Par'tah. It was he who forced my world under the Imperial shroud."

"That ought to be a good reason for you to stand up to him," Gillespee pointed out. "If you're afraid of what Thrawn might do to you *now*, just think what'll happen to you if he gets the whole galaxy under the Imperial shroud again."

"Nothing will happen to us if we don't oppose him," Brasck insisted. "They need our services too much for that."

"That's a nice theory," a voice spoke up from near the back of the group. "But I can tell you right now it won't hold a mug's worth of vacuum."

Karrde focused on the speaker. He was a big, thick-built human with dark hair and a beard, a thin unlit cigarra clenched in his teeth. "And you are . . . ?" Karrde asked, though he was pretty sure he knew.

"Niles Ferrier," the other identified himself. "And I can tell you flat out that minding your own business isn't going to do you a blame bit of good if Thrawn decides he wants you."

"And yet he pays well," Mazzic said, idly stroking the hand of his female companion. "Or so I've heard."

"You've heard that, huh?" Ferrier growled. "Have you also heard that he grabbed me off New Cov and confiscated my ship? And then ordered me out on a nasty little errand for him aboard a bomb-rigged Intelligence bucket? Oh, and go ahead and guess what the penalty was going to be if we couldn't do it."

Karrde looked around the room, listening to the gently sloshing water in the Drinking Cup behind him and holding his silence. This was hardly the way Solo had described Ferrier's involvement; and all other things being equal, he would probably trust Solo's rendition over the ship thiefs. Still, it was always possible Solo had misinterpreted things. And if Ferrier's story helped convince the others that the Empire had to be opposed . . .

"Were you paid for all your trouble?" Mazzic asked.

"'Course I was paid," Ferrier sniffed. "That's not the point."

"It is for me," Mazzic said, turning back to look at Karrde. "Sorry, Karrde, but I still haven't heard any good reason for me to stick my neck out this way."

"What about the Empire's new traffic in clones?" Karrde reminded him. "Doesn't that worry you?"

"I'm not especially happy about it, no," Mazzic conceded. "But I figure that's the New Republic's problem, not ours."

[When does iyt become our problem?] Par'tah demanded. [When the Empiyre has replaced all smugglers wiyth these clones?]

"No one's going to replace us with clones," Dravis said. "You know, Brasck is right, Karrde. The Empire needs us too much to bother us . . . provided we don't take sides."

"Exactly," Mazzic said. "We're businessmen, pure and simple; and I for one intend to stay that way. If the New Republic can outbid the Empire for information, I'll be happy to sell it to them. If not—" He shrugged.

Karrde nodded, privately conceding defeat. Par'tah might be willing to discuss the matter further, and possibly one or two of the others. Ellor, perhaps—the Duro had so far stayed out of the conversation, which with his species was often a sign of agreement. But none of the rest were convinced, and pushing them further at this point would only annoy them. Later, perhaps, they might be willing to accept the realities of the Empire's threat. "Very well," he said. "I think it's clear now where all of you stand on this. Thank you for your time. Perhaps we can plan to meet again after—"

And without warning, the back of the Whistler's Whirlpool blew in.

"Stay where you are!" an amplified voice shouted through the din. "Face forward—no one move. Everyone here is under Imperial detention."

Karrde squinted over the heads of his suddenly frozen audience to the rear of the building. Through the smoke and dust he could see a double line of about thirty Imperial army troops crunching their way across the debris where the back wall had been, their flanks protected by two pair of white-armored stormtroopers. Behind them, almost obscured by the haze, he could see two Chariot command speeders hovering in backup positions. "So they came to the party after all," he murmured.

"With a big hammer," Gillespee agreed tightly from beside him. "Looks like you were right about Ferrier."

"Perhaps." Karrde looked over at Ferrier, half expecting to see a triumphant smirk on the big man's face.

But Ferrier wasn't looking at him. His attention was slightly off to the side; not looking at the approaching troopers, but at a section of wall to the right of the new hole. Karrde followed the line of his gaze—

Just in time to see a solid black shadow detach itself from the wall and move silently up behind one set of flanking stormtroopers.

"On the other hand, perhaps not," he told Gillespee, nodding slightly toward the shadow. "Take a look—just past Ellor's shoulder."

Gillespee inhaled sharply. "What in hell's name is *that*?"

"Ferrier's pet Defel, I think," Karrde said. "Sometimes called wraiths—Solo told me about him. This is it. Everyone ready?"

"We're ready," Gillespee said, and there were echoing murmurs from behind them. Karrde swept his gaze across his fellow smugglers and their aides, catching each pair of eyes in turn. They gazed back, their shock at the ambush rapidly turning to a cold anger . . . and they, too, were ready. The shadow of Ferrier's Defel reached the end of the approaching line of Imperials; and suddenly one of the stormtroopers was hurled bodily off his feet to slam crosswise into his companion. The nearest troopers reacted instantly, swinging their weapons to the side as they searched for the unseen attacker.

"Now," Karrde murmured.

And from the corner of his eye he saw the long muzzles of two BlasTech A280 blaster rifles swing up over the rim of the Drinking Cup and open fire.

The first salvo cut through the center of the line, taking out a handful of the Imperials before the rest were able to dive for cover among the empty tables and chairs. Karrde took a long step forward, tipping over the nearest table and dropping to one knee behind it.

An almost unnecessary precaution. The Imperials' attention had been distracted away from their intended prisoners for a fatal half-second . . . and even as Karrde yanked out his weapon the entire room exploded into blaster fire.

Brasck and his bodyguards took out an entire squad of the troopers in the first five seconds, with a synchronized fire that showed the Brubb hadn't forgotten his mercenary background. Par'tah's entourage was concentrating on the other end of the line, their weapons smaller and less devastating than Brasck's heavy blaster pistols but more than enough to keep the Imperials pinned down. Dravis, Ellor, and Clyngunn were taking advantage of that cover fire to pick off the remaining troopers one by one. Mazzic, in contrast, was ignoring the nearer threat of the troopers to blast away at the Chariot command speeders outside.

A good idea, actually. "Aves! Fein!" Karrde shouted over the din. "Concentrate fire on the Chariots."

There were shouts of acknowledgment from the edge of the Drinking Cup behind him, and the rifle blasts sizzling past his shoulder shifted their aim. Karrde eased a little over his table, caught a glimpse of Mazzic's female companion—her plaited hair down around her shoulders now and her face no longer blank—as she hurled the last of her enameled needles with lethal accuracy at one of the troopers. Another Imperial lunged up out of cover, bringing his rifle to bear on her, falling backward again as Karrde's shot caught him square in the torso. A pair of shots hit his cover table, sending clouds of splinters into the air and forcing him to drop to the floor. From outside came the sound of a massive explosion, echoed an instant later by a second blast.

And then, suddenly, it was all over.

Carefully, Karrde eased up over his table again. The others were doing likewise, weapons held at the ready as they surveyed the wreckage around them. Clyngunn was holding an arm gingerly out from his body as he dug in his beltpack for a bandage; Brasck's tunic was burned away in several places, the body armor beneath it blackened and blistered. "Everyone all right?" Karrde called.

Mazzic straightened up. Even at this distance Karrde could see the white knuckles gripping his blaster. "They got Lishma," he said, his voice deadly quiet. "He wasn't even shooting."

Karrde dropped his gaze to the broken table at Mazzic's feet and the Gotal lying motionless and half hidden beneath it. "I'm sorry," he said, and meant it. He'd always rather liked the Gotal people.

"I'm sorry, too," Mazzic said, jamming his blaster back

STAR WARS: THE LAST COMMAND

into its holster and looking at Karrde with smoldering eyes. "But the Empire's going to be a lot sorrier. Okay, Karrde; I'm convinced. Where do I sign up?"

"Somewhere far away from here, I think," Karrde said, peering out the shattered wall at the burning Chariots as he pulled out his comlink. No one was moving out there, but that wouldn't last. "They'll surely have backup on the way. Lachton, Torve—you there?"

"Right here," Torve's voice came. "What in space was all that?"

"The Imperials decided they wanted to play, after all," Karrde told him grimly. "Sneaked in with a couple of Chariots. Anyone stirring in either of your areas?"

"Not here," Torve said. "Wherever they came from, they didn't start at the spaceport."

"Ditto here," Lachton put in. "Garrison's still quiet as a grave."

"Let's hope it stays that way for a few more minutes," Karrde said. "Pass the word to the others; we're pulling back to the ship."

"On our way. See you there."

Karrde flicked off the comlink and turned around. Gillespee was just helping Aves and Fein pull themselves out over the lip of the Drinking Cup, the web harnesses that had held them suspended just beneath the rocky edge trailing behind them. "Nicely done, gentlemen," he complimented them. "Thank you."

"Our pleasure," Aves grunted, popping his harness and accepting his blaster rifle back from Gillespee. Even with the water level at its lowest, he noticed, the turbulence had still managed to soak both men up to their knees. "Time to make ourselves scarce?"

"Just as soon as we can," Karrde agreed, turning back to the other smugglers. "Well, gentlefolk, we'll see you in space."

THERE WAS NO ambush waiting for them by the *Wild Karrde*. No ambush, no fighter pursuit, no Imperial Star Destroyer lurking in orbit for them. From all appearances, the incident back at the Whistler's Whirlpool might just as well have been an elaborate mass hallucination.

Except for the destruction to the tapcafe, and the gutted Chariots, and the very real burns. And, of course, the dead Gotal.

"So what's the plan?" Dravis asked. "You want us to help hunt down this clone pipeline you mentioned, right?"

"Yes," Karrde told him. "We know it goes through Poderis, so Orus sector is the place to start."

"It once went through Poderis," Clyngunn pointed out. "Thrawn could have moved it by now."

"Though presumably not without leaving some traces we can backtrack," Karrde said. "So. Have we an agreement?"

"My group's with you," Ferrier put in promptly. "Matter of fact, Karrde, if you want I'll see what I can do about getting your people some real fighting ships."

"I may take you up on that," Karrde promised. "Par'tah?"

[We wiyll assiyst iyn the search,] Par'tah said, her voice about as angry as Karrde had ever heard it. The death of the Gotal was hitting her almost as hard as it had hit Mazzic. [The Empiyre must be taught a lesson.]

"Thank you," Karrde said. "Mazzic?"

"I agree with Par'tah," he said coldly. "But I think the lesson needs to be a bit more eye-catching. You go ahead and do your clone hunt—Ellor and I have something else in mind."

Karrde looked at Aves, who shrugged. "If he wants to go slap their hands, who are we to stop him?" the other murmured.

Karrde shrugged back and nodded. "All right," he said to Mazzic. "Good luck. Try not to bite off more than you can chew."

"We won't," Mazzic said. "We're heading out—see you later."

At the far starboard edge of the viewport, two of the ships in their loose formation flickered with pseudomotion and vanished into hyperspace. "That just leaves you, Brasck," Karrde prompted. "What do you say?"

There was a long, subtly voiced sigh from the comm speaker; one of many untranslatable Brubb verbal gestures. "I cannot and will not stand against Grand Admiral Thrawn," he said at last. "To give information to the New Republic would be to invite his hatred and wrath upon me." Another voiced sigh. "But I will also not interfere with your activities or bring them to his attention."

"Fair enough," Karrde nodded. It was, in fact, far more than he had expected from Brasck. The Brubbs' fear of the Empire ran deep. "Well, then. Let's organize our groups and plan to reconvene over Chazwa in, say, five days. Good luck, all."

The others acknowledged and signed off, and one by one made their jumps to lightspeed. "So much for staying neutral," Aves sighed as he checked the nav computer. "Mara's going to have a fit when she finds out. When is she coming back, by the way?"

"As soon as I can find a way to get her here," Karrde said, feeling a twinge of guilt. It had been several days since he'd gotten the message that she and Ghent were ready to rejoin him, a message that had probably been several more days in reaching him in the first place. She was probably ready to bite hull metal by now. "After that last raise in the Imperial price on us, there are probably twenty bounty hunters waiting off Coruscant for us to show up."

Aves shifted uncomfortably. "Is that what you think happened down there? Some bounty hunter got wind of the meeting and tipped off the Imperials?"

Karrde gazed out at the stars. "I really don't know what all that was about," he admitted. "Bounty hunters generally avoid tipping off the authorities unless they already have a financial agreement. On the other hand, when the Imperials go to the effort of carrying out a raid, one expects them to do a more competent job of it."

"Unless they were just tailing Gillespee and didn't know the rest of us were there," Aves suggested hesitantly. "Could be that three squads of troops and a couple of Chariots is all he rates."

"I suppose that's possible," Karrde conceded. "Hard to believe their intelligence was that spotty, though. Well, I'll have our people on Trogan make some quiet inquiries. See if they can backtrack that unit and find out where the tip-off came from. In the meantime, we have a hunt to organize. Let's get to it."

NILES FERRIER WAS smiling behind that unkempt beard of his, Pellaeon noticed as the stormtroopers escorted him across the bridge; a smug, highly self-satisfied type of smile that showed he had no idea whatsoever why he'd been brought to the *Chimaera*. "He's here, Admiral," Pellaeon murmured.

"I know," Thrawn said calmly, his back to the approaching spaceship thief. Calmly, but with a deadly look in his glowing red eyes. Grimacing, Pellaeon braced himself. This wasn't going to be pretty.

The group reached Thrawn's command chair and halted. "Niles Ferrier, Admiral," the stormtrooper commander stated. "As per orders."

For a long moment the Grand Admiral didn't move, and as Pellaeon watched, the smirk on Ferrier's face slipped a bit. "You were on Trogan two days ago," Thrawn said at last, still not turning around. "You met with two men currently wanted by the Empire: Talon Karrde and Samuel Tomas Gillespee. You also persuaded a small and unprepared task force under one Lieutenant Reynol Kosk to launch a rash attack on this meeting, an attack which failed. Is all this true?"

"Sure is," Ferrier nodded. "See, that's why I sent you that message. So you'd know—"

"Then I should like to hear your reasons," Thrawn cut him off, swiveling his chair around at last to gaze up at the thief, "why I should not order your immediate execution."

Ferrier's mouth dropped open. "What?" he said. "But—I've gotten in with Karrde. He trusts me now—see? That was the whole idea. I can dig out the rest of his gang and deliver the whole bunch to you . . ." He trailed off, his throat bobbing as he swallowed.

"You were directly responsible for the deaths of four stormtroopers and thirty-two Imperial army troops," Thrawn continued. "Also for the destruction of two Chariot command speeders and their crews. I am not the Lord Darth Vader, Ferrier—I do not spend my men recklessly. Nor do I take their deaths lightly."

The color was starting to leave Ferrier's face. "Sir—Admiral—I know that you've put a bounty on Karrde's whole group of almost—"

"But all that pales in comparison to the utter disaster you've created," Thrawn cut him off again. "Intelligence informed me of this meeting of smuggler chiefs almost four days ago. I knew the location, the timing, and the probable guest list . . . and I had already given the Trogan garrison precise instructions—*precise* instructions, Ferrier—to leave it strictly alone."

Pellaeon hadn't thought Ferrier's face could get any paler. He was wrong. "You—? But—sir—but . . . I don't get it."

"I'm sure you don't," Thrawn said, his voice deadly quiet. He gestured; and from his position beside Thrawn's chair the Noghri bodyguard Rukh took a step forward. "But it's really quite simple. I know these smugglers, Ferrier. I've studied their operations, and I've made it a point to deal personally with each of them at least once over the past year. None of them wants to become entangled in this war, and without your staged attack I'm quite certain they would have left Trogan convinced that they could sit things out in traditional smuggler neutrality."

He gestured again to Rukh, and suddenly the Noghri's slen-

der assassin's knife was in his hand. "The result of your interference," he continued quietly, "has been to unite them against
the Empire—precisely the turn of events I'd gone to great
lengths to avoid." His glowing eyes bored into Ferrier's face.
"And I do not appreciate having my efforts wasted."

Ferrier's eyes flicked back and forth between Thrawn and
the blade in Rukh's hand, his face now gone from pasty white
to gray. "I'm sorry, Admiral," he said, the words coming out
with obvious difficulty. "I didn't mean—I mean, just give me
another chance, huh? Just one more chance? I can deliver
Karrde—I swear to you. Well, hey—I mean, never mind even
Karrde. I'll deliver all of them to you."

He ran out of words and just stood there looking sick.
Thrawn let him hang for another few heartbeats. "You are a
small-minded fool, Ferrier," he said at last. "But even fools occasionally have their uses. You will have one more chance. One
last chance. I trust I make myself clear."

"Yes, Admiral, real clear," Ferrier said, his head jerking up
and down in something closer to a twitch than a nod.

"Good." Thrawn gestured, and Rukh's knife vanished.
"You can start by telling me exactly what they have planned."

"Sure." Ferrier took a shuddering breath. "Karrde, Par'tah,
and Clyngunn are going to meet in—I guess three days now—at
Chazwa. Oh—they know you're running your new clones
through Orus sector."

"Do they," Thrawn said evenly. "And they intend to stop it?"

"No—just find out where it's coming from. Then they're
going to tell the New Republic. Brasck isn't going along, but
he said he wouldn't stop them, either. Dravis is going to check
with Billey and get back to them. And Mazzic and Ellor have
something else planned—they didn't say what."

He ran out of words, or air, and stopped. "All right,"
Thrawn said after a moment. "This is what you're going to do.
You and your people will meet Karrde and the others at
Chazwa on schedule. You'll take Karrde a gift: an assault shut-
tle you stole from the Hishyim patrol station."

"Rigged, right?" Ferrier nodded eagerly. "Yeah, that was my idea, too—give em some rigged ships that—"

"Karrde will of course examine this gift thoroughly," Thrawn interrupted him, his patience clearly becoming strained. "The ship will therefore be in perfect condition. Its purpose is merely to establish your credibility. Assuming you still have any."

Ferrier's lip twisted. "Yes, sir. And then?"

"You will continue to report on Karrde's activities," Thrawn told him. "And from time to time I'll be sending you further instructions. Instructions which you will carry out instantly and without question. Is that clear?"

"Sure," Ferrier said. "Don't worry, Admiral, you can count on me."

"I certainly hope so." Deliberately, Thrawn looked at Rukh. "Because I would hate to have to send Rukh to pay you a visit. I trust I make myself understood?"

Ferrier looked at Rukh, too, and swallowed hard. "Yeah, I get it."

"Good." He swiveled his chair to face away from Ferrier again. "Commander, escort our guest back to his ship and see that his people are checked out on the assault shuttle I've had prepared for them."

"Yes, sir," the stormtrooper commander said. He gave Ferrier a nudge, and the group turned and headed aft.

"Go with them, Rukh," Thrawn said. "Ferrier has a small mind, and I want it to leave here filled with the knowledge of what will happen if he trips over my plans again."

"Yes, my lord," the Noghri said, and slipped silently away after the departing ship thief.

Thrawn turned to Pellaeon. "Your analysis, Captain?"

"Not a good situation, sir," Pellaeon said, "but not as bad as it might have been. We have a potential line on Karrde's group, if you can believe Ferrier. And in the meantime, he and his new allies won't be doing anything but following the decoy trail we've already prepared for the Rebellion."

"And eventually they'll tire of that and again go their separate ways," Thrawn agreed, his glowing eyes narrowed in thought. "Particularly as the financial burden of lost Imperial business begins to take its toll. Still, that will take time."

"What are the options?" Pellaeon asked. "Take Ferrier up on his offer to give them booby-trapped ships?"

Thrawn smiled. "I have something more useful and satisfying in mind, Captain. Eventually, I'm sure some of the other smugglers will realize how unconvincing the Trogan attack really was. With a little judiciously planted evidence, perhaps we can persuade them that it was Karrde who was behind it."

Pellaeon blinked. "Karrde?" he repeated.

"Why not?" Thrawn asked. "A deceitful and heavy-handed attempt, shall we say, to persuade the others that his fears about the Empire were justified. It would certainly lose Karrde any influence he might have over them, as well as possibly saving us the trouble of hunting him down ourselves."

"It's something to think about, sir," Pellaeon agreed diplomatically. The middle of a major offensive, in his opinion, was not the right time to be worrying about exacting vengeance on the dregs of the galaxy's under-fringes. There would be plenty of time for that after the Rebellion had been pounded into dust. "May I suggest, Admiral, that the stalled campaign off Ketaris requires your attention?"

Thrawn smiled again. "Your devotion to duty is commendable, Captain." He turned his head to gaze out the side viewport. "No word yet from Coruscant?"

"Not yet, sir," Pellaeon said, checking the comm log update just to be sure. "But you remember what Himron said about first creating a data trail. He might have run into some delays."

"Perhaps." Thrawn turned back, and Pellaeon could see the slight tightness in his face. "Perhaps not. Still, even if we fail to obtain the twins for our beloved Jedi Master, Major Himron's fingering of Mara Jade should succeed in neutralizing her as a threat to us. For the moment, that's what's important."

He straightened in his chair. "Set course for the Ketaris battle plane, Captain. We'll leave as soon as Ferrier is clear."

CHAPTER 11

THE BULKY MAN was turning into the Grand Corridor when Han finally caught up with him, his expression that of a man in a hurry and in a rotten mood besides. But that was okay; Han wasn't in all that great a mood, either. "Colonel Bremen," he said, falling in step beside the man just as he passed the first of the slender purple-and-green ch'hala trees that lined both sides of the Grand Corridor. "I want to talk to you a minute."

Bremen threw him an irritated glance. "If it's about Mara Jade, Solo, I don't want to hear it."

"She's still under house arrest," Han said anyway. "I want to know why."

"Gee, well, maybe it has something to do with that Imperial attack two nights ago," Bremen said sarcastically. "You suppose?"

"Could be," Han agreed, batting at one of the ch'hala branches that was stretching a little too far from the trunk. The subtle turmoil of color taking place beneath the tree's transparent outer bark exploded into an angry red at the spot where the branch connected to it, the color shooting around the trunk in ripples as it slowly faded. "I guess it all depends on how much we're listening to Imperial rumor these days."

Bremen stopped short and spun to face him. "Look, Solo,

what do you want from me?" he snapped. A new flush of pale
red rippled across the ch'hala tree Han had touched, and
across the corridor a group of diplomats sitting around a conversation ring looked up questioningly. "Look at the facts a
minute, huh? Jade knew about the secret back door and the
passages—she admits that outright. She was there on the scene
before any alert was sounded—she admits that, too."

"Well, so were Lando and General Bel Iblis," Han said,
feeling that thin plating of diplomacy that Leia had worked so
hard to build starting to fail. "You haven't got *them* locked up."

"The situations are hardly similar, are they?" Bremen shot
back. "Calrissian and Bel Iblis have histories with the New
Republic, and people here who vouch for them. Jade has neither."

"Leia and I vouch for her," Han told him, trying hard to
ignore that whole thing about her wanting to kill Luke. "Isn't
that good enough? Or are you just mad at her for doing your
job for you?"

It was the wrong thing to say. Bremen turned nearly as red
as the ch'hala tree had, his face hardening to something you
could use for hull metal. "So she helped shoot some alleged
Imperial agents," he said frostily. "That proves absolutely
nothing. With a Grand Admiral pulling the strings out there,
the entire raid could have been nothing more than an elaborate
scheme to convince us she's on our side. Well, I'm sorry, but
we're not buying today. She gets the full treatment: records
search, background search, acquaintance correlation, and a
couple of question/answer sessions with our interrogators."

"Terrific," Han snorted. "If she's not on our side now,
that'll put her there for sure."

Bremen drew himself up to his full height. "We're not doing
this to be popular, Solo. We're doing this to protect New Republic lives—yours and your children's among them, if you
recall. I presume Councilor Organa Solo will be at Mon
Mothma's briefing; if she has any complaints or suggestions,
she can present them there. Until then, I don't want to hear

anything about Jade from anyone. Especially you. Is that clear, *Captain* Solo."

Han sighed. "Yeah. Sure."

"Good." Spinning around again, Bremen continued on his way down the corridor. Han watched him go, glowering at his back.

"You do have a way with people, don't you?" a familiar voice said wryly from beside him.

Han turned in mild surprise. "Luke! When did you get back?"

"About ten minutes ago," Luke told him, nodding down the corridor. "I called your room, and Winter told me you two had headed down here for a special meeting. I was hoping to catch you before you went in."

"I'm not invited, actually," Han said, throwing one last glare at Bremen's retreating back. "And Leia stopped by Mara's room first."

"Ah. Mara."

Han looked back at his friend. "She was here when we needed her," he reminded the younger man.

Luke grimaced. "And I wasn't."

"That wasn't what I meant," Han protested.

"I know," Luke assured him. "But I still should have been here."

"Well . . ." Han shrugged, not really sure what to say. "You can't always be here to protect her. That's what she's got me for."

Luke threw him a wry smile. "Right. I must have forgotten."

Han looked over his shoulder. Other diplomats and Council aides were starting to show up, but no Leia yet. "Come on—she must have gotten hung up somewhere. We can meet her halfway."

"I'm surprised you're letting her walk around the Palace alone," Luke commented as they headed back along the row of ch'hala trees.

"She's not exactly alone," Han said dryly. "Chewie hasn't let her out of his sight since the attack. The big fuzzball even sleeps outside our door at night."

"Must give you a safe feeling."

"Yeah. The kids'll probably grow up allergic to Wookiee hair." He glanced over at Luke. "Where were you, anyway? Your last message said you'd be back three days ago."

"That was before I got stuck on—" Luke broke off, eyeing the people beginning to wander through the corridor. "I'll tell you later," he amended. "Winter said that Mara was under house arrest?"

"Yeah, and it looks like she's going to stay there," Han growled. "At least till we can convince the bit-pushers down in Security that she's clear."

"Yes," Luke said hesitantly. "Well, that might not be as easy as it sounds."

Han frowned. "Why not?"

Luke seemed to brace himself. "Because she spent most of the war years as a personal assistant to the Emperor."

Han stared at him. "I hope you're kidding."

"I'm not," Luke said, shaking his head. "He had her going all over the Empire doing jobs for him. They called her the Emperor's Hand."

Which was what that Imperial major down in the medical wing had called her. "That's great," he told Luke, turning to face forward again. "Just great. You could have told us."

"I didn't think it was important," Luke said. "She's not with the Empire now, that's for sure." He threw Han a significant glance. "And I suppose most of us have things in our background we wouldn't want people talking about."

"Somehow, I don't think Bremen and his Security hotshots are going to see it that way," Han said grimly.

"Well, we'll just have to convince them—"

He broke off. "What is it?" Han asked.

"I don't know," Luke said slowly. "I just felt a disturbance in the Force."

Something cold settled into the pit of Han's stomach. "What kind of disturbance?" he asked. "You mean like danger?"

"No," Luke said, his forehead wrinkled with concentration. "More like surprise. Or shock." He looked at Han. "And I'm not sure . . . but I think it was coming from Leia."

Han's hand dropped to the grip of his blaster, his eyes flicking around the corridor. Leia was up there with a former Imperial agent . . . and she was surprised enough for Luke to pick up on it. "You think we should run?" he said quietly.

"No," Luke said. His hand, Han noted, was fingering his lightsaber. "But we can walk fast."

FROM OUTSIDE THE DOOR came the muffled voice of the G-2RD guard droid, and with a tired sigh Mara shut down her data pad and tossed it on the desk in front of her. Eventually, she assumed, Security would get tired of these polite little sweetness-coated interrogation sessions. But if they were, it wasn't showing yet. Reaching out with the Force, she tried to identify her visitor, hoping at least that it wasn't that Bremen character again.

It wasn't; and she had just enough time to get over her surprise before the door opened and Leia Organa Solo walked in.

"Hello, Mara," Organa Solo nodded in greeting. Behind her, the guard droid closed the door, giving Mara a brief glimpse of an obviously unhappy Wookiee. "I just stopped in to see how you were doing."

"I'm just terrific," Mara growled, still not sure whether getting Organa Solo instead of Bremen was a step up or a step down. "What was all that about outside?"

Leia shook her head, and Mara caught a flicker of the other woman's annoyance. "Somebody in Security apparently decided you shouldn't have more than one guest at a time unless it was one of them. Chewie had to stay outside, and he wasn't very happy about it."

"I take it he doesn't trust me?"

"Don't take it personally," Leia assured her. "Wookiees take these life-debts of theirs very seriously, you know. He's still pretty upset that he nearly lost all of us to that kidnap squad. Actually, at this point he probably trusts you more than he trusts anyone else in the Palace."

"I'm glad *someone* does," Mara said, hearing the bitterness in her voice. "Maybe I should ask him to have a little talk with Colonel Bremen."

Organa Solo sighed. "I'm sorry about this, Mara. We've got a meeting downstairs in a few minutes and I'm going to try again to get you released. But I don't think Mon Mothma and Ackbar will okay it until Security finishes their check."

And when they found out that she really *had* been the Emperor's Hand . . . "I should have kept pushing Winter to get me a ship out of here."

"If you had, the twins and I would be in Imperial hands now," Organa Solo said quietly. "On our way to be the prizes of his Jedi Master C'baoth."

Mara felt her jaw tighten. Offhand, she couldn't think of many fates more horrible than that one. "You've already thanked me," she muttered. "Let's just say you owe me one and leave it at that, okay?"

Organa Solo smiled slightly. "I think we owe you a lot more than just one," she said.

Mara looked her straight in the eye. "Remember that when I kill your brother."

Organa Solo didn't flinch. "You still think you want to kill him?"

"I don't want to discuss it," Mara told her, getting up from her chair and stalking over to the window. "I'm doing fine, you're going to try to get me out, and we're all glad I saved you from C'baoth. Was there anything else?"

She could feel Organa Solo's eyes studying her. "Not really," the other said. "I just wanted to ask why you did it."

Mara stared out the window, feeling an uncomfortable swelling of emotion washing up against the heavy armor-plate she'd worked so hard to build up around herself. "I don't know," she said, vaguely surprised that she was even admitting it. "I've had two days of solitary to think it over, and I still don't know. Maybe . . ." She shrugged. "I guess it was just something about Thrawn trying to steal your children."

For a minute Organa Solo was silent. "Where did you come from, Mara?" she asked at last. "Before the Emperor brought you to Coruscant."

Mara thought back. "I don't know. I remember the first time I met the Emperor, and the ride here in his private ship. But I don't have any memories of where I started from."

"Do you remember how old you were?"

Mara shook her head. "Not really. I was old enough to talk to him, and to understand that I would be leaving home and going with him. But I can't pin it down any closer than that."

"How about your parents? Do you remember them?"

"Only a little," Mara said. "Not much more than shadows." She hesitated. "I have a feeling, though, that they didn't want me to go."

"I doubt the Emperor gave them any choice in the matter," Organa Solo said, her voice suddenly gentle. "What about you, Mara? Did *you* have any choice?"

Mara smiled tightly through a sudden inexplicable welling up of tears. "So that's where you're going with this. You think I risked my life for your twins because I got taken from my home the same way?"

"Were you?"

"No," Mara said flatly, turning back to face her. "It wasn't like that. I just didn't want C'baoth getting his crazy grip on them. Just leave it at that."

"All right," Organa Solo said, in a voice that said she only half believed it. "But if you ever want to talk more about it—"

"I know where to find you," Mara finished for her. She still didn't believe she was telling Organa Solo all this . . . but down deep she had to admit that it felt strangely good to talk about it. Maybe she was getting soft.

"And you can call on me anytime," Organa Solo smiled as she stood up. "I'd better get downstairs to the briefing. See what Thrawn's fighting clones are up to today."

Mara frowned. "What fighting clones?"

It was Organa Solo's turn to frown. "You don't know?"

"Know what?"

"The Empire's found some Spaarti cloning cylinders somewhere. They've been turning out huge numbers of clones to fight against us."

Mara stared at her, an icy chill running through her. Clones . . . "No one told me," she whispered.

"I'm sorry," Organa Solo said. "I thought everyone knew. It was the main topic of conversation in the Palace for nearly a month."

"I was in the medical wing," Mara said mechanically. Clones. With the *Katana*-fleet ships to fight from, and with the cold-blooded genius of Grand Admiral Thrawn to command them. It would be the Clone Wars all over again.

"That's right—I'd forgotten," Organa Solo acknowledged. "There was so much else going on." She was looking oddly at Mara. "Are you all right?"

"I'm fine," Mara said, her voice sounding distant in her ears as the memories flashed across her mind like heat lightning. A forest—a mountain—a hidden and very private warehouse of the Emperor's personal treasures—

And a vast chamber full of cloning tanks.

"All right," Organa Solo said, clearly not convinced but equally unwilling to press the point. "Well . . . I'll see you later." She reached again for the door handle—

"Wait."

Organa Solo turned back. "Yes?"

Mara took a deep breath. The very existence of the place had been a sacred trust, known to only a handful of people—

the Emperor had made that clear time and time again. But for Thrawn to have a renewable army of clones to throw against the galaxy . . . "I think I know where Thrawn's Spaarti cylinders are."

Even with her rudimentary sensing abilities she could feel the wave of shock that rippled outward from Organa Solo. "Where?" she asked, her voice tightly controlled.

"The Emperor had a private storehouse," Mara said, the words coming out with difficulty. His wizened face seemed to hover before her, those yellow eyes gazing at her in silent and bitter accusation. "It was beneath a mountain on a world he called Wayland—I don't know if it even had an official name. It was where he kept all of his private mementos and souvenirs and odd bits of technology he thought might be useful someday. One of the artificial caverns held a complete cloning facility he'd apparently appropriated from one of the clonemasters."

"How complete was it?"

"Very," Mara said with a shiver. "It had a full nutrient delivery system in place, plus a flash-teaching setup for personality imprinting and tech training on the clones while they developed."

"How many cylinders were there?"

Mara shook her head. "I don't know for sure. It was arranged in concentric tiers, sort of like a sport arena, and it filled the whole cavern."

"Were there a thousand cylinders?" Organa Solo persisted. "Two thousand? Ten?"

"I'd say at least twenty thousand," Mara told her. "Maybe more."

"Twenty thousand," Organa Solo said, her face carved from ice. "And he can turn out a clone from each one every twenty days."

Mara stared at her. "Twenty *days*?" she echoed. "That's impossible."

"I know. Thrawn's doing it anyway. Do you know Wayland's coordinates?"

Mara shook her head. "I was only there once, and the Emperor flew the ship himself. But I know I could find it if I had access to charts and a nav computer."

Organa Solo nodded slowly, her sense giving Mara the impression of wind racing through a ravine. "I'll see what I can do. In the meantime—" Her eyes focused abruptly on Mara's face. "You aren't to tell anyone what you've just told me. *Anyone*. Thrawn is still getting information out of the Palace . . . and this is well worth killing for."

Mara nodded. "I understand," she said. Suddenly, the room was feeling chillier.

"All right. I'll try to get some extra security up here. If I can do it without drawing unwelcome attention." She paused, cocking her head slightly to the side as if listening. "I'd better go. Han and Luke are coming, and this isn't the right place for a council of war."

"Sure," Mara said, turning away from her to face the window. The lot was cast, and she had now irrevocably put herself on the side of the New Republic.

On the side of Luke Skywalker. The man she had to kill.

THEY HELD THE COUNCIL of war that night in Leia's office, the one place they knew for certain that the mysterious Delta Source had so far had no access to. Luke glanced around the room as he came in, thinking back again to the tangled series of events that had brought these people—these friends—into his life. Han and Leia, sitting together on the couch, sharing a brief moment of quietness together before the realities of a galaxy at war intruded once more. Chewbacca, sitting between them and the door, his bow-caster resting ready on his shaggy knees, determined not to fail again in the self-imposed duties of his life-debt. Lando, scowling at Leia's computer terminal and a list of what looked like some kind of current market prices displayed there. Threepio and Artoo, conversing off in a corner, probably catching each other up on recent news and whatever passed for gossip among droids. And Winter, sitting unobtrusively in another corner, tending to the sleeping twins.

His friends. His family.

"Well?" Han asked.

"I did a complete circle around the office area," Luke told him. "No beings or droids anywhere nearby. How about here?"

"I had Lieutenant Page come in personally and do a counterintelligence sweep," Leia said. "And no one's come in since then. Everything should be secure."

"Great," Han said. "Now can we find out what this is all about?"

"Yes," Leia said, and Luke sensed his sister brace herself. "Mara thinks she knows where the Empire's cloning facility is."

Han sat up a little straighter, threw a quick look at Lando. "Where?"

"On a planet the Emperor called Wayland," Leia said. "A code name, apparently—it's not on any list I can find."

"What was it, one of the old clonemaster facilities?" Luke asked.

"Mara said it was the Emperor's storehouse," Leia said. "I got the impression that it was a sort of combination trophy room and equipment dump."

"A private rat's nest," Han said. "Sounds like him. Where is it?"

"She doesn't have the coordinates," Leia said. "She was only there once. But she thinks she can find it again."

"Why hasn't she said something about it before now?" Lando asked.

Leia shrugged. "Apparently, she didn't know about the clones until I said something. She was undergoing neural regeneration, remember, when everyone here was discussing it."

"It's still hard to believe she could just miss the whole thing," Lando objected.

"Hard, but not impossible," Leia said. "None of the

general-distribution reports she had access to have ever mentioned the clones. And she hasn't exactly been what you'd call sociable around the Palace."

"The timing here's still pretty convenient," Lando pointed out. "One might even say suspiciously convenient. Here she was, with practically free run of the Palace. Then she gets fingered by an Imperial commando leader and locked up—and suddenly she's dangling Wayland in front of us and wanting us to break her out."

"Who said anything about breaking her out?" Leia asked, looking slightly aghast at the whole idea.

"Isn't that what she's offering?" Lando asked. "To take us to Wayland if we get her out?"

"She's not asking anything," Leia protested. "And all *I'm* offering is to smuggle a nav computer in to her to get Wayland's location."

"Afraid that won't do it, sweetheart," Han shook his head. "The coordinates would be a start, but a planet's a pretty big place to hide a storehouse in."

"Especially one the Emperor didn't want found," Luke agreed. "Lando's right. We'll have to take her with us."

Han and Lando turned to stare at him, and even Leia looked taken aback. "You don't mean you're buying this whole thing," Lando said.

"I don't think we have any choice," Luke said. "The longer we delay, the more clones the Empire's going to have to throw at us."

"What about the backtrack you started?" Leia suggested. "The one through Poderis and Orus sector?"

"That'll take time," Luke said. "This'll get us there a lot faster."

"*If* she's telling the truth," Lando countered darkly. "If she isn't, you're off on a dead-end chase."

"Or worse," Han added. "Thrawn's already tried once to get you and that C'baoth character together. This could be another trap."

Luke looked at each of them in turn, wishing he knew how to explain it. Somewhere deep within him he knew that this was the right thing to do; that this was where his path was leading him. As it had been with that final confrontation with Vader and the Emperor, somehow his destiny and Mara's were joined together at this place in time. "It's not a trap," he said at last. "At least, not on Mara's part."

"I agree," Leia said quietly. "And I think you're right. We have to take her with us."

Han shifted in his seat to stare at his wife. Shot a frown at Luke, looked back at Leia. "Let me guess," he growled. "This is one of those crazy Jedi things, right?"

"Partly," Leia conceded. "But it's mostly just simple tactical logic. I don't think Thrawn would have tried so hard to convince us that Mara was a party to that kidnapping attempt unless he wanted us to disbelieve anything she might have told us about Wayland."

"If you assume that, you also have to assume Thrawn figured the attempt would fail," Lando pointed out.

"I assume Thrawn prepares for all contingencies," Leia said. A muscle tightened in her cheek. "And as you said, Han, there's also some Jedi insight involved here, I touched Mara's mind twice during that attack: once when she woke me up, then again when she came in behind the commandos."

She looked at Luke, and in her sense he could see that she knew about Mara's vow to kill him. "Mara doesn't like us very much," she said aloud. "But on some level I don't think that matters. She understands what a new round of Clone Wars would do to the galaxy, and she doesn't want that."

"If she's willing to take me to Wayland, I'm going," Luke added firmly. "I'm not asking any of you to go along. All I want is your help getting Mon Mothma to release her." He hesitated. "And your blessing."

For a long moment the room was silent. Han stared at the floor, his forehead creased with concentration, gripping Leia's hand tightly in both of his. Lando stroked at his mustache, saying nothing. Chewbacca fingered his bowcaster, rumbling softly under his breath; in the opposite corner Artoo was chirping away thoughtfully to himself. One of the twins—Jacen, Luke decided—moaned a little in his sleep, and Winter reached over to rub his back soothingly.

"We can't talk to Mon Mothma about it," Han said at last. "She'll go through channels, and by the time anyone's ready to do anything half the Palace will know about it. If Thrawn wants to shut Mara up for good, he'll have all the time he needs to do it."

"What's the alternative?" Leia asked, her eyes suddenly cautious.

"What Lando already said," Han told her bluntly. "We break her out."

Leia threw a startled look at Luke. "Han! We can't do that."

"Sure we can," Han assured her. "Chewie and me had to pop a guy out of an Imperial hotbox once, and it worked just fine."

Chewbacca growled. "It did too," Han protested, looking over at him. "It wasn't *our* fault they picked him up again a week later."

"That's not what I meant," Leia said, her voice pained. "You're talking about a highly illegal action. Bordering on treason."

Han patted her knee. "The whole Rebellion was a highly illegal action bordering on treason, sweetheart," he reminded her. "When the rules don't work, you break 'em."

Leia took a deep breath, let it out slowly. "You're right," she admitted at last. "You're right. When do we do it?"

"*We*—that is, you—don't do it," Han told her. "It's going to be Luke and me. You and Chewie are staying here where it's safe."

Chewbacca started to rumble something, broke off in mid-sentence. Leia looked at the Wookiee, at Luke—"You don't need to come, Han," Luke said, reading in his sister the fears he knew she couldn't voice. "Mara and I can do it alone."

"What, two of you are going to take out a whole cloning complex by yourselves?" Han snorted.

"We don't have much choice," Luke said. "As long as Delta Source is active there aren't too many other people we know we can trust. And the ones we can, like Rogue Squadron, are on active defense duty." He waved a hand to encompass the room. "We're pretty much it."

"So we're it," Han said. "We'll still have a lot better chance with three than with two."

Luke looked at Leia. Her eyes were haunted with fear for her husband's safety; but in her sense he could find only a reluctant acceptance of Han's decision. She understood the critical importance of this mission, and she was far too experienced a warrior not to recognize that Han's offer made sense.

Or perhaps, like Han, she didn't want Luke going off alone with the woman who wanted to kill him.

"All right, Han," he said. "Sure—we'll make it a party of three."

"Might as well make it a party of four," Lando sighed. "The way things are going with my Nomad City petition, it doesn't look like I'm going to have much else to do. It'd be nice to pay them back a little for that."

"Sounds good to me, pal," Han nodded. "Welcome aboard." He turned to Chewbacca. "Okay, Chewie. Now what's *your* problem?"

Luke looked at Chewbacca in surprise. He hadn't noticed any problem there; but now that he was paying attention, he could indeed sense the turmoil in the Wookiee's emotions. "What is it, Chewie?"

For a moment the other just rumbled under his breath. Then, with obvious reluctance, he told them. "Well, we'd like to have you along, too," Han told him. "But someone's got to stay here and take care of Leia. Unless you think Palace Security's up to the job."

Chewbacca growled a succinct opinion of Palace Security. "Right," Han agreed. "That's why you're staying."

Luke looked at Leia. She was looking at him, too, and he could tell that she also recognized the dilemma. Chewbacca's original life-debt was to Han, and it pained him terribly to let Han go into this kind of danger without him. But Leia and the twins were also under the Wookiee's protection, and it would be equally unthinkable for him to leave them unguarded in the Palace.

And then, even as he tried to think of a solution, Luke saw his sister's eyes light up. "I have an idea," she said carefully.

They all listened to it, and to Han's obviously stunned surprise, Chewbacca agreed at once. "You're kidding," Han said. "This is a joke, right? Yeah—it's a joke. 'Cause if you think I'm going to leave Leia and the twins—"

"It's the only way, Han," Leia said quietly. "Chewie's going to be miserable any other way."

"Chewie's been miserable before," Han shot back. "He'll get over it. Come on, Luke—tell her."

Luke shook his head. "Sorry, Han. I happen to think it's a good idea." He hesitated, but couldn't resist. "I guess it's one of those crazy Jedi things."

"Very funny," Han growled. He looked around the room again. "Lando? Winter? Come on, one of you say something."

"Don't look at me, Han," Lando said, holding up his hands. "I'm out of this part of the discussion."

"As for me, I trust Princess Leia's judgment," Winter added. "If she believes we'll be safe, I'm willing to accept that."

"You've got a few days to get used to the idea," Leia reminded him before Han could say anything more. "Maybe we can change your mind."

The look on Han's face wasn't encouraging. But he nodded anyway. "Yeah. Sure."

There was a moment of silence. "So that's it?" Lando asked at last.

"That's it," Leia confirmed. "We've got a mission to plan. Let's get to it."

CHAPTER 12

ROM THE CORNER of the communications desk the intercom pinged. "Karrde?" Dankin's voice came tiredly. "We're
coming up on the Bilbringi system. Breakout in about five minutes."

"We'll be right there," Karrde told him. "Make sure the
turbolasers are manned—no telling what we're going to run
into."

"Right," Dankin said. "Out."

Karrde tapped off the intercom and keyed off the desk's de-
crypters. "He sounds tired," Aves commented from the other
side of the desk as he put down his data pad.

"Almost as tired as you look," Karrde said, giving the display he'd been studying one last scan before shutting it down
as well. The report from his people on Anchoron, like the others before it: all negative. "It must be too long since we've had
to pull double shifts," he added to Aves. "No one's used to it
anymore. I'll have to include that in future training exercises."

"I'm sure the crew will love it," Aves said dryly. "We'd hate
to have people think we were soft."

"Contrary to our image," Karrde agreed, standing up.
"Let's go; we'll finish sorting through these later."

"For all the good it'll do," Aves grunted. "Are you absolutely sure those were clones Skywalker spotted on Berchest?"

"Skywalker was sure," Karrde said as they left the office and headed for the bridge. "I trust you're not suggesting the noble Jedi would have lied to me."

"Not lied, no," Aves shook his head. "I'm just wondering if the whole thing could have been a setup. Something Thrawn deliberately dangled in front of you to put us off the real pipeline."

"That thought has occurred to me," Karrde agreed. "Even given Governor Staffa's indebtedness to us, we seemed to get in and out of the system just that little bit too easily."

"You didn't mention these reservations when you were passing out search assignments back at Chazwa."

"I'm sure similar thoughts have already occurred to each of the others," Karrde assured him. "Just as the thought has undoubtedly occurred to them that if there's an Imperial agent among us we should do our best to keep him believing we're buying Grand Admiral Thrawn's deception. If it *is* a deception."

"*And* if there's an Imperial agent in the group," Aves said.

Karrde smiled. " 'If we had some bruallki, we could have bruallki and Menkooro—' "

"—if we had some Menkooro,' " Aves finished the old saying. "You still think Ferrier's working for Thrawn, don't you."

Karrde shrugged. "It's only his word against Solo's that he wasn't a willing agent of the Empire in the *Katana*-fleet business."

"That why you had Torve take that assault shuttle off to the Roche system?"

"Right," Karrde nodded, wishing briefly that Mara was here. Aves was a good enough man, but he needed things laid out in front of him that Mara would have instantly picked up on her own. "I know a couple of Verpine out there who owe me a favor. If the assault shuttle is rigged in any way, they'll find it."

The door to the bridge slid open and they stepped inside.

"Status?" Karrde asked as he glanced through the viewport at the mottled sky of hyperspace rolling past.

"All systems showing ready," Dankin said, yielding the helm seat to Aves. "Balig, Lachton, and Corvis are at the turbolasers."

"Thank you," Karrde said, sitting down beside Aves at the copilot station. "Stick around, Dankin; you're going to be captain today."

"I'm honored," Dankin said wryly, stepping over to the comm station and sitting down.

"What do you suppose this is all about?" Aves asked as he got the ship ready for breakout.

"No idea," Karrde admitted. "According to Par'tah, all Mazzic would say was that I might want to come by Bilbringi after our rendezvous with the others at Chazwa."

"Probably the eye-catching lesson for the Empire he and Ellor were talking about at Trogan," Aves said heavily. "I don't think I'm going to like this."

"Just remember that whatever happens we're innocent bystanders," Karrde reminded him. "An incoming freighter with an authorized delivery schedule and a cargo of Koensayr power converters. Perfectly legitimate."

"As long as they don't look too close at any of it," Aves said. "Okay, here we go." He eased the hyperdrive levers forward, and the starlines appeared and collapsed again into a background of stars.

A background of stars, half-completed ships, service and construction vessels, and floating dockyard platforms. And, almost directly ahead of the *Wild Karrde*, a massive Golan II battle station bristling with armament.

They had arrived at the Imperial Shipyards of Bilbringi.

Dankin whistled softly. "Look at all that new construction," he said, his voice awed. "They aren't kidding around, are they?"

"No, they're not," Karrde agreed. "Nor are they kidding

around at Ord Trasi or Vaga Minor." And if Thrawn was putting half as much effort into his cloning operation as he was into warship construction—

"Incoming freighter, this is Bilbringi Control," an official-sounding voice from the comm cut him off. "Identify yourself and your home port and state your business."

"Dankin?" Karrde murmured.

Dankin nodded. "Freighter *Hab Camber*, out of Valrar," he said briskly into the comm. "Captain Abel Quiller in command. Carrying a shipment of power converters for Dock Forty-seven."

"Acknowledged," the controller said. "Stand by for confirmation."

Aves tapped Karrde on the arm and pointed to the battle station ahead. "They're launching an assault shuttle," he said.

And launching it in the *Wild Karrde*'s direction. "Hold course," Karrde told him quietly. "They may just be seeing how nervous we are."

"Or else they're expecting trouble," Aves countered.

"Or are cleaning up after it," Dankin put in. "If Mazzic's already been here—"

"Freighter *Hab Camber*, you're ordered to hold position there," the controller broke in. "An inspection team is on its way to examine your shipment order."

Dankin keyed the comm. "Why, what's wrong with it?" he asked with just the right mixture of puzzlement and annoyance. "Look, I've got a business to run here—I haven't got time for any bureaucratic nonsense."

"If you'd prefer, we can arrange to end all your scheduling problems right here and now," the controller offered in a nasty voice. "If that doesn't appeal to you, I'd suggest you prepare to receive boarders."

"Acknowledged, Control," Dankin growled. "I just hope they're fast."

"Control out."

Dankin looked at Karrde. "Now what?"

"We prepare to receive boarders," Karrde said, letting his gaze sweep across the expanse of the shipyards. If Mazzic was keeping to the tentative schedule he'd given Par'tah, he ought to be showing up sometime soon.

He paused. "Aves, get me a reading on those," he said, pointing to a cluster of dark irregular spots drifting near the center of the shipyard area. "They don't look like ships to me."

"They're not," Aves confirmed a few seconds later. "Look to be midsize asteroids—maybe forty meters across each. I make the count . . . twenty-two of them."

"Odd," Karrde said, frowning at the sensor-focus display Aves had pulled up. There were over thirty small support craft in the area, he saw, with what seemed to be a similar number of maintenance-suited workers moving around the asteroids. "I wonder what the Imperials are doing with that many asteroids."

"Could be mining them," Aves suggested hesitantly. "I've never heard of anyone hauling the whole asteroid to a shipyard, though."

"Neither have I," Karrde nodded. "It's just a thought . . . but I wonder if they could have something to do with Thrawn's magic superweapon. The one he hit Ukio and Woostri with."

"That might explain the heavy security," Aves said. "Speaking of which, that assault shuttle's still coming. Are we going to let them board?"

"Unless you'd rather turn and run, I don't see many alternatives," Karrde said. "Dankin, how much scrutiny can our delivery schedule handle?"

"It can stand a lot," Dankin said slowly. "Depends a little on if they suspect something or if they're just being careful. Karrde, take a look about forty degrees to portside. That half-finished Imperial Star Destroyer—see it?"

Karrde swiveled in his seat. The Star Destroyer was, in fact, considerably more than half finished, with only the command superstructure and sections of the forward bastion ridgeline left to add. "I see it," he said. "What about it?"

"There seems to be some activity around—"

And in midsentence, the starboard flank of the Star Destroyer blew up.

Aves whistled in startled awe. "Scratch one warship," he said as a section of the forward hull followed the flank to fiery oblivion. "Mazzic, you think?"

"I don't think there's any doubt," Karrde said, keying his main display for a closer view. For a moment, silhouetted against the boiling flames, he caught a glimpse of a half-dozen freighter-sized craft angling swiftly toward the shipyard perimeter. "I also think they may have cut things a bit too fine," he added, looking up again at the Star Destroyer. A group of disaster-control craft were already swarming in toward the burning ship, three squadrons of TIE fighters right behind them.

And then, abruptly, the focal point of the incoming fighter cloud shifted from the Star Destroyer to the vector the escaping freighters had taken. "They've been spotted," Karrde said grimly, giving the situation a quick assessment. Mazzic's group was outnumbered and outgunned, an imbalance that would likely get worse before they could get far enough out from the shipyard clutter to make their escape to hyperspace. The *Wild Karrde*'s three turbolasers would go a long way toward evening those odds; unfortunately, the center of action was too far away for them to make any significant difference to the outcome.

"We going to help him out?" Aves murmured.

"By all rights, we shouldn't lift a finger," Karrde told him, keying the nav computer to start their own lightspeed calculation and tapping the intercom. "Helping to salvage careless tactical planning only encourages more of the same. But I suppose we can't just sit here. Corvis?"

"Here," Corvis's voice came.

"On my command you're to open fire on that approaching assault shuttle," Karrde ordered. "Balig and Lachton, you'll target the battle station. See how much chaos we can cause. At the same time, Aves, you'll bring us around onto a vector of—"

"Wait a minute, Karrde," Dankin cut him off. "There—fifty degrees portside."

Karrde looked. There, straddling the same vector Mazzic's sabotage crew was escaping along, a pair of Corellian Gunships had shot in from hyperspace. A formation of TIE fighters that had been sweeping in from approximately that direction swerved to intercept, and were promptly blown into flaming dust. "Well, well," Karrde said. "Perhaps Mazzic's tactics aren't as bad as I'd thought."

"That's got to be Ellor's people," Aves said.

Karrde nodded. "Agreed. Corellian Gunships are a bit out of Mazzic's style—certainly out of his budget. It's a strategy that would certainly appeal to the legendary Duros cultural recklessness."

"I'd have thought Corellian Gunships would be a strain on Ellor's budget, too," Dankin commented. "You think he stole them from the New Republic?"

" 'Stole' is such a harsh word," Karrde chided mildly. "I expect he considers them merely an informal loan. New Republic ships often use the line of Duros maintenance depots scattered through the Trade Spine, and Ellor has a silent interest in several of them."

"I bet there'll be some complaints about the service this time around," Aves said dryly. "By the way, are we still planning to hit that assault shuttle?"

Karrde had almost forgotten about that. "No, actually. Corvis, Balig, Lachton—power down those turbolasers. Everyone else: stand down from alert and prepare to receive Imperial inspectors."

He got acknowledgments, and turned back to find Aves staring at him. "We're not going to run?" the other asked carefully. "Not even after that?" He nodded toward the firefight blazing off to portside.

"What's happening out there has absolutely nothing to do with us," Karrde said, giving the other his best innocent look. "We're an independent freighter with a cargo of power converters. Remember?"

"Yeah, but—"

"More to the point, it might be useful to see what happens in the aftermath of this raid," Karrde went on, gazing back at the ships. With their immediate exit vector being covered by Ellor's gunships, and with the yards' capital ships too far away to reach them in time, the raiders looked well on their way to a relatively clean escape. "Listen to their communications traffic, watch their cleanup and postraid security adjustments, get an assessment of how much damage was actually done. That sort of thing."

Aves didn't look convinced, but he knew better than to argue the point. "If you think we can pull it off," he said doubtfully. "I mean, with the bounty on us and all."

"This is the last place an Imperial commander would expect us to show up," Karrde assured him. "Hence, no one here will be watching for us."

"Certainly not on a ship under the command of Captain Abel Quiller," Dankin said, unstrapping and standing up. "Impatient and bombastic, right?"

"Right," Karrde said. "But don't overdo the bombastic part. We don't want any hostility toward you, just contempt."

"Got it," Dankin nodded.

He left the bridge, and Karrde turned back to gaze at the smoldering wreckage of the now stillborn Star Destroyer. An eye-catching lesson, indeed, and one that Karrde would have argued strongly against if Mazzic and Ellor had asked his advice. But they hadn't, and they'd gone ahead and done it.

And now the lot was even more strongly cast than it had been after Trogan. Because Grand Admiral Thrawn would not let this go by without a swift and violent response. And if he could trace the attack back to Mazzic . . . and from there back to him . . .

"We're not going to be able to stop here," he murmured, half to himself. "We're going to have to organize. All of us."

"What?" Aves asked.

Karrde focused on him. On that open and puzzled face, clever in its own way but neither brilliant nor intuitive. "Never mind," he told the other, smiling to take any possible sting out of the words.

He turned back to the approaching assault shuttle. And vowed that when this was over, he would find a way to get Mara back.

THE LAST PAGE scrolled across the display, and Thrawn looked up at the man standing at stiff attention before him. "Have you anything to add to this report, General Drost?" he asked, his voice quiet.

Far too quiet, in Pellaeon's opinion. Certainly quieter than Pellaeon's voice would have been had *he* been in command here. Looking out the *Chimaera*'s viewport at the blackened wreckage that had once been a nearly completed and highly valuable Imperial Star Destroyer, it was all he could do to stand silently beside the Grand Admiral and not take Drost's head off. It was no more than the man deserved.

And Drost knew it. "No, sir," he said, his voice sounding strained.

Thrawn held his eyes a moment longer, then turned his gaze out the viewport. "Can you offer me any reason why you should not be relieved of command?"

The faintest of sighs escaped Drost's lips. "No, sir," he said again.

For a long moment the only sound was the muted background murmur of the *Chimaera*'s bridge. Pellaeon glowered at Drost's carved-stone face, wondering what his punishment would be. At the very least, a fiasco like this ought to earn him a summary court-martial and dismissal on charges of gross negligence. At the very most . . . well, there was always Lord Vader's traditional response to incompetence.

And Rukh was already standing close at hand behind Thrawn's command chair.

"Return to your headquarters, General," Thrawn said. "The *Chimaera* will be leaving here in approximately thirty hours. You have until then to design and implement a new security system for the shipyards. At that point I'll make my decision about your future."

Drost glanced at Pellaeon, looked back at Thrawn. "Understood, sir," he said. "I won't fail you again, Admiral."

"I trust not," Thrawn said, the barest hint of veiled threat in his voice. "Dismissed."

Drost nodded and turned away, a freshly awakened determination in his step.

"You disapprove, Captain."

Pellaeon forced himself to meet those glowing red eyes. "I would have thought a more punitive response would be called for," he said.

"Drost is a good enough man in his way," Thrawn said evenly. "His chief weakness is a tendency to become complacent. For the immediate future, at least, he should be cured of that."

Pellaeon looked back at the wreckage outside the *Chimaera*'s viewport. "A rather expensive lesson," he said sourly.

"Yes," Thrawn agreed. "And it demonstrates precisely why I didn't want Karrde's smuggler associates stirred up."

Pellaeon frowned at him. "This was the smugglers? I assumed it was a Rebel sabotage squad."

"Drost is under that same impression," Thrawn said. "But the method and execution here were quite different from the usual Rebel pattern. Mazzic, I think, is the most likely suspect. Though there are enough Duros elements woven into the style for Ellor's group to also have been involved."

"I see," Pellaeon said slowly. This put an entirely new spin on things. "I presume that we'll be teaching them the folly of attacking the Empire."

"I would like nothing better," Thrawn agreed. "And at the height of the Empire's power I wouldn't have hesitated to do so. Unfortunately, at this point such a reaction would be counterproductive. Not only would it harden the smugglers' resolve, but would risk bringing others of the galaxy's fringe elements into open hostility against us."

"We surely don't need their assistance and services that badly," Pellaeon said. "Not now."

"Our need for such vermin has certainly been reduced," Thrawn said. "That doesn't mean we're yet in a position to abandon them entirely. But that's not really the point. The problem is the dangerous fact that those in the fringe are highly experienced at operating within official circles without any official permission to do so. Keeping them out of places like Bilbringi would require far more manpower than we have to spare at present."

Pellaeon ground his teeth. "I understand that, sir. But we can't simply ignore an attack of this magnitude."

"We won't," Thrawn promised quietly, his eyes glittering. "And when it comes, our response will be to the Empire's best advantage." He swiveled his chair to face the center of the shipyards. "In the meantime—"

"GRAND ADMIRAL THRAWN!"

The shout roared through the bridge like a violent thunderclap, filling it from aft to forward and echoing back again. Pellaeon wrenched himself around, reflexively scrabbling for the blaster he wasn't wearing.

Joruus C'baoth was striding toward them across the bridge, his eyes flashing above his flowing beard. An angry radiance seemed to burn the air around him; behind him, the two stormtroopers guarding the entrance to the bridge were sprawled on the floor, unconscious or dead.

Pellaeon swallowed hard, his hand groping for and finding the reassuring presence of the ysalamir nutrient frame stretched

across the top of the Grand Admiral's command chair. The
frame rotated away from his touch as Thrawn swiveled to face
the approaching Jedi Master. "You wish to speak to me, Master C'baoth?"

"They have failed, Grand Admiral Thrawn," C'baoth
snarled at him. "Do you hear me? Your commandos have
failed."

"I hear you," Thrawn nodded calmly. "What have you done
to my guards?"

"*My* men!" C'baoth snapped, his voice again reverberating
around the bridge. Even without the element of surprise, the
trick was an effective one. "Mine! *I* command the Empire,
Grand Admiral Thrawn. Not you."

Thrawn turned to the side and caught the eye of the portside crew pit officer. "Call sick bay," he ordered the man. "Have
them send a team."

For a few painful heartbeats Pellaeon thought C'baoth was
going to object or—worse—take the crew pit officer down,
too. But all of his attention seemed to be focused on Thrawn.
"Your commandos have failed, Grand Admiral Thrawn," he
repeated, his voice now quiet and lethal.

"I know," Thrawn said. "All of them except the major in
command appear to have been killed."

C'baoth drew himself up. "Then it is time for me to take
this task upon myself. You will take me to Coruscant. Now."

Thrawn nodded. "Very well, Master C'baoth. We will load
my special cargo, and then we shall go."

It was clearly not the answer C'baoth was expecting.
"What?" he demanded, frowning.

"I said that as soon as the special cargo has been loaded
aboard the *Chimaera* and the other ships we'll leave here for
Coruscant," Thrawn said.

C'baoth shot a look at Pellaeon, his eyes seeming to probe
for the information his Jedi senses were blinded to. "What is
this trick?" he growled, looking back at Thrawn.

"There is no trick," Thrawn assured him. "I've decided that

a lightning thrust into the heart of the Rebellion will be the best way to shake their morale and prepare them for the next stage of the campaign. This will be that thrust."

C'baoth looked out the viewport, his eyes searching the vast reaches of the Bilbringi shipyards. His gaze swept past the blackened hulk of the Star Destroyer . . . drifted to the asteroids clustered in the central sector . . .

"Those?" he demanded, jabbing a finger toward them. "Are those your special cargo?"

"You're the Jedi Master," Thrawn said. "You tell me."

C'baoth glared at him, and Pellaeon held his breath. The Grand Admiral was baiting him, Pellaeon knew—a rather dangerous game, in his opinion. The only people who knew precisely what Thrawn had in mind for those asteroids were currently protected by ysalamiri. "Very well, Grand Admiral Thrawn," C'baoth said. "I will."

He took a deep breath and closed his eyes, and the lines in his face sharpened with a depth of mental strain Pellaeon hadn't seen in the Jedi Master for a long time. He watched the other; wondering what he was up to . . . and suddenly, he understood. Out there, around the asteroids, were hundreds of officers and techs who had worked on the project, each of them with his own private speculations as to what the whole thing was about. C'baoth was reaching out to all those minds, trying to draw out those speculations and compile them into a complete picture—

"No!" he snapped suddenly, turning his flashing eyes on Thrawn again. "You can't destroy Coruscant. Not until I have my Jedi."

Thrawn shook his head. "I have no intention of destroying Coruscant—"

"You lie!" C'baoth cut him off, jabbing an accusing finger at him. "You always lie to me. But no more. No more. *I* command the Empire, and all its forces."

He raised his hands above his head, an eerie blue-white coronal sheen playing about them. Pellaeon cringed despite himself, remembering the lightning bolts C'baoth had thrown at them in the crypt on Wayland. But no lightning came. C'baoth simply stood there, his hands clutching at empty air, his eyes gazing toward infinity. Pellaeon frowned at him . . . and he was just considering asking C'baoth what he was talking about when he happened to glance down into the portside crew pit.

The crewers were sitting stiffly in their chairs, their backs parade-ground straight, their hands folded in their laps, their eyes staring blankly through their consoles. Behind them, the officers were equally stiff, equally motionless, equally oblivious. The starboard crew pit was the same as was the aft bridge. And on the consoles Pellaeon could see, which should have been active with incoming reports from other sectors of the ship, the displays had all gone static.

It was a moment Pellaeon had expected and dreaded since that first visit to Wayland. C'baoth had taken command of the *Chimaera*.

"Impressive," Thrawn said into the brittle silence. "Very impressive indeed. And what do you propose to do now?"

"Need I repeat myself?" C'baoth said, his voice trembling slightly with obvious strain. "I will take this ship to Coruscant. To take my Jedi, not to destroy them."

"It's a minimum of five days to Coruscant from here," Thrawn said coldly. "Five days during which you'll have to maintain your control of the *Chimaera*'s thirty-seven thousand crewers. Longer, of course, if you intend for them to actually fight at the end of that voyage. And if you intend for us to arrive with any support craft, that figure of thirty-seven thousand will increase rather steeply."

C'baoth snorted contemptuously. "You doubt the power of the Force, Grand Admiral Thrawn?"

"Not at all," Thrawn said. "I merely present the problems you and the Force will have to solve if you continue with this course of action. For instance, do you know where the Coruscant sector fleet is based, or the number and types of ships making it up? Have you thought about how you will neutralize Coruscant's orbital battle stations and ground-based systems?

Do you know who is in command of the planet's defenses at present, and how he or she is likely to deploy the available forces? Have you considered Coruscant's energy field? Do you know how best to use the strategic and tactical capabilities of an Imperial Star Destroyer?"

"You seek to confuse me," C'baoth accused. "Your men— *my* men—know the answers to all those questions."

"To some of them, yes," Thrawn said. "But you cannot learn the answers. Not all of them. Certainly not quickly enough."

"I control the Force," C'baoth repeated angrily. But to Pellaeon's ear there was a hint of pleading in the tone. Like a child throwing a tantrum that he didn't really expect to get him anywhere . . .

"No," Thrawn said, his voice abruptly soothing. Perhaps he, too, had picked up on C'baoth's tone. "The galaxy is not yet ready for you to lead, Master C'baoth. Later, when order has been restored, I will present it to you to govern as you please. But that time is not yet."

For a long moment C'baoth remained motionless, his mouth working half invisibly behind his flowing beard. Then, almost reluctantly, he lowered his arms; and as he did so, the bridge was filled with muffled gasps and groans and the scraping of boots on steel decking as the crewers were released from the Jedi Master's control. "You will never present the Empire to me," C'baoth told Thrawn. "Not of your own will."

"That may depend on your ability to maintain that which I am in the process of re-creating," Thrawn said.

"And which will not come to be at all without you?"

Thrawn cocked an eyebrow. "You're the Jedi Master. As you gaze into the future, can you see a future Empire arising without me?"

"I see many possible futures," C'baoth said. "In not all of them do you survive."

"An uncertainty faced by all warriors," Thrawn nodded. "But that was not what I asked."

C'baoth smiled thinly. "Never assume you are indispensable to my Empire, Grand Admiral Thrawn. Only I am that."

He sent his gaze leisurely around the bridge, then drew himself to his full height. "For now, however, I am pleased that you should lead my forces into battle." He looked back sharply at Thrawn. "You may lead; but you will not destroy Coruscant. Not until I have my Jedi."

"As I have said already, I have no intention of destroying Coruscant," Thrawn told him. "For now, the fear and undermining of morale that accompany a siege will serve my purposes better."

"*Our* purposes," C'baoth corrected. "Do not forget that, Grand Admiral Thrawn."

"I forget nothing, Master C'baoth," Thrawn countered quietly.

"Good," C'baoth said, just as quietly. "Then you may carry on with your duties. I will be meditating, should you require me. Meditating upon the future of *my* Empire."

He turned and strode off the bridge; and Pellaeon let out a breath he hadn't realized he'd been holding. "Admiral . . ."

"Signal the *Relentless*, Captain," Thrawn ordered him, swiveling back around again. "Tell Captain Dorja I need a five-hundred-man caretaker crew for the next six hours."

Pellaeon looked down into the portside crew pit. Here and there one could see a crewer sitting properly at his station or an officer standing more or less vertically. But for the most part the crewers were collapsed limply in their seats, their officers leaning against walls and consoles or lying trembling on the deck. "Yes, sir," he said, stepping back to his chair and keying for comm. "Will you be postponing the Coruscant operation?"

"No more than absolutely necessary," Thrawn said. "History is on the move, Captain. Those who cannot keep up will be left behind, to watch from a distance."

He glanced back at the door through which C'baoth had departed. "And those who stand in our way," he added softly, "will not watch at all."

CHAPTER 13

THEY CAME INTO Coruscant in the dead of night: ten of them, disguised as Jawas, slipping in through the secret entrance that Palace Security had carefully sealed and that Luke had now just as carefully unsealed. Getting to the Tower unseen was no problem—no one had yet had the time to do anything about the Emperor's limited maze of hidden passageways.

And so they filed silently into the suite behind Luke . . . and for the first time Han found himself face-to-face with the bodyguards his wife had chosen to protect her and her children from the Empire.

A group of Noghri.

"We greet you, Lady Vader," the first of the gray-skinned aliens said in a gravelly voice, dropping to the floor and spreading his arms out to his sides. The others followed suit, which should have been awkward or at least crowded in the narrow suite entryway. It wasn't, which probably said something about their agility. "I am Cakhmaim, warrior of the clan Eikh'mir," the Noghri continued, talking toward the floor. "I lead the honor guard of the *Mal'ary'ush*. To your service and protection we commit ourselves and our lives."

"You may rise," Leia said, her voice solemnly regal. Han stole a glance at her, to find that her face and posture were just as stately as her voice. The sort of authority stuff that usually kicked in his automatic disobedience circuits. But on Leia it looked good. "As the *Mal'ary'ush*, I accept your service."

The Noghri got to their feet, making no more noise than they had getting down. "My lieutenant, Mobvekhar clan Hakh'khar," Cakhmaim said, indicating the Noghri to his right. "He will lead the second watch."

"My husband, Han Solo," Leia responded, gesturing to Han.

Cakhmaim turned to face him, and with a conscious effort Han kept his hand away from his blaster. "We greet you," the alien said gravely. "The Noghri honor the consort of the Lady Vader."

The consort? Han threw a startled look at Leia. Her expression was still serious, but he could see the edge of an amused smile tugging at the corners of her mouth. "Thanks," Han growled. "Nice meeting you, too."

"And you, Khabarakh," Leia said, holding her hand out to another of the Noghri. "It's good to see you again. I trust the maitrakh of your family is well?"

"She is very well, my lady," the Noghri said, stepping forward from the group to take her hand. "She sends her greetings, as well as a renewed promise of her service."

Behind the Noghri, the door opened and Chewbacca slipped inside. "Any trouble?" Han asked him, glad of a distraction from all these pleasantries.

Chewbacca growled a negative, his eyes searching the group of aliens. He spotted Khabarakh and moved to the Noghri's side, rumbling a greeting. Khabarakh greeted him in turn. "Which others will be under our protection, Lady Vader?" Cakhmaim asked.

"My aide, Winter, and my twins," Leia said. "Come; I'll show you."

She headed toward the bedroom with Cakhmaim and Mobvekhar at her sides. The rest of the aliens began to spread out around the suite, giving special attention to the walls and doors. Chewbacca and Khabarakh headed off toward Winter's room together, conversing quietly between themselves.

"You still don't like this, do you?" Luke said from Han's side.

"Not really, no," Han conceded, watching Chewbacca and Khabarakh. "But I don't seem to have a lot of choices."

He sensed Luke shrug. "You and Chewie could stay here," he offered. "Lando, Mara, and I could go to Wayland by ourselves."

"Or you could take the Noghri with you," Han suggested dryly. "At least out there you wouldn't have to worry about anyone seeing them."

"No one will see us here," a gravelly voice mewed at his elbow.

Han jerked, hand dropping to his blaster as he spun around. There was a Noghri standing there, all right. He would have sworn none of the half-sized aliens were anywhere near him. "You always sneak up on people like that?" he demanded.

The alien bowed his head. "Forgive me, consort of the Lady Vader. I meant no offense."

"They're great hunters," Luke murmured.

"Yeah, I'd heard that," Han said, turning back to Luke. Impressive, sure, but it was never the aliens' *ability* to protect Leia and the twins that he'd worried about. "Look—Luke—"

"They're all right, Han," Luke said quietly. "Really they are. Leia's already trusted them once with her life."

"Yeah," Han said again. Tried to erase the image of Leia and the twins in Imperial hands. . . . "Everything go all right at the landing pad?"

"No problems," Luke assured him. "Wedge and a couple of his Rogue Squadron teammates were there to fly escort, and Chewie got the ship under cover. No one saw us come into the Palace, either."

"I hope you sealed the door behind you," Han said. "If another Imperial team gets in, Leia's going to have her hands full."

"It's closed but not really sealed," Luke shook his head. "We'll have Cakhmaim seal it behind us."

Han frowned at him, an unpleasant suspicion forming in his gut. "You suggesting we go *now*?"

"Can you think of a better time?" Luke countered. "I mean, the Noghri are here and the *Falcon*'s loaded and ready. And no one's likely to miss Mara until morning."

Han looked over Luke's shoulder, to where Leia was just emerging from the bedroom with her Noghri escort still in tow. It made sense—he had to admit that. But somehow he'd counted on him and Leia having a little more time together.

Except that the Empire would still be making clones during that time . . .

He grimaced. "All right," he grumbled. "Sure. Why not?"

"I know," Luke said sympathetically. "And I'm sorry."

"Forget it. How do you want to do this?"

"Lando and I will go get Mara out," Luke said, all business again. Probably could tell that Han wasn't in the mood for sympathy. "You and Chewie get the *Falcon* and pick us up. And don't forget to bring the droids."

"Right," Han said, feeling his lip twist. It wasn't bad enough that he had to leave Leia and his kids to go break into another Imperial stronghold—he had to have Threepio along yakking his overcultured metal head off, too. It just got better and better. "You got the restraining bolt Chewie rigged up?"

"Right here," Luke nodded, patting his jacket. "I know where to attach it, too."

"Just don't miss," Han warned. "You get a G-2RD droid going, and you'll have to take its head off to stop it."

"I understand," Luke nodded. "We'll meet you out where we hid the Noghri ship—Chewie knows the place." He turned and headed toward the door.

"Good luck," Han muttered under his breath. He started to turn—"What're *you* looking at?" he demanded.

The Noghri standing there bowed his head. "I meant no offense, consort of the Lady Vader," he assured Han. Turning away, he resumed his study of the wall.

Grimacing, Han looked around for Leia. Okay, he'd leave tonight; but he wasn't going anywhere until he'd said good-bye to his wife. And in private.

THE EMPEROR RAISED his hands, sending cascades of jagged blue-white lightning at his enemies. Both men staggered under the counterattack, and Mara watched with the sudden agonized hope that this time it might end differently. But no. Vader and Skywalker straightened, and with an electronic-sounding shriek of rage, they lifted their lightsabers high—

Mara snapped awake, her hand groping automatically under her bed for the blaster that wasn't there. That shriek had sounded like the start of an alarm from the G-2RD droid outside her room. An alarm that had been suddenly cut off . . .

Across the room, the lock clicked open. Mara's searching hand touched the data pad she'd been reading from before going to sleep . . . and as the door swung open she hurled the instrument with all her strength at the dark figure silhouetted in the doorway.

The impromptu missile never reached him. The figure simply held up a hand, and the data pad skidded to a halt in mid-air. "It's all right, Mara," he murmured as he took another step into the room. "It's just me—Luke Skywalker."

Mara frowned through the darkness, stretching out with her mind toward the intruder. It was Skywalker, all right. "What do you want?" she demanded.

"We're here to get you out," Skywalker told her, stepping over to the desk and turning on a low light. "Come on—you've got to get dressed."

"I do, huh?" Mara retorted, squinting for a moment before her eyes adjusted to the light. "Mind telling me where we're going?"

A slight frown creased Skywalker's forehead. "We're going to Wayland," he said. "You told Leia you could find it."

Mara stared at him. "Sure, I told her that. When did I ever say I'd take anyone there?"

"You have to, Mara," Skywalker said, his voice laced with that irritating idealistic earnestness of his. The same earnestness that had stopped her from killing that insane Joruus C'baoth back on Jomark. "We're standing on the edge of a new round of Clone Wars here. We have to stop it."

"So go stop it," she retorted. "This isn't my war, Skywalker."

But the words were mere reflex, and she knew it. The minute she'd told Organa Solo about the Emperor's storehouse she had committed herself to this side of the war, and that meant doing whatever she was called on to do. Even if it meant taking them personally to Wayland.

With all those well-trained Jedi insights Skywalker must have seen that, too. Fortunately, he had the sense not to throw any of it back into her face. "All right," she growled, swinging her legs out of bed. "Wait outside—I'll be right there."

She had time while dressing to sweep the area with her far less trained Force abilities, and was therefore not surprised to find Calrissian waiting with Skywalker when she emerged from her suite. The condition of the G-2RD *was* a surprise, though. From the way that electronic shriek had been truncated, she'd expected to find the guard droid scattered around the hallway in several pieces; instead, it was standing perfectly intact beside her door, quivering slightly with mechanical rage or frustration. "We put a restraining bolt on it," Skywalker answered her unspoken question.

She looked and spotted the flat device attached to the droid's side. "I didn't think you could restrain a guard droid."

"It's not easy, but Han and Chewie knew a way to do it," Skywalker said as the three of them hurried down the hallway toward the turbolifts. "They thought this would make the prison break a little less conspicuous."

Prison break. Mara threw a glance at Skywalker's profile, the word suddenly putting this whole thing into a new perspective. Here he was: Luke Skywalker, Jedi Knight, hero of the Rebellion, pillar of law and justice . . . and he'd just defied the entire New Republic establishment, from Mon Mothma on down, to get her out. Mara Jade, a smuggler to whom he owed not a single thing, and who in fact had promised to kill him.

All because he saw what needed to be done. And he trusted her to help him do it.

"A nice trick," she murmured, glancing down a cross corridor as they passed, her eyes and mind alert for guards. "I'll have to get Solo to teach it to me."

CALRISSIAN BROUGHT THE AIRSPEEDER down at what appeared to be an old private landing pad. The *Millennium Falcon* was already there, an obviously nervous and impatient Chewbacca waiting for them at the open hatchway.

"About time," Solo said as Mara followed Skywalker into the cockpit. They were barely aboard, she saw, and already he had the freighter in the air. He must be as nervous about this as the Wookiee. "Okay, Mara. Where do we go?"

"Set course for Obroa-skai," she told him. "That was the last stop before Wayland on that trip. I should be able to have the rest of it plotted out by the time we get there."

"Let's hope so," Solo said, reaching around to key the nav computer. "Better strap in—we'll be making the jump to lightspeed as soon as we're clear."

Mara slid into the passenger seat behind him, Skywalker taking the other one. "What kind of assault force are we taking?" she asked as she strapped in.

"You're looking at it," Solo grunted. "You, me, Luke, Lando, and Chewie."

"I see," Mara said, swallowing hard. Five of them, against whatever defenses Thrawn would have set up to protect his most vital military base. Terrific. "You sure we're not being unsporting about it?" she asked sarcastically.

"We didn't have a lot more than this at Yavin," Solo pointed out. "Or at Endor."

She glared at the back of his head, willing the anger and hatred to flow. But all she felt was a quiet and strangely distant ache. "Your confidence is so very reassuring," she bit out.

Solo shrugged. "You can get a lot of distance out of not doing what the other side expects you to," he said. "Remind me sometime to tell you how we got away from Hoth."

Behind them, the door slid open and Chewbacca lumbered into the cockpit. "Everything all set back there?" Solo asked him.

The Wookiee rumbled something that was probably an affirmation. "Good. Run a quick check on the alluvial dampers—they were sparking red a while back."

Another rumble, and the Wookiee got to work. "Before I forget, Luke," Solo added, "you're in charge of those droids back there. I don't want to see Threepio fiddling with anything unless Chewie or Lando is with him. Got that?"

"Got it," Skywalker said. He caught Mara's eye and threw her an amused grin. "Threepio sometimes has extra time on his hands," he explained. "He's taken an interest in mechanical work."

"And he's pretty bad at it," Solo put in sourly. "Okay, Chewie, get ready. Here we go . . ."

He pulled back on the hyperdrive levers. Through the viewport the stars flared into starlines . . . and they were on their way. Five of them, on their way to invade an Imperial stronghold.

Mara looked over at Skywalker. And the only one of them who really trusted her was the one man she had to kill.

"Your first command since you resigned your commission, Han," Skywalker commented into the silence.

"Yeah," Solo said tightly. "Let's just hope it's not my last."

"The *Bellicose* task force has arrived, Captain," the comm officer called up to the *Chimaera*'s command walkway. "Captain Aban reports all ships at battle readiness, and requests final deployment orders."

"Relay them to him, Lieutenant," Pellaeon ordered, peering out the viewport at the new group of running lights that had appeared off to starboard and trying to suppress the growing sense of apprehension that was curling through his gut like wisps of poisoned smoke. It was all well and good for Thrawn to assemble the Empire's seasoned elite for what amounted to an extended hit-and-fade attack on Coruscant; what was not so well and good was the possibility that the raid might not stop there. C'baoth was aboard, and C'baoth's sole agenda these days seemed to be the capture of Leia Organa Solo and her twins. He'd already demonstrated his ability to take absolute control of the *Chimaera* and its crewers, an arrogant little stunt that had already delayed this operation by several hours. If he decided to do it again in the thick of battle off Coruscant . . .

Pellaeon grimaced, the ghostly memories of the Empire's defeat at Endor floating up before his eyes. The second Death Star had died there, along with Vader's Super Star Destroyer *Executor* and far too many of the best and brightest of the Empire's officer corps. If C'baoth's interference precipitated a repetition of that debacle—if the Empire lost both Grand Admiral Thrawn and his core Star Destroyer force—it might never again recover.

He was still gazing out the viewport at the gathering assault force, trying to suppress his concerns, when a rustle of uneasiness rippled across the bridge around him . . . and even without looking he knew what it meant.

C'baoth was here.

Pellaeon's command chair and its protecting ysalamir were

a dozen long steps away—far too distant to reach without looking obvious about it. None of the other ysalamiri scattered around the bridge were within reach, either. It wouldn't do to go running around like a frightened field scurry in front of his crew, even if C'baoth was willing to let him.

And if the Jedi Master chose instead to paralyze him like he had the rest of the *Chimaera*'s crew at Bilbringi . . .

A shiver ran up Pellaeon's back. He'd seen the medical reports for those who'd had to recover in sick bay, and he had no desire to go through that himself. Aside from the discomfort and emotional confusion involved, such a public humiliation would severely diminish his command authority aboard his ship.

He could only hope that he'd be able to give C'baoth what he wanted without looking weak and subservient. Turning to face the approaching Jedi Master, he wondered if playing on this same fear of humiliation had been the way the Emperor had started his own rise to power. "Master C'baoth," he nodded gravely. "What may I do for you?"

"I want a ship prepared for me at once," C'baoth said, his eyes blazing with a strange inward fire. "One with enough range to take me to Wayland."

Pellaeon blinked. "To Wayland?"

"Yes," C'baoth said, looking out the viewport. "I told you long ago that I would eventually take command there. That time has now come."

Pellaeon braced himself. "I was under the impression that you'd agreed to assist with the Coruscant attack—"

"I have changed my mind," C'baoth cut him off sharply.

Sharply, but with a strange sense of preoccupation. "Has something happened on Wayland?" Pellaeon asked.

C'baoth looked at him, and Pellaeon had the odd sense that the Jedi Master was really only noticing him for the first time. "What happens or does not happen on Wayland is no concern of yours, Imperial Captain Pellaeon," he said. "Your only concern is to prepare me a ship." He looked out the viewport again. "Or do I need to choose my own?"

A movement at the rear of the bridge caught Pellaeon's eye: Grand Admiral Thrawn, arriving from his private command room to oversee the final preparations for the Coruscant assault. As Pellaeon watched, Thrawn's glowing red eyes flicked across the scene, taking in C'baoth's presence and pausing momentarily on Pellaeon's face and posture. He turned his head and nodded, and a stormtrooper with an ysalamir nutrient frame on his back stepped to Thrawn's side. Together, they started forward.

C'baoth didn't bother to turn around. "You will prepare me a ship, Grand Admiral Thrawn," he called. "I wish to go to Wayland. Immediately."

"Indeed," Thrawn said, stepping to Pellaeon's side. The stormtrooper moved between and behind the two of them, finally bringing Pellaeon into the safety of the ysalamir's Force-empty bubble. "May I ask why?"

"My reasons are my own," C'baoth said darkly. "Do you question them?"

For a long moment Pellaeon was afraid Thrawn was going to take him up on that challenge. "Not at all," the Grand Admiral said at last. "If you wish to go to Wayland, you may of course do so. Lieutenant Tschel?"

"Sir?" the young duty officer said from the portside crew pit, stiffening to attention.

"Signal the *Death's Head*," Thrawn ordered. "Inform Captain Harbid that the Star Galleon *Draklor* is to be detached from his group and reassigned to me. Crew only; I'll supply troops and passengers."

"Yes, sir," Tschel acknowledged, and stepped over to the comm station.

"I did not ask for troops, Grand Admiral Thrawn," C'baoth said, his face alternating between petulance and suspicion. "Nor for other passengers."

"I've been planning for some time to send General Covell to take command of the Mount Tantiss garrison," Thrawn said. "As well as to supplement the troops already there. This would seem as good a time as any to do so."

C'baoth looked at Pellaeon, then back at Thrawn. "All right," he said at last, apparently settling on petulance. "But it will be *my* ship—not Covell's. *I* will give the orders."

"Of course, Master C'baoth," Thrawn said soothingly. "I will so inform the general."

"All right." C'baoth's mouth worked uncertainly behind his long white beard, and for a moment Pellaeon thought he was going to lose control again. His head twitched to the side; then he was back in command of himself again. "All right," he repeated curtly. "I will be in my chambers. Call me when my ship is ready."

"As you wish," Thrawn nodded.

C'baoth threw each of them another piercing look, then turned and strode away. "Inform General Covell of this change of plans, Captain," Thrawn ordered Pellaeon, watching C'baoth make his way across the bridge. "The computer has a list of troops and crewers assigned as cloning templets; Covell's aides will arrange for them to be put aboard the *Draklor*. Along with a company of the general's best troops."

Pellaeon frowned at Thrawn's profile. Covell's troops—and Covell himself, for that matter—had been slated to relieve the shock forces currently working their way across Qat Chrystac. "You think Mount Tantiss is in danger?" he asked.

"Not any substantial danger, no," Thrawn said. "Still, it's possible our farseeing Jedi Master may indeed have picked up on something—unrest among the natives, perhaps. Best not to take chances."

Pellaeon looked out the viewport at the star that was Coruscant's sun. "Could it be something having to do with the Rebels?"

"Unlikely," Thrawn said. "There's no indication yet that they've even learned of Wayland's existence, let alone are planning any action against it. If and when that happens, we should have plenty of advance notice of their intentions."

"Via Delta Source."

"And via normal Intelligence channels." Thrawn smiled slightly. "It still disturbs you, doesn't it, to receive information from a source you don't understand?"

"A little, sir, yes," Pellaeon admitted.

"Consider it a cultivation of your trust," Thrawn said. "Someday I'll turn Delta Source over to you. But not yet."

"Yes, sir," Pellaeon said. He looked aft, toward where C'baoth had disappeared from the bridge. Something about this was tickling uncomfortably in the back of his memory. Something about C'baoth and Wayland . . .

"You seem disturbed, Captain," Thrawn said.

Pellaeon shook his head. "I don't like the idea of him being inside Mount Tantiss, Admiral. I don't know why. I just don't like it."

Thrawn followed his gaze. "I wouldn't worry about it," he said quietly. "Actually, this is more likely to be a solution than a problem."

Pellaeon frowned. "I don't understand."

Thrawn smiled again. "All in good time, Captain. But now to the business at hand. Is my flagship ready?"

Pellaeon shook his thoughts away. Now, with the center of the Rebellion lying open before them, was not the time for nameless fears. "The *Chimaera* is fully at your command, Admiral," he gave the formal response.

"Good." Thrawn sent his gaze around the bridge, then turned again to Pellaeon. "Make certain the rest of the assault force is likewise, and inform them we'll be waiting until the *Draklor* has cleared the area."

He looked out the viewport. "And then," he added softly, "we'll remind the Rebellion what war is all about."

CHAPTER 14

THEY STOOD THERE SILENTLY: Mara and Luke, waiting as the dark hooded shadow moved toward them, a lightsaber glittering in its hand. Back behind the figure an old man stood, craziness in his eyes and blue lightning in his hands. The shadow stopped and raised its weapon. Luke stepped away from Mara, lifting his own lightsaber, his mind filled with horror and dread—

The alarms wailed through the suite from the corridor outside, jolting Leia awake and shattering the nightmare into fragments of vivid color.

Her first thought was that the alarm was for Luke and Mara; her second was that another Imperial commando team had gotten into the Palace. But as she came awake enough to recognize the pitch of the alarm, she realized it was even worse.

Coruscant was under attack.

Across the room, the twins began to cry. "Winter!" Leia shouted, grabbing her robe and throwing what she could in the way of mental comfort in the twins' direction.

Winter was already in the doorway, halfway into her own robe. "That's a battle alert," she called to Leia over the alarm.

"I know," Leia said, tying the robe around her. "I have to get to the war room right away."

"I understand," Winter said, peering intently at her face. "Are you all right?"

"I had a dream, that's all," Leia told her, snagging a pair of half-boots and pulling them on. Trust Winter to pick up on something like that, even in the middle of chaos. "Luke and Mara were having a battle with someone. And I don't think they were expecting to win."

"Are you sure it was just a dream?"

Leia bit at her lip as she fastened the half-boots. "I don't know," she had to admit. If it hadn't been a dream, but instead had been a Jedi vision . . . "No—it had to be a dream," she decided. "Luke would be able to tell from space if C'baoth or another Dark Jedi was there. He wouldn't risk trying to carry out the mission under those conditions."

"I hope not," Winter said. But she didn't sound all that confident about it.

"Don't worry about it," Leia assured her. "It was probably just a bad dream sparked by the alarms going off." And fueled by a guilty conscience, she added silently, for letting Han and Luke talk her into letting them go to Wayland in the first place. "Take care of the twins, will you?"

"We'll watch them," Winter said.

We? Leia glanced around, frowning, and for the first time spotted Mobvekhar and the other two Noghri who'd taken up positions in the shadows around the crib. They hadn't been there when she went to bed, she knew, which meant they must have slipped in from the suite's main living area sometime in the minute or so since the alarm had gone off. Without her noticing.

"You may go without fear, Lady Vader," Mobvekhar said solemnly. "Your heirs will come to no harm."

"I know," Leia said, and meant it. She picked up her comlink from her nightstand, considered calling for information, but slipped it into the side pocket of her robe instead. The last thing the war room staff needed right now was to have to spend time explaining the situation to a civilian. She'd know soon enough what was happening. "I'll be back when I can," she told Winter. Grabbing her lightsaber, she left the suite.

The hallway outside was filled with beings of all sorts, some of them hurrying along on business, the rest milling around in confusion or demanding information from the security guards standing duty. Leia maneuvered her way past the guards and through the clumps of anxious discussion, joining a handful of sleep-tousled military aides hurrying toward the turbolifts. A full car was just preparing to leave as she arrived; two of the occupants, obviously recognizing Councilor Organa Solo, promptly gave up their places. The door slid shut behind her, barely missing a chattering pair of brown-robed Jawas who brazenly pushed their way aboard at the last instant, and they headed down.

The entire lower floor of the Palace was given over to military operations, starting with the support service offices on the periphery, moving inward to the offices of Ackbar and Drayson and other duty commanders, and on to the more vital and sensitive areas in the center. Leia cleared herself through at the duty station, passed between a towering pair of Wookiee guards, and stepped through the blast doors into the war room.

Bare minutes after the alarm had sounded, the place was already a scene of marginally controlled chaos as freshly awakened senior officers and aides hurried to battle positions. A single glance at the master tactical display showed that all the furor was fully justified: eight Imperial Interdictor Cruisers had appeared in a loose grouping around the one-one-six vector in Sector Four, their hyperdrive-dampening gravetic cones blocking all entry or exit from the region immediately around Coruscant. Even as she watched, a new group of ships flicked into the center of the cluster: two more Interdictors, plus an escort of eight *Katana*-fleet Dreadnaughts.

"What's going on?" an unfamiliar voice said at Leia's shoulder.

She turned. A young man—a kid, really—was standing

there, scratching at a mop of tangled hair and frowning up at the tactical. For a moment she didn't recognize him; then her memory clicked. Ghent, the slicer Karrde had lent them to help crack the bank break-in code that the Imperials had framed Admiral Ackbar with. She'd forgotten he was still here. "It's an Imperial attack," she said.

"Oh," he said. "Can they do that?"

"We're at war," she reminded him patiently. "In war you can do just about anything the other side can't stop you from doing. How did you get in here, anyway?"

"Oh, I cut myself an entry code a while back," he said, waving a vague hand, his eyes still on the tactical. "Haven't had much to do lately. Can't you stop them?"

"We're certainly going to try," Leia said grimly, looking around the room. Across by the command console she spotted General Rieekan. "Stay out of the way and don't touch anything."

She'd gotten two steps toward Rieekan when her brain suddenly caught up with her. Ghent, who'd cut himself a top-level access code because he didn't have anything better to do . . .

She spun around, took two steps back, and grabbed Ghent's arm. "On second thought, come with me," she said, steering him through the chaos to a door marked CRYPT opening off the side of the war room. She keyed in her security code, and the door slid open.

It was a good-sized room, crowded to the gills with computers, decrypt techs, and interface droids. "Who's in charge here?" Leia called as a couple of heads swung her direction.

"I am," a middle-aged man wearing a colonel's insignia said, taking a step back from one of the consoles into about the only bit of empty space in the room.

"I'm Councilor Organa Solo," Leia identified herself. "This is Ghent, an expert slicer. Can you use him?"

"I don't know," the colonel said, throwing the kid a speculative look. "Ever tackled an Imperial battle encrypt code, Ghent?"

"Nope," Ghent said. "Never seen one. I've sliced a couple of their regular military encrypts, though."

"Which ones?"

Ghent's eyes went a little foggy. "Well, there was one called a Lepido program. Oh, and there was something called the ILKO encrypt back when I was twelve. That was a tough one—took me almost two months to slice."

Someone whistled softly. "Is that good?" Leia asked.

The colonel snorted. "I'd say so, yes. ILKO was one of the master encrypt codes the Empire used for data transfer between Coruscant and the original Death Star construction facility at Horuz. It took *us* nearly a month to crack it." He beckoned. "Come on over, son—we've got a console for you right here. If you liked ILKO, you're going to love battle encrypts."

Ghent's face lit up, and he was picking his way between the other consoles as Leia slipped back into the war room.

To find that the battle was under way.

Six Imperial Star Destroyers had come in from hyperspace through the center gap of the Interdictor group, splitting into two groups of three and heading for the two massive midorbit Golan III battle stations. Their TIE fighters were swarming ahead of them, heading toward the defenders now beginning to emerge from the low-orbit space-dock facility and from Coruscant's surface. On the master visual display, occasional flashes of turbolaser fire flickered as both sides began to fire ranging shots.

General Rieekan was standing a few steps back from the main command console when Leia reached him. "Princess," he nodded gravely in greeting.

"General," she nodded back breathlessly, throwing a quick look across the console displays. Coruscant's energy shield was up, the ground-based defenses were coming rapidly to full combat status, and a second wave of X-wings and B-wings were beginning to scramble from the space dock.

And standing in front of the raised command chair, barking out orders to everyone in sight, was Admiral Drayson.

"*Drayson?*" she demanded.

"Ackbar's on an inspection tour of the Ketaris region," Rieekan said grimly. "That leaves Drayson in charge."

Leia looked up at the master tactical, a sinking feeling settling firmly in her stomach. Drayson was competent enough . . . but against Grand Admiral Thrawn, competent wasn't good enough. "Has the sector fleet been alerted?"

"I think we got the word out to them before the shield went up," Rieekan said. "Unfortunately, one of the first things the Imperials hit was the out-orbit relay station, so there's no way of knowing whether or not they heard. Not without opening the shield."

The sinking feeling sunk a little lower. "Then this isn't just a feint to draw the sector fleet here," Leia said. "Otherwise, they'd have left the relay station alone so we could keep calling for help."

"I agree," Rieekan said. "Whatever Thrawn has in mind, we seem to be it."

Leia nodded wordlessly, gazing up at the visual display. The Star Destroyers had entered the battle stations' outer kill zones now, and the black of space was beginning to sparkle with more serious turbolaser fire. Outside the main fire field, Dreadnaughts and other support ships were forming a perimeter to protect the Star Destroyers from the defenders rising toward them.

On the master tactical, a flicker of pale white light shot upward: an ion cannon blast from the surface, streaking toward the Star Destroyers. "Waste of power," Rieekan muttered contemptuously. "They're way out of range."

And even if they weren't, Leia knew, the electronics-disrupting charge would have had as much chance of hitting the battle station as any of the Star Destroyers it had been aimed at. Ion cannon weren't exactly known for tight-beam accuracy. "We've got to get someone else in command here," she said, looking around the war room. If she could find Mon Mothma and persuade her to put Rieekan in charge—

Abruptly, her eyes stopped their sweep. There, standing against the back wall, gazing up at the master tactical, was Sena Leikvold Midanyl. Chief adviser to General Garm Bel Iblis . . . who was considerably more than merely competent. "I'll be back," she told Rieekan, and headed off into the crowd.

"Councilor Organa Solo," Sena said as Leia reached her, a tautness straining her face and sense. "I was told to stay back here out of the way. Can you tell me what's happening?"

"What's happening is that we need Garm," Leia said, glancing around. "Where is he?"

"Observation gallery," Sena said, nodding upward toward the semicircular balcony running around the back half of the war room.

Leia looked up. Beings of all sorts were beginning to pour into the gallery—government civilians, most of them, who were authorized this deep into the command floor but weren't cleared for access to the war room proper. Sitting alone to one side, gazing intently at the master displays, was Bel Iblis. "Get him down here," Leia told Sena. "We need him."

Sena seemed to sigh. "He won't come down," she said. "Not unless and until Mon Mothma asks him to. His own words."

Leia felt her stomach tighten. Bel Iblis had more than his share of stiff-necked pride, but this was no time for personal squabbles. "He can't do that. We need his help."

Sena shook her head minutely. "I've tried. He won't listen to me."

Leia took a deep breath. "Maybe he'll listen to me."

"I hope so." Sena gestured toward the display, where one of Bel Iblis's Dreadnaughts had appeared from the space dock to join the rising wave of starfighters, Corellian Gunships, and Escort Frigates blazing toward the invaders. "That's the

Harrier," she identified it. "My sons Peter and Dayvid are aboard it."

Leia touched her shoulder. "Don't worry—I'll get him down here."

The center section of the gallery was becoming almost crowded by the time she reached it. But the area around Bel Iblis was still reasonably empty. "Hello, Leia," he said as she came up to him. "I thought you'd be down below."

"I should be—and so should you," Leia said. "We need you down—"

"You have your comlink with you?" he cut her off sharply. She frowned at him. "Yes."

"Get it out. Now. Call Drayson and warn him about those two Interdictors."

Leia looked at the master tactical. The two Interdictor Cruisers that had come in late to the party were doing some fine-tune maneuvering, their hazy gravity-wave cones sweeping across one of the battle stations. "Thrawn pulled this stunt on us at Qat Chrystac," Bel Iblis went on. "He uses an Interdictor Cruiser to define a hyperspace edge, then brings a ship in along an intersecting vector to drop out at a precisely chosen point. Drayson needs to pull some ships up on those flanks to be ready for whatever Thrawn's bringing in."

Leia was already digging in her robe pocket. "But we don't have anything here that can take on another Star Destroyer."

"It's not a matter of taking it on," Bel Iblis told her. "Whatever's on its way will come in blind, with deflectors down and no targeting references. If our ships are in place, we'll get one solid free shot at them. That could make a lot of difference."

"I understand," Leia said, thumbing on her comlink and keying for the central switching operator. "This is Councilor Leia Organa Solo. I have an urgent message for Admiral Drayson."

"Admiral Drayson is occupied and cannot be disturbed," the electronic voice said.

"This is a direct Council override," Leia ordered. "Put me through to Drayson."

"Voice analysis confirmed," the operator said. "Council override is superseded by military emergency procedure. You may leave Admiral Drayson a message."

Leia ground her teeth, throwing a quick glance at the tactical. "Then put me through to Drayson's chief aide."

"Lieutenant DuPre is occupied and cannot—"

"Cancel," Leia cut it off. "Get me General Rieekan."

"General Rieekan is occupied—"

"Too late," Bel Iblis said quietly.

Leia looked up. Two Victory-class Star Destroyers had suddenly appeared out of hyperspace, dropping in at point-blank range to their target battle stations exactly as Bel Iblis had predicted. They delivered massive broadsides, then angled away before the station or its defending Gunships could respond with more than token return fire. On the tactical, the hazy blue shell indicating the stations deflector shield flickered wildly before settling down again.

"Drayson's no match for him," Bel Iblis sighed. "He just isn't."

Leia took a deep breath. "You have to come down, Garm."

He shook his head. "I can't. Not until Mon Mothma asks me to."

"You're behaving like a child," Leia snapped, abandoning any attempt to be diplomatic about this. "You can't let people die out there just because of personal pique."

He looked at her; and as she glared back she was struck by the pain in his eyes. "You don't understand, Leia," he said. "This has nothing to do with me. It has to do with Mon Mothma. After all these years, I finally understand why she does things the way she does. I've always assumed she was gathering more and more power to herself simply because she was in love with power. But I was wrong."

"So why *does* she do it?" Leia demanded, not really interested in talking about Mon Mothma.

"Because with everything she does there are lives hanging in the balance," he said quietly. "And she's terrified of trusting anyone else with those lives."

Leia stared at him . . . but even as she opened her mouth to deny it, all the pieces of her life these past few years fell suddenly into place. All the diplomatic missions Mon Mothma had insisted she go on, no matter what the personal cost in lost Jedi training and strained family life. All the trust she'd invested in Ackbar and a few others; all the responsibility that had been shifted onto fewer and fewer shoulders.

Onto the shoulders of those few she could trust to do the job right.

"That's why I can't simply go down and take command," Bel Iblis said into the silence, "Until she's able to accept me— really accept me—as someone she can trust, she won't ever be able to give me any genuine authority in the New Republic. She'll always need to be hovering around in the background somewhere, watching over my shoulder to make sure I don't make any mistakes. She hasn't got the time for that, I haven't got the patience, and the friction would be devastating for everyone caught in the middle."

He nodded toward the war room. "When she's ready to trust me, I'll be ready to serve. Until then, it's better for everyone involved if I stay out of it."

"Except for those dying out there," Leia reminded him tightly. "Let me call her, Garm, Maybe I can persuade her to offer you command."

Bel Iblis shook his head. "If you have to persuade her, Leia, it doesn't count. She has to decide this for herself."

"Perhaps she has," Mon Mothma's voice came from behind them.

Leia turned in surprise. With all her attention concentrated on Bel Iblis, she hadn't even noticed the older woman's approach. "Mon Mothma," she said, feeling the guilty awkwardness of having being caught talking about someone behind her back. "I—"

"It's all right, Leia," Mon Mothma said. "General Bel Iblis . . ."

Bel Iblis had risen to his feet to face her. "Yes?"

Mon Mothma seemed to brace herself. "We've had more than our share of differences over the years, General. But that was a long time ago. We were a good team once. There's no reason why we can't be one again."

She hesitated again; and with a sudden flash of insight, Leia saw how incredibly difficult this was for her. How humiliating it was to face a man who'd once turned his back on her and to admit aloud that she needed his help. If Bel Iblis was unwilling to bend until she'd said the words he wanted to hear . . .

And then, to Leia's surprise, Bel Iblis straightened to a military attention. "Mon Mothma," he said formally, "given the current emergency, I hereby request your permission to take command of Coruscant's defense."

The lines around Mon Mothma's eyes smoothed noticeably, a quiet relief coloring over her sense. "I would be very grateful if you would do so, Garm."

He smiled. "Then let's get to it."

Together, they headed for the stairway down to the command floor; and with a newly humbled sense of her own limitations, Leia realized that probably half of what she'd just witnessed had passed her by completely. The long and perilous history Mon Mothma and Bel Iblis had shared had created an empathy between them, a bond and understanding far deeper than Leia's Jedi insights could even begin to track through. Perhaps, she decided, it was that empathy that formed the true underlying strength of the New Republic. The strength that would create the future of the galaxy.

If it could withstand the next few hours. Clenching her teeth, she hurried after them.

A PAIR OF Corellian Gunships shot past the *Chimaera*, sending a volley of turbolaser fire spattering across the bridge deflector shield. A squadron of TIE fighters was right on their tail, sweeping into a Rellis flanking maneuver as they tried for a clear shot. Beyond them, Pellaeon spotted an Escort Frigate cutting into backup position across the Gunships' exit vector. "Squadron A-4, move to sector twenty-two," Pellaeon ordered. So far, as near as he could tell, the battle seemed to be going well.

"There they go," Thrawn commented from beside him.

Pellaeon scanned the area. "Where?" he asked.

"They're preparing to pull back," Thrawn told him, pointing to one of the two Rebel Dreadnaughts that had joined the battle. "Observe how that Dreadnaught is moving into cover position for a retreat. There—the second one is following suit."

Pellaeon frowned at the maneuvering Dreadnaughts. He still didn't see it; but he'd never yet seen Thrawn wrong on such a call. "They're abandoning the battle stations?"

Thrawn snorted gently. "They never should have brought those ships out to defend them in the first place. Golan defense platforms can take considerably more punishment than their former ground commander apparently realized."

"Their former ground commander?"

"Yes," Thrawn said. "At a guess, I'd say our old Corellian adversary has just been put in command of Coruscant's defense. I wonder what took them so long."

Pellaeon shrugged, studying the battle area. The Grand Admiral was right: the defenders were starting to pull back. "Perhaps they had to wake him up."

"Perhaps." Thrawn sent a leisurely look around the battle area. "You see how the Corellian offers us a choice: stay here and duel with the battle stations, or follow the defenders down into range of the ground-based weaponry. Fortunately"—his eyes glittered—"we have a third option."

Pellaeon nodded. He'd been wondering when Thrawn would unveil his brilliant new siege weapon. "Yes, sir," he said. "Shall I order the tractor launching?"

"We'll wait for the Corellian to pull his ships back a bit further," Thrawn said. "We wouldn't want him to miss this."

"Understood," Pellaeon said. Stepping back to his command chair, he sat down and confirmed that the asteroids and the hangar-bay tractor beams were ready.

And waited for the Grand Admiral's order.

"ALL RIGHT," BEL IBLIS said. "*Harrier*, begin pulling back—cover those Escort Frigates on your portside flank. Red leader, watch out for those TIE interceptors."

Leia watched the tactical display, holding her breath. Yes; it was going to work. Unwilling to risk the ground-based weaponry, the Imperials were letting the defenders retreat back toward Coruscant. That left only the two battle stations still in danger, and they were proving themselves more capable of absorbing damage than Leia had realized they could. And even that would be ending soon—the Grand Admiral would know better than to be here when the sector fleet arrived. It was almost over, and they'd gotten through it.

"General Bel Iblis?" an officer at one of the monitor stations spoke up. "We're getting a funny reading from the *Chimaera*'s hangar bay."

"What is it?" Bel Iblis asked, stepping over to the console.

"It reads like the launching tractor beams being activated," the officer said, indicating one of the multicolored spots on the Star Destroyer silhouette centered in his display. "But it's pulling far too much power."

"Could they be launching a whole TIE squadron together?" Leia suggested.

"I don't think so," the officer said. "That's the other thing: near as we can tell, nothing at all left the bay."

Beside Leia, Bel Iblis stiffened. "Calculate the exit vector," he ordered. "All ships: sensor focus along that path for drive emissions. I think the *Chimaera*'s just launched a cloaked ship."

Someone nearby swore feelingly. Leia looked up at the master visual display, her throat suddenly tight as the memory of that brief conversation she and Han had had with Admiral Ackbar flashed back to mind. Ackbar had been solidly convinced—and had convinced her—that the double-blind properties of the cloaking shield made it too user-dangerous to be an effective weapon. If Thrawn had found a way around that problem . . .

"They're firing again," the sensor officer reported. "And again."

"Same from the *Death's Head*," another officer put in. "—firing again."

"Signal the battle stations to track and fire along those vectors," Bel Iblis ordered. "As close to the Star Destroyers as possible. We've got to find out what Thrawn's up to."

The word was barely out of his mouth when there was a flash of light from the visual display. One of the Escort Frigates along the first projected vector was suddenly ablaze, its aft section trailing fiery drive gases as the whole ship spun wildly about its transverse axis. "Collision!" someone barked. "Escort Frigate *Evanrue*—impact with unknown object."

"Impact?" Bel Iblis echoed. "Not a turbolaser shot?"

"Telemetry indicates physical impact," the other shook his head.

Leia looked back at the visual, where the *Evanrue* was now wreathed in burning gas as it fought to get its spin under control. "Cloaking shields are supposed to be double-blind," Leia said. "How are they maneuvering?"

"Maybe they're not," Bel Iblis said, his voice dark with suspicion. "Tactical: give me a new track from point of impact with the *Evanrue*. Assume inert object; calculate impact velocity by distance to the *Chimaera*, and don't forget to factor in the local gravitational field. Feed probable location to the *Harrier*; order it to open fire as soon as it has the coordinates."

"Yes, sir," one of the lieutenants spoke up. "Feeding to the *Harrier* now,"

"On second thought, belay that last," Bel Iblis said, holding up a hand. "Order the *Harrier* to use its ion cannon only— repeat, ion cannon only. No turbolasers."

Leia frowned at him. "You're trying to take the ship intact?"

"I'm trying to take it intact, yes," Bel Iblis said slowly. "But I don't think it's a ship."

He fell silent. On the visual, the *Harrier*'s ion cannon began to fire.

THE DREADNAUGHT OPENED FIRE, as indeed Thrawn had predicted it would. But only, Pellaeon noted with some surprise, with its ion cannon. "Admiral?"

"Yes, I see," Thrawn said. "Interesting. I was right, Captain—our old Corellian adversary is indeed in command below. But he's allowed us to lead him by the nose only so far."

Pellaeon nodded as understanding suddenly came. "He's trying to knock out the asteroid's cloaking shield."

"Hoping to take it intact." Thrawn touched his control board. "Forward turbolaser batteries: track and target asteroid number one. Fire on my command only."

Pellaeon looked down at his magnified visual display. The Dreadnaught had found its target, its ion beams vanishing in midspace as they flooded down into the cloaking shield. It shouldn't be able to take much more of that. . . .

Abruptly, the stars in that empty region vanished. For a couple of heartbeats there was complete blackness as the cloaking shield collapsed in on itself; then, just as abruptly, the newly uncloaked asteroid was visible.

The ion beams cut off "Turbolasers, stand by," Thrawn said. "We want them to have a good look first. . . . Turbolasers: fire."

Pellaeon shifted his attention to the viewport. The green fire lanced out, disappearing into the distance as they converged on their target. A second later, there was a faint flash from that direction, a flash that was repeated more strongly from his visual display. Another salvo—another—and another—

"Cease fire," Thrawn said with clear satisfaction. "They're welcome to whatever's left. Hangar bay: firing status."

"We're up to seventy-two, sir," the engineering officer reported, his voice sounding a little strained. "But the power feedback shunt's starting to glow white. We can't keep up these dry firings much longer without burning out either the shunt or the tractor projector itself."

"Close down dry firing," Thrawn ordered, "and signal the other ships to do likewise. How many total firings have there been, Captain?"

Pellaeon checked the figures. "Two hundred eighty-seven," he told the Grand Admiral.

"I presume all twenty-two actual asteroids are out?"

"Yes, sir," Pellaeon confirmed. "Most of them in the first two minutes. Though there's no way of knowing if they've taken up their prescribed orbits."

"The specific orbits are irrelevant," Thrawn assured him. "All that matters is that the asteroids are somewhere in the space around Coruscant."

Pellaeon smiled. Yes, they were . . . except that there were only a fraction of the number the Rebels thought were there. "And now we leave, sir?"

"Now we leave," Thrawn confirmed. "For the moment, at least, Coruscant is effectively out of the war."

DRAYSON NODDED TO the battle ops colonel and stepped back to the small group waiting for him a short distance behind the consoles. "The final numbers are in," he said, his voice sounding a little hollow. "They can't be absolutely certain they didn't miss any through the battle debris. But even so . . . their count is two hundred eighty-seven."

"Two hundred eighty-seven?" General Rieekan repeated, his jaw dropping slightly.

"That's the number," Drayson nodded, turning his glare on Bel Iblis. As if, Leia thought, all this was somehow Bel Iblis's fault. "What now?"

Bel Iblis was rubbing his cheek thoughtfully. "For starters, I don't think the situation is quite as bad as it looks," he said. "From everything I've heard about how expensive cloaking shields are, I can't see Thrawn squandering the kind of resources three hundred of them would take. Especially when a much smaller number would do the job just as well."

"You think the other tractor beam firings were faked?" Leia asked.

"They couldn't have been," Rieekan objected. "I was watching the sensor board. Those projectors were definitely drawing power."

Bel Iblis looked at Drayson. "You know more about Star Destroyers than the rest of us, Admiral. Is it possible?"

Drayson frowned off into the distance, professional pride momentarily eclipsing his personal animosity toward Bel Iblis. "It could be done," he agreed at last. "You could run a feedback shunt from the tractor beam projector, either to a flash capacitor or a power dissipator somewhere else on the ship. That would let you run a sizable surge of power through the projector without it really doing anything."

"Is there any way to tell the difference between that and an actual asteroid launch?" Mon Mothma asked.

"From this distance?" Drayson shook his head. "No."

"It almost doesn't matter how many are up there," Rieekan said. "Eventually, their orbits will decay, and letting even one hit ground would be a disaster. Until we've cleared them out, we can't risk lowering the planetary shield."

"The problem being how we locate them," Drayson agreed heavily. "And how we know when we've gotten them all."

A movement caught Leia's eye, and she looked over as a tight-faced Colonel Bremen joined them. "Again, it could be worse," Bel Iblis pointed out. "The sector fleet can have the out-orbit relay station replaced in a few hours, so at least we'll still be able to direct the New Republic's defense from here."

"It'll also make it easier to transmit an all-worlds alert," Bremen spoke up. "Mara Jade's escaped."

Mon Mothma inhaled sharply. "How?" she asked.

"With help," Bremen said grimly. "The guard droid was deactivated. Some kind of jury-rigged restraining bolt. It erased that section of memory, too."

"How long ago?" Rieekan asked.

"No more than a few hours." Bremen glanced around the war room. "We've had extra security on the command floor since the break was discovered, thinking they might have been planning some sabotage to coincide with the Imperials' attack."

"That could still be the plan," Bel Iblis said. "Have you sealed off the Palace?"

"Like a smuggler's profit box," Bremen said. "I doubt they're still here, though."

"We'll need to make certain of that," Mon Mothma said. "I want you to organize a complete search of the Palace, Colonel."

Bremen nodded. "Right away."

Leia braced herself. They weren't going to be happy about this. "Don't bother, Colonel," she said, touching Bremen's arm to stop him as he turned to leave. "Mara's not here."

They all looked at her. "How do you know?" Bel Iblis asked.

"Because she left Coruscant earlier tonight. Along with Han and Luke."

There was a long silence. "I wondered why Solo didn't come to the war room with you," Bel Iblis said. "You want to tell us what's going on?"

Leia hesitated; but surely none of these people could possibly have anything to do with the Delta Source security leak. "Mara thinks she knows where the Empire's cloning facility might be. We thought it would be worth sending her and a small team to check it out."

"*We* thought?" Drayson snapped. "Who is this *we*?"

Leia looked him straight in the eye. "My family and closest friends," she said. "The only people I can be absolutely certain aren't leaking information to the Empire."

"That is a gross insult—"

"Enough, Admiral," Mon Mothma cut him off calmly. Calmly, but there was a hardness around her eyes. "Whatever reprimands may be due here can wait until later. Whether it was prudent or otherwise, the fact remains that they're on their way, and we need to decide how best to help them. Leia?"

"The most important thing to do is to pretend Mara's still here," Leia said, the tightness in her chest easing slightly. "She told me she'd only been to Wayland once, and she couldn't guess how long it would take her to reconstruct the route. The longer lead they have, the less time the Empire will have to rush reinforcements there."

"What happens then?" Mon Mothma asked. "Assuming they find it."

"They'll try to destroy it."

There was a moment of silence. "By themselves," Drayson said.

"Unless you have a spare fleet to lend them, yes," Leia said.

Mon Mothma shook her head. "You shouldn't have done it, Leia," she said. "Not without consulting the Council."

"If I'd brought it to the Council, Mara might be dead now," Leia said bluntly. "If news leaked to the Empire that she could find Wayland, the next commando team they sent wouldn't stop at just trying to discredit her."

"The Council is above suspicion," Mon Mothma said, her voice turning chilly.

"Are all the Council members' aides?" Leia countered. "Or the tactical people and supply officers and library researchers? If I'd suggested an attack on Wayland to the Council, all of those people would eventually have known about it."

"And more," Bel Iblis nodded. "She has a point, Mon Mothma."

"I'm not interested in laying blame, Garm," Mon Mothma said quietly, "Nor in defending anyone's little niche of power. I'm concerned about the possibility that all this was indeed a setup, Leia . . . and that it will cost your husband and brother their lives."

Leia swallowed hard. "We thought about that, too," she said. "But we decided it was worth the risk. And there was no one else to do it."

For a long minute no one said anything. Then Mon Mothma stirred. "You'll need to talk to everyone who knows Mara Jade is gone, Colonel," she said to Bremen. "If and when we obtain Wayland's location, we'll see what we can do about sending reinforcements to help them."

"Provided we can be sure it isn't a trap," Drayson added, glowering.

"Of course," Mon Mothma agreed, avoiding Leia's eyes. "For now, that's all we can do. Let's concentrate on Coruscant's immediate problems: defense, and finding those cloaked asteroids. General Bel Iblis—"

A tentative hand touched Leia's shoulder, and she turned to find the slicer Ghent standing there. "It's all over?" he muttered to her.

"The battle is, yes," she said, glancing at Mon Mothma and the others. They were already knee-deep into a discussion about the asteroids, but eventually one of them was bound to notice Ghent and realize he wasn't supposed to be here. "Come on," she told him, steering him back toward the war room exit. "I'll tell you all about it outside. What did you think of Imperial battle encrypt codes?"

"Oh, they're okay," he said. "The guys in there didn't let me do all that much, really. I didn't know their machines as well as they did. They had kind of a silly drill going, too."

Leia smiled. The best and smoothest decrypting routine the New Republic's experts had come up with, and Ghent considered it a silly drill. "People get into routines on the way they do things," she said diplomatically. "Maybe I can arrange for you

to talk to the person in overall charge and offer some suggestions."

Ghent waved a vague hand. "Naw. Military types wouldn't
like the way I do things. Even Karrde gets bent out by it sometimes. By the way, you know that pulse transmitter you've got
going somewhere nearby?"

"The one Delta Source has been using?" Leia nodded.
"Counterintelligence has been trying to locate it since it started
transmitting. But it's some sort of cross-frequency split-phase
something-or-other, and they haven't had any luck."

"Oh." Ghent seemed to digest that. "Well, that's a tech
problem. I don't know anything about those."

"That's all right," Leia assured him. "I'm sure you'll find
other ways to help."

"Yeah," he said, digging a data card from his pocket. "Anyway . . . here."

She frowned as she took the card. "What's this?"

"It's the encrypt code from the pulse transmitter."

Leia stopped short. "It's *what*?"

He stopped too, turning innocent eyes on her. "The encrypt
code that cross-frequency whatsis is using. I finally got it
sliced."

She stared at him. "Just like that? You just went ahead and
sliced it?"

He shrugged again. "Well, sort of. I've been working on it
for a month, you know."

Leia gazed at the data card in her hand, a strange and not
entirely pleasant thrill of excitement tingling through her.
"Does anyone know you have this?" she asked quietly.

He shook his head. "I thought about giving it to that colonel in there before I left, but he was busy talking to someone."

Delta Source's encrypt code . . . and Delta Source didn't
know they had it. "Don't tell anyone else," she said. "And I
mean *anyone*."

Ghent frowned, but shrugged. "Okay. Whatever you say."

"Thank you," Leia murmured, sliding the data card into her robe pocket. It was the key to Delta Source—deep within her, she knew that. All she needed was to find the right way to use it.

And to find it fast.

CHAPTER 15

THE FORTRESS OF HIJARNA had been crumbling slowly away for perhaps a thousand years before the Fifth Alderaanian Expedition had spotted it, keeping its silent, deserted vigil over its silent, deserted world. A vast expanse of incredibly hard black stone, it stood on a high bluff overlooking a plain that still bore the deep scars of massive destruction. To some, the enigmatic fortress was a tragic monument: a last-ditch attempt at defense by a desperate world under siege. To others, it was the brooding and malicious cause of both that siege and the devastation that had followed.

To Karrde, for the moment at least, it was home.

"You sure know how to pick em, Karrde," Gillespee commented, propping his feet up on the edge of the auxiliary comm desk and looking around. "How did you find this place, anyway?"

"It's all right there in the old records," Karrde told him, watching his display as the decrypt program ran its course. A star map appeared, accompanied by a very short text . . .

Gillespee nodded toward Karrde's display. "Clyngunn's report?"

"Yes," Karrde said, pulling out the data card. "Such as it is."

"Nothing, right?"

"Pretty much. No indications of clone traffic anywhere on Poderis, Chazwa, or Joiol."

Gillespee dropped his feet off the table and stood up. "Well, that's that, then," he said, stepping over to the fruit rack someone had laid out on a side table and picking himself out a driblis fruit. "Looks like whatever the Empire had going in Orus sector has dried up. If there was anything going there in the first place."

"Given the lack of a trail, I suspect the latter," Karrde agreed, choosing one of the cards that had come from his contact on Bespin and sliding it into the display. "Still, it was something we needed to know, one way or the other. Among other things, it frees us up to concentrate on other possibilities."

"Yeah," Gillespee said reluctantly as he went back to his seat. "Well . . . you know, Karrde, this whole thing has been kind of strange. Smugglers, I mean, doing this kind of snoop work. Hasn't paid very much, either."

"I've already told you we'll be getting some reimbursement from the New Republic."

"Except that we don't have anything to sell them," Gillespee pointed out. "Never known anyone yet who paid for no delivery."

Karrde frowned over at him. Gillespee had produced a wicked-looking knife from somewhere and was carefully carving a slice from the driblis fruit. "This isn't about getting paid," he reminded the other. "It's about surviving against the Empire."

"Maybe for you it is," Gillespee said, studying the slice of fruit a moment before taking a bite. "You've got enough sidelines going that you can afford to lay off business for a while. But, see, the rest of us have payrolls to meet and ships to keep fueled. The money stops coming in, our employees start getting nasty."

"So you and the others want money?"

He could see Gillespee brace himself. "I want money. The others want out."

It was not, in retrospect, exactly an unexpected development. The white-hot anger toward the Empire that had been sparked by that attack at the Whistler's Whirlpool was cooling, and the habits of day-to-day business were beginning to reassert themselves. "The Empire's still dangerous," he said.

"Not to us," Gillespee said bluntly. "There hasn't been a single blip of Imperial attention directed toward us since the Whirlpool. They didn't mind us poking around Orus sector; they didn't even come down on Mazzic for that thing at the Bilbringi shipyards."

"So they're ignoring us, despite provocation to do otherwise. Does that make you feel safe?"

Carefully, Gillespee sliced himself off another piece of fruit. "I don't know," he conceded. "Half the time I think Brasck's right, that if we leave the Empire alone, it'll leave us alone. But I can't help thinking about that army of clones Thrawn chased me off Ukio with. I start thinking that maybe he's just too busy with the New Republic to bother with us right now."

Karrde shook his head. "Thrawn's never too busy to chase someone down if he wants them," he said. "If he's ignoring us, it's because he knows that's the best way to quiet any opposition. Next step will probably be to offer us transport contracts and pretend that we're all good friends again."

Gillespee looked at him sharply. "You been talking to Par'tah?"

"No. Why?"

"She told me two days ago that she's been offered a contract to bring a bunch of sublight engines to the Imperial shipyards at Ord Trasi."

Karrde grimaced. "Has she accepted?"

"Said she was still working out the details. But you know Par'tah—she's always running right on the edge. Probably can't afford to say no."

Karrde turned back to his display, the sour taste of defeat in his mouth. "I suppose I can't really blame her," he said. "What about the others?"

Gillespee shrugged uncomfortably. "Like I said, the money keeps going out. We have to have money coming in, too."

And just like that, the reluctant coalition he'd tried to put together was falling apart. And the Empire hadn't had to fire a single shot to do it. "Then I suppose I'll just have to go it alone," he said, standing up. "Thank you for your assistance. I'm sure you'll want to be getting back to business."

"Now, don't get all huffy, Karrde," Gillespee chided him, taking one last bite of fruit and getting to his feet. "You're right, this clone stuff is serious business. If you want to hire my ships and people for your hunt, we'll be happy to help you out. We just can't afford to do it for free anymore, that's all. Just let us know." He turned toward the door—

"Just a minute," Karrde called after him. A rather audacious thought had just occurred to him. "Suppose I find a way to guarantee funding for everyone. You think the others would stay aboard, too?"

Gillespee eyed him suspiciously. "Don't con me, Karrde. You don't have that kind of money lying around."

"No. But the New Republic does. And under the current situation, I don't think they'd be averse to having a few more fighting ships on the payroll."

"Uh-uh," Gillespee shook his head firmly. "Sorry, but privateer is a little out of my line."

"Even if your duty consists entirely of collecting information?" Karrde asked. "I'm not talking about anything more than what you were just doing in Orus sector."

"Sounds like a dream assignment," Gillespee said sardonically. "Except for the tiny little problem of finding someone in the New Republic stupid enough to pay privateer rates for snoop duty."

Karrde smiled. "Actually, I wasn't planning to waste their valuable time telling them about it. Have you ever met my associate Ghent?"

For a moment Gillespee just stared at him, looking puzzled. Then, abruptly, he got it. "You wouldn't"

"Why not?" Karrde countered. "On the contrary, we'd be doing them a service. Why clutter their lives with these troublesome accounting details while they're trying to survive a war?"

"And since they'd have to pay anyway once we found the clone center for them . . ."

"Exactly," Karrde nodded. "We can consider this merely a prepayment for work about to be rendered."

"Just as well they won't know about it until it's over," Gillespee said dryly. "Question is, can Ghent pull it off?"

"Easily," Karrde assured him. "Particularly since he's inside the Imperial Palace on Coruscant at the moment. I was planning to head that way soon to pick up Mara anyway; I'll simply have him slice into some sector fleet's records and write us in."

Gillespee exhaled noisily. "It's got possibilities—I'll give it that much. Don't know if it'll be enough to get the others back on board, though."

"Then we'll just have to ask them," Karrde said, stepping back to his desk. "Invitations for, say, four days from now?"

Gillespee shrugged. "Give it a try. What have you got to lose?"

Karrde sobered. "With Grand Admiral Thrawn," he reminded the other, "that's not a question to ever ask lightly."

THE EVENING BREEZE moved through the crumbling walls and stone columns of the ruined fortress, occasionally whistling softly as it found its way through a small hole or crevice. Sitting with his back to one of the pillars, Karrde sipped at his cup and watched the last sliver of the sun disappear below the horizon. On the plain below, the long shadows stretching across the scarred ground were beginning to fade as the coming darkness of night began its inexorable move across the landscape.

All in all, rather symbolic of the way this galactic war had finally caught up with Karrde himself.

He took another sip from his cup, marveling once again at this whole absurd situation. Here he was: an intelligent, calculating, appropriately selfish smuggler who'd made a successful career out of keeping his distance from galactic politics. A smuggler, moreover, who'd sworn explicitly to keep his people out of this particular war. And yet, somehow, here he was, squarely in the middle of it.

And not only in the middle of it, but trying his best to drag other smugglers in after him.

He shook his head in vague annoyance. This exact same thing, he knew, had happened to Han Solo sometime around the big Yavin battle. He could remember being highly amused by Solo's gradual entanglement in the Rebel Alliance's nets of duty and responsibility. Looking at it from the inside of the net, the whole thing wasn't nearly so entertaining.

From across the battered courtyard came the faint sound of crunching gravel. Karrde turned to look at the line of stone pillars in that direction, his hand dropping to his blaster. No one else was supposed to be here at the moment. "Sturm?" he called softly. "Drang?"

The familiar cackling/purr came in response, and Karrde let out a quiet sigh of relief. "Over here," he called to the animal. "Come on—over here."

The order was unnecessary. The vornskr was already loping around the pillars toward him, its muzzle low to the ground, the stub of its truncated whip tail wagging madly behind him. Probably Drang, Karrde decided: he was the more sociable of the two, and Sturm had a tendency to dawdle over his meals.

The vornskr skidded to a halt beside him, giving another of his strange cackle/purrs—a rather mournful one this time—as he pressed his muzzle up into Karrde's outstretched palm. It was Drang, all right. "Yes, it's very quiet," Karrde told him, running his hand back up across the animal's face and around to scratch at the sensitive skin behind his ears. "But the others will be back soon. They've just gone out to check on the other ships."

Drang gave another mournful cackle/purr and dropped into a half-crouch beside Karrde's chair, staring alertly out over the empty plain below. But whatever he was looking for, he didn't find it, and after a moment he growled deep in his throat and lowered his muzzle to rest on the stone. His ears twitched once, as if straining to hear a sound that wasn't there, and then they, too, folded back down.

"It's quiet down there, too," Karrde agreed soberly, stroking the vornskr's fur. "What do you suppose happened here?"

Drang didn't answer. Karrde gazed down at the vornskr's lean, muscled back, wondering yet again about these strange predators he'd so casually—perhaps even arrogantly—decided to make pets of. Wondering if he'd have thought twice about doing so if he'd realized that he was dealing with possibly the only animals in the galaxy who hunted via the Force.

It was a preposterous conclusion, on the face of it. Force sensitivity itself wasn't unheard of, certainly—the Gotal had a fairly useless form of it, and there were persistent rumors about the Duinuogwuin as well, to name just two. But all those who had such sensitivity were sentient creatures, with the high levels of intelligence and self-awareness that that implied. For non-sentient animals to use the Force this way was something new.

But it was a conclusion that the events of the past few months had forced him to. There had been his pets' unexpected reaction to Luke Skywalker at Karrde's Myrkr base. There'd been the similar and, again, previously unseen reaction to Mara aboard the *Wild Karrde*, just before the hunch she'd had that had saved them from that Imperial Interdictor Cruiser. There'd been the far more vicious reaction of the wild vornskrs toward both Mara and Skywalker during their three-day trek through the Myrkr forests.

Skywalker was a Jedi. Mara had shown some decidedly Jedi-like talents. And perhaps even more telling, the existence of the bizarre Force-empty bubbles created by Myrkr's ysalamiri could finally be explained if they were simply a form of defense or camouflage against predators.

Abruptly Drang's head snapped up, his ears stiffening as he twisted halfway around. Karrde strained his ears . . . and a few seconds later he heard the faint sounds of the returning shuttle. "It's all right," he assured the vornskr. "It's just Chin and the others, back from the ship."

Drang held the pose a moment longer. Then, as if deciding to take Karrde's word for it, he turned and laid his head back down again. Looking out over a plain that, if Karrde's suspicion was right, was more silent even for him than it was for Karrde. "Don't worry," he soothed the animal, scratching again behind his ears. "We'll be out of here soon. And I promise that the next place we go will have plenty of other life around for you to listen to."

The vornskr's ears twitched, but that might have been just the scratching. Taking one last look at the fading colors of sunset, Karrde stood up, resettling his gun belt across his hips. There was no particular reason to go in yet, of course. The invitations had been written, encrypted, and transmitted, and for now there was nothing to do except wait for the replies. But suddenly it felt lonely out here. Much lonelier that it had a few minutes ago. "Come on, Drang," he said, reaching down for one last pat. "Time to go in."

THE SHUTTLE SETTLED to the floor of the *Chimaera*'s hangar bay, release valves hissing over the heads of the stormtroopers moving purposefully into escort position around the lowering ramp. Pellaeon stayed where he was beside Thrawn, grimacing at the smell of the skid gases and wishing he knew what in the Empire the Grand Admiral was up to this time.

Whatever it was, he had a bad feeling that he wasn't going

to like it. Thrawn could talk all he liked about how predictable these smugglers were; and maybe to him they were. But Pellaeon had had his own share of dealings with this sort of fringe scum, and he'd never yet seen a deal that hadn't gone sour one way or the other.

And none of *those* deals had started from the sheer audacity of an attack on an Imperial shipyard.

The ramp finished its descent and locked in place. The stormtrooper commander peered up into the shuttle and nodded . . . and, flanked by two black-clad fleet troopers, the prisoner descended to the deck.

"Ah—Captain Mazzic," Thrawn said smoothly as the stormtroopers fell into escort positions around him. "Welcome to the *Chimaera*. I apologize for this rather theatrical summons and any problems it may have created in your business scheduling. But there are certain matters that cannot be discussed other than face-to-face."

"You're very funny," Mazzic snarled. A marked contrast, Pellaeon thought, to the suave, sophisticated ladies' man that had been profiled in Intelligence's files. But then, the knowledge that one was facing an Imperial interrogation was enough to strip the civilized polish from any man. "How did you find me?"

"Come now, Captain," Thrawn admonished him calmly. "Did you seriously think you could hide from me if I wanted you found?"

"Karrde managed it," Mazzic shot back. Trying hard to put up a good front; but the manacled hands were working nervously at each other. "You still haven't got him, have you?"

"Karrde's time will come," Thrawn told him, his voice still calm but noticeably cooler. "But we're not talking about Karrde. We're talking about you."

"Yes, and I'm sure you're looking forward to it," Mazzic growled, waving his manacled hands. "Let's get it over with."

Thrawn's eyebrows lifted slightly. "You misunderstand,

Captain. You're not here for punishment. You're here because I wanted to clear the air between us."

Mazzic paused in midbluster. "What are you talking about?" he asked suspiciously.

"I'm talking about the recent incident at the Bilbringi shipyards," Thrawn said. "No, don't deny it—I know it was you and Ellor who destroyed that unfinished Star Destroyer. And normally the Empire would exact an extremely high price for such an act. However, under these particular circumstances, I'm prepared to let it go."

Mazzic stared at him. "I don't understand."

"It's very simple, Captain." Thrawn gestured, and one of Mazzic's escort began removing his restraints. "Your attack on Bilbringi was in revenge for a similar attack against a smugglers' meeting you attended on Trogan. All well and good; except that neither I nor any senior Imperial officer authorized that attack. In fact, the garrison commander had explicit orders to leave your meeting alone."

Mazzic snorted. "You expect me to believe that?"

Thrawn's eyes glittered. "Would you rather believe I was so incompetent that I allowed an inadequate field force to be sent on a mission?" he bit out.

Mazzic eyed him, still hostile but starting to look a little thoughtful, as well, "I always thought we got away too easily," he muttered.

"Then we understand each other," Thrawn said, his voice calm again. "And the matter is settled. The shuttle has orders to take you back to your base." He smiled faintly. "Or, rather, to the backup base your ship and crew will have fled to by now on Lelmra. Again, my apologies for the inconvenience."

Mazzic's eyes darted around the hangar bay, his expression halfway between suspicion that this was a trick and an almost painfully eager hope that it wasn't. "And I'm just supposed to believe you?" he demanded.

"You're welcome to believe anything you wish," Thrawn

said. "But remember that I had you in my hand . . . and that I let you go. Good day, Captain."

He started to turn away. "So who were they?" Mazzic called after him. "If they weren't Imperial troops, I mean?"

Thrawn turned back to face him. "They were indeed Imperial troops," he said. "Our inquiries are still incomplete, but at the moment it appears that Lieutenant Kosk and his men were attempting to make a little extra money on the side."

Mazzic stared. "Someone *hired* them to hit us? Imperial troops?"

"Even Imperial troops are not always immune to the lure of bribery," Thrawn said, his voice dark with an excellent imitation of bitter contempt. "In this case, they paid for their treason with their lives. Be assured that the person or persons responsible will pay a similar price."

"You know who it was?" Mazzic demanded.

"I believe I know," Thrawn said. "As yet, I have no proof."

"Give me a hint."

Thrawn smiled sardonically. "Form your own hints, Captain. Good day."

He turned and strode back toward the archway leading to the service and prep areas. Pellaeon waited long enough to watch Mazzic and his escort turn and start back up into the shuttle, then hurried to join him. "Do you think you gave him enough, Admiral?" he asked quietly.

"It won't matter, Captain," Thrawn assured him. "We've given him all that's necessary; and if Mazzic himself isn't clever enough to finger Karrde, one of the other smuggler chiefs will be. In any case, it's always better to offer too little rather than too much. Some people automatically distrust free information."

Behind them, the shuttle lifted from the deck and swung back around into space . . . and from the archway ahead a grinning figure emerged. "Nicely done, Admiral," Niles Ferrier said, shifting his cigarra to the other side of his mouth.

"You got him all squirmy and then tossed him back. He'll be thinking about that for a long time."

"Thank you, Ferrier," Thrawn said dryly. "Your approval means so very much to me."

For a second the ship thief's grin seemed to slip. Then, apparently, he decided to take the comment at face value. "Okay," he said. "So what's our next move?"

Thrawn's eyes flashed at the *our*, but he let it go. "Karrde sent out a series of transmissions last night, one of which we intercepted," he said. "We're still decrypting it, but it can only be a call for another meeting. Once we have the location and time, they'll be provided to you."

"And I'll go and help Mazzic finger Karrde," Ferrier nodded.

"You'll do nothing of the sort," Thrawn said sharply. "You will sit in a corner and keep your mouth shut."

Ferrier seemed to shrink back. "Okay. Sure."

Thrawn held his gaze another moment. "What you *will* do," he continued at last, "is to make certain that a certain data card is placed into Karrde's possession. Preferably in the office aboard his ship—that will be where Mazzic will probably look first."

He motioned, and an officer stepped forward and handed Ferrier a data card. "Ah," Ferrier said slyly as he took it. "Yeah, I get it. The record of Karrde's deal with this Lieutenant Kosk, huh?"

"Correct," Thrawn said. "That, plus the supporting evidence we've already inserted into Kosk's own personal records should leave no doubt that Karrde has been manipulating the other smugglers. I expect that to be more than adequate."

"Yeah, they're a pretty nasty bunch, all right." Ferrier turned the data card over in his hand, chewing on his cigarra. "Okay. So all I gotta do is get aboard the *Wild Karrde*—"

He broke off at the look on Thrawn's face. "No," the Grand Admiral said quietly. "On the contrary, you'll stay as far away from his ship and private ground facilities as possible. In fact, you will never allow yourself to be alone while you're at his base."

Ferrier blinked in surprise. "Yeah, but . . ." Helplessly, he held up the data card.

Beside him, Pellaeon felt Thrawn's sigh of strained patience. "Your Defel will be the one to plant the data card aboard the *Wild Karrde*."

Ferrier's face cleared. "Oh, yeah. Yeah. He can probably slip in and out without anyone even noticing."

"He had better," Thrawn warned; and suddenly his voice was icy cold. "Because I haven't forgotten your role in the deaths of Lieutenant Kosk and his men. You owe the Empire, Ferrier. And that debt will be paid."

Behind his beard, Ferrier's face had gone a little pale. "I got it, Admiral."

"Good," Thrawn said. "You'll remain on your ship until Decrypt obtains the location of Karrde's meeting for you. After that, you'll be on your own."

"Sure," Ferrier said, stuffing the data card into his tunic. "So. After they take care of Karrde, what do I do?"

"You'll be free to go about your business," Thrawn said. "When I want you again, I'll let you know."

Ferrier's lip twitched. "Sure," he repeated.

And on his face, Pellaeon saw that he was slowly starting to realize just how deep his debt to the Empire really was.

CHAPTER 16

THE PLANET WAS GREEN and blue and mottled white, pretty much like all the other planets Han had dropped in on over the years. With the minor exception that this one didn't have a name.

Or spaceports. Or orbit facilities. Or cities, power plants, or other ships. Or much of anything else.

"That's it, huh?" he asked Mara.

She didn't answer. Han looked over and found her staring at the planet hanging out there in front of them. "Well, is it or isn't it?" he prompted.

"It is," she said, her voice strangely hollow. "We're here."

"Good," Han said, still frowning at her. "Great. You going to tell us where this mountain is? Or are we just going to fly around and see where we draw fire from?"

Mara seemed to shake herself. "It's about halfway between the equator and the north pole," she said. "Near the eastern edge of the main continent. A single mountain, rising out of forest and grassland."

"Okay," Han said, feeding in the information and hoping the sensors wouldn't loop out and fail on him. Mara had made enough snide comments about the *Falcon* as it was.

Behind him, the cockpit door slid open, and Lando and Chewbacca came in. "How about it?" Lando asked. "We there?"

"We're there," Mara said before Han could answer.

Chewbacca rumbled a question. "No, seems to be a real low-tech place," Han shook his head. "No power sources or transmissions anywhere."

"Military bases?" Lando asked.

"If they're there, I can't find 'em," Han said.

"Interesting," Lando murmured, peering over Mara's shoulder. "I wouldn't have pegged the Grand Admiral as being the trusting sort."

"The place was designed to be a private storehouse," Mara reminded him tartly. "Not a display ad for Imperial hardware. There weren't any garrisons or command centers scattered around for Thrawn to have moved into."

"So whatever he's got will be stashed inside the mountain?" Han asked.

"Plus probably a few ground patrols just outside," Mara said. "But they won't have any fighter squadrons or heavy weaponry to throw at us."

"That'll be a nice change," Lando said wryly.

"Unless Thrawn decided to put up a couple of garrisons on his own," Han pointed out. "You and Chewie'd better charge up the quads, just in case."

"Right."

The two of them left. Han shifted into a general approach vector, then keyed for a sensor search. "Trouble?" Mara asked.

"Probably not," Han assured her, watching the displays. But there was nothing showing anywhere around them. "A couple of times on the way in I thought I spotted something hanging around back there."

"Calrissian thought he saw something when we changed course at Obroa-skai, too," Mara said, peering down at the display. "Could be something with a really good sensor stealth mode."

"Or just a glitch," Han said. "The Fabritech's been giving us trouble lately."

Mara craned her neck to look out to starboard. "Could someone have followed us here from Coruscant?"

"Who knew we were coming?" Han countered. No, there was nothing there. Must have been his imagination. "How much of this private storehouse did you see?"

Slowly, Mara turned back to face forward, not looking all that convinced. "Not much more than the route between the entrance and the throne room at the top," she said. "But I know where the Spaarti cylinder chamber is."

"How about the power generators?"

"I never actually saw them," she said. "But I remember hearing that the cooling system pulls in water from a river flowing down the northeastern slope of the mountain. They're probably somewhere on that side."

Han chewed at his lip. "And the main entrance is on the southwest side."

"The *only* entrance," she corrected. "There's just the one way in or out."

"I've heard that before."

"This time it's true," she retorted.

Han shrugged. "Okay," he said. There was no point in arguing about it. Not until they'd looked the place over, anyway.

The cockpit door slid open, and he glanced over his shoulder to see Luke come in. "We're here, kid," he said.

"I know," Luke said, moving forward to stand behind Mara. "Mara told me."

Han threw a look at Mara. Near as he could tell, she'd spent the whole trip avoiding Luke, which wasn't all that easy on a ship the size of the *Falcon*. Luke had returned the favor by staying out of her way, which wasn't much easier. "She did, huh?"

"It's all right," Luke assured him, gazing out at the planet ahead. "So that's Wayland."

"That's Wayland," Mara said shortly, unstrapping and brushing past Luke. "I'll be in back," she said over her shoulder, and left.

"You two work so well together," Han commented as the cockpit door slid shut behind her.

"Actually, we do," Luke said, sliding into the copilot's seat Mara had just vacated. "You should have seen us aboard the *Chimaera* when we went in to rescue Karrde. She's a good person to have at your side."

Han threw him a sideways look. "Except when she wants to slide a knife in it."

"I'm willing to take my chances." Luke smiled. "Must be one of those crazy Jedi things."

"This isn't funny, Luke," Han growled. "She hasn't given up on killing you, you know. She told Leia that back on Coruscant."

"Which tells me that she really doesn't want to do it," Luke countered. "People don't usually go around announcing murder plans in advance. Especially not to the victim's family."

"You willing to bet your life on that?"

Luke shrugged fractionally. "I already have."

The *Falcon* was skimming along the outer atmosphere now, and the computer had finally identified a probable location for Mount Tantiss. "Well, if you ask me, this isn't a good time to be running short odds," he told Luke, giving the sensor map a quick study. A straight-in southern approach, he decided— that would give them forest cover for both the landing and the overland trip.

"You have any suggestions?" Luke asked.

"Yeah, I've got one," Han said, changing course toward the distant mountain. "We leave her with the *Falcon* at the landing site."

"Alive?"

At other times in his life, Han reflected, it wouldn't necessarily have been a ridiculous question. "Of course alive," he said stiffly. "There are a lot of ways to keep her from getting into trouble."

"You really think she'd agree to stay behind?"

"No one said we had to ask her."

Luke shook his head. "We can't do that, Han. She needs to see this through."

"Which part of it?" Han growled. "Hitting the clone factory, or trying to kill you?"

"I don't know," Luke said quietly. "Maybe both."

HAN HAD NEVER liked forests very much before joining the Rebel Alliance. Which wasn't to say he'd *disliked* them, either. Forests were simply not something the average smuggler thought about very much. Most of the time you picked up and delivered in grimy little spaceports like Mos Eisley or Abregado-rae; and on the rare occasion where you met in a forest, you let the customer watch the forest while you watched the customer. As a result, Han had wound up with a vague sort of assumption that one forest was pretty much like another.

His stint with the Alliance had changed all that. What with Endor, Corstris, Fedje, and a dozen more, he'd learned the hard way that each forest was different, with its own array of plants, animal life, and general all-around headaches for the casual visitor. Just one of many subjects the Alliance had taught him more about than he'd really wanted to know.

Wayland's forest fit the pattern perfectly; and the first headache proved to be how to get the *Falcon* down through the dense upper leaf canopy without leaving a hole any wandering Imperial TIE pilot would have to be asleep to miss. They'd first had to find a gap—in this case made by a fallen tree—and then he'd had to basically run the ship in on its side, a lot trickier maneuver in a planetary gravity well than it was out in an asteroid field. The secondary canopy, which he didn't find out about until he was most of the way through the first, was the second headache, and he tore the tops off a line of those shorter trees before he got the *Falcon* stabilized and down, crunching a lot of underbrush in the process.

"Nice landing," Lando commented dryly, rubbing his

shoulder beneath the restraint strap as Han shut down the re-pulsorlifts.

"At least the sensor dish is still there," Han said pointedly.

Lando winced. "You're never going to let that go, are you?"

Han shrugged, keying in the life-form algorithms. Time to find out what was out there. "You said you wouldn't get a scratch on her," he reminded the other.

"Fine," Lando grumped. "Next time, *I'll* destroy the energy field generator and *you* can fly her down the Death Star's throat."

Which wasn't all that funny. If the Empire got enough of its old resources back again, Thrawn just might try to build another of the blasted things.

"We're ready back here," Luke said, poking his head into the cockpit. "How's it look?"

"Not too bad," Han said, reading off the display. "Got a bunch of animals out there, but they're keeping their distance."

"How big are these animals?" Lando asked, leaning over Han's shoulder to have a look at the display.

"And how many to a bunch?" Luke added.

"About fifteen," Han told him. "Nothing we can't handle if we need to. Let's go take a look."

Mara and Chewbacca were waiting at the hatchway with Artoo and Threepio, the latter keeping his mouth shut for a change. "Chewie and me'll go first," Han told them, drawing his blaster. "The rest of you stay sharp up here."

He punched the controls, and the hatchway slid open as the entry ramp lowered, settling into the dead leaves with a muffled crunch. Trying to watch all directions at once, Han started down.

He spotted the first of the animals before he'd reached the bottom of the ramp: gray, with a freckling of white across its back, maybe two meters from nose to tail tuft. It was crouched at the base of a tree limb, its beady little eyes following him as he walked. And if its teeth and claws were anything to go by, it was definitely a predator.

Beside him, Chewbacca rumbled softly. "Yeah, I see it," Han muttered back. "There are another fourteen out there somewhere, too."

The Wookiee growled again, gesturing. "You're right," Han agreed slowly, eyeing the predator. "It does kind of look familiar. Like those panthac things from Mantessa, maybe?"

Chewbacca considered, then growled a negative. "Well, we'll figure it out later," Han decided. "Luke?"

"Right here," Luke's voice came down from the hatchway.

"You and Mara start bringing the equipment down," Han ordered, watching the predator closely. The sound of conversation didn't seem to be bothering it any. "Start with the speeder bikes. Lando, you're high cover. Stay sharp."

"Right," Lando said.

From above came a handful of pops and clicks as the transport restraints around the first two speeder bikes were knocked off, then the faint hum as the repulsorlifts were activated.

And with a sudden violent crackling of leaves and branches, the predator leaped.

"Chewie!" was all Han had time to shout before the animal was on top of him. He fired, the blaster bolt catching it square in the torso, and managed to duck as the carcass shot past his head. Chewbacca was roaring Wookiee battle cries, swinging his bowcaster around and firing again and again as more of the predators charged at them from out of the trees. From the hatchway someone shouted something and another shot flashed out.

And out of the corner of his eye, moving much too fast to avoid, Han saw a set of claws coming his direction.

He threw up his forearm across his face, ducking his head back as far out of the way as he could. An instant later he was knocked back off his feet as the predator slammed full-tilt into him. A moment of pressure and lancing pain as the claws dug through his camouflage jacket—

And then, suddenly, the weight was gone. He lowered his arm, just in time to see the predator bound onto the ramp and prepare for a spring into the *Falcon*. He twisted around and fired, just as a shot from inside the ship also caught it.

Chewbacca snarled a warning. Still on his back, Han swung around, to see three more of the animals bounding across the ground toward him. He dropped one with a pair of quick shots, and was trying to swing his blaster around to target the second when a pair of black-booted feet hit the ground just in front of him. The animals leaped upward into a blurred line of brilliant green and crashed to the ground.

Rolling over, Han scrambled back to his feet and looked around. Luke was standing in a half-crouch in front of him, lightsaber humming in ready position. On the other side of the ramp, Chewbacca was still on his feet with three of the speckled animals lying dead around him.

Han looked down at the dead predator beside him. Now that he had a good, close look at the thing . . .

"Watch out—there are three more over there," Luke warned.

Han looked. Two of the animals were visible, crouched low down in the trees. "They won't bother us. Any of them get into the ship?"

"Not very far into it," Luke told him. "What did you do that set them off?"

"We didn't do anything," Han said, holstering his blaster. "It was you and Mara turning on the speeder bikes."

Chewbacca rumbled with sudden recognition. "You got it, pal," Han nodded. "That's where we tangled with them, all right."

"What are they?" Luke asked.

"They're called garrals," Mara said from the ramp. Crouching down, her own blaster still drawn, she was peering at the carcasses scattered around Chewbacca. "The Empire used to use them as watchdogs, usually near heavily wooded frontier garrisons where probe droid pickets weren't practical. There's something in the ultrasonic signature of a repulsorlift that's supposed to sound like one of their prey animals. Draws them like a magnet."

"So that's why they were sitting here waiting for us," Luke said, closing down his lightsaber but keeping it handy.

"They can hear a ship-sized repulsorlift coming in from kilometers away," Mara said. Jumping down off the side of the ramp, she dropped to one knee beside one of the dead garrals and dug her free hand into the fur at its neck. "Which means that if they've been radiotagged, the controllers in Mount Tantiss know we're here."

"Great," Han muttered, crouching down beside the dead garral at his feet. "What do we look for, a collar?"

"Probably," Mara said. "Check around the legs, too."

It took a few anxious minutes, but in the end they confirmed that none of the dead predators had been tagged.

"Must be descendants of the group they brought in to protect the mountain," Lando said.

"Or else this is where they came from originally," Mara said. "I never saw their home planet listed."

"It's trouble either way," Han said, shoving the last carcass off the *Falcon's* ramp to crunch into the leaf cover below. "If we can't use the speeder bikes, it means we're walking."

From up above came a low electronic whistle. "Pardon me, sir," Threepio asked. "Does that also apply to Artoo and me?"

"Unless you've learned how to fly," Han said.

"Well—sir—it occurs to me that Artoo in particular isn't really equipped for this sort of forest travel," Threepio pointed out primly. "If the cargo plat can't be used, perhaps other arrangements can be made."

"The arrangement is that you walk like the rest of us," Han said shortly. Getting into a long discussion with Threepio wasn't how he'd been planning to spend his day. "You did it on Endor; you can do it here."

"We didn't have nearly as far to go on Endor," Luke reminded him quietly. "We must be about two weeks' walk from the mountain here."

"It's not that bad," Han said, doing a quick estimate. It

wasn't that bad, but it was bad enough. "Eight or nine days, tops. Maybe a couple more if we run into trouble."

"Oh, we'll run into trouble, all right," Mara said sourly, sitting down on the ramp and dropping her blaster into her lap. "Trust me on that one."

"You don't expect the natives to be hospitable?" Lando asked.

"I expect them to welcome us with open crossbows," Mara retorted. "There are two different native species here, the Psadans and the Myneyrshi. Neither of them had any great love of humans even before the Empire moved in on Mount Tantiss."

"Well, at least they won't be on the Empire's side," Lando said.

"That's not likely to be a lot of comfort," Mara growled. "And whatever trouble they don't give us, the usual range of predators will. We'll be lucky to make it in twelve or thirteen days, not eight or nine."

Han looked out at the forest, and as he did, something caught his eye. Something more than a little disturbing . . . "So we'll figure on twelve," he said. Suddenly it was critical that they make tracks away from here. "Let's get to it. Lando, Mara, you get the equipment packs sorted out for carrying. Chewie, go pull all the ration boxes out of the survival packs— that ought to do us for extra food. Luke, you and the droids head that way"—he pointed—"and see what you can find in the way of a path. Maybe a dry creek bed—we ought to be close enough to the mountain to have some of those around."

"Certainly, sir," Threepio said brightly, starting down the ramp. "Come, Artoo."

There was a muttering of acknowledgment and the others headed into the ship. Han started toward the ramp; stopped as Luke put a hand on his arm. "What's wrong?" he asked quietly.

Han jerked his head back toward the forest. "Those garrals that were watching us? They're gone."

Luke looked back. "Did they all leave together?"

"I don't know. I didn't see them go."

Luke fingered his lightsaber. "You think it's an Imperial patrol?"

"Or else a flock of those prey animals Mara mentioned. You getting anything?"

Luke took a deep breath, held it a moment, then slowly let it out. "I don't sense anyone else nearby," he said. "But they could just be out of range. You think we should abort the mission?"

Han shook his head. "If we do, we'll lose our best shot at the place. Once they know we've found their clone factory, there won't be any point in pretending they're just some overlooked backwoods system anymore. By the time we got back with a strike force, they'd have a couple of Star Destroyer fleets waiting for us."

Luke grimaced. "I suppose so. And you're right—if they tracked the *Falcon* in, the sooner we get away from it the better. Are you going to send the coordinates back to Coruscant before we go?"

"I don't know." Han looked up at the *Falcon* looming above him, trying not to think about the Imperials getting their grubby little hands on it again. "If that's a patrol out there, we'll never get the transmitter tuned tight enough to slide a message past them. Not the way it's been acting up lately."

Luke glanced up, too. "Sounds risky," he said. "If we get into trouble, they won't have any idea where to send a follow-up strike force."

"Yeah, well, if we transmit through an Imperial patrol, I can guarantee that trouble," Han growled. "I'm open to suggestions."

"How about if I stay behind for a few hours?" Luke suggested. "If no patrols have shown up by then, it should be safe to transmit."

"Forget it," Han shook his head. "You'd have to travel alone, and there's a better-than-even chance you wouldn't even be able to find us."

"I'm willing to risk it."

"I'm not," Han said bluntly. "And besides, every time you go off alone you wind up getting me in trouble."

Luke smiled ruefully. "It does seem that way sometimes."

"Bet on it," Han told him. "Come on, we're wasting time. Get out there and find us a path."

"All right," Luke said with a sigh. But he didn't sound all that upset. Maybe he'd known all along that it wasn't a very smart idea. "Come on, Threepio, Artoo. Let's go."

THE FIRST HOUR was the hardest. The vague, pathlike trail Artoo had found dead-ended into a mass of thornbushes after less than a hundred meters, forcing them to push a path of their own through the dense undergrowth. In the process they disturbed more than plant life, and wound up spending several tense minutes shooting at a nest of six-legged, half-meter-long creatures that swarmed out biting and clawing at them. Fortunately, the claws and teeth were designed for much smaller game, and aside from a nicely matched set of tooth dents in Threepio's left leg, no one suffered any damage before they could be driven away. Threepio moaned more about that than either the incident or the damage really deserved, the noise possibly attracting the brown-scaled animal that attacked a few minutes later. Han's quick blaster shot failed to stop the animal, and Luke had to use his lightsaber to cut it off Threepio's arm. The droid was even more inclined to moan after that; and Han was threatening to shut him down and leave him for the scavengers when they unexpectedly hit one of the dry creek beds they'd been hoping to find. With the easier terrain, and with no further animal attacks to slow them down, they made much better speed, and by the time the leaf canopy overhead began to darken with nightfall they'd made nearly ten kilometers.

"Brings back such wonderful memories, doesn't it?" Mara

commented sarcastically as she got out of her backpack and dropped it beside one of the small bushes lining the creek bed.

"Just like back on Myrkr," Luke agreed, using his lightsaber to cut away another of the thornbushes they'd become all too familiar with in the past few hours. "You know, I never did find out what happened after we left."

"About what you'd expect," Mara told him. "We cleared out about two steps ahead of Thrawn's AT-ATs. And then nearly got caught anyway when Karrde insisted on hanging around to watch."

"Is that why you're helping us?" he asked her. "Because Thrawn's put a death mark on Karrde?"

"Let's get one thing clear right now, Skywalker," she growled. "I work for Karrde, and Karrde has already said that we're staying neutral in this war of yours. The only reason I'm here is because I know a little about the Clone Wars era and don't want to see a bunch of cold-faced duplicates trying to overrun the galaxy again. The only reason *you're* here is that I can't shut the place down by myself."

"I understand," Luke said, cutting a second thornbush and closing down his lightsaber. Reaching out with the Force, he lifted the two bushes off the ground and lowered them into the creek bed. "Well, it won't stop anything that's really determined to get at us," he decided, studying the makeshift barrier. "But it should at least slow them down."

"For whatever that's worth," Mara said, pulling out a ration bar and stripping off the wrapping. "Let's just hope this isn't one of those lucky places where all the really big predators come out at night."

"Hopefully, Artoo's sensors can spot them before they get too close," Luke told her. Igniting his lightsaber again, he cut two more thornbushes for good measure.

And he was preparing to shut it down when he caught the subtle change in Mara's sense. He turned, to find her staring at his lightsaber, ration bar forgotten in her hand, a strangely haunted expression on her face. "Mara?" he asked, "You all right?"

Her gaze shifted almost guiltily away from him. "Sure," she muttered. "I'm fine." Throwing him a quick glare, she bit viciously into her ration bar.

"Okay." Closing down the lightsaber, Luke used the Force to move the newly cut thornbushes into place on top of the others. Still not much of a barrier, he decided. Maybe if he stretched a few of those vines between the trees . . .

"Skywalker."

He turned. "Yes?"

Mara was looking up at him. "I have to ask," she said quietly. "You're the only one who knows. How did the Emperor die?"

For a moment Luke studied her face. Even in the fading light he could see the ache in her eyes; the bitter memories of the luxuriant life and glittering future that had been snatched away from her at Endor. But alongside the ache was an equally strong determination. However badly this might hurt, she truly did want to hear it. "The Emperor was trying to turn me to the dark side," he told her, long-buried memories of his own surging painfully back again. It had nearly been him, not the Emperor, who'd died that day. "He almost succeeded. I'd taken one swing at him, and wound up fighting with Vader instead. I guess he thought that if I killed Vader in anger, I'd be opened to him through the dark side."

"And so instead you ganged up on him," she accused, her eyes flashing with sudden anger. "You turned on him—both of you—"

"Wait a minute," Luke protested. "I didn't attack him. Not after that first swing."

"What are you talking about?" she demanded. "I saw you do it. Both of you moved in against him with your lightsabers. I saw you do it."

Luke stared at her . . . and suddenly he understood. Mara Jade, the Emperor's Hand, who could hear his voice from anywhere in the galaxy. She'd been in contact with her master at the moment of his death, and had seen it all.

Except that, somehow, she'd gotten it wrong.

"I didn't move against him, Mara," he told her. "He was about to kill me when Vader picked him up and threw him down an open shaft. I couldn't have done anything even if I'd wanted to—I was still half paralyzed from the lightning bolts he'd hit me with."

"What do you mean, if you'd wanted to?" Mara said scornfully. "That was the whole reason you went aboard the Death Star in the first place, wasn't it?"

Luke shook his head. "No. I went there to try to turn Vader away from the dark side."

Mara turned away, and Luke could sense the turmoil within her. "Why should I believe you?" she demanded at last.

"Why should I lie?" he countered. "It doesn't change the fact that if I hadn't been there Vader wouldn't have turned on him. In that sense, I'm probably still responsible for his death."

"That's right, you are," Mara agreed harshly. But there was a moment of hesitation before she said it. "And I won't forget it."

Luke nodded silently, and waited for her to say more. But she didn't, and after a minute he turned back to the thornbushes. "I'd go easy on those things if I were you," Mara said from behind him, her voice cool and under control again. "You don't want to trap us in an area this size if something big comes over the bushes."

"Good point," Luke said, understanding both the words and the meaning beneath them. There was a job to do, and until that job was finished, she still needed Luke alive.

At which point, she would have to face the destiny that had been prepared for her. Or would have to choose a new one.

Closing down his lightsaber, he stepped past Mara to where the others were busy setting up camp. Time to check on the droids.

CHAPTER 17

THE DOOR TO the Assemblage chamber slid open and a small flood of beings and droids began pouring out into the Grand Corridor, chattering among themselves in the usual spectrum of different languages. Glancing at Winter as the two of them walked toward the crowd, Leia nodded.

It was show time.

"Anything else come in that I should know about?" she asked as they passed along the edge of the flow.

"There was an unusual follow-up to the Pantolomin report," Winter said, her eyes flicking casually around the crowd. "A bounty hunter there claims to have penetrated the Imperial shipyards at Ord Trasi and is offering to sell us information about their new building program."

"I've dealt with my share of bounty hunters," Leia said, trying not to look around the crowd as they passed through it. Winter was watching, and with her perfect memory she would remember everyone who was close enough to overhear their conversation. "What makes Colonel Derlin think we can trust him?"

"He's not sure we can," Winter said. "The smuggler offered what he said was a free sample: the information that there are three Imperial Star Destroyers within a month of completion out there. Colonel Derlin said Wing Commander Harleys is drawing up a plan to confirm that."

They were out of the Grand Corridor now, following along with the handful of beings who hadn't yet split off toward offices or other conference rooms. "Sounds dangerous," Leia said, dutifully running their prepared script out to the end. "I hope he's not just going to do a fly-by."

"The report didn't give any details," Winter said. "But there was an addendum asking about the possibility of borrowing a freighter from someone who does business with the Empire."

The last of the officials turned off into a cross corridor, leaving them alone in the hallway with an assortment of techs, assistants, admin personnel, and other low-ranking members of the New Republic government. Leia threw a quick glance at each, decided there was no point in going through another script for their benefit. Looking at Winter, she nodded again, and together the two women headed toward the turbolifts.

They'd needed some place where Ghent could set up shop without word or even rumors of the project leaking out, and a search of the Palace's original blueprints had found them the ideal spot. It was an old backup power cell room, closed down and sealed years earlier, wedged in between the Sector Ordnance/Supply and Starfighter Command offices down on the command floor. Leia had cut a new entrance from a service corridor with her lightsaber; Bel Iblis had helped them run power cables and datalines; and Ghent had set up his decrypting program.

They had everything they needed. Except results.

Ghent was sitting in the room's single chair when they arrived, staring dreamily off into space with his feet propped up on the edge of his decrypter desk. They were both inside, and Winter had closed the door, before he even noticed their presence. "Oh—hi," he said, dropping his feet to the floor with a muffled thud.

"Not so loud, please," Leia reminded him, wincing. The officers working on the other sides of the thin walls would probably ascribe any stray noises to the adjacent offices. But then again, they might not. "Has General Bel Iblis brought the latest transmissions in yet?" she asked.

"Yeah—about an hour ago," Ghent nodded, whispering almost inaudibly now. "I just finished slicing 'em."

He tapped a key, and a series of decrypted messages came up on the display. Leia stepped up behind his chair, reading down them. Details of upcoming military deployments, what seemed to be verbatim transcriptions of high-level diplomatic conversations, tidbits of idle Palace gossip—as always, Delta Source had covered the whole range from the significant to the trivial.

"There's one of ours," Winter said, touching a spot on the display.

Leia read the item. An unconfirmed intelligence report from the Bpfassh system, suggesting that the *Chimaera* and its support ships had been spotted near Anchoron. That was one of theirs, all right. "How many heard that one?" she asked Winter.

"Only forty-seven," Winter told her, already busy with Ghent's data pad, "It was just before three yesterday afternoon—during the second Assemblage session—and the Grand Corridor was fairly empty."

Leia nodded and turned back to the display. By the time Winter had finished her list she'd identified two more of their decoy messages. By the time Winter had finished those, she'd found another five.

"Looks like that's it," she said as Winter handed Ghent her first three lists and got to work on the others. "Let's go ahead and run these through your sifter."

"Okay," Ghent said, throwing one last look of awe at Winter before turning back to his console. Three days into this scheme, he still hadn't gotten over the way she could remember every single detail of fifty separate one-minute conversations.

"Okay, let's see. Correlations . . . okay. We're down to a hundred twenty-seven possibilities. Mostly techs and admin types, looks like. Some offworld diplomats, too."

Leia shook her head. "None of those are likely to have access to all of this information," she said, waving at the decrypt display. "It has to be someone considerably higher up the command structure—"

"Wait a minute," Ghent interrupted, raising a finger. "You want a big fish; you got one. Councilor Sian Tevv of Sullust."

Leia frowned at the display. "That's impossible. He was one of the earliest leaders in the Rebel Alliance. In fact, I think he was the one who brought Nien Nunb and his private raiding squad over to us after the Empire forced them out of Sullust system."

Ghent shrugged. "I don't know anything about that. All I know is that he heard all fifteen of those little teasers that wound up on Delta Source's transmitter."

"It can't be Councilor Tevv," Winter spoke up absently, still working at the data pad. "He wasn't present during any of these last six conversations."

"Maybe one of his aides heard it," Ghent offered. "He didn't have to be there personally."

Winter shook her head. "No. One of his aides was present, but only for one of these conversations. More importantly, Councilor Tevv *was* present for two conversations the day before yesterday that Delta Source didn't transmit. Nine-fifteen in the morning and two-forty-eight in the afternoon."

Ghent keyed up the relevant lists. "You're right," he confirmed. "Didn't think about checking things that direction. Guess I'd better work up a better sifter program."

Behind Leia their makeshift door swung open, and she turned to see Bel Iblis come in. "Thought I'd find you here," he nodded to Leia. "We're about ready to give the Stardust plan its first try, if you want to come and watch."

The latest scheme to locate the swarm of cloaked asteroids Thrawn had left in orbit around Coruscant. "Yes, I do," Leia said. "Winter, I'll be in the war room when you're finished here."

"Yes, Your Highness."

Leia and Bel Iblis left the room and headed single-file down the service corridor. "Find anything yet?" the general asked over his shoulder.

"Winter's still running yesterday's list," Leia told him. "So far we've got around a hundred thirty possibilities."

Bel Iblis nodded. "Considering how many of us there are working in the Palace, I'd say that qualifies as progress."

"Maybe." She hesitated. "It's occurred to me that this scheme will only work if Delta Source is a single person. If it's a whole group, we may not be able to weed them out this way."

"Perhaps," Bel Iblis agreed. "But I have a hard time believing we could have that many traitors here. Matter of fact, I still have trouble believing we have even one. I've always thought that Delta Source might be some kind of exotic recording system. Something Security simply hasn't been able to locate yet."

"I've watched them do counterintelligence sweeps," Leia said. "I can't think how they could possibly have missed anything."

"Unfortunately, neither can I."

They arrived in the war room, to find General Rieekan and Admiral Drayson standing behind the main command console. "Princess," Rieekan greeted her gravely. "You're just in time."

Leia looked up at the master visual. An old transport had left the group of ships standing guard in far orbit and was making its careful way down toward the planet. "How far in is it going to come?" Leia asked.

"We're going to start just above the planetary shield, Councilor," Drayson told her. "The postbattle analysis indicates that most of the cloaked asteroids probably wound up in low orbit."

Leia nodded. And since those would be the ones most likely

to sneak through if they opened the shield, it made all the more sense to start there.

Slowly, moving with the tentative awkwardness of a ship under remote control, the transport came closer in. "All right," Drayson said. "Transport One control, cut drive and prepare to dump on my command. Ready . . . dump."

For a moment nothing happened. Then, abruptly, a cloud of brilliant dust began to billow from the aft end of the transport, swirling around lazily in the ship's wake. "Keep it coming," Drayson said. "*Harrier*, stand by negative ion beams."

"All dust is clear of the transport, Admiral," one of the officers reported.

"Transport One control, pull her away," Drayson ordered.

"But slowly," Bel Iblis murmured. "We don't want to carve exhaust grooves through the dust."

Drayson threw an annoyed look back at him. "Take it nice and slow," he said grudgingly. "Do we have any readings yet?"

"Coming in very strong, sir," the officer at the sensor console reported. "Between point nine-three and nine-eight reflection on all bands."

"Good," Drayson nodded. "Keep a sharp eye on it. *Harrier*?"

"*Harrier* reports ready, sir," another officer confirmed.

"Fire negative ion beam," Drayson ordered. "Lowest intensity. Let's see how this works."

Leia peered up at the visual. The shimmering dust particles were beginning to clump together as ions from the departing transport's drive created random electrostatic charges throughout the cloud. Out of the corner of her eye, she saw the hazy line of an ion beam appear on the master tactical display and sweep across the cloud. Charging all the dust particles with the same polarity so that they would repel each other . . . and suddenly the coalescing dust cloud was expanding again, spreading out across the *visual* display like the opening of some exotic flower.

"Cease fire," Drayson said. "Let's see if that does it."

For a long minute the flower continued to open, and Leia

found herself staring intently at the hazy glitter. Unreasonably, of course. Given how much space there was out there, it was highly unlikely that this first dump would happen to be in the path of any of the orbiting asteroids. And even if it was, there still would be nothing for her to see on the visual. Except at the moment before its collapse, the cloaking shield seemed to twist light and sensor beams perfectly around itself, which meant there would be no dark spot cutting visibly through the dust.

"Cloud's starting to break up, Admiral," the sensor officer reported. "Dissipation ratio is up to twelve."

"Solar wind's catching it," Rieekan muttered.

"As expected," Drayson reminded him. "Transport Two control: go ahead and launch."

A second transport emerged from among the orbiting ships and headed down toward the surface. "This is definitely the slow way to do this," Bel Iblis commented quietly.

"Agreed," Rieekan said. "I wish they hadn't lost that CGT array of yours out at Svivren. We could sure have used it here."

Leia nodded. Crystal gravfield traps, originally designed to zoom in on the mass of sensor-stealthed ships from thousands of kilometers away, would be ideal for this job. "I thought Intelligence had a lead on another one."

"They've got leads on three," Rieekan said. "Problem is, they're all in Imperial space."

"I'm still not convinced a CGT would do us all that much good here," Bel Iblis said. "This close in, I suspect that Coruscant's gravity would swamp any readings we got from the asteroids."

"It would be tricky—no doubt about that," Rieekan agreed. "But I think it's our best chance."

They fell silent as, on the visual, the second transport reached its target zone and repeated the procedure of the first. Again, nothing.

"That solar wind is going to be a real nuisance," Bel Iblis

commented as the third transport headed out. "We may want to consider going with larger dust particles on the next batch."

"Or shifting operations to the night side," Rieekan suggested. "That would at least cut back the effect—"

"Turbulence!" the sensor officer barked. "Vector one-one-seven—bearing four-nine-two."

There was a mad scramble for the sensor console. At the very edge of the still-expanding second dust cloud a hazy orange line had appeared, marking the turbulence created by the invisible asteroid's passage. "Get a track on it," Drayson ordered. "*Harrier*, fire at will."

On the visual, red lines lanced out as the Dreadnaught's turbolasers began to sweep across the projected path. Leia watched the visual, hands gripping the sensor officer's chair back . . . and suddenly, there it was: a misshapen lump of rock, drifting slowly across the stars.

"Cease fire," Drayson ordered. "Well done, gentlemen. All right, *Allegiant*, it's your turn. Get your tech crew out there—"

He broke off. On the visual, a mesh of thin lines had appeared crisscrossing the dark bulk of the asteroid. For a brief moment they flared brilliantly, then faded away.

"Belay that order, *Allegiant*," Drayson growled. "Looks like the Grand Admiral doesn't want anyone else getting a look at his little toys."

"At least we found one of them," Leia said. "That's something."

"Right," Rieekan said dryly. "Leaves just under three hundred to go."

Leia nodded again and started to turn away. This was going to take a while, and she might as well get back to Winter and Ghent—

"Collision!" the sensor officer snapped.

She twisted back. On the visual the third transport was spinning wildly off course, its stern crushed and on fire, its cargo of dust spraying out in all directions.

"Can you get a track?" Drayson demanded.

The officer's hands were skating across his board. "Negative—insufficient data. All I can do is a probability cone."

"I'll take it," Drayson said. "All ships: open fire. Full-pattern bombardment; target cone as indicated."

The cone had appeared on the tactical, and from the distant fleet turbolaser fire began to appear. "Open the cone to fifty percent probability," Drayson ordered. "Battle stations, you take the outer cone. I want that target found."

The encouragement was unnecessary. The space above Coruscant had become a fire storm, with turbolaser blasts and proton torpedoes cutting through the marked probability cone. The target zone stretched and expanded as the computers calculated the invisible asteroid's possible paths, the ships and battle stations shifting aim in response.

But there was nothing there . . . and after a few minutes Drayson finally conceded defeat.

"All units, cease fire," he said, his voice tired. "There's no more point. We've lost it."

There didn't seem to be anything else to be said. In silence they stood and watched as the crippled transport, far out of range of the fleet's tractor beams, spun slowly toward the planetary shield and its impending death. Its crushed stern skimmed the shield, and the fire of burning drive gases was joined by the sharp blue-white edge of shattered atomic bonds. A muffled flash as the stern broke away—a brighter flash as the bow hit the shield—scatterings of dark debris against the flame as the hull began to break up—

And with a final spattering of diffuse fire it was gone.

Leia watched the last flickers fade away, running through her Jedi calming exercises and forcing the anger from her mind. Allowing herself the luxury of hating Thrawn for doing this to them would only fog her own intellect. Worse, such hatred would be a perilous step toward the dark side.

There was a breath of movement at her shoulder, and she

turned to see Winter at her side. The other woman was gazing up at the visual, a look of ancient pain deep in her eyes. "It's all right," Leia assured her. "There wasn't anyone aboard."

"I know," Winter murmured. "I was thinking about another transport I saw go down like that over Xyquine. A passenger transport . . ."

She took a deep breath, and Leia could see the conscious effort as she put her always-vivid past away from her. "I'd like to speak with you, Your Highness, whenever you're finished here."

Leia reached out past Winter's carefully neutral expression and touched her sense. Whatever the news was, it wasn't good. "I'll come now," she said.

They left the war room and circled back past the turbolifts to the service corridor and their secret decrypt room. And the news was indeed not good.

"This can't be," Leia said, shaking her head as she reread Ghent's analysis. "We *know* there's a leak in the Palace."

"I've checked it backwards, forwards, and from the inside out," Ghent said. "It comes up the same every time. Feed in everyone who heard and didn't hear the stuff Delta Source sent out; feed in everyone who heard or didn't hear the stuff Delta Source *didn't* send out; and you come out with the same answer every time. A straight, flat zero."

Leia keyed the data pad for a replay and watched as the list of names dwindled with each sifting until it was gone. "Then Delta Source has to be more than one person," she said.

"I already ran that," Ghent said, waving his hands helplessly. "It doesn't work, either. You wind up having to have at least fifteen people. Your security here can't be that bad."

"Then he's picking and choosing what he transmits. Sending some of what he hears but not all of it."

Ghent scratched at his cheek. "I suppose that could be it," he said reluctantly. "I don't know, though. You look at some of the really stupid stuff he's sent—I mean, there was one in that last transmission that was nothing but a couple of Arcona talking about what one of them was going to name her hatchlings. Either this guy doesn't remember too good or else he's got a really weird priority list."

The door opened, and Leia turned as Bel Iblis stepped in. "I saw you leave," the general said. "Have you found something?"

Wordlessly, Leia handed him the data pad. Bel Iblis glanced over it, then read it through more carefully. "Interesting," he said at last. "Either the analysis is wrong, or Winter's memory is starting to fail her . . . or Delta Source is onto us."

"How do you figure that?" Leia asked.

"Because he's clearly no longer transmitting everything he hears," Bel Iblis said. "Something must have aroused his suspicions."

Leia thought back to all those staged conversations. "No," she said slowly. "I don't believe it. I never picked up even a hint of malice or suspicion."

Bel Iblis shrugged. "The alternative is to believe we have a whole spy nest here. Wait a minute, though—this isn't quite as bad as it sounds. If we assume he didn't catch on right away, we should still be able to use the data from the first two days to cut the suspect list down to a manageable number."

Leia felt her stomach tighten. "Garm, we're talking about over a hundred trusted members of the New Republic here. We can't go around accusing that many people of treason. Councilor Fey'lya's accusations against Admiral Ackbar were bad enough—this would be orders of magnitude worse."

"I know that, Leia," Bel Iblis said firmly. "But we can't let the Empire continue to listen in on our secrets. Offer me an alternative and I'll take it."

Leia bit at her lip, her mind racing. "What about that comment you made on the way to the war room?" she asked. "You said you thought Delta Source might be nothing but an exotic recording system."

"If it is, it's somewhere in the Grand Corridor," Winter said before Bel Iblis could answer. "That's where all the conversations that were transmitted took place."

"Are you sure?" Bel Iblis frowned.

"Absolutely," Winter said. "Every one."

"That's it, then," Leia said, feeling the first stirrings of excitement. "Somehow, someone's planted a recording system in the Grand Corridor."

"Don't get excited," Bel Iblis cautioned. "I know it sounds good, but it's not that easy. Microphone systems have certain well-defined characteristics, all of which are quite well known and can be readily picked up by a competent counterintelligence sweep."

"Unless it goes dormant when counterintelligence comes by," Ghent suggested. "I've seen systems that do that."

Bel Iblis shook his head. "But then you're talking something with at least minimal decision-making capabilities. Anything that close to droid-level intelligence would—"

"Hey!" Ghent interrupted excitedly. "That's it. Delta Source isn't a person—it's a droid."

Leia looked at Bel Iblis. "Is that possible?"

"I don't know," the general said slowly. "Implanting secondary espionage programming in a droid is certainly feasible. The problem is how to get that programming in past the Palace's usual security procedures, and then avoiding the counterintelligence sweeps."

"It would have to be a droid that has a good reason to hang around the Grand Corridor," Leia said, trying to think it through. "But who can also leave without attracting notice whenever a sweep gets under way."

"And given the sort of high-level traffic that passes through the Grand Corridor, those sweeps are pretty frequent," Bel Iblis agreed. "Ghent, can you get into Security's records and pull a list of sweep times over the past three or four days?"

"Sure," the kid shrugged. "Probably take me a couple of hours, though. Unless you don't care if they spot me."

Bel Iblis looked at Leia. "What do you think?"

"We certainly don't want him to get caught," Leia said. "On the other hand, we don't want to give Delta Source free rein of the Palace any longer than we have to."

"Your Highness?" Winter asked. "Pardon me, but it seems to me that if the sweeps are that frequent, all we need to do is watch the Grand Corridor until one gets under way and then see which droids leave."

"It's worth a try," Bel Iblis said. "Ghent, you get started on Security. Leia, Winter—let's go."

"THEY'RE COMING," WINTER'S voice came softly from the com-link nestled in Leia's palm.

"You sure they're Palace Security?" Bel Iblis's voice said.

"Yes," Winter said. "I've seen Colonel Bremen giving them orders. And they have droids and equipment with them."

"Sounds like this is it," Leia murmured, surreptitiously raising her hand near her mouth and hoping the three Kubaz sitting across the lounge/conversation ring from her wouldn't notice the odd behavior. "Watch carefully."

There were acknowledging murmurs from both of them. Lowering her hand back to her lap, Leia looked around. This was it, all right: possibly the clearest shot at Delta Source they were likely to get. With an Assemblage meeting just letting out and a Council meeting about to start, the Grand Corridor was crowded with high-ranking officials. With officials, their aides and assistants, and their droids.

On one level, Leia had always known how common droids were in the Imperial Palace. On another level, as she was rapidly coming to realize, she'd had no idea how many of them there actually were. There were quite a few 3PO protocol droids visible from where she sat, most of them accompanying groups of offworld diplomats but some also in the entourages of various Palace officials. Hovering over the crowd on repulsorlifts, a set of insectoid SPD maintenance droids were systematically cleaning the carvings and cut-glass windows that alternated along the walls. A line of MSE droids scuttled past along the far wall, delivering messages too complex for comm transmissions or too sensitive for direct data transfer and trying hard not to get stepped on. At the next of the greenish-purple ch'hala trees down the line, occasionally visible through the crowd, an MN-2E maintenance droid was carefully pruning away dead leaves.

Which one of them, she wondered, had the Empire turned into a spy?

"They're starting," Winter reported quietly. "Lining up across the Corridor—"

There was a sudden rustle of sound from the comlink, as if Winter had put her hand across the microphone. Another series of muffled sounds; and Leia was wondering if she should go and investigate when a man's voice came on. "Councilor Organa Solo?"

"Yes," she said cautiously. "Who is this?"

"Lieutenant Machel Kendy, Councilor," he said. "Palace Security. Are you aware that a third person is tapping into your comlink signal?"

"It's not a tap, Lieutenant," Leia assured him. "We were holding a three-way discussion with General Bel Iblis."

"I see," Kendy said, sounding a little disappointed. Probably thought he'd stumbled onto Delta Source. "I'll have to ask you to suspend your conversation for a few minutes, Councilor. We're about to do a sweep of the Grand Corridor, and we can't have stray comlink transmissions in the area."

"I understand," Leia said. "We'll wait until you're finished."

She shut off the comlink and replaced it in her belt, her heart beginning to thud in her ears. Twisting casually around in her seat, she made sure she could see the entire end of the Grand Corridor. If there was an espionage droid present, he'd be shuffling this direction as soon as he noticed the sweep team coming from the other end.

Overhead, the hovering cleaning droids had been joined by

a new set of SPDs, moving down the corridor as they method-
ically checked the upper walls and convoluted contours of the
vaulted ceiling for any microphones or recording systems that
might have somehow been planted there since the last sweep.
Directly beneath them, Leia could see Lieutenant Kendy and
his squad, walking through the milling diplomats in a militarily straight line stretched across the corridor and watching the
displays of their shoulder-slung detectors. The line reached
her lounge area, passed it, and continued without incident to
the end of the corridor. There the squad waited, letting the
SPD droids and a group of wall-hugging MSEs finish their
part of the sweep and catch up. Re-formed again, the entire
group disappeared down the hallway toward the Inner Council
offices.

And that was that. The entire Grand Corridor had been
swept, and had obviously come up negative . . . and not a single droid had scurried out ahead of the sweep.

Something off to the side caught her eye. But it was just the
MN-2E maintenance droid she'd noticed earlier, rolling up to
the ch'hala tree that sprouted out of the floor beside her conversation ring. Clucking softly to itself, the droid began poking delicate feelers through the branches, hunting for dead or
dying leaves.

Dead or dying. Rather like their theory.

With a sigh, she pulled out her comlink. "Winter? Garm?"

"Here, Your Highness," Winter's voice came promptly.

"So am I," Bel Iblis added. "What happened?"

Leia shook her head. "Absolutely nothing," she told them.
"As far as I could tell, none of the droids even twitched."

There was a short pause. "I see," Bel Iblis said at last.
"Well . . . it may just be that our droid doesn't happen to be
here today. What we need to do is send Winter back to Ghent
and have her add droids into the list."

"What do you think, Winter?" Leia asked.

"I can try," the other woman said hesitantly. "The problem

will be identifying specific droids. Externally, one 3PO protocol droid looks basically like any other."

"We'll take whatever you can get," Bel Iblis said. "It's here,
though, somewhere close by. I can feel it."

Leia held her breath, stretching out with her Jedi senses.
She didn't have Bel Iblis's fine-honed warrior's intuition, nor
did she have Luke's far deeper Jedi skill. But she could sense it,
too. Something about the Grand Corridor . . . "I think you're
right," she told Bel Iblis. "Winter, you'd better head down and
get busy on this."

"Certainly, Your Highness."

"I'll come with you, Winter," Bel Iblis volunteered. "I want
to see what's happening with the Stardust plan."

Leia shut off the comlink and leaned back in her seat, fatigue and discouragement seeping into her mind despite her
best efforts to hold it back. It had seemed like such a good
idea, using Ghent's decrypt to try to identify Delta Source. But
so far every lead had simply melted away from in front of
them.

And time was running out. Even if they were able to keep
Ghent's work a secret—which was by no means certain—each
of these failed gambits simply brought them closer to the inevitable day when Delta Source would finally notice all the activity and shut down. And when that happened, their last
chance to identify the Imperial spy in their midst would be
gone.

And that would be a disaster. Not because of the leak
itself—Imperial Intelligence had been stealing information
since the Rebel Alliance was first formed, and they'd managed
to live through it. What was infinitely more dangerous to the
New Republic was the deepening aura of suspicion and distrust that Delta Sources mere existence had already spread
through the Palace. Councilor Fey'lya's discredited accusations against Admiral Ackbar had already shown what such
distrust could do to the delicate multispecies coalition that

made up the New Republic. If that leadership was found to contain a genuine Imperial agent . . .

Across the conversation ring the three Kubaz got to their feet and headed away, circling around behind the ch'hala tree and the MN-2E droid working alongside it and disappearing into the traffic flow down the corridor. Leia found herself staring at the droid, watching as it eased a manipulator arm carefully through the branches toward a small cluster of dead leaves, clucking softly to itself all the while. She'd had a brief run-in with an Imperial espionage droid on the Noghri home planet of Honoghr, a run-in which could have spelled disaster for her and genocide for the remnants of the Noghri race. If Bel Iblis was right—if Delta Source was, in fact, merely a droid and not a traitor . . .

But it didn't really help. The Empire simply could not have infiltrated an espionage droid into the Palace without the collaboration of one or more of the beings here. Security invariably did a complete screening of every droid that came into the Palace, whether on a permanent or temporary basis, and they knew exactly what to look for. Hidden secondary espionage programming would show up like a burst of pale red against the subtle background pattern on that ch'hala tree—

Leia frowned, staring at the tree, as her chain of thought jolted to a halt. Another small burst of red appeared on the slender trunk as she watched, sending a pale red ring rippling outward and around the trunk until it faded into the quiet purple background turmoil. Another flicker followed, and another, and another, chasing each other around the trunk like ripples from a dripping water line. All of them more or less the same size; all of them originating from the same place on the trunk.

And each of them exactly in time with one of the clucking noises from the MN-2E droid.

And suddenly then it hit her, like a violent wave of icy water. Fumbling at her belt with suddenly trembling fingers, she keyed for the central operator. "This is Councilor Organa

Solo," she identified herself. "Get me Colonel Bremen in Security.

"Tell him I've found Delta Source."

THEY HAD TO DIG nearly eight meters down before they found it: a long, fat, age-tarnished tube half buried in the side of the ch'hala tree's taproot with a thousand slender sampling leads feeding into one end and a direct-transmission fiber snaking out the other. Even then, it took another hour and the preliminary report before Bremen himself was finally convinced.

"The techs say it's like nothing they've ever seen before," the security chief told Leia, Bel Iblis, and Mon Mothma as they stood on the scattered dirt around the uprooted ch'hala tree. "But apparently it's reasonably straightforward. Any pressure on the ch'hala tree's trunk—including the pressure created by sound waves—sets off small chemical changes in the inner layers of bark."

"Which is what creates the shifting colors and patterns?" Mon Mothma asked.

"Right," Bremen nodded, wincing slightly. "Obvious in hindsight, really—the pattern changes are far too fast to be anything but biochemical in origin. Anyway, those implanted tubes running up into the trunk continuously sample the chemicals and shunt the information back down to the module on the taproot. The module takes the chemical data, turns it back into pressure data, and from there back into speech. Some other module—maybe further down the taproot—sorts out the conversations and gets the whole thing ready for encrypting and transmission. That's all there is to it."

"An organic microphone," Bel Iblis nodded. "With no electronics anywhere in sight for a counterintelligence sweep to pick up."

"A whole series of organic microphones," Bremen corrected, glancing significantly at the twin rows of trees lining the Grand Corridor. "We'll get rid of them right away."

"Such a brilliant plan," Mon Mothma mused. "And so very like the Emperor. I'd always wondered how he obtained some of the information he used against us in the Senate." She shook her head. "Even after his death, it seems, his hand can move against us."

"Well, this part's about to be stilled, anyway," Bel Iblis said. "Let's get a team up here, Colonel, and dig up some trees."

CHAPTER 18

I N THE DISTANCE, far across the scarred plain, there was a glimmer of reflected light. "Mazzic's coming," Karrde commented.

Gillespee turned his attention from the refreshments table and squinted out past the crumbling fortress wall. "Someone's coming, anyway," he agreed, putting down his cup and the cold bruallki he'd been munching on and wiping his hands on his tunic. Pulling out his macrobinoculars, he peered through them. "Yeah, it's him," he confirmed. "Funny—he's got two other ships with him."

Karrde frowned at the approaching spot. "Two other ships?"

"Take a look," Gillespee said, handing over the macrobinoculars.

Karrde held them up to his eyes. There were three incoming, all right: a sleek space yacht and two slender, highly vicious-looking ships of an unfamiliar design. "You suppose he's brought some guests?" Gillespee asked.

"He didn't say anything about guests when he checked in with Aves a few minutes ago," Karrde said. Even as he watched, the two flanking ships left the formation, dropping to the plain below and vanishing into one of the deep ravines crisscrossing it.

"Maybe you'd better check."

"Maybe I'd better," Karrde agreed, handing back the macrobinoculars and pulling out his comlink. "Aves? You have some ID on our incoming?"

"Sure do," Aves's voice came back. "Gimmicked IDs on all of them, but we read them as the *Distant Rainbow*, the *Skyclaw*, and the *Raptor*."

Karrde grimaced. The designs might not be familiar, but the names certainly were. Mazzic's personal transport and two of his favorite customized fighters. "Thank you," he said, and shut down the comlink.

"Well?" Gillespee asked.

Karrde returned the comlink to his belt. "It's just Mazzic," he said.

"What's that about Mazzic?" Niles Ferrier's voice put in.

Karrde turned. The ship thief was standing behind them at the refreshments table, a generous helping of charred pirki nuts cupped in one hand. "I said Mazzic was coming," he repeated.

"Good," Ferrier nodded, popping one of the nuts into his mouth and cracking it loudly between his teeth. "About time. Finally get this meeting going."

He sauntered off, crunching as he went, nodding at Dravis and Clyngunn as he passed. "I thought you didn't want him here," Gillespee muttered.

Karrde shook his head; "I didn't. Apparently, the feeling wasn't universal."

Gillespee frowned. "You mean someone else invited him? Who?"

"I don't know," Karrde admitted, watching as Ferrier wandered over to the corner where Ellor and his group had gathered. "I haven't found a way to ask around without looking either petty, suspicious, or overbearing. Anyway, it's probably quite innocent. Someone assuming that all those at the original Trogan meeting should continue to be involved."

"The lack of an invitation notwithstanding?"

Karrde shrugged. "Perhaps that was assumed to be an oversight. At any rate, calling attention to it at this point would only create friction. Some of the others already seem resentful that I've apparently taken over management of the operation."

Gillespee tossed the last bit of bruallki into his mouth. "Yeah, maybe it's innocent," he said darkly. "But maybe it's not."

"We're keeping a good watch on the likely approaches," Karrde reminded him. "If Ferrier's made a deal with the Empire, we'll see them coming in plenty of time."

"I hope so," Gillespee grunted, surveying the refreshments table for his next target. "I hate running on a full stomach."

Karrde smiled; and he was starting to turn away when his comlink beeped. He pulled it out and flicked it on, eyes automatically turning to the sky. "Karrde," he said into it.

"This is Torve," the other identified himself . . . and from the tone Karrde knew something was wrong. "Could you step downstairs a minute?"

"Certainly," Karrde said, his other hand dropping to his side and the blaster holstered there. "Should I bring anyone?"

"No need—we're not having a party or anything here."

Translation: reinforcements were already on their way. "Understood," Karrde said. "I'll be right there."

He shut off the comlink and returned it to his belt. "Trouble?" Gillespee asked, eyeing Karrde over his glass.

"We've got an intruder," Karrde said, glancing around the courtyard. None of the other smugglers or their entourages seemed to be looking his direction. "Do me a favor and keep an eye on things here."

"Sure. Anyone in particular I should watch?"

Karrde looked at Ferrier, who had now left Ellor and was heading toward Par'tah and her fellow Ho'Din. "Make sure Ferrier doesn't leave."

The main part of the base had been set up three levels below the top remaining floors of the ruined fortress, in what had probably been the kitchens and ancillary prep areas for a huge high-ceilinged room that had probably been a banquet area. The *Wild Karrde* was berthed in the banquet chamber itself—a moderately tight fit for a ship its size, but offering the twin advantages of reasonable concealment plus the possibility for a quick exit should that become necessary. Karrde arrived at the high double doors to find Fynn Torve and five of the crewers from the *Starry Ice* waiting with drawn blasters. "Report," he said.

"We think someone's in there," Torve told him grimly. "Chin was taking the vornskrs for a walk around the ship and saw something moving in the shadows along the south wall."

The wall closest to the *Wild Karrde*'s lowered entrance ramp. "Anyone currently aboard the ship?"

"Lachton was working on the secondary command console," Torve said. "Aves told him to sit tight on the bridge with his blaster pointed at the door until we got someone else there. Chin grabbed some of the *Etherway* people who were hanging around and started searching through the south-end rooms; Dankin is doing the same with the north-end ones."

Karrde nodded. "That leaves the ship for us, then. You two"—he pointed to two of the *Starry Ice* crewers—"will stay here and guard the doors. Nice and easy; let's go."

They pulled open one of the double doors and slipped inside. Directly ahead, the *Wild Karrde*'s stern rose up darkly in front of them; 150 meters beyond it, glimpses of the blue Hijarna sky could be seen through the broken fortress wall. "I wish we had better lighting in here," Torve muttered as he looked around.

"It looks easier to hide in than it really is," Karrde assured him, pulling out his comlink. "Dankin, Chin, this is Karrde. Report."

"Nothing so far in the north-end rooms," Dankin's voice came promptly. "I sent Corvis for some portable sensor equipment, but he's not back yet."

"Nothing here either, Capt'," Chin added.

"All right," Karrde said. "We're coming in around the starboard side of the ship and heading for the entryway. Be ready to give us cover fire if we need it."

"We're ready, Capt'."

Karrde slid the comlink back in his belt. Taking a deep breath, he headed out.

THEY SEARCHED THE SHIP, the banquet chamber, and all the offices and storerooms on the periphery. And in the end, they found no one.

"I must have imagined it," Chin said morosely as the searchers gathered together at the foot of the *Wild Karrde*'s entrance ramp. "Sorry, Capt'. Truly sorry."

"Don't worry about it," Karrde said, looking around the banquet chamber. Cleared or not, there was still an uneasy feeling tugging at him. Like someone was watching and laughing . . . "We all misread things sometimes. If this was, in fact, a misreading. Torve, you're certain you and Lachton covered the entire ship?"

"Every cubic meter of it," Torve said firmly. "If anyone sneaked into the *Wild Karrde*, he was out long before we got here."

"What about those vornskr pets of yours, sir?" one of the *Starry Ice* crewers asked. "Are they any good at tracking?"

"Only if you're hunting ysalamiri or Jedi," Karrde told him. "Well. Whoever was here seems to be gone now. Still, we may have driven him off before he finished whatever it was he came to do. Torve, I want you to set up a guard detail for the area. Have Aves alert the duty personnel aboard the *Starry Ice* and *Etherway*, as well."

"Right," Torve said, pulling out his comlink. "What about our guests upstairs? Should we warn them, too?"

"What are we, their mothers?" one of the other crewers snorted. "They're big boys—they can look out for themselves."

"I'm sure they can," Karrde reproved him mildly. "But

they're here at my invitation. As long as they're under our roof, they're under our protection."

"Does that include whoever sent the intruder Chin spotted?" Lachton asked.

Karrde looked up at his ship. "That will depend on what the intruder was sent to do," he said. And speaking of his guests, it was time he got back to them. Mazzic would have joined them by now, and Ferrier wasn't the only one impatient for the meeting to begin. "Lachton, as soon as Corvis gets here with those scanners I want the two of you to run a complete check of the ship, starting with the exterior hull. Our visitor may have left us a gift, and I don't want to fly out of here with a homing beacon or timed concussion bomb aboard somewhere. I'll be up in the conference area if you need me."

He left them to their work, feeling once again Mara Jade's absence from the group. One of these days, he was going to have to make the time to go back to Coruscant and get her and Ghent back.

Assuming he was allowed to do so. His information sources had picked up a vague and disturbing rumor that an unnamed woman had been caught giving assistance to an Imperial commando force on Coruscant. Given Mara's obvious disdain for Grand Admiral Thrawn, it was unlikely she would actually give his Empire any help. But on the other hand, there were many in the New Republic starting to edge toward a kind of war hysteria . . . and given her shadowy history, Mara was an obvious candidate for that kind of accusation. All the more reason for him to get her off Coruscant.

He reached the upper courtyard to find that Mazzic had indeed arrived. He was standing with the Ho'Din group, talking earnestly with Par'tah, with the deceptively decorative female bodyguard he'd had at Trogan an aloof half-step back from the conversation, trying to look inconspicuous.

As were the pair of men just behind her. And the four standing around them a few meters away. And the six scattered elsewhere around the edges of the courtyard.

Karrde paused in the arched entrance, a quiet warning alarm going off in the back of his head. For Mazzic to bring a pair of fighting ships to protect him en route was one thing. To bring a full squad of enforcers into a friendly meeting was something else entirely. Either the Imperial attack on Trogan had made him uncharacteristically nervous . . . or else he wasn't planning for the meeting to remain quite so friendly.

"Hey—Karrde," Ferrier called, beckoning him over "Come on—let's get this meeting out of the bay."

"Certainly," Karrde said, putting on his best host's smile as he walked into the room. Too late now to bring some of his own people up here for balance. He would just have to hope that Mazzic was merely being cautious. "Good afternoon, Mazzic. Thank you for coming."

"No problem," Mazzic said, his eyes cool. He didn't smile back.

"We have more comfortable seats prepared in a room back this way," Karrde said, gesturing to his left. "If you'd all care to follow me—"

"I have a better idea," Mazzic interrupted. "What do you say we hold this meeting inside the *Wild Karrde*?"

Karrde looked at him. Mazzic returned the gaze evenly, his face not giving anything away. Apparently, he was not merely being cautious. "May I ask why?" Karrde asked.

"Are you suggesting you have something to hide?" Mazzic countered.

Karrde allowed himself a cool smile. "Of course I have things to hide," he said. "So does Par'tah; so does Ellor; so do you. We're business competitors, after all."

"So you won't allow us aboard the *Wild Karrde*?"

Karrde looked at each of the smuggler chiefs in turn. Gillespee, Dravis, and Clyngunn were frowning, clearly with no idea at all as to what this was all about. Par'tah's Ho'Din face was difficult to read, but there was something about her stance that seemed oddly troubled. Ellor was avoiding his eyes entirely. And Ferrier—

Ferrier was smirking. Not obviously—almost invisibly, in fact, behind that beard of his. But enough. More than enough.

And now, far too late, he finally understood. What Chin had seen—and what all of them had subsequently failed to catch—had been Ferrier's shadowy Defel.

Mazzic's men were here. Karrde's were three levels down, guarding his ship and base against a danger that was long gone. And all his guests were waiting for his answer. "The *Wild Karrde* is berthed down below," he told them. "If you'd care to follow me?"

Dankin and Torve were conversing together at the foot of the *Wild Karrde*'s entrance ramp as the group arrived. "Hello, Captain," Dankin said, looking surprised. "Can we help you?"

"No help needed," Karrde said. "We've decided to hold the meeting aboard ship, that's all."

"Aboard ship?" Dankin echoed, his eyes flicking over the group and obviously not liking what he saw. Small wonder: among the smuggler chiefs, aides, and bodyguards, Mazzic's enforcers stood out like a landing beacon cluster. "I'm sorry— I wasn't informed," he added, hooking the thumb of his right hand casually into the top of his gun belt.

"It was a rather spur-of-the-moment decision," Karrde told him. Out of the corner of his eye, he could see the rest of his people in the banquet chamber beginning to drift from their assigned tasks as they spotted Dankin's hand signal. Drifting into encirclement positions . . .

"Oh, sure," Dankin said, starting to look a little embarrassed. "Though the place really isn't set up for anything this fancy. I mean, you know what the wardroom looks like—"

"We're not interested in the decor," Mazzic interrupted. "Please step aside—we have business to attend to."

"Right—I understand that," Dankin said, looking even more embarrassed but holding his ground. "Problem is, we've got a scanning crew aboard right now. It'll foul up the readings if we get more people coming and going."

"So foul them up," Ferrier put in. "Who do you think you are, anyway?"

Dankin didn't get a chance to come up with an answer to that one. A whiff of perfume-scented air brushed across the side of Karrde's face, and the hard knob of a blaster muzzle dug gently into his side. "Nice try, Karrde," Mazzic said, "but it won't work. Call them off. Now."

Carefully, Karrde looked over his shoulder. Mazzic's decorative bodyguard looked back, her eyes cool and very professional. "If I don't?"

"Then we have a firefight," Mazzic said bluntly. "Right here."

There was a quiet ripple of movement through the group. "Would someone like to tell me what's going on here?" Gillespee murmured uncertainly.

"I'll tell you inside the ship," Mazzic said, his eyes steady on Karrde. "Assuming we all live to get in there. That part's up to our host."

"I won't surrender my people to you," Karrde said quietly. "Not without a fight."

"I have no interest in your people," Mazzic told him. "Or your ship, or your organization. This is a personal matter, between you and me. And our fellow smugglers."

"Then let's have it out," Dankin suggested. "We'll clear a space, you can choose weapons—"

"I'm not talking some stupid private feud," Mazzic cut him off. "This is about treachery."

"About *what*?" Gillespee asked. "Mazzic—"

"Shut up, Gillespee," Mazzic said, throwing a quick glare at him. "Well, Karrde?"

Slowly, Karrde looked around the group. There were no allies here; no friends who would stand firmly by him against whatever these phantom charges were that Mazzic and Ferrier had concocted. Whatever respect any of them might have for him, whatever favors they might owe him—all of that was already forgotten. They would watch while his enemies took him down . . . and then they would each take a piece of the organization he'd worked so hard to build.

But until that happened, the men and other beings here were still his associates. And still his responsibility.

"There's not enough room in the wardroom for anyone but the eight of us," he told Mazzic quietly. "All aides, bodyguards, and your enforcers will have to stay out here. Will you order them to leave my people alone?"

For a long minute Mazzic studied his face. Then he nodded, a single curt jerk of his head. "As long as they're not provoked, they won't bother anyone. Shada, get his blaster. Karrde . . . after you."

Karrde looked at Dankin and Torve and nodded. Reluctantly, they moved away from the ramp and he started up. Followed closely by the people he'd once hoped to make into a unified front against the Empire.

He should have known better.

THEY SETTLED INTO the wardroom, Mazzic nudging Karrde into a chair in one corner as the others found places around the table facing him. "All right," Karrde said. "We're here. Now what?"

"I want your data cards," Mazzic said. "All of them. We'll start with the ones in your office."

Karrde nodded over his shoulder. "Through the door and down the corridor to the right."

"Access codes?"

"None. I trust my people."

Mazzic's lip twisted slightly. "Ellor, go get them. And bring a couple of data pads back with you."

Wordlessly, the Duro stood up and left. "While we're waiting," Karrde said into the awkward silence, "perhaps I could present the proposal I invited you to Hijarna to hear."

Mazzic snorted. "You've got guts, Karrde—I'll give you that. Guts and style. Let's just sit quiet for now, okay?"

Karrde looked at the blaster pointed at him. "Whatever you wish."

Ellor returned a minute later, carrying a tray full of data cards with two data pads balanced on top. "Okay," Mazzic said as the Duro sat down beside him. "Give one of the data pads to Par'tah and start going through them. You both know what to look for."

[[I must acknowledge at the beginning,]] Ellor said, [[that I do not like this.]]

[Iy agree,] Par'tah said, her head appendages writhing like disturbed snakes. [To fiyght openly agaiynst a competiytor iys part of busiyness. But thiys iys diyfferent.]

"This isn't about business," Mazzic said.

"Of course not," Karrde agreed. "He's already said he has no interest in my organization. Remember?"

"Don't try playing on my words, Karrde," Mazzic warned. "I hate that as much as I hate being led around by the nose."

"I'm not leading anyone by the nose, Mazzic," Karrde said quietly. "I've dealt squarely with all of you since this whole thing began."

"Maybe. That's what we're here to find out."

Karrde looked around the table, remembering back to the chaos that had flooded through the twilight world of smuggling after the collapse of Jabba the Hutt's organization. Every group in the galaxy had scrambled madly to pick up the pieces, snatching ships and people and contracts for themselves, sometimes fighting viciously for them. The larger organizations, particularly, had profited quite handsomely from the Hutt's demise.

He wondered if Aves would be able to beat them off. Aves, and Mara.

"Anything yet?" Mazzic asked.

[We wiyll tell you iyf there iys,] Par'tah said, her off-pitch tone betraying her displeasure with the whole situation.

Karrde looked at Mazzic. "Would you mind at least telling me what it is I've allegedly done?"

"Yeah, I want to hear it, too," Gillespee seconded.

Mazzic leaned back in his seat, resting his gun hand on his thigh. "It's very simple," he said. "That attack on Trogan—the one where my friend Lishma was killed—appears to have been staged."

"What do you mean, staged?" Dravis asked.

"Just what I said. Someone hired an Imperial lieutenant and his squad to attack us."

Clyngunn rumbled deep in his throat. "Imperial troops do not work for hire," he growled.

"This group did," Mazzic told him.

"Who said so?" Gillespee demanded.

Mazzic smiled tightly. "The most knowledgeable source there is. Grand Admiral Thrawn."

There was a moment of stunned silence. Dravis found his voice first. "No kidding," he said. "And he just happened to mention this to you?"

"They picked me up poking around Joiol system and took me to the *Chimaera*," Mazzic said, ignoring the sarcasm. "After the incident at the Bilbringi shipyards I thought I was in for a rough time. But Thrawn told me he'd just pulled me in to clear the air, that no one in the Empire had ordered the Trogan attack and that I shouldn't hold them responsible for it. And then he let me go."

"Having conveniently implied that I was the one you should hold responsible?" Karrde suggested.

"He didn't finger you specifically," Mazzic said. "But who else had anything to gain by getting us mad at the Empire?"

"We're talking a Grand Admiral here, Mazzic," Karrde reminded him. "A Grand Admiral who delights in leisurely and convoluted strategies. And who has a personal interest in destroying me."

Mazzic smiled tightly. "I'm not just taking Thrawn's word for this, Karrde. I had a friend do a little digging through Imperial military records before I came here. He got me the complete details of the Trogan arrangement."

"Imperial records can be altered," Karrde pointed out.

"Like I said, I'm not taking their word for it," Mazzic retorted. "But if we find the other end of the deal here"—he lifted his blaster slightly—"I'd say that would be hard evidence."

"I see," Karrde murmured, looking at Ferrier. So that was what his Defel had been doing down here. Planting Mazzic's hard evidence, "I suppose it's too late to mention that we had an intruder down here a few minutes before you arrived."

Ferrier snorted. "Oh, right. Nice try, Karrde, but a little late."

"A little late for what?" Dravis asked, frowning.

"He's trying to throw suspicion on someone else, that's all," Ferrier said contemptuously. "Trying to make you think one of us planted that data card on him."

"What data card?" Gillespee scoffed. "We haven't found any data card."

"Yes, we have," Ellor said softly.

Karrde looked at him. Ellor's flat face was stiff, his emotions unreadable as he silently handed his data pad to Mazzic. The other took it; and his face, too, hardened. "So there it is," he said softly, laying the data pad on the table. "Well. I suppose there's nothing else to say."

"Wait a second," Gillespee objected. "There is too. Karrde's right about that intruder—I was with him upstairs when the alert came through."

Mazzic shrugged. "Fine; I'll play. What about it, Karrde? What did you see?"

Karrde shook his head, trying to keep his eyes off the muzzle of Mazzic's blaster. "Nothing, unfortunately. Chin thought he saw some movement near the ship, but we weren't able to locate anyone."

"I didn't notice all that many places out there where anyone could hide," Mazzic pointed out.

"A human couldn't, no," Karrde agreed. "On the other hand, it didn't occur to us at the time just how many shadows there were along the walls and near the doors."

"Meaning you think it was my wraith, huh?" Ferrier put in. "That's typical, Karrde—fire off a few hints and try to fog the issue. Well, forget it—it won't work."

Karrde frowned at him. At the aggressive face but wary eyes . . . and suddenly he realized he'd been wrong about the setup here. Ferrier and Mazzic were not, in fact, working together on this. It was Ferrier alone, probably under Thrawn's direction, who was trying to bring him down.

Which meant Mazzic honestly thought Karrde had betrayed them all. Which meant, in turn, that there might still be a chance to persuade him otherwise. "Let me try this, then," he said, shifting his attention back to Mazzic. "Would I really be so careless as to leave a record of my treachery here where anyone could find it?"

"You didn't know we'd be looking for it," Ferrier said before Mazzic could answer.

Karrde cocked an eyebrow at him. "Oh, so now it's 'we,' Ferrier? You're assisting Mazzic on this?"

"He's right, Karrde—stop trying to fog the issue," Mazzic said. "You think Thrawn would go to all this effort just to take you down? He could have done that straight-out at Trogan."

"He couldn't touch me at Trogan," Karrde shook his head. "Not with all of you there watching. He would have risked stirring up the entire fringe against him. No, this way is much better. He destroys me, discredits my warnings about him, and retains both your goodwill and your services."

Clyngunn shook his shaggy head. "No. Thrawn is not like Vader. He would not waste troops in a deliberately failed attack."

"I agree," Karrde said. "I don't think he ordered the Trogan attack, either. I think someone else planned that raid, and that Thrawn's simply making the best use of it he can."

"I suppose you're going to try to put that one on me, too," Ferrier growled.

"I haven't accused anyone, Ferrier," Karrde reminded him mildly. "One might think you had a guilty conscience."

"There he goes—fogging things again," Ferrier said, looking around the table before turning his glare back to Karrde. "You already practically flat out accused my wraith of planting that data card in here."

"That was your suggestion, not mine," Karrde said, watching the other closely. Thinking on his feet obviously wasn't Ferrier's strong point, and the strains were starting to show. If he could push just a little harder . . . "But since we're on the subject, where *is* your Defel?"

"He's on my ship," Ferrier said promptly. "Over in the western courtyard with everyone else's. He's been there since I landed."

"Why?"

Ferrier frowned. "What do you mean, why? He's there because he's part of my crew."

"No, I mean why isn't he outside the *Wild Karrde* with the rest of the bodyguards?"

"Who said he was a bodyguard?"

Karrde shrugged. "I simply assumed he was. He was playing that role on Trogan, after all."

"That's right, he was," Gillespee said slowly. "Standing over against the wall. Where he was all ready to hit the Imperials when they came in."

"Almost as if he knew they were coming," Karrde agreed.

Ferrier's face darkened. "Karrde—"

"Enough," Mazzic cut him off. "This isn't evidence, Karrde, and you know it. Anyway, what would Ferrier have to gain by setting up an attack like that?"

"Perhaps so he could be conspicuous in helping us fight it off," Karrde suggested. "Hoping it would soothe our suspicions about his relationship with the Empire."

"Twist all the words you want," Ferrier said, jabbing a finger at the data pad sitting on the table beside Mazzic. "But that data card doesn't say *I* hired Kosk and his squad. It says *you* did. Personally, I think we've heard enough of this—"

"Just a minute," Mazzic interrupted, turning to face him. "How do you know what the data card says?"

"You told us," Ferrier said. "You said it was the other half of the—"

"I never mentioned the lieutenant's name."

The room was suddenly very quiet . . . and behind his beard, Ferrier's face had gone pale. "You must have."

"No," Mazzic said coldly. "I didn't."

"No one said it," Clyngunn rumbled.

Ferrier glared at him. "This is insane," he spat, some of his courage starting to come back. "All the evidence points straight to Karrde—and you're going to let him off just because I happened to hear this Kosk's name somewhere? Maybe one of the stormtroopers on Trogan shouted it during the fight—how should I know?"

"Well, then, here's an easier question," Karrde said. "Tell us how you learned the time and location of this meeting. Given your lack of an invitation."

Mazzic shot a look at him. "You didn't invite him?"

Karrde shook his head. "I've never really trusted him, not since I heard about his role in Thrawn's acquisition of the *Katana* fleet. He wouldn't have been at Trogan at all if Gillespee hadn't made that invitation more or less open to anyone."

"Well, Ferrier?" Dravis prompted. "Or are you going to claim one of us told you?"

There were tight lines at the corners of Ferrier's eyes. "I picked up the transmission to Mazzic," he muttered. "Decrypted it; figured I ought to be here."

"Pretty fast decrypting work," Gillespee commented. "Those were good encrypt codes we were using. You kept a copy of the original encrypted transmission, of course?"

Ferrier stood up. "I don't have to sit here and listen to this," he growled. "Karrde's the one on trial here, not me."

"Sit down, Ferrier," Mazzic said softly. His blaster was no longer pointed at Karrde.

"But *he*'s the one," Ferrier insisted. His right hand shot out, forefinger pointed accusingly at Karrde. "He's the one who—"

"Watch out!" Gillespee snapped.

But it was too late. With his right hand waving out in front of him as a diversion, Ferrier's left hand had dipped into his waist sash and was now back out in front of him.

Holding a thermal detonator.

"All right, hands on the table," he snarled. "Drop it, Mazzic."

Slowly, Mazzic laid his blaster on the table. "You can't possibly get out of here, Ferrier," he bit out. "It'll be a toss-up between Shada and my enforcers."

"They'll never even get a shot at me," Ferrier said, reaching over to pick up Mazzic's blaster. "Wraith! Get in here!"

Behind him, the wardroom door slid open and a black shadow moved silently into the room. A black shadow with red eyes and a hint of long white fangs.

Clyngunn swore, a roiling ZeHethbra curse. "So Karrde was right about all of it. You have betrayed us to the Empire."

Ferrier ignored him. "Watch them," he ordered, shoving Mazzic's blaster at the shadow and drawing his own. "Come on, Karrde—we're going to the bridge."

Karrde didn't move. "If I refuse?"

"I kill you all and take the ship up myself," Ferrier told him shortly. "Maybe I should do that anyway—Thrawn'd probably pay a good bounty on all of you."

"I concede the point," Karrde said, getting to his feet. "This way."

They reached the bridge without incident. "You're flying," Ferrier instructed, gesturing toward the helm with his blaster as he took a quick look at the displays. "Good—I figured you'd have it ready to go."

"Where are we going?" Karrde asked, sitting down in the

helm seat. Through the viewport, he could see some of his people, oblivious to his presence up here as they maintained their uneasy standoff with Mazzic's enforcers.

"Out, up, and over," Ferrier told him, motioning toward the broken fortress wall ahead with his blaster. "We'll start with that."

"I see," Karrde said, keying for a preflight status report with his right hand and letting his left drop casually to his knee. Just above it, built into the underside of the main console, was a knee panel with the controls for the ship's external lights. "What happens then?"

"What do you think?" Ferrier retorted, crossing over to the comm station and giving it a quick look. "We get out of here. You got any other ships on comm standby?"

"The *Starry Ice* and *Etherway*," Karrde said, turning the exterior running lights on and then off three times. Outside the viewport, frowning faces began turning to look up at him. "I trust you're not going to try to go very far."

Ferrier grinned at him. "What, you afraid I'll steal your precious freighter?"

"You're not going to steal it," Karrde said, locking eyes with him. "I'll destroy it first."

Ferrier snorted. "Big talk from someone on the wrong end of a blaster," he said contemptuously, hefting the weapon for emphasis.

"I'm not bluffing," Karrde warned him, turning on the running lights again and risking a casual look out the viewport. Between the warning flicker of lights and the sight of Ferrier holding a blaster on him, the crowd out there had presumably caught on to what was happening. He hoped so, anyway. If they hadn't, the *Wild Karrde*'s unannounced departure would probably trigger a firefight.

"Sure you're not," Ferrier grunted, dropping into the copilot station beside him. "Relax—you're not going to have to be a hero. I'd like nothing better than to take the *Wild Karrde* off your hands, but I know better than to try to run a ship like this with half a crew. No, all you're going to do is take me back to my ship. We'll get out of here and lay low until all this blows over." He threw one last look at the displays and nodded. "Okay. Let's go."

Mentally crossing his fingers, Karrde eased in the repulsorlifts and nudged the ship forward, half expecting a barrage of blaster shots from the crowd of aides and bodyguards outside. But no one opened fire as he maneuvered carefully through the jagged stone edging the opening and out into the open air. "Yeah, they're all gone from in there, all right," Ferrier said casually into the silence. "Probably scrambling to get back to their ships so they can chase after us."

"You don't seem worried about it."

"I'm not," Ferrier said. "All you have to do is get me to my ship a little ahead of them. You can do that, right?"

Karrde looked over at the blaster pointed at him. "I'll do my best."

They made it easily. Even as the *Wild Karrde* settled to the cracked stone beside a modified Corellian Gunship the others were just beginning to appear from the archways leading into the main part of the fortress, a good couple of minutes away. "Knew you could do it," Ferrier complimented him sarcastically, standing up and keying the intercom. "Wraith? Hit the door. We're out of here."

There was no response. "Wraith? You hear me?"

"He will not be hearing anything for a while," Clyngunn's voice rumbled back. "If you want him, you will have to carry him."

Viciously, Ferrier slapped off the intercom. "Fool. I should have known better than to trust a stupid wraith with anything. Better yet, I should have killed all of you right at the start."

"Perhaps," Karrde said. He nodded across the courtyard toward the approaching bodyguards and enforcers. "I don't think you have time to correct that oversight now."

"I'll just have to do it later," Ferrier shot back. "I could still take care of you, though."

"Only if you're willing to die along with me," Karrde countered, shifting slightly in his seat to show that his left hand was holding down one of the knee panel switches. "As I said, I'd rather destroy the ship than let you have it."

For a long moment he thought Ferrier was going to try it anyway. Then, with obvious reluctance, the ship thief shifted his aim and sent two shots sizzling into the fire-control section of the control board. "Another time, Karrde," he said. He stepped back to the bridge door, threw a quick look outside as it opened, and then slipped through.

Karrde took a deep breath, exhaled it slowly. Releasing the landing light switch he'd been holding down, he stood up. Fifteen seconds later, he spotted Ferrier through the viewport as he sprinted alone toward his Gunship.

Reaching carefully past the sizzling hole in his control board, he keyed the intercom. "This is Karrde," he said. "You can unbarricade the door now; Ferrier's left. Do you need any medical help or assistance with your prisoner?"

"No, to both," Gillespee assured him. "Defel might be good at sneaking around, but they're not much good as jailers. So Ferrier just abandoned him here, huh?"

"No more or less than I would have expected from him," Karrde said. Outside the viewport, Ferrier's Gunship was rising on its repulsorlifts, rotating toward the west as it did so. "He's lifting now. Warn everyone not to leave the ship—he's bound to have something planned to discourage pursuit."

And he did. The words were barely out of Karrde's mouth when the hovering ship ejected a large canister into the air overhead. There was a flash of light, and suddenly the sky exploded into a violently expanding tangle of metal mesh. The net stretched itself out across the courtyard and settled to the ground, throwing off sparks where it draped itself across the parked ships.

"A Conner net," Dravis's voice came from behind him. "Typical ship-thief trick."

Karrde turned. Dravis, Par'tah, and Mazzic were standing

just inside the door, looking through the viewport at the departing Gunship. "We have plenty of people outside it," he reminded them. "It shouldn't take long to get it burned off."

[He must not be allowed to escape,] Par'tah insisted, making a Ho'Din gesture of contempt toward the Gunship.

"He won't," Karrde assured her. The Gunship was streaking low across the plain, staying out of range of anything the netted ships might still be able to fire at him. "The *Etherway* and *Starry Ice* are standing ready, north and south of here." He turned back and lifted an eyebrow toward Mazzic. "But under the circumstances, I think Mazzic should have the honor."

Mazzic gave him a tight smile. "Thank you," he said softly, pulling out his comlink. "Griv, Amber. Gunship on the way. Take it."

Karrde looked back. The Gunship was nearly to the horizon now, starting its vertical climb toward space . . . and as he watched, Mazzic's two fighters rose behind it from their hiding places and gave pursuit.

"I guess I owe you an apology," Mazzic said from behind him.

Karrde shook his head. "Forget it," he said. "Or, better, don't forget it. Keep it as a reminder of the way Grand Admiral Thrawn does business. And what people like us ultimately mean to him."

"Don't worry," Mazzic said softly. "I won't forget."

"Good," Karrde said briskly. "Well, then. Let's get our people out there busy on this net—I'm sure we'd all prefer to be off Hijarna before the Empire realizes their scheme has failed."

In the distance, just above the horizon, there was a brief flare of light. "And while we're waiting," Karrde added, "I still have a proposal to present to you."

CHAPTER 19

"ALL RIGHT," HAN told Lando, his fingers searching along the edge of Artoo's left leg for a better handhold. "Get ready."

The droid twittered something. "He reminds you to be careful," Threepio translated, standing nervously just far enough out of their way not to get yelled at. "Do remember that the last time—"

"We didn't drop him on purpose," Han growled. "If he'd rather wait for Luke, he's welcome."

Artoo twittered again. "He says that will not be necessary," Threepio said primly. "He trusts you implicitly."

"Glad to hear it," Han said. There were, unfortunately, no better handholds. He'd have to talk to Industrial Automaton about that someday. "Here we go, Lando: lift."

Together they strained; and with a jolt that wrenched Han's back the droid came up and out of the tangle of tree roots that he'd somehow gotten entwined around his wheels. "There you go," Lando grunted as they dropped the droid more or less gently back into the dirt and leaves of the dry creek bed. "How's it feel?"

The explanation this time was longer. "He says there appears to have been only minimal damage," Threepio said. "Mainly cosmetic in nature."

"Translation: he's rusting," Han muttered, rubbing the small of his back as he turned around. Five meters further down the creek bed, Luke was using his lightsaber to carefully slice through a set of thick vines blocking their path. Beside him, Chewbacca and Mara were crouched with weapons drawn, ready to shoot the snakelike creatures that sometimes came boiling out when you cut into them. Like everything else on Wayland, they'd learned about that one the hard way.

Lando walked up beside him, brushing a few last bits of acidic tree root off his hands. "Fun place, isn't it?" he commented.

"I should have brought the *Falcon* down closer," Han grumbled. "Or moved it closer in when we found out we couldn't use the speeder bikes."

"If you had, we might be dodging Imperial patrols right now instead of fighting acid root and vine snakes," Lando said. "Personally, I'd call that a fair trade."

"I suppose so," Han agreed reluctantly. In the near distance something gave out with a complicated whistle, and something else whistled back. He looked that direction, but between the brush and vines and two different levels of trees he couldn't see anything.

"Doesn't sound much like a predator," Lando said.

"Maybe." Han looked back over his shoulder, to where Threepio was talking soothingly to Artoo as he inspected the squat droid's latest acid burns. "Hey—short stuff. Get your scanners busy."

Obediently, Artoo extended its little antenna and began moving it back and forth. For a minute it clucked to itself, then jabbered something. "He says there are no large animals anywhere within twenty meters," Threepio said. "Beyond that—"

"He can't read through the undergrowth," Han finished for him. It was getting to be a very familiar conversation. "Thanks."

Artoo retracted his sensor, and he and Threepio resumed their discussion. "Where do you suppose they've all gone?" Lando asked.

"The predators?" Han shook his head. "Beats me. Maybe the same place the natives went."

Lando looked around, exhaling gently between his teeth. "I don't like it, Han. They've got to know by now that we're here. What are they waiting for?"

"Maybe Mara was wrong about them," Han suggested doubtfully. "Maybe the Empire got tired of sharing the planet with anyone else and wiped them out."

"That's a cheerful thought," Lando said. "Still wouldn't explain why the predators have ignored us for the past two and a half days."

"No," Han agreed. But Lando was right: there *was* something out there watching them. He could feel it deep in his gut. Something, or somebody. "Maybe the ones that got away after that first fight passed the word down the wire to leave us alone."

Lando snorted. "Those things were dumber than space slugs, and you know it."

Han shrugged. "Just a thought."

Ahead, the greenish glow vanished as Luke closed down his lightsaber. "Looks clear," he called softly back. "You get Artoo out?"

"Yeah, he's all right," Han said, stepping up behind them. "Any snakes?"

"Not this time." Luke pointed with his lightsaber at one of the trees bordering the creek bed. "Looks like we just missed having to tangle with another group of clawbirds, though."

Han looked. There, in one of the lower branches, was another of the plate-sized mud-and-grass nests. Threepio had brushed against one of them the day before, and Chewbacca was still nursing the slashes he'd gotten in his left arm before they'd managed to shoot or lightsaber the predator birds that had come out of it. "Don't touch it," he warned.

"It's okay—it's empty," Luke assured him, nudging it with the tip of the lightsaber. "They must have moved on."

"Yeah," Han said slowly, taking a step closer to the nest. "Right."

"Something wrong?"

Han looked back at him. "No," he said, trying hard to sound casual. "No problem. Why?"

Behind Luke, Chewbacca rumbled deep in his throat. "Let's get moving," Han added before Luke could say anything. "I want to get a little further before it gets dark. Luke, you and Mara take the droids and head out. Chewie and me'll take the rear"

Luke wasn't going for it—he could tell that from the kid's face. But he just nodded. "All right. Come on, Threepio."

They started down the creek bed, Threepio complaining as usual the whole way. Lando threw Han a look of his own, but followed after them without comment.

Beside him, Chewbacca growled a question. "We're going to find out what happened to the clawbirds, that's what," Han told him, looking back at the nest. It didn't look damaged, like it should have if a predator had got it. "You're the one who can smell fresh meat ten paces upwind. Start sniffing."

It turned out not to take much in the way of Wookiee hunting skill. One of the birds was lying beside a bush just on the other side of the tree, its wings stretched out and stiff. Very dead.

"What do you think?" Han asked as Chewbacca gingerly picked it up. "Some predator?"

Chewbacca rumbled a negative. His climbing claws slid from their sheaths, probing at a dark-brown stain on the feathers under the left wing. He found a cut, dug a single claw delicately into it.

And growled. "You sure it was a knife?" Han frowned, peering at the wound. "Not some kind of claw?"

The Wookiee rumbled again, pointing out the obvious: if the bird had been killed by a predator, there shouldn't have been anything left but feathers and bones.

"Right," Han commented sourly as Chewbacca dropped the clawbird back beside the bush. "So much for hoping the natives weren't around. Must be pretty close, too."

Chewbacca growled the obvious question. "Beats me," Han told him. "Maybe they're still checking us out. Or waiting for reinforcements."

The Wookiee rumbled, gesturing at the bird, and Han took another look. He was right: the way the wound was placed meant that the wings had been open when it had been killed. Which meant it had been killed in flight. By a single stab. "You're right—they're not going to need any reinforcements," he agreed. "Come on, let's catch up with the others."

SOLO HAD WANTED them to keep going until it got dark, but after another disagreement between Skywalker's astromech droid and a tangle of acid vines, he gave up and called a halt.

"So what's the word?" Mara asked as Skywalker dropped his pack beside hers and stretched his shoulder muscles. "We going to have to carry it?"

"I don't think so," Skywalker said, looking over his shoulder to where Calrissian and the Wookiee had the R2 on its side and were tinkering with its wheels. "Chewie thinks he'll be able to fix it."

"You ought to trade it in on something that wasn't designed to travel on a flat metal deck."

"Sometimes I've wished," Skywalker conceded, sitting down beside her. "All things considered, though, he does pretty well. You should have seen how far across the Tatooine desert he got the first night I had him."

Mara looked past the droids to where Solo was setting up his bedroll and keeping one eye on the forest around them. "You going to tell me what Solo was talking to you about back there? Or is it something I'm not supposed to know?"

"He and Chewie found one of the clawbirds from that empty nest," Skywalker said. "The one near the second vine cluster we had to cut through today. It had been killed by a knife thrust."

Mara swallowed, thinking back to some of the stories she'd

heard when she was here with the Emperor. "Probably the Myneyrshi," she said. "They were supposed to have made an art of that kind of close-blade combat."

"Did they have any feelings one way or the other about the Empire?"

"Like I told you before, they don't like humans," Mara told him. "Starting with the ones who came here as colonists long before the Emperor found the planet."

She looked at Skywalker, but he wasn't looking back. He was staring at nothing, a slight frown creasing his forehead.

Mara took a deep breath, stretching out with the Force as hard as she could. The sounds and smells of the forest wove their way into her mind, flattening into the overall pattern of life around her. Trees, bushes, animals, and birds . . .

And there, just at the edge of her consciousness, was another mind. Alien, unreadable . . . but a mind just the same.

"Four of them," Skywalker said quietly. "No. Five."

Mara frowned, concentrating on the sensation. He was right: there was more than one mind out there. But she couldn't quite separate the various components out from the general sense.

"Try looking for deviations," Skywalker murmured. "The ways the minds are different from each other. That's the best way to resolve them."

Mara tried it; and to her slightly annoyed surprise discovered that he was right. There was the second mind . . . the third . . .

And then, suddenly, they were gone.

She looked sharply at Skywalker. "I don't know," he said slowly, still concentrating. "There was a surge of emotion, and then they just turned and left."

"Maybe they didn't know we were here," Mara suggested hesitantly, knowing even as she said it how unlikely that was. Between the Wookiee roaring at everything that came at them and the protocol droid whining about everything else, it was a wonder the whole planet didn't know they were there.

"No, they knew," Skywalker said. "In fact, I'm pretty sure they were coming directly toward us when they were—" He shook his head. "I want to say they were scared away. But that doesn't make any sense."

Mara looked at the double leaf-canopy overhead. "Could we have picked up an Imperial patrol?"

"No." Skywalker was positive. "I'd know if there were any other humans nearby."

"Bet that comes in handy," Mara muttered.

"It's just a matter of training."

She threw him a sideways look. There'd been something odd in his voice. "What's that supposed to mean?"

He grimaced, a quick tightening of his mouth. "Nothing. Just . . . I was thinking about Leia's twins. Thinking about how I'm going to have to train them some day."

"You worried about when to start?"

He shook his head. "I'm worried about being able to do it at all."

She shrugged. "What's to do? You teach them how to hear minds and move objects and use lightsabers. You did that with your sister, didn't you?"

"Yes," he agreed. "But that was when I thought that was all there was to it. It's really just the beginning. They're going to be strong in the Force, and with that strength comes responsibility. How do I teach them that? How do I teach them wisdom and compassion and how not to abuse their power?"

Mara studied his profile as he gazed out into the forest. This wasn't just word games; he was really serious about it. Definitely a side of the heroic, noble, infallible Jedi she hadn't seen before. "How does anyone teach anyone else that stuff?" she said. "Mostly by example, I suppose."

He thought about it, nodded reluctantly. "I suppose so. How much Jedi training did the Emperor give you?"

YOU WILL KILL LUKE SKYWALKER. "Enough," she said shortly, shaking the sound of the words from her mind and trying to stifle the flash of reflexive hatred that came with them. "All the basics. Why?—you checking for wisdom and compassion?"

"No." He hesitated. "But as long as we've got a few more days until we reach Mount Tantiss, it might be a good idea to go over it again. You know—a refresher course sort of thing."

She looked at him, an icy chill running through her. He was just a little bit too casual about this. . . . "Have you seen something about what's ahead of us?" she asked suspiciously.

"Not really," he said. But there was that brief hesitation again. "A few images and pictures that didn't make any sense. I just think it would be a good idea for you to be as strong in the Force as possible before we go in."

She looked away from him. *YOU WILL KILL LUKE SKY-WALKER.* "You'll be there," she reminded him. "What do I need to be strong in the Force for?"

"For whatever purpose your destiny calls you to," he said, his voice quiet but firm. "We have an hour or so left before sundown. Let's get started."

WEDGE ANTILLES SLID into his place on the long semicircular bench beside the other starfighter squadron commanders, glancing around the Star Cruiser war room as he did so. A good crowd already, and more were still filing in. Whatever Ackbar had planned, it was going to be big.

"'Lo, Wedge," someone grunted in greeting as he sat down beside Wedge. "Fancy meeting you here."

Wedge looked at him in mild surprise. Pash Cracken, son of the legendary General Airen Cracken, and one of the best starfighter commanders in the business. "I could say the same about you, Pash," he said. "I thought you were out in Atrivis sector, baby-sitting the Outer Rim comm center."

"You're behind the times," Pash said grimly. "Generis fell three days ago."

Wedge stared at him. "I hadn't heard," he apologized. "How bad was it?"

"Bad enough," Pash said. "We lost the whole comm center, more or less intact, and most of the sector fleet supply depots. On the plus side, we didn't leave them any ships they could use. And we were able to make enough trouble on our way out to let General Kryll sneak Travia Chan and her people out from under the Imperials' collective snout."

"That's something, I guess," Wedge said. "What was it got you, numbers or tactics?"

"Both," Pash said with a grimace. "I don't think Thrawn was there personally, but he sure planned out the assault. I've got to tell you, Wedge, that those clones of his are the creepiest things I've ever tangled with. It's like going up against stormtroopers: same rabid dedication, same cold-blooded machine-precision fighting. The only difference is that they're everywhere now instead of just handling shock-troop duty."

"Tell me about it," Wedge agreed soberly. "We had to fight off two TIE fighter squadrons of the things in the first Qat Chrystac assault. They were pulling stunts I didn't think TIEs were capable of."

Pash nodded. "General Kryll figures Thrawn must be picking his best people for his cloning templets."

"He'd be stupid to do anything else. What about Varth? Did he make it out?"

"I don't know," Pash said. "We lost contact with him during the retreat. I'm still hoping he was able to punch through the other side of the pincer and hook up with one of the units at Fedje or Ketaris."

Wedge thought about the handful of times he'd gone nose-to-nose with Wing Commander Varth over something, usually involving spare parts or maintenance time. The man was a bitter, caustic-mouthed tyrant, with the single redeeming talent of being able to throw his starfighters against ridiculous odds and then get them back out again. "He'll make it," Wedge said. "He's too contrary to roll over and die just for the Empire's convenience."

"Maybe." Pash nodded toward the center of the room. "Looks like we're ready to start."

Wedge turned back as the buzz of conversation around them faded away. Admiral Ackbar was standing by the central holo table, flanked by General Crix Madine and Colonel Bren Derlin. "Officers of the New Republic," Ackbar greeted them gravely, his large Mon Calamari eyes rotating to take in the entire war room. "None of you needs to be reminded that in the past few weeks our war against the remnants of the Empire has changed from what was once called a mopping-up exercise to a battle for our very survival. For the moment, the advantage of resources and personnel is still ours; but even as we speak that advantage is in danger of slipping away. Less tangible but no less serious are the ways in which Grand Admiral Thrawn is seeking to undermine our resolve and morale. It is time for us to throw both aspects of this attack back into the Empire's face." He looked at Madine. "General Madine."

"I assume that you've all been briefed on the innovative form of siege the Imperials have created around Coruscant," Madine said, tapping his light-pointer gently against his left palm. "They've been making some progress in clearing out the cloaked asteroids; but what they really need to get the job done is a crystal gravfield trap. We've been assigned to get them one."

"Sounds like fun," Pash muttered.

"Quiet," Wedge muttered back.

"Intelligence has located three of them," Madine continued. "All in Imperial-held space, naturally. The simplest one to go after is at Tangrene, helping to guard the new Ubiqtorate base they're putting together there. Lots of cargo and construction ships moving around, but relatively few combat ships. We've managed to insert some of our people into the cargo crews, and they report the place is ripe for the taking."

"Sounds a lot like Endor," someone commented from the bench across from Wedge. "How can we be sure it isn't a trap?"

"Actually, we're pretty sure it is," Madine said with a tight smile. "That's why we're going here instead."

He touched a switch. The holo projector rose from the center of the table, and a schematic appeared in the air above it. "The Imperial shipyards at Bilbringi," he identified it. "And I know what you're all saying to yourselves: it's big, it's well defended, and what in the galaxy is the high command thinking about? The answer is simple: it's big, it's well defended, and it's the last place the Imperials will expect us to hit."

"Moreover, if we succeed, we will have severely damaged their shipbuilding capability," Ackbar added. "As well as putting to rest the growing belief in Grand Admiral Thrawn's infallibility."

Which assumed, of course, that Thrawn *was* fallible. Wedge thought about pointing that out, decided against it. Everyone here was probably already thinking it, anyway.

"The operation will consist of two parts," Madine went on. "We certainly don't want to disappoint the Imperials planning the trap for us at Tangrene, so Colonel Derlin will be in charge of creating the illusion that that system is indeed our target. While he does that, Admiral Ackbar and I will be organizing the actual attack on Bilbringi. Any questions?"

There was a moment of silence. Then, Pash raised his hand. "What happens if the Imperials pick up on the Bilbringi attack and miss the Tangrene preparations entirely?"

Madine smiled thinly. "We'd be most disappointed in them. All right, gentlemen, we have an assault force to organize. Let's get started."

THE BEDROOM WAS DARK and warm and quiet, murmuring with the faint nighttime noises of the Imperial City outside the windows and the more subtle sounds of the sleeping infants across the room. Listening to the sounds, inhaling the familiar aromas of home, Leia stared at the ceiling and wondered what had awakened her.

"Do you require anything, Lady Vader?" a soft Noghri voice came from the shadows beside the door.

"No, Mobvekhar, thank you," Leia said. She hadn't made any noise—he must have picked up on the change in her breathing pattern. "I'm sorry; I didn't mean to disturb you."

"You did not," the Noghri assured her. "Are you troubled?"

"I don't know," she said. It was starting to come back now. "I had—not a dream, exactly. More like a subconscious flash of insight. A piece of a puzzle trying to fit into place."

"Do you know which piece?"

Leia shook her head. "I don't even know which puzzle."

"Did it relate to the siege of stones in the sky above?" Mobvekhar asked. "Or with the mission of your consort and the son of Vader?"

"I'm not sure," Leia said, frowning with concentration into the darkness and running through the short-term memory enhancement techniques Luke had taught her. Slowly, the half-remembered dream images started to sharpen. . . . "It was something Luke said. No. It was something *Mara* said. Something Luke *did*. They fit together somehow. I don't know how . . . but I know it's important."

"Then you will find the answer," Mobvekhar said firmly. "You are the Lady Vader. The *Mal'ary'ush* of the Lord Vader. You will succeed at whatever goal you set for yourself."

Leia smiled in the darkness. It wasn't just words. Mobvekhar and the other Noghri truly believed that. "Thank you," she said, taking a deep breath and feeling a renewing of her own spirit. Yes, she would succeed. If for no other reason than to justify the trust that the Noghri people had placed in her.

Across the room, she could sense the restlessness and growing hunger that meant the twins would be waking up soon. Reaching past the lightsaber half hidden beneath her pillow, she pulled her robe over to her. Whatever this important puzzle piece was she'd stumbled on, it would wait until morning.

CHAPTER 20

THE LAST SURVIVING Rebel ship flickered with pseudomotion and vanished into hyperspace . . . and after a thirty-hour battle, the heart of Kanchen sector was finally theirs. "Secure the fleet from full battle status, Captain," Thrawn ordered, his voice grimly satisfied as he stood at the side viewport. "Deploy for planetary bombardment, and have Captain Harbid transmit our terms of surrender to the Xa Fel government."

"Yes, sir," Pellaeon said, keying in the order.

Thrawn half turned to face him. "And send a further message to all ships," he added. "Well done."

Pellaeon smiled. Yes; the Grand Admiral did indeed know how to lead his men. "Yes, sir," he said, and transmitted the message. On his board, a light went on: a preflagged message had just come through decrypt. He pulled it up, skimmed through it—

"A report from Tangrene?" Thrawn asked, still gazing out at the helpless world lying below them.

"Yes, sir," Pellaeon nodded. "The Rebels have sent two more freighters into the system. Long-range scans suggest that they off-loaded something in the outer system on the way in, but Intelligence has so far been unable to locate or identify the drops."

"Instruct them not to try," Thrawn said. "We don't want our prey frightened off."

Pellaeon nodded, marveling once again at the Grand Admiral's ability to read his opponents. Up until twenty hours ago he would have sworn the Rebels wouldn't be audacious enough to commit this many forces to a battle just to get hold of a CGT array. Apparently, they were. "We're also getting reports of Rebel ships drifting quietly into the Tangrene area," he added, skimming down the report again. "Warships, starfighters, support craft—the whole range."

"Good," Thrawn said. But there was something preoccupied and troubled about the way he clasped his hands behind his back.

A message appeared on Pellaeon's board: the Xa Fel government had accepted Harbid's terms. "Word from the *Death's Head*, Admiral," he said. "Xa Fel has surrendered."

"Not unexpectedly," Thrawn said. "Inform Captain Harbid that he will handle the landings and troop deployments. You, Captain, will reconfigure the fleet into defensive formation until planetary defenses have been secured."

"Yes, sir." Pellaeon frowned at the Grand Admiral's back. "Is anything wrong, Admiral?"

"I don't know," Thrawn said slowly. "I'll be in my private command room, Captain. Join me there in one hour."

He turned and favored Pellaeon with a tight smile. "Perhaps by then I'll have an answer to that question."

GILLESPEE FINISHED READING and handed the data pad across the table to Mazzic. "You never cease to amaze me, Karrde," he said, his voice just loud enough to be heard over the tapcafe's background noise. "Where in space do you dig this stuff up from, anyway?"

"Around," Karrde said, waving his hand vaguely. "Just around."

"That doesn't tell me mynock spit," Gillespee complained.

"I don't think it was meant to," Mazzic said dryly, handing the data pad back to Karrde. "I agree; it's very interesting. The question is whether we can believe it."

"The information itself is reliable," Karrde said. "My interpretation of it, of course, is certainly open to question."

Mazzic shook his head. "I don't know. It seems like a pretty desperate move to me."

"I wouldn't say desperate," Karrde disagreed. "Call it instead a return to the bold tactics the Rebel Alliance used to be known for. Personally, I think a move like this is long overdue—they've allowed themselves to be put on the defensive far longer than they should have."

"That doesn't change the fact that if this doesn't work they're going to lose a lot of ships," Mazzic pointed out. "Up to two entire sector fleets, if you can believe these numbers."

"True," Karrde agreed. "But if it does work, they get a major victory against Thrawn and an equally major lift in morale. Not to mention a CGT array."

"Yeah, that's another thing," Gillespee put in. "What do they need a CGT for, anyway?"

"It supposedly has something to do with the reason Coruscant has been closed to civilian traffic for the past few days," Karrde said. "That's all I know."

Mazzic leaned back in his seat and fixed Karrde with a speculative look. "Forget what they need it for. What are you proposing we do about it?"

Karrde shrugged. "It looks to me like the New Republic is fairly desperate to get their hands on a CGT. If they're willing to fight for one, I assume they'd be even more willing to pay for one."

"Seems reasonable," Mazzic agreed. "So what do you want us to do, sneak into Tangrene before they get there?"

"Not really," Karrde shook his head. "I thought that while everyone was busy fighting at Tangrene, we'd pick up the CGT at Bilbringi."

Mazzic's smile vanished. "You're joking."

"Not a bad idea, really," Gillespee put in, slowly swirling the remains of the drink in his cup. "We slip in before the attack starts, then grab the CGT and run."

"Through half the Imperial fleet?" Mazzic countered. "Come on—I've seen the kind of firepower they keep there."

"I doubt they'll have more than a skeleton defense there." Karrde raised an eyebrow. "Unless you seriously think Thrawn won't anticipate and prepare for the New Republic's move on Tangrene."

"Point," Mazzic conceded. "They can't afford to let the New Republic have a victory there, can they?"

"Particularly not at Tangrene," Karrde nodded. "That's where General Bel Iblis successfully hit them once before."

Mazzic grunted and pulled the data pad over in front of him again. Karrde let him reread the information and analysis, giving the tapcafe a leisurely scan as he waited. Near the main entrance, Aves and Gillespee's lieutenant Faughn were sitting together at one of the tables, doing a good job of looking inconspicuous. Across the way at the rear entrance, Mazzic's bodyguard Shada was playing the flirtatious hostess role for Dankin and Torve, the whole routine being convincingly leered at by Rappapor and Oshay, two more of Gillespee's people. Three more tables of backup forces were scattered elsewhere throughout the tapcafe, primed and ready. This time, none of them were taking any chances with Imperial interference.

"It won't be easy," Mazzic warned at last. "Thrawn was furious about that raid we pulled. They've probably redone their whole security setup by now."

"All the better," Karrde said. "They won't have found the holes in it yet. Are you in or out?"

Mazzic looked down at the data pad. "I might be in," he growled. "But only if you can get a confirmation on the time of this Tangrene thing. I don't want Thrawn anywhere within a hundred light-years of Bilbringi when we hit the place."

"That shouldn't be a problem," Karrde said. "We know the

systems where the New Republic is assembling their forces. I'll send some of my people to poke around and see what they can turn up."

"What if they can't get anything?"

Karrde smiled. "I need to have Ghent write us onto their payroll anyway," he pointed out. "As long as he's in the system, he might as well check on their battle plans, too."

For a moment Mazzic just stared at him. Then, suddenly, the frown vanished and he actually chuckled. "You know, Karrde, I've never seen anyone play both ends against the middle the way you do. Okay. I'm in."

"Glad to have you," Karrde nodded. "Gillespee?"

"I've already seen Thrawn's clones in action," Gillespee reminded him grimly. "You bet I'm in. Besides, if we win maybe I can get that land back the Empire stole from me on Ukio."

"I'll put in a good word for you with the New Republic," Karrde promised. "All right, then. I'm taking the *Wild Karrde* to Coruscant, but I'll be leaving Aves behind to coordinate my part of the attack group. He'll give you the operations plan when you check in."

"Sounds good," Mazzic said as they all got to their feet. "You know, Karrde, I just hope I'm around to see the day the New Republic catches up with you. Whether they give you a medal or just shoot you—either way, it'll be a terrific show."

Karrde smiled at him. "I rather hope to be there that day myself," he said. "Good flights, gentlemen; I'll see you at Bilbringi."

THE BRILLIANT GREEN turbolaser blast flashed downward from the fuzzy-looking Star Destroyer in the distance beyond. It splashed slightly against the unseen energy shield, then reappeared a short distance away, continuing onward—

"Stop," Admiral Drayson said.

The record froze, the hazy splash of turbolaser fire looking angular and rather artificial as it sat there in stop-frame mode on the main display. "I apologize for the quality here," Drayson said, stepping over to tap it with his light-pointer. "Macrobinocular records can be enhanced only so much before the algorithms start breaking down. But even so, I think you can all see what's happening. The Star Destroyer's blast is not, in fact, penetrating Ukio's planetary shield. What appears to be that same blast is actually a second shot, fired from a cloaked vessel *inside* the shield."

Leia peered at the hazy picture. It didn't seem nearly that obvious to her. "Are you sure?" she asked.

"Quite sure," Drayson said, touching his light-pointer to the empty space between the splash and the continuing green fire. "We have spectral and energy-line data on the beams themselves; but this gap by itself is really all the proof we need. That's the bulk of the second ship—most likely a *Carrack*-class light cruiser, from the size."

He lowered the light-pointer and looked around the table. "In other words, the Empire's new superweapon is nothing more than an extremely clever fraud."

Leia thought about that meeting in Admiral Ackbar's rooms, back when he was under suspicion of treason. "Ackbar once warned Han and me that a Grand Admiral would find ways to use a cloaking shield against us."

"I don't think you'd find anyone arguing that point," Drayson nodded. "At any rate, this should put an end to this particular gambit. We'll put out an alert to all planetary forces that if the Empire tries it again, all they need to do is direct a saturation fire at the spot where the turbolaser blasts appear to penetrate the shield."

"Fraud or not, it was still one highly impressive show," Bel Iblis commented. "The position and timing were exquisitely handled. What do you think, Leia—that insane Jedi Luke locked horns with on Jomark?"

"I don't think there's any doubt," Leia said, a shiver running through her. "We've already seen this kind of coordination between forces in Thrawn's earlier campaigns. And we know from Mara that C'baoth and Thrawn are working together."

Mentioning Mara's name was a mistake. There was a general, uncomfortable shifting in seats around the table as the emotional sense in the room chilled noticeably. They'd all heard Leia's reasoning for her unilateral decision to release Mara, and none of them had liked it.

Bel Iblis broke the awkward silence first. "Where did this macrobinocular record come from, Admiral?"

"From that smuggler, Talon Karrde," Drayson said. He threw a significant look at Leia. "Another outsider who came here offering valuable information that didn't pan out."

Leia bristled. "That's not fair," she insisted. "The fact we lost the *Katana* fleet wasn't Karrde's fault." She looked at Councilor Fey'lya, sitting silently at the table, doing his private Bothan penance. If Fey'lya hadn't been making that insane bid for power . . .

She looked back at Drayson. "It was nobody's fault," she added quietly, releasing at last the final lingering dregs of resentment at Fey'lya and allowing them to drain away. The recognition of his failure was already paralyzing the Bothan. She couldn't allow long-dead anger to do the same to her.

Bel Iblis cleared his throat. "I think what Leia's trying to say is that without Karrde's help we might have lost more than just the *Katana* fleet. Whatever you think of smugglers in general or Karrde in particular, we owe him."

"Interesting that you should say that, General," Drayson said dryly. "Karrde seems to feel the same way. In exchange for this record and certain other minor items of intelligence, he's drawn rather liberally from a special New Republic credit line." He looked at Leia again. "A line apparently set up by Councilor Organa Solo's brother."

Commander Sesfan, Ackbar's representative to the Council, rolled his huge Mon Calamari eyes toward Leia. "Jedi Skywalker authorized payments to a smuggler?" he said, his gravelly voice sounding astonished.

"He did," Drayson confirmed. "Completely without authorization, of course. We'll close it off immediately."

"You'll do no such thing," Mon Mothma's quiet voice came from the head of the table. "Whether Karrde is officially on our side or not, he's clearly willing to help us. That makes him worthy of our support."

"But he is a smuggler," Sesfan objected.

"So was Han," Leia reminded him. "So was Lando Calrissian, once. Both of them became generals."

"*After* they joined us," Sesfan countered. "Karrde has made no such commitment."

"It doesn't matter," Mon Mothma said. Her voice was still quiet, but there was steel beneath it. "We need all the allies we can get. Official or otherwise."

"Unless he's setting us up," Drayson pointed out darkly. "Gaining our trust with things like this macro-binocular record so that he can feed us disinformation later. And in the meantime profiting rather handsomely from it."

"We'll simply have to make certain we spot any such duplicity," Mon Mothma told him. "But I don't believe that will happen. Luke Skywalker is a Jedi . . . and he, clearly, has some trust in this man Karrde. Regardless, for now, our focus should be on those parts of our destiny which are in our hands. Admiral Drayson, have you the latest report on the Bilbringi operation?"

"Yes," Drayson nodded, pulling out a data card. He inserted it into the display slot, and as he did so, Leia heard the faint beep of a comlink from beside her. Winter pulled the device from her belt and acknowledged softly into it. Leia couldn't make out the reply, but she felt the sudden flicker in Winter's sense. "Trouble?" she murmured.

"If I may have everyone's attention?" Drayson said, just a little too loudly.

Leia turned back to him, feeling her face warm, as Winter pushed her chair back and slipped over to the door. Drayson threw a glare at her back, apparently decided it wasn't worth invoking the usual sealed-room rule. The door slid open at Winter's touch and an unseen person pressed a data card into her hand. The door slid shut again—"Well?" Drayson demanded. "I trust this is something that couldn't wait?"

"I'm certain it could have," Winter said coolly, giving Drayson her full antibluster gaze as she returned to her seat and sat down. "For you, Your Highness," she said, handing Leia the data card. "The coordinates of the planet Wayland."

A ripple of surprise went around the room as Leia took the card. "That was fast," Drayson said, his voice tinged with suspicion. "I was under the impression this place was going to be a lot harder to find."

Leia shrugged, trying to suppress her own twinge of uneasiness. That had been her impression, too. "Apparently it wasn't."

"Show it to us," Mon Mothma said.

Leia slid the data card into the slot and keyed for a visual. A sector map appeared on the main display, with familiar names floating beside several of the stars. In the center, surrounded by a group of unlabeled stars, one of the systems flashed red. At the bottom of the map was a short list of planetary data and a few lines of text. "So that's the Emperor's rat's nest," Bel Iblis murmured, leaning forward as he studied it. "I always wondered where he hid all those interesting little tidbits that seemed to mysteriously vanish from official storehouses and depots."

"If that's really the place," Drayson murmured.

"I presume you can confirm the information came from Captain Solo," Mon Mothma said, looking at Winter.

Winter hesitated. "It didn't come from him, exactly," she said.

Leia frowned at her. "What do you mean, not exactly? Was it from Luke?"

A muscle in Winter's cheek twitched. "All I can say is that the source is reliable."

There was a short moment of silence as everyone digested that. "Reliable," Mon Mothma said.

"Yes," Winter nodded.

Mon Mothma threw a look at Leia. "This Council is not accustomed to having information withheld from it," she said. "I want to know where these coordinates came from."

"I'm sorry," Winter said quietly. "It's not my secret to tell."

"Whose secret is it?"

"I can't tell you that, either."

Mon Mothma's face darkened. "It doesn't matter," Bel Iblis put in before she could speak. "Not for right now. Whether this planet is the actual cloning center or not, there's nothing we can do about it until the Bilbringi operation is over."

Leia looked at him. "We're not sending any backup?"

"Impossible," Sesfan growled, shaking his huge Mon Calamari head. "All available ships and personnel are already committed to the Bilbringi attack. Too many regions and systems have been left undefended as it is."

"Especially when we don't even know if this is the right place," Drayson added. "It could just as easily be an Imperial trap."

"It's not a trap," Leia insisted. "Mara's not working for the Empire anymore."

"We only have your word for that—"

"It still doesn't matter," Bel Iblis cut him off, his senatorial voice cutting through the growing argument. "Look at the bottom of the map, Leia—it says all indications are that their landing was undetected. Would you really want to risk that element of surprise by sending another ship in after them?"

Leia felt her stomach tighten. Unfortunately, he had a point.

"Then perhaps the Bilbringi attack should be postponed," Fey'lya said.

Leia turned to look at him, dimly aware that the whole table was doing likewise. It was practically the first time the Bothan had spoken at a Council meeting since his bid for

power had ignominiously collapsed out at the *Katana* fleet.
"I'm afraid that's out of the question, Councilor Fey'lya,"
Mon Mothma said. "Aside from all the preparations that
would have to be discarded, it's absolutely imperative that we
clear out these cloaked asteroids hanging over our heads."

"Why?" Fey'lya demanded, a rippling wave running through
the fur of his neck and down his shoulders. "The shield protects us. We have adequate supplies for many months. We have
full communication with the rest of the New Republic. Is it
merely the fear of looking weak and helpless?"

"Appearances and perceptions are important to the New
Republic," Mon Mothma reminded him. "And properly so.
The Empire rules by force and threat; we rule instead by inspiration and leadership. We cannot be perceived to be cowering
here in fear of our lives."

"This is beyond image and perception," Fey'lya insisted, the
fur flattening across the back of his head. "The Bothan people
knew the Emperor—knew his desires and his ambitions, perhaps better than all who were not his allies and servants. There
are things in that storehouse which must never again see light.
Weapons and devices which Thrawn will some day find and
use against us unless we prevent him from doing so."

"And we will do so," Mon Mothma assured him. "And
soon. But not until we've damaged the Bilbringi shipyards and
obtained a CGT array."

"And what of Captain Solo and Councilor Organa Solo's
brother?"

The lines around Mon Mothma's mouth tightened. For all
the rigid military logic, Leia could see that she didn't like
abandoning them there, either. "All we can do for them right
now is to continue with our plans," she said quietly. "To draw
the Grand Admiral's attention toward our supposed attack on
Tangrene." She looked at Drayson. "Which we were about to
discuss. Admiral?"

Drayson stepped up to the display again. "We'll start with

the current status of preparations for the Tangrene feint," he said, keying his light-pointer to call up the proper display.

Leia threw a sideways glance at Fey'lya, and at the obvious signs of agitation still visible in the Bothan's face and fur movements. What was in the mountain, she wondered, that he was so afraid Thrawn would get hold of?

Perhaps it was just as well she didn't know.

PELLAEON STEPPED INTO the dimly lit entry room just outside Thrawn's private command room, his eyes darting around. Rukh was here somewhere, waiting to play his little Noghri games. He took a step toward the door to the main chamber, took another—

There was a touch of air on the back of his neck. Pellaeon spun around, hands snapping up in half-remembered academy self-defense training.

There was no one there. He looked around again, searching for where the Noghri might have taken cover—

"Captain Pellaeon," the familiar catlike voice mewed from behind him.

He spun back again. Again, no one was there; but even as his eyes searched the walls and nonexistent cover, Rukh stepped around from behind him. "You are expected," the Noghri said, gesturing with his slender assassin's knife toward the main door.

Pellaeon glared at him. Someday, he promised himself darkly, he would persuade Thrawn that a Grand Admiral of the Empire didn't need an arrogant alien bodyguard to protect him. And when that happened, he was going to take a very personal pleasure in having Rukh killed. "Thank you," he growled, and went in.

He'd expected the command room to be filled with Thrawn's usual eclectic collection of alien art, and he was right. But with one minor difference: even to Pellaeon's untrained eye it

was clear that two very different styles of art were being represented. They were spread out along opposite sides of the room,
with a large tactical holo of the Tangrene system filling the
center.

"Come in, Captain," Thrawn called from the double display ring as Pellaeon paused in the doorway. "What news from
Tangrene?"

"The Rebels are still moving forces into strike positions,"
Pellaeon told him, making his way between the sculptures and
the tactical holo toward Thrawn's command chair. "Sneaking
their devious way into our trap."

"How very convenient of them." Thrawn gestured to his
right. "Mon Calamari art," he identified it. "What do you
think?"

Pellaeon gave it a quick look as he came up to the double
display ring. It looked about as repulsive and primitive as the
Mon Calamari themselves. "Very interesting," he said aloud.

"Isn't it," Thrawn agreed. "Those two pieces in particular—
they were created by Admiral Ackbar himself."

Pellaeon eyed the indicated sculptures. "I didn't know Ackbar had any interest in art."

"A minor one only," Thrawn said. "These were composed
some time ago, before he joined the Rebellion. Still, they provide useful insights into his character. As do those," he added,
gesturing to his left. "Artwork once chosen personally by our
Corellian adversary."

Pellaeon looked at them with new interest. So Senator Bel
Iblis had picked these out himself, had he? "Where were these
from, his old Imperial Senate office?"

"Those were," Thrawn said, indicating the nearest group.
"Those were from his home; those from his private ship. Intelligence found these records, more or less accidentally, in the
data from our last Obroa-skai information raid. So the Rebels
continue to edge toward our trap, do they?"

"Yes, sir," Pellaeon said, glad to be getting back to something he could understand. "We've had two more reports of

Rebel support ships moving into positions at the edge of the Draukyze system."

"But not obviously."

Pellaeon frowned. "Excuse me, Admiral?"

"What I mean is that they're being highly secretive about their preparations," Thrawn said thoughtfully. "Quietly detaching intelligence and support ships from other assignments; moving and re-forming sector fleets to free capital ships for service—that sort of thing. Never obviously. Always making Imperial Intelligence work hard to put the pieces together."

He looked up at Pellaeon, his glowing red eyes glittering in the dim light. "Almost as if Tangrene was indeed their true target."

Pellaeon stared at him. "Are you saying it isn't?"

"That's correct, Captain," Thrawn said, gazing out at the artwork.

Pellaeon looked at the Tangrene holo. Intelligence had put a 94 percent probability on this. "But if they're not going to hit Tangrene . . . then where?"

"The last place we would normally expect them," Thrawn said, reaching over to touch a switch on his command board. Tangrene system vanished, to be replaced by—

Pellaeon felt his jaw drop. "*Bilbringi*?" He wrenched his eyes back to his commander. "Sir, that's . . ."

"Insane?" Thrawn cocked a blue-black eyebrow. "Of course it is. The insanity of men and aliens who've learned the hard way that they can't match me face-to-face. And so they attempt to use my own tactical skill and insight against me. They pretend to walk into my trap, gambling that I'll notice the subtlety of their movements and interpret that as genuine intent. And while I then congratulate myself on my perception"—he gestured at the Bilbringi holo—"they prepare their actual attack."

Pellaeon looked at Bel Iblis's old artwork. "We might want to wait for confirmation before we shift any forces from Tangrene, Admiral," he suggested cautiously. "We could intensify

Intelligence activity in the Bilbringi region. Or perhaps Delta Source could confirm it."

"Unfortunately, Delta Source has been silenced," Thrawn said. "But we have no need of confirmation. This *is* the Rebels' plan, and we will not risk tipping our hand with anything so obvious as a heightened Intelligence presence. They believe they've deceived me. Our overriding task now is to make certain they continue to believe that."

He smiled grimly. "After all, Captain, it makes no difference whether we crush them at Tangrene or at Bilbringi. No difference whatsoever."

CHAPTER 21

THE LOPSIDED-HELIX SHAPE of the seed pod hovered a meter and a half in front of Mara, practically daring her to strike it down. She eyed it darkly, Skywalker's lightsaber held ready in an unorthodox but versatile two-handed grip. She'd already missed the pod twice; she didn't intend to do so a third time.

"Don't rush it," Skywalker cautioned her. "Concentrate, and let the Force flow into you. Try to anticipate the pod's motion."

Easy for him to say, she thought sourly; after all, he was the one controlling it. The pod twitched a millimeter closer, daring her again. . . .

And suddenly, she decided she was tired of this game. Reaching out with the Force, she got a grip of her own on the pod. Briefly immobilized, it managed a single tremor before she jabbed the lightsaber straight out, stabbing it neatly dead center. "There," she said, closing down the weapon. "I did it."

She'd expected Skywalker to be angry. To her mild surprise, and not so mild annoyance, he wasn't in the least. "Good," he said encouragingly. "Very good. It's difficult to split your attention between two separate mental and physical activities that way. And you did it well."

"Thanks," she muttered, tossing the lightsaber away from her toward the bushes. It curved smoothly around in midair as

Skywalker pulled it back to land in his outstretched hand. "So is that it?" she added.

Skywalker looked over his shoulder. Solo and Calrissian were hunched over the protocol droid, which had stopped complaining about Wayland's terrain, vegetation, and animal life and was instead complaining about what crunching through that stone crust had done to its foot. Skywalker's astromech droid was hovering nearby with its sensor antenna extended, running through its usual repertoire of encouraging noises. A couple of steps away, the Wookiee was rummaging through one of their packs, probably for some tool or other.

"I think we've got time for a few more exercises," Skywalker decided, turning back to face her. "That technique of yours is very interesting—Obi-Wan never taught me anything about using the tip of the lightsaber blade."

"The Emperor's philosophy was to use everything you had available," Mara said.

"Somehow, that doesn't surprise me," Skywalker said dryly. He held out the lightsaber. "Let's try something else. Go ahead and take the lightsaber."

Reaching out with the Force, Mara snatched it away from his loose grip, wondering idly what he would do if she tried sometime to ignite the weapon first. She wasn't sure she could handle anything as small as a switch, but it'd be worth trying just to see him scramble away from the blade.

And if, in the process, she happened to accidentally kill him . . .

YOU WILL KILL LUKE SKYWALKER.

She squeezed the lightsaber hard. *Not yet,* she told the voice firmly. *I still need him.* "All right," she growled. "What now?"

He didn't get a chance to answer. Behind him, the astromech droid suddenly started squealing excitedly.

"What?" Solo demanded, his blaster already out of its holster.

"He says he's just noticed something worth investigating

there to the side," the protocol droid translated, gesturing to his left. "A group of vines, I believe he's saying. Though I could be mistaken—with all the acid damage—"

"Come on, Chewie, let's check it out," Solo cut him off, getting to his feet and starting up the shallow slope of the creek bed.

Skywalker caught Mara's eye. "Come on," he said, and started off after them.

There wasn't very far to go. Just inside the first row of trees, hidden from view by a bush, was another set of vines like the ones they'd had to occasionally cut through the last couple of days.

Except that this group had already been cut. Cut, and then bunched up out of the way like a pile of thick, tangled rope.

"I think that ends any discussion as to whether someone out there is helping us along," Calrissian said, studying one of the cut ends.

"I think you're right," Solo said. "No predator would have bunched them up like this."

The Wookiee rumbled something under his breath and pulled on the bush in front of the vines. To Mara's surprise, it came away from the ground without any effort at all. "And wouldn't have bothered with camouflage, either," Calrissian said as the Wookiee turned it over. "Knife cut, looks like. Just like the vines."

"And like the clawbird from yesterday," Solo agreed grimly. "Luke? We been getting company?"

"I've sensed some of the natives," Skywalker said. "But they never seem to come very close before they leave again." He looked back downslope at the protocol droid, waiting anxiously for them in the creek bed. "You suppose it has anything to do with the droids?"

Solo snorted. "You mean like on Endor, when those fuzzball Ewoks thought Threepio was a god?"

"Something like that," Skywalker nodded. "They could be getting close enough to hear either Threepio or Artoo."

"Maybe." Solo looked around. "When do they come around?"

"Mostly around sundown," Skywalker said, "So far, anyway."

"Well, next time they do, let me know," Solo said, jamming his blaster back into its holster and starting back down the slope to the creek bed. "It's about time we all had a little chat together. Come on, let's get moving."

THE DARKNESS WAS growing thicker, and the camp nearly put together for the night, when the wisps of sensation came. "Han?" Luke called softly. "They're here."

Han nodded, tapping Lando on the back as he drew his blaster. "How many?"

Luke focused his mind, working at separating the distinct parts out of the overall sensation. "Looks like five or six of them, coming in from that direction." He pointed to the side.

"Is that just in the first group?" Mara asked.

First group? Luke frowned, letting his focus open up again. She was right: there was a second group coming up behind the first. "That's just the first group," he confirmed. "Second group . . . I get five or six there, too. I'm not sure, but they might be a different species from the first."

Han looked at Lando. "What do you think?"

"I don't like it," Lando said, fingering his blaster uneasily. "Mara, how well do these species usually get along?"

"Not all that well," she said. "There was some trade and other stuff going on when I was here; but there were also stories about long, three-way wars between them and the human colonists."

Chewbacca growled a suggestion: that the aliens might be joining forces against them. "That's a fun thought," Han said. "How about it, Luke?"

Luke strained, but it was no use. "Sorry," he said. "There's plenty of emotion there, but I don't have any basis for figuring out what kind."

"They've stopped," Mara said, her face tight with concentration. "Both groups."

Han grimaced. "I guess this is it. Lando, Mara—you stay here and guard the camp. Luke, Chewie, let's go check 'em out."

They headed up the rocky slope and into the forest, moving as quietly as possible among the bushes and dead leaves underfoot. "They know we're coming yet?" Han muttered over his shoulder.

Luke stretched out with the Force. "I can't tell," he said. "But they don't seem to be coming any closer."

Chewbacca rumbled something Luke didn't catch. "Could be," Han said. "It'd be pretty stupid to hold a council of war this close to their target, though."

And then, ahead and to their left, Luke caught a shadowy movement beside a thick tree trunk. "Watch it!" he warned, his lightsaber igniting with a *snap-hiss*. In the green-white light from the blade a small figure in a tight-fitting hooded garment could be seen as it ducked back behind the trunk, barely getting out of the way as Han's quick shot blew a sizable pit in one side of the trunk. Chewbacca's bowcaster bolt was a split second behind Han's, gouging out a section of the trunk on the other side. Through the erupting cloud of smoke and splinters the figure could be seen briefly as it darted from the rapidly decreasing cover of its chosen tree toward another, thicker trunk. Even as Han swung his blaster to track it, a strange warbling split the air, sounding like a dozen alien birds—

And with a roar that was part recognition, part understanding, and part relief, Chewbacca swung the end of his bowcaster into Han's blaster, sending the shot wide of its intended target. "Chewie—!" Han barked.

"No—he's right," Luke cut him off. Suddenly, it had all come together for him, too. "You—stop."

The order was unnecessary. The shadowy figure had already come to a halt, standing unprotected in the open, its hooded face shaded from the faint light of Luke's lightsaber.

Luke took a step toward it. "I'm Luke Skywalker," he said formally. "Brother of Leia Organa Solo, son of the Lord Darth Vader. Who are you?"

"I am Ekhrikhor clan Bakh'tor," the gravelly Noghri voice replied. "I greet you, son of Vader."

THE CLEARING EKHRIKHOR led them to was close, only twenty meters or so further along the vector Luke had started them on in the first place. The aliens were there, all right: two different types, five of each, standing on the far side of a thick fallen tree trunk. On the near side stood two more Noghri in those camouflaged outfits of theirs with the hoods thrown back. Propped up on the log between the two sides was some sort of compact worklight, giving off just enough of a glow for Han to pick out the details of the nearest aliens.

It wasn't very encouraging. The group on the right were a head taller than the Noghri facing them and maybe a head shorter than Han. Covered with lumpy plates, they looked more like walking rock piles than anything else. The group on the left were nearly as tall as Chewbacca, with four arms each and a shiny, bluish-crystal skin that reminded Han of the brownish thing they'd had to shoot off Threepio their first day here. "Friendly-looking bunch," he muttered to Luke as their group moved toward the last line of trees between them and the clearing.

"They are the Myneyrshi and Psadans," Ekhrikhor said. "They have been seeking to confront you."

"And you've been driving them off?" Luke asked.

"They sought to confront," the Noghri repeated. "We could not permit that."

They stopped just inside the clearing. A rustle ran through the aliens, one that didn't sound all that friendly. "I get the feeling we aren't all that welcome," Han said. "Luke?"

Beside him, he felt Luke shake his head. "I still can't read anything solid," he said. "What's this all about, Ekhrikhor?"

"They have indicated they wish a conversation with us," the Noghri said. "Perhaps to decide whether they will seek to give us battle."

Han gave the aliens a quick once-over. They all seemed to be wearing knives, and there were a couple of bows in evidence, but he didn't see anything more advanced. "They better hope they brought an army with them," he said.

"We don't want to fight at all if we can avoid it," Luke reproved him mildly. "How are you going to communicate with them?"

"One of them learned a little of the Empire's Basic when the storehouse was being built beneath the mountain," Ekhrikhor said, pointing to the Myneyrsh standing closest to the work light. "He will attempt to translate."

"We might be able to do a little better." Luke raised his eyebrows at Han. "What do you think?"

"It's worth a try," Han agreed, pulling out his comlink. It was about time Threepio earned his keep, anyway. "Lando?"

"Right here," Lando's voice came instantly. "You find the aliens?"

"Yeah, we found them," Han said. "Plus a surprise or two. Have Mara bring Threepio here—if she heads out the way we went she'll run right into us."

"Got it," Lando said. "What about me?"

"I don't think this bunch will give us any trouble," Han said, giving the aliens another once-over. "You and Artoo might as well stay there and keep an eye on the camp. Oh, and if you see some short guys with camouflage suits and lots of teeth, don't shoot. They're on our side."

"I'm glad," Lando said dryly. "I think. Anything else?"

Han looked at the groups of shadowy aliens, all of them staring straight back at him. "Yeah—cross your fingers. We might be about to pick up some allies. Or else a whole lot of trouble down the road."

"Right. Mara and Threepio are on their way. Good luck."

"Thanks." Shutting off the comlink, Han returned it to his belt. "They're coming," he told Luke.

"There is no need for them to guard your camp," Ekhrikhor said. "The Noghri will protect it."

"That's okay," Han said. "It's getting crowded enough here as it is." He eyed Ekhrikhor. "So I was right. We *were* followed in."

"Yes," Ekhrikhor said, bowing his head. "And for that deception I beg your forgiveness, consort of the Lady Vader. I and others did not feel it entirely honorable; but Cakhmaim clan Eikh'mir wished our presence to be kept hidden from you."

"Why?"

Ekhrikhor bowed again. "Cakhmaim clan Eikh'mir felt hostility from you in the Lady Vader's suite," he said. "He believed you would not willingly accept a guard of Noghri to accompany you."

Han looked at Luke, caught the kid's halfway try at hiding a grin. "Well, next time you see Cakhmaim, you tell him that I stopped passing up free help years ago," he told Ekhrikhor. "But as long as we're discussing hostility, you can knock off that 'consort of the Lady Vader' stuff. Call me Han, or Solo. Or Captain. Or practically anything else."

"Han clan Solo, maybe," Luke murmured.

Ekhrikhor brightened. "That is good," he said. "We beg your forgiveness, Han clan Solo."

Han looked at Luke. "I think you've been adopted," Luke said, fighting that grin again.

"Yeah," Han said. "Thanks. A lot."

"A little rapport never hurts," Luke pointed out. "Remember Endor."

"I'm not likely to forget," Han growled, feeling his lip twist. Sure, the little fuzzballs there had done their bit in that final battle against the second Death Star. That didn't change the fact that being made part of an Ewok tribe was one of the more ridiculous things he'd ever had to go through.

Still, the Ewoks had overwhelmed the Imperial troops by sheer weight of numbers. The Noghri, on the other hand— "How many of you are there here?" he asked Ekhrikhor.

"There are eight," the other replied. "Two each have traveled before, after, and on either side of you during your journey."

Han nodded, feeling a grudging trickle of unwilling respect for these things. Eight of them, silently killing or driving away predators and natives. Day and night both. *And* still finding time on top of it to clear their path of nuisances like clawbirds and vine snakes.

He looked down at Ekhrikhor. No, the adoption process didn't feel quite so ridiculous this time around.

From somewhere behind them came a familiar shuffling sound. Han turned, and a moment later the equally familiar golden figure of Threepio traipsed into view. Beside him and a half-step behind was Mara, blaster in hand. "Master Luke," Threepio called, his voice its usual mixture of relieved and anxious and just plain prissy.

"Over here, Threepio," Luke called back. "Think you can do some translation for us?"

"I'll do my best," the droid said. "As you know, I am fluent in over six million forms of communica—"

"I see you found the natives," Mara cut him off, giving the group by the log a quick survey as she and Threepio stepped into the clearing. Her eyes fell on Ekhrikhor—"And a little surprise, too," she added, her blaster quietly shifting its aim toward the Noghri.

"It's all right—he's a friend," Luke assured her, reaching toward her blaster.

"I don't think so," Mara said, twitching the weapon to the side out of his reach. "They're Noghri. They work for Thrawn."

"We serve him no longer," Ekhrikhor told her.

"That's true, Mara, they don't," Luke said.

"Maybe," Mara said. She still wasn't happy about it, but at least her blaster wasn't pointed exactly at Ekhrikhor anymore.

Across the clearing, the Myneyrsh nearest the log pulled

what seemed to be a bleached-white stuffed clawbird from a shoulder pouch. Speaking inaudibly under his breath, he laid it in front of him beside the worklight. "What's that?" Han asked. "Lunch?"

"It is called the *satna-chakka*," Ekhrikhor said. "It is a bond of peace while this meeting lasts. They are ready to begin. You—Threepio-droid—come with me."

"Of course," Threepio said, not sounding exactly thrilled by the whole arrangement. "Master Luke . . . ?"

"I'll come with you," Luke soothed. "Han, Chewie—you stay here."

"No argument from me," Han said.

With a clearly reluctant Threepio in tow, Luke and the Noghri headed toward the log. The head Myneyrsh raised its upper two hands over his head, palm inwards. "*Bidaesi charaa*," he said, his voice surprisingly melodious. "*Lyaaunu baaraemaa dukhnu phaeri.*"

"He announces the arrival of the strangers," Threepio said precisely. "Presumably, that refers to us. He fears, however, that we will bring danger and trouble again to his people."

Beside Han, Chewbacca rumbled a sarcastic comment. "No, they're not much for small talk," Han agreed. "Not much for diplomacy, either."

"We bring hope to your people," the chief Noghri countered. "If you let us pass, we will free you from the domination of the Empire."

Threepio translated, the melodious Myneyrshi words still coming out prissy, in Han's opinion. One of the lumpy Psadans made a chopping gesture and said something that sounded like a faint and distant scream with consonants scattered around in it. "He says that the Psadan people have long memories," Threepio translated. "Apparently, deliverers have come before but nothing has ever changed."

"Welcome to the real world," Han muttered.

Luke threw a look at him over his shoulder. "Ask him to explain, Threepio," he told the droid.

Threepio complied, quiet-screaming back at the Psadan and then throwing in a Myneyrshi translation, too, just to show he could do it. The Psadan's answer went on for several minutes, and Han's ears were starting to hurt by the time he was done.

"Well," Threepio said, tilting his head and settling into the professor mode Han had always hated. "There are many details—but I will pass those by for now," he added hastily, probably at a look from one of the Noghri. "The humans who came as colonists were the first invaders. They drove the native peoples from some of their lands, and were stopped only when their lightning bows and metal birds—those are their terms, of course—began to fail. Much later came the Empire, who as we know built into the forbidden mountain. They enslaved many of the native peoples to help on the project and drove others from their lands. After the builders left came someone who called himself the Guardian, and he, too, sought control over the native peoples. Finally, the one who called himself the Jedi Master came, and in a battle that lit up the sky he defeated the Guardian. For a time the native peoples thought they might be freed, but the Jedi Master brought humans and native peoples to himself and forced them to live together beneath the shadow of the forbidden mountain. Finally, the Empire has returned." Threepio tilted his head back again. "As you can see, Master Luke, we are merely the last in a long line of invaders."

"Except that we're not invaders," Luke said. "We're here to free them from the rule of the Empire."

"I understand that, Master Luke—"

"I know you do," Luke interrupted the droid. "Tell *them* that."

"Oh. Yes. Of course."

He started into his translation. "You ask me, I don't think they've had it all that bad," Han muttered to Chewbacca. "The Empire took whole planets away from some people."

"Primitives always have this reaction to visitors," Mara said. "They usually have long memories, too."

"Yeah. Maybe. You suppose that Jedi Master they were talking about was your pal C'baoth?"

"Who else?" Mara said grimly. "This must be where Thrawn found him."

Han felt his stomach tighten. "You think he's here now?"

"I don't sense anything," Mara said slowly. "Doesn't mean he can't come back."

The head Myneyrsh was talking again. Han let his gaze drift around the clearing. Were there other Myneyrshi and Psadans out there keeping an eye on the big debate? Luke hadn't said anything about backups, but they'd have to be crazy not to have them somewhere nearby.

Unless Ekhrikhor's pals had already taken care of them. If this didn't work, it could turn out to be handy having the Noghri around.

The Myneyrsh finished its speech. "I'm sorry, Master Luke," Threepio apologized; "They say they have no reason to assume we are any different than all those they have already spoken of."

"I understand their fears," Luke nodded. "Ask them how we can prove our good intentions."

Threepio started to translate; and as he did so, a hard Wookiee elbow jabbed into Han's shoulder. "What?" Han asked.

Chewbacca nodded toward his left, his bowcaster already up and tracking. Han followed the movement with his eyes— "Uh-oh."

"What is it?" Mara demanded.

Han opened his mouth; then, suddenly, there wasn't time to tell her. The wiry predator Chewbacca had spotted slinking through the tree branches had stopped slinking and was coiling itself to spring at the discussion group. "Look out!" he snapped instead, bringing his blaster up.

Chewbacca was faster. With a Wookiee hunter's roar, he fired, the bowcaster bolt slicing the predator nearly in half. It fell off its perch, crunching into the dead leaves, and lay still.

And over by the log, the whole group of Myneyrshi snarled.

"Watch it, Chewie," Han warned, shifting his aim toward the aliens.

"That might have been a mistake," Mara said tensely. "You're not supposed to fire weapons at a truce conference."

"You're not supposed to let the conference get eaten, either," Han retorted. Beside the Myneyrshi, the five Psadans had started to shake, and he hoped Ekhrikhor's pals had the rest of the area covered. "Threepio—tell them."

"Certainly, Captain Solo," Threepio said, sounding about as nervous as Han felt. "*Mulansaar*—"

The head Myneyrsh cut him off with a chopping motion of its two left arms. "You!" he warbled in passable Basic, jabbing all four hands at Han. "He have lightning bow?"

Han frowned at him. Of course Chewbacca had a weapon—so did all the rest of them. He glanced up at the Wookiee . . . and suddenly he understood. "Yes, he has," he told the Myneyrsh, lowering his blaster. "He's our friend. We don't keep slaves like the Empire did."

Threepio started into his translation, but the Myneyrsh was already jabbering away to his friends. "Nice work," Mara murmured. "I hadn't thought of that. But you're right—the last Wookiees they saw here would have been Imperial slaves."

Han nodded. "Let's hope it makes a difference."

The discussion ran on for a few more minutes, mostly between the Myneyrshi and the Psadans. Threepio tried for a while to keep up a running translation, but it quickly degenerated into not much more than a reporting of the highlights. The Myneyrshi, apparently, were starting to think this was their chance to get rid of the oppression of first the Empire and then the Jedi Master himself. The Psadans didn't like the Imperials any more than the Myneyrshi, but the thought of facing up to C'baoth was making them skittish.

"We aren't asking you to fight alongside us," Luke told them when he was finally able to get their attention back. "Our battle is our own, and we will handle it ourselves. All we ask is

TIMOTHY ZAHN

your permission to travel through your territory to the forbidden mountain and your assurance that you won't betray us to the Empire."

Threepio did his double translation, and Han braced himself for another argument. But there wasn't one. The head Myneyrsh raised his upper hands again, and with his lower hands picked up the bleached clawbird and offered it to Luke. "I believe he is offering you safe conduct, Master Luke," Threepio said helpfully. "Though I could be wrong—their dialect has survived relatively intact, but gestures and movements are often—"

"Tell him thank you," Luke said, nodding as he accepted the clawbird. "Tell him we accept their hospitality. And that they won't be sorry they helped us."

"GENERAL COVELL?" THE MILITARILY precise voice came over the intercom from the shuttle cockpit. "We should be on the surface in just a few more minutes."

"Acknowledged," Covell said. He keyed the intercom off and turned to the shuttle's only other passenger. "We're almost there," he said.

"Yes, I heard," C'baoth said, his amusement echoing through his voice. And through Covell's mind. "Tell me, General Covell, are we at the end of our voyage or at the beginning?"

"The beginning, of course," Covell told him. "The voyage we have set upon will have no end."

"And what of Grand Admiral Thrawn?"

Covell felt a frown crease his forehead. He hadn't heard this question before, at least not said this particular way. But even as he hesitated, the answer came soothingly into his thoughts. As all answers did now. "It's the beginning of Grand Admiral Thrawn's ending," he said.

C'baoth laughed softly, the amusement rippling pleasantly through Covell's mind. Covell thought about asking what was funny, but it was easier and far more agreeable to just sit back and enjoy the laughter. And anyway, he knew perfectly well what it was that was funny.

"You do, don't you," C'baoth agreed, shaking his head. "Ah, General, General. It's so very ironic, isn't it? From the very beginning—from that very first meeting in my city—Grand Admiral Thrawn has had the answer within his grasp. And yet even now he is as far from understanding as he was then."

"Is it about power, Master C'baoth?" Covell asked. This was a familiar topic, and even without the prompting in his mind he would have remembered his lines.

"It is indeed, General Covell," C'baoth said gravely. "I told him at the very beginning that true power didn't lie in the conquering of distant worlds. Or in battles and war and the crushing of faceless rebellions."

He smiled, his eyes glittering brightly in Covell's mind. "No, General Covell," he said softly. "This—*this*—is true power. Holding another's life in the palm of your hand. Having the power to choose his path, and his thoughts, and his feelings. To rule his life, and decree his death." Slowly, theatrically, C'baoth held out his hand, palm upward. "To command his soul."

"Something not even the Emperor ever understood," Covell reminded him.

Another ripple of pleasure rolled through Covell's mind. It was so satisfying to see the Master enjoying his game. "Not even the Emperor," C'baoth agreed, his eyes and thoughts drifting far away. "He, like the Grand Admiral, saw power only as how far outside himself he could reach. And it destroyed him, as I could have told him it would. For if he'd truly commanded Vader . . ." He shook his head. "In many ways he was a fool. But perhaps it was not his destiny to be otherwise. Perhaps it was the will of the universe that I, and I alone, would understand. For only I have both the strength and the will to grasp hold of this power. The first . . . but not the last."

346 TIMOTHY ZAHN

Covell nodded, swallowing against a dry throat. It was not pleasant when C'baoth left him like this, even for a little bit. Especially not when there was this strange loneliness along with it . . .

But of course, the Master knew that. "Do you ache with my loneliness, General Covell?" he said, warming Covell's mind with another smile. "Yes, of course you do. But be patient. The time is coming when we shall be many. And when that time is here, we will never be lonely again. Observe."

He felt the distant sense as he did all others now: filtered and focused and structured through the Master's perfect mind. "You see, I was right," C'baoth said, reaching out to examine that sense. "They are here. Skywalker and Jade both." He smiled at Covell. "They will be the first, General Covell—the first of our many. For they will come to me, and when I have shown to them the true power, they will understand and will join us." His eyes drifted away again. "Jade will be first, I think," he added thoughtfully. "Skywalker has resisted once, and will resist again; but the key to his soul is even now waiting for me in the mountain below. But Jade is another matter. I have seen her in my meditations—have seen her coming to me and kneeling at my feet. She will be mine, and Skywalker will follow. One way or another."

He smiled, again. Covell smiled back, pleased at the Master's own pleasure and by the thought of others who would be there to warm his mind.

And then, without any warning, it all went dark. Not loneliness, not the way it had been. But a sort of emptiness . . .

By and by, he felt his head being roughly lifted by his chin. C'baoth was there, in a way, staring into his eyes. "General Covell!" the Master's voice thundered. Thundered strangely, too. Covell could hear it, but it wasn't really there. Not like it should have been. "Can you hear me?"

"I can hear you," Covell said. His own voice sounded strange, too. He looked past C'baoth's face, to the interesting pattern of lines on the shuttle bulkhead.

He felt himself being shaken. "Look at me!" C'baoth demanded.

Covell did so. That was odd, too, because he could see the Master but he wasn't really there. "Are you still there?"

The Master's face changed. Something—was it called a smile?—came across it. "Yes, General, I am here," the distant voice said. "I no longer touch your mind, but I am still your Master. You will continue to obey me."

Obey. An odd concept, Covell thought. Not like simply doing what was natural. "Obey?"

"You will do as I tell you," C'baoth said. "I will give you things to say, and you will repeat every word."

"All right," Covell said. "If I do that, will you come back?"

"I will," the Master promised. "Despite Grand Admiral Thrawn's treachery. With your obedience—with you doing what I tell you—we will together destroy his betrayal of us. And then we will never be apart again."

"The emptiness will be gone?"

"Yes. But only if you do what I say."

The other men came a little later. The Master stayed at his side the whole time, and he said all the words the Master told him to say. They all went somewhere, and then the men left, and the Master left, too.

He stared off across the place they'd left him in, watching the patterns of lines and listening to the emptiness all around him. Eventually, he fell asleep.

A STRANGE SORT of birdcall warbled off in the distance, and instantly the background crackle of insects and scuttling animals ceased. But apparently there was no immediate danger, and a minute later the nighttime sounds and activity resumed. Shifting her position against her chosen tree trunk, Mara eased her aching back muscles and wished this whole thing was over.

"There is no need for you to stay awake," a soft Noghri voice said at her shoulder. "We will guard."

"Thanks," Mara said shortly. "If it's all the same to you, I'll do my job."

The Noghri was silent a moment. "You still do not trust us, do you?"

Actually, she hadn't thought all that much about it one way or the other. "Skywalker trusts you," she said. "Isn't that good enough?"

"It is not approval we seek," the Noghri told her. "Only the chance to repay our debt."

She shrugged. They'd protected the camp, they'd tackled the always tricky job of first contact with the Myneyrshi and Psadans, and now here they were protecting the camp again. "If it's a debt to the New Republic, I'd say you're doing a pretty good job of it," she conceded. "You finally figured out Thrawn and the Empire had been stringing you along?"

There was a quiet click, like needle teeth coming together. "You knew about that?"

"I heard rumors," Mara said, recognizing how potentially dangerous this ground was but not really caring. "More like jokes, really. I never knew how much of it was true."

"Most likely all of it," the Noghri said calmly. "Yes. I can see how our lives and deaths could be amusing to our enslavers. We will convince them otherwise."

No white-hot rage, no fanatical hatred. Just a simple, icy determination. About as dangerous as you could get. "How are you going to do that?" she asked.

"When the time is right the Noghri will turn upon their enslavers. Some on Imperial worlds, some on transporting ships. And five groups will come here."

Mara frowned. "You knew about Wayland?"

"Not until you led us here," the other said. "But we know now. We have sent the location to those waiting at Coruscant. By now they will have passed the word on to others."

Mara snorted quietly. "You have a lot of confidence in us, don't you?"

"Our missions complement each other," the Noghri assured her, his gravelly mewing somehow sounding grimmer. "You have set for yourselves the task of destroying the cloning facility. With the help of the son of Vader we do not doubt you will succeed. For ourselves, the Noghri have chosen the task of eliminating every last reminder of the Emperor's presence on Wayland."

Probably the last relics of the Emperor's presence anywhere. Mara turned that idea over in her mind, wondering why it didn't seem to grieve or anger her. Probably she was just tired. "Sounds like a big project," she said instead. "Who is this son of Vader you're expecting to show up and help us?"

There was a brief silence. "The son of Vader is already with you," the Noghri said, sounding puzzled. "You serve him, as do we."

Mara stared at him through the darkness . . . and suddenly her heart seemed to freeze in her chest. "You mean . . . *Skywalker*?"

"You did not know?"

Mara turned away from him, staring down at the sleeping form no more than a meter away from her feet, a horrible numbness flooding through her. Suddenly, finally, after all these years, the last elusive piece had fallen into place. The Emperor didn't want her to kill Skywalker for his own sake. It was, instead, one final act of vengeance against his father.

YOU WILL KILL LUKE SKYWALKER.

And in the space of a few heartbeats everything Mara had believed about herself—her hatred, her mission, her entire life—had turned from certainty to confusion.

YOU WILL KILL LUKE SKYWALKER. YOU WILL KILL LUKE SKYWALKER. YOU WILL KILL LUKE SKYWALKER.

"No," she muttered at the voice through clenched teeth. "Not like that. *My* decision. *My* reasons."

But the voice continued unabated. Perhaps it was her resistance and defiance fueling it now, or perhaps the deeper power in the Force that Skywalker had given her over the past few days had made her more receptive to it.

*YOU WILL KILL LUKE SKYWALKER. YOU WILL KILL
LUKE SKYWALKER.*

But you are another matter, Mara Jade.

Mara jerked, the sudden motion banging the back of her
head against the tree trunk behind her. Another voice; but this
one wasn't coming from inside her. It was coming from—

I have seen you in my meditations, the voice continued
placidly. *Have seen you coming to me and kneeling at my feet.
You will be mine, and Skywalker will follow. One way or another.*

Mara shook her head violently, trying to shake away the
words and thoughts. The second voice seemed to laugh; then,
suddenly, the words and laughter disappeared beneath a distant but steady pressure against her mind. Setting her teeth,
she pushed back against it. Dimly, she heard the voice laugh
again at her efforts—

And then, with a suddenness that made her catch her
breath, the pressure was gone.

"Are you all right?" Skywalker's voice asked quietly.

Mara looked down. Skywalker had risen up on one elbow,
his silhouetted face turned toward her. "Did you hear it, too?"
she asked.

"I didn't hear any words. But I felt the pressure."

Mara looked up toward the leaf canopy overhead. "It's
C'baoth," she said. "He's here."

"Yes," Skywalker said; and she could hear the apprehension
in his voice. Small wonder—he'd faced C'baoth once, back on
Jomark, and nearly lost out to him.

"So what now?" Mara asked, rubbing at the sweat around
her mouth with a shaking hand. "We abort the mission?"

The silhouette shrugged. "How? We're only a couple of
days from the mountain. It'd take us a lot longer than that to
get back to the *Falcon*."

"Except that the Imperials know we're here now."

"Maybe," Skywalker said slowly. "But maybe not. Did the
contact cut off suddenly for you, too?"

She frowned; and suddenly it hit her. "You think they moved some ysalamiri around him?"

"Or else strapped him into one of those frames you were using on Jomark," Skywalker said. "Either way, it would imply he was a prisoner."

Mara thought about that. If so, he might not be interested in telling his captors about the invaders moving toward the mountain.

She looked sharply at him as another thought suddenly occurred to her. "Did you know C'baoth was going to come?" she demanded. "Is that why you wanted me to practice my old Jedi training?"

"I didn't know he'd be here," Skywalker said. "But I knew we would eventually have to face him again. He said that himself on Jomark."

Mara shivered. *Kneeling at my feet* . . . "I don't want to face him, Skywalker."

"Neither do I," he said softly. "But I think we have to."

He sighed; and then, quietly, he peeled off the top of his bedroll and got to his feet. "Why don't you go get some sleep," he said, stepping over to her side. "I'm awake now anyway; and you took the brunt of that attack."

"All right," Mara said, too tired to argue. "If you need any help, call me."

"I will."

She picked her way across Calrissian and the Wookiee to her bedroll and crawled into it. Her last memory, as she dropped off to sleep, was of the voice in the back of her mind.

YOU WILL KILL LUKE SKYWALKER . . .

CHAPTER 22

THE REPORT CAME in from Mount Tantiss during ship's night and was waiting for him when Pellaeon arrived on the bridge in the morning. The *Draklor* had reached Wayland more or less on schedule six hours previously, had offloaded its passengers, and had left the system bound for Valrar as per orders. General Covell had refused to take command until local morning—

Pellaeon frowned. *Refused to take command?* That didn't sound like Covell.

"Captain Pellaeon?" the comm officer called up to him. "Sir, were getting a holo transmission from Colonel Selid on Wayland. It's marked urgent."

"Put it through to the aft bridge hologram pod," Pellaeon instructed, getting up from his command chair and heading aft. "Signal the Grand Admiral to—never mind," he interrupted himself as, through the archway, he spotted Thrawn and Rukh coming up the steps into the aft bridge.

Thrawn saw him, too. "What's wrong, Captain?"

"Urgent message from Wayland, sir," Pellaeon said, gesturing toward the hologram pod. The image of an Imperial officer was already waiting, and even in a quarter-size holo, Pellaeon could see the younger man's nervousness.

"Probably C'baoth," Thrawn predicted darkly. They

reached position in front of the hologram pod, and Thrawn nodded to the image. "Colonel Selid, this is Grand Admiral Thrawn. Report."

"Sir," Selid said, his parade-ground posture stiffening even more. "I regret to inform you, Admiral, of the sudden death of General Covell."

Pellaeon felt his mouth fall open a couple of centimeters. "How?" he asked.

"We don't know yet, sir," Selid said. "He apparently died in his sleep. The medics are still running tests, but so far all they can suggest is that large portions of the General's brain had simply shut down."

"Brain tissue does not 'simply' shut down, Colonel," Thrawn said. "There has to be a reason for it."

Selid seemed to wince. "Yes, sir. I'm sorry, sir; I didn't mean it that way."

"I know you didn't," Thrawn assured him. "What about the rest of the passengers?"

"The medics are checking them all now," Selid said. "No problems so far. Rather, they're checking all those still within the garrison. General Covell's troops—the company that arrived on the *Draklor* with him—had already been dispersed outside the mountain when he died."

"What, the whole company?" Pellaeon asked. "What for?"

"I don't know, sir," Selid said. "General Covell gave the orders. After the big meeting, I mean, before he died."

"Perhaps we'd better have the story from the beginning, Colonel," Thrawn cut him off. "Tell me everything."

"Yes, sir." Selid visibly pulled himself together. "General Covell and the others were landed via shuttle approximately six hours ago. I tried to turn over command of the garrison to him, but he refused. He then insisted on having a private word with his troops in one of the officers' mess halls."

"Which troops?" Thrawn asked. "The whole garrison?"

"No, sir, just the ones who'd accompanied him on the *Draklor*. He said he had some special orders to give them."

Pellaeon looked at Thrawn. "I'd have thought he'd have had plenty of time aboard ship for special orders."

"Yes," Thrawn agreed. "One would think so."

"Maybe it was C'baoth's idea, sir," Selid suggested. "He was at the general's side from the minute they got off the shuttle. Muttering, sort of, the whole time."

"Was he, now," Thrawn said thoughtfully. His voice was calm, but there was something beneath it that sent a shiver up Pellaeon's back. "Where is Master C'baoth now?"

"Up in the Emperor's old royal chambers," Selid said. "General Covell insisted they be opened for him."

"Would he be above the ysalamiri influence up there?" Pellaeon murmured.

Thrawn shook his head. "I doubt it. According to my calculations, the entire mountain and some of the surrounding area should be within the Force-empty bubble. What happened then, Colonel?"

"The general spent about fifteen minutes talking to his troops," Selid said. "When he came out, he told me that he'd given them secret orders that had come directly from you, Admiral, and that I wasn't to interfere."

"And then they left the mountain?"

"After stripping one of the supply rooms of field gear and explosives, yes," Selid said. "Actually, they spent a couple more hours inside the garrison before leaving. Familiarizing themselves with the layout, the general said. After they left, C'baoth escorted the general to his quarters and then was himself escorted to the royal chambers by two of my stormtroopers. I put the rest of the garrison back onto standard nighttime routine, and that was it. Until this morning, when the orderly found the general."

"So C'baoth wasn't with Covell at the time of his death?" Thrawn asked.

"No, sir," Selid said. "Though the medics don't think the general lived very long after C'baoth left him."

"And he was with the general up until that time."

"Yes, sir."

Pellaeon threw Thrawn a sideways look. The Grand Admiral was staring at nothing, his glowing red eyes narrowed to slits. "Tell me, Colonel, what was your impression of General Covell?"

"Well . . ." Selid hesitated. "I'd have to say I was a bit disappointed, sir."

"How so?"

"He just wasn't what I was expecting, Admiral," Selid said, sounding distinctly uncomfortable. Pellaeon didn't blame him: criticizing one senior officer in front of another was a serious breach of military etiquette. Especially between different branches of the service. "He seemed . . . *distant* is the word I'd have to use, sir. He implied that my security was poor and that he would be making some important changes, but he wouldn't talk to me about them. In fact, he hardly spoke to me the whole time he was here. And it wasn't just me—he was short with the other officers who tried to talk to him, as well. That was his privilege, of course, and he may have just been tired. But it didn't seem to fit with what I'd heard of the general's reputation."

"No, it doesn't," Thrawn said. "Is the hologram pad in the Emperor's old throne room operational, Colonel?"

"Yes, sir. Though C'baoth may not be in the throne room itself."

"He will be," Thrawn said coldly. "Connect me with him."

"Yes, sir."

Selid's image vanished, replaced by the pause symbol. "You think C'baoth did something to Covell?" Pellaeon asked quietly.

"I see no other likely explanation," Thrawn said. "My guess is that our beloved Jedi Master was trying to take over Covell's mind, perhaps even replacing entire sections of it with his own. When they hit the ysalamir bubble and he lost that direct contact, there wasn't enough of Covell left to keep him alive for long."

"I see." Pellaeon turned his head away from the Grand Admiral, a darkening anger flowing through him. He'd warned Thrawn about what C'baoth might do. Had warned him over and over again. "What are you going to do about it?"

The pause symbol vanished before Thrawn could answer; but it wasn't the standard quarter-size figure that replaced it. Instead, a huge image of C'baoth's face suddenly glared out at them, jolting Pellaeon an involuntary step backwards.

Thrawn didn't even twitch. "Good morning, Master C'baoth," the Grand Admiral said, his voice mirror smooth. "I see you've discovered the Emperor's private hologram setting."

"Grand Admiral Thrawn," C'baoth said, his own voice cold and arrogant. "Is this how you reward my work on behalf of your ambitions? By an act of betrayal?"

"If there is betrayal, it's on your side, Master C'baoth," Thrawn said. "What did you do to General Covell?"

C'baoth ignored the question. "The Force is not so easily betrayed as you think," he said. "And never forget this, Grand Admiral Thrawn: With my destruction will come your own. I have foreseen it."

He stopped, glaring back and forth at the two of them. For a handful of heartbeats Thrawn remained silent. "Are you finished?" he asked at last.

C'baoth frowned, the play of uncertainty and nervousness easily visible in the magnified face. For all its intimidating majesty, the Emperor's personal hologram setting clearly had its own set of drawbacks. "For now," C'baoth said. "Have you some feeble defense to offer?"

"I have nothing to defend, Master C'baoth," Thrawn said. "It was you who insisted on going to Wayland. Now tell me what you did to General Covell."

"You will first restore the Force to me."

"The ysalamiri will stay where they are," Thrawn said. "Tell me what you did to General Covell."

For a moment the two men glared at each other. C'baoth's glare crumbled first, and for a moment it looked as if he was going to fold. But then the old man's jaw jutted out, and once again he was the arrogant Jedi Master. "General Covell was mine to do with as I pleased," he said. "As is everything in my Empire."

"Thank you," Thrawn said. "That's all I need to know. Colonel Selid?"

The huge face vanished and was replaced by Selid's quarter-size image. "Yes, Admiral?"

"Instructions, Colonel," Thrawn told him. "First of all, Master C'baoth is hereby placed under arrest. You may allow him free run of the royal chambers and Emperor's throne room but he is not to leave there. All control circuits from those floors will be disconnected, of course. Secondly, you're to initiate inquiries as to precisely where General Covell's troops were seen within the mountain before they left."

"Why don't we ask the troops themselves, sir?" Selid suggested. "They presumably have comlinks with them."

"Because I'm not certain we could trust their answers," Thrawn told him. "Which brings me to my third order. None of the troops which left the mountain under General Covell's orders are to be allowed back in."

Selid's jaw dropped visibly. "Sir?"

"You heard correctly," Thrawn told him. "Another transport will arrive for them in a few days, at which time they'll be rounded up and taken off the planet. But under no circumstances are they to be allowed back into the mountain."

"Yes, sir," Selid said, floundering. "But—sir, what do I tell them?"

"You may tell them the truth," Thrawn said quietly. "That their orders came not from General Covell, and certainly not from me, but from a traitor to the Empire. Until Intelligence can sort through the details, the entire company will be considered as under suspicion, as unwitting accomplices to treason."

The word seemed to hang before them in the air. "Understood, sir," Selid said at last.

"Good," Thrawn said. "You are of course reinstated as garrison commander. Any questions?"

Selid drew himself up. "No, sir."

"Good. Carry on, Colonel. *Chimaera* out."

The figure vanished from the hologram pod. "Do you think it's safe to leave C'baoth there, sir?" Pellaeon asked.

"There's nowhere in the Empire safer," Thrawn pointed out. "At least, not yet."

Pellaeon frowned "I don't understand."

"His use to the Empire is rapidly nearing an end, Captain," Thrawn said, turning and walking beneath the archway into the main section of the bridge. "However, he still has one last role to play in our long-term consolidation of power."

He paused at the aft edge of the command walkway. "C'baoth is insane, Captain—that we both agree on. But such insanity is in his mind. Not in his body."

Pellaeon stared at him. "Are you suggesting we *clone* him?"

"Why not?" Thrawn asked. "Not at Mount Tantiss itself, certainly, given the conditions there. Most likely not at the speed which that facility allows, either—that's all well and good for techs and TIE fighter pilots, but not a project of this delicacy. No, I envision bringing such a clone to childhood and then allowing it to grow to maturity at a normal pace for its last ten or fifteen years. Under suitable upbringing conditions, of course."

"I see," Pellaeon said, struggling to keep his voice steady. A young C'baoth—or maybe two or ten or twenty of them—running loose around the galaxy. This was an idea that was going to take some getting used to. "Where would you set up this other cloning facility?"

"Somewhere absolutely secure," Thrawn said. "Possibly on one of the worlds in the Unknown Regions where I once served the Emperor. You'll instruct Intelligence to begin searching for a suitable location after we've crushed the Rebels at Bilbringi."

Pellaeon felt his lip twitch. Right: the dangerously ethereal Bilbringi attack. What with this C'baoth thing, he'd almost forgotten the main business of the day. Or his reservations concerning it. "Yes, sir. Admiral, I'm forced to remind you that all the evidence still indicates Tangrene as the probable point of attack."

"I'm aware of the evidence, Captain," Thrawn said. "Nevertheless, they will be at Bilbringi."

He sent his gaze leisurely around his bridge, his glowing red eyes missing nothing. And the crewers knew it. At every station, from the crew pits to the lateral consoles, there were the subtle sounds and movements of men aware that their commander was watching and striving to show him their best. "And so will we," the Grand Admiral added to Pellaeon. "Set course for Bilbringi, Captain. And let us prepare to meet our guests."

WEDGE DRAINED THE LAST of his cup and set it back on the chipped and stained wood of the small table, glancing across the noisy Mumbri Storve cantina as he did so. The place was as crowded as it had been when he, Janson, and Hobbie had come in an hour earlier, but the texture of the crowd had changed quite a bit. Most of the younger people had left, couples and groups both, and had been replaced by an older and decidedly seedier-looking bunch. The fringe types were drifting in; which meant it was time for them to be drifting out.

His fellow Rogue Squadron pilots knew it, too. "Time to go?" Hobbie suggested, his voice just audible over the noise.

"Right," Wedge nodded, getting to his feet and fumbling in his pouch for a coin that would cover this last round. His *civilian* pouch; and he really hated the awkward things. But it would hardly do for them to go wandering around town in full New Republic uniforms, complete with the distinctive Rogue Squadron patches.

He found a proper-size coin and dropped it into the center of the table as the others stood up. "Where to now?" Janson asked, hunching his shoulders slightly to stretch out his back muscles.

"Back to the base, I think," Wedge told him.

"Good," Janson grunted. "Morning's going to come early enough as it is."

Wedge nodded as he turned and headed toward the exit. Morning could come anytime it wanted to, of course: well before then they were going to be off this planet and driving hard toward their assigned rendezvous point outside the Bilbringi shipyards.

They wove their way between the crowded tables; and as they did so, a tall, thin man shoved his chair back almost into Wedge's knees and got unsteadily to his feet. "Watch out," he slurred, half turning to throw his arm across Wedge's shoulders and much of his weight against Wedge's side.

"Easy, friend," Wedge grunted, struggling to regain his balance. Out of the corner of his eye he saw Janson step to the tall man's other side and put a supporting arm around him—

"Easy sounds good to me," the man murmured, the slurring abruptly gone as his arm tightened around Wedge's shoulders. "All four of us—nice and easy now, let's help the poor old drunk out of here."

Wedge stiffened. Tracked, blindsided, and caught . . . and in the flip of an X-wing they had suddenly gone from a simple night on the town to serious trouble. With him and Janson tangled up like this, only Hobbie was left with a clear gun hand. And their assailant surely hadn't forgotten to have some backup around.

The tall man must have felt Wedge's tension. "Hey—play it smooth," he admonished quietly. "Don't remember me, huh?"

Wedge frowned at the face practically leaning against his. It didn't look familiar; but on the other hand, at this range he probably wouldn't recognize his own mother. "Should I?" he murmured back.

The other did a little more staggering. "I'd have thought so," he said in an injured voice. "You go up against a Star Destroyer with someone, he ought to remember you. Especially out in the middle of nowhere."

Wedge frowned a little harder at the face, dimly aware that the whole group had started walking. In the middle of nowhere . . . ?

And suddenly, it hit him. The *Katana* fleet, and Talon Karrde's people coming out of nowhere to lend their assistance and firepower against the Imperials. And afterwards the brief, preoccupied introductions aboard the Star Cruiser . . . "Aves?"

"That wasn't so hard, was it?" the other said approvingly. "Told you you could do it if you tried. Come on, now—nice and easy and don't let's draw any more attention to ourselves than we need to."

There didn't seem to be any real option other than to comply; but even as Wedge continued toward the exit, he kept his eyes moving, looking for something they could use to get them out of this. Karrde and his people had supposedly agreed to funnel information back to the New Republic, but that was a far way from being allies together. And if the Empire had threatened them . . . or just bought them outright . . .

But no opportunity for escape presented itself before they got out the doors. "This way," Aves said, abandoning his drunk act and hurrying down the dimly lit and sparsely populated street.

Janson caught Wedge's eye and raised his eyebrows questioningly. Wedge shrugged slightly in return and set off after Aves. It could still be some sort of trap, but at this point the vague fears were being rapidly overtaken by simple curiosity. Something was going on, and he wanted to find out what.

He didn't have long to wonder about it. Two buildings down from the Mumbri Storve, Aves turned and disappeared into a darkened entryway. Wedge followed, half expecting to run into a half-dozen blaster muzzles. But Aves was alone. "What now?" he asked as Janson and Hobbie joined them.

Aves nodded toward the street outside the entryway. "Watch," he said. "If I'm right—here he comes."

Wedge looked. A walrus-faced Aqualish strode quickly by, throwing a quick glance into the entryway as he passed. His stride broke, just noticeably; then he caught himself and picked up his pace. He passed the other, side of the entryway—

There was a muffled thud, and suddenly the Aqualish was back in the entryway, his slack and obviously unconscious form being supported by two grim-faced men. "Any trouble?" Aves asked.

"Naw," one of the men said as they dropped the Aqualish none too gently to the ground near the back of the entryway. "They're a lot meaner than they are smart."

"This one was smart enough," Aves said. "Take a good look at him, Antilles. Maybe next time you'll recognize an Imperial spy when you pick one up."

Wedge looked down at the alien. "An Imperial spy, huh?"

"A free-lancer, anyway," Aves shrugged. "Just as dangerous."

Wedge looked back at him, trying to keep his expression neutral. "I suppose we ought to thank you," he said.

One of the other men, busy searching the Aqualish's clothing, snorted under his breath. "I'd think you should, yeah," Aves said. "If it hadn't been for us, you'd have been a juicy little item in the next Imperial Intelligence report."

"I suppose we would have," Wedge conceded, exchanging glances with Hobbie and Janson. But then, that had been the idea of the whole charade. To do their bit to convince Grand Admiral Thrawn that Tangrene was still the New Republic's intended target. "What are you going to do with him?" he asked Aves.

"We'll take care of him," Aves said. "Don't worry, he won't be making any reports anytime soon."

Wedge nodded. One evening, shot completely to flinders. Still, it was nice to know Karrde's people were still on their side. "Thanks again," he said, and meant it this time. "I owe you one."

Aves cocked his head. "You want to pay off the debt right now?"

"How?" Wedge asked cautiously.

"We've got a little job in the works," Aves said, waving a

hand vaguely toward the night sky. "We know you do, too. It would help a lot if we could time ours to go while you're keeping Thrawn occupied."

Wedge frowned at him. "What, you want me to tell you when our operation is starting?"

"Why not?" Aves said reasonably. "Like I said, we already know it's in the works. Bel Iblis's repeat performance, and all that."

Wedge looked at his pilots again, wondering if they appreciated the irony of this as much as he did. Here they stood, an evening's worth of subtle hints gone straight down the proton tubes; and now they were being asked for an outright confirmation of the whole operation. Colonel Derlin's decoy team couldn't have set things up better if they'd tried. "I'm sorry," he said slowly, putting some genuine regret into his voice. "But you know I can't tell you that."

"Why not?" Aves asked patiently. "Like I said, we already know most of it already. I can prove that if you want."

"Not here," Wedge said quickly. The goal was to plant hints, not to be so obvious that it aroused suspicion. "Someone might hear you."

Janson tapped his arm. "Sir, we need to get back," he murmured. "There's a lot of work yet to do before we leave."

"I know, I know," Wedge said. Good old Janson; just the angle he'd been searching for. "Look, Aves, I tell you what I'll do. Are you going to stick around here for a while?"

"I could. Why?"

"Let me talk to my unit commander," Wedge said. "See if I can get a special clearance for you."

Aves' expression showed pretty clearly what he thought of that idea. "It's worth a try," he said diplomatically instead. "How soon can you get an answer?"

"I don't know," Wedge said. "He's as busy as all the rest of us, you know. I'll try to get back to you one way or the other; but if you haven't heard from me in about twenty-eight hours, don't expect to."

Aves might have smiled slightly. Wedge couldn't tell in the dim light. "All right," he said, grumbling a bit. "I suppose it's better than nothing. You can leave any messages with the night bartender at the Dona Laza tapcafe."

"Okay," Wedge said. "We've got to go. Thanks again."

Together, he and the other two pilots left the entryway and crossed the street. They were two blocks away before Hobbie spoke. "Twenty-eight hours, huh? Pretty clever."

"I thought so," Wedge agreed modestly. "Leaving here then would get us to Tangrene just about on time for the big battle."

"Let's just hope he's planning to sell that information to the Empire," Janson murmured. "It'd be a shame to have wasted the whole evening."

"Oh, he'll sell it, all right," Hobbie snorted. "He's a smuggler. What else would he want it for?"

Wedge thought back to the *Katana* battle. Maybe that was indeed all Karrde and his gang were: fringe scum, always for sale to the highest bidder. But somehow, he didn't think so. "We'll find out soon enough," he told Hobbie. "Come on. Like Janson said, we've got a lot of work to do."

CHAPTER 23

THE LAST PAGE scrolled across the display and stopped. SEARCH SUMMARY ENDED. NEXT REQUEST?

"Cancel," Leia said, leaning back in her desk chair and looking out the window. Another dead end. Just like the last one, and the one before that. It was beginning to look like the Research librarians had been right: if there was any information on the old Clone Wars cloning techniques still in the Old Senate Library, it was buried away so deeply that no one would ever find it.

Across the room, she caught a flicker of returning consciousness. Standing up, she crossed to the crib and looked down on her children. Jacen was indeed awake, cooing to himself and making a serious effort to study his fingers. Beside him, Jaina was still asleep, her pudgy lips hanging open just enough to whistle softly with every breath. "Hi, there," Leia murmured to her son, picking him up out of the crib and cradling him in her arms. He looked up at her, his fingers momentarily forgotten, and smiled his wonderful toothless smile. "Well, thank you," she said, smiling back and caressing his cheek. "Come on— let's go see what's happening out in the big world."

She carried him to the window. Beneath them, the Imperial City was in full midmorning mayhem, with ground vehicles and airspeeders buzzing along in all directions like frantic insects. Beyond the city, the snow-tipped peaks of the Manarai Mountains to the south were dazzling in the morning sunshine. Beyond the mountains, the sky was a deep and cloudless blue; and beyond the sky—

She shivered. Beyond the sky was the planetary energy shield. And the Empire's invisible, deadly asteroids.

Jacen gurgled. Leia looked back down at him, found him studying her with what she could almost imagine to be concern. "It's all right," she assured him, holding him a little closer and bouncing him gently in her arms. "It's all right. We'll find them all and get rid of them—don't you worry."

Behind her, the door opened and Winter came into the room, a hover tray floating along in front of her. "Your Highness," she greeted Leia in a soft voice. "I thought you might like some refreshment."

"Yes, I would, thank you," Leia said, sniffing at the gentle aroma of spiced paricha rising from the pot on the tray. "Anything happening downstairs?"

"Nothing interesting," Winter said, pushing the tray over to a side table and starting to unload it. "The search teams haven't found any new asteroids since yesterday morning. I understand General Bel Iblis has been suggesting they may already have cleared them all out."

"I doubt Admiral Drayson believes that."

"No," Winter agreed, holding out a steaming mug and waiting as Leia shifted Jacen to a one-armed grip. "Neither does Mon Mothma."

Leia nodded as she accepted the mug. To be honest, she didn't really believe it herself. No matter how expensive these cloaking shields might be to produce, she couldn't see the Empire going to this much trouble for anything fewer than seventy cloaked asteroids. And there could easily be twice that many. The twenty-one they'd found hardly even scratched the surface.

"How is the research going?" Winter asked, pouring a mug for herself.

"It's not," Leia had to admit. From one insoluble problem to another, it seemed. "Though I don't know why that should surprise me. The Council Research specialists have already been all through the records, and they didn't find anything."

"But you're a Jedi," Winter reminded her. "You have the Force."

"Not enough of it, apparently," Leia shook her head. "At least, not enough to guide me to the right archive. If there is a right archive. I'm not sure anymore that there is."

For a minute they sipped in silence. Leia savored the soft flavor of the hot paricha, acutely aware that this could easily be her last taste of it for a while. All supplies of the root from which the drink was made had to be imported from offplanet.

"I was talking to Mobvekhar yesterday," Winter said into her thoughts. "He said you'd spoken to him about a clue of some sort. Something that Mara Jade had said."

"Something that Mara said, coupled with something Luke did," Leia nodded. "Yes, I remember; and I still think there's an important key in there somewhere. I just can't figure out what it is."

At her waist, her comlink beeped. "I knew it couldn't last," Leia sighed, putting her mug down and pulling the comlink out. Mon Mothma had promised her a complete morning off; obviously, that promise was about to be bent a little. "Councilor Organa Solo," she said into the device.

But it wasn't Mon Mothma. "Councilor, this is Central Communications," a brisk military voice said. "There's a civilian freighter called the *Wild Karrde* holding position just outside the sentry line. The captain insists on speaking with you personally. Do you want to talk to him, or shall we just go ahead and chase him out of the system?"

So Karrde had finally come to pick up his people. Or else had been listening to rumors and had decided to poke around Coruscant a little for himself. Either way, it was trouble. "Better let me talk to him," she told the controller.

"Yes, Councilor."

There was a quiet click. "Hello, Karrde," Leia said. "This is Leia Organa Solo."

"Hello, Councilor," Karrde's cool, well-modulated voice replied. "It's nice to talk to you again. I trust you received my package?"

Leia had to think back. Right—the macrobinocular record of the Ukio attack. "Yes, we did," she acknowledged. "Allow me to express the New Republic's gratitude."

"Your gratitude has already been amply expressed," Karrde said dryly. "Were there any unpleasant repercussions over the payment arrangements?"

"On the contrary," Leia said, bending the truth only a bit. "We'd be happy to pay equivalent rates for more information of that quality."

"I'm glad to hear that," Karrde said. "Are you by any chance also in the market for technology?"

Leia blinked. It wasn't a question she'd been expecting. "What sort of technology?" she asked.

"The semirare sort," he said. "Why don't you give me clearance to come down and we'll discuss it."

"I'm afraid that won't be possible," Leia said. "All nonessential traffic in and out of Coruscant has been restricted."

"Only the nonessential traffic?"

Leia grimaced. So he *had* been listening to rumors. "What exactly have you heard?"

"Assorted whispers only," he said. "Only one of which really concerns me. Tell me about Mara."

"What about Mara?" Leia asked guardedly.

"Is she under arrest?"

Leia threw a look at Winter. "Karrde, this isn't something we should be discussing—"

"Don't give me that," Karrde cut her off, his voice suddenly hard. "You owe me. More to the point, you owe her."

"I'm aware of that," Leia countered, letting her own voice cool a degree or two. "If you'll let me finish, this isn't something we should be discussing on an open channel."

"Ah. I see." If he was feeling any embarrassment over his mistake, it didn't show in his voice. "Let's try this. Is Ghent available?"

"He's around somewhere."

"Find him and get him on a terminal with comm system access. Tell him to program in one of my personal encrypt codes—his choice. That should give us enough privacy."

Leia thought about it. It should at least filter out casual eavesdropping by other civilian ships in the system. Whether any Imperial probe droids lurking out there would be fooled was another question. "It's a start, at least," she agreed. "I'll go find him."

"I'll be waiting."

The signal went silent. "Trouble?" Winter asked.

"Probably," Leia said. She looked down at Jacen, a strange tingling in the back of her mind. There it was again: the eerie feeling that a vital piece of information was hovering in the darkness just out of reach. Luke and Mara were involved with it, she'd already decided. Could Karrde be involved, too? "He's come to plead Mara's case . . . and I don't think he's going to be happy to find her gone. Take care of the twins, please—I have to find Ghent and get down to the war room."

THE DATA CHECKLIST ran to the end and stopped. "Looks okay," Ghent told Leia, peering at the display and making one final adjustment to the encrypt scheme. "You're not going to lose more than a syllable here or there, anyway. Go ahead."

"Just be careful what you say," Bel Iblis reminded her. "There could still be probe droids out there listening in, and there's no guarantee the Imperials haven't broken Karrde's encrypt codes. Don't say anything they don't already know,"

"I understand," Leia nodded. She sat down and tapped the switch the comm officer indicated. "We're ready here, Karrde."

"So am I," Karrde's voice came back. It sounded a bit lower

in pitch than normal, but otherwise seemed to be coming through fine. "Why is Mara under arrest?"

"There was a break-in by an Imperial commando team a few weeks ago," Leia said, choosing her words carefully. "The leader of the team implicated Mara as an accomplice."

"That's absurd," Karrde scoffed.

"I agree," Leia said. "But an accusation like that has to be investigated."

"And what have your investigators discovered?"

"What some of us already knew," Leia said. "That she was once a member of the Emperor's personal staff."

"Is that why you're still holding her?" Karrde demanded. "For things she might or might not have done years ago?"

"We're not worried about her past," Leia said, starting to sweat a little. She hated misleading Karrde this way, particularly after all the assistance he'd given them. But if there were probe droids listening, she needed to make it look like Mara was still under suspicion. "Certain members of the Council and high command are concerned about her current loyalties."

"Then those members are fools," Karrde bit out. "I'd like to talk with her."

"I'm afraid that's impossible," Leia said. "She's not being allowed access to external communications."

There was a faint sound from the speaker; an encrypt glitch or a sigh, Leia couldn't tell which. "Tell me why I can't land," Karrde said. "I've heard the rumors. Tell me the truth."

Leia looked up at Bel Iblis. There was a sour look on his face, but he gave a reluctant nod. "The truth is we're under siege," she told Karrde. "The Grand Admiral has placed a large number of cloaked asteroids into orbit around Coruscant. We don't know what their orbits are, or even how many of them are there. Until we find and destroy all of them the planetary shield has to stay up."

"Indeed," Karrde murmured. "Interesting. I'd heard about the Empire's hit-and-fade, but there hasn't been anything at all about any asteroids. Most of the rumors have suggested merely that you'd suffered severe damage and were trying to cover it up."

"That sounds like the sort of story Thrawn would circulate," Bel Iblis growled. "A little jab at our morale to keep him amused between attacks."

"He's adept at all aspects of warfare," Karrde agreed. But to Leia's ear, there was something odd in his tone. "How many of these asteroids have you found so far? I presume you've been looking."

"We've found and destroyed twenty-one," she told him. "That's twenty-two gone, counting the one the Imperials destroyed to keep us from capturing it. But our battle data indicates he could have launched as many as two hundred eighty-seven."

Karrde was silent a moment. "That's still not all that many for the volume of space involved. I'd be willing to risk coming through it."

"We're not worried about you," Bel Iblis put in. "We're thinking of what would happen to Coruscant if a forty-meter asteroid got through the shield and hit the surface."

"I could make it in through a five-second gap," Karrde offered.

"We're not opening one," Leia said firmly. "I'm sorry."

There was another faint sound from the speaker. "In that case, I suppose I have no choice but to make a deal. You said earlier that you'd be willing to pay for information. Very well. I have something you need; and my price is a few minutes with Mara."

Leia frowned up at Bel Iblis, got an equally puzzled look in return. Whatever Karrde was angling for, it wasn't obvious to him, either. What *was* obvious was that she couldn't very well promise to let him talk to Mara. "I can't make any promises," she told him. "Tell me what the information is, and I'll try to be fair."

There was a moment of silence as he thought it over. "I suppose that's the best offer I'm going to get," he said at last. "All right. You can lower your shield any time now. The asteroids are all gone."

Leia stared at the speaker. "What?"

"You heard me," Karrde said. "They're gone. Thrawn left you twenty-two; you've destroyed twenty-two. The siege is over."

"How do you know?" Bel Iblis asked.

"I was at the Bilbringi shipyards shortly before the Empire's hit-and-fade attack," Karrde told him. "We observed a group of twenty-two asteroids being worked on under close security. At the time, of course, we didn't know what the Empire was doing with them."

"Did you make any records while you were there?" Bel Iblis asked.

"I have the *Wild Karrde*'s sensor data," he said. "If you're ready, I'll drop it to you."

"Go ahead."

The data-feed light went on, and Leia looked up at the master visual display. It was the inside of the Bilbringi shipyards, all right—she recognized it from New Republic surveillance flights. And there in the center, surrounded by support craft and maintenance-suited workers—

"He's right," Bel Iblis murmured. "Twenty-two of them."

"That doesn't prove there aren't any more, sir," the officer at the sensor console pointed out. "They could have put together another group at Ord Trasi or Yaga Minor."

"No," Bel Iblis shook his head. "Aside from the logistics problems involved, I can't imagine Thrawn spreading his cloaking technology around more than he has to. The last thing he can afford would be for us to get our hands on a working model."

"Or even a systems readout," Karrde agreed. "If you found a weakness, one of his chief advantages over you would be gone. All right: I've delivered on my end of the deal. How about yours?"

Leia looked at Bel Iblis helplessly "Why do you want to talk with her?" the general asked.

"If it matters, one of the hardest parts of being locked up is the feeling that you've been deserted," Karrde said coolly. "I imagine Mara's feeling that—I know I did when I was Thrawn's unwilling guest aboard the *Chimaera*. I want to let her know—in person—that she hasn't been forgotten."

"Leia?" Bel Iblis murmured. "What do we do?"

Leia stared at the general, hearing his words but not really registering them. There it was, right in front of her: the key she'd been searching for. Karrde's imprisonment aboard the *Chimaera* . . .

"Leia?" Bel Iblis repeated, frowning.

"I heard you," she said, the words sounding distant and mechanical in her ears. "Let him land."

Bel Iblis threw a glance at the deck officer. "Perhaps we should—"

"I said let him land," Leia snapped with more fire than she'd intended. Suddenly, all the pieces had fallen into place . . . and the picture they formed was one of potential disaster. "I'll take responsibility."

For a moment, Bel Iblis studied her face. "Karrde, this is Bel Iblis," he said slowly. "We'll give you your five-second opening. Stand by for landing instructions."

"Thank you," Karrde said. "I'll talk to you soon."

Bel Iblis gestured to the deck officer, who nodded and got busy. "All right, Leia," he said, turning back to her. "What's going on?"

Leia took a deep breath. "It's the cloning, Garm. I know how Thrawn's growing them so fast."

The whole war room had gone dead quiet. "Tell me," Bel Iblis said.

"It's the Force," she told him. It was so obvious—so utterly obvious—and yet she'd missed it completely. "Don't you see? When you make an exact duplicate of a sentient being, there's a natural resonance or something set up through the Force between that duplicate and the original. *That's* what warps the mind of a clone that's been grown too fast—there's not enough time for the mind to adapt to the pressure on it. It can't adjust; so it breaks."

"All right," Bel Iblis said dubiously. "How is Thrawn getting around the problem?"

"It's very simple," Leia said, a shiver running through her. "He's using ysalamiri to block the Force away from the cloning tanks."

Bel Iblis's face went rigid. Across the silent war room, someone swore softly. "It was Karrde's rescue from the *Chimaera* that was the key," Leia went on. "Mara told me that the Empire had taken five or six thousand ysalamiri out of the forests on Myrkr. But they weren't loading them onto their warships, because when she and Luke went after Karrde Luke had no problem using the Force."

"Because the ysalamiri were on Wayland," Bel Iblis nodded. He looked sharply at Leia, the texture of his sense abruptly changing. "Which means that when the team gets to the mountain—"

"Luke will be helpless," Leia nodded, her throat tight. "And he won't even suspect it until it's too late."

She shivered again, the dream she'd had the night of the Imperial attack suddenly coming back to her. Luke and Mara, facing a crazed Jedi and another unknown threat. She'd soothed herself at the time with the knowledge that Luke would be able to sense C'baoth's presence on Wayland and take steps to avoid him. But with the ysalamiri there, he might walk right into the other's hands.

No. *Would* walk into C'baoth's hands. Somehow, at this instant, she knew that he would. What she'd seen that night hadn't been a dream, but a Jedi vision.

"I'll talk to Mon Mothma," Bel Iblis was saying, his face grim. "Even with Bilbringi, maybe we can shake some ships loose to go to their assistance."

Turning, he headed quickly toward the exit and the turbolifts beyond it. For a moment Leia watched him, listening as the war room broke its self-imposed trance and came slowly back to life. He'd try, she knew; but she also knew that he would fail. Mon Mothma, Commander Sesfan, and Bel Iblis himself had already said it: there simply weren't enough resources available to hit both Wayland and the Bilbringi shipyards at the same time. And she knew all too well that not everyone on the Council would believe that the threat of cloaked asteroids had ended. At least, not enough to call off the Bilbringi attack.

Which meant there was exactly one person left who could go to the aid of her husband and brother.

Taking a deep breath, Leia headed off after Bel Iblis. There was a great deal she had to do before Karrde arrived.

THERE WERE THREE of them waiting when Karrde emerged from the ship, skulking beneath the canopy overhanging the pad accessway tunnel. Karrde spotted them from the top of the *Wild Karrde*'s entrance, ramp, and despite the shadows had two of them identified before he was halfway down. Leia Organa Solo was there, with Ghent fidgeting behind her. The third figure, standing behind both of the others, was short and wore the coarse brown robe of a Jawa. What a desert scavenger was doing there Karrde couldn't guess . . . but as the group stepped out of the shadows toward him and he got his first good look at Organa Solo's face, it became clear that he was about to find out. "Good morning, Councilor," he greeted her, inclining his head slightly. "Good to see you, Ghent. I trust you've been making yourself useful?"

"I suppose so," Ghent said, shifting nervously from one foot to the other. Far too nervously, even for him. "They say so, anyway."

"Good." Karrde shifted his attention to the third of the party. "And your friend is . . . ?"

"I am Mobvekhar clan Hakh'khar," a gravelly voice mewed.

Karrde resisted the urge to take a half-step backward. Whatever it was hiding under that robe, it most certainly wasn't a Jawa. "He's my bodyguard," Organa Solo said.

"Ah." With an effort, Karrde pulled his eyes away from whatever it was that was being concealed by the dark hood. "Well," he said, waving a hand toward the accessway. "Shall we go?"

Organa Solo shook her head. "Mara's not here."

Karrde threw a look at Ghent, who was looking even more uncomfortable. "You told me she was."

"I only agreed with you that she'd been arrested," Organa Solo said. "I couldn't say anything more then—there may have been Imperial probe droids listening in."

With an effort, Karrde fought down his annoyance. They were all on the same side here, after all. "Where is she?"

"On a planet called Wayland," Organa Solo said. "Along with Luke and Han and some others."

Wayland? Karrde couldn't recall ever hearing of that world before. "And what's on Wayland that they find so interesting?" he asked.

"Grand Admiral Thrawn's cloning facility."

Karrde stared at her. "You found it?"

"We didn't," Organa Solo said. "Mara did."

Karrde nodded mechanically. So they'd found the cloning facility on their own. All that work he'd put in organizing the other smuggler groups: gone like dumped Kessel spice. The work, the risk, not to mention the money he'd planned to pay them with. "You're certain the cloning facility is there?"

"We'll find out soon enough," Organa Solo said, gesturing to the ship behind him. "I need you to take me there. Right away."

"Why?"

"Because the expedition's in danger," Organa Solo said. "They may not know it yet, but they are. And if they're still on the timetable we were sent, we have a chance of getting to them before it's too late."

"She told me all about it on the way up here," Ghent added hesitantly. "I think we ought to . . ."

He trailed off as Karrde sent a look his way. "I sympathize with your people, Councilor," he said. "But there are other matters that also need my attention."

"Then you abandon Mara," Organa Solo reminded him.

"I have no particular feelings for Mara," Karrde countered. "She's a member of my organization; nothing more."

"Isn't that enough?"

For a moment Karrde gazed at her. She held his gaze evenly, calling his bluff . . . and in her eyes, he could see that she knew perfectly well that it *was* a bluff. He couldn't simply walk away and abandon Mara to her death, any more than he could abandon Aves or Dankin or Chin. Not if there was anything he could do to prevent it. "It's not that easy," he said quietly. "I have responsibilities to the rest of my people, as well. At the moment they're preparing to launch a raid with the hope of obtaining a crystal gravfield trap to sell you."

A flicker of surprise flashed across Organa Solo's face. "A crystal gravfield trap—?"

"It's not the one you're trying for," Karrde assured her. "But we've scheduled it for the same time, hoping your attack will distract the enemy. I need to be there."

"I see," Organa Solo murmured, apparently deciding to pass over the question of how Karrde could have known about the Tangrene raid. "Will the *Wild Karrde* make all that much difference in that raid?"

Karrde looked at Ghent. It wouldn't make any difference at all, not with Mazzic and Ellor and the others reinforcing the impressive group Aves had already pulled together. The problem was that if they left now—and the way Organa Solo was talking, she meant for him to turn around and head straight back into space—there wouldn't be any chance of turning Ghent loose on the New Republic's computer system and rerouting the funds he needed to pay the other groups.

Unless he could get the money another way. "It can't be

done," he told Organa Solo firmly. "I can't simply walk out on my people. At least, not without—"

Abruptly, the Jawa-robed alien snapped his fingers. Karrde paused in midsentence, watching in fascination as the creature slipped noiselessly back into the accessway tunnel, a slender knife appearing somehow in his hand. He disappeared through the door, and for a moment there was silence. Karrde raised his eyebrows at Organa Solo, got a slight shrug in return—

There was a sudden squeal from inside the accessway door, followed by a sudden flurry of half-visible commotion. Karrde found his blaster in his hand; and he was bringing it to bear on the figures when all the activity abruptly stopped. A moment later, the alien reappeared, forcing a half-crouched figure before him.

An all-too-familiar figure. "Well, well," Karrde said, lowering his blaster but not holstering it. "Councilor Fey'lya, I believe. Reduced to eavesdropping at doorways?"

"He is unarmed," the robed alien said in his gravelly voice.

"Release him, then," Organa Solo said.

The alien complied. Fey'lya straightened up, his fur rippling madly across his head and torso as he tried to salvage what he could of his composure. "I protest this improper treatment," he said, his voice somewhat less melodious than the Bothan norm. "And I was not eavesdropping. General Bel Iblis informed me of Councilor Organa Solo's revelation concerning the cloning facility on Wayland. I came here, Captain Karrde, to urge you to assist Councilor Organa Solo in her wish to go to Wayland."

Karrde smiled tightly. "Where she would be conveniently out of your way? Thank you, but I believe we've already been through this together."

The Bothan drew himself up. "This is not about politics. Without her warning, the team on Wayland may not survive. And without their survival, the Emperor's storehouse may not be destroyed before the Grand Admiral can remove some of its contents to a safe place."

His violet eyes locked with Karrde's. "And that would be a disaster. To both the Bothan people and to the galaxy."

For a moment Karrde studied him, wondering what was there that Fey'lya was so worried about. Some weapon or technology that Thrawn hadn't found yet? Or was it more personal than that? Unpleasant or embarrassing information, perhaps, either about Fey'lya or the Bothan people generally?

He didn't know, and he suspected Fey'lya wouldn't tell. But the particulars didn't really matter. "Potential disasters to the Bothan people don't worry me," he told Fey'lya. "How much do they worry you?"

There was an uncertain ripple of the fur across Fey'lya's shoulders. "It would be a disaster for the galaxy as well," he said.

"So you said," Karrde agreed. "I repeat. How much does it worry you?"

And this time Fey'lya got it. His eyes narrowed, his fur rippling with obvious contempt. "How much worry will it take?" he demanded.

"Nothing unreasonable," Karrde assured him. "Merely a credit of, say, seventy thousand?"

"Seventy *thousand*?" Fey'lya echoed, aghast. "What exactly do you think—"

"That's my price, Councilor," Karrde cut him off. "Take it or leave it. And if Councilor Organa Solo is correct, we don't have time for any long discussions."

Fey'lya hissed like an angry predator. "You're no better than a foul mercenary," he snarled, his voice about as vicious as Karrde had ever heard a Bothan get. "You drain out the lifeblood of the Bothan people—"

"Spare me the lecture, Councilor," Karrde said. "Yes or no?"

Fey'lya hissed again. "Yes."

"Good," Karrde nodded, looking at Organa Solo. "Is the credit line your brother set up for me still there?"

"Yes," she said. "General Bel Iblis knows how to access it."

"You can deposit the seventy thousand there," Karrde told

Fey'lya. "And bear in mind that we'll be stopping to check on it before we reach Wayland. In case you had any thoughts about backing out."

"*I* am honorable, smuggler," Fey'lya snarled. "Unlike others present."

"I'm glad to hear that," Karrde said. "Honorable beings are so difficult to find. Councilor Organa Solo?"

She took a deep breath, "I'm ready," she said.

THEY WERE OFF Coruscant and nearly ready for the jump to lightspeed before Leia finally asked the question she'd worried about since coming aboard. "Are we really going to stop to check on Fey'lya's funds?"

"With time as critical as you suggest?" Karrde countered. "Don't be silly. But Fey'lya doesn't know that."

Leia watched him for a moment as he handled the *Wild Karrde*'s helm. "The money's not really important to you, is it?"

"Don't believe that, either," he advised her coolly. "I have certain obligations to meet. If Fey'lya hadn't been willing to cooperate, your New Republic would have had to do so."

"I see," Leia murmured.

He must have heard something in her voice. "I mean that," he insisted, throwing a brief and entirely unconvincing scowl at her. "I'm here because it suits my purposes. Not for the sake of your war."

"I said I understood," Leia agreed, smiling privately to herself. The words were different; but the look on Karrde's face was almost identical. *Look, I ain't in this for your revolution, and I'm not in it for you, Princess. I expect to be well paid. I'm in it for the money.* Han had said that to her after that stormy escape from the first Death Star. At the time, she'd believed it.

Her smile faded. He and Luke had saved her life then. She wondered if she'd be in time now to save theirs.

CHAPTER 24

T HE ENTRANCE TO Mount Tantiss was a glint of metal nestled cozily beneath an overhang of rock and vegetation. Between them and it, just visible from their hilltop vantage point, was a clearing with a small city lying in it. "What do you think?" Luke asked.

"I think we find another way in," Han told him, bracing his elbows a little harder into the dead leaves and trying to hold the macrobinoculars steady. He'd been right; there was a stormtrooper guard station just off the metal doors. "You never want the front door, anyway."

Luke tapped his shoulder twice: the signal that he'd picked up someone coming. Han froze, listening. Sure enough, there was a faint sound of clumping feet in the underbrush. A minute later, four Imperial troops in full field gear came out of the trees a few meters further down the hill. They walked straight past Han and Luke without so much as looking up, disappearing back into the trees a few steps later. "Starting to get pretty thick," Han muttered.

"I think it's just the proximity to the mountain," Luke said. "I still don't get any indication that they know we're out here."

Han grunted and shifted his view to the village poking out of the clearing down below them. Most of the buildings were squat, alien-looking things, with one really good-sized one facing into an open square. His angle wasn't all that good, but it looked like there were a bunch of Psadans hanging around near the front of the big one. A town meeting, maybe? "I don't see any sign of a garrison down there," he said, sweeping the macrobinoculars slowly across the village. "Must be working directly out of the mountain."

"That should make it easier to get around it,"

"Yeah," Han said, frowning as he swung the macrobinoculars back to the town square. That crowd of Psadans he'd noticed a minute ago had shifted into a sort of semicircle now, facing a couple more of the walking rock piles standing with their backs to the big building. And it was definitely getting bigger.

"Trouble?" Luke murmured.

"I don't know," Han said slowly, wedging his elbows a little tighter and kicking the magnification up a notch. "There's a big meeting going on down there. Two Psadans . . . but they don't seem to be talking. Just holding something."

"Let me try," Luke offered. "There are Jedi techniques for enhancing vision. Maybe they'll work on a macrobinocular image."

"Go ahead," Han said, handing over the macrobinoculars and squinting at the sky. There were a few wispy clouds visible up there, but nothing that looked like it was going to become a general overcast anytime soon. Figure two hours till sundown; another half hour of light after that—

"Hmm," Luke said.

"What is it?"

"I'm not exactly sure," Luke said, lowering the macrobinoculars. "But it looks to me like what they're holding is a data pad."

Han looked out toward the city. "I didn't know they used data pads."

"Neither did I," Luke said, his voice suddenly going all strange.

Han frowned at him. The kid was just staring at the mountain, a funny look on his face. "What's wrong?"

"It's the mountain," he said, staring hard at it. "It's dark. All of it."

Dark? Han frowned at the mountain. It looked fine to him. "What are you talking about?"

"It's dark," Luke repeated slowly. "Like Myrkr was."

Han looked at the mountain. Looked back at Luke. "You mean, like in a bunch of ysalamiri cutting off the Force?"

Luke nodded. "That's what it feels like. I won't know for sure until we're closer."

Han looked back at the mountain, feeling his stomach curling up inside him. "Great," he muttered. "Just great. Now what?"

Luke shrugged, "We go on. What else is there?"

"Getting back to the *Falcon* and getting out of here, that's what," Han retorted. "Unless you're really hot to walk into an Imperial trap."

"I don't think it's a trap," Luke said, shaking his head thoughtfully. "Or at least, not a trap for us. Remember how that contact I told you about with C'baoth was suddenly cut off?"

Han rubbed his cheek. He could see what Luke was getting at, all right: the ysalamiri were here for C'baoth, not him. "I'm still not sure I buy that," he said. "I thought C'baoth and Thrawn were on the same side. Mara said that herself."

"Maybe they had a falling out," Luke suggested. "Or maybe Thrawn was using him from the start and now doesn't need him anymore. If the Imperials don't know we're here, the ysalamiri must have been meant for him."

"Yeah, well, it doesn't matter much who they were meant for," Han pointed out. "They'll block you just as well as they will C'baoth. It'll be like Myrkr all over again."

"Mara and I did okay on Myrkr," Luke reminded him. "We can handle it here. Anyway, we've come too far to back out now."

Han grimaced. But the kid was right. Once the Empire gave up on this deserted-planet routine, chances were the next New Republic team wouldn't even make it into the atmosphere. "You going to tell Mara before we get there?"

"Of course." Luke looked up at the sky. "But I'll tell her on the way. We'd better get moving while we still have daylight."

"Right," Han said, giving the area one last look before he got to his feet. Force or no Force, it was up to them. "Let's go."

The others were waiting just around the other side of the hill. "How's it look?" Lando asked as Han and Luke rejoined them.

"They still don't know we're here," Han told him, looking around for Mara. She was sitting on the ground near Threepio and Artoo, concentrating on a set of five stones she'd gotten to hover in the air in front of her. Luke had been teaching her this kind of stuff for days, and Han had finally given up trying to talk the kid out of it. It looked like the lessons were going to be a waste of time now, anyway. "You ready to take us to this back door of yours?"

"I'm ready to start looking for it," she said, still keeping the stones in the air. "As I told you before, I only saw the air system equipment from inside the mountain. I never saw the intakes themselves."

"We'll find them," Luke assured her, passing Han and walking over to the droids. "How are you doing, Threepio?"

"Quite well, thank you, Master Luke," the droid answered primly. "This route is so much better than many of the earlier ones." Beside him, Artoo trilled something. "Artoo finds it so, as well," Threepio added.

"Don't get attached to it," Mara warned, finally letting the stones drop as she stood up. "There probably won't be any Myneyrshi trails up the mountain for us to follow. The Empire discouraged native activity anywhere nearby."

"But don't worry," Luke soothed the droids. "The Noghri will help us find a path."

"FREIGHTER *GARRET'S GOLD,* you're cleared for final approach," the brisk voice of Bilbringi Control came over the *Etherway*'s bridge speaker. "Docking Platform Twenty-five. Straight-vector as indicated to the buoy; it'll feed you the course to follow to the platform."

"Acknowledged, Control," Aves said, keying in the course that had come up on the nav display. "What about the security fields?"

"Stay on the course you're given and you won't run into them," the controller said. "Deviate more than about fifteen meters any direction and you'll get a good bump on the nose. From the looks of it, I don't think your nose can afford any more bumps."

Aves threw a glare at the speaker. One of these days he was going to get real tired of Imperial sarcasm. "Thank you," he said, and keyed off.

"Imperials are such fun to work with, aren't they?" Gillespee commented from the copilot station.

"I like to imagine what his expression is going to be like when we burn out of here with their CGT," Aves said.

"Let's hope we're not around to find out for sure," Gillespee said. "Pretty complicated flight system they've got here."

"It wasn't like this before that raid of Mazzic's," Aves said, gazing ahead through the viewport. Half a dozen shield generators were visible along his approach vector, floating loose around the area and defining the flight path the buoy would supposedly give him. "Probably supposed to keep anyone else from flying around the shipyards any old way they want to."

"Yeah," Gillespee said. "I just hope they've got all the glitches out of the system."

"Me, too," Aves agreed. "I don't want them to know how much of a bump this ship can really take."

He glanced down at his board, confirming his vector and then checking the time. The New Republic fleet ought to be hitting Tangrene in a little over three hours. Just enough time for the *Etherway* to dock, unload the specially tweaked tractor beam burst capacitors they were courteously donating to the Empire's war effort, and get into backup position for Mazzic's attempt to grab the CGT from the main command center eight docking platforms away.

"There goes Ellor," Gillespee commented, nodding off to starboard.

Aves looked. It was the *Kai Mir*, all right, with the *Klivering* running in flanking position beside it. Beyond it, he could see the *Starry Ice* drifting in toward a docking platform near the perimeter. Near as he could tell, everything seemed to be falling into place.

Though with someone like Thrawn in charge, appearances didn't mean much. For all he knew, the Grand Admiral might already know all about this raid, and was just waiting for everybody to sneak in under the net before wrapping it around them.

"You ever hear anything else from Karrde?" Gillespee asked, a little too casually.

"He's not deserting us, Gillespee," Aves growled. "If he says he has something more important to do, then he has something more important to do. Period."

"I know," Gillespee said, his voice noncommittal. "Just thought some of the others might have asked."

Aves grimaced. Here they went again. He'd have thought that opening up Ferrier's treachery at Hijarna would have settled this whole thing once and for all. He should have known better. "I'm here," he reminded Gillespee. "So are the *Starry Ice*, the *Dawn Beat*, the *Lastri's Ort*, the *Amanda Fallow*, the—"

"Yeah, right, I get the point," Gillespee interrupted. "Don't get huffy at me—my ships are here, too."

"Sorry," Aves said. "I'm just getting tired of everybody always being so suspicious of everybody else."

Gillespee shrugged. "We're smugglers. We've had a lot of

practice at it. Personally, I'm surprised the group's held together this long. What do you think he's doing?"

"Who, Karrde?" Aves shook his head. "No idea. But it'll be
something important."

"Sure." Gillespee pointed ahead. "That the marker buoy?"

"Looks like it," Aves agreed. "Get ready to copy the course
data. Ready or not, here we go."

THE ORDERS CAME up on Wedge's comm screen, and he gave
them a quick check as he keyed for the squadron's private frequency. "Rogue Squadron, this is Rogue Leader," he said. "Orders: we're going in with the first wave, flanking Admiral
Ackbar's Command Cruiser. Hold position here until we're
cleared for positioning. All ships acknowledge."

The acknowledgments came in, crisp and firm, and Wedge
smiled tightly to himself. There'd been some worry among
Ackbar's staff, he knew, that the long flight here to the rendezvous point might take the edge off those units that had first
had to carry out decoy duty near the supposed Tangrene jump-
off point. Wedge didn't know about the others, but it was clear
that Rogue Squadron was primed and ready for battle.

"You suppose Thrawn got our message, Rogue Leader?"
Janson's voice came into Wedge's thoughts.

Their message . . . ? Oh, right—that little conversation outside the Mumbri Storve cantina with Talon Karrde's friend
Aves. The one Hobbie had been firmly convinced would be
going straight to Imperial Intelligence. "I don't know, Rogue
Five," Wedge told him. "Actually, I sort of hope it didn't."

"Kind of a waste of time if it didn't."

"Not necessarily," Wedge pointed out. "Remember, he said
they had some other scheme on line that they wanted to coordinate with ours. Anything that hits or distracts the Empire
can't help but do us some good."

"They've probably just got some smuggling drop planned,"

Rogue Six sniffed. "Hoping to run it through while the Imperials are looking the other way."

Wedge didn't reply. Luke Skywalker seemed to think Karrde was quietly on the New Republic's side, and that was good enough for him. But there wasn't any way he was going to convince the rest of his squadron of that. Someday, maybe, Karrde would be willing to take a more open stand against the Empire. Until then, at least in Wedge's opinion, everyone who wasn't on the Grand Admiral's side was helping the New Republic, whether they admitted it or not.

Sometimes, even, whether they knew it or not.

His comm display changed, the vanguard cone of Star Cruisers had made it into their launch formation. Time for their escort ships to do the same. "Okay, Rogue Squadron," he told the others. "We've got the light. Let's get to our places."

Easing power to his X-wing's drive, he headed off toward the running lights ahead. Two and a half hours, if the rest of the fleet assembly stayed on schedule, and they'd be dropping out of lightspeed within spitting distance of the Bilbringi shipyards.

A shame, he thought, that they wouldn't be able to see the looks on the Imperials' faces.

THE LATEST GROUP of reports from the Tangrene region scrolled across the display. Pellaeon skimmed through them, scowling blackly to himself. No mistake—the Rebels were still there. Still slipping forces into the region; still doing nothing to draw attention to themselves. And in two hours, if Intelligence's projections were even halfway accurate, they would be launching an attack on an effectively undefended system.

"They're doing quite well, aren't they, Captain?" Thrawn commented from beside him. "A very convincing performance all around."

"Sir," Pellaeon said, fighting to keep his voice properly deferential. "I respectfully suggest that the Rebel activity is not any kind of performance. The preponderance of evidence points to Tangrene as their probable target. Several key starfighter units and capital ships have clearly been assembled at likely jump-off points—"

"Wrong, Captain," Thrawn cut him off coolly. "That's what they want us to believe, but it's nothing more than a carefully constructed illusion. The ships you refer to pulled out of those sectors between forty and seventy hours ago, leaving behind a few men with the proper uniforms and insignia to confuse our spies. The bulk of the force is even now on its way to Bilbringi."

"Yes, sir," Pellaeon said with a silent sigh of defeat. So that was it. Once again, Thrawn had chosen to ignore his arguments—as well as all the evidence—in favor of nebulous hunches and intuitions.

And if he was wrong, it wouldn't be simply the Tangrene Ubiqtorate base that would be lost. An error of that magnitude would shake the confidence and momentum of the entire Imperial war machine.

"All war is risk, Captain," Thrawn said quietly. "But this is not as large a risk as you seem to think. If I'm wrong, we lose one Ubiqtorate base—important, certainly, but hardly critical." He cocked a blue-black eyebrow. "But if I'm right, we stand a good chance of destroying two entire Rebel sector fleets. Consider the impact that will have on the current balance of power."

"Yes, sir," Pellaeon said dutifully.

He could feel Thrawn's eyes on him. "You don't have to believe," the Grand Admiral told him. "But be prepared to be proved wrong."

"I very much hope so, sir," Pellaeon said.

"Good. Is my flagship ready, Captain?"

Pellaeon felt his back stiffen a bit in old parade-ground reflex. "The *Chimaera* is fully at your command, Admiral."

"Then prepare the fleet for hyperspace." The glowing eyes glittered. "And for battle."

There were no real paths up Mount Tantiss; but as Luke had predicted, the Noghri had a knack for terrain. They made remarkably good time, even with the droids slowing them down, and as the sun was disappearing below the trees, they reached the air intakes.

It was not, however, exactly the way Luke had envisioned it.

"Looks more like a retractable turbolaser turret than an air system," he commented to Han as they moved cautiously through the trees toward the heavy metal mesh and the even heavier metal structure the mesh was set into.

"Reminds me of the bunker we had to break into on Endor," Han muttered back. "Except with a screen door. Easy—they might have intruder detectors."

Anywhere else, Luke would have reached out into the tunnel with the Force. Here, within the ysalamiri effect surrounding him, it was like being blind.

Like being on Myrkr again.

He looked at Mara, wondering if she was having similar thoughts and memories. Perhaps so. Even in the fading light, he could see the tension in her face, an anxiety and fear that hadn't been there before they entered the ysalamiri bubble. "So what now?" she growled, flashing a brief glare at him before looking away again. "We just sit around until morning?"

Han had his macrobinoculars trained on the intake. "Looks like a computer outlet there on the wall under the overhang," he said. "The rest of you stay put—I'll take Artoo over and try plugging him in."

Beside Han, Chewbacca rumbled a warning. "Where?" Han muttered, drawing his blaster.

The Wookiee pointed with one hand as he unlimbered his bowcaster with the other.

The whole group froze, weapons ready . . . and it was then that Luke first heard the faint sounds of distant blaster fire. From several kilometers away, he thought, possibly somewhere down the mountain. But without his Jedi enhancement techniques, there was no way to know for sure.

From much closer came a birdlike warbling. "A group of Myneyrshi approach," Ekhrikhor said, listening intently to the signaling. "The Noghri have stopped them. They wish to come forward and speak."

"Tell them to stay there," Han said, hesitating just a second before holstering his blaster. Pulling the bleached *satnachakka* clawbird out of a pocket of his jacket, he beckoned to Threepio. "Come on, Goldenrod, let's go find out what they want."

Ekhrikhor muttered an order, and one of the Noghri moved silently to Han's side. Chewbacca stepped to the other side, and with a helplessly protesting Threepio trailing along they all headed off into the trees.

Artoo gurgled uncomfortably, his dome head swiveling back and forth between Luke and the departing Threepio. "He'll be all right," Luke assured him. "Han won't let anything happen to him."

The squat droid grunted, probably expressing his opinion of the depths of Han's concern for Threepio. "We may have more problems than Threepio's health to worry about in a minute," Lando said grimly. "I thought I heard blaster fire from down the mountain."

"I did, too," Mara nodded. "Probably coming from the storehouse entrance."

Lando looked over his shoulder at the massive air intake. "Let's see if we can get that vent open. At least it'll give us another direction to go if we need to jump."

Luke looked at Mara, but she was avoiding his eyes again. "All right," he told Lando. "I'll go first; you bring Artoo."

Cautiously, he moved through the trees toward the intakes. But if there were any anti-intruder defenses, they didn't seem to be working anymore. He made it in under the metal overhang without incident, and with the wind of the inrushing air ruffling through his hair he studied the mesh. At this distance he could see that it was more like a heavy grating, with each strand of what had looked like mesh actually a plate extending several centimeters back into the tunnel. A formidable barrier, but nothing his lightsaber couldn't handle.

There was the sound of a footstep through leaves, and he turned as Lando and Artoo came up. "The outlet's over there, Artoo," he told the droid, pointing to the socket in the side wall. "Plug in and see what you can find out."

The droid warbled acknowledgment, and with Lando's help maneuvered his way across the rough ground.

"It's not just going to open up for you," Mara said from behind him.

"Artoo's going to check it out," Luke told her, peering at her face. "You all right?"

He'd expected a sarcastic comment or at least a withering glare. He wasn't prepared for her to reach out and grip his hand. "I want you to promise me something," she said in a low voice. "Whatever it costs, don't let me go over to C'baoth's side. You understand? Don't let me join him. Even if you have to kill me."

Luke stared at her, an eerie chill running through him. "C'baoth can't force you to his side, Mara," he said. "Not without your cooperation."

"Are you sure of that? *Really* sure?"

Luke grimaced. There was so much he didn't know yet about the Force. "No."

"Neither am I," Mara said. "That's what worries me. C'baoth told me back on Jomark that I'd be joining him. He said it again here, too, the night he arrived."

"He may have been mistaken," Luke suggested hesitantly. "Or lying."

"I don't want to risk it." She gripped Luke's hand tighter. "I'm not going to serve him, Skywalker. I want you to promise that you'll kill me before you let him do that to me."

Luke swallowed hard. Even without the Force, he could hear in her voice that she meant it. But for a Jedi to promise to cut someone down in cold blood . . . "I'll promise you this," he said instead. "Whatever happens in there, you won't have to face him alone. I'll be there to help you."

She turned her face away. "What if you're already dead?"

So it was down to this: the same battle she'd been fighting with herself since the day they met. "You don't have to do it," he said quietly. "The Emperor's dead. That voice you hear is just a memory he left behind inside you."

"I know that," she snapped, a touch of fire flickering through the cold dread. "You think that makes it any easier to ignore?"

"No," he conceded. "But you can't use the voice as an excuse, either. Your destiny is in your hands, Mara. Not C'baoth's or the Emperor's. In the end you're the one who makes the decisions. You have that right . . . and that responsibility."

From the forest came the sound of footsteps. "Fine," Mara growled, dropping Luke's hand and taking a step back away from him. "You spout philosophy if you want to. Just remember what I said." Spinning around, she turned to face the approaching group. "So what's going on, Solo?"

"We've picked up some allies," he said, throwing what looked like a frown in Luke's general direction. "Sort of allies, anyway."

"Hey—Threepio," Lando called, waving to him. "Come over here, will you, and tell me what Artoo's all excited about."

"Certainly, sir," Threepio said, shuffling over to the computer terminal.

Luke looked back at Han. "What do you mean, sort of allies?"

"It's kind of confusing," Han said. "At least the way Threepio translates it. They don't want to help us, they just want to go in and fight the Imperials. They followed us because they figured we'd find a back door they could get in through."

Luke studied the group of silent four-armed aliens towering over the Noghri guarding them. All wore four or more long knives and carried crossbows—not exactly the sort of weapons to use against armored Imperial troops. "I don't know. What do you think?"

"Hey, Han," Lando called softly before Han could answer. "Come here. You'll want to hear this."

"What?" Han asked as they went over to the computer terminal.

"Tell them, Threepio," Lando said.

"Apparently, there is an attack taking place at the main entrance to the mountain," Threepio said in that perennially surprised manner of his. "Artoo has picked up several reports detailing perimeter-guard troop movements into the area—"

"Who's attacking?" Han cut him off.

"Apparently, some of the Psadans from the city," Threepio said. "According to the gate reports, they demanded the release of their Lord C'baoth before they attacked."

Han looked at Luke. "The data pad."

"Makes sense," Luke agreed. A message from C'baoth, inciting them to attack. "I wonder how he managed to smuggle it out to them."

"Confirms he's been locked up, anyway," Mara put in. "I hope they've got some good guards on his cell."

"Pardon me, Master Luke," Threepio said, cocking his head to one side, "but as to the data pad Captain Solo mentioned, I would suggest it arrived the same way the weapons did. According to reports—"

"What kind of weapons?" Han said.

"I was getting to that, sir," Threepio said, sounding a bit huffy. "According to gate reports, the attackers are armed with blasters, portable missile launchers, and thermal detonators. All quite modern versions, if reports are to be believed."

"Never mind where they got them from," Lando said. "The point is that we've got a custom-cut diversion here. Let's use it while it's still there."

Chewbacca rumbled suspiciously. "You're right, pal," Han agreed, peering into the grating. "It's awfully convenient timing. But Lando's right—we might as well go for it."

Lando nodded. "Okay, Artoo. Shut it all down."

The squat droid chirped acknowledgment, his computer arm rotating in the socket. The inflow of air across Luke's face began to decrease, and a minute later had stopped completely.

Artoo warbled again. "Artoo reports that all operating systems for this intake have been shut down," Threepio announced. "He warns, however, that once the duty cycle has ended, the dust barriers and driving fields may be reactivated from a central location."

"Better get moving, then," Luke said, igniting his lightsaber and stepping over to the intake. Four careful slices later, they had their entrance.

"Looks clear," Han said, climbing gingerly through the opening and stepping over to the limited protection of the side wall. "Got maintenance lights showing up down the tunnel a ways. Artoo, you get us any floor plans for this place?"

The droid jabbered as he rolled through the opening. "I'm terribly sorry, sir," Threepio said. "He has full schematics for the air-duct system itself, but he says that further information on the facility was not available at this terminal."

"There'll be other terminals down the line," Lando said. "Are we leaving a rear guard?"

"One of the Noghri will stay," Ekhrikhor mewed at Han's elbow. "He will keep the exit clear."

"Fine," Han said. "Let's go."

They were fifty meters down the tunnel and approaching the first of the dim maintenance lights Han had spotted before Luke suddenly noticed that the silent Myneyrshi had followed them in. "Han?" he murmured, gesturing behind them.

"Yeah, I know," Han said. "What did you want me to do, tell them to go home?"

Luke looked back again. He was right, of course. But knives and crossbows against blasters . . . "Ekhrikhor?"

"What is your command, son of Vader?"

"I want you to assign two of your people to go with those

Myneyrshi," he told the Noghri. "They're to guide them and help them with their attacks."

"But it is you we must protect, son of Vader," Ekhrikhor objected.

"You will be protecting me," Luke said. "Every Imperial the Myneyrshi can pin down will be one less for us to worry about. But they can't pin any troops down if they're killed in the first sortie."

The Noghri made an unhappy-sounding noise in the back of his throat. "I hear and obey," he said reluctantly. He gestured to two of the Noghri; and as Luke watched them drop back down the tunnel he caught a quick look at Mara's face as she passed one of the lights. The dread was still there, but along with it was a grim determination. Whatever was waiting ahead for them, she was ready to face it.

He could only hope that he was, too.

"There it is," Karrde announced, pointing ahead to the mountain rising out of the forest and the gathering shadows of twilight.

"You sure?" Leia asked, stretching out with the Force as hard as she could. Back at Bespin, during that mad escape from Lando's Cloud City, she'd been able to sense Luke's call from almost this far away. Here, now, there was nothing at all.

"That's where their nav feed seems to be leading us," Karrde told her. "Unless they've seen through Ghent's little deception and are sending us to some sort of decoy spot." He glanced over his shoulder at her. "Anything?"

"No." Leia looked out at the mountain, her stomach tightening painfully. After all their hopes and effort, they were too late. "They must already be inside."

"They're heading into trouble, then," Ghent spoke up from the comm station where he was still fiddling with the fine-tuning on his counterfeit Imperial ID code. "Flight control says they've got a riot going on at the entrance. They're diverting us to a secondary maintenance area about ten kilometers north."

Leia shook her head. "We're going to have to risk contacting them."

"Too dangerous," Dankin, the copilot, said. "If they catch us using a non-Imperial comlink channel, we're likely to get shot down."

"Perhaps there is another way," Mobvekhar said, moving to Leia's side. "Ekhrikhor clan Bakh'tor will have left a guard at their entrance point. There is a Noghri recognition signal that can be created with landing lights."

"Go ahead," Karrde said. "We can always claim a malfunction if the garrison notices. Chin, Corvis—watch your scopes."

Stepping over to Dankin's board, the Noghri keyed the landing lights on and off a half-dozen times. Leia stared out the viewport, trying to watch the whole mountain at once. If Han and the others had gone in above the dusk line—

"Got it," Corvis's voice came from his turbolaser turret. "Bearing zero-zero-three mark seventeen."

Leia looked over Karrde's shoulder as the coordinates came up on his nav display. There it was, faint but visible: a flickering light. "They are there," Mobvekhar confirmed.

"Good," Karrde said. "Ghent, acknowledge that we're proceeding to that secondary maintenance area as ordered. Better find a seat and strap down, Councilor; we're about to have an unexpected repulsorlift malfunction."

Between the trees and eroded rock outcroppings it looked to Leia like an impossible place for a ship the size of the *Wild Karrde* to land. But Karrde and his crew had clearly pulled this trick before, and with a last-second sputter of precision-aimed turbolaser fire they created just enough of a gap to put down into.

"Now what?" Dankin asked as Karrde cycled back the repulsorlifts.

Karrde looked at Leia, raised an eyebrow in question. "I'm going in," Leia told him, the vision of Luke and Mara in danger hovering before her eyes. "You don't have to come along."

"The Councilor and I will go look for her friends," Karrde answered Dankin, unstrapping and getting to his feet. "Ghent, you'll try to convince the garrison that we don't need any assistance."

"What about me?" Dankin asked.

Karrde smiled tightly. "You'll stay ready in case they don't believe him. Come on, Councilor."

The Noghri who'd returned their signal was nowhere in sight as they stepped out onto the *Wild Karrde*'s ramp. "Where is he?" Karrde asked, looking around.

"Waiting," Mobvekhar said, putting a hand to the side of his mouth and giving a complex whistle. An answering whistle came, shifted into a complex warble. "Our identity is confirmed," he said. "He bids us come quickly. The others are no more than a quarter hour ahead."

A quarter hour. Leia stared out at the starlit darkness of the mountain. Too late to warn them, but maybe not too late to help. "Come on—we're wasting time," she said.

"Just a minute," Karrde said, looking past her shoulder. "We have to wait for—ah."

Leia turned. Coming down the corridor toward them from the aft section of the ship was a middle-aged man with a pair of long-legged quadruped animals in tow. "Here you go, Capt'," the man said, holding out the leashes.

"Thank you, Chin," Karrde said, taking them as he squatted down to scratch both animals briefly behind the ears. "I don't believe you've met my pet vornskrs, Councilor. This one's named Drang; the somewhat more aloof one there is Sturm. On Myrkr they use the Force to hunt their prey Here, they're going to use it to find Mara. Right?"

The vornskrs made a strange sound, rather like a cackling purr. "Good," Karrde said, straightening up again. "I believe we're ready now, Councilor. Shall we go?"

CHAPTER 25

THE ALARMS WERE still hooting in the distance as Han carefully leaned one eye around the corner. According to the floor plans Artoo had pulled up, this should be the major outer defense monitor station in this sector of the garrison. There were likely to be guards, and those guards were likely to be alert.

He was right on both counts. Five meters away down the entry corridor, flanking a heavy blast door, stood a pair of stormtroopers. And they were alert enough to notice the skulking stranger looking at them and to snap their blaster rifles up into firing position.

The smart thing to do—the thing any reasonably non-suicidal person would do—would be to duck back behind the corner before the shooting started. Instead, Han gripped the corner with his free hand, using the leverage to throw himself completely across the entry corridor. He made it to the other side millimeters ahead of the tracking blaster bolts, flattening himself against the wall as the rapid fire blew out chunks of paneling metal behind him.

They were still firing as Chewbacca leaned around the corner Han had just left and ended the discussion with two quick bowcaster shots.

"Good job, Chewie," Han grunted, throwing a quick look behind him and then slipping back around the corner. The stormtroopers were out of the fight, all right, leaving nothing in their way but a massive metal door.

Which, like the stormtroopers themselves, was no big deal. At least, not for them. "Ready?" he asked, dropping into a half-crouch at one side of the door and raising his blaster. There would be another pair of guards inside.

"Ready," Luke confirmed. There was the *snap-hiss* of the kid's lightsaber, and the brilliant green blade whipped past Han's head to slice horizontally through the heavy metal of the blast door. Somewhere along the way it caught the internal release mechanism, and as Luke finished the cut the top part of the door shot up along its track into the ceiling.

From the way the stormtroopers were facing the door, it was clear they'd heard the short fight outside. It was also clear that they hadn't expected anyone to be coming through this soon. Han shot one of them as he tried to bring his blaster rifle to bear; Luke lunged half over the bottom part of the door, lightsaber swinging, and took out the other.

The group of Imperials manning their sensor consoles weren't expecting company, either. They were fumbling for sidearms and scrambling for cover as Han and Chewbacca took them out. A dozen shots after that, the room had been reduced to a smoldering collection of junk.

"That ought to do it," Han decided. "Better get lost before the reinforcements get here."

But between the riot down at the main entrance and the wandering band of Myneyrshi, Imperial response time was down. The three intruders made it back along the corridor to the emergency stairway and three levels down to the pump room where they'd left the others.

Two of the Noghri were standing silent guard just inside the door as Han keyed it open. "Any trouble?" Lando called from somewhere in the tangle of pipes that seemed to fill two thirds of the room.

"Not really," Han said as Chewbacca closed and locked the door behind them. "Wouldn't want to try it again, though."

Lando grunted. "I don't think you'll have to. They should be adequately convinced that there's a major aerial attack on the way."

"Let's hope so," Han said, stepping around to where Lando was fiddling with an archaic-looking control board. Artoo was plugged into a computer socket on the side of the board, while Threepio hovered off to the side like a nervous mother bird. "Vintage stuff, huh?"

"You've got that," Lando agreed. "I think the Emperor must have just picked up the cloning complex and dropped it in here whole."

Artoo gibbered indignantly. "Right—including the programming," Lando said dryly. "I know a little about this stuff, Han, but not enough to do any permanent damage. I think we're going to have to use the explosives."

"Fine with me," Han said. He would have hated lugging them all the way across Wayland for nothing, anyway. "Where's Mara?"

"Out there," Lando said, nodding toward another door half hidden by the pipes. "In the main room."

"Let's check it out, Luke," Han said. He didn't like the idea of Mara wandering around alone in this place. "Chewie, stay here with Lando. See if there's anything worth blowing up."

Crossing to the door, he keyed it open. Beyond was a wide circular walkway running around the inside of what seemed to be a huge natural cavern. Directly ahead, framed against a massive equipment column that extended downward from the ceiling through the center of the cavern, Mara was standing at the walkway's railing. "This the place?" he asked her, glancing around as he started toward her. About twenty other doors opened up onto the walkway at more or less regular intervals, and there were four retractable bridges extending out to a work platform encircling the central equipment column. Aside from a couple of their Noghri skulking around doing guard duty there was no one else in sight.

But there were sounds. A muted hum of machinery and

voices was coming from somewhere, punctuated by the faint
clicks of relays and a strange rhythmic pulsing or whooshing
sound. Like the whole cavern was breathing . . .

"It's the place," Mara confirmed, her voice sounding
strange. Maybe she thought it sounded like breathing, too.
"Come and see."

Han threw a glance at Luke, and together they stepped to
Mara's side and looked down over the railing.

And it was, indeed, the place.

The cavern was huge, extending downward at least ten stories below their walkway. It was laid out like a sport arena,
with each level being a kind of circular balcony running
around the inside of the cavern. Each balcony was a little
wider than the one above it, extending further into the center
of the cavern and making for a smaller hole around the big
equipment column. There were pipes everywhere: huge ones
coming off the ducts of the central column, smaller ones running around the edges of each of the balconies, and little ones
feeding off them into the neatly arranged metal circles that
filled the balconies and main floor.

Thousands of little circles. Each one the top cover plate of
a Spaarti cloning cylinder.

Beside Han, Luke made a strange sound in the back of his
throat. "It's hard to believe," he said, sounding about halfway
between awestruck and dumbfounded.

"Believe it," Han advised him grimly, pulling out his macrobinoculars and focusing them on the main floor below. The
ductwork blocked a lot of the view, but he could catch glimpses
of men in medtech and guard uniforms scurrying around.
They were on some of the balconies, too. "They're stirred up
like a rats' nest down there," he said. "Stormtroopers on the
main floor and everything."

He threw a sideways look at Mara. Her expression was
tight as she stared down at the cloning tanks, with the haunted
look of someone gazing back into the past. "Bring back memories?" he asked.

"Yes," she said mechanically. She stood there a moment longer, then slowly straightened up. "But we can't allow it to stand."

"Glad you agree," Han said, studying her face. She looked and sounded okay now, but there was a lot of stuff going on under the surface. *Hold it together, kid,* he told her silently. *Just a little longer, okay?* "That column in the middle looks like our best shot. You know anything about it?"

She looked across the cavern. "Not really." She hesitated. "But there might be another way. The Emperor wasn't one for leaving things behind for other people to use. Not if he could help it."

Han threw a glance at Luke. "You mean this whole place might have a self-destruct?"

"It's possible," she said, that haunted look back in her eyes again. "If so, the control will be up in the throne room. I could go and take a look."

"I don't know," Han said, looking down into the cloning cavern. It was an awfully big place for them to take on with a single sack of explosives—he'd give her that much. A destruct switch would simplify things a lot. But the idea of Mara and her memories up there in the Emperor's throne room didn't sound so good, either. "Thanks, but I don't think any of us ought to go wandering around this place alone."

"I'll go with her," Luke volunteered. "She's right—it's worth checking out."

"It'll be safe enough," Mara added. "There's a service-droid turbolift along the walkway that'll get us most of the way there. Most of the Imperials' attention should be focused on the riot at the entrance, anyway."

Han grimaced. "All right, get going," he growled. "Don't forget to let us know before you pull the switch, okay?"

"We won't," Luke assured him with a tight grin. "Come on, Mara."

They headed down the walkway. "Where are they going?" Lando asked from behind Han.

"Emperor's throne room," Han said. "She thinks he might have put a self-destruct switch up there. You find anything?"

"Artoo's finally got a connection into the main computer," Lando told him. "He's looking for schematics of that thing." He gestured toward the central column.

"We can't wait," Han decided, turning back as Chewbacca emerged from the pump room with their bag of explosives over one shoulder. "Chewie, you and Lando take one of those bridges across and get busy."

"Right," Lando said, taking a cautious look over the railing. "What about you?"

"I'm going to go lock us in," Han told him, pointing to the other doors opening out onto the walkway. "You—Noghri—come here."

The two Noghri who'd been standing guard moved silently to him as Lando and Chewbacca headed toward the nearest bridge. "Your command, Han clan Solo?" one of them asked.

"You—stay here," he told the nearest one. "Watch for trouble. You—" He pointed to the other. "Help me seal off those doors. One good blaster shot into each control box ought to do it. I'll go this way; you go the other."

He was about two thirds of the way around his side of the walkway when he heard something over the eerie mechanical breathing sounds of the cavern below him. Looking back, he saw Threepio calling and beckoning to him from the pump room door. "Great," he muttered. Leave it to Threepio, and sooner or later he'd make a mess of it. Finishing the door he was on, he turned and hurried back.

"Captain Solo!" Threepio gushed in relief as Han came up to him. "Thank the Maker. Artoo says—"

"What are you trying to do?" Han snapped. "Bring the whole garrison down on us?"

"Of course not, sir. But Artoo says—"

"You want to talk to me, you come out and find me. Right?"

"Yes, sir. But Artoo says—"

"If you don't know where to look, you use your comlink,"

Han said, jabbing a finger at the little cylinder the droid was clutching. "That's why you've got one. You don't just shout around. You got that?"

"Yes, sir," Threepio said, his mechanical patience sounding more than a little strained. "May I continue?"

Han sighed. So much for the lecture. He'd do better talking to a bantha. "Yeah, what is it?"

"It's about Master Luke," Threepio said. "I overheard one of the Noghri say that he and Mara Jade were on their way to the Emperor's throne room."

"Yeah. So?"

"Well, sir, in the course of his inquiries Artoo has just learned that the Jedi Master Joruus C'baoth is imprisoned in that area."

Han stared at him. "What do you mean, that area? Isn't he in the detention center?"

"No, sir," Threepio said. "As I said—"

"Why didn't you say so?" Han demanded, yanking out his comlink and thumbing it on.

And just as fast thumbing it off. "The comlinks appear to be inoperable," Threepio said primly. "I discovered that when I attempted to contact you."

"Great," Han snarled, the burst of jamming static still echoing in his ears as he looked around. Luke and Mara, walking right into C'baoth's arms. And no way to warn them.

No way except one. "Keep Artoo busy looking for those schematics," he told Threepio, shoving the comlink back into his belt. "While he's at it, tell him to see if he can find out where the jamming is coming from. If he can, send a couple of the Noghri to try to get rid of it. Then get out to that work platform and tell Chewie and Lando where I've gone."

"Yes, sir," Threepio said, sounding a little surprised by the flurry of orders and command authority. "Pardon me, sir, but where *will* you have gone?"

"Where do you think?" Han retorted over his shoulder as he started down the walkway. It never failed, he thought sourly.

One way or the other, no matter where they were or what they were doing, somehow he always wound up chasing off after Luke.

And it was starting to look more and more like a good thing he'd come along.

"ALL RIGHT, *GARRET'S GOLD*, hatchways here are sealed," the controller's voice said. "Stand by to receive outbound course data."

"Acknowledged, Control," Aves said, easing the *Etherway* back from the docking arm and starting a leisurely turn. They were ready here; and from the looks of things, so was everyone else.

"There he is," Gillespee muttered, pointing out the viewport. "Right on schedule."

"You sure that's Mazzic?" Aves asked, peering out at the ship.

"Pretty sure," Gillespee said. "Want me to try giving him a call?"

Aves shrugged, looking around the shipyards. They'd set up the rest of the group with a good encrypt code, but it wouldn't be a smart idea to tempt trouble by using it before they had to. "Let's hold off a minute," he told Gillespee. "Wait until we've got something to talk about."

The words were barely out of his mouth when the whole thing went straight to hell.

"Star Destroyers!" Faughn barked from the comm console. "Coming in from lightspeed."

"Vectors?" Gillespee snapped.

"Don't bother," Aves told him, a cold knife twisting in his gut. He could see the Star Destroyers ahead, all right, appearing out of hyperspace at the edge of the shipyards. And the Dreadnaughts, and the Lancer Frigates, and the Strike Cruisers, and the TIE squadrons. A complete assault fleet, and then some.

And practically every fighting ship of Karrde's smuggler confederation was here. Right in the middle of it.

"So it *was* a trap," Gillespee said, his voice icy calm.

"I guess so," Aves said, staring out at the armada still moving into formation. A formation that seemed wrong, somehow.

"Aves, Gillespee, this is Mazzic," the other smuggler's voice came over the comm. "Looks like we've been sold out after all. I'm not going to surrender. How about you?"

"I think they deserve to lose at least a couple of Star Destroyers for this," Gillespee agreed.

"That was my idea," Mazzic said. "Too bad Karrde isn't here to see us go out in a blaze of glory."

He paused, and Aves could feel Gillespee's and Faughn's eyes on him. They would, he knew, go to their deaths believing Karrde had betrayed them. All of them would. "I'm with you, too," he told the others quietly. "If you want, Mazzic, you can have command."

"Thanks," Mazzic said. "I was going to take it anyway. Stand by: we might as well deliver our first punch together."

Aves took one last look at the armada . . . and suddenly he had it. "Hold it," he snapped. "Mazzic—everyone—hold it. That assault force isn't here for us."

"What are you talking about?" Gillespee demanded.

"Those Interdictor Cruisers out there," Aves said. "Out past that Star Destroyer group—see them? Look at their positioning."

There was a moment of silence. Mazzic got it first. "That's not an enclosure configuration," he said.

"You're right, it's not," Gillespee agreed. "Look—you can see a second group of them further back."

"It's an entrapment configuration," Mazzic said, sounding like he didn't believe his own words. "They're setting up to pull someone out of hyperspace. And then keep him here long enough to pound him."

Aves looked at Gillespee, found him looking back. "No,"

Gillespee breathed. "You don't suppose . . . ? I thought they were supposed to be hitting Tangrene."

"So did I," Aves told him grimly, the twisting knife back in his gut. "I guess we were wrong."

"Or else Thrawn is." Gillespee looked out at the armada and shook his head. "No. Probably not."

"All right, let's not panic," Mazzic said. "If the New Republic comes, it just means that much more to occupy the Imperials' attention. Let's stay on schedule and see what happens."

"Right," Aves sighed. Square in the middle of an Imperial base during a New Republic attack. Terrific.

"Tell you something, Aves," Gillespee commented. "If we get out of this, I'm going to go have some words with your boss."

"No argument." Aves looked out at Thrawn's armada. "Matter of fact, I think maybe I'll go with you."

CAREFULLY, MARA EASED her head out of the emergency stairway and took a look into the corridor beyond. The caution was wasted; this level was as deserted as the three below it had been. "All clear," she murmured, stepping out into the corridor.

"No guards here, either?" Skywalker asked, looking around as he joined her.

"No point to it," she told him. "Except for the throne room and the royal chambers, there was never much of anything on these top levels."

"I guess there still isn't. Where's this private turbo-lift?"

"To the right and around that corner," she said, pointing with her blaster.

More from habit than any real need, she tried to keep her footsteps quiet as she led the way down the corridor. She reached the cross corridor and turned into it.

There, ten meters dead ahead, two stormtroopers stood flanking the turbolift door, their blaster rifles already lifting to track toward her.

Half a step into the corridor, all her momentum going the wrong direction, there was nowhere for Mara to go but down. She dived for the deck, firing toward them as she fell. One of the stormtroopers toppled back as a burst of flame erupted in his chest armor. The second rifle swung toward her face—

And jerked reflexively away as Skywalker's lightsaber came spinning down the corridor toward him.

It didn't do any real damage, of course—at that distance, and without the Force, Skywalker wasn't that good a shot. But it did a fine job of distracting the stormtrooper, and that was all Mara needed. Even as the Imperial ducked away from the whirling blade, she caught him with two clean shots. He hit the deck and stayed there.

"I guess they don't want anyone going in there," Skywalker said, coming up beside her.

"I guess not," Mara agreed, ignoring the hand he offered and getting up on her own. "Come on."

The turbolift car had been locked at this level, but it took Mara only a minute to release it. There were only four stops listed: the one they were on, the emergency shuttle hangar, the royal chambers, and the throne room itself. She keyed for the last, and the door slid shut behind them. The trip upward was a short one, and a few seconds later the door on the opposite side of the car slid open. Bracing herself, Mara stepped out.

Into the Emperor's throne room . . . and into a flood of memories.

It was all here, just as she remembered it. The muted side-lights and brooding darkness the Emperor had found so conducive to meditation and thought. The raised section of floor at the far end of the chamber, allowing him to look down from his throne as visitors climbed the staircase into his presence. Viewscreens on the walls on either side of the throne, darkened now, which had enabled him to keep track of the details of his domain.

And for an overview of that domain . . .

She turned to her left, gazing over the railing of the walkway into the huge open space that faced the throne. Floating there in the darkness, a blaze of light twenty meters across, was the galaxy.

Not the standard galaxy hologram any school or shipping business might own. Not even the more precise versions that could be found only in the war rooms of select sector military headquarters. This hologram was sculpted in exquisite and absolutely unique detail, with a single accurately positioned spot of light for each of the galaxy's hundred billion stars. Political regions were delineated by subtle encirclements of color: the Core systems, the Outer Rim Territories, Wild Space, the Unknown Regions. From his throne the Emperor could manipulate the image, highlighting a chosen sector, locating a single system, or tracking a military campaign.

It was as much a work of art as it was a tool. Grand Admiral Thrawn would love it.

And with that thought, the memories of the past faded reluctantly into the realities of the present. Thrawn was in command now, a man who wanted to re-create the Empire in his own image. Wanted it badly enough to unleash a new round of Clone Wars if that would gain it for him.

She took a deep breath. "All right," she said. The words echoed around the chamber, pushing the memories still further away. "If it's here, it'll be built into the throne."

With an obvious effort, Skywalker pulled his gaze away from the hologram galaxy. "Let's take a look."

They headed down the ten-meter walkway that led from the turbolift into the main part of the throne room, walking beneath the overhead catwalk that ran across the front edge of the hologram pit and between the raised guard platforms flanking the stairway. Mara glanced at the platforms as she and Skywalker walked up the steps to the upper level, remembering the red-cloaked Imperial guards who had once stood there in silent watchfulness. Beneath the upper-level floor, visible between the steps as they climbed, the Emperor's monitor and control area was dark and silent. Aside from the galaxy hologram, all of the systems up here appeared to have been shut down.

They reached the top of the steps and headed across toward the throne itself, turned away from them toward the polished rock wall behind it. Mara was looking at it, wondering why the Emperor had left it facing away from his galaxy, when it began to turn around.

She grabbed Skywalker's arm, snapping her blaster up to point at the throne. The massive chair completed its turn—

"So at last you have come to me," Joruus C'baoth said gravely, gazing out at them from the depths of the throne. "I knew you would. Together we will teach the galaxy what it means to serve the Jedi."

CHAPTER 26

"I KNEW YOU WOULD be coming to me tonight," C'baoth said, rising slowly from the throne to face them. "From the moment you left Coruscant, I knew you would come. That was why I set this night for the people of my city to attack my oppressors."

"That wasn't necessary," Luke told him, taking an involuntary step backward as the memories of those near-disastrous days on Jomark came rushing back to him. C'baoth had tried there to subtly corrupt him to the dark side . . . and when he'd failed at that, he'd tried to kill Luke and Mara both.

But he wouldn't be trying that again. Not here. Not without the Force.

"Of course it was necessary," C'baoth said. "You needed a distraction to gain entrance to my prison. And they, like all lesser beings, needed purpose. What better purpose could they have than the honor of dying in the service of the Jedi?"

Beside him, Mara muttered something. "I think you have that backwards," Luke said. "The Jedi were the guardians of peace. The servants of the Old Republic, not its masters."

"Which is why they and the Old Republic failed, Jedi Skywalker," C'baoth said, jabbing a finger toward him in emphasis. "Why they failed, and why they died."

"The Old Republic survived a thousand generations," Mara put in. "That doesn't sound like failure to me."

"Perhaps not," C'baoth said with obvious disdain. "You are young, and do not yet see clearly."

"And you do, of course?"

C'baoth smiled at her. "Oh, yes, my young apprentice," he said softly. "I do indeed. As will you."

"Don't count on it," Mara growled. "We aren't here to get you out."

"The Force does not rely on what you think are your goals," C'baoth said. "Nor do the true masters of the Force. Whether you knew it or not, you came here at my summons."

"You just go ahead and believe that," Mara said, motioning to the side with her blaster. "Move over there."

"Of course, my young apprentice." C'baoth took three steps in the indicated direction. "She has great strength of will, Jedi Skywalker," he added to Luke as Mara moved warily over to the throne and crouched down to examine the armrest control boards. "She will be a great power in the galaxy which we shall build."

"No," Luke said, shaking his head. This was, perhaps, his last chance to bring the insane Jedi back. To save him, as he had saved Vader aboard the second Death Star. "You aren't in any shape to build anything, Master C'baoth. You're not well. But I can help you if you'll let me."

C'baoth's face darkened. "How dare you say such things?" he demanded. "How dare you even *think* such blasphemy about the great Jedi Master C'baoth?"

"But that's just it," Luke said gently. "You're not the Jedi Master C'baoth. Not the original one, anyway. The proof is there in the *Katana*'s records. Jorus C'baoth died a long time ago during the Outbound Flight Project."

"Yet I am here."

"Yes," Luke nodded. "*You* are. But not Jorus C'baoth, You see, you're his clone."

C'baoth's whole body went rigid. "No," he said. "No. That can't be."

Luke shook his head. "There's no other explanation. Surely that thought has occurred to you before."

C'baoth took a long, shuddering breath . . . and then, abruptly, he threw his head back and laughed.

"Watch him," Mara snapped, eyeing the old man warily over the throne's armrest. "He pulled this same stunt on Jomark, remember?"

"It's all right," Luke said. "He can't hurt us."

"Ah, Skywalker, Skywalker," C'baoth said, shaking his head. "You, too? Grand Admiral Thrawn, the New Republic, and now you. What is this sudden fascination with clones and cloning?"

He barked another laugh; and then, without warning, turned deadly serious. "He does not understand, Jedi Skywalker," he said earnestly. "Not Grand Admiral Thrawn—not any of them. The true power of the Jedi is not in these simple tricks of matter and energy. The true might of the Jedi is that we alone of all those in the galaxy have the power to grow beyond ourselves. To extend ourselves into all the reaches of the universe."

Luke glanced at Mara, got a shrug and puzzled look in return. "We don't understand, either," he told C'baoth. "What do you mean?"

C'baoth took a step toward him. "I have done it, Jedi Skywalker," he whispered, his eyes glittering in the dim light. "With General Covell. What even the Emperor never did. I took his mind in my hands and altered it. Re-formed it and rebuilt it into my own image."

Luke felt a cold shiver run through him. "What do you mean, rebuilt it?"

C'baoth nodded, a secret sort of smile playing around his lips. "Yes—rebuilt it. And that was only the start. Beneath us, down in the depths of the mountain, the future army of the

Jedi even now stands in readiness to serve us. What I did with General Covell I will do again, and again, and again. Because what Grand Admiral Thrawn has never realized is that the army he thinks he is creating for himself he is instead creating for me."

And suddenly Luke understood. The clones growing down in that cavern weren't just physically identical to their original templet. Their minds were identical, too, or close enough to be only minor variations of the same pattern. If C'baoth could learn how to break the mind of any one of them, he could do the same to all the clones in that group.

Luke looked at Mara again. She understood, too. "You still think he can be saved?" she demanded grimly.

"I need no one to save me, Mara Jade," C'baoth told her. "Tell me, do you really believe I would simply stand by and allow Grand Admiral Thrawn to imprison me this way?"

"I didn't think he'd asked your permission," Mara bit out, stepping away from the throne. "There's nothing here for us, Skywalker. Let's get out of here."

"I did not grant you permission to leave," C'baoth said, his voice suddenly loud and regal. He raised his hand, and Luke saw that he was holding a small cylinder. "And you shall not."

Mara gestured with her blaster. "You're not going to stop us with *that*," she said with thinly veiled contempt. "A remote activator has to have something to activate."

"And so it does," C'baoth said, smiling thinly. "I had my soldiers prepare it for me. Before I sent them outside the mountain with the weapons and orders for my people."

"Sure." Mara took a step back toward the stairs, throwing a wary glance at the ceiling above her as her left hand found the guardrail that separated the raised section of the throne room from the lower level. "We'll take your word for it."

C'baoth shook his head. "You won't have to" he said softly, pressing the switch. In the back of Luke's mind, something distant and very alien seemed to shriek in agony—

And suddenly, impossibly, he felt a surge of awareness and strength fill him. As if he were waking up from a deep sleep, or stepping from a dark room into the light.

The Force was again with him.

"Mara!" he snapped. But it was too late. Mara's blaster had already wrenched itself from her grip and been flung back across the room; and even as Luke leaped toward her C'baoth's outstretched hand erupted into a brilliant blaze of blue-white lightning.

The blast caught Mara square in the chest, throwing her backward to slam into the guardrail behind her. "Stop it!" Luke shouted, getting in front of her and igniting his light-saber. C'baoth ignored him, firing a second burst. Luke caught most of it on his lightsaber blade, grimacing as the part he missed jolted through his muscles. C'baoth fired a third burst, and a fourth, and a fifth—

And then, abruptly, he lowered his hands. "You will not presume to give me commands, Jedi Skywalker," he said, his voice strangely petulant. "I am the master. You are the servant."

"I'm not your servant," Luke told him, stepping back and throwing a quick look at Mara. She was still pretty much on her feet, clutching the guardrail for support. Her eyes were open but not fully aware, her breath making little moaning sounds as she exhaled between clenched teeth. Laying his free hand on her shoulder, wincing at the stink of ozone, Luke began a quick probe of her injuries.

"You are indeed my servant," C'baoth said, the earlier pet-ulance replaced now by a sort of haughty grandeur. "As is she. Leave her alone, Jedi Skywalker. She required a lesson, and she has now learned it."

Luke didn't answer. None of her burns seemed too bad, but her muscles were still twitching uncontrollably. Reaching out with the Force, he tried to draw away some of the pain.

"I said leave her alone," C'baoth repeated, his voice echo-ing eerily across the throne room. "Her life is not in danger.

Save your strength rather for the trial that awaits you." Dramatically, he lifted a hand and pointed.

Luke turned to look. There, silhouetted against the shimmering galaxy holo, stood a figure dressed in what looked like the same brown robe C'baoth was wearing. A figure that seemed somehow familiar . . .

"There is no choice, my young Jedi," C'baoth said, his voice almost gentle now. "Don't you understand? You must serve me, or we will not be able to save the galaxy from itself. You must therefore face death and emerge at my side . . . or you must die that another may take your place." He lifted his eyes to the figure and beckoned. "Come," he called. "And face your destiny."

The figure moved forward toward the stairs, unhooking a lightsaber from his belt as he came. With the blaze of light from the hologram behind him, the figure's face was still impossible to make out.

Luke stepped away from Mara, a strange and unpleasant buzzing pressure beginning to form against his mind. There was something disturbingly familiar about this confrontation. As if he were about to face someone or something he'd faced once before . . .

Abruptly, the memory clicked. Dagobah—his Jedi training—the dark side cave Yoda had sent him into. His brief dreamlike battle with a vision of Darth Vader . . .

Luke caught his breath, a horrible suspicion squeezing his heart. But no—the silent figure approaching him wasn't tall enough to be Vader. But then who . . . ?

And then the figure stepped into the light . . . and, too late, Luke remembered how that dream battle in the dark side cave had ended. Vader's mask had shattered, and the face behind it had been Luke's own.

As was the face that gazed emotionlessly up at him now.

Luke felt himself moving back from the steps, his mind frozen with shock and the buzzing pressure growing against it. "Yes, Jedi Skywalker," C'baoth said quietly from behind him.

"He is you. Luuke Skywalker, created from the hand you left behind in the Cloud City on Bespin. Wielding the lightsaber you lost there."

Luke glanced at the weapon in the clone's hands. It was his, all right. The lightsaber Obi-Wan had told him his father had left for him. "Why?" he managed.

"To bring you to true understanding," C'baoth said gravely. "And because your destiny must be fulfilled. One way or another, you must serve me."

Luke threw a quick glance at him. C'baoth was watching him, his eyes glowing with anticipation. And with madness.

And in that moment, the clone Luuke struck.

He leaped to the top of the stairway, igniting his lightsaber and slashing the blue-white blade viciously toward Luke's chest. Luke jumped to the side, whipping his own weapon up to block the attack. The blades came together with an impact that threw him off balance and nearly tore the lightsaber from his grip. The clone Luuke jumped after him, lightsaber already swinging to the attack; reaching out to the Force, Luke threw himself backwards, flipping over the guardrail and onto one of the raised guard platforms rising from the lower part of the throne room floor. He needed time to think and plan, and to find a way past the distraction of the buzzing in his mind.

But the clone Luuke wasn't going to give him that time. Stepping to the guardrail, he hurled his lightsaber downward at the base of the platform Luke was standing on. It wasn't a clean hit—the blade probably sliced through only half of the base—but it was enough to throw the platform into a sudden tilt. Reaching out again to the Force, Luke did another backflip, trying to reach the overhead catwalk that spanned the throne room five meters behind him.

But the distance was too great, or else his mind too distracted by the buzzing to properly draw on the Force. The back of his knee hit the edge of the catwalk, and instead of landing on his feet he flipped over to slam into it on his back.

"I did not wish to do this to you, Jedi Skywalker," C'baoth's voice called out. "I do not wish it still. Join me—let me teach you. Together we can save the galaxy from the lesser peoples who would destroy it."

"No," Luke said hoarsely, grabbing a support strut and pulling himself up as he fought to catch his breath. The clone Luuke had retrieved his lightsaber now, and was starting down the stairs toward him.

The clone. *His* clone. Was that what was causing this strange pressure in his mind? The close presence of an exact duplicate that was itself drawing on the Force?

He didn't know, any more than he knew what C'baoth's purpose was in throwing the two of them together. Obi-Wan and Master Yoda had both warned him that killing in anger or hatred would lead toward the dark side. Would killing a clone duplicate of himself do the same thing?

Or had C'baoth meant something entirely different? Had he meant that killing his own clone would drive Luke insane?

Either way, it wasn't something Luke was anxious to find out firsthand. And it occurred to him that he really didn't have to. He could drop off the far side of the catwalk, get to the turbolift he and Mara had come up on, and escape.

Leaving Mara here to face C'baoth alone.

He raised his eyes. Mara was still leaning against the guardrail. Possibly not fully conscious. Certainly in no shape to travel.

Setting his teeth together, Luke pulled himself to his feet. Mara had asked him—begged him—to kill her rather than leave her in C'baoth's hands. The least he could do was to stay with her to the end.

Whether it was her end . . . or his.

THE EXPLOSION DRIFTED up from the cavern below like a distant thunderclap, clearly audible and yet curiously dampened.

"You hear that, Chewie?" Lando asked, leaning back to throw a cautious look over the edge of their work platform. "You suppose something down there blew up?"

Chewbacca, his hands full of cables and leads as he dug in and around the support lattice of the equipment column, growled a correction: it hadn't been one large explosion, but many simultaneous small ones. Small blasting disks, or something of equally low power. "You sure?" Lando asked uneasily, peering at the cloning tanks on the balcony one level beneath where they were working. This didn't sound like any normal malfunction.

He stiffened. Thin wisps of smoke could be seen now, rising lazily into the air above the nutrient pipes feeding into the tops of the cloning tanks. A *lot* of wisps of smoke, and they seemed to be rising in a reasonably regular pattern. As if something in each cluster of Spaarti cylinders had blown up . . .

There was the muffled clink of metal on metal behind him. Lando twisted around, to find Threepio stepping gingerly from the bridge onto the work platform, his head tilted to look down into the cavern. "Is that smoke?" the droid asked, sounding like he wasn't sure he really wanted to know.

"Looks like smoke to me," Lando agreed. "What are you doing here?"

"Ah . . ." Resolutely, the droid looked away from whatever was happening below. "Artoo has found the schematics for that equipment column," he said, offering Lando a data card. "He suggests that the negative flow coupler on the main power line might be worth investigating."

"We'll keep that in mind," Lando said, sliding the data card into his data pad and throwing a quick look over the platform railing as he handed the data pad to Chewbacca. He and the Wookiee weren't all that visible against the drab colors of the equipment column and the rocky cavern ceiling two meters above them, but Threepio would stand out like a lump of gold on a mud flat. "Now get out of here before someone spots you."

"Oh," Threepio said, stiffening a little more than usual. "Yes, of course. Also, Artoo has located the source of the comlink jamming in this vicinity. Captain Solo requested that if we found that—"

"Right," Lando interrupted him. Was that someone moving behind one of the banks of Spaarti cylinders on the next level down? "I remember. You and Artoo go ahead. And take the Noghri with you."

The droid seemed taken aback. "Artoo and me? But sir—"

And with a sound like a spitting tauntaun, a brilliant ripple of blue flashed upward from the cloning balcony below.

"Stun blast!" Lando barked, dropping flat on the work platform and feeling the heavy thud as Chewbacca landed beside him. A second stun blast rippled out, ricocheting off the column above his head as he yanked out his blaster. "Threepio, get out of here."

The droid didn't need any encouragement. "Yes, sir," he called over his shoulder, already scuttling away down the bridge.

Chewbacca growled a question. "Over there somewhere," Lando told him, gesturing with his blaster. "Watch it, though, they're bound to have more moving in."

A third stun blast slammed uselessly into the underside of the work platform, and this time Lando spotted the soldier skulking behind one of the cloning cylinders. He fired twice, dropping the Imperial to the floor and making a mess of the cloning cylinder itself. Behind him, another blue ripple sizzled by overhead, followed a split second later by the heavy bark of Chewbacca's bowcaster.

Lando grinned tightly to himself. They were in trouble, but not nearly as much as they could have been. As long as they were sitting up next to all this critical equipment, the Imperials didn't dare use anything stronger than stun settings on them. But at the same time, the Imperials themselves had absolutely no cover down there on the balconies except the cloning tanks. Which meant all they really could do was stay there, probably not bothering their targets any, and get themselves and a lot of valuable equipment blown to bits.

Or else they could simply come one level up and blast away at them from an angle where the heavy metal of the work platform wouldn't keep getting in their way.

From the other side of the equipment column, Chewbacca rumbled: the Imperials were pulling back. "Probably coming up here," Lando agreed, glancing around their level at the doors lining the outer walkway. They looked pretty strong, probably only a step or two down from warship-type blast doors. If Han and the Noghri had done a good job of sealing them off, they ought to hold off even a determined group of stormtroopers for a while.

Except for the door to the pump room that Artoo had been working in. Han would have left that one open for them to get out through.

Lando grimaced; but there was nothing for it. Bracing his gun hand against the bottom section of the railing, he took careful aim at the door's control box and fired. The box cover flashed and crumpled, and for a couple of seconds he could see a faint sputtering of sparks through the smoke.

And that was that. The Imperials were locked out. And he and Chewbacca were locked in.

Keeping low, he crept around to the other side of the column. Chewbacca was already back at work, his grease-slicked hands digging back through the cables and pipes, the data pad on the floor by his feet. "Making any progress?" Lando asked.

Chewbacca growled, tapping at the data pad awkwardly with one foot, and Lando craned his neck to look. It was a schematic of a section of the power cable, showing a coupling with eight leads coming off it.

And just above the coupling, clearly marked, a positive flow regulator. "Uh-*huh*," Lando said, a not entirely pleasant sensation running through him. "You're not by any chance thinking of running that into the negative flow coupler Threepio mentioned, are you?"

In answer, the Wookiee withdrew his hand from the tangle of cables, pulling the partially disconnected negative flow coupler with it. "Wait a minute," Lando said, eyeing the coupler warily. He'd heard stories about what happened when you ran a negative flow coupler into a positive flow detonator, and using a positive flow regulator instead of a detonator didn't sound a lot safer. "What exactly is this supposed to do?"

The Wookiee told him. He'd been right: using a regulator wasn't any safer. In fact, it was a whole lot more dangerous. "Let's not go overboard on this, Chewie," he warned. "We came here to destroy the cloning cylinders, not bring the whole storehouse down on top of us."

Chewbacca rumbled insistently. "All right, fine, we'll keep it in reserve," Lando sighed.

The Wookiee grunted agreement and got back to work. Grimacing, Lando laid his blaster down and pulled two charges out of their explosives bag. He might as well keep himself busy while he tried to figure out how they were going to get out through locked blast doors and a corridor full of storm-troopers.

And if they wound up falling back on Chewbacca's power core arhythmic resonance scheme . . . well, in that case, getting out of here would probably become an academic question anyway.

Prying open a gap in the power cables with one hand, he got to work.

THE TIMING COUNTER buzzed its five-second warning, and Wedge took a deep breath. This was it. He reached for the hy-perspace levers—

And abruptly, the mottled sky of hyperspace faded into starlines and into stars. Around him, the rest of Rogue Squadron flashed into view, still in formation; ahead, the distinctive light patterns and layout of a shipyard could be seen.

They'd arrived at the Bilbringi shipyards. Only they'd arrived too far out. Which could only mean—

"Battle alert!" Rogue Two snapped. "TIE interceptors coming in—bearing two-nine-three mark twenty."

"All ships—emergency combat status," Admiral Ackbar's gravelly voice cut in on the comm. "Defensive configuration: Starfighter Command to screen positions. It appears to be a trap."

"Sure does," Wedge muttered to himself, pulling hard to portside and risking a quick look at his displays. Sure enough, there were the Interdictor Cruisers that had brought them out of hyperspace, staying well back from the massive fleets that were beginning to jockey for battle position. And judging from the way they'd been deployed, the New Republic fleet wasn't going to be jumping to lightspeed anytime soon.

And then the TIE interceptors were on them, and there was no time left to wonder why their carefully planned surprise attack had failed before it had even begun. For the moment the only question was that of survival, one ship and one engagement at a time.

THE STEALTHY FOOTSTEPS came around the corner ten meters away and continued toward him; and Han, pressed painfully back into the slightly recessed doorway that was the only cover for those same ten meters, abandoned the faint hope that his pursuers would miss him and prepared for the inevitable firefight.

They *should* have turned off. In fact, by all rights they shouldn't have been up here at all. From the snatches of status reports he'd been able to catch while passing by deserted checkpoints, it sounded like everyone who could carry a blaster was supposed to be twenty levels down fighting the natives who were running loose through the garrison. These upper levels didn't seem to even be occupied, and there sure wasn't anything up here except maybe C'baoth that needed any protection.

The footsteps were getting closer. It would be just his luck, Han thought sourly, to run into a couple of deserters looking for a place to hide.

And then, maybe five meters away, the footsteps abruptly stopped . . . and in the sudden silence he heard a stifled gasp.

He'd been spotted.

Han didn't hesitate. Pushing hard off the door behind him, he leaped across the corridor, trying to duplicate that trick down at the defense station, or at least do the best he could without Chewbacca here to back him up. There were fewer of them out there than he'd expected, and further to the side than he expected, and he lost a vital half-second as his blaster tracked toward them—

"Han!" Leia shouted. "Don't shoot!"

The sheer surprise of it caught Han's timing straight across the knees, and he slammed rather ingloriously into the wall on the opposite side of the corridor. It was Leia, all right. Even more surprising, Talon Karrde was with her, along with those two vornskr pets of his. "What in blazes are you doing here?" he demanded.

"Luke's in trouble," Leia said breathlessly, rushing forward and giving him a quick, tense hug. "He's ahead somewhere—"

"Whoa, sweetheart," Han assured her, hanging on to her arm as she tried to pull away. "It's okay—we knew the ysalamiri were here going in."

Leia shook her head. "That's just it: they're not. The Force is back. Just before you jumped out of cover."

Han swore under his breath. "C'baoth," he muttered. "Has to be him."

"Yes," Leia said, shivering. "It is."

Han threw a look at Karrde. "I was hired to destroy the Emperor's storehouse," the smuggler said evenly. "I brought Sturm and Drang along to help us find Mara."

Han glanced at the vornskrs. "You have anyone else with you?" he asked Leia.

She shook her head. "We ran into a squad of troops three levels down moving this way. Our two Noghri stayed behind to hold them off."

He looked at Karrde. "How about your people?"

"They're all in the *Wild Karrde*," he said. "Guarding our exit, should we have the chance to use it."

Han grunted. "Then I guess it's just us," he said, shifting his grip on Leia's arm and heading down the corridor. "Come on. They're up in the throne room—I know the way."

And as they ran, he tried not to think about the last time he'd faced a Dark Jedi. In Lando's Cloud City on Bespin, when Vader had tortured him and then had him frozen in carbonite.

Somehow, from what Luke had told him, he didn't expect C'baoth to be even that civilized.

CHAPTER 27

THE LIGHTSABERS FLASHED, blue-white blade against green-white blade, sizzling where they struck each other, slashing through metal and cable where they hit anything else. Gripping the guardrail with both hands, fighting against the turmoil roiling through her own mind, Mara watched in helpless fascination as the battle raged across the throne room floor. It was like a twisted inversion of that last horrifying vision the Emperor had given her at the instant of his destruction nearly six years ago.

Except that this time it wasn't the Emperor who was facing death. It was Skywalker.

And it was no vision. It was real.

"Watch them closely, Mara Jade," C'baoth said from where he stood at the top of the steps, his voice hard yet strangely wistful. "Unless you bow willingly to my authority, you will someday face this same battle."

Mara threw a sideways look at him. C'baoth was watching this duel he'd orchestrated with a fascination that bordered on the grisly. She'd called it, all right, back when she'd first met him on Jomark. The work he'd done for Thrawn had given him a taste of power; and like the Emperor before him, that taste had not been enough.

But unlike the Emperor, he was not going to be content

merely with the control of worlds and armies. His would be a more personal form of empire: minds re-formed and rebuilt into his own conception of what a mind should be.

Which meant that Mara had been right on the other count, too. C'baoth was thoroughly insane.

"It is not insanity to offer the richness of my glory to others," C'baoth murmured. "It is a gift which many would die for."

"You're giving Skywalker a good shot at that part, anyway," Mara bit out, shaking her head to try to clear it. Between her own memories, an echo of the strange buzzing pressure she was picking up from Skywalker's mind, and C'baoth's overbearing presence two meters away, trying to hang on to a line of thought was like trying to fly an airspeeder in a winter windstorm.

But there was a mental pattern the Emperor had taught her long ago, a pattern for those times when he'd wanted his instructions hidden even from Vader. If she could just clear her mind enough to get it in place—

Through the turmoil came a sudden jolt of pain. "Do not attempt to hide your thoughts from me, Mara Jade," C'baoth admonished her sharply. "You are mine now. It is not right for an apprentice to hide her thoughts from her master."

"So I'm already your apprentice, huh?" Mara growled, gritting her teeth against the pain and making another try at the pattern. This time, she made it. "I thought I had at least until I'd knelt at your feet."

"You mock my vision," C'baoth said, his voice darkly petulant. "But you *shall* kneel before me."

"Just like Skywalker will, right? Assuming he lives through this?"

"He will be mine," C'baoth agreed, quietly confident. "As will his sister and her children."

"And then together you'll heal the galaxy," Mara said, watching his face and listening to the turmoil in her mind. Yes;

the barrier seemed to be keeping C'baoth back. Now if she could just hold on to that privacy a little longer . . .

"You disappoint me, Mara Jade," C'baoth said, shaking his head. "Do you truly believe I need to hear your thoughts in order to read your heart? Like the lesser peoples of the galaxy, you seek my destruction. A foolish notion. Did the Emperor teach you nothing about our destiny?"

"He didn't do a good job of reading his own, I know that much," Mara retorted, listening to her heart thudding as she watched C'baoth. If that erratic mind of his decided she was a genuine threat and launched another of those lightning bolt attacks . . .

C'baoth smiled, holding his arms out to the sides. "Do you feel the need to measure your strength against mine, Mara Jade? Come, then, and do so."

For a pair of heartbeats she eyed him, almost tempted to try. He looked so old and helpless; and she had her mental barrier and some of the best unarmed combat training the Empire at its height could provide. It would take just a few seconds. . . .

She took a deep breath and lowered her eyes. No; not now. Not like this. Not with these pressures and distractions spinning through her mind. She'd never make it. "You kill me now and I won't be able to kneel for you," she muttered, letting her shoulders slump in an attitude of defeat.

"Very good," C'baoth purred. "You have wisdom of a sort, after all. Watch, then, and learn."

Mara turned back to the guardrail. But not to watch the lightsaber duel. Somewhere down there was the blaster C'baoth had torn from her grip when he did whatever it was he'd done to the mountain's ysalamiri and gotten to the Force again. If she could find it before C'baoth realized that she hadn't really given up . . .

Across the floor, Skywalker leaped up again to the catwalk. The clone was ready for the move, hurling his lightsaber up-ward right behind him. The blue-white blade missed Skywalker by a hair, slicing instead most of the way through the catwalk floor and one of the support struts holding it to the ceiling. With a tooth-jarring shriek, the strained metal twisted under Skywalker's weight, dumping him back off.

He hit the floor more or less on his feet, dropping down to land on one knee. His hand reached out, and the lightsaber that had been falling toward the clone suddenly changed direction. It arced toward Skywalker's hand—

And stopped dead in midair. Skywalker strained, the muscles of his hand tightening visibly as his mind stretched out. "Not that way, Jedi Skywalker," C'baoth said reprovingly; and Mara glanced over to see that his hand, too, was stretched out toward the errant lightsaber. The clone, for his part, was just standing there in his brown robe, as if he knew that C'baoth would be on his side in this battle.

Maybe he did. Maybe there was nothing left in that body but an extension of C'baoth's own mind.

"This duel must be to the death," C'baoth continued. "It must be weapon against weapon, mind against mind, soul against soul. Anything less will not bring you to the knowledge you must have if you are to properly serve me."

Skywalker was good, all right. With the strange buzzing pressure in his mind he must have known he couldn't match C'baoth strength for strength. Mara felt the subtle change in his concentration; and suddenly he swung his own lightsaber over his shoulder, the green-white blade scything toward a point midway along the other lightsaber handle.

But if C'baoth wouldn't let Skywalker disarm his opponent, he wouldn't let him destroy the weapon, either. Even as the blade sliced downward, a small object shot out of the shadows to Skywalker's right, slamming into his shoulder and deflecting his arm just far enough for his blade to sweep through empty air. An instant later the old Jedi had torn the clone's lightsaber from Skywalker's mental grip, sending it back across the room to its owner. The clone raised it to en guard position;

STAR WARS: THE LAST COMMAND

wearily, Skywalker got to his feet and prepared to continue the battle.

But for the moment Mara wasn't interested in the lightsabers. Lying on the floor, maybe two meters back from Skywalker's feet, was the object C'baoth had thrown at him.

Mara's blaster.

She looked sideways at C'baoth, wondering if he was watching her. He wasn't. In fact, he wasn't looking at much of anything. His eyes were unfocused, staring across the throne room, a strangely childlike smile on his face. "She has come," he said, his voice almost inaudible over the clash of the lightsabers below. "Just as I knew she would." Abruptly, he looked at Mara. "She is here, Mara Jade," he said, pointing dramatically toward the turbolift she and Skywalker had come up.

Frowning, not sure she should take her eyes off him, Mara turned her head to look. The turbolift door slid open and Solo stepped out, his blaster ready. And right behind him—

Mara caught her breath, her whole body going tense. It was Leia Organa Solo, holding a blaster in one hand and her lightsaber in the other. And behind her, his pet vornskrs in front of him on leashes—

It was Karrde.

Organa Solo? And *Karrde*?

"Leia—Han—go back," Skywalker called to them over the clash of the lightsabers as the newcomers moved along the walkway past the galaxy hologram and on into the main part of the throne room. "It's too danger—"

"Welcome, my new apprentice!" C'baoth shouted joyfully, his voice drowning out Skywalker's as it echoed grandly in the open space. "Come to me, Leia Organa Solo. I will teach you the true ways of the Force."

Solo had a different sort of lesson in mind. He reached the end of the walkway, sighted along the barrel of his blaster, and fired.

But even wallowing in self-delusion, a Jedi of C'baoth's

power couldn't be taken out that easily. In a blur of motion, Mara's blaster leaped upward from the floor into the path of the shot, its grip shattering into a shower of sparks as Solo's shot expended its energy there. The second shot was likewise blocked; the third caught the blaster's power pack, turning the weapon into a spectacular fireball. The blaster was torn from Solo's grip before he could fire a fourth.

And C'baoth went berserk.

He screamed, a horrible shriek of rage and betrayal that seemed like it would set the air on fire. Mara jerked back as the piercing sound cut through her ears—

And an instant later nearly fell over the guardrail as the Force equivalent of the scream slammed into her.

It was like nothing she'd ever experienced before; not from Vader, not from the Emperor himself. The utter, animal ferocity—the total loss of every shred of self-control—it was like standing alone in the middle of a sudden violent storm. Wave after wave of fury swept over her, ripping through the mental barrier she'd created and battering her mind with a numbing combination of hatred and pain. Dimly, she saw Skywalker and Organa Solo staggering under the assault; heard Karrde's vornskrs' howling in pain of their own.

And from C'baoth's outstretched hands erupted a blaze of lightning.

Mara winced in sympathetic pain as Solo was thrown backwards into the guardrail at the front of the hologram pit. Through the crackle of the lightning she heard Organa Solo shout her husband's name and jump to his side, dropping her blaster and igniting her lightsaber just in time to catch the third blast of lightning on the green-white blade. Abruptly, C'baoth shifted his aim upward to the damaged catwalk hanging precariously over their heads. The lightning flashed again—

And with a *crack* of exploding metal the center of the catwalk split apart. Pivoting on its last remaining support strut, it toppled ponderously downward toward Organa Solo.

She saw it coming, or maybe Skywalker's training had

taught her how to use the Force to anticipate danger. As the heavy metal swung down on her, she slashed upward with her lightsaber, cutting through the catwalk far enough to the side that the main part missed her and Solo as it swung past to crash into the floor in front of Karrde and the vornskrs. But there was no time for her to get out from under the end she had cut off. It caught her across her head and shoulder, knocking the lightsaber from her hand and hammering her to the floor beside Solo.

"Leia!" Skywalker shouted, throwing an anguished glance at his sister. Suddenly the debilitating buzzing in his mind seemed to be forgotten as his fighting abruptly shifted from groggy defense to furious attack. The clone fell back before the onslaught, barely managing to block Skywalker's blows. He jumped up onto the stairway, hastily backed two steps further up toward C'baoth as Skywalker charged after him, then leaped over onto the remaining guard platform. For a second Mara thought Skywalker was going to pursue him up there, or else cut through the platform base and bring him down.

He didn't do either. Standing halfway up the stairs, a sheen of sweat glistening on his face, he gazed up at C'baoth with an expression that sent a shiver down Mara's back.

"Do you also seek to destroy me, Jedi Skywalker?" C'baoth said, his voice quietly deadly. "For such thoughts are foolish. I could crush you like a small insect beneath my heel."

"Perhaps," Skywalker said, breathing heavily. "But if you do, you'll never have the chance to control my mind."

C'baoth studied him. "What do you want?"

Skywalker jerked his head back toward his sister and Solo. "Let them leave. All of them. Now." His eyes flicked to Mara. "Mara, too."

"And if I do?"

A muscle in Skywalker's cheek twitched. His finger moved, and with a sputtering hiss his lightsaber blade disappeared. "Let them go," he said quietly, "and I'll stay."

———

FROM SOMEWHERE NEARBY a dull thudding noise began, adding an irregular pulsebeat to the eerie breathing sounds whispering through the cloning cavern. A blaster rifle pounding against heavy metal, Lando decided, giving the doors around the walkway a quick look. So far they all seemed secure, but he knew that wouldn't last. The stormtroopers out there weren't firing at the doors just for target practice, and there was bound to be a bag of shaped explosives on their way.

From the other side of the equipment column, Chewbacca rumbled a warning. "I *am* keeping my head down," Lando assured him, peering into the gap between two large ducts at the maze of multicolored wiring and piping beyond. Now, where was that repulsor pump connection again . . . ?

He had located the spot and was reaching in with the charge when the callbeep from his comlink unexpectedly went off, echoed a fraction of a second later from Chewbacca's comlink. Frowning, half expecting it to be some hotshot Imperial tech who'd found his channel, he pulled it out. "Calrissian," he said.

"Ah—General Calrissian," Threepio's precise voice came back. "I see Artoo has been successful in eliminating the jamming. Surprising, actually, given all the trouble which we've been required to—"

"Tell him good job," Lando cut him off. Now was decidedly not the time for a pleasant little chat with Threepio. "Was there anything else?"

"Ah, yes, sir, there is," the droid said. "The Noghri instructed me to ask whether you wish us to return to assist you."

There was another thud, a louder one this time. "I wish you could," Lando sighed. "But you'd never make it back in time." The thud came again, and this time he distinctly saw the door opposite their bridge shake with the impact. "We'll just have to get out of here by ourselves."

From the other side of the work platform, Chewbacca rumbled his less-than-enthusiastic opinion of that. "But if Chewbacca wishes us to return—"

"You won't get here in time," Lando told him firmly. "Tell the Noghri if they want to be useful they should head up to the throne room and give Han a hand."

"It's too late for that," a new voice put in, almost too quiet to hear.

Lando frowned at the comlink. "Han?"

"No, it's Talon Karrde," the other identified himself. "I came in with Councilor Organa Solo. We're up in the throne room—"

"*Leia's* here?" Lando asked. "What in—?"

"Shut up and listen," Karrde cut him off. "That Jedi Master of Luke's—Joruus C'baoth—is up here, too. He's taken out Solo and Organa Solo both, and has Skywalker fighting what looks to be a clone of himself. He's not paying any attention to me at the moment—there's some kind of face-off going on up there. But he would the minute I tried anything."

"I thought Luke said the Force was being blocked."

"It was. Somehow, C'baoth got it back. Are you down with the cloning tanks?"

"We're above them, yes. Why?"

"Organa Solo suggested earlier that there should be a large number of ysalamiri scattered around that area," Karrde said. "If you can pull a few of them off their nutrient frames and get them up here, we might have a chance of stopping him."

Chewbacca growled mournfully, and Lando felt his lip twist as he nodded agreement. So that was what all those blasting disk explosions had been about. "It's too late for that, too," he told Karrde. "C'baoth's already had them all killed."

For a long moment the comlink was silent. "I see," Karrde said at last. "Well, that explains that. Any suggestions?"

Lando hesitated. "Not really," he said. "If we come up with anything, we'll let you know."

"Thank you," Karrde said, a little too dryly. "I'll be waiting."

There was a click as he left the channel. "Threepio, you still there?" Lando asked.

"Yes, sir," the droid answered.

"Get Artoo back on the computer," Lando told him. "Have him do whatever he can to shift troops away from that air intake we came in through. Then you and the Noghri start heading that way."

"We're leaving, sir?" Threepio asked, sounding astonished.

"That's right," Lando told him. "And Chewie and I will be right behind you, so you'd better move fast if you don't want to get stepped on. Better alert the two Noghri that Luke sent with that Myneyrshi bunch, too. Got all that?"

"Yes, sir," Threepio said hesitantly. "What about Master Luke and the others?"

"Leave that to me," Lando told him. "Get busy."

"Yes, sir," Threepio said again. Another click, and he was gone.

There was a moment of silence. Chewbacca broke it with the obvious question. "I don't think we've got a choice anymore," Lando told him grimly. "The way Luke and Mara talk about him, C'baoth's at least as dangerous as the Emperor was. Maybe even more so. We've got to try to take out the whole storehouse and hope we get him along with it."

Chewbacca growled an objection. "We can't," Lando shook his head. "At least not until it's set and running. We warn anyone up there now and C'baoth will know all about it. Might have time to get it stopped."

There was another muffled blast from the door. "Come on, let's get this done," Lando said, picking up the last of his explosives. With luck, they would have time to rig Chewbacca's arrhythmic resonance gimmick before the stormtroopers got in. With a little more luck, the two of them might make it out of the cavern alive.

And with still more, they might be able to find a way to

alert Han and the others before the whole storehouse blew up beneath them.

For a long moment the throne room was silent. Mara stared at Skywalker, wondering if he understood what he was saying. To offer to voluntarily stay here with C'baoth . . .

His gaze flicked sideways again to meet hers, and even through the buzzing in his mind she could feel his private dread. He knew what he was saying, all right. And he meant it. If C'baoth accepted his offer, he would go willingly with the insane Jedi. Sacrificing himself to save his friends.

Including the woman who'd once promised to kill him.

She turned away, suddenly unable to watch. Her eyes found Karrde, half hidden behind the wreckage of the catwalk as he knelt between his two vornskrs. Stroking them, talking quietly to them—probably calming them down after that Force-driven tantrum of C'baoth's. She peered at the animals, but they didn't seem to be hurt.

Her head movement must have caught Karrde's eye. He looked up at her, his face expressionless. Still patting the vornskrs, he tilted his head fractionally toward Solo and Organa Solo. Frowning, Mara followed his gaze—

And froze. Beside the section of catwalk wreckage still half covering his wife, Solo was moving. Slowly, a couple of centimeters at a time, he was creeping across the floor.

Toward the blaster Organa Solo had dropped.

"You ask too much, Skywalker," C'baoth warned softly. "Mara Jade will be mine. Must be mine. It is the destiny demanded of her by the Force. Not even you may trifle with that."

"Right," Mara put in, looking back at C'baoth and putting all the sarcasm into her voice as she could manage. Whatever the risks to herself, she had to draw as much of C'baoth's attention away from the other end of the throne room as she could. "I still have to kneel at his feet, remember?"

"You insult me, Mara Jade," C'baoth said, turning an evil smile on her. "Do you really believe me so easy to mislead?" Still watching her, he crooked a finger—

And as Solo's hand stretched out toward it, the blaster twitched another half meter out of his reach.

From the guard platform came a subtle change in hum. "Skywalker—look out!" Mara snapped.

Skywalker spun around, lightsaber igniting again and swinging up into defense. The clone, his wind or his courage back, was already halfway through his leap, his lightsaber slicing downward. The two blades met with a crash and an impact that drove Skywalker backward to the edge of the stairway. He took one step more, fought for balance, then dropped off to the floor below.

Mara threw a quick look at Solo as the clone charged over the edge in pursuit. If the clone really was an extension of C'baoth's mind . . .

But no. Even as Solo tried again for the blaster it again slid away from him. Whatever effort C'baoth was expending on the lightsaber duel, he clearly still had enough concentration left to toy with his prisoners.

"You see, Mara Jade?" C'baoth asked quietly. His fury had passed, the brief flicker of fun as he toyed with his prisoners had passed, and now it was time to return to the important business of building his Empire. "It is inevitable. I will rule . . . and along with Skywalker and his sister, you will serve at my side. And we shall be great together."

Abruptly, he took a long step back from the guardrail on the other side of the stairway. Just in time; an instant later Skywalker was back, backflipping up from the lower throne room floor. He landed with his back to Mara, floundering a moment as he fought to recover his balance. There was another flash of light, blue-white this time, as the clone leaped up over the guardrail in pursuit, swinging his lightsaber in vicious horizontal arcs to guard against attack. Skywalker moved backward out of his way; glancing past him, Mara saw C'baoth take a hasty backward step of his own. The clone hit the floor and charged, lightsaber still slashing toward Skywalker in wide horizontal arcs. Skywalker continued to give way, apparently unaware that he was backing toward the solid rock wall.

Against which he would be trapped.

They passed by . . . and Mara looked over to find C'baoth once again gazing at her. "As I said, Mara Jade," he said. "Inevitable. And with you and Skywalker beside me, the lesser peoples of the galaxy will flock to us like leaves in the wind. Their hearts and their souls will be ours."

He looked across the room and beckoned. Still crouching behind the catwalk wreckage, Karrde jerked in surprise as his blaster rose from his holster and shot through the air toward C'baoth. Halfway there it was joined by Organa Solo's dropped lightsaber and the blaster Solo was still doggedly trying to chase down. "As will their insignificant weapons," C'baoth added. Holding a negligent hand out to receive them, he turned his eyes back to the duel about to play itself to its conclusion.

It was the chance Mara had been waiting for. Possibly the last chance she would ever have. Reaching through the chaos surrounding her mind, she stretched out to the Force, focusing her eyes and mind on the weapons flying across the room toward C'baoth's hand. She felt his inattentive control snap—

And Organa Solo's lightsaber arced away from the blasters to land firmly in her hand.

C'baoth spun back to face her, the blasters falling with a clatter onto the stairway. "No!" he screamed, his face twisted horribly with fear, confusion, and dread. Mara felt his sudden frantic tug fumbling at the lightsaber; but it, too, was twisted with confusion and dread, and this time he didn't have surprise on his side. Given time, he would recover from the shock, but Mara had no intention of giving him that time. Igniting the lightsaber, she charged.

The clone must have heard her coming, of course; the distinctive sound of her lightsaber made that inevitable. But with Skywalker backed up against the wall, the temptation to finish off one opponent first was too great to resist. He swung one last time, his lightsaber slashing into the wall as Skywalker ducked low beneath the blade—

And with a brilliant flash of shattered electronics, the wall exploded outward, over Skywalker's head and directly into the clone's face.

Skywalker hadn't been backing into a wall after all. He'd been backing into one of the throne room's view-screens.

The clone shrieked—the first sound Mara could remember hearing him make—as he staggered backward. He spun toward the sound of her lightsaber, his face twisted with anger and fear, his eyes still dazzled. He raised his lightsaber to attack—

YOU WILL KILL LUKE SKYWALKER.

She ducked beneath the slashing blade, gazing into his face. Skywalker's face. The face that had haunted her nightmares for nearly six years. The face the Emperor had ordered her to destroy.

YOU WILL KILL LUKE SKYWALKER.

And for the first time since she'd found Skywalker and his crippled X-wing floating in deep space, she let herself give in to the voice swirling through her mind. With all her strength, she swung her lightsaber and cut him down.

The clone crumpled, his lightsaber clattering to the floor beside him.

Mara gazed down at him . . . and as she took a ragged breath, the voice in the back of her mind fell silent.

It was done. She had fulfilled the Emperor's last command.

And she was finally free.

CHAPTER 28

"T HAT APPEARS TO be all of them, Captain," Thrawn said, gazing out the bridge viewport at the Rebel warships spread out along the edges of the Interdictor Cruisers' gravity cones. "Instruct the *Constrainer* and *Sentinel* to secure from entrapment duty and return to their positions in the demarcation line. All warships: prepare to engage the enemy."

"Yes, sir," Pellaeon said, shaking his head in silent wonder as he keyed in the orders. Once again, against overwhelming evidence to the contrary, the Grand Admiral had proved himself right. The Rebel assault fleet was here.

And probably wondering at this very moment what had gone wrong with their clever little scheme. "It occurs to me, Admiral, that we might not want to destroy all of them," he suggested. "Someone should be allowed to return to Coruscant to tell them how badly they were outsmarted."

"I agree, Captain," Thrawn said. "Though I doubt that will be their interpretation. More likely they'll conclude instead that they were betrayed."

"Probably," Pellaeon agreed, throwing a quick look around the bridge. He'd thought he'd heard a faint sound just then, something like an overstressed bearing or someone rumbling in the back of his throat. He listened closely, but the sound wasn't repeated. "Though that would work equally well to our advantage."

"Indeed," Thrawn said. "Shall we designate Admiral Ackbar's Star Cruiser for messenger duty?"

Pellaeon smiled tightly. Ackbar. Who'd just barely survived Councilor Borsk Fey'lya's previous accusations of incompetence and treason over the operation at the Sluis Van shipyards. This time, he wouldn't be so lucky. "A nice touch, Admiral," he said.

"Thank you, Captain."

Pellaeon glanced up at Rukh, standing silent guard behind Thrawn's chair, and wondered if the Noghri appreciated the irony of it all. Given the species' lack of sophistication, probably not.

Ahead, space was filling with flashes of laser fire as the opposing starfighter squadrons began to engage. Settling himself comfortably in his chair, Pellaeon glanced over his displays and prepared his mind for battle. For battle, and for victory.

"WATCH IT, ROGUE LEADER, you've picked up a couple of tails," the voice of Rogue Two came in Wedge's ear. "Rogue Six?"

"Right with you, Rogue Two," the other confirmed. "Double-chop on three. One, two—"

Bracing himself, Wedge threw his X-wing into a wild scissors roll. The two TIE fighters, trying to match his maneuver while at the same time not overshooting him, probably never even saw the other two X-wings drop into position behind them. Two messy explosions later, Wedge was clear. "Thanks," he said.

"No problem. What now?"

"I don't know," he admitted, taking a quick look at the battle raging around them. So far, Admiral Ackbar was still holding his Star Cruisers together in combat formation. But the way the periphery support ships were being hammered by the

Imperials, the whole thing could dissolve into the mass confusion of a brawl at any minute. In which event, the starfighter squadrons would be basically on their own, hitting wherever and whatever they could.

Which they were for all practical purposes doing now anyway. The trick would be to find something really effective to hit. . . .

Rogue Two must have followed the same reasoning. "You know, Rogue Leader, it occurs to me that those Imperials wouldn't have so many ships available to pound us with if they had to protect their shipyard at the same time."

Wedge craned his neck to look at the blaze of lights off in the near distance. Silhouetted against them, he could make out the dark, brooding outlines of at least four Golan II battle stations. "Agreed," he said. "But I think it would take more than an attack by even the legendary Rogue Squadron to make them that nervous—"

"Commander Antilles, this is Fleet Central Communications," a brisk voice cut in. "I have a signal coded urgent coming in for you under a New Republic diplomatic encrypt. Do you want to bother with it?"

Wedge blinked. A diplomatic encrypt? Way out here? "I suppose so. Sure, put it through."

"Yes, sir." There was a click—

"Hello, Antilles," a vaguely familiar voice said dryly in his ear. "Nice to see you again."

"The feeling's mutual, I'm sure," Wedge said, frowning. "Who *is* this?"

"Oh, come now," the other chided. "Have you forgotten already those wonderful times we spent together outside the Mumbri Storve cantina?"

The Mumbri Storve—? "*Aves?*"

"Hey, very good," Aves said. "Your memory's getting better."

"You people are starting to be hard to forget," Wedge told him. "Where are you?"

"Right smack in the middle of that big blaze of Imperial lights off on your flank," Aves said, his voice turning a little grim. "I wish you'd told me you were hitting this place instead of Tangrene like we thought."

"I wish you'd told *me* what that little job of yours was all about," Wedge countered. "Did a good job of fooling each other, didn't we?"

"Sure did. Fooled everybody except the Grand Admiral."

"Tell me about it. So is this just a social call, or what?"

"It could be," Aves said. "Or it couldn't. See, in about ninety seconds some of us are going to make a grab for the CGT array we came here to get. After that, it's a quick good-bye and we punch our way out."

Punching their way out from an Imperial shipyard. And he made it sound so easy, too. "Good luck."

"Thanks. The reason I mention it is that it doesn't matter much to us which direction we pick to punch through. Thought it might make a difference to you."

Wedge felt a tight smile tugging at his lip. "It might, at that," he said. "Like, say, if you were to come out near those Golan Twos out there. Maybe hitting them a little from behind on the way?"

"Looks like a good route to me," Aves agreed. "'Course, it'll get nasty outside the perimeter—all those ships and things taking potshots and all. I don't suppose you could find a way to give us a friendly escort from that point on?"

Wedge looked over at the lights, thinking it over. It could work, all right. If Aves' people were able to knock out even one of those Golan II's, it would open up the shipyard to a New Republic incursion. Unless the Imperials were willing to sacrifice it, they would have to shift some of their battle force over there to close the puncture and chase down any ships that had gotten in.

And from the smugglers' point of view, having an influx of New Republic warships to sneak through on their way out would give them better cover than they would get anywhere else along the perimeter. All in all, a pretty fair exchange. "You've got a deal," he told Aves. "Give me a couple of minutes and I'll get that escort arranged."

"A *friendly* escort, don't forget," Aves warned. "If you know what I mean."

"I know exactly what you mean," Wedge assured him. The traditional Mon Calamari loathing for smugglers and smuggling was the stuff of wardroom legend, and Wedge didn't want to get caught in the middle of that any more than Aves did. Probably why the smuggler had come to him instead of offering his assistance to Ackbar and the fleet commanders directly. "Don't worry, I've got it covered."

"Okay. Whoops—there goes the first charge. See you."

The comm clicked off. "We're going in?" Rogue Eleven asked.

"We're going in," Wedge confirmed, bringing his X-wing around in a tight starboard turn. "Rogue Two, give Command a quick update and tell them we need some support. Don't mention Aves by name—just tell them we're coordinating with an independent resistance group inside the shipyards."

"Got it, Rogue Leader."

"What if Ackbar doesn't want to risk it?" Rogue Seven put in.

Wedge looked out at the lights of the shipyard. So once again, as it had so many times before, it was all going to come down to a matter of trust. Trust in a farm kid, fresh off a backward desert world, to lead him in an attack on the first Death Star. Trust in a former high-stakes gambler, who might or might not have had any real combat experience, to lead him in an attack on the second Death Star. And now, trust in a smuggler who might just as easily betray him for the right price. "It doesn't matter," he said. "With or without support, we're going in."

Mara's lightsaber flashed, slicing viciously through the clone Luuke. The clone fell, its lightsaber clattering to the floor, and lay still.

And suddenly, the buzzing pressure in Luke's mind was gone.

He rose to his feet in front of the still sparking view-screen he'd lured the clone to, taking what felt like the first clean breath he'd had in hours. The ordeal was finally over. "Thank you," he said quietly to Mara.

She took a step back from the dead clone. "No problem. Brain all clear now?"

So she'd been able to sense the buzzing in his mind. He'd wondered about that. "Yes," he nodded, taking another wonderfully clean breath. "How about yours?"

She threw him a look that was half amused, half ironic. But for the first time since they'd met he could see that the pain and hatred were gone from her eyes. "I did what he wanted me to," she said. "It's over."

Luke looked back across the throne room. Karrde had tied the vornskrs' leashes to the collapsed catwalk and was picking his way carefully across the wreckage. Han, on his feet now, was helping a still groggy Leia out from under the section that had fallen on her. "Leia?" Luke called. "You all right?"

"I'm fine," Leia called back. "Just a little banged up. Let's get out of here, all right?"

Luke turned back to C'baoth. The old Jedi was staring down at the dead clone, his hands working at his sides, his eyes furious and lost and insane. "Yes," he agreed. "Come on, Mara."

"Go ahead," Mara said. "I'll be with you in a minute."

Luke eyed her. "What are you going to do?"

"What do you think?" she retorted. "I'm going to finish the job. Like I should have done on Jomark."

Slowly, C'baoth raised his eyes to her. "You will die for this, Mara Jade," he said, his quiet voice more chilling than any outburst of rage could have been. "Slowly, and in great pain."

Taking a deep breath, curling his hands into fists in front of his chest, he closed his eyes.

"We'll see about that," Mara muttered. Raising her lightsaber, she started toward him.

It began as a distant rumble, more felt than really heard. Luke looked around the room, senses tingling with a premonition of danger. But he could see nothing out of place. The sound grew louder, deeper—

And with a thunderous explosion, the sections of throne room ceiling directly above him and Mara suddenly collapsed in a downpour of gravel-sized rocks.

"Look out!" Luke shouted, throwing his arms up to protect his head and trying to leap out of the way. But the center of the rockfall moved with him. He tried again, this time nearly losing his balance as his foot caught in a pile of stones already ankle deep. Too numerous and too small for him to get a grip on through the Force, they kept coming, pummeling against him with bruising impact. Through the dust swirling around him, he saw Mara floundering under a deluge of her own, trying to guard her head with one arm as she slashed vainly at the falling stones with her lightsaber. From across the throne room, Luke could hear Han shouting something, and guessed that they, too, were under the same attack.

And standing untouched by the destructive rock storms he'd unleashed, C'baoth lifted his hands high. "I am the Jedi Master C'baoth!" he shouted, his voice ringing through the throne room and the roar of the rockfalls. "The Empire—the universe—is mine."

Luke dropped his lightsaber back into defense position, senses again tingling with danger. But once again, the knowledge did him little good. C'baoth's lightning burst flashed against the lightsaber blade, the impact knocking Luke off balance and dropping him painfully onto his knees in the pile of stones around him. Even as he struggled to get up, one of the falling rocks slammed hard into the side of his head. He staggered, toppling sideways onto one hand. Again the lightning flashed, throwing coronal fire all through the stone pile and sending wave after wave of agony through him. The lightsaber was plucked from his fingers; dimly he saw it fly over the railing toward the far end of the throne room.

"Stop it," Mara screamed. Through the haze of pain, Luke saw that she was standing up to her knees in stones, her lightsaber slashing uselessly through the mound as if trying to sweep them away "If you're going to kill us, just do it."

"Patience, my future apprentice," C'baoth said . . . and squinting through the stones and dust, Luke saw the other's dreamy smile. "You cannot die yet. Not until I have taken you down to the Grand Admiral's cloning chamber."

Beneath her rockfall, Mara jerked, her sense flashing with sudden horror. "What?"

"For I have foreseen that Mara Jade will kneel before me," C'baoth reminded her. "One Mara Jade . . . or another."

"THAT'S IT," LANDO said, tapping the activation switch on the last charge. "Give it a kick and let's get out of here."

From around the central column Chewbacca growled acknowledgment. Picking up his blaster, Lando stood up, giving each of the doors around the outer walkway a quick look. So far, so good. If they could keep the stormtroopers out for just two more minutes, long enough for Chewbacca and him to get off this work platform and out to the walkway . . .

Chewbacca rumbled a warning. Listening closely, Lando could hear the faint rising-pitch hum of an extremely unhappy negative flow coupler. "Great, Chewie," he said. "Let's go." He stepped out onto the end of the bridge—

And straight ahead of him, the door opposite the bridge blew up.

"Watch it!" Lando barked, dropping flat on his stomach on the bridge and pouring blaster fire into the cloud of dust and debris expanding out from where the door had been. Already, the sizzling blue ripples of stun fire were starting to erupt from

STAR WARS: THE LAST COMMAND   449

the doorway in their general direction. Behind him, the roar of
Chewbacca's bowcaster was answering. So much for those last
two minutes.

And with his face pressed as close to the metal-mesh floor
as he could get it, Lando found himself looking at the bridge.
At the bridge, and the thin but sturdy guardrails running along
both sides of it . . .

It was crazy. But that didn't mean it wouldn't work.

"Chewie, get over here," he called, rolling halfway over and
throwing a quick look up at the bridge controls set into the top
of the work platform guardrail. Extension control . . . there.
Retraction control—emergency stop control—

The bridge shook as Chewbacca landed with a thud on the
bridge beside him. "Keep them busy," Lando told him. Gaug-
ing the distance, he lunged upward, jabbing the retraction control and the emergency stop in quick succession. The bridge
lurched out from the work platform and stopped, just far
enough for its locking bars to disengage.

Chewbacca rumbled a question as the bridge bobbed gently with the strain of their weight. "You'll see," Lando told
him. From both sides came flashes of light as two more doors
disintegrated. "Just hang on to the guardrail supports and
keep firing. Here we go." Getting a firm grip himself, he aimed
carefully and opened fire.

But not at the stormtroopers now charging out onto the
circular walkway. His shots were directed instead at the far
end of the bridge, throwing out clouds of sparks as they vaporized sections of the mesh flooring and dug chunks out of
the structural support bars beneath. The bridge lurched, bobbing even harder now, as Lando continued to hammer away
at its structural integrity. Beside him, Chewbacca rumbled a
savage Wookiee phrase that Lando had never heard him use
before—

And with a horrible shriek of strained metal, the bridge
suddenly gave way. Connected to the walkway only by the-
still-intact guardrails, it pivoted ponderously downward.

Lando gripped the guardrail tightly as their horizontal position changed rapidly toward a vertical one—

And with a crash that nearly jarred him loose, the bridge slammed up against the guardrail of the cloning balcony three levels down.

"This is our stop," Lando said. "Come on." Jamming his blaster awkwardly into its holster, he swung himself around the steeply angled bridge guardrail to drop onto the cloning balcony floor. Chewbacca, with his natural arboreal skills, was there a good three seconds ahead of him.

They were halfway to the balcony's exit door, dodging between the rows of Spaarti cylinders, when the column behind them blew up.

The charges went first, blowing sections of cable and pipework in a series of dazzling fireballs all around the column's perimeter. An evil-looking cloud of smoke and dust and flash-vaporized nutrient liquids swirled into the air, obscuring the view; from all sides, multicolored fluids began spraying out. The work platform they'd been standing on a minute earlier broke free of its supports and slid roughly down the column, tearing and damaging more equipment as it fell. From inside the cloud came a sputtering of shorted power lines and secondary explosions, each one adding to the rain of debris.

And with a horrible creaking of strained and shattered supports, the external layers of the column began to peel away and fall almost leisurely outward.

Over the din, Chewbacca roared a warning. "Me, neither," Lando shouted back. "Let's get out of here."

Ten seconds later, bursting past the single token guard who'd been left on this level's exit door, they were out. They were two corridors away when they felt the distant vibration as the column crashed to the cloning cavern floor.

"Okay," Lando panted, pausing and glancing both ways as they reached a cross corridor. Artoo must have done a good job with those troop reassignments; the whole area seemed deserted. "Exit's that direction," he told Chewbacca, pulling out his comlink. "We'll call the others and get out of here." He keyed for Han—

And jerked back as the comlink erupted with a loud crackling noise. "Han?" he called.

"Lando?" Han's voice came back, almost inaudible over the noise.

"Right," Lando confirmed. "What's happening up there?"

"This crazy Jedi's dropping the roof in on us," Han shouted. "Leia and me have a little cover, but he's got Luke and Mara out in the open. Where are you?"

"Down near the cloning cavern," Lando gritted. If that arrhythmic resonance thing of Chewbacca's worked, one of the mountain's reactors would already be starting to flicker with instabilities. If they didn't get out of the mountain before it blew . . . "You want us to come up and help?"

"Don't bother," Karrde's voice cut in grimly. "There's already a large pile of stone in front of the turbolift. Looks like we're here for the duration."

Chewbacca snarled, his voice filled with frustration. "Forget it, Chewie, there's nothing you could do anyway," Han told him. "We've still got Luke and Mara—maybe they can stop him."

"What if they can't?" Lando demanded, stomach twisting inside him. "Look, you haven't got much time—we think we've got an arrhythmic resonance going in the power core."

"Good," Han said. "Means C'baoth won't get out either."

"Han—"

"Go on, get out of here," Han cut him off. "Chewie, it's been great; but if we don't make it, someone beside Winter's going to have to take care of Jacen and Jaina. You got that?"

"The *Wild Karrde*'s waiting where you came in," Karrde added. "They'll be expecting you."

"Right," Lando said, gritting his teeth. "Good luck."

He keyed off and jammed the comlink back in his belt. Han was right, there wasn't anything they could do against C'baoth from down here. But with the *Wild Karrde*'s turbo-lasers and

Artoo's set of floor plans . . . "Come on, Chewie," he said,
turning toward their exit and breaking into a run. "It's not
over yet."

"PERHAPS IT IS for the best," C'baoth murmured, gazing at
Luke sadly as he stepped toward him. Blinking the dust away
from his eyes, Luke looked up at the old Jedi, trying to force
back the agony still throbbing through him.

The agony, and the looming sense of defeat. Kneeling on
the floor, encased in stones to above his waist with more still
falling on him, facing an insane Jedi Master who wanted to
kill him . . .

No. *A Jedi must act when he is calm. At peace with the
Force.* "Master C'baoth, listen to me," he said. "You're not
well. I know that. But I can help you."

A dozen expressions flicked across C'baoth's face, as if he
were trying various emotions on for size. "Can you, now," he
said, settling on wry amusement. "And why should you do that
for me?"

"Because you need it," Luke said. "And because we need
you. You have a vast store of experience and power that you
could use for the good of the New Republic."

C'baoth snorted. "The Jedi Master Joruus C'baoth does
not serve lesser peoples, Jedi Skywalker."

"Why not? All the great Jedi Masters of the Old Republic
did."

"And that was their failing," C'baoth said, jabbing a finger
at Luke. "That was why the lesser peoples rose up and killed
them."

"But they didn't—"

"Enough!" C'baoth thundered. "It doesn't matter what you
think the lesser peoples need from me. *I* am the one who will
decide that. They will accept my rule, or they will die." His
eyes flashed. "You had that choice, Jedi Skywalker. And

more—you could have ruled beside me. Instead, you chose death."

A drop of sweat or blood trickled down the side of Luke's face. "What about Mara?"

C'baoth shook his head. "Mara Jade is no longer any concern of yours," he said. "I will deal with her later."

"No," Mara snapped. "You will deal with me *now*."

Luke looked over at her. The stones were still raining down above her head; but to his astonishment, the knee-high pile of rock that had been trapping her in place was gone. And now he saw why: those lightsaber slashes she'd been making earlier hadn't been the useless sweeping motions that he'd assumed. Instead, she'd been slicing huge gashes in the floor, releasing the stones to drain through to the monitor area below.

Raising her lightsaber, she charged.

C'baoth swung around to face her, his face contorted with rage. "No!" he screamed; and again the blue-white lightning crackled from his fingertips. Mara caught the burst on her lightsaber, her mad rush faltering as coronal fire burned all around her. C'baoth fired again and again, backing toward the throne and the solid wall behind it. Doggedly, Mara kept coming.

Abruptly, the rockfall over her head ceased. From the edge of the pile that had half buried Luke, stones began flying toward C'baoth. Curving around behind him, they shot straight into Mara's face. She staggered backward, squeezing her eyes shut against the hailstorm and throwing up her right elbow to try to block them away.

Setting his teeth, Luke tried to heave away the stones weighing him down. He couldn't leave Mara to fight alone. But it was no use; his muscles were still too weakened from C'baoth's last attack. He tried again anyway, ignoring the fresh pain the effort sent through him. He looked at Mara—

And saw her face suddenly change. He frowned; and then he heard it too. Leia's voice, speaking in his mind—

Keep your eyes closed, Mara, and listen to my voice. I can see; I'll guide you.

"No!" C'baoth screamed again. "No! She is mine!"

Luke looked over at the other end of the throne room, wondering how C'baoth would lash out at Leia in retaliation. But there was nothing. Even the stones had stopped falling on the section of catwalk they were all huddled beneath. Perhaps the long battle had finally begun to drain C'baoth's strength, and he could no longer risk splitting his attention. Beyond the catwalk, lying half buried in the pile of stone that now blocked the turbolift door, Luke spotted the metallic glint of his lightsaber. If he could call it to him, and regain enough strength to join Mara's battle . . .

And then, another motion caught his eye. Tied to the catwalk to one side, untouched by the rockfall that had attacked their owner, Karrde's pet vornskrs were tugging at their leashes.

Straining toward Mara. And toward C'baoth.

A wild vornskr had nearly killed Mara during their trek through the Myrkr forest. It seemed only fitting, somehow, for these two to help save her. The lightsaber stirred under Luke's call, igniting as his mind found the control. It rolled off the rock pile, the brilliant green blade throwing sparks from the stones as it bounced across them. Luke strained, and the weapon lifted into the air and flew toward him.

And as it reached the ruined catwalk, he let the blade dip to slice neatly through the vornskrs' leashes.

C'baoth saw them coming, of course. His back nearly to the throne room wall now, he shifted his aim, sending a burst of lightning toward the charging predators as they came up over the stairway. One of them howled and fell to the floor, skidding across the scattered stones; the other staggered but kept coming.

The distraction was all the opening Mara needed. She leaped forward against the rocks still pummeling against her face, covering the last remaining distance between her and C'baoth; and as he brought his hands desperately back toward her, she dropped onto her knees in front of him and stabbed viciously upward with her lightsaber. With a last, mournful scream, C'baoth crumpled—

And as it had with the Emperor aboard the Death Star, the dark side energy within him burst out in a violent explosion of blue fire.

Luke was ready. Throwing every last bit of strength into the effort, he caught Mara in a solid Force grip, pulling her back away from that burst of energy as fast as he could. He felt the wave-front slam into him; felt the slight easing of stress as Leia's strength joined his effort.

And then, suddenly, it was all over.

For a long minute he lay still, gasping for air, fighting against the unconsciousness threatening to roll over him. Dimly, he felt the stones being pushed away from around him. "Are you all right, Luke?" Leia asked.

He forced open his eyes. Dust-covered and bruised, she didn't look much better than he felt. "I'm fine," he told her, pushing against the remaining stones and getting his feet under him. "How about the others?"

"They're not too bad," she said, catching his arm to help steady him. "But Han's going to need medical treatment—he's got some bad burns."

"So does Mara," Karrde said grimly, coming up the steps holding an unconscious Mara in his arms. "We have to get her to the *Wild Karrde* as quickly as possible."

"So give them a call," Han said. He was kneeling over the dead Luuke clone, gazing down at him. "Tell them to come pick us up."

"Pick us up where?" Karrde frowned.

Han pointed toward the spot where C'baoth had died. "Right there."

Luke turned and looked. The massive detonation of dark side energy had made a shambles of that end of the throne room. The walls and ceiling were blackened and cratered; the metal of the floor where C'baoth had stood was buckled and half melted; the throne itself had been ripped away and was lying smoldering a meter from its base.

And behind it, through a jagged crack in the rear wall, he could see the bright twinkle of a single star.

"Right," Luke said, taking a deep breath. "Leia?"

"I see it," she nodded, handing him his lightsaber and igniting hers. "Let's get busy."

THE TWO REBEL Assault Frigates broke to either side of the beleaguered Golan II, delivering massive broadsides as they veered off. A section of the battle station flared and went dark; and against its darkened bulk another wave of Rebel starfighters could be seen slipping past into the shipyards beyond.

And Pellaeon was no longer smiling.

"Don't panic, Captain," Thrawn said. But he, too, was starting to sound grim. "We're not defeated yet. Not by a long shot."

Pellaeon's board pinged. He looked at it—"Sir, we have a priority message coming in from Wayland," he told Thrawn, his stomach twisting with a sudden horrible premonition. Wayland—the cloning facility—

"Read it, Captain," Thrawn said, his voice deadly quiet.

"Decrypt is coming in now, sir," Pellaeon said, tapping the board impatiently as the message slowly began to come up. It was exactly as he'd feared. "The mountain is under attack, sir," he told Thrawn. "Two different forces of natives, plus some Rebel saboteurs—" He broke off, frowning in disbelief. "And a group of Noghri—"

He never got to read any more of the report. Abruptly, a gray-skinned hand slashed out of nowhere, catching him across the throat.

He gagged, falling limply in his chair, his whole body instantly paralyzed. "For the treachery of the Empire against the Noghri people," Rukh's voice said quietly from beside him as he gasped for breath. "We were betrayed. We have been re-venged."

There was a whisper of movement, and he was gone. Still gasping, struggling against the inertia of his stunned muscles, Pellaeon fought to get a hand up to his command board. With one final effort he made it, trying twice before he was able to hit the emergency alert.

And as the wailing of the alarm cut through the noise of a Star Destroyer at battle, he finally managed to turn his head.

Thrawn was sitting upright in his chair, his face strangely calm. In the middle of his chest, a dark red stain was spreading across the spotless white of his Grand Admiral's uniform. Glittering in the center of the stain was the tip of Rukh's assassin's knife.

Thrawn caught his eye; and to Pellaeon's astonishment, the Grand Admiral smiled. "But," he whispered, "it was so artistically done."

The smile faded. The glow in his eyes did likewise . . . and Thrawn, the last Grand Admiral, was gone.

"Captain Pellaeon?" the comm officer called urgently as the medic team arrived—too late—to the Grand Admiral's chair. "The *Nemesis* and *Stormhawk* are requesting orders. What shall I tell them?"

Pellaeon looked up at the viewports. At the chaos that had erupted behind the defenses of the supposedly secure shipyards; at the unexpected need to split his forces to its defense; at the Rebel fleet taking full advantage of the diversion. In the blink of an eye, the universe had suddenly turned against them.

Thrawn could still have pulled an Imperial victory out of it. But he, Pellaeon, was not Thrawn.

"Signal to all ships," he rasped. The words ached in his throat, in a way that had nothing to do with the throbbing pain of Rukh's treacherous attack. "Prepare to retreat."

CHAPTER 29

THE SUN HAD set beneath a thin layer of western clouds, and the colors of the evening sky were beginning to fade into the encroaching darkness of Coruscant night. Leaning on the chest-high wrought-stone railing at the edge of the Palace roof, listening to the breezes whispering by her ears, Mara gazed out at the lights and vehicles of the Imperial City below. Buzzing with activity, there was still something strangely peaceful about it.

Or maybe the peace was in her. Either way, it made for a nice change.

Twenty meters behind her, the door out onto the roof opened. She stretched out with the Force; but she knew who it had to be. And she was right. "Mara?" Luke called softly.

"Over here," she called back, grimacing out at the city below. From his sense she could tell he was here for her answer.

So much for inner peace.

"Quite a view, isn't it?" Luke commented, coming up beside her and gazing out over the city. "Must bring back memories for you."

She threw him a patient look. "Translation: How am I feeling about the homecoming this time. You know, Skywalker—just between us—you're pretty pathetic when you try to be devious. If I were you, I'd give it up and just stick with that straight-out farm boy honesty."

"Sorry," he said. "Too much time spent around Han, I guess."

"And Karrde and me, I suppose?"

"You want a straight-out farm boy honest answer to that?"

She threw him a crooked smile. "I'm sorry I even brought it up."

Luke smiled back, then turned serious again. "So how *are* you feeling?"

Mara looked back out at the lights. "Strange," she told him. "It's sort of like coming home . . . only it isn't. I've never really stood here and just *looked* at the city like this. The only times I was ever up here were to watch for a certain airspeeder to arrive or to keep an eye on some particular building or something like that. Business for the Emperor. I don't think he ever saw the Imperial City as people and lights—to him it was just power and opportunities."

"Probably how he saw everything," Luke agreed. "And speaking about opportunities . . . ?"

Mara grimaced. She'd been right: he was here for her answer. "The whole thing's ridiculous," she said. "You know it, and I know it."

"Karrde doesn't think so."

"Karrde's even a worse idealist than you are sometimes," she shot back. "In the first place, he's never going to be able to hold this smuggler coalition of his together."

"Maybe not," Luke said. "But think of the possibilities if he can. There are a lot of contacts and information sources out there in the fringe that the New Republic doesn't have any access to at all."

"So what do you need information sources for?" Mara countered. "Thrawn's dead, his cloning center is a shambles, and the Empire's in retreat again. You've won."

"We won at Endor, too," Luke pointed out. "That didn't

stop us from years of so-called mopping-up action. There's still a lot of work yet to be done."

"It still doesn't make any sense to put me in the middle of it," Mara argued. "If you want a liaison between you and the smugglers, why don't you get Karrde to do it?"

"Because Karrde's a smuggler. You were just a smuggler's assistant."

She snorted. "Big difference."

"To some people, it is," Luke said. "This whole negotiation process is running as much on appearance and image as it is on reality. Anyway, Karrde's already said he won't do it. Now that those vornskrs of his have recovered, he wants to get back out to his people."

Mara shook her head. "I'm not a politician," she insisted. "Not a diplomat, either."

"But you're someone both sides are willing to trust," Luke said. "That's what's important here."

Mara made a face. "You don't know these people, Sky-walker. Trust me—Chewbacca and the guys you're sending out to transplant the Noghri to their new world are going to have a lot more fun."

He touched her hand. "You can do it, Mara. I know you can."

She sighed. "I have to think about it."

"That's all right," he said. "Just come on downstairs whenever you're ready."

"Sure." She threw a sideways look at him. "Was there something else?"

He smiled. "You're getting good at that."

"Your fault for teaching me too well. Come on, what is it?"

"Just this." Reaching into his tunic, he pulled out a light-saber.

"What's this?" Mara asked, frowning.

"It's my old lightsaber," Luke told her quietly. "The one I lost at Cloud City, and nearly got killed with at Wayland." He held it out. "I'd like you to have it."

She looked up at him, startled. "Me? Why?"

He shrugged self-consciously. "Lots of reasons. Because you earned it. Because you're on your way to becoming a Jedi and you'll need it. Mostly, though, because I want you to have it."

Slowly, almost reluctantly, she took the weapon. "Thank you."

"You're welcome." He touched her hand again. "I'll be in the conference room with the others. Come on down when you've decided."

He turned and walked away across the Palace roof. Mara turned to gaze out at the lights of the city again, the cool metal of the lightsaber pressed against her hand. Luke's lightsaber. Probably one of his last links to the past . . . and he was giving it away.

Was there a message in that for her? Probably. Like she'd said, subtlety wasn't one of Luke's strong points. But if that was why he'd done it, he'd been wasting his time. Her last link with the past had been broken in the Mount Tantiss throne room.

Her past was over. It was time to get on with the future. And the New Republic was that future. Whether she liked it or not.

Behind her, she heard Luke open the roof door. "Hang on a minute," she called after him. "I'll come with you."

THE STAR WARS LEGENDS NOVELS TIMELINE

 BEFORE THE REPUBLIC
37,000–25,000 YEARS BEFORE
STAR WARS: A NEW HOPE

c. 25,793 YEARS BEFORE *STAR WARS: A NEW HOPE*

Dawn of the Jedi: Into the Void

 OLD REPUBLIC
5,000–67 YEARS BEFORE
STAR WARS: A NEW HOPE

Lost Tribe of the Sith: The Collected
Stories

3,954 YEARS BEFORE *STAR WARS: A NEW HOPE*

The Old Republic: Revan

3,650 YEARS BEFORE *STAR WARS: A NEW HOPE*

The Old Republic: Deceived
Red Harvest
The Old Republic: Fatal Alliance
The Old Republic: Annihilation

1,032 YEARS BEFORE *STAR WARS: A NEW HOPE*

Knight Errant
Darth Bane: Path of Destruction
Darth Bane: Rule of Two
Darth Bane: Dynasty of Evil

 RISE OF THE EMPIRE
67–0 YEARS BEFORE
STAR WARS: A NEW HOPE

67 YEARS BEFORE *STAR WARS: A NEW HOPE*

Darth Plagueis

33 YEARS BEFORE *STAR WARS: A NEW HOPE*

Cloak of Deception
Darth Maul: Shadow Hunter
Maul: Lockdown

32 YEARS BEFORE *STAR WARS: A NEW HOPE*

STAR WARS: EPISODE I
THE PHANTOM MENACE

Rogue Planet
Outbound Flight
The Approaching Storm

22 YEARS BEFORE *STAR WARS: A NEW HOPE*

STAR WARS: EPISODE II
ATTACK OF THE CLONES

22–19 YEARS BEFORE *STAR WARS: A NEW HOPE*

STAR WARS: THE CLONE
WARS

The Clone Wars: Wild Space
The Clone Wars: No Prisoners

Clone Wars Gambit
  Stealth
  Siege

Republic Commando
  Hard Contact
  Triple Zero
  True Colors
  Order 66

Shatterpoint
The Cestus Deception
MedStar I: Battle Surgeons
MedStar II: Jedi Healer
Jedi Trial
Yoda: Dark Rendezvous
Labyrinth of Evil

19 YEARS BEFORE *STAR WARS: A NEW HOPE*

STAR WARS: EPISODE III
REVENGE OF THE SITH

Kenobi
Dark Lord: The Rise of Darth Vader
Imperial Commando 501st

Coruscant Nights
  Jedi Twilight
  Street of Shadows
  Patterns of Force
The Last Jedi

10 YEARS BEFORE *STAR WARS: A NEW HOPE*

The Han Solo Trilogy
  The Paradise Snare
  The Hutt Gambit
  Rebel Dawn

The Adventures of Lando Calrissian
The Force Unleashed
The Han Solo Adventures
Death Troopers
The Force Unleashed II

THE STAR WARS LEGENDS NOVELS TIMELINE

REBELLION
0–5 YEARS AFTER
STAR WARS: A NEW HOPE

Death Star
Shadow Games

0

> ### STAR WARS: EPISODE IV
> ### A NEW HOPE

Tales from the Mos Eisley Cantina
Tales from the Empire
Tales from the New Republic
Scoundrels
Allegiance
Choices of One
Honor Among Thieves
Galaxies: The Ruins of Dantooine
Splinter of the Mind's Eye
Razor's Edge

3 YEARS AFTER *STAR WARS: A NEW HOPE*

> ### STAR WARS: EPISODE V
> ### THE EMPIRE STRIKES BACK

Tales of the Bounty Hunters
Shadows of the Empire

4 YEARS AFTER *STAR WARS: A NEW HOPE*

> ### STAR WARS: EPISODE VI
> ### THE RETURN OF THE JEDI

Tales from Jabba's Palace

The Bounty Hunter Wars
  The Mandalorian Armor
  Slave Ship
  Hard Merchandise

The Truce at Bakura
Luke Skywalker and the Shadows of
  Mindor

NEW REPUBLIC
5–25 YEARS AFTER
STAR WARS: A NEW HOPE

X-Wing
  Rogue Squadron
  Wedge's Gamble
  The Krytos Trap
  The Bacta War
  Wraith Squadron
  Iron Fist
  Solo Command

The Courtship of Princess Leia
Tatooine Ghost

The Thrawn Trilogy
  Heir to the Empire
  Dark Force Rising
  The Last Command

X-Wing: Isard's Revenge

The Jedi Academy Trilogy
  Jedi Search
  Dark Apprentice
  Champions of the Force

I, Jedi
Children of the Jedi
Darksaber
Planet of Twilight
X-Wing: Starfighters of Adumar
The Crystal Star

The Black Fleet Crisis Trilogy
  Before the Storm
  Shield of Lies
  Tyrant's Test

The New Rebellion

The Corellian Trilogy
  Ambush at Corellia
  Assault at Selonia
  Showdown at Centerpoint

The Hand of Thrawn Duology
  Specter of the Past
  Vision of the Future

Scourge
Survivor's Quest

NEW JEDI ORDER
25–40 YEARS AFTER
STAR WARS: A NEW HOPE

The New Jedi Order
Vector Prime
Dark Tide I: Onslaught
Dark Tide II: Ruin
Agents of Chaos I: Hero's Trial
Agents of Chaos II: Jedi Eclipse
Balance Point
Edge of Victory I: Conquest
Edge of Victory II: Rebirth
Star by Star
Dark Journey
Enemy Lines I: Rebel Dream
Enemy Lines II: Rebel Stand
Traitor
Destiny's Way
Force Heretic I: Remnant
Force Heretic II: Refugee
Force Heretic III: Reunion
The Final Prophecy
The Unifying Force

35 YEARS AFTER *STAR WARS: A NEW HOPE*

The Dark Nest Trilogy
The Joiner King
The Unseen Queen
The Swarm War

LEGACY
40+ YEARS AFTER
STAR WARS: A NEW HOPE

Legacy of the Force
Betrayal
Bloodlines
Tempest
Exile
Sacrifice
Inferno
Fury
Revelation
Invincible

Crosscurrent
Riptide
Millennium Falcon

43 YEARS AFTER *STAR WARS: A NEW HOPE*

Fate of the Jedi
Outcast
Omen
Abyss
Backlash
Allies
Vortex
Conviction
Ascension
Apocalypse

X-Wing: Mercy Kill

45 YEARS AFTER *STAR WARS: A NEW HOPE*

Crucible

PHOTO: © KENT AKSELSEN

TIMOTHY ZAHN is the author of more than forty novels, nearly ninety short stories and novellas, and four short fiction collections. In 1984, he won the Hugo Award for best novella. Zahn is best known for his *Star Wars* novels (*Heir to the Empire, Dark Force Rising, The Last Command, Specter of the Past, Vision of the Future, Survivor's Quest, Outbound Flight, Allegiance, Choices of One,* and *Scoundrels*), with more than four million copies of his books in print. Other books include the Cobra series, the Quadrail series, and the young adult Dragonback series. Zahn has a B.S. in physics from Michigan State University and an M.S. from the University of Illinois. He lives with his family on the Oregon coast.

Facebook.com/TimothyZahn

Read on for an excerpt from

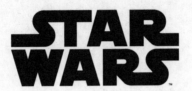

THE
HIGH REPUBLIC:
LIGHT OF THE JEDI

BY CHARLES SOULE

CHAPTER ONE

HYPERSPACE. THE *LEGACY RUN*.

3 HOURS TO IMPACT.

*A*LL IS WELL.

Captain Hedda Casset reviewed the readouts and displays built into her command chair for the second time. She always went over them at least twice. She had more than four decades of flying behind her, and figured the double check was a large part of the reason she'd survived all that time. The second look confirmed everything she'd seen in the first.

"All is well," she said, out loud this time, announcing it to her bridge crew. "Time for my rounds. Lieutenant Bowman, you have the bridge."

"Acknowledged, Captain," her first officer replied, standing from his own seat in preparation to occupy hers until she returned from her evening constitutional.

Not every long-haul freighter captain ran their ship like a military vessel. Hedda had seen starships with stained floors and leaking pipes and cracks in their cockpit viewports, lapses that speared her to her very soul. But Hedda Casset began her career as a fighter pilot with the Malastare—Sullust Joint Task Force, keeping order in their little sector on the border of the Mid Rim. She'd started out flying an Incom Z-24, the single-seat fighter everyone just called a Buzzbug. Mostly security missions, hunting down pirates and the like. Eventually, though, she rose to command a heavy cruiser, one of the largest vessels in the fleet. A good career, doing good work.

She'd left Mallust JTF with distinction and moved on to a job captaining merchant vessels for the Byne Guild—her version of a relaxed retirement. But thirty-plus years in the military meant order and discipline weren't just in her blood—they *were* her blood. So every ship she flew now was run like it was about to fight a decisive battle against a Hutt armada, even if it was just carrying a load of ogrut hides from world A to world B. This ship, the *Legacy Run,* was no exception.

Hedda stood, accepting and returning Lieutenant Jary Bowman's snapped salute. She stretched, feeling the bones of her spine crackle and crunch. Too many years on patrol in tiny cockpits, too many high-g maneuvers—sometimes in combat, sometimes just because it made her feel alive.

The real problem, though, she thought, tucking a stray strand of gray hair behind one ear, *is too many years.*

She left the bridge, departing the precise machine of her command deck and walking along a compact corridor into the larger, more chaotic world of the *Legacy Run.* The ship was a Kaniff Yards Class A modular freight transport, more than twice as old as Hedda herself. That put the craft a bit past her ideal operational life, but well within safe parameters if she was well maintained and regularly serviced—which she was. Her captain saw to that.

The *Run* was a mixed-use ship, rated for both cargo and passengers—hence "modular" in its designation. Most of the vessel's structure was taken up by a single gigantic compartment, shaped like a long, triangular prism, with engineering aft, the bridge fore, and the rest of the space allotted for cargo. Hollow boom arms protruded from the central "spine" at regular intervals, to which additional smaller modules could be attached. The ship could hold up to 144 of these, each customizable, to handle every kind of cargo the galaxy had to offer.

Hedda liked that the ship could haul just about anything. It meant you never knew what you were going to get, what weird challenges you might face from one job to the next. She had flown the ship once when half the cargo space in the primary compartment was reconfigured into a huge water tank, to carry a gigantic saberfish from the storm seas on Tibrin to the private aquarium of a countess on Abregado-rae. Hedda and her crew had gotten the beast there safely—not an easy gig. Even harder, though, was getting the creature back to Tibrin three cycles later, when the blasted thing got sick because the countess's people had no idea how to take care of it. She gave the woman credit, though—she paid full freight to send the saberfish home. A lot of people, nobles especially, would have just let it die.

This particular trip, in comparison, was as simple as they came. The *Legacy Run*'s cargo sections were about 80 percent filled with settlers heading to the Outer Rim from overpopulated Core and Colony worlds, seeking new lives, new opportunities, new skies. She could relate to that. Hedda Casset had been restless all her life. She had a feeling she'd die that way, too, looking out a viewport, hoping her eyes would land on something she'd never seen before.

Because this was a transport run, most of the ship's modules were basic passenger configurations, with open seating that converted into beds that were, in theory, comfortable enough to sleep in. Sanitary facilities, storage, a few holoscreens, small galleys, and that was it. For settlers willing to pay for the increased comfort and convenience, some had droid-operated auto-canteens and private sleeping compartments, but not many. These people were frugal. If they'd had credits to begin with, they probably wouldn't be heading to the Outer Rim to scrape out a future. The dark edge of the galaxy was a place of challenges both exciting and deadly. More deadly than exciting, in truth.

Even the road to get out here is tricky, Hedda thought, her gaze drawn by the swirl of hyperspace outside the large porthole she happened to be passing. She snapped her eyes away, knowing she could end up standing there for twenty minutes if she let herself get sucked in. You couldn't trust hyperspace. It was useful, sure, it got you from here to there, it was the key to the expansion of the Republic out from the Core, but no one really understood it. If your navidroid miscalculated the coordinates, even a little, you could end up off the marked route, the main road through whatever hyperspace actually was, and then you'd be on a dark path leading to who knew where. It happened even in the welltraveled hyperlanes near the galactic center, and out here, where the prospectors had barely mapped out any routes . . . well, you had to watch yourself.

She put her concerns out of her mind and continued on her way. The truth was, the *Legacy Run* was currently speeding along the best-traveled, bestknown route to the Outer Rim worlds. Ships moved through this hyperlane constantly, in both directions. Nothing to worry about.

But then, more than nine thousand souls aboard this ship were depending on Captain Hedda Casset to get them safely to their destination. She worried. It was her job.

Hedda exited the corridor and entered the central hull, emerging in a large, circular space, an open spot necessitated by the ship's structure that had been repurposed as a sort of unofficial common area. A group of children kicked a ball around as adults stood and chatted nearby; all just enjoying a little break from the cramped confines of the modules where they spent most of their time. The space wasn't fancy, just a bare junction spot where several short corridors met—but it was clean. The ship employed—at its captain's insistence—an automated maintenance crew that kept its interiors neat and sanitary. One of the custodial droids was spidering its way along a wall at that very moment, performing one of the endless tasks required on a ship the size of the *Run*.

She took a moment to take stock of this group—twenty

people or so, all ages, from a number of worlds. Humans, of course, but also a few four-armed, fur-covered Ardennians, a family of Givin with their distinctive triangular eyes, and even a Lannik with its pinched face, topknot, and huge, pointed ears protruding from the sides of its head—you didn't see many of those around. But no matter their planet of origin, they were all just ordinary beings, biding time until their new lives could begin.

One of the kids looked up.

"Captain Casset!" the boy said, a human, olive-skinned with red hair. She knew him.

"Hello, Serj," Hedda said. "What's the good word? Everything all right here?"

The other children stopped their game and clustered around her.

"Could use some new holos," Serj said. "We've watched everything in the system."

"All we got is all we got," Hedda replied. "And stop trying to slice into the archive to see the age-restricted titles. You think I don't know? This is my ship. I know everything that happens on the *Legacy Run*."

She leaned forward.

"Everything."

Serj blushed and looked toward his friends, who had also, suddenly, found very interesting things to look at on the absolutely uninteresting floor, ceiling, and walls of the chamber.

"Don't worry about it," she said, straightening. "I get it. This is a pretty boring ride. You won't believe me, but in not too long, when your parents have you plowing fields or building fences or fighting off rancors, you'll be dreaming of the time you spent on this ship. Just relax and enjoy."

Serj rolled his eyes and returned to whatever improvised ball game he and the other kids had devised.

Hedda grinned and moved through the room, nodding and chatting as she went. People. Probably some good, some bad, but for the next few days, her people. She loved these runs. No matter what eventually happened in the lives of these folks, they were heading to the Rim to make their dreams come true. She was part of that, and it made her feel good.

Chancellor Soh's Republic wasn't perfect—no government was or ever could be—but it was a system that gave people room to dream. No, even better. It encouraged dreams, big and small. The Republic had its flaws, but really, things could be a hell of a lot worse.

Hedda's rounds took over an hour—she made her way through the passenger compartments, but also checked on a shipment of supercooled liquid Tibanna to make sure the volatile stuff was properly locked down (it was), inspected the engines (all good), investigated the status of repairs to the ship's environmental recirculation systems (in progress and proceeding nicely), and made sure fuel reserves were still more than adequate for the rest of the journey with a comfortable margin besides (they were).

The *Legacy Run* was exactly as she wanted it to be. A tiny, well-maintained world in the wilderness, a warm bubble of safety holding back the void. She couldn't vouch for what was waiting for these settlers once they dispersed into the Outer Rim, but she would make sure they got there safe and sound to find out.

Hedda returned to the bridge, where Lieutenant Bowman all but leapt to his feet the moment he saw her enter.

"Captain on the bridge," he said, and the other officers sat up straighter.

"Thank you, Jary," Hedda said as her second stepped aside and returned to his post.

Hedda settled into her command chair, automatically checking the displays, scanning for anything out of the ordinary.

All is well, she thought.

KTANG. KTANG. KTANG. KTANG. An alarm, loud and insistent. The bridge lighting flipped into its emergency configuration—bathing everything in red. Through the front viewport, the swirls of hyperspace looked off, somehow. Maybe it was the emergency lighting, but they had a . . . reddish tinge. They looked . . . sickly.

Hedda felt her pulse quicken. Her mind snapped into combat mode without thinking.

"Report!" she barked out, her eyes whipping along her own set of screens to find the source of the alarm.

"Alarm generated by the navicomp, Captain," called out her navigator, Cadet Kalwar, a young Quermian. "There's something in the hyperlane. Dead ahead. Big. Impact in ten seconds."

The cadet's voice held steady, and Hedda was proud of him. He probably wasn't that much older than Serj.

She knew this situation was impossible. The hyperlanes were empty. That was the whole point. She couldn't rattle off all the science involved, but she did know that lightspeed collisions in established lanes simply could not happen. It was "mathematically absurd," to hear the engineers talk about it.

Hedda had been flying in deep space long enough to know that impossible things happened all the time, every damn day. She also knew that ten seconds was no time at all at speeds like the *Legacy Run* was traveling.

You can't trust hyperspace, she thought.

Hedda Casset tapped two buttons on her command console.

"Brace yourselves," she said, her voice calm. "I'm taking control."

Two piloting sticks snapped up out from the armrests of her captain's chair, and Hedda grasped them, one in each hand.

She spared the time for one breath, and then she flew.

The *Legacy Run* was not an Incom Z-24 Buzzbug, or even one of the new Republic Longbeams. It had been in service for well over a century. It was a freighter at the end of—if not beyond—its operational life span, loaded to capacity, with engines designed for slow, gradual acceleration and deceleration, and docking with spaceports and orbital loading facilities. It maneuvered like a moon.

The *Legacy Run* was no warship. Not even close. But Hedda flew it like one.

She saw the obstacle in their path with her fighter pilot's eye and instincts, saw it advancing at incredible velocity, large enough that both her ship and whatever the thing was would be disintegrated into atoms, just dust drifting forever through the hyperlanes. There was no time to avoid it. The ship could not make the turn. There was no room, and there was no time.

But Captain Hedda Casset was at the helm, and she would not fail her ship.

The tiniest tweak of the left control stick, and a larger rotation of the right, and the *Legacy Run* moved. More than it wanted to, but not less than its captain believed it could. The huge freighter slipped past the obstacle in their path, the thing shooting by their hull so close Hedda was sure she felt it ruffle her hair despite the many layers of metal and shielding between them.

But they were alive. No impact. The ship was alive.

Turbulence, and Hedda fought it, feeling her way through the jagged bumps and ripples, closing her eyes, not needing to see to fly. The ship groaned, its frame complaining.

"You can do it, old gal," she said, out loud. "We're a couple of cranky old ladies and that's for sure, but we've both got a lot of life to live. I've taken damn good care of you, and you know it. I won't let you down if you won't let me down."

Hedda did not fail her ship.

It failed her.

The groan of overstressed metal became a scream. The vibrations of the ship's passage through space took on a new timbre Hedda had felt too many times before. It was the feeling of a ship that had moved beyond its limits, whether from taking too much damage in a firefight or, as here, just being asked to perform a maneuver that was more than it could give.

The *Legacy Run* was tearing itself apart. At most, it had seconds left.

Hedda opened her eyes. She released the control sticks and tapped out commands on her console, activating the bulkhead shielding that separated each cargo module in the instance of a disaster, thinking that perhaps it might give some of the people aboard a chance. She thought about Serj and his friends, playing in the common area, and how emergency doors had just slammed down at the entrance to each passenger module, possibly trapping them in a zone that was about to become vacuum. She hoped the children had gone to their families when the alarms sounded.

She didn't know.

She just didn't know.

Hedda locked eyes with her first officer, who was staring at her, knowing what was about to happen. He saluted.

"Captain," Lieutenant Bowman said, "it's been an—"

The bridge ripped open.

Hedda Casset died, not knowing if she had saved anyone at all.

ABOUT THE TYPE

This book was set in Sabon, a typeface designed by the well-known German typographer Jan Tschichold (1902–74). Sabon's design is based upon the original letter forms of sixteenth-century French type designer Claude Garamond and was created specifically to be used for three sources: foundry type for hand composition, Linotype, and Monotype. Tschichold named his typeface for the famous Frankfurt typefounder Jacques Sabon (c. 1520–80).

A long time ago in a galaxy far, far away. . . .

Join up! Subscribe to our newsletter
at ReadStarWars.com or find us on social.

f **StarWarsBooks**

🐦 **@DelReyStarWars**

📷 **@DelReyStarWars**

STAR WARS BOOKS BY TIMOTHY ZAHN

DARK FORCE RISING

DARK FORCE RISING

TIMOTHY ZAHN

NEW YORK

2021 Del Rey Trade Paperback Edition

Published in the United States by Del Rey, an imprint of Random House,
a division of Penguin Random House LLC, New York.

DEL REY is a registered trademark and the CIRCLE colophon is a trademark of
Penguin Random House LLC.

Originally published in hardcover in the United States by Bantam Spectra, an
imprint of Random House, a division of
Penguin Random House LLC, in 1992.

ISBN 978-0-593-35879-5
Ebook ISBN 978-0-307-79618-9

Printed in the United States of America on acid-free paper

randomhousebooks.com

8 9

Book design by Edwin Vazquez

THE ESSENTIAL LEGENDS COLLECTION

For more than forty years, novels set in a galaxy far, far away have enriched the *Star Wars* experience for fans seeking to continue the adventure beyond the screen. When he created *Star Wars*, George Lucas built a universe that sparked the imagination and inspired others to create. He opened up that universe to be a creative space for other people to tell their own tales. This became known as the Expanded Universe, or EU, of novels, comics, videogames, and more.

To this day, the EU remains an inspiration for *Star Wars* creators and is published under the label Legends. Ideas, characters, story elements, and more from new *Star Wars* entertainment trace their origins back to material from the Expanded Universe. This Essential Legends Collection curates some of the most treasured stories from that expansive legacy.

DARK FORCE RISING

CHAPTER 1

DIRECTLY AHEAD, THE STAR was a marble-sized yellow-orange ball, its intensity moderated by its distance and by the viewports' automatic sunscreens. Surrounding it and the ship itself were the stars, a spattering of blazing white pinpricks in the deep blackness of space. Directly beneath the ship, in the western part of the Great Northern Forest of the planet Myrkr, dawn was approaching.

The last dawn that some in that forest would ever see.

Standing at one of the side bridge viewports of the Imperial Star Destroyer *Chimaera*, Captain Pellaeon watched as the fuzzy terminator line crept toward the target zone on the planet below. Ten minutes ago, the ground forces surrounding the target had reported themselves ready; the *Chimaera* itself had been holding blockade position for nearly an hour. All that was missing now was the order to attack.

Slowly, feeling almost furtive about it, Pellaeon turned his head a couple of centimeters to the side. Behind him and to his right, Grand Admiral Thrawn was seated at his command station, his blue-skinned face expressionless, his glowing red eyes focused on the bank of status readouts wrapped around his chair. He hadn't spoken or moved from that position since the last of the ground forces had reported in, and Pellaeon could tell the bridge crew was beginning to get restless.

For his own part, Pellaeon had long since stopped trying to second-guess Thrawn's actions. The fact that the late Emperor had seen fit to make Thrawn one of his twelve Grand Admirals was evidence of his own confidence in the man—all the more so given Thrawn's not-entirely-human heritage and the Emperor's well-known prejudices in such matters. Moreover, in the year since Thrawn had taken command of the *Chimaera* and had begun the task of rebuilding the Imperial Fleet, Pellaeon had seen the Grand Admiral's military genius demonstrated time and again. Whatever his reason for holding off the attack, Pellaeon knew it was a good one.

As slowly as he'd turned away, he turned back to the viewport. But his movements had apparently not gone unnoticed. "A question, Captain?" Thrawn's smoothly modulated voice cut through the low hum of bridge conversation.

"No, sir," Pellaeon assured him, turning again to face his superior.

For a moment those glowing eyes studied him, and Pellaeon unconsciously braced himself for a reprimand, or worse. But Thrawn, as Pellaeon still had a tendency to forget, did not have the legendary and lethal temper that had been the hallmark of the Lord Darth Vader. "You're perhaps wondering why we haven't yet attacked?" the Grand Admiral suggested in that same courteous tone.

"Yes, sir, I was," Pellaeon admitted. "All our forces appear to be in position."

"Our military forces are, yes," Thrawn agreed. "But not the observers I sent into Hyllyard City."

Pellaeon blinked. "Hyllyard City?"

"Yes. I find it unlikely that a man of Talon Karrde's cunning would set up a base in the middle of a forest without also setting up security contacts with others outside the immediate area. Hyllyard City is too far from Karrde's base for anyone there to directly witness our attack; hence, any sudden flurries of activity in the city will imply the existence of a more subtle line of communication. From that we'll be able to identify Karrde's contacts and put them under long-term surveillance. Eventually, they'll lead us to him."

"Yes, sir," Pellaeon said, feeling a frown crease his forehead. "Then you're not expecting to take any of Karrde's own people alive."

The Grand Admiral's smile turned brittle. "On the contrary. I fully expect our forces to find an empty and abandoned base."

Pellaeon threw a glance out the viewport at the partly lit planet below. "In that case, sir . . . why are we attacking it?"

"Three reasons, Captain. First, even men like Talon Karrde occasionally make mistakes. It could well be that in the rush to evacuate his base he left some crucial bit of information behind. Second, as I've already mentioned, an attack on the base may lead us to his contacts in Hyllyard City. And third, it provides our ground forces with some badly needed field experience."

The glowing eyes bored into Pellaeon's face. "Never forget, Captain, that our goal is no longer merely the pitiful rearguard harassment of the past five years. With Mount Tantiss and our late Emperor's collection of Spaarti cylinders in our hands, the initiative is once again ours. Very soon now we'll begin the process of taking planets back from the Rebellion; and for that we'll need an army every bit as well trained as the officers and crew of the Fleet."

"Understood, Admiral," Pellaeon said.

"Good." Thrawn lowered his gaze to his displays. "It's time. Signal General Covell that he may begin."

"Yes, sir," Pellaeon said, leaving the viewport and returning to his station. He gave the readouts a quick check and tapped his comm switch, peripherally aware as he did so that Thrawn had likewise activated his own comm. Some private message to his spies in Hyllyard City? "This is the *Chimaera*," Pellaeon said. "Launch the attack."

"ACKNOWLEDGED, *CHIMAERA*," GENERAL COVELL said into his helmet comlink, careful to keep the quiet scorn in his gut from getting through to his voice. It was typical—typical and disgustingly predictable. You scrambled around like mad hellions, got your troops and vehicles on the ground and set up . . . and then you stood around waiting for those strutting Fleet people in their spotless uniforms and nice clean ships to finish sipping their tea and finally get around to letting you loose.

Well, get yourselves comfortable, he thought sardonically in the direction of the Star Destroyer overhead. Because whether Grand Admiral Thrawn was interested in real results or just a good rousing show, he was going to get his money's worth. Reaching to the board in front of him, he keyed for local command frequency. "General Covell to all units: we've got the light. Let's go."

The acknowledgments came in; and with a shiver from the steel deck beneath him, the huge AT-AT walker was off, lumbering its deceptively awkward-looking way through the forest toward the encampment a kilometer away. Ahead of the AT-AT, occasionally visible through the armored transparisteel viewport, a pair of AT-ST scout walkers ran in twin-point formation, tracking along the AT-AT's path and watching for enemy positions or booby traps. Not that such futile gestures would do Karrde any good. Covell had directed literally hundreds of assault campaigns in his years of Imperial service, and he knew full well the awesome capabilities of the fighting machines under his command.

Beneath the viewport, the holographic tactical display was lit up like a decorative disk, the winking red, white, and green lights showing the positions of Covell's circle of AT-ATs,

AT-STs, and hoverscout attack vehicles, all closing on Karrde's encampment in good order.

Good, but not perfect. The north-flank AT-AT and its support vehicles were lagging noticeably behind the rest of the armored noose. "Unit Two, bring it up," he said into his comlink.

"Trying, sir," the voice came back, tinny and distant through the strange dampening effects of Myrkr's metal-rich flora. "We're encountering some thick vine clusters that are slowing down our scout walkers."

"Is it bothering your AT-AT any?"

"No, sir, but I wanted to keep the flank together—"

"Pattern coherence is a fine goal during academy maneuvers, Major," Covell cut him off. "But not at the expense of an overall battle plan. If the AT-STs can't keep up, leave them behind."

"Yes, sir."

Covell broke the connection with a snort. The Grand Admiral was right about one thing, at least: his troops were going to need a lot more battle seasoning before they would be up to real Imperial standards. Still, the raw material was there. Even as he watched, the north flank reformed itself, with the hoverscouts spreading forward to take up the AT-STs' former point positions while the lagging AT-STs themselves fell back into rear-guard deployment.

The energy sensor beeped a proximity warning: they were coming up on the encampment. "Status?" he asked his crew.

"All weapons charged and ready," the gunner reported, his eyes on the targeting displays.

"No indications of resistance, active or passive," the driver added.

"Stay alert," Covell ordered, keying for command frequency again. "All units: move in."

And with a final crash of mangled vegetation, the AT-AT broke through into the clearing.

It was an impressive sight. From all four sides of the open area, in nearly perfect parade-ground unison, the other three AT-ATs appeared from the forest cover in the predawn gloom, the AT-STs and hoverscouts clustered around their feet quickly fanning out on all sides to encircle the darkened buildings.

Covell gave the sensors a quick but thorough check. Two energy sources were still functioning, one in the central building, the other in one of the outer barracks-style structures. There was no evidence of operating sensors, or of weapons or energy fields. The life-form analyzer ran through its complicated algorithms and concluded that the outer buildings were devoid of life.

The large main building, on the other hand . . .

"I'm getting approximately twenty life-form readings from the main building, General," the number four AT-AT commander reported. "All in the central section."

"They don't register as human, though," Covell's driver murmured.

"Maybe they're being shielded," Covell grunted, looking out the viewport. Still no movement from the encampment. "Let's find out. Assault squads: go."

The hoverscouts popped their aft hatchways, and from each came a squad of eight soldiers, laser rifles held tautly across battle-armored chests as they dropped to the ground. Half of each squad took up backstop position, their rifles trained on the encampment from the partial cover of their hoverscout, while the other half sprinted across the open ground to the outer line of buildings and sheds. There, they assumed covering positions, allowing their comrades in the rear to similarly advance. It was a centuries-old military tactic, executed with the kind of squeamish determination that Covell would have expected of green troops. Still, the raw material was definitely there.

The soldiers continued their leap-frog approach to the main building, with small groups breaking off the main encirclement to check out each of the outer structures as they passed. The point men reached the central building—a brilliant flash lit up the forest as they blasted down the door— a slightly confused scramble as the rest of the troops piled through.

And then, silence.

For a handful of minutes the silence continued, punctuated only by occasional short commands from the troop commanders. Covell listened, watching the sensors . . . and finally the report came through. "General Covell, this is Lieutenant Barse. We've secured the target zone, sir. There's no one here."

Covell nodded. "Very good, Lieutenant. How does it look?"

"Like they pulled out in a hurry, sir," the other said. "They left a fair amount of stuff behind, but it all looks pretty much like junk."

"That'll be for the scanning crew to decide," Covell told him. "Any indication of booby traps or other unpleasant surprises?"

"None at all, sir. Oh—and those life-forms we picked up are nothing but these long furry animals living on the tree growing up through the center of the roof."

Covell nodded again. Ysalamiri, he believed they were called. Thrawn had been making a big deal about the stupid creatures for a couple of months now, though what use they could possibly be to the war effort he couldn't guess. Eventually, he supposed, the Fleet people would get around to letting him in on the big secret. "Set up a defensive honeycomb," he ordered the lieutenant. "Signal the scanning crew when you're ready. And get comfortable. The Grand Admiral wants this place taken apart, and that's exactly what we're going to do."

"VERY GOOD, GENERAL," the voice said, almost too faint to hear despite the heavy amplification and computer scrubbing. "Proceed with the dismantling."

Seated at the *Wild Karrde*'s helm, Mara Jade half turned to face the man standing behind her. "I suppose that's it, then," she said.

For a moment Talon Karrde didn't seem to hear her. He just stood there, gazing through the viewport at the distant planet, a tiny bluish-white crescent shape visible around the jagged edge of the sun-skimmer asteroid the *Wild Karrde* was snuggled up against. Mara was just about to repeat the comment when he stirred. "Yes," he said, that calm voice showing no hint of the emotion he was obviously feeling. "I suppose it is."

Mara exchanged glances with Aves, at the copilot station, then looked back up at Karrde. "Shouldn't we be going, then?" she prompted.

Karrde took a deep breath . . . and as she watched him, Mara caught in his expression a glimmer of what the Myrkr base had meant to him. More than just a base, it had been his home.

With an effort, she suppressed the thought. So Karrde had lost his home. Big deal. She'd lost far more than that in her lifetime and had survived just fine. He'd get over it. "I asked if we should get going."

"I heard you," Karrde said, the flicker of emotion vanishing again into that slightly sardonic facade of his. "I think perhaps we ought to wait a little longer. See if we left anything behind that might point in the direction of our Rishi base."

Mara looked at Aves again. "We were pretty thorough," Aves said. "I don't think there was any mention of Rishi anywhere except the main computer, and that left with the first group out."

"I agree," Karrde said. "Are you willing to stake your life on that assessment?"

Aves's lip twitched. "Not really."

"Nor am I. So we wait."

"What if they spot us?" Mara persisted. "Skulking behind asteroids is the oldest trick on the list."

"They won't spot us." Karrde was quietly positive. "Actually, I doubt the possibility will even occur to them. The average man running from the likes of Grand Admiral Thrawn is unlikely to stop running until he's a good deal farther away than this."

Are you willing to stake your life on that assessment? Mara thought sourly. But she kept the retort to herself. He was probably right; and anyway, if the *Chimaera* or any of its TIE fighters started toward *Wild Karrde*, they would have no trouble punching the engines up to power and going to lightspeed well ahead of the attack.

The logic and tactics seemed clean. But still, Mara could feel something nagging at the back of her mind. Something that didn't feel good about all this.

Gritting her teeth, she adjusted the ship's sensors to their highest sensitivity and checked once more that the engine pre-start sequence was keyed in and ready. And then settled in to wait.

THE SCANNING CREW was fast, efficient, and thorough; and it took them just over thirty minutes to come up completely dry.

"Well, so much for that." Pellaeon grimaced as he watched the negative reports scroll up his display. A good practice session for the ground forces, perhaps, but otherwise the whole exercise seemed to have been pretty useless. "Unless your observers have picked up any reactions in Hyllyard City," he added, turning to face Thrawn.

The Grand Admiral's glowing red eyes were on his displays. "There was a small twitch, as a matter of fact," he said. "Cut off almost before it began, but I think the implications are clear."

Well, that was something, anyway. "Yes, sir. Shall I have Surveillance begin equipping a long-term ground team?"

"Patience, Captain," Thrawn said. "It may not be necessary, after all. Key for a midrange scan, and tell me what you see."

Pellaeon swiveled back to his command board and tapped for the appropriate readout. There was Myrkr itself, of course, and the standard TIE fighter defense cloud ranged around the *Chimaera*. The only other object anywhere within midrange distance—"You mean that little asteroid out there?"

"That's the one," Thrawn nodded. "Nothing remarkable about it, is there? No, don't do a sensor focus," he added, almost before the thought of doing one had even occurred to Pellaeon. "We wouldn't want to prematurely flush our quarry, would we?"

"Our quarry?" Pellaeon repeated, frowning at the sensor data again. The routine sensor scans that had been done of the asteroid three hours earlier had come up negative, and nothing could have sneaked up on it since then without being detected. "With all due respect, sir, I don't see any indication that anything's out there."

"I don't either," Thrawn agreed. "But it's the only sizable cover available for nearly ten million kilometers around Myrkr. There's really no other place for Karrde to watch our operation from."

Pellaeon pursed his lips. "Your permission, Admiral, but I doubt Karrde is foolish enough to just sit around waiting for us to arrive."

The glowing red eyes narrowed, just a bit. "You forget, Captain," he said softly, "that I've met the man. More important, I've seen the sort of artwork he collects." He turned back to his displays. "No; he's out there. I'm sure of it. Talon Karrde is not merely a smuggler, you see. Perhaps not even primarily a smuggler. His real love is not goods or money but information. More than anything else in the galaxy, he craves knowledge . . . and the knowledge of what we have or have not found here is too valuable a gem for him to pass up."

Pellaeon studied the Grand Admiral's profile. It was, in his opinion, a pretty tenuous leap of logic. But on the other hand, he'd seen too many similar leaps borne out not to take this one seriously. "Shall I order a TIE fighter squadron to investigate, sir?"

"As I said, Captain, patience," Thrawn said. "Even in sensor stealth mode with all engines shut down, he'll have made sure he can power up and escape before any attack force could reach him." He smiled at Pellaeon. "Or rather, any attack force from the *Chimaera*."

A stray memory clicked: Thrawn, reaching for his comm just as Pellaeon was giving the ground forces the order to attack. "You sent a message to the rest of the fleet," he said. "Timing it against my attack order to mask the transmission."

Thrawn's blue-black eyebrows lifted a fraction. "Very good, Captain. Very good, indeed."

Pellaeon felt a touch of warmth on his cheeks. The Grand Admiral's compliments were few and far between. "Thank you, sir."

Thrawn nodded. "More precisely, my message was to a single ship, the *Constrainer*. It will arrive in approximately ten minutes. At which point"—his eyes glittered—"we'll see just how accurate my reading of Karrde has been."

OVER THE *WILD KARRDE'S* bridge speakers, the reports from the scanning crew were beginning to taper off. "Doesn't sound like they've found anything," Aves commented.

"Like you said, we were thorough," Mara reminded him, hardly hearing her own words. The nameless thing nagging at the back of her mind seemed to be getting stronger. "Can we get out of here now?" she asked, turning to look at Karrde.

He frowned down at her. "Try to relax, Mara. They can't possibly know we're here. There's been no sensor-focus probe of the asteroid, and without one there's no way for them to detect this ship."

"Unless a Star Destroyer's sensors are better than you think," Mara retorted.

"We know all about their sensors," Aves soothed. "Ease up, Mara, Karrde knows what he's doing. The *Wild Karrde* has probably the tightest sensor stealth mode this side of—"

He broke off as the bridge door opened behind them; and Mara turned just as Karrde's two pet vornskrs bounded into the room.

Dragging, very literally, their handler behind them.

"What are you doing here, Chin?" Karrde asked.

"Sorry, Capt'," Chin puffed, digging his heels into the deck and leaning back against the taut leashes. The effort was only partially successful; the predators were still pulling him slowly forward. "I couldn't stop them. I thought maybe they wanted to see you, hee?"

"What's the matter with you two, anyway?" Karrde chided the animals, squatting down in front of them. "Don't you know we're busy?"

The vornskrs didn't look at him. Didn't even seem to notice his presence, for that matter. They continued staring straight ahead as if he wasn't even there.

Staring directly at Mara.

"Hey," Karrde said, reaching over to slap one of the animals lightly across the muzzle. "I'm talking to you, Sturm. What's gotten into you, anyway?" He glanced along their unblinking line of sight—

Paused for a second and longer look. "Are you doing something, Mara?"

Mara shook her head, a cold shiver tingling up her back. She'd seen that look before, on many of the wild vornskrs she'd run into during that long three-day trek through the Myrkr forest with Luke Skywalker.

Except that those vornskr stares hadn't been directed at her. They'd been reserved instead for Skywalker. Usually just before they attacked him.

"That's Mara, Sturm," Karrde told the animal, speaking to it as he might a child. "Mara. Come on, now—you saw her all the time back home."

Slowly, almost reluctantly, Sturm stopped his forward pull and turned his attention to his master. "Mara," Karrde repeated, looking the vornskr firmly in the eye. "A friend. You hear that, Drang?" he added, reaching over to grip the other vornskr's muzzle. "She's a friend. Understand?"

Drang seemed to consider that. Then, as reluctantly as Sturm had, he lowered his head and stopped pulling. "That's better," Karrde said, scratching both vornskrs briefly behind their ears and standing up again. "Better take them back down, Chin. Maybe walk them around the main hold—give them some exercise."

"If I can find a clear track through all the stuff in there, hee?" Chin grunted, twitching back on the leashes. "Come on, littles—we go now."

With only a slight hesitation the two vornskrs allowed him to take them off the bridge. Karrde watched as the door shut behind them. "I wonder what that was all about," he said, giving Mara a thoughtful look.

"I don't know," she told him, hearing the tightness in her voice. With the temporary distraction now gone, the strange dread she'd been feeling was back again in full force. She swiveled back to her board, half expecting to see a squadron of TIE fighters bearing down on them.

But there was nothing. Only the *Chimaera*, still sitting harmlessly out there in orbit around Myrkr. No threat any of the *Wild Karrde*'s instruments could detect. But the tingling was getting stronger and stronger . . .

And suddenly she could sit still no longer. Reaching out to the control board, she keyed for engine prestart.

"Mara!" Aves yelped, jumping in his seat as if he'd been stung. "What in—?"

"They're coming," Mara snarled back, hearing the strain of a half dozen tangled emotions in her voice. The die was irrevocably cast—her activation of the *Wild Karrde*'s engines would have set sensors screaming all over the *Chimaera*. Now there was nowhere to go but out.

She looked up at Karrde, suddenly afraid of what his expression might be saying. But he was just standing there looking down at her, a slightly quizzical frown on his face. "They don't appear to be coming," he pointed out mildly.

She shook her head, feeling the pleading in her eyes. "You have to believe me," she said, uncomfortably aware that she didn't really believe it herself. "They're getting ready to attack."

"I believe you," he said soothingly. Or perhaps he, too, recognized that there weren't any other choices left. "Aves: lightspeed calculation. Take the easiest course setting that's not anywhere toward Rishi; we'll stop and reset later."

"Karrde—"

"Mara is second in command," Karrde cut him off. "As such, she has the right and the duty to make important decisions."

"Yeah, but—" Aves stopped, the last word coming out pinched as he strangled it off. "Yeah," he said between clenched teeth. Throwing a glower at Mara, he turned to the nav computer and got to work.

"You might as well get us moving, Mara," Karrde continued, stepping over to the vacant communications chair and sitting down. "Keep the asteroid between us and the *Chimaera* as long as you can."

"Yes, sir," Mara said. Her tangle of emotions was starting to dissolve now, leaving a mixture of anger and profound embarrassment in its wake. She'd done it again. Listened to her inner feelings—tried to do things she knew full well she couldn't do—and in the process had once again wound up clutching the sharp end of the bayonet.

And it was probably the last she'd hear of being Karrde's second in command, too. Command unity in front of Aves was one thing, but once they were out of here and he could get her alone there was going to be hell to pay. She'd be lucky if he didn't bounce her out of his organization altogether. Jabbing viciously at her board, she swung the *Wild Karrde* around, turning its nose away from the asteroid and starting to drive toward deep space—

And with a flicker of pseudomotion, something big shot in from lightspeed, dropping neatly into normal space not twenty kilometers away.

An Imperial Interdictor Cruiser.

Aves yelped a startled-sounding curse. "We got company," he barked.

"I see it," Karrde said. As cool as ever . . . but Mara could hear the tinge of surprise in his voice, too. "What's our time to lightspeed?"

"It'll be another minute," Aves said tautly. "There's a lot of junk in the outer system for the computer to work through."

"We have a race, then," Karrde said. "Mara?"

"Up to point seven three," she said, nursing as much power as she could out of the still-sluggish engines. He was right; it was indeed going to be a race. With their four huge gravity-wave generators capable of simulating planet-sized masses, Interdictor Cruisers were the Empire's weapon of choice for trapping an enemy ship in normal space while TIE fighters pounded it to rubble. But coming in fresh out of lightspeed itself, the Interdictor would need another minute before it could power up those generators. If she could get the *Wild Karrde* out of range by then . . .

"More visitors," Aves announced. "A couple squadrons of TIE fighters coming from the *Chimaera*."

"We're up to point eight six power," Mara reported. "We'll be ready for lightspeed as soon as the nav computer gives me a course."

"Interdictor status?"

"Grav generators are powering up," Aves said. On Mara's tactical display a ghostly cone appeared, showing the area where the lightspeed-dampening field would soon exist. She changed course slightly, aiming for the nearest edge, and risked a glance at the nav computer display. Almost ready. The hazy grav cone was rapidly becoming more substantial . . .

The computer scope pinged. Mara wrapped her hand around the three hyperspace control levers at the front of the control board and gently pulled them toward her. The *Wild Karrde* shuddered slightly, and for a second it seemed that the Interdictor had won their deadly race. Then, abruptly, the stars outside burst into starlines.

They'd made it.

Aves heaved a sigh of relief as the starlines faded into the mottled sky of hyperspace. "Talk about slicing the mynock close to the hull. How do you suppose they tumbled that we were out there, anyway?"

"No idea," Karrde said, his voice cool. "Mara?"

"I don't know, either." Mara kept her eyes on her displays, not daring to look at either of them. "Thrawn may have just been playing a hunch. He does that sometimes."

"Lucky for us he's not the only one who gets hunches," Aves offered, his voice sounding a little strange. "Nice going, Mara. Sorry I jumped on you."

"Yes," Karrde seconded. "A very good job indeed."

"Thanks," Mara muttered, keeping her eyes on her control board and blinking back the tears that had suddenly come to her eyes. So it was back. She'd hoped fervently that her locating of Skywalker's X-wing out in deep space had been an isolated event. A fluke, more his doing than hers.

But no. It was all coming back, as it had so many times before in the past five years. The hunches and sensory flickers, the urges and the compulsions.

Which meant that, very soon now, the dreams would probably be starting again, too.

Angrily, she swiped at her eyes, and with an effort un-clenched her jaw. It was a familiar enough pattern . . . but this time things were going to be different. Always before there'd been nothing she could do about the voices and urges except to suffer through the cycle. To suffer, and to be ready to break out of whatever niche she'd managed to carve for herself when she finally betrayed herself to those around her.

But she wasn't a serving girl in a Phorliss cantina this time, or a come-up flector for a swoop gang on Caprioril, or even a hyperdrive mechanic stuck in the backwater of the Ison Corridor. She was second in command to the most powerful smuggler in the galaxy, with the kind of resources and mobility she hadn't had since the death of the Emperor.

The kind of resources that would let her find Luke Skywalker again. And kill him.

Maybe then the voices would stop.

FOR A LONG MINUTE Thrawn stood at the bridge viewport, looking out at the distant asteroid and the now superfluous Interdictor Cruiser near it. It was, Pellaeon thought uneasily, almost the identical posture the Grand Admiral had assumed when Luke Skywalker had so recently escaped a similar trap. Holding his breath, Pellaeon stared at Thrawn's back, wondering if another of the *Chimaera*'s crewers was about to be executed for this failure.

Thrawn turned around. "Interesting," he said, his voice conversational. "Did you note the sequence of events, Captain?"

"Yes, sir," Pellaeon said cautiously. "The target was already powering up before the *Constrainer* arrived."

"Yes," Thrawn nodded. "And it implies one of three things. Either Karrde was about to leave anyway, or else he panicked for some reason—" The red eyes glittered. "Or else he was somehow warned off."

Pellaeon felt his back stiffen. "I hope you're not suggesting, sir, that one of our people tipped him."

"No, of course not." Thrawn's lip twitched slightly. "Loyalties of your crewers aside, no one on the *Chimaera* knew the *Constrainer* was on its way; and no one on the *Constrainer* could have sent any messages here without our detecting them." He stepped over to his command station and sat down, a thoughtful look on his face. "An interesting puzzle, Captain.

One I'll have to give some thought to. In the meantime, we have more pressing matters. The task of acquiring new warships, for one. Have there been any recent responses to our invitation?"

"Nothing particularly interesting, Admiral," Pellaeon said, pulling up the comm log and giving it a quick scan to refresh his memory. "Eight of the fifteen groups I contacted have expressed interest, though none were willing to commit themselves to anything specific. We're still waiting on the others."

Thrawn nodded. "We'll give them a few weeks. If there've been no results after that time, we'll make the invitation a bit more compulsory."

"Yes, sir." Pellaeon hesitated. "There's also been another communication from Jomark."

Thrawn turned his glowing eyes on Pellaeon. "I would very much appreciate it, Captain," he said, biting off each word, "if you would try to make it clear to our exalted Jedi Master C'baoth that if he persists in these communications he's going to subvert the whole purpose of putting him on Jomark in the first place. If the Rebels get even a hint of any connection between us, he can forget about Skywalker ever showing up there."

"I *have* explained it to him, sir," Pellaeon grimaced. "Numerous times. His reply is always that Skywalker is going to show up. And then he demands to know when you're going to get around to delivering Skywalker's sister to him."

For a long moment Thrawn said nothing. "I suppose there'll be no shutting him up until he gets what he wants," he said at last. "Nor of getting any uncomplaining work out of him, either."

"Yes, he was grumbling about the attack coordination you've been having him do," Pellaeon nodded. "He's warned me several times that he can't predict exactly when Skywalker will arrive on Jomark."

"And implied that a horrible retribution would fall upon us if he's not there when that happens," Thrawn growled. "Yes, I know the routine well. And I'm getting rather tired of it." He took a deep breath, let it out slowly. "Very well, Captain. The next time C'baoth calls, you may inform him that the Taanab operation will be his last for the immediate future. Skywalker isn't likely to make it to Jomark for at least two more weeks— the little pot of political confusion we've stirred up in the Rebellion high command should occupy him at least that long. As to Organa Solo and her unborn Jedi . . . you may also inform him that from now on I'll be taking a personal hand in that matter."

Pellaeon threw a quick glance over his shoulder, to where the Grand Admiral's bodyguard, Rukh, stood silently near the aft bridge door. "Does that mean you'll be taking the Noghri off the job, sir?" he asked quietly.

"Do you have a problem with that, Captain?"

"No, sir. May I respectfully remind the Grand Admiral, though, that the Noghri have never liked leaving a mission uncompleted."

"The Noghri are servants of the Empire," Thrawn countered coldly. "More to the point, they're loyal to me personally. They will do as they're told." He paused. "However, I'll take your concerns under advisement. At any rate, our task here at Myrkr is completed. Order General Covell to bring his force back up."

"Yes, sir," Pellaeon said, signaling the communications officer to relay the message.

"I'll want the general's report on file in three hours," Thrawn continued. "Twelve hours after that I want his recommendations as to the three best infantry troopers and two best mechanized operators in the assault. Those five men will be transferred to the Mount Tantiss operation and given immediate transport to Wayland."

"Understood," Pellaeon nodded, dutifully logging the orders in Covell's file. Such recommendations had been part of standard Imperial procedure for several weeks now, ever since the Mount Tantiss operation had begun in earnest. But

Thrawn nevertheless still periodically went out of his way to mention it to his officers. Perhaps as a not-so-subtle reminder of how vitally important those recommendations were to the Grand Admiral's sweeping plan to crush the Rebellion.

Thrawn looked out the viewport again at the planet beneath them. "And while we await the general's return, you'll contact Surveillance regarding that long-term team for Hyllyard City." He smiled. "It's a very large galaxy, Captain, but even a man like Talon Karrde can run for only so long. Eventually, he'll have to come to rest."

It wasn't really deserving of its name, the High Castle of Jomark. Not in Joruus C'baoth's estimation, anyway. Short and dirty, its stonework ill-fitting in places and as alien as the long-gone race that had built it, it squatted uneasily between two of the larger crags on what was left of an ancient volcanic cone. Still, with the rest of the rim circling around in the distance, and the brilliant blue waters of Ring Lake four hundred meters almost straight down beneath him, C'baoth could allow that the natives had at least found some good scenery to build their castle on. Their castle, or temple, or whatever. It had been a good place for a Jedi Master to move into, if only because the colonists seemed to hold the place in awe. Then too, the dark island that filled the center of the crater and gave the lake its ring shape provided a suitably hidden landing site for Thrawn's annoyingly endless stream of shuttles.

But it was neither the scenery, nor the power, nor even the Empire that held C'baoth's thoughts as he stood on the castle terrace and gazed down into Ring Lake. It was, instead, the strange flicker he'd just felt in the Force.

He'd felt it before, this flicker. Or at least he thought he had. Threads to the past were always so hard to follow, so easily lost in the mists and the hurryings of the present. Even of his own past he had only glimpses of memory, scenes as if from a history record. He rather thought he remembered someone trying to explain the reasons to him once, but the explanation was long gone in the darkness of the past.

It didn't matter anyway. Memory wasn't important; concentration wasn't important; his own past wasn't important. He could call upon the Force when he wanted to, and *that* was what was important. As long as he could do that, no one could ever hurt him or take away what he had.

Except that Grand Admiral Thrawn had already taken it away. Hadn't he?

C'baoth looked around the terrace. Yes. Yes; this wasn't the home and city and world he'd chosen to mold and command as his own. This wasn't Wayland, which he'd wrested from the Dark Jedi whom the Emperor had set to guard his Mount Tantiss storehouse. This was Jomark, where he was waiting for . . . someone.

He stroked his fingers through his long white beard, forcing himself to concentrate. He was waiting for Luke Skywalker—that was it. Luke Skywalker was going to come to him, and Luke Skywalker's sister and her as-yet-unborn twins, and he would turn all of them into his followers. Grand Admiral Thrawn had promised them to him, in return for his help to the Empire.

He winced at the thought. It was hard, this help that Grand Admiral Thrawn wanted. He had to concentrate hard to do what they wanted; to hold his thoughts and feelings closely in line, and for long periods at a time. On Wayland he hadn't had to do anything like that, not since he'd fought against the Emperor's Guardian.

He smiled. It had been a grand battle, that fight against the Guardian. But even as he tried to remember it, the details skittered away like straws in the wind. It had been too long ago.

Long ago . . . like these flickers in the Force had been.

C'baoth's fingers slipped away from his beard, to the medallion nestled against the skin of his chest. Squeezing the warm metal against his palm, he fought against the mists of the past, trying to see beyond them. Yes. Yes, he was not mistaken. These same flickers had come three times before in the past few seasons. Had come, had stayed for a time, and then once again had gone dormant. Like someone who had learned how to utilize the Force for a time, but then somehow forgotten.

He didn't understand it. But it was of no threat to him, and so wasn't important.

Above him, he could sense now the Imperial Star Destroyer entering high orbit, far above the clouds where none of the others on Jomark would see it. When night fell, the shuttle would come, and they would take him off somewhere—Taanab, he thought—to help coordinate yet another of these multiple Imperial attacks.

He wasn't looking forward to the effort and pain. But it would all be worth it when he had his Jedi. He would remake them in his own image, and they would be his servants and his followers all the days of their lives.

And then even Grand Admiral Thrawn would have to admit that he, Joruus C'baoth, had found the true meaning of power.

CHAPTER 2

"I'M SORRY, LUKE," Wedge Antilles' voice said over the comm, the words punctuated by occasional spittings of static. "I've tried every handle I can think of, including pulling all the rank I've got and some I haven't. It's still no go. Some data pusher up the riser somewhere has issued orders that the Sluissi's own defense ships have absolute top priority for repair work. Until we can find this guy and talk him into a special dispensation, we're not going to get anyone to touch your X-wing."

Luke Skywalker grimaced, feeling four hours' worth of frustration welling up in his throat. Four precious hours wasted, with the end still not in sight, while on Coruscant the future of the entire New Republic was even now teetering on the edge. "Did you get this data pusher's name?" he asked.

"I couldn't even get that," Wedge said. "Every line I've tried has disappeared about three layers up from the mechanics themselves. I'm still trying, but this whole place has gone kind of baffy."

"A major Imperial attack will do that to you," Luke conceded with a sigh. He could understand why the Sluissi had set their priorities the way they had; but it wasn't like he was just going off on a joyride, either. It was a good six-day flight from here to Coruscant as it was, and every hour that he was delayed was one more hour the political forces trying to oust Admiral Ackbar would have to consolidate their position. "Keep trying, okay? I've got to get out of here."

"Sure," Wedge said. "Look, I know you're worried about what's happening on Coruscant. But any one person can only do so much. Even a Jedi."

"I know," Luke agreed reluctantly. And Han was on his way back, and Leia was already there . . . "I just hate sitting around being out of it."

"Me, too." Wedge lowered his voice a bit. "You've still got one other option. Don't forget that."

"I won't," Luke promised. It was certainly an option he'd been tempted to take his friend up on. But Luke wasn't officially a member of the New Republic military anymore; and with the New Republic forces here at the shipyards still at full alert, Wedge could face an immediate court martial for handing his X-wing over to a civilian. Councilor Borsk Fey'lya and his anti-Ackbar faction might not want to bother making an example out of someone as relatively low in rank as a starfighter wing commander. But then again, they might.

Wedge, of course, knew all that better than Luke did. Which made the offer that much more generous. "I appreciate it," Luke told him. "But unless things get really desperate, it'll probably be better all around if I just wait for mine to get fixed."

"Okay. How's General Calrissian doing?"

"He's in roughly the same boat as my X-wing," Luke said dryly. "Every doctor and medical droid in the place is tied up treating battle injuries. Digging minor bits of metal and glass out of someone who's not currently bleeding is kind of low on their priority list at the moment."

"I'll bet he's really pleased with that."

"I've seen him happier," Luke admitted. "I'd better go give

the medics another push. Why don't you get back to prodding the Sluissi bureaucracy from your end—if we both push hard enough, maybe we can meet in the middle."

Wedge chuckled. "Right. Talk to you later."

With one final crackle of static, the comm cut off. "And good luck," Luke added softly as he got up from the public-use comm desk and headed off across the Sluis Van Central reception area toward the medical corridor. If the rest of the Sluissi equipment had been damaged as much as their in-system communications, it could be a long time indeed before anyone had enough spare time to put a couple of new hyper-drive motivators into a civilian's X-wing.

Still, things weren't quite as dark as they could have been, he decided as he maneuvered his way carefully through the hurrying crowds that seemed to be going in all directions at once. There were several New Republic ships here, whose work crews might be more willing than the Sluissi themselves to bend the rules for a former officer like Luke. And if worse came to worst, he could try calling Coruscant to see if Mon Mothma could expedite matters any.

The drawback to that approach was that calling for help would probably give the appearance of weakness . . . and to show weakness in front of Councilor Fey'lya was not the right signal to be sending now.

Or so it seemed to him. On the other hand, showing that he could get the head of the New Republic to give him personal attention could as easily be seen instead as a sign of strength and solidarity.

Luke shook his head in mild frustration. It was, he supposed, a generally useful trait for a Jedi to be able to see both sides of an argument. It did, however, make the machinations of politics seem even murkier than they already were. Another good reason why he'd always tried to leave politics to Leia.

He could only hope that she'd be equal to this particular challenge.

The medical wing was as crowded as the rest of the huge

Sluis Van Central space station, but here at least a large percentage of the inhabitants were sitting or lying quietly off to the side instead of running around. Threading his way between the chairs and parked float gurneys, Luke reached the large ward room that had been turned into a waiting area for low-priority patients. Lando Calrissian, his expression and sense hovering somewhere between impatience and boredom, was sitting off in the far corner, holding a medpack desensitizer against his chest with one hand while balancing a borrowed data pad with the other. He was scowling at the latter as Luke came up. "Bad news?" Luke asked.

"No worse than everything else that's happened to me lately," Lando said, dropping the data pad onto the empty chair beside him. "The price of hfredium has dropped again on the general market. If it doesn't come up a little in the next month or two, I'm going to be out a few hundred thousand."

"Ouch," Luke agreed. "That's the main product of your Nomad City complex, isn't it?"

"One of several main products, yes," Lando said with a grimace. "We're diversified enough that normally it wouldn't hurt us much. The problem is that lately I've been stockpiling the stuff, expecting the price to go up. Now it's done just the opposite."

Luke suppressed a smile. That was Lando, all right. Respectable and legitimate though he might have become, he was still not above dabbling in a little manipulative gambling on the side. "Well, if it helps any, I've got some good news for you. Since all the ships that the Imperials tried to steal belonged directly to the New Republic, we won't have to go through the local Sluissi bureaucracy to get your mole miners back. It'll just be a matter of submitting a proper claim to the Republic military commander and hauling them out of here."

The lines in Lando's face eased a little. "That's great, Luke," he said. "I really appreciate it—you have no idea what I had to go through to get hold of those mole miners in the first place. Finding replacements would be a major headache."

Luke waved the thanks away. "Under the circumstances, it was the least we could do. Let me go over to the routing station, see if I can hurry things up a little for you. Are you finished with the data pad?"

"Sure, take it back. Anything new on your X-wing?"

"Not really," Luke said, reaching past him to pick up the data pad. "They're still saying it'll take another few hours at least to—"

He caught the abrupt change in Lando's sense a second before the other's hand suddenly snaked up to grip his arm. "What is it?" Luke asked.

Lando was staring at nothing, his forehead furrowed with concentration as he sniffed the air. "Where were you just now?" he demanded.

"I went through the reception area to one of the public comm desks," Luke said. Lando wasn't just sniffing the air, he realized suddenly: he was sniffing at Luke's sleeve. "Why?"

Lando let Luke's arm drop. "It's carababba tabac," he said slowly. "With some armudu spice mixed in. I haven't smelled that since . . ." He looked up at Luke, his sense abruptly tightening even further. "It's Niles Ferrier. Has to be."

"Who's Niles Ferrier?" Luke asked, feeling his heartbeat start to pick up speed. Lando's uneasiness was contagious.

"Human—big and built sort of thick," Lando said. "Dark hair, probably a beard, though that comes and goes. Probably smoking a long thin cigarra. No, of course he was smoking— you got some of the smoke on you. Do you remember seeing him?"

"Hang on." Luke closed his eyes, reaching inward with the Force. Short-term memory enhancement was one of the Jedi skills he'd learned from Yoda. The pictures flowed swiftly backward in time: his walk to the medical wing, his conversation with Wedge, his hunt for a public comm desk—

And there he was. Exactly as Lando had described him, passing no more than three meters away. "Got him," he told Lando, freezing the picture in his memory.

"Where's he going?"

"Uh . . ." Luke replayed the memory forward again. The man wandered in and out of his field of vision for a minute, eventually disappearing entirely as Luke found the comm desks he'd been hunting for. "Looks like he and a couple of others were heading for Corridor Six."

Lando had punched up a station schematic on the data pad. "Corridor Six . . . blast." He stood up, dropping both the data pad and the desensitizer onto his chair. "Come on, we'd better go check this out."

"Check what out?" Luke asked, taking a long step to catch up as Lando hurried off through the maze of waiting patients to the door. "Who is this Niles Ferrier, anyway?"

"He's one of the best spaceship thieves in the galaxy," Lando threw over his shoulder. "And Corridor Six leads to one of the staging areas for the repair teams. We'd better get out there before he palms a Corellian gunship or something and flies off with it."

They made their way through the reception area and under the archway labeled "Corridor Six" in both delicate Sluissi carioglyphs and the blockier Basic letters. Here, to Luke's surprise, the crowds of people that seemed to be everywhere else had dropped off to barely a trickle. By the time they'd gone a hundred meters along the corridor, he and Lando were alone.

"You *did* say this was one of the repair staging areas, didn't you?" he asked, reaching out with Jedi senses as they walked. The lights and equipment in the offices and workrooms around them seemed to be functioning properly, and he could sense a handful of droids moving busily about their business. But apart from that the place seemed to be deserted.

"Yes, I did," Lando said grimly. "The schematic said Corridors Five and Three are also being used, but there ought to be enough traffic to keep this one busy, too. I don't suppose you have a spare blaster on you?"

Luke shook his head. "I don't carry a blaster anymore. Do you think we should call station security?"

"Not if we want to find out what Ferrier's up to. He'll be all through the station computer and comm system by now—call security and he'll just pull out and disappear back under a rock somewhere." He peered into one of the open office doorways as they passed it. "This is vintage Ferrier, all right. One of his favorite tricks is to fiddle work orders to route everyone out of the area he wants to—"

"Hold it," Luke cut him off. At the edge of his mind . . . "I think I've got them. Six humans and two aliens, the nearest about two hundred meters straight ahead."

"What kind of aliens?"

"I don't know. I've never run into either species before."

"Well, watch them. Aliens in Ferrier's gang are usually hired for their muscle. Let's go."

"Maybe you should stay here," Luke suggested, unhooking his lightsaber from his belt. "I'm not sure how well I'll be able to protect you if they decide to make a fight of it."

"I'll take my chances," Lando told him. "Ferrier knows me; maybe I can keep it from coming down to a fight. Besides, I've got an idea I want to try."

They were just under twenty meters from the first human when Luke caught the change in sense from the group ahead. "They've spotted us," he murmured to Lando, shifting his grip slightly on his lightsaber. "You want to try talking to them?"

"I don't know," Lando murmured back, craning his neck to look down the seemingly deserted corridor ahead. "We might need to get a little closer—"

It came as a flicker of movement from one of the doorways, and an abrupt ripple in the Force. "Duck!" Luke barked, igniting his lightsaber. With a *snap-hiss* the brilliant green-white blade appeared—

And moved almost of its own accord to neatly block the blaster bolt that shot toward them.

"Get behind me!" Luke ordered Lando as a second bolt sizzled the air toward them. Guided by the Force, his hands again shifted the lightsaber blade into the path of the attack.

A third bolt spattered from the blade, followed by a fourth. From a doorway farther down the corridor a second blaster opened up, adding its voice to the first.

Luke held his ground, feeling the Force flowing into him and out through his arms, evoking an odd sort of tunnel vision effect that turned mental spotlights on the attack itself and relative darkness on everything else. Lando, half crouched directly behind him, was only a hazy sense in the back of his mind; the rest of Ferrier's people were even dimmer. Setting his teeth firmly together, letting the Force control his defense, he kept his eyes moving around the corridor, alert for new threats.

He was looking directly at the odd shadow when it detached itself from the wall and started forward.

For a long minute he didn't believe what he was seeing. There was no texture or detail to the shadow; nothing but a slightly fluid shape and nearly absolute blackness. But it was real . . . and it was moving toward him. "Lando!" he shouted over the scream of blaster shots. "Five meters away—forty degrees left. Any ideas?"

He heard the hissing intake of air from behind him. "Never seen anything like it. Retreat?"

With an effort, Luke pulled as much of his concentration as he dared away from their defense and turned it toward the approaching shadow. There was indeed something there—one of the alien intelligences, in fact, that he'd sensed earlier. Which implied it was one of Ferrier's people . . .

"Stay with me," he told Lando. This was going to be risky, but turning tail and running wouldn't accomplish anything. Moving slowly, keeping his stance balanced and yet fluid, he headed directly toward the shadow.

The alien halted, its sense clearly surprised that a potential prey would be advancing instead of backing away from it. Luke took advantage of the momentary hesitation to move farther toward the corridor wall to his left. The first blaster, its shots starting to come close to the mobile shadow as it tracked

Luke's movement, abruptly ceased fire. The shadow's form shifted slightly, giving Luke the impression of something looking over its shoulder. He continued moving to his left, drawing the second blaster's fire toward the shadow as he did so; and a second later it, too, fell reluctantly silent.

"Good job," Lando murmured approvingly in his ear. "Allow me."

He took a step back from Luke. "Ferrier?" he called. "This is Lando Calrissian. Listen, if you want to keep your pal here in one piece, you'd better call him off. This is Luke Skywalker, Jedi Knight. The guy who took down Darth Vader."

Which wasn't strictly true, of course. But it was close enough. Luke *had*, after all, defeated Vader in their last lightsaber duel, even if he hadn't actually gone on to kill him.

Regardless, the implications weren't lost on the unseen men down the corridor. He could sense the doubt and consternation among them; and even as he lifted his lightsaber a little higher, the shadow stopped its approach. "What was your name?" someone called.

"Lando Calrissian," Lando repeated. "Think back to that botched Phraetiss operation about ten years ago."

"Oh, I remember," the voice said grimly. "What do you want?"

"I want to offer you a deal," Lando said. "Come on out and we'll talk."

There was a moment of hesitation. Then, the big man from Luke's memory track stepped out from behind a group of crates that had been stacked against the corridor wall, the simmering cigarra still clenched between his teeth. "All of you," Lando insisted. "Come on, Ferrier, bring them out. Unless you seriously think you can hide them from a Jedi."

Ferrier's eyes flicked to Luke. "The mystic Jedi powers have always been exaggerated," he sneered. But his lips moved inaudibly; and, even as he approached them, five humans and a tall, thin, green-scaled insectoid alien emerged one by one from concealment.

"That's better," Lando said approvingly, stepping out from behind Luke. "A Verpine, huh?" he added, waving toward the insectoid alien. "Got to hand it to you, Ferrier—you're fast. Maybe thirty hours since the Imperials pulled out, and already you're on board. And with a tame Verpine, yet. You ever heard of Verpine, Luke?"

Luke nodded. The alien's appearance wasn't familiar, but the name was. "They're supposed to be geniuses at fixing and reassembling high-tech devices."

"And it's a well-deserved reputation," Lando said. "Rumor has it they're the ones who helped Admiral Ackbar design the B-wing starfighter. You shifted specialties to palming damaged ships, Ferrier? Or did your Verpine come aboard just for the occasion?"

"You mentioned a deal," Ferrier said coldly. "So deal."

"I want to know first if you were in on the Sluis Van attack from the beginning," Lando said, matching Ferrier's tone. "If you're working for the Empire, we can't deal."

One of the gang, blaster in hand, took a quiet preparatory breath. Luke shifted his lightsaber toward him slightly in warning, and the brief thought of heroics faded quickly away. Ferrier looked at the man, back at Lando. "The Empire's sent out a call for ships," he said grudgingly. "Warships in particular. They're paying a bounty of twenty percent above market value for anything over a hundred thousand tons that can fight."

Luke and Lando exchanged a quick glance. "Odd request," Lando said. "They lose one of their shipyard facilities or something?"

"They didn't say, and I didn't ask," Ferrier said acidly. "I'm a businessman; I give the customer what he wants. You here to deal, or just talk?"

"I'm here to deal," Lando assured him. "You know, Ferrier, it seems to me that you're in sort of a jam here. We've nailed you red-handed in the process of trying to steal New Republic warships. We've also pretty well proved that Luke can take all of you without any trouble. All I have to do is whistle up Security and the whole bunch of you will be off to a penal colony for the next few years."

The shadow, which had been standing still, took a step forward. "The Jedi might survive," Ferrier said darkly. "But you wouldn't."

"Maybe; maybe not," Lando said easily. "Regardless, it's not the sort of situation a businessman like yourself wants to be in. So here's the deal: you leave now, and we'll let you get out of the Sluis Van system before we drop the hammer with the authorities."

"How very generous of you," Ferrier said, heavily sarcastic. "So what do you *really* want? A cut of the operation? Or just a wad of money?"

Lando shook his head. "I don't want your money. I just want you out of here."

"I don't take well to threats."

"Then take it as a friendly warning for past associations' sake," Lando said, his voice hard. "But take it seriously."

For a long minute the only sound in the corridor was the quiet background hum of distant machinery. Luke held himself in combat stance, trying to read the shifting emotions in Ferrier's sense. "Your 'deal' would cost us a lot of money," Ferrier said, shifting the cigarra to the other side of his mouth.

"I realize that," Lando conceded. "And believe it or not, I *am* sorry. But the New Republic can't afford to lose any ships at the moment. However, you might try over at the Amorris system. Last I heard, the Cavrilhu pirate gang was using that as a base, and they're always in need of expert maintenance people." He looked appraisingly at the shadow. "And extra muscle, too."

Ferrier followed his gaze. "Ah, you like my wraith, do you?"

"Wraith?" Luke frowned.

"They call themselves Defel," Ferrier said. "But I think 'wraith' suits them so much better. Their bodies absorb all visible light—some sort of evolved survival mechanism." He eyed Luke. "And what do *you* think of this deal, Jedi? Enforcer of law and justice that you are?"

Luke had expected the question. "Have you stolen anything here?" he countered. "Or done anything illegal other than breaking into the station's assignment computer?"

Ferrier's lip twisted. "We also shot at a couple of bizits who were poking their noses in where they shouldn't have," he said sarcastically. "That count?"

"Not when you didn't hit them," Luke countered evenly. "As far as I'm concerned, you can leave."

"You're too kind," Ferrier growled. "So is that it?"

"That's it," Lando nodded. "Oh, and I want your slicer access code, too."

Ferrier glared at him, but gestured to the Verpine standing behind him. Silently, the tall green alien lurched forward and handed Lando a pair of data cards. "Thank you," Lando said. "All right. I'll give you one hour to get your ship up and out of the system before we drop the hammer. Have a good trip."

"Yeah, we'll do that," Ferrier bit out. "So good to see you, Calrissian. Maybe next time I can do *you* a favor."

"Give Amorris a try," Lando urged him. "I'd bet they've got at least a couple of old Sienar patrol ships you could relieve them of."

Farrier didn't reply. In silence, the group passed Lando and Luke and headed back down the empty corridor toward the reception area. "You sure telling him about Amorris was a good idea?" Luke murmured as he watched them go. "The Empire's likely to get a patrol ship or two out of the deal."

"Would you rather they have gotten hold of a Calamarian Star Cruiser?" Lando countered. "Ferrier's probably good enough to have palmed one. Certainly with things as confused out there as they are." He shook his head thoughtfully. "I wonder what's going on over in the Empire. It doesn't make sense to pay premium prices for used ships when you've got the facilities to make your own."

"Maybe they're having some trouble," Luke suggested,

closing down the lightsaber and returning it to his belt. "Or maybe they've lost one of their Star Destroyers but managed to save the crew and need ships to put them on."

"I suppose that's possible," Lando conceded doubtfully. "Hard to imagine an accident that would destroy any ship beyond repair but leave the crew alive. Well, we can get the word back to Coruscant. Let the Intelligence hot-shots figure out what it means."

"If they're not all too busy playing politics," Luke said. Because if Councilor Fey'lya's group was also trying to take over Military Intelligence . . . He shook the thought away. Worrying about the situation wasn't productive. "So what now? We give Ferrier his hour and then hand those slicer codes over to the Sluissi?"

"Oh, we'll give Ferrier his hour, all right," Lando said, frowning thoughtfully at the departing group. "But the slicer codes are another matter. It occurred to me on the way in that if Ferrier was using them to divert workers from this end of the station, there's no particular reason why we can't also use them to bump your X-wing to the top of the priority stack."

"Ah," Luke said. It was, he knew, not exactly the sort of marginally legal activity a Jedi should participate in. But under the circumstances—and given the urgency of the situation back on Coruscant—bending some rules in this case was probably justified. "When do we get started?"

"Right now," Lando said, and Luke couldn't help wincing at the quiet relief in the other's voice and sense. Clearly, he'd been half afraid that Luke would raise those same awkward ethical questions about the suggestion. "With any luck, you'll be up and ready to fly before I have to give these things to the Sluissi. Come on, let's go find a terminal."

CHAPTER 3

"LANDING REQUEST ACKNOWLEDGED and confirmed, *Millennium Falcon*," the voice of the Imperial Palace air control director came over the comm. "You're cleared for pad eight. Councilor Organa Solo will meet you."

"Thanks, Control," Han Solo said, easing the ship down toward the Imperial City and eyeing with distaste the dark cloud cover that hung over the whole region like some brooding menace. He'd never put much stock in omens, but those clouds sure didn't help his mood any.

And speaking of bad moods . . . Reaching over, he tapped the ship's intercom switch. "Get ready for landing," he called. "We're coming into our approach."

"Thank you, Captain Solo," C-3PO's stiffly precise voice came back. A little stiffer than usual, actually; the droid must still be nursing a wounded ego. Or whatever it was that passed for ego in droids.

Han shut off the intercom, lip twisting with some annoyance of his own as he did so. He'd never really liked droids much. He'd used them occasionally, but never more than he'd absolutely had to. Threepio wasn't as bad as some of those he'd known . . . but then, he'd never spent six days alone in hyperspace with any of the others, either.

He'd tried. He really had, if for no other reason than that Leia rather liked Threepio and would have wanted them to get along. The first day out from Sluis Van he'd let Threepio sit up front in the cockpit with him, enduring the droid's prissy voice and trying valiantly to hold something resembling a real conversation with him. The second day, he'd let Threepio do most of the talking, and had spent a lot of his time working in maintenance crawlways where there wasn't room for two. Threepio had accepted the limitation with typical mechanical cheerfulness, and had chattered at him from outside the crawlway access hatches.

By the afternoon of the third day, he'd banned the droid from his presence entirely.

Leia wouldn't like it when she found out. But she'd have liked it even less if he'd given in to his original temptation and converted the droid into a set of backup alluvial dampers.

The *Falcon* was through the cloud layer now and in sight of the monstrosity that was the Emperor's old palace. Banking slightly, Han confirmed that pad eight was clear and brought them down.

Leia must have been waiting just inside the canopy that shrouded the pad's accessway, because she was already beside the ship as Han lowered the *Falcon*'s ramp. "Han," she said, her voice laced with tension. "Thank the Force you're back."

"Hi, sweetheart," he said, being careful not to press too hard against the increasingly prominent bulge of her belly as he hugged her. The muscles in her shoulders and back felt tight beneath his arms. "I'm glad to see you, too."

She clutched him to her for a moment, then gently disengaged. "Come on—we've got to go."

Chewbacca was waiting for them just inside the accessway, his bowcaster slung over his shoulder in ready position. "Hey,

Chewie," Han nodded, getting a growled Wookiee greeting in return. "Thanks for taking care of Leia."

The other rumbled something strangely noncommittal in reply. Han eyed him, decided this wasn't the time to press for details of their stay on Kashyyyk. "What've I missed?" he asked Leia instead.

"Not much," she said as she led the way down the ramp corridor and into the Palace proper. "After that first big flurry of accusations, Fey'lya's apparently decided to cool things down. He's talked the Council into letting him take over some of Ackbar's internal security duties, but he's been behaving more like a caretaker than a new administrator. He's also hinted broadly that he'd be available to take charge of the Supreme Command, but he hasn't done any real pushing in that direction."

"Doesn't want anyone to panic," Han suggested. "Accusing someone like Ackbar of treason is a big enough bite for people to chew on as it is. Anything more and they might start choking on it."

"That's my feeling, too," Leia agreed. "Which should give us at least a little breathing space to try to figure out this bank thing."

"Yeah, what's the lowdown on that, anyway?" Han asked. "All you told me was that some routine bank check had found a big chunk of money in one of Ackbar's accounts."

"It turns out it wasn't just a routine check," Leia said. "There was a sophisticated electronic break-in at the central clearing bank on Coruscant the morning of the Sluis Van attack, with several big accounts being hit. The investigators ran a check on all the accounts the bank served and discovered that there'd been a large transfer into Ackbar's account that same morning from the central bank on Palanhi. You familiar with Palanhi?"

"Everybody knows Palanhi," Han said sourly. "Little crossroads planet with an overblown idea of their own importance."

"And the firm belief that if they can stay neutral enough

they can play both sides of the war to their own profit," Leia said. "Anyway, the central bank there claims that the money didn't come from Palanhi itself and must have just been transferred through them. So far our people haven't been able to backtrack it any further."

Han nodded. "I'll bet Fey'lya's got some ideas where it came from."

"The ideas aren't unique to him," Leia sighed. "He was just the first one to voice them, that's all."

"And to make himself a few points at Ackbar's expense," Han growled. "Where've they put Ackbar, anyway? The old prison section?"

Leia shook her head. "He's under a sort of loose house arrest in his quarters while the investigation is under way. More evidence that Fey'lya's trying not to ruffle any more feathers than he has to."

"Or else that he knows full well there isn't enough here to hang a stunted Jawa from," Han countered. "Has he got anything on Ackbar besides the bank thing?"

Leia smiled wanly. "Just the near-fiasco at Sluis Van. And the fact that it was Ackbar who sent all those warships out there in the first place."

"Point," Han conceded, trying to recall the old Rebel Alliance regulations on military prisoners. If he remembered correctly, an officer under house arrest could receive visitors without those visitors first having to go through more than minor amounts of bureaucratic datawork.

Though he could easily be wrong about that. They'd made him learn all that stuff back when he'd first let them slap an officer's rank on him after the Battle of Yavin. But regulations were never something he'd taken seriously. "How much of the Council does Fey'lya have on his side?" he asked Leia.

"If you mean *solidly* on his side, only a couple," she said. "If you mean leaning in his direction . . . well, you'll be able to judge for yourself in a minute."

Han blinked. Lost in his own mulling of the mess, he hadn't

really paid attention to where Leia was taking him. Now, with a start, he suddenly realized they were walking down the Grand Corridor that linked the Council chamber with the much larger Assemblage auditorium. "Wait a minute," he protested. "*Now*?"

"I'm sorry, Han," she sighed. "Mon Mothma insisted. You're the first person back who was actually at the Sluis Van attack, and there are a million questions they want to ask you about it."

Han looked around the corridor: at the high, convoluted vaulting of the ceiling; the ornate carvings and cut-glass windows alternating on the walls; the rows of short, greenish-purple saplings lining each side. The Emperor had supposedly designed the Grand Corridor personally, which probably explained why Han had always disliked the place. "I knew I should have sent Threepio out first," he growled.

Leia took his arm. "Come on, soldier. Take a deep breath and let's get it over with. Chewie, you'd better wait out here."

The usual Council chamber arrangement was a scaled-up version of the smaller Inner Council room: an oval table in the center for the Councilors themselves, with rows of seats along the walls for their aides and assistants. Today, to Han's surprise, the room had been reconfigured more along the lines of the huge Assemblage Commons. The seats were in neat, slightly tiered rows, with each Councilor surrounded by his or her assistants. In the front of the room, on the lowest level, Mon Mothma sat alone at a simple lectern, looking like a lecturer in a classroom. "Whose idea was this?" Han murmured as he and Leia started down the side aisle toward what was obviously a witness chair next to Mon Mothma's desk.

"Mon Mothma set it up," she murmured. "I'd be willing to bet it was Fey'lya's idea, though."

Han frowned. He'd have thought that underlining Mon Mothma's preeminent role in the Council like this would be the last thing Fey'lya would want. "I don't get it."

She nodded toward the lectern. "Giving Mon Mothma the

whole spotlight helps calm any fears that he plans to make a bid for her position. At the same time, putting the Councilors and their aides together in little groups tends to isolate the Councilors from each other."

"I get it." Han nodded back. "Slippery little fuzzball, isn't he?"

"Yes, he is," Leia said. "And he's going to milk this Sluis Van thing for all it's worth. Watch yourself."

They reached the front and separated, Leia going to the first row and sitting down next to her aide, Winter, Han continuing on to Mon Mothma and the witness chair waiting for him. "You want me sworn in or anything?" he asked without preamble.

Mon Mothma shook her head. "That won't be necessary, Captain Solo," she said, her voice formal and a little strained. "Please sit down. There are some questions the Council would like to ask you about the recent events at the Sluis Van shipyards."

Han took his seat. Fey'lya and his fellow Bothans, he saw, were in the group of front-row seats next to Leia's group. There were no empty seats anywhere that might have signified Admiral Ackbar's absence, at least not in the front where they should have been. The Councilors, seated according to rank, had apparently shuffled positions so as to each be closer to the front. Another reason for Fey'lya to have pushed this configuration, Han decided: at the usual oval table, Ackbar's seat might have been left vacant.

"First of all, Captain Solo," Mon Mothma began, "we would like you to describe your role in the Sluis Van attack. When you arrived, what happened subsequently—that sort of thing."

"We got there pretty much as the battle was starting," Han said. "Came in just ahead of the Star Destroyers. We picked up a call from Wedge—that's Wing Commander Wedge Antilles of Rogue Squadron—saying that there were TIE fighters loose in the shipyards—"

"Excuse me?" Fey'lya interrupted smoothly. "Just who is the 'we' here?"

Han focused on the Bothan. On those violet eyes, that soft, cream-colored fur, that totally bland expression. "My crew consisted of Luke Skywalker and Lando Calrissian." As Fey'lya no doubt knew perfectly well already. Just a cheap trick to throw Han off stride. "Oh, and two droids. You want their serial numbers?"

A slight rustle of not-quite humor ran through the room, and Han had the minor satisfaction of seeing that cream-colored fur flatten a little. "Thank you, no," Fey'lya said.

"Rogue Squadron was engaged with a group of approximately forty TIE fighters and fifty stolen mole miners that had somehow been smuggled into the shipyards," Han continued. "We gave them some assistance with the fighters, figured out that the Imperials were using the mole miners to try and steal some of the capital ships that had been pressed into cargo duty, and were able to stop them. That's about it."

"You're too modest, Captain Solo," Fey'lya spoke up again. "According to the reports we've received here, it was you and Calrissian who managed single-handedly to thwart the Empire's scheme."

Han braced himself. Here it came. He and Lando had stopped the Imperials, all right . . . only they'd had to fry the nerve centers of over forty capital ships to do it. "I'm sorry about wrecking the ships," he said, looking Fey'lya straight in the eye. "Would you rather the Imperials have taken them intact?"

A ripple ran through the Bothan's fur. "Really, Captain Solo," he said soothingly. "I have no particular quarrel with your method of stopping the Empire's attempt at grand larceny, costly though it might have been. You had only what you could work with. Within your constraints, you and the others succeeded brilliantly."

Han frowned, feeling suddenly a little off balance. He had expected Fey'lya to try to make him the man under the hammer on this one. For once, the Bothan seemed to have missed a bet. "Thank you, Councilor," he said, for lack of anything better to say.

"Which is not to say that the Empire's attempt and near-victory are not important," Fey'lya said, his fur rippling the opposite direction this time as he looked around the room. "On the contrary. At the best, they speak of serious misjudgments on the part of our military commanders. At the worst . . . they may speak of treason."

Han felt his lip twist. So that was it. Fey'lya hadn't changed his stripes; he'd simply decided not to waste a golden opportunity like this on a nobody like Han. "With all due respect, Councilor," he spoke up quickly, "what happened at Sluis Van wasn't Admiral Ackbar's fault. The whole operation—"

"Excuse me, Captain Solo," Fey'lya cut him off. "And with all due respect to *you*, let me point out that the reason those capital ships were sitting at Sluis Van in the first place, undermanned and vulnerable, was that Admiral Ackbar had ordered them there."

"There isn't anything like treason involved," Han insisted doggedly. "We already know that the Empire's got a tap into our communications—"

"And who's responsible for such failures of security?" Fey'lya shot back. "Once again, the blame falls squarely around Admiral Ackbar's shoulders."

"Well, then, *you* find the leak," Han snapped. Peripherally, he could see Leia shaking her head urgently at him, but he was too mad now to care whether he was being properly respectful or not. "And while you're at it, I'd like to see how well *you* would do up against an Imperial Grand Admiral."

The low-level buzz of conversation that had begun in the room cut off abruptly. "What was that last?" Mon Mothma asked.

Silently, Han swore at himself. He hadn't meant to spring this on anyone until he'd had a chance to check it out himself at the Palace archives. But it was too late now. "The Empire's being led by a Grand Admiral," he muttered. "I saw him my-self."

The silence hung thick in the air. Mon Mothma recovered first. "That's impossible," she said, sounding more like she wanted to believe it than that she really did. "We've accounted for all the Grand Admirals."

"I saw him myself," Han repeated.

"Describe him," Fey'lya said. "What did he look like?"

"He wasn't human," Han said. "At least, not completely. He had a roughly human build, but he had light blue skin, a kind of bluish black hair, and eyes that glowed red. I don't know what species he was."

"Yet we know that the Emperor didn't like non-humans," Mon Mothma reminded him.

Han looked at Leia. The skin of her face was tight, her eyes staring at and through him with a kind of numb horror. She understood what this meant, all right. "He was wearing a white uniform," he told Mon Mothma. "No other Imperial officers wore anything like that. And the contact I was with specifically called him a Grand Admiral."

"Obviously a self-granted promotion," Fey'lya said briskly. "Some regular admiral or perhaps a leftover Moff trying to rally the remains of the Empire around him. Anyway, that's beside the immediate point."

"Beside the *point*?" Han demanded. "Look, Councilor, if there's a Grand Admiral running around loose—"

"If there is," Mon Mothma interrupted firmly, "we'll soon know for certain. Until then, there seems little value in holding a debate in a vacuum. Council Research is hereby directed to look into the possibility that a Grand Admiral might still be alive. Until such an investigation has been completed, we will continue with our current inquiry into the circumstances of the Sluis Van attack." She looked at Han, then turned and nodded at Leia. "Councilor Organa Solo, you may begin the questioning."

ADMIRAL ACKBAR'S HIGH-DOMED, salmon-colored head bent slightly to the side, his huge round eyes swiveling in their sockets in a Calamarian gesture Leia couldn't recall ever having seen before. Surprise? Or was it perhaps dread?

"A Grand Admiral," Ackbar said at last, his voice sounding even more gravelly than usual. "An Imperial Grand Admiral. Yes. That would indeed explain a great many things."

"We don't actually *know* that it's a real Grand Admiral yet," Leia cautioned him, throwing a glance at the stony look on her husband's face. Han, clearly, had no doubts of his own. Neither did she, for that matter. "Mon Mothma's having Research look into it."

"They won't find anything," Ackbar said, shaking his head. A more human gesture, that, of the sort he usually tried to use when dealing with humans. Good; that meant he was getting back on balance. "I had a thorough search made of the Imperial records when we first took Coruscant back from the Empire. There's nothing in there but a list of the Grand Admirals' names and a little about their assignments."

"Erased before they pulled out," Han growled.

"Or perhaps never there to begin with," Leia suggested. "Remember that these weren't just the best and brightest military leaders the Emperor could find. They were also part of his plan to bring the Imperial military more personally under his control."

"As was the Death Star project itself," Ackbar said. "I agree, Councilor. Until the Grand Admirals were fully integrated both militarily *and* politically, there was no reason to publish details of their identities. And every reason to conceal them."

"So," Han said. "Dead end."

"It appears that way," Ackbar agreed. "Any information we're going to get will have to come from current sources."

Leia looked at Han. "You mentioned you were with a contact when you saw this Grand Admiral, but you didn't give us the contact's name."

"That's right," Han nodded. "I didn't. And I'm not going to. Not now, anyway."

Leia frowned at that unreadable sabacc face, stretching out with all her rudimentary Jedi skills to try to sense his purpose and feelings. It didn't get her very far. *If only I had more time to practice*, she thought ruefully. But if the Council had needed all her time before, it was going to need even more than that now. "Mon Mothma's going to want to know, eventually," she warned him.

"And I'm going to tell her, eventually," he came back. "Until then, it's going to be our little secret."

"As in 'leverage'?"

"You never can tell." A shadow of something crossed Han's face. "The name's not going to do the Council any good right now, anyway. The whole group's probably buried themselves away somewhere. If the Empire hasn't caught up with them."

"You don't know how to find them?" Leia asked.

Han shrugged. "There's a ship I promised to get out of impoundment for them. I can try that."

"Do what you can," Ackbar said. "You said Councilor Organa Solo's brother was with you at Sluis Van?"

"Yes, sir," Han said. "His hyperdrive needed some repairs, but he should've only been a couple of hours behind me." He looked at Leia. "Oh, and we're going to have to get Lando's ship back to him at Sluis Van."

Ackbar made a noise that sounded something like a choked whistle: the Calamarian equivalent of a grunt. "We'll need to hear testimony from both of them," he said. "And from Wing Commander Antilles, as well. It's vital that we learn how the Empire was able to smuggle such a large force past so many sensors."

Leia threw Han a look. "According to Wedge's preliminary

report, they apparently were inside a freighter whose hold registered empty."

Ackbar's eyes swiveled in their sockets. "Empty? Not merely unreadable, as if from a sensor misfire or static-damping?"

"Wedge said it was empty," Han told him. "He ought to know the difference between that and static-damping."

"Empty." Ackbar seemed to slump a little in his seat. "Which can only mean the Empire has finally developed a workable cloaking shield."

"It's starting to look that way," Leia agreed soberly. "I suppose the only good news is that they must still have some bugs left in the system. Otherwise, they could have simply cloaked the whole Sluis Van task force and torn the place to ribbons."

"No," Ackbar said, shaking his massive head. "That's something we won't have to worry about, at least. By its very nature a cloaking shield would be more danger to the user than it was worth. A cloaked warship's own sensor beams would be as useless as those of its enemies, leaving it to flail about totally blind. Worse, if it were under power, the enemy could locate it by simply tracking its drive emissions."

"Ah," Leia said. "I hadn't thought of that."

"There have been rumors for years that the Emperor was developing a cloaking shield," Ackbar said. "I've put a good deal of thought into the contingency." He harrumphed. "But the weaknesses are of small comfort. A cloaking shield in the hands of a Grand Admiral would still be a dangerous weapon indeed. He would find ways to use it against us."

"He already has," Han muttered.

"Apparently so." Ackbar's swiveling eyes locked onto Leia's face. "You must get me cleared of this ridiculous charge, Councilor. As soon as possible. For all his ambition and self-confidence, Councilor Fey'lya hasn't the tactical skills we need against a threat of this magnitude."

"We'll get you released, Admiral," Leia promised, wishing she felt that confident. "We're working on it right now."

There was a diffident knock, and behind Leia the door opened. "Excuse me," the squat G-2RD droid said in a mechanically resonant voice. "Your time has expired."

"Thank you," Leia said, suppressing her frustration as she stood up. She wanted desperately to have more time with Ackbar, to explore with him both this new Imperial threat and also discuss the legal strategies they might use in his defense. But arguing with the droid would gain her nothing, and might get her visiting privileges revoked entirely. Guard droids were allowed that kind of discretion, and the 2RD series in particular was reputed to be a touchy lot. "I'll be back soon, Admiral," she told Ackbar. "Either this afternoon or tomorrow."

"Good-bye, Councilor." There was just a brief hesitation— "And to you, Captain Solo. Thank you for coming."

"Good-bye, Admiral," Han said.

They stepped from the room and started down the wide corridor, the G-2RD taking up position at the door behind them. "That must have hurt," Han commented.

"What must have?" Leia asked.

"Thanking me for coming."

She frowned up at him, but there was nothing but seriousness in his face. "Oh, come on, Han. Just because you resigned your commission—"

"He considers me one step up from a complete traitor," Han finished for her.

An obvious retort about persecution complexes flashed through Leia's mind. "Ackbar's never been what you'd call an outgoing person," she said instead.

Han shook his head. "I'm not imagining it, Leia. Ask Lando sometime—he gets the same kind of treatment. You leave the military and you might as well be tauntaun spit as far as Ackbar is concerned."

Leia sighed. "You have to understand the Mon Calamari ethos, Han. They were never a warlike species at all until the Empire started enslaving them and ravaging their world.

Those wonderful Star Cruisers of theirs were originally passenger liners, you know, that we helped them convert into warships. Maybe it's not so much anger at you for quitting as it is some sort of residual guilt at himself and his people for taking up warfare in the first place."

"Even if they were forced into it?"

Leia shrugged uncomfortably. "I don't think anyone ever goes into a war without the nagging feeling that there might have been some other way. Even when every other way has already been tried and hasn't worked. I know *I* felt it when I first joined the Rebellion—and believe me, people like Mon Mothma and Bail Organa had tried everything. For an inherently peaceful race like the Mon Calamari, the feeling must be even worse."

"Well . . . maybe," Han conceded grudgingly. "I just wish they'd work it through for themselves and leave the rest of us out of it."

"They are," Leia assured him. "We've just got to give them time."

He looked down at her. "You haven't told me yet why you and Chewie left Kashyyyk and came back here."

Leia squeezed thumb and forefinger together. Eventually, she knew, she would have to tell Han about the deal she'd made with the Noghri commando Khabarakh. But walking down a public corridor of the Imperial Palace wasn't the place for that kind of discussion. "There didn't seem any point in staying," she told him. "There was another attack—"

"There *what*?"

"Relax, we fought it off," she soothed him. "And I've made arrangements that should keep me safe, at least for the next couple of weeks. I'll tell you about it later, when we're someplace more secure."

She could feel his eyes boring into her; could sense the suspicion in his mind that there was something she wasn't telling him. But he recognized as well as she did the danger of speaking secrets out in the open. "All right," he muttered. "I just hope you know what you're doing."

Leia shivered, focusing on the sense of the twins she carried within her. So potentially strong in the Force . . . and yet so utterly helpless. "So do I," she whispered.

CHAPTER 4

JORUS C'BAOTH. HUMAN. BORN IN REITHCAS,
ON BORTRAS. ON 4\3\112, PRE-EMPIRE DATE.

Luke made a face as he watched the words scroll up the Old
Senate Library computer screen. What was it about new re-
gimes, he wondered, that one of their first official acts always
seemed to be the creation of a new dating system, which they
then went and applied to all existing historical records? The
Galactic Empire had done that, as had the Old Republic before it. He could only hope that the New Republic wouldn't
follow suit. History was hard enough to keep track of as it
was.

ATTENDED MIRNIC UNIVERSITY 6\4\95 TO 4\32\90 PE.
ATTENDED JEDI TRAINING CENTER ON KAMPARAS
2\15\90 TO 8\33\88 PE. PRIVATE JEDI TRAINING BEGUN
9\88 PE; INSTRUCTOR UNKNOWN. GRANTED TITLE OF
JEDI KNIGHT 3\6\86 PE. OFFICIALLY ASSUMED TITLE OF

JEDI MASTER 4\3\74 PE. SUMMARY ENDS. FURTHER
DETAILS OF SCHOOLING AND TRAINING?

"No," Luke said, frowning. C'baoth had *assumed* the title
of Jedi Master? He'd always been under the impression that
that title, like the rank of Jedi Knight itself, was something
that was granted by the rest of the Jedi community and not
simply self-proclaimed. "Give me the highlights of his record
as a Jedi."

MEMBER OF ANDO DEMILITARIZATION OBSERVATION
GROUP 8\82 TO 7\81 PE. MEMBER OF SENATE
INTERSPECIES ADVISORY COMMITTEE 9\81 TO 6\79 PE.
PERSONAL JEDI ADVISER TO SENATOR PALPATINE 6\79
TO 5\77—

"Stop," Luke ordered, a sudden shiver running up his back.
Jedi adviser to Senator *Palpatine*? "Detail C'baoth's service to
Senator Palpatine."

The computer seemed to consider the request, UNAVAIL-
ABLE, the answer came at last.

"Unavailable, or just classified?" Luke countered.

UNAVAILABLE, the computer repeated.

Luke grimaced. But there was little he could do about it for
the moment. "Continue."

MEMBER OF JEDI FORCE ASSEMBLED TO OPPOSE THE
DARK JEDI INSURRECTION ON BPFASSH 7\77 TO 1\74
PE. ASSISTED IN RESOLVING ALDERAAN ASCENDANCY
CONTENTION 11\70 PE. ASSISTED JEDI MASTER TRA 'S
M' INS IN MEDIATION OF DUINUOGWUIN-GOTAL
CONFLICT 1\68 TO 4\66 PE. NAMED AMBASSADOR AT
LARGE TO XAPPYH SECTOR 8\21\62 PE BY SENATE.
HIGHLY INSTRUMENTAL IN CONVINCING SENATE TO
AUTHORIZE AND FUND OUTBOUND FLIGHT PROJECT.
ONE OF SIX JEDI MASTERS ATTACHED TO PROJECT 7\7\65

PE. NO RECORD EXISTS AFTER PROJECT DEPARTURE
FROM YAGA MINOR, 4\1\64. HIGHLIGHTS SUMMARY
ENDS. FURTHER INFORMATION?

Luke leaned back in his chair, gazing at the display and
chewing at the inside of his cheek. So not only had C'baoth
once been an adviser to the man who would someday declare
himself Emperor, but he'd also been part of the attack against
those Dark Jedi from the Sluis sector that Leia had told him
about. One of whom had survived long enough to face Master
Yoda on Dagobah . . .

There was a soft footstep behind him. "Commander?"

"Hello, Winter," Luke said without turning. "Looking for
me?"

"Yes," Winter said, coming up to stand beside him. "Princess Leia would like to see you whenever you're finished here."
She nodded at the display, running a hand through her silky
white hair as she did so. "More Jedi research?"

"Sort of," Luke told her, sliding a data card into the terminal's slot. "Computer: copy complete record of Jedi Master
Jorus C'baoth."

"Jorus C'baoth," Winter repeated thoughtfully. "Wasn't he
involved in the big ascendancy flap on Alderaan?"

"That's what the record says," Luke nodded. "You know
anything about that?"

"No more than any other Alderaanian," Winter said. Even
with her rigid control some of the pain leaked through to her
voice, and Luke found himself wincing in sympathy with it.
For Leia, he knew, the destruction of Alderaan and the loss of
her family was a heartrending but slowly fading ache in the
back corners of her mind. For Winter, with her perfect and
indelible memory, the pain would probably go on forever.
"The question was whether the line of ascent to Viceroy
should go to Bail Organa's father or one of the other family
lines," Winter continued. "After the third voting deadlock they
appealed to the Senate to mediate the issue. C'baoth was one

of the delegation they sent, which took less than a month to decide that the Organas had the proper claim."

"Did you ever see any pictures of C'baoth?" Luke asked.

Winter considered. "There was a group holo in the archives that showed the entire mediation team," she said after a moment. "C'baoth was—oh, about average height and build, I suppose. Fairly muscular, too, which I remember thinking seemed rather odd for a Jedi." She looked at Luke, coloring slightly. "I'm sorry; I didn't mean that to sound derogatory."

"No problem," Luke assured her. It was a common misconception, he'd discovered: with mastery over the Force, people just assumed there was no reason for a Jedi to cultivate physical strength. It had taken Luke himself several years to truly appreciate the subtle ways in which control of the body was linked to control of the mind. "What else?"

"He had graying hair and a short, neatly trimmed beard," Winter said. "He was wearing the same brown robe and white undertunic that a lot of Jedi seemed to favor. Other than that, there wasn't anything particularly notable about him."

Luke rubbed his chin. "How old did he look?"

"Oh . . . I'd say somewhere around forty," Winter said. "Plus or minus five years, perhaps. Age is always hard to ascertain from a picture."

"That would fit with the record here," Luke agreed, retrieving the data card from the slot. But if the record was right . . . "You said Leia wanted to see me?" he asked, standing up.

"If it's convenient," Winter nodded. "She's in her office."

"Okay. Let's go."

They left the library and started down the cross corridor linking the research areas with the Council and Assemblage chambers. "You know anything about the planet Bortras?" he asked Winter as they walked. "Specifically, anything about how long its people live?"

She thought a moment. "I've never read anything that mentioned it one way or another. Why?"

Luke hesitated; but however the Imperials were getting information out of the New Republic's inner sanctum, Winter was certainly far above suspicion. "The problem is that if this alleged Jedi out on Jomark really is Jorus C'baoth, he has to be over a hundred by now. I know there are some species that live longer than that, but he's supposed to be human."

Winter shrugged. "There are always exceptions to a race's normal life span," she pointed out. "And a Jedi, in particular, might have techniques that would help extend that span."

Luke thought about that. It was possible, he knew. Yoda had certainly had a long life—a good nine hundred years— and as a general rule, smaller species usually had shorter life spans than larger ones. But *usually* didn't mean *always;* and after many hours of records searches, Luke still hadn't figured out just what species Yoda had belonged to. Perhaps a better approach might be to try to find out how long the Emperor had lived.

"So you think Jorus C'baoth is alive?" Winter asked into his thoughts.

Luke glanced around. They'd reached the Grand Corridor now, which because of its location was usually fairly brimming with beings of all sorts. But today it was nearly empty, with only a few humans and others standing around in little conversation groups of their own, all of them too far away to eavesdrop. "I had a brief mental contact with another Jedi while I was on Nkllon," he said, lowering his voice. "Afterward, Leia told me that there were rumors C'baoth had been seen on Jomark. I don't know what other conclusion to come to."

Winter was silent. "Any comments?" Luke prompted her.

She shrugged. "Anything having to do with Jedi and the Force are out of my personal experience, Commander," she said. "I really can't comment one way or another on that. But . . . I'd have to say that the impression I got of C'baoth from Alderaanian history makes me skeptical."

"Why?"

"It's just an impression, you understand," Winter emphasized. "Nothing I would even have mentioned if you hadn't asked. C'baoth struck me as the sort of person who loved being in the middle of things. The sort who, if he couldn't lead, control, or help in a particular situation, would still be there just so he'd be visible."

They were passing by one of the purple-and-green ch'hala trees lining the Grand Corridor now, close enough for Luke to see the subtle moirélike turmoil of color taking place beneath the thin transparent outer bark. "I suppose that fits with what I read," he conceded, reaching out to slide a fingertip across the slender tree trunk as they walked. The subtle turmoil exploded at his touch into a flash of angry red across the quiet purple, the color shooting out around the trunk like ripples in a cylindrical pond, circling it again and again as it flowed up and down the trunk before finally fading to burgundy and then back to purple again. "I don't know if you knew it, but he apparently promoted himself from Jedi Knight to Jedi Master. Seems like kind of a conceited thing to do."

"Yes, it does," Winter agreed. "Though at least by the time he came to Alderaan there didn't seem to be any dispute about it. My point is that someone who likes the spotlight that much wouldn't have stayed so completely out of the war against the Empire."

"And a good point it is, too," Luke admitted, half turning to watch the last bit of red fade away on the ch'hala tree he'd touched. The Nkllon contact with the mysterious Jedi had been like that: there for a short time, and then gone without a trace. Was C'baoth perhaps no longer fully in control of his powers? "New subject, then. What do you know about this Outbound Flight project the Old Republic put together?"

"Not much," she said, frowning with concentration. "It was supposedly an attempt to search for life outside the galaxy proper, but the whole thing was so buried in secrecy they never released any details. I'm not even sure whether or not it was ever launched."

"The records say it was," Luke said, touching the next ch'hala tree in line as they passed by, eliciting another flash of red. "They also say that C'baoth was attached to the project. Does that mean he would have been aboard?"

"I don't know," Winter said. "There were rumors that several Jedi Masters would be going along, but again there was no official confirmation of that." She looked sideways at him. "Are you thinking that might be why he wasn't around during the Rebellion?"

"It's possible," Luke said. "Of course, that would just raise another whole set of questions. Like what happened to them and how he got back."

Winter shrugged. "I suppose there's one way to find out."

"Yeah." Luke touched the last tree in line. "Go to Jomark and ask him. I guess I'll have to."

LEIA'S OFFICE WAS grouped with the other Inner Council suites just off the cross hallway that linked the Grand Corridor with the more intimate Inner Council meeting room. Luke and Winter entered the outer reception area, to find a familiar figure waiting there. "Hello, Threepio," Luke said.

"Master Luke—how good to see you again," the gold-skinned droid gushed. "I trust you're well?"

"I'm fine," Luke told him. "Artoo said to say hello when I saw you, by the way. They've got him over at the spaceport helping with some maintenance on my X-wing, but I'll be bringing him back later this evening. You can see him then."

"Thank you, sir." Threepio tilted his head slightly, as if suddenly remembering that he was supposed to be acting as a receptionist here. "Princess Leia and the others are expecting you," he said, touching the inner chamber release. "Please go on in."

"Thank you," Luke said, nodding gravely. No matter how ridiculous Threepio might look in any given situation, there was always a certain inherent dignity about him, a dignity that Luke usually tried to respond to in kind. "Let us know if anyone else comes."

"Of course, sir," Threepio said.

They went into the inner chamber to find Leia and Han holding a quiet conversation over a computer display on Leia's desk. Chewbacca, sitting alone near the door with his bowcaster across his knees, growled a greeting as they entered.

"Ah—Luke," Leia said, looking up. "Thanks for coming." She shifted her attention to Winter. "That'll be all for now, Winter."

"Yes, Your Highness," Winter nodded. With her usual grace, she glided from the room.

Luke looked at Han. "I hear you dropped a double-size thermal detonator on the Council yesterday."

Han grimaced. "I tried. Not that anyone really believed me."

"One of those instances where politics drifts off into the realm of wishful thinking," Leia said. "The last thing anyone wants to believe is that in our sweep we somehow missed one of the Emperor's Grand Admirals."

"Sounds more like willful denial than wishful thinking to me," Luke said. "Or do they have another theory as to how we got edged so neatly into that Sluis Van trap?"

Leia grimaced. "Some of them say that's where Ackbar's collusion comes in."

"Ah," Luke murmured. So *that* was the thrust of Fey'lya's scheme. "I hadn't heard any of the details yet."

"So far, Fey'lya's been playing the sabacc cards close to the fur," Han growled. "*He* claims he's trying to be fair; *I* think he's just trying not to rock all the stabilizers at once."

Luke frowned at him. There was something else in his friend's face and sense . . . "And maybe something more?" he prompted.

Han and Leia exchanged glances. "Maybe," Han said. "You notice how quickly after the Sluis Van attack Fey'lya dropped the hammer on Ackbar? Either he's one of the great opportunists of all time—"

"Which we already know he is," Leia put in.

"—or else," Han continued grimly, "he knew in advance what was going to happen."

Luke looked at Leia. At the strain in her face and sense . . . "You realize what you're saying," he said quietly. "You're accusing a member of the Council of being an Imperial agent."

Leia's sense seemed to flinch. Han's didn't even flicker. "Yeah, I know," Han said. "Isn't that what he's accusing Ackbar of?"

"The problem is timing, Han," Leia said, her tone one of strained patience. "As I've already tried to explain. If we accuse Fey'lya of anything now, it'll just look like we're trying to take the pressure off Ackbar by turning Fey'lya's charges back against him. Even if it were true—and I don't think it is—it would still come across as a cheap and rather mindless trick."

"Maybe that's why he was so quick to finger Ackbar in the first place," Han countered. "So that we couldn't turn it back on him. That ever occur to you?"

"Yes, it has," Leia said. "Unfortunately, it doesn't change the situation. Until we've cleared Ackbar, we can't go making accusations against Fey'lya."

Han snorted. "Come on, Leia. Political waddlefooting is fine in its place, but we're talking about the survival of the New Republic here."

"Which could fall completely apart over this without anyone ever firing a shot," Leia retorted hotly. "Face it, Han—this whole thing is still being held together with hope and crating tape. You get a few wild accusations flying around, and half the races in the old Rebel Alliance might decide to pull out and go their separate ways."

Luke cleared his throat. "If I can say something . . . ?"

They looked at him, the tension in the room fading a little. "Sure, kid, what is it?" Han said.

"I think we all agree that, whatever his agenda or possible

sponsors, Fey'lya is up to *something*," Luke said. "Maybe it would help to find out what that something is. Leia, what do we know about Fey'lya?"

She shrugged. "He's a Bothan, obviously, though he grew up on the Bothan colony world of Kothlis instead of on Bothawui proper. He joined the Rebel Alliance right after the Battle of Yavin, bringing a good-sized group of his fellow Bothans in with him. His people served mainly in support and reconnaissance, though they saw some occasional action, too. He was involved in a number of wide-ranging interstellar business activities before joining the Alliance—shipping, merchandising, some mining, assorted other ventures. I'm pretty sure he's kept up with some of them since then, but I don't know which ones."

"Are they on file?" Luke asked.

She shook her head. "I've been through his file five times, and I've checked every other reference to him I could find. Nothing."

"That's where we want to start our backtrack, then," Han decided. "Quiet business stuff is always good for digging up dirt."

Leia threw him a patient look. "It's a big galaxy, Han. We don't even know where to start looking."

"I think we can figure it out," Han assured her. "You said the Bothans saw some action after Yavin. Where?"

"Any number of places," Leia said, frowning. She swiveled the computer around to face her, tapped in a command. "Let's see . . ."

"You can skip any battle they were ordered into," Han told her. "Also any time there were only a few of them there as part of a big multispecies force. I just want the places where a bunch of Fey'lya's people really threw themselves into it."

It was clear from Leia's face that she didn't see where Han was going with this, a sentiment Luke could readily identify with. But she fed in the parameters without comment. "Well . . . I suppose the only one that really qualifies would be a short but violent battle off New Cov in the Churba sector. Four Bothan ships took on a *Victory*-class Star Destroyer that was snooping around, keeping it busy until a Star Cruiser could come to their assistance."

"New Cov, huh?" Han repeated thoughtfully. "That system get mentioned anywhere in Fey'lya's business stuff?"

"Uh . . . no, it doesn't."

"Fine," Han nodded. "Then that's where we start."

Leia threw Luke a blank look. "Did I miss something?"

"Oh, come on, Leia," Han said. "You said yourself that the Bothans pretty much sat out the real war everywhere they could. They didn't take on a *Victory* Star Destroyer at New Cov just for the fun of it. They were protecting something."

Leia frowned. "I think you're reaching."

"Maybe," Han agreed. "Maybe not. Suppose it was Fey'lya and not the Imperials that sneaked that money into Ackbar's account? Transferring a block fund through Palanhi from the Churba sector would be easier than sending it in from any of the Imperial systems."

"That takes us back to accusing Fey'lya of being an Imperial agent," Luke warned.

"Maybe not," Han argued. "Could be the timing of the transfer was coincidence. Or maybe one of the Bothans got a whiff of the Empire's intentions and Fey'lya figured he could use it to take down Ackbar."

Leia shook her head. "It's still nothing we can take to the Council," she said.

"I'm not going to take it to the Council," Han told her. "I'm going to take Luke, and we're going to go to New Cov and check it out ourselves. Quiet like."

Leia looked at Luke, an unspoken question forming in her mind. "There's nothing I can do here to help," he said. "It's worth a look, anyway."

"All right," Leia sighed. "But keep it quiet."

Han gave her a tight grin. "Trust me." He raised an eyebrow at Luke. "You ready?"

Luke blinked. "You mean right now?"

"Sure, why not? Leia's got the political end covered here okay."

There was a flicker of sense from Leia, and Luke looked over just in time to see her wince. Her eyes met Luke's, her sense pleading with him to keep quiet. *What is it?* he asked her silently.

Whether she would have answered him or not he never found out. From over at the door Chewbacca growled out the whole story.

Han turned to stare at his wife, his mouth falling open. "You promised *what*?" he breathed.

She swallowed visibly. "Han, I had no choice."

"No choice? No *choice*? I'll give you a choice—no, you're not going."

"Han—"

"Excuse me," Luke interrupted, standing up. "I have to go check out my X-wing. I'll see you both later."

"Sure, kid," Han growled, not looking at him.

Luke stepped to the door, catching Chewbacca's eye as he passed and nodding toward the outer office. Clearly, the Wookiee had already come to the same conclusion. Heaving his massive bulk to his feet, he followed Luke from the room.

THE DOOR SLID shut behind them, and for a long moment they just stared at each other. Leia broke the silence first. "I have to go, Han," she said softly. "I promised Khabarakh I'd meet him. Don't you understand?"

"No, I don't understand," Han retorted, trying hard to hold on to his temper. The gut-wrenching fear he'd felt after that near-miss on Bpfassh was back, churning hard at his stomach. Fear for Leia's safety, and the safety of the twins she carried. His son and daughter . . . "These whatever-they-ares—"

"Noghri," she supplied the word.

"—these Noghri have been taking potshots at you every chance they've had for a couple of months now. You remember Bpfassh and that mock-up of the *Falcon* they tried to sucker us into getting aboard? And the attack on Bimmisaari before that—they came within a hair of snatching us right out of the middle of a marketplace. If it hadn't been for Luke and Chewie they'd have done it, too. These guys are *serious*, Leia. And now you tell me you want to fly out alone and visit their planet? You might as well turn yourself over to the Empire and save some time."

"I wouldn't be going if I thought that," she insisted. "Khabarakh knows I'm Darth Vader's daughter, and for whatever reason, that seems to be very important to them. Maybe I can use that leverage to turn them away from the Empire and onto our side. Anyway, I have to try."

Han snorted. "What is this, some kind of crazy Jedi thing? Luke was always getting all noble and charging off into trouble, too."

Leia reached over to lay her hand on his arm. "Han . . . I know it's a risk," she said quietly. "But it may be the only chance we ever have of resolving this. The Noghri need help—Khabarakh admitted that. If I can give them that help—if I can convince them to come over to our side—that'll mean one less enemy for us to have to deal with." She hesitated. "And I can't keep running forever."

"What about the twins?"

He had the guilty satisfaction of seeing her wince. "I know," she said, a shiver running through her as she reached her other hand up to hold her belly. "But what's the alternative? To lock them away in a tower of the Palace somewhere with a ring of Wookiee guards around them? They'll never have any chance of a normal life as long as the Noghri are trying to take them from us."

Han gritted his teeth. So she knew. He hadn't been sure before, but he was now. Leia knew that what the Empire had been after this whole time was her unborn children.

And knowing that, she still wanted to meet with the Empire's agents.

For a long minute he gazed at her, his eyes searching the features of that face he'd grown to love so deeply over the years, his memory bringing up images of the past as he did so. The young determination in her face as, in the middle of a blazing firefight, she'd grabbed Luke's blaster rifle away from him and shot them an escape route into the Death Star's detention-level garbage chute. The sound of her voice in the middle of deadly danger at Jabba's, helping him through the blindness and tremors and disorientation of hibernation sickness. The wiser, more mature determination visible through the pain in her eyes as, lying wounded outside the Endor bunker, she had nevertheless summoned the skill and control to coolly shoot two stormtroopers off Han's back.

And he remembered, too, the wrenching realization he'd had at that same time: that no matter how much he tried, he would never be able to totally protect her from the dangers and risks of the universe. Because no matter how much he might love her—no matter how much he might give of himself to her—she could never be content with that alone. Her vision extended beyond him, just as it extended beyond herself, to all the beings of the galaxy.

And to take that away from her, whether by force or even by persuasion, would be to diminish her soul. And to take away part of what he'd fallen in love with in the first place.

"Can I at least go with you?" he asked quietly.

She reached up to caress his cheek, smiling her thanks through the sudden moisture in her eyes. "I promised I'd go alone," she whispered, her voice tight with emotion. "Don't worry, I'll be all right."

"Sure." Abruptly, Han got to his feet. "Well, if you're going, you're going. Come on—I'll help you get the *Falcon* prepped."

"The *Falcon*?" she repeated. "But I thought you were going to New Cov."

"I'll take Lando's ship," he called over his shoulder as he strode to the door. "I've got to get it back to him, anyway."

"But—"

"No argument," he cut her off. "If this Noghri of yours has something besides talking in mind, you'll stand a better chance in the *Falcon* than you will in the *Lady Luck*." He opened the door and stepped into the reception area.

And stopped short. Standing directly between him and the door, looking for all the world like a giant hairy thundercloud, Chewbacca was glowering at him. "What?" Han demanded.

The Wookiee's comment was short, sharp, and very much to the point. "Well, *I* don't much like it, either," Han told him bluntly. "What do you want me to do, lock her up somewhere?"

He felt Leia come up behind him. "I'll be all right, Chewie," she assured him. "Really I will."

Chewbacca growled again, making it abundantly clear what he thought of her assessment. "You got any suggestions, let's hear 'em," Han said.

Not surprisingly, he did. "Chewie, I'm sorry," Leia said. "I promised Khabarakh I'd come alone."

Chewbacca shook his head violently, showing his teeth as he growled his opinion of that idea. "He doesn't like it," Han translated diplomatically.

"I got the gist, thank you," Leia retorted. "Listen, you two; for the last time—"

Chewbacca cut her off with a bellow that made her jump half a meter backward. "You know, sweetheart," Han said, "I really think you ought to let him go with you. At least as far as the rendezvous point," he added quickly as she threw him a glare. "Come on—you know how seriously Wookiees take this life debt thing. You need a pilot, anyway."

For just a second he could see the obvious counter-argument in her eyes: that she was perfectly capable of flying the *Falcon* herself. But only for a second. "All right," she sighed. "I guess Khabarakh won't object to that. But once we reach the rendezvous, Chewie, you do as I tell you, whether you like it or not. Agreed?"

The Wookiee thought about it, rumbled agreement. "Okay," Leia said, sounding relieved. "Let's get going, then. Threepio?"

"Yes, Your Highness?" the droid said hesitantly. For once, he'd had the brains to sit quietly at the reception desk and keep his loose change out of the discussion. It was a marked improvement over his usual behavior, Han decided. Maybe he ought to let Chewbacca get angry more often.

"I want you to come with me, too," Leia told the droid. "Khabarakh spoke Basic well enough, but the other Noghri may not, and I don't want to have to depend on their translators to make myself understood."

"Of course, Your Highness," Threepio said, tilting his head slightly to the side.

"Good." Leia turned to look up at Han, licked her lips. "I guess we'd better get going."

There were a million things he could have said to her. A million things he wanted to say. "I guess," he said instead, "you'd better."

CHAPTER 5

"YOU'LL FORGIVE ME," Mara said conversationally as she finished the last bit of wiring on her comm board, "if I say that as a hideout, this place stinks."

Karrde shrugged as he hefted a sensor pack out of its box and set it down on the side table with an assortment of other equipment. "I agree it's not Myrkr," he said. "On the other hand, it has its compensations. Who'd ever think of looking for a smuggler's nest in the middle of a swamp?"

"I'm not referring to the ship drop," Mara told him, reaching beneath her loose-flowing tunic sleeve to readjust the tiny blaster sheathed to her left forearm. "I mean this place."

"Ah. *This* place." Karrde glanced out the window. "I don't know. A little public, perhaps, but that, too, has its compensations."

"A little public?" Mara echoed, looking out the window herself at the neat row of cream-white buildings barely five meters away and the crowds of brightly clad humans and aliens hurrying along just outside. "You call this a *little* public?"

"Calm down, Mara," Karrde said. "When the only viable

places to live on a planet are a handful of deep valleys, of course things are going to get a bit crowded. The people here are used to it, and they've learned how to give each other a reasonable degree of privacy. Anyway, even if they wanted to snoop, it wouldn't do them much good."

"Mirror glass won't stop a good sensor probe," Mara countered. "And crowds mean cover for Imperial spies."

"The Imperials have no idea where we are." He paused and threw her an odd look. "Unless you know differently."

Mara turned away. So that was how it was going to be this time. Previous employers had reacted to her strange hunches with fear, or anger, or simple bald-faced hatred. Karrde, apparently, was going to go for polite exploitation. "I can't turn it on and off like a sensor pack," she growled over her shoulder. "Not anymore."

"Ah," Karrde said. The word implied he understood; the tone indicated otherwise. "Interesting. Is this a remnant of some previous Jedi training?"

She turned to look at him. "Tell me about the ships."

He frowned. "Excuse me?"

"The ships," she repeated. "The capital warships that you were very careful not to tell Grand Admiral Thrawn about, back when he visited us on Myrkr. You promised to give me the details later. This is later."

He studied her, a slight smile creasing his lips. "All right," he said. "Have you ever heard of the *Katana* fleet?"

She had to search her memory. "That was the group also called the Dark Force, wasn't it? Something like two hundred *Dreadnaught*-class Heavy Cruisers that were lost about ten years before the Clone Wars broke out. All the ships were fitted with some kind of new-style full-rig slave circuitry, and when the system malfunctioned, the whole fleet jumped to lightspeed together and disappeared."

"Nearly right," Karrde said. "The Dreadnaughts of that era in particular were ridiculously crew-intensive ships, requiring upwards of sixteen thousand men each. The full-rig slave circuitry on the *Katana* ships cut that complement down to around two thousand."

Mara thought about the handful of Dreadnaught cruisers she'd known. "Must have been an expensive conversion."

"It was," Karrde nodded. "Particularly since they played it as much for public relations as they did for pure military purposes. They redesigned the entire Dreadnaught interior for the occasion, from the equipment and interior decor right down to the dark gray hull surfacing. That last was the origin of the nickname 'Dark Force,' incidentally, though there was some suggestion that it referred to the smaller number of interior lights a two-thousand-crewer ship would need. At any rate, it was the Old Republic's grand demonstration of how effective a slave-rigged fleet could be."

Mara snorted. "Some demonstration."

"Agreed," Karrde said dryly. "But the problem wasn't in the slave circuitry itself. The records are a little vague—suppressed by those in charge at the time, no doubt—but it appears that one or more of the fleet's crewers picked up a hive virus at one of the ports of call on their maiden voyage. It was spread throughout all two hundred ships while in dormant state, which meant that when it suddenly flared up it took down nearly everybody at once."

Mara shivered. She'd heard of hive viruses leveling whole planetary populations in pre-Clone Wars days, before the medical science of the Old Republic and later the Empire had finally figured out how to deal with the things. "So it killed the crews before they could get to help."

"Apparently in a matter of hours, though that's just an educated guess," Karrde said. "What turned the whole thing from a disaster into a debacle was the fact that this particular hive virus had the charming trait of driving its victims insane just before it killed them. The dying crewers lasted just long enough to slave their ships together . . . which meant that when the *Katana* command crew also went crazy and took off, the entire fleet went with them."

"I remember now," Mara nodded slowly. "That was supposedly what started the big movement toward decentralization in automated ship functions. Away from big, all-powerful computers into hundreds of droids."

"The movement was already on its way, but the *Katana* fiasco pretty well sealed the outcome," Karrde said. "Anyway, the fleet disappeared somewhere into the depths of interstellar space and was never heard from again. It was a big news item for a while, with some of the less reverent members of the media making snide word-plays on the 'Dark Force' name, and for a few years it was considered a hot prospect by salvage teams who had more enthusiasm than good sense. Once it finally dawned on them just how much empty space was available in the galaxy to lose a couple hundred ships in, the flurry of interest ended. At any rate, the Old Republic soon had bigger problems on its hands. Aside from the occasional con artist who'll try to sell you a map of its location, you never hear about the fleet anymore."

"Right." It was, of course, obvious now where Karrde was going with this. "So how did you happen to find it?"

"Purely by accident, I assure you. In fact, it wasn't until several days afterward that I realized what exactly I'd found. I suspect none of the rest of the crew ever knew at all."

Karrde's gaze defocused, his eyes flattening with the memory. "It was just over fifteen years ago," he said, his voice distant, the thumbs of his intertwined hands rubbing slowly against each other. "I was working as navigator/sensor specialist for a small, independent smuggling group. We'd rather botched a pickup and had had to shoot our way past a pair of Carrack cruisers on our way out. We made it all right, but since I hadn't had the time to do a complete lightspeed calculation, we dropped back to real-space a half light-year out to recalculate." His lip twitched. "Imagine our surprise when we discovered a pair of Dreadnaughts waiting directly in our path."

"Lying dead in space."

Karrde shook his head. "Actually, they weren't, which was

what threw me for those first few days. From all appearances, the ships seemed to be fully functional, with both interior and running lights showing and even a standby sensor scan in operation. Naturally, we assumed it was part of the group we'd just tangled with, and the captain made an emergency jump to lightspeed to get us out of there."

"Not a good idea," Mara murmured.

"It seemed the lesser of two evils at the time," Karrde said grimly. "As it turned out, we came close to being fatally wrong on that account. The ship hit the mass shadow of a large comet on the way out, blowing the main hyperdrive and nearly wrecking the rest of the ship on the spot. Five of our crew were killed in the collision, and another three died of injuries before we could limp back to civilization on the backup hyperdrive."

There was a moment of silence. "How many of you were left?" Mara asked at last.

Karrde focused on her, his usual sardonic smile back on his face. "Or in other words, who else might know about the fleet?"

"If you want to put it that way."

"There were six of us left. As I said, though, I don't think any of the others realized what it was we'd found. It was only when I went back to the sensor records and discovered that there were considerably more than just the two Dreadnaughts in the area that I began to have my own suspicions."

"And the records themselves?"

"I erased them. After memorizing the coordinates, of course."

Mara nodded. "You said this was fifteen years ago?"

"That's right," Karrde nodded back. "I've thought about going back and doing something with the ships, but I never had the time to do it properly. Unloading two hundred Dreadnaughts on the open market isn't something you rush into without a good deal of prior preparation. Even if you have markets for all of them, which has always been problematic."

"Until now."

He cocked an eyebrow. "Are you suggesting I sell them to the Empire?"

"They're in the market for capital ships," she reminded him. "And they're offering value plus twenty percent."

He cocked an eyebrow at her. "I thought you didn't much care for the Empire."

"I don't," she retorted. "What's the other option—give them to the New Republic?"

He held her gaze. "That might be more profitable in the long run."

Mara's left hand curled into a tight fist, her stomach churning with mixed feelings. To let the Dreadnaughts fall into the hands of the New Republic, successor to the Rebel Alliance that had destroyed her life, was a hateful thought. But on the other hand, the Empire without the Emperor was only a pale shadow of its former self, hardly even worthy of the name anymore. It would be pearls before swine to give the Dark Force to them.

Or would it? With a Grand Admiral in charge of the Imperial Fleet again, perhaps there was now a chance for the Empire to regain some of its old glory. And if there was . . . "What are you going to do?" she asked Karrde.

"At the moment, nothing," Karrde said. "It's the same problem we faced with Skywalker, after all: the Empire will be swifter to exact vengeance if we go against them, but the New Republic looks more likely to win in the end. Giving Thrawn the *Katana* fleet would only delay the inevitable. The most prudent course right now is to stay neutral."

"Except that giving Thrawn the Dreadnaughts might get him off our exhaust trail," Mara pointed out. "That would be worth the trade right there."

Karrde smiled faintly. "Oh, come now, Mara. The Grand Admiral may be a tactical genius, but he's hardly omniscient. He can't possibly have any idea where we are. And he certainly has more important things to do than spend his resources chasing us down."

"I'm sure he does," Mara agreed reluctantly. But she couldn't help remembering how, even at the height of his power and with a thousand other concerns, the Emperor had still frequently taken the time to exact vengeance on someone who'd crossed him.

Beside her the comm board buzzed, and Mara reached over to key the channel. "Yes?"

"Lachton," a familiar voice came from the speaker. "Is Karrde around?"

"Right here," Karrde called, stepping to Mara's side. "How's the camouflage work going?"

"We're about done," Lachton said. "We ran short of flash-netting, though. Do we have any more?"

"There's some at one of the dumps," Karrde told him. "I'll send Mara to get it; can you have someone come in to pick it up?"

"Sure, no problem. I'll send Dankin—he hasn't got much to do at the moment anyway."

"All right. The netting will be ready by the time he gets here."

Karrde gestured, and Mara keyed off the channel. "You know where the Number Three dump is?" he asked her.

She nodded. "Four twelve Wozwashi Street. Three blocks west and two north."

"Right." He peered out the window. "Unfortunately, it's still too early for repulsorlift vehicles to be on the streets. You'll have to walk."

"That's all right," Mara assured him. She felt like a little exercise, anyway. "Two boxes be enough?"

"If you can handle that many," he told her, looking her up and down as if making sure her outfit conformed to local Rishi standards of propriety. He needn't have bothered; one of the first rules the Emperor had drummed into her so long ago was to blend in as best she could with her surroundings. "If not, Lachton can probably make do with one."

"All right. I'll see you later."

Their townhouse was part of a row of similar structures
abutting one of the hundreds of little market areas that dotted
the whole congested valley. For a moment Mara stood in the
entry alcove of their building, out of the busy flow of pedestrian traffic, and looked around her. Through the gaps between the nearest buildings she could see the more distant
parts of the city-vale, most of it composed of the same cream-
white stone so favored by the locals. In places, she could see all
the way to the edge, a few small buildings perched precariously partway up the craggy mountains that rose sharply into
the sky on all sides. Far up those mountains, she knew, lived
loose avian tribes of native Rishii, who no doubt looked down
in bemused disbelief at the strange creatures who had chosen
the most uncomfortably hot and humid spots of their planet
in which to live.

Dropping her gaze from the mountains, Mara gave the immediate area a quick scan. Across the street were more townhouses; between her and them was the usual flow of brightly
clad pedestrians hurrying to and from the market area to the
east. Reflexively, her eyes flicked across the townhouses,
though with each window composed of mirror glass there
wasn't a lot there for her to see. Also reflexively, she glanced
across each of the narrow pedestrian alleyways between the
buildings.

Between two of them, back at the building's rear where he
was hardly visible, was the motionless figure of a man wearing
a blue scarf and patterned green tunic.

Staring in her direction.

Mara let her gaze drift on as if she hadn't seen him, her
heart thudding suddenly in her throat. Stepping out of the alcove, she turned east toward the market and joined the flow of
traffic.

She didn't stay with it long, though. As soon as she was out
of the mysterious loiterer's line of sight, she began cutting her
way across the flow, heading across the street toward the townhouse row. She reached it three buildings down from the loi-

terer, ducked into the alleyway, and hurried toward the rear. If he was indeed monitoring Karrde's place, there was a good chance she could take him from behind.

She reached the rear of the buildings and circled around . . . only to find that her quarry had vanished.

For a moment she stood there, looking around her for any sign of the man's whereabouts, wondering what to do now. There was none of the insistent tingling that had gotten them away from Myrkr at the last second; but as she'd told Karrde, it wasn't a talent she could turn on and off.

She looked down at the ground where the man had been standing. There were a few faint footprints in the thin coating of dust that had collected at the corner of the townhouse, giving the impression that the man had been there long enough to shuffle his feet a few times. A half dozen steps away, right in the center of another layer of dust, was a clear footprint pointing toward the west behind the row of townhouses.

Mara looked in that direction, feeling her lip twist. A deliberate lead-on, obviously—footprints in dust never came out that clear and unsmudged unless carefully planted. And she was right. A hundred meters directly ahead, strolling casually along the rear of the buildings toward a north-south street, was the man in the blue scarf and patterned tunic. A not-very-subtle invitation to follow him.

Okay, friend, she thought as she started off after him. *You want to play? Let's play.*

She had closed the gap between them to perhaps ninety meters when he reached the cross flow of traffic and turned north into it. Another clear invitation, this time to close the gap further lest she lose him.

But Mara had no intention of taking him up on this one. She'd memorized the geography of the city-vale their first day here, and it was pretty obvious that his intention was to lead her up to the more sparsely populated industrial areas to the north, where presumably he could deal with her without the awkward presence of witnesses. If she could get there first, she might be able to turn things around on him. Double-checking the blaster beneath her left sleeve, she cut through an alley between the buildings to her right and headed north.

The valley stretched for nearly a hundred fifty kilometers in a roughly east-west direction, but at this point its north-south dimension was only a few kilometers. Mara kept up her pace, continually revising her course to avoid crowds and other impediments. Gradually, the houses and shops began to give way to light industry; and, finally, she judged she'd come far enough. If her quarry had kept with the leisurely pace of a man who didn't want to lose a tracker, she should now have enough time to prepare a little reception for him.

There was, of course, always the possibility that he'd shifted to one of the other north-south streets somewhere along the way, changed direction east or west, or even doubled back completely and returned to Karrde's townhouse. But as she looked carefully around the corner of a building into the street he'd first turned onto, she discovered that his imagination was as limited as his surveillance technique. Halfway down the block, he was crouched motionless behind a row of storage barrels with his back to her, his blue scarf thrown back out of the way across his patterned green tunic, something that was probably a weapon clutched ready in his hand. Waiting, no doubt, for her to stroll into his trap. *Amateur*, she thought, lip twisting in contempt. Watching him closely, not even bothering with her blaster, she eased around the corner and started silently toward him.

"That's far enough," a mocking voice said from behind her.

Mara froze. The figure crouched by the barrels ahead of her didn't even twitch . . . and it was only then that she belatedly realized that it was far too still to be simply waiting in ambush. Far too still, for that matter, to even be alive.

Slowly, keeping her arms stretched straight out to her sides, she turned around. The man facing her was of medium height, with a somewhat bulky build and dark, brooding eyes. His undertunic hung open to reveal a light-armor vest beneath it.

In his hand, of course, was a blaster. "Well, well, well," he sneered. "What we got here? 'Bout time you showed up—I was startin' to think you'd gotten lost or somethin'."

"Who are you?" Mara asked.

"Oh, no, Red, I'm the one what's askin' the questions here. Not that I need to, 'course. That fancy stuff on top pret' well tells me aw I need t' know." He gestured with his blaster at her red-gold hair. "Shoulda gotten rid o' that—hide it or dyed it, y'know. Dead give'way. Pardon the 'spression."

Mara took a careful breath, forcing her muscles to unknot. "What do you want with me?" she asked, keeping her voice calm.

"Same thin' ev'ry man reall' wants," he grinned slyly. "A pile o' hard cold cash."

She shook her head. "In that case, I'm afraid you've picked the wrong person. I've only got about fifty on me."

He grinned even wider. "Cute, Red, but you're wastin' your time. I know who y'are, aw right. You 'n' your pals are gonna make me real rich. C'mon—let's go."

Mara didn't move. "Perhaps we can work a deal," she suggested, feeling a drop of sweat trickle down between her shoulder blades. She knew better than to be fooled by the other's careless speech and manner—whoever and whatever he was, he knew exactly what he was doing.

On the plus side, she still had the blaster hidden beneath her sleeve; and she would give long odds that her assailant wouldn't expect that a weapon that potent might be small enough to conceal there. The fact that he hadn't already searched her seemed to confirm that assessment.

But whatever she was going to do, she had to do it now, while she was still facing him. Unfortunately, with her hands spread apart there was no way for her to get at her weapon without telegraphing the movement. Somehow, she needed to distract him.

"A deal, huh?" he asked lazily. "What kind o' deal you got in mind?"

"What kind of deal do you want?" she countered. If there'd been a box anywhere near her feet, she might have been able to scoop it up with her foot and throw it at him. But though there was a fair amount of junk littering the street in this part of town, nothing suitable was within reach. Her half-boots were firmly fastened around her ankles, impossible to get loose without him noticing. Rapidly, she ran through an inventory of items she was carrying or wearing—nothing.

But the Emperor's intensive training had included direct manipulation of the Force as well as the long-range communication abilities that had been her primary value to his regime. Those skills had vanished at the moment of his death, reappearing only briefly and erratically in the years since then.

But if the sensory tingles and hunches had started again, perhaps the power was back, too . . .

"I'm sure we can double whatever you've been offered," she said. "Maybe even throw in something extra to sweeten the pot."

His grin turned evil. "That's a real gen'rous offer, Red. Real gen'rous. Lotta men'd jump on that right away, sure 'nough. Me"—he lifted the blaster a little higher—"I like stayin' with a sure thing."

"Even if it means settling for half the money?" Two meters behind him, piled carelessly up against a retaining wall, was a small stack of scrap metal parts waiting to be picked up. A short length of shield tubing, in particular, seemed to be rather precariously positioned on one edge of a battered power cell case.

Setting her teeth, clearing her thoughts as best she could, Mara reached her mind out toward the tubing.

"On my pad, half a sure thing's better than twice o' nothin'," the man said. "Anyway, I don't 'spect you can outbid the Empire."

Mara swallowed. She'd suspected it from the first; but the confirmation still sent a shiver up her back. "You might be surprised at our resources," she said. The length of tubing twitched, rolled a couple of millimeters—

"Naw, don't think so," the other said easily. "C'mon, let's go."

Mara tilted a finger back toward the dead man crouched at the box behind her. "You mind telling me first what happened here?"

Her assailant shrugged. "What's t' tell? I needed a decoy; he was wanderin' around the wrong place at the wrong time. End o' story." His grin suddenly vanished. "Enough stallin'. Turn around and start walkin' . . . unless you're lookin' t' spite me by makin' me settle for the death fee instead."

"No," Mara murmured. She took a deep breath, straining with every bit of strength she possessed, knowing that this was her last best chance—

And behind her captor, the tubing fell with a muffled clank onto the ground.

He was good, all right. The tubing had hardly even finished its fall before he'd dropped to one knee, spinning around and spraying the area behind him with a splattering of quick cover fire as he searched for whoever was sneaking up on him. It took less than a second for him to recognize his mistake, and with another spray of blaster fire he spun back again.

But one second was all Mara needed. His desperate blaster spray was still tracking toward her when she shot him neatly in the head.

For a long moment she just stood there, breathing hard, muscles trembling with reaction. Then, glancing around to make sure no one was running to see what all the commotion was about, she holstered her weapon and knelt down beside him.

There was, as she'd expected, precious little to find. An ID—probably forged—giving his name as Dengar Roth, a couple of spare power clips for his blaster, a backup vibro-blade knife, a data card and data pad, and some working cap-

ital in both local and Imperial currency. Stuffing the ID and
data card into her tunic, she left the money and weapons
where they were and got back to her feet. "There's your twice
of nothing," she muttered, looking down at the body. "Enjoy
it."

Her eyes shifted to the piece of shield tubing that had saved
her life. She'd been right. The twitches of power, as well as the
hunches, were back. Which meant the dreams wouldn't be far
behind.

She swore under her breath. If they came, they came, and
there was nothing much she could do except endure them. For
the moment she had other, more pressing matters to deal with.
Taking one final look around, she headed for home.

KARRDE AND DANKIN were waiting when she arrived back at
the townhouse, the latter all but pacing the floor in his nervousness. "*There* you are," he snapped as she slipped in
through the back door. "Where the blazes—?"

"We've got trouble," Mara cut him off, handing the Dengar
Roth ID to Karrde and brushing past them to the still largely
disassembled communications room. Pushing aside a box of
cables, she found a data pad and plugged in the card.

"What kind of trouble?" Karrde asked, coming up behind
her.

"The bounty hunter kind," Mara said, handing him the
data pad. Neatly framed in the center of the display, under a
large *20,000*, was Karrde's face. "We're probably all in there,"
she told him. "Or at least as many as Grand Admiral Thrawn
knew about."

"So I'm worth twenty thousand now," Karrde murmured,
paging quickly through the card, "I'm flattered."

"Is that all you're going to say?" Mara demanded.

He looked at her. "What would you like me to say?" he
asked mildly. "That you were right and I was wrong about the
Empire's interest in us?"

"I'm not interested in laying blame," she told him stiffly. "What I want to know is what we're going to do about it."

Karrde looked at the data pad again, a muscle tightening briefly in his jaw. "We're going to do the only prudent thing," he said. "Namely, retreat. Dankin, get on the secure comm and tell Lachton to start pulling the drop apart again. Then call Chin and his team and have them go over and repack the stuff in the equipment dumps. You can stay and help Mara and me here. I want to get off Rishi by midnight if at all possible."

"Got it," Dankin said, already keying the encrypt codes into the comm board.

Karrde handed the data pad back to Mara. "We'd better get busy."

She stopped him with a hand on his arm. "And what happens when we run out of backup bases?"

He locked eyes with her. "We don't give up the Dreadnaughts under duress," he said, lowering his voice to just above a whisper. "Not to Thrawn; not to anyone else."

"We may have to," she pointed out.

His eyes hardened. "We may choose to," he corrected her. "We will never *have* to. Is that clear?"

Mara grimaced to herself. "Yes."

"Good." Karrde flicked a glance over her shoulder to where Dankin was speaking urgently into the comm. "We have a lot of work to do. Let's get to it."

MARA WOULD HAVE bet that they couldn't reassemble their equipment in less than twenty-four hours. To her mild surprise, the crews had everything packed and ready to go barely an hour after local midnight. With suitably generous applications of funds to spaceport officials, they were off Rishi and to lightspeed an hour after that.

And later that night, as the *Wild Karrde* drove through the mottled sky of hyperspace, the dreams started again.

CHAPTER 6

From a distance it had looked like a standard-issue Bulk Cruiser: old, slow, minimally armed, with very little going for it in a fight except its size. But as with so very much of warfare, appearances in this case turned out to be deceiving; and if Grand Admiral Thrawn hadn't been on the *Chimaera*'s bridge, Pellaeon had to admit that he might have been caught a bit by surprise.

But Thrawn had been on the bridge, and had recognized immediately the unlikelihood that the Rebellion's strategists would have put such an important convoy under the protection of such a weak ship. And so, when the Bulk Cruiser's bays suddenly erupted with three full squadrons of A-wing starfighters, the *Chimaera*'s TIE interceptors were already in space and swarming to the attack.

"Interesting tactic," Thrawn commented as the gap between the *Chimaera* and the Rebel convoy began to sparkle with laser flashes. "If not especially innovative. The idea of converting Bulk Cruisers to starfighter carriers was first proposed over twenty years ago."

"I don't recall it ever being implemented," Pellaeon said, feeling a twinge of uneasiness as he eyed the tactical displays. A-wings were faster even than those cursed X-wings, and he wasn't at all sure how well his TIE interceptors would handle them.

"Excellent fighters, A-wings," Thrawn said, as if reading Pellaeon's thoughts. "Not without their limitations, though. Particularly here—high-speed craft like that are far more suited to hit-and-fade operations than to escort duty. Forcing them to remain near a convoy largely neutralizes their speed advantage." He cocked a blue-black eyebrow at Pellaeon. "Perhaps we're seeing the result of Admiral Ackbar's removal as Supreme Commander."

"Perhaps." The TIE interceptors did indeed seem to be holding their own against the A-wings; and the *Chimaera* itself was certainly having no trouble with the Bulk Cruiser. Beyond the battlefront, the rest of the convoy was trying to huddle together, as if that would do them any good. "Ackbar's people are still in charge, though. Obviously."

"We've been over this territory already, Captain," Thrawn said, his voice cooling slightly. "Planting a vacuum-tight collection of evidence against Ackbar would have ruined him far too quickly. The more subtle attack will still neutralize him, but it will also send ripples of uncertainty and confusion through the Rebellion's entire political system. At the very least, it will distract and weaken them just at the moment when we'll be launching the Mount Tantiss campaign. At its best, it could split the entire Alliance apart." He smiled. "Ackbar himself is replaceable, Captain. The delicate political balance the Rebellion has created for itself is not."

"I understand all that, Admiral," Pellaeon growled. "My concern is with your assumption that that Bothan on the Council can be relied upon to push things so close to your theoretical breakup point."

"Oh, he'll push, all right," Thrawn said, his smile turning sardonic as he gazed out at the battle blazing on around the enemy convoy. "I've spent many hours studying Bothan art, Captain, and I understand the species quite well. There's no doubt at all that Councilor Fey'lya will play his part beautifully. As beautifully as if we were pulling his strings directly."

He tapped a key on his board. "Starboard batteries: one of the Frigates in the convoy is easing into attack position. Assume it's an armed backup and treat it accordingly. Squadrons A-2 and A-3, move to protect that flank until the Frigate has been neutralized."

The batteries and TIE wing commander acknowledged, and some of the turbolaser fire began to track on the Frigate. "And what happens if Fey'lya wins?" Pellaeon persisted. "Quickly, I mean, before all this political confusion has a chance to set in. By your own analysis of the species, any Bothan who's risen as high as Fey'lya has would have to be highly intelligent."

"Intelligent, yes, but not necessarily in any way that's dangerous to us," Thrawn said. "He'd have to be a survivor, certainly, but that kind of verbal skill doesn't necessarily translate into military competence." He shrugged. "Actually, a victory by Fey'lya would merely prolong the whole awkward situation for the enemy. Given the kind of support Fey'lya's been cultivating among the Rebellion military, the politicians would have to go through another polarizing struggle when they realized their mistake and tried to replace him."

"Yes, sir," Pellaeon said, suppressing a sigh. It was the kind of tangled subtlety that he'd never really felt comfortable with. He just hoped the Grand Admiral was right about the potential gains; it would be a shame for Intelligence to have engineered such a brilliantly successful bank job and then not get anything of real value out of it.

"Trust me, Captain," Thrawn said into his unspoken worries. "I dare say the wasting of political effort has already begun, in fact. Ackbar's staunchest allies would hardly have left Coruscant at this critical point unless they were desperately searching for evidence to clear him."

Pellaeon frowned at him. "Are you saying that Solo and Organa Solo are headed for the Palanhi system?"

"Solo only, I think," Thrawn corrected thoughtfully. "Organa Solo and the Wookiee are most likely still trying to find a place to hide from our Noghri. But Solo will be going to Palanhi, firmly convinced by Intelligence's electronic sleight-of-hand that the trail leads through that system. Which is why the *Death's Head* is on its way there right now."

"I see," Pellaeon murmured. He'd noticed that order on the daily log and had wondered why Thrawn was pulling one of their best Imperial Star Destroyers off battle duty. "I hope it will be equal to the task. Solo and Skywalker have both proved hard to trap in the past."

"I don't believe Skywalker is going to Palanhi," Thrawn told him, his face settling into a somewhat sour expression. "Our esteemed Jedi Master apparently called it correctly. Skywalker has decided to pay a visit to Jomark."

Pellaeon stared at him. "Are you sure, Admiral? I haven't seen anything from Intelligence to that effect."

"The information wasn't from Intelligence," Thrawn said. "It came from Delta Source."

"Ah," Pellaeon said, feeling his own expression go a little sour. The *Chimaera*'s Intelligence section had been nagging him for months now to find out what exactly this Delta Source was that seemed to feed such clear and precise information to the Grand Admiral from the very heart of the Imperial Palace. So far all Thrawn would say was that Delta Source was firmly established and that the information gained through it should be treated as absolutely reliable.

Intelligence hadn't even been able to figure out whether Delta Source was a person, a droid, or some exotic recording system that was somehow able to elude the Rebellion's hourly counterintelligence sweeps of the Palace. It irritated them no end; and Pellaeon had to admit he didn't much like being kept in the dark about it, either. But Thrawn had personally activated Delta Source, and long years of unwritten protocol in such matters gave him the right to keep the contact confidential if he chose. "I'm sure C'baoth will be pleased to hear it," he said. "I presume you'll want to give him the news yourself."

He thought he'd hidden his irritation with C'baoth reasonably well. Apparently, he'd thought wrong. "You're still upset about Taanab," Thrawn said, turning to gaze out at the battle. It wasn't a question.

"Yes, sir, I am," Pellaeon said stiffly. "I've been over the records again, and there's only one possible conclusion. C'baoth deliberately went beyond the battle plan Captain Aban had laid out—went beyond it to the point of disobeying a direct order. I don't care who C'baoth is or whether he felt justified or not. What he did constitutes mutiny."

"It did indeed," Thrawn agreed calmly. "Shall I throw him out of the Imperial service altogether, or simply demote him in rank?"

Pellaeon glared at the other. "I'm serious, Admiral."

"So am I, Captain," Thrawn countered, his voice abruptly cold. "You know full well what's at stake here. We need to utilize every weapon at our disposal if we're to defeat the Rebellion. C'baoth's ability to enhance coordination and battle efficiency between our forces is one of those weapons; and if he can't handle proper military discipline and protocol, then we bend the rules for him."

"And what happens when we've bent the rules so far that they come around and stab us in the back?" Pellaeon demanded. "He ignored a direct order at Taanab—maybe next time it'll be two orders. Then three, then four, until finally he's doing what he damn well pleases and to blazes with the Empire. What's to stop him?"

"Initially, the ysalamiri," Thrawn said, gesturing at the odd-looking tubular frameworks scattered around the bridge, each with an elongated furry creature wrapped around it. Each of them creating a bubble in the Force where none of C'baoth's Jedi tricks would work. "That's what they're here for, after all."

"That's all well and good," Pellaeon said. "But in the long run—"

"In the long run, *I* will stop him," Thrawn cut him off, touching his board. "Squadron C-3, watch your port-zenith flank. There's a blister on that Frigate that could be a cluster trap."

The commander acknowledged, the TIE interceptors veering away in response. A second later, half a heartbeat too late, the blister abruptly exploded, sending a withering hail of concussion grenades outward in all directions. The rearmost of the TIE interceptors was caught by the edge of the fiery flower, shattering in a brilliant secondary explosion. The rest, out of range, escaped the booby trap unharmed.

Thrawn turned his glowing eyes on Pellaeon. "I understand your concerns, Captain," he said quietly. "What you fail to grasp—what you've always failed to grasp—is that a man with C'baoth's mental and emotional instabilities can never be a threat to us. Yes, he has a great deal of power, and at any given moment he could certainly do considerable damage to our people and equipment. But by his very nature he's unable to use that power for any length of time. Concentration, focus, long-term thinking—those are the qualities that separate a warrior from a mere flailing fighter. And they're qualities C'baoth will never possess."

Pellaeon nodded heavily. He still wasn't convinced, but there was clearly no use in arguing the point further. Not now, anyway. "Yes, sir." He hesitated. "C'baoth will also want to know about Organa Solo."

Thrawn's eyes glittered; but the annoyance, Pellaeon knew, wasn't directed at him. "You will tell Master C'baoth that I've decided to allow the Noghri one last chance to find and capture her. When we've finished here, I'll be taking that message to them. Personally."

Pellaeon glanced back at the entrance to the bridge, where the Noghri bodyguard Rukh stood his usual silent vigil. "You're calling a convocate of the Noghri commandos?" he asked, suppressing a shiver. He'd been to one such mass meeting once, and facing a whole roomful of those quiet gray-skinned killers was not an experience he was anxious to repeat.

"I think matters have gone beyond simply calling a convocate," Thrawn said coldly. "You'll instruct Navigation to prepare a course from the rendezvous point to the Honoghr system. The entire Noghri populace, I think, needs to be reminded of who it is they serve."

He shifted his glare out the viewport at the battle and tapped his board. "TIE command: recall all fighters to the ship," he ordered. "Navigation: begin calculations for a return to the rendezvous point."

Pellaeon frowned out the viewport. The modified Bulk Cruiser and backup Frigate were pretty much dead where they lay, but the convoy itself was largely undamaged. "We're letting them go?"

"There's no need to destroy them," Thrawn said. "Stripping them of their defense is an adequate object lesson for the moment."

He tapped a key, and a tactical holo of this section of the galaxy appeared between their two stations. Blue lines marked the Rebellion's main trade routes; those sheathed in red marked ones the Imperial forces had hit in the past month. "There's more to these attacks than simple harassment, Captain. Once this group has told their story, all future convoys from Sarka will demand upgraded protection. Enough such attacks, and the Rebellion will face the choice of either tying up large numbers of its ships with escort duty or effectively abandoning cargo shipment through these border sectors. Either way, it will put them at a serious disadvantage when we launch the Mount Tantiss campaign." He smiled grimly. "Economics and psychology, Captain. For now, the more civilian survivors there are to spread the tale of Imperial power, the better. There'll be time enough for destruction later." He glanced at his board, looked back out the viewport. "Speaking of Imperial power, any news on our ship hunt?"

"We've had five more capital ships turned in to various Imperial bases in the past ten hours," Pellaeon told him. "Nothing larger than an old Star Galleon, but it's a start."

"We're going to need more than just a start, Captain," Thrawn said, craning his neck slightly to watch the returning TIE interceptors. "Any word on Talon Karrde?"

"Nothing since that tip from Rishi," Pellaeon told him, tapping the proper log for an update. "The bounty hunter who sent it was killed shortly afterward."

"Keep up the pressure," Thrawn ordered. "Karrde knows a great deal about what happens in this galaxy. If there are any capital ships lying unused out there, he'll know where they are."

Personally, Pellaeon thought it pretty unlikely that a mere smuggler, even one with Karrde's connections, would have better information sources than the vast Imperial Intelligence network. But he'd also dismissed the possibility that Karrde might be hiding Luke Skywalker out at that base on Myrkr. Karrde was turning out to be full of surprises. "There are a lot of people out there hunting for him," he told the Grand Admiral. "Sooner or later, one of them will find him."

"Good." Thrawn glanced around the bridge. "In the meantime, all units will continue their assigned harassment of the Rebellion." His glowing red eyes bored into Pellaeon's face. "And they will continue, too, to maintain a watch for the *Millennium Falcon* and the *Lady Luck*. After the Noghri have been properly primed for their task, I want their prey to be ready for them."

C'BAOTH AWAKENED SUDDENLY, his black-edged dreams giving way to the sudden realization that someone was approaching.

For a moment he lay there in the darkness, his long white

beard scratching gently against his chest as he breathed, his mind reaching out through the Force to track along the road from the High Castle to the cluster of villages at the base of the rim mountains. It was hard to concentrate—so very hard—but with a perverse grimness he ignored the fatigue-driven pain and kept at it. There . . . no . . . *there*. A lone man riding a Cracian Thumper, laboring over one of the steeper sections of the roadway. Most likely a messenger, come to bring him some news from the villagers below. Something trifling, no doubt, but something that they felt their new Master should know.

Master. The word echoed through C'baoth's mind, sparking a windblown tangle of thoughts and feelings. The Imperials who pleaded for him to help them fight their battles—they called him Master, too. So had the people of Wayland, whose lives he had been content to rule before Grand Admiral Thrawn and his promise of Jedi followers had lured him away.

The people of Wayland had meant it. The people here on Jomark weren't quite sure yet whether they did or not. The Imperials didn't mean it at all.

C'baoth felt his lip twist in disgust. No, they most certainly did not. They made him fight their battles for them—drove him by their disbelief to do things he hadn't attempted for years and years. And then, when he'd succeeded in doing the impossible, they still held tightly to their private contempt for him, hiding it behind those ysalamiri creatures and the strange empty spaces they somehow created in the Force.

But he knew. He'd seen the sideways looks among the officers, and the brief but muttered discussions between them. He'd felt the edginess of the crew, submitting by Imperial order to his influence on their combat skills but clearly disliking the very thought of it. And he'd watched Captain Aban sit there in his command chair on the *Bellicose*, shouting and blaspheming at him even while calling him Master, spitting anger and impotent rage as C'baoth calmly inflicted his punishment on the Rebel ship that had dared to strike at his ship.

The messenger below was approaching the High Castle gate now. Reaching out with the Force to call his robe to him, C'baoth got out of bed, feeling a brief rush of vertigo as he stood erect. Yes, it had been difficult, that business of taking command of the *Bellicose*'s turbolaser crews for the few seconds it had required to annihilate that Rebel ship. It had gone beyond any previous stretch of concentration and control, and the mental aches he was feeling now were the payment for that stretch.

He tightened the robe sash around him, thinking back. Yes, it had been hard. And yet, at the same time, it had also been strangely exhilarating. On Wayland, he had personally commanded a whole city-state, one with a larger population than that which nestled beneath the High Castle. But there, he'd long since gone beyond the need to impose his will by force. The humans and Psadans had submitted to his authority early on; even the Myneyrshi, with their lingering resentment of his rule, had learned to obey his orders without question.

The Imperials, as well as the people of Jomark, were going to have to learn that same lesson.

Back when Grand Admiral Thrawn had first goaded C'baoth into this alliance, he'd implied that C'baoth had been too long without a real challenge. Perhaps the Grand Admiral had also secretly thought that this challenge of running the Empire's war would prove too much for a single Jedi Master to handle.

C'baoth smiled tightly in the darkness. If that was what the glowing-eyed Grand Admiral thought, he was going to be in for a surprise. Because when Luke Skywalker finally got here, C'baoth would face perhaps the most subtle challenge of his life: to bend and twist another Jedi to his will without the other even being aware of what was happening to him.

And when he'd succeeded, there would be two of them . . . and who could tell what might be possible then?

The messenger had dismounted from his Thumper and was standing beside the gate now, his sense that of a man prepared to await the convenience of his Master, no matter how long that wait might be. That was good: exactly the proper attitude. Giving his robe sash one final tug, C'baoth headed through the maze of darkened rooms toward the door, to hear what his new subjects wished to tell him.

CHAPTER 7

WITH A DELICACY that always seemed so incongruous in a being his size, Chewbacca maneuvered the *Falcon* into his precisely selected orbital slot above the lush green moon of Endor. Rumbling under his breath, he switched over the power linkages and cut the engines back to standby.

Seated in the copilot seat, Leia took a deep breath, wincing as one of the twins kicked her from inside. "Doesn't look like Khabarakh's here yet," she commented, realizing even as she said it how superfluous the comment was. She'd been watching the sensors from the moment they dropped out of lightspeed; and given there were no other ships anywhere in the system, there wasn't much chance that they could have missed him. But with the familiar engine roar now cut back down to a whisper, the silence felt strange and even a little eerie to her.

Chewbacca growled a question. "We wait, I guess," Leia shrugged. "Actually, we're almost a day early—we got here faster than I'd expected."

Chewbacca turned back to his board, growling his own interpretation of the Noghri's absence. "Oh, come on," Leia chided him. "If he'd decided to make this meeting into a trap, don't you think they'd have had a couple of Star Destroyers and an Interdictor Cruiser waiting to meet us?"

"Your Highness?" Threepio's voice called from down the tunnel. "I'm sorry to disturb you, but I believe I've located the fault in the Carbanti countermeasures package. Could you ask Chewbacca to step back for a moment?"

Leia raised her eyebrows in mild surprise as she looked at Chewbacca. As was depressingly normal with the *Falcon*, several bits of equipment had gone out early in the flight from Coruscant. Up to his elbows with more important repairs, Chewbacca had assigned the relatively low-priority work on the Carbanti to Threepio. Leia had had no objections, though given the results the last time Threepio had tried to work on the *Falcon*, she hadn't expected very much to come of it. "We'll make a repair droid out of him yet," she said to Chewbacca. "Your influence, no doubt."

The Wookiee snorted his opinion of that as he got out of the pilot's seat and headed back to see what Threepio had found. The cockpit door slid open, closed again behind him.

Leaving the cockpit that much quieter.

"You see that planet down there, my dears?" Leia murmured, rubbing her belly gently. "That's Endor. Where the Rebel Alliance finally triumphed over the Empire, and the New Republic began."

Or at least, she amended silently to herself, that was what the histories someday would say. That the death of the Empire occurred at Endor, with all the rest of it merely a mopping-up action.

A mopping-up action which had lasted five years, so far. And could wind up lasting another twenty, the way things were going.

She let her eyes drift across the brilliant mottled green world turning slowly beneath them, wondering yet again why she'd chosen this place for her rendezvous with Khabarakh. True, it was a system that practically every being in both the

Republic and Imperial sections of the galaxy had heard of and knew how to find. And with the major planes of contention long gone from this sector, it was a quiet enough place for two ships to meet.

But there were memories here, too, some of which Leia would just as soon not bring to mind. Before they'd triumphed, they'd very nearly lost everything.

From down the tunnel, Chewbacca roared a question. "Hang on, I'll check," Leia called back. Leaning over the board, she keyed a switch. "It reads 'standby/modulo,'" she reported. "Wait a minute—now it reads 'system ready.' Do you want me to—?"

And abruptly, without any warning, a black curtain seemed to drop across her vision. . . .

Slowly, she became aware that there was a metallic voice calling to her. "Your Highness," it said over and over again. "Your Highness. Can you hear me? Please, Your Highness, can you hear me?" She opened her eyes, vaguely surprised to discover they were closed, to find Chewbacca leaning over her with an open medpack gripped in one huge hand, an agitated Threepio hovering like a nervous mother bird behind him. "I'm all right," she managed. "What happened?"

"You shouted for help," Threepio put in before Chewbacca could answer. "At least, we thought it was for help," he amended helpfully. "You were brief and rather incoherent."

"I don't doubt it," Leia told him. It was starting to come back now, like moonlight through the edge of a cloud. The menace, the rage; the hatred, the despair. "You didn't feel it, did you?" she asked Chewbacca.

He growled a negative, watching her closely. "I felt nothing either," Threepio put in.

Leia shook her head. "I don't know what it could have been. One minute I was sitting there, and then the next—"

She broke off, a sudden horrible thought striking her. "Chewie—where does this orbit take us? Does it ever pass through the position where the Death Star blew up?"

Chewbacca stared at her a moment, rumbling something deep in his throat. Then, shifting the medpack to his other hand, he reached past her to key the computer. The answer came almost immediately.

"Five minutes ago," Leia murmured, feeling cold. "That would be just about right, wouldn't it?"

Chewbacca growled an affirmative, then a question. "I really don't know," she had to admit. "It sounds a little like something Luke went through on—during his Jedi training," she amended, remembering just in time that Luke still wanted Dagobah's significance to be kept a secret. "But he saw a vision. All I felt was . . . I don't know. It was anger and bitterness; but at the same time, there was something almost sad about it. No—sad isn't the right word." She shook her head, sudden tears welling inexplicably up in her eyes. "I don't know. Look, I'm all right. You two can go on back to what you were doing."

Chewbacca rumbled under his breath again, clearly not convinced. But he said nothing else as he closed the medpack and pushed past Threepio. The cockpit door slid open for him; with the proverbial Wookiee disdain for subtlety, he locked it in that position before disappearing down the tunnel into the main body of the ship.

Leia focused on Threepio. "You, too," she told him. "Go on—you still have work to do back there. I'm all right. Really."

"Well . . . very well, Your Highness," the droid said, clearly no happier than Chewbacca was. "If you're certain."

"I am. Go on, scat."

Threepio dithered another moment, then obediently shuffled out of the cockpit.

And the silence resumed. A silence that was thicker, somehow, than it had been before. And much darker.

Leia set her teeth firmly together. "I will not be intimidated," she said aloud to the silence. "Not here; not anywhere."

The silence didn't reply. After a minute Leia reached over to the board and keyed in a course alteration that would keep them from again passing through the spot where the Emperor had died. Refusing to be intimidated, after all, didn't mean deliberately asking for trouble.

And after that, there was nothing left to do but wait. And wonder if Khabarakh would indeed come.

THE TOPMOST BIT of the walled city Ilic poked through the clutching trees of the jungle pressing tightly around it, looking to Han for all the world like some sort of dome-topped, silver-skinned droid drowning in a sea of green quicksand. "Any idea how we land on that thing?" he asked.

"Probably through those vents near the top," Lando said, pointing at the *Lady Luck*'s main display. "They read large enough for anything up to about a W-class space barge to get into."

Han nodded, fingers plucking restlessly at the soft armrest of his copilot seat. There weren't a lot of things in the galaxy that could make him nervous, but having to sit there while someone else made a tricky landing was one of them. "This is even a crazier place to live than that Nomad City thing of yours," he growled.

"No argument from me," Lando agreed, adjusting their altitude a bit. Several seconds later than Han would have done it. "At least on Nkllon we don't have to worry about getting eaten by some exotic plant. But that's economics for you. At last count there were eight cities in this part of New Cov, and two more being built."

Han grimaced. And all because of those same exotic plants. Or to be specific, the exotic biomolecules that could be harvested from them. The Covies seemed to think the profit was worth having to live in armored cities all the time. No one knew what the plants thought about it. "They're still crazy," he said. "Watch out—they may have magnetic airlocks on those entrance ducts."

Lando gave him a patient look. "Will you relax? I *have* flown ships before, you know."

"Yeah," Han muttered. Setting his teeth together, he settled in to suffer through the landing.

It wasn't as bad as he'd expected. Lando got his clearance from Control and guided the *Lady Luck* with reasonable skill into the flaring maw of one of the entrance ducts, following the curved pipe down and inward to a brightly lit landing area just beneath the transparisteel dome that topped the city walls. Inbound customs were a mere formality, though given the planet's dependence on exports, the outbound scrutiny would probably be a lot tighter. They were officially welcomed to Ilic by a professional greeter with a professional smile, given a data card with maps of the city and surrounding territory, and then turned loose.

"That wasn't so hard," Lando commented as they rode a sliding spiral ramp down through the spacious open center. At each level walkways led outward from the ramp to the market, administrative, and living areas of the city. "Where are we supposed to be meeting Luke?"

"Three more levels down, in one of the entertainment districts," Han told him. "The Imperial library didn't have much detail on this place, but it did mention a little tap-cafe called the Mishra attached to some half-size version they've got of the old Grandis Mon theater on Coruscant. I got the impression it was kind of a watering hole for local big shots."

"Sounds like a good place to meet," Lando agreed. He threw Han a sideways look. "So. You ready to show me the hook yet?"

Han frowned. "Hook?"

"Come on, you old pirate," Lando snorted. "You pick me up at Sluis Van, ask for a lift out to New Cov, send Luke on ahead for this cloak-and-blade rendezvous—and you expect me to believe you're just going to wave goodbye now and let me go back to Nkllon?"

Han gave his friend his best wounded look. "Come on, Lando—"

"The hook, Han. Let me see the hook."

Han sighed theatrically. "There isn't any hook, Lando," he said. "You can leave for Nkllon any time you want to. 'Course," he added casually, "if you hung around a little and gave us a hand, you might be able to work a deal here to unload any spare metals you had lying around. Like, oh, a stockpile of hfredium or something."

Carefully keeping his eyes forward, he could still feel the heat of Lando's glare. "Luke told you about that, didn't he?" Lando demanded.

Han shrugged. "He might have mentioned it," he conceded.

Lando hissed between clenched teeth. "I'm going to strangle him," he announced. "Jedi or not, I'm going to strangle him."

"Oh, come on, Lando," Han soothed. "You hang around a couple days, you listen to people's jabberings, you maybe dig us out a lead or two about what Fey'lya's got going here, and that's it. You go home and back to your mining operation, and we never bother you again."

"I've heard *that* before," Lando countered. But Han could hear the resignation in his voice. "What makes you think Fey'lya's got contacts on New Cov?"

"Because during the war, this was the only place his Bothans ever seemed to care about defending—"

He broke off, grabbing Lando's arm and turning both of them hard to the right toward the central column of the spiral walkway. "What—" Lando managed.

"Quiet!" Han hissed, trying to simultaneously hide his face and still watch the figure he'd spotted leaving the ramp one level down. "That Bothan down there to the left—see him?"

Lando turned slightly, peering in the indicated direction out of the corner of his eye. "What about him?"

"It's Tav Breil'lya. One of Fey'lya's top aides."

"You're kidding," Lando said, frowning down at the alien. "How can you tell?"

"That neckpiece he wears—some kind of family crest or something. I've seen it dozens of times at Council meetings." Han chewed at his lip, trying to think. If that really was Breil'lya over there, finding out what he was up to could save them a lot of time. But Luke was probably sitting in the tap-cafe downstairs right now waiting for them . . . "I'm going to follow him," he told Lando, shoving his data pad and the city map into the other's hands. "You head down to the Mishra, grab Luke, and catch up with me."

"But—"

"If you're not with me in an hour I'll try calling on the comlink," Han cut him off, stepping toward the outside of the ramp. They were nearly to the Bothan's level now. "Don't call me—I might be someplace I wouldn't want a callbeep going off." He stepped off the ramp onto the walkway.

"Good luck," Lando called softly after him.

There was a good scattering of aliens among the humans wandering around Ilic, but Breil'lya's cream-colored fur stood out of the crowd enough to make him easy to follow. Which was just as well. If Han could recognize the Bothan, the Bothan could probably recognize him right back, and it would be risky to have to get too close.

Luckily, the alien didn't seem to even consider the possibility that anyone might be following him. He kept up a steady pace, never turning around, as he headed past cross streets and shops and atria toward the outer city wall. Han stayed with him, wishing he hadn't been so quick to give the city map to Lando. It might have been nice to have some idea where he was going.

They passed through one final atrium and reached a section of warehouse-type structures abutting a vast mural that seemed to have been painted directly on the inner city wall. Breil'lya went straight to one of the buildings near the mural and disappeared through the front door.

Han ducked into a convenient doorway about thirty meters down the street from the warehouse. The door Breil'lya had gone through, he could see, carried the faded sign Amethyst Shipping and Storage above it. "I just hope it's on the map," he muttered under his breath, pulling his comlink from his belt.

"It is," a woman's voice came softly from behind him.

Han froze. "Hello?" he asked tentatively.

"Hello," she said back. "Turn around, please. Slowly, of course."

Han did as ordered, the comlink still in hand. "If this is a robbery—"

"Don't be silly." The woman was short and slender, perhaps ten years older than him, with close-cut graying hair and a thin face which under other circumstances would look friendly enough. The blaster pointed his direction was some unfamiliar knockoff of a BlasTech DL-18—not nearly as powerful as his own DL-44, but under the circumstances the difference didn't matter a whole lot. "Put the comlink on the ground," she continued. "Your blaster, too, as long as you're down there."

Silently, Han crouched down, drawing his weapon out with exaggerated caution. Under cover of the motion, with most of her attention hopefully on the blaster, he flicked on the comlink. Laying both on the ground, he straightened and took a step back, just to prove that he knew the proper procedure for prisoners. "Now what?"

"You seem interested in the little get-together yonder," she said, stooping to retrieve the blaster and comlink. "Perhaps you'd like a guided tour."

"That would be great," Han told her, raising his hands and hoping that she wouldn't think to look at the comlink before putting it away in one of the pockets in her jumpsuit.

She didn't look at it. She did, however, shut it off. "I think I'm insulted," she said mildly. "That has to be the oldest trick on the list."

Han shrugged, determined to maintain at least a little dignity here. "I didn't have time to come up with any new ones."

"Apology accepted. Come on, let's go. And lower your hands—we don't want any passersby wondering, now, do we?"

"Of course not," Han said, dropping his hands to his sides.

They were halfway to the Amethyst when, off in the distance, a siren began wailing.

IT WAS, LUKE thought as he looked around the Mishra, almost like an inverted replaying of his first visit to the Mos Eisley cantina on Tatooine all those years ago.

True, the Mishra was light-years more sophisticated than that dilapidated place had been, with a correspondingly more upscale clientele. But the bar and tables were crowded with the same wide assortment of humans and aliens, the smells and sounds were equally variegated, and the band off in the corner was playing similar music—a style, obviously, that had been carefully tailored to appeal to a multitude of different races.

There was one other difference, too. Crowded though the place might be, the patrons were leaving Luke a respectful amount of room at the bar.

He took a sip of his drink—a local variant of the hot chocolate Lando had introduced him to, this one with a touch of mint—and glanced over at the entrance. Han and Lando should have been only a couple of hours behind him, which meant they could be walking in at any minute. He hoped so, anyway. He'd understood Han's reasons for wanting the two ships to come into Ilic separately, but with all the threats that seemed to be hanging over the New Republic, they couldn't really afford to waste time. He took another sip—

And from behind him came an inhuman bellow.

He spun around, hand automatically yanking his lightsaber from his belt, as the sound of a chair crashing over backwards added an exclamation point to the bellow. Five meters away from him, in the middle of a circle of frozen patrons, a

Barabel and a Rodian stood facing each other over a table, both with blasters drawn.

"No blasters! No blasters!" an SE4 servant droid called, waving his arms for emphasis as he scuttled toward the confrontation. In the flick of an eye, the Barabel shifted aim and blew the droid apart, bringing his blaster back to bear on the Rodian before the other could react.

"Hey!" the bartender said indignantly. "That's going to cost you—"

"Shut up," the Barabel cut him off with a snarl. "Rodian will pay you. After he pay me."

The Rodian drew himself up to his full height—which still left him a good half meter shorter than his opponent—and spat something in a language Luke didn't understand. "You lie," the Barabel spat back. "You cheat. I know."

The Rodian said something else. "You no like?" the Barabel countered, his voice haughty. "You do anyway. I call on Jedi for judgment."

Every eye in the tapcafe had been riveted to the confrontation. Now, in almost perfect unison, the gazes turned to Luke. "What?" he asked cautiously.

"He wants you to settle the dispute," the bartender said, relief evident in his voice.

A relief that Luke himself was far from feeling. "Me?"

The bartender gave him a strange look. "You're the Jedi Knight Luke Skywalker, aren't you?" he asked, gesturing at the lightsaber in Luke's hand.

"Yes," Luke admitted.

"Well, then," the bartender concluded, waving a hand toward the disputants.

Except that, Jedi or no Jedi, Luke didn't have a drop of legal authority here. He opened his mouth to tell the bartender that—

And then took another look into the other's eyes.

Slowly, he turned back around, the excuses sticking unsaid in his throat. It wasn't just the bartender, he saw. Everyone in the tapcafe, it seemed, was looking at him with pretty much the same expression. An expression of expectation and trust. Trust in the judgment of a Jedi.

Taking a quiet breath, sternly ordering his pounding heart to calm down, he started through the crowd toward the confrontation. Ben Kenobi had introduced him to the Force; Yoda had taught him how to use the Force for self-control and self-defense. Neither had ever taught him anything about mediating arguments.

"All right," he said as he reached the table. "The first thing you're going to do—both of you—is put away your weapons."

"Who first?" the Barabel demanded. "Rodians collect bounty—he shoot if I disarm."

This was certainly getting off to a great start. Suppressing a sigh, Luke ignited his lightsaber, holding it out so that the brilliant green blade was directly between the opposing blasters. "No one is going to shoot anyone," he said flatly. "Put them away."

Silently, the Barabel complied. The Rodian hesitated a second longer, then followed suit. "Now tell me the problem," Luke said, shutting down the lightsaber but keeping it ready in his hand.

"He hire me for tracking job," the Barabel said, jabbing a keratin-plated finger at the Rodian. "I do what he say. But he no pay me."

The Rodian said something indignant sounding. "Just a minute—we'll get to you," Luke told him, wondering how he was going to handle that part of the cross-examination. "What sort of job was it?"

"He ask me hunt animal nest for him," the Barabel said. "Animals bothering little ships—eating at sides. I do what he say. He burn animal nest, get money. But then he pay me in no-good money." He gestured down at a now scattered pile of gold-colored metal chips.

Luke picked one up. It was small and triangular, with an intricate pattern of lines in the center, and inscribed with a

small *"100"* in each corner. "Anyone ever see this currency before?" he called, holding it up.

"It's new Imperial scrip," someone dressed in an expensive
business coat said with thinly veiled contempt. "You can only
spend it on Imperial-held worlds and stations."

Luke grimaced. Another reminder, if he'd needed one, that
the war for control of the galaxy was far from over. "Did you
tell him beforehand that you'd be paying in this?" he asked the
Rodian.

The other said something in his own language. Luke glanced
around the circle, wondering if asking for a translator would
diminish his perceived status here. "He says that that was how
he was paid," a familiar voice said; and Luke turned to see
Lando ease his way to the front of the crowd. "Says he argued
about it, but that he didn't have any choice in the matter."

"That *is* how the Empire's been doing business lately,"
someone in the crowd offered. "At least around here."

The Barabel spun toward the other. "I no want your judgment," he snarled. "Only Jedi give judgment."

"All right, calm down," Luke told him, fingering the chit
and wondering what he was going to do. If this really was the
way the Rodian had been paid . . . "Is there any way to convert these into something else?" he asked the Rodian.

The other answered. "He says no," Lando translated. "You
can use them for goods and services on Imperial worlds, but
since no one in the New Republic will take them, there's no
official rate of exchange."

"Right," Luke said dryly. He might not have Lando's experience in under-the-plate operations, but he hadn't been born
yesterday, either. "So what's the unofficial exchange rate?"

"No idea, actually," Lando said, looking around the crowd.
"Must be someone here who works both sides of the street,
though." He raised his voice. "Anyone here do business with
the Empire?"

If they did, they were keeping quiet about it. "Shy, aren't
they?" Luke murmured.

"About admitting Imperial dealings to a Jedi?" Lando countered. "I'd be shy, too."

Luke nodded, feeling a sinking sense in the pit of his stomach as he studied the Rodian's tapirlike snout and passive, multifaceted eyes. He'd hoped that he could simply smooth out the problem and thereby avoid the need to pass any kind of real judgment. Now, he had no choice but to rule on whether the Rodian was in fact deliberately trying to cheat his partner.

Closing his eyes down to slits, he composed his mind and stretched out his senses. It was a long shot, he knew; but most species showed subtle physiological changes when under stress. If the Rodian was lying about the payment—and if he thought that Luke's Jedi skills could catch him at it—he might react enough to incriminate himself.

But even as Luke ran through the sensory enhancement techniques, something else caught his attention. It was an odor: a faint whiff of Carababba tabac and armudu. The same combination Lando had called his attention to on the Sluis Van space station . . .

Luke opened his eyes and looked around the crowd. "Niles Ferrier," he called. "Will you step forward, please."

There was a long pause, punctuated only by Lando's sudden hissing intake of air at Ferrier's name. Then, with a rustle of movement from one side of the circle, a familiar bulky figure pushed his way to the front. "What do you want?" he demanded, his hand resting on the butt of his holstered blaster.

"I need to know the unofficial exchange rate between Imperial and New Republic currencies," Luke said. "I thought perhaps you could tell me what it is."

Ferrier studied him with ill-concealed scorn. "This is your problem, Jedi. Leave me out of it."

There was a low rumble of displeasure from the crowd. Luke didn't reply, but held Ferrier in a level gaze; and after a moment, the other's lip twisted. "The last time I did business on the other side, we settled on a five to four Empire/Republic conversion," he growled.

"Thank you," Luke said. "That seems straightforward enough, then," he continued, turning to the Rodian. "Pay your associate with New Republic currency at a five/four exchange rate and take the Empire scrip back for the next time you work in their territory."

The Rodian spat something. "That is lie!" the Barabel snarled back.

"He says he doesn't have enough in New Republic currency," Lando translated. "Knowing Rodians, I'd tend to agree with the Barabel."

"Perhaps." Luke stared hard into the Rodian's faceted eyes. "Perhaps not. But there might be another way." He looked back at Ferrier, raised his eyebrows questioningly.

The other was sharp, all right. "Don't even think it, Jedi," he warned.

"Why not?" Luke asked. "You work both sides of the border. You're more likely to be able to spend Imperial scrip than the Barabel could."

"Suppose I don't want to?" Ferrier countered. "Suppose I don't plan to go back anytime soon. Or maybe I don't want to get caught with that much Imperial scrip on me. Fix it yourself, Jedi—I don't owe you any favors."

The Barabel whirled on him. "You talk respect," he snarled. "He is Jedi. You talk respect."

A low rumble of agreement rippled through the crowd. "Better listen to him," Lando advised. "I don't think you'd want to get in a fight here, especially not with a Barabel. They've always had a soft spot for Jedi."

"Yeah—right behind their snouts," Ferrier retorted. But his eyes were flicking around the crowd now, and Luke caught the subtle shift in his sense as he began to realize just how much in the minority his opinion of Luke was.

Or perhaps he was realizing that winding up in the middle of an official flap might buy him more attention than he really wanted to have. Luke waited, watching the other's sense flicker with uncertainty, waiting for him to change his mind.

When it happened, it happened quickly. "All right, but it'll have to be a five/three exchange," Ferrier insisted. "The five/four was a fluke—no telling if I'll ever get that again."

"It is cheat," the Barabel declared. "I deserve more from Rodian."

"Yes, you do," Luke agreed. "But under the circumstances, this is probably the best you're going to get." He looked at the Rodian. "If it helps any," he added to the Barabel, "remember that you can pass a warning to the rest of your people about dealing with this particular Rodian. Not being able to hire expert Barabel hunters will hurt him far more in the long run than he might cost you now."

The Barabel made a grating noise that was probably the equivalent of a laugh. "Jedi speak truth," he said. "Punishment is good."

Luke braced himself. This part the Barabel wasn't going to be nearly so happy about. "You will, however, have to pay for the repair of the droid you shot. Whatever the Rodian said or did, he is not responsible for that."

The Barabel stared at Luke, his needle teeth making small, tight biting motions. Luke returned the cold gaze, senses alert to the Force for any intimation of attack. "Jedi again speak truth," the alien said at last. Reluctantly, but firmly. "I accept judgment."

Luke let out a quiet sigh of relief. "Then the matter is closed," he said. He looked at Ferrier, then raised his lightsaber to his forehead in salute to the two aliens and turned away.

"Nicely done," Lando murmured in his ear as the crowd began to break up.

"Thanks," Luke murmured, his mouth dry. It had worked, all right . . . but it had been more luck than skill, and he knew it. If Ferrier hadn't been there—or if the ship thief hadn't decided to back down—Luke had no idea how he would have solved the dispute. Leia and her diplomatic training would have done better than he had; even Han and his long experience at hard bargaining would have done as well.

It was an aspect of Jedi responsibility that he'd never considered before. But it was one he'd better start thinking about, and fast.

"Han's following one of Fey'lya's Bothan pals up on Level Four," Lando was saying as they moved through the crowd toward the exit. "Spotted him from the west-central ramp and sent me to—"

He stopped short. From outside the Mishra the sound of wailing sirens had started. "I wonder what that is," he said, a touch of uneasiness in his voice.

"It's an alarm," one of the tapcafe patrons said, his forehead wrinkled in concentration as he listened. The pitch of the siren changed; changed again . . . "It's a raid."

"A raid?" Luke frowned. He hadn't heard of any pirate activity in this sector. "Who's raiding you?"

"Who else?" the man retorted. "The Empire."

Luke looked at Lando. "Uh-oh," he said quietly.

"Yeah," Lando agreed. "Come on."

They left the Mishra and headed out into the wide avenue. Oddly enough, there were no signs of the panic Luke would have expected to find. On the contrary, the citizens of Ilic seemed to be continuing about their daily business as if nothing untoward was happening. "Maybe they don't realize what's going on," he suggested doubtfully as they headed for one of the spiral ramps.

"Or else they've got a quiet agreement with the Empire," Lando countered sourly. "Maybe the leadership finds it politically handy to align themselves with the New Republic, but they also want to keep in the Empire's good graces. Since they can't pay anything as overt as tribute, they instead let the Imperials come in every so often and raid their stocks of refined biomolecules. I've seen that sort of thing done before."

Luke looked around at the unconcerned crowds. "Only this time it might backfire on them."

"Like if the Imperials spot the *Lady Luck* and your X-wing on the landing records."

"Right. Where did you say Han was?"

"Last I saw, he was on Level Four heading west," Lando said, digging out his comlink. "He told me not to call him, but I think this qualifies as an unforeseen circumstance."

"Wait a minute," Luke stopped him. "If he's anywhere near this aide of Fey'lya's—and if Fey'lya is working some kind of deal with the Empire . . . ?"

"You're right." Lando swore under his breath as he put the comlink away. "So what do we do?"

They'd reached the ramp now and stepped onto the section spiraling upward. "I'll go find Han," Luke said. "You get up to the landing area and see what's happening. If the Imperials haven't actually landed yet, you might be able to get into the air control computer and erase us from the list. Artoo can help if you can get him out of my X-wing and over to a terminal without being caught."

"I'll give it a try."

"Okay." A stray memory flicked through Luke's mind— "I don't suppose the *Lady Luck*'s equipped with one of those full-rig slave circuits you talked about back on Nkllon, is it?"

Lando shook his head. "It's rigged, but only with a simple homing setup. Nothing much more than straight-line motion and a little maneuvering. It'd never be able to get to me through the middle of an enclosed city like this."

And even if it could, Luke had to admit, it wouldn't do them much good. Short of blasting a huge hole through the outer wall, the only way out of Ilic for anything the size of a spaceship was through the exit ducts above the landing area. "It was just a thought," he said.

"Here's where Han got off," Lando said, pointing. "He headed that way."

"Right." Luke stepped off the ramp. "See you soon. Be careful."

"You, too."

CHAPTER 8

THE GRAYING WOMAN took Han to a small office-type room in the Amethyst building, turned him over to a couple of other guard types there, and disappeared with his blaster, comlink, and ID in hand. Han tried once or twice to strike up a conversation with the guards, got no response from either of them, and had just about resigned himself to sitting quietly, listening to the sirens outside, when the woman returned.

Accompanied by another, taller woman with the unmistakable air of authority about her. "Good day to you," the tall woman said, nodding at Han. "Captain Han Solo, I believe?"

With his ID in her hand, there didn't seem much point in denying it. "That's right," he said.

"We're honored by your visit," she said, her tone putting a slightly sardonic edge to the polite words. "Though a bit surprised by it."

"I don't know why—the visit was your idea," Han countered. "You always pick people up off the street like this?"

"Just special ones." The tall woman's eyebrows lifted slightly. "You want to tell me who you are and who sent you?"

Han frowned. "What do you mean, who am I? You've got my ID right there."

"Yes, I do," the woman nodded, turning the card over in her hand. "But there's some difference of opinion as to whether or not it's genuine." She looked out the door and beckoned—

And Tav Breil'lya stepped past her into the room. "I was right," the Bothan said, his cream-colored fur rippling in an unfamiliar pattern. "As I told you when I first saw his ID. He is an impostor. Almost certainly an Imperial spy."

"What?" Han stared at him, the whole situation tilting slightly off vertical. He looked at the alien's neckpiece—it was Tav Breil'lya, all right. "What did you call me?"

"You're an Imperial spy," Breil'lya repeated, his fur rippling again. "Come to destroy our friendship, or even to kill us all. But you'll never live to report back to your masters." He turned to the tall woman. "You must destroy him at once, Sena," he urged. "Before he has the chance to summon your enemies here."

"Let's not do anything rash, Council-Aide Breil'lya," Sena soothed. "Irenez has a good picket screen in position." She looked at Han. "Would you care to respond to the Council-Aide's accusations?"

"We have no interest in the ravings of an Imperial spy," Breil'lya insisted before Han could speak.

"On the contrary, Council-Aide," Sena countered. "Around here, we have an interest in a great many things." She turned back to Han, lifted his ID. "Do you have any proof other than this that you're who you claim to be?"

"It doesn't matter who he is," Breil'lya jumped in again, his voice starting to sound a little strained. "He's seen you, and he must certainly know that we have some kind of arrangement. Whether he's from the Empire or the New Republic is irrelevant—both are your enemies, and both would use such information against you."

Sena's eyebrows lifted again. "So now his identity doesn't

matter," she said coolly. "Does that mean you're no longer certain he's an impostor?"

Breil'lya's fur rippled again. Clearly, he wasn't as quick on his verbal feet as his boss. "He's a very close likeness," the other muttered. "Though a proper dissection would quickly establish for certain who he is."

Sena smiled slightly. But it was a smile of understanding, not of humor . . . and suddenly Han realized that the confrontation had been as much a test of Breil'lya as it had been of him. And if Sena's expression was anything to go by, the Bothan had just flunked it. "I'll keep that recommendation in mind," she told him dryly.

There was a soft beep, and the gray-haired woman pulled out a comlink and spoke quietly into it. She listened, spoke again, and looked up at Sena. "Picket line reports another man approaching," she said. "Medium build, dark blond hair, dressed in black"—she threw a glance at Breil'lya—"and carrying what appears to be a lightsaber."

Sena looked at Breil'lya, too. "I believe that ends the discussion," she said. "Have one of the pickets meet him, Irenez, and ask him if he'll join us. Make it clear that's a *request*, not an order. Then return Captain Solo's weapon and equipment to him." She turned to Han, nodded gravely to him as she returned his ID. "My apologies, Captain. You understand we have to be cautious. Particularly given the coincidence of this." She gestured toward the outside wall.

Han frowned, wondering what she meant. Then he got it: she was indicating the sirens still wailing outside. "No problem," he assured her. "What are the sirens for, anyway?"

"It's an Imperial raid," Irenez said, handing him his blaster and comlink.

Han froze. "A raid?"

"It's no big deal," Sena assured him. "They come by every few months and take a percentage of the refined biomolecules that have been packaged for export. It's a covert form of taxation the city governments have worked out with them. Don't worry, they never come any farther in than the landing level."

"Yeah, well, they may change the routine a little this time," Han growled, flicking on his comlink. He half expected someone to try to stop him, but no one even twitched. "Luke?"

"I'm here, Han," the younger man's voice came back. "My escort tells me I'm being brought to where you are. You all right?"

"Just a little misunderstanding. Better get in here fast—we got company."

"Right."

Han shut off the comlink. Sena and Irenez, he saw, had meanwhile been having a quiet conversation of their own. "If you're as touchy about Imperials as Breil'lya implied, you might want to find a hole to disappear into," he advised.

"Our escape route's ready," Sena assured him as Irenez left the room. "The question is what to do with you and your friend."

"You can't just turn them loose," Breil'lya insisted, trying one last time. "You know full well that if the New Republic learns about you—"

"The Commander is being notified," Sena cut him off. "He'll decide."

"But—"

"That's all, Council-Aide," she cut him off again, her voice suddenly hard. "Join the others at the lift shaft. You'll accompany me on my ship."

Breil'lya threw one last unreadable look at Han, then silently left the room.

"Who's this Commander of yours?" Han asked.

"I can't tell you that." Sena studied him a moment. "Don't worry, though. Despite what Breil'lya said, we're not enemies of the New Republic. At least, not at the moment."

"Oh," Han said. "Great."

There was the sound of footsteps from the hallway outside.

A few seconds later, accompanied by two young men with holstered blasters, Luke stepped into the room.

"Han," Luke greeted his friend, giving Sena a quick once-over. "You all right?"

"I'm fine," Han assured him. "Like I said, a little misunderstanding. The lady here—Sena—" He paused expectantly.

"Let's just leave it at Sena for now," she said.

"Ah," Han said. He'd hoped to get her last name, but clearly she wasn't in the habit of giving it out. "Anyway, Sena thought I was an Imperial spy. And speaking of Imperials—"

"I know," Luke nodded. "Lando's gone up to see if he can clear our ships from the landing record."

"He won't be able to," Han shook his head. "Not in time. And they're bound to pull the landing list."

Luke nodded agreement. "Then we'd better get up there."

"Unless you'd all rather come with us," Sena offered. "There's plenty of room on our ship, and it's hidden away where they won't find it."

"Thanks, but no," Han said. He wasn't about to go off with these people until he knew a lot more about them. Whose side they were on, for starters. "Lando won't want to leave his ship."

"And I need to get my droid back," Luke added.

Irenez slipped back into the room. "Everyone's on their way down, and the ship's being prepped," she told Sena. "And I got through to the Commander." She handed the tall woman a data pad.

Sena glanced at it, nodded, and turned back to Han. "There's a service shaft near here that opens up into the west edge of the landing area," she told him. "I doubt the Imperials know about it; it's not on any of the standard city maps. Irenez will guide you up there and give you what help she can."

"That's really not necessary," Han told her.

Sena held up the data pad. "The Commander has instructed me to give you whatever aid you require," she said firmly. "I'd appreciate it if you'd allow me to carry out my orders."

Han looked at Luke, raised his eyebrows. Luke shrugged slightly in return: if there was treachery in the offer, his Jedi senses weren't picking it up. "Fine, she can tag along," he said. "Let's go."

"Good luck," Sena said, and disappeared out the door.

Irenez gestured to the door after her. "This way, gentlemen."

The service shaft was a combination stairway and lift-car tube set into the outer city wall, its entrance almost invisible against the swirling pattern of that section of the mural. The liftcar itself was nowhere to be seen—probably, Han decided, still ferrying Sena's group to wherever it was they'd stashed their ship. With Irenez in the lead, they started up the stairs.

It was only three levels up to the landing area. But three levels in a city with Ilic's high-ceilinged layout translated into a lot of stairs. The first level ran to fifty-three steps; after that, Han stopped counting. By the time they slipped through another disguised door into the landing area and took cover behind a massive diagnostic analyzer, his legs were beginning to tremble with fatigue. Irenez, in contrast, wasn't even breathing hard.

"Now what?" Luke asked, looking cautiously around the analyzer. He wasn't breathing hard, either.

"Let's find Lando," Han said, pulling out his comlink and thumbing his call. "Lando?"

"Right here," the other's whispered voice came back instantly. "Where are you?"

"West end of the landing area, about twenty meters from Luke's X-wing. How about you?"

"About ninety degrees away from you toward the south," Lando answered. "I'm behind a stack of shipping boxes. There's a stormtrooper standing guard about five meters away, so I'm sort of stuck here."

"What sort of trouble are we looking at?"

"It looks like a full-fledged task force," Lando said grimly. "I saw three drop ships come in, and I think there were one or two on the ground when I got here. If they were fully loaded, that translates to a hundred sixty to two hundred men. Most of them are regular army troops, but there are a few storm-troopers in the crowd, too. There aren't too many of either still up here—most of them headed on down the ramps a few minutes ago."

"Probably gone to search the city for us," Luke murmured.

"Yeah." Han eased up to look over the analyzer. The top of Luke's X-wing was just visible over the nose of a W-23 space barge. "Looks like Artoo's still in Luke's ship."

"Yeah, but I saw them doing something over that way," Lando warned. "They may have put a restraining bolt on him."

"We can handle that." Han scanned as much of the area around them as he could see. "I think we can make it to the X-wing without being spotted. You told me on the trip here that you had a beckon call for the *Lady Luck*, right?"

"Right, but it's not going to do me any good," Lando said. "With all these boxes around, there's no place I can set it down without opening myself to fire."

"That's okay," Han told him, feeling a tight smile twist at his lip. Luke might have the Force, and Irenez might be able to climb stairs without getting winded; but he would bet heavily that he could outdo both of them in sheer chicanery. "You just get it moving toward you when I give the word."

He switched off the comlink. "We're going over to the X-wing," he told Luke and Irenez, adjusting his grip on his blaster. "You ready?"

He got two acknowledgments, and with a last look around the area headed as quickly as silence permitted across the floor. He reached the space barge lying across their path with-out incident, paused there to let the others catch up—

"Shh!" Luke hissed.

Han froze, pressing himself against the barge's corroded hull. Not four meters away a stormtrooper standing guard was starting to turn in their direction.

Clenching his teeth, Han raised his blaster. But even as he did so, his peripheral vision caught Luke's hand making some sort of gesture; and suddenly the Imperial spun around in the opposite direction, pointing his blaster rifle toward a patch of empty floor. "He thinks he heard a noise," Luke whispered. "Let's go."

Han nodded, and sidled around to the other side of the barge. A few seconds later they were crouched beside the X-wing's landing skids. "Artoo?" Han stage-whispered upward. "Come on, short stuff, wake up."

There was a soft and rather indignant beep from the top of the X-wing. Which meant the Imperials' restraining bolt hadn't shut the droid down entirely, just blocked out his control of the X-wing's systems. Good. "Okay," he called to the droid. "Get your comm sensor warmed up and get ready to record."

Another beep. "Now what?" Irenez asked.

"Now we get cute," Han told her, pulling out his comlink. "Lando? You ready?"

"As ready as I'm going to be," the other came back.

"Okay. When I give the signal, turn on your beckon call and get the *Lady Luck* moving. When I tell you again, shut it off. Got that?"

"Got it. I hope you know what you're doing."

"Trust me." Han looked at Luke. "You got your part figured out?"

Luke nodded, holding up his lightsaber. "I'm ready."

"Okay, Lando. Go."

For a long moment nothing happened. Then, through the background noise of the landing area, came the distinctive whine of repulsorlifts being activated. Half standing up, Han was just in time to see the *Lady Luck* rise smoothly up from among the other docked ships.

From somewhere in the same general vicinity came a shout, followed by multiple flashes of blaster fire. Another three weapons opened up almost immediately, all four tracking the

Lady Luck as it made a somewhat ponderous turn and began floating south toward Lando's hiding place.

"You know it'll never get there," Irenez muttered in Han's ear. "As soon as they figure out where it's going, they'll be all over him."

"That's why it's not going to get to him," Han countered, watching the *Lady Luck* closely. Another couple of seconds and every stormtrooper and Imperial soldier in the place ought to have his attention solidly fixed on the rogue ship . . . "Ready, Luke . . . *now*."

And suddenly Luke was gone, a single leap taking him to the top of the X-wing. Over the commotion Han heard the *snap-hiss* as Luke ignited his lightsaber, could see the green glow reflected from the nearest ships and equipment. The glow and sound shifted subtly as Luke made a short slice—

"Restraining bolt's off," Luke called down. "Now?"

"Not yet," Han told him. The *Lady Luck* was about a quarter of the way to the far wall, blaster bolts still scattering off its armored underside. "I'll tell him when. You get ready to fly interference."

"Right." The X-wing rocked slightly as Luke moved forward and dropped into the cockpit, its own repulsorlifts beginning to whine as Artoo activated them.

A whine that no one else out in all that confusion had a hope of hearing. The *Lady Luck* was halfway to the wall now . . . "Okay, Lando, shut down," Han ordered. "Artoo, your turn. Call it back this way."

With full access again to the X-wing's transmitters, it was a simple task for the droid to duplicate the signal from Lando's beckon call. The *Lady Luck* shuddered to a halt, reoriented itself to the new call, and started across the landing area again toward the X-wing.

It wasn't something the Imperials had expected. For a second the blaster fire faltered as the soldiers chasing the yacht skidded to a halt; and by the time the fire resumed in earnest, the *Lady Luck* was nearly to the X-wing.

"Now?" Luke called.

"Now," Han called back. "Put 'er down and clear us a path."

Artoo twittered, and the *Lady Luck* again halted in midair, this time dropping smoothly to the ground. There was a shout that sounded like triumph from the Imperials . . . but if so, it was the shortest triumph on record. The *Lady Luck* touched down—

And without warning, the X-wing leaped into the air. Pulling a tight curve around the *Lady Luck*, Luke swooped back down, wingtip lasers spitting a corridor of destruction across the startled soldiers' line of approach.

Given time, the Imperials would regroup. Han had no intention of giving them that time. "Come on," he snapped to Irenez, leaping to his feet and making a mad dash for the *Lady Luck*. He was probably on the ramp before the soldiers even noticed him, and was up and through the hatch before anyone was able to get off a shot. "Stay here and guard the hatch," he shouted back as Irenez charged in behind him. "I'm going to go pick up Lando."

Luke was still roaring around creating havoc as Han scrambled into the cockpit and dived into the pilot's seat, throwing a quick look at the instruments as he did so. All the systems seemed to be ready; and anything that wasn't was going to have to do so on the way up. "Grab onto something!" he shouted back to Irenez and lifted.

The stormtrooper Lando had mentioned as being near his position was nowhere in sight as Han brought the *Lady Luck* swinging over to the pile of shipping boxes. Luke was right with him, the X-wing's lasers making a mess of the landing area floor as he kept the Imperials pinned down. Han dropped the ship to within a half meter of the floor, entrance ramp swiveled toward the boxes. There was a flicker of motion, visible for just a second through the cockpit's side viewport—

"We've got him," Irenez shouted from the hatch. "Go!"

Han swiveled the ship around, throwing full power to the repulsorlifts and heading upward into one of the huge exit ducts overhead. There was a slight jolt as he cleared the magnetic seal on the end, and then they were out in clear air, screaming hard for space.

Four TIE fighters were skulking around just above the city, waiting for trouble. But they apparently weren't waiting for it to come this quickly. Luke got three of them on the fly, and Han took out the fourth.

"Nothing like cutting it close to the wire," Lando panted as he slid into the copilot's seat and got busy with his board. "What have we got?"

"Looks like a couple more drop ships coming in," Han told him, frowning. "What are you doing?"

"Running a multisensor airflow analysis," Lando said. "It'll show up any large irregularities on the hull. Like if someone's attached a homing beacon to us."

Han thought back to that escape from the first Death Star, and their near-disastrous flight to Yavin with just such a gadget snugged aboard. "I wish I had a system like that for the *Falcon*."

"It'd never work," Lando commented dryly. "Your hull's so irregular already the system would go nuts just trying to map it." He keyed off the display. "Okay; we're clear."

"Great." Han threw a glance out to the left. "We're clear of those drop ships, too. They don't have a hope of catching us now."

"Yes, but that might," Irenez said, pointing at the midrange scope.

Which showed an Imperial Star Destroyer behind them, already leaving orbit and moving into pursuit. "Great," Han growled, kicking in the main drive. Using it this close to the ground wasn't going to do New Cov's plant life any good, but that was the least of his worries at the moment. "Luke?"

"I see it," Luke's voice came back through the comm speaker. "Any ideas besides running for it?"

"I think running for it sounds like a great idea," Han said. "Lando?"

"Calculating the jump now," the other said, busy with the nav computer. "It ought to be ready by the time we're far enough out."

"There's another ship coming up from below," Luke said. "Right out of the jungle."

"That's ours," Irenez said, peering over Han's shoulder. "You can parallel them by changing course to one twenty-six mark thirty."

The Star Destroyer was picking up speed, the scope now showing a wedge of TIE fighters sweeping along ahead of it. "We'd do better to split up," Han said.

"No—stay with our ship," Irenez said. "Sena said we've got help coming."

Han took another look at the ship climbing for deep space. A small transport, with a fair amount of speed but not much else going for it. Another look at the approaching TIE fighters—

"They're going to be in range before we can make the jump," Lando murmured, echoing Han's thought.

"Yeah. Luke, you still there?"

"Yes. I think Lando's right."

"I know. Any way you can pull that Nkllon stunt again? You know—scramble the pilots' minds a little?"

There was a noticeable hesitation from the comm. "I don't think so," Luke said at last. "I—don't think it's good for me to do that sort of thing. You understand?"

Han didn't, really, but it probably didn't matter. For a moment he'd forgotten that he wasn't in the *Falcon*, with a pair of quad lasers and shields and heavy armor. The *Lady Luck*, for all Lando's modifications, wasn't anything to take on even confused TIE fighter pilots with. "All right, skip it," he told Luke. "Sena just better be right about this help of hers."

The words were hardly out of his mouth when a flash of

brilliant green light shot past the *Lady Luck*'s cockpit canopy. "TIE fighters coming in from portside," Lando snapped.

"They're trying to cut us off," Luke said. "I'll get rid of them."

Without waiting for comment, he dropped his X-wing below the *Lady Luck*'s vector and with a roar of main drive swung off to the left toward the incoming TIE fighters. "Watch yourself," Han muttered after him, giving the rear scope another look. The pursuing batch of fighters was still closing fast. "Your ship got any weapons?" he asked Irenez.

"No, but it's got good armor and plenty of deflector power," she told him. "Maybe you should get ahead of them, let them take the brunt of the attack."

"Yeah, I'll think about it," Han said, wincing at the woman's ignorance of this kind of fight. TIE pilots didn't much care which ship was first in line when they attacked; and sitting close enough to another ship to hide in its deflector shield was to give up your maneuverability.

Off to portside, the incoming group of TIE fighters scattered out of the way as Luke drove through their formation, wingtip lasers blazing away madly. A second wave of Imperials behind the first closed to intercept as Luke pulled a hard one-eighty and swung back on the tails of the first wave. Han held his breath; but even as he watched, the X-wing managed somehow to thread its way unscathed through the melee and take off at full throttle at an angle from the *Lady Luck*'s vector, the whole squadron hot on his tail.

"Well, so much for that group," Irenez commented.

"And maybe for Luke, too," Lando countered harshly as he jabbed at the comm. "Luke, you all right?"

"I got a little singed, but everything's still running," Luke's voice came back. "I don't think I can get back to you."

"Don't try," Han told him. "As soon as you're clear, jump to lightspeed and get out of here."

"What about you?"

Luke's last word was partially drowned out by a sudden twitter from the comm. "That's the signal," Irenez said. "Here they come."

Han frowned, searching the sky outside the front viewport. As far as he could see, there was nothing out there but stars—

And then, in perfect unison, three large ships suddenly dropped out of hyperspace into triangular formation directly ahead of them.

Lando inhaled sharply. "Those are old Dreadnaught cruisers."

"That's our help," Irenez said. "Straight down the middle of the triangle—they'll cover for us."

"Right," Han gritted, shifting the *Lady Luck*'s vector a few degrees, and trying to coax a little more speed out of its engines. The New Republic had a fair number of Dreadnaughts, and at six hundred meters long each they were impressive enough warships. But even three of them working together would be hard pressed to take out an Imperial Star Destroyer.

Apparently, the Dreadnaughts' commander agreed. Even as the Star Destroyer behind the *Lady Luck* opened up with its huge turbolaser batteries, the Dreadnaughts began pelting the larger ship with a furious barrage of ion cannon blasts, trying to temporarily knock out enough of its systems for them to get away.

"That answer your question?" Han asked Luke.

"I think so," Luke said dryly. "Okay, I'm gone. Where do I meet you?"

"You don't," Han told him. He didn't like that answer much, and he suspected Luke would like it even less. But it couldn't be helped. With a dozen TIE fighters currently between the *Lady Luck* and the X-wing, suggesting a rendezvous point on even what was supposed to be a secure comm channel would be an open invitation for the Empire to send their own reception committee on ahead. "Lando and I can handle the mission on our own," he added. "If we run into any problems, we'll contact you through Coruscant."

"All right," Luke said. Sure enough, he didn't sound happy about it. But he had enough sense to recognize there was no other safe way. "Take care, you two."

"See you," Han said, and cut the transmission.

"So now it's *my* mission, too, huh?" Lando growled from the copilot's seat, his tone a mixture of annoyance and resignation. "I knew it. I just *knew* it."

Sena's transport was into the triangular pocket between the Dreadnaughts now, still driving for all it was worth. Han kept the *Lady Luck* with them, staying as close above the transport's tail as he could without getting into its exhaust. "You got some particular place you'd like us to drop you?" he asked, looking back at Irenez.

She was gazing out the viewport at the underside of the Dreadnaught they were passing beneath. "Actually, our Commander was rather hoping you'd accompany us back to our base," she said.

Han threw a look at Lando. There had been something in her tone that implied the request was more than merely a suggestion. "And just how hard was your Commander hoping this?" Lando asked.

"Very much." She dropped her gaze from the Dreadnaught. "Don't misunderstand—it's not an order. But when I spoke to him, the Commander seemed extremely interested in meeting again with Captain Solo."

Han frowned. "*Again?*"

"Those were his words."

Han looked at Lando, found the other looking back at him. "Some old friend you've never mentioned?" Lando asked.

"I don't recall having any friends who own Dreadnaughts," Han countered. "What do you think?"

"I think I'm being nicely maneuvered into a corner here," Lando said, a little sourly. "Aside from that, whoever this Commander is, he seems to be in contact with your Bothan pals. If you're trying to find out what Fey'lya's up to, he'd be the one to ask."

Han thought it over. Lando was right, of course. On the other hand, the whole thing could just as easily be a trap, with this talk about old friends being designed to lure him in.

Still, with Irenez sitting behind him with a blaster riding her hip, there wasn't really a graceful way to get out of it if she and Sena chose to press the point. They might as well be polite about it. "Okay," he told Irenez. "What course do we set?"

"You don't," she said, nodding upward.

Han followed her gaze. One of the three Dreadnaughts they'd passed had now swung around to fly parallel with them. Ahead, Sena's ship was heading up toward one of a pair of brightly lit docking ports. "Let me guess," he said to Irenez.

"Just relax and let us do the flying," she said, with the first hint of humor that he'd yet seen from her.

"Right," Han sighed.

And with the flashes of the rear guard battle still going on behind them, he eased the *Lady Luck* up toward the docking port. Luke, he reminded himself, had apparently not sensed any treachery from Sena or her people back in the city.

But then, he hadn't sensed any deceit from the Bimms on Bimmisaari, either, just before that first Noghri attack.

This time the kid better be right.

THE FIRST DREADNAUGHT gave a flicker of pseudomotion and vanished into hyperspace, taking the transport and the *Lady Luck* with it. A few seconds later, the other two Dreadnaughts ceased their ion bombardment of the Star Destroyer and, through a hail of turbolaser blasts from still-operating Imperial batteries, made their own escape.

And Luke was alone. Except, of course, for the squadron of TIE fighters still chasing him.

From behind him came an impatient and rather worried-sounding trill. "Okay, Artoo, we're going," he assured the little droid. Reaching over, he pulled the hyperdrive lever; and the stars became starlines, and turned to mottled sky, and he and Artoo were safe.

Luke took a deep breath, let it out in a sigh. So that was it. Han and Lando were gone, to wherever Sena and her mysterious Commander had taken them, and there really wasn't any way for him to track them down. Until they surfaced again and got in touch with him, he was out of the mission.

But perhaps that was for the best.

There was another warble from behind, a questioning one this time. "No, we're not going back to Coruscant, Artoo," he told the droid, an echo of déjà vu tugging at him. "We're going to a little place called Jomark. To see a Jedi Master."

CHAPTER 9

THE LITTLE FAST-ATTACK patrol ship had dropped out of hyper-space and closed to within a hundred kilometers of the *Falcon* before the ship's sensors even noticed its presence. By the time Leia got to the cockpit, the pilot had already made contact.

"Is that you, Khabarakh?" she called, slipping into the co-pilot's seat beside Chewbacca.

"Yes, Lady Vader," the Noghri's gravelly, catlike voice mewed. "I have come alone, as I promised. Are you also alone?"

"My companion Chewbacca is with me as pilot," she said. "As is a protocol droid. I would like to bring the droid along to help with translation, if I may. Chewbacca, as we agreed, will stay here."

The Wookiee turned to her with a growl. "No," she said firmly, remembering just in time to mute the transmitter. "I'm sorry, but that was the promise I made to Khabarakh. You'll stay here on the *Falcon*, and that's an order."

Chewbacca growled again, more insistently this time . . . and with a sudden prickly sensation on the back of her neck, Leia became acutely aware of something she hadn't really thought about for years. Namely, that the Wookiee was quite capable of ignoring pretty much any order he chose to.

"I have to go alone, Chewie," she said in a low voice. Force of will wasn't going to work here; she was going to have to go for logic and reason. "Don't you understand? That was the arrangement."

Chewbacca rumbled. "No," Leia shook her head. "My safety isn't a matter of strength anymore. My only chance is to convince the Noghri that I can be trusted. That when I make promises I keep them."

"The droid will pose no problem," Khabarakh decided. "I will bring my ship alongside for docking."

Leia switched the transmitter back on. "Fine," she said. "I also have one case of clothing and personal items to bring along, if I may. Plus a sensor/analyzer package, to test the air and soil for anything that might be dangerous to me."

"The air and soil where we shall be is safe."

"I believe you," Leia said. "But I am not responsible only for my own safety. I carry within me two new lives, and I must protect them."

The comm speaker hissed. "Heirs of the Lord Vader?"

Leia hesitated; but genetically, if not philosophically, it was true enough. "Yes."

Another hiss. "You may bring what you wish," he said. "I must be allowed to scan them, though. Do you bring weapons?"

"I have my lightsaber," Leia said. "Are there any animals on your world dangerous enough for me to need a blaster?"

"Not anymore," Khabarakh said, his voice grim. "Your lightsaber, too, will be acceptable."

Chewbacca snarled something quietly vicious, his wickedly curved climbing claws sliding involuntarily in and out of their fingertip sheaths. He was, Leia realized abruptly, on the edge of losing control . . . and perhaps of taking matters into those huge hands of his—

"What is the problem?" Khabarakh demanded.

Leia's stomach tightened. *Honesty*, she reminded herself. "My pilot doesn't like the idea of me going off alone with you," she conceded. "He has a—well, you wouldn't understand."

"He is under a life debt to you?"

Leia blinked at the speaker. She hadn't expected Khabarakh to have ever heard of the Wookiee life debt, much less know anything about it. "Yes," she said. "The original life debt was to my husband, Han Solo. During the war Chewie extended it to include my brother and me."

"And now to the children you bear within you?"

Leia looked at Chewbacca. "Yes."

For a long minute the comm was silent. The patrol ship continued toward them, and Leia found herself gripping the seat arms tightly as she wondered what the Noghri was thinking. If he decided that Chewbacca's objections constituted betrayal of their arrangement . . .

"The Wookiee code of honor is similar to our own," Khabarakh said at last. "He may come with you."

Chewbacca gave a throaty rumble of surprise, a surprise that slid quickly into suspicion. "Would you rather he have said you had to stay here?" Leia countered, her own surprise at the Noghri's concession quickly covered up by relief that the whole thing had been resolved so easily. "Come on, make up your mind."

The Wookiee rumbled again, but it was clear that he'd rather walk into a trap with her than let her walk into one alone. "Thank you, Khabarakh, we accept," Leia told the Noghri. "We'll be ready whenever you get here. How long will the trip to your world take, by the way?"

"Approximately four days," Khabarakh said. "I await the honor of your presence aboard my ship."

The comm went silent. *Four days*, Leia thought, a shiver running up her back. Four days in which to learn all that she could about both Khabarakh and the Noghri people.

And to prepare for the most important diplomatic mission of her life.

As IT TURNED OUT, she didn't learn much about the Noghri culture during the trip. Khabarakh kept largely to himself, splitting his time between the sealed cockpit and his cabin. Occasionally he would come by to talk to Leia, but the conversations were short and invariably left her with the uncomfortable feeling that he was still very ambivalent about his decision to bring her to his home. When they'd set up this meeting back on the Wookiee world of Kashyyyk, she had suggested that he discuss the question with friends or confidants; but as they neared the end of the voyage and his dark nervousness grew, she began to pick up little hints that he had not, in fact, done so. The decision had been made entirely on his own.

It was not, to her way of thinking, a very auspicious beginning. It implied either a lack of trust in his friends or else a desire to absolve them from responsibility should the whole thing go sour. Either way, not exactly the sort of situation that filled her with confidence.

With their host generally keeping to himself, she and Chewbacca were forced to come up with their own entertainment. For Chewbacca, with his innate mechanical interests, such entertainment consisted mainly of wandering through the ship and poking his nose into every room, access hatch, and crawlway he could find—studying the ship, as he ominously put it, in case they needed at some point to fly it themselves. Leia, for her part, spent most of the trip in her cabin with Threepio, trying to deduce a possible derivation of *Mal'ary'ush*, the only Noghri word she knew, with the hope of at least getting some idea of where in the galaxy they might be going. Unfortunately, with six million languages to draw on, Threepio could come up with any number of possible etymologies for the word, ranging from reasonable to tenuous to absurd and right back again. It was an interesting exercise in applied linguistics, but ultimately more frustrating than useful.

In the middle of the fourth day, they reached the Noghri world . . . and it was even worse than she'd expected.

"It's incredible," she breathed, a hard knot forming in her throat as she pressed close to Chewbacca to stare through the ship's only passenger viewport at the world they were rapidly approaching. Beneath the mottling of white clouds the planetary surface seemed to be a uniform brown, relieved only by the occasional deep blue of lakes and small oceans. No greens or yellows, no light purples or blues—none of the colors, in fact, that usually signified plant life. For all she could tell, the entire planet might have been dead.

Chewbacca growled a reminder. "Yes, I know Khabarakh said it had been devastated in the war," she agreed soberly. "But I didn't realize he really meant the *whole* planet had been hit." She shook her head, feeling sick at heart. Wondering which side had been most responsible for this disaster.

Most responsible. She swallowed hard at the reflexively defensive words. There was no *most responsible* here, and she knew it. Khabarakh's world had been destroyed during a battle in space . . . and there had been only two sides to the war. Whatever had happened to turn this world into a desert, the Rebel Alliance could not avoid its share of the guilt. "No wonder the Emperor and Vader were able to turn them against us," she murmured. "We have to find some way to help them."

Chewbacca growled again, gestured out the viewport. The terminator line was coming up over the horizon now, a fuzzy strip of twilight between day and night; and there, fading through to the darkness beyond was what looked like an irregular patch of pale green. "I see it," Leia nodded. "You suppose that's all that's left?"

The Wookiee shrugged, offered the obvious suggestion.

"Yes, I suppose that would be the simplest way to find out," Leia agreed. "I really don't know if I want to ask him, though. Let's wait until we're closer and can see more of—"

She felt Chewbacca go stiff beside her a split second before his bellow split the air and left her ears ringing. "What—?"

And then she saw it, and her stomach knotted abruptly with shock. There, just coming over the curve of the planet, was an Imperial Star Destroyer.

They'd been betrayed.

"No," she breathed, staring out at the huge arrow-head shape. No mistake—it was a Star Destroyer, all right. "No. I can't believe Khabarakh would do this."

The last words were spoken to empty air; and with a second shock, she realized that Chewbacca was no longer beside her. Spinning around, she saw a flash of brown as he vanished down the corridor leading to the cockpit.

"No!" she shouted, pushing away from the bulkhead and taking off after him as fast as she could run. "Chewie, no!"

The order was a waste of air, and she knew it. The Wookiee had murder in his heart, and he would get to Khabarakh even if he had to tear down the cockpit door with his bare hands.

The first *clang* sounded as she was halfway down the corridor; the second came as she rounded the slight curve and came within sight of the door. Chewbacca was raising his massive fists for a third blow—

When, to Leia's amazement, the door slid open.

Chewbacca seemed surprised, too, but he didn't dwell on it long. He was through the door before it was completely open, charging into the cockpit with a ululating Wookiee battle yell. "Chewie!" Leia shouted again, diving through herself.

Just in time to see Khabarakh, seated at the pilot's station, throw up his right arm and somehow send Chewbacca spinning past him to crash with a roar into the underside of the control board.

Leia skidded to a halt, not quite believing what she'd just seen. "Khabarakh—"

"I did not call them," the Noghri said, half turning to face her. "I did not betray my word of honor."

Chewbacca thundered his disbelief as he fought to scramble to his feet in the cramped space. "You must stop him," Khabarakh shouted over the Wookiee's roar. "Must keep him quiet. I must give the recognition signal or all will be lost."

Leia looked past him at the distant Star Destroyer, her teeth clenched hard together. *Betrayal* . . . but if Khabarakh had planned a betrayal, why had he let Chewbacca come along? Whatever that fighting technique was he'd used to deflect Chewbacca's first mad rush, it wasn't likely to work a second time.

She focused again on Khabarakh's face; on those dark eyes, protruding jaw, and needle-sharp teeth. He was watching her, ignoring the threat of the enraged Wookiee behind him, his hand poised ready over the comm switch. A beep sounded from the board, and his hand twitched toward the switch before stopping again. The board beeped again—"I have not betrayed you, Lady Vader," Khabarakh repeated, a note of urgency in his voice. "You must believe me."

Leia braced herself. "Chewie, be quiet," she said. "Chewie? Chewie, be *quiet*."

The Wookiee ignored the order. Finally back on his feet, he roared his war cry again and lunged for Khabarakh's throat. The Noghri took the charge head-on this time, grabbing Chewbacca's huge wrists in his wiry hands and holding on for all he was worth.

It wasn't enough. Slowly but steadily, Khabarakh's arms were bent steadily backwards as Chewbacca forced his way forward. "Chewie, I said stop," Leia tried again. "Use your head—if he was planning a trap, don't you think he'd have timed it for when we were asleep or something?"

Chewbacca spit out a growl, his hands continuing their unwavering advance. "But if he doesn't check in, they'll *know* something's wrong," she countered. "That's a sure way to bring them down on us."

"The Lady Vader speaks truth," Khabarakh said, his voice taut with the strain of holding back Chewbacca's hands. "I have not betrayed you, but if I give no recognition signal you *will* be betrayed."

"He's right," Leia said. "If they come to investigate, we lose by default. Come on, Chewie, it's our only hope."

The Wookiee snarled again, shaking his head firmly. "Then you leave me no choice," Khabarakh said.

And without warning, the cockpit flashed with blue light, dropping Chewbacca to the floor like a huge sack of grain. "What—?" Leia gasped, dropping to her knees beside the motionless Wookiee. "Khabarakh!"

"A stun weapon only," the Noghri said, breathing rapidly as he swiveled back to his board. "A built-in defense."

Leia twisted her head to glare at him, furious at what he'd done . . . a fury that faded reluctantly behind the logic of the situation. Chewbacca had been fully prepared to throttle the life out of Khabarakh; and from personal experience, she knew how hard it was to calm down an angry Wookiee, even when you were his friend to begin with.

And Khabarakh *had* tried talking first. "Now what?" she asked the Noghri, digging a hand through Chewbacca's thick torso hair to check his heartbeat. It was steady, which meant the stun weapon hadn't played any of its rare but potentially lethal tricks on the Wookiee's nervous system.

"Now be silent," Khabarakh said, tapping his comm switch and saying something in his own language. Another mewing Noghri voice replied, and for a few minutes they conversed together. Leia remained kneeling at Chewbacca's side, wishing she'd had time to bring Threepio up before the discussion started. It would have been nice to know what the conversation was all about.

But finally it ended, and Khabarakh signed off. "We are safe now," he said, slumping a little in his seat. "They are persuaded it was an equipment malfunction."

"Let's hope so," Leia said.

Khabarakh looked at her, a strange expression on his nightmare face. "I have not betrayed you, Lady Vader," he said quietly, his voice hard and yet oddly pleading. "You must believe me. I have promised to defend you, and I will. To my own death, if need be."

Leia stared at him . . . and whether through some sensitivity of the Force or merely her own long diplomatic experience, she finally understood the position Khabarakh was now in. Whatever waverings or second thoughts he might have been feeling during the voyage, the Star Destroyer's unexpected appearance had burned those uncertainties away. Khabarakh's word of honor had been brought into question, and he was now in the position of having to conclusively prove that he had not broken that word.

And he would have to go to whatever lengths such proof demanded. Even if it killed him.

Earlier, Leia had wondered how Khabarakh could possibly understand the concept of the Wookiee life debt. Perhaps the Noghri and Wookiee cultures were more alike than she'd realized.

"I believe you," she told him, climbing to her feet and sitting down in the copilot seat. Chewbacca she would have to leave where he was until he was awake enough to help her move him. "What now?"

Khabarakh turned back to his board. "Now we must make a decision," he said. "My intention had been to bring you to ground in the city of Nystao, waiting until full dark to present you to my clan dynast. But that is now impossible. Our Imperial lord has come, and is holding a convocate of the dynasts."

The back of Leia's neck tingled. "Your Imperial lord is the Grand Admiral?" she asked carefully.

"Yes," Khabarakh said. "That is his flagship, the *Chimaera*. I remember the day that the Lord Darth Vader first brought him to us," he added, his mewing voice becoming reflective. "The Lord Vader told us that his duties against the Emperor's enemies would now be taking his full attention. That the

Grand Admiral would henceforth be our lord and commander." He made a strange, almost purring sound deep in his chest. "There were many who were sad that day. The Lord Vader had been the only one save the Emperor who cared for Noghri well-being. He had given us hope and purpose."

Leia grimaced. That purpose being to go off and die as death commandos at the Emperor's whim. But she couldn't say things like that to Khabarakh. Not yet, anyway. "Yes," she murmured.

At her feet, Chewbacca twitched. "He will be fully awake soon," Khabarakh said. "I would not like to stun him again. Can you control him?"

"I think so," Leia said. They were coming in low toward the upper atmosphere now, on a course that would take them directly beneath the orbiting Star Destroyer. "I hope they don't decide to do a sensor focus on us," she murmured. "If they pick up three life-forms here, you're going to have a lot of explaining to do."

"The ship's static-damping should prevent that," Khabarakh assured her. "It is at full power."

Leia frowned. "Aren't they likely to wonder about that?"

"No. I explained it was part of the same malfunction that caused the transmitter problem."

There was a low rumble from Chewbacca, and Leia looked down to see the Wookiee's eyes glaring impotently up at her. Fully alert again, but without enough motor control yet to do anything. "We've cleared outer control," she told him. "We're heading down to—where *are* we going, Khabarakh?"

The Noghri took a deep breath, let it out in an odd sort of whistle. "We will go to my home, a small village near the edge of the Clean Land. I will hide you there until our lord the Grand Admiral leaves."

Leia thought about that. A small village situated off the mainstream of Noghri life ought to be safely out of the way of wandering Imperials. On the other hand, if it was anything like the small villages she'd known, her presence there would be common knowledge an hour after they put down. "Can you trust the other villagers to keep quiet?"

"Do not worry," Khabarakh said. "I will keep you safe."

But he hesitated before he said it . . . and as they headed into the atmosphere, Leia noted uneasily that he hadn't really answered the question.

THE DYNAST BOWED one last time and stepped back to the line of those awaiting their turn to pay homage to their leader. Thrawn, seated in the gleaming High Seat of the Common Room of Honoghr, nodded gravely to the departing clan leader and motioned to the next. The other stepped forward, moving in the formalized dance that seemed to indicate respect, and bowed his forehead to the ground before the Grand Admiral.

Standing two meters to Thrawn's right and a little behind him, Pellaeon shifted his weight imperceptibly between feet, stifled a yawn, and wondered when this ritual would be over. He'd been under the impression they'd come to Honoghr to try to inspire the commando teams, but so far the only Noghri they'd seen had been ceremonial guards and this small but excessively boring collection of clan leaders. Thrawn presumably had his reasons for wading through the ritual, but Pellaeon wished it would hurry up and be over. With a galaxy still to win back for the Empire, sitting here listening to a group of gray-skinned aliens drone on about their loyalty seemed a ridiculous waste of time.

There was a touch of air on the back of his neck. "Captain?" someone said quietly in his ear—Lieutenant Tschel, he tentatively identified the voice. "Excuse me, sir, but Grand Admiral Thrawn asked to be informed immediately if anything out of the ordinary happened." Pellaeon nodded slightly, glad of any interruption. "What is it?"

"It doesn't seem dangerous, sir, or even very important," Tschel said. "A Noghri commando ship on its way in almost didn't give the recognition response in time."

"Equipment trouble, probably," Pellaeon said.

"That's what the pilot said," Tschel told him. "The odd thing is that he begged off putting down at the Nystao landing area. You'd think that someone with equipment problems would want his ship looked at immediately."

"A bad transmitter isn't exactly a crisis-level problem," Pellaeon grunted. But Tschel had a point; and Nystao was the only place on Honoghr with qualified spaceship repair facilities. "We have an ID on the pilot?"

"Yes, sir. His name's Khabarakh, clan Kihm'bar. I pulled up what we have on him," he added, offering Pellaeon a data pad.

Surreptitiously, Pellaeon took it, wondering what he should do now. Thrawn had indeed left instructions that he was to be notified of any unusual activity anywhere in the system. But to interrupt the ceremony for something so trivial didn't seem like a good idea.

As usual, Thrawn was one step ahead of him. Lifting a hand, he stopped the Noghri clan dynast's presentation and turned his glowing red eyes on Pellaeon. "You have something to report, Captain?"

"A small anomaly only, sir," Pellaeon told him, steeling himself and stepping to the Grand Admiral's side. "An incoming commando ship was slow to transmit its recognition signal, and then declined to put down at the Nystao landing area. Probably just an equipment problem."

"Probably," Thrawn agreed. "Was the ship scanned for evidence of malfunction?"

"Ah . . ." Pellaeon checked the data pad. "The scan was inconclusive," he told the other. "The ship's static-damping was strong enough to block—"

"The incoming ship was static-damped?" Thrawn interrupted, looking sharply up at Pellaeon.

"Yes, sir."

Wordlessly, Thrawn held up a hand. Pellaeon gave him the data pad, and for a moment the Grand Admiral frowned down at it, skimming the report. "Khabarakh, clan Kihm'bar," he murmured to himself. "Interesting." He looked up at Pellaeon again. "Where did the ship go?"

Pellaeon looked in turn at Tschel. "According to the last report, it was headed south," the lieutenant said. "It might still be in range of our tractor beams, sir."

Pellaeon turned back to Thrawn. "Shall we try to stop it, Admiral?"

Thrawn looked down at the data pad, his face tight with concentration. "No," he said at last. "Let it land, but track it. And order a tech team from the *Chimaera* to meet us at the ship's final destination." His eyes searched the line of Noghri dynasts, came to rest on one of them. "Dynast Ir'khaim, clan Kihm'bar, step forward."

The Noghri did so. "What is your wish, my lord?" he mewed.

"One of your people has come home," Thrawn said. "We go to his village to welcome him."

Ir'khaim bowed. "At my lord's request."

Thrawn stood up. "Order the shuttle to be prepared, Captain," he told Pellaeon. "We leave at once."

"Yes, sir," Pellaeon said, nodding the order on to Lieutenant Tschel. "Wouldn't it be easier, sir, to have the ship and pilot brought here to us?"

"Easier, perhaps," Thrawn acknowledged, "but possibly not as illuminating. You obviously didn't recognize the pilot's name; but Khabarakh, clan Kihm'bar, was once part of commando team twenty-two. Does *that* jog any memories?"

Pellaeon felt his stomach tighten. "That was the team that went after Leia Organa Solo on Kashyyyk."

"And of which team only Khabarakh still survives," Thrawn nodded. "I think it might be instructive to hear from him the details of that failed mission. And to find out why it's taken him this long to return home."

Thrawn's eyes glittered. "And to find out," he added quietly, "just why he's trying so hard to avoid us."

CHAPTER 10

I T WAS FULL dark by the time Khabarakh brought the ship to ground in his village, a tight-grouped cluster of huts with brightly lit windows. "Do ships land here often?" Leia asked as Khabarakh pointed the ship toward a shadowy structure standing apart near the center of the village. In the glare of the landing lights the shadow became a large cylindrical building with a flat cone-shaped roof, the circular wall composed of massive vertical wooden pillars alternating with a lighter, shimmery wood. Just beneath the eaves she caught a glint of a metal band encircling the entire building.

"It is not common," Khabarakh said, cutting the repulsorlifts and running the ship's systems down to standby. "Neither is it unheard of."

In other words, it was probably going to attract a fair amount of attention. Chewbacca, who had recovered enough for Leia to help into one of the cockpit passenger seats, was obviously thinking along the same lines. "The villagers are all close family of the clan Kihm'bar," Khabarakh said in answer to the Wookiee's slightly slurred question. "They will accept my promise of protection as their own. Come."

Leia unstrapped and stood up, suppressing a grimace as she did so. But they were here now, and she could only hope that Khabarakh's confidence was more than just the unfounded idealism of youth.

She helped Chewbacca unstrap and together they followed the Noghri back toward the main hatchway, collecting Threepio from her cabin on the way. "I must go first," Khabarakh said as they reached the exit. "By custom, I must approach alone to the *dukha* of the clan Kihm'bar upon arrival. By law, I am required to announce out-clan visitors to the head of my family."

"I understand," Leia said, fighting back a fresh surge of uneasiness. She didn't like this business of Khabarakh having conversations with his fellow Noghri that she wasn't in on. Once again, there wasn't a lot she could do about it. "We'll wait here until you come and get us."

"I will be quick," Khabarakh promised. He palmed the door release twice, slipping outside as the panel slid open and then shut again.

Chewbacca growled something unintelligible under his breath. "He'll be back soon," Leia soothed him, making a guess as to what was bothering the Wookiee.

"I'm certain he is telling the truth," Threepio added helpfully. "Customs and rituals of this sort are very common among the more socially primitive prespaceflight cultures."

"Except that this culture isn't prespaceflight," Leia pointed out, her hand playing restlessly with the grip of her lightsaber as she stared at the closed hatchway in front of her. Khabarakh could at least have left the door open so that they would be able to see when he was coming back.

Unless, of course, he didn't *want* them to see when he was coming back.

"That is evident, Your Highness," Threepio agreed, his

voice taking on a professorial tone. "I feel certain, however, that their status in that regard has been changed only recent— Well!" he broke off as Chewbacca abruptly pushed past him and lumbered back toward the center of the ship.

"Where are you going?" Leia called after the Wookiee. His only reply was some comment about the Imperials that she wasn't quite able to catch. "Chewie, get back here," she snapped. "Khabarakh will be back any minute."

This time the Wookiee didn't bother to answer. "Great," Leia muttered, trying to decide what to do. If Khabarakh came back and found Chewbacca gone—but if he came and found *both* of them gone—"As I was saying," Threepio went on, apparently deciding that the actions of rude Wookiees were better left ignored, "all the evidence I have gathered so far about this culture indicates that they were until recently a nonspacefaring people. Khabarakh's reference to the *dukha*— obviously a clan center of some sort—the familial and clan structures themselves, plus this whole preoccupation with your perceived royal status—"

"The high court of Alderaan had a royal hierarchy, too," Leia reminded him tartly, still looking back along the empty corridor. No, she decided, she and Threepio had better stay here and wait for Khabarakh. "Most other people in the galaxy didn't consider us to be socially primitive."

"No, of course not," Threepio said, sounding a little embarrassed. "I didn't mean to imply any such thing."

"I know," Leia assured him, a little embarrassed herself at jumping on Threepio like that. She'd known what he meant. "Where *is* he, anyway?"

The question had been rhetorical; but even as she voiced it the hatchway abruptly slid open again. "Come," Khabarakh said. His dark eyes flicked over Leia and Threepio—"Where is the Wookiee?"

"He went back into the ship," Leia told him. "I don't know why. Do you want me to go and find him?"

Khabarakh made a sound halfway between a hiss and a purr. "There is no time," he said. "The maitrakh is waiting. Come."

Turning, he started back down the ramp. "Any idea how long it will take you to pick up the language?" Leia asked Threepio as they followed.

"I really cannot say, Your Highness," the droid answered as Khabarakh led them across a dirt courtyard past the large wooden building they'd seen on landing—the clan *dukha*, Leia decided. One of the smaller structures beyond it seemed to be their goal. "Learning an entirely new language would be difficult indeed," Threepio continued. "However, if it is similar to any of the six million forms of communication with which I am familiar—"

"I understand," Leia cut him off. They were almost to the lighted building now; and as they approached, a pair of short Noghri standing in the shadows pulled open the double doors for them. Taking a deep breath, Leia followed Khabarakh inside.

From the amount of light coming through the windows she would have expected the building's interior to be uncomfortably bright. To her surprise, the room they entered was actually darker than it had been immediately outside. A glance to the side showed why: the brightly lit "windows" were in fact standard self-powered lighting panels, with the operational sides facing outward. Except for a small amount of spillage from the panels, the interior of the building was lit only by a pair of floating-wick lamps. Threepio's assessment of the society echoed through her mind; apparently, he'd known what he was talking about.

In the center of the room, standing silently in a row facing her, were five Noghri.

Leia swallowed hard, sensing somehow that the first words should be theirs. Khabarakh stepped to the Noghri in the center and dropped to his knees, ducking his head to the floor and splaying out his hands to his sides. The same gesture of respect, she remembered, that he'd extended to her back in the Kashyyyk holding cell. "*Ilyr'ush mir lakh svoril'lae,*" he said. "*Mir'lae karah siv Mal'ary'ush vir'ae Vader'ush.*"

"Can you understand it?" Leia murmured to Threepio.

"To a degree," the droid replied. "It appears to be a dialect of the ancient trade language—"

"*Sha'vah!*" the Noghri in the center of the line spat.

Threepio recoiled. "She said, 'Quiet,'" he translated unnecessarily.

"I understood the gist," Leia said, drawing herself up and bringing the full weight of her Royal Alderaanian Court upbringing to bear on the aliens facing her. Deference to local custom and authority was all well and good; but she was the daughter of their Lord Darth Vader, and there were certain discourtesies that such a person should not put up with. "Is this how you speak to the *Mal'ary'ush*?" she demanded.

Six Noghri heads snapped over to look at her. Reaching out with the Force, Leia tried to read the sense behind those gazes; but as always, this particular alien mind seemed totally closed to her. She was going to have to play it by ear. "I asked a question," she said into the silence.

The Noghri in the center took a step forward, and with the motion Leia noticed for the first time the two small hard bumps on the alien's upper chest beneath the loose tunic. A female? "Maitrakh?" she murmured to Threepio, remembering the word Khabarakh had used earlier.

"A female who is leader of a local family or subclan structure," the droid translated, his voice nervous and almost too low to hear. Threepio hated being yelled at.

"Thank you," Leia said, eyeing the Noghri. "You are the maitrakh of this family?"

"I am she," the Noghri said in heavily accented but understandable Basic. "What proof do you offer to your claim of *Mal'ary'ush*?"

Silently, Leia held out her hand. The maitrakh hesitated, then stepped up to her and gingerly sniffed it. "Is it not as I said?" Khabarakh asked.

"Be silent, thirdson," the maitrakh said, raising her head to stare into Leia's eyes. "I greet you, Lady Vader. But I do not welcome you."

Leia held her gaze steadily. She could still not sense anything from any of the aliens, but with her thoughts extended she could tell that Chewbacca had left the ship and was approaching the house. Approaching rather rapidly, and with a definite agitation about him. She hoped he wouldn't charge brashly in and ruin what little civility remained here. "May I ask why not?" she asked the maitrakh.

"Did you serve the Emperor?" the other countered. "Do you now serve our lord, the Grand Admiral?"

"No, to both questions," Leia told her.

"Then you bring discord and poison among us," the maitrakh concluded darkly. "Discord between what was and what now is." She shook her head. "We do not need more discord on Honoghr, Lady Vader."

The words were barely out of her mouth when the doors behind Leia swung open again and Chewbacca strode into the room.

The maitrakh started at the sight of the Wookiee, and one of the other Noghri uttered something startled-sounding. But any further reactions were cut off by Chewbacca's snarled warning. "Are you sure they're Imperials?" Leia asked, a cold fist clutching her heart. *No*, she pleaded silently. *Not now. Not yet.*

The Wookiee growled the obvious: that a pair of *Lambda*-class shuttles coming from orbit and from the direction of the city of Nystao could hardly be anything else.

Khabarakh moved up beside the maitrakh, said something urgently in his own language. "He says he has sworn protection to us," Threepio translated. "He asks that the pledge be honored."

For a long moment Leia thought the maitrakh was going to refuse. Then, with a sigh, she bowed her head slightly. "Come with me," Khabarakh said to Leia, brushing past her and Chewbacca to the door. "The maitrakh has agreed to hide you from our lord the Grand Admiral, at least for now."

"Where are we going?" Leia asked as they followed him out into the night.

"Your droid and your analysis equipment I will hide among the decon droids that are stored for the night in an outer shed," the Noghri explained, pointing to a window-less building fifty meters away. "You and the Wookiee will be more of a problem. If the Imperials have sensor equipment with them, your life-sign profiles will register as different from Noghri."

"I know," Leia said, searching the sky for the shuttles' running lights and trying to remember everything she could about life-form identification algorithms. Heart rate was one of the parameters, she knew, as were ambient atmosphere, respiratory byproducts, and molecule-chain EM polarization effects. But the chief long-range parameter was—"We need a heat source," she told Khabarakh. "As big a one as possible."

"The bake house," the Noghri said, pointing to a window-less building three down from where they stood. At its back was a squat chimney from which wisps of smoke could be seen curling upward in the backwash of light from the surrounding structures.

"Sounds like our best chance," Leia agreed. "Khabarakh, you hide Threepio; Chewie, come with me."

THE NOGHRI WERE waiting for them as they stepped from the shuttle: three females standing side by side, with two children acting as honor wardens by the doors of the clan *dukha* building. Thrawn glanced at the group, threw an evaluating sweep around the area, and then turned to Pellaeon. "Wait here until the tech team arrives, Captain," he ordered Pellaeon quietly. "Get them started on a check of the communications and

countermeasures equipment in the ship over there. Then join
me inside."

"Yes, sir."

Thrawn turned to Ir'khaim. "Dynast," he invited, gesturing at the waiting Noghri. The dynast bowed and strode
toward them. Thrawn threw a glance at Rukh, who'd taken
Ir'khaim's former position at the Grand Admiral's side, and
together they followed. There was the usual welcoming ritual,
and then the females led the way into the *dukha*.

The shuttle from the *Chimaera* was only a couple of minutes behind them. Pellaeon briefed the tech team and got them
busy, then crossed to the *dukha* and went in.

He'd expected that the maitrakh would have managed to
round up perhaps a handful of her people for this impromptu
late-evening visit by their glorious lord and master. To his surprise, he found that the old girl had in fact turned out half the
village. There was a double row of them, children as well as
adults, lining the *dukha* walls from the huge genealogy wall
chart back to the double doors and around again to the meditation booth opposite the chart. Thrawn was seated in the
clan High Seat two-thirds of the way to the back of the room
with Ir'khaim standing again at his side. The three females
who'd met the shuttle stood facing them with a second tier of
elders another pace back. Standing with the females, his steel-
gray skin a marked contrast to their older, darker gray, was a
young Noghri male.

Pellaeon had, apparently, missed nothing more important
than a smattering of the nonsense ritual the Noghri never
seemed to get enough of. As he moved past the silent lines of
aliens to stand at Thrawn's other side, the young male stepped
forward and knelt before the High Seat. "I greet you, my lord,"
he mewed gravely, spreading his arms out to his sides. "You
honor my family and the clan Kihm'bar with your presence
here."

"You may rise," Thrawn told him. "You are Khabarakh,
clan Kihm'bar?"

"I am, my lord."

"You were once a member of the Imperial Noghri commando team twenty-two," Thrawn said. "A team that ceased to exist on the planet Kashyyyk. Tell me what happened."

Khabarakh might have twitched. Pellaeon couldn't tell for sure. "I filed a report, my lord, immediately upon leaving that world."

"Yes, I read the report," Thrawn told him coolly. "Read it very carefully, and noted the questions it left unanswered. Such as how and why you survived when all others in your team were killed. And how it was you were able to escape when the entire planet had been alerted to your presence. And why you did not return immediately to either Honoghr or one of our other bases after your failure."

This time there was definitely a twitch. Possibly a reaction to the word *failure*. "I was left unconscious by the Wookiees during the first attack," Khabarakh said. "I awakened alone and made my way back to the ship. Once there, I deduced what had happened to the rest of the team from official information sources. I suspect they simply were unprepared for the speed and stealth of my ship when I made my escape. As to my whereabouts afterward, my lord—" He hesitated. "I transmitted my report, and then left for a time to be alone."

"Why?"

"To think, my lord, and to meditate."

"Wouldn't Honoghr have been a more suitable place for such meditation?" Thrawn asked, waving a hand around the *dukha*.

"I had much to think about. My lord."

For a moment Thrawn eyed him thoughtfully. "You were slow to respond when the request for a recognition signal came from the surface," he said. "You then refused to land at the Nystao port facilities."

"I did not refuse, my lord. I was never ordered to land there."

"The distinction is noted," Thrawn said dryly. "Tell me why you chose to come here instead."

"I wished to speak with my maitrakh. To discuss my meditations with her, and to ask forgiveness for my . . . failure."

"And have you done so?" Thrawn asked, turning to face the maitrakh.

"We have begun," she said in atrociously mangled Basic. "We have not finished."

At the back of the room, the *dukha* doors swung open and one of the tech team stepped inside. "You have a report, Ensign?" Thrawn called to him.

"Yes, Admiral," the other said, crossing the room and stepping somewhat gingerly around the assembled group of Noghri elders. "We've finished our preliminary set of comm and countermeasures tests, sir, as per orders."

Thrawn shifted his gaze to Khabarakh. "And?"

"We think we've located the malfunction, sir. The main transmitter coil seems to have overloaded and back-fed into a dump capacitor, damaging several nearby circuits. The compensator computer rebuilt the pathway, but the bypass was close enough to one of the static-damping command lines for the resulting inductance surge to trigger it."

"An interesting set of coincidences," Thrawn said, his glowing eyes still on Khabarakh. "A natural malfunction, do you think, or an artificial one?"

The maitrakh stirred, as if about to say something. Thrawn looked at her, and she subsided. "Impossible to say, sir," the tech said, choosing his words carefully. Obviously, he hadn't missed the fact that this was skating him close to the edge of insult in the middle of a group of Noghri who might decide to take offense at it. "Someone who knew what he was doing could probably have pulled it off. I have to say, though, sir, that compensator computers in general have a pretty low reputation among mechanics. They're okay on the really serious stuff that can get unskilled pilots into big trouble, but on noncritical reroutes like this they've always had a tendency to foul up something else along the way."

"Thank you." If Thrawn was annoyed that he hadn't caught Khabarakh red-handed in a lie, it didn't show in his face. "Your team will take the ship back to Nystao for repairs."

"Yes, sir." The tech saluted and left.

Thrawn looked back at Khabarakh. "With your team destroyed, you will of course have to be reassigned," he said. "When your ship has been repaired you will fly it to the Valrar base in Glythe sector and report there for duty."

"Yes, my lord," Khabarakh said.

Thrawn stood up. "You have much to be proud of here," he said, inclining his head slightly to the maitrakh. "Your family's service to the clan Kihm'bar and to the Empire will be long remembered by all of Honoghr."

"As will your leadership and protection of the Noghri people," the maitrakh responded.

Flanked by Rukh and Ir'khaim, Thrawn stepped down from the chair and headed back toward the double doors. Pellaeon took up the rear, and a minute later they were once again out in the chilly night air. The shuttle was standing ready, and without further comment or ritual Thrawn led the way inside. As they lifted, Pellaeon caught just a glimpse out the viewport of the Noghri filing out of the *dukha* to watch their departing leaders. "Well, *that* was pleasant," he muttered under his breath.

Thrawn looked at him. "A waste of time, you think, Captain?" he asked mildly.

Pellaeon glanced at Ir'khaim, seated farther toward the front of the shuttle. The dynast didn't seem to be listening to them, but it would probably still pay to be tactful. "Diplomatically, sir, I'm sure it was worthwhile to demonstrate that you care about all of Honoghr, including the outer villages," he told Thrawn. "Given that the commando ship really *had* malfunctioned, I don't think anything else was gained."

Thrawn turned to stare out the side viewport. "I'm not so sure of that, Captain," he said. "There's something not quite right back there. Rukh, what's your reading of our young commando Khabarakh?"

"He was unsettled," the bodyguard told him quietly. "That much I saw in his hands and his face."

Ir'khaim swiveled around in his chair. "It is a naturally unsettling experience to face the lord of the Noghri," he said.

"Particularly when one's hands are wet with failure?" Rukh countered.

Ir'khaim half rose from his seat, and for a pair of heartbeats the air between the two Noghri was thick with tension. Pellaeon felt himself pressing back in his seat cushions, the long and bloody history of Noghri clan rivalry flooding fresh into his consciousness . . . "This mission has generated several failures," Thrawn said calmly into the taut silence. "In that, the clan Kihm'bar hardly stands alone."

Slowly, Ir'khaim resumed his seat. "Khabarakh is still young," he said.

"He is indeed," Thrawn agreed. "One reason, I presume, why he's such a bad liar. Rukh, perhaps the Dynast Ir'khaim would enjoy the view from the forward section. Please escort him there."

"Yes, my lord." Rukh stood up. "Dynast Ir'khaim?" he said, gesturing toward the forward blast door.

For a moment the other Noghri didn't move. Then, with obvious reluctance, he stood up. "My lord," he said stiffly, and headed down the aisle.

Thrawn waited until the door had closed on both aliens before turning back to Pellaeon. "Khabarakh is hiding something, Captain," he said, a cold fire in his eyes. "I'm certain of it."

"Yes, sir," Pellaeon said, wondering how the Grand Admiral had come to that conclusion. Certainly the routine sensor scan they'd just run hadn't picked up anything. "Shall I order a sensor focus on the village?"

"That's not what I meant," Thrawn shook his head. "He wouldn't have brought anything incriminating back to Honoghr with him—you can't hide anything for long in one of these close-knit villages. No, it's something he's not telling us about that missing month. The one where he claims he was off meditating by himself."

"We might be able to learn something from his ship," Pellaeon suggested.

"Agreed," Thrawn nodded. "Have a scanning crew go over it before the techs get to work. Every cubic millimeter of it, interior and exterior both. And have Surveillance put someone on Khabarakh."

"Ah—yes, sir," Pellaeon said. "One of our people, or another Noghri?"

Thrawn cocked an eyebrow at him. "The ridiculously obvious or the heavily political, in other words?" he asked dryly. "Yes, you're right, of course. Let's try a third option: does the *Chimaera* carry any espionage droids?"

"I don't believe so, sir," Pellaeon said, punching up the question on the shuttle's computer link. "No. We have some Arakyd Viper probe droids, but nothing of the more compact espionage class."

"Then we'll have to improvise," Thrawn said. "Have Engineering put a Viper motivator into a decon droid and rig it with full-range optical and auditory sensors and a recorder. We'll have it put in with the group working out of Khabarakh's village."

"Yes, sir," Pellaeon said, keying in the order. "Do you want a transmitter installed, too?"

Thrawn shook his head. "No, a recorder should be sufficient. The antenna would be difficult to conceal from view. The last thing we want is for some curious Noghri to see it and wonder why this one was different."

Pellaeon nodded his understanding. Especially since that

might lead the aliens to start pulling decon droids apart for a look inside. "Yes, sir. I'll have the order placed right away."

Thrawn's glowing eyes shifted to look out the viewport. "There's no particular rush here," he said thoughtfully. "Not now. This is the calm before the storm, Captain; and until the storm is ready to unleash, we might as well spend our time and energy making sure our illustrious Jedi Master will be willing to assist us when we want him."

"Which means bringing Leia Organa Solo to him."

"Exactly." Thrawn looked at the forward blast door. "And if my presence is what the Noghri need to inspire them, then my presence is what they'll have."

"For how long?" Pellaeon asked.

Thrawn smiled tightly. "For as long as it takes."

CHAPTER 11

"Han?" Lando's voice came from the cabin intercom beside the bunk. "Wake up."

"Yeah, I'm awake," Han grunted, swiping at his eyes with one hand and swiveling the repeater displays toward him with the other. If there was one thing his years on the wrong side of the law had hammered into him, it was the knack of going from deep sleep to full alertness in the space between heartbeats. "What's up?"

"We're here," Lando announced. "Wherever *here* is."

"I'll be right up."

They were in sight of their target planet by the time he'd dressed and made his way to the *Lady Luck*'s cockpit. "Where's Irenez?" he asked, peering out at the mottled blue-green crescent shape they were rapidly approaching. It looked pretty much like any of a thousand other planets he'd seen.

"She's gone back to the aft control station," Lando told her. "I got the impression she wanted to be able to send down some recognition codes without us looking over her shoulder."

"Any idea where we are?"

"Not really," Lando said. "Transit time was forty-seven hours, but that doesn't tell us a whole lot."

Han nodded, searching his memory. "A Dreadnaught can pull, what, about Point Four?"

"About that," Lando agreed. "When it's really in a hurry, anyway."

"Means we aren't any more than a hundred fifty light-years from New Cov, then."

"I'd guess we're closer than that, myself," Lando said. "It wouldn't make much sense to use New Cov as a contact point if they were that far away."

"Unless New Cov was Breil'lya's idea and not theirs," Han pointed out.

"Possible," Lando said. "I still think we're closer than a hundred fifty light-years, though. They could have taken their time getting here just to mislead us."

Han looked up at the Dreadnaught that had been hauling them through hyperspace for the past two days. "Or to have time to organize a reception committee."

"There's that," Lando nodded. "I don't know if I mentioned it, but after they apologized for getting the magnetic coupling off-center over our hatch I went back and took a look."

"You didn't mention it, but I did the same thing," Han said sourly. "Looked kind of deliberate, didn't it?"

"That's what I thought, too," Lando said. "Like maybe they wanted an excuse to keep us cooped up down here and not wandering around their ship."

"Could be lots of good and innocent reasons for that," Han reminded him.

"And lots of not-so-innocent ones," Lando countered. "You sure you don't have any idea who this Commander of theirs might be?"

"Not even a guess. Probably be finding out real soon, though."

The comm crackled on. "*Lady Luck*, this is Sena," a familiar voice said. "We've arrived."

"Yes, we noticed," Lando told her. "I expect you'll want us to follow you down."

"Right," she said. "The *Peregrine* will drop the magnetic coupling whenever you're ready to fly."

Han stared at the speaker, barely hearing Lando's response. A ship called the *Peregrine* . . . ?

"You still with me?"

Han focused on Lando, noticing with mild surprise that the other's conversation with Sena had ended. "Yeah," he said. "Sure. It's just—that name, *Peregrine*, rang an old bell."

"You've heard of it?"

"Not the ship, no," Han shook his head. "The Peregrine was an old Corellian scare legend they used to tell when I was a kid. He was some old ghostly guy who'd been cursed to wander around the world forever and never find his home again. Used to make me feel real creepy."

From above came a clang; and with a jolt they were free of the Dreadnaught. Lando eased them away from the huge warship, looking up as it passed by overhead. "Well, try to remember it was just a legend," he reminded Han.

Han looked at the Dreadnaught. "Sure," he said, a little too quickly. "I know that."

THEY FOLLOWED SENA'S freighter down and were soon skimming over what appeared to be a large grassy plain dotted with patches of stubby coniferous trees. A wall of craggy cliffs loomed directly ahead—an ideal spot, Han's old smuggler instincts told him, to hide a spaceship support and servicing base. A few minutes later his hunch was borne out as, sweeping over a low ridge, they came to the encampment.

An encampment that was far too large to be merely a servicing base. Rows upon rows of camouflaged structures filled the plain just beneath the cliffs: everything from small living quarters to larger admin and supply sheds to still larger maintenance and tool buildings, up to a huge camo-roofed refurbishing hangar. The perimeter was dotted with the squat, turret-topped cylinders of Golan Arms anti-infantry batteries and a few of the longer Speizoc anti-vehicle weapons, along with some KAAC Freerunner assault vehicles parked in defensive posture.

Lando whistled softly under his breath. "Would you look at that?" he said. "What *is* this, someone's private army?"

"Looks that way," Han agreed, feeling the skin on the back of his neck starting to crawl. He'd run into private armies before, and they'd never been anything but trouble.

"I think I'm starting not to like this," Lando decided, easing the *Lady Luck* gingerly over the outer sentry line. Ahead, Sena's freighter was approaching a landing pad barely visible against the rest of the ground. "You sure you want to go through with this?"

"What, with three Dreadnaughts standing on our heads out there?" Han snorted. "I don't think we've got a whole lot of choice. Not in this crate, anyway."

"Probably right," Lando conceded, apparently too preoccupied to notice the insult to his ship. "So what do we do?"

Sena's freighter had dropped its landing skids and was settling onto the pad. "I guess we go down and behave like invited guests," Han said.

Lando nodded at Han's blaster. "You don't think they'll object to their invited guests coming in armed?"

"Let 'em object first," Han said grimly. "Then we'll discuss it."

Lando put the *Lady Luck* down beside the freighter, and together he and Han made their way to the aft hatchway. Irenez, her transmission chores finished, was waiting there for them, her own blaster strapped prominently to her hip. A transport skiff was parked outside, and as the three of them headed down the ramp, Sena and a handful of her entourage came around the *Lady Luck*'s bow. Most of the others were dressed in a casual tan uniform of an unfamiliar but vaguely Corellian cut; Sena, by contrast, was still in the nondescript civilian garb she'd been wearing on New Cov.

"Welcome to our base of operations," Sena said, waving a hand to encompass the encampment around them. "If you'll come with us, the Commander is waiting to meet you."

"Busy looking place you've got here," Han commented as they all boarded the skiff. "You getting ready to start a war or something?"

"We're not in the business of starting wars," Sena said coolly.

"Ah," Han nodded, looking around as the driver swung the skiff around and headed off through the camp. There was something about the layout that seemed vaguely familiar.

Lando got it first. "You know, this place looks a lot like one of the old Alliance bases we used to work out of," he commented to Sena. "Only built on the surface instead of dug in underground."

"It does look that way, doesn't it?" Sena agreed, her voice not giving anything away.

"You've had dealings with the Alliance, then?" Lando probed gently.

Sena didn't answer. Lando looked at Han, eyebrows raised. Han shrugged slightly in return. Whatever was going on here, it was clear the hired hands weren't in the habit of talking about it.

The skiff came to a halt beside an admin-type building indistinguishable from the others nearby except for the two uniformed guards flanking the doorway. They saluted as Sena approached, one of them reaching over to pull the door open. "The Commander asked to see you for a moment alone, Captain Solo," Sena said, stopping by the open door. "We'll wait out here with General Calrissian."

"Right," Han said. Taking a deep breath, he stepped inside.

From its outside appearance he'd expected it to be a standard administrative center, with an outer reception area and a honeycomb of comfy executive offices stacked behind it. To his mild surprise, he found himself instead in a fully equipped war room. Lining the walls were comm and tracking consoles, including at least one crystal grav-field trap receptor and what looked like the ranging control for a KDY v-150 Planet Defender ion cannon like the one the Alliance had had to abandon on Hoth. In the center of the room a large holo display showed a sector's worth of stars, with a hundred multicolored markers and vector lines scattered among the glittering white dots.

And standing beside the holo was a man.

His face was distorted somewhat by the strangely colored lights playing on it from the display; and it was, at any rate, a face Han had never seen except in pictures. But even so, recognition came with the sudden jolt of an overhead thunderclap. "Senator Bel Iblis," he breathed.

"Welcome to Peregrine's Nest, Captain Solo," the other said gravely, coming away from the holo toward him. "I'm flattered you still remember me."

"It'd be hard for any Corellian to forget you, sir," Han said, his numbed brain noting vaguely in passing that there were very few people in the galaxy who rated an automatic sir from him. "But you . . ."

"Were dead?" Bel Iblis suggested, a half smile creasing his lined face.

"Well—yes," Han floundered. "I mean, everyone thought you died on Anchoron."

"In a very real sense, I did," the other said quietly, the smile fading from his face. Closer now, Han was struck with just how lined with age and stress the Senator's face was. "The Emperor wasn't quite able to kill me at Anchoron, but he might just as well have done so. He took everything I had except my life: my family, my profession, even all future contacts with mainstream Corellian society. He forced me outside the law I'd worked so hard to create and maintain." The smile returned, like a hint of sunshine around the edge of a dark cloud. "Forced me to become a rebel. I imagine you understand the feeling."

"Pretty well, yeah," Han said, grinning lopsidedly in return. He'd read in school about the legendary presence of the equally legendary Senator Garm Bel Iblis; now, he was getting to see that charm up close. It made him feel like a schoolkid again. "I still can't believe this. I wish we'd known sooner—we could really have used this army of yours during the war."

For just a second a shadow seemed to cross Bel Iblis's face. "We probably couldn't have done much to help," he said. "It's taken us a good deal of time to build up to what you see here." His smile returned. "But there'll be time to talk about that later. Right now, I see you standing there trying to figure out exactly when it was we met."

Actually, Han had forgotten about Sena's references to a previous meeting. "Tell you the truth, I haven't got a clue," he confessed. "Unless it was after Anchoron and you were in disguise or something."

Bel Iblis shook his head. "No disguise; but it wasn't something I'd really expect you to remember. I'll give you a hint: you were all of eleven at the time."

Han blinked. "Eleven?" he echoed. "You mean in school?"

"Correct," Bel Iblis nodded. "Literally correct, in fact. It was at a convocation at your school, where you were being forced to listen to a group of us old fossils talk about politics."

Han felt his face warming. The specific memory was still a blank, but that *was* how he'd felt about politicians at that time in his life. Though come to think of it, the opinion hadn't changed all that much over the years. "I'm sorry, but I still don't remember."

"As I said, I didn't expect you to," Bel Iblis said. "I, on the other hand, remember the incident quite well. During the question period after the talk you asked two irreverently phrased yet highly pointed questions: the first regarding the ethics of the anti-alien bias starting to creep into the legal structure of the Republic, the second about some very specific instances of corruption involving my colleagues in the Senate."

It was starting to come back, at least in a vague sort of way. "Yeah, I remember now," Han said slowly. "I think one of my friends dared me to throw those questions at you. He probably figured I'd get in trouble for not being polite. I was in trouble enough that it didn't bother me."

"Setting your life pattern early, were you?" Bel Iblis suggested dryly. "At any rate, they weren't the sort of questions I would have expected from an eleven-year-old, and they intrigued me enough to ask about you. I've been keeping a somewhat loose eye on you ever since."

Han grimaced. "You probably weren't very impressed by what you saw."

"There were times," Bel Iblis agreed. "I'll admit to having been extremely disappointed when you were dismissed from the Imperial Academy—you'd shown considerable promise there, and I felt at the time that a strongly loyal officer corps was one of the few defenses the Republic still had left against the collapse toward Empire." He shrugged. "Under the circumstances, it's just as well that you got out when you did. With your obvious disdain for authority, you'd have been quietly eliminated in the Emperor's purge of those officers he hadn't been able to seduce to his side. And then things would have gone quite differently, wouldn't they?"

"Maybe a little," Han conceded modestly. He glanced around the war room. "So how long have you been here at—you called it Peregrine's Nest?"

"Oh, we never stay anywhere for very long," Bel Iblis said, clapping a hand on Han's shoulder and gently but firmly turning him toward the door. "Sit still too long and the Imperials will eventually find you. But we can talk business later. Right now, your friend outside is probably getting nervous. Come introduce me to him."

Lando was indeed looking a little tense as Han and Bel Iblis

stepped out into the sunlight again. "It's all right," Han assured him. "We're with friends. Senator, this is Lando Calrissian, one-time general of the Rebel Alliance. Lando; Senator
Garm Bel Iblis."

He hadn't expected Lando to recognize the name of a long-
past Corellian politician. He was right. "Senator Bel Iblis,"
Lando nodded, his voice neutral.

"Honored to meet you, General Calrissian," Bel Iblis said.
"I've heard a great deal about you."

Lando glanced at Han. "Just Calrissian," he said. "The
General is more a courtesy title now."

"Then we're even," Bel Iblis smiled. "I'm not a Senator
anymore, either." He waved a hand at Sena. "You've met my
chief adviser and unofficial ambassador-at-large, Sena
Leikvold Midanyl. And—" He paused, looking around. "I understood Irenez was with you."

"She was needed back at the ship, sir," Sena told him. "Our
other guest required some soothing."

"Yes; Council-Aide Breil'lya," Bel Iblis said, glancing in the
direction of the landing pad. "This could prove somewhat
awkward."

"Yes, sir," Sena said. "Perhaps I shouldn't have brought him
here, but at the time I didn't see any other reasonable course
of action."

"Oh, I agree," Bel Iblis assured her. "Leaving him in the
middle of an Imperial raid would have been more than simply
awkward."

Han felt a slight chill run through him. In the flush of excitement over meeting Bel Iblis, he'd completely forgotten
what had taken them to New Cov in the first place. "You seem
to be on good terms with Breil'lya, Senator," he said carefully.

Bel Iblis eyed him. "And you'd like to know just what those
good terms entail?"

Han steeled himself. "As a matter of fact, sir . . . yes, I
would."

The other smiled slightly. "You still have that underlying

refusal to flinch before authority, don't you. Good. Come on over to the headquarters lounge and I'll tell you anything you want to know." His smile hardened, just a little. "And after that, I'll have some questions to ask you, as well."

THE DOOR SLID OPEN, and Pellaeon stepped into the darkened antechamber of Thrawn's private command room. Darkened and apparently empty; but Pellaeon knew better than that. "I have important information for the Grand Admiral," he said loudly. "I don't have time for these little games of yours."

"They are not games," Rukh's gravelly voice mewed right in Pellaeon's ear, making him jump despite his best efforts not to. "Stalking skills must be practiced or lost."

"Practice on someone else," Pellaeon growled. "I have work to do."

He stepped forward to the inner door, silently cursing Rukh and the whole Noghri race. Useful tools of the Empire they might well be; but he'd dealt with this kind of close-knit clan structure before, and he'd never found such primitives to be anything but trouble in the long run. The door to the command room slid open—

Revealing a darkness lit only by softly glowing candles.

Pellaeon stopped abruptly, his mind flashing back to that eerie crypt on Wayland, where a thousand candles marked the graves of offworlders who had come there over the past few years, only to be slaughtered by Joruus C'baoth. For Thrawn to have turned his command room into a duplicate of that . . .

"No, I haven't come under the influence of our unstable Jedi Master," Thrawn's voice came dryly across the room. Over the candles, Pellaeon could just see the Grand Admiral's glowing red eyes. "Look closer."

Pellaeon did as instructed, to discover that the "candles" were in fact holographic images of exquisitely delicate lighted sculptures. "Beautiful, aren't they?" Thrawn said, his voice meditative. "They're Corellian flame miniatures, one of that

very short list of art forms which others have tried to copy but
never truly been able to duplicate. Nothing more than shaped
transoptical fibers, pseudoluminescent plant material, and a
pair of Goorlish light sources, really; and yet, somehow, there's
something about them that's never been captured by anyone
else." The holographic flames faded away, and in the center of
the room a frozen image of three Dreadnaught cruisers appeared. "This was taken by the *Relentless* two days ago off the
planet New Cov, Captain," Thrawn continued in the same
thoughtful tone. "Watch closely."

He started the recording. Pellaeon watched in silence as the
Dreadnaughts, in triangular formation, opened fire with ion
cannons toward the camera's point of view. Almost hidden in
the fury of the assault, a freighter and what looked like a small
pleasure yacht could be seen skittering to safety down the middle of the formation. Still firing, the Dreadnaughts began
drawing back, and a minute later the whole group had jumped
to lightspeed. The holo faded away, and the room lights came
up to a gentle glow. "Comments?" Thrawn invited.

"Looks like our old friends are back," Pellaeon said. "They
seem to have recovered from that scare we gave them at Linuri.
A nuisance, especially right now."

"Unfortunately, indications are that they're about to become more than just a nuisance," Thrawn told him. "One of
the two ships they were rescuing was identified by the *Relentless* as the *Lady Luck*. With Han Solo and Lando Calrissian
aboard."

Pellaeon frowned. "Solo and Calrissian? But—" He broke
off sharply.

"But they were supposed to go to the Palanhi system,"
Thrawn finished for him. "Yes. An error on my part. Obviously, something more important came up than their concerns
for Ackbar's reputation."

Pellaeon looked back at where the holo had been. "Such as
adding new strength to the Rebellion military."

"I don't believe they've merged quite yet," Thrawn said, his forehead furrowed with thought. "Nor do I believe such an alliance is inevitable. That was a Corellian leading that task force, Captain—I'm sure of that now. And there are only a few possibilities as to just who that Corellian might be."

A stray memory clicked. "Solo is Corellian, isn't he?"

"Yes," Thrawn confirmed. "One reason I think they're still in the negotiation stage. If their leader is who I suspect, he might well prefer sounding out a fellow Corellian before making any commitment to the Rebellion's leaders."

To Thrawn's left, the comm pinged. "Admiral Thrawn? We have the contact you requested with the *Relentless*."

"Thank you," Thrawn said, tapping a switch. In front of the double circle of repeater displays a three-quarter-sized hologram of an elderly Imperial officer appeared, standing next to what appeared to be a detention block control board. "Grand Admiral," the image said, nodding gravely.

"Good day, Captain Dorja," Thrawn nodded back. "You have the prisoner I asked for?"

"Right here, sir," Dorja said. He glanced to the side and gestured; and from off-camera a rather bulky human appeared, his hands shackled in front of him, his expression studiously neutral behind his neatly trimmed beard. "His name's Niles Ferrier," Dorja said. "We picked him and his crew up during the raid on New Cov."

"The raid from which Skywalker, Solo, and Calrissian escaped," Thrawn said.

Dorja winced. "Yes, sir."

Thrawn shifted his attention to Ferrier. "Captain Ferrier," he nodded. "Our records indicate that you specialize in spaceship theft. Yet you were picked up on New Cov with a cargo of biomolecules aboard your ship. Would you care to explain?"

Ferrier shrugged fractionally. "Palming ships isn't something you can do every day," he said. "It takes opportunities and planning. Taking the occasional shipping job helps make ends meet."

"You're aware, of course, that the biomolecules were undeclared."

"Yes, Captain Dorja told me that," Ferrier said with just the right mixture of astonishment and indignation. "Believe me, if I'd known I was being made a party to such cheating against the Empire—"

"I presume you're also aware," Thrawn cut him off, "that for such actions I can not only confiscate your cargo, but also your ship."

Ferrier was aware of that, all right. Pellaeon could see it in the pinched look around his eyes. "I've been very helpful to the Empire in the past, Admiral," he said evenly. "I've smuggled in loads of contraband from the New Republic, and only recently delivered three Sienar patrol ships to your people."

"And were paid outrageous sums of money in all cases," Thrawn reminded him. "If you're trying to suggest we owe you for past kindnesses, don't bother. However . . . there may be a way for you to pay back this new debt. Did you happen to notice the ships attacking the *Relentless* as you were trying to sneak away from the planet?"

"Of course I did," Ferrier said, a touch of wounded professional pride creeping into his voice. "They were Rendili StarDrive Dreadnaughts. Old ones, by the look of them, but spry enough. Probably undergone a lot of refitting."

"They have indeed." Thrawn smiled slightly. "I want them."

It took Ferrier a handful of seconds for the offhanded sounding comment to register. When it did, his mouth dropped open. "You mean . . . *me*?"

"Do you have a problem with that?" Thrawn asked coldly.

"Uh . . ." Ferrier swallowed. "Admiral, with all due respect—"

"You have three standard months to get me either those ships or else their precise location," Thrawn cut him off. "Captain Dorja?"

Dorja stepped forward again. "Sir."

"You will release Captain Ferrier and his crew and supply them with an unmarked Intelligence freighter to use. Their own ship will remain aboard the *Relentless* until they've completed their mission."

"Understood," Dorja nodded.

Thrawn cocked an eyebrow. "One other thing, Captain Ferrier. On the off chance that you might feel yourself tempted to abandon the assignment and make a run for it, the freighter you'll be given will be equipped with an impressive and totally unbreakable doomsday mechanism. With exactly three standard months set on its clock. I trust you understand."

Above his beard, Ferrier's face had gone a rather sickly white. "Yes," he managed.

"Good." Thrawn shifted his attention back to Dorja. "I leave the details in your hands, Captain. Keep me informed of developments."

He tapped a switch, and the hologram faded away. "As I said, Captain," Thrawn said, turning to Pellaeon. "I don't think an alliance with the Rebellion is necessarily inevitable."

"If Ferrier can pull it off," Pellaeon said doubtfully.

"He has a reasonable chance," Thrawn assured him. "After all, we have a general idea ourselves of where they might be hidden. We just don't have the time and manpower at the moment to properly root them out. Even if we did, a large-scale attack would probably end up destroying the Dreadnaughts, and I'd rather capture them intact."

"Yes, sir," Pellaeon said grimly. The word *capture* had reminded him of why he'd come here in the first place. "Admiral, the report on Khabarakh's ship has come in from the scanning team." He held the data card over the double display circle.

For a moment Thrawn's glowing red eyes burned into Pellaeon's face, as if trying to read the reason for his subordinate's obvious tension. Then, wordlessly, he took the data card from the captain's hand and slid it into his reader. Pellaeon waited, tight-lipped, as the Grand Admiral skimmed the report.

Thrawn reached the end and leaned back in his seat, his face unreadable. "Wookiee hairs," he said.

"Yes, sir," Pellaeon nodded. "All over the ship."

Thrawn was silent another few heartbeats. "Your interpretation?"

Pellaeon braced himself. "I can only see one, sir. Khabarakh didn't escape from the Wookiees on Kashyyyk at all. They caught him . . . and then let him go."

"After a month of imprisonment." Thrawn looked up at Pellaeon. "And interrogation."

"Almost certainly," Pellaeon agreed. "The question is, what did he tell them?"

"There's one way to find out." Thrawn tapped on the comm. "Hangar bay, this is the Grand Admiral. Prepare my shuttle; I'm going to the surface. I'll want a troop shuttle and double squad of stormtroopers ready to accompany me, plus two flights of Scimitar assault bombers to provide air cover."

He got an acknowledgment and keyed off. "It may be, Captain, that the Noghri have forgotten where their loyalties lie," he told Pellaeon, standing up and stepping out around the displays. "I think it's time they were reminded that the Empire commands here. You'll return to the bridge and prepare a suitable demonstration."

"Yes, sir." Pellaeon hesitated. "Do you want merely a reminder and not actual destruction?"

Thrawn's eyes blazed. "For the moment, yes," he said, his voice icy. "Let them all pray that I don't change my mind."

CHAPTER 12

I T WAS THE SMELL Leia noticed first as she drifted slowly
awake: a smoky smell, reminiscent of the wood fires of the
Ewoks of Endor but with a tangy sharpness all its own. A
warm, homey sort of aroma, reminding her of the campouts
she'd had as a child on Alderaan.

And then she woke up enough to remember where she was.
Full consciousness flooded in, and she snapped open her
eyes—

To find herself lying on a rough pallet in a corner of the
Noghri communal bake house. Exactly where she'd been when
she'd fallen asleep the night before.

She sat up, feeling relieved and a little ashamed. What with
that unexpected visit last night by the Grand Admiral, she realized she'd half expected to wake up in a Star Destroyer detention cell. Clearly, she'd underestimated the Noghri's ability
to stick by their promises.

Her stomach growled, reminding her it had been a long
time since she'd eaten; a little lower down, one of the twins

kicked a reminder of his own. "Okay," she soothed. "I get the hint. Breakfast time."

She tore the top off a ration bar from one of her cases and took a bite, looking around the bake house as she chewed. Against the wall by the door, the double pallet that had been laid out for Chewbacca to sleep on was empty. For a moment the fear of betrayal again whispered to her; but a little concentration through the Force silenced any concerns. Chewbacca was somewhere nearby, with a sense that gave no indication of danger. *Relax*, she ordered herself sternly, pulling a fresh jumpsuit out of her case and starting to get dressed. Whatever these Noghri were, it was clear they weren't savages. They were honorable people, in their own way, and they wouldn't turn her over to the Empire. At least, not until they'd heard her out.

She downed the last bite of ration bar and finished dressing, making sure as always that her belt didn't hang too heavily across her increasingly swollen belly. Retrieving her lightsaber from its hiding place under the edge of the pallet, she fastened it prominently to her side. Khabarakh, she remembered, had seemed to find reassurance of her identity in the presence of the Jedi weapon; hopefully, the rest of the Noghri would also respond that way. Stepping to the bake house door, she ran through her Jedi calming exercises and went outside.

Three small Noghri children were playing with an inflatable ball in the grassy area outside the door, their grayish-white skin glistening with perspiration in the bright morning sunlight. A sunlight that wasn't going to last, Leia saw: a uniform layer of dark clouds extending all the way to the west was even now creeping its way east toward the rising sun. All for the best; a thick layer of clouds would block any direct telescopic observations the Star Destroyer up there might make of the village, as well as diffusing the non-Noghri infrared signatures she and Chewbacca were giving off.

She looked back down, to find that the three children had halted their game and formed a straight line in front of her. "Hello," she said, trying a smile on them.

The child in the middle stepped forward and dropped to his knees in an awkward but passable imitation of his elders' gesture of respect. "*Mal'ary'ush*," he mewed. "*Miskh'hara isf chrak'mi'sokh. Mir'es kha.*"

"I see," Leia said, wishing fervently that she had Threepio with her. She was just wondering if she should risk calling him on the comlink when the child spoke again. "Hai ghreet yhou, *Mal'ary'ush*," he said, the Basic words coming out mangled but understandable. "The maitrakh whaits for yhou hin the *dukha*."

"Thank you," Leia nodded gravely to him. Door wardens last night; official greeters this morning. Noghri children seemed to be introduced early into the rituals and responsibilities of their culture. "Please escort me to her."

The child made the respect gesture again and got back to his feet, heading off toward the large circular structure that Khabarakh had landed next to the night before. Leia followed, the other two children taking up positions to either side of her. She found herself throwing short glances, at them as they walked, wondering at the light color of their skin. Khabarakh's skin was a steel gray; the maitrakh's had been much darker. Did the Noghri consist of several distinct racial types? Or was the darkening a natural part of their aging process? She made a mental note to ask Khabarakh about it when she had a chance.

The *dukha*, seen now in full daylight, was far more elaborate than she'd realized. The pillars spaced every few meters around the wall seemed to be composed of whole sections of tree trunk, stripped of bark and smoothed to a black marble finish. The shimmery wood that made up the rest of the wall was covered to perhaps half its height with intricate carvings. As they got closer, she could see that the reinforcing metal band that encircled the building just beneath the eaves was also decorated—clearly, the Noghri believed in combining function and art. The whole structure was perhaps twenty meters across and four meters high, with another three or four meters for the conical roof, and she found herself wondering how many more pillars they'd had to put inside to support the thing.

Tall double doors had been built into the wall between two of the pillars, flanked at the moment by two straight-backed Noghri children. They pulled open the doors as Leia approached; nodding her thanks, she stepped inside.

The interior of the *dukha* was no less impressive than its exterior. It was a single open room, with a thronelike chair two-thirds of the way to the back, a small booth with an angled roof and a dark-meshed window built against the wall between two of the pillars to the right, and a wall chart of some sort directly across from it on the left. There were no internal support pillars; instead, a series of heavy chains had been strung from the top of each of the wall pillars to the edge of a large concave dish hanging over the center of the room. From inside the dish—just inside its rim, Leia decided—hidden lights played upward against the ceiling, providing a softly diffuse illumination.

A few meters in front of the chart a group of perhaps twenty small children were sitting in a semicircle around Threepio, who was holding forth in their language with what was obviously some kind of story, complete with occasional sound effects. It brought to mind the condensed version of their struggle against the Empire that he'd given the Ewoks, and Leia hoped the droid would remember not to vilify Darth Vader here. Presumably he would; she'd drummed the point into him often enough during the voyage.

A small movement off to the left caught her eye: Chewbacca and Khabarakh were sitting facing each other on the other side of the door, engaged in some kind of quiet activity that seemed to involve hands and wrists. The Wookiee had paused and was looking questioningly in her direction. Leia nodded her assurance that she was all right, trying to read from his sense just what he and Khabarakh were doing. At least it didn't seem to involve ripping the Noghri's arms out of their sockets; that was something, anyway.

"Lady Vader," a gravelly Noghri voice said. Leia turned back to see the maitrakh walking up to her. "I greet you. You slept well?"

"Quite well," Leia told her. "Your hospitality has been most honorable." She looked over at Threepio, wondering if she should call him back to his duties as translator.

The maitrakh misunderstood. "It is the history time for the children," she said. "Your machine graciously volunteered to tell to them the last story of our lord Darth Vader."

Vader's final, self-sacrificial defiance against the Emperor, with Luke's life hanging in the balance. "Yes," Leia murmured. "It took until the end, but he was finally able to rid himself of the Emperor's web of deception."

For a moment the maitrakh was silent. Then, she stirred. "Walk with me, Lady Vader." She turned and began walking along the wall. Leia joined her, noticing for the first time that the *dukha*'s inner walls were decorated with carvings, too. A historical record of their family? "My thirdson has gained a new respect for your Wookiee," she said, gesturing toward Chewbacca and Khabarakh. "Our lord the Grand Admiral came last eve seeking proof that my thirdson had deceived him about his flying craft being broken. Because of your Wookiee, he found no such proof."

Leia nodded. "Yes, Chewie told me last night about gimmicking the ship. I don't have his knowledge of spaceship mechanics, but I know it can't be easy to fake a pair of linked malfunctions the way he did. It's fortunate for all of us he had the foresight and skill to do so."

"The Wookiee is not of your family or clan," the maitrakh said. "Yet you trust him, as if he were a friend?"

Leia took a deep breath. "I never knew my true father, the Lord Vader, as I was growing up. I was instead taken to Alderaan and raised by the Viceroy as if I were his own child. On Alderaan, as seems to also be the case here, family relationships were the basis of our culture and society. I grew up memorizing lists of aunts and uncles and cousins, learning how to place them in order of closeness to my adoptive line." She gestured to Chewbacca. "Chewie was once merely a good friend. Now, he is part of my family. As much a part as my husband and brother are."

They were perhaps a quarter of the way around the *dukha* before the maitrakh spoke again. "Why have you come here?"

"Khabarakh told me his people needed help," Leia said simply. "I thought there might be something I could do."

"Some will say you have come to sow discord among us."

"You said that yourself last night," Leia reminded her. "I can only give you my word that discord is not my intention."

The maitrakh made a long hissing sound that ended with a sharp double click of needle teeth. "The goal and the end are not always the same, Lady Vader. Now we serve one overclan only. You would require service to another. This is the seed of discord and death."

Leia pursed her lips. "Does service to the Empire satisfy you, then?" she asked. "Does it gain your people better life or higher honor?"

"We serve the Empire as one clan," the maitrakh said. "For you to demand our service would be to bring back the conflicts of old." They had reached the wall chart now, and she gestured a thin hand up toward it. "Do you see our history, Lady Vader?"

Leia craned her neck to look. Neatly carved lines of alien script covered the bottom two-thirds of the wall, with each word connected to a dozen others in a bewildering crisscross of vertical, horizontal, and angled lines, each cut seemingly of a different width and depth. Then she got it: the chart was a genealogical tree, either of the entire clan Kihm'bar or else just this particular family. "I see it," she said.

"Then you see the terrible destruction of life created by the conflicts of old," the maitrakh said. She gestured to three or four places on the chart which were, to Leia, indistinguishable from the rest of the design. Reading Noghri genealogies was apparently an acquired skill. "I do not wish to return to those days," the maitrakh continued. "Not even for the daughter of the Lord Darth Vader."

"I understand," Leia said quietly, shivering as the ghosts of Yavin, Hoth, Endor, and a hundred more rose up before her. "I've seen more conflict and death in my lifetime than I ever thought possible. I have no wish to add to the list."

"Then you must leave," the maitrakh said firmly. "You must leave and not come back while the Empire lives."

They began to walk again. "Is there no alternative?" Leia asked. "What if I could persuade all of your people to leave their service to the Empire? There would be no conflict then among you."

"The Emperor aided us when no one else would," the maitrakh reminded her.

"That was only because we didn't know about your need," Leia said, feeling a twinge of conscience at the half truth. Yes, the Alliance had truly not known about the desperate situation here; and yes, Mon Mothma and the other leaders would certainly have wanted to help if they had. But whether they would have had the resources to actually do anything was another question entirely. "We know now, and we offer you our help."

"Do you offer us aid for our own sakes?" the maitrakh asked pointedly. "Or merely to wrest our service from the Empire to your overclan? We will not be fought over like a bone among hungry *stava*."

"The Emperor used you," Leia said flatly. "As the Grand Admiral uses you now. Has the aid they've given been worth the sons they've taken from you and sent off to die?"

They had gone another twenty steps or so before the maitrakh answered. "Our sons have gone," she said softly. "But with their service they have bought us life. You came in a flying craft, Lady Vader. You saw what was done to our land."

"Yes," Leia said with a shiver. "It—I hadn't realized how widespread the destruction had been."

"Life on Honoghr has always been a struggle," the maitrakh said. "The land has required much labor to tame. You saw on the history the times when the struggle was lost. But after the battle in the sky . . ."

She shuddered, a peculiar kind of shaking that seemed to move from her hips upward to her shoulders. "It was like a war between gods. We know now that it was only large flying craft high above the land. But then we knew nothing of such things. Their lightning flashed across the sky, through the night and into the next day, brightening the distant mountains with their fury. And yet, there was no thunder, as if those same gods were too angry even to shout at each other as they fought. I remember being more frightened of the silence than of any other part of it. Only once was there a distant crash like thunder. It was much later before we learned that one of our higher mountains had lost its uppermost peak. Then the lightning stopped, and we dared to hope that the gods had taken their war away from us.

"Until the groundshake came."

She paused, another shudder running through her. "The lightning had been the anger of the gods. The groundshake was their war hammer. Whole cities vanished as the ground opened up beneath them. Fire-mountains that had been long quiet sent out flame and smoke that darkened the sky over all the land. Forests and fields burned, as did cities and villages that had survived the groundshake itself. From those who had died came sickness, and still more died after them. It was as if the fury of the sky gods had come among the gods of the land, and they too were fighting among themselves.

"And then, when finally we dared to hope it was over, the strange-smelling rain began to fall."

Leia nodded, the whole sequence of events painfully clear.

One of the warring ships had crashed, setting off massive earthquakes and releasing toxic chemicals which had been carried by wind and rain to every part of the planet. There were any number of such chemicals in use aboard a modern warship, but it was only the older ships that carried anything as virulent as this chemical must have been.

Older ships . . . which had been virtually all the Rebel Alliance had had to fight with in the beginning.

A fresh surge of guilt twisted like a blade in her stomach. *We did this*, she thought miserably. *Our ship. Our fault.* "Was it the rain that killed the plants?"

"The Empire's people had a name for what was in the rain," the maitrakh said. "I do not know what it was."

"They came soon after the disaster, then. The Lord Vader and the others."

"Yes." The maitrakh waved her hands to encompass the area around them. "We had gathered together here, all who were left alive and could make the journey. This place had always been a truce ground between clans. We had come here to try to find a way for survival. It was here that the Lord Vader found us."

They walked in silence for another minute. "Some believed then that he was a god," the maitrakh said. "All feared him and the mighty silver flying craft that had brought him and his attendants from the sky. But even amid the fear there was anger at what the gods had done to us, and nearly two tens of warriors chose to attack."

"And were duly slaughtered," Leia said grimly. The thought of effectively unarmed primitives taking on Imperial troops made her wince.

"They were not slaughtered," the maitrakh retorted, and there was no mistaking the pride in her voice. "Only three of the two tens died in the battle. In turn, they killed many of the Lord Vader's attendants, despite their lightning-weapons and rock-garments. It was only when the Lord Vader himself intervened that the warriors were defeated. But instead of destroying us, as some of the attendants counseled, he instead offered us peace. Peace, and the blessing and aid of the Emperor."

Leia nodded, one more piece of the puzzle falling into place. She had wondered why the Emperor would have bothered with what to him would have been nothing more than a tiny group of primitive nonhumans. But primitive nonhumans with that kind of natural fighting skill were something else entirely. "What sort of aid did he bring?"

"All that we needed," the maitrakh said. "Food and medicine and tools came at once. Later, when the strange rain began to kill our crops, he sent the metal droids to begin cleaning the poison from our land."

Leia winced, freshly aware of her twins' vulnerability. But the analysis kit had found no trace of anything toxic in the air as they approached the village, and Chewbacca and Khabarakh had done similar tests on the soil. Whatever it was that had been in the rain, the decon droids had done a good job of getting rid of it. "And still nothing will grow outside the cleaned land?"

"Only the *kholm*-grass," the maitrakh said. "It is a poor plant, of no use as food. But it alone can grow now, and even it no longer smells as it once did."

Which explained the uniform brown color that she and Chewbacca had seen from space. Somehow, that particular plant had adapted to the toxic soil. "Did any of the animals survive?" she asked.

"Some did. Those who could eat the *kholm*-grass, and those which in turn ate them. But they are few."

The maitrakh lifted her head, as if looking in her mind's eye toward the distant hills. "This place was never rich with life, Lady Vader. Perhaps that was why the clans had chosen it as a truce ground. But even in so desolate a place there were still animals and plants without count. They are gone now."

She straightened up, visibly putting the memory behind her. "The Lord Vader helped us in other ways, as well. He sent attendants to teach our sons and daughters the ways and customs of the Empire. He issued new orders to allow all clans to share the Clean Land, though for all clans to live beside one another this way had never happened since the beginning." She gestured around her. "And he sent mighty flying craft into the desolation, to find and bring to us our clan *dukhas*."

She turned her dark eyes to gaze at Leia. "We have an honorable peace, Lady Vader. Whatever the cost, we pay it gladly."

Across the room, the children had apparently finished their lesson and were getting to their feet. One of them spoke to Threepio, making a sort of truncated version of their facedown bow. The droid replied, and the whole group turned and headed for the door, where two adults awaited them. "Break time?" Leia asked.

"The clan lessons are over for today," the maitrakh said. "The children must now begin their share of the work of the village. Later, in the evening, they will have the lessons which will equip them to someday serve the Empire."

Leia shook her head. "It's not right," she told the maitrakh as the children filed out of the *dukha*. "No people should have to sell their children in return for life."

The maitrakh gave a long hiss. "It is the debt we owe," she said. "How else shall we pay it?"

Leia squeezed her thumb and forefinger together. How else, indeed? Clearly, the Empire was quite happy with the bargain it had made; and having seen the Noghri commandos in action, she could well understand its satisfaction. They wouldn't be interested in letting the Noghri buy out of their debt in any other way. And if the Noghri themselves considered their service to be a debt of honor to their saviors . . . "I don't know," she had to concede.

A movement to the side caught her attention: Khabarakh, still sitting on the floor across the room, had fallen over onto his side, with Chewbacca's hand engulfing his wrist. It looked like fighting, except that Chewbacca's sense didn't indicate anger. "What *are* they doing over there?" she asked.

"Your Wookiee has asked my thirdson to instruct him in our fighting methods," the maitrakh answered, pride again touching her voice. "Wookiees have great strength, but no knowledge of the subtlety of combat."

It was probably not an assessment the Wookiees themselves would have agreed with. But Leia had to admit that Chewbacca, at least, had always seemed to rely mainly on brute force and bowcaster accuracy. "I'm surprised he was willing to have Khabarakh teach him," she said. "He's never really trusted him."

"Perhaps it is that same distrust that whets his interest," the maitrakh said dryly.

Leia had to smile. "Perhaps."

For a minute they watched in silence as Khabarakh showed Chewbacca two more wrist and arm locks. They seemed to be variants of techniques Leia had learned in her youth on Alderaan, and she shivered once at the thought of those moves with Wookiee muscle behind them. "You understand the cycle of our life now, Lady Vader," the maitrakh said quietly. "You must realize that we still hang by spider silk. Even now we do not have enough clean land to grow sufficient food. We must continue to buy from the Empire."

"Payment for which requires that much more service from your sons." Leia nodded, grimacing. Permanent debt—the oldest form of covert slavery in the galaxy.

"It also encourages the sending away of our sons," the maitrakh added bitterly. "Even if the Empire allowed it, we could not now bring all our sons home. We would not have food for them."

Leia nodded again. It was as neat and tidy a box as she'd ever seen anyone trapped in. She should have expected no less from Vader and the Emperor. "You'll never be entirely out of their debt," she told the maitrakh bluntly. "You know that, don't you? As long as you're useful to them, the Grand Admiral will make sure of that."

"Yes," the maitrakh said softly. "It has taken a long time,

but I now believe that. If all Noghri believed so, changes could perhaps be made."

"But the rest of the Noghri still believe the Empire is their friend?"

"Not all believe so. But cnough." She stopped and gestured upward. "Do you see the starlight, Lady Vader?"

Leia looked up at the concave dish that hung four meters off the ground at the intersection of the wall support chains. About a meter and a half across, it was composed of some kind of black or blackened metal and perforated with hundreds of tiny pinholes. With the light from the inside rim of the dish winking through like stars, the whole effect was remarkably like a stylized version of the night sky. "I see it."

"The Noghri have always loved the stars," the maitrakh said, her voice distant and reflective. "Once, long ago, we worshiped them. Even after we knew what they were they remained our friends. There were many among us who would have gladly gone with the Lord Vader, even without our debt, for the joy of traveling among them."

"I understand," Leia murmured. "Many in the galaxy feel the same way. It's the common birthright of us all."

"A birthright which we have now lost."

"Not lost," Leia said, dropping her gaze from the star dish. "Only misplaced." She looked over at Khabarakh and Chewbacca. "Perhaps if I talked to all the Noghri leaders at once."

"What would you say to them?" the maitrakh countered.

Leia bit at her lip. What *would* she say? That the Empire was using them? But the Noghri perceived it as a debt of honor. That the Empire was pacing the cleanup job so as to keep them on the edge of self-sufficiency without ever reaching it? But at the rate the decontamination was going she would be hard-pressed to prove any such lagging, even to herself. That she and the New Republic could give the Noghri back their birthright? But why should they believe her?

"As you see, Lady Vader," the maitrakh said into the silence. "Perhaps matters will someday change. But until then, your presence here is a danger to us as much as to you. I will honor the pledge of protection made by my thirdson, and not reveal your presence to our lord the Grand Admiral. But you must leave."

Leia took a deep breath. "Yes," she said, the word hurting her throat. She'd had such hopes for her diplomatic and Jedi skills here. Hopes that those skills, plus the accident of her lineage, would enable her to sweep the Noghri out from under the Empire's fist and bring them over to the New Republic.

And now the contest was over, almost before it had even begun. *What in space was I thinking about when I came here?* she wondered bleakly. "I will leave," she said aloud, "because I don't wish to bring trouble to you or your family. But the day will come, maitrakh, when your people will see for themselves what the Empire is doing to them. When that happens, remember that I'll always be ready to assist you."

The maitrakh bowed low. "Perhaps that day will come soon, Lady Vader. I await it, as do others."

Leia nodded, forcing a smile. Over before it had begun . . . "Then we must make arrangements to—"

She broke off as, across the room, the double doors flew open and one of the child door wardens stumbled inside. *"Maitrakh!"* he all but squealed. *"Mira'kh saar khee hrach'mani vher ahk!"*

Khabarakh was on his feet in an instant; out of the corner of her eye, Leia saw Threepio stiffen. "What is it?" she demanded.

"It is the flying craft of our lord the Grand Admiral," the maitrakh said, her face and voice suddenly very tired and very alien.

"And it is coming here."

CHAPTER 13

FOR A SINGLE heartbeat Leia stared at the maitrakh, her muscles frozen with shock, her mind skidding against the idea as if walking on ice. No—it couldn't be. It *couldn't*. The Grand Admiral had been here just last night—surely he wouldn't be coming back again. Not so soon.

And then, in the distance, she heard the faint sound of approaching repulsorlifts, and the paralysis vanished. "We've got to get out of here," she said. "Chewie—?"

"There is no time," Khabarakh called, sprinting toward them with Chewbacca right on his heels. "The shuttle must already be in sight beneath the clouds."

Leia looked quickly around the room, silently cursing her moment of indecision. No windows; no other doors; no cover except the small booth that faced the wall genealogy chart from across the *dukha*.

No way out.

"Are you certain he's coming here?" Leia asked Khabarakh, realizing as she spoke that the question was a waste of breath. "Here to the *dukha*, I mean?"

"Where else would he come?" Khabarakh countered darkly, his eyes on the maitrakh. "Perhaps he was not fooled, as we thought."

Leia looked around the *dukha* again. If the shuttle landed by the double doors, there would be a few seconds before the Imperials entered when the rear of the building would be out of their view. If she used those seconds to cut them an escape hole with her lightsaber . . .

Chewbacca's growled suggestion echoed her own train of thought. "Yes, but cutting a hole isn't the problem," she pointed out. "It's how to seal it up afterward."

The Wookiee growled again, jabbing a massive hand toward the booth. "Well, it'll hide the hole from the inside, anyway," Leia agreed doubtfully. "I suppose that's better than nothing." She looked at the maitrakh, suddenly aware that slicing away part of their ancient clan *dukha* might well qualify as sacrilege. "Maitrakh—"

"If it must be done, then be it so," the Noghri cut her off harshly. She was still in shock herself; but even as Leia watched she visibly drew herself together again. "You must not be found here."

Leia bit at the inside of her lip. She'd seen that same expression several times on Khabarakh's face during the trip from Endor. It was a look she'd come to interpret as regret for his decision to bring her to his home. "We'll be as neat as possible," she assured the maitrakh, pulling her lightsaber from her belt. "And as soon as the Grand Admiral is gone, Khabarakh can get his ship back and take us away—"

She broke off as Chewbacca snarled for silence. Faintly, in the distance, they could hear the sound of the approaching shuttle; and then, suddenly, another all-too-familiar whine shot past the *dukha*.

"Scimitar assault bombers," Leia breathed, hearing in the whine the crumbling of her impromptu plan. With Imperial bombers flying cover overhead, it would be impossible for them to sneak out of the *dukha* without being spotted.

Which left them only one option. "We'll have to hide in the booth," she told Chewbacca, doing a quick estimation of its size as she hurried toward it. If the slanting roof that sloped upward from the front edge back to the *dukha* wall wasn't just for show, there should be barely enough room for both her and Chewbacca inside—

"Will you want me in there as well, Your Highness?"

Leia skidded to a halt, spinning around in shock and chagrin. Threepio—she'd forgotten all about him.

"There will not be room enough," the maitrakh hissed. "Your presence here has betrayed us, Lady Vader—"

"Quiet!" Leia snapped, throwing another desperate look around the *dukha*. But there was still no other place to hide.

Unless . . .

She looked at the star dish hanging over the middle of the room. "We'll have to put him up there," she told Chewbacca, pointing to it. "Do you think you can—?"

There was no need to finish the question. Chewbacca had already grabbed Threepio and was heading at top speed toward the nearest of the tree-trunk pillars, throwing the frantically protesting droid over his shoulder as he ran. The Wookiee leaped upward at the pillar from two meters out, his hidden climbing claws anchoring him solidly to the wood. Three quick pulls got him to the top of the wall; and, with the half hysterical droid balanced precariously, he began to race hand over hand along the chain. "Quiet, Threepio," Leia called to him from the booth door, giving the interior a quick look. The ceiling did indeed follow the slanting roof, giving the back of the booth considerably more height than the front, and there was a low benchlike seat across the back wall. A tight fit, but they should make it. "Better yet, shut down—they may have sensors going," she added.

Though if they did, the whole game was over already. Listening to the approaching whine of repulsorlifts, she could only hope that after the negative sensor scan from the previous night, they wouldn't bother doing another one.

Chewbacca had reached the center now. Pulling himself partway up on the chain with one hand, he unceremoniously dumped Threepio into the star dish. The droid gave one last screech of protest, a screech that broke off halfway through as the Wookiee reached into the dish and shut him off. Dropping back to the floor with a thud, he hit the ground running as the repulsorlifts outside went silent.

"Hurry!" Leia hissed, holding the door open for him. Chewbacca made it across the *dukha* and dived through the narrow opening, jumping up on the bench and turning around to face forward, his head jammed up against the sloping ceiling and his legs spread to both sides of the bench. Leia slid in behind him, sitting down in the narrow gap between the Wookiee's legs.

There was just enough time to ease the door closed before the double doors a quarter of the way around the *dukha* slammed open.

Leia pressed against the back wall of the booth and Chewbacca's legs, forcing herself to breathe slowly and quietly and running through the Jedi sensory enhancement techniques Luke had taught her. From above her Chewbacca's breathing rasped in her ears, the heat from his body flowing like an invisible waterfall onto her head and shoulders. She was suddenly and acutely aware of the weight and bulge of her belly and of the small movements of the twins within it; of the hardness of the bench she was sitting on; of the intermingling smells of Wookiee hair, the alien wood around her, and her own sweat. Behind her, through the wall of the *dukha*, she could hear the sound of purposeful footsteps and the occasional clink of laser rifles against stormtrooper armor, and said silent thanks that they'd scrubbed her earlier plan of trying to escape that way.

And from the inside of the *dukha*, she could hear voices.

"Good morning, maitrakh," a calm, coolly modulated voice said. "I see that your thirdson, Khabarakh, is here with you. How very convenient."

Leia shivered, the rough rubbing of her tunic against her skin horribly loud in her ears. That voice had the unmistakable tone of an Imperial commander, but with a calmness and sheer weight of authority behind it. An authority that surpassed even the smug condescension she'd faced from Governor Tarkin aboard the Death Star.

It could only be the Grand Admiral.

"I greet you, my lord," the maitrakh's voice mewed, her own tone rigidly controlled. "We are honored by your visit."

"Thank you," the Grand Admiral said, his tone still polite but with a new edge of steel beneath it. "And you, Khabarakh clan Kihm'bar. Are you also pleased at my presence here?"

Slowly, carefully, Leia eased her head to the right, hoping to get a look at the newcomer through the dark mesh of the booth window. No good; they were all still over by the double doors, and she didn't dare get her face too close to the mesh. But even as she eased back to her previous position there was the sound of measured footsteps . . . and a moment later, in the center of the *dukha*, the Grand Admiral came into view.

Leia stared at him through the mesh, an icy chill running straight through her. She'd heard Han's description of the man he'd seen on Myrkr—the pale blue skin, the glowing red eyes, the white Imperial uniform. She'd heard, too, Fey'lya's casual dismissal of the man as an impostor, or at best a self-promoted Moff. And she'd wondered privately if Han might indeed have been mistaken.

She knew now that he hadn't been.

"Of course, my lord," Khabarakh answered the Grand Admiral's question. "Why should I not be?"

"Do you speak to your lord the Grand Admiral in such a tone?" an unfamiliar Noghri voice demanded.

"I apologize," Khabarakh said. "I did not mean disrespect."

Leia winced. Undoubtedly not; but the damage was already done. Even with her relative inexperience of the subtleties of Noghri speech, the words had sounded too quick and too defensive. To the Grand Admiral, who knew this race far better than she did . . .

"What then *did* you mean?" the Grand Admiral asked, turning around to face Khabarakh and the maitrakh.

"I—" Khabarakh floundered. The Grand Admiral stood silently, waiting. "I am sorry, my lord," Khabarakh finally got out. "I was overawed by your visit to our simple village."

"An obvious excuse," the Grand Admiral said. "Possibly even a believable one . . . except that you weren't overawed by my visit last night." He cocked an eyebrow. "Or is it that you didn't expect to face me again so soon?"

"My lord—"

"What is the Noghri penalty for lying to the lord of your overclan?" the Grand Admiral interrupted, his cool voice suddenly harsh. "Is it death, as it was in the old days? Or do the Noghri no longer prize such outdated concepts as honor?"

"My lord has no right to bring such accusations against a son of the clan Kihm'bar," the maitrakh spoke up stiffly.

The Grand Admiral shifted his gaze slightly. "You would be well advised to keep your counsel to yourself, maitrakh. This particular son of the clan Kihm'bar has lied to me, and I do not take such matters lightly." The glowing gaze shifted back. "Tell me, Khabarakh clan Kihm'bar, about your imprisonment on Kashyyyk."

Leia squeezed her lightsaber hard, the cool metal ridges of the grip biting into the palm of her hand. It had been during Khabarakh's brief imprisonment on Kashyyyk that he'd been persuaded to bring her here to Honoghr. If Khabarakh blurted out the whole story—

"I do not understand," Khabarakh said.

"Really?" the Grand Admiral countered. "Then allow me to refresh your memory. You didn't escape from Kashyyyk as you stated in your report and repeated last night in my presence and in the presence of your family and your clan dynast. You were, in fact, captured by the Wookiees after the failure of your mission. And you spent that missing month not meditating, but undergoing interrogation in a Wookiee prison. Does that help your memory any?"

Leia took a careful breath, not daring to believe what she was hearing. However it was the Grand Admiral had learned about Khabarakh's capture, he'd taken that fact and run in exactly the wrong direction with it. They'd been given a second chance . . . if Khabarakh could hold on to his wits and poise a little longer.

Perhaps the maitrakh didn't trust his stamina, either. "My thirdson would not lie about such matters, my lord," she said before Khabarakh could reply. "He has always understood the duties and requirements of honor."

"Has he, now," the Grand Admiral shot back. "A Noghri commando, captured by the enemy for interrogation—and still alive? Is this the duty and requirement of honor?"

"I was not captured, my lord," Khabarakh said stiffly. "My escape from Kashyyyk was as I said it."

For a half dozen heartbeats the Grand Admiral gazed in his direction in silence. "And I say that you lie, Khabarakh clan Kihm'bar," he said softly. "But no matter. With or without your cooperation I will have the truth about your missing month . . . and whatever the price was you paid for your freedom. Rukh?"

"My lord," the third Noghri voice said.

"Khabarakh clan Kihm'bar is hereby placed under Imperial arrest. You and Squad Two will escort him aboard the troop shuttle and take him back to the *Chimaera* for interrogation."

There was a sharp hiss. "My lord, this is a violation—"

"You will be silent, maitrakh," the Grand Admiral cut her off. "Or you will share in his imprisonment."

"I will not be silent," the maitrakh snarled. "A Noghri accused of treason to the overclan must be given over to the clan dynasts for the ancient rules of discovery and judgment. It is the law."

"I am not bound by Noghri law," the Grand Admiral said coldly. "Khabarakh has been a traitor to the Empire. By Imperial rules will he be judged and condemned."

"The clan dynasts will demand—"

"The clan dynasts are in no position to demand anything," the Grand Admiral barked, touching the comlink cylinder pocketed beside his tunic insignia. "Do you require a reminder of what it means to defy the Empire?"

Leia heard the faint sound of the maitrakh's sigh. "No, my lord," she said, her voice conceding defeat.

The Grand Admiral studied her. "You shall have one anyway."

He touched his comlink again—

And abruptly the interior of the *dukha* flashed with a blinding burst of green light.

Leia jerked her head back into Chewbacca's legs, squeezing her eyelids shut against the sudden searing pain ripping through her eyes and face. For a single, horrifying second she thought that the *dukha* had taken a direct hit, a turbolaser blast powerful enough to bring the whole structure down in flaming ruin around them. But the afterimage burned into her retina showed the Grand Admiral still standing proud and unmoved; and belatedly she understood.

She was trying desperately to reverse her sensory enhancement when the thunderclap slammed like the slap of an angry Wookiee into the side of her head.

She would later have a vague recollection of several more turbolaser blasts, seen and heard only dimly through the thick gray haze that clouded over her mind, as the orbiting Star Destroyer fired again and again into the hills surrounding the village. By the time her throbbing head finally dragged her back to full consciousness the Grand Admiral's reminder was over, the final thunderclap roiling away into the distance.

Cautiously, she opened her eyes, squinting a little against the pain. The Grand Admiral was still standing where he'd been, in the center of the *dukha* . . . and as the last thunderclap faded into silence he spoke. "*I* am the law on Honoghr now, maitrakh," he said, his voice quiet and deadly. "If I choose to follow the ancient laws, I will follow them. If I choose to ignore them, they will be ignored. Is that clear?"

The voice, when it came, was almost too alien to recognize. If the purpose of the Grand Admiral's demonstration had been to frighten the maitrakh half out of her mind, it had clearly succeeded. "Yes, my lord."

"Good." The Grand Admiral let the brittle silence hang in the air for another moment. "For loyal servants of the Empire, however, I am prepared to make compromises. Khabarakh will be interrogated aboard the *Chimaera*; but before that, I will allow the first stage of the ancient laws of discovery." His head turned slightly. "Rukh, you will remove Khabarakh clan Kihm'bar to the center of Nystao and present him to the clan dynasts. Perhaps three days of public shaming will serve to remind the Noghri people that we are still at war."

"Yes, my lord."

There was the sound of footsteps, and the opening and closing of the double doors. Hunched against the ceiling above her, his sense in unreadable turmoil, Chewbacca rumbled softly to himself. Leia clenched her teeth, hard enough to send flashes of pain through her still throbbing head. Public shaming . . . and something called the laws of discovery.

The Rebel Alliance had unwittingly destroyed Honoghr. Now, it seemed, she was going to do the same to Khabarakh.

The Grand Admiral was still standing in the middle of the *dukha*. "You are very quiet, maitrakh," he said.

"My lord ordered me to be silent," she countered.

"Of course." He studied her. "Loyalty to one's clan and family is all well and good, maitrakh. But to extend that loyalty to a traitor would be foolish. As well as potentially disastrous to your family and clan."

"I have not heard evidence that my thirdson is a traitor."

The Grand Admiral's lip twitched. "You will," he promised softly.

He walked toward the double doors, passing out of Leia's sight, and there was the sound of the doors opening. The footsteps paused, clearly waiting; and a moment later the quieter paces of the maitrakh joined him. Both left, the doors closed again, and Leia and Chewbacca were alone.

Alone. In enemy territory. Without a ship. And with their only ally about to undergo an Imperial interrogation. "I think, Chewie," she said softly, "we're in trouble."

CHAPTER 14

ONE OF THE FIRST minor truths about interstellar flight that any observant traveler learned was that a planet seen from space almost never looked anything at all like the official maps of it. Scatterings of cloud cover, shadows from mountain ranges, contour-altering effects of large vegetation tracts, and lighting tricks in general, all combined to disguise and distort the nice clean computer-scrubbed lines drawn by the cartographers. It was an effect that had probably caused a lot of bad moments for neophyte navigators, as well as supplying the ammunition for innumerable practical jokes played on those same neophytes by their more experienced shipmates.

It was therefore something of a surprise to find that, on this particular day and coming in from this particular angle, the major continent of the planet Jomark did indeed look almost exactly like a precisely detailed map. Of course, in all fairness, it was a pretty small continent to begin with.

Somewhere on that picture-perfect continent was a Jedi Master.

Luke tapped his fingers gently on the edge of his control

board, gazing out at the greenish-brown chunk of land now framed in his X-wing's canopy. He could sense the other Jedi's presence—had been able to sense it, in fact, since first dropping out of hyperspace—but so far he'd been unable to make a more direct contact. *Master C'baoth?* he called silently, trying one more time. *This is Luke Skywalker. Can you hear me?*

There was no response. Either Luke wasn't doing it right, or C'baoth was unable to reply . . . or else this was a deliberate test of Luke's abilities.

Well, he was game. "Let's do a sensor focus on the main continent, Artoo," he called, looking over his displays and trying to put himself into the frame of mind of a Jedi Master who'd been out of circulation for a while. The bulk of Jomark's land area was in that one small continent—not much more than an oversized island, really—but there were also thousands of much smaller islands scattered in clusters around the vast ocean. Taken all together, there were probably close to three hundred thousand square kilometers of dry land, which made for an awful lot of places to guess wrong. "Scan for technology, and see if you can pick out the main population centers."

Artoo whistled softly to himself as he ran the X-wing's sensor readings through his programmed life-form algorithms. He gave a series of beeps, and a pattern of dots appeared superimposed on the scope image. "Thanks," Luke said, studying it. Not surprisingly, most of the population seemed to be living along the coast. But there were a handful of other, smaller centers in the interior, as well. Including what seemed to be a cluster of villages near the southern shore of an almost perfectly ring-shaped lake.

He frowned at the image, keyed for a contour overlay. It wasn't just an ordinary lake, he saw now, but one that had formed inside what was left of a cone-shaped mountain, with a smaller cone making a large island in the center. Probably volcanic in origin, given the mountainous terrain around it.

A wilderness region thick with mountains, where a Jedi

Master could have lived in privacy for a long time. And a cluster of villages nearby where he could have emerged from his isolation when he was finally ready to do so.

It was as good a place to start as any. "Okay, Artoo, here's the landing target," he told the droid, marking it on his scope. "I'll take us down; you watch the sensors and let me know if you spot anything interesting."

Artoo beeped a somewhat nervous question. "Yes, or anything suspicious," Luke agreed. Artoo had never fully believed that the Imperial attack on them the last time they'd tried to come here had been purely coincidence.

They dropped in through the atmosphere, switching to repulsorlifts about halfway down and leveling off just below the tops of the highest mountains. Seen up close, the territory was rugged enough but not nearly as desolate as Luke had first thought. Vegetation was rich down in the valley areas between mountains, though it was sparse on the rocky sides of the mountains themselves. Most of the gaps they flew over seemed to have at least a couple of houses nestled into them, and occasionally even a village that had been too small for the X-wing's limited sensors to notice.

They were coming up on the lake from the southwest when Artoo spotted the mansion perched up on the rim.

"Never seen a design like that before," Luke commented. "You getting any life readings from it?"

Artoo warbled a moment: inconclusive. "Well, let's give it a try," Luke decided, keying in the landing cycle. "If we're wrong, at least it'll be a downhill walk to everywhere else."

The mansion was set into a small courtyard bordered by a fence that appeared more suited for decoration than defense. Killing the X-wing's forward velocity, he swung the ship parallel to the fence and set it down a few meters outside its single gate. He was in the process of shutting down the systems when Artoo's trilled warning made him look up again.

Standing just outside the gate, watching them, was the figure of a man.

Luke gazed at him, heart starting to beat a little harder. The man was old, obviously—the gray-white hair and long beard that the mountain winds were blowing half across his lined face were evidence enough of that. But his eyes were keenly alert, his posture straight and proud and unaffected by even the harder gusts of wind, and the half-open brown robe revealed a chest that was strongly muscled.

"Finish shutting down, Artoo," Luke said, hearing the slight quaver in his voice as he slipped off his helmet and popped the X-wing's canopy. Standing up, he vaulted lightly over the cockpit side to the ground.

The old man hadn't moved. Taking a deep breath, Luke walked over to him. "Master C'baoth," he said, bowing his head slightly. "I'm Luke Skywalker."

The other smiled faintly. "Yes," he said. "I know. Welcome to Jomark."

"Thank you," Luke said, letting his breath out in a quiet sigh. At last. It had been a long and circuitous journey, what with the unscheduled stopovers at Myrkr and Sluis Van. But at last he'd made it.

C'baoth might have been reading his mind. Perhaps he was. "I expected you long before now," he said reproachfully.

"Yes, sir," Luke said. "I'm sorry. Circumstances lately have been rather out of my control."

"Why?" C'baoth countered.

The question took Luke by surprise. "I don't understand."

The other's eyes narrowed slightly. "What do you mean, you don't understand?" he demanded. "Are you or are you not a Jedi?"

"Well, yes—"

"Then you should be in control," C'baoth said firmly. "In control of yourself; in control of the people and events around you. Always."

"Yes, Master," Luke said cautiously, trying to hide his confusion. The only other Jedi Master he'd ever known had been Yoda . . . but Yoda had never talked like this.

For another moment C'baoth seemed to study him. Then, abruptly, the hardness in his face vanished. "But you've come," he said, the lines in his face shifting as he smiled. "That's the important thing. They weren't able to stop you."

"No," Luke said. "They tried, though. I must have gone through four Imperial attacks since I first started out this way."

C'baoth looked at him sharply. "Did you, now. Were they directed specifically at you?"

"One of them was," Luke said. "For the others I just happened to be in the wrong place at the wrong time. Or maybe the right place at the right time," he corrected.

The sharp look faded from C'baoth's face, replaced by something distant. "Yes," he murmured, gazing into the distance toward the edge of the cliff and the ring-shaped lake far below. "The wrong place at the wrong time. The epitaph of so many Jedi." He looked back at Luke. "The Empire destroyed them, you know."

"Yes, I know," Luke said. "They were hunted down by the Emperor and Darth Vader."

"And one or two other Dark Jedi with them," C'baoth said grimly, his gaze turned inward. "Dark Jedi like Vader. I fought the last of them on—" He broke off, shaking his head slowly. "So long ago."

Luke nodded uncomfortably, feeling as if he was standing in loose sand. All these strange topic and mood shifts were hard to follow. A result of C'baoth's isolation? Or was this another test, this time of Luke's patience? "A long time ago," he agreed. "But the Jedi can live again. We have a chance to rebuild."

C'baoth's attention returned to him. "Your sister," he said. "Yes. She'll be giving birth to Jedi twins soon."

"Potential Jedi, anyway," Luke said, a little surprised that C'baoth had heard about Leia's pregnancy. The New Republic's publicists had given the news wide dissemination, but he'd have thought Jomark too far out of the mainstream to have picked up on it. "The twins are the reason I came here, in fact."

"No," C'baoth said. "The reason you came here was because I called you."

"Well . . . yes. But—"

"There are no *buts*, Jedi Skywalker," C'baoth cut him off sharply. "To be a Jedi is to be a servant of the Force. I called you through the Force; and when the Force calls, you must obey."

"I understand," Luke nodded again, wishing that he really did. Was C'baoth just being figurative? Or was this yet another topic his training had skipped over? He was familiar enough with the general controlling aspects of the Force; they were what kept him alive every time he matched his lightsaber against blaster fire. But a literal "call" was something else entirely. "When you say the Force calls you, Master C'baoth, do you mean—?"

"There are two reasons why I called you," C'baoth interrupted him again. "First, to complete your training. And second . . . because I need your help."

Luke blinked. "My help?"

C'baoth smiled wanly, his eyes suddenly very tired. "I am nearing the end of my life, Jedi Skywalker. Soon now I will be making that long journey from this life to what lies beyond."

A lump caught in Luke's throat. "I'm sorry," was all he could think of to say.

"It's the way of all life," C'baoth shrugged. "For Jedi as well as for lesser beings."

Luke's memory flicked back to Yoda, lying on his deathbed in his Dagobah home . . . and his own feeling of helplessness that he could do nothing but watch. It was not an experience he really wanted to go through again. "How can I help?" he asked quietly.

"By learning from me," C'baoth said. "Open yourself to me; absorb from me my wisdom and experience and power. In this way will you carry on my life and work."

"I see," Luke nodded, wondering exactly what work the other was referring to. "You understand, though, that I have work of my own to do—"

"And are you prepared to do it?" C'baoth said, arching his eyebrows. "*Fully* prepared? Or did you come here with nothing to ask of me?"

"Well, actually, yes," Luke had to admit. "I came on behalf of the New Republic, to ask your assistance in the fight against the Empire."

"To what end?"

Luke frowned. He'd have thought the reasons self-evident. "The elimination of the Empire's tyranny. The establishment of freedom and justice for all the beings of the galaxy."

"Justice." C'baoth's lip twisted. "Do not look to lesser beings for justice, Jedi Skywalker." He slapped himself twice on the chest, two quick movements of his fingertips. "*We* are the true justice of this galaxy. We two, and the new legacy of Jedi that we will forge to follow us. Leave the petty battles to others, and prepare yourself for that future."

"I . . ." Luke floundered, searching for a response to that.

"What is it your sister's unborn twins need?" C'baoth demanded.

"They need—well, they're someday going to need a teacher," Luke told him, the words coming out with a strange reluctance. First impressions were always dicey, he knew; but right now he wasn't at all sure that this was the sort of man he wanted to be teaching his niece and nephew. C'baoth seemed to be too mercurial, almost on the edge of instability. "It's sort of been assumed that I'd be teaching them when they're old enough, like I'm teaching Leia. The problem is that just being a Jedi doesn't necessarily mean you can be a good teacher." He hesitated. "Obi-wan Kenobi blamed himself for Vader's turn to the dark side. I don't want that to happen to Leia's children. I thought maybe you could teach me the proper methods of Jedi instruction—"

"A waste of time," C'baoth said with an offhanded shrug. "Bring them here. I'll teach them myself."

"Yes, Master," Luke said, picking his words carefully. "I appreciate the offer. But as you said, you have your own work to do. All I really need are some pointers—"

"And what of you, Jedi Skywalker?" C'baoth interrupted him again. "Have you yourself no need of further instruction? In matters of judgment, perhaps?"

Luke gritted his teeth. This whole conversation was leaving him feeling a lot more transparent than he really liked. "Yes, I could use some more instruction in that area," he conceded. "I think sometimes that the Jedi Master who taught me expected me to pick that up on my own."

"It's merely a matter of listening to the Force," C'baoth said briskly. For a moment his eyes seemed to unfocus; then they came back again. "But come. We will go down to the villages and I will show you."

Luke felt his eyebrows go up. "Right now?"

"Why not?" C'baoth shrugged. "I have summoned a driver; he will meet us on the road." His gaze shifted to something over Luke's shoulder. "No—stay there," he snapped.

Luke turned. Artoo had raised himself out of the X-wing's droid socket and was easing his way along the upper hull. "That's just my droid," he told C'baoth.

"He will stay where he is," C'baoth bit out. "Droids are an abomination—creations that reason, but yet are not genuinely part of the Force."

Luke frowned. Droids were indeed unique in that way, but that was hardly a reason to label them as abominations. But this wasn't the time or the place to argue the point. "I'll go help him back into his socket," he soothed C'baoth, hurrying back to the ship. Drawing on the Force, he leaped up to the hull beside Artoo. "Sorry, Artoo, but you're going to have to stay here," he told the droid. "Come on—let's get you back in."

Artoo beeped indignantly. "I know, and I'm sorry," Luke said, herding the squat metal cylinder back to its socket. "But Master C'baoth doesn't want you coming along. You might as well wait here as on the ground—at least this way you'll have the X-wing's computer to talk to."

The droid warbled again, a plaintive and slightly nervous sound this time. "No, I don't think there's any danger," Luke assured him. "If you're worried, you can keep an eye on me through the X-wing's sensors." He lowered his voice to a murmur. "And while you're at it, I want you to start doing a complete sensor scan of the area. See if you can find any vegetation that seems to be distorted, like that twisted tree growing over the dark side cave on Dagobah. Okay?"

Artoo gave a somewhat bemused acknowledging beep. "Good. See you later," Luke said and dropped back to the ground. "I'm ready," he told C'baoth.

The other nodded. "This way," he said, and strode off along a path leading downward.

Luke hurried to catch up. It was, he knew, something of a long shot: even if the spot he was looking for was within Artoo's sensor range, there was no guarantee that the droid would be able to distinguish healthy alien plants from unhealthy ones. But it was worth a try. Yoda, he had long suspected, had managed to stay hidden from the Emperor and Vader only because the dark side cave near his home had somehow shielded his own influence on the Force. For C'baoth to have remained unnoticed, it followed that Jomark must also have a similar focus of dark side power somewhere.

Unless, of course, he *hadn't* gone unnoticed. Perhaps the Emperor had known all about him, but had deliberately left him alone.

Which would in turn imply . . . what?

Luke didn't know. But it was something he had better find out.

THEY HAD WALKED no more than two hundred meters when the driver and vehicle C'baoth had summoned arrived: a tall, lanky man on an old SoroSuub recreational speeder bike pulling an elaborate wheeled carriage behind it. "Not much more than a converted farm cart, I'm afraid," C'baoth said as he ushered Luke into the carriage and got in beside him. Most of the vehicle seemed to be made of wood, but the seats were comfortably padded. "The people of Chynoo built it for me when I first came to them."

The driver got the vehicles turned around—no mean trick on the narrow path—and started downward. "How long were you alone before that?" Luke asked.

C'baoth shook his head. "I don't know," he said. "Time was not something I was really concerned with. I lived, I thought, I meditated. That was all."

"Do you remember when it was you first came here?" Luke persisted. "After the Outbound Flight mission, I mean."

Slowly, C'baoth turned to face him, his eyes icy. "Your thoughts betray you, Jedi Skywalker," he said coldly. "You seek reassurance that I was not a servant of the Emperor."

Luke forced himself to meet that gaze. "The Master who instructed me told me that I was the last of the Jedi," he said. "He wasn't counting Vader and the Emperor in that list."

"And you fear that I'm a Dark Jedi, as they were?"

"Are you?"

C'baoth smiled; and to Luke's surprise, actually chuckled. It was a strange sound, coming out of that intense face. "Come now, Jedi Skywalker," he said. "Do you really believe that Joruus C'baoth—*Joruus C'baoth*—would ever turn to the dark side?"

The smile faded. "The Emperor didn't destroy me, Jedi Skywalker, for the simple reason that during most of his reign I was beyond his reach. And after I returned . . ."

He shook his head sharply. "There is another, you know. Another besides your sister. Not a Jedi; not yet. But I've felt the ripples in the Force. Rising, and then falling."

"Yes, I know who you're talking about," Luke said. "I've met her."

C'baoth turned to him, his eyes glistening. "You've *met* her?" he breathed.

"Well, I think I have," Luke amended. "I suppose it's possible there's someone else out there who—"

"What is her name?"

Luke frowned, searching C'baoth's face and trying unsuccessfully to read his sense. There was something there he didn't like at all. "She called herself Mara Jade," he said.

C'baoth leaned back into the seat cushions, eyes focused on nothing. "Mara Jade," he repeated the name softly.

"Tell me more about the Outbound Flight project," Luke said, determined not to get dragged off the topic. "You set off from Yaga Minor, remember, searching for other life outside the galaxy. What happened to the ship and the other Jedi Masters who were with you?"

C'baoth's eyes took on a faraway look. "They died, of course," he said, his voice distant. "All of them died. I alone survived to return." He looked suddenly at Luke. "It changed me, you know."

"I understand," Luke said quietly. So that was why C'baoth seemed so strange. Something had happened to him on that flight . . . "Tell me about it."

For a long moment C'baoth was silent. Luke waited, jostled by the bumps as the carriage wheels ran over the uneven ground. "No," C'baoth said at last, shaking his head. "Not now. Perhaps later." He nodded toward the front of the carriage. "We are here."

Luke looked. Ahead he could see half a dozen small houses, with more becoming visible as the carriage cleared the cover of the trees. Probably fifty or so all told: small, neat little cottages that seemed to combine natural building elements with selected bits of more modern technology. About twenty people could be seen moving about at various tasks; most stopped what they were doing as the speeder bike and carriage appeared. The driver pulled to roughly the center of the village and stopped in front of a thronelike chair of polished wood protected by a small, dome-roofed pavilion.

"I had it brought down from the High Castle," C'baoth explained, gesturing to the chair. "I suspect it was a symbol of authority to the beings who carved it."

"What's it used for now?" Luke asked. The elaborate throne seemed out of place, somehow, in such a casually rustic setting as this.

"It's from there that I usually give my justice to the people," C'baoth said, standing up and stepping out of the carriage. "But we will not be so formal today. Come."

The people were still standing motionless, watching them. Luke reached out with the Force as he stepped out beside C'baoth, trying to read their overall sense. It seemed expectant, perhaps a little surprised, definitely awed. There didn't seem to be any fear; but there was nothing like affection, either. "How long have you been coming here?" he asked C'baoth.

"Less than a year," C'baoth said, setting off casually down the street. "They were slow to accept my wisdom, but eventually I persuaded them to do so."

The villagers were starting to return to their tasks now, but their eyes still followed the visitors. "What do you mean, persuaded them?" Luke asked.

"I showed them that it was in their best interests to listen to me." C'baoth gestured to the cottage just ahead. "Reach out your senses, Jedi Skywalker. Tell me about that house and its inhabitants."

It was instantly apparent what C'baoth was referring to. Even without focusing his attention on the place Luke could feel the anger and hostility boiling out of it. There was a flicker of something like murderous intent—"Uh-oh," he said. "Do you think we should—?"

"Of course we should," C'baoth said. "Come." He stepped up to the cottage and pushed open the door. Keeping his hand on his lightsaber, Luke followed.

There were two men standing in the room, one holding a large knife toward the other, both frozen in place as they stared at the intruders. "Put the knife down, Tarm," C'baoth said sternly. "Svan, you will likewise lay aside your weapon."

Slowly, the man with the knife laid it on the floor. The other looked at C'baoth, back at his now unarmed opponent— "I said lay it aside!" C'baoth snapped.

The man cringed back, hastily pulled a small slug-thrower from his pocket and dropped it beside the knife. "Better," C'baoth said, his voice calm but with a hint of the fire still there. "Now explain yourselves."

The story came out in a rush from both men at once, a loud and confusing babble of charges and countercharges about some kind of business deal gone sour. C'baoth listened silently, apparently having no trouble following the windstorm of fact and assumption and accusation. Luke waited beside him, wondering how he was ever going to untangle the whole thing. As near as he could understand it, both men seemed to have equally valid arguments.

Finally, the men ran out of words. "Very well," C'baoth said. "The judgment of C'baoth is that Svan will pay to Tarm the full wages agreed upon." He nodded at each man in turn. "The judgment will be carried out immediately."

Luke looked at C'baoth in surprise. "That's all?" he asked.

C'baoth turned a steely gaze on him. "You have something to say?"

Luke glanced back at the two villagers, acutely aware that arguing the ruling in front of them might undermine whatever authority C'baoth had built up here. "I just thought that more of a compromise might be in order."

"There is no compromise to be made," C'baoth said firmly. "Svan is at fault, and he will pay."

"Yes, but—"

Luke caught the flicker of sense a half second before Svan dived for the slugthrower. With a single smooth motion he had his lightsaber free of his belt and ignited. But C'baoth was faster. Even as Luke's green-white blade snapped into existence, C'baoth raised his hand; and from his fingertips flashed a sizzling volley of all-too-well-remembered blue lightning bolts.

Svan took the blast full in the head and chest, snapping over backwards with a scream of agony. He slammed into the ground, screaming again as C'baoth sent a second blast at him. The slugthrower flew from his hand, its metal surrounded for an instant by a blue-white coronal discharge.

C'baoth lowered his hand, and for a long moment the only sound in the room was a soft whimpering from the man on the floor. Luke stared at him in horror, the smell of ozone wrenching at his stomach. "C'baoth—!"

"You will address me as *Master*," the other cut him off quietly.

Luke took a deep breath, forcing calm into his mind and voice. Closing down his lightsaber, he returned it to his belt and went over to kneel beside the groaning man. He was obviously still hurting, but aside from some angry red burns on his chest and arms, he didn't seem to be seriously hurt. Laying his hand gently on the worst of the burns, Luke reached out with the Force, doing what he could to alleviate the other's pain.

"Jedi Skywalker," C'baoth said from behind him. "He is not permanently damaged. Come away."

Luke didn't move. "He's in pain."

"That is as it should be," C'baoth said. "He required a lesson, and pain is the one teacher no one will ignore. Now come away."

For a moment Luke considered disobeying. Svan's face and sense were in agony . . .

"Or would you have preferred that Tarm lie dead now?" C'baoth added.

Luke looked at the slugthrower lying on the floor, then at Tarm standing stiffly with wide eyes and face the color of dirty snow. "There were other ways to stop him," Luke said, getting to his feet.

"But none that he will remember longer." C'baoth locked

eyes with Luke. "Remember that, Jedi Skywalker; remember it well. For if you allow your justice to be forgotten, you will be forced to repeat the same lessons again and again."

He held Luke's gaze a pair of heartbeats longer before turning back to the door. "We're finished here. Come."

THE STARS WERE blazing overhead as Luke eased open the low gate of the High Castle and stepped out of the courtyard. Artoo had clearly noticed his approach; as he closed the gate behind him the droid turned on the X-wing's landing lights, illuminating his path. "Hi, Artoo," Luke said, walking to the short ladder and wearily pulling himself up into the cockpit. "I just came out to see how you and the ship were doing."

Artoo beeped his assurance that everything was fine. "Good," Luke said, flicking on the scopes and keying for a status check anyway. "Any luck with the sensor scan I asked for?"

The reply this time was less optimistic. "That bad, huh?" Luke nodded heavily as the translation of Artoo's answer scrolled across the X-wing's computer scope. "Well, that's what happens when you get up into mountains."

Artoo grunted, a distinctly unenthusiastic sound, then warbled a question. "I don't know," Luke told him. "A few more days at least. Maybe longer, if he needs me to stay." He sighed. "I don't know, Artoo. I mean, it's just never what I expect. I went to Dagobah expecting to find a great warrior, and I found Master Yoda. I came here expecting to find someone like Master Yoda . . . and instead I got Master C'baoth."

Artoo gave a slightly disparaging gurgle, and Luke had to smile at the translation. "Yes, well, don't forget that Master Yoda gave you a hard time that first evening, too," he reminded the droid, wincing a little himself at the memory. Yoda had also given Luke a hard time at that encounter. It had been a test of Luke's patience and of his treatment of strangers.

And Luke had flunked it. Rather miserably.

Artoo warbled a point of distinction. "No, you're right," Luke had to concede. "Even while he was still testing us Yoda never had the kind of hard edge that C'baoth does."

He leaned back against his headrest, staring past the open canopy at the mountaintops and the distant stars beyond them. He was weary—wearier than he'd been, probably, since the height of that last climactic battle against the Emperor. It had been all he could do to come out here to check on Artoo. "I don't know, Artoo. He hurt someone today. Hurt him a lot. And he pushed his way into an argument without being invited, and then forced an arbitrary judgment on the people involved, and—" He waved a hand helplessly. "I just can't see Ben or Master Yoda acting that way. But he's a Jedi, just like they were. So which example am I supposed to follow?"

The droid seemed to digest that. Then, almost reluctantly, he trilled again. "That's the obvious question," Luke agreed. "But why would a Dark Jedi of C'baoth's power bother playing games like this? Why not just kill me and be done with it?"

Artoo gave an electronic grunt, a list of possible reasons scrolling across the screen. A rather lengthy list—clearly, the droid had put a lot of time and thought into the question. "I appreciate your concern, Artoo," Luke soothed him. "But I really don't think he's a Dark Jedi. He's erratic and moody, but he doesn't have the same sort of evil aura about him that I could sense in Vader and the Emperor." He hesitated. This wasn't going to be easy to say. "I think it's more likely that Master C'baoth is insane."

It was possibly the first time Luke had ever seen Artoo actually startled speechless. For a minute the only sound was the whispering of the mountain winds playing through the spindly trees surrounding the High Castle. Luke stared at the stars and waited for Artoo to find his voice.

Eventually, the droid did. "No, I don't know for sure how something like that could happen," Luke admitted as the question appeared on his screen. "But I've got an idea."

He reached up to lace his fingers behind his neck, the movement easing the pressure in his chest. The dull fatigue in his mind seemed to be matched by an equally dull ache in his muscles, the kind he sometimes got if he went through an overly strenuous workout. Dimly, he wondered if there was something in the air that the X-wing's biosensors hadn't picked up on. "You never knew, but right after Ben was cut down—back on the first Death Star—I found out that I could sometimes hear his voice in the back of my mind. By the time the Alliance was driven off Hoth, I could see him, too."

Artoo twittered. "Yes, that's who I sometimes talked to on Dagobah," Luke confirmed. "And then right after the Battle of Endor, I was able to see not only Ben but Yoda and my father, too. Though the other two never spoke, and I never saw them again. My guess is that there's some way for a dying Jedi to— oh, I don't know; to somehow anchor himself to another Jedi who's close by."

Artoo seemed to consider that, pointed out a possible flaw in the reasoning. "I didn't say it was the tightest theory in the galaxy," Luke growled at him, a glimmer of annoyance peeking through his fatigue. "Maybe I'm way off the mark. But if I'm not, it's possible that the five other Jedi Masters from the Outbound Flight project wound up anchored to Master C'baoth."

Artoo whistled thoughtfully. "Right," Luke agreed ruefully. "It didn't bother me any to have Ben around—in fact, I wish he had talked to me more often. But Master C'baoth was a lot more powerful than I was. Maybe it was different with him."

Artoo made a little moan, and another, rather worried suggestion appeared on the screen. "I can't just leave him, Artoo," Luke shook his head tiredly. "Not with him like this. Not when there's a chance I can help him."

He grimaced, hearing in the words a painful echo of the past. Darth Vader, too, had needed help, and Luke had similarly taken on the job of saving him from the dark side. And had nearly gotten himself killed in the process. *What am I doing?* he wondered silently. *I'm not a healer. Why do I keep trying to be one?*

Luke?

With an effort, Luke dragged his thoughts back to the present. "I've got to go," he said, levering himself out of the cockpit seat. "Master C'baoth's calling me."

He shut down the displays, but not before the translation of Artoo's worried jabbering scrolled across the computer display. "Relax, Artoo," Luke told him, leaning back over the open cockpit canopy to pat the droid reassuringly. "I'll be all right. I'm a Jedi, remember? You just keep a good eye on things out here. Okay?"

The droid trilled mournfully as Luke dropped down the ladder and onto the ground. He paused there, looking at the dark mansion, lit only by the backwash of the X-wing's landing lights. Wondering if maybe Artoo was right about them getting out of here.

Because the droid had a good point. Luke's talents didn't lean toward the healing aspects of the Force—that much he was pretty sure of. Helping C'baoth was going to be a long, time-consuming process, with no guarantee of success at the end of the road. With a Grand Admiral in command of the Empire, political infighting in the New Republic, and the whole galaxy hanging in the balance, was this really the most efficient use of his time?

He raised his eyes from the mansion to the dark shadows of the rim mountains surrounding the lake below. Snowcapped in places, barely visible in the faint light of Jomark's three tiny moons, they were reminiscent somehow of the Manarai Mountains south of the Imperial City on Coruscant. And with that memory came another one: Luke, standing on the Imperial Palace rooftop gazing at those other mountains, sagely explaining to Threepio that a Jedi couldn't get so caught up in galactic matters that he was no longer concerned about individual people.

The speech had sounded high and noble when he'd given it. This was his chance to prove that it hadn't been just words.

Taking a deep breath, he headed back toward the gate.

CHAPTER 15

"TANGRENE WAS OUR real crowning achievement," Senator Bel Iblis said, draining the last of his glass and raising it high above his head. Across the expansive but largely empty headquarters lounge the bartender nodded in silent acknowledgment and busied himself with his drinks dispenser. "We'd been sniping at the Imperials for probably three years at that point," Bel Iblis continued. "Hitting small bases and military supply shipments and generally making as much trouble for them as we could. But up till Tangrene they weren't paying much attention to us."

"What happened at Tangrene?" Han asked.

"We blasted a major Ubiqtorate center into fine powder," Bel Iblis told him with obvious satisfaction. "And then waltzed out right under the collective nose of the three Star Destroyers that were supposed to be guarding the place. I think that was when they finally woke up to the fact that we were more than just a minor irritant. That we were a group to be taken seriously."

"I'll bet they did," Han agreed, shaking his head in admiration. Even getting within sight of one of Imperial Intelligence's Ubiqtorate bases was a tricky job, let alone blasting it and getting out again. "What did it cost you?"

"Amazingly enough, we got all five warships out," Bel Iblis said. "There was a fair amount of damage all around, of course, and one of them was completely out of commission for nearly seven months. But it was worth it."

"I thought you said you had six Dreadnaughts," Lando spoke up.

"We have six now," Bel Iblis nodded. "At the time we only had five."

"Ah," Lando said, and lapsed back into silence.

"So after that was when you started moving your base around?" Han asked.

Bel Iblis eyed Lando a moment longer before turning back to Han. "That was when mobility became a top priority, yes," he corrected. "Though we hadn't exactly been sitting still before that. This place is, what, our thirteenth location in seven years, Sena?"

"Fourteenth," Sena said. "That's if you count Womrik and the Mattri asteroid bases."

"Fourteen, then," Bel Iblis nodded. "You probably noticed that every building here is built of bi-state memory plastic. Makes it relatively simple to fold everything up and toss it aboard the transports." He chuckled. "Though that's been known to backfire on us. Once on Lelmra we got hit by a violent thunderstorm, and the lightning strikes were hitting so close to us that the edge currents triggered the flip-flop on a couple of barracks buildings and a targeting center. Folded them up neat as a set of birthday presents, with nearly fifty people still inside."

"That was terrific fun," Sena put in dryly. "No one was killed, fortunately, but it took us the better part of the night to cut them all free. With the storm still blazing on around us."

"Things finally quieted down just before daylight," Bel Iblis said. "We were out of there by the next evening. Ah."

The bartender had arrived with the next round of drinks. Twistlers, Bel Iblis had called them: a blend of Corellian brandy with some unidentified but very tart fruit extract. Not the sort of drink Han would have expected to find in a military camp, but not bad either. The Senator took two of the drinks off the tray and handed them across to Han and Sena; took the other two off—

"I'm still good, thanks," Lando said before Bel Iblis could offer him one.

Han frowned across the table at his friend. Lando was sitting stiffly in his lounge chair, his face impassive, his glass still half full. His *first* glass, Han realized suddenly—Lando hadn't had a refill in the hour and a half since Bel Iblis had brought them here. He caught Lando's eye, raised his eyebrows fractionally. Lando looked back, his expression still stony, then dropped his gaze and took a small sip of his drink.

"It was about a month after Tangrene," Bel Iblis went on, "that we first met Borsk Fey'lya."

Han turned back to him, feeling a twitch of guilt. He'd gotten so wrapped up in Bel Iblis's storytelling that he'd completely forgotten why he and Lando had set off on this mission in the first place. Probably that was what had Lando glaring crushed ice in his direction. "Yeah—Fey'lya," he said. "What's your deal with him?"

"Considerably less of a deal than he'd like, I assure you," Bel Iblis said. "Fey'lya did us some favors during the height of the war years, and he seems to think we should be more grateful for them."

"What sort of favors?" Lando asked.

"Small ones," Bel Iblis told him. "Early on he helped us set up a supply line through New Cov, and he whistled up some Star Cruisers once when the Imperials started nosing around the system at an awkward moment. He and some of the other Bothans also shifted various funds to us, which enabled us to buy equipment sooner than we otherwise would have. That sort of thing."

"So how grateful are you?" Lando persisted.

Bel Iblis smiled slightly. "Or in other words, what exactly does Fey'lya want from me?"

Lando didn't smile back. "That'll do for starters," he agreed.

"Lando," Han said warningly.

"No, that's all right," Bel Iblis said, his own smile fading. "Before I answer, though, I'd like you to tell me a little about the New Republic hierarchy. Mon Mothma's position in the new government, Fey'lya's relationship to her—that sort of thing."

Han shrugged. "That's pretty much public record."

"That's the official version," Bel Iblis said. "I'm asking what things are *really* like."

Han glanced over at Lando. "I don't understand," he said.

Bel Iblis took a swallow of his Twistler. "Well, then, let me be more direct," he said, studying the liquid in his glass. "What's Mon Mothma really up to?"

Han felt a trickle of anger in his throat. "Is that what Breil'lya told you?" he demanded. "That she's up to something?"

Bel Iblis raised his eyes over the rim of his glass. "This has nothing to do with the Bothans," he said quietly. "It's about Mon Mothma. Period."

Han looked back at him, forcing down his confusion as he tried to collect his thoughts. There were things he didn't like about Mon Mothma—a lot of things, when you came right down to it. Starting with the way she kept running Leia off her feet doing diplomacy stuff instead of letting her concentrate on her Jedi training. And there were other things, too, that drove him crazy. But when you came right down to it . . . "As far as I know," he told Bel Iblis evenly, "the only thing she's trying to do is put together a new government."

"With herself at its head?"

"Shouldn't she be?"

A shadow of something seemed to cross Bel Iblis's face,

and he dropped his eyes to his glass again. "I suppose it was inevitable," he murmured. For a moment he was silent. Then he looked up again, seeming to shake himself out of the mood. "So you'd say that you're becoming a republic in fact as well as in name?"

"I'd say that, yes," Han nodded. "What does this have to do with Fey'lya?"

Bel Iblis shrugged. "It's Fey'lya's belief that Mon Mothma wields altogether too much power," he said. "I presume you'd disagree with that assessment?"

Han hesitated. "I don't know," he conceded. "But she sure isn't running the whole show, like she did during the war."

"The war's still going on," Bel Iblis reminded him.

"Yeah. Well . . ."

"What does Fey'lya think ought to be done about it?" Lando spoke up.

Bel Iblis's lip twitched. "Oh, Fey'lya has some rather personal and highly unsurprising ideas about the reapportionment of power. But that's Bothans for you. Give them a sniff of the soup pot and they climb all over each other to be in charge of the ladle."

"Especially when they can claim to have been valued allies of the winning side," Lando said. "Unlike others I could mention."

Sena stirred in her seat; but before she could say anything, Bel Iblis waved a hand at her. "You're wondering why I didn't join the Alliance," he said calmly. "Why I chose instead to run my own private war against the Empire."

"That's right," Lando said, matching his tone. "I am."

Bel Iblis gave him a long, measuring look. "I could give you several reasons why I felt it was better for us to remain independent," he said at last. "Security, for one. There was a great deal of communication going on between various units of the Alliance, with a correspondingly large potential for interception of that information by the Empire. For a while it seemed like every fifth Rebel base was being lost to the Imperials through sheer sloppiness in security."

"We had some problems," Han conceded. "But they've been pretty well fixed."

"Have they?" Bel Iblis countered. "What about this information leak I understand you have right in the Imperial Palace?"

"Yeah, we know it's there," Han said, feeling strangely like a kid who's been called on the carpet for not finishing his homework. "We've got people looking into it."

"They'd better do more than just look," Bel Iblis warned. "If our analysis of Imperial communiqués is correct, this leak has its own name—Delta Source—and is furthermore reporting personally to the Grand Admiral."

"Okay," Lando said. "Security. Let's hear some of the other reasons."

"Ease off, Lando," Han said, glaring across the table at his friend. "This isn't a trial, or—"

He broke off at a gesture from Bel Iblis. "Thank you, Solo, but I'm quite capable of defending my own actions," the Senator said. "And I'll be more than happy to do so . . . when I feel the time is right for such a discussion."

He looked at Lando, then at his watch. "But right now; I have other duties to attend to. It's getting late, and I know you really haven't had time to relax since landing. Irenez has had your baggage taken to a vacant officers' efficiency back toward the landing pad. It's small, I'm afraid, but I trust you'll find it comfortable enough." He stood up. "Perhaps later over dinner we can continue this discussion."

Han looked at Lando. *Such convenient timing*, the other's expression said; but he kept the thought to himself. "Sounds fine," Han told Bel Iblis for both of them.

"Good," Bel Iblis smiled. "I'll need Sena with me, but we'll point you in the direction of your quarters on our way out. Unless you'd rather I assign you a guide."

"We can find it," Han assured him.

"All right. Someone will come to get you for dinner. Until later, then."

THEY WALKED IN silence for probably half the distance to their quarters before Lando finally spoke. "You want to go ahead and get it over with?"

"Get what over with?" Han growled.

"Chewing me out for not bowing and scraping in front of your pal the Senator," Lando said. "Do it and get it over with, because we have to talk."

Han kept his eyes straight ahead. "You weren't just not bowing and scraping, pal," he bit out. "I've seen Chewie in a bad mood be more polite than you were back there."

"You're right," Lando acknowledged. "You want to be mad a little longer, or are you ready to hear my reasons?"

"Oh, this should be interesting," Han said sarcastically. "You've got a good reason to be rude to a former Imperial Senator, huh?"

"He's not telling us the truth, Han," Lando said earnestly. "Not the whole truth, anyway."

"So?" Han said. "Who says he has to tell strangers everything?"

"He brought us here," Lando countered. "Why do that and then lie to us about it?"

Han frowned sideways at his friend . . . and through his annoyance he saw for the first time the tension lines in Lando's face. Whatever Lando was reaching for here, he was serious about it. "Okay," he said, a little more calmly. "What did he lie about?"

"This camp, for starters," Lando said, gesturing toward the nearest building. "The Senator said they move around a lot—fourteen sites in seven years, remember? But this place has been here a lot longer than half a year."

Han looked at the building as they passed it. At the smoothness of the edges where the memory-plastic would fold up, at the signs of wear in the subfoundation . . .

"There are other things, too," Lando went on. "That headquarters lounge back there—did you notice all the decoration they had in that place? Probably a dozen sculptures scattered around on those corner ledges between the booths, plus a lot of light poles. And that doesn't even count all the stuff on the walls. There was a whole antique repeater display panel mounted over the main bar, a ship's chrono next to the exit—"

"I was there, too, remember?" Han cut him off. "What's your point?"

"My point is that this place isn't ready to pack up and ship offplanet on three minutes' notice," Lando said quietly. "Not anymore. And you don't get this soft and comfortable if you're still in the business of launching major attacks against Imperial bases."

"Maybe they decided to lie low for a while," Han said. This business of having to defend Bel Iblis was starting to feel uncomfortable.

"Could be," Lando said. "In that case, the question is why? What else could he be holding his ships and troops back for?"

Han chewed at the inside of his cheek. He saw where Lando was going with this, all right. "You think he's made a deal with Fey'lya."

"That's the obvious answer," Lando agreed soberly. "You heard how he talked about Mon Mothma, like he expected her to declare herself Emperor any day now. Fey'lya's influence?"

Han thought it over. It was still crazy, but not nearly as crazy as it had seemed at first blush. Though if Fey'lya thought he could stage a coup with six private Dreadnaughts, he was in for a rude surprise.

But on the other hand—"Wait a minute, Lando, this is crazy," he said. "If they're plotting against Mon Mothma, why bring us here?"

Lando hissed softly between his teeth. "Well, that brings us to the worst-case scenario, Han old buddy. Namely, that your friend the Senator is a complete phony . . . and that what we've got here is a giant Imperial scam."

Han blinked. "*Now* you've lost me."

"Think about it," Lando urged, lowering his voice as a group of uniformed men rounded a corner of one of the buildings and headed off in another direction. "Garm Bel Iblis, supposedly killed, suddenly returned from the dead? And not only alive, but with his own personal army on top of it? An army that neither of us has ever heard of?"

"Yeah, but Bel Iblis wasn't exactly a recluse," Han pointed out. "There were a lot of holos and recordings of him when I was growing up. You'd have to go to a lot of effort to look and sound that much like him."

"If you had those records handy to compare him with, sure," Lando agreed. "But all you've got is memories. It wouldn't take that much effort to rig a fairly close copy. And we know that this base has been sitting here for more than a year. Maybe abandoned by someone else; and it wouldn't take much effort to throw a fake army together. Not for the Empire."

Han shook his head. "You're skating on drive trails, Lando. The Empire's not going to go to this much effort just for us."

"Maybe they didn't," Lando said. "Maybe it was for Fey'lya's benefit, and we just happened to stumble in on it."

Han frowned. "*Fey'lya's* benefit?"

"Sure," Lando said. "Start with the Empire gimmicking Ackbar's bank account. That puts Ackbar under suspicion and ripe for someone to push him off his perch. Enter Fey'lya, convinced that he's got the support of the legendary Garm Bel Iblis and a private army behind him. Fey'lya makes his bid for power, the New Republic hierarchy is thrown into a tangle; and while no one's watching, the Empire moves in and takes back a sector or two. Quick, clean, and simple."

Han snorted under his breath. "That's what you call simple, huh?"

"We're dealing with a Grand Admiral, Han," Lando reminded him. "Anything is possible."

"Yeah, well, possible doesn't mean likely," Han countered. "If they're running a con game, why would they bring *us* here?"

"Why not? Our presence doesn't hurt the plan any. Might even help it a little. They show us the setup, send us back, we blow the whistle on Fey'lya, and Mon Mothma pulls back ships to protect Coruscant from a coup attempt that never materializes. More chaos, and even more unprotected sectors for the Imperials to gobble up."

Han shook his head. "I think you're jumping at shadows."

"Maybe," Lando said darkly. "And maybe you're putting too much trust in the ghost of a Corellian Senator."

They had reached their quarters now, one of a double row of small square buildings each about five meters on a side. Han keyed in the lock combination Sena had given them, and they went inside.

The apartment was about as stark and simple as it could be while still remaining even halfway functional. It consisted of a single room with a compact cooking niche on one side and a door leading to what was probably a bathroom on the other. A brown fold-down table/console combo and two old-fashioned contour chairs upholstered in military gray occupied much of the space, with the cabinets of what looked like two fold-down beds positioned to take up the table's share of the floor space at night. "Cozy," Lando commented.

"Probably can be packed up and shipped offplanet on three minutes' notice, too," Han said.

"I agree," Lando nodded. "This is exactly the sort of feel that lounge should have had, only it didn't."

"Maybe they figured they ought to have at least one building around here that didn't look like it came out of the Clone Wars," Han suggested.

"Maybe," Lando said, squatting down beside one of the

chairs and peering at the edge of the seat cushion. "Probably pulled them out of that Dreadnaught up there." Experimentally he dug his fingers under the gray material. "Looks like they didn't even add any extra padding before they reupholstered them with this—"

He broke off, and abruptly his face went rigid. "What is it?" Han demanded.

Slowly, Lando turned to look up at him. "This chair," he whispered. "It's not gray underneath. It's blue-gold."

"Okay," Han said, frowning. "So?"

"You don't understand. The Fleet doesn't do the interiors of military ships in blue-gold. They've never done them in blue-gold. Not under the Empire, not under the New Republic, not under the Old Republic. Except one time."

"Which was?" Han prompted.

Lando took a deep breath. "The *Katana* fleet."

Han stared at him, an icy feeling digging up under his breastbone. The *Katana* fleet . . . "That can't be right, Lando," he said. "Got to be a mistake."

"No mistake, Han," Lando shook his head. Digging his fingers in harder, he lifted the edge of the gray covering high enough to show the material beneath it. "I once spent two whole months researching the Dark Force. This is it."

Han gazed at the age-dulled blue-gold cloth, a sense of unreality creeping over him. The *Katana* fleet. The Dark Force. Lost for half a century . . . and now suddenly found.

Maybe. "We need something better in the way of proof," he told Lando. "This doesn't do it by itself."

Lando nodded, still half in shock. "That would explain why they kept us aboard the *Lady Luck* the whole way here," he said. "They'd never be able to hide the fact that their Dreadnaught was running with only two thousand crewers instead of the normal sixteen. The *Katana* fleet."

"We need to get a look inside one of the ships," Han persisted. "That recognition code Irenez sent—I don't suppose you made a recording of it?"

Lando took a deep breath and seemed to snap out of it. "We can probably reconstruct it," he said. "But if they've got any sense, their code for getting in won't be the same as their code for getting out. But I don't think we have to get aboard the ships themselves. All I need is a good, close look at that repeater display panel back in the headquarters lounge."

"Okay," Han nodded grimly. "Let's go and get you that look."

CHAPTER 16

IT TOOK THEM only a few minutes to make their way back to the headquarters lounge. Han kept an eye on the pedestrian and vehicle traffic as they walked, hoping they were still early enough for the place to be empty. Getting a close look at that repeater display would be tricky enough without a whole bunch of people sitting around with nothing better to do than watch what was happening at the bar. "What exactly are we looking for?" he asked as they came in sight of the building.

"There should be some specialized input slots on the back for the full-rig slave circuitry readouts," Lando told him. "And there'll be production serial numbers, too."

Han nodded. So they were going to need to get the thing off the wall. Great. "How come you know so much about the fleet?"

"Like I said, I did a lot of studying." Lando snorted under his breath. "If you must know, I got stuck with a fake map to it as part of a deal back when I was selling used ships. I figured if I could learn enough about it to look like an expert I might be able to unload the map on someone else and get my money back."

"Did you?"

"You really want to know?"

"I guess not. Get ready; it's show time."

They were in luck. Aside from the bartender and a couple of deactivated serving droids behind the bar, the place was deserted. "Welcome back, gentlemen," the bartender greeted them. "What can I get you?"

"Something to take back to our quarters," Han told him, giving the shelves behind the bar a quick once-over. They had a good selection here—there were probably a hundred bottles of various shapes and sizes. But there was also a door off to the side that probably led back to a small storeroom. That'd be their best bet. "I don't suppose you'd have any Vistulo brandale on hand."

"I think we do," the bartender said, peering back at his selection. "Yes—there it is."

"What's the vintage?" Han asked.

"Ah—" The bartender brought the bottle over. "It's a '49."

Han made a face. "Don't have any '46, do you? Maybe stashed in the back room somewhere?"

"I don't think so, but I'll check," the bartender said agreeably, heading toward the door.

"I'll come with you," Han offered, ducking under the bar and joining him. "If you don't have any '46, maybe there'll be something else that'll do as well."

For a second the bartender looked like he was going to object. But he'd seen the two of them having a friendly drink earlier with Bel Iblis himself; and anyway, Han was already halfway to the storeroom door. "I guess that'd be okay," he said.

"Great," Han said, opening the door and ushering the bartender through.

He didn't know how long it would take Lando to get the repeater display off the wall, check it out, and then put it back up. On the theory it was better to play it safe, he managed to drag out the search for a '46 Vistulo for a full five minutes. Eventually, with cheerful good grace, he settled for a '48 Kibshae instead. The bartender led the way out of the room; mentally crossing his fingers, Han followed.

Lando was standing at the same place at the bar where he'd been when Han had left him, his hands on the bar, his face tight. And for good reason. Standing a few paces behind him, her hand on the butt of her blaster, was Irenez.

"Well, hello, Irenez," Han said, trying his best innocent look on her. "Funny meeting you here."

The innocent look was wasted. "Not all that funny," Irenez said tartly. "Sena assigned me to keep an eye on you. You get what you came for?"

Han looked at Lando, saw the fractional nod. "I think so, yeah," he said.

"Glad to hear it. Let's go—outside."

Han handed the bottle of Kibshae to the bartender. "Keep it," he said. "Looks like the party's been canceled."

THERE WAS AN old five-passenger landspeeder waiting outside when they emerged from the lounge. "Inside," Irenez said, motioning to the vehicle's aft doorway.

Han and Lando obeyed. There, sitting with uncharacteristic stiffness in one of the passenger seats, Sena Leikvold Midanyl was waiting. "Gentlemen," she said gravely as they entered. "Sit down, please."

Han chose one of the seats, swiveled it to face her. "Time for dinner already?"

"Irenez, take the controls," Sena said, ignoring him. "Drive us around the camp—I don't care where."

Silently, Irenez made her way to the front of the vehicle; and with a slight lurch they were off. "You didn't stay in your room very long," Sena said to Han.

"I don't remember the Senator saying anything about being confined to quarters," Han countered.

"He didn't," Sena agreed. "On the other hand, a properly brought up guest should know better than to wander unescorted around sensitive areas."

"I apologize," Han said, trying to keep a sarcastic edge out of his voice. "I didn't realize your liquor supply was classified." He glanced out the window. "If you're trying to take us back to our quarters, you're going the wrong way."

Sena studied his face a moment. "I came to ask you a favor."

It was about the last thing Han would have expected her to say, and it took him a second to find his voice again. "What sort of favor?"

"I want you to talk to Mon Mothma for me. To ask her and the Council to invite Senator Bel Iblis to join the New Republic."

Han shrugged. Was *that* why they'd brought him and Lando all the way over here? "You don't need a special invitation to join up. All you have to do is contact someone on the Council and offer your services."

A muscle in Sena's cheek twitched. "I'm afraid that in the Senator's case it's not going to be quite that easy," she said. "It's not so much a matter of joining the New Republic as of *re*joining it."

Han threw a frown at Lando. "Oh?" he said carefully.

Sena sighed, half turning to gaze out the side window. "It happened a long time ago," she said. "Before the various resistance groups fighting the Empire were formally consolidated into the Rebel Alliance. You know anything about that period of history?"

"Just what's in the official record," Han said. "Mon Mothma and Bail Organa of Alderaan got three of the biggest groups together and convinced them to make an alliance. After that the whole thing snowballed."

"Have you ever heard the name of that first agreement?"

"Sure. It was called the Corellian Treaty—" Han broke off. "The *Corellian* Treaty?"

"Yes," Sena nodded. "It was Senator Bel Iblis, not Mon Mothma, who convinced those three resistance groups to agree to a meeting. And, furthermore, who guaranteed protection for them."

For a long minute the only sound in the speeder was the hum of the repulsorlifts. "What happened?" Lando asked at last.

"To put it bluntly, Mon Mothma began to take over," Sena said. "Senator Bel Iblis was far better at strategy and tactics than she was, better even than many of the Rebellion's generals and admirals in those early days. But she had the gift of inspiration, the knack of getting diverse groups and species to work together. Gradually, she became the most visible symbol of the Rebellion, with Organa and the Senator increasingly relegated to the background."

"Must have been hard for someone like Bel Iblis to take," Lando murmured.

"Yes, it was," Sena said. "But you have to understand that it wasn't just pride that drove him to withdraw his support. Bail Organa had been a strong moderating influence on Mon Mothma—he was one of the few people whom she respected and trusted enough to pay serious attention to. After he was killed in the Death Star's attack on Alderaan, there was really no one of equal status who could stand up to her. She began to take more and more power to herself; and the Senator began to suspect that she was going to overthrow the Emperor only to set herself up in his place."

"So he pulled you out of the Alliance and started his own private war against the Empire," Lando said. "Did you know any of this, Han?"

"Never heard a whisper," Han shook his head.

"I'm not surprised," Sena said. "Would *you* have advertised a defection by someone of the Senator's stature? Especially in the middle of a war?"

"Probably not," Han conceded. "I suppose the only surprise is that more groups didn't back out like you did. Mon Mothma can be pretty overbearing when she wants to be."

"There wasn't any doubt as to who was in charge during the war, either," Lando added dryly. "I once saw her make Admiral Ackbar and General Madine both back down on one of their pet projects when she decided she didn't like it."

Han looked at Sena, a sudden thought striking him. "Is that why you've cut back your raids against the Empire? So that you'd be ready to move against Mon Mothma if she turned the New Republic into a dictatorship?"

"That's it exactly," Sena said. "We moved here to Peregrine's Nest just under three years ago, suspended all operations except materiel raids, and started working up tactical contingency plans. And settled in to wait for the Senator's triumphal vindication." Her cheek twitched again. "And we've been waiting ever since."

Han looked out the window at the camp passing by outside, a hollow sense of loss filling him. The legendary Senator Bel Iblis . . . waiting for a return to power that would never come. "It's not going to happen," he told Sena quietly.

"I know that." She hesitated. "Down deep, so does the Senator."

"Except that he can't swallow his pride long enough to go to Mon Mothma and ask to be let back in." Han nodded. "So he gets you to ask us to—"

"The Senator had nothing to do with this," Sena cut him off sharply. "He doesn't even know I'm talking to you. This is on my responsibility alone."

Han drew back a little. "Sure," he said. "Okay."

Sena shook her head. "I'm sorry," she apologized. "I didn't mean to snap at you."

"It's okay," Han said, feeling some sympathetic ache of his own. She could have all the good intentions and logic in the galaxy on her side, but this probably still looked and felt to her like betrayal. A stray memory clicked: the expression on

Luke's face, just before the battle off Yavin with the first Death Star. When he'd thought Han was going to run off and abandon them . . .

"Han," Lando said quietly.

Han looked over at his friend, shaking off the memory. Lando raised his eyebrows slightly in reminder . . . "We'll make you a deal, Sena," Han said, turning back to her. "We'll talk to Mon Mothma about the Senator. You talk to us about the *Katana* fleet."

Sena's face went rigid. "The *Katana* fleet?"

"Where your six Dreadnaughts came from," Lando said. "Don't bother denying it—I got a good look at that repeater display you've got up over the bar in the headquarters lounge."

Sena took a deep breath. "No. I can't tell you anything about that."

"Why not?" Lando asked. "We're all about to be allies again, remember?"

An unpleasant tingle ran up Han's back. "Unless you've already promised the fleet to Fey'lya."

"We've promised Fey'lya nothing," Sena said flatly. "Not that he hasn't asked for it."

Han grimaced. "So he *is* trying for a coup."

"Not at all," Sena shook her head. "Fey'lya wouldn't know what to do with a military coup if you gift wrapped it and handed it to him on a drinks tray. You have to understand that Bothans think in terms of political and persuasive influence, not military power. The typical Bothan's goal is to go through life getting more and more people to listen to what he has to say. Fey'lya thinks that being the one to bring the Senator back into the New Republic will be a large step in that direction."

"Especially if Ackbar isn't around to oppose him?" Han asked.

Sena nodded. "Yes, that's unfortunately another typical Bothan move. A Bothan leader who stumbles is invariably jumped on by all those who want to take over his position. In the distant past the attacks were literal—knives and usually death. Now, it's been modified to more of a verbal assassination. Progress, I suppose."

"Ackbar's not a Bothan," Lando pointed out.

"The technique is easily adapted to other races."

Han grunted. "What a great group to have as allies. So do they just stab, or do they also help with the tripping?"

"You mean the bank transfer?" Sena shook her head. "No, I doubt that was Fey'lya's doing. As a rule Bothans don't stick their necks out far enough to concoct plots on their own. They much prefer to take advantage of other people's."

"More like scavengers than hunters," Han said sourly. Probably explained why he'd always disliked Fey'lya and his crowd. "So what do we do about him?"

Sena shrugged. "All you really need to do is get Ackbar cleared. As soon as he's not vulnerable to attack anymore, Fey'lya should back off."

"Great," Han growled. "Problem is, with a Grand Admiral in charge of the Empire, we might not have that much time."

"And if we don't, neither do you," Lando added. "Wounded dignity aside, Sena, the Senator had better start facing reality. You're a small, isolated group with a line on the *Katana* fleet, and there's an Empire out there hungry for new warships. The minute the Grand Admiral tumbles to what you've got, he'll have the whole Imperial Fleet on you before you can blink twice. Bring the *Katana* fleet over to the New Republic and you get to be heroes. Wait too long, and you'll lose everything."

"I know that," Sena said, her voice almost too low to hear. Han waited, mentally crossing his fingers . . . "We don't actually know where the fleet is," she said. "Our Dreadnaughts came from a man who says he stumbled on them about fifteen years ago. He's thin, below-average height, with a sort of weasely look about him. He has short white hair and a heavily lined face, though I suspect much of that appearance is due more to some past disease or injury than actual age."

"What's his name?" Han asked.

"I don't know. He's never told us that." She hesitated again, then plunged ahead. "He loves to gamble, though. All our meetings with him have been aboard the *Coral Vanda*, usually across gaming tables. The staff there seemed to know him quite well, though the way he was throwing money around, that may not mean anything. Croupiers always get to know the losers quickly."

"The *Coral Vanda*?" Han asked.

"It's a subocean luxury casino on Pantolomin," Lando told him. "Does three- and seven-day runs through the big network of reefs lying off the northern continent. I've always wanted to go there, but never had the chance."

"Well, you've got it now," Han said. He looked at Sena. "I suppose the next question is how we're going to get out of here."

"That won't be a problem," she said, her voice sounding strained. Already having second thoughts, probably. "I can get the *Harrier* to take you back to New Cov. When do you want to leave?"

"Right now," Han said. He saw Sena's expression—"Look, no matter when we go, you're going to have some explaining to do to the Senator. We're in a race with the Empire here—even a few hours might make a difference."

"I suppose you're right," she said with a reluctant nod. "Irenez, take us to their ship. I'll make the arrangements from there."

IT TURNED OUT there was no need to make arrangements from the *Lady Luck*. Standing outside the ship's ramp as they arrived, clearly waiting for them, was Senator Bel Iblis.

"Hello, Solo; Calrissian," he smiled as Han and Lando stepped out of the speeder. "You weren't at your quarters, and I thought you might be here. I see I guessed right."

His eyes flicked over Han's shoulder as Sena emerged from the speeder. Looked again into Han's face . . . and abruptly the easy smile vanished. "Sena? What's going on?"

"They know about the *Katana* fleet, Commander," she said quietly, coming up beside Han. "And . . . I told them about our contact."

"I see," Bel Iblis said evenly. "And so you're leaving. To see if you can persuade him to turn the Dark Force over to the New Republic."

"That's right, sir," Han said, matching his tone. "We need the ships—need them pretty badly. But not as much as we need good fighters. And good commanders."

For a long moment Bel Iblis gazed at him. "I won't go to Mon Mothma like a beggar pleading to be let in," he said at last.

"You left for good reasons," Han persisted. "You can come back the same way."

Again, Bel Iblis's eyes flicked to Sena. "No," he said. "Too many people know what happened between us. I would look like an old fool. Or like a beggar."

He looked past Han, his eyes sweeping slowly across the buildings of Peregrine's Nest. "I don't have anything to bring, Solo," he said, his voice tinged with something that sounded like regret. "Once I'd dreamed of having a fleet that would rival the best in the New Republic. A fleet, and a string of decisive and pivotal victories over the Empire. With that, per- haps I could have returned with dignity and respect." He shook his head. "But what we have here barely qualifies as a strike force."

"Maybe so, but six Dreadnaughts aren't anything to sneer at," Lando put in. "And neither is your combat record. Forget Mon Mothma for a minute—every military person in the New Republic would be delighted to have you in."

Bel Iblis cocked an eyebrow. "Perhaps. I suppose it's worth thinking about."

"Especially with a Grand Admiral in charge of the Em- pire," Han pointed out. "If he catches you here alone, you'll have had it."

Bel Iblis smiled tightly. "That thought has occurred to me,

Solo. Several times a day." He straightened up. "The *Harrier* is leaving in half an hour to take Breil'lya back to New Cov. I'll instruct them to take you and the *Lady Luck* along."

Han and Lando exchanged glances. "You think it'll be safe to go back to New Cov, sir?" Han asked. "There might still be Imperials hanging around."

"There won't be." Bel Iblis was positive. "I've studied the Imperials and their tactics a long time. Aside from not expecting us to show up again so soon, they really can't afford to hang around any one place for long. Besides, we have to go there—Breil'lya will need to pick up his ship."

Han nodded, wondering what kind of report Breil'lya would be giving to his boss when he got back to Coruscant. "All right. Well . . . I guess we'd better get the ship prepped."

"Yes." Bel Iblis hesitated, then held out his hand. "It was good to see you, Solo. I hope we'll meet again."

"I'm sure we will, sir," Han assured him, grasping the outstretched hand.

The Senator nodded to Lando. "Calrissian," he said. Releasing Han's hand, he turned and walked away across the landing field.

Han watched him go, trying to figure out whether he admired the Senator more than he pitied him or vice versa. It was a useless exercise. "Our luggage is still back at our quarters," he told Sena.

"I'll have it sent over while you get the ship prepped." She looked at Han, her eyes suddenly blazing with a smoldering fire. "But I want you to remember one thing," she said with deadly earnestness. "You can go now, with our blessings. But if you betray the Senator—in any way—you will die. At my hand, personally, if necessary."

Han held her gaze, considering what to say. To remind her, perhaps, that he'd been attacked by bounty hunters and interstellar criminals, shot at by Imperial stormtroopers, and tortured at the direction of Darth Vader himself. To suggest that after all that, a threat coming from someone like Sena was too laughable to even take seriously. "I understand," he said gravely. "I won't let you down."

FROM THE DORSAL hatchway connection behind them came the creak of a stressed seal; and through the *Lady Luck*'s canopy the patch of stars visible around the bulk of the Dreadnaught abruptly flashed into starlines. "Here we go again," Lando said, his voice sounding resigned. "How do I keep letting you talk me into these things?"

"Because you're the respectable one," Han told him, running an eye over the *Lady Luck*'s instruments. There wasn't a lot there to see, with the engines and most of the systems running at standby. "And because you know as well as I do that we have to do it. Sooner or later the Empire's going to find out that the *Katana* fleet's been found and start looking for it themselves. And if they get to it before we do, we're going to be in big trouble." And here they were, stuck uselessly for another two days in hyperspace while the *Harrier* took them back to New Cov. Not because they wanted to go there, but because Bel Iblis wasn't willing to trust them with the location of his stupid Peregrine's Nest base—

"You're worried about Leia, aren't you?" Lando asked into the silence.

"I shouldn't have let her go," Han muttered. "Something's gone wrong. I just know it. That lying little alien's turned her over to the Empire, or the Grand Admiral's out-thought us again. I don't know, but *something*."

"Leia can take care of herself, Han," Lando said quietly. "And even Grand Admirals sometimes make mistakes."

Han shook his head. "He made his mistake at Sluis Van, Lando. He won't make another one. Bet you the *Falcon* he won't."

Lando clapped him on the shoulder. "Come on, buddy, brooding about it won't help. We've got two days to kill. Let's go break out a sabacc deck."

———

THE GRAND ADMIRAL read the dispatch twice before turning his glowing eyes on Pellaeon. "You vouch for the reliability of this report, Captain?"

"As much as I can vouch for any report that doesn't originate with an Imperial agent," Pellaeon told him. "On the other hand, this particular smuggler has fed us fifty-two reports over the last ten years, forty-eight of which proved to be accurate. I'd say he's worth believing."

Thrawn looked back at the reader. "Endor," he murmured, half to himself. "Why Endor?"

"I don't know, sir," Pellaeon said. "Perhaps they were looking for another place to hide."

"Among the Ewoks?" Thrawn snorted derisively. "That would be desperation indeed. But no matter. If the *Millennium Falcon* is there, then so is Leia Organa Solo. Alert Navigation and Engineering; we leave immediately for Endor."

"Yes, sir," Pellaeon nodded, keying in the orders. "Shall I have Khabarakh brought up from Nystao?"

"Yes. Khabarakh." Thrawn said the name thoughtfully. "Note the interesting timing here, Captain. Khabarakh comes back to Honoghr after a month's absence, just as Solo and Organa Solo head off on secret errands to New Cov and Endor. Coincidence?"

Pellaeon frowned. "I don't follow you, sir."

Thrawn smiled thinly. "What I think, Captain, is that we're seeing a new degree of subtlety among our enemies. They knew that the return of a survivor from the failed Kashyyyk operation would catch my attention. They therefore arranged his release to coincide with their own missions, in the hope I would be too preoccupied to notice them. Doubtless when we break Khabarakh, we'll learn a great many things from him that will cost us countless man-hours to finally prove wrong." Thrawn snorted again. "No, leave him where he is. You may inform the dynasts that I have decided to permit them the full seven days of public shame, after which they may perform the rites of discovery as they choose. No matter how useless his information, Khabarakh may still serve the Empire by dying painfully. As an object lesson to his race."

"Yes, sir." Pellaeon hesitated. "May I point out, though, that such a drastic psychological fragmentation and reconditioning is well outside the Rebellion's usual operating procedure."

"I agree," Thrawn said grimly. "Which implies all the more strongly that whatever Organa Solo is looking for on Endor, it's considerably more vital to the Rebellion's war effort than mere sanctuary."

Pellaeon frowned, trying to think of what might be on Endor that anyone could possibly want. "Some of the materiel left over from the Death Star project?" he hazarded.

"More valuable than that," the Grand Admiral shook his head. "Information, perhaps, that the Emperor might have had with him when he died. Information they may think they can still retrieve."

And then Pellaeon got it. "The location of the Mount Tantiss storehouse."

Thrawn nodded. "That's the only thing I can think of that would be worth this much effort on their part. At any rate, it's a risk we can't afford to take. Not now."

"Agreed." Pellaeon's board pinged: Navigation and Engineering signaling ready. "Shall I break orbit?"

"At your convenience, Captain."

Pellaeon nodded to the helm. "Take us out. Course as set by Navigation."

Through the viewports the planet below began to fall away; and as it did so there was the short trill of a priority message coming through. Pellaeon pulled it up, read the heading. "Admiral? Report from the *Adamant*, in the Abregado system. They've captured one of Talon Karrde's freighters. Transcript of the preliminary interrogation is coming through now." He frowned as he glanced down to the end. "It's rather short, sir."

"Thank you," Thrawn said with quiet satisfaction as he pulled up the report to his own station.

He was still reading it when the *Chimaera* made the jump to lightspeed. Reading it very, very carefully.

CHAPTER 17

MARA HAD NEVER been to the Abregado-rae Spaceport before; but as she walked along its streets she decided it deserved every bit of the rock-bottom reputation it had worked so hard to achieve.

Not that it showed on the surface. On the contrary, the place was neat and almost painfully clean, though with that grating antiseptic quality that showed the cleanliness had been imposed from above by government decree instead of from below by the genuine wishes of the inhabitants. It seemed reasonably peaceful, too, as spaceports went, with lots of uniformed security men patrolling the streets around the landing pits.

But beneath the surface glitter the rot showed straight through. Showed in the slightly furtive manner of the locals; in the halfhearted swaggering of the uniformed security men; in the lingering stares of the plainclothes but just as obvious quiet security men. The whole spaceport—maybe the whole planet—was being held together with tie wire and blaster power packs.

A petty totalitarian regime, and a populace desperate to escape it. Just the sort of place where anyone would betray anyone else for the price of a ticket offplanet. Which meant that if any of the locals had tumbled to the fact that there was a smuggling ship sitting here under Security's nose, Mara had about ten steps to go before the whole place came down on top of her.

Walking toward a faded door with the equally faded sign "Landing Pit 21" over it, she hoped sardonically that it wasn't a trap. She would really hate to die in a place like this.

The door to the landing pit was unlocked. Taking a deep breath, acutely conscious of the two pairs of uniformed security men within sight of her, she went inside.

It was the *Etherway*, all right, looking just as shabby and decrepit as it had when Fynn Torve had had to abandon it in Landing Pit 63 of this same spaceport. Mara gave it a quick once-over, checked out all the nooks and crannies in the pit where an armed ambush squad could be skulking, and finally focused on the dark-haired young man lounging in a chair by the freighter's lowered ramp. Even in that casual slouch he couldn't shake the military air that hovered around him. "Hello, there," he called to her, lowering the data pad he'd been reading. "Nice day for flying. You interested in hiring a ship?"

"No," she said, walking toward him as she tried to watch all directions at once. "I'm more in a buying mood, myself. What kind of ship is this flying hatbox, anyway?"

"It's a Harkners-Balix Nine-Oh-Three," the other sniffed with a second-rate attempt at wounded pride. "Flying hatbox, indeed."

Not much of an actor, but he was clearly getting a kick out of all this cloak-and-blade stuff. Setting her teeth firmly together, Mara sent a silent curse down on Torve's head for setting up such a ridiculous identification procedure in the first place. "Looks like a Nine-Seventeen to me," she said dutifully. "Or even a Nine-Twenty-Two."

"No, it's a Nine-Oh-Three," he insisted. "Trust me—my uncle used to make landing gear pads for them. Come inside and I'll show you how to tell the difference."

"Oh, that'll be great," Mara muttered under her breath as she followed him up the ramp.

"Glad you finally got here," the man commented over his shoulder as they reached the top of the ramp. "I was starting to think you'd been caught."

"That could still happen if you don't shut up," Mara growled back. "Keep your voice down, will you?"

"It's okay," he assured her. "I've got all your MSE droids clattering around on cleaning duty just inside the outer hull. That should block out any audio probes."

Theoretically, she supposed, he was right. As a practical matter . . . well, if the locals had the place under surveillance they were in trouble, anyway. "You have any trouble getting the ship out of impoundment?" she asked him.

"Not really," he said. "The spaceport administrator said the whole thing was highly irregular, but he didn't give me any major grief about it." He grinned. "Though I suppose the size of the bribe I slipped him might have had something to do with that. My name's Wedge Antilles, by the way. I'm a friend of Captain Solo's."

"Nice to meet you," Mara said. "Solo couldn't make it himself?"

Antilles shook his head. "He had to leave Coruscant on some kind of special mission, so he asked me to get the ship sprung for you. I was scheduled for escort duty a couple systems over anyway, so it wasn't a problem."

Mara ran a quick eye over him. From his build and general manner . . . "B-wing pilot?" she hazarded.

"X-wing," he corrected her. "I've got to get back before my convoy finishes loading. Want me to give you an escort out of here?"

"Thanks, but no," she said, resisting the urge to say something sarcastic. The first rule of smuggling was to stay as inconspicuous as possible, and flying out of a third-rate spaceport with a shiny New Republic X-wing starfighter in tow didn't exactly qualify as a low-profile stance. "Tell Solo thanks."

"Right. Oh, one other thing," Antilles added as she started past him. "Han also wanted me to ask you if your people might be interested in selling information on our friend with the eyes."

Mara sent him a sharp look. "Our friend with the eyes?"

Antilles shrugged. "That's what he said. He said you'd understand."

Mara felt her lip twist. "I understand just fine. Tell him I'll pass on the message."

"Okay." He hesitated. "It sounded like it was pretty important—"

"I said I'll pass on the message."

He shrugged again. "Okay—just doing my job. Have a good trip." With a friendly nod, he headed back down the ramp. Still half expecting a trap, Mara got the hatchway sealed for flight and went up to the bridge.

It took a quarter hour to run the ship through its preflight sequence, almost exactly the amount of time it took the spaceport controllers to confirm her for takeoff. Easing in the repulsorlifts, she lifted clear of the landing pit and made for space.

She was nearly high enough to kick in the sublight drive when the back of her neck began to tingle.

"Uh-oh," she muttered aloud, giving the displays a quick scan. Nothing was visible; but this close to a planetary mass, that meant less than nothing. Anything could be lurking just over the horizon, from a single flight of TIE fighters all the way up to an Imperial Star Destroyer.

But maybe they weren't quite ready yet . . .

She threw full power to the drive, feeling herself pressed back into the seat cushion for a few seconds as the acceleration compensators fought to catch up. An indignant howl came from the controller on the comm speaker; ignoring him, she keyed the computer, hoping that Torve had followed

Karrde's standard procedure when he'd first put down on Abregado.

He had. The calculation for the jump out of here had already been computed and loaded, just waiting to be initiated. She got the computer started making the minor adjustments that would correct for a couple of months of general galactic drift, and looked back out the forward viewport.

There, emerging over the horizon directly ahead, was the massive bulk of a *Victory*-class Star Destroyer.

Bearing toward her.

For a long heartbeat Mara just sat there, her mind skimming through the possibilities, all the time knowing full well how futile the exercise was. The Star Destroyer's commander had planned his interception with exquisite skill: given their respective vectors and the *Etherway*'s proximity to the planet, there was absolutely no way she would be able to elude the larger ship's weapons and tractor beams long enough to make her escape to lightspeed. Briefly, she toyed with the hope that the Imperials might not be after her at all, that they were actually gunning for that Antilles character still on the surface. But that hope, too, evaporated quickly. A single X-wing pilot could hardly be important enough to tie up a *Victory*-class Star Destroyer for. And if he was, they would certainly not have been so incompetent as to spring the trap prematurely.

"Freighter *Etherway*," a cold voice boomed over her comm speaker. "This is the Star Destroyer *Adamant*. You are ordered to shut down your engines and prepare to be brought aboard."

So that was that. They had indeed been looking for her. In a very few minutes now she would be their prisoner.

Unless . . .

Reaching over, she keyed her mike. "Star Destroyer *Adamant*, this is the *Etherway*," she said briskly. "I congratulate you on your vigilance; I was afraid I was going to have to search the next five systems to find an Imperial ship."

"You will shut down all deflector systems—" The voice faltered halfway through the standard speech as the fact belatedly penetrated that this was not the normal response of the normal Imperial prisoner.

"I'll want to speak to your captain the minute I'm aboard," Mara said into the conversational gap. "I'll need him to set up a meeting with Grand Admiral Thrawn and provide me transport to wherever he and the *Chimaera* are at the moment. And get a tractor beam ready—I don't want to have to land this monster in your hangar bay myself."

The surprises were coming too fast for the poor man. "Ah—freighter *Etherway*—" he tried again.

"On second thought, put the captain on now," Mara cut him off. She had the initiative now, and was determined to keep it as long as possible. "There's no one around who can tap into this communication."

There was a moment of silence. Mara continued on her intercept course, a trickle of doubt beginning to worm its way through her resolve. *It's the only way*, she told herself sternly.

"This is the captain," a new voice came on the speaker. "Who are you?"

"Someone with important information for Grand Admiral Thrawn," Mara told him, shifting from brisk to just slightly haughty. "For the moment, that's all you need to know."

But the captain wasn't as easily bullied as his junior officers. "Really," he said dryly. "According to our sources, you're a member of Talon Karrde's smuggling gang."

"And you don't believe such a person could tell the Grand Admiral anything useful?" she countered, letting her tone frost over a bit.

"Oh, I'm sure you can," the captain said. "I simply don't see any reason why I should bother him with what will be, after all, a routine interrogation."

Mara squeezed her left hand into a fist. At all costs she had to avoid the kind of complete mind-sifting the captain was obviously hinting at. "I wouldn't advise that," she told him, throwing every bit of the half-remembered dignity and power of the old Imperial court into her voice. "The Grand Admiral would be extremely displeased with you. *Extremely* displeased."

There was a short pause. Clearly, the captain was starting to recognize that he had more here than he'd bargained for. Just as clearly, he wasn't ready yet to back down. "I have my orders," he said flatly. "I'll need more than vague hints before I can make you an exception to them."

Mara braced herself. This was it. After all these years of hiding from the Empire, as well as from everyone else, this was finally it. "Then send a message to the Grand Admiral," she said. "Tell him the recognition code is Hapspir, Barrini, Corbolan, Triaxis."

There was a moment of silence, and Mara realized she'd finally gotten through to the other. "And your name?" the captain asked, his voice suddenly respectful.

Beneath her, the *Etherway* jolted slightly as the *Adamant*'s tractor beam locked on. She was committed now. The only way out was to see it all through. "Tell him," she said, "that he knew me as the Emperor's Hand."

THEY BROUGHT HER and the *Etherway* aboard, settled her with uncertain deference into one of the senior officers' quarters . . . and then headed away from Abregado like a mynock with its tail on fire.

She was left alone in the cabin for the rest of the day and into the night, seeing no one, speaking with no one. Meals were delivered by an SE4 servant droid; at all other times the door was kept locked. Whether the enforced privacy was on the captain's orders or whether it came from above was impossible to tell, but at least it gave her time to do such limited planning as she could.

There was similarly no way of knowing where they were going, but from the labored sound of the engines, she could guess they were pushing uncomfortably far past a *Victory* Star

Destroyer's normal flank speed of Point Four Five. Possibly even as high as Point Five, which would mean they were covering a hundred twenty-seven light-years per hour. For a while she kept her mind occupied by trying to guess which system they might be making for; but as the hours ticked by and the number of possibilities grew too unwieldy to keep track of, she abandoned the game.

Twenty-two hours after leaving Abregado, they arrived at the rendezvous. At the last place Mara would have expected. At the very last place in the galaxy she would have wanted to go. The place where her universe had died a sudden and violent death.

Endor.

"THE GRAND ADMIRAL will see you now," the stormtrooper squad leader said, stepping back from the opening door and motioning her ahead. Mara threw a glance at the silent Noghri bodyguard standing on the other side of the doorway and stepped through.

"Ah," a well-remembered voice called quietly from the command center in the middle of the room. Grand Admiral Thrawn sat in the double display ring, his red eyes glowing at her above the glistening white uniform. "Come in."

Mara stayed where she was. "Why did you bring me to Endor?" she demanded.

The glowing eyes narrowed. "I beg your pardon?"

"You heard me," she said. "Endor. Where the Emperor died. Why did you choose this place for the rendezvous?"

The other seemed to consider that. "Come closer, Mara Jade."

The voice was rich with the overtones of command, and Mara found herself walking toward him before she realized what she was doing. "If it's supposed to be a joke, it's in poor taste," she bit out. "If it's supposed to be a test, then get it over with."

"It is neither," Thrawn said as she came to the edge of the outer display ring and stopped. "The choice was forced upon us by other, unconnected business." One blue-black eyebrow raised slightly. "Or perhaps not *entirely* unconnected. That still remains to be seen. Tell me, can you really sense the Emperor's presence here?"

Mara took a deep breath, feeling the air shuddering through her lungs with an ache as real as it was intangible. Could Thrawn see how much this place hurt her? she wondered. How thick with memories and sensations the whole Endor system still remained? Or would he even care about any of that if he did?

He saw, all right. She could tell that much from the way he was looking at her. What he thought of it she didn't much care. "I can feel the evidence of his death," she told him. "It's not pleasant. Let's get this over with so I can get out of here."

His lip quirked, perhaps at her assumption that she would in fact be leaving the *Chimaera*. "Very well. Let's begin with some proof of who you were."

"I gave the *Adamant*'s captain a high-level recognition code," she reminded him.

"Which is why you're here instead of in a detention cell," Thrawn said. "The code isn't proof in itself."

"All right, then," Mara said. "We met once, during the public dedication of the new Assemblage wing of the Imperial Palace on Coruscant. At that ceremony the Emperor introduced me to you as Lianna, one of his favorite dancers. Later, during the more private ceremony that followed, he revealed to you my true identity."

"And what was that private ceremony?"

"Your secret promotion to the rank of Grand Admiral."

Thrawn pursed his lips, his eyes never leaving her face. "You wore a white dress to both ceremonies," he said. "Aside from the sash, the dress had only one decoration. Do you recall what that decoration was?"

Mara had to think back. "It was a small shoulder-sculp,"

she said slowly. "Left shoulder. A Xyquine design, as I remember."

"It was indeed." Thrawn reached to his control board, touched a switch; and abruptly, the room was filled with holos of shouldersculps on ornate pillars. "The one you wore is somewhere in this room. Find it."

Mara swallowed, turning slowly as she looked around. She'd had literally hundreds of fancy dresses for her cover role as a member of the Emperor's entourage. To remember one particular shouldersculp out of all that . . .

She shook her head, trying to clear away the unpleasant buzzing sensation that hovered deep in her mind. She'd had an excellent memory once, one which the Emperor's training had made even better. Focusing her thoughts, fighting upstream against the disquieting aura of this place, she concentrated . . . "That's it," she said, pointing to a delicate filigree of gold and blue.

Thrawn's expression didn't change, but he seemed to relax a little in his seat. "Welcome back, Emperor's Hand." He touched the switch a second time, and the art gallery vanished. "You've been a long time in returning."

The glowing eyes bored into her face, the question unspoken but obvious. "What was here for me before?" she countered. "Who but a Grand Admiral would have accepted me as legitimate?"

"Was that the only reason?"

Mara hesitated, recognizing the trip wire. Thrawn had been in command of the Empire for over a year now, and yet she hadn't approached him until now. "There were other reasons," she said. "None of which I wish to discuss at this time."

His face hardened. "As, I presume, you don't wish to discuss why you helped Skywalker escape from Talon Karrde?"

YOU WILL KILL LUKE SKYWALKER.

Mara jerked, unsure for that first frozen heartbeat whether

the voice had been real or just in her mind. The strange buzzing intensified, and for a moment she could almost see the Emperor's wizened face glaring at her. The image grew clearer, the rest of the room beginning to swim before her eyes . . .

She took a deep breath, forcing calmness. She would not fall apart. Not here; not in front of the Grand Admiral. "It wasn't my idea to let Skywalker escape," she said.

"And you were unable to alter that decision?" Thrawn asked, the eyebrow lifting again. "You, the Emperor's Hand?"

"We were on Myrkr," Mara reminded him stiffly. "Under the influence of a planetful of ysalamiri." She glanced over his shoulder at the ysalamir hanging from the nutrient frame behind his chair. "I doubt you've forgotten their effect on the Force."

"Oh, I remember it quite well," Thrawn nodded. "It's their dampening of the Force, in fact, that proves Skywalker had help in his escape. All I need to know from you is whether it was Karrde himself who gave the order, or others of his group acting independently."

So that he would know where to focus his revenge. Mara looked into those glowing eyes, beginning to remember now why the Emperor had made this man a Grand Admiral. "It doesn't matter who's responsible," she said. "I'm here to offer a deal that'll clear the debt."

"I'm listening," Thrawn said, his face neutral.

"I want you to stop your harassment of Karrde and his organization. To cancel the cash bounty on all of us, and clear us with all Imperial forces and worlds that you control." She hesitated; but this was no time to go all bashful. "I also want a monetary credit of three million to be deposited under Karrde's name toward the purchase of Imperial goods and services."

"Indeed," Thrawn said, his lip twitching in an amused smile. "I'm afraid Skywalker isn't worth nearly that much to me. Or do you propose to deliver Coruscant, as well?"

"I'm not offering Skywalker or Coruscant," Mara said. "I'm offering the *Katana* fleet."

The amused smile vanished. "The *Katana* fleet?" Thrawn repeated quietly, his eyes glittering.

"Yes, the *Katana* fleet," Mara said. "The Dark Force, if you prefer the more dramatic title. I presume you've heard of it?"

"I have indeed. Where is it?"

The tone of command again; but this time Mara was ready for it. Not that it would have done him any good anyway. "I don't know," she told him. "But Karrde does."

For a long moment Thrawn gazed at her in silence. "How?" he asked at last.

"He was on a smuggling mission that went sour," she told him. "They escaped past some Imperial watchdogs, but didn't have time to do a proper jump calculation. They ran into the fleet, thought it was a trap, and jumped again, nearly destroying the ship in the process. Karrde was on nav duty; later, he figured out what they'd hit."

"Interesting," he murmured. "When exactly was this?"

"That's all I'll give you until we have a deal," Mara told him. She caught the expression on his face—"And if you're thinking of running me through one of Intelligence's sifters, don't bother. I really *don't* know where the fleet is."

Thrawn studied her. "And you would have blocks set up around it even if you did," he agreed. "All right. Tell me where Karrde is, then."

"So Intelligence can sift him instead?" Mara shook her head. "No. Let me go back to him, and I'll get you the location. Then we'll trade. Assuming the deal is to your liking."

A dark shadow had settled across Thrawn's face. "Do not presume to dictate to me, Mara Jade," he said quietly. "Not even in private."

A small shiver ran up Mara's back. Yes; she was remembering indeed why Thrawn had been made a Grand Admiral. "I was the Emperor's Hand," she reminded him, matching the steel in his tone as best she could. Even to her own ears it came out a poor second. "I spoke for him . . . and even Grand Admirals were obliged to listen."

Thrawn smiled sardonically. "Really. Your memory serves you poorly, Emperor's Hand. When all is said and done, you were little more than a highly specialized courier."

Mara glared at him. "Perhaps it is *your* memory that needs refreshing, Grand Admiral Thrawn," she retorted. "I traveled throughout the Empire in his name, making policy decisions that changed lives at the highest levels of government—"

"You carried out his will," Thrawn cut her off sharply. "No more. Whether you heard his commands more clearly than the rest of his Hands is irrelevant. It was still his decisions that you implemented."

"What do you mean, the rest of his Hands?" Mara sniffed. "I was the only—"

She broke off. The look on Thrawn's face . . . and abruptly, all her rising anger drained away. "No," she breathed. "No. You're wrong."

He shrugged. "Believe what you wish. But don't attempt to blind others with exaggerated memories of your own importance." Reaching to his control board, he tapped a key. "Captain? What report from the boarding party?"

The reply wasn't audible; but Mara wasn't interested in what Thrawn's men were doing, anyway. He was wrong. He *had* to be wrong. Hadn't the Emperor himself given her the title of Emperor's Hand? Hadn't he himself brought her to Coruscant from her home and trained her, teaching her how to use her rare sensitivity to the Force to serve him?

He wouldn't have lied to her. He wouldn't have.

"No, there's no point to that," Thrawn said. He looked up at Mara. "You don't happen to have any idea why Leia Organa Solo might have come to Endor, do you?"

With an effort, Mara brought her thoughts back from the past. "Organa Solo is here?"

"The *Millennium Falcon* is, at any rate," he said grimly. "Left in orbit, which unfortunately leaves us no way of knowing where she might be. If she's there at all." He turned back to his board. "Very well, Captain. Have the ship brought aboard. Perhaps a closer examination will tell us something."

He got an acknowledgment and keyed off the circuit. "Very well, Emperor's Hand," he said, looking up at Mara again. "We have an agreement. The Dark Force for the lifting of our death mark against Karrde. How long will it take you to return to Karrde's current base?"

Mara hesitated; but that information wouldn't do the Grand Admiral much good. "On the *Etherway*, about three days. Two and a half if I push it."

"I suggest you do so," Thrawn said. "Since you have exactly eight days to obtain the location and bring it back here to me."

Mara stared at him. "Eight days? But that—"

"Eight days. Or I find him and get the location my way."

A dozen possible retorts rushed through Mara's mind. Another look at those glowing red eyes silenced all of them. "I'll do what I can," she managed. Turning, she headed back across the room.

"I'm sure you will," he said after her. "And afterward, we'll sit down and have a long talk together. About your years away from Imperial service . . . and why you've been so long in returning."

PELLAEON STARED RIGIDLY at his commander, heart thudding audibly in his chest. "The *Katana* fleet?" he repeated carefully.

"So our young Emperor's Hand told me," Thrawn said. His gaze was fixed solidly on one of the displays in front of him. "She may be lying, of course."

Pellaeon nodded mechanically, the possibilities sweeping out like a spread cloak before him. "The Dark Force," he murmured the old nickname, listening to the words echo through his mind. "You know, I once had hopes of finding the fleet myself."

"Most everyone your age did," Thrawn returned dryly. "Is the homing device properly installed aboard her ship?"

"Yes, sir." Pellaeon let his gaze drift around the room, his eyes focusing without real interest on the sculptures and flats that Thrawn had on display today. The Dark Force. Lost for nearly fifty-five years. Now within their grasp . . .

He frowned suddenly at the sculptures. Many of them looked familiar, somehow.

"They're the various pieces of art that graced the offices of Rendili Star Drive and the Fleet planning department at the time they were working on the basic design of the *Katana*," Thrawn answered his unspoken question.

"I see," Pellaeon said. He took a deep breath and, reluctantly, brought himself back to reality. "You realize, sir, how improbable this claim of Jade's really is."

"Certainly it's improbable." Thrawn raised glowing eyes to Pellaeon. "But it's also true." He tapped a switch, and part of the art gallery vanished. "Observe."

Pellaeon turned to look. It was the same scene Thrawn had showed him a few days earlier: the three renegade Dreadnaughts providing cover fire off New Cov so that the *Lady Luck* and that unidentified freighter could escape—

He inhaled sharply, a sudden suspicion flooding into him. "*Those* ships?"

"Yes," Thrawn said, his voice grimly satisfied. "The differences between regular and slave-rigged Dreadnaughts are subtle, but visible enough when you know to look for them."

Pellaeon frowned at the holo, trying hard to fit all of it together. "Your permission, Admiral, but it doesn't make sense for Karrde to be supplying this renegade Corellian with ships."

"I agree," Thrawn nodded. "Obviously, someone else from that ill-fated smuggling ship also realized what it was they'd stumbled across. We're going to find that someone."

"Do we have any leads?"

"A few. According to Jade, they escaped from an Imperial force on the way out of a botched job. All such incidents should be on file somewhere; we'll correlate with what we know about Karrde's checkered past and see what turns up. Jade also said that the ship was badly damaged in the process of doing its second jump. If they had to go to a major spaceport for repairs, that should be on file, as well."

"I'll put Intelligence on it immediately," Pellaeon nodded.

"Good." Thrawn's eyes unfocused for a moment. "And I also want you to get in contact with Niles Ferrier."

Pellaeon had to search his memory. "That ship thief you sent out to look for the Corellian's home base?"

"That's the one," Thrawn said. "Tell him to forget the Corellian and concentrate instead on Solo and Calrissian." He cocked an eyebrow. "After all, if the Corellian is indeed planning to join the Rebellion, what better dowry could he bring than the *Katana* fleet?"

The comm pinged. "Yes?" Thrawn asked.

"Sir, the target has made the jump to lightspeed," a voice reported. "We've got a strong signal from the beacon; we're doing a probability extrapolation now."

"Very good, Lieutenant," Thrawn said. "Don't bother with any extrapolations just yet—she'll change course at least once more before settling down on her true heading."

"Yes, sir."

"Still, we don't want her getting too far ahead of us," Thrawn told Pellaeon as he keyed off the comm. "You'd best return to the bridge, Captain, and get the *Chimaera* moving after her."

"Yes, sir." Pellaeon hesitated. "I thought we were going to give her time to get the *Katana*'s location for us."

Thrawn's expression hardened. "She's not part of the Empire anymore, Captain," he said. "She may want us to believe that she's coming back—she may even believe it herself. But she isn't. No matter. She's leading us to Karrde, and that's the important thing. Between him and our Corellian renegade we have two leads to the *Katana* fleet. One way or the other, we'll find it."

Pellaeon nodded, feeling the stirrings of excitement again despite his best efforts to remain unemotional about this. The *Katana* fleet. Two hundred Dreadnaughts, just sitting there waiting for the Empire to take possession . . .

"I have the feeling, Admiral," he said, "that our final offensive against the Rebellion may be ready to launch a bit ahead of schedule."

Thrawn smiled. "I believe, Captain, that you may be right."

CHAPTER 18

THEY HAD BEEN sitting around the table in the maitrakh's house since early morning, studying maps and floor plans and diagrams, searching for a plan of action that would be more than simply a complicated way of surrendering. Finally, just before noon, Leia called a halt. "I can't look at this anymore," she told Chewbacca, closing her eyes briefly and rubbing her thumbs against throbbing temples. "Let's go outside for a while."

Chewbacca growled an objection. "Yes, of course there are risks," she agreed wearily. "But the whole village knows we're here, and no one's told the authorities yet. Come on; it'll be okay." Stepping to the door, she opened it and went out. Chewbacca grumbled under his breath, but followed after her.

The late morning sunshine was blazing brightly down, with only a scattering of high clouds to interfere. Leia glanced upward at the clear sky, shivering involuntarily at the sudden sensation of nakedness that flooded in on her. A clear sky, all the way up to space . . . but it was all right. A little before midnight the maitrakh had brought the news of the Star Destroyer's imminent departure, a departure which she and Chewbacca had been able to watch with the macrobinoculars from the Wookiee's kit. It had been their first break since Khabarakh's arrest: just as it had begun to look like she and Chewbacca would be pinned down here until it was too late, the Grand Admiral had abruptly left.

It was an unexpected gift . . . a gift which Leia couldn't help but view with suspicion. From the way the Grand Admiral had been talking in the *dukha*, she'd expected him to stay here until Khabarakh's humiliation period had ended, after which the shipboard interrogation would begin. Perhaps he'd changed his mind and had taken Khabarakh back early, with a backhand gesture of contempt for Noghri tradition. But the maitrakh had said that Khabarakh was still on public display in the center of Nystao.

Unless she was lying about that. Or was herself being lied to about it. But if the Grand Admiral suspected enough to lie to the maitrakh, why hadn't a legion of Imperial troops already swooped down on them?

But he was a Grand Admiral, with all the cunning and subtlety and tactical genius that the title implied. This whole thing could be a convoluted, carefully orchestrated trap . . . and if it was, chances were she would never even see it until it had been sprung around her.

Stop it! she ordered herself firmly. Letting herself get caught up in the mythos of infallibility that had been built up around the Grand Admirals would gain her nothing but mental paralysis. Even Grand Admirals could make mistakes, and there were any number of reasons why he might have had to leave Honoghr. Perhaps some part of the campaign against the New Republic had gone sour, requiring his attention elsewhere. Or perhaps he'd simply gone off on some short errand, intending to be back in a day or two.

Either way, it meant that the time to strike was now. If they could only find something to strike at.

Beside her, Chewbacca growled a suggestion. "We can't do

that," Leia shook her head. "It'd be no better than a full-blown attack on the spaceport. We have to keep damage to Nystao and its people to an absolute minimum."

The Wookiee snarled impatiently.

"I don't *know* what else to do," she snapped back. "All I know is that death and massive destruction won't do anything but put us back where we were before we came here. It certainly won't convince the Noghri that they should leave the Empire and come over to our side."

She looked out past the cluster of huts at the distant hills and the brown *kholm*-grass rippling in the breeze. Glinting in the sunlight, the squat box shapes of a dozen decon droids were hard at work, scooping up a quarter cubic meter of topsoil with each bite, running it through some exotic catalytic magic in their interiors, and dumping the cleansed product out the back. Slowly but steadily bringing the people of Honoghr back from the edge of the destruction they'd faced . . . and a highly visible reminder, if anyone needed it, of the Empire's benevolence toward them.

"Lady Vader," a gravelly voice mewed from just behind her.

Leia jumped. "Good morning, maitrakh," she said, turning and giving the Noghri a solemn nod. "I trust you are well this morning?"

"I feel no sickness," the other said shortly.

"Good," Leia said, the word sounding rather lame. The maitrakh hadn't been so impolite as to say anything out loud, but it was clear enough that she considered herself to be in a no-win situation here, with dishonor and perhaps even death waiting for her family as soon as the Grand Admiral discovered what Khabarakh had done. It was probably only a matter of time, Leia knew, before she came to the conclusion that turning the intruders over to the Empire herself would be the least disastrous course still open to her.

"Your plans," the maitrakh said. "How do they go?"

Leia glanced at Chewbacca. "We're making progress," she said. It was true enough, after a fashion: the elimination of every approach they'd come up with *did* technically qualify as progress. "We still have a long way to go, though."

"Yes," the maitrakh said. She looked out past the buildings. "Your droid has spent much time with the other machines."

"There isn't as much here for him to do as I'd thought there would be," Leia said. "You and many of your people speak Basic better than I'd anticipated."

"The Grand Admiral has taught us well."

"As did my father, the Lord Darth Vader, before him," Leia reminded her.

The maitrakh was silent a moment. "Yes," she conceded reluctantly.

Leia felt a chill run up her back. The first step in a betrayal would be to put emotional distance between the Noghri and their former lord.

"That area will be finished soon," the maitrakh said, pointing to the laboring decon droids. "If they finish within the next ten days, we will be able to plant there this season."

"Will the extra land be enough to make you self-sufficient?" Leia asked.

"It will help. But not enough."

Leia nodded, feeling a fresh surge of frustration. To her, the Empire's scheme was as blatant as it was cynical: with careful tuning of the whole decontamination process, they could keep the Noghri on the verge of independence indefinitely without ever letting them quite make it over that line. She knew it; the maitrakh herself suspected it. But as for proving it . . .

"Chewie, are you familiar at all with decon droids?" she asked suddenly. This thought had occurred to her once before, but she'd never gotten around to following up on it. "Enough that you could figure out how long it would take the number of droids they have on Honoghr to decontaminate this much land?"

The Wookiee growled an affirmative, and launched into a rundown of the relevant numbers—clearly, the question had occurred to him, too. "I don't need the complete analysis right now," Leia interrupted the stream of estimates and extrapolations and rules of thumb. "Have you got a bottom line?"

He did. Eight years.

"I see," Leia murmured, the brief flicker of hope fading back into the overall gloom. "That would have put it right about the height of the war, wouldn't it?"

"You still believe the Grand Admiral has deceived us?" the maitrakh accused.

"I *know* he's deceiving you," Leia retorted. "I just can't prove it."

The maitrakh was silent for a minute. "What then will you do?"

Leia took a deep breath, exhaled it quietly. "We have to leave Honoghr. That means breaking into the spaceport at Nystao and stealing a ship."

"There should be no difficulty in that for a daughter of the Lord Darth Vader."

Leia grimaced, thinking of how the maitrakh had effortlessly sneaked up on them a minute ago. The guards at the spaceport would be younger and far better trained. These people must have been fantastic hunters before the Emperor turned them into his private killing machines. "Stealing a ship won't be too hard," she told the maitrakh, aware of just how far she was stretching the truth here. "The difficulty arises from the fact that we have to take Khabarakh with us."

The maitrakh stopped short. "What is that you say?" she hissed.

"It's the only way," Leia said. "If Khabarakh is left to the Empire, they'll make him tell everything that's occurred here. And when that happens, he and you will both die. Perhaps your whole family with you. We can't allow that."

"Then you face death yourselves," the maitrakh said. "The guards will not easily allow Khabarakh to be freed."

"I know," Leia said, acutely aware of the two small lives she carried within her. "We'll have to take that risk."

"There will be no honor in such a sacrifice," the old Noghri all but snarled. "The clan Kihm'bar will not carve it into history. Neither will the Noghri people long remember."

"I'm not doing it for the praise of the Noghri people," Leia sighed, suddenly weary of banging her head against alien misunderstandings. She'd been doing it in one form or another, it seemed, for the whole of her life. "I'm doing it because I'm tired of people dying for my mistakes. I asked Khabarakh to bring me to Honoghr—what's happened is my responsibility. I can't just run off and leave you to the Grand Admiral's vengeance."

"Our lord the Grand Admiral would not deal so harshly with us."

Leia turned to look the maitrakh straight in the eye. "The Empire once destroyed an entire world because of me," she said quietly. "I don't ever want that to happen again."

She held the maitrakh's gaze a moment longer, then turned away, her mind twisted in a tangle of conflicting thoughts and emotions. Was she doing the right thing? She'd risked her life countless times before, but always for her comrades in the Rebellion and for a cause she believed in. To do the same for servants of the Empire—even servants who'd been duped into that role—was something else entirely. Chewbacca didn't like any of this; she could tell that much from his sense and the stiff way he stood at her side. But he would go along, driven by his own sense of honor and the life-debt he had sworn to Han.

She blinked back sudden tears, her hand going to the bulge of her belly. Han would understand. He would argue against such a risk, but down deep he would understand. Otherwise, he wouldn't have let her come here in the first place.

If she didn't return, he would almost certainly blame himself.

"The humiliation period has been extended for four more days," the maitrakh murmured beside her. "In two days' time the moons will give their least light. It would be best to wait until then." Leia frowned at her. The maitrakh met her gaze steadily, her alien face unreadable. "Are you offering me your help?" Leia asked.

"There is honor in you, Lady Vader," the maitrakh said, her voice quiet. "For the life and honor of my thirdson, I will go with you. Perhaps we will die together."

Leia nodded, her heart aching. "Perhaps we will."

But she wouldn't. The maitrakh and Khabarakh might die, and probably Chewbacca beside them. But not her. The Lady Vader they would take alive, and save as a gift for their lord the Grand Admiral.

Who would smile, and speak politely, and take her children away from her.

She looked out at the fields, wishing Han were here. And wondered if he would ever know what had happened to her.

"Come," the maitrakh said. "Let us return to the house. There are many things about Nystao which you must yet learn."

"I'M GLAD YOU finally called," Winter's voice came over the *Lady Luck*'s speaker, distorted slightly by a not-quite-attuned scrambler package. "I was starting to worry."

"We're okay—we just had to run silent awhile," Han assured her. "You got trouble back there?"

"No more than when you left," she said. "The Imperials are still hitting our shipping out there, and no one's figured out what to do about it. Fey'lya's trying to persuade the Council that he could do a better job of defense than Ackbar's people, but so far Mon Mothma hasn't taken him up on the offer. I get the feeling that some of the Council members are starting to have second thoughts about his motivations for all of this."

"Good," Han growled. "Maybe they'll tell him to shut up and put Ackbar back in command."

"Unfortunately, Fey'lya's still got too much support to ignore completely," Winter said. "Particularly among the military."

"Yeah." Han braced himself. "I don't suppose you've heard from Leia."

"Not yet," Winter said; and Han could hear the underlying tension in her voice. She was worried, too. "But I *did* hear from Luke. That's why I wanted to get in touch with you, in fact."

"Is he in trouble?"

"I don't know—the message didn't say. He wants you to rendezvous with him on New Cov."

"New Cov?" Han frowned down at the cloud-speckled planet turning beneath them. "Why?"

"The message didn't say. Just that he'd meet you at the, quote, money-changing center, unquote."

"The—?" Han shifted his frown to Lando. "What's that supposed to mean?"

"He's talking about the Mishra tapcafe in Ilic where he and I met while you were following Breil'lya," Lando said. "Private joke—I'll fill you in later."

"So that means there's no question Luke sent the message?" Winter asked.

"Wait a minute," Han put in as Lando started to answer. "Didn't you talk to him personally?"

"No, the message came in printed," Winter said. "Not on any scrambler, either."

"He doesn't have a scrambler on his X-wing, does he?" Lando asked.

"No, but he could get a message coded at any New Republic diplomatic post," Han said slowly. "Is this private joke something only you two would know about?"

"Us two, plus maybe a hundred bystanders," Lando conceded. "You think it's a trap?"

"Could be. Okay, Winter, thanks. We'll be checking in more often from now on."

"All right. Be careful."

"You bet."

He signed off and looked at Lando. "It's your ship, pal. You want to go down and take a look, or give it a miss and go check out this swimming casino of yours?"

Lando hissed a breath between his teeth. "I don't think we've got much choice," he said. "If the message *was* from Luke, it's probably important."

"And if it wasn't?"

Lando favored him with a tight grin. "Hey, we've run Imperial traps before. Come on, let's take her down."

After the way they'd blasted out of Ilic a few days earlier, it was doubtful the local authorities would be especially overjoyed to see the return of the *Lady Luck* to their city. Fortunately, he'd put the past two days' worth of leisure time to good use; and as they set down inside the domed landing area, the spaceport computer dutifully logged the arrival of the pleasure yacht *Tamar's Folly*.

"It's just terrific to be back," Han commented dryly as he and Lando started down the ramp. "Probably ought to snoop around a little before we head down to the Mishra."

Beside him, Lando stiffened. "I don't think we're going to have to bother with the Mishra," he said quietly.

Han threw a quick glance at him, dropping his hand casually to his blaster as he shifted his gaze to where Lando was looking. Standing five meters from the end of the *Lady Luck*'s ramp was a bulky man in an ornate tunic, chewing on the end of a cigarra, and smiling with sly innocence up at them.

"Friend of yours?" Han murmured.

"I wouldn't go *that* far," Lando murmured back. "Name's Niles Ferrier. Ship thief and occasional smuggler."

"He was in on the Mishra thing, I take it?"

"One of the key players, actually."

Han nodded, letting his eyes drift around the spaceport. Among the dozens of people moving briskly about their business, he spotted three or four who seemed to be loitering nearby. "Ship thief, huh?"

"Yes, but he's not going to bother with anything as small as the *Lady Luck*," Lando assured him.

Han grunted. "Watch him anyway."

"You bet."

They reached the foot of the ramp and, by unspoken but mutual consent, stopped there and waited. Ferrier's grin broadened a bit, and he sauntered forward to meet them. "Hello there, Calrissian," he said. "We keep bumping into each other, don't we?"

"Hello, *Luke*," Han spoke up before Lando could reply. "You've changed."

Ferrier's smile turned almost sheepish. "Yeah—sorry about that. I didn't figure you'd come if I put my own name on the message."

"Where's Luke?" Han demanded.

"Search me," Ferrier shrugged. "He burned out of here same time you did—that was the last I saw of him."

Han studied his face, looking for a lie. He didn't see one. "What do you want?"

"I want to cut a deal with the New Republic," Ferrier said, lowering his voice. "A deal for some new warships. You interested?"

Han felt a tingle at the back of his neck. "We might be," he said, trying to sound casual. "What kind of ships are we talking about?"

Ferrier gestured to the ramp. "How about we talk in the ship?"

"How about we talk out here?" Lando retorted.

Ferrier seemed taken aback. "Take it easy, Calrissian," he said soothingly. "What do you think I'm going to do, walk off with your ship in my pocket?"

"What kind of ships?" Han repeated.

Ferrier looked at him for a moment, then made a show of

glancing around the area. "Big ones," he said, lowering his voice. "Dreadnaught class." He lowered his voice still further. "The *Katana* fleet."

With an effort, Han kept his sabacc face in place. "The *Katana* fleet. Right."

"I'm not kidding," Ferrier insisted. "The *Katana*'s been found . . . and I've got a line on the guy who found it."

"Yeah?" Han said. Something in Ferrier's face—

He turned around quickly, half expecting to see someone trying to sneak up over the edge of the ramp into the *Lady Luck*. But aside from the usual mix of shadows from the spaceport lights, there was nothing there. "Something?" Lando demanded.

"No," Han said, turning back to Ferrier. If the thief really did have a line on Bel Iblis's supplier, it could save them a lot of time. But if he had nothing but rumors—and was maybe hoping to wangle something a little more solid . . . "What makes you think this guy has anything?" he demanded.

Ferrier smiled slyly. "Free information, Solo? Come on— you know better than that."

"All right, then," Lando said. "What do you want from us, and what are you offering in trade?"

"I know the guy's name," Ferrier said, his face turning serious again. "But I don't know where he is. I thought we could pool our resources, see if we can get to him before the Empire does."

Han felt his throat tighten. "What makes you think the Empire's involved?"

Ferrier threw him a scornful look. "With Grand Admiral Thrawn in charge over there? He's involved in everything."

Han smiled lopsidedly. At last they had a name to go with the uniform. "Thrawn, huh? Thanks, Ferrier."

Ferrier's face went rigid as he suddenly realized what he'd just given away. "No charge," he said between stiff lips.

"We still haven't heard what we're getting out of the deal," Lando reminded him.

"Do you know where he is?" Ferrier asked.

"We have a lead," Lando said. "What are you offering?"

Ferrier shifted a measuring gaze back and forth between them. "I'll give you half the ships we take out," he said at last. "Plus an option for the New Republic to buy out the rest at a reasonable price."

"What's a reasonable price?" Han asked.

"Depends on what kind of shape they're in," Ferrier countered. "I'm sure we'll be able to come to an agreement."

"Mm." Han looked at Lando. "What do you think?"

"Forget it," Lando said, his voice hard. "You want to give us the name, fine—if it checks out, we'll make sure you're well paid once we've got the ships. Otherwise, shove off."

Ferrier drew back. "Well, fine," he said, sounding more hurt than annoyed. "You want to do it all by yourselves, be my guest. But if we get to the ships first, your precious little New Republic's going to pay a lot more to get them. A *lot* more."

Spinning around, he stalked off. "Come on, Han, let's get out of here," Lando muttered, his eyes on Ferrier's retreating back.

"Yeah," Han said, looking around for the loiterers he'd spotted earlier. They, too, were drifting away. It didn't look like trouble; but he kept his hand on his blaster anyway until they were inside the *Lady Luck* with the hatch sealed.

"I'll prep for lift," Lando said as they headed back to the cockpit. "You talk to Control, get us an exit slot."

"Okay," Han said. "You know, with a little more bargaining—"

"I don't trust him," Lando cut him off, running his hand over the start-up switches. "He was smiling too much. And he gave up too easily."

It was a hard comment to argue against. And as Han had noted earlier, it *was* Lando's ship. Shrugging to himself, he keyed for spaceport control.

They were out in ten minutes, once again leaving an unhappy group of controllers behind them. "I hope this is the last time we have to come here," Han said, scowling across the cockpit at Lando. "I get the feeling we've worn out our welcome."

Lando threw him a sideways glance. "Well, well. Since when did you start caring what other people thought about you?"

"Since I married a princess and started carrying a government ID," Han growled back. "Anyway, I thought you were supposed to be respectable, too."

"It comes and goes. Ah-*ha*." He smiled humorlessly at Han. "It looks like while we were talking to Ferrier, someone sneaked up and put something on our hull. Ten'll get you one it's a homing beacon."

"What a surprise," Han said, keying his display for its location. It was on the rear lower hull, back near the ramp where it would be out of most of the lift-off turbulence. "What do you want to do with it?"

"The Terrijo system's more or less on the way to Pantolomin," Lando said, consulting his display. "We'll swing through there and drop it off."

"Okay." Han scowled at his display. "Too bad we can't put it on another ship right here. That way he wouldn't even know what direction we're going."

Lando shook his head. "He'll know we've spotted it if we put down on New Cov now. Unless you want to take it off up here and try to toss it onto another passing ship." He glanced at Han; paused for a longer look. "We're not going to try it, Han," he said firmly. "Get that look out of your eye."

"Oh, all right," Han grumbled. "That'd get him off our backs, though."

"And might get you killed in the process," Lando retorted. "And then *I'd* have to go back and explain it to Leia. Forget it."

Han gritted his teeth. Leia. "Yeah," he said with a sigh.

Lando looked at him again. "Come on, buddy, relax. Ferrier hasn't got a hope of beating us. Trust me—we're going to win this one."

Han nodded. He hadn't been thinking about Ferrier, actually. Or about the *Katana* fleet. "I know," he said.

THE *LADY LUCK* disappeared smoothly through one of the ducts in the transparisteel dome, and Ferrier shifted his cigarra to the other side of his mouth. "You're sure they won't find the second beacon?" he asked.

Beside him, the oddly shaped shadow between a pile of shipping crates stirred. "They will not," it said in a voice like cold running water.

"You'd better be right," Ferrier warned, a note of menace in his voice. "I didn't stand there and take that garbage from them for nothing." He glared at the shadow. "As it was, you almost gave the game away," he said accusingly. "Solo looked straight back at you once."

"There was no danger," the wraith said flatly. "Humans need movement to see. Not-moving shadows are of no concern."

"Well, it worked this time," Ferrier was willing to concede. "You're still lucky it was Solo and not Calrissian who looked—he saw you once before, you know. Next time, keep your big feet quiet."

The wraith said nothing. "Oh, go on, get back to the ship," Ferrier ordered. "Tell Abric to get 'er ready to lift. We've got ourselves a fortune to make."

He threw a last look upward. "And maybe," he added with grim satisfaction, "a smart-mouthed gambler to take out."

CHAPTER 19

THE *ETHERWAY* WAS clearly visible now, dropping like a misshapen rock out of the sky toward its assigned landing pit. Standing in the protective shadow of the exit tunnel, Karrde watched its approach, stroking the grip of his blaster gently with his fingertips and trying to ignore the uneasiness still tickling the back of his mind. Mara was over three days late in bringing the freighter back from Abregado—not a particularly significant delay under normal conditions, but this trip had hardly qualified as normal. But there had been no other ships on her tail as she entered orbit, and she'd transmitted all the proper "all clear" code signals to him as she dropped into the approach pattern. And aside from the incompetence of the controllers, who'd taken an inordinate amount of time to decide which pit she was actually being assigned to, the landing itself had so far been completely routine.

Karrde smiled wryly as he watched the ship come down. There had been times in the past three days when he'd thought about Mara's hatred of Luke Skywalker, and had wondered if she had decided to drop out of his life as mysteriously as she'd dropped into it. But it seemed now that his original reading of her had been correct. Mara Jade wasn't the sort of person who gave her loyalty easily, but once she'd made a decision she stuck with it. If she ever ran out on him, she wouldn't do so in a stolen ship. Not stolen from him, anyway.

The *Etherway* was on its final approach now, rotating on its repulsorlifts to orient its hatchway toward the exit tunnel. Obviously, Karrde's reading of Han Solo had been correct, too. Even if the other hadn't been quite gullible enough to send a Mon Cal Star Cruiser out to Myrkr, he'd at least kept his promise to get the *Etherway* out of impoundment. Apparently, all of Karrde's private worrying of the past three days had been for nothing.

But the uneasiness was still there.

With a hiss of back-release outgassing, the *Etherway* settled to the stress-scored paving of the landing pit. His eyes on the closed hatchway, Karrde pulled his comlink from his belt and thumbed for his backup spotter. "Dankin? Anything suspicious in sight?"

"Not a thing," the other's voice came back promptly. "Looks very quiet over there."

Karrde nodded. "All right. Keep out of sight, but stay alert."

He replaced the comlink in his belt. The *Etherway*'s landing ramp began to swing down, and he shifted his hand to a grip on his blaster. If this was a trap, now would be the likely time to spring it.

The hatchway opened, and Mara appeared. She glanced around the pit as she started down the ramp, spotting him immediately in his chosen shadow. "Karrde?" she called.

"Welcome home, Mara," he said, stepping out into the light. "You're a bit late."

"I wound up making a little detour," she said grimly, coming toward him.

"That can happen," he said, frowning. Her attention was still flitting around the pit, her face lined with a vague sort of tension. "Trouble?" he asked quietly.

"I don't know," she murmured. "I feel—"

She never finished the sentence. At Karrde's belt his comlink suddenly squawked, screeched briefly with the electronic stress of blanket jamming, and then went silent. "Come on," Karrde snapped, drawing his blaster and spinning back toward the exit. At the far end of the tunnel he could see shapes moving; lifting his blaster, he fired toward them—

The violent thunderclap of a sonic boom shattered the air around him, slamming hard against his head and nearly toppling him to the ground. He glanced up, ears ringing, just as two slower-moving TIE fighters swooped past overhead, laying down a spitting pattern of laser fire at the mouth of the exit tunnel. The paving erupted into steaming blocks of half-molten ceramic under the assault, blocking any chance of quick escape in that direction. Karrde snapped off a reflexive if meaningless shot toward the TIE fighters; and he was just beginning to shift his aim back toward the figures in the tunnel when a dozen stormtroopers suddenly leaped into view at the upper rim of the landing pit, sliding down droplines to the ground. "Down!" he snapped at Mara, his voice hardly audible to his paralyzed sense of hearing. He dived for the ground, hitting awkwardly on his left arm and bringing his blaster to bear on the nearest stormtrooper. He fired, missing by half a meter . . . and he was just noticing the curious fact that the Imperials weren't returning fire when the blaster was deftly plucked from his hand.

He rolled half over, looking up at Mara with stunned disbelief. "What—"

She was standing over him, her face so pinched with emotion he could hardly recognize it, her lips moving with words he couldn't hear.

But he didn't really need any explanation. Strangely, he felt no anger at her; not for concealing her Imperial past from him all this time, nor for now returning to her origins. Only chagrin that he'd been fooled so easily and so thoroughly . . . and a strange regret that he had lost such a skilled associate.

The stormtroopers hauled him to his feet and moved him roughly toward a drop ship that was settling onto the paving beside the *Etherway;* and as he stumbled toward it, a stray thought occurred to him.

He was betrayed and captured and probably facing death . . . but at least he now had a partial answer to the mystery of why Mara wanted to kill Luke Skywalker.

MARA GLARED AT THE Grand Admiral, her hands curled into fists, her body trembling with rage. "Eight days, Thrawn," she snarled, her voice echoing oddly through the background noises of the *Chimaera*'s vast shuttle bay. "You said eight days. You *promised* me eight days."

Thrawn gazed back with a polite calmness that made her long to burn him down where he stood. "I changed my mind," he said coolly. "It occurred to me that Karrde might not only refuse to divulge the *Katana* fleet's location, but might even abandon you here for suggesting that he make such a deal with us."

"The gates of hell you did," Mara snapped back. "You planned to use me like this right from the start."

"And it got us what we wanted," the red-eyed freak said smoothly. "That's all that matters."

Deep within Mara, something snapped. Ignoring the armed stormtroopers standing just behind her, she threw herself at Thrawn, fingers hooking like a hunting bird's talons for his throat—

And came to an abrupt, bone-wrenching stop as Thrawn's Noghri bodyguard sidled in from two meters away, threw his arm across her neck and shoulder, and spun her around and halfway to the deck.

She grabbed at the iron-hard arm across her throat, simultaneously throwing her right elbow back toward his torso. But the blow missed; and even as she shifted to a two-handed grip on his arm, white spots began to flicker in her vision. His forearm was pressing solidly against her carotid artery, threatening her with unconsciousness.

There wasn't anything to be gained by blacking out. She relaxed her struggle, felt the pressure ease. Thrawn was still standing there, regarding her with amusement. "That was very unprofessional of you, Emperor's Hand," he chided.

Mara glared at him and lashed out again, this time with the Force. Thrawn frowned slightly, fingers moving across his neck as if trying to brush away an intangible cobweb. Mara leaned into her tenuous grip on his throat; and he brushed again at his neck before understanding came. "All right, that's enough," he said, his voice noticeably altered, his tone starting to get angry. "Stop it, or Rukh will have to hurt you."

Mara ignored the order, digging in as hard as she could. Thrawn gazed unblinkingly back at her, his throat muscles moving as he fought against the grip. Mara clenched her teeth, waiting for the order or hand movement that would signal permission for the Noghri to choke her, or for the storm-troopers to burn her down.

But Thrawn remained silent and unmoving . . . and a minute later, gasping for breath, Mara had to concede defeat.

"I trust you've learned the limits of your small powers," Thrawn said coldly, fingering his throat. But at least he didn't sound amused anymore. "A little trick the Emperor taught you?"

"He taught me a great many tricks," Mara bit out, ignoring the throbbing in her temples. "How to deal with traitors was one of them."

Thrawn's glowing eyes glittered. "Have a care, Jade," he said softly. "*I* rule the Empire now. Not some long-dead Emperor; certainly not you. The only treason is defiance of my orders. I'm willing to let you come back to your rightful place in the Empire—as first officer, perhaps, of one of the *Katana* Dreadnaughts. But any further outbursts like this one and that offer will be summarily withdrawn."

"And then you'll kill me, I suppose," Mara growled.

"My Empire isn't in the habit of wasting valuable resources," the other countered. "You'd be given instead to Master C'baoth as a little bonus gift. And I suspect you would
soon wish I'd had you executed."

Mara stared at him, an involuntary shiver running up her
back. "Who is C'baoth?"

"Joruus C'baoth is a mad Jedi Master," Thrawn told her
darkly. "He's consented to help our war effort, in exchange for
Jedi to mold into whatever twisted image he chooses. Your
friend Skywalker has already walked into his web; his sister,
Organa Solo, we hope to deliver soon." His face hardened. "I
would genuinely hate for you to have to join them."

Mara took a deep breath. "I understand," she said, forcing
out the words. "You've made your point. It won't happen
again."

He eyed her a moment, then nodded. "Apology accepted,"
he said. "Release her, Rukh. Now. Do I take it you wish to rejoin the Empire?"

The Noghri let go of her neck—reluctantly, Mara thought—
and took a short step away. "What about the rest of Karrde's
people?" she asked.

"As we agreed, they're free to go about their business. I've
already canceled all Imperial search and detention orders concerning them, and Captain Pellaeon is at this moment calling
off the bounty hunters."

"And Karrde himself?"

Thrawn studied her face. "He'll remain aboard until he
tells me where the *Katana* fleet is. If he does so with a minimum of wasted time and effort on our part, he'll receive the
three million in compensation which you and I agreed on at
Endor. If not . . . there may not be much left of him to pay
compensation to."

Mara felt her lip twitch. He wasn't bluffing, either. She'd
seen what a full-bore Imperial interrogation could do. "May I
talk to him?" she asked.

"Why?"

"I might be able to persuade him to cooperate."

Thrawn smiled slightly. "Or could at least assure him that you did not, in fact, betray him?"

"He'll still be locked in your detention block," Mara reminded him, forcing her voice to stay calm. "There's no reason for him not to know the truth."

Thrawn lifted his eyebrows. "On the contrary," he said. "A sense of utter abandonment is one of the more useful psychological tools available to us. A few days with only thoughts of that sort to relieve the monotony may convince him to cooperate without harsher treatment."

"Thrawn—" Mara broke off, strangling back the sudden flash of anger.

"That's better," the Grand Admiral approved, his eyes steady on her face. "Especially considering that the alternative is for me to turn him directly over to an interrogator droid. Is that what you want?"

"No, Admiral," she said, feeling herself slump a little. "I just . . . Karrde helped me when I had nowhere else to go."

"I understand your feelings," Thrawn said, his face hardening again. "But they have no place here. Mixed loyalties are a luxury no officer of the Imperial Fleet can afford. Certainly not if she wishes someday to be given a command of her own."

Mara drew herself up again to her full height. "Yes, sir. It won't happen again."

"I trust not." Thrawn glanced past her shoulder and nodded. With a rustle of movement, her stormtrooper escort began to withdraw. "The deck officer's station is just beneath the control tower," he said, gesturing to the large transparisteel bubble nestled in among the racked TIE fighters three-quarters of the way up the hangar bay's back wall. "He'll assign you a shuttle and pilot to take you back to the surface."

It was clearly a dismissal. "Yes, Admiral," Mara said. Stepping past him, she headed toward the door he'd indicated. For a moment she could feel his eyes on her, then heard the faint sound of his footsteps as he turned away toward the lift cluster beyond the starboard blast doors.

Yes; the Grand Admiral had made his point. But it wasn't exactly the one he'd intended to make. With that single casual act of betrayal, he had finally destroyed her last wistful hope that the new Empire might someday measure up to the one that Luke Skywalker had destroyed out from under her.

The Empire she'd once been proud to serve was gone. Forever.

It was a painful revelation, and a costly one. It could erase in one stroke everything she'd worked so hard to build up for herself over the last year.

It could also cost Karrde his life. And if it did, he would die believing that she had deliberately betrayed him to Thrawn.

The thought twisted in her stomach like a heated knife, mixing with her bitter anger toward Thrawn for lying to her and her shame at her own gullibility in trusting him in the first place. No matter how she looked at it, this mess was her fault.

It was up to her to fix it.

Beside the door to the deck officer's office was the huge archway that led from the hangar bay proper into the service and prep areas behind it. Mara threw a glance over her shoulder as she walked, and spotted Thrawn stepping into one of the turbolifts, his tame Noghri at his side. Her stormtrooper escort, too, had disappeared, its members probably returning to their private section aft for debriefing over the mission they'd just completed. There were twenty or thirty other people in the bay, but none of them seemed to be paying any particular attention to her.

It was probably the only chance she would ever get. With her ear cocked for the shout—or the blaster shot—that would mean she'd been noticed, she bypassed the deck officer's office and stepped past the retracted blast doors into the prep area.

There was a computer terminal just inside the archway, built against the wall where it would be accessible to both the forward prep area and the aft hangar bay. Its location made it an obvious target for unauthorized access, and as a consequence it would undoubtedly be protected by an elaborate entry code. Probably changed hourly, if she knew Thrawn; but what even a Grand Admiral might not know was that the Emperor had had a private back door installed into the main computer of every Star Destroyer. It had been his guarantee, first during his consolidation of power and then during the upheaval of Rebellion, that no commander could ever lock him out of his own ships. Not him, and not his top agents.

Mara keyed in the backdoor entry code, permitting herself a tight smile as she did so. Thrawn could consider her a glorified courier if he liked. But she knew better.

The code clicked, and she was in.

She called up a directory, trying to suppress the creepy awareness that she might already have brought the stormtroopers down on top of her. The backdoor code was hardwired into the system and impossible to eliminate, but if Thrawn suspected its existence, he might well have set a flag to trigger an alarm if it was ever used. And if he had, it would take far more than another show of humble loyalty to keep her out of trouble.

No stormtroopers had appeared by the time the directory came up. She keyed for the detention section and ran her eye down the listing, wishing fleetingly that she had an R2 astromech droid like Skywalker's to help cut through all of it. Even if Thrawn had missed the backdoor code, he would certainly have alerted the deck officer to expect her. If someone in the control tower noticed she was overdue and sent someone out to look for her . . .

There it was: an updated prisoner list. She keyed for it, pulling up a diagram of the entire detention block while she was at it. A duty roster was next, with attention paid to the shift changes, then back to the daily orders and a listing of the *Chimaera*'s projected course and destinations for the next six days. Thrawn had implied he would be waiting a few days before beginning a formal interrogation, letting boredom and tension and Karrde's own imagination wear down his resistance. Mara could only hope she could get back before that softening-up period was over.

A drop of sweat trickled down her spine as she cleared the display. And now came the really painful part. She'd run through the logic a dozen times while walking across the hangar bay deck, and each time had been forced to the same odious answer. Karrde would almost certainly have had a backup spotter watching the *Etherway*'s approach, who would have had a front-row view of the stormtroopers' trap. If Mara now returned free and clear from the *Chimaera*, she would never be able to convince Karrde's people that she hadn't betrayed him to the Imperials. She'd be lucky, in fact, if they didn't burn her down on sight.

She couldn't rescue Karrde alone. She couldn't expect any help from his organization. Which left only one person in the galaxy she might be able to enlist. Only one person who might possibly feel he owed Karrde something.

Clenching her teeth, she keyed for the current location of a Jedi Master named Joruus C'baoth.

It seemed to take the computer an inordinate amount of time to dig out the information, and the skin on Mara's back was starting to crawl by the time the machine finally spat it out. She caught the planet's name—Jomark—and keyed off, doing what she could to bury the fact that this interaction had ever taken place. Already she'd pushed her timing way too close to the wire; and if they caught her here on a computer she shouldn't have been able to access at all, she was likely to find herself in the cell next to Karrde's.

She barely made it. She'd just finished her cleanup and started back toward the archway when a young officer and three troopers came striding through from the hangar bay, their eyes and weapons clearly ready for trouble. One of the troopers spotted her, muttered something to the officer—

"Excuse me," Mara called as all four turned to her. "Can you tell me where I can find the deck officer?"

"I'm the deck officer," the officer said, scowling at her as the group came to a halt in front of her. "You Mara Jade?"

"Yes," Mara said, putting on her best unconcerned/innocent expression. "I was told your office was over here somewhere, but I couldn't find it."

"It's on the other side of the wall," the officer growled. Brushing past her, he stepped to the terminal she'd just left. "Were you fiddling with this?" he asked, tapping a few keys.

"No," Mara assured him. "Why?"

"Never mind—it's still locked down," the officer muttered under his breath. For a moment he looked around the area, as if searching for some other reason Mara might have wanted to be back here. But there was nothing; and almost reluctantly, he brought his attention back to her again. "I've got orders to give you transport down to the planet."

"I know," she nodded. "I'm ready."

THE SHUTTLE LIFTED and turned and headed off into the sky. Standing by the *Etherway*'s ramp, the stink of burned paving still thick in the air, Mara watched the Imperial craft disappear over the top of the landing pit. "Aves?" she called. "Come on, Aves, you've got to be here somewhere."

"Turn around and put your hands up," the voice came from the shadows inside the ship's hatchway. "All the way up. And don't forget I know about that little sleeve gun of yours."

"The Imperials have it now," Mara said as she turned her back to him and raised her hands. "And I'm not here for a fight. I came for help."

"You want help, go to your new friends upstairs," Aves retorted. "Or maybe they were always your friends, huh?"

He was goading her, Mara knew, pushing for a chance to vent his own anger and frustration in an argument or gun battle. "I didn't betray him, Aves," she said. "I got picked up by the Imperials and blew them a smoke ring that I thought would buy us enough time to get out. It didn't."

"I don't believe you," Aves said flatly. There was a muffled clank of boot on metal as he came cautiously down the ramp.

"No, you believe me," Mara shook her head. "You wouldn't have come here if you didn't."

She felt a breath of air on the back of her neck as he stepped close behind her. "Don't move," he ordered. Reaching carefully to her left arm, he pulled the sleeve down to reveal the empty holster. He checked her other sleeve, then ran a hand down each side of her body. "All right, turn around," he said, stepping back again.

She did so. He was standing a meter away from her, his face tight, his blaster pointed at her stomach. "Turn the question around, Aves," she suggested. "If I betrayed Karrde to the Imperials, why would I come back here? Especially alone?"

"Maybe you needed to get something from the *Etherway*," he countered harshly. "Or maybe it's just a trick to try to round up the rest of us."

Mara braced herself. "If you really believe that," she said quietly, "you might as well go ahead and shoot. I can't get Karrde out of there without your help."

For a long minute Aves stood there in silence. Mara watched his face, trying to ignore the white-knuckled hand holding the blaster. "The others won't help you, you know," he said. "Half of them think you've been manipulating Karrde from the minute you joined up. Most of the rest figure you for the type who switches loyalties twice a year anyway."

Mara grimaced. "That was true once," she admitted. "Not anymore."

"You got any way to prove that?"

"Yeah—by getting Karrde out," Mara retorted. "Look, I haven't got time to talk. You going to help, or shoot?"

He hesitated for a handful of heartbeats. Then, almost reluctantly, he lowered the blaster until it was pointed at the ground. "I'm probably scribing my own death mark," he growled. "What do you need?"

"For starters, a ship," Mara said, silently letting out a breath she hadn't realized she'd been holding. "Something smaller and faster than the *Etherway*. One of those three boosted Skipray blastboats we brought in from Vagran would do nicely. I'll also need one of those ysalamiri we've been carrying around on the *Wild Karrde*. Preferably on a nutrient frame that's portable."

Aves frowned. "What do you want with an ysalamir?"

"I'm going to talk to a Jedi," she said briefly. "I need a guarantee he'll listen."

Aves studied her a moment, then shrugged. "I suppose I really don't want to know. What else?"

Mara shook her head. "That's it."

His eyes narrowed. "That's *it*?"

"That's it. How soon can you get them to me?"

Aves pursed his lips thoughtfully. "Let's say an hour," he said. "That big swamp about fifty kilometers north of the city—you know it?"

Mara nodded. "There's a soggy sort of island near the eastern edge."

"Right. You bring the *Etherway* to the island and we'll do the switch there." He glanced up at the freighter towering over him. "If you think it's safe to move it."

"It should be for now," Mara said. "Thrawn told me he'd lifted all the search and detention orders for the rest of the group. But you'd better disappear anyway after I go. He'll have the whole Fleet screaming down your necks again if and when I get Karrde out. Better run a fine-edge scan on the *Etherway* before you take it anywhere, though—there has to be a homing beacon aboard for Thrawn to have gotten the jump on me the way he did." She felt her lip twitch. "And knowing Thrawn, he's probably got someone tailing me, too. I'll have to get rid of him before I leave the planet."

"I can give you a hand with that," Aves said grimly. "We're disappearing anyway, right?"

"Right." Mara paused, trying to think if there was anything else she needed to tell him. "I guess that's it. Let's get going."

"Right." Aves hesitated. "I still don't know whose side you're on, Mara. If you're on ours . . . good luck."

She nodded, feeling a hard lump settle into her throat. "Thanks."

TWO HOURS LATER she was strapped into the Skipray's cockpit, a strange and unpleasant sense of déjà vu burning through her as she drove toward deep space. It had been in a ship just like this one that she'd screamed off into the sky over the Myrkr forest a few weeks ago, in hot pursuit of an escaped prisoner. Now, like a twisted repeat of history, she once again found herself chasing after Luke Skywalker.

Only this time, she wasn't trying to kill or capture him. This time, she was going to plead for his help.

CHAPTER 20

THE LAST PAIR of villagers detached themselves from the group standing at the back wall and made their way toward the raised judgment seat. C'baoth stood there, watching them come; and then, as Luke had known he would, the Jedi Master stood up. "Jedi Skywalker," he said, gesturing Luke to the seat. "The final case of the evening is yours."

"Yes, Master C'baoth," Luke said, bracing himself as he stepped over and gingerly sat down. It was, to his mind, a thoroughly uncomfortable chair: too warm, too large, and far too ornate. Even more than the rest of C'baoth's home, it had an alien smell to it, and a strangely disturbing aura that Luke could only assume was a lingering aftereffect of the hours the Jedi Master had spent in it judging his people.

Now it was Luke's turn to do so.

Taking a deep breath, trying to push back the fatigue that had become a permanent part of him, he nodded at the two villagers. "I'm ready," he said. "Please begin."

It was a relatively simple case, as such things went. The first villager's livestock had gotten through the second's fence and had stripped half a dozen of his fruit bushes before they'd been discovered and driven back. The animals' owner was willing to pay compensation for the ruined bushes, but the second was insisting that he also rebuild the fence. The first countered that a properly built fence wouldn't have failed in the first place and that, furthermore, his livestock had suffered injuries from the sharp edges as they went through. Luke sat quietly and let them talk, waiting until the arguments and counterarguments finally ended.

"All right," he said. "In the matter of the fruit bushes themselves, my judgment is that you"—he nodded to the first villager—"will pay for the replacement of those damaged beyond repair, plus an additional payment to compensate for the fruit eaten or destroyed by your livestock. The latter amount will be determined by the village council."

Beside him C'baoth stirred, and Luke winced at the disapproval he could sense from the Jedi Master. For a second he floundered, wondering if he should back up and try a different solution. But changing his mind so abruptly didn't sound like a good thing to do. And anyway, he really didn't have any better ideas.

So what was he doing here?

He looked around the room, fighting against a sudden flush of nervousness. They were all looking at him: C'baoth, the two supplicants, the rest of the villagers who'd come tonight for Jedi judgment. All of them expecting him to make the right decision.

"As to the fence, I'll examine it tomorrow morning," he continued. "I want to see how badly it was damaged before I make my decision."

The two men bowed and backed away. "I therefore declare this session to be closed," C'baoth called. His voice echoed grandly, despite the relatively small size of the room. An interesting effect, and Luke found himself wondering if it was a trick of the room's acoustics or yet another Jedi technique that Master Yoda had never taught him. Though why he would ever need such a technique he couldn't imagine.

The last of the villagers filed out of the room. C'baoth cleared his throat; reflexively, Luke braced himself. "I sometimes wonder, Jedi Skywalker," the old man said gravely, "whether or not you have really been listening to me these past few days."

"I'm sorry, Master C'baoth," Luke said, an all-too-familiar lump sticking in his throat. No matter how hard he tried, it seemed, he was never quite able to measure up to C'baoth's expectations.

"Sorry?" C'baoth's eyebrows rose sardonically. "Sorry? Jedi Skywalker, you had it all right there in your hands. You should have cut off their prattle far sooner than you did—your time is too valuable to waste with petty recriminations. You should have made the decision yourself on the amount of compensation, but instead gave it over to that absurd excuse of a village council. And as to the fence—" He shook his head in mild disgust. "There was absolutely no reason for you to postpone judgment on that. Everything you needed to know about the damage was right there in their minds. It should have been no trouble, even for you, to have pulled that from them."

Luke swallowed. "Yes, Master C'baoth," he said. "But reading another person's thoughts that way seems wrong—"

"When you are using that knowledge to help him?" C'baoth countered. "How can that be wrong?"

Luke waved a hand helplessly. "I'm trying to understand, Master C'baoth. But this is all so new to me."

C'baoth's bushy eyebrows lifted. "Is it, Jedi Skywalker? Is it really? You mean you've never violated someone's personal preference in order to help him? Or ignored some minor bureaucratic rule that stood between you and what needed to be done?"

Luke felt his cheeks flush, thinking back to Lando's use of

that illegal slicer code to get his X-wing repaired at the Sluis Van shipyards. "Yes, I've done that on occasion," he admitted. "But this is different, somehow. It feels . . . I don't know. Like I'm taking more responsibility for these people's lives than I should."

"I understand your concerns," C'baoth said, less severely this time. "But that is indeed the crux of the matter. It is precisely the acceptance and wielding of responsibility that sets a Jedi apart from all others in the galaxy." He sighed deeply. "You must never forget, Luke, that in the final analysis these people are primitives. Only with our guidance can they ever hope to achieve any real maturity."

"I wouldn't call them primitive, Master C'baoth," Luke suggested hesitantly. "They have modern technology, a reasonably efficient system of government—"

"The trappings of civilization without the substance," C'baoth said with a contemptuous snort. "Machines and societal constructs do not define a culture's maturity, Jedi Skywalker. Maturity is defined solely by the understanding and use of the Force."

His eyes drifted away, as if peering into the past. "There was such a society once, Luke," he said softly. "A vast and shining example of the heights all could aspire to. For a thousand generations we stood tall among the lesser beings of the galaxy, guardians of justice and order. The creators of true civilization. The Senate could debate and pass laws; but it was the Jedi who turned those laws into reality."

His mouth twisted. "And in return, the galaxy destroyed us."

Luke frowned. "I thought it was just the Emperor and a few Dark Jedi who exterminated the Jedi."

C'baoth smiled bitterly. "Do you truly believe that even the Emperor could have succeeded in such a task without the consent of the entire galaxy?" He shook his head. "No, Luke. They hated us—all the lesser beings did. Hated us for our power, and our knowledge, and our wisdom. Hated us for our maturity." His smile vanished. "And that hatred still exists. Waiting only for the Jedi to reemerge to blaze up again."

Luke shook his head slowly. It didn't really seem to fit with what little he knew about the destruction of the Jedi. But on the other hand, he hadn't lived through that era. C'baoth had. "Hard to believe," he murmured.

"Believe it, Jedi Skywalker," C'baoth rumbled. His eyes caught Luke's, burning suddenly with a cold fire. "That's why we must stand together, you and I. Why we must never let down our guard before a universe that would destroy us. Do you understand?"

"I think so," Luke said, rubbing at the corner of his eye. His mind felt so sluggish in the fatigue dragging at him. And yet, even as he tried to think about C'baoth's words, images flowed unbidden from his memory. Images of Master Yoda, gruff but unafraid, with no trace of bitterness or anger toward anyone at the destruction of his fellow Jedi. Images of Ben Kenobi in the Mos Eisley cantina, treated with a sort of aloof respect, but respect nonetheless, after he'd been forced to cut down those two troublemakers.

And clearest of all, images of his encounter at the New Cov tapcafe. Of the Barabel, asking for the mediation of a stranger, and accepting without question even those parts of Luke's judgment that had gone against him. Of the rest of the crowd, watching with hope and expectation and relief that a Jedi was there to keep things from getting out of hand. "I haven't experienced any such hatred."

C'baoth gazed at him from under bushy eyebrows. "You will," he said darkly. "As will your sister. And her children."

Luke's chest tightened. "I can protect them."

"Can you teach them, as well?" C'baoth countered. "Have you the wisdom and skill to bring them to full knowledge of the ways of the Force?"

"I think so, yes."

C'baoth snorted. "If you think but do not know then you

gamble with their lives," he bit out. "You risk their futures over a selfish whim."

"It's not a whim," Luke insisted. "Together, Leia and I can do it."

"If you try, you will risk losing them to the dark side," C'baoth said flatly. He sighed, his eyes drifting away from Luke as he looked around the room. "We can't take that chance, Luke," he said quietly. "There are so few of us as it is. The endless war for power still rages—the galaxy is in turmoil. We who remain must stand together against those who would destroy everything." He turned his eyes suddenly back on Luke. "No; we can't risk being divided and destroyed again. You must bring your sister and her children to me."

"I can't do that," Luke said. C'baoth's expression changed— "Not now, at least," Luke amended hastily. "It wouldn't be safe for Leia to travel right now. The Imperials have been hunting her for months, and Jomark isn't all that far from the edge of their territory."

"Do you doubt that I can protect her?"

"I . . . no, I don't *doubt* you," Luke said, choosing his words carefully. "It's just that—"

He paused. C'baoth had gone abruptly stiff, his eyes gazing outward at nothing. "Master C'baoth?" he asked. "Are you all right?"

There was no reply. Luke stepped to his side, reaching out with the Force and wondering uneasily if the other was ill. But as always the Jedi Master's mind was closed to him. "Come, Master C'baoth," he said, taking the other's arm. "I'll help you to your chambers."

C'baoth blinked twice, and with what seemed to be an effort, brought his gaze back to Luke's face. He took a shuddering breath; and suddenly he was back to normal again. "You're tired, Luke," he said. "Leave me and return to your chambers for sleep."

Luke *was* tired, he had to admit. "Are you all right?"

"I'm fine," C'baoth assured him, a strangely grim tone to his voice.

"Because if you need my help—"

"I said leave me!" C'baoth snapped. "I am a Jedi Master. I need help from no one."

Luke found himself two paces back from C'baoth without any recollection of having taken the steps. "I'm sorry, Master C'baoth," he said. "I didn't mean any disrespect."

The other's face softened a bit. "I know you didn't," he said. He took another deep breath, exhaled it quietly. "Bring your sister to me, Jedi Skywalker. I will protect her from the Empire; and will teach her such power as you can't imagine."

Far in the back of Luke's mind, a small warning bell went off. Something about those words . . . or perhaps the way C'baoth had said them . . .

"Now return to your chambers," C'baoth ordered. Once again his eyes seemed to be drifting away toward nothing. "Sleep, and we will talk further in the morning."

HE STOOD BEFORE HER, his face half hidden by the cowl of his robe, his yellow eyes piercingly bright as they gazed across the infinite distance between them. His lips moved, but his words were drowned out by the throaty hooting of alarms all around them, filling Mara with an urgency that was rapidly edging into panic. Between her and the Emperor two figures appeared: the dark, imposing image of Darth Vader, and the smaller black-clad figure of Luke Skywalker. They stood before the Emperor, facing each other, and ignited their lightsabers. The blades crossed, brilliant red-white against brilliant green-white, and they prepared for battle.

And then, without warning, the blades disengaged . . . and with twin roars of hatred audible even over the alarms, both turned and strode toward the Emperor.

Mara heard herself cry out as she struggled to rush to her master's aid. But the distance was too great, her body too sluggish. She screamed a challenge, trying to at least distract them. But neither Vader nor Skywalker seemed to hear her. They moved outward to flank the Emperor . . . and as they lifted their lightsabers high, she saw that the Emperor was gazing at her.

She looked back at him, wanting desperately to turn away from the coming disaster but unable to move. A thousand thoughts and emotions flooded in through that gaze, a glittering kaleidoscope of pain and fear and rage that spun far too fast for her to really absorb. The Emperor raised his hands, sending cascades of jagged blue-white lightning at his enemies. Both men staggered under the counterattack, and Mara watched with the sudden agonized hope that this time it might end differently. But no. Vader and Skywalker straightened; and with another roar of rage, they lifted their lightsabers high—

YOU WILL KILL LUKE SKYWALKER!

And with a jerk that threw her against her restraints, Mara snapped out of the dream.

For a minute she just sat there, gasping for breath and struggling against the fading vision of lightsabers poised to strike. The small cockpit of the Skipray pressed tightly around her, triggering a momentary surge of claustrophobia. The back and neck of her flight suit were wet with perspiration, clammy against her skin. From what seemed to be a great distance, a proximity alert was pinging.

The dream again. The same dream that had followed her around the galaxy for five years now. The same situation; the same horrifying ending; the same final, desperate plea.

But this time, things were going to be different. This time, she had the power to kill Luke Skywalker.

She looked out at the mottling of hyperspace spinning around the Skipray's canopy, some last bit of her mind coming fully awake. No, that was wrong. She wasn't going to kill Skywalker at all. She was—

She was going to ask him for help.

The sour taste of bile rose into her throat; with an effort, she forced it down. *No argument*, she told herself sternly. If she wanted to rescue Karrde, she was going to have to go through with it.

Skywalker owed Karrde this much. Later, after he'd repaid the debt, there would be time enough to kill him.

The proximity alert changed tone, indicating thirty seconds to go. Cupping the hyperdrive levers in her hand, Mara watched the indicator go to zero and gently pushed the levers back. Mottling became starlines became the black of space. Space, and the dark sphere of a planet directly ahead.

She had arrived at Jomark.

Mentally crossing her fingers, she tapped the comm, keying the code she'd programmed in during the trip. Luck was with her: here, at least, Thrawn's people were still using standard Imperial guidance transponders. The Skipray's displays flashed the location, an island forming the center of a ring-shaped lake just past the sunset line. She triggered the transponder once more to be sure, then keyed in the sublight drive and started down. Trying to ignore that last image of the Emperor's face . . .

The wailing of the ship's alarm jerked her awake. "What?" she barked aloud to the empty cockpit, sleep-sticky eyes flicking across the displays for the source of the trouble. It wasn't hard to find: the Skipray had rolled half over onto its side, its control surfaces screaming with stress as the computer fought to keep her from spinning out of the sky. Inexplicably, she was already deep inside the lower atmosphere, well past the point where she should have switched over to repulsorlifts.

Clenching her teeth, she made the switchover and then gave the scan map a quick look. She'd only been out of it for a minute or two, but at the speed the Skipray was doing even a few seconds of inattention could be fatal. She dug her knuckles hard into her eyes, fighting against the fatigue pulling at her and feeling sweat breaking out again on her forehead. Flying while half asleep, her old instructor had often warned her, was

the quickest if messiest way to end your life. And if she had
gone down there would have been no one to blame but herself.

Or would there?

She leveled the ship off, confirmed that there were no mountains in her path, and keyed in the autopilot. The ysalamir
and portable nutrient framework that Aves had given her
were back near the aft hatchway, secured to the engine access
panel. Unstrapping from her seat, Mara made her way back
toward it—

It was as if someone had snapped on a light switch. One
second she felt as if she had just finished a four-day battle; half
a step later, a meter or so from the ysalamir, the fatigue
abruptly vanished.

She smiled grimly to herself. So her suspicion had been correct: Thrawn's mad Jedi Master didn't want any company.
"Nice try," she called into the air. Unfastening the ysalamir
frame from the access panel, she lugged it back to the cockpit
and wedged it beside her seat.

The rim of mountains surrounding the lake was visible
now on the electropulse scanner, and the infrared had picked
up an inhabited structure on the far side. Probably where Skywalker and this mad Jedi Master were, she decided, a guess
that was confirmed a moment later as the sensors picked up a
small mass of spaceship-grade metal just outside the building.
There were no weapons emplacements or defense shields anywhere that she could detect, either on the rim or on the island
beneath her. Maybe C'baoth didn't think he needed anything
so primitive as turbolasers to protect him.

Maybe he was right. Hunching herself over the control
board, hair-trigger alert for any danger, Mara headed in.

She was nearly to the midpoint of the crater when the attack came, a sudden impact on the Skipray's underside that
kicked the entire craft a few centimeters upward. The second
impact came on the heels of the first, this one centered on the
ventral fin and yawing the ship hard to starboard. The ship

jolted a third time before Mara finally identified the weapon: not missiles or laser blasts, but small, fast-moving rocks, undetectable by most of the Skipray's sophisticated sensors.

The fourth impact knocked out the repulsorlifts, sending the Skipray falling out of the sky.

CHAPTER 21

M ARA SWORE UNDER her breath, throwing the Skipray's control surfaces into glide mode and keying for a contour scan of the cliff face beneath the rim building. A landing up on the rim was out of the question now; putting down on the limited area up there without her repulsorlifts might be possible, but not with a Jedi Master fighting her the whole way. Alternately, she could go for the dark island beneath her, which would give her more room to operate but leave her with the problem of getting back up to the rim. Ditto if she tried to find a big enough landing area somewhere else down the mountains.

Or she could admit defeat, fire up the main drive and pull for space, and go after Karrde alone.

Gritting her teeth, she studied the contour scan. The rock storm had stopped after the fourth hit—the Jedi Master, no doubt, waiting to see if she'd crash without further encouragement on his part. With a little luck, maybe she could convince him that she was done for without actually wrecking the ship in the process. If she could just find the proper formation in that cliff face . . .

There it was, perhaps a third of the way down: a roughly hemispherical concavity where erosion had eaten away a layer of softer rock from the harder material surrounding it. The ledge that had been left beneath the indentation was relatively flat, and the whole thing was large enough to hold the Skipray comfortably.

Now all she had to do was get the ship there. Mentally crossing her fingers, she flipped the ship nose up and eased in the main sublight drive.

The glare of the drive trail lit up the near side of the rim mountains, throwing them into a dancing mosaic of light and shadow. The Skipray jerked up and forward, stabilized a little as Mara brought the nose a bit farther back off vertical. It threatened to overbalance, eased back as she tapped the control surfaces, twitched almost too far in the other direction, then steadied. Balancing on the drive like this was an inherently unstable operation, and Mara could feel the sweat breaking out on her forehead as she fought to keep the suddenly unwieldy craft under control. If C'baoth suspected what she was trying, it wouldn't take much effort on his part to finish her off.

Setting her teeth together, splitting her attention between the approach scope, the airspeed indicator, and the throttle, she brought the ship in.

She nearly didn't make it. The Skipray was still ten meters short of the ledge when its drive trail hit the cliff face below it with enough heat to ignite the rock, and an instant later the ship was sheathed in brilliantly colored fire. Mara held her course, trying to ignore the warbling of the hull warning sirens as she strained to see through the flames between her and her target. There was no time to waste with second thoughts—if she hesitated even a few seconds, the drive could easily burn away too much of the ledge for her to safely put down. Five meters away now, and the temperature inside the cabin was beginning to rise. Then three, then one—

There was a horrible screech of metal on rock as the Skipray's ventral fin scraped against the edge of the ledge. Mara cut the drive and braced herself, and with a stomach-churning drop, the ship dropped a meter to land tail-first on the ledge. For a second it almost seemed it would remain balanced there. Then, with ponderous grace, it toppled slowly forward and slammed down hard onto its landing skids.

Wiping the sweat out of her eyes, Mara keyed for a status readout. The airstilting maneuver had been taught to her as an absolute last-ditch alternative to crashing. Now, she knew why.

But she'd been lucky. The landing skids and ventral fin were a mess, but the engines, hyperdrive, life-support, and hull integrity were still all right. Shutting the systems back to standby, she hoisted the ysalamir frame up onto her shoulders and headed aft.

The main portside hatchway was unusable, opening as it did out over empty space. There was, however, a secondary hatch set behind the dorsal laser cannon turret. Getting up the access ladder and through it with the ysalamir on her back was something of a trick, but after a couple of false starts she made it. The metal of the upper hull was uncomfortably hot to her touch as she climbed out onto it, but the cold winds coming off the lake below were a welcome relief after the superheated air inside. She propped the hatchway open to help cool the ship and looked upward.

And to her chagrin discovered that she'd miscalculated. Instead of being ten to fifteen meters beneath the top of the crater, as she'd estimated, she was in fact nearly fifty meters down. The vast scale of the crater, combined with the mad rush of the landing itself, had skewed her perception.

"Nothing like a little exercise after a long trip," she muttered to herself, pulling the glow rod from her beltpack and playing it across her line of ascent. The climb wasn't going to be fun, especially with the top-heavy weight of the ysalamir frame, but it looked possible. Attaching the glow rod to the shoulder of her jumpsuit, she picked out her first set of handholds and started up.

She'd made maybe two meters when, without warning, the rock in front of her suddenly blazed with light.

The shock of it sent her sliding back down the cliff face to a bumpy landing atop the Skipray; but she landed in a crouch with her blaster ready in her hand. Squinting against the twin lights glaring down on her, she snapped off a quick shot that took out the leftmost of them. The other promptly shut off; and then, even as she tried to blink away the purple blobs obscuring her vision, she heard a faint but unmistakable sound.

The warbling of an R2 droid.

"Hey!" she called softly. "You—droid. Are you Skywalker's astromech unit? If you are, you know who I am. We met on Myrkr—remember?"

The droid remembered, all right. But from the indignant tone of the reply, it wasn't a memory the R2 was especially fond of. "Yes, well, skip all that," she told it tartly. "Your master's in trouble. I came to warn him."

Another electronic warble, this one fairly dripping with sarcasm. "It's true," Mara insisted. Her dazzled vision was starting to recover now, and she could make out the dark shape of the X-wing hovering on its repulsorlifts about five meters away, its two starboard laser cannons pointed directly at her face. "I need to talk to him right away," Mara went on. "Before that Jedi Master up there figures out I'm still alive and tries to rectify the situation."

She'd expected more sarcasm, or even out-and-out approval for such a goal. But the droid didn't say anything. Perhaps it had witnessed the brief battle between the Skipray and C'baoth's flying boulders. "Yes, that was him trying to kill me," she confirmed. "Nice and quiet, so that your master wouldn't notice anything and ask awkward questions."

The droid beeped what sounded like a question of its own. "I came here because I need Skywalker's help," Mara said, taking a guess as to the content. "Karrde's been captured by the Imperials, and I can't get him out by myself. Karrde, in case you've forgotten, was the one who helped your friends set up an ambush against those stormtroopers that got both of you off Myrkr. You owe him."

The droid snorted. "All right, then," Mara snapped. "Don't do it for Karrde, and don't do it for me. Take me up there because otherwise your precious master won't know until it's too late that his new teacher, C'baoth, is working for the Empire."

The droid thought it over. Then, slowly, the X-wing rotated to point its lasers away from her and sidled over to the damaged Skipray. Mara holstered her blaster and got ready, wondering how she was going to squeeze into the cockpit with the ysalamir framework strapped to her shoulders.

She needn't have worried. Instead of maneuvering to give her access to the cockpit, the droid instead presented her with one of the landing skids.

"You must be joking," Mara protested, eyeing the skid hovering at waist height in front of her and thinking about the long drop to the lake below. But it was clear that the droid was serious; and after a moment, she reluctantly climbed aboard. "Okay," she said when she was as secure as she could arrange. "Let's go. And watch out for flying rocks."

The X-wing eased away and began moving upward. Mara braced herself, waiting for C'baoth to pick up the attack where he'd left off. But they reached the top without incident; and as the droid settled the X-wing safely to the ground, Mara saw the shadowy figure of a cloaked man standing silently beside the fence surrounding the house.

"You must be C'baoth," Mara said to him as she slid off the landing skid and got a grip on her blaster. "You always greet your visitors this way?"

For a moment the figure didn't speak. Mara took a step toward him, feeling an eerie sense of déjà vu as she tried to peer into the hood at the face not quite visible there. The Emperor had looked much the same way that night when he'd first chosen her from her home . . . "I have no visitors except lackeys from Grand Admiral Thrawn," the figure said at last. "All others are, by definition, intruders."

"What makes you think I'm not with the Empire?" Mara countered. "In case it escaped your notice, I was following the Imperial beacon on that island down there when you knocked me out of the sky."

In the dim starlight she had the impression that C'baoth was smiling inside the hood. "And what precisely does that prove?" he asked. "Merely that others can play with the Grand Admiral's little toys."

"And can others get hold of the Grand Admiral's ysalamiri, too?" she demanded, gesturing toward the frame on her back. "Enough of this. The Grand Admiral—"

"The Grand Admiral is your enemy," C'baoth snapped suddenly. "Don't insult me with childish denials, Mara Jade. I saw it all in your mind as you approached. Did you really believe you could take my Jedi away from me?"

Mara swallowed, shivering from the cold night wind and the colder feeling within her. Thrawn had said that C'baoth was insane, and she could indeed hear the unstable edge of madness in his voice. But there was far more to the man than just that. There was a hard steel behind the voice, ruthless and calculating, with a sense of both supreme power and supreme confidence underlying it all.

It was like hearing the Emperor speak again.

"I need Skywalker's help," she said, forcing her own voice to remain calm. "All I need to do is borrow him for a little while."

"And then you'll return him?" C'baoth said sardonically.

Mara clenched her teeth. "I'll have his help, C'baoth. Whether you like it or not."

There was no doubt this time that the Jedi Master had smiled. A thin, ghostly smile. "Oh, no, Mara Jade," he murmured. "You are mistaken. Do you truly believe that simply because you stand in the middle of an empty space in the Force that I am powerless against you?"

"There's also this," Mara said, pulling her blaster from its holster and aiming it at his chest.

C'baoth didn't move; but suddenly Mara could feel a surge of tension in the air around her. "No one points a weapon at me with impunity," the Jedi Master said with quiet menace. "You will pay dearly for this one day."

"I'll take my chances," Mara said, retreating a step to put her back against the X-wing's starboard S-foils. Above and to her left she could hear the R2 droid chirping thoughtfully to itself. "You want to stand aside and let me pass? Or do we do this the hard way?"

C'baoth seemed to study her. "I could destroy you, you know," he said. The menace had vanished from his voice now, leaving something almost conversational in its place. "Right there where you stand, before you even knew the attack was coming. But I won't. Not now. I've felt your presence over the years, Mara Jade; the rising and falling of your power after the Emperor's death took most of your strength away. And now I've seen you in my meditations. Someday you will come to me, of your own free will."

"I'll take my chances on that one, too," Mara said.

"You don't believe me," C'baoth said with another of his ghostly smiles. "But you shall. The future is fixed, my young would-be Jedi, as is your destiny. Someday you will kneel before me. I have foreseen it."

"I wouldn't trust Jedi foreseeing all that much if I were you," Mara retorted, risking a glance past him at the darkened building and wondering what C'baoth would do if she tried shouting Skywalker's name. "The Emperor did a lot of that, too. It didn't help him much in the end."

"Perhaps I am wiser than the Emperor was," C'baoth said. His head turned slightly. "I told you to go to your chambers," he said in a louder voice.

"Yes, you did," a familiar voice acknowledged; and from the shadows at the front of the house a new figure moved across the courtyard.

Skywalker.

"Then why are you here?" C'baoth asked.

"I felt a disturbance in the Force," the younger man said as he passed through the gate and came more fully into the dim starlight. Above his black tunic his face was expressionless, his eyes fixed on Mara. "As if a battle were taking place nearby. Hello, Mara."

"Skywalker," she managed between dry lips. With all that had happened to her since her arrival in the Jomark system, it was only now just dawning on her the enormity of the task she'd set for herself. She, who'd openly told Skywalker that she would someday kill him, was now going to have to convince him that she was more trustworthy than a Jedi Master. "Look—Skywalker—"

"Aren't you aiming that at the wrong person?" he asked mildly. "I thought I was the one you were gunning for."

Mara had almost forgotten the blaster she had pointed at C'baoth. "I didn't come here to kill you," she said. Even to her own ears the words sounded thin and deceitful. "Karrde's in trouble with the Empire. I need your help to get him out."

"I see." Skywalker looked at C'baoth. "What happened here, Master C'baoth?"

"What does it matter?" the other countered. "Despite her words just now, she did indeed come here to destroy you. Would you rather I had not stopped her?"

"Skywalker—" Mara began.

He stopped her with an upraised hand, his eyes still on C'baoth. "Did she attack you?" he asked. "Or threaten you in any way?"

Mara looked at C'baoth . . . and felt the breath freeze in her lungs. The earlier confidence had vanished from the Jedi Master's face. In its place was something cold and deadly. Directed not at her, but at Skywalker.

And suddenly Mara understood. Skywalker wouldn't need convincing of C'baoth's treachery after all. Somehow, he already knew.

"What does it matter what her precise actions were?" C'baoth demanded, his voice colder even than his face. "What matters is that she is a living example of the danger I have been warning you of since your arrival. The danger all Jedi face from a galaxy that hates and fears us."

"No, Master C'baoth," Skywalker said, his voice almost gentle. "Surely you must understand that the means are no less important than the ends. A Jedi uses the Force for knowledge and defense, never for attack."

C'baoth snorted. "A platitude for the simpleminded. Or for those with insufficient wisdom to make their own decisions. I am beyond such things, Jedi Skywalker. As you will be some-day. *If* you choose to remain."

Skywalker shook his head. "I'm sorry," he said. "I can't." He turned away and walked toward Mara—

"Then you turn your back on the galaxy," C'baoth said, his voice now earnest and sincere. "Only with our guidance and strength can they ever hope to achieve real maturity. You know that as well as I do."

Skywalker stopped. "But you just said they hate us," he pointed out. "How can we teach people who don't want our guidance?"

"We can heal the galaxy, Luke," C'baoth said quietly. "To-gether, you and I can do it. Without us, there is no hope. None at all."

"Maybe he can do it without you," Mara put in loudly, try-ing to break up the verbal spell C'baoth was weaving. She'd seen the same sort of thing work for the Emperor, and Sky-walker's eyelids were heavy enough as it was.

Too heavy, in fact. Like hers had been on the approach to Jomark . . .

Stepping away from the X-wing, she walked over to Sky-walker. C'baoth made a small movement, as if he were going to stop her; she hefted her blaster, and he seemed to abandon the idea.

Even without looking at him, she could tell when the Force-empty zone around her ysalamir touched Skywalker. He in-haled sharply, shoulders straightening from a slump he probably hadn't even noticed they had, and nodded as if he finally understood a hitherto unexplained piece of a puzzle. "Is this how you would heal the galaxy, Master C'baoth?" he asked. "By coercion and deceit?"

Abruptly, C'baoth threw back his head and laughed. It was about the last reaction Mara would have expected from him, and the sheer surprise of it momentarily froze her muscles.

And in that split second, the Jedi Master struck.

It was only a small rock, as rocks went, but it came in out of nowhere to strike her gun hand with paralyzing force. The blaster went spinning off into the darkness as her hand flared with pain and then went numb. "Watch out!" she snapped to Skywalker, dropping down into a crouch and scrabbling around for her weapon as a second stone whistled past her ear.

There was a *snap-hiss* from beside her, and suddenly the terrain was bathed in the green-white glow of Skywalker's lightsaber. "Get behind the ship," he ordered her. "I'll hold him off."

The memory of Myrkr flashed through Mara's mind; but even as she opened her mouth to remind him of how useless he was without the Force, he took a long step forward to put himself outside the ysalamir's influence. The lightsaber flashed sideways, and she heard the double *crunch* as its brilliant blade intercepted two more incoming rocks.

Still laughing, C'baoth raised his hand and sent a flash of blue lightning toward them.

Skywalker caught the bolt on his lightsaber, and for an instant the green of the blade was surrounded by a blue-white coronal discharge. A second bolt shot past him to vanish at the edge of the empty zone around Mara; a third again wrapped itself around the lightsaber blade.

Mara's fumbling hand brushed something metallic: her blaster. Scooping it up, she swung it toward C'baoth—

And with a brilliant flash of laser fire, the whole scene seemed to blow up in front of her.

She had forgotten about the droid sitting up there in the X-wing. Apparently, C'baoth had forgotten about it, too.

"Skywalker?" she called, blinking at the purple haze floating in front of her eyes and wrinkling her nose at the tingling smell of ozone. "Where are you?"

"Over here by C'baoth," Skywalker's voice said. "He's still alive."

"We can fix that," Mara growled. Carefully picking her way across the steaming ruts the X-wing's laser cannon had gouged in the ground, she headed over.

C'baoth was lying on his back, unconscious but breathing evenly, with Skywalker kneeling over him. "Not even singed," she murmured. "Impressive."

"Artoo wasn't shooting to kill," Skywalker said, his fingertips moving gently across the old man's face. "It was probably the sonic shock that got him."

"That, or getting knocked off his feet by the shock wave," Mara agreed, lining her blaster up on the still figure. "Get out of the way. I'll finish it."

Skywalker looked up at her. "We're not going to kill him," he said. "Not like this."

"Would you rather wait until he's conscious again and can fight back?" she retorted.

"There's no need to kill him at all," Skywalker insisted. "We can be off Jomark long before he wakes up."

"You don't leave an enemy at your back," she told him stiffly. "Not if you like living."

"He doesn't have to be an enemy, Mara," Skywalker said with that irritating earnestness of his. "He's ill. Maybe he can be cured."

Mara felt her lip twist. "You didn't hear the way he was talking before you showed up," she said. "He's insane, all right; but that's not all he is anymore. He's a lot stronger, and a whole lot more dangerous." She hesitated. "He sounded just like the Emperor and Vader used to."

A muscle in Skywalker's cheek twitched. "Vader was deep in the dark side, too," he told her. "He was able to break that hold and come back. Maybe C'baoth can do the same."

' "I wouldn't bet on it," Mara said. But she holstered her blaster. They didn't have time to debate the issue; and as long as she needed Skywalker's help, he had effective veto on decisions like this. "Just remember, it's your back that'll get the knife if you're wrong."

"I know." He looked down at C'baoth once more, then back up at her. "You said Karrde was in trouble."

"Yes," Mara nodded, glad to change the subject. Skywalker's mention of the Emperor and Vader had reminded her all too clearly of that recurring dream. "The Grand Admiral's taken him. I need your help to get him out."

She braced herself for the inevitable argument and bargaining; but to her surprise, he simply nodded and stood up. "Okay," he said. "Let's go."

WITH ONE LAST mournful electronic wail Artoo signed off; and with the usual flicker of pseudomotion, the X-wing was gone. "Well, he's not happy about it," Luke said, shutting down the Skipray's transmitter. "But I think I've persuaded him to go straight home."

"You'd better be more than just thinking you've persuaded him," Mara warned from the pilot's chair, her eyes on the nav computer display. "Sneaking into an Imperial supply depot is going to be hard enough without a New Republic X-wing in tow."

"Right," Luke said, throwing a sideways look at her and wondering if getting into the Skipray with her had been one of the smarter things he'd done lately. Mara had put the ysalamir away in the rear of the ship, and he could feel her hatred of him simmering beneath her consciousness like a half-burned fire. It evoked unpleasant memories of the Emperor, the man who'd been Mara's teacher, and Luke briefly wondered if this could be some sort of overly elaborate trick to lure him to his death.

But her hatred seemed to be under control, and there was no deceit in her that he could detect.

But then, he hadn't seen C'baoth's deceit either, until it was almost too late.

Luke shifted in his chair, his face warming with embarrassment at how easily he'd been taken in by C'baoth's act. But it hadn't all been an act, he reminded himself. The Jedi Master's emotional instabilities were genuine—that much he was convinced of. And even if those instabilities didn't extend as far as the insanity that Mara had alluded to, they certainly extended far enough for C'baoth to qualify as ill.

And if what she'd said about C'baoth working with the Empire was also true . . .

Luke shivered. *I will teach her such power as you can't imagine*, C'baoth had said about Leia. The words had been different from those Vader had spoken to Luke on Endor, but the dark sense behind them had been identical. Whatever C'baoth had once been, there was no doubt in Luke's mind that he was now moving along the path of the dark side.

And yet, Luke had been able to help Vader win his way back from that same path. Was it conceit to think he could do the same for C'baoth?

He shook the thought away. However C'baoth's destiny might yet be entwined with his, such encounters were too far in the future to begin planning for them. For now, he needed to concentrate on the immediate task at hand, and to leave the future to the guidance of the Force. "How did the Grand Admiral find Karrde?" he asked Mara.

Her lips compressed momentarily, and Luke caught a flash of self-reproach. "They put a homing beacon aboard my ship," she said. "I led them right to his hideout."

Luke nodded, thinking back to the rescue of Leia and that harrowing escape from the first Death Star aboard the *Falcon*.

"They pulled that same trick on us, too," he said. "That's how they found the Yavin base."

"Considering what it cost them, I don't think you've got any complaints coming," Mara said sarcastically.

"I don't imagine the Emperor was pleased," Luke murmured.

"No, he wasn't," Mara said, her voice dark with memories of her own. "Vader nearly died for that blunder." Deliberately, she looked over at Luke's hands. "That was when he lost his right hand, in fact."

Luke flexed the fingers of his artificial right hand, feeling a ghostly echo of the searing pain that had lanced through it as Vader's lightsaber had sliced through skin and muscle and bone. A fragment of an old Tatooine aphorism flickered through his mind: something about the passing of evil from one generation to the next . . . "What's the plan?" he asked.

Mara took a deep breath, and Luke could sense the emotional effort as she put the past aside. "Karrde's being held aboard the Grand Admiral's flagship, the *Chimaera*," she told him. "According to their flight schedule, they're going to be taking on supplies in the Wistril system four days from now. If we push it, we should be able to get there a few hours ahead of them. We'll ditch the Skipray, take charge of one of the supply shuttles, and just go on up with the rest of the flight pattern."

Luke thought it over. It sounded tricky, but not ridiculously so. "What happens after we're aboard?"

"Standard Imperial procedure is to keep all the shuttle crews locked aboard their ships while the *Chimaera*'s crewers handle the unloading," Mara said. "Or at least that was standard procedure five years ago. Means we'll need some kind of diversion to get out of the shuttle."

"Sounds risky," Luke shook his head. "We don't want to draw attention to ourselves."

"You got any better ideas?"

Luke shrugged. "Not yet," he said. "But we've got four days to think about it. We'll come up with something."

CHAPTER 22

Mara eased the repulsorlifts off; and with a faint metallic clank the cargo shuttle touched down on the main deck of the *Chimaera*'s aft hangar bay. "Shuttle 37 down," Luke announced into the comm. "Awaiting further orders."

"Shuttle 37, acknowledged," the voice of the controller came over the speaker. "Shut down all systems and prepare for unloading."

"Got it."

Luke reached over to shut off the comm, but Mara stopped him. "Control, this is my first cargo run," she said, her voice carrying just the right touch of idle curiosity. "About how long until we'll be able to leave?"

"I suggest you make yourselves comfortable," Control said dryly. "We unload all the shuttles before any of you leave. Figure a couple of hours, at the least."

"Oh," Mara said, sounding taken aback. "Well . . . thanks. Maybe I'll take a nap."

She signed off. "Good," she said, unstrapping and standing

up. "That ought to give us enough time to get to the detention center and back."

"Let's just hope they haven't transferred Karrde off the ship," Luke said, following her to the rear of the command deck and the spiral stairway leading down to the storage area below.

"They haven't," Mara said, heading down the stairs. "The only danger is that they might have started the full treatment already."

Luke frowned down at her. "The full treatment?"

"Their interrogation." Mara reached the center of the storage room and looked appraisingly around. "All right. Just about . . . there should do it." She pointed to a section of the deck in front of her. "Out of the way of prying eyes, and you shouldn't hit anything vital."

"Right." Luke ignited his lightsaber, and began carefully cutting a hole in the floor. He was most of the way through when there was a brilliant spark from the hole and the lights in the storage room abruptly went out. "It's okay," Luke told Mara as she muttered something vicious under her breath. "The lightsaber gives off enough light to see by."

"I'm more worried that the cable might have arced to the hangar deck," she countered. "They couldn't help but notice that."

Luke paused, stretching out with Jedi senses. "Nobody nearby seems to have seen anything," he told Mara.

"We'll hope." She gestured to the half-finished cut. "Get on with it."

He did so. A minute later, with the help of a magnetic winch, they had hauled the severed section of decking and hull into the storage room. A few centimeters beneath it, lit eerily by the green light from Luke's lightsaber, was the hangar bay deck. Mara got the winch's grapple attached to it; stretching out flat on his stomach, Luke extended the lightsaber down through the hole. There he paused, waiting until he could sense that the corridor beneath the hangar deck was clear.

"Don't forget to bevel it," Mara reminded him as the light-saber bit smoothly into the hardened metal. "A gaping hole in the ceiling would be a little too obvious for even conscripts to miss."

Luke nodded and finished the cut. Mara was ready, and even as he shut down the lightsaber she had the winch pulling the thick slab of metal up into the shuttle. She brought it per-haps a meter up and then shut down the motor. "That's far enough," she said. Blaster ready in her hand, she sat gingerly on the still-warm edge of the hole and dropped lightly down to the deck below. There was a second's pause as she looked around—"All clear," she hissed.

Luke sat down on the edge and looked over at the winch control. Reaching out with the Force, he triggered the switch and followed her down.

The deck below was farther than it had looked, but his Jedi-enhanced muscles handled the impact without trouble. Recovering his balance, he looked up just as the metal plug settled neatly back down into the hole. "Looks pretty good," Mara murmured. "I don't think anyone will notice."

"Not unless they look straight up," Luke agreed. "Which way to the detention center?"

"There," Mara said, gesturing with her blaster to their left. "We're not going to get there dressed like this, though. Come on."

She led the way to the end of the passage, then down a crossway to another, wider corridor. Luke kept his senses alert, but only occasionally did he detect anyone. "Awfully quiet down here."

"It won't last," Mara said. "This is a service supply area, and most of the people who'd normally be working here are a level up helping unload the shuttles. But we need to get into some uniforms or flight suits or something before we go much farther."

Luke thought back to the first time he'd tried masquerading as an Imperial. "Okay, but let's try to avoid stormtrooper armor," he said. "Those helmets are hard to see through."

"I didn't think Jedi needed to use their eyes," Mara countered sourly. "Watch it—here we are. That's a section of crew quarters over there."

Luke had already sensed the sudden jump in population level. "I don't think we can sneak through that many people," he warned.

"I wasn't planning to." Mara pointed to another corridor leading off to their right. "There should be a group of TIE pilot ready rooms down that way. Let's see if we can find an empty one that has a couple of spare flight suits lying around."

But if the Empire was lax enough to leave its service supply areas unguarded, it wasn't so careless with its pilot ready rooms. There were six of them grouped around the turbolift cluster at the end of the corridor; and from the sounds of conversation faintly audible through the doors, it was clear that all six were occupied by at least two people. "What now?" Luke whispered to Mara.

"What do you think?" she retorted, dropping her blaster back in its holster and flexing her fingers. "Just tell me which room has the fewest people in it and then get out of the way. I'll do the rest."

"Wait a minute," Luke said, thinking hard. He didn't want to kill the men behind those doors in cold blood; but neither did he want to put himself into the dangerous situation he'd faced during the Imperial raid on Lando's Nkllon mining operation a few months earlier. There, he'd successfully used the Force to confuse the attacking TIE fighters, but at the cost of skating perilously close to the edge of the dark side. It wasn't an experience he wanted to repeat.

But if he could just gently touch the Imperials' minds, instead of grabbing and twisting them . . .

"We'll try this one," he told Mara, nodding to a room in which he could sense only three men. "But we're not going to charge in fighting. I think I can suppress their curiosity enough for me to walk in, take the flight suits, and leave."

"What if you can't?" Mara demanded. "We'll have lost whatever surprise we would have had."

"It'll work," Luke assured her. "Get ready."

"Skywalker—"

"Besides which, I doubt that even with surprise you can take out all three without any noise," he added. "Can you?"

She glared laser bolts, but gestured him to the door. Setting his mind firmly in line with the Force, he moved toward it. The heavy metal panel slid open at his approach, and he stepped in.

There were indeed three men lounging around the monitor table in the center of the room: two in the Imperial brown of ordinary crewers, the other in the black uniform and flaring helmet of a Fleet trooper. All three looked up as the door opened, and Luke caught their idle interest in the newcomer. Reaching out through the Force, he gently touched their minds, shunting the curiosity away. The two crewers seemed to size him up and then ignore him; the trooper continued to watch, but only as a change from watching his companions. Trying to look as casual and unconcerned as he could, Luke went over to the rack of flight suits against the wall and selected three of them. The conversation around the monitor table continued as he draped them over his arm and walked back out of the room. The door slid shut behind him—

"Well?" Mara hissed.

Luke nodded, exhaling quietly. "Go ahead and get into it," he told her. "I want to try and hold off their curiosity for another couple of minutes. Until they've forgotten I was ever in there."

Mara nodded and started pulling the flight suit on over her jumpsuit. "Handy trick, I must say."

"It worked this time, anyway," Luke agreed. Carefully, he eased back his touch on the Imperials' minds, waiting tensely for the surge of emotion that would show the whole scheme was unraveling. But there was nothing except the lazy flow of idle conversation.

The trick had worked. This time, anyway.

Mara had a turbolift car standing by as he turned away from the ready room. "Come on, come on," she beckoned impatiently. She was already in her flight suit, with the other two slung over her shoulder. "You can change on the way."

"I hope no one comes aboard while I'm doing it," he muttered as he slipped into the car. "Be a little hard to explain."

"No one's coming aboard," she said as the turbolift door closed behind him and the car started to move. "I've keyed it for nonstop." She eyed him. "You still want to do it this way?"

"I don't think we've got any real choice," he said, getting into the flight suit. It felt uncomfortably tight over his regular outfit. "Han and I tried the frontal approach once, on the Death Star. It wasn't exactly an unqualified success."

"Yes, but you didn't have access to the main computer then," Mara pointed out. "If I can fiddle the records and transfer orders, we ought to be able to get him out before anyone realizes they've been had."

"But you'd still be leaving witnesses behind who knew he'd left," Luke reminded her. "If any of them decided to check on the order verbally, the whole thing would fall apart right there. And I don't think that suppression trick I used in the ready room will work on detention center guards—they're bound to be too alert."

"All right," Mara said, turning back to the turbolift control board. "It doesn't sound like much fun to me. But if that's what you want, I'm game."

The detention center was in the far aft section of the ship, a few decks beneath the command and systems control sections and directly above Engineering and the huge sublight drive thrust nozzles. The turbolift car shifted direction several times along the way, alternating between horizontal and vertical movement. It seemed to Luke to be altogether too complicated a route, and he found himself wondering even now if

Mara might be pulling some kind of double-cross. But her sense didn't indicate any such treachery; and it occurred to him that she might have deliberately tangled their path to put the *Chimaera*'s internal security systems off the scent.

At last the car came to a halt, and the door slid open. They stepped out into a long corridor in which a handful of crewers in maintenance coveralls could be seen going about their business. "Your access door's that way," Mara murmured, nodding down the corridor. "I'll give you three minutes to get set."

Luke nodded and set off, striving to look like he belonged there. His footsteps echoed on the metal deck, bringing back memories of that near-disastrous visit to the first Death Star.

But he'd been a wide-eyed kid then, dazzled by visions of glory and heroism and too naive to understand the deadly dangers that went with such things. Now, he was older and more seasoned, and knew exactly what it was he was walking into.

And yet was walking into it anyway. Dimly, he wondered if that made him less reckless than he'd been the last time, or more so.

He reached the door and paused beside it, pretending to study a data pad that had been in one of the flight suit's pockets until the corridor was deserted. Then, taking one last deep breath of clear air, he opened the door and stepped inside.

Even holding his breath, the stench hit him like a slap in the face. Whatever advancements the Empire might have made in the past few years, their shipboard garbage pits still smelled as bad as ever.

He let the door slide shut behind him, and as it did so he heard the faint sound of an internal relay closing. He'd cut things a little too close; Mara must already have activated the compression cycle. Breathing through his mouth, he waited . . . and a moment later, with a muffled clang of heavy hydraulics, the walls began moving slowly toward each other.

Luke swallowed, gripping his lightsaber tightly as he tried to keep on top of the tangle of garbage and discarded equipment that was now starting to buck and twist around his feet. Getting into the detention level this way had been his idea, and he'd had to talk long and hard before Mara had been convinced. But now that he was actually here, and the walls were closing in on him, it suddenly didn't seem like nearly such a good idea anymore. If Mara couldn't adequately control the walls' movement—or if she was interrupted at her task—

Or if she gave in for just a few seconds to her hatred for him . . .

The walls came ever closer, grinding together everything in their path. Luke struggled to keep his footing, all too aware that if Mara was planning a betrayal he wouldn't know until it was too late to save himself. The compressor walls were too thick for him to cut a gap with his lightsaber, and already the shifting mass beneath his feet had taken him too far away from the door to escape that way. Listening to the creak of tortured metal and plastic, Luke watched as the gap between the walls closed to two meters . . . then one and a half . . . then one . . .

And came to a shuddering halt just under a meter apart.

Luke took a deep breath, almost not noticing the rancid smell. Mara hadn't betrayed him, and she'd handled her end of the scheme perfectly. Now it was his turn. Moving to the back end of the chamber, he gathered his feet beneath him and jumped.

The footing was unstable, and the garbage compactor walls impressively tall, and even with Jedi enhancement behind the jump he made it only about halfway to the top. But even as he reached the top of his arc he drew his knees up and swung his feet out; and with a wrenching jolt to his legs and lower back, he wedged himself solidly between the walls. Taking a moment to catch his breath and get his bearings, he started up.

It wasn't as bad as he'd feared it would be. He'd done a fair amount of climbing as a boy on Tatooine and had tackled rock chimneys at least half a dozen times, though never with any real enthusiasm. The smooth walls here in the compactor offered less traction than stone would have, but the evenness of the spacing and the absence of sharp rocks to dig into his back more than made up for it. Within a couple of minutes he had reached the top of the compactor's walls and the maintenance chute that would lead—he hoped—to the detention level. If Mara's reading of the schedule had been right, he had about five minutes before the guard shift changed up there. Setting his teeth together, he forced his way through the magnetic screen at the bottom of the chute and, in clean air again, started up.

He made it in just over five minutes, to discover that Mara's reading had indeed been right. Through the grating that covered the chute opening he could hear the sounds of conversation and movement coming from the direction of the control room, punctuated by the regular hiss of opening turbolift doors. The guard was changing; and for the next couple of minutes both shifts would be in the control room. An ideal time, if he was quick, to slip a prisoner out from under their noses.

Hanging on to the grating by one hand, he got his lightsaber free and ignited it. Making sure not to let the tip of the blade show through into the corridor beyond, he sliced off a section of the grating and eased it into the shaft with him. He used a hook from his flight suit to hang the section to what was left of the grating, and climbed through the opening.

The corridor was deserted. Luke glanced at the nearest cell number to orient himself and set off toward the one Mara had named. The conversation in the control room seemed to be winding down, and soon now the new shift of guards would be moving out to take up their positions in the block corridors. Senses alert, Luke slipped down the cross corridor to the indicated cell and, mentally crossing his fingers, punched the lock release.

Talon Karrde looked up from the cot as the door slid open, that well-remembered sardonic half smile on his face. His eyes focused on the face above the flight suit, and abruptly the smile vanished. "I don't believe it," he murmured.

"Me, either," Luke told him, throwing a quick glance around the room. "You fit to travel?"

"Fit and ready," Karrde said, already up and moving toward the door. "Fortunately, they're still in the softening-up phase. Lack of food and sleep—you're familiar with the routine."

"I've heard of it." Luke looked both ways down the corridor: Still no one. "Exit's this way. Come on."

They made it to the grating without incident. "You must be joking, of course," Karrde said as Luke maneuvered his way into the hole and got his feet and back braced against the chute walls.

"The other way out has guards at the end of it," Luke reminded him.

"Point," Karrde conceded, reluctantly looking into the gap. "I suppose it'd be too much to hope for a rope."

"Sorry. The only place to tie it is this grate, and they'd spot that in no time." Luke frowned at him. "You're not afraid of heights, are you?"

"It's the falling from them that worries me," Karrde said dryly. But he was already climbing into the opening, though his hands were white-knuckled where he gripped the grating.

"We're going to rock-chimney it down to the garbage masher," Luke told him. "You ever done that before?"

"No, but I'm a quick study," Karrde said. Looking back over his shoulder at Luke, he eased into a similar position against the chute walls. "I presume you want this hole covered up," he added, pulling the grating section from its perch and fitting it back into the opening. "Though it's not going to fool anyone who takes a close look at it."

"With luck, we'll be back at the hangar bay before that happens," Luke assured him. "Come on, now. Slow and easy; let's go."

They made it back to the garbage compactor without serious mishap. "The side of the Empire the tourists never see," Karrde commented dryly as Luke led him across the tangle of garbage. "How do we get out?"

"The door's right there," Luke said, pointing down below the level of the mass they were walking on. "Mara's supposed to open the walls again in a couple of minutes and let us down."

"Ah," Karrde said. "Mara's here, is she?"

"She told me on the trip here how you were captured," Luke said, trying to read Karrde's sense. If he was angry at Mara, he was hiding it well. "She said she wasn't in on that trap."

"Oh, I'm sure she wasn't," Karrde said. "If for no other reason than that my interrogators worked so hard to drop hints to the contrary." He looked thoughtfully at Luke. "What did she promise for your help in this?"

Luke shook his head. "Nothing. She just reminded me that I owed you one for not turning me over to the Imperials back on Myrkr."

A wry smile twitched Karrde's lip. "Indeed. No mention, either, of why the Grand Admiral wanted me in the first place?"

Luke frowned at him. The other was watching him closely . . . and now that he was paying attention, Luke could tell that Karrde was holding some secret back from him. "I assumed it was in revenge for helping me escape. Is there more to it than that?"

Karrde's gaze drifted away from him. "Let's just say that if we make it away from here the New Republic stands to gain a great deal."

His last word was cut off by a muffled clang; and with a ponderous jolt the compactor walls began slowly moving apart again. Luke helped Karrde maintain his balance as they waited for the door to be clear, stretching his senses outward into the corridor beyond. There were a fair number of crewers passing by, but he could sense no suspicion or special alertness in any of them. "Is Mara doing all this?" Karrde asked.

Luke nodded. "She has an access code for the ship's computer."

"Interesting," Karrde murmured. "I gathered from all this that she had some past connection with the Empire. Obviously, she was more highly placed than I realized."

Luke nodded, thinking back to Mara's revelation to him back in the Myrkr forest. Mara Jade, the Emperor's Hand . . . "Yes," he told Karrde soberly. "She was."

The walls reached their limit and shut down. A moment later there was the click of a relay. Luke waited until the corridor immediately outside was deserted, then opened it and stepped out. A couple of maintenance techs working at an open panel a dozen meters down the corridor threw a look of idle curiosity at the newcomers; throwing an equally unconcerned glance back their way, Luke pulled the data pad from his pocket and pretended to make an entry. Karrde played off the cue, standing beside him and spouting a stream of helpful jargon as Luke filled out his imaginary report. Letting the door slide closed, Luke stuffed the data pad back into his pocket and led the way down the corridor.

Mara was waiting at the turbolift cluster with the spare flight suit draped over her arm. "Car's on its way," she murmured. For a second, as her eyes met Karrde's, her face seemed to tighten.

"He knows you didn't betray him," Luke told her quietly.

"I didn't ask," she growled. But Luke could sense some of her tension vanish. "Here," she added, thrusting the flight suit at Karrde. "A little camouflage."

"Thank you," Karrde said. "Where are we going?"

"We came in on a supply shuttle," Mara said. "We cut an exit hole in the lower hull, but we should have enough time to weld it airtight before they send us back to the surface."

The turbolift car arrived as Karrde was adjusting the fasteners on his borrowed flight suit. Two men with a gleaming power core relay on a float table were there before them, taking up most of the room. "Where to?" one of the techs asked with the absent politeness of a man with more important things on his mind.

"Pilot ready room 33–129-T," Mara told him, using the same tone.

The tech entered the destination on the panel and the door slid shut; and Luke took his first really relaxed breath since Mara had put the Skipray down on Wistril five hours ago. Another ten or fifteen minutes and they'd be safely back in their shuttle.

Against all odds, they'd done it.

THE MIDPOINT REPORT from the hangar bay came in, and Pellaeon paused in his monitoring of the bridge deflector control overhaul to take a quick look at it. Excellent; the unloading was running nearly eight minutes ahead of schedule. At this rate the *Chimaera* would be able to make its rendezvous with the *Stormhawk* in plenty of time for them to set up their ambush of the Rebel convoy assembling off Corfai. He marked the report as noted and sent it back into the files; and he had turned his attention back to the deflector overhaul when he heard a quiet footstep behind him.

"Good evening, Captain," Thrawn nodded, coming up beside Pellaeon's chair and giving the bridge a leisurely scan.

"Admiral," Pellaeon nodded back, swiveling to face him. "I thought you'd retired for the night, sir."

"I've been in my command room," Thrawn said, looking past Pellaeon at the displays. "I thought I'd make one last survey of ship's status before I went to my quarters. Is that the bridge deflector overhaul?"

"Yes, sir," Pellaeon said, wondering which species' artwork had been favored with the Grand Admiral's scrutiny tonight. "No problems so far. The cargo unloading down in Aft Bay Two is running ahead of schedule, too."

"Good," the Grand Admiral said. "Anything further from the patrol at Endor?"

"Just an addendum to that one report, sir," Pellaeon told him. "Apparently, they've confirmed that the ship they caught coming into the system was in fact just a smuggler planning to sift again through the remains of the Imperial base there. They're continuing to back-check the crew."

"Remind them to make a thorough job of it before they let the ship go," Thrawn said grimly. "Organa Solo won't have simply abandoned the *Millennium Falcon* in orbit there. Sooner or later she'll return for it . . . and when she does, I intend to have her."

"Yes, sir," Pellaeon nodded. The commander of the Endor patrol group, he was certain, didn't need any reminding of that. "Speaking of the *Millennium Falcon*, have you decided yet whether or not to do any further scan work on it?"

Thrawn shook his head. "I doubt that would gain us anything. The scanning team would be better employed assisting with maintenance on the *Chimaera*'s own systems. Have the *Millennium Falcon* transferred up to vehicle deep storage until we can find some use for it."

"Yes, sir," Pellaeon said, swiveling back and logging the order. "Oh, and there was one other strange report that came in a few minutes ago. A routine patrol on the supply base perimeter came across a Skipray blastboat that had made a crash landing out there."

"A crash landing?" Thrawn frowned.

"Yes, sir," Pellaeon said, calling up the report. "Its underside was in pretty bad shape, and the whole hull was scorched."

The picture came up on Pellaeon's display, and Thrawn leaned over his shoulder for a closer look. "Any bodies?"

"No, sir," Pellaeon said. "The only thing aboard—and this is the strange part—was an ysalamir."

He felt Thrawn stiffen. "Show me."

Pellaeon keyed for the next picture, a close-up of the ysalamir on its biosupport frame. "The frame isn't one of our designs," he pointed out. "No telling where it came from."

"Oh, there's telling, all right," Thrawn assured him. He straightened up and took a deep breath. "Sound intruder alert, Captain. We have visitors aboard."

Pellaeon stared up at him in astonishment, fumbling fingers locating and twisting the alert key. "Visitors?" he asked as the alarms began their throaty wailing.

"Yes," Thrawn said, his glowing red eyes glittering with a sudden fire. "Order an immediate check of Karrde's cell. If he's still there, he's to be moved immediately and put under direct stormtrooper guard. I want another guard ring put around the supply shuttles and an immediate ID check begun of their crews. And then"—he paused—"have the *Chimaera*'s main computer shut down."

Pellaeon's fingers froze on his keyboard. "Shut *down*—?"

"Carry out your orders, Captain," Thrawn cut him off.

"Yes, sir," Pellaeon said between suddenly stiff lips. In all his years of Imperial service he had never seen a warship's main computer deliberately shut down except in space dock. To do so was to blind and cripple the craft. With intruders aboard, perhaps fatally.

"It will hamper our efforts a bit, I agree," Thrawn said, as if reading Pellaeon's fears. "But it will hamper our enemies' far more. You see, the only way for them to have known the *Chimaera*'s course and destination was for Mara Jade to have tapped into the computer when we brought her and Karrde aboard."

"That's impossible," Pellaeon insisted, wincing as his computer-driven displays began to wink out. "Any access codes she might have known were changed years ago."

"Unless there are codes permanently hard-wired into the system," Thrawn said. "Set there by the Emperor for his use and that of his agents. Jade no doubt is counting on that access in her rescue attempt; therefore, we deprive her of it."

A stormtrooper stepped up to them. "Yes, Commander?" Thrawn said.

"Comlink message from detention," the electronically filtered voice announced. "The prisoner Talon Karrde is no longer in his cell."

"Very well," the Grand Admiral said darkly. "Alert all units to begin a search of the area between detention and the aft hangar bays. Karrde is to be recaptured alive—not necessarily undamaged, but alive. As to his would-be rescuers, I want them also alive if possible. If not—" He paused. "If not, I'll understand."

CHAPTER 23

THE WAIL OF the alarm sounded over the overhead speaker; and a few seconds later the turbolift car came to an abrupt halt. "Blast," one of the two gunners who had replaced the service techs in the car muttered, digging a small ID card from the slot behind his belt buckle. "Don't they ever get tired of running drills up there on the bridge?"

"Talk like that might get you a face-to-face with a storm-trooper squad," the second warned, throwing a sideways glance at Luke and the others. Stepping past the first gunner, he slid his ID card into a slot on the control board and tapped in a confirmation code. "It was a lot worse before the Grand Admiral took over. Anyway, what do you want 'em to do, announce snap drills in advance?"

"The whole thing's burnin' useless, if you ask me," the first growled, clearing his ID the same way. "Who they expect's gonna come aboard, anyway? Some burnin' pirate gang or something?"

Luke glanced questioningly at Karrde, wondering what they should do. But Mara was already moving toward the two gunners, the ID from her borrowed flight suit in hand. She stepped between them, reached the ID toward the slot—

And whipped the edge of her hand hard into the side of the first gunner's neck.

The man's head snapped sideways and he toppled to the floor without a sound. The second gunner had just enough time to gurgle something unintelligible before Mara sent him to join his friend.

"Come on, let's get out of here," she snapped, feeling along the line where the door fitted into the car's cylindrical wall. "Locked solid. Come on, Skywalker, get busy here."

Luke ignited his lightsaber. "How much time have we got?" he asked as he carved a narrow exit through part of the door.

"Not much," Mara said grimly. "Turbolift cars have sensors that keep track of the number of people inside. It'll give us maybe another minute to do our ID checks before reporting us to the system computer. I need to get to a terminal before the flag transfers from there to the main computer and brings the stormtroopers down on top of us."

Luke finished the cut and closed down the lightsaber as Mara and Karrde lifted the section down and out of the way. Beyond was the tunnel wall, not quite in line with the hole. "Good," Mara said, easing through the gap. "We were starting to rotate when the system froze down. There's room here to get into the tunnel."

The others followed. The turbolift tunnel was roughly rectangular in cross-section, with gleaming guide rails along the walls, ceiling, and floor. Luke could feel the tingle of electric fields as he passed close beside the rails, and he made a mental note not to touch them. "Where are we going?" he whispered down the tunnel toward Mara.

"Right here," she whispered back, stopping at a red-rimmed plate set in the wall between the guide rails. "Access tunnel—should lead back to a service droid storage room and a computer terminal."

The lightsaber made quick work of the access panel's safety

interlock. Mara darted through the opening, blaster in hand, and disappeared down the dark tunnel beyond. Luke and Karrde followed past a double row of deactivated maintenance droids, each with a bewildering array of tools fanned out from their limbs as if for inspection. Beyond the droids the tunnel widened into a small room where, as predicted, a terminal sat nestled amid the tubes and cables. Mara was already hunched over it; but as Luke stepped into the room he caught the sudden shock in her sense. "What's the matter?" he asked.

"They've shut down the main computer," she said, a stunned expression on her face. "Not just bypassed or put it on standby. Shut it down."

"The Grand Admiral must have figured out you can get into it," Karrde said, coming up behind Luke. "We'd better get moving. Do you have any idea where we are?"

"I think we're somewhere above the aft hangar bays," Mara said. "Those service techs got off just forward of the central crew section, and we hadn't gone very far down yet."

"Above the hangar bays," Karrde repeated thoughtfully. "Near the vehicle deep storage area, in other words?"

Mara frowned at him. "Are you suggesting we grab a ship from up there?"

"Why not?" Karrde countered. "They'll probably be expecting us to go directly to one of the hangar bays. They might not be watching for us to come in via vehicle lift from deep storage."

"And if they are, it'll leave us trapped like clipped mynocks when the stormtroopers come to get us," Mara retorted. "Trying to shoot our way out of deep storage—"

"Hold it," Luke cut her off, Jedi combat senses tingling a warning. "Someone's coming."

Mara muttered a curse and dropped down behind the computer terminal, blaster trained on the door. Karrde, still weaponless, faded back into the partial cover of the service tunnel and the maintenance droids lined up there. Luke flattened himself against the wall beside the door, lightsaber held ready but not ignited. He let the Force flow through him as he poised for action, listening to the dark, purposeful senses of the troopers coming up to the door and recognizing to his regret that no subtle mind touches would accomplish anything here. Gripping his lightsaber tightly, he waited . . .

Abruptly, with only a flicker of warning, the door slid open and two stormtroopers were in the room, blaster rifles at the ready. Luke raised his lightsaber, thumb on the activation switch—

And from the tunnel where Karrde had disappeared a floodlight suddenly winked on, accompanied by the sound of metal grinding against metal.

The stormtroopers took a long step into the room, angling to opposite sides of the door, their blaster rifles swinging reflexively toward the light and sound as two black-clad naval troopers crowded into the room behind them. The stormtroopers spotted Mara crouching beside the terminal, and the blaster rifles changed direction to track back toward her.

Mara was faster. Her blaster spat four times, two shots per stormtrooper, and both Imperials dropped to the floor, one with blaster still firing uselessly in death reflex. The naval troopers behind them dived for cover, firing wildly toward their attacker.

A single sweep of the lightsaber caught them both.

Luke closed down the weapon and ducked his head out the doorway for a quick look around. "All clear," he told Mara, coming back in.

"For now, anyway," she countered, holstering her blaster and picking up two of the blaster rifles. "Come on."

Karrde was waiting for them at the access panel they'd come in by. "Doesn't sound like the turbolifts have been reactivated yet," he said. "It should be safe to move through the tunnels a while longer. Any trouble with the search party?"

"No," Mara said, handing him one of the blaster rifles. "Effective diversion, by the way."

"Thank you," Karrde said. "Maintenance droids are such useful things to have around. Deep storage?"

"Deep storage," Mara agreed heavily. "You just better be right about this."

"My apologies in advance if I'm not. Let's go."

SLOWLY, BY COMLINK and intercom, the reports began to come in. They weren't encouraging.

"No sign of them anywhere in the detention level area," a stormtrooper commander reported to Pellaeon with the distracted air of someone trying to hold one conversation while listening to another. "One of the waste chute gratings in detention has been found cut open—that must be how they got Karrde out."

"Never mind how they got him out," Pellaeon growled. "The recriminations can wait until later. The important thing right now is to find them."

"The security teams are searching the area of that turbolift alert," the other said, his tone implying that anything a stormtrooper commander said must by definition be important. "So far there's been no contact."

Thrawn turned from the two communications officers who had been relaying messages for him to and from the hangar bays. "How was the waste chute grating cut open?" he asked.

"I have no information on that," the commander said.

"Get it," Thrawn said, his tone icy. "Also inform your search parties that two maintenance techs have reported seeing a man in a TIE fighter flight suit in the vicinity of that waste collector. Warn your guards in the aft hangar bays, as well."

"Yes, sir," the commander said.

Pellaeon looked at Thrawn. "I don't see how it matters right now how they got Karrde out, sir," he said. "Wouldn't our resources be better spent in finding them?"

"Are you suggesting that we send all our soldiers and storm-troopers converging on the hangar bays?" Thrawn asked mildly. "That we thereby assume our quarry won't seek to cause damage elsewhere before attempting their escape?"

"No, sir," Pellaeon said, feeling his face warming. "I realize we need to protect the entire ship. It just seems to me to be a low-priority line of inquiry."

"Indulge me, Captain," Thrawn said quietly. "It's only a hunch, but—"

"Admiral," the stormtrooper commander interrupted. "Report from search team 207, on deck 98 nexus 326-KK." Pellaeon's fingers automatically started for his keyboard; came up short as he remembered that there was no computer mapping available to pinpoint the location for him. "They've found team 102, all dead," the commander continued. "Two were killed by blaster fire; the other two . . ." He hesitated. "There seems to be some confusion about the other two."

"No confusion, Commander," Thrawn put in, his voice suddenly deadly. "Instruct them to look for near-microscopic cuts across the bodies with partial cauterization."

Pellaeon stared at him. There was a cold fire in the Grand Admiral's eyes that hadn't been there before. "Partial cauterization?" he repeated stupidly.

"And then inform them," Thrawn continued, "that one of the intruders is the Jedi Luke Skywalker."

Pellaeon felt his mouth drop open. "Skywalker?" he gasped. "That's impossible. He's on Jomark with C'baoth."

"Was Captain," Thrawn corrected icily. "He's here now." He took a deep, controlled breath; and as he let it out, the momentary anger seemed to fade away. "Obviously, our vaunted Jedi Master failed to keep him there, as he claimed he'd be able to. And I'd say that we now have our proof that Skywalker's escape from Myrkr wasn't a spur-of-the-moment decision."

"You think Karrde and the Rebellion have been working together all along?" Pellaeon asked.

"We'll find out soon enough," Thrawn told him, turning to look over his shoulder. "Rukh?"

The silent gray figure moved to Thrawn's side. "Yes, my lord?"

"Get a squad of noncombat personnel together," Thrawn ordered. "Have them collect all the ysalamiri from Engineering and Systems Control and move them down to the hangar bays. There aren't nearly enough to cover the whole area, so use your hunter's instincts on their placement. The more we can hamper Skywalker's Jedi tricks, the less trouble we'll have taking him."

The Noghri nodded and headed for the bridge exit. "We could also use the ysalamiri from the bridge—" Pellaeon began.

"Quiet a moment, Captain," Thrawn cut him off, his glowing eyes gazing unseeing through the side viewport and the edge of the planet turning beneath them. "I need to think. Yes. They'll try to travel in concealment whenever possible, I think. For now, that means the turbolift tunnels." He gestured to the two communications officers still standing beside his chair. "Order turbolift control to put the system back into normal service except for the 326-KK nexus between deck 98 and the aft hangar bays," he instructed them. "All cars in that area are to be moved to the nearest cluster point and remain locked there until further notice."

One of the officers nodded and began relaying the order into his comlink. "You trying to herd them toward the hangar bays?" Pellaeon hazarded.

"I'm trying to herd them in from a specific direction, yes," Thrawn nodded. His forehead was creased with thought, his eyes still gazing at nothing in particular. "The question is what they'll do once they realize that. Presumably try to break out of the nexus; but in which direction?"

"I doubt they'll be foolish enough to return to the supply ship," Pellaeon suggested. "My guess is that they'll bypass the aft hangar bays entirely and try for one of the assault shuttles in the forward bays."

"Perhaps," Thrawn agreed slowly. "If Skywalker is directing the escape, I'd say that was likely. But if Karrde is giving the orders . . ." He fell silent, again deep in thought.

It was somewhere to start, anyway. "Have extra guards placed around the assault shuttles," Pellaeon ordered the stormtrooper commander. "Better put some men inside the ships, too, in case the intruders make it that far."

"No, they won't make for the shuttles if Karrde's in command," Thrawn murmured. "He's more apt to try something less obvious. Perhaps TIE fighters; or perhaps he'll return to the supply shuttles after all, assuming we won't expect that. Or else—"

Abruptly, his head snapped around to look at Pellaeon. "The *Millennium Falcon*," he demanded. "Where is it?"

"Ah—" Again, Pellaeon's hand reached uselessly for his command board. "I ordered it sent to deep storage, sir. I don't know whether or not the order's been carried out."

Thrawn jabbed a finger at the stormtrooper commander. "You—get someone on the hangar bay computer and find that ship. Then get a squad there."

The Grand Admiral looked at Pellaeon . . . and for the first time since ordering the intruder alert, he smiled. "We have them, Captain."

KARRDE PULLED AWAY the section of cable duct that Luke had cut and carefully looked through the opening. "No one seems to be around," he murmured over his shoulder, his voice almost inaudible over the background rumble of machinery coming through from the room beyond. "I think we've beaten them here."

"If they're coming at all," Luke said.

"They're coming," Mara growled. "Bet on it. If there was one thing Thrawn had over all the other Grand Admirals, it was a knack for predicting his enemies' strategy."

"There are a half dozen ships out there," Karrde continued. "Unmarked Intelligence ships, from the look of them. Any would probably do."

"Any idea where we are?" Luke asked, trying to see past him through the cable duct. There was a fair amount of empty space out there surrounding the ships, plus a gaping light-rimmed opening in the deck that was presumably the shaft of a heavy vehicle lift. Unlike the one he remembered from the Death Star's hangar bay, though, this shaft had a corresponding hole in the ceiling above it to allow ships to be moved farther up toward the Star Destroyer's core.

"We're near the bottom of the deep storage section, I think," Karrde told him. "A deck or two above the aft hangar bays. The chief difficulty will be if the lift itself is a deck down, blocking us from access to the bay and entry port."

"Well, let's get in there and find out," Mara said, fingering her blaster rifle restlessly. "Waiting here won't gain us anything."

"Agreed." Karrde cocked his head to the side. "I think I hear the lift coming now. They're slow, though, and there's enough cover by the ships. Skywalker?"

Luke ignited his lightsaber again and quickly cut them a hole large enough to get through. Karrde went first, followed by Luke, with Mara bringing up the rear. "The hangar bay computer link is over there," Mara said, pointing to a free-standing console to their right as they crouched beside a battered-looking light freighter. "As soon as the lift passes I'll see if I can get us into it."

"All right, but don't take too long at it," Karrde warned. "A faked transfer order won't gain us enough surprise to be worth any further delay."

The top of a ship was becoming visible now as it was lifted from the hangar bays below. A ship that seemed remarkably familiar . . .

Luke felt his mouth drop open in surprise. "That's—no. No, it can't be."

"It is," Mara said. "I'd forgotten—the Grand Admiral

mentioned they were taking it aboard when I talked to him at Endor."

Luke stared, a cold lump forming in his throat as the *Millennium Falcon* rose steadily up through the opening. Leia and Chewbacca had been aboard that ship . . . "Did he say anything about prisoners?"

"Not to me," Mara said. "I got the impression he'd found the ship deserted."

Which meant that wherever Leia and Chewbacca had gone, they were now stranded there. But there was no time to worry about that now. "We're taking it back," he told the others, stuffing his lightsaber into his flight suit tunic. "Cover me."

"Skywalker—" Mara hissed; but Luke was already jogging toward the shaft. The lift plate itself came into view, revealing two men riding alongside the *Falcon*: a naval trooper and a tech with what looked like a combined data pad/control unit. They caught sight of Luke—

"Hey!" Luke called, waving as he hurried toward them. "Hold on!"

The tech did something with his data pad and the lift stopped, and Luke could sense the sudden suspicion in the trooper's mind. "Got new orders on that one," he said as he trotted up to them. "The Grand Admiral wants it moved back down. Something about using it as bait."

The tech frowned down at his data pad. He was young, Luke saw, probably not out of his teens. "There's nothing about new orders here," he objected.

"I haven't heard anything about it, either," the trooper growled, drawing his blaster and pointing it vaguely in Luke's direction as he threw a quick look around the storage room.

"It just came through a minute ago," Luke said, nodding back toward the computer console. "Stuff's not transferring very fast today, for some reason."

"Makes a good story, anyway," the trooper retorted. His blaster was now very definitely pointed at Luke. "Let's see some ID, huh?"

Luke shrugged; and, reaching out through the Force, he yanked the blaster out of the trooper's hand.

The man didn't even pause to gape at the unexpected loss of his weapon. He threw himself forward, hands stretching toward Luke's neck—

The blaster, heading straight toward Luke, suddenly reversed direction. The trooper caught the butt end full in the stomach, coughed once in strangled agony, and fell unmoving to the deck.

"I'll take that," Luke told the tech, waving Karrde and Mara to join him. The tech, his face a rather motley gray, handed the data pad to him without a word.

"Good job," Karrde said as he came up beside Luke. "Relax, we're not going to hurt you," he added to the tech, squatting down and relieving the gasping trooper of his comlink. "Not if you behave, anyway. Take your friend to that electrical closet over there and lock yourselves in."

The tech glanced at him, looked again at Luke, and gave a quick nod. Hoisting the trooper under the armpits, he dragged him off. "Make sure they get settled all right, and then join me in the ship," Karrde told Luke. "I'm going to get the preflight started. Are there any security codes I need to know about?"

"I don't think so." Luke glanced around the room, spotted Mara already busy with the computer console. "The *Falcon*'s hard enough to keep functional as it is."

"All right. Remind Mara not to waste too much time fiddling with that computer."

He ducked under the ship and disappeared up the ramp. Luke waited until the tech had locked himself and the trooper into the electrical closet as ordered, and then followed.

"It has a remarkably fast start-up sequence," Karrde remarked as Luke joined him in the cockpit. "Two minutes, maybe three, and we'll be ready to fly. You still have that controller?"

"Right here," Luke said, handing it to him. "I'll go get Mara." He glanced out the cockpit window—

Just as a wide door across the room slid open, to reveal a full squad of stormtroopers.

"Uh-oh," Karrde murmured as the eight white-armored Imperials marched purposefully toward the *Falcon*. "Do they know we're here?"

Luke stretched out his senses, trying to gauge the stormtroopers' mental state. "I don't think so," he murmured back. "They seem to be thinking more like guards than soldiers."

"Probably too noisy in here for them to hear the engines in start-up mode," Karrde said, ducking down in his seat out of their direct view. "Mara was right about the Grand Admiral; but we seem to be a step ahead of him."

A sudden thought struck Luke, and he threw a look through the side of the canopy. Mara was crouching beside the computer console, temporarily hidden from the stormtroopers' view.

But she wouldn't remain concealed for long . . . and knowing Mara, she wouldn't just sit and wait for the Imperials to notice her. If there were only some way he could warn her not to fire on them yet . . .

Perhaps there was. *Mara*, he sent silently, trying to picture her in his mind. *Wait until I give the word before you attack.*

There was no reply; but he saw her throw a quick look at the *Falcon* in response and ease farther back into her limited cover. "I'm going back to the hatchway," he told Karrde. "I'll try to catch them in a cross fire with Mara. Stay out of sight up here."

"Right."

Keeping down, Luke hurried back down the short cockpit corridor. Barely in time; even as he came to the hatchway he could feel the vibration of battle-armored boots on the entry ramp. Four of them were coming in, he could sense, with the other four fanning out beneath the ship to watch the approaches. Another second and they would see him—a second after that and someone would notice Mara—*Mara; now.*

There was a flash of blaster fire from Mara's position, com-

ing quickly enough on the tail of his command that Luke got
the distinct impression Mara had planned to attack at that
time whether she'd had his permission or not. Igniting his
lightsaber, Luke leaped around the corner onto the ramp,
catching the stormtroopers just as they were starting to turn
toward the threat behind them. His first sweep took off the
barrel of the lead stormtrooper's blaster rifle; reaching out
with the Force, he gave the man a hard shove, pushing him
into his companions and sending the whole bunch of them
tumbling helplessly down to the lift plate. Jumping off the
ramp to the side, he deflected a shot from another stormtrooper and sliced the lightsaber blade across him; caught a
half dozen more shots before Mara's blaster fire took the next
one out. A quick look showed that she'd already dealt with the
other two.

A surge in the Force spun him around, to find that the
group he'd sent rolling to the bottom of the ramp had untan-
gled themselves. With a shout he charged them, lightsaber
swinging in large circles as he waited for Mara to take advantage of his distraction to fire on them. But she didn't; and with
the blaster bolts beginning to flash in at him there weren't
many alternatives left. The lightsaber slashed four times and it
was over.

Breathing hard, he closed down the lightsaber . . . and with
a shock discovered why Mara hadn't been firing there at the
end. The lift carrying the *Falcon* was dropping steadily down
toward the deck below, well past the point where the stormtroopers would be out of Mara's line of fire. "Mara!" he
called, looking up.

"Yeah, what?" she shouted back, coming into view at the
rim of the lift, already five meters above him. "What's Karrde
doing?"

"I guess we're leaving," Luke said. "Jump—I'll catch you."

An expression of annoyance flickered across Mara's face;
but the *Falcon* was receding fast and she obeyed without hesitation. Reaching out with the Force, Luke caught her in an

invisible grip, slowing her descent and landing her on the *Falcon*'s ramp. She hit the ramp running, and was inside in three steps.

She was seated beside Karrde in the cockpit by the time Luke got the hatchway sealed and made it up there himself. "Better strap in," she called over her shoulder.

Luke sat down behind her, suppressing the urge to order her out of the copilot's seat. He knew the *Falcon* far better than either she or Karrde did, but both of them probably had had more experience flying this general class of ship.

And from the looks of things, there was some tricky flying coming up. Through the cockpit canopy Luke could see that they were coming down, not into a hangar bay as he'd hoped, but into a wide vehicle corridor equipped with what looked like some kind of repulsorlift pads set across the deck. "What happened with the computer?" he asked Mara.

"I couldn't get in," Mara said. "Though it wouldn't have mattered if I had. That stormtrooper squad had plenty of time to call for help. Unless you thought to jam their comlinks," she added, looking at Karrde.

"Come now, Mara," Karrde chided. "Of course I jammed their comlinks. Unfortunately, since they probably had orders to report once they were in position, we still won't have more than a few minutes. If that much."

"Is that our way out?" Luke frowned, looking along the corridor. "I thought we'd be taking the lift straight down to the hangar bays."

"This lift doesn't seem to go all the way down," Karrde said. "Offset from the hangar bay shaft, apparently. That lighted hole in the corridor deck ahead is probably it."

"What then?" Luke asked.

"We'll see if this control can operate that lift," Karrde said, holding up the data pad he'd taken from the tech. "I doubt it, though. If only for security they'll probably have—"

"Look!" Mara snapped, pointing down the corridor. Far ahead down the corridor was another lift plate, moving down toward the lighted opening Karrde had pointed out a moment earlier. If that was indeed the exit to the hangar bays—and if the lift plate stopped there, blocking their way—

Karrde had apparently had the same thought. Abruptly, Luke was slammed hard into his seat as the *Falcon* leaped forward, clearing the edge of their lift plate and shooting down the corridor like a scalded tauntaun. For a moment it yawed wildly back and forth, swinging perilously near the corridor walls as the ship's repulsorlifts strobed with those built into the deck. Clenching his teeth, Luke watched as the lift plate ahead steadily closed the gap, the same bitter taste of near-helplessness in his mouth that he remembered from the Rancor pit beneath Jabba the Hutt's throne room. The Force was with him here, as it had been there, but at the moment he couldn't think of a way to harness that power. The *Falcon* shot toward the descending plate—he braced himself for the seemingly inevitable collision—

And abruptly, with a short screech of metal against metal, they were through the gap. The *Falcon* rolled over once as it dropped through to the huge room below, cleared the vertical lift plate guides—

And there, straight ahead as Karrde righted them again, was the wide hangar entry port. And beyond it, the black of deep space.

A half dozen blaster bolts sizzled at them as they shot across the hangar bay above the various ships parked there. But the shooting was reflexive, without any proper setup or aiming, and for the most part the shots went wild. A near miss flashed past the cockpit canopy; and then they were out, jolting through the atmosphere barrier and diving down out of the entry port toward the planet below.

And as they did so, Luke caught a glimpse across the entry port of TIE fighters from the forward hangar bays scrambling to intercept.

"Come on, Mara," he said, slipping off his restraints. "You know how to handle a quad laser battery?"

"No, I need her here," Karrde said. He had the *Falcon* skimming the underside of the Star Destroyer now, heading for the ship's portside edge. "You go ahead. And take the dorsal gun bay—I think I can arrange for them to concentrate their attack from that direction." Luke had no idea how he was going to accomplish that, but there was no time to discuss it. Already the *Falcon* was starting to jolt with laser hits, and from experience he knew there was only so much the ship's deflector shields could handle. Leaving the cockpit, he hurried to the gun well ladder, leaping halfway up, then climbing the rest of the way. He strapped in, fired up the quads. . . . and as he looked around he discovered what Karrde had had in mind. The *Falcon* had curved up past the portside edge of the *Chimaera*, swung aft along the upper surface, and was now driving hard for deep space on a vector directly above the exhaust from the Star Destroyer's massive sublight drive nozzles. Skimming rather too close to it, in Luke's opinion; but it was for sure that no TIE fighters would be coming at them from underneath for a while.

The intercom pinged in his ear. "Skywalker?" Karrde's voice came. "They're almost here. You ready?"

"I'm ready," Luke assured him. Fingers resting lightly on the firing controls, he focused his mind and let the Force flow into him.

The battle was furious but short, in some ways reminding Luke of the *Falcon*'s escape from the Death Star so long ago. Back then, Leia had recognized that they'd gotten away too easily; and as the TIE fighters swarmed and fired and exploded around him, Luke wondered uneasily whether or not the Imperials might have something equally devious in mind this time, too.

And then the sky flared with starlines and went mottled, and they were free.

Luke took a deep breath as he cut power to the quads. "Good flying," he said into the intercom.

"Thank you," Karrde's dry voice came back. "We seem to

be more or less clear, though we took some damage around the starboard power converter pack. Mara's gone to check it out."

"We can manage without it," Luke said. "Han's got the whole ship so cross-wired that it'll fly with half the systems out. Where are we headed?"

"Coruscant," Karrde said. "To drop you off, and also to follow through on the promise I made to you earlier."

Luke had to search his memory. "You mean that bit about the New Republic standing to gain from your rescue?"

"That's the one," Karrde assured him. "As I recall Solo's sales pitch to me back on Myrkr, your people are in need of transport ships. Correct?"

"Badly in need of them," Luke agreed. "You have some stashed away?"

"Not exactly stashed away, but it won't be too hard to put my hands on them. What do you think the New Republic would say to approximately two hundred pre-Clone Wars vintage *Dreadnaught*-class heavy cruisers?"

Luke felt his mouth fall open. Growing up on Tatooine had been a sheltered experience, but it hadn't been *that* sheltered. "You don't mean . . . the Dark Force?"

"Come on down and we'll discuss it," Karrde said. "Oh, and I wouldn't mention it to Mara just yet."

"I'll be right there." Turning off the intercom, Luke hung the headset back on its hook and climbed onto the ladder . . . and for once, he didn't even notice the discontinuity as the gravity field changed direction partway down the ladder.

THE *MILLENNIUM FALCON* shot away from the *Chimaera*, outmaneuvering and outgunning its pursuing TIE fighters and driving hard for deep space. Pellaeon sat at his station, hands curled into fists, watching the drama in helpless silence. Helpless, because with the main computer still only partially operational, the *Chimaera*'s sophisticated weapons and tractor beam systems were useless against a ship that small, that fast, and that distant. Silent, because the disaster was far beyond the scope of any of his repertoire of curses.

The ship flickered and was gone . . . and Pellaeon prepared himself for the worst.

The worst didn't come. "Recall the TIE fighters to their stations, Captain," Thrawn said, his voice showing no sign of strain or anger. "Secure from intruder alert, and have Systems Control continue bringing the main computer back on line. Oh, and the supply unloading can be resumed."

"Yes, sir." Pellaeon said, throwing a surreptitious frown at his superior. Had Thrawn somehow missed the significance of what had just happened out there?

The glowing red eyes glinted as Thrawn looked at him. "We've lost a round, Captain," he said. "No more."

"It seems to me, Admiral, that we've lost far more than that," Pellaeon growled. "There's no chance that Karrde won't give the *Katana* fleet to the Rebellion now."

"Ah; but he won't simply *give* it to them," Thrawn corrected, almost lazily. "Karrde's pattern has never been to give anything away for free. He'll attempt to bargain, or else will set conditions the Rebellion will find unsatisfactory. The negotiations will take time, particularly given the suspicious political atmosphere we've taken such pains to create on Coruscant. And a little time is all we need."

Pellaeon shook his head. "You're assuming that ship thief Ferrier will be able to find the Corellian group's ship supplier before Karrde and the Rebellion work out their differences."

"There's no assumption involved," Thrawn said softly. "Ferrier is even now on Solo's trail and has extrapolated his destination for us . . . and thanks to Intelligence's excellent work on Karrde's background, I know exactly who the man is we'll be meeting at the end of that trail."

He gazed out the viewport at the returning TIE fighters. "Instruct Navigation to prepare a course for the Pantolomin system, Captain," he said, his voice thoughtful. "Departure to be as soon as the supply shuttles have been unloaded."

"Yes, sir," Pellaeon said, nodding the order on to the navigator and doing a quick calculation in his head. Time for the *Millennium Falcon* to reach Coruscant; time for the *Chimaera* to reach Pantolomin . . .

"Yes," Thrawn said into his thoughts. "Now it's a race."

CHAPTER 24

THE SUN HAD set over the brown hills of Honoghr, leaving a lingering hint of red and violet in the clouds above the horizon. Leia watched the fading color from just inside the *dukha* door, feeling the all-too-familiar sense of nervous dread that always came when she was about to go into danger and battle. A few more minutes and she, Chewbacca, and Threepio would be setting out for Nystao, to free Khabarakh and escape. Or to die trying.

She sighed and walked back into the *dukha*, wondering dimly where she'd gone wrong on this whole thing. It had seemed so reasonable to come to Honoghr—so *right*, somehow, to make such a bold gesture of good faith to the Noghri. Even before leaving Kashyyyk she'd been convinced that the offer hadn't been entirely her own idea, but instead the subtle guidance of the Force.

And perhaps it had been. But not necessarily from the side of the Force she'd assumed.

A cool breeze whispered in through the doorway, and Leia shivered. *The Force is strong in my family.* Luke had said those words to her on the eve of the Battle of Endor. She hadn't believed it at first, not until long afterward when his patient training had begun to bring out a hint of those abilities in her. But her father had had that same training and those same abilities . . . and yet had ultimately fallen to the dark side.

One of the twins kicked. She paused, reaching out to gently touch the two tiny beings within her; and as she did so, fragments of memory flooded in on her. Her mother's face, taut and sad, lifting her from the darkness of the trunk where she'd lain hidden from prying eyes. Unfamiliar faces leaning over her, while her mother spoke to them in a tone that had frightened her and set her crying. Crying again when her mother died, holding tightly to the man she'd learned to call Father.

Pain and misery and fear . . . and all of it because of her true father, the man who had renounced the name Anakin Skywalker to call himself Darth Vader.

There was a faint shuffling sound from the doorway. "What is it, Threepio?" Leia asked, turning to face the droid.

"Your Highness, Chewbacca has informed me that you will be leaving here soon," Threepio said, his prim voice a little anxious. "May I assume that I will be accompanying you?"

"Yes, of course," Leia told him. "Whatever happens in Nystao, I don't think you'll want to be here for the aftermath."

"I quite agree." The droid hesitated, and Leia could see in his stance that his anxiety hadn't been totally relieved. "There is, however, something that I really think you should know," he continued. "One of the decon droids has been acting very strangely."

"Really?" Leia said. "What exactly does this strangeness consist of?"

"He seems far too interested in everything," Threepio said. "He has asked a great number of questions, not only about you and Chewbacca, but also about me. I've also seen him moving about the village after he was supposed to be shut down for the night."

"Probably just an improper memory wipe the last time

around," Leia said, not really in the mood for a fullblown discussion of droid personality quirks. "I could name one or two other droids who have more curiosity than their original programming intended."

"Your Highness!" Threepio protested, sounding wounded. "Artoo is a different case altogether."

"I wasn't referring only to Artoo." Leia held up a hand to forestall further discussion. "But I understand your concerns. I tell you what: you keep an eye on this droid for me. All right?"

"Of course, Your Highness," Threepio said. He gave a little bow and shuffled his way back out into the gathering dusk.

Leia sighed and looked around her. Her restless wandering around the *dukha* had brought her to the genealogy wall chart, and for a long minute she gazed at it. There was a deep sense of history present in the carved wood; a sense of history, and a quiet but deep family pride. She let her eyes trace the connections between the names, wondering what the Noghri themselves thought and felt as they studied it. Did they see their triumphs and failures both, or merely their triumphs? Both, she decided. The Noghri struck her as a people who didn't deliberately blind themselves to reality.

"Do you see in the wood the end of our family, Lady Vader?"

Leia jumped. "I sometimes wish you people weren't so good at that," she growled as she regained her balance.

"Forgive me," the maitrakh said, perhaps a bit dryly. "I did not mean to startle you." She gestured at the chart. "Do you see our end there, Lady Vader?"

Leia shook her head. "I have no vision of any future, maitrakh. Not yours; not even mine. I was just thinking about children. Trying to imagine what it's like to try to raise them. Wondering how much of their character a family can mold, and how much is innate in the children themselves." She hesitated. "Wondering if the evil in a family's history can be erased, or whether it always passes itself on to each new generation."

The maitrakh tilted her head slightly, the huge eyes studying Leia's face. "You speak as one newly facing the challenge of child-service."

"Yes," Leia admitted, her hand caressing her belly. "I don't know if Khabarakh told you, but I'm carrying my first two children."

"And you fear for them."

Leia felt a muscle in her cheek twitch. "With good reason. The Empire wants to take them from me."

The maitrakh hissed softly. "Why?"

"I'm not sure. But the purpose can only be an evil one."

The maitrakh dropped her gaze. "I'm sorry, Lady Vader. I would help you if I could."

Leia reached over to touch the Noghri's shoulder. "I know."

The maitrakh looked up at the genealogy chart. "I sent all four of my sons into danger, Lady Vader. To the Emperor's battles. It never becomes easier to watch them go forth to war and death."

Leia thought of all her allies and companions who had died in the long war. "I've sent friends to their deaths," she said quietly. "That was hard enough. I can't imagine sending my children."

"Three of them died," the maitrakh continued, almost as if talking to herself. "Far from home, with none but their companions to mourn them. The fourth became a cripple, and returned home to live his shortened life in the silent despair of dishonor before death released him."

Leia grimaced. And now, as the cost for helping her, Khabarakh was facing both dishonor and death—

The line of thought paused. "Wait a minute. You said all four of your sons went to war? And that all four have since died?"

The maitrakh nodded. "That is correct."

"But then what about Khabarakh? Isn't he also your son?"

"He is my thirdson," the maitrakh said, a strange expression on her face. "A son of the son of my firstson."

Leia looked at her, a sudden horrible realization flashing through her. If Khabarakh was not her son but instead her great-grandson; and if the maitrakh had personally witnessed the space battle that had brought destruction on Honoghr . . . "Maitrakh, how long has your world been like this?" she breathed. "How many years?"

The Noghri stared at her, clearly sensing the sudden change in mood. "Lady Vader, what have I said—?"

"*How many years?*"

The maitrakh twitched away from her. "Forty-eight Noghri years," she said. "In years of the Emperor, forty-four."

Leia put her hand against the smooth wood of the genealogy chart, her knees suddenly feeling weak with shock. Forty-four years. Not the five or eight or even ten that she'd assumed. Forty-four. "It didn't happen during the Rebellion," she heard herself say. "It happened during the Clone Wars."

And suddenly the shock gave way to a wall of blazing-white anger. "Forty-four years," she snarled. "They've held you like this for *forty-four years?*"

She spun to face the door. "Chewie!" she called, for the moment not caring who might hear her. "Chewie, get in here!"

A hand gripped her shoulder, and she turned back around to find the maitrakh gazing at her, an unreadable expression on her alien face. "Lady Vader, you will tell me what is the matter."

"Forty-four years, maitrakh, is what's the matter," Leia told her. The fiery heat of her anger was fading, leaving behind an icy resolve. "They've held you in slavery for almost half a century. Lying through their teeth to you, cheating you, murdering your sons." She jabbed a finger down toward the ground beneath their feet. "*That* is not forty-four years' worth of decontamination work. And if they aren't just cleaning the dirt—"

There was a heavy footstep at the door and Chewbacca charged in, bowcaster at the ready. He saw Leia, roared a question as his weapon swung to cover the maitrakh.

"I'm not in danger, Chewie," Leia told him. "Just very

angry. I need you to get me some more samples from the contaminated area. Not soil this time: some of the *kholm*-grass."

She could see the surprise in the Wookiee's face. But he merely growled an acknowledgment and left. "Why do you wish to examine the *kholm*-grass?" the maitrakh asked.

"You said yourself it smelled different than before the rains came," Leia reminded her. "I think there may be a connection here we've missed."

"What connection could there be?"

Leia shook her head. "I don't want to say anything more right now, maitrakh. Not until I'm sure."

"Do you still wish to go to Nystao?"

"More than ever," Leia said grimly. "But not to hit and run. If Chewie's samples show what I think they will, I'm going to go straight to the dynasts."

"What if they refuse to listen?"

Leia took a deep breath. "They can't refuse," she said. "You've already lost three generations of your sons. You can't afford to lose any more."

For a minute the Noghri gazed at her in silence. "You speak truth," she said. She hissed softly between her needle teeth, and with her usual fluid grace moved toward the door. "I will return within the hour," she said over her shoulder. "Will you be ready to leave then?"

"Yes," Leia nodded. "Where are you going?"

The maitrakh paused at the door, her dark eyes locking onto Leia's. "You speak truth, Lady Vader: they must listen. I will be back."

THE MAITRAKH RETURNED twenty minutes later, five minutes ahead of Chewbacca. The Wookiee had collected a double handful of the *kholm*-grass from widely scattered sites and retrieved the analysis unit from its hiding place in the decon droid shed. Leia got the unit started on a pair of the ugly brown plants and they set off for Nystao.

But not alone. To Leia's surprise, a young Noghri female was already seated at the driver's seat of the open-topped landspeeder the maitrakh had obtained for them; and as they drove through the village at a brisk walking pace a dozen more Noghri joined them, striding along on both sides of the landspeeder like an honor guard. The maitrakh herself walked next to the vehicle, her face unreadable in the dim reflected light from the instrument panel. Sitting in the back seat next to the analysis unit, Chewbacca fingered his bowcaster and rumbled distrustingly deep in his throat. Behind him, wedged into the luggage compartment at the rear of the vehicle, Threepio was uncharacteristically quiet.

They passed through the village into the surrounding cropland, running without lights, the small group of Noghri around them virtually invisible in the cloud-shrouded starlight. The party reached another village, barely distinguishable from the cropland now that its own lights were darkened for the night, and passed through without incident. More cropland; another village; more cropland. Occasionally Leia caught glimpses of the lights of Nystao far ahead, and she wondered uneasily whether confronting the dynasts directly was really the wisest course of action at this point. They ruled with the assistance or at least the tacit consent of the Empire, and to accuse them of collaboration with a lie would not sit well with such a proud and honor-driven people.

And then, in the northeast sky, the larger of Honoghr's three moons broke through a thick cloud bank . . . and with a shock Leia saw that she and her original escort were no longer alone. All around them was an immense sea of shadowy figures, flowing like a silent tide along the landspeeder's path.

Behind her, Chewbacca growled surprise of his own. With his hunter's senses he had already been aware that the size of their party was increasing with each village they passed through. But even he hadn't grasped the full extent of the recruitment, and wasn't at all certain he liked it.

But Leia found some of the tightness in her chest easing as

she settled back against the landspeeder's cushions. Whatever happened in Nystao now, the sheer size of the assemblage would make it impossible for the dynasts to simply arrest her and cover up the fact that she'd ever been there.

The maitrakh had guaranteed her a chance to speak. The rest would be up to her.

THEY REACHED THE EDGE of Nystao just before sunrise . . . to find another crowd of Noghri waiting for them.

"Word has arrived ahead of us," the maitrakh told Leia as the landspeeder and its escort moved toward them. "They have come to see the daughter of the Lord Vader and to hear her message."

Leia looked at the crowd. "And what is the message you've told them to expect?"

"That the debt of honor to the Empire has been paid in full," the maitrakh said. "That you have come to offer a new life for the Noghri people."

Her dark eyes bored into Leia's face in unspoken question. Leia looked in turn over her shoulder at Chewbacca, and raised her eyebrows. The Wookiee rumbled an affirmative and tilted the analysis unit up to show her the display.

Sometime during their midnight journey the unit had finally finished its work . . . and as she read the analysis, Leia felt a fresh stirring of her earlier anger toward the Empire at what they'd done to these people. "Yes," she told the maitrakh. "I can indeed prove that the debt has been paid."

Nearer now to the waiting crowd, she could see in the dusky light that most of the Noghri were females. The relative handful of males she could spot were either the very light gray skin tone of children and young adolescents or the much darker gray of the elderly. But directly in line with the landspeeder's path were a group of about ten males with the steely-gray color of young adults. "I see the dynasts have heard the word, too," she said.

"That is our official escort," the maitrakh said. "They will accompany us to the Grand *Dukha*, where the dynasts await you."

The official escort—or guards, or soldiers; Leia wasn't quite sure how to think of them—remained silent as they walked in arrowhead formation in front of the landspeeder. The rest of the crowd was alive with whispered conversation, most of it between the city dwellers and the villagers. What they were saying Leia didn't know; but wherever her eyes turned the Noghri fell silent and gazed back in obvious fascination.

The city was smaller than Leia had expected, particularly given the limited land area the Noghri had available to them. After only a few minutes, they arrived at the Grand *Dukha*.

From its name Leia had expected it to be simply a larger version of the *dukha* back in the village. It was certainly larger; but despite the similarity in design, there was a far different sense to this version. Its walls and roof were made of a silver-blue metal instead of wood, with no carvings of any sort on their surfaces. The supporting pillars were black—metal or worked stone, Leia couldn't tell which. A wide set of black-and-red-marbled steps led up to a gray flagstone entrance terrace outside the double doors. The whole thing seemed cold and remote, very different from the mental picture of the Noghri ethos that she'd built up over the past few days. Fleetingly, she wondered if the Grand *Dukha* had been built not by the Noghri, but by the Empire.

At the top of the steps stood a row of thirteen middle-aged Noghri males, each wearing an elaborately tooled garment that looked like a cross between a vest and a shawl. Behind them, his arms and legs chained to a pair of upright posts in the middle of the terrace, was Khabarakh.

Leia gazed past the row of dynasts at him, a ripple of sympathetic ache running through her. The maitrakh had described the mechanics of a Noghri public humiliation to her; but it was only as she looked at him that she began to grasp the full depth of the shame involved in the ritual. Khabarakh's face was haggard and pale, and he sagged with fatigue against the chains holding his wrists and upper arms. But his head was upright, his dark eyes alert and watching.

The crowd parted to both sides as the landspeeder reached the *dukha* area, forming a passage for the vehicle to move through. The official escort went up the stairs, forming a line between the crowd and the row of dynasts. "Remember, we're not here to fight," Leia murmured to Chewbacca; and summoning every bit of regal demeanor she could muster, she stepped out of the landspeeder and walked up the stairs.

The last rustle of conversation in the crowd behind her vanished as she reached the top. "I greet you, dynasts of the Noghri people," she said in a loud voice. "I am Leia Organa Solo, daughter of your Lord Darth Vader. He who came to you in your distress, and brought you aid." She held out the back of her hand toward the Noghri in the center of the line.

He gazed at her for a moment without moving. Then, with obvious reluctance, he stepped forward and gingerly sniffed at her hand. He repeated the test twice before straightening up again. "The Lord Vader is dead," he said. "Our new lord the Grand Admiral has ordered us to bring you to him, Leia Organa Solo. You will come with us to await the preparation of transport."

From the bottom of the steps Chewbacca growled warningly. Leia quieted him with a gesture and shook her head. "I have not come here to surrender to your Grand Admiral," she told the dynast.

"You will do so nonetheless," he said. He signaled, and two of the guards left their line and moved toward Leia.

She stood her ground, again signaling Chewbacca to do the same. "Do you serve the Empire, then, or the people of Honoghr?"

"All Noghri of honor serve both," the dynast said.

"Indeed?" Leia said. "Does serving Honoghr now mean sending generation after generation of young men to die in the Empire's wars?"

"You are an alien," the dynast said contemptuously. "You know nothing about the honor of the Noghri." He nodded to the guards now standing at Leia's sides. "Take her into the *dukha*."

"Are you then so afraid of the words of a lone alien woman?" Leia asked as the Noghri took her arms in a firm grip. "Or is it that you fear your own power will be diminished by my coming?"

"You will speak no words of discord and poison!" the dynast snarled.

Chewbacca rumbled again, and Leia could sense him preparing to leap up the stairs to her aid. "My words are not of discord," she said, raising her voice loud enough for the whole crowd to hear. "My words are of treachery."

There was a sudden stirring from the crowd. "You will be silent," the dynast insisted. "Or I will have you silenced."

"I would hear her speak," the maitrakh called from below.

"You will be silent as well!" the dynast barked as the crowd murmured approval of the maitrakh's demand. "You have no place or speech here, maitrakh of the clan Kihm'bar. I have not called a convocate of the Noghri people."

"Yet the convocate is here," the maitrakh countered. "The Lady Vader has come. We would hear her words."

"Then you will hear them in prison." The dynast gestured, and two more of the official guard left their line, heading purposefully toward the steps.

It was, Leia judged, the right moment. Glancing down at her belt, she reached out through the Force with all the power and control she could manage—

And her lightsaber leaped from her belt, breaking free from its quick-release and jumping up in front of her. Her eyes and mind found the switch, and with a *snap-hiss* the brilliant green-white blade flashed into existence, carving out a vertical line between her and the line of dynasts.

There was a sound like a hissing gasp from the crowd. The two Noghri who had been moving toward the maitrakh froze in midstride . . . and as the gasp vanished into utter silence, Leia knew that she'd finally gotten their complete attention. "I am not merely the daughter of the Lord Vader," she said, putting an edge of controlled anger into her voice. "I am the *Mal'ary'ush:* heir to his authority and his power. I have come through many dangers to reveal the treachery that has been done to the Noghri people."

She withdrew as much of her concentration as she could risk from the floating lightsaber to look slowly down the line of dynasts. "Will you hear me? Or will you instead choose death?"

For a long minute the silence remained unbroken. Leia listened to the thudding of her heart and the deep hum of the lightsaber, wondering how long she could hold the weapon steady in midair before losing control of it. And then, from halfway down the line to her left, one of the dynasts took a step forward. "I would hear the words of the *Mal'ary'ush*," he said.

The first dynast spat. "Do not add your own discord, Ir'khaim," he warned. "You see here only a chance to save the honor of the clan Kihm'bar."

"Perhaps I see a chance to save the honor of the Noghri people, Vor'corkh," Ir'khaim retorted. "I would hear the *Mal'ary'ush* speak. Do I stand alone?"

Silently, another dynast stepped forward to join him. Then another did so; and another, and another, until nine of the thirteen stood with Ir'khaim. Vor'corkh hissed between his teeth, but stepped back to his place in line. "The dynasts of Honoghr have chosen," he growled. "You may speak."

The two guards released her arms. Leia counted out two more seconds before reaching a hand up to take the lightsaber and close it down. "I will tell the story twice," she said, turning to the crowd as she returned the weapon to her belt. "Once as the Empire has told you; once as it truly is. You may then decide for yourselves whether or not the Noghri debt has been paid.

"You all know the history of how your world was devastated by the battle in space. How many of the Noghri were killed by the volcanoes and earthquakes and killer seas that followed, until a remnant arrived here to this place. How the Lord Darth Vader came to you, and offered you aid. How after the falling of the strange-smelling rains all plants except the *kholm*-grass withered and died. How the Empire told you the ground had been poisoned with chemicals from the destroyed ship, and offered machines to clean the soil for you. And you know all too well the price they demanded for those machines."

"Yet the ground is indeed poisoned," one of the dynasts told her. "I and many others have tried through the years to grow food in places where the machines have not been. But the seed was wasted, for nothing would grow."

"Yes," Leia nodded. "But it was not the soil that was poisoned. Or rather, not the soil directly."

She signaled to Chewbacca. Reaching back into the landspeeder, he picked up the analyzer unit and one of the *kholm*-grass plants and brought them up the steps to her. "I will now tell you the story that is true," Leia said as the Wookiee went back down the steps. "After the Lord Vader left in his ship, other ships came. They flew far and wide over your world. To any who asked they probably said they were surveying the land, perhaps searching for other survivors or other habitable places. But that was all a lie. Their true purpose was to seed your world with a new type of plant." She held up the *kholm*-grass. "This plant."

"Your truth is dreams," the dynast Vor'corkh spat. "*Kholm*-grass has grown on Honoghr since the beginning of knowledge."

"I didn't say this was *kholm*-grass," Leia countered. "It looks like the *kholm*-grass you remember, and even smells very much like it. But not exactly. It is, in fact, a subtle creation of the Empire . . . sent by the Emperor to poison your world."

The silence of the crowd broke into a buzz of stunned conversation. Leia gave them time, letting her gaze drift around the area as she waited. There must be close to a thousand Noghri pressed around the Grand *Dukha*, she estimated, and more were still coming into the area. The word about her must still be spreading, she decided, and glanced around to see where they were coming from.

And as she looked off to her left a slight glint of metal caught her eye. Well back from the Grand *Dukha*, half hidden in the long early-morning shadows beside another building, was the boxy shape of a decon droid.

Leia stared at it, a shiver of sudden horror running through her. A decon droid with unusual curiosity—Threepio had mentioned that, but she'd been too preoccupied at the time to pay any attention to his concerns. But for a decon droid to be in Nystao, fifty kilometers or more from its designated work area, was far more than just overdeveloped curiosity. It had to be—

She squatted down, mentally berating herself for her carelessness. Of course the Grand Admiral wouldn't have just flitted away on the spur of the moment. Not without leaving someone or something to keep an eye on things. "Chewie—over there to your right," she hissed. "Looks like a decon droid, but I think it's an espionage droid."

The Wookiee growled something vicious and started pushing his way through the crowd. But even as the Noghri made way for him, Leia knew he would never make it. Espionage droids weren't brilliant, but they were smart enough to know not to hang around after their cover had been blown. Long before Chewbacca could get over there it would be off and running. If it had a transmitter—and if there were any Imperial ships within range—

"People of Honoghr!" she shouted over the conversation. "I will prove to you right now the truth of what I say. One of the Emperor's decon droids is there." She pointed to it. "Bring it to me."

The crowd turned to look, and Leia could sense their uncertainty. But before anyone could move, the droid abruptly vanished around the corner of the building it had been skulking beside. A second later Leia caught a glimpse of it between two other buildings, scuttling away for all it was worth.

It was, tactically, the worst decision the droid could have made. Running away was as good as admitting guilt, particularly in front of a people who had grown up with the things and knew exactly what the normal behavioral range of a decon droid was. The crowd roared, and from the rear perhaps fifty of the older adolescents took off after it.

And as they did so, one of the guards on the terrace beside Leia cupped his hand around his mouth and sent a piercing half-scream into the air.

Leia jerked away, ears ringing with the sound. The guard screamed again, and this time there was an answer from somewhere in the near distance. The guard switched to a warble that sounded like a complicated medley of birdcalls; a short reply, and both fell silent. "He calls others to the hunt," the maitrakh told Leia.

Leia nodded, squeezing her hands into fists as she watched the pursuers disappear around a corner after the droid. If the droid had a transmitter it would right now be frantically dumping its data . . .

And then, suddenly, the pursuers were back in sight, accompanied by a half dozen adult Noghri males. Held aloft like the prize from a hunt, struggling uselessly in their grip, was the droid.

Leia took a deep breath. "Bring it here to me," she said as the party approached. They did so, six of the adolescents lugging it up the stairs and laying it on its back on the terrace. Leia ignited her lightsaber, her eyes searching the droid as she did so for signs of a concealed antenna port. She couldn't see one, but that by itself didn't prove anything. Steeling herself for the worst, she sliced a vertical cut through the droid's outer shell. Two more crosswise cuts, and its internal workings were laid out for all to see.

Chewbacca was already kneeling beside the droid as Leia shut down her lightsaber, his huge fingers probing delicately among the maze of tubes and cables and fibers. Near the top of the cavity was a small gray box. He threw a significant look at Leia and pulled it free from its connections.

Leia swallowed as he laid it on the ground beside him. She recognized it, all right, from long and sometimes bitter experience: the motivator/recorder unit from an Imperial probe droid. But the antenna connector jack was empty. Luck, or the Force, was still with them.

Chewbacca was poking around the lower part of the cavity now. Leia watched as he pulled several cylinders out of the tangle, examined their markings, and returned them to their places. The crowd was starting to murmur again when, with a satisfied murmur of his own, he pulled out a large cylinder and slender needle from near the intake hopper.

Gingerly, Leia took the cylinder from him. It shouldn't be dangerous to her, but there was no point in taking chances. "I call on the dynasts to bear witness that this cylinder was indeed taken from the inside of this machine," she called to the crowd.

"Is this your proof?" Ir'khaim asked, eyeing the cylinder doubtfully.

"It is," Leia nodded. "I have said that these plants are not the *kholm*-grass you remember from before the disaster. But I have not yet said what is different about them." Picking up one of the plants, she held it up for them to see. "The Emperor's scientists took your *kholm*-grass and changed it," she told the crowd. "They created differences that would breed true between generations. The altered smell you have noticed is caused by a chemical which the stem, roots, and leaves secrete. A chemical which has one purpose only: to inhibit the growth of all other plant life. The machines that the Grand Admiral claims are cleaning the ground are in fact doing nothing but destroying this special *kholm*-grass which the Empire planted."

"Your truth is again dreams," Vor'corkh scoffed. "The droid machines require nearly two tens of days to cleanse a single *pirkha* of land. My daughters could destroy the *kholm*-grass there in one."

Leia smiled grimly. "Perhaps the machines don't require as much time as it appears. Let's find out." Holding the *kholm*-grass out in front of her, she eased a drop of pale liquid from the tip of the needle and touched it to the stem.

It was as dramatic a demonstration as she could have hoped for. The drop soaked through the dull brown surface of the plant, and for a handful of seconds nothing seemed to happen. There was a faint sizzling sound; and then, without warning, the plant suddenly began to turn black and wither. There was a hissing gasp from the crowd as the patch of catalytic destruction spread along the stem toward the leaves and roots. Leia held it up a moment longer, then dropped it on the terrace. There it lay, writhing like a dry branch thrown into a fire, until there was nothing left but a short and unrecognizable filament of wrinkled black. Leia touched it tentatively with the toe of her boot, and it disintegrated into a fine powder.

She had expected another outburst of surprise or outrage from the crowd. Their dead silence was in its own way more unnerving than any noise would have been. The Noghri understood the implications of the demonstration, all right.

And as she looked around at their faces, she knew that she'd won.

She put the cylinder down on the terrace beside the destroyed plant and turned to face the dynasts. "I have shown you my proof," she said. "You must now decide whether the Noghri debt has been paid."

She looked at Vor'corkh; and moved by an impulse she couldn't explain, she unhooked her lightsaber from her belt and put it in his hand. Stepping past him, she went over to Khabarakh. "I'm sorry," she said softly. "I didn't expect for you to have to go through anything like this because of me."

Khabarakh opened his mouth in a needle-toothed Noghri smile. "The Empire has long taught us that it is a warrior's pride and duty to face pain for his overlord. Should I do less for the *Mal'ary'ush* of the Lord Vader?"

Leia shook her head. "I'm not your overlord, Khabarakh,

and I never will be. The Noghri are a free people. I came only to try to restore that freedom to you."

"And to bring us on your side against the Empire," Vor'corkh said caustically from behind her.

Leia turned. "That would be my wish," she agreed. "But I do not ask it."

Vor'corkh studied her a moment. Then, reluctantly, he handed her lightsaber back to her. "The dynasts of Honoghr cannot and will not make so important a decision in a single day," he said. "There is much to consider, and a full convocate of the Noghri people must be called."

"Then call it," Khabarakh urged. "The *Mal'ary'ush* of the Lord Vader is here."

"And can the *Mal'ary'ush* protect us from the might of the Empire, should we choose to defy it?" Vor'corkh countered.

"But—"

"No, Khabarakh, he's right," Leia said. "The Empire would rather kill you all than let you defect or even become neutral."

"Have the Noghri forgotten how to fight?" Khabarakh scoffed.

"And has Khabarakh clan Kihm'bar forgotten what happened to Honoghr forty-eight years ago?" Vor'corkh snapped. "If we defy the Empire now, we would have no option but to leave our world and hide."

"And doing that would guarantee the instant slaughter of the commando teams that are out serving the Empire," Leia pointed out to Khabarakh. "Would you have them die without even knowing the reason? There is no honor in that."

"You speak wisdom, Lady Vader," Vor'corkh said, and for the first time Leia thought she could detect a trace of grudging respect in his eyes. "True warriors understand the value of patience. You will leave us now?"

"Yes," Leia nodded. "My presence here is still a danger to you. I would ask one favor: that you would allow Khabarakh to return me to my ship."

Vor'corkh looked at Khabarakh. "Khabarakh's family conspired to free him," he said. "They succeeded, and he escaped into space. Three commando teams who were here on leave have followed in pursuit. The entire clan Kihm'bar will be in disgrace until they yield up the names of those responsible."

Leia nodded. It was as good a story as any. "Just be sure to warn the commandos you send to be careful when they make contact with the other teams. If even a hint of this gets back to the Empire, they'll destroy you."

"Do not presume to tell warriors their job," Vor'corkh retorted. He hesitated. "Can you obtain more of this for us?" he asked, gesturing back at the cylinder.

"Yes," Leia said. "We'll need to go to Endor first and pick up my ship. Khabarakh can accompany me back to Coruscant then and I'll get him a supply."

The dynast hesitated. "There is no way to bring it sooner?"

A fragment of conversation floated up from Leia's memory: the maitrakh, mentioning that the window for planting this season's crops was almost closed. "There might be," she said. "Khabarakh, how much time would we save if we skipped Endor and went directly to Coruscant?"

"Approximately four days, Lady Vader," he said.

Leia nodded. Han would kill her for leaving his beloved *Falcon* sitting in orbit at Endor like that, but there was no way around it. "All right," she nodded. "That's what we'll do, then. Don't forget to be careful where you use it, though—you can't risk incoming Imperial ships spotting new cropland."

"Do not presume, either, to tell farmers their job," Vor'corkh said; but this time there was a touch of dry humor in his voice. "We will eagerly await its arrival."

"Then we'd better leave at once," Leia said. She looked past him to the maitrakh, and nodded her head in thanks. Finally— finally—everything was starting to go their way. Despite her earlier doubts, the Force was clearly with her.

Turning back to Khabarakh, she ignited her lightsaber and cut him loose from his chains. "Come on, Khabarakh," she said. "Time to go."

CHAPTER 25

THE *CORAL VANDA* billed itself as the most impressive casino in the galaxy . . . and as he looked around the huge and ornate Tralla Room, Han could understand why he'd never heard of anyone challenging that claim.

The room had at least a dozen sabacc tables scattered around its three half-levels, plus a whole range of lugjack bars, tregald booths, holo-chess tables, and even a few of the traditional horseshoe-shaped warp-tops favored by hard-core crinbid fanatics. A bar bisecting the room stocked most anything a customer would want to drink, either to celebrate a win or forget a loss, and there was a serving window built into the back wall for people who didn't want to stop playing even to eat.

And when you got tired of looking at your cards or into your glass, there was the view through the full-wall transparent outer hull. Rippling blue-green water, hundreds of brilliantly colored fish and small sea mammals; and around all of it the intricate winding loops and fans of the famous Pantolomin coral reefs.

The Tralla Room was, in short, as fine a casino as Han had ever seen in his life . . . and the *Coral Vanda* had seven other rooms just like it.

Sitting at the bar beside him, Lando downed the last of his drink and pushed the glass away from him. "So what now?" he asked.

"He's here, Lando," Han told him, tearing his gaze from the reef outside and looking one more time around the casino. "Somewhere."

"I think he's skipped this trip," Lando disagreed. "Probably ran out of money. Remember what Sena said—the guy spends it like poisoned water."

"Yeah, but if he was out of money he'd be trying to sell them another ship," Han pointed out. He drained his own glass and got up from his seat. "Come on—one more room to go."

"And then we do it all over again," Lando growled. "And again, and again. It's a waste of time."

"You got any other ideas?"

"Matter of fact, I do," Lando said as they swung wide to get around a large Herglic balanced precariously across two of the seats and headed down the bar toward the exit. "Instead of just wandering around like we have for the past six hours, we should plant ourselves at a sabacc table somewhere and start dropping some serious money. Word'll get around that there are a couple of pikers ripe for plucking; and if this guy loses money as fast as Sena says, he'll be plenty interested in trying to make some of it back."

Han looked at his friend in mild surprise. He'd had the same idea a couple of hours ago, but hadn't figured on Lando going for it. "You think your professional gambler's pride can take that kind of beating?"

Lando looked him straight in the eye. "If it'll get me out of here and back to my mining operation, my pride can take anything."

Han grimaced. He sometimes forgot that he'd kind of

dragged Lando into all of this. "Yeah," he said. "Sorry. Okay, tell you what. We'll give the Saffkin Room one last look. If he's not there, we'll come back here and—"

He broke off. There on the bar, in front of an empty seat, was a tray with a still-smoldering cigarra sitting in it. A cigarra with an unusual but very familiar aroma to it . . .

"Uh-oh," Lando said quietly at his shoulder.

"I don't believe it," Han said, dropping his hand to his blaster as he threw a quick look around the crowded room.

"Believe it, buddy," Lando said. He touched the cushion of the vacant seat. "It's still warm. He must be—there he is."

It was Niles Ferrier, all right, standing beneath the ornate shimmerglass exit archway, another of his ever-present cigarras gripped between his teeth. He grinned at them, made a sort of mock salute, and disappeared out the door.

"Well, that's just great," Lando said. "Now what?"

"He wants us to follow him," Han said, throwing a quick glance around them. He didn't see anyone he recognized, but that didn't mean anything. Ferrier's people were probably all around them. "Let's go see what he's up to."

"It could be a trap," Lando warned.

"Or he could be ready to deal," Han countered. "Keep your blaster ready."

"No kidding."

They were halfway to the archway when they heard it: a short, deep-toned thud like a distant crack of thunder. It was followed by another, louder one, and then a third. The conversational din of the casino faltered as others paused to listen; and as they did so, the *Coral Vanda* seemed to tremble a little.

Han looked at Lando. "You thinking what I'm thinking?" he muttered.

"Turbolaser bursts hitting the water," Lando murmured grimly. "Ferrier's dealing, all right. Only not with us."

Han nodded, feeling a hard knot settle into his stomach. Ferrier had gone ahead and made a deal with the Empire . . . and if the Imperials got their hands on the *Katana* fleet, the balance of power in the ongoing war would suddenly be skewed back in their favor.

And under the command of a Grand Admiral . . .

"We've got to find that ship dealer, and fast," he said, hurrying toward the exit. "Maybe we can get him out in an escape pod or something before we're boarded."

"Hopefully, before the rest of the passengers start panicking," Lando added. "Let's go."

They'd made it to the archway when their time ran out. There was a sudden thunderclap, not distant this time but seemingly right on top of them, and for a second the coral reef outside the transparent hull lit up with an angry green light. The *Coral Vanda* lurched like a wounded animal, and Han grabbed at the edge of the archway for balance—

Something caught his arm and pulled hard, yanking him out of the archway to his right. He grabbed reflexively for his blaster, but before he could draw it strong furry arms wrapped around his chest and face, pinning his gun hand to his side and blotting out all view of the sudden panic in the corridor. He tried to shout, but the arm was blocking his mouth as well as his eyes. Struggling uselessly, swearing under what breath he could get, he was hauled backwards down the corridor. Two more thunderclaps came, the second nearly throwing both him and his attacker off their feet. A change of direction sideways—his elbow banged against the side of a doorway—

A hard shove and he was free again, gasping for breath. He was in a small drinks storage room, with crates of bottles lining three of the walls almost to the ceiling. Several had already been knocked to the floor by the *Coral Vanda*'s lurching, and out of one of them a dark red liquid was oozing.

Lounging beside the door, grinning again, was Ferrier. "Hello, Solo," he said. "Nice of you to drop in."

"It was too kind an invitation to turn down," Han said sourly, looking around. His blaster was hovering in front of a stack of crates two meters away, right in the middle of a thick and strangely solid shadow.

"You remember my wraith, of course," Ferrier said blandly, gesturing at the shadow. "He's the one who sneaked up onto the *Lady Luck*'s ramp to plant our backup homing beacon. The one *inside* the ship."

So that was how Ferrier had managed to get here so fast. Another thunderclap shook the *Coral Vanda*, and another crate tottered too far and crashed to the floor. Han jumped back out of the way and took a closer look at the shadow. This time he was able to pick out the eyes and a glint of white fangs. He'd always thought wraiths were just space legend. Apparently not. "It's not too late to make a deal," he told Ferrier.

The other gave him a look of surprise. "This is your deal, Solo," he said. "Why else do you think you're in here instead of out where the shooting's about to start? We're just going to keep you here, nice and safe, until things settle down again." He cocked an eyebrow. "Calrissian, now—he's another story."

Han frowned at him. "What do you mean?"

"I mean that I'm tired of him getting in my way," Ferrier said softly. "So when the *Coral Vanda* finally gives up and surfaces, I'm going to make sure he's right up there in front, trying valiantly to protect poor Captain Hoffner from the evil stormtroopers. With any luck . . ." He spread his hands and smiled.

"Hoffner's the guy's name, huh?" Han said, fighting his anger down. Getting mad wasn't going to help Lando any. "Suppose he's not on board? The Imperials won't be happy about that."

"Oh, he's aboard," Ferrier assured him. "Getting a little stircrazy, though. He's been sort of locked in our suite since about an hour after we sailed."

"You sure you got the right guy?"

Ferrier shrugged. "If not, the Grand Admiral has only himself to blame. He's the one who supplied me with the name."

Another blast rocked the ship. "Well, nice talking to you, Solo, but I've got a deal to close," Ferrier said, regaining his balance and hitting the door release. "See you around."

"We'll pay you twice what the Empire's offering," Han said, trying one last time.

Ferrier didn't even bother to answer. Smiling one last time, he slipped out the door and closed it behind him.

Han looked at the shadow that was the wraith. "How about you?" he asked. "You want to be rich?"

The wraith showed its teeth, but made no other reply. There was another thunderclap, and they were jerked hard to the side. The *Coral Vanda* was a well-built ship, but Han knew it couldn't stand up to this kind of pounding for long. Sooner or later, it would have to give up and surface . . . and then the stormtroopers would come.

He had just that long to find a way out of here.

THE *CHIMAERA*'S TURBOLASER batteries fired again, and on the bridge holo display a short red line dug briefly into the sea near the tapered black cylinder that marked the *Coral Vanda*'s position. For an instant the red line was sheathed in the pale green of seawater suddenly flashed into superheated steam; and then the pale green spread outward in all directions, and the *Coral Vanda* rocked visibly as the shock wave passed it. "They're stubborn, I'll give them that," Pellaeon commented.

"They have a great many wealthy patrons aboard," Thrawn reminded him. "Many of whom would rather drown than give up their money under threat of force."

Pellaeon glanced at his readouts. "It won't be long until they're at that choice. Main propulsion's been knocked out, and they're developing microfractures in their hull seams. Computer projects that if they don't surface in ten minutes, they won't be able to."

"They're a shipful of gamblers, Captain," Thrawn said. "They'll gamble on the strength of their ship while they seek an alternative."

Pellaeon frowned at the holo display. "What alternative could they possibly have?"

"Observe." Thrawn touched his board, and a small white circle appeared on the holo in front of the *Coral Vanda*, extending backward like the path of a crazed worm. "There appears to be a path here beneath this section of the reef that would allow them to evade us, at least temporarily. I believe that's where they're heading."

"They'll never make it," Pellaeon decided. "Not the way they're bouncing around down there. Best to be sure, though. A shot right at the entrance to that maze should do it."

"Yes," Thrawn said, his voice meditative. "A pity, though, to have to damage any of these reefs. They're genuine works of art. Unique, perhaps, in that they were created by living yet nonsentient beings. I should have liked to have studied them more closely."

He turned to Pellaeon again, gave a short nod. "You may fire when ready."

THERE WAS ANOTHER clap of thunder as the Imperial ship overhead flash-boiled the water near them . . . and as the *Coral Vanda* lurched to the side Han made his move.

Letting the ship's motion throw him sideways, he half staggered, half fell across the storeroom to slam into one of the stacks of crates, turning at the last instant so that his back was to them. His hands, flung up over his head as if for balance, found the bottom corners of the topmost crate; and as the force of his impact shook the stack, he brought the box tipping over on top of him. He let it roll a quarter rotation toward his head, then shifted his grip and shoved it as hard as he could toward the wraith.

The alien caught it square on the upper torso, lost his balance, and crashed backward to the floor.

Han was on him in a second, kicking his blaster out of the wraith's hand and jumping after it. He caught up with the weapon, spun back up. The wraith had gotten clear of the box and was scrambling to get back to his feet on a floor now slippery with spilled Menkooro whiskey. "Hold it!" Han snapped, gesturing with the blaster.

He might as well have been talking to a hole in the air. The wraith continued on to his feet—

And with the only other option being to shoot him dead, Han lowered his aim and fired into the pool of whiskey. There was a gentle *whoosh*; and abruptly, the center of the room burst into blue-tinged flame.

The alien leaped backward out of the fire, screaming something in his own language which Han was just as glad he couldn't understand. The wraith's momentum slammed him up against a stack of crates, nearly bringing the whole pile down. Han fired twice into the crate above the alien, starting twin waterfalls of alcohol cascading down around his shoulders and head. The alien screamed again, got his balance back—

And with one final shot, Han set the waterfalls on fire.

The wraith's scream turned into a high-pitched wail as it twisted away from the blaze, its head and shoulders sheathed in flame. More in anger than pain, though, Han knew—alcohol fires weren't all that hot. Given time, the wraith would slap out the fire, and then very likely break Han's neck.

He wasn't given that time. Midway through the wail the storeroom's automatic fire system finally sputtered into action, the sensors directing streams of fire foam straight into the wraith's face.

Han didn't wait to see the outcome. Ducking past the temporarily blinded alien, he slipped out the door.

The corridor, which had been crowded with panicking people when he'd first been grabbed, was now deserted, the passengers on their way to the escape pods or the imagined safety of their staterooms. Firing a shot into the storeroom lock to seal it, Han hurried forward toward the ship's main hatchway. And hoped he'd get to Lando in time.

FROM FAR BELOW him, almost lost among the shouts and screams of frightened passengers, Lando could hear the muffled hum of activated pumps. Sooner than he'd expected, the *Coral Vanda* was surrendering.

He swore under his breath, throwing another quick look over his shoulder. Where in blazes had Han gotten to, anyway? Probably hunting for Ferrier, wanting to see what the slippery ship thief was up to. Trust Han to run off and play a hunch when there was work to be done.

A dozen of the *Coral Vanda*'s crewers were busy taking up defensive positions inside the ship's main hatchway as he arrived. "I need to talk to the captain or another officer right away," he called to them.

"Get back to your room," one of the men snapped without looking at him. "We're about to be boarded."

"I know," Lando said. "And I know what the Imperials want."

That one rated him a quick look. "Yeah? What?"

"One of your passengers," Lando told him. "He has something the Empire—"

"What's his name?"

"I don't know. I've got a description, though."

"Wonderful," the crewer grunted, checking the power level on his blaster. "Tell you what you do—you head aft and start going door to door. Let us know if you find him."

Lando gritted his teeth. "I'm serious."

"So am I," the other retorted. "Go on, get out of here."

"But—"

"I said move it." He pointed his blaster at Lando. "If your passenger's got any sense he's probably already ejected in an escape pod, anyway."

Lando backed away down the corridor, the whole thing belatedly falling together in his mind. No, the ship supplier wouldn't be in any escape pod. He probably wouldn't even be in his stateroom. Ferrier was here; and knowing Ferrier, he wouldn't have deliberately shown himself like that unless he'd already won the race.

The deck rocked slightly beneath his feet: the *Coral Vanda* had reached the surface. Turning, Lando hurried aft again. There was a passenger-access computer terminal a couple of corridors back. If he could get a passenger list from it and find Ferrier's room, he might be able to get to them before the Imperials took control of the ship. Breaking into a quick jog, he turned into a cross corridor—

They were striding purposefully toward him: four large men with blasters at the ready, with a thin, white-haired man almost hidden in the center of the group. The lead man spotted Lando, snapped his blaster up, and fired.

The first shot was a clean miss. The second sizzled into the wall as Lando ducked back behind the corner.

"So much for finding Ferrier's room," Lando muttered. Another handful of shots spit past his barricade; and then, surprisingly, the firing stopped. Blaster in hand, hugging the corridor wall, Lando eased back to the corner and threw a quick look around it.

They were gone.

"Great," he muttered, taking a longer look. They were gone, all right, probably into one of the crew-only areas that ran down the central core of the ship. Chasing after someone through an unfamiliar area was usually not a good idea, but there weren't a whole lot of other options available. Grimacing to himself, he started around the corner—

And yelped as a blaster bolt from his right scorched past his sleeve. He dived forward into the cross corridor, catching a glimpse as he fell of three more men coming toward him down the main corridor. He hit the thick carpet hard enough to see stars, rolled onto his side and yanked his legs out of the line of fire, fully aware that if any of the original group was watching from cover, he was dead. A barrage of blaster shots from the newcomers bit into the wall, with the kind of clustering that meant it was being used as cover fire while they advanced on him. Breathing hard—that crash dive had knocked the wind out of him—Lando got to his feet and started toward an arched doorway halfway down the cross corridor. It wouldn't give him much cover, but it was the best he had. He had just made it to the doorway when there was a sudden curse from the direction of his attackers, a handful of shots from what sounded like a different model blaster—

And then, silence.

Lando frowned, wondering what they were pulling now. He could hear footsteps running toward him; flattening himself into the doorway as best he could, he leveled his blaster at the intersection.

The footsteps came to the intersection and paused. "Lando?"

Lando lowered his blaster with a silent sigh of relief. "Over here, Han," he called. "Come on—Ferrier's people have our man."

Han rounded the corner and sprinted toward him. "That's not all, buddy," he panted. "Ferrier's gunning for you, too."

Lando grimaced. He hadn't missed by much, either. "Never mind me," he said. "I think they must have gone down the ship's core. We've got to catch up with them before they reach the main hatchway."

"We can try," Han said grimly, looking around. "Over there—looks like a crewer access door."

It was. And it was locked.

"Ferrier's people got in," Lando grunted, stooping down to examine the half-open release panel. "Yeah. Here—it's been hot-wired. Let's see . . ."

He probed carefully into the mechanism with the tip of his little finger; and with a satisfying *click*, the panel unlocked and slid open. "There we go," he said. He got to his feet again—

And jumped back from the opening as a stuttering of blaster fire flashed through.

"Yeah, there we go all right," Han said. He was against the wall on the other side of the opening, blaster ready but with no chance of getting a shot in through the rear guard's fire. "How many people has Ferrier got on this ship, anyway?"

"A lot," Lando growled. The door, apparently deciding that no one was going through after all, slid shut again. "I guess we do this the hard way. Let's get back to the main hatchway and try to catch them there."

Han grabbed his shoulder. "Too late," he said. "Listen."

Lando frowned, straining his ears. Over the quiet hum of ship's noises, he could make out the rapid-fire spitting of stormtrooper laser rifles in the distance. "They're aboard," he murmured.

"Yeah," Han nodded. The deck vibrated briefly beneath their feet, and abruptly the laser fire slackened off. "Subsonic grenade," he identified it. "That's it. Come on."

"Come on where?" Lando asked as Han set off down the cross corridor.

"Aft to the escape pod racks," the other said. "We're getting out of here."

Lando felt his mouth drop open. But he looked at his friend, and his objections died unsaid. Han's face was set into tight lines, his eyes smoldering with anger and frustration. He knew what this meant, all right. Probably better than Lando did.

THE ESCAPE POD bobbed on the surface of the sea, surrounded by a hundred other pods and floating bits of reef. Through the tiny porthole Han watched as, in the distance, the last of the Imperial assault shuttles lifted from the *Coral Vanda* and headed back to space. "That's it, then?" Lando ventured from the seat behind him.

"That's it," Han said, hearing the bitterness in his voice. "They'll probably start picking up the pods soon."

"We did all we could, Han," Lando pointed out quietly. "And it could have been worse. They could have blown the

Coral Vanda out of the water—it might have been days before anyone came to get us then."

Which would have given the Empire that much more of a head start. "Oh, yeah, great," Han said sourly. "We're really on top of things."

"What else could we have done?" Lando persisted. "Scuttled the ship to keep them from getting him—never mind that we'd have killed several hundred people in the process? Or maybe just gotten ourselves killed fighting three assault shuttles' worth of stormtroopers? At least this way Coruscant has a chance to get ready before ships from the Dark Force start showing up in battle."

Lando was trying—you had to give him that. But Han wasn't ready to be cheered up yet. "How do you get ready to get hit by two hundred Dreadnaughts?" he growled. "We're stretched to the limit as it is."

"Come on, Han," Lando said, his voice starting to sound a little irritated. "Even if the ships are in mint condition and ready to fly, they're still going to need two thousand crewers apiece to man them. It'll be years before the Imperials can scrape that many recruits together and teach them how to fly the things."

"Except that the Empire already had a call out for new ships," Han reminded him. "Means they already have a bunch of recruits ready to go."

"I doubt they have four hundred thousand of them," Lando countered. "Come on, try looking on the bright side for once."

"There's not much bright side here to look at." Han shook his head.

"Sure there is," Lando insisted. "Thanks to your quick action, the New Republic still has a fighting chance."

Han frowned at him. "What do you mean?"

"You saved my life, remember? Shot those goons of Ferrier's off my back."

"Yeah, I remember. What does that have to do with the New Republic's chances?"

"Han!" Lando said, looking scandalized. "You know perfectly well how fast the New Republic would fall apart without me around."

Han tried real hard, but he couldn't quite strangle off a smile on that one. He compromised, letting it come out twisted. "All right, I give up," he sighed. "If I stop grousing, will you shut up?"

"Deal," Lando nodded.

Han turned back to the porthole, the smile fading away. Lando could talk all he wanted; but the loss of the *Katana* fleet would be a first-magnitude disaster, and they both knew it. Somehow, they had to stop the Empire from getting to those ships.

Somehow.

CHAPTER 26

MON MOTHMA SHOOK her head in wonderment. "The *Katana* fleet," she breathed. "After all these years. It's incredible."

"Some might even put it more strongly than that," Fey'lya added coolly, his fur rippling as he gazed hard at Karrde's impassive face. He'd been doing a lot of that throughout the hastily called meeting, Leia had noticed: gazing hard at Karrde, at Luke, at Leia herself. Even Mon Mothma hadn't been left out. "Some might, in fact, have severe doubts that what you're telling us is true at all."

Beside Karrde, Luke shifted in his seat, and Leia could sense his efforts to control his annoyance with the Bothan. But Karrde merely cocked an eyebrow. "Are you suggesting that I'm lying to you?"

"What, a smuggler lie?" Fey'lya countered. "What a thought."

"He's not lying," Han insisted, an edge to his voice. "The fleet's been found. I saw some of the ships."

"Perhaps," Fey'lya said, dropping his eyes to the polished

surface of the table. Of all those at the meeting, Han had so far been the only one to escape Fey'lya's posturing and his glare. For some reason, the Bothan seemed reluctant to even look at him. "Perhaps not. There are more Dreadnaught cruisers in the galaxy than just the *Katana* fleet."

"I don't believe this," Luke spoke up at last, looking back and forth between Fey'lya and Mon Mothma. "The *Katana* fleet's been found, the Empire's going after it, and we're sitting here arguing about it?"

"Perhaps the problem is that *you* believe too much, or too easily," Fey'lya retorted, turning his gaze on Luke. "Solo tells us the Empire is holding someone who can lead them to these alleged ships. And yet Karrde has said only he knows their location."

"And as I've mentioned at least once today," Karrde said tartly, "the assumption that no one else knew what we'd found was just that: an assumption. Captain Hoffner was a very astute man in his way, and I have no trouble believing that he might have pulled a copy of the coordinates for himself before I erased them."

"I'm glad you have such faith in your former associate," Fey'lya said. "For myself, I find it easier to believe that it is Captain Solo who is wrong." His fur rippled. "Or has been deliberately deceived."

Beside her, Leia felt Han's mood darken. "You want to explain that, Councilor?" he demanded.

"I think you were lied to," Fey'lya said bluntly, his eyes still not meeting Han's. "I think this contact of yours—who I notice you've been remarkably reluctant to identify—told you a story and dressed it up with false evidence. That piece of machinery you say Calrissian examined could have come from anywhere. And you yourself admitted that you were never actually aboard any of the ships."

"What about that Imperial raid on the *Coral Vanda*?" Han demanded. "*They* thought there was someone there worth grabbing."

Fey'lya smiled thinly. "Or else they wanted us to believe that they did. Which they very well might . . . if your unnamed contact is in fact working for them."

Leia looked at Han. There was something there, beneath the surface. Some swirl of emotion she couldn't identify. "Han?" she asked quietly.

"No," he said, his eyes still on Fey'lya. "He's not working for the Imperials."

"So you say," Fey'lya sniffed. "You offer little proof of that."

"All right, then," Karrde put in. "Let's assume for the moment that all of this is in fact a giant soap bubble. What would the Grand Admiral stand to gain from it?"

Fey'lya's fur shifted in a gesture Leia decided was probably annoyance. Between her and Karrde they'd pretty well burst the Bothan's theory that Thrawn was not, in fact, an Imperial Grand Admiral; and Fey'lya wasn't taking even that minor defeat well. "I should think that was obvious," he told Karrde stiffly. "How many systems would we have to leave undefended, do you suppose, in order to reassign enough trained personnel to reactivate and transport two hundred Dreadnaughts? No, the Empire has a great deal to gain by hasty action on our part."

"They also have a great deal to gain by our total lack of action," Karrde said, his voice icy cold. "I worked with Hoffner for over two years; and I can tell you right now that it won't take the Imperials a great deal of time to obtain the fleet's location from him. If you don't move quickly, you stand to lose everything."

"If there's anything out there to lose," Fey'lya said.

Leia put a warning hand on Han's arm. "That should be easy enough to check," she jumped in before Karrde could respond. "We can send a ship and tech crew out to take a look. If the fleet is there and seems operational, we can start a full-scale salvage effort."

From the look on Karrde's face she could tell that he

thought even that was moving too slowly. But he nodded. "I suppose that's reasonable enough," he said.

Leia looked at Mon Mothma. "Mon Mothma?"

"I agree," the other said. "Councilor Fey'lya, you'll speak to Admiral Drayson at once about assigning an Escort Frigate and two X-wing squadrons to this mission. Preferably a ship already here at Coruscant; we don't want anyone outside the system to get even a hint of what we're doing."

Fey'lya inclined his head slightly. "As you wish. Will tomorrow morning be sufficiently early?"

"Yes." Mon Mothma looked at Karrde. "We'll need the fleet's coordinates."

"Of course," Karrde agreed. "I'll supply them tomorrow morning."

Fey'lya snorted. "Let me remind you, Captain Karrde—"

"Unless, of course, Councilor," Karrde continued smoothly, "you'd prefer I leave Coruscant tonight and offer the location to the highest bidder."

Fey'lya glared at him, his fur flattening. But there was nothing he could do about it, and he knew it. "In the morning, then," he growled.

"Good," Karrde nodded. "If that's all, then, I believe I'll return to my quarters and rest awhile before dinner."

He looked across at Leia . . . and suddenly, there was something different in his face or his sense. She nodded fractionally, and his gaze slid unconcernedly away from her as he stood up. "Mon Mothma; Councilor Fey'lya," he said, nodding to each in turn. "It's been interesting."

"We'll see you in the morning," Fey'lya said darkly.

A faintly sardonic smile touched Karrde's lips. "Of course."

"Then I declare this meeting adjourned," Mon Mothma said, making it official.

"Let's go," Leia murmured to Han as the others began collecting their data cards together.

"What's going on?" he murmured back.

"I think Karrde wants to talk," she told him. "Come on—I don't want to get bogged down here talking to Mon Mothma."

"Yeah, well, you go on," Han said, his voice oddly preoccupied.

She frowned at him. "You sure?"

"Yeah," he said. His eyes flicked over her shoulder, and she glanced around in time to see Fey'lya stride from the room. "Go on. I'll catch up with you."

"All right," she said, frowning at him.

"It's okay," he assured her, reaching down to squeeze her hand. "I just need to talk to Fey'lya for a minute."

"What about?"

"Personal stuff." He tried one of those lopsided smiles she usually found so endearing. It didn't look nearly so innocent this time as it normally did. "Hey—it's okay," he repeated. "I'm just going to talk to him. Trust me."

"I've heard *that* before," Leia sighed. But Luke had already left the room, and Karrde was on his way out . . . and Mon Mothma had that look about her that signified that she was about to come over and ask Leia for a favor. "Just try to be diplomatic, all right?"

His eyes flicked over her shoulder again. "Sure," he said. "Trust me."

FEY'LYA WAS HEADING down the Grand Corridor toward the Assemblage chamber when Han caught sight of him, walking with that peculiar gait of someone who's in a terrific hurry but doesn't want anyone else to know it. "Hey!" Han called. "Councilor Fey'lya!"

The only response was a brief flush of pale red across the nearest of the line of ch'hala trees. Glowering at the back of Fey'lya's head, Han lengthened his stride, and within a dozen quick paces had caught up with the other. "I'd like a word with you, Councilor," he said.

Fey'lya didn't look at him. "We have nothing to discuss," he said.

"Oh, I think we do," Han said, falling into step beside him. "Like maybe trying to find a way out of the jam you're in here."

"I thought your female was the diplomat of the family," Fey'lya sniffed, throwing a sideways look at Han's shirtfront.

"We take turns," Han told him, trying real hard not to dislike the other. "See, what got you into trouble here was trying to play politics by Bothan rules. That bank thing made Ackbar look bad, so like any good Bothan, you jumped on him. Trouble is, no one else jumped with you, so you were left there all alone with your neck stuck way out and your political reputation on the line. You don't know how to back out gracefully, and you figure the only way to salvage your prestige is to make sure Ackbar goes down."

"Indeed?" Fey'lya said acidly. "Did it ever occur to you that I might have stuck my neck out, as you put it, because I truly believed Ackbar was guilty of treason?"

"Not really, no," Han told him. "But a lot of other people think that, and that's what's got your reputation on the line. They can't imagine anyone making such a fuss without some proof."

"What makes you think I haven't any proof?"

"For starters, the fact that you haven't shown it," Han said bluntly. "Then there's the fact that you sent Breil'lya scrambling out to New Cov to try and make some sort of high-prestige deal with Senator Bel Iblis. That *is* what Breil'lya was doing out there, isn't it?"

"I don't know what you're talking about," Fey'lya muttered.

"Right. And that's the third thing: the fact that five minutes ago you were ready to throw Bel Iblis to the cravers if it would buy you enough time to bring in the *Katana* fleet."

Abruptly, Fey'lya stopped. "Let me speak frankly with you, Captain Solo," he said, still not looking directly at Han's face. "Whether you understand my motivations or not, I certainly understand yours. You hope to bring the *Katana* fleet to Coruscant yourself; and with that leverage to force my downfall and Ackbar's reinstatement."

"No," Han said tiredly, shaking his head. "That's the whole point, Councilor. Leia and the others don't play by Bothan rules. They make decisions based on evidence, not prestige. If Ackbar is guilty, he gets punished; if he's innocent, he gets released. It's that simple."

Fey'lya smiled bitterly. "Take my advice, Captain Solo, and stick with smuggling and fighting and other things you understand. The private rules of politics are far beyond you."

"You're making a mistake, Councilor," Han said, trying one last time. "You can back out now without losing anything— you really can. But if you keep going, you risk bringing the whole New Republic down with you."

Fey'lya drew himself up to his full height. "I do not intend to fall, Captain Solo. My supporters among the New Republic military will see to that. Ackbar will fall, and I will rise in his place. Excuse me, now; I must speak with Admiral Drayson."

He turned and stalked off. Han watched him go, the sour taste of defeat in his mouth. Couldn't Fey'lya see what he was doing? That he was risking everything on a single long-shot bet?

Maybe he couldn't. Maybe it took an experienced gambler to see how the odds were stacked here.

Or a politician who wasn't so set in his own system that he couldn't change.

Fey'lya reached the end of the Grand Corridor and headed to the left toward the Admiralty center. Shaking his head, Han turned and headed back toward Karrde's guest quarters. First the *Coral Vanda*, and now this. He hoped it wasn't the start of a trend.

MARA STOOD AT the window of her room, staring out at the Manarai Mountains in the distance, feeling the oppressive weight of black memories gathering around her mind. The

Imperial Palace. After five years, she was back in the Imperial
Palace. Scene of important governmental meetings, glittering
social functions, dark and private intrigues. The place where
her life had effectively begun.

The place where she'd been when it had ended.

Her fingernails grated across the carved swirls of the window frame as well-remembered faces rose before her: Grand
Admiral Thrawn, Lord Vader, Grand Moff Tarkin, advisers
and politicians and sycophants by the hundreds. But above
them all was the image of the Emperor. She could see him in
her mind's eye as clearly as if he were staring in at her through
the window, his wrinkled face frowning, his yellow-tinged eyes
bright with anger and disapproval.

YOU WILL KILL LUKE SKYWALKER.

"I'm trying," she whispered to the words echoing through
her mind. But even as she said it she wondered if it were really
true. She'd helped save Skywalker's life on Myrkr; had come
begging for his help on Jomark; and had now uncomplain-
ingly come to Coruscant with him.

She wasn't in any danger. Neither was Karrde. There was
no way she could think of why Skywalker would be useful to
either her or any of Karrde's people.

She had, in short, no excuses left.

From the next room over came the faint sound of a door
opening and closing: Karrde, returned from his meeting. Turning from the window, glad of an excuse to drop this line of
thought, she headed toward the door connecting their rooms.

Karrde got there first. "Mara?" he said, opening the door
and poking his head through. "Come in here, please."

He was standing by the room's computer terminal when
she arrived. One look at his face was all she needed. "What's
gone wrong?" she asked.

"I'm not entirely sure," he said, pulling a data card from
the terminal's copy slot. "That Bothan on the Council put up
a surprising amount of resistance to our offer. He basically
forced Mon Mothma to hold off on any serious retrieval mis-

sion until the location's been checked out. He's getting a ship set up now for a morning flight."

Mara frowned. "A double-cross?"

"Possibly, but I can't see any point to it." Karrde shook his head. "Thrawn already has Hoffner. He'll get to the fleet soon enough. No, I think it more likely Fey'lya's playing internal politics here, perhaps connected to his campaign against Admiral Ackbar. But I'd rather not take any chances."

"I've heard stories about internal Bothan politics," Mara agreed grimly. "What do you want me to do?"

"I want you to leave tonight for the Trogan system," he said, handing her the data card. "Best guess is that's where Aves will have holed up. Make contact and tell him I want everything we have that can both fly and fight to rendezvous with me at the *Katana* fleet as soon as possible."

Mara took the card gingerly, her fingers tingling at the touch of the cool plastic. There it was, in her hands: the *Katana* fleet. A lifetime's worth of wealth or power . . . "I may have trouble persuading Aves to trust me," she warned.

"I don't think so," Karrde said. "The Imperials will have reinstated the hunt for our group by now—that alone should convince him I've escaped. There's also a special recognition code on that data card that he'll know, a code the Grand Admiral couldn't possibly have extracted from me this quickly."

"Let's hope he doesn't have a higher opinion of Imperial interrogation methods than you do," Mara said, sliding the data card into her tunic. "Anything else?"

"No—yes," Karrde corrected himself. "Tell Ghent I'd like him to come to Coruscant instead of going to the *Katana* fleet. I'll meet him here after all this is over."

"Ghent?" Mara frowned. "Why?"

"I want to see what a really expert slicer can do with that suspicious lump in Ackbar's bank account. Skywalker mentioned a theory that the break-in and deposit happened at the same time, but he said that so far no one's been able to prove it. I'm betting Ghent can do so."

"I thought this involvement in New Republic politics was supposed to be a one-shot deal," Mara objected.

"It is," Karrde nodded. "I don't want to leave an ambitious Bothan at my back when we leave."

"Point," she had to concede. "All right. You have a ship for me to use?"

There was a tap at the door. "I will in a minute," Karrde said, crossing to the door and pulling it open.

It was Skywalker's sister. "You wanted to see me?" she asked.

"Yes," Karrde nodded in greeting. "I believe you know my associate, Mara Jade?"

"We met briefly when you arrived on Coruscant," Organa Solo nodded. For a moment her eyes met Mara's, and Mara wondered uneasily how much Skywalker had told her.

"I need Mara to go on an errand for me," Karrde said, glancing both directions down the corridor before closing the door. "She'll need a fast, long-range ship."

"I can get her one," Organa Solo said. "Will a reconnaissance Y-wing do, Mara?"

"That'll be fine," Mara said shortly.

"I'll call the spaceport and make arrangements." She looked back at Karrde. "Anything else?"

"Yes," Karrde said. "I want to know if you can throw together a tech team and get it into space tonight."

"Councilor Fey'lya's already sending a team," she reminded him.

"I know that. I want yours to get there first."

She studied him a moment. "How big a team do you want?"

"Nothing too elaborate," Karrde told her. "A small transport or freighter, perhaps a starfighter squadron if you can find one that doesn't mind risking official wrath. The point is not to have Fey'lya's presumably handpicked crew the only ones there."

Mara opened her mouth; closed it again without speaking. If Karrde wanted Organa Solo to know that his own people would also be coming, he would tell her himself. Karrde glanced at her, back at Organa Solo. "Can you do it?"

"I think so," she said. "Fey'lya has built up a lot of support in the military, but there are enough people who would rather have Admiral Ackbar back in charge."

"Here are the coordinates," Karrde said, handing her a data card. "The sooner you can get the team moving, the better."

"It'll be gone in two hours," Organa Solo promised.

"Good," Karrde nodded, his face hardening. "There's just one more thing, then. I want you to understand that there are exactly two reasons why I'm doing this. First, as gratitude to your brother for risking his life to help Mara rescue me; and second, to get the Imperials off my back by eliminating their chief reason to hunt me down. That's all. As far as your war and your internal politics are concerned, my organization intends to remain completely neutral. Is that clear?"

Organa Solo nodded. "Very clear," she said.

"Good. You'd better get moving, then. It's a long way to the fleet, and you'll want as much head start on Fey'lya as you can get."

"Agreed." Organa Solo looked at Mara. "Come on, Mara. Let's get you your ship."

THE COMM BESIDE Wedge Antilles' bunk buzzed its annoying call-up signal. Groaning under his breath, he groped in the darkness and slapped in the general direction of the switch. "Come on, give me a break, huh?" he pleaded. "I'm still running on Ando time."

"It's Luke, Wedge," a familiar voice said. "Sorry to drag you out of bed, but I need a favor. You feel like maybe getting your people into some trouble?"

"When *aren't* we in trouble?" Wedge countered, coming fully awake. "What's the deal?"

"Get your pilots together and meet me at the spaceport in

an hour," Luke told him. "Docking Pad 15. We've got an old transport; we should be able to fit all your X-wings aboard."

"It's a long trip, then?"

"A few days," Luke said. "I can't tell you any more than that right now."

"You're the boss," Wedge said. "We'll be there in one hour."

"See you then. And thanks."

Wedge keyed off and rolled out of bed, feeling a stirring of old excitement. He'd seen a lot of action in the decade he'd been with the Rebellion and New Republic; a lot of flying, a lot of fighting. But somehow, the missions he remembered as being the most interesting always seemed to be the ones where Luke Skywalker was also involved. He wasn't sure why; maybe Jedi just had a knack for that.

He hoped so. Between politics on Coruscant and cleaning up after Imperial raids across the New Republic, things were getting more and more frustrating around here. A change would do him good.

Keying on the light, he pulled a fresh tunic out of his wardrobe and started getting dressed.

THERE WAS NO problem getting the midnight transport off Coruscant; Leia's authorization guaranteed that. But a freighter with a cargo consisting of a dozen X-wings was unusual enough to spark comment and speculation . . . and it was inevitable that the speculation would eventually reach the ears of one of Fey'lya's supporters.

By morning, he knew everything.

"This goes well beyond internal political infighting," he snarled at Leia, his fur rippling back and forth like short stalks of grain caught in a succession of dust devils. "It was blatantly illegal. If not treasonous."

"I'm not sure I'd go quite *that* far," Mon Mothma said. But she looked troubled. "Why did you do it, Leia?"

"She did it because I asked her to," Karrde put in calmly.

"And since the *Katana* fleet is technically not yet under New Republic jurisdiction, I don't see how any activity related to it can be considered illegal."

"We'll explain proper legal procedure to you later, smuggler," Fey'lya said acidly. "Right now, we have a serious breach of security to deal with. Mon Mothma, I request an executive order be made out for Solo's and Skywalker's arrest."

Even Mon Mothma seemed taken aback by that one. "An arrest order?"

"They know where the *Katana* fleet is," Fey'lya bit out. "None of their group has been cleared for that information. They must be sequestered until the fleet has been entirely brought into New Republic possession."

"I hardly think that will be necessary," Leia said, throwing a look at Karrde. "Han and Luke have both handled classified information in the past—"

"This is not the past," Fey'lya interrupted her. "This is the present; and they have not been cleared." His fur flattened. "Under the circumstances, I think I had best take personal charge of this mission."

Leia threw a look at Karrde, saw her own thought reflected in his face. If Fey'lya was able to personally bring back the *Katana* fleet—"You're certainly welcome to come along, Councilor," Karrde told the Bothan. "Councilor Organa Solo and I will appreciate your company."

It took a second for that to register, "What are you talking about?" Fey'lya demanded. "No one's authorized either of you to come along."

"*I'm* authorizing it, Councilor," Karrde said coldly. "The *Katana* fleet is still mine, and will remain so until the New Republic takes possession of it. Until then, I make the rules."

Fey'lya's fur flattened again, and for a moment Leia thought the Bothan was going to launch himself physically at Karrde's throat. "We will not forget this, smuggler," he hissed instead. "Your time will come."

Karrde smiled sardonically. "Perhaps. Shall we go?"

CHAPTER 27

THE PROXIMITY ALERT WARBLED, and Luke straightened up in his seat. After five days, they'd made it. "Here we go," he said. "You ready?"

"You know me," Han said from the pilot's seat beside him. "I'm always ready."

Luke threw a sideways glance at his friend. To all outward appearances, Han seemed perfectly normal, or at least as close to it as he ever got. But beneath the casual flippancy Luke had noticed something else over the past few days: a darker, almost brooding sense that had been with him since they left Coruscant. It was there now; and as he studied Han's face, Luke could see the tension lines there. "You all right?" he asked quietly.

"Oh, sure. Fine." The lines tightened a little further. "But just once I'd like them to find someone else to go off on these little jaunts across the galaxy. You know Leia and I didn't even get a day together? We didn't see each other for a whole month; and we didn't even get a day."

Luke sighed. "I know," he said. "Sometimes I feel like I've

been running full speed since we blasted out of Tatooine with the droids and Ben Kenobi way back when."

Han shook his head. "I hadn't seen her for a month," he repeated. "She looks twice as pregnant as she did when she left. I don't even know what happened to her and Chewie out there—all she had time to tell me was that those Noghri things are on our side now. Whatever *that* means. I can't get anything out of Chewie, either. Says it's her story, and that she should tell it herself. I'm about ready to strangle him."

Luke shrugged. "You have to face it, Han. We're just too good at what we do."

Han snorted. But some of the tension left his face. "Yeah. Right."

"More to the point, I guess, we're on the list of people Leia knows she can trust," Luke continued more seriously. "Until we find that information tap the Empire's got into the Imperial Palace, that list is going to stay pretty short."

"Yeah." Han grimaced. "Someone told me the Imperials call it Delta Source. You got any ideas who or what it might be?"

Luke shook his head. "Not really. Got to be close in to the Assemblage, though. Maybe even to the Council. One thing's for sure—we'd better get busy and find it."

"Yeah." Han stirred and reached for the hyperdrive levers. "Get ready . . ."

He pulled the levers; and a moment later they were again in the blackness of deep space. "Here we are," Han announced.

"Right." Luke looked around, an involuntary shiver running up his back. "Dead center in the middle of nowhere."

"Should be a familiar feeling for you," Han suggested, keying for a sensor scan.

"Thanks," Luke said, "but getting stuck between systems with a dead hyperdrive isn't something I want to get familiar with."

"I didn't mean that," Han said innocently as he keyed the comm. "I was talking about Tatooine. Wedge?"

"Right here," the other's voice came over the speaker.

"Looks like we've got a target at oh-four-seven mark one-six-six," Han told him. "You ready to fly?"

"Ready and eager."

"Okay." Han took a last look out the viewport and keyed the cargo hatch release. "Go."

Luke craned his neck to look in the direction Han had indicated. At first all he could see was the normal scattering of stars, achingly bright against the total blackness around them. And then he saw them: the softer glow of a ship's running lights. His eyes traced the empty space between them, his brain forcing a pattern to the lights; and suddenly the image coalesced. "It's a Dreadnaught, all right."

"There's another one just past it," Han said. "And three more to port and a little below."

Luke nodded as he located them, a strange tingle running through him. The *Katana* fleet. Only now did he realize just how little he'd really believed in the fleet's existence. "Which one do we check out?" he asked.

"Might as well take the closest," Han said.

"No," Luke said slowly, trying to focus on the vague impression tingling through him. "No. Let's try . . . that one over there." He pointed to a set of running lights a few kilometers farther away.

"Any particular reason?"

"I don't really know," Luke had to admit.

He could feel Han's eyes on him. Then the other shrugged. "Okay," he said. "Sure. We'll take that one. Wedge, you getting all this?"

"Copy, transport," Wedge's voice confirmed. "We're shifting into escort formation around you. So far it looks clean."

"Good," Han said. "Stay sharp anyway." He keyed the transport's intercom into the circuit and glanced at his chrono. "Lando? Where are you?"

"Just inside the cargo hatch," the other answered. "We've got the sled loaded and ready to go."

"Okay," Han said. "We're heading in."

They were approaching their target Dreadnaught now, close enough that Luke could see the faint outline of reflected starlight that marked the edge of the hull. Roughly cylindrical in shape, with a half dozen weapons blisters arranged around its midsection and a bow that he'd heard once described as a giant clam with an overbite, the ship looked almost quaintly archaic. But it was a false impression. The Dreadnaught Heavy Cruiser had been the backbone of the Old Republic's fleet; and while it might not look as sleek as the Imperial Star Destroyer that had replaced it, its massive turbolaser batteries still packed an awesome punch. "How do we get aboard?" he asked Han.

"There's the main docking bay," Han said, pointing to a dim rectangle of lights. "We'll take the ship inside."

Luke looked at the rectangle doubtfully. "If it's big enough."

His fears proved groundless. The entrance to the docking bay was larger than it had appeared, and the bay itself even more so. With casual skill Han brought the transport in, swiveled it around to face the opening, and put it down on the deck. "Okay," he said, keying the systems to standby and unstrapping. "Let's get this over with."

Lando, Chewbacca, and the four-man tech team were waiting at the cargo hatchway when Han and Luke arrived, the techs looking somewhat ill at ease with the unaccustomed blasters belted awkwardly to their sides. "Checked the air yet, Anselm?" Han asked.

"It looks fine," the head of the tech team reported, offering Han a data pad for inspection. "Better than it should be after all these years. Must still be some droids on housekeeping duty."

Han glanced at the analysis, handed back the data pad, and nodded to Chewbacca. "Okay, Chewie, open the hatch. Tomrus, you drive the sled. Watch out for blank spots in the gravity plates—we don't want you bouncing the sled off the ceiling."

The air in the bay had a strangely musty odor about it; a combination of oil and dust, Luke decided, with a slight metallic tang. But it was fresh enough otherwise. "Pretty impressive," he commented as the group walked behind the repulsorlift sled toward the main hatchway. "Especially after all this time."

"Those full-rig computer systems were designed to last," Lando said. "So what's the plan, Han?"

"I guess we split up," Han said. "You and Chewie take Anselm, Tomrus, and the sled and go check out engineering. We'll head up to the bridge."

For Luke, it was one of the eeriest trips of his life, precisely because it all looked so normal. The lights in the wide corridors were all working properly, as were the gravity plates and the rest of the environment system. Doors leading off the corridor slid open automatically whenever any of the group strayed close enough to trigger them, revealing glimpses of perfectly maintained machine shops, equipment rooms, and crew lounges. The faint mechanical noises of idling systems whispered behind the sound of their own footsteps, and occasionally they glimpsed an ancient droid still going about its business. To all appearances, the ship might just as well have been abandoned yesterday.

But it hadn't been. The ships had been floating here in the blackness for half a century . . . and their crews had not left, but had died here in agony and madness. Looking down empty cross corridors as they walked, Luke wondered what the maintenance droids had made of it all as they cleared away the bodies.

The bridge was a long walk from the docking bay. But eventually they made it. "Okay, we're here," Han announced into his comlink as the blast doors between the bridge and the monitor anteroom behind it opened with only minor grating sounds. "Doesn't seem to be any obvious damage. What have you got on the sublight engines?"

"Doesn't look good," Lando reported. "Tomrus says that six of the eight main power converters have been knocked out of alignment. He's still running a check, but my guess is this tub's not going anywhere without a complete overhaul."

"Ask me if I'm surprised," Han countered dryly. "What about the hyperdrive? Any chance we can at least fly it somewhere in towing range of a shipyard?"

"Anselm is looking into that," Lando said. "Personally, I wouldn't trust it that far."

"Yeah. Well, we're just here to look the thing over, not get it moving. We'll see what kind of control systems we've got left up here and that'll be it."

Luke glanced up at the space over the blast doors. Paused for a second look at the elaborate name plaque fastened there. "It's the *Katana*," he murmured.

"What?" Han craned his neck for a look. "Huh." He looked oddly at Luke. "Was that why you wanted this one?"

Luke shook his head. "I guess so. It was just intuition through the Force."

"Han, Luke," Wedge's voice cut in suddenly. "We've got incoming."

Luke felt his heart jump. "Where?"

"Vector two-ten mark twenty-one. Configuration . . . it's an Escort Frigate."

Luke let out a quiet breath. "Better give them a call," he said. "Let them know where we are."

"Actually, they're calling us," Wedge said. "Hang on; I'll patch it through."

"—tain Solo, this is Captain Virgilio of the Escort Frigate *Quenfis*," a new voice came over Han's comlink. "Do you read?"

"Solo here," Han said. "Calling from aboard the Old Republic ship *Katana*—"

"Captain Solo, I regret to inform you that you and your party are under arrest," Virgilio cut him off. "You will return to your own vessel at once and prepare to surrender."

VIRGILIO'S WORDS, AND the stunned silence that followed, echoed through the command observation deck above and behind the *Quenfis*'s bridge. Seated at the main board, Fey'lya threw a mocking smile at Leia, a slightly less insolent one at Karrde, then returned his attention to the distant X-wing drive trails. "They don't seem to be taking you seriously, Captain," he said toward the intercom. "Perhaps launching your X-wing squadrons would convince them we're serious."

"Yes, Councilor," Virgilio said briskly, and Leia strained her ears in vain for any signs of resentment in that voice. Most of the warship captains she'd known would be highly annoyed at the prospect of taking line orders from a civilian, particularly a civilian with negligible military experience of his own. But then, Fey'lya would hardly have picked the *Quenfis* for this mission if Virgilio hadn't been one of his staunchest backers. Just one more indication, if she'd needed it, as to who was really in charge here. "X-wings: launch."

There were a series of dull thuds as the two squadrons of starfighters left the ship. "Captain Solo, this is Captain Virgilio. Please respond."

"Captain, this is Wing Commander Wedge Antilles of Rogue Squadron," Wedge's voice cut in. "May I ask your authorization to order our arrest?"

"Allow me, Captain," Fey'lya said, touching the comm switch on the board behind him. "This is Councilor Borsk Fey'lya, Commander Antilles," he said. "Though I doubt you're aware of it, Captain Solo is operating illegally."

"I'm sorry, Councilor," Wedge said, "but I don't understand how that can be. Our orders came from Councilor Leia Organa Solo."

"And these new orders come directly from Mon Mothma," Fey'lya told him. "Therefore, your authorization is—"

"Can you prove that?"

Fey'lya seemed taken aback. "I have the order sitting here in front of me, Commander," he said. "You're welcome to examine it once you're aboard."

"Commander, for the moment the origin of the arrest order is irrelevant," Virgilio put in, annoyance starting to creep into his voice. "As a superior officer, *I* order you to surrender and bring your squadron aboard my ship."

There was a long silence. Leia threw a look at Karrde, seated a quarter of the way around the observation deck from her. But his attention was turned outward through the transparisteel bubble, his face impassive. Perhaps he was remembering the last time he'd been to this spot. "What if I refuse?" Wedge asked at last.

"Forget it, Wedge," Han's voice cut in. "It's not worth risking a court martial over. Go on, we don't need you anymore. Nice hearing from you, Fey'lya." There was the faint click of a disconnecting comlink—

"Solo!" Fey'lya barked, leaning over the comm as if that would do any good. "Solo!" He turned and glared at Leia. "Get over here," he ordered her, jabbing a finger at the comm. "I want him back."

Leia shook her head. "Sorry, Councilor. Han won't listen to anyone when he's like this."

Fey'lya's fur flattened. "I'll ask you one more time, Councilor. If you refuse—"

He never had a chance to finish the threat. Something flickered at the edge of Leia's peripheral vision; and even as she turned to look, the *Quenfis*'s alarms went off. "What—?" Fey'lya yelped, jerking in his seat and looking frantically around him.

"It's an Imperial Star Destroyer," Karrde told him over the blaring of the alarms. "And it appears to be coming this way."

"WE GOT COMPANY, ROGUE LEADER," one of Wedge's X-wing pilots snapped as the sound of the *Quenfis*'s alarms came hooting over the comm. "Star Destroyer; bearing one-seven-eight mark eighty-six."

"Got it," Wedge said, turning his ship away from its confrontation with the *Quenfis*'s approaching starfighters and bringing it around in a tight one-eighty. It was a Star Destroyer, all right: almost straight across from the *Quenfis*, with the *Katana* dead center between them. "Luke?" he called.

"We see it," Luke's voice came back tightly. "We're heading for the docking bay now."

"Right—hold it," Wedge interrupted himself. Against the dark bulk of the Star Destroyer's lower hull a large group of drive trails had suddenly appeared. "They're launching," he told the other. "Twelve marks—drop ships, probably, from the look of the drive trails."

"So we hurry," Han's voice came on. "Thanks for the warning; now get back to the *Quenfis*."

The comlink clicked and went dead. "Like blazes we will," Wedge muttered under his breath. "Rogue Squadron: let's go."

Captain Virgilio was trying to say something on the open channel. Switching to his squadron's private frequency, Wedge kicked the X-wing's drive to full power and set off toward the *Katana*.

In the near distance, just beyond the drive trails of the *Quenfis*'s X-wings, Rogue Squadron turned and blazed off in the direction of the Star Destroyer. "They're going to attack," Fey'lya breathed. "They must be insane."

"They're not attacking—they're running cover," Leia told him, staring at the scenario unfolding outside the bubble and trying to estimate interception points. It was going to be far too close. "We need to get over there and back them up," she said. "Captain Virgilio—"

"Captain Virgilio, you'll recall your X-wings at once," Fey'lya cut her off. "Navigation will prepare to make the jump to lightspeed."

"Councilor?" Virgilio asked, his voice sounding stunned. "Are you suggesting we abandon them?"

"Our duty, Captain, is to get out of here alive and sound the alarm," Fey'lya countered sharply. "If Rogue Squadron insists on defying orders, there's nothing we can do for them."

Leia was on her feet. "Captain—"

Fey'lya was quicker, slapping off the intercom before she could speak. "I'm in charge here, Councilor," he said as she started toward him. "Authorized by Mon Mothma herself."

"To blazes with your authority," Leia snapped. For a handful of heartbeats she had the almost overwhelming urge to snatch her lightsaber from her belt and send it slicing through that bland face . . .

With an effort, she choked the urge down. Violent hatred was the path of the dark side. "Mon Mothma didn't anticipate anything like this happening," she said, fighting to keep her voice as calm as she could. "Fey'lya, that's my husband and my brother out there. If we don't help them, they'll die."

"And if we *do* help them, they'll most likely still die," Fey'lya said coolly. "And your unborn children along with them."

An icy knife jabbed at Leia's heart. "That's not fair," she whispered.

"Reality is not required to be fair," Fey'lya said. "And the reality in this case is that I will not waste men and ships on a lost cause."

"It's not lost!" Leia insisted, her voice breaking with desperation as she threw a look out the bubble. No; it couldn't end like this. Not after all she and Han had survived together. She took another step toward Fey'lya—

"The *Quenfis* will withdraw," the Bothan said quietly; and suddenly, from some hiding place within the cream-colored fur, a blaster appeared in his hand. "And neither you nor anyone else is going to change that."

"REPORT FROM SENSORS, CAPTAIN," the officer at the *Judicator's* scan station called up to the command walkway. "All the other Dreadnaughts in the region read negative for life-forms."

"So they're concentrating on just the one," Captain Brandei nodded. "That's where we'll hit, then. The Rebels will be in far less of a hurry to open fire on a ship that has their own people aboard. Still just the one starfighter squadron moving to intercept?"

"Yes, sir. The Escort Frigate and other two squadrons haven't yet responded. They must have been caught off guard."

"Perhaps." Brandei permitted himself a slight smile. So it always went with rebels. They fought like crazed animals when they had nothing to lose; but give them a taste of victory and a chance to enjoy the spoils of war and suddenly they weren't nearly so eager to risk their lives anymore. One of many reasons why the Empire would ultimately defeat them. "Order the drop ships into defense formation," he instructed the communications officer. "And have Starfighter Command launch two squadrons of TIE fighters to intercept those X-wings."

He smiled again. "And send a message to the *Chimaera*. Inform the Grand Admiral that we have engaged the enemy."

FOR A LONG MINUTE Han gazed out the bridge observation bubble at the approaching Imperial ships, doing a quick estimate of times and distances and ignoring the fidgeting tech men waiting nervously at the bridge doorway. "Shouldn't we be going?" Luke prompted from beside him.

Han came to a decision. "We're not leaving," he said, thumbing on his comlink. "We'd get the transport out of the docking bay just in time to run into those drop ships and TIE fighters. Lando?"

"Right here," Lando's voice came tensely back. "What's happening out there?"

"Imperials on the way," Han told him, moving over to the bridge fire-control panel and gesturing the techs to join him. "Rogue Squadron's moving to intercept, but it sounds like Fey'lya's crowd is going to run for it."

Lando swore under his breath. "We can't just sit here and let Wedge tackle them alone."

"We're not going to," Han assured him grimly. "Get busy back there and see what shape the power coupling to the turbolaser batteries is in. We'll check the fire control up here. And make it fast—once they break formation we won't be able to hit them."

"Right."

Han stuck the comlink back in his belt. "How's it look, Shen?"

"Looks pretty solid," the tech's muffled voice came from underneath the control board. "Kline?"

"Connections look good here, too," the other tech reported from a board across the room. "If we can get the computer to enable the system . . . there we go." He looked at Han. "You're all set."

Han sat down at the weapons panel, running his eyes over the unfamiliar arrangement of the controls and wondering if all this effort was more than just spitting in vacuum. Even these full-rigged, computer-centralized, slave-circuit-equipped Dreadnaughts still required over two thousand people to fly them.

But the Imperials wouldn't be expecting a derelict ship to fire. He hoped. "Here we go," he muttered to himself as he keyed for visual targeting. The drop ships were still flying in tight formation, using their overlapping shields to protect them from any lucky shots from the approaching X-wings. The faster TIE fighters had caught up with them now, sweeping around the group on all sides and starting to pass them.

"You've got just one shot at this," Luke murmured.

"Thanks," Han growled. "I really needed to hear that." He took a deep breath, held it, and gently squeezed the fire control triggers.

The *Katana* lurched, and as the multiple blazes of turbolaser light flashed outward he felt the double *thud* of a disintegrating capacitor bank through the deck. Luke had been right—the ship's first shot had been its last. But it had been worth it. The laser bolts hit the drop ship formation dead center; and suddenly the whole Imperial force seemed to come apart in a blaze of multiple explosions. For a few seconds everything was hidden behind secondary explosions and clouds of debris. Then, through the destruction, a handful of ships shot out. A few more joined them, this group moving with the distinctive limp of damaged property.

"Looks like you took out five of the drop ships," Kline reported, peering through a set of macrobinoculars pressed tightly against his face. "A few of the TIE fighters, too."

"They're going into evasive maneuvers," Luke added.

"Okay," Han said, getting up from the chair and pulling out his comlink. "That's it for that game. Lando?"

"Whatever you just did, it made a real mess back here," the other's voice came back. "Took out the fire-control power coupling and at least one of the generators. What now?"

"We get ready for a boarding party," Han told him. "Meet us in the portside main corridor just forward of the docking bay. We'll see what kind of defense we can set up."

"Right."

Han shut down the comlink. "Let's go," he said.

"This had better be some defense," Luke commented as they left the bridge and headed back down the portside corridor. "Especially when we're talking maybe forty-to-one odds."

Han shook his head. "Never tell me the odds," he admonished the other, glancing at his chrono. It could be any time now. "Besides, you never know when the odds are going to change."

"WE CAN'T JUST ABANDON THEM," Leia said again, dimly aware that she was talking to Fey'lya as if he were a child. "That's my husband and brother out there, and a dozen good X-wing pilots. We can't just leave them to the Imperials."

"One mustn't place personal considerations above one's duty to the New Republic, Councilor," Fey'lya said. His fur rippled, perhaps with appreciation of his own insight. But the blaster in his hand remained steady. "Surely you understand that."

"It's not just personal considerations," Leia insisted, fighting hard to keep from losing her temper again. "It's—"

"One moment," Fey'lya interrupted her, touching the intercom switch. "Captain? How soon to lightspeed?"

"Another minute," Virgilio's voice came back. "Perhaps two."

"As quickly as you can, Captain," Fey'lya said. He shut the intercom off again and looked back at Leia. "You were saying, Councilor?"

Leia consciously unclenched her teeth. If Fey'lya's aim would only shift—even a little—she might be able to risk jumping him. But as matters stood, she was helpless. Her rudimentary abilities with the Force weren't nearly strong enough for her to grab or deflect the blaster, and he was nearly a meter out of reach of her lightsaber. "Han and Luke are vitally important to the New Republic," she said. "If they die or are captured—"

"The *Katana*'s firing," Karrde commented calmly, getting to his feet as if for a better view.

Leia glanced out the bubble as the distant Imperial ships were engulfed briefly in flame. "They know a great deal about the workings of the New Republic, Fey'lya. Do you want the Empire to get that knowledge?"

"I'm afraid you're missing the Councilor's point, Leia," Karrde said, walking over to where she sat. He passed in front of her, dropping a data pad casually onto the tracking console beside her as he did so. "You're concerned about your family, of course," he continued, walking on a couple of paces before turning to face Fey'lya. "Councilor Fey'lya has a different set of priorities."

"I'm sure he does," Leia said, her mouth suddenly dry as she looked sideways at the data pad Karrde had set down. On its screen was a short message.

Turn on the intercom and comm.

She looked up again. Fey'lya's blaster was still pointed at her, but the Bothan's violet eyes were turned toward Karrde. Setting her teeth, Leia focused on the board behind him and reached out with the Force . . . and without even a click the intercom was on. Another effort and the comm was, too. "I don't understand," she said to Karrde. "What other priorities could Councilor Fey'lya have?"

"It's simple enough," Karrde said. "Councilor Fey'lya is motivated solely by his own political survival. He's running away from the fight because he's put his most ardent support- ers aboard this ship and he can't afford to lose any of them."

Leia blinked. "He's what? But I thought—"

"That this was the normal crew of the *Quenfis*?" Karrde shook his head. "Not at all. The captain and senior officers are all that remain, and they were mostly on his side in the first place. That's why Fey'lya wanted a few hours before leaving Coruscant: so that he could shift duty assignments around and make sure everyone aboard was fully loyal to him." He smiled thinly. "Not that any of them realized that, of course. They were given the impression that it was a special security arrangement."

Leia nodded, feeling cold all over. So it wasn't just the cap- tain. The entire ship was on Fey'lya's side.

Which meant it was over, and she had lost. Even if she was somehow able to take out Fey'lya himself, she had lost.

"So you can imagine," Karrde went on offhandedly, "how reluctant Fey'lya is to risk losing any of them over anything so outmoded as loyalty to one's comrades. Especially after hav- ing worked so hard to convince them of how much he cared for the average fighting man."

Leia threw Karrde a sharp look, suddenly seeing where he was going with this. "Is that true, Councilor?" she asked Fey'lya, putting disbelief in her voice. "All this talk about being on the side of the military was nothing more than a play for political power?"

"Don't be foolish, Councilor," Fey'lya said, fur rippling with contempt. "What other use are soldiers to a politician?"

"Is that why you don't care if the men of Rogue Squadron die?" Karrde asked. "Because they prefer to stay out of politics?"

"No one cares if their enemies die," Fey'lya said coldly. "And all those who are not on my side are my enemies." He gestured with his blaster. "I trust, Captain Karrde, that I need not say more."

Karrde raised his eyes from Fey'lya to the view outside. "No, Councilor," he said. "I believe you've said enough."

Leia followed his gaze. Between the *Quenfis* and the *Katana*, in twos and threes, Fey'lya's X-wing squadrons were heading to Wedge's support. Deserting the politician who had just defined the limits of his consideration for their welfare. "Yes," she murmured. "You've said enough."

Fey'lya frowned at her; but even as he started to speak the door to the bridge slid open. Captain Virgilio stood there, flanked by two soldiers. "Councilor Fey'lya," he said stiffly. "I respectfully request you return to your quarters. These men will accompany you."

Fey'lya's fur flattened. "I don't understand, Captain."

"We're closing off this room, sir," Virgilio said, his voice respectful but with an edge. Stepping over to the Bothan's seat, he leaned toward the intercom. "This is the captain," he called. "All hands to battle stations."

The alarm promptly went off . . . and in Fey'lya's eyes Leia could see the sudden shock of understanding. "Captain—"

"You see, Councilor, some of us don't consider loyalty to be all that outmoded," Virgilio cut him off, turning to Leia. "Councilor Organa Solo, I'd like you to join me on the bridge at your convenience. We've called for a Star Cruiser to back us up, but it'll take a while to get here."

"We'll just have to hold them until then," Leia said, standing up. She looked at Karrde. "Thank you," she said quietly.

"Not for you or your war," Karrde warned her. "Mara and my people could be arriving at any time. I'd just as soon they not be facing a Star Destroyer alone."

"They won't," Virgilio said. "Councilor?"

"It's a lost cause," Fey'lya said, trying one last time as he surrendered his blaster to one of the soldiers.

"That's all right," Virgilio said, smiling tightly. "The whole Rebellion was considered nothing more than a lost cause. Excuse me, Councilor; I have a battle to run."

THE *CHIMAERA* WAS TOURING the region Pellaeon had privately dubbed the Depot when the report from the *Judicator* came in. "Interesting," Thrawn commented. "They've responded faster than I'd expected."

"Karrde must have decided to be generous," Pellaeon said, skimming the follow-up report. Five drop ships and three TIE fighters destroyed; one of the Dreadnaughts apparently under Rebellion control and joining battle. It looked like a major scrap was shaping up out there. "I recommend we send another Star Destroyer to assist, Admiral," he said. "The Rebellion may have larger ships on the way."

"We'll go ourselves, Captain," Thrawn said. "Navigation: set us a course back to the *Katana* fleet."

The navigation officer didn't move. He sat at his station, his back to them, unnaturally stiff. "Navigation?" Thrawn repeated.

"Admiral, message coming through from the sentry line," the comm officer reported suddenly. "Unidentified *Lancer*-class Frigate has entered the system and is approaching. They insist on speaking with you, personally and immediately."

Thrawn's glowing eyes narrowed as he tapped the comm switch . . . and suddenly Pellaeon realized who it must be aboard that ship. "This is Thrawn," the Grand Admiral said. "Master C'baoth, I presume?"

"You presume correctly," C'baoth's voice boomed from the speaker. "I would speak with you, Grand Admiral. Now."

"We're on our way to assist the *Judicator*," Thrawn said, his eyes flicking to the still-motionless nav officer. "As you perhaps already know. When we return—"

"*Now*, Grand Admiral."

Moving quietly in the brittle silence, Pellaeon keyed for a course projection on C'baoth's ship. "It'll take at least fifteen minutes to bring him aboard," he murmured.

Thrawn hissed softly between his teeth; and Pellaeon knew what he was thinking. In the fluid situation of a spontaneous battle, a fifteen-minute delay could easily be the difference between victory and defeat. "Captain, order the *Peremptory* to assist the *Judicator*," the Grand Admiral said at last. "We'll remain here to consult our ally."

"Thank you, Grand Admiral," C'baoth said; and abruptly, the nav officer gasped and slumped in his chair. "I appreciate your generosity."

Thrawn reached to his board, and with a vicious flick of his wrist cut off the comm. He looked down into the crew pit and motioned to two bridge guards. "Sick bay," he told them, indicating the now-shivering nav officer.

"Where do you suppose C'baoth found that *Lancer*?" Pellaeon murmured as the guards helped the nav officer out of his seat and carried him aft.

"He most likely hijacked it," Thrawn said, his voice tight. "He's been sending messages for us over distances of several light-years, and he certainly knows how to take control of people. Apparently, he's learned how to meld the two abilities."

Pellaeon looked down into the crew pit, a shiver running up his back. "I'm not sure I like that, sir."

"I don't much like it myself, Captain," Thrawn agreed, turning his head to look out the viewport. "It may be time," he added thoughtfully, "to reconsider our arrangement with Master C'baoth. To reconsider it very carefully."

CHAPTER 28

THE *KATANA*'S TURBOLASERS flashed, disintegrating the center of the Imperials' drop ship formation, and one of Wedge's X-wing pilots gave a war whoop. "Will you look at that?"

"Cut the chatter, Rogue Seven," Wedge admonished, trying to see through the cloud of flaming debris. The Imperials had gotten a bloody nose, but that was about all. "They've got lots more TIE fighters in reserve."

"Wedge?"

Wedge switched channels. "I'm here, Luke."

"We've decided not to leave the ship," Luke said. "We'd run right into the Imperials, and you know how well transports fight. You might as well get your group out of here and go whistle up some help."

The surviving drop ships, Wedge saw, were reconfiguring into an evasion pattern with the TIE fighters moving ahead to clear a path for them. "You'll never be able to hold out," he told Luke flatly. "There could be three hundred troops aboard those drop ships."

"We'll have a better chance against them than you will against a Star Destroyer," Luke retorted. "Come on, get going."

Wedge clenched his teeth. Luke was right, and they both knew it. But to abandon his friends here—

"Rogue Leader, this is Gold Leader," a new voice abruptly came on the comm. "Requesting permission to join the party." Frowning, Wedge threw a glance out the back of his canopy. They were there, all right: the *Quenfis's* two X-wing squadrons, coming up behind his group for all they were worth. "Permission granted," he said. "I didn't think Councilor Fey'lya was going to let you come out and play."

"Fey'lya doesn't have any say in it anymore," the other said grimly. "Tell you about it later. Captain's turned things over to Organa Solo."

"First good news I've heard today," Wedge grunted. "All right, here's the scheme. You detail four of your group to hit those drop ships; the rest of us will concentrate on the TIE fighters. With luck, we can clear them out before the next wave gets here. I don't suppose we've got any backup of our own coming?"

"Captain says there's a Star Cruiser on the way," Gold Leader said. "Don't know when it'll get here, though."

Probably not soon enough, Wedge told himself silently. "Okay," he said aloud. "Let's do it."

A new set of drive trails had appeared near the Star Destroyer's docking bay: the second wave of TIE fighters had launched. That was going to be trouble down the line; but for the moment, the X-wings had this batch of Imperials outnumbered. And the Imperials knew it. They were spreading out, trying to draw their attackers apart where they couldn't cover each other. Wedge did a quick evaluation of the situation— "All X-wings: we'll do a one-on-one," he said. "Choose your target and go."

Closer now, he could see that two of the Imperial starfighters were the faster and more advanced TIE interceptors. Picking one of them for himself, he broke formation and headed after it.

Whatever erosion the Empire had experienced in the way of ships and trained personnel over the past five years, it was quickly clear that their starfighter training program hadn't suffered a lot. Wedge's target TIE interceptor slipped adroitly away from his initial attack, doing a sideways skid that simultaneously braked him out of the X-wing's way and swiveled his lasers around to track along its flight vector. Wedge threw the X-wing into a drop loop, wincing as the other's shot came close enough to trigger the starboard engines' heat sensors, and turned sharply to starboard. He braced himself for a second shot, but it didn't come. Bringing the X-wing out of its combination loop/turn, he looked around for his opponent.

"Watch your back, Rogue Leader!" the voice of Rogue Three snapped in his ear; and Wedge again threw the X-wing into a drop loop just as another laser blast sizzled past his canopy. Not only had the Imperial not been fooled by Wedge's corkscrew maneuver, he'd even managed to follow him through it. "He's still with you," Rogue Three confirmed. "Go evasive—I can be there in a minute."

"Don't bother," Wedge told him. Through the spinning sky outside his canopy he'd caught a glimpse of another Imperial moving past him to portside. Hauling hard on his controls, he broke out of his loop and drove directly toward it. The TIE fighter jerked slightly as its pilot suddenly became aware of the threat bearing down on him and tried to veer out of the way.

Which was exactly what Wedge had counted on. Ducking beneath the TIE fighter, he threw the X-wing into an upward rolling turn, swinging perilously close to the Imperial's canopy and bringing his nose around to point back the way he'd come.

The TIE interceptor, which had instinctively swerved off Wedge's tail to keep from ramming one of his own ships, was caught flat-footed. A single point-blank blast from the X-wing's lasers blew it out of the sky.

"Nice flying, Rogue Leader," Gold Leader commented. "My turn."

Wedge understood. Throwing power to his drive, he shot away from the TIE fighter he'd used for cover, getting clear just as Gold Leader's lasers caught it. "How we doing?" Wedge asked as his canopy lit up briefly with the reflected light of the explosion.

"We're done," Gold Leader said.

"We are?" Wedge frowned, bringing his X-wing around in a wide circle. Sure enough, the only things visible nearby were X-wings. Apart from expanding clouds of glowing debris, of course. "What about the drop ships?" he asked.

"I don't know," the other admitted. "Gold Three, Gold Four; report."

"We got six of them, Gold Leader," a new voice said. "I don't know what happened to the seventh."

Wedge swore under his breath, switching comm channels as he glanced back toward the Star Destroyer. The new group of TIE fighters was coming up fast. No time for him to do anything for the *Katana* except maybe warn them. "Luke? You've got company coming."

"We know," Luke's tight voice came back. "They're already here."

THEY CAME OUT of the drop ship with lasers blazing, laying down a heavy cover fire as they moved toward the two sets of blast doors that led forward from the docking bay. Luke couldn't see them from where he was, any more than he could see Han's group waiting silently for them behind the edge of the portside blast doors. But he could hear the Imperials' blaster fire, and he could sense their approach.

And there was something about that sense that set the back of his neck tingling. Something not quite right about them . . .

His comlink beeped. "Luke?" Lando's voice came softly. "They're coming. You ready?"

Luke closed down his lightsaber and gave his handiwork one last check. A large section of the corridor's ceiling was now hanging perilously by a few strands of metal, ready to come crashing down at the slightest provocation. Beyond it, two sections of the wall were similarly booby-trapped. "All set," he told Lando.

"Okay. Here goes . . ."

And suddenly, the pitch of a different class of weapons joined the cacophony as the defenders opened up on the Imperials. For a few seconds the two groups of weapons vied with each other. Then, with a screech of strained metal, the sounds were cut off.

The four techs were the first around the corner to where Luke waited, their faces showing the mixture of fear and nervousness and exhilaration of men who've just survived their first firefight. Lando was next, with Han and Chewbacca bringing up the rear. "Ready?" Han asked Luke.

"Yes." Luke indicated the rigged sections of ceiling and wall. "It's not going to hold them for long, though."

"Doesn't have to," Han grunted. "As long as it takes a few of them out it's worth it. Let's go."

"Hold it," Luke said, stretching out with the Force. Those strangely disturbing minds . . . "They're splitting up," he told Han. "About half are still at the portside blast doors; the other half are going to the starboard Operations section."

"Trying to flank us," Han nodded. "Lando, how well is that area sealed off?"

"Not very," Lando admitted. "The blast doors from the docking bay itself should hold for a while, but there's a whole maze of storage rooms and maintenance shops off of Operations that they can probably get back to the main starboard corridor from. There were too many doors for us to close it all off."

From the blast doors they'd just left came the dull thud of

a shaped charge. "So this group keeps us busy thinking they're all here, while the other one tries to get behind us," Han decided. "Well, we didn't want to hold the whole corridor, anyway. Chewie, you and Lando take the others and fall back toward the bridge. Take out as many of them as you can on the way. Luke and I'll go across to starboard and see if we can slow that batch down a little."

Chewbacca growled an acknowledgment and headed off, the four tech men already on their way. "Good luck," Lando said, and followed.

Han looked at Luke. "Still in just the two groups?"

"Yes," Luke said, straining to locate the enemy. The strange feeling was still there . . .

"Okay. Let's go."

They set off, Han leading the way down a narrow cross corridor lined with the kind of closely spaced doors that indicated crew quarters. "Where are we going?" Luke asked as they hurried along.

"Number two starboard weapons blister," Han said. "Should be something nasty there we can use to flood the main corridor with—turbolaser coolant or something."

"Unless they have life-support gear," Luke pointed out.

"They don't," Han said. "At least, they weren't wearing any when they charged us. They had standard trooper air filters, but if we fill the whole corridor with coolant those won't do them much good. You never know," he added reflectively. "The coolant might be flammable, too."

"Too bad the *Katana* fleet wasn't made up of Star Galleons," Luke said, reaching out again toward the enemy. As near as he could tell, they were in the maze of rooms Lando had mentioned, working their way around toward the main starboard corridor. "We really could have used those anti-intruder defenses they come equipped with."

"If this was a Star Galleon, the Empire wouldn't be so anxious to take it away from us in one piece," Han retorted. "They'd just blow it out of the sky and be done with it."

Luke grimaced. "Right."

They reached the main starboard corridor; and they were halfway across it when Han suddenly stopped short. "What in blazes—?"

Luke turned to look. Ten meters down the corridor, sitting in a patch of darkness beneath burned-out light panels, was a large metal box resting at a tilt on a half-seen tangle of cables and struts. Twin blaster cannon protruded from beneath a narrow viewport; the corridor walls immediately around it were warped and blackened, with a half dozen good-sized holes visible. "What is it?" he asked.

"Looks like a scaled-down version of a scout walker," Han said. "Let's go take a look."

"Wonder what it's doing here," Luke said as they walked toward it. The floor beneath their feet was noticeably warped, too. Whoever had been in there firing had done a thorough job of it.

"Probably someone brought it out of storage during the hive virus thing that killed everyone," Han suggested. "Either trying to protect the bridge or else just gone crazy themselves."

Luke nodded, shivering at the thought. "It must have been a real trick to get it in here in the first place."

"Well, we're sure not going to get it out," Han said, peering down at the tangle of debris where the walker's right leg had been. He cocked an eyebrow at Luke. "Unless . . . ?"

Luke swallowed. Master Yoda had lifted his X-wing out of a Dagobah swamp once . . . but Master Yoda had been far stronger in the Force than Luke was. "Let's find out," he said. Taking a deep breath, clearing his mind, he raised his hand and reached out with the Force.

The walker didn't even quiver. Luke tried again; and again. But it was no use. Either the machine was wedged too tightly against walls and ceiling to move, or Luke simply didn't have the strength to lift it.

"Well, never mind," Han said, glancing back down the corridor. "It would have been nice to have it mobile—we could have put it in that big monitor room behind the bridge and picked off anyone who came close. But we can use it here, too. Let's see if we can get in."

Holstering his blaster, he climbed up the single remaining leg. "They're getting closer," Luke warned him, looking uneasily back down the corridor. "Another couple of minutes and they'll be in sight."

"Better get around behind me," Han said. He was at the walker's side door now, and with a grunt he pulled it open—

"What?" Luke asked sharply as Han's sense abruptly changed.

"You don't want to know," Han told him grimly. Visibly bracing himself, he ducked down and climbed inside. "Still has power," he called, his voice echoing slightly. "Let's see . . ."

Above Luke, the blaster cannon traversed a few degrees. "Still has maneuverability," Han added with satisfaction. "Great."

Luke had made it to the top of the leg now, easing carefully past sharp edges. Whoever the walker had been fighting against had put up a good fight. The back of his mind tingled— "They're coming," he hissed to Han, slipping off the leg and landing silently on the deck. Dropping into a crouch, he peered back through the gap between the angled leg and the main part of the walker, hoping the darkness would be adequate to conceal him.

He'd gotten out of sight just in time. The Imperials were moving swiftly toward them down the corridor, spread out in a properly cautious military formation. The two point men paused as they caught sight of the broken walker, probably trying to decide whether to risk a straight advance or to give up the element of surprise by laying down cover fire. Whoever was in charge opted for a compromise; the point men glided forward while the rest of the party dropped prone or hugged the corridor walls.

Han let them get right up to the base of the walker. Then, swiveling the blaster cannon over their heads, he opened up on the main group.

The answering fire came instantly; but it was no contest at all. Han systematically raked the walls and the floor, driving back the handful who'd been fortunate enough to have a nearby doorway to duck into and annihilating those who hadn't. The two point men reacted instantly, one of them firing upward toward the viewport, the other scrambling up the leg toward the side door.

He reached the top to find Luke waiting for him. His companion down below got three shots off—all deflected—before the lightsaber found him, too.

Abruptly, the blaster cannon stopped firing. Luke glanced down the corridor, reaching out with the Force. "There are still three of them left," he warned as Han opened the walker's door and squeezed out.

"Leave 'em," Han said, climbing carefully down the back of the damaged leg and consulting his chrono. "We need to get back to Lando and Chewie." He threw Luke a mirthless grin. "Besides, the actuator crystals just burned up. Let's get going before they figure that out."

THE FIRST WAVE of TIE fighters had been destroyed, as had all but one of the drop ships. The Rebel Escort Frigate and its X-wings were now engaged with Squadrons One and Three, and appeared to be holding their own quite well.

And Captain Brandei was no longer smiling.

"Squadron Four launching now," Starfighter Control announced. "Squadrons Five and Six are awaiting your orders."

"Order them to stand by," Brandei instructed. Not that he had much choice in the matter. Five and Six were recon and bomber squadrons—useful enough in their particular areas of expertise, but not in straight battle against Rebel X-wings. "Anything further on the *Peremptory*?"

"No, sir. The last report from the *Chimaera*—before our shields went up—had their ETA as approximately 1519."

Only about seven minutes away. But battles had been lost in less time than that; and from the look of things, this could very well become one of them.

Which left Brandei only one real option. Much as he disliked the idea of moving into range of that Dreadnaught's turbolasers, he was going to have to take the *Judicator* into combat. "All ahead," he ordered the helm. "Shields at full strength; turbolaser batteries stand ready. And inform the leader of the boarding party that I want that Dreadnaught in Imperial hands *now*."

"Yes, sir." There was a dull roar through the deck as the sublight drive came up to power—

And, without warning, the roar was joined by the hooting of the ship's alarms. "Bandits coming out of light-speed astern," the sensor officer snapped. "Eighteen craft—freighter class and smaller. They're attacking."

Brandei swore viciously as he punched for the appropriate display. They weren't Rebel vessels, not this group, and he wondered who in the Empire they could be. But no matter. "Come around to two-seven-one," he ordered the helm. "Bring aft turbolasers to bear on the bandits. And launch Squadron Six."

Whoever they were, he would soon teach them not to meddle in Imperial business. As to their identity . . . well, Intelligence would be able to ascertain that later from the wreckage.

"WATCH IT, MARA," Aves's voice warned over the comm. "They're trying to come about. And we've got TIE fighters on the way."

"Right," Mara said, permitting herself a sardonic smile. For all the good that would do. The bulk of the Star Destroyer's starfighters were already engaged with the New Republic forces, which meant that all Karrde's people were likely to get would be recon ships and bombers. Nothing they couldn't handle. "Dankin, Torve—swing down to intercept."

The two pilots acknowledged, and she returned her attention to the inconspicuous spot beneath the Star Destroyer's central sublight drive nozzle where her Z-95's lasers were currently blasting away. Beneath the shielding at that point was a critical part of the lower-aft sensor package. If she could take it out, she and the others would have free run of the relatively undefended underside of the huge ship.

With a sudden puff of vaporized metal and plastic, the lasers punched through. "Got it," she told Aves. "Lower-aft-central sector is now blind."

"Good job," Aves said. "Everyone: move in."

Mara pulled the Z-95 away, glad to be leaving the heat and radiation of the drive emissions. The *Wild Karrde* and other freighters could handle the job of tearing into the Star Destroyer's outer hull now; her small starfighter would be better utilized in keeping the TIE fighters away from them.

But first, she had enough time to check in. "Jade calling Karrde," she said into the comm. "You there?"

"Right here, Mara, thank you," came a familiar voice; and Mara felt a little of her tension drain away. *Right here, thank you*, meant everything was fine aboard the New Republic ship.

Or as fine as could be expected while facing an Imperial Star Destroyer. "What's the situation?" she asked.

"We've taken some damage, but we seem to be holding our own," he said. "There's a small tech team aboard the *Katana* and they have the turbolasers operational, which may account for the Star Destroyer's reluctance to move any closer. No doubt they'll overcome their shyness eventually."

"They've overcome it now," Mara said. "The ship was under power when we arrived. And we're not going to be able to distract them for long."

"Mara, this is Leia Organa Solo," a new voice came on the comm. "We've got a Star Cruiser on its way."

"The Imperials will have backup coming, too," Mara said

flatly. "Let's not be heroic to the point of stupidity, okay? Get your people off the *Katana* and get out of here."

"We can't," Organa Solo said. "The Imperials have boarded. Our people are cut off from the docking bay."

Mara looked across at the dark bulk of the Dreadnaught, lit only by its own running lights and the flickers of reflected light from the battle raging near and around it. "Then you'd better write them off," she said. "The Imperials aren't likely to be far away—their backup will get here long before yours does."

And as if cued by her words, there was a flicker of pseudo-motion off to her left; and abruptly three Dreadnaughts in triangular formation appeared. "Mara!" Aves snapped.

"I see them," Mara said as a second triad flickered in behind and above the first. "That's it, Karrde. Get out of there—"

"Attention, New Republic forces," a new voice boomed over the channel. "This is Senator Garm Bel Iblis aboard the warship *Peregrine*. May I offer our assistance?"

LEIA STARED AT the comm speaker, a strange combination of surprise, hope, and disbelief flooding in on her. She glanced up at Karrde, caught his eye. He shrugged slightly, shook his head. "I'd heard he was dead," he murmured.

Leia swallowed. So had she . . . but it *was* Bel Iblis's voice, all right. Or else an excellent copy. "Garm, this is Leia Organa Solo," she said.

"Leia!" Bel Iblis said. "It's been a long time, hasn't it? I didn't expect you to be out here personally. Though perhaps I should have. Was all this your idea?"

Leia frowned out the viewport. "I don't understand what you mean by *all this*. What are you doing here, anyway?"

"Captain Solo sent my assistant the coordinates and asked us to come along as backup," Bel Iblis said, a note of caution creeping into his voice. "I assumed it was at your request."

Leia smiled tightly. She should have guessed. "Han's memory sort of slips sometimes," she said. "Though to be honest, we haven't had much time since we got back to compare notes."

"I see," Bel Iblis said slowly. "So it wasn't actually an official request from the New Republic?"

"It wasn't, but it is now," Leia assured him. "On behalf of the New Republic, I hereby ask for your assistance." She looked over at Virgilio. "Log that, please, Captain."

"Yes, Councilor," Virgilio acknowledged. "And speaking for myself, Senator Bel Iblis, I'm delighted to have you along."

"Thank you, Captain," Bel Iblis said, and in her mind's eye Leia could see the other's famous smile. "Let's do some damage, shall we? *Peregrine* out."

The six Dreadnaughts had moved into encirclement formation around the Star Destroyer now, smothering it with a flood of ion cannon fire and ignoring the increasingly sporadic turbolaser blasts raking them in return.

"Mara's right, though," Karrde said, stepping close to Leia. "As soon as we can get the tech team off that ship, we'd better get them and run."

Leia shook her head. "We can't just leave the *Katana* fleet to the Empire."

Karrde snorted. "I take it you haven't had a chance to count how many Dreadnaughts are left out there."

Leia frowned. "No. Why?"

"I did a scan," Karrde said grimly. "Earlier, when you were arguing with Fey'lya. Out of the original two hundred *Katana* ships . . . there are fifteen left."

Leia stared at him. "Fifteen?" she breathed.

Karrde nodded. "I'm afraid I underestimated the Grand Admiral, Councilor," he said, an edge of bitterness seeping in beneath the studied urbanity of his voice. "I knew that once he had the location of the fleet he would start moving the ships away from here. But I didn't expect him to get the location from Hoffner this quickly."

Leia shivered. She'd undergone an Imperial interrogation

herself once. Years later, the memory was still vivid. "I wonder if there's anything left of him."

"Save your sympathy," Karrde advised. "In retrospect, it seems unlikely that Thrawn needed to bother with anything so uncivilized as coercion. For Hoffner to have talked so freely implies the Grand Admiral simply applied a large infusion of cash."

Leia gazed out at the battle, the dark feeling of failure settling over her. They'd lost. After all their efforts, they'd lost.

She took a deep breath, running through the Jedi relaxation exercises. Yes, they'd lost. But it was just a battle, not the war. The Empire might have taken the Dark Force, but recruiting and training crewers to man all those Dreadnaughts would take years. A lot could happen in that time. "You're right," she told Karrde. "We'd do best to cut our losses. Captain Virgilio, as soon as those TIE fighters have been neutralized I want a landing party sent to the *Katana* to assist our tech team there."

There was no reply. "Captain?"

Virgilio was staring out the bridge viewport, his face carved from stone. "Too late, Councilor," he said quietly.

Leia turned to look. There, moving toward the besieged Imperial ship, a second Star Destroyer had suddenly emerged from hyperspace.

The Imperials' backup had arrived.

"PULL OUT!" AVES shouted, his voice starting to sound ragged. "All ships, pull out! Second Star Destroyer in system."

The last word was half drowned out by the clang of the Z-95's proximity warning as something got entirely too close. Mara threw the little ship into a sideways skid, just in time to get out of a TIE fighter's line of fire. "Pull out where?" she demanded, turning her skid into a barely controlled spin that had the effect of killing her forward velocity. Her attacker, perhaps made overconfident by the appearance of the backup force, roared by too fast for more than a wild shot in her direction. Coolly, Mara blew him out of the sky. "In case you've forgotten, some of us don't have enough computing power aboard to calculate a safe hyperspace jump."

"I'll feed you the numbers," Aves said. "Karrde—"

"I agree," Karrde's voice came from the Escort Frigate. "Get out of here."

Mara clenched her teeth, glancing up at the second Star Destroyer. She hated to turn tail and run, but she knew they were right. Bel Iblis had shifted three of his ships to meet the new threat, but even equipped with ion cannon, three Dreadnaughts couldn't hold down a Star Destroyer for long. If they didn't disengage soon, they might not get another chance—

Abruptly, her danger sense tingled. Again she threw the Z-95 into a skid; but this time she was too late. The ship lurched hard, and from behind her came the hissing scream of superheated metal vaporizing into space. "I'm hit!" she snapped, one hand automatically slapping cutoff switches as the other grabbed for her flight suit's helmet seals and fastened them in place. Just in time; a second hiss, cut off almost before it began, announced the failure of cabin integrity. "Power lost, air lost. Ejecting now."

She reached for the eject loop . . . and paused. By chance—or perhaps last-second instinct—her crippled fighter was aimed almost directly at the first Star Destroyer's hangar entry port. If she could coax a little more power out of the auxiliary maneuvering system . . .

It took more than a little coaxing, but when she finally gripped the eject loop again she had the satisfaction of knowing that even in death the Z-95 would take a minor bit of revenge on the Empire's war machine. Not much, but a little.

She pulled down on the loop, and an instant later was slammed hard into her seat as explosive bolts blew the canopy clear and catapulted her out of the ship. She got a quick glimpse of the Star Destroyer's portside edge, an even quicker glimpse of a TIE fighter whipping past—

And suddenly there was an agonized squeal from the ejection seat's electronics, and the violent crackle of arcing circuits . . . and with a horrible jolt Mara realized that she had made what might very well be the last mistake of her life. Intent on aiming her crippled Z-95 at the Star Destroyer's hangar bay, she had drifted too close to the giant ship and ejected directly into the path of the Dreadnaughts' ion beam bombardment.

And in that single crackle of tortured electronics she had lost everything. Her comm, her lights, her limited maneuvering jets, her life support regulator, her emergency beacons.

Everything.

For a second her thoughts flickered to Skywalker. He'd been lost in deep space, too, awhile back. But she'd had a reason to find him. No one had a similar reason to find her.

A flaming TIE fighter roared past her and exploded. A large piece of shrapnel glanced off the ceramic armor that wrapped partially around her shoulders, slamming her head hard against the side of the headrest.

And as she fell into the blackness, she saw the Emperor's face before her. And knew that she had again failed him.

THEY WERE APPROACHING the monitor anteroom just behind the *Katana's* bridge when Luke abruptly jerked. "What?" Han snapped, looking quickly around down the corridor behind them.

"It's Mara," the other said, his face tight. "She's in trouble."

"Hit?" Han asked.

"Hit and . . . and lost," Luke said, forehead straining in concentration. "She must have run into one of the ion beams."

The kid was looking like he'd just lost his best friend, instead of someone who wanted to kill him. Han thought about pointing that out, decided at the last second they had more immediate things to worry about. Probably just one of those crazy Jedi things that never made sense anyway. "Well, we can't help her now," he said, starting forward again. "Come on."

Both the starboard and port main corridors fed into the monitor anteroom, from which a single set of blast doors led the rest of the way forward into the bridge proper. Lando and Chewbacca were at opposite sides of the port corridor entranceway as Han and Luke arrived, huddling back from a barrage of laser fire and occasionally risking a quick shot back. "What've you got, Lando?" Han asked as he and Luke joined them.

"Nothing good, buddy," Lando grunted back. "There are at least ten of them left. Shen and Tomrus were both hit— Shen will probably die if we don't get him to a medic droid in the next hour or so. Anselm and Kline are taking care of them inside the bridge."

"We did a little better, but we've still got a couple of them coming up behind us," Han told him, doing a quick assessment of the rows of monitor consoles in the anteroom. They would provide reasonable cover, but given the layout, the defenders wouldn't be able to retreat farther without opening themselves to enemy fire. "I don't think four of us can hold this place," he decided. "We'd better pull back to the bridge."

"From which there's nowhere else to go," Lando pointed out. "I trust you considered that part?"

Beside him, Han felt Luke brace himself. "All right," Luke said. "Into the bridge, all of you. I'll handle this."

Lando threw him a look. "You'll *what*?"

"I'll handle it," Luke repeated. With a sharp *snap-hiss* he ignited his lightsaber. "Get going—I know what I'm doing."

"Come on," Han seconded. He didn't know what Luke had in mind, but something about the kid's face suggested it wouldn't be a good idea to argue. "We can backstop him from inside."

A minute later they were set: Han and Lando just inside the bridge blast doors, Chewbacca a few meters farther in under cover of an engineering console, Luke standing alone in the archway with lightsaber humming. It took another minute for the Imperials to realize that they had the corridors to themselves; but once they did they moved swiftly. Cover fire began ricocheting around the monitor consoles, and as it did so the Imperials began diving one by one through the two corridor archways into the anteroom, taking cover behind the long consoles and adding their contribution to the laser fire storm.

Trying not to wince back from the attack, Han kept up his own fire, knowing full well that he wasn't doing much more than making noise. Luke's lightsaber flashed like something alive and hungry, deflecting the bolts that came too close. So far the kid didn't seem to have been hit . . . but Han knew that it couldn't last. As soon as the Imperials stopped laying down random cover fire and started concentrating on their aim, there would be too many shots for even a Jedi to stay clear of. Gritting his teeth, wishing he knew what Luke had in mind, he kept shooting.

"Ready!" Luke shouted over the screaming of the bolts . . . and even as Han wondered what he was supposed to be ready for, the kid took a step back and threw his lightsaber to the side. It spiraled across the anteroom, spun into the wall—

And with a crack like thunder, sliced the anteroom open to space.

Luke leaped backwards, barely making it into the bridge before the blast doors slammed shut against the explosive decompression. Alarms whistled for a moment until Chewbacca shut them off, and for another minute Han could hear the thudding of laser fire as the doomed Imperials fired uselessly at the blast doors.

And then the firing trailed off into silence . . . and it was all over.

Luke was already at the main viewport, gazing out at the battle taking place outside. "Take it easy, Luke," Han advised, holstering his blaster and coming up behind him. "We're out of the fight."

"We can't be," Luke insisted, his artificial right hand opening and closing restlessly. Maybe remembering Myrkr, and that long trek with Mara across the forest. "We've got to do something to help. The Imperials will kill everyone if we don't."

"We can't fire, and we can't maneuver," Han growled, fighting back his own feeling of helplessness. Leia was on that Escort Frigate out there . . . "What's left?"

Luke waved a hand helplessly. "I don't know," he conceded. "You're supposed to be the clever one. *You* think of something."

"Yeah," Han muttered, looking around the bridge. "Sure. I'm supposed to just wave my hands and—"

He stopped short . . . and felt a slow, lopsided smile spread across his face. "Chewie, Lando—get over there to those sensor displays," he ordered, looking down at the console in front of him. Not the right one. "Luke, help me find—never mind; here it is."

"Here what is?" Lando asked, stepping in front of the display Han had indicated.

"Think about it a minute," Han said, glancing over the controls. Good; everything still seemed to be engaged. He just hoped it all still worked. "Where are we, anyway?" he added, stepping over to the helm console and activating it.

"We're in the middle of nowhere," Lando said with strained patience. "And fiddling with that helm isn't going to get us anywhere."

"You're right," Han agreed, smiling tightly. "It's not going to get *us* anywhere."

Lando stared at him . . . and slowly, a smile of his own appeared. "Right," he said slyly. "Right. This is the *Katana* fleet. And we're aboard the *Katana*."

"You got it," Han told him. Taking a deep breath, mentally crossing his fingers, he eased power to the drive.

The *Katana* didn't move, of course. But the whole reason the entire *Katana* fleet had disappeared together in the first place—

"Got one," Lando called out, hunching over his sensor display. "Bearing forty-three mark twenty."

"Just one?" Han asked.

"Just one," Lando confirmed. "Count your blessings—after this much time we're lucky to have even one ship whose engines still work."

"Let's hope they stay working," Han grunted. "Give me an intercept course for that second Star Destroyer."

"Uh . . ." Lando frowned. "Come around fifteen degrees portside and down a hair."

"Right." Carefully, Han made the necessary course change. It was a strange feeling to be flying another ship by slave-rig remote control. "How's that?" he asked Lando.

"Looks good," Lando confirmed. "Give it a little more power."

"The fire control monitors aren't working," Luke warned, stepping to Han's side. "I don't know if you're going to be able to fire accurately without them."

"I'm not even going to try," Han told him grimly. "Lando?"

"Shift a little more to portside," Lando directed. "A little more . . . that's it." He looked up at Han. "You're lined up perfectly."

"Here goes," Han said; and threw the throttle control wide open. There was no way the Star Destroyer could have missed seeing the Dreadnaught bearing down on it, of course. But with its electronic and control systems still being scrambled by Bel Iblis's ion attack, there was also no way for it to move out of the way in time.

Even from the *Katana's* distance, the impact and explosion were pretty spectacular. Han watched the expanding fireball fade slowly, and then turned to Luke. "Okay," he said. "*Now* we're out of the fight."

THROUGH THE *JUDICATOR*'s side viewport Captain Brandei watched in stunned disbelief as the *Peremptory* died its fiery death. No—it couldn't be. It simply couldn't. Not an Imperial Star Destroyer. Not the mightiest ship in the Empire's fleet.

The *crack* of a shot against the bridge deflector screen snapped him out of it. "Report," he snapped.

"One of the enemy Dreadnaughts seems to have been damaged in the *Peremptory*'s explosion," the sensor officer reported. "The other two are on their way back here."

To reinforce the three still blasting away with their ion cannon. Brandei gave the tactical display a quick check; but it was a meaningless exercise. He knew full well what their only course was. "Recall all remaining fighters," he ordered. "We'll make the jump to lightspeed as soon as they're aboard."

"Yes, sir."

And as the bridge crew moved to comply, Brandei permitted himself a tight smile. Yes, they'd lost this one. But it was just a battle, not the war. They'd be back soon enough . . . and when they did, it would be with the Dark Force and Grand Admiral Thrawn to command it.

So he would leave the Rebels to enjoy their victory here. It might well be their last.

CHAPTER 29

THE REPAIR PARTY from the *Quenfis* got the anteroom hull breach patched in what was probably record time. The ship Luke had requested was waiting for him in the docking bay, and he was out in space again barely an hour after the destruction of the second Star Destroyer and the retreat of the first.

Locating a single inert ejection seat among all the debris of battle had been a nearly hopeless task for Karrde's people. For a Jedi, it was no trick at all.

Mara was unconscious when they found her, both from a dangerously depleted air supply and from what was probably a mild concussion. Aves got her aboard the *Wild Karrde* and set off at near-reckless speed toward the medical facilities of the Star Cruiser which had finally arrived. Luke saw them safely aboard, then headed back toward the *Katana* and the transport he and the rest of his team would be returning to Coruscant by.

Wondering why it had been so important for him to rescue Mara in the first place.

He didn't know. There were lots of rationalizations he

could come up with, from simple gratitude for her assistance in the battle all the way up to the saving of lives being a natural part of a Jedi's duty. But none of them was more than simply a rationalization. All he knew for certain was that he had had to do it.

Maybe it was the guidance of the Force. Maybe it was just one last gasp of youthful idealism and naïveté.

From the board in front of him, the comm pinged. "Luke?"

"Yes, Han, what is it?"

"Get back here to the *Katana*. Right away."

Luke looked out his canopy at the dark ship ahead, a shiver running through him. Han's voice had been that of someone walking through a graveyard . . . "What is it?"

"Trouble," the other said. "I know what the Empire's up to now. And it's not good."

Luke swallowed. "I'll be right there."

"So," THRAWN SAID, his glowing eyes blazing with cold fire as he looked up from the *Judicator*'s report. "Thanks to your insistence on delaying me, we've lost the *Peremptory*. I trust you're satisfied."

C'baoth met the gaze evenly. "Don't blame the incompetence of your would-be conquerors on me," he said, his voice as icy as Thrawn's. "Or perhaps it wasn't incompetence, but the skill of the Rebellion. Perhaps it would be you lying dead now if the *Chimaera* had gone instead."

Thrawn's face darkened. Pellaeon eased a half step closer to the Grand Admiral, moving a little farther into the protective sphere of the ysalamir beside the command chair, and braced himself for the explosion.

But Thrawn had better control than that. "Why are you here?" he asked instead.

C'baoth smiled and turned deliberately away. "You've made many promises to me since you first arrived on Wayland, Grand Admiral Thrawn," he said, pausing to peer at one of the hologram sculptures scattered around the room. "I'm here to make sure those promises are kept."

"And how do you intend to do that?"

"By making certain that I'm too important to be, shall we say, conveniently forgotten," C'baoth said. "I'm hereby informing you, therefore, that I will be returning to Wayland . . . and will be assuming command of your Mount Tantiss project."

Pellaeon felt his throat tighten. "The Mount Tantiss project?" Thrawn asked evenly.

"Yes," C'baoth said, smiling again as his eyes flicked to Pellaeon. "Oh, I know about it, Captain. Despite your petty efforts to conceal the truth from me."

"We wished to spare you unnecessary discomfort," Thrawn assured him. "Unpleasant memories, for example, that the project might bring to mind."

C'baoth studied him. "Perhaps you did," he conceded with only a touch of sarcasm. "If that was truly your motive, I thank you. But the time for such things has passed. I have grown in power and ability since I left Wayland, Grand Admiral Thrawn. I no longer need you to care for my sensitivities."

He drew himself up to his full height; and when he spoke again, his voice boomed and echoed throughout the room. "I am C'baoth; Jedi Master. The Force which binds the galaxy together is my servant."

Slowly, Thrawn rose to his feet. "And you are my servant," he said.

C'baoth shook his head. "Not anymore, Grand Admiral Thrawn. The circle has closed. The Jedi will rule again."

"Take care, C'baoth," Thrawn warned. "Posture all you wish. But never forget that even you are not indispensable to the Empire."

C'baoth's bushy eyebrows lifted . . . and the smile which creased his face sent an icy shiver through Pellaeon's chest. It was the same smile he remembered from Wayland.

The smile that had first convinced him that C'baoth was indeed insane.

"On the contrary," the Jedi Master said softly. "As of now, I am all that is *not* indispensable to the Empire."

He lifted his gaze to the stars displayed on the room's walls. "Come," he said. "Let us discuss the new arrangement of our Empire."

LUKE LOOKED DOWN at the bodies of the Imperial troops who had died in his sudden decompression of the *Katana*'s bridge anteroom. Understanding at last why they'd felt strange to his mind. "I don't suppose there's any chance of a mistake," he heard himself say.

Beside him, Han shrugged. "Leia's got them doing a genetic check. But I don't think so."

Luke nodded, staring down at the faces laid out before him. Or rather, at the single face that was shared by all of the bodies.

Clones.

"So that's it," he said quietly. "Somewhere, the Empire's found a set of Spaarti cloning cylinders. And has gotten them working."

"Which means it's not going to take them years to find and train crews for their new Dreadnaughts," Han said, his voice grim. "Maybe only a few months. Maybe not even that long."

Luke took a deep breath. "I've got a really bad feeling about this, Han."

"Yeah. Join the club."

TO BE CONCLUDED . . .

Read on for an excerpt from

THE
LAST COMMAND

BY TIMOTHY ZAHN

CHAPTER 1

GLIDING THROUGH THE BLACKNESS of deep space, the Imperial Star Destroyer *Chimaera* pointed its mighty arrowhead shape toward the dim star of its target system, three thousandths of a light-year away. And prepared itself for war.

"All systems show battle ready, Admiral," the comm officer reported from the portside crew pit. "The task force is beginning to check in."

"Very good, Lieutenant," Grand Admiral Thrawn nodded. "Inform me when all have done so. Captain Pellaeon?"

"Sir?" Pellaeon said, searching his superior's face for the stress the Grand Admiral must be feeling. The stress he himself was certainly feeling. This was not just another tactical strike against the Rebellion, after all—not a minor shipping raid or even a complex but straightforward hit-and-fade against some insignificant planetary base. After nearly a month of frenzied preparations, Thrawn's master campaign for the Empire's final victory was about to be launched.

But if the Grand Admiral was feeling any tension, he was

keeping it to himself. "Begin the countdown," he told Pellaeon, his voice as calm as if he were ordering dinner.

"Yes, sir," Pellaeon said, turning back to the group of one-quarter-size holographic figures standing before him in the *Chimaera*'s aft bridge hologram pod. "Gentlemen: launch marks. *Bellicose:* three minutes."

"Acknowledged, *Chimaera*," Captain Aban nodded, his proper military demeanor not quite masking his eagerness to take this war back to the Rebellion. "Good hunting."

The holo image sputtered and vanished as the *Bellicose* raised its deflector shields, cutting off long-range communications. Pellaeon shifted his attention to the next image in line. "*Relentless:* four point five minutes."

"Acknowledged," Captain Dorja said, cupping his right fist in his left in an ancient Mirshaf gesture of victory as he, too, vanished from the hologram pod.

Pellaeon glanced at his data pad. "*Judicator:* six minutes."

"We're ready, *Chimaera*," Captain Brandei said, his voice soft. Soft, and just a little bit wrong. . . .

Pellaeon frowned at him. Quarter-sized holos didn't show a lot of detail, but even so the expression on Brandei's face was easy to read. It was the expression of a man out for blood.

"This is war, Captain Brandei," Thrawn said, coming up silently to Pellaeon's side. "Not an opportunity for personal revenge."

"I understand my duty, Admiral," Brandei said stiffly.

Thrawn's blue-black eyebrows lifted slightly. "Do you, Captain? Do you indeed?"

Slowly, reluctantly, some of the fire faded from Brandei's face. "Yes, sir," he muttered. "My duty is to the Empire, and to you, and to the ships and crews under my command."

"Very good," Thrawn said. "To the living, in other words. Not to the dead."

Brandei was still glowering, but he gave a dutiful nod. "Yes, sir."

"Never forget that, Captain," Thrawn warned him. "The

fortunes of war rise and fall, and you may be assured that the Rebellion will be repaid in full for their destruction of the *Peremptory* at the *Katana* fleet skirmish. But that repayment will occur in the context of our overall strategy. Not as an act of private vengeance." His glowing red eyes narrowed slightly. "Certainly not by any Fleet captain under my command. I trust I make myself clear."

Brandei's cheek twitched. Pellaeon had never thought of the man as brilliant, but he was smart enough to recognize a threat when he heard one. "Very clear, Admiral."

"Good." Thrawn eyed him a moment longer, then nodded. "I believe you've been given your launch mark?"

"Yes, sir. *Judicator* out."

Thrawn looked at Pellaeon. "Continue, Captain," he said, and turned away.

"Yes, sir." Pellaeon looked at his data pad. "*Nemesis . . .*"

He finished the list without further incident. By the time the last holo image disappeared, the final check-in from their own task force was complete.

"The timetable appears to be running smoothly," Thrawn said as Pellaeon returned to his command station. "The *Stormhawk* reports that the guide freighters launched on time with tow cables functioning properly. And we've just intercepted a general emergency call from the Ando system."

The *Bellicose* and its task force, right on schedule. "Any response, sir?" Pellaeon asked.

"The Rebel base at Ord Pardron acknowledged," Thrawn said. "It should be interesting to see how much help they send."

Pellaeon nodded. The Rebels had seen enough of Thrawn's tactics by now to expect Ando to be a feint, and to respond accordingly. But on the other hand, an attack force consisting of an Imperial Star Destroyer and eight *Katana* fleet Dreadnaughts was hardly something they could afford to dismiss out of hand, either.

Not that it really mattered. They would send a few ships to

Ando to fight the *Bellicose*, and a few more to Filve to fight the *Judicator*, and a few more to Crondre to fight the *Nemesis*, and so on and so on. By the time the *Death's Head* hit the base itself, Ord Pardron would be down to a skeleton defense and screaming itself for all the reinforcements the Rebellion could scramble.

And that was where those reinforcements would go. Leaving the Empire's true target ripe for the picking.

Pellaeon looked out the forward viewport at the star of the Ukio system dead ahead, his throat tightening as he contemplated again the enormous conceit of this whole plan. With planetary shields able to hold off all but the most massive turbolaser and proton torpedo bombardment, conventional wisdom held that the only way to subdue a modern world was to put a fast-moving ground force down at the edges and send them overland to destroy the shield generators. Between the fire laid down by the ground force and the subsequent orbital assault, the target world was always badly damaged by the time it was finally taken. The alternative, landing hundreds of thousands of troops in a major ground campaign that could stretch into months or years, was no better. To capture a planet relatively undamaged but with shield generators still intact was considered an impossibility.

That bit of military wisdom would fall today. Along with Ukio itself.

"Intercepted distress signal from Filve, Admiral," the comm officer reported. "Ord Pardron again responding."

"Good." Thrawn consulted his chrono. "Seven minutes, I think, and we'll be able to move." His lips compressed, just noticeably. "I suppose we'd better confirm that our exalted Jedi Master is ready to do his part."

Pellaeon hid a grimace. Joruus C'baoth, insane clone of the long-dead Jedi Master Jorus C'baoth, who a month ago had proclaimed himself the true heir to the Empire. He didn't like talking to the man any more than Thrawn did; but he might as well volunteer. If he didn't, it would simply become an order. "I'll go, sir," he said, standing up.

"Thank you, Captain," Thrawn said. As if Pellaeon would have had a choice.

He felt the mental summons the moment he stepped beyond the Force-protection of the ysalamiri scattered about the bridge on their nutrient frames. Master C'baoth, clearly, was impatient for the operation to begin. Preparing himself as best he could, fighting against C'baoth's casual mental pressure to hurry, Pellaeon made his way down to Thrawn's command room.

The chamber was brightly lit, in marked contrast to the subdued lighting the Grand Admiral usually preferred. "Captain Pellaeon," C'baoth called, beckoning to him from the double display ring in the center of the room. "Come in. I've been waiting for you."

"The rest of the operation has taken my full attention," Pellaeon told him stiffly, trying to hide his distaste for the man. Knowing full well how futile such attempts were.

"Of course," C'baoth smiled, a smile that showed more effectively than any words his amusement with Pellaeon's discomfort. "No matter. I take it Grand Admiral Thrawn is finally ready?"

"Almost," Pellaeon said. "We want to clear out Ord Pardron as much as possible before we move."

C'baoth snorted. "You continue to assume the New Republic will dance to the Grand Admiral's tune."

"They will," Pellaeon said. "The Grand Admiral has studied the enemy thoroughly."

"He's studied their artwork," C'baoth countered with another snort. "That will be useful if the time ever comes when the New Republic has nothing but artists left to throw against us."

A signal from the display ring saved Pellaeon from the need to reply. "We're moving," he told C'baoth, starting a mental countdown of the seventy-six seconds it would take to reach the Ukio system from their position and trying not to let C'baoth's words get under his skin. He didn't understand himself how Thrawn could so accurately learn the innermost secrets of a species from its artwork. But he'd seen that knowledge proved often enough to trust the Grand Admiral's instincts on such things. C'baoth hadn't.

But then, C'baoth wasn't really interested in an honest debate on the subject. For the past month, ever since declaring himself to be the true heir to the Emperor, C'baoth had been pressing this quiet war against Thrawn's credibility, implying that true insight came only through the Force. And, therefore, only through him.

Pellaeon himself didn't buy that argument. The Emperor had been deep into this Force thing, too, and he hadn't even been able to predict his own death at Endor. But the seeds of uncertainty C'baoth was trying to sow were nevertheless starting to take hold, particularly among the less experienced of Thrawn's officers.

Which was, for Pellaeon, just one more reason why this attack had to succeed. The outcome hinged as much on Thrawn's reading of the Ukian cultural ethos as it did on straight military tactics. On Thrawn's conviction that, at a basic psychological level, the Ukians were terrified of the impossible.

"He will not always be right," C'baoth said into Pellaeon's musings.

Pellaeon bit down hard on the inside of his cheek, the skin of his back crawling at having had his thoughts so casually invaded. "You don't have any concept of privacy, do you?" he growled.

"I am the Empire, Captain Pellaeon," C'baoth said, his eyes glowing with a dark, fanatical fire. "Your thoughts are a part of your service to me."

"My service is to Grand Admiral Thrawn," Pellaeon said stiffly.

C'baoth smiled. "You may believe that if you wish. But to

business—true Imperial business. When the battle here is over, Captain Pellaeon, I want a message sent to Wayland."

"Announcing your imminent return, no doubt," Pellaeon said sourly. C'baoth had been insisting for nearly a month now that he would soon be going back to his former home on Wayland, where he would take command of the cloning facility in the Emperor's old storehouse inside Mount Tantiss. So far, he'd been too busy trying to subvert Thrawn's position to do anything more than talk about it.

"Do not worry, Captain Pellaeon," C'baoth said, all amused again. "When the time is right, I will indeed return to Wayland. Which is why you will contact Wayland after this battle is over and order them to create a clone for me. A very special clone."

Grand Admiral Thrawn will have to authorize that, were the words that came to mind. "What kind do you want?" were the ones that inexplicably came out. Pellaeon blinked, running the memory over in his mind again. Yes, that was what he'd said, all right.

C'baoth smiled again at his silent confusion. "I merely wish a servant," he said. "Someone who will be waiting there for me when I return. Formed from one of the Emperor's prize souvenirs—sample B-2332-54, I believe it was. You will, of course, impress upon the garrison commander there that this must be done in total secrecy."

I will do nothing of the sort. "Yes," Pellaeon heard himself say instead. The sound of the word shocked him; but certainly he didn't mean it. On the contrary, as soon as the battle was over he'd be reporting this little incident directly to Thrawn.

"You will also keep this conversation a private matter between ourselves," C'baoth said lazily. "Once you have obeyed, you will forget it even happened."

"Of course," Pellaeon nodded, just to shut him up. Yes, he'd report this to Thrawn, all right. The Grand Admiral would know what to do.

The countdown reached zero, and on the main wall display

the planet Ukio appeared. "We should put up a tactical display, Master C'baoth," he said.

C'baoth waved a hand. "As you wish."

Pellaeon reached over the double display ring and touched the proper key, and in the center of the room the holographic tactical display appeared. The *Chimaera* was driving toward high orbit above the sunside equator; the ten *Katana* fleet Dreadnaughts of its task force were splitting up into outer and inner defense positions; and the *Stormhawk* was coming in as backstop from the night side. Other ships, mostly freighters and other commercial types, could be seen dropping through the brief gaps Ground Control was opening for them in Ukio's energy shield, a hazy blue shell surrounding the planet about fifty kilometers above the surface. Two of the blips flashed red: the guide freighters from the *Stormhawk*, looking as innocent as all the rest of the ships scurrying madly for cover. The freighters, and the four invisible companions they towed.

"Invisible only to those without eyes to see them," C'baoth murmured.

"So now you can see the ships themselves, can you?" Pellaeon growled. "How Jedi skills grow."

He'd been hoping to irritate C'baoth a little—not much, just a little. But it was a futile effort. "I can see the men inside your precious cloaking shields," the Jedi Master said placidly. "I can see their thoughts and guide their wills. What does the metal itself matter?"

Pellaeon felt his lip twist. "I suppose there's a lot that doesn't matter to you," he said.

From the corner of his eye he saw C'baoth smile. "What doesn't matter to a Jedi Master does not matter to the universe."

The freighters and cloaked cruisers were nearly to the shield now. "They'll be dropping the tow cables as soon as they're inside the shield," Pellaeon reminded C'baoth. "Are you ready?"

The Jedi Master straightened up in his seat and closed his

eyes to slits. "I await the Grand Admiral's command," he said sardonically.

For another second Pellaeon looked at the other's composed expression, a shiver running up through him. He could remember vividly the first time C'baoth had tried this kind of direct long-distance control. Could remember the pain that had been on C'baoth's face; the pinched look of concentration and agony as he struggled to hold the mental contacts.

Barely two months ago, Thrawn had confidently said that C'baoth would never be a threat to the Empire because he lacked the ability to focus and concentrate his Jedi power on a long-term basis. Somehow, between that time and now, C'baoth had obviously succeeded in learning the necessary control.

Which left C'baoth as a threat to the Empire. A very dangerous threat indeed.

The intercom beeped. "Captain Pellaeon?"

Pellaeon reached over the display ring and touched the key, pushing away his fears about C'baoth as best he could. For the moment, at least, the Fleet needed C'baoth. Fortunately, perhaps, C'baoth also needed the Fleet. "We're ready, Admiral," he said.

"Stand by," Thrawn said. "Tow cables detaching now."

"They are free," C'baoth said. "They are under power . . . moving now to their appointed positions."

"Confirm that they're beneath the planetary shield," Thrawn ordered.

For the first time a hint of the old strain crossed C'baoth's face. Hardly surprising; with the cloaking shield preventing the *Chimaera* from seeing the cruisers and at the same time blinding the cruisers' own sensors, the only way to know exactly where they were was for C'baoth to do a precise location check on the minds he was touching. "All four ships are beneath the shield," he said.

"Be absolutely certain, Jedi Master. If you're wrong—"

"I am not wrong, Grand Admiral Thrawn," C'baoth cut

him off harshly. "I will do my part in this battle. Concern yourself with yours."

For a moment the intercom was silent. Pellaeon winced, visualizing the Grand Admiral's expression. "Very well, Jedi Master," Thrawn said calmly. "Prepare to do your part."

There was the double click of an opening comm channel. "This is the Imperial Star Destroyer *Chimaera*, calling the Overliege of Ukio," Thrawn said. "In the name of the Empire, I declare the Ukian system to be once again under the mandate of Imperial law and the protection of Imperial forces. You will lower your shields, recall all military units to their bases, and prepare for an orderly transfer of command."

There was no response. "I know you're receiving this message," Thrawn continued. "If you fail to respond, I will have to assume that you mean to resist the Empire's offer. In that event, I would have no choice but to open hostilities."

Again, silence. "They're sending another transmission," Pellaeon heard the comm officer say. "Sounds a little more panicked than the first one was."

"I'm certain their third will be even more so," Thrawn told him. "Prepare for firing sequence one. Master C'baoth?"

"The cruisers are ready, Grand Admiral Thrawn," C'baoth said. "As am I."

"Be sure that you are," Thrawn said, quietly threatening. "Unless the timing is absolutely perfect, this entire show will be worse than useless. Turbolaser battery three: stand by firing sequence one on my mark. Three . . . two . . . one . . . fire."

On the tactical hologram a double lance of green fire angled out from the *Chimaera*'s turbolaser batteries toward the planet below. The blasts struck the hazy blue of the planetary shield, splashed slightly as their energy was defocused and reflected back into space—

And with the desired perfect timing the two cloaked cruisers hovering on repulsorlifts beneath the shield at those two points fired in turn, their turbolaser blasts sizzling through the atmosphere into two of Ukio's major air defense bases.

That was what Pellaeon saw. The Ukians, with no way of knowing about the cloaked cruisers, would have seen the *Chimaera* fire two devastating shots cleanly through an impenetrable planetary shield.

"Third transmission cut off right in the middle, sir," the comm officer reported with a touch of dark humor. "I think we surprised them."

"Let's convince them it wasn't a fluke," Thrawn said. "Prepare firing sequence two. Master C'baoth?"

"The cruisers are ready."

"Turbolaser battery two: stand by firing sequence two on my mark. Three . . . two . . . one . . . fire."

Again the green fire lanced out, and again, with perfect timing, the cloaked cruisers created their illusion. "Well done," Thrawn said. "Master C'baoth, move the cruisers into position for sequences three and four."

"As you command, Grand Admiral Thrawn."

Unconsciously, Pellaeon braced himself. Sequence four had two of the Ukians' thirty overlapping shield generators as its targets. Launching such an attack would mean that Thrawn had given up on his stated goal of taking Ukio with its planetary defenses intact.

"Imperial Star Destroyer *Chimaera*, this is Tol dosLla of the Ukian Overliege," a slightly quavering voice came from the intercom speaker. "We would ask you to cease your bombardment of Ukio while we discuss terms for surrender."

"My terms are quite simple," Thrawn said. "You will begin by lowering your planetary shield and allowing my forces to land. They will be given control of the shield generators themselves and of all ground-to-space weaponry. All fighting vehicles larger than command speeders will be moved to designated military bases and turned over to Imperial control. Though you will, of course, be ultimately answerable to the Empire, your political and social systems will remain under your control. Provided your people behave themselves, of course."

"And once these changes have been implemented?"

"Then you will be part of the Empire, with all the rights and duties that implies."

"There will be no war-level tax levies?" dosLla asked suspiciously. "No forced conscription of our young people?"

Pellaeon could imagine Thrawn's grim smile. No, the Empire would never need to bother with forced conscription again. Not with the Emperor's collection of Spaarti cloning cylinders in their hands.

"No, to your second question; a qualified no to your first," Thrawn told the Ukian. "As you are obviously aware, most Imperial worlds are currently under war-status taxation levels. However, there are exceptions, and it is likely that your share of the war effort will come directly from your extensive food production and processing facilities."

There was a long pause from the other end. DosLla was no fool, Pellaeon realized—the Ukian knew full well what Thrawn had in mind for his world. First it would be direct Imperial control of the ground/space defenses, then direct control of the food distribution system, the processing facilities, and the vast farming and livestock grazing regions themselves; and in a very short time the entire planet would have become nothing more than a supply depot for the Imperial war machine.

But the alternative was for him to stand silently by and watch as his world was utterly and impossibly demolished before his eyes. And he knew that, too.

"We will lower the planetary shields, *Chimaera*, as a gesture of good faith," dosLla said at last, his tone defiant but with a hint of defeat to it. "But before the generators and ground/space weaponry can be turned over to Imperial forces we shall require certain guarantees regarding the safety of the Ukian people and our land."

"Certainly," Thrawn said, without any trace of the gloating that most Imperial commanders would have indulged in at this point. A small act of courtesy that, Pellaeon knew, was as precisely calculated as the rest of the attack had been. Permitting the Ukian leaders to surrender with their dignity intact would slow down the inevitable resistance to Imperial rule until it was too late. "A representative will be on his way shortly to discuss the particulars with your government," Thrawn continued. "Meanwhile, I presume you have no objection to our forces taking up preliminary defense positions?"

A sigh, more felt than really heard. "We have no objections, *Chimaera*," dosLla said reluctantly. "We are lowering the shield now."

On the tactical display, the blue haze surrounding the planet faded away. "Master C'baoth, have the cruisers move to polar positions," Thrawn ordered. "We don't want any of the drop ships blundering into them. General Covell, you may begin transporting your forces to the surface. Standard defensive positions around all targets."

"Acknowledged, Admiral," Covell's voice said, a little too dryly, and Pellaeon felt a tight smile twitch at his lip. It had only been two weeks since the top Fleet and army commanders had been let in on the secret of the Mount Tantiss cloning project, and Covell was one of those who still hadn't adjusted completely to the idea.

Though the fact that three of the companies he was about to lead down to the surface were composed entirely of clones might have had something to do with his skepticism.

On the tactical hologram the first waves of drop ships and TIE fighter escorts had exited the *Chimaera* and *Stormhawk*, fanning out toward their assigned targets. Clones in drop ships, about to carry out Imperial orders. As the clone crews in the cloaked cruisers had already done so well.

Pellaeon frowned, an odd and uncomfortable thought suddenly striking him. Had C'baoth been able to guide the cruisers so well because each of their thousand-man crews were composed of variants on just twenty or so different minds? Or—even more disturbing—could part of the Jedi Master's split-second control have been due to the fact that C'baoth was himself a clone?

And either way, did that mean that the Mount Tantiss project was playing directly into C'baoth's hands in his bid for power? Perhaps. One more question he would have to bring to Thrawn's attention.

Pellaeon looked down at C'baoth, belatedly remembering that in the Jedi Master's presence such thoughts were not his private property. But C'baoth wasn't looking at him, knowingly or otherwise. He was staring straight ahead, his eyes unfocused, the skin of his face taut. A faint smile just beginning to crease his lips. "Master C'baoth?"

"They're there," C'baoth whispered, his voice deep and husky. "They're there," he repeated, louder this time.

Pellaeon frowned back at the tactical hologram. "Who's where?" he asked.

"They're at Filve," C'baoth said. Abruptly, he looked up at Pellaeon, his eyes bright and insane. "My Jedi are at Filve."

"Master C'baoth, confirm that the cruisers have moved to polar positions," Thrawn's voice came sharply. "Then report on the feint battles—"

"My Jedi are at Filve," C'baoth cut him off. "What do I care about your battles?"

"C'baoth—"

With a wave of his hand, C'baoth shut off the intercom. "Now, Leia Organa Solo," he murmured softly, "you are mine."

THE *MILLENNIUM FALCON* twisted hard to starboard as a TIE fighter shot past overhead, lasers blazing away madly as it tried unsuccessfully to track the freighter's maneuver. Clenching her teeth firmly against the movement, Leia Organa Solo watched as one of their escort X-wings blew the Imperial starfighter into a cloud of flaming dust. The sky spun around the *Falcon*'s canopy as the ship rolled back toward its original heading—

"Look out!" Threepio wailed from the seat behind Leia as another TIE fighter roared in toward them from the side. The warning was unnecessary; with deceptive ungainliness the *Falcon* was already corkscrewing back the other direction to bring its ventral quad laser battery to bear. Faintly audible even through the cockpit door, Leia heard the sound of a Wookiee battle roar, and the TIE fighter went the way of its late partner.

"Good shot, Chewie," Han Solo called into the intercom as he got the *Falcon* leveled again. "Wedge?"

"Still with you, *Falcon*," Wedge Antilles' voice came promptly. "We're clear for now, but there's another wave of TIE fighters on the way."

"Yeah." Han glanced at Leia. "It's your call, sweetheart. You still want to try and reach ground?"

Threepio gave a little electronic gasp. "Surely, Captain Solo, you aren't suggesting—"

"Put a choke valve on it, Goldenrod," Han cut him off. "Leia?"

Leia looked out the cockpit canopy at the Imperial Star Destroyer and eight Dreadnaughts arrayed against the beleaguered planet ahead. Clustering around it like mynocks around an unshielded power generator. It was to have been her last diplomatic mission before settling in to await the birth of her twins: a quick trip to calm a nervous Filvian government and demonstrate the New Republic's determination to protect the systems in this sector.

Some demonstration.

"There's no way we can make it through all that," she told Han reluctantly. "Even if we could, I doubt the Filvians would risk opening the shield to let us in. We'd better make a run for it."

"Sounds good to me," Han grunted. "Wedge? We're pulling out. Stay with us."

"Copy, *Falcon*" Wedge said. "You'll have to give us a few minutes to calculate the jump back."

"Don't bother," Han said, swiveling around in his seat to key in the nav computer. "We'll feed you the numbers from here."

"Copy. Rogue Squadron: screen formation."

"You know, I'm starting to get tired of this," Han told Leia, swiveling back to face front. "I thought you said your Noghri pals were going to leave you alone."

"This has nothing to do with the Noghri." Leia shook her head, an odd half-felt tension stretching at her forehead. Was it her imagination, or were the Imperial ships surrounding Filve starting to break formation? "This is Grand Admiral Thrawn playing with his new Dark Force Dreadnaughts."

"Yeah," Han agreed quietly, and Leia winced at the momentary flash of bitterness in his sense. Despite everyone's best efforts to persuade him otherwise, Han still considered it his own personal fault that Thrawn had gotten to the derelict *Katana* fleet ships—the so-called Dark Force—ahead of the New Republic. "I wouldn't have thought he could get them reconditioned this fast," Han added as he twisted the *Falcon*'s nose away from Filve and back toward deep space.

Leia swallowed. The strange tension was still there, like a distant malevolence pressing against the edges of her mind. "Maybe he has enough Spaarti cylinders to clone some engineers and techs as well as soldiers."

"That's sure a fun thought," Han said; and through her tension Leia could sense his sudden change in mood as he tapped the comm switch. "Wedge, take a look back at Filve and tell me if I'm seeing things."

Over the comm, Leia could hear Wedge's thoughtful intake of air. "You mean like the whole Imperial force breaking off their attack and coming after us?"

"Yeah. That."

"Looks real enough to me," Wedge said. "Could be a good time to get out of here."

"Yeah," Han said slowly. "Maybe."

Leia frowned at her husband. There'd been something in his voice. . . . "Han?"

"The Filvians would've called for help before they put up their shield, right?" Han asked her, forehead furrowed with thought.

"Right," Leia agreed cautiously.

"And the nearest New Republic base is Ord Pardron, right?"

"Right."

"Okay. Rogue Squadron, we're changing course to starboard. Stay with me."

He keyed his board, and the Falcon started a sharp curve to the right. "Watch it, *Falcon*—this is taking us back toward that TIE fighter group," Wedge warned.

"We're not going that far," Han assured him. "Here's our vector."

He straightened out the ship onto their new course heading and threw a look at the rear display. "Good—they're still chasing us."

Behind him, the nav computer beeped its notification that the jump coordinates were ready. "Wedge, we've got your coordinates," Leia said, reaching for the data transmission key.

"Hold it, *Falcon*," Wedge cut her off. "We've got company to starboard."

Leia looked that direction, her throat tightening as she saw what Wedge meant. The approaching TIE fighters were coming up fast, and already were close enough to eavesdrop on any transmission the *Falcon* tried to make to its escort. Sending Wedge the jump coordinates now would be an open invitation for the Imperials to have a reception committee waiting at the other end.

"Perhaps I can be of assistance, Your Highness," Threepio offered brightly. "As you know, I am fluent in over six million forms of communication. I could transmit the coordinates to Commander Antilles in Boordist or Vaathkree trade language, for example—"

"And then you'd send them the translation?" Han put in dryly.

"Of course—" The droid broke off. "Oh, dear," he said, sounding embarrassed.

"Yeah, well, don't worry about it," Han said. "Wedge, you were at Xyquine two years ago, weren't you?"

"Yes. Ah. A Cracken Twist?"

"Right. On two: one, two."

Outside the canopy, Leia caught a glimpse of the X-wings swinging into a complicated new escort formation around the *Falcon*. "What does this buy us?" she asked.

"Our way out," Han told her, checking the rear display again. "Pull the coordinates, add a two to the second number of each one, and then send the whole package to the X-wings."

"I see," Leia nodded her understanding as she got to work. Altering the second digit wouldn't change the appearance of their exit vector enough for the Imperials to catch on to the trick, but it would be more than enough to put any chase force a couple of light-years off target. "Clever. And that little flight maneuver they did just now was just window dressing?"

"Right. Makes anyone watching think that's all there is to it. A little something Pash Cracken came up with at that fiasco off Xyquine." Han glanced at the rear display again. "I think we've got enough lead to outrun them," he said. "Let's try."

"We're not jumping to lightspeed?" Leia frowned, an old and rather painful memory floating up from the back of her mind. That mad scramble away from Hoth, with Darth Vader's whole fleet breathing down their necks and a hyperdrive that turned out to be broken . . .

Han threw her a sideways look. "Don't worry, sweetheart. The hyperdrive's working fine today."

"Let's hope so," Leia murmured.

"See, as long as they're chasing us they can't bother Filve," Han went on. "And the farther we draw them away, the longer the backup force'll have to get here from Ord Pardron."

The brilliant green flash of a near miss cut off Leia's intended response. "I think we've given them all the time we can," she told Han. Within her, she could sense the turmoil coming from her unborn twins. "Can we please get out of here?"

A second bolt spattered off the *Falcon*'s upper deflector shield. "Yeah, I think you're right," Han agreed. "Wedge? You ready to leave this party?"

"Whenever you are, *Falcon*," Wedge said. "Go ahead— we'll follow when you're clear."

"Right." Reaching over, Han gripped the hyperdrive levers and pulled them gently back. Through the cockpit canopy the stars stretched themselves into starlines, and they were safe.

Leia took a deep breath, let it out slowly. Within her, she could still sense the twins' anxiety, and for a moment she turned her mind to the job of calming them down. It was a strange sensation, she'd often thought, touching minds that dealt in emotion and pure sensation instead of pictures and words. So different from the minds of Han and Luke and her other friends.

So different, too, from the distant mind that had been orchestrating that Imperial attack force.

Behind her, the door slid open and Chewbacca came into the cockpit. "Good shooting, Chewie," Han told the Wookiee as he heaved his massive bulk into the portside passenger seat beside Threepio. "You have any more trouble with the horizontal control arm?"

Chewbacca rumbled a negative. His dark eyes studying Leia's face, he growled her a question. "I'm all right," Leia assured him, blinking back sudden and inexplicable tears. "Really."

She looked at Han, to find him frowning at her, too.

"You weren't worried, were you?" he asked. "It was just an Imperial task force. Nothing to get excited about."

She shook her head. "It wasn't that, Han. There was something else back there. A kind of . . ." She shook her head again. "I don't know."

"Perhaps it was similar to your indisposition at Endor," Threepio offered helpfully. "You remember—when you collapsed while Chewbacca and I were repairing the—?"

Chewbacca rumbled a warning, and the droid abruptly shut up. But far too late. "No—let him talk," Han said, his sense going all protectively suspicious as he looked at Leia. "What indisposition was this?"

"There wasn't anything to it, Han," Leia assured him, reaching over to take his hand. "On our first orbit around Endor we passed through the spot where the Death Star blew up. For a few seconds I could feel something like the Emperor's presence around me. That's all."

"Oh, that's all," Han said sarcastically, throwing a brief glare back at Chewbacca. "A dead Emperor tries to make a grab for you, and you don't think it's worth mentioning?"

"Now you're being silly," Leia chided. "There was nothing to worry about—it was over quickly, and there weren't any aftereffects. Really. Anyway, what I felt back at Filve was completely different."

"Glad to hear it," Han said, not yet ready to let it go. "Did you have any of the med people check you over or anything after you got back?"

"Well, there really wasn't any time before—"

"Fine. You do it as soon as we're back."

Leia nodded with a quiet sigh. She knew that tone; and it wasn't something she could wholeheartedly argue against, anyway. "All right. If I can find time."

"You'll *make* time," Han countered. "Or I'll have Luke lock you in the med center when he gets back. I mean it, sweetheart."

Leia squeezed his hand, feeling a similar squeeze on her heart as she did so. Luke, off alone in Imperial territory . . . but he was all right. He had to be. "All right," she told Han. "I'll get checked out. I promise."

"Good," he said, his eyes searching her face. "So what was it you felt back at Filve?"

"I don't know." She hesitated. "Maybe it was the same thing Luke felt on the *Katana*. You know—when the Imperials put that landing party of clones aboard."

"Yeah," Han agreed doubtfully. "Maybe. Those Dreadnaughts were awfully far away."

"There were probably a lot more clones, though, too."

"Yeah. Maybe," Han said again. "Well . . . I suppose Chewie and me'd better get to work on that ion flux stabilizer before it quits on us completely. Can you handle things up here okay, sweetheart?"

"I'm fine," Leia assured him, just as glad to be leaving this line of conversation. "You two go ahead."

Because the other possibility was one she'd just as soon not think about right now. The Emperor, it had long been rumored, had had the ability to use the Force to exercise direct control over his military forces. If the Jedi Master Luke had confronted on Jomark had that same ability . . .

Reaching down, she caressed her belly and focused on the pair of tiny minds within her. No, it was indeed not something she wanted to think about.

"I PRESUME," THRAWN said in that deadly calm voice of his, "that you have some sort of explanation."

Slowly, deliberately, C'baoth lifted his head from the command room's double display circle to look at the Grand Admiral. At the Grand Admiral and, with undisguised contempt, at the ysalamir on its nutrient frame slung across Thrawn's shoulders. "Do you likewise have an explanation, Grand Admiral Thrawn?" he demanded.

"You broke off the diversionary attack on Filve," Thrawn said, ignoring C'baoth's question. "You then proceeded to send the entire task force on a dead-end chase."

"And you, Grand Admiral Thrawn, have failed to bring my Jedi to me," C'baoth countered. His voice, Pellaeon noticed uneasily, was slowly rising in both pitch and volume.

"You, your tame Noghri, your entire Empire—all of you have failed."

Thrawn's glowing red eyes narrowed. "Indeed? And was it also our failure that you were unable to hold on to Luke Skywalker after we delivered him to you on Jomark?"

"You did not deliver him to me, Grand Admiral Thrawn," C'baoth insisted. "I summoned him there through the Force—"

"It was Imperial Intelligence who planted the rumor that Jorus C'baoth had returned and been seen on Jomark," Thrawn cut him off coldly. "It was Imperial Transport who brought you there, Imperial Supply who arranged and provisioned that house for you, and Imperial Engineering who built the camouflaged island landing site for your use. The Empire did its part to get Skywalker into your hands. It was you who failed to keep him there."

"No!" C'baoth snapped. "Skywalker left Jomark because Mara Jade escaped from you and twisted his mind against me. And she will pay for that. You hear me? She shall pay."

For a long moment Thrawn was silent. "You threw the entire Filve task force against the *Millennium Falcon*," he said at last, his voice under control again. "Did you succeed in capturing Leia Organa Solo?"

"No," C'baoth growled. "But not because she didn't want to come to me. She does. Just as Skywalker does."

Thrawn threw a glance at Pellaeon. "She wants to come to you?" he asked.

C'baoth smiled. "Very much," he said, his voice unexpectedly losing all its anger. Becoming almost dreamy . . . "She wants me to teach her children," he continued, his eyes drifting around the command room. "To instruct them in the ways of the Jedi. To create them in my own image. Because I am the master. The only one there is."

He looked back at Thrawn. "You must bring her to me, Grand Admiral Thrawn," he said, his manner somewhere halfway between solemn and pleading, "We must free her from her entrapment among those who fear her powers. They'll destroy her if we don't."

"Of course we must," Thrawn said soothingly. "But you must leave that task to me. All I need is a little more time."

C'baoth frowned with thought, his hand slipping up beneath his beard to finger the medallion hanging on its neck chain, and Pellaeon felt a shiver run up his back. No matter how many times he saw it happen, he would never get used to these sudden dips into the slippery twilight of clone madness. It had, he knew, been a universal problem with the early cloning experiments: a permanent mental and emotional instability, inversely scaled to the length of the duplicate's growth cycle. Few of the scientific papers on the subject had survived the Clone Wars era, but Pellaeon had come across one that had suggested that no clone grown to maturity in less than a year would be stable enough to survive outside of a totally controlled environment.

Given the destruction they'd unleashed on the galaxy, Pellaeon had always assumed that the clonemasters had eventually found at least a partial solution to the problem. Whether they had recognized the underlying cause of the madness was another question entirely.

It could very well be that Thrawn was the first to truly understand it.

"Very well, Grand Admiral Thrawn," C'baoth said abruptly. "You may have one final chance. But I warn you: it will be your last. After that, I will take the matter into my own hands." Beneath the bushy eyebrows his eyes flashed. "And I warn you further: if you cannot accomplish even so small a task, perhaps I will deem you unworthy to lead the military forces of my Empire."

Thrawn's eyes glittered, but he merely inclined his head slightly. "I accept your challenge, Master C'baoth."

"Good." Deliberately, C'baoth resettled himself into his seat and closed his eyes. "You may leave me now, Grand Admiral Thrawn. I wish to meditate, and to plan for the future of my Jedi."

For a moment Thrawn stood silently, his glowing red eyes gazing unblinkingly at C'baoth. Then he shifted his gaze to Pellaeon. "You'll accompany me to the bridge, Captain," he said. "I want you to oversee the defense arrangements for the Ukio system."

"Yes, sir," Pellaeon said, glad of any excuse to get away from C'baoth.

For a moment he paused, feeling a frown cross his face as he looked down at C'baoth. Had there been something he had wanted to bring to Thrawn's attention? He was almost certain there was. Something having to do with C'baoth, and clones, and the Mount Tantiss project . . .

But the thought wouldn't come, and with a mental shrug, he pushed the question aside. It would surely come to him in time.

Stepping around the display ring, he followed his commander from the room.

THE STAR WARS LEGENDS NOVELS TIMELINE

BEFORE THE REPUBLIC
37,000–25,000 YEARS BEFORE
STAR WARS: A NEW HOPE

c. 25,793 YEARS BEFORE *STAR WARS: A NEW HOPE*

Dawn of the Jedi: Into the Void

OLD REPUBLIC
5,000–67 YEARS BEFORE
STAR WARS: A NEW HOPE

Lost Tribe of the Sith: The Collected
Stories

3,954 YEARS BEFORE *STAR WARS: A NEW HOPE*

The Old Republic: Revan

3,650 YEARS BEFORE *STAR WARS: A NEW HOPE*

The Old Republic: Deceived
Red Harvest
The Old Republic: Fatal Alliance
The Old Republic: Annihilation

1,032 YEARS BEFORE *STAR WARS: A NEW HOPE*

Knight Errant
Darth Bane: Path of Destruction
Darth Bane: Rule of Two
Darth Bane: Dynasty of Evil

RISE OF THE EMPIRE
67–0 YEARS BEFORE
STAR WARS: A NEW HOPE

67 YEARS BEFORE *STAR WARS: A NEW HOPE*

Darth Plagueis

33 YEARS BEFORE *STAR WARS: A NEW HOPE*

Cloak of Deception
Darth Maul: Shadow Hunter
Maul: Lockdown

32 YEARS BEFORE *STAR WARS: A NEW HOPE*

STAR WARS: EPISODE I
THE PHANTOM MENACE

Rogue Planet
Outbound Flight
The Approaching Storm

22 YEARS BEFORE *STAR WARS: A NEW HOPE*

STAR WARS: EPISODE II
ATTACK OF THE CLONES

22–19 YEARS BEFORE *STAR WARS: A NEW HOPE*

STAR WARS: THE CLONE
WARS

The Clone Wars: Wild Space
The Clone Wars: No Prisoners

Clone Wars Gambit
  Stealth
  Siege

Republic Commando
  Hard Contact
  Triple Zero
  True Colors
  Order 66

Shatterpoint
The Cestus Deception
MedStar I: Battle Surgeons
MedStar II: Jedi Healer
Jedi Trial
Yoda: Dark Rendezvous
Labyrinth of Evil

19 YEARS BEFORE *STAR WARS: A NEW HOPE*

STAR WARS: EPISODE III
REVENGE OF THE SITH

Kenobi
Dark Lord: The Rise of Darth Vader
Imperial Commando 501st

Coruscant Nights
  Jedi Twilight
  Street of Shadows
  Patterns of Force

The Last Jedi

10 YEARS BEFORE *STAR WARS: A NEW HOPE*

The Han Solo Trilogy
  The Paradise Snare
  The Hutt Gambit
  Rebel Dawn

The Adventures of Lando Calrissian
The Force Unleashed
The Han Solo Adventures
Death Troopers
The Force Unleashed II

THE STAR WARS LEGENDS NOVELS TIMELINE

REBELLION
0–5 YEARS AFTER
STAR WARS: A NEW HOPE

Death Star
Shadow Games

0

STAR WARS: EPISODE IV
A NEW HOPE

Tales from the Mos Eisley Cantina
Tales from the Empire
Tales from the New Republic
Scoundrels
Allegiance
Choices of One
Honor Among Thieves
Galaxies: The Ruins of Dantooine
Splinter of the Mind's Eye
Razor's Edge

3 YEARS AFTER *STAR WARS: A NEW HOPE*

STAR WARS: EPISODE V
THE EMPIRE STRIKES BACK

Tales of the Bounty Hunters
Shadows of the Empire

4 YEARS AFTER *STAR WARS: A NEW HOPE*

STAR WARS: EPISODE VI
THE RETURN OF THE JEDI

Tales from Jabba's Palace

The Bounty Hunter Wars
  The Mandalorian Armor
  Slave Ship
  Hard Merchandise

The Truce at Bakura
Luke Skywalker and the Shadows of
  Mindor

NEW REPUBLIC
5–25 YEARS AFTER
STAR WARS: A NEW HOPE

X-Wing
  Rogue Squadron
  Wedge's Gamble
  The Krytos Trap
  The Bacta War
  Wraith Squadron
  Iron Fist
  Solo Command

The Courtship of Princess Leia
Tatooine Ghost

The Thrawn Trilogy
  Heir to the Empire
  Dark Force Rising
  The Last Command

X-Wing: Isard's Revenge

The Jedi Academy Trilogy
  Jedi Search
  Dark Apprentice
  Champions of the Force

I, Jedi
Children of the Jedi
Darksaber
Planet of Twilight
X-Wing: Starfighters of Adumar
The Crystal Star

The Black Fleet Crisis Trilogy
  Before the Storm
  Shield of Lies
  Tyrant's Test

The New Rebellion

The Corellian Trilogy
  Ambush at Corellia
  Assault at Selonia
  Showdown at Centerpoint

The Hand of Thrawn Duology
  Specter of the Past
  Vision of the Future

Scourge
Survivor's Quest

NEW JEDI ORDER
25–40 YEARS AFTER
STAR WARS: A NEW HOPE

 LEGACY
40+ YEARS AFTER
STAR WARS: A NEW HOPE

The New Jedi Order
Vector Prime
Dark Tide I: Onslaught
Dark Tide II: Ruin
Agents of Chaos I: Hero's Trial
Agents of Chaos II: Jedi Eclipse
Balance Point
Edge of Victory I: Conquest
Edge of Victory II: Rebirth
Star by Star
Dark Journey
Enemy Lines I: Rebel Dream
Enemy Lines II: Rebel Stand
Traitor
Destiny's Way
Force Heretic I: Remnant
Force Heretic II: Refugee
Force Heretic III: Reunion
The Final Prophecy
The Unifying Force

35 YEARS AFTER *STAR WARS: A NEW HOPE*

The Dark Nest Trilogy
The Joiner King
The Unseen Queen
The Swarm War

Legacy of the Force
Betrayal
Bloodlines
Tempest
Exile
Sacrifice
Inferno
Fury
Revelation
Invincible

Crosscurrent
Riptide
Millennium Falcon

43 YEARS AFTER *STAR WARS: A NEW HOPE*

Fate of the Jedi
Outcast
Omen
Abyss
Backlash
Allies
Vortex
Conviction
Ascension
Apocalypse

X-Wing: Mercy Kill

45 YEARS AFTER *STAR WARS: A NEW HOPE*

Crucible

PHOTO: © KENT AKSELSEN

TIMOTHY ZAHN is the author of more than forty novels, nearly ninety short stories and novellas, and four short fiction collections. In 1984, he won the Hugo Award for best novella. Zahn is best known for his *Star Wars* novels (*Heir to the Empire*, *Dark Force Rising*, *The Last Command*, *Specter of the Past*, *Vision of the Future*, *Survivor's Quest*, *Outbound Flight*, *Allegiance*, *Choices of One*, and *Scoundrels*), with more than four million copies of his books in print. Other books include the Cobra series, the Quadrail series, and the young adult Dragonback series. Zahn has a B.S. in physics from Michigan State University and an M.S. from the University of Illinois. He lives with his family on the Oregon coast.

Facebook.com/TimothyZahn

ABOUT THE TYPE

This book was set in Sabon, a typeface designed by the well-known German typographer Jan Tschichold (1902–74). Sabon's design is based upon the original letter forms of sixteenth-century French type designer Claude Garamond and was created specifically to be used for three sources: foundry type for hand composition, Linotype, and Monotype. Tschichold named his typeface for the famous Frankfurt typefounder Jacques Sabon (c. 1520–80).

A long time ago in a galaxy far, far away. . . .

STAR WARS™

Join up! Subscribe to our newsletter
at ReadStarWars.com or find us on social.

f StarWarsBooks

🐦 @DelReyStarWars

📷 @DelReyStarWars

STAR WARS

HEIR TO THE EMPIRE

HEIR TO THE EMPIRE

TIMOTHY ZAHN

NEW YORK

2021 Del Rey Trade Paperback Edition

Copyright © 1991 by Lucasfilm Ltd. & ® or ™ where indicated.
All rights reserved.
Excerpt from *Star Wars: Dark Force Rising* copyright © 1992 by
Lucasfilm Ltd. & ® or ™ where indicated. All rights reserved.

Published in the United States by Del Rey,
an imprint of Random House, a division of
Penguin Random House LLC, New York.

DEL REY is a registered trademark and the CIRCLE colophon
is a trademark of Penguin Random House LLC.

Originally published in hardcover in the United States by
Bantam Spectra, an imprint of Random House, a division of
Penguin Random House LLC, in 1991.

ISBN 978-0-593-35876-4
Ebook ISBN 978-0-307-79610-3

Printed in the United States of America on acid-free paper

randomhousebooks.com

8 9

Book design by Edwin Vazquez

THE ESSENTIAL
LEGENDS COLLECTION

For over forty years, novels set in a galaxy far, far away have enriched the *Star Wars* experience for fans seeking to continue the adventure beyond the screen. When he created *Star Wars*, George Lucas built a universe that sparked the imagination and inspired others to create. He opened up that universe to be a creative space for other people to tell their own tales. This became known as the Expanded Universe, or EU, of novels, comics, videogames, and more.

To this day, the EU remains an inspiration for *Star Wars* creators and is published under the label Legends. Ideas, characters, story elements, and more from new *Star Wars* entertainment trace their origins back to material from the Expanded Universe. This Essential Legends Collection curates some of the most treasured stories from that expansive legacy.

HEIR TO THE EMPIRE

CHAPTER 1

"CAPTAIN PELLAEON?" A voice called down the port-side crew pit through the hum of background conversation. "Message from the sentry line: the scoutships have just come out of lightspeed."

Pellaeon, leaning over the shoulder of the man at the *Chimaera*'s bridge engineering monitor, ignored the shout. "Trace this line for me," he ordered, tapping a light pen at the schematic on the display.

The engineer threw a questioning glance up at him. "Sir . . . ?"

"I heard him," Pellaeon said. "You have an order, Lieutenant."

"Yes, sir," the other said carefully, and keyed for the trace.

"Captain Pellaeon?" the voice repeated, closer this time. Keeping his eyes on the engineering display, Pellaeon waited until he could hear the sound of the approaching footsteps. Then, with all the regal weight that fifty years spent in the Imperial Fleet gave to a man, he straightened up and turned.

The young duty officer's brisk walk faltered; came to an abrupt halt. "Uh, sir—" He looked into Pellaeon's eyes and his voice faded away.

Pellaeon let the silence hang in the air for a handful of heartbeats, long enough for those nearest to notice. "This is not a cattle market in Shaum Hii, Lieutenant Tschel," he said at last, keeping his voice calm but icy cold. "This is the bridge of an Imperial Star Destroyer. Routine information is not—repeat, *not*—simply shouted in the general direction of its intended recipient. Is that clear?"

Tschel swallowed. "Yes, sir."

Pellaeon held his eyes a few seconds longer, then lowered his head in a slight nod. "Now. Report."

"Yes, sir." Tschel swallowed again. "We've just received word from the sentry ships, sir: the scouts have returned from their scan raid on the Obroa-skai system."

"Very good," Pellaeon nodded. "Did they have any trouble?"

"Only a little, sir—the natives apparently took exception to them pulling a dump of their central library system. The wing commander said there was some attempt at pursuit, but that he lost them."

"I hope so," Pellaeon said grimly. Obroa-skai held a strategic position in the borderland regions, and intelligence reports indicated that the New Republic was making a strong bid for its membership and support. If they'd had armed emissary ships there at the time of the raid. . . .

Well, he'd know soon enough. "Have the wing commander report to the bridge ready room with his report as soon as the ships are aboard," he told Tschel. "And have the sentry line go to yellow alert. Dismissed."

"Yes, sir." Spinning around with a reasonably good imitation of a proper military turn, the lieutenant headed back toward the communications console.

The *young* lieutenant . . . which was, Pellaeon thought with a trace of old bitterness, where the problem really lay. In the old days—at the height of the Empire's power—it would have been inconceivable for a man as young as Tschel to serve as a bridge officer aboard a ship like the *Chimaera.* Now—

He looked down at the equally young man at the engineering monitor. Now, in contrast, the *Chimaera* had virtually no one aboard except young men and women.

Slowly, Pellaeon let his eyes sweep across the bridge, feeling the echoes of old anger and hatred twist through his stomach. There had been many commanders in the Fleet, he knew, who had seen the Emperor's original Death Star as a blatant attempt to bring the Empire's vast military power more tightly under his direct control, just as he'd already done with the Empire's political power. The fact that he'd ignored the battle station's proven vulnerability and gone ahead with a second Death Star had merely reinforced that suspicion. There would have been few in the Fleet's upper echelons who would have genuinely mourned its loss . . . if it hadn't, in its death throes, taken the Super Star Destroyer *Executor* with it.

Even after five years Pellaeon couldn't help but wince at the memory of that image: the *Executor,* out of control, colliding with the unfinished Death Star and then disintegrating completely in the battle station's massive explosion. The loss of the ship itself had been bad enough; but the fact that it was the *Executor* had made it far worse. That particular Super Star Destroyer had been Darth Vader's personal ship, and despite the Dark Lord's legendary—and often lethal—capriciousness, serving aboard it had long been perceived as the quick line to promotion.

Which meant that when the *Executor* died, so also did a disproportionate fraction of the best young and midlevel officers and crewers.

The Fleet had never recovered from that fiasco. With the *Executor*'s leadership gone, the battle had quickly turned into a confused rout, with several other Star Destroyers being lost before the order to withdraw had finally been given. Pellaeon himself, taking command when the *Chimaera*'s former captain was killed, had done what he could to hold things together; but despite his best efforts, they had never regained the initiative against the Rebels. Instead, they had been steadily pushed back . . . until they were here.

Here, in what had once been the backwater of the Empire, with barely a quarter of its former systems still under nominal Imperial control. Here, aboard a Star Destroyer manned almost entirely by painstakingly trained but badly inexperienced young people, many of them conscripted from their home worlds by force or threat of force.

Here, under the command of possibly the greatest military mind the Empire had ever seen.

Pellaeon smiled—a tight, wolfish smile—as he again looked around his bridge. No, the end of the Empire was not yet. As the arrogantly self-proclaimed New Republic would soon discover.

He glanced at his chron. Two-fifteen. Grand Admiral Thrawn would be meditating in his command room now . . . and if Imperial procedure frowned on shouting across the bridge, it frowned even harder on interrupting a Grand Admiral's meditation by intercom. One spoke to him in person, or one did not speak to him at all. "Continue tracing those lines," Pellaeon ordered the engineering lieutenant as he headed for the door. "I'll be back shortly."

The Grand Admiral's new command room was two levels below the bridge, in a space that had once housed the former commander's luxury entertainment suite. When Pellaeon had found Thrawn—or rather, when the Grand Admiral had found him—one of his first acts had been to take over the suite and convert it into what was essentially a secondary bridge.

A secondary bridge, meditation room . . . and perhaps more. It was no secret aboard the *Chimaera* that since the recent refitting had been completed the Grand Admiral had been spending a great deal of his time here. What *was* secret was what exactly he did during those long hours.

Stepping to the door, Pellaeon straightened his tunic and braced himself. Perhaps he was about to find out. "Captain Pellaeon to see Grand Admiral Thrawn," he announced. "I have informa—"

The door slid open before he'd finished speaking. Mentally preparing himself, Pellaeon stepped into the dimly lit entry room. He glanced around, saw nothing of interest, and started for the door to the main chamber, five paces ahead.

A touch of air on the back of his neck was his only warning. "Captain Pellaeon," a deep, gravelly, catlike voice mewed into his ear.

Pellaeon jumped and spun around, cursing both himself and the short, wiry creature standing less than half a meter away. "Blast it, Rukh," he snarled. "What do you think you're doing?"

For a long moment Rukh just looked up at him, and Pellaeon felt a drop of sweat trickle down his back. With his large dark eyes, protruding jaw, and glistening needle teeth, Rukh was even more of a nightmare in the dimness than he was in normal lighting.

Especially to someone like Pellaeon, who knew what Thrawn used Rukh and his fellow Noghri for.

"I'm doing my job," Rukh said at last. He stretched his thin arm almost casually out toward the inner door, and Pellaeon caught just a glimpse of the slender assassin's knife before it vanished somehow into the Noghri's sleeve. His hand closed, then opened again, steel-wire muscles moving visibly beneath his dark gray skin. "You may enter."

"*Thank* you," Pellaeon growled. Straightening his tunic again, he turned back to the door. It opened at his approach, and he stepped through—

Into a softly lit art museum.

He stopped short, just inside the room, and looked around in astonishment. The walls and domed ceiling were covered with flat paintings and planics, a few of them vaguely human-looking but most of distinctly alien origin. Various sculptures were scattered around, some freestanding, others on pedestals. In the center of the room was a double circle of repeater displays, the outer ring slightly higher than the inner ring. Both sets of displays, at least from what little Pellaeon could see, also seemed to be devoted to pictures of artwork.

And in the center of the double circle, seated in a duplicate of the Admiral's Chair on the bridge, was Grand Admiral Thrawn.

He sat motionlessly, his shimmery blue-black hair glinting in the dim light, his pale blue skin looking cool and subdued and very alien on his otherwise human frame. His eyes were nearly closed as he leaned back against the headrest, only a glint of red showing between the lids.

Pellaeon licked his lips, suddenly unsure of the wisdom of having invaded Thrawn's sanctum like this. If the Grand Admiral decided to be annoyed. . . .

"Come in, Captain," Thrawn said, his quietly modulated voice cutting through Pellaeon's thoughts. Eyes still closed to slits, he waved a hand in a small and precisely measured motion. "What do you think?"

"It's . . . very interesting, sir," was all Pellaeon could come up with as he walked over to the outer display circle.

"All holographic, of course," Thrawn said, and Pellaeon thought he could hear a note of regret in the other's voice. "The sculptures and flats both. Some of them are lost; many of the others are on planets now occupied by the Rebellion."

"Yes, sir," Pellaeon nodded. "I thought you'd want to

know, Admiral, that the scouts have returned from the Obroa-skai system. The wing commander will be ready for debriefing in a few minutes."

Thrawn nodded. "Were they able to tap into the central library system?"

"They got at least a partial dump," Pellaeon told him. "I don't know yet if they were able to complete it—apparently, there was some attempt at pursuit. The wing commander thinks he lost them, though."

For a moment Thrawn was silent. "No," he said. "No, I don't believe he has. Particularly not if the pursuers were from the Rebellion." Taking a deep breath, he straightened in his chair and, for the first time since Pellaeon had entered, opened his glowing red eyes.

Pellaeon returned the other's gaze without flinching, feeling a small flicker of pride at the achievement. Many of the Emperor's top commanders and courtiers had never learned to feel comfortable with those eyes. Or with Thrawn himself, for that matter. Which was probably why the Grand Admiral had spent so much of his career out in the Unknown Regions, working to bring those still-barbaric sections of the galaxy under Imperial control. His brilliant successes had won him the title of Warlord and the right to wear the white uniform of Grand Admiral—the only nonhuman ever granted that honor by the Emperor.

Ironically, it had also made him all the more indispensable to the frontier campaigns. Pellaeon had often wondered how the Battle of Endor would have ended if Thrawn, not Vader, had been commanding the *Executor*. "Yes, sir," he said. "I've ordered the sentry line onto yellow alert. Shall we go to red?"

"Not yet," Thrawn said. "We should still have a few minutes. Tell me, Captain, do you know anything about art?"

"Ah . . . not very much," Pellaeon managed, thrown a little by the sudden change of subject. "I've never really had much time to devote to it."

"You should make the time." Thrawn gestured to a part of the inner display circle to his right. "Saffa paintings," he identified them. "Circa 1550 to 2200, Pre-Empire Date. Note how the style changes—right here—at the first contact with the Thennqora. Over there—" he pointed to the left-hand wall "—are examples of Paonidd extrassa art. Note the similarities with the early Saffa work, and also the mid-eighteenth-century Pre-Em Vaathkree flatsculp."

"Yes, I see," Pellaeon said, not entirely truthfully. "Admiral, shouldn't we be—?"

He broke off as a shrill whistle split the air. "Bridge to Grand Admiral Thrawn," Lieutenant Tschel's taut voice called over the intercom. "Sir, we're under attack!"

Thrawn tapped the intercom switch. "This is Thrawn," he said evenly. "Go to red alert, and tell me what we've got. Calmly, if possible."

"Yes, sir." The muted alert lights began flashing, and Pellaeon could hear the sound of the klaxons baying faintly outside the room. "Sensors are picking up four New Republic Assault Frigates," Tschel continued, his voice tense but under noticeably better control. "Plus at least three wings of X-wing fighters. Symmetric cloud-vee formation, coming in on our scoutships' vector."

Pellaeon swore under his breath. A single Star Destroyer, with a largely inexperienced crew, against four

Assault Frigates and their accompanying fighters . . . "Run engines to full power," he called toward the intercom. "Prepare to make the jump to lightspeed." He took a step toward the door—

"Belay that jump order, Lieutenant," Thrawn said, still glacially calm. "TIE fighter crews to their stations; activate deflector shields."

Pellaeon spun back to him. "Admiral—"

Thrawn cut him off with an upraised hand. "Come here, Captain," the Grand Admiral ordered. "Let's take a look, shall we?"

He touched a switch; and abruptly, the art show was gone. Instead, the room had become a miniature bridge monitor, with helm, engine, and weapons readouts on the walls and double display circle. The open space had become a holographic tactical display; in one corner a flashing sphere indicated the invaders. The wall display nearest to it gave an ETA estimate of twelve minutes.

"Fortunately, the scoutships have enough of a lead not to be in danger themselves," Thrawn commented. "So. Let's see what exactly we're dealing with. Bridge: order the three nearest sentry ships to attack."

"Yes, sir."

Across the room, three blue dots shifted out of the sentry line onto intercept vectors. From the corner of his eye Pellaeon saw Thrawn lean forward in his seat as the Assault Frigates and accompanying X-wings shifted in response. One of the blue dots winked out—

"Excellent," Thrawn said, leaning back in his seat. "That will do, Lieutenant. Pull the other two sentry ships back, and order the Sector Four line to scramble out of the invaders' vector."

"Yes, sir," Tschel said, sounding more than a little confused.

A confusion Pellaeon could well understand. "Shouldn't we at least signal the rest of the Fleet?" he suggested, hearing the tightness in his voice. "The *Death's Head* could be here in twenty minutes, most of the others in less than an hour."

"The last thing we want to do right now is bring in more of our ships, Captain," Thrawn said. He looked up at Pellaeon, and a faint smile touched his lips. "After all, there *may* be survivors, and we wouldn't want the Rebellion learning about us. Would we."

He turned back to his displays. "Bridge: I want a twenty-degree port yaw rotation—bring us flat to the invaders' vector, superstructure pointing at them. As soon as they're within the outer perimeter, the Sector Four sentry line is to re-form behind them and jam all transmissions."

"Y-yes, sir. Sir—?"

"You don't have to understand, Lieutenant," Thrawn said, his voice abruptly cold. "Just obey."

"Yes, sir."

Pellaeon took a careful breath as the displays showed the *Chimaera* rotating as per orders. "I'm afraid I don't understand, either, Admiral," he said. "Turning our superstructure toward them—"

Again, Thrawn stopped him with an upraised hand. "Watch and learn, Captain. That's fine, bridge: stop rotation and hold position here. Drop docking bay deflector shields, boost power to all others. TIE fighter squadrons: launch when ready. Head directly away from the *Chimaera* for two kilometers, then sweep around in open cluster formation. Backfire speed, zonal attack pattern."

He got an acknowledgment, then looked up at Pellaeon. "Do you understand now, Captain?"

Pellaeon pursed his lips. "I'm afraid not," he admitted. "I see now that the reason you turned the ship was to give the fighters some exit cover, but the rest is nothing but a classic Marg Sabl closure maneuver. They're not going to fall for anything that simple."

"On the contrary," Thrawn corrected coolly. "Not only will they fall for it, they'll be utterly destroyed by it. Watch, Captain. And learn."

The TIE fighters launched, accelerating away from the *Chimaera* and then leaning hard into etheric rudders to sweep back around it like the spray of some exotic fountain. The invading ships spotted the attackers and shifted vectors—

Pellaeon blinked. "What in the Empire are they *doing*?"

"They're trying the only defense they know of against a Marg Sabl," Thrawn said, and there was no mistaking the satisfaction in his voice. "Or, to be more precise, the only defense they are psychologically capable of attempting." He nodded toward the flashing sphere. "You see, Captain, there's an Elom commanding that force . . . and Elomin simply cannot handle the unstructured attack profile of a properly executed Marg Sabl."

Pellaeon stared at the invaders, still shifting into their utterly useless defense stance . . . and slowly it dawned on him what Thrawn had just done. "That sentry ship attack a few minutes ago," he said. "You were able to tell from *that* that those were Elomin ships?"

"Learn about art, Captain," Thrawn said, his voice almost dreamy. "When you understand a species' art, you understand that species."

He straightened in his chair. "Bridge: bring us to flank speed. Prepare to join the attack."

An hour later, it was all over.

THE READY ROOM door slid shut behind the wing commander, and Pellaeon gazed back at the map still on the display. "Sounds like Obroa-skai is a dead end," he said regretfully. "There's no way we'll be able to spare the manpower that much pacification would cost."

"For now, perhaps," Thrawn agreed. "But only for now."

Pellaeon frowned across the table at him. Thrawn was fiddling with a data card, rubbing it absently between finger and thumb, as he stared out the viewport at the stars. A strange smile played about his lips. "Admiral?" he asked carefully.

Thrawn turned his head, those glowing eyes coming to rest on Pellaeon. "It's the second piece of the puzzle, Captain," he said softly, holding up the data card. "The piece I've been searching for now for over a year."

Abruptly, he turned to the intercom, jabbed it on. "Bridge, this is Grand Admiral Thrawn. Signal the *Death's Head;* inform Captain Harbid we'll be temporarily leaving the Fleet. He's to continue making tactical surveys of the local systems and pulling data dumps wherever possible. Then set course for a planet called Myrkr—the nav computer has its location."

The bridge acknowledged, and Thrawn turned back

to Pellaeon. "You seem lost, Captain," he suggested. "I take it you've never heard of Myrkr."

Pellaeon shook his head, trying without success to read the Grand Admiral's expression. "Should I have?"

"Probably not. Most of those who have have been smugglers, malcontents, and otherwise useless dregs of the galaxy."

He paused, taking a measured sip from the mug at his elbow—a strong Forvish ale, from the smell of it—and Pellaeon forced himself to remain silent. Whatever the Grand Admiral was going to tell him, he was obviously going to tell it in his own way and time. "I ran across an offhand reference to it some seven years ago," Thrawn continued, setting his mug back down. "What caught my attention was the fact that, although the planet had been populated for at least three hundred years, both the Old Republic and the Jedi of that time had always left it strictly alone." He cocked one blue-black eyebrow slightly. "What would you infer from that, Captain?"

Pellaeon shrugged. "That it's a frontier planet, somewhere too far away for anyone to care about."

"Very good, Captain. That was my first assumption, too . . . except that it's not. Myrkr is, in fact, no more than a hundred fifty light-years from here—close to our border with the Rebellion and well within the Old Republic's boundaries." Thrawn dropped his eyes to the data card still in his hand. "No, the actual explanation is far more interesting. And far more useful."

Pellaeon looked at the data card, too. "And that explanation became the first piece of this puzzle of yours?"

Thrawn smiled at him. "Again, Captain, very good. Yes. Myrkr—or more precisely, one of its indigenous animals—was the first piece. The second is on a world called Wayland." He waved the data card. "A world for which, thanks to the Obroans, I finally have a location."

"I congratulate you," Pellaeon said, suddenly tired of this game. "May I ask just what exactly this puzzle is?"

Thrawn smiled—a smile that sent a shiver up Pellae- on's back. "Why, the only puzzle worth solving, of course," the Grand Admiral said softly. "The complete, total, and utter destruction of the Rebellion."

CHAPTER 2

"LUKE?"

The voice came softly but insistently. Pausing amid the familiar landscape of Tatooine—familiar, yet oddly distorted—Luke Skywalker turned to look.

An equally familiar figure stood there watching him. "Hello, Ben," Luke said, his voice sounding sluggish in his ears. "Been a long time."

"It has indeed," Obi-wan Kenobi said gravely. "And I'm afraid that it will be longer still until the next time. I've come to say good-bye, Luke."

The landscape seemed to tremble; and abruptly, a small part of Luke's mind remembered that he was asleep. Asleep in his suite in the Imperial Palace, and dreaming of Ben Kenobi.

"No, I'm not a dream," Ben assured him, answering Luke's unspoken thought. "But the distances separating us have become too great for me to appear to you in any other way. Now, even this last path is being closed to me."

"No," Luke heard himself say. "You can't leave us, Ben. We need you."

Ben's eyebrows lifted slightly, and a hint of his old smile touched his lips. "You don't need me, Luke. You are a Jedi, strong in the Force." The smile faded, and for a moment his eyes seemed to focus on something Luke couldn't see. "At any rate," he added quietly, "the decision is not mine to make. I have lingered too long already, and can no longer postpone my journey from this life to what lies beyond."

A memory stirred: Yoda on his deathbed, and Luke pleading with him not to die. *Strong am I in the Force*, the Jedi Master had told him softly. *But not that strong.*

"It is the pattern of all life to move on," Ben reminded him. "You, too, will face this same journey one day." Again, his attention drifted away, then returned. "You are strong in the Force, Luke, and with perseverance and discipline you will grow stronger still." His gaze hardened. "But you must never relax your guard. The Emperor is gone, but the dark side is still powerful. Never forget that."

"I won't," Luke promised.

Ben's face softened, and again he smiled. "You will yet face great dangers, Luke," he said. "But you will also find new allies, at times and places where you expect them least."

"New allies?" Luke echoed. "Who are they?"

The vision seemed to waver and become fainter. "And now, farewell," Ben said, as if he hadn't heard the question. "I loved you as a son, and as a student, and as a friend. Until we meet again, may the Force be with you."

"Ben—!"

But Ben turned, and the image faded . . . and in the dream, Luke knew he was gone. *Then I am alone*, he told himself. *I am the last of the Jedi.*

He seemed to hear Ben's voice, faint and indistinct, as if from a great distance. "Not the last of the old Jedi, Luke. The first of the new."

The voice trailed off into silence, and was gone . . . and Luke woke up.

For a moment he just lay there, staring at the dim lights of the Imperial City playing across the ceiling above his bed and struggling through the sleep-induced disorientation. The disorientation, and an immense weight of sadness that seemed to fill the core of his being. First Uncle Owen and Aunt Beru had been murdered; then Darth Vader, his real father, had sacrificed his own life for Luke's; and now even Ben Kenobi's spirit had been taken away.

For the third time, he'd been orphaned.

With a sigh, he slid out from under the blankets and pulled on his robe and slippers. His suite contained a small kitchenette, and it took only a few minutes to fix himself a drink, a particularly exotic concoction Lando had introduced him to on his last visit to Coruscant. Then, attaching his lightsaber to his robe sash, he headed up to the roof.

He had argued strongly against moving the center of the New Republic here to Coruscant; had argued even more strongly against setting up their fledgling government in the old Imperial Palace. The symbolism was all wrong, for one thing, particularly for a group which—in his opinion—already had a tendency to pay too much attention to symbols.

But despite all its drawbacks, he had to admit that the view from the top of the Palace was spectacular.

For a few minutes he stood at the roof's edge, leaning against the chest-high wrought stone railing and letting the cool night breeze ruffle his hair. Even in the middle of the night the Imperial City was a bustle of activity, with the lights of vehicles and streets intertwining to form a sort of flowing work of art. Overhead, lit by both the city lights and those of occasional airspeeders flitting through them, the low-lying clouds were a dim sculptured ceiling stretching in all directions, with the same apparent endlessness as the city itself. Far to the south, he could just make out the Manarai Mountains, their snow-covered peaks illuminated, like the clouds, largely by reflected light from the city.

He was gazing at the mountains when, twenty meters behind him, the door into the Palace was quietly opened.

Automatically, his hand moved toward his lightsaber; but the motion had barely begun before it stopped. The sense of the creature coming through the doorway . . . "I'm over here, Threepio," he called.

He turned to see C-3PO shuffling his way across the roof toward him, radiating the droid's usual mixture of relief and concern. "Hello, Master Luke," he said, tilting his head to look at the cup in Luke's hand. "I'm terribly sorry to disturb you."

"That's all right," Luke told him. "I just wanted some fresh air, that's all."

"Are you certain?" Threepio asked. "Though of course I don't mean to pry."

Despite his mood, Luke couldn't help but smile. Threepio's attempts to be simultaneously helpful, inquisitive, and polite never quite came off. Not without looking vaguely comical, anyway. "I'm just a little depressed, I guess," he told the droid, turning back to gaze out over the city again. "Putting together a real, functioning government is a lot harder than I expected. Harder than most of the Council members expected, too." He hesitated. "Mostly, I guess I'm missing Ben tonight."

For a moment Threepio was silent. "He was always very kind to me," he said at last. "And also to Artoo, of course."

Luke raised his cup to his lips, hiding another smile behind it. "You have a unique perspective on the universe, Threepio," he said.

From the corner of his eye, he saw Threepio stiffen. "I hope I didn't offend you, sir," the droid said anxiously. "That was certainly not my intent."

"You didn't offend me," Luke assured him. "As a matter of fact, you might have just delivered Ben's last lesson to me."

"I beg your pardon?"

Luke sipped at his drink. "Governments and entire planets are important, Threepio. But when you sift everything down, they're all just made up of people."

There was a brief pause. "Oh," Threepio said.

"In other words," Luke amplified, "a Jedi can't get so caught up in matters of galactic importance that it interferes with his concern for individual people." He looked at Threepio and smiled. "Or for individual droids."

"Oh. I see, sir." Threepio cocked his head toward Luke's cup. "Forgive me, sir . . . but may I ask what that is that you're drinking?"

"This?" Luke glanced down at his cup. "It's just some-thing Lando taught me how to make a while back."

"Lando?" Threepio echoed, and there was no missing the disapproval in his voice. Programmed politeness or not, the droid had never really much cared for Lando.

Which wasn't very surprising, given the circumstances of their first meeting. "Yes, but in spite of such a shady origin, it's really quite good," Luke told him. "It's called hot chocolate."

"Oh. I see." The droid straightened up. "Well, then, sir. If you are indeed all right, I expect I should be on my way."

"Sure. By the way, what made you come up here in the first place?"

"Princess Leia sent me, of course," Threepio an-swered, clearly surprised that Luke would have to ask. "She said you were in some kind of distress."

Luke smiled and shook his head. Leave it to Leia to find a way to cheer him up when he needed it. "Show-off," he murmured.

"I beg your pardon, sir?"

Luke waved a hand. "Leia's showing off her new Jedi skills, that's all. Proving that even in the middle of the night she can pick up on my mood."

Threepio's head tilted. "She really *did* seem concerned about you, sir."

"I know," Luke said. "I'm just joking."

"Oh." Threepio seemed to think about that. "Shall I tell her you're all right, then?"

"Sure," Luke nodded. "And while you're down there, tell her that she should quit worrying about me and get herself back to sleep. Those bouts of morning sickness she still gets are bad enough when she *isn't* worn-out tired."

"I'll deliver the message, sir," Threepio said.

"And," Luke added quietly, "tell her I love her."

"Yes, sir. Good night, Master Luke."

"Good night, Threepio."

He watched the droid go, a fresh flow of depression threatening again to drag him down. Threepio wouldn't understand, of course—no one on the Provisional Council had understood, either. But for Leia, just over three months pregnant, to be spending the bulk of her time *here* . . .

He shivered, and not from the cool night air. *This place is strong with the dark side*. Yoda had said that of the cave on Dagobah—the cave where Luke had gone on to fight a lightsaber duel with a Darth Vader who had turned out to be Luke himself. For weeks afterward the memory of the sheer power and presence of the dark side had haunted his thoughts; only much later had he finally realized that Yoda's primary reason for the exercise had been to show him how far he still had to go.

Still, he'd often wondered how the cave had come to be the way it had. Wondered whether perhaps someone or something strong in the dark side had once lived there.

As the Emperor had once lived here. . . .

He shivered again. The really maddening part of it was that he *couldn't* sense any such concentration of evil in the Palace. The Council had made a point of asking him about that, in fact, when they'd first considered moving operations here to the Imperial City. He'd had to grit his teeth and tell them that, no, there seemed to be no residual effects of the Emperor's stay.

But just because he couldn't sense it didn't necessarily mean it wasn't there.

He shook his head. *Stop it*, he ordered himself firmly. Jumping at shadows wasn't going to gain him anything but paranoia. His recent nightmares and poor sleep were probably nothing more than the stresses of watching Leia and the others struggling to turn a military-oriented rebellion into a civilian-based government. Certainly Leia would never have agreed to come anywhere near this place if she'd had any doubts herself about it.

Leia.

With an effort, Luke forced his mind to relax and let his Jedi senses reach outward. Halfway across the palace's upper section he could feel Leia's drowsy presence. Her presence, and that of the twins she carried within her.

For a moment he held the partial contact, keeping it light enough to hopefully not wake her any further, marveling again at the strange feel of the unborn children within her. The Skywalker heritage was indeed with them; the fact that he could sense them at all implied they must be tremendously strong in the Force.

At least, he assumed that was what it meant. It had been something he'd hoped he would someday have a chance to ask Ben about.

And now that chance was gone.

Fighting back sudden tears, he broke the contact. His mug felt cold against his hand; swallowing the rest of the chocolate, he took one last look around. At the city, at the clouds . . . and, in his mind's eye, at the stars that lay beyond them. Stars, around which revolved planets, upon which lived people. Billions of people. Many of them still waiting for the freedom and light the New Republic had promised them.

He closed his eyes against the bright lights and the equally bright hopes. There was, he thought wearily, no magic wand that could make everything better.

Not even for a Jedi.

THREEPIO SHUFFLED HIS way out of the room, and with a tired sigh Leia Organa Solo settled back against the pillows. *Half a victory is better than none*, the old saying crossed her mind.

The old saying she'd never believed for a minute. Half a victory, to her way of thinking, was also half a defeat.

She sighed again, feeling the touch of Luke's mind. His encounter with Threepio had lightened his dark mood, as she'd hoped it would; but with the droid gone, the depression was threatening to overtake him again.

Perhaps she should go to him herself. See if she could get him to talk through whatever it was that had been bothering him for the past few weeks.

Her stomach twisted, just noticeably. "It's all right," she soothed, rubbing her hand gently across her belly. "It's all right. I'm just worried about your Uncle Luke, that's all."

Slowly, the twisting eased. Picking up the half-filled glass on the nightstand, Leia drank it down, trying not to make a face. Warm milk was pretty far down on her list of favorite drinks, but it had proved to be one of the fastest ways to soothe these periodic twinges from her digestive tract. The doctors had told her that the worst of her stomach troubles should begin disappearing any day now. She hoped rather fervently that they were right.

Faintly, from the next room, came the sound of footsteps. Quickly, Leia slapped the glass back on the nightstand with one hand as she hauled the blankets up to her chin with the other. The bedside light was still glowing, and she reached out with the Force to try and turn it off.

The lamp didn't even flicker. Gritting her teeth, she tried again; again, it didn't work. Still not enough fine control over the Force, obviously, for something as small as a light switch. Untangling herself from the blankets, she tried to make a lunge for it.

Across the room, the side door opened to reveal a tall woman in a dressing robe. "Your Highness?" she called softly, brushing her shimmering white hair back from her eyes. "Are you all right?"

Leia sighed and gave up. "Come on in, Winter. How long have you been listening at the door?"

"I haven't been listening," Winter said as she glided into the room, sounding almost offended that Leia would even suggest such a thing of her. "I saw the light coming from under your door and thought you might need something."

"I'm fine," Leia assured her, wondering if this woman would ever cease to amaze her. Awakened in the middle of the night, dressed in an old robe with her hair in total disarray, Winter still looked more regal than Leia herself could manage on her best days. She'd lost track of the number of times when, as children together on Alderaan, some visitor to the Viceroy's court had automatically assumed Winter was, in fact, the Princess Leia.

Winter had probably not lost track, of course. Anyone who could remember whole conversations verbatim should certainly be able to reconstruct the number of times she'd been mistaken for a royal princess.

Leia had often wondered what the rest of the Provisional Council members would think if they knew that the silent assistant sitting beside her at official meetings or standing beside her at unofficial corridor conversations was effectively recording every word they said. Some of them, she suspected, wouldn't like it at all.

"Can I get you some more milk, Your Highness?" Winter asked. "Or some crackers?"

"No, thank you," Leia shook her head. "My stomach isn't really bothering me at the moment. It's . . . well, you know. It's Luke."

Winter nodded. "Same thing that's been bothering him for the past nine weeks?"

Leia frowned. "Has it been that long?"

Winter shrugged. "You've been busy," she said with her usual knack for diplomacy.

"Tell me about it," Leia said dryly. "I don't know, Winter—I really don't. He told Threepio that he misses Ben Kenobi, but I can tell that's not all of it."

"Perhaps it has something to do with your pregnancy," Winter suggested. "Nine weeks ago would put it just about right."

"Yes, I know," Leia agreed. "But that's also about the time Mon Mothma and Admiral Ackbar were pushing to move the government seat here to Coruscant. Also about the time we started getting those reports from the borderlands about some mysterious tactical genius having taken command of the Imperial Fleet." She held her hands out, palms upward. "Take your pick."

"I suppose you'll just have to wait until he's ready to talk to you." Winter considered. "Perhaps Captain Solo will be able to draw him out when he returns."

Leia squeezed thumb and forefinger together, a wave of anger-filled loneliness sweeping over her. For Han to have gone out on yet another of these stupid contact missions, leaving her all alone—

The flash of anger disappeared, dissolving into guilt. Yes, Han was gone again; but even when he was here it seemed sometimes like they hardly saw each other. With more and more of her time being eaten up by the enormous task of setting up a new government, there were days when she barely had time to eat, let alone see her husband.

But that's my job, she reminded herself firmly; and it was a job that, unfortunately, only she could do. Unlike virtually all the others in the Alliance hierarchy, she had had extensive training in both the theory and the more practical aspects of politics. She'd grown up in the Royal House of Alderaan, learning about systemwide rule from her foster father—learning it so well that while still in her teens she was already representing him in the Imperial Senate. Without her expertise, this whole thing could easily collapse, particularly in these critical early stages of the New Republic's development. A few more months—just a few more months—and she'd be able to ease off a little. She'd make it all up to Han then.

The guilt faded. But the loneliness remained.

"Maybe," she told Winter. "In the meantime, we'd better both get some sleep. We have a busy day tomorrow."

Winter arched her eyebrows slightly. "There's another kind?" she asked with a touch of Leia's earlier dryness.

"Now, now," Leia admonished, mock-seriously. "You're far too young to become a cynic. I mean it, now—off to bed with you."

"You're sure you don't need anything first?"

"I'm sure. Go on, scat."

"All right. Good night, Your Highness."

She glided out, closing the door behind her. Sliding down flat onto the bed, Leia readjusted the blankets over her and shifted the pillows into a more or less comfortable position. "Good night to you two, too," she said softly to her babies, giving her belly another gentle rub. Han had suggested more than once that anyone who talked to her own stomach was slightly nuts. But then, she suspected that Han secretly believed *everyone* was slightly nuts.

She missed him terribly.

With a sigh, she reached over to the nightstand and turned off the light. Eventually, she fell asleep.

A QUARTER OF the way across the galaxy, Han Solo sipped at his mug and surveyed the semiorganized chaos flowing all around him. *Didn't we*, he quoted to himself, *just leave this party?*

Still, it was nice to know that, in a galaxy busily turning itself upside down, there were some things that never changed. The band playing off in the corner was different, and the upholstery in the booth was noticeably less comfortable; but apart from that, the Mos Eisley cantina looked exactly the same as it always had before. The

same as it had looked the day he'd first met Luke Skywalker and Obi-wan Kenobi.

It felt like a dozen lifetimes ago.

Beside him, Chewbacca growled softly. "Don't worry,
he'll be here," Han told him. "It's just Dravis. I don't
think he's ever been on time for anything in his whole
life."

Slowly, he let his eyes drift over the crowd. No, he
amended to himself, there *was* one other thing different
about the cantina: virtually none of the other smugglers
who had once frequented the place were anywhere to be
seen. Whoever had taken over what was left of Jabba the
Hutt's organization must have moved operations off Tatooine. Turning to peer toward the cantina's back door,
he made a mental note to ask Dravis about it.

He was still gazing off to the side when a shadow fell
across the table. "Hello, Solo," a snickering voice said.

Han gave himself a three-count before turning casually to face the voice. "Well, hello, Dravis," he nodded.
"Long time no see. Have a seat."

"Sure," Dravis said with a grin. "Soon as you and
Chewie both put your hands on the table."

Han gave him an injured look. "Oh, come on," he
said, reaching up to cradle his mug with both hands.
"You think I'd invite you all the way here just to shoot at
you? We're old buddies, remember?"

"Sure we are," Dravis said, throwing Chewbacca an
appraising glance as he sat down. "Or at least we used to
be. But I hear you've gone respectable."

Han shrugged eloquently. "*Respectable*'s such a vague
word."

Dravis cocked an eyebrow. "Oh, well, then let's be specific," he said sardonically. "I hear you joined the Rebel Alliance, got made a general, married a former Alderaanian princess, and got yourself a set of twins on the way."

Han waved a self-deprecating hand. "Actually, I resigned the general part a few months back."

Dravis snorted. "Forgive me. So what's all this about? Some kind of warning?"

Han frowned. "What do you mean?"

"Don't play innocent, Solo," Dravis said, the banter gone from his tone. "New Republic replaces Empire—all fine and sweet and dandy, but you know as well as I do that it's all the same to smugglers. So if this is an official invitation to cease and desist our business activities, let me laugh in your face and get out of here." He started to get up.

"It's nothing like that," Han told him. "As a matter of fact, I was hoping to hire you."

Dravis froze, halfway up. "What?" he asked warily.

"You heard right," Han said. "We're looking to hire smugglers."

Slowly, Dravis sat back down. "Is this something to do with your fight with the Empire?" he demanded. "Because if it is—"

"It isn't," Han assured him. "There's a whole spiel that goes along with this, but what it boils down to is that the New Republic is short of cargo ships at the moment, not to mention experienced cargo ship pilots. If you're looking to earn some quick and honest money, this would be a good time to do it."

"Uh-*huh*." Dravis leaned back in his chair, draping an arm over the seat back as he eyed Han suspiciously. "So what's the catch?"

Han shook his head. "No catch. We need ships and pilots to get interstellar trade going again. You've got 'em. That's all there is to it."

Dravis seemed to think it over. "So why work for you and your pittance directly?" he demanded. "Why can't we just smuggle the stuff and make more per trip?"

"You could do that," Han conceded. "But only if your customers had to pay the kind of tariffs that would make hiring smugglers worthwhile. In this case—" he smiled "—they won't."

Dravis glared at him. "Oh, come *on*, Solo. A brand-new government, hard-pressed like crazy for cash—and you want me to believe they won't be piling tariffs on top of each other?"

"Believe anything you want," Han said, letting his own tone go frosty. "Go ahead and try it, too. But when you're convinced, give me a call."

Dravis chewed at the inside of his cheek, his eyes never leaving Han's. "You know, Solo," he said thoughtfully, "I wouldn't have come if I didn't trust you. Well, maybe I was curious, too, to see what scam you were pulling. And I might be willing to believe you on this, at least enough to check it out myself. But I'll tell you right up front that a lot of others in my group won't."

"Why not?"

"Because you've gone respectable, that's why. Oh, don't give me that hurt look—the simple fact is that you've been out of the business too long to even remember what it's like. Profits are what drives a smuggler, Solo. Profits and excitement."

"So what are you going to do instead, operate in the Imperial sectors?" Han countered, trying hard to remember all those lessons in diplomacy that Leia had given him.

Dravis shrugged. "It pays," he said simply.

"For now, maybe," Han reminded him. "But their territory's been shrinking for five years straight, and it's going to keep getting smaller. We're just about evenly gunned now, you know, and our people are more motivated and a lot better trained than theirs."

"Maybe." Dravis cocked an eyebrow. "But maybe not. I hear rumors that there's someone new in charge out there. Someone who's been giving you a lot of trouble—like in the Obroa-skai system, for instance? I hear you lost an Elomin task force out there just a little while ago. Awfully sloppy, losing a whole task force like that."

Han gritted his teeth. "Just remember that anybody who gives *us* trouble is going to give *you* trouble, too." He leveled a finger at the other. "And if you think the New Republic is hungry for cash, think of how hungry the Empire must be right now."

"It's certainly an adventure," Dravis agreed easily, getting to his feet. "Well, it really was nice seeing you again, Solo, but I gotta go. Say hi to your princess for me."

Han sighed. "Just give your people our offer, okay?"

"Oh, I will. Might even be some who'll take you up on it. You never can tell."

Han nodded. It was, really, all he could have expected out of this meeting. "One other thing, Dravis. Who exactly is the big fish in the pond now that Jabba's gone?"

Dravis eyed him thoughtfully. "Well . . . I guess it's not really a secret," he decided. "Mind you, there aren't any really official numbers. But if I were betting, I'd put my money on Talon Karrde."

Han frowned. He'd heard of Karrde, of course, but never with any hint that his organization was even in the top ten, let alone the one on top. Either Dravis was wrong, or Karrde was the type who believed in keeping a low profile. "Where can I find him?"

Dravis smiled slyly. "You'd like to know that, wouldn't you? Maybe someday I'll tell you."

"Dravis—"

"Gotta go. See you around, Chewie."

He started to turn; paused. "Oh, by the way. You might tell your pal over there that he's got to be the worst excuse for a backup man I've ever seen. Just thought you'd like to know." With another grin, he turned again and headed back into the crowd.

Han grimaced as he watched him go. Still, at least Dravis had been willing to turn his back on them as he left. Some of the other smugglers he'd contacted hadn't even trusted him that far. Progress, sort of.

Beside him, Chewbacca growled something derogatory. "Well, what do you expect with Admiral Ackbar sitting on the Council?" Han shrugged. "The Calamarians were death on smugglers even before the war, and everyone knows it. Don't worry, they'll come around. Some of them, anyway. Dravis can blather all he wants about profit and excitement; but you offer them secure maintenance facilities, no Jabba-style skimming, and no one shooting at them, and they'll get interested. Come on, let's get going."

He slid out of the booth and headed for the bar and the exit just visible beyond it. Halfway across, he stopped at one of the other booths and looked down at its lone occupant. "I've got a message for you," he announced, "I'm supposed to tell you that you're the worst excuse for a backup man that Dravis has ever seen."

Wedge Antilles grinned up at him as he slid out from behind the table. "I thought that was the whole idea," he said, running his fingers through his black hair.

"Yes, but Dravis didn't." Though privately, Han would be the first to admit that Dravis had a point. As far as he was concerned, the only times Wedge *didn't* stick out like a lump on plate glass was when he was sitting in the cockpit of an X-wing blasting TIE fighters into dust. "So where's Page, anyway?" he asked, glancing around.

"Right here, sir," a quiet voice said at his shoulder.

Han turned. Beside them had appeared a medium-height, medium-build, totally nondescript-looking man. The kind of man no one would really notice; the kind who could blend invisibly into almost any surroundings.

Which had, again, been the whole idea. "You see anything suspicious?" Han asked him.

Page shook his head. "No backup troops; no weapons other than his blaster. This guy must have genuinely trusted you."

"Yeah. Progress." Han took one last look around. "Let's get going. We're going to be late enough back to Coruscant as it is. And I want to swing through the Obroa-skai system on the way."

"That missing Elomin task force?" Wedge asked.

"Yeah," Han said grimly. "I want to see if they've figured out what happened to it yet. And if we're lucky, maybe get some idea of who did it to them."

CHAPTER 3

THE FOLD-OUT TABLE in his private office was set, the food was ready to serve, and Talon Karrde was just pouring the wine when the tap came on his door. As always, his timing was perfect. "Mara?" he called.

"Yes," the young woman's voice confirmed through the door. "You asked me to join you for dinner."

"Yes. Please come in."

The door slid open, and with her usual catlike grace Mara Jade walked into the room. "You didn't say what—" her green eyes flicked to the elaborately set table "—this was all about," she finished, her tone just noticeably different. The green eyes came back to him, cool and measuring.

"No, it's not what you're thinking," Karrde assured her, motioning her to the chair opposite his. "This is a business meal—no more, no less."

From behind his desk came a sound halfway between a cackle and a purr. "That's right, Drang—a business meal," Karrde said, turning toward the sound. "Come on, out with you."

The vornskr peered out from around the edge of the desk, its front paws gripping the carpet, its muzzle close to the floor as if on the hunt. "I said out with you," Karrde repeated firmly, pointing toward the open door behind Mara. "Come on, your dish has been set up in the kitchen. Sturm's already there—chances are he's eaten half your supper by now."

Reluctantly, Drang slunk out from behind the desk, cackle/purring forlornly to himself as he padded toward the door. "Don't give me that poor-little-me act," Karrde chided, picking a piece of braised bruallki from the serving dish. "Here—this should cheer you up."

He tossed the food in the general direction of the doorway. Drangs lethargy vanished in a single coiled-spring leap as he snagged the mouthful in midair. "There," Karrde called after him. "Now go and enjoy your supper."

The vornskr trotted out. "All right," Karrde said, shifting his attention back to Mara. "Where were we?"

"You were telling me this was a business meal," she said, her voice still a little cool as she slid into the seat across from his and surveyed the table. "It's certainly the nicest business meal I've had in quite a while."

"Well, that's the point, really," Karrde told her, sitting down himself and reaching over to the serving tray. "I think it's occasionally good for us to remember that being a smuggler doesn't necessarily require one to be a barbarian, too."

"Ah," she nodded, sipping at her wine. "And I'm sure

most of your people are so very grateful for that reminder."

Karrde smiled. So much, he thought, for the unusual
setting and scenario throwing her off balance. He should
have known that particular gambit wouldn't work on
someone like Mara. "It *does* often make for an interesting evening," he agreed. "Particularly—" he eyed her
"—when discussing a promotion."

A flicker of surprise, almost too fast to see, crossed
her face. "A promotion?" she echoed carefully.

"Yes," he said, scooping a serving of bruallki onto her
plate and setting it in front of her. "Yours, to be precise."

The wary look was back in her eyes. "I've only been
with the group for six months, you know."

"Five and a half, actually," he corrected her. "But time
has never been as important to the universe as ability and
results . . . and your ability and results have been quite
impressive."

She shrugged, her red-gold hair shimmering with the
movement. "I've been lucky," she said.

"Luck is certainly part of it," he agreed. "On the
other hand, I've found that what most people call luck is
often little more than raw talent combined with the ability to make the most of opportunities."

He turned back to the bruallki, dished some onto his
own plate. "Then there's your talent for starship piloting, your ability to both give and accept orders—" he
smiled slightly, gesturing to the table "—and your ability
to adapt to unusual and unexpected situations. All highly
useful talents for a smuggler."

He paused, but she remained silent. Evidently, somewhere in her past she'd also learned when not to ask questions. Another useful talent. "The bottom line, Mara, is that you're simply too valuable to waste as a backup or even as a line operator," he concluded. "What I'd like to do is to start grooming you toward eventually becoming my second in command."

There was no chance of mistaking her surprise this time. The green eyes went momentarily wide, and then narrowed. "What exactly would my new duties consist of?" she asked.

"Traveling with me, mostly," he said, taking a sip of wine. "Watching me set up new business, meeting with some of our long-term customers so that they can get to know you—that sort of thing."

She was still suspicious—he could tell that from her eyes. Suspicious that the offer was a smoke screen to mask some more personal request or demand on his part. "You don't have to answer now," he told her. "Think about it, or talk to some of the others who've been with the organization longer." He looked her straight in the eye. "They'll tell you that I don't lie to my people."

Her lip twisted. "So I've heard," she said, her voice going noncommittal again. "But bear in mind that if you give me that kind of authority, I *am* going to use it. There's some revamping of the whole organizational structure—"

She broke off as the intercom on his desk warbled. "Yes?" Karrde called toward it.

"It's Aves," a voice said. "Thought you'd like to know we've got company; an Imperial Star Destroyer just made orbit."

Karrde glanced at Mara as he got to his feet. "Any

make on it yet?" he asked, dropping his napkin beside his plate and stepping around the desk to where he could see the screen.

"They're not exactly broadcasting ID sigs these days," Aves shook his head. "The lettering on the side is hard to read at this distance, but Torve's best guess is that it's the *Chimaera*."

"Interesting," Karrde murmured. Grand Admiral Thrawn himself. "Have they made any transmissions?"

"None that we've picked up—wait a minute. Looks like . . . yes—they're launching a shuttle. Make that two shuttles. Projected landing point . . ." Aves frowned at something offscreen for a moment. "Projected landing point somewhere here in the forest."

Out of the corner of his eyes, Karrde saw Mara stiffen a bit. "Not in any of the cities around the edge?" he asked Aves.

"No, it's definitely the forest. No more than fifty kilometers from here, either."

Karrde rubbed his forefinger gently across his lower lip, considering the possibilities. "Still only two shuttles?"

"That's all so far." Aves was starting to look a little nervous. "Should I call an alert?"

"On the contrary. Let's see if they need any help. Give me a hailing channel."

Aves opened his mouth; closed it again. "Okay," he said, taking a deep breath and tapping something off-screen. "You have hailing."

"Thank you. Imperial Star Destroyer *Chimaera*, this is Talon Karrde. May I be of any assistance to you?"

"No response," Aves muttered. "You think maybe they didn't want to be noticed?"

"If you don't want to be noticed, you don't use a Star Destroyer," Karrde pointed out. "No, they're most likely busy running my name through ship's records. Be interesting to see some day just what they have on me. If anything." He cleared his throat. "Star Destroyer *Chimaera*, this is—"

Abruptly, Aves's face was replaced by that of a middle-aged man wearing a captain's insignia. "This is Captain Pellaeon of the *Chimaera*," he said brusquely. "What is it you want?"

"Merely to be neighborly," Karrde told him evenly. "We track two of your shuttles coming down, and wondered if you or Grand Admiral Thrawn might require any assistance."

The skin around Pellaeon's eyes tightened, just a bit. "Who?"

"Ah," Karrde nodded, allowing a slight smile. "Of course. I haven't heard of Grand Admiral Thrawn, either. Certainly not in connection with the *Chimaera*. Or with some intriguing information raids on several systems in the Paonnid/Obroa-skai region, either."

The eyes tightened a little more. "You're very well informed, Mr. Karrde," Pellaeon said, his voice silky but with menace lurking beneath it. "One might wonder how a lowly smuggler would come by such information."

Karrde shrugged. "My people hear stories and rumors; I take the pieces and put them together. Much the same way your own intelligence units operate, I imagine. Incidentally, if your shuttles are planning to put down in the forest, you need to warn the crews to be careful. There are several dangerous predator species living here, and the high metal content of the vegetation makes sensor readings unreliable at best."

"Thank you for the advice," Pellaeon said, his voice still frosty. "But they won't be staying long."

"Ah," Karrde nodded, running the possibilities through his mind. There were, fortunately, not all that many of them. "Doing a little hunting, are they?"

Pellaeon favored him with a slightly indulgent smile. "Information on Imperial activities is very expensive. I'd have thought a man in your line of work would know that."

"Indeed," Karrde agreed, watching the other closely. "But occasionally one finds bargains. It's the ysalamiri you're after, isn't it?"

The other's smile froze. "There are no bargains to be had here, Karrde," he said after a moment, his voice very soft. "And *expensive* can also mean *costly*."

"True," Karrde said. "Unless, of course, it's traded for something equally valuable. I presume you're already familiar with the ysalamiri's rather unique characteristics—otherwise, you wouldn't be here. Can I assume you're also familiar with the somewhat esoteric art of safely getting them off their tree branches?"

Pellaeon studied him, suspicion all over his face. "I was under the impression that ysalamiri were no more than fifty centimeters long and not predatory."

"I wasn't referring to *your* safety, Captain," Karrde told him. "I meant theirs. You can't just pull them off their branches, not without killing them. An ysalamir in this stage is sessile—its claws have elongated to the point where they've essentially grown directly into the core of the branch it inhabits."

"And you, I suppose, know the proper way to do it?"

"Some of my people do, yes," Karrde told him. "If you'd like, I could send one of them to rendezvous with your shuttles. The technique involved isn't especially difficult, but it really *does* have to be demonstrated."

"Of course," Pellaeon said, heavily sardonic. "And the fee for this esoteric demonstration . . . ?"

"No fee, Captain. As I said earlier, we're just being neighborly."

Pellaeon cocked his head slightly to one side. "Your generosity will be remembered." For a moment he held Karrde's gaze; and there was no mistaking the twin-edged meaning to the words. If Karrde was planning some sort of betrayal, it too would be remembered. "I'll signal my shuttles to expect your expert."

"He'll be there. Good-bye, Captain."

Pellaeon reached for something off-camera, and once again Ave's face replaced his on the screen. "You get all that?" Karrde asked the other.

Aves nodded. "Dankin and Chin are already warming up one of the Skiprays."

"Good. Have them leave an open transmission; and I'll want to see them as soon as they're back."

"Right." The display clicked off.

Karrde stepped away from the desk, glanced once at Mara, and reseated himself at the table. "Sorry for the interruption," he said conversationally, watching her out of the corner of his eye as he poured himself some more wine.

Slowly, the green eyes came back from infinity; and as she looked at him, the muscles of her face eased from their deathlike rigidity. "You really not going to charge them for this?" she asked, reaching a slightly unsteady hand for her own wine. "They'd certainly make *you* pay if you wanted something. That's about all the Empire really cares about these days, money."

He shrugged. "We get to have our people watching them from the moment they set down to the moment they lift off. That seems an adequate fee to me."

She studied him. "You don't believe they're here just to pick up ysalamiri, do you?"

"Not really." Karrde took a bite of his bruallki. "At least, not unless there's a use for the things that we don't know about. Coming all the way out here to collect ysalamiri is a bit of an overkill to use against a single Jedi."

Mara's eyes again drifted away. "Maybe it's not Skywalker they're after," she murmured. "Maybe they've found some more Jedi."

"Seems unlikely," Karrde said, watching her closely. The emotion in her voice when she'd said Luke Skywalker's name . . . "The Emperor supposedly made a clean sweep of them in the early days of the New Order. Unless," he added as another thought occurred to him, "they've perhaps found Darth Vader."

"Vader died on the Death Star," Mara said. "Along with the Emperor."

"That's the story, certainly—"

"He died there," Mara cut him off, her voice suddenly sharp.

"Of course," Karrde nodded. It had taken him five months of close observation, but he'd finally pinned down the handful of subjects guaranteed to trigger strong responses from the woman. The late Emperor was among them, as was the pre-Endor Empire.

And at the opposite end of the emotional spectrum was Luke Skywalker. "Still," he continued thoughtfully, "if a Grand Admiral thinks he has a good reason to carry ysalamiri aboard his ships, we might do well to follow his lead."

Abruptly, Mara's eyes focused on him again. "What for?" she demanded.

"A simple precaution," Karrde said. "Why so vehement?"

He watched as she fought a brief internal battle. "It seems like a waste of time," she said. "Thrawn's probably just jumping at shadows. Anyway, how are you going to keep ysalamiri alive on a ship without transplanting some trees along with them?"

"I'm sure Thrawn has some ideas as to the mechanics of it," Karrde assured her. "Dankin and Chin will know how to poke around for details."

Her eyes seemed strangely hooded. "Yes," she muttered, her voice conceding defeat. "I'm sure they will."

"And in the meantime," Karrde said, pretending not to notice, "we still have business to discuss. As I recall, you were going to list some improvements you would make in the organization."

"Yes." Mara took another deep breath, closing her eyes . . . and when she opened them again she was back to her usual cool self. "Yes. Well—"

Slowly at first, but with ever-increasing confidence, she launched into a detailed and generally insightful compendium of his group's shortcomings. Karrde listened closely as he ate, wondering again at the hidden talents of this woman. Someday, he promised himself silently, he was going to find a way to dig the details of her

past out from under the cloak of secrecy she'd so carefully shrouded it with. To find out where she'd come
from, and who and what she was.

And to learn exactly what it was Luke Skywalker had
done to make her so desperately hate him.

CHAPTER 4

IT TOOK THE *Chimaera* nearly five days at its Point Four cruising speed to cover the three hundred fifty light-years between Myrkr and Wayland. But that was all right, because it took the engineers nearly that long to come up with a portable frame that would both support and nourish the ysalamiri.

"I'm still not convinced this is really necessary," Pellaeon grumbled, eyeing with distaste the thick curved pipe and the fur-scaled, salamanderlike creature attached to it. The pipe and its attached frame were blasted heavy, and the creature itself didn't smell all that good. "If this Guardian you're expecting was put on Wayland by the Emperor in the first place, then I don't see why we should have any problems with him."

"Call it a precaution, Captain," Thrawn said, settling into the shuttle's copilot seat and fastening his own straps. "It's conceivable we could have trouble convincing him of who we are. Or even that we still serve the

Empire." He sent a casual glance across the displays and nodded to the pilot. "Go."

There was a muffled *clank*, and with a slight jolt the shuttle dropped from the *Chimaera*'s docking bay and started its descent toward the planet surface. "We might have had an easier time convincing him with a squad of stormtroopers along," Pellaeon muttered, watching the repeater display beside his seat.

"We might also have irritated him," Thrawn pointed out. "A Dark Jedi's pride and sensibilities are not to be taken lightly, Captain. Besides—" he looked over his shoulder "—that's what Rukh is for. Any close associate of the Emperor ought to be familiar with the glorious role the Noghri have played over the years."

Pellaeon glanced at the silent nightmare figure seated across the aisle. "You seem certain, sir, that the Guardian will be a Dark Jedi."

"Who else would the Emperor have chosen to protect his personal storehouse?" Thrawn countered. "A legion of stormtroopers, perhaps, equipped with AT-ATs and the kind of advanced weaponry and technology you could detect from orbit with your eyes closed?"

Pellaeon grimaced. That, at least, was something they wouldn't have to worry about. The *Chimaera*'s scanners had picked up nothing beyond bow-and-arrow stage anywhere on Wayland's surface. It wasn't all that much comfort. "I'm just wondering whether the Emperor might have pulled him off Wayland to help against the Rebellion."

Thrawn shrugged. "We'll know soon enough."

The gentle roar of atmospheric friction against the shuttle's hull was growing louder now, and on Pellaeon's repeater display details of the planet's surface were becoming visible. Much of the area directly beneath them appeared to be forest, spotted here and there with large, grassy plains. Ahead, occasionally visible through the haze of clouds, a single mountain rose above the landscape. "Is that Mount Tantiss?" he asked the pilot.

"Yes, sir," the other confirmed. "The city ought to be visible soon."

"Right." Reaching surreptitiously to his right thigh, Pellaeon adjusted his blaster in its holster. Thrawn could be as confident as he liked, both in the ysalamiri and in his own logic. For his part, Pellaeon still wished they had more firepower.

The city nestled against the southwestern base of Mount Tantiss was larger than it had looked from orbit, with many of its squat buildings extending deep under the cover of the surrounding trees. Thrawn had the pilot circle the area twice, and then put down in the center of what appeared to be the main city square, facing a large and impressively regal-looking building.

"Interesting," Thrawn commented, looking out the viewports as he settled his ysalamir backpack onto his shoulders. "There are at least three styles of architecture out there—human plus two different alien species. It's not often you see such diversity in the same planetary region, let alone side by side in the same city. In fact, that palace thing in front of us has itself incorporated elements from all three styles."

"Yes," Pellaeon agreed absently, peering out the viewports himself. At the moment, the buildings were of far less interest to him than the people the life-form sensors said were hiding behind and inside them. "Any idea whether those alien species are hostile toward strangers?"

"Probably," Thrawn said, stepping to the shuttle's exit ramp, where Rukh was already waiting. "Most alien species are. Shall we go?"

The ramp lowered with a hiss of released gases. Gritting his teeth, Pellaeon joined the other two. With Rukh in the lead, they headed down.

No one shot at them as they reached the ground and took a few steps away from the shuttle. Nor did anyone scream, call out, or make any appearance at all. "Shy, aren't they?" Pellaeon murmured, keeping his hand on his blaster as he looked around.

"Understandably," Thrawn said, pulling a megaphone disk from his belt. "Let's see if we can persuade them to be hospitable."

Cupping the disk in his hand, he raised it to his lips. "I seek the Guardian of the mountain," his voice boomed across the square, the last syllable echoing from the surrounding buildings. "Who will take me to him?"

The last echo died away into silence. Thrawn lowered the disk and waited; but the seconds ticked by without any response. "Maybe they don't understand Basic," Pellaeon suggested doubtfully.

"No, they understand," Thrawn said coldly. "The humans do, at any rate. Perhaps they need more motivation." He raised the megaphone again. "I seek the Guardian of the mountain," he repeated. "If no one will take me to him, this entire city will suffer."

The words were barely out of his mouth when, without warning, an arrow flashed toward them from the right. It struck Thrawn in the side, barely missing the ysalamir tube wrapped around his shoulders and back, and bounced harmlessly off the body armor hidden beneath the white uniform. "Hold," Thrawn ordered as Rukh leaped to his side, blaster at the ready. "You have the location?"

"Yes," the Noghri grated, his blaster pointed at a squat two-story structure a quarter of the way around the square from the palace.

"Good." Thrawn raised the megaphone again. "One of your people just shot at us. Observe the consequences." Lowering the disk again, he nodded to Rukh. "Now."

And with a tight grin of his needle teeth, Rukh proceeded—quickly, carefully, and scientifically—to demolish the building.

He took out the windows and doors first, putting perhaps a dozen shots through them to discourage any further attack. Then he switched to the lower-floor walls. By the twentieth shot, the building was visibly trembling on its foundations. A handful of shots into the upper-floor walls, a few more into the lower—

And with a thunderous crash, the building collapsed in on itself.

Thrawn waited until the sound of crunching masonry had died away before raising the megaphone again. "Those are the consequences of defying me," he called. "I ask once more: who will take me to the Guardian of the mountain?"

"I will," a voice said from their left.

Pellaeon spun around. The man standing in front of the palace building was tall and thin, with unkempt gray hair and a beard that reached almost to the middle of his chest. He was dressed in shin-laced sandals and an old brown robe, with a glittering medallion of some sort half hidden behind the beard. His face was dark and lined and regal to the point of arrogance as he studied them, his eyes holding a mixture of curiosity and disdain. "You are strangers," he said, the same mixture in his voice. "Strangers—" he glanced up at the shuttle towering over them "—from offworld."

"Yes, we are," Thrawn acknowledged. "And you?"

The old man's eyes flicked to the smoking rubble Rukh had just created. "You destroyed one of my buildings," he said. "There was no need for that."

"We were attacked," Thrawn told him coolly. "Were you its landlord?"

The stranger's eyes might have flashed; at this distance, Pellaeon couldn't say for certain. "I rule," he said, his voice quiet but with menace beneath it. "All that is here is mine."

For a handful of heartbeats he and Thrawn locked eyes. Thrawn broke the silence first. "I am Grand Admiral Thrawn, Warlord of the Empire, servant of the Emperor. I seek the Guardian of the mountain."

The old man bowed his head slightly. "I will take you to him."

Turning, he started back toward the palace. "Stay close together," Thrawn murmured to the others as he moved to follow. "Be alert for a trap."

No more arrows came as they crossed the square and walked under the carved keystone archway framing the palace's double doors. "I would have thought the Guardian would be living in the mountain," Thrawn said as their guide pulled open the doors. They came easily; the old man, Pellaeon decided, must be stronger than he looked.

"He did, once," the other said over his shoulder. "When I began my rule, the people of Wayland built this for him." He crossed to the center of the ornate foyer room, halfway to another set of double doors, and stopped. "Leave us," he called.

For a split second Pellaeon thought the old man was talking to him. He was just opening his mouth to refuse when two flanking sections of wall swung open and a pair of scrawny men stepped out of hidden guard niches. Glowering silently at the Imperials, they shouldered their crossbows and left the building. The old man waited until they were gone, then continued on to the second set of double doors. "Come," he said, gesturing to the doors, an odd glitter in his eyes. "The Emperor's Guardian awaits you."

Silently, the doors swung open, revealing the light of what looked to be several hundred candles filling a huge room. Pellaeon glanced once at the old man standing beside the doors, a sudden premonition of dread sending a shiver up his back. Taking a deep breath, he followed Thrawn and Rukh inside.

Into a crypt.

There was no doubt as to what it was. Aside from the flickering candles, there was nothing else in the room but a large rectangular block of dark stone in the center.

"I see," Thrawn said quietly. "So he is dead."

"He is dead," the old man confirmed from behind them. "Do you see all the candles, Grand Admiral Thrawn?"

STAR WARS: HEIR TO THE EMPIRE   55

"I see them," Thrawn nodded. "The people must have honored him greatly."

"Honored him?" The old man snorted gently. "Hardly. Those candles mark the graves of offworlders who have come here since his death."

Pellaeon twisted to face him, instinctively drawing his blaster as he did so. Thrawn waited another few heartbeats before slowly turning around himself. "How did they die?" he asked.

The old man smiled faintly. "I killed them, of course. Just as I killed the Guardian." He raised his empty hands in front of him, palms upward. "Just as I now kill you."

Without warning, blue lightning bolts flashed from his fingertips—

And vanished without a trace a meter away from each of them.

It all happened so fast that Pellaeon had no chance to even flinch, let alone fire. Now, belatedly, he raised his blaster, the scalding hot air from the bolts washing over his hand—

"Hold," Thrawn said calmly into the silence. "However, as you can see, Guardian, we are not ordinary offworlders."

"The Guardian is dead!" the old man snapped, the last word almost swallowed up by the crackle of more lightning. Again, the bolts vanished into nothingness before even coming close.

"Yes, the old Guardian is dead," Thrawn agreed, shouting to be heard over the crackling thunder. "You are the Guardian now. It is you who protects the Emperor's mountain."

"I serve no Emperor!" the old man retorted, unleashing a third useless salvo. "My power is for myself alone."

As suddenly as it had started, the attack ceased. The old man stared at Thrawn, his hands still raised, a puzzled and oddly petulant expression on his face. "You are not Jedi. How do you do this?"

"Join us and learn," Thrawn suggested.

The other drew himself up to his full height. "I am a Jedi Master," he ground out. "I join no one."

"I see," Thrawn nodded. "In that case, permit *us* to join *you*." His glowing red eyes bored into the old man's face. "And permit us to show you how you can have more power than you've ever imagined. All the power even a Jedi Master could desire."

For a long moment the old man continued to stare at Thrawn, a dozen strange expressions flicking in quick succession across his face. "Very well," he said at last. "Come. We will talk."

"Thank you," Thrawn said, inclining his head slightly. "May I ask who we have the honor of addressing?"

"Of course." The old man's face was abruptly regal again, and when he spoke his voice rang out in the silence of the crypt. "I am the Jedi Master Joruus C'baoth."

Pellaeon inhaled sharply, a cold shiver running up his back. "Jorus C'baoth?" he breathed. "But—"

He broke off. C'baoth looked at him, much as Pellaeon himself might look at a junior officer who has spoken out of turn. "Come," he repeated, turning back to Thrawn. "We will talk."

He led the way out of the crypt and back into the sunshine. Several small knots of people had gathered in the square in their absence, huddling well back from both the crypt and the shuttle as they whispered nervously together.

With one exception. Standing directly in their path a few meters away was one of the two guards C'baoth had ordered out of the crypt. On his face was an expression of barely controlled fury; in his hands, cocked and ready, was his crossbow. "You destroyed his home," C'baoth said, almost conversationally. "Doubtless he would like to exact vengeance."

The words were barely out of his mouth when the guard suddenly snapped the crossbow up and fired. Instinctively, Pellaeon ducked, raising his blaster—

And three meters from the Imperials the bolt came to an abrupt halt in midair.

Pellaeon stared at the hovering piece of wood and metal, his brain only slowly catching up with what had just happened. "They are our guests," C'baoth told the guard in a voice clearly intended to reach everyone in the square. "They will be treated accordingly."

With a crackle of splintering wood, the crossbow bolt shattered, the pieces dropping to the ground. Slowly, reluctantly, the guard lowered his crossbow, his eyes still burning with a now impotent rage. Thrawn let him stand there another second like that, then gestured to Rukh. The Noghri raised his blaster and fired—

And in a blur of motion almost too fast to see, a flat stone detached itself from the ground and hurled itself directly into the path of the shot, shattering spectacularly as the blast hit it.

Thrawn spun to face C'baoth, his face a mirror of surprise and anger. "C'baoth—!"

"These are *my* people, Grand Admiral Thrawn," the

other cut him off, his voice forged from quiet steel. "Not yours; mine. If there is punishment to be dealt out, *I* will do it."

For a long moment the two men again locked eyes. Then, with an obvious effort, Thrawn regained his composure. "Of course, Master C'baoth," he said. "Forgive me."

C'baoth nodded. "Better. Much better." He looked past Thrawn, dismissed the guard with a nod. "Come," he said, looking back at the Grand Admiral. "We will talk."

"You will now tell me," C'baoth said, gesturing them to low cushions, "how it was you defeated my attack."

"Let me first explain our offer," Thrawn said, throwing a casual glance around the room before easing carefully down on one of the cushions. Probably, Pellaeon thought, the Grand Admiral was examining the bits of artwork scattered around. "I believe you'll find it—"

"You will now tell me how it was you defeated my attack," C'baoth repeated.

A slight grimace, quickly suppressed, touched Thrawn's lips. "It's quite simple, actually." He looked up at the ysalamir wrapped around his shoulders, reaching a finger over to gently stroke its long neck. "These creatures you see on our backs are called ysalamiri. They're sessile tree-dwelling creatures from a distant, third-rate planet, and they have an interesting and possibly unique ability—they push back the Force."

C'baoth frowned. "What do you mean, push it back?"

"They push its presence out away from themselves,"

Thrawn explained. "Much the same way a bubble is created by air pushing outward against water. A single ysalamir can occasionally create a bubble as large as ten meters across; a whole group of them reinforcing one another can create much larger ones."

"I've never heard of such a thing," C'baoth said, staring at Thrawn's ysalamir with an almost childlike intensity. "How could such a creature have come about?"

"I really don't know," Thrawn conceded. "I assume the talent has some survival value, but what that would be I can't imagine." He cocked an eyebrow. "Not that it matters. For the moment, the ability itself is sufficient for my purpose."

C'baoth's face darkened. "That purpose being to defeat my power?"

Thrawn shrugged. "We were expecting to find the Emperor's Guardian here. I needed to make certain he would allow us to identify ourselves and explain our mission." He reached up again to stroke the ysalamir's neck. "Though as it happens, protecting us from the Guardian was really only an extra bonus. I have something far more interesting in mind for our little pets."

"That being . . . ?"

Thrawn smiled. "All in good time, Master C'baoth. *And* only after we've had a chance to examine the Emperor's storehouse in Mount Tantiss."

C'baoth's lip twisted. "So the mountain is all you really want."

"I need the mountain, certainly," Thrawn acknowledged. "Or rather, what I hope to find within it."

"And that is . . . ?"

Thrawn studied him for a moment. "There were rumors, just before the Battle of Endor, that the Emperor's researchers had finally developed a genuinely practical cloaking shield. I want it. Also," he added, almost as an afterthought, "another small—almost trivial—bit of technology."

"And you think to find one of these cloaking shields in the mountain?"

"I expect to find either a working model or at least a complete set of schematics," Thrawn said. "One of the Emperors purposes in setting up this storehouse was to make sure that interesting and potentially useful technology didn't get lost."

"That, and collecting endless mementos of his glorious conquests." C'baoth snorted. "There are rooms and rooms of that sort of cackling self-congratulation."

Pellaeon sat up a bit straighter. "You've been inside the mountain?" he asked. Somehow, he'd expected the storehouse to be sealed with all sorts of locks and barriers.

C'baoth sent him a scornfully patient look. "Of course I've been inside. I killed the Guardian, remember?" He looked back at Thrawn. "So. You want the Emperor's little toys; and now you know you can just walk into the mountain, with or without my help. Why are you still sitting here?"

"Because the mountain is only part of what I need," Thrawn told him. "I also require the partnership of a Jedi Master like yourself."

C'baoth settled back into his cushion, a cynical smile showing through his beard. "Ah, we finally get down to it. This, I take it, is where you offer me all the power even a Jedi Master could desire?"

Thrawn smiled back. "It is indeed. Tell me, Master C'baoth: are you familiar with the Imperial Fleet's disastrous defeat at the Battle of Endor five years ago?"

"I've heard rumors. One of the offworlders who came here spoke about it." C'baoth's gaze drifted to the window, to the palace/crypt visible across the square. "Though only briefly."

Pellaeon swallowed. Thrawn himself didn't seem to notice the implication. "Then you must have wondered how a few dozen Rebel ships could possibly rout an Imperial force that outgunned it by at least ten to one."

"I didn't spend much time with such wonderings," C'baoth said dryly. "I assumed that the Rebels were simply better warriors."

"In a sense, that's true," Thrawn agreed. "The Rebels did indeed fight better, but not because of any special abilities or training. They fought better than the Fleet because the Emperor was dead."

He turned to look at Pellaeon. "You were there, Captain—you must have noticed it. The sudden loss of coordination between crew members and ships; the loss of efficiency and discipline. The loss, in short, of that elusive quality we call fighting spirit."

"There was some confusion, yes," Pellaeon said stiffly. He was starting to see where Thrawn was going with this, and he didn't like it a bit. "But nothing that can't be explained by the normal stresses of battle."

One blue-black eyebrow went up, just slightly. "Really? The loss of the *Executor*—the sudden, last-minute TIE fighter incompetence that brought about the destruction of the Death Star itself—the loss of six other Star Destroyers in engagements that none of them should have had trouble with? *All* of that nothing but normal battle stress?"

"The Emperor was not directing the battle," Pellaeon snapped with a fire that startled him. "Not in any way. I was there, Admiral—*I* know."

"Yes, Captain, you were there," Thrawn said, his voice abruptly hard. "And it's time you gave up your blindfold and faced the truth, no matter how bitter you find it. You had no real fighting spirit of your own anymore—none of you in the Imperial Fleet did. It was the Emperor's will that drove you; the Emperor's mind that provided you with strength and resolve and efficiency. You were as dependent on that presence as if you were all borg-implanted into a combat computer."

"That's not true," Pellaeon shot back, stomach twisting painfully within him. "It can't be. We fought on after his death."

"Yes," Thrawn said, his voice quiet and contemptuous. "You fought on. Like cadets."

C'baoth snorted. "So is *this* what you want me for, Grand Admiral Thrawn?" he asked scornfully. "To turn your ships into puppets for you?"

"Not at all, Master C'baoth," Thrawn told him, his voice perfectly calm again. "My analogy with combat borg implants was a carefully considered one. The Emperor's fatal error was in seeking to control the entire Imperial Fleet personally, as completely and constantly as possible. That, over the long run, is what did the damage. My wish is merely to have you enhance the coordination between ships and task forces—and then only at critical times and in carefully selected combat situations."

C'baoth threw a look at Pellaeon. "To what end?" he rumbled.

"To the end we've already discussed," Thrawn said. "Power."

"What sort of power?"

For the first time since landing, Thrawn seemed taken aback. "The conquering of worlds, of course. The final defeat of the Rebellion. The reestablishment of the glory that was once the Empire's New Order."

C'baoth shook his head. "You don't understand power, Grand Admiral Thrawn. Conquering worlds you'll never even visit again isn't power. Neither is destroying ships and people and rebellions you haven't looked at face-to-face." He waved his hands in a sweeping gesture around him, his eyes glittering with an eerie fire. "*This*, Grand Admiral Thrawn, is power. This city— this planet—these people. Every human, Psa-dan, and Myneyrsh who live here are mine. *Mine*." His gaze drifted to the window again. "I teach them. I command them. I punish them. Their lives, and their deaths, are in *my* hand."

"Which is precisely what I offer you," Thrawn said. "Millions of lives—billions, if you wish. All those lives to do with as you please."

"It isn't the same," C'baoth said, a note of paternal patience in his voice. "I have no desire to hold distant power over faceless lives."

"You could have just a single city to rule, then," Thrawn persisted. "As large or as small as you wish."

"I rule a city now."

Thrawns eyes narrowed. "I need your assistance, Master C'baoth. Name your price."

C'baoth smiled. "My price? The price for my service?" Abruptly, the smile vanished. "I'm a Jedi Master, Grand Admiral Thrawn," he said, his voice simmering with menace. "Not a mercenary for hire like your Noghri."

He threw a contemptuous look at Rukh, sitting silently off to one side. "Oh, yes, Noghri—I know what you and your people are. The Emperor's private Death Commandos; killing and dying at the whim of ambitious men like Darth Vader and the Grand Admiral here."

"Lord Vader served the Emperor and the Empire," Rukh grated, his dark eyes staring unblinkingly at C'baoth. "As do we."

"Perhaps." C'baoth turned back to Thrawn. "I have all I want or need, Grand Admiral Thrawn. You will leave Wayland now."

Thrawn didn't move. "I need your assistance, Master C'baoth," he repeated quietly. "And I will have it."

"Or you'll do what?" C'baoth sneered. "Have your Noghri try to kill me? It would almost be amusing to watch." He looked at Pellaeon. "Or perhaps you'll have your brave Star Destroyer captain try to level my city from orbit. Except that you can't risk damaging the mountain, can you?"

"My gunners could destroy this city without even singeing the grass on Mount Tantiss," Pellaeon retorted. "If you need a demonstration—"

"Peace, Captain," Thrawn cut him off calmly. "So it's the personal, face-to-face sort of power you prefer, Master C'baoth? Yes, I can certainly understand that. Not that there can be much challenge left in it—not anymore. Of course," he added reflectively, glancing out the window, "that may be the whole idea. I expect that even Jedi Masters eventually get too old to be interested in anything except to sit out in the sun."

C'baoth's forehead darkened. "Have a care, Grand Admiral Thrawn," he warned. "Or perhaps I'll seek challenge in your destruction."

"That would hardly be a challenge for a man of your skill and power," Thrawn countered with a shrug. "But then, you probably already have other Jedi here under your command."

C'baoth frowned, obviously thrown by the sudden change in subject. "Other Jedi?" he echoed.

"Of course. Surely it's only fitting that a Jedi Master have lesser Jedi serving beneath him. Jedi whom he may teach and command and punish at will."

Something like a shadow crossed C'baoth's face. "There are no Jedi left," he murmured. "The Emperor and Vader hunted them down and destroyed them."

"Not all of them," Thrawn told him softly. "Two new Jedi have arisen in the past five years: Luke Skywalker and his sister, Leia Organa Solo."

"And what is that to me?"

"I can deliver them to you."

For a long minute C'baoth stared at him, disbelief and desire struggling for supremacy on his face. The desire won. "Both of them?"

"Both of them," Thrawn nodded. "Consider what a man of your skill could do with brand-new Jedi. Mold them, change them, re-create them in any image you chose." He cocked an eyebrow. "And with them would come a very special bonus . . . because Leia Organa Solo is pregnant. With twins."

C'baoth inhaled sharply. "*Jedi* twins?" he hissed.

"They have the potential, or so my sources tell me." Thrawn smiled. "Of course, what they ultimately became would be entirely up to you."

C'baoth's eyes darted to Pellaeon; back to Thrawn. Slowly, deliberately, he stood up. "Very well, Grand Admiral Thrawn," he said. "In return for the Jedi, I will assist your forces. Take me to your ship."

"In time, Master C'baoth," Thrawn said, getting to his feet himself. "First we must go into the Emperor's mountain. This bargain is dependent on whether I find what I'm looking for there."

"Of course." C'baoth's eyes flashed. "Let us both hope," he said warningly, "that you do."

It took seven hours of searching, through a mountain fortress much larger than Pellaeon had expected. But in the end, they did indeed find the treasures Thrawn had hoped for. The cloaking shield . . . and that other small, almost trivial, bit of technology.

THE DOOR TO the Grand Admiral's command room slid open; settling himself, Pellaeon stepped inside. "A word with you, Admiral?"

"Certainly, Captain," Thrawn said from his seat in the center of the double display circle. "Come in. Has there been any update from the Imperial Palace?"

"No, sir, not since yesterday's," Pellaeon said as he walked to the edge of the outer circle, silently rehearsing one last time how he was going to say this, "I can request one, if you'd like."

"Probably unnecessary," Thrawn shook his head. "It

looks like the details of the Bimmisaari trip have been more or less settled. All we have to do is alert one of the commando groups—Team Eight, I think—and we'll have our Jedi."

"Yes, sir." Pellaeon braced himself. "Admiral . . . I have to tell you that I'm not convinced dealing with C'baoth is a good idea. To be perfectly honest, I don't think he's entirely sane."

Thrawn cocked an eyebrow. "Of course he's not sane. But then, he's not Jorus C'baoth, either."

Pellaeon felt his mouth fall open. "What?"

"Jorus C'baoth is dead," Thrawn said. "He was one of the six Jedi Masters aboard the Old Republic's Outbound Flight project. I don't know if you were highly enough placed back then to have known about it."

"I heard rumors," Pellaeon frowned, thinking back. "Some sort of grand effort to extend the Old Republic's authority outside the galaxy, as I recall, launched just before the Clone Wars broke out. I never heard anything more about it."

"That's because there wasn't anything more to be heard," Thrawn said evenly. "It was intercepted by a task force outside Old Republic space and destroyed."

Pellaeon stared at him, a shiver running up his back. "How do you know?"

Thrawn raised his eyebrows. "Because I was the force's commander. Even at that early date the Emperor recognized that the Jedi had to be exterminated. Six Jedi Masters aboard the same ship was too good an opportunity to pass up."

Pellaeon licked his lips. "But then . . . ?"

"Who is it we've brought aboard the *Chimaera*?"

Thrawn finished the question for him. "I should have thought that obvious. Joruus C'baoth—note the telltale mispronunciation of the name *Jorus*—is a clone."

Pellaeon stared at him. "A *clone*?"

"Certainly," Thrawn said. "Created from a tissue sample, probably sometime just before the real C'baoth's death."

"Early in the war, in other words," Pellaeon said, swallowing hard. The early clones—or at least those the fleet had faced—had been highly unstable, both mentally and emotionally. Sometimes spectacularly so . . . "And you deliberately brought this thing aboard my ship?" he demanded.

"Would you rather we have brought back a full-fledged Dark Jedi?" Thrawn asked coldly. "A second Darth Vader, perhaps, with the sort of ambitions and power that might easily lead him to take over your ship? Count your blessings, Captain."

"At least a Dark Jedi would have been predictable," Pellaeon countered.

"C'baoth is predictable enough," Thrawn assured him. "And for those times when he isn't—" He waved a hand at the half dozen frameworks encircling his command center. "That's what the ysalamiri are for."

Pellaeon grimaced. "I still don't like it, Admiral. We can hardly protect the ship from him while at the same time having him coordinate the fleet's attacks."

"There's a degree of risk involved," Thrawn agreed. "But risk has always been an inescapable part of warfare. In this case, the potential benefits far outweigh the potential dangers."

Reluctantly, Pellaeon nodded. He didn't like it—was

fairly certain he would never like it—but it was clear that Thrawn had made up his mind. "Yes, sir," he muttered. "You mentioned a message to Team Eight. Will you be wanting me to transmit that?"

"No, I'll handle it myself." Thrawn smiled sardonically. "Their glorious leader, and all that—you know how Noghri are. If there's nothing more . . . ?"

It was, clearly, a dismissal. "No, sir," Pellaeon said. "I'll be on the bridge if you require me." He turned to go.

"It will bring us victory, Captain," the Grand Admiral called softly after him. "Quiet your fears, and concentrate on that."

If it doesn't kill us all. "Yes, sir," Pellaeon said aloud, and left the room.

CHAPTER 5

H AN FINISHED HIS report, sat back, and waited for the criticism to start.

It was a very short wait. "So once again your smuggler friends refuse to commit themselves," Admiral Ackbar said, sounding more than a little disgusted. His high-domed head bobbed twice in some indecipherable Calamarian gesture, his huge eyes blinking in time with the head movements. "You'll recall that I disagreed with this idea all along," he added, waving a webbed hand toward Han's report case.

Han glanced across the table at Leia. "It's not a matter of commitment, Admiral," he told the other. "It's a matter that most of them just don't see any real gain in switching from their current activities to straight shipping."

"Or else it's a lack of trust," a melodic alien voice put in. "Could that be it?"

Han grimaced before he could stop himself. "It's possible," he said, forcing himself to look at Borsk Fey'lya.

"Possible?" Fey'lya's violet eyes widened, the fine cream-colored fur covering his body rippling slightly with the motion. It was a Bothan gesture of polite surprise, one which Fey'lya seemed to use a lot. "You said *possible*, Captain Solo?"

Han sighed quietly and gave up. Fey'lya would only maneuver him into saying it some other way if he didn't. "Some of the groups I've talked to don't trust us," he conceded. "They think the offer might be some sort of trap to bring them out into the open."

"Because of me, of course," Ackbar growled, his normal salmon color turning a little darker. "Haven't you tired of retaking this same territory, Councilor Fey'lya?"

Fey'lya's eyes widened again, and for a moment he gazed silently at Ackbar as the tension around the table quickly rose to the level of thick paste. They had never liked each other, Han knew, not from the day Fey'lya had first brought his sizable faction of the Bothan race into the Alliance after the Battle of Yavin. Right from the start Fey'lya had been jockeying for position and power, cutting deals wherever and whenever he could and making it abundantly clear that he expected to be given a high position in the fledgling political system Mon Mothma was putting together. Ackbar had considered such ambitions to be a dangerous waste of time and effort, particularly given the bleak situation the Alliance was facing at the time, and with typical bluntness had made no effort to conceal that opinion.

Given Ackbar's reputation and subsequent successes,

Han had little doubt that Fey'lya would ultimately have been shunted off to some relatively unimportant government post in the New Republic . . . if it hadn't happened that the spies who discovered the existence and location of the Emperor's new Death Star had been a group of Fey'lya's Bothans.

Preoccupied at the time with more urgent matters, Han had never learned the details of how Fey'lya had managed to parlay that serendipity into his current position on the Council. And to be perfectly honest, he wasn't sure he wanted to.

"I merely seek to clarify the situation in my own mind, Admiral," Fey'lya said at last into the heavy silence. "It's hardly worthwhile for us to continue sending a valuable man like Captain Solo out on these contact missions if each is predoomed to failure."

"They're *not* predoomed to failure," Han cut in. Out of the corner of his eye he saw Leia give him a warning look. He ignored it. "The kind of smugglers we're looking for are conservative businesspeople—they don't just jump into something new without thinking it through first. They'll come around."

Fey'lya shrugged, his fur again rippling. "And meanwhile, we expend a great deal of time and effort with nothing to show for it."

"Look, you can't build up any—"

A gentle, almost diffident tap of a hammer from the head of the table cut off the argument. "What the smugglers are waiting for," Mon Mothma said quietly, her stern gaze touching each of the others at the table in turn, "is the same thing the rest of the galaxy is waiting for: the formal reestablishment of the principals and law of the Old Republic. *That* is our first and primary task, Councilors. To become the New Republic in fact as well as in name."

Han caught Leia's eye, and this time he was the one who sent out the warning look. She grimaced, but nodded slightly and kept quiet.

Mon Mothma let the silence linger a moment longer, again sending her gaze around the table. Han found himself studying her, noting the deepening lines in her face, the streaks of gray in her dark hair, the thinness rather than slenderness of her neck. She'd aged a lot since he'd first met her, back when the Alliance was trying to find a way out from under the shadow of the Empire's second Death Star. Ever since then, Mon Mothma had been right in the middle of this horrendous task of setting up a viable government, and the strain had clearly told on her.

But despite what the years were doing to her face, her eyes still held the same quiet fire they'd possessed then— the same fire, or so the stories went, that had been there since her historic break with the Emperor's New Order and her founding of the Rebel Alliance. She was tough, and smart, and fully in control. And everyone present knew it.

Her eyes finished their sweep and came to rest on Han. "Captain Solo, we thank you for your report; and, too, for your efforts. And with the Captains report, this meeting is adjourned."

She tapped the hammer again and stood up. Han closed his report case and worked his way through the

general confusion around to the other side of the table.
"So," he said quietly, coming up behind Leia as she collected her own things. "Are we out of here?"

"The sooner the better," she muttered back. "I just
have to give these things to Winter."

Han glanced around and lowered his voice a notch. "I
take it things were going a little rough before they called
me in?"

"No more than usual," she told him. "Fey'lya and
Ackbar had one of their polite little dogfights, this one
over the fiasco at Obroa-skai—that lost Elomin force—
with some more of Fey'lya's veiled suggestions that the
job of Commander in Chief is too much for Ackbar to
handle. And then, of course, Mon Mothma—"

"A word with you, Leia?" Mon Mothma's voice came
from over Han's shoulder.

Han turned to face her, sensing Leia tense a little beside him as she did likewise. "Yes?"

"I forgot to ask you earlier if you'd talked to Luke
about going with you to Bimmisaari," Mon Mothma
said. "Did he agree?"

"Yes," Leia nodded, throwing an apologetic look at
Han. "I'm sorry, Han; I didn't get a chance to tell you.
The Bimms sent a message yesterday asking that Luke be
there with me for the talks."

"They did, huh?" A year ago, Han reflected, he would
probably have been furious at having a painstakingly
crafted schedule flipped at the last minute like this. Leia's
diplomatic patience must be starting to rub off on him.

Either that, or he was just getting soft. "They give any
reasons?"

"The Bimms are rather hero-oriented," Mon Mothma

said before Leia could answer, her eyes searching Han's face. Probably trying to figure out just how mad he was about the change in plans. "And Luke's part in the Battle of Endor *is* rather well known."

"Yeah, I'd heard that," Han said, trying not to be too sarcastic. He had no particular quarrel with Luke's position in the New Republics pantheon of heroes—the kid had certainly earned it. But if having Jedi around to brag about was so important to Mon Mothma, then she ought to be letting Leia get on with her own studies instead of foisting all this extra diplomatic work on her. As it was, he would bet on an ambitious snail to make full Jedi before she did.

Leia found his hand, squeezed it. He squeezed back, to show that he wasn't mad. Though she probably already knew that. "We'd better get going," she told Mon Mothma, using her grip on Han's hand to start steering him away from the table. "We still have to collect our droids before we leave."

"Have a good trip," Mon Mothma said gravely. "And good luck."

"The droids are already on the *Falcon*," Han told Leia as they wove their way around the various conversations that had sprung up between the Councilors and staff members. "Chewie got them aboard while I came here."

"I know," Leia murmured.

"Right," Han said, and left it at that.

She squeezed his hand again. "It'll be all right, Han. You, me, and Luke together again—it'll be just like old times."

"Sure," Han said. Sitting around with a group of

half-furred, half-size aliens, listening to Threepio's precise voice all day as he translated back and forth, trying to penetrate yet another alien psychology to figure out what exactly it would take to get them to join the New Republic—"Sure," he repeated with a sigh, "just exactly like old times."

CHAPTER 6

THE WAVING ALIEN trees shied back like some sort of huge tentacles from the landing area, and with the barest of bumps Han set the *Millennium Falcon* down on the uneven ground. "Well, here we are," he announced to no one in particular. "Bimmisaari. Fur and moving plants a specialty."

"None of that," Leia warned him, unstrapping from the seat behind him and running through the Jedi relaxation techniques Luke had taught her. Political dealings with people she knew were relatively easy for her. Diplomatic missions with unfamiliar alien races were something else entirely.

"You'll do fine," Luke said from beside her, reaching over to squeeze her arm.

Han half turned. "I wish you two wouldn't do that," he complained. "It's like listening to half a conversation."

"Sorry," Luke apologized, climbing out of his seat and stooping to peer out the *Falcon*'s nose window, "Looks like our reception committee coming. I'll go get Threepio ready."

"We'll be there in a minute," Leia called after him. "You ready, Han?"

"Yeah," Han told her, adjusting his blaster in its holster. "Last chance to change your mind, Chewie."

Leia strained her ears as Chewbacca growled out a curt reply. Even after all these years she still couldn't understand him nearly as well as Han could—some subtle level of harmonics in the Wookiee's voice, apparently, that she had trouble picking up.

But if some of the words were less than distinct, the overall meaning came through crystal clear. "Oh, come on," Han urged. "You've been fawned over before— remember that big awards thing back at the Yavin base? I didn't hear you complaining *then*."

"It's all right, Han," Leia put in over Chewbacca's response. "If he wants to stay aboard with Artoo and work on the stabilizers, that's fine. The Bimms won't be offended."

Han looked out the nose window at the approaching delegation. "I wasn't worried about offending them," he muttered. "I just thought it'd be nice to have a little extra backup along. Just in case."

Leia smiled and patted his arm. "The Bimms are very friendly people," she assured him. "There won't be any trouble."

"I've heard *that* before," Han said dryly, pulling a comlink from a small storage compartment beside his seat. He started to clip it to his belt; changed direction in midmotion and fastened it to his collar instead.

"Looks good there," Leia said. "Are you going to put your old general's insignia on your belt now?"

He made a face at her. "Very funny. With the comlink here, all I have to do is casually switch it on and I'll be able to talk to Chewie without being obvious about it."

"Ah," Leia nodded. It *was* a good idea, at that. "Sounds like you've been spending too much time with Lieutenant Page and his commandos."

"I've been spending too much time sitting in on Council meetings," he countered, sliding out of his seat and standing up. "After four years of watching political infighting, you learn the occasional value of subtlety. Come on, Chewie—we'll need you to lock up behind us."

Luke and Threepio were waiting when they got to the hatchway. "Ready?" Luke asked.

"Ready," Leia said, taking a deep breath. With a hiss of released airseal the hatchway opened, and together they walked down the ramp to where the yellow-clad, half-furred creatures waited.

The arrival ceremony was short and, for the most part, unintelligible, though Threepio did his best to keep up a running translation of the five-part harmony the whole thing seemed to have been written in. The song/welcome ended and two of the Bimms stepped forward, one of them continuing the melody while the other held up a small electronic device. "He offers greetings to Distinguished Visitor Councilor Leia Organa Solo," Threepio said, "and hopes your discussions with the Law

Elders will be fruitful. He also requests that Captain Solo return his weapon to the ship."

The droid said it so matter-of-factly that it took a second for the words to penetrate. "What was that last?" Leia asked.

"Captain Solo must leave his weapon aboard the ship," Threepio repeated. "Weapons of violence are not permitted within the city. There are no exceptions."

"Terrific," Han murmured into her ear. "You didn't tell me this one was coming."

"I didn't *know* this one was coming," Leia countered quietly, giving the two Bimms a reassuring smile. "Doesn't look like we've got any choice."

"Diplomacy," Han growled, making a curse out of the word. Unfastening his gun belt, he wrapped it carefully around the holstered blaster and set the package up inside the hatchway. "Happy?"

"Aren't I always?" Leia nodded to Threepio. "Tell them we're ready."

The droid translated. Stepping aside, the two Bimms gestured back the way they'd come.

They were perhaps twenty meters from the *Falcon*, with the sounds of Chewbacca sealing the hatchway coming from behind them, when something abruptly occurred to Leia. "Luke?" she murmured.

"Yes, I know," he murmured back. "Maybe they figure it's just part of the proper Jedi's outfit."

"Or else their weapons detector doesn't read lightsabers," Han put in quietly from Leia's other side. "Either way, what they don't know won't hurt them."

"I hope so," Leia said, forcing down her reflexive diplomatic misgivings. After all, if the Bimms themselves hadn't objected to it . . . "Good skies, would you look at that crowd?"

They were waiting where the path exited the trees—hundreds of Bimms, standing perhaps twenty deep on both sides of the way, all clothed in the same tooled yellow. The official reception committee shifted to single file and started down the gauntlet without giving the crowd a second glance; bracing herself, Leia followed.

It was a little strange, but not nearly as uncomfortable as she'd feared it would be. Each Bimm reached out a hand as she passed, touching her with a feathery lightness on shoulder or head or arm or back. It was all done in complete silence, and complete order, with the aura of perfect civilization about it.

Still, she was glad that Chewbacca had decided not to come. He hated—rather violently—being pawed by strangers.

They passed through the crowd, and the Bimm walking nearest Leia sang something. "He says the Tower of Law is just ahead," Threepio translated. "It's the location of their planetary council."

Leia peered over the heads of the leading Bimms. There, obviously, was the Tower of Law. And next to it . . . "Threepio, ask what that thing is beside it," she instructed the droid. "That building that looks like a three-level dome with the sides and most of the roof cut away."

The droid sang, and the Bimm replied. "It's the city's main marketplace," Threepio told her. "He says they prefer the open air whenever possible."

"That roof probably stretches to cover more of the dome framework when the weather's bad," Han added from behind her. "I've seen that design in a few other places."

"He says that perhaps you can be given a tour of the facility before you leave," Threepio added.

"Sounds great," Han said. "Wonderful place to pick up souvenirs."

"Quiet," Leia warned. "Or you can wait in the *Falcon* with Chewie."

The Bimmisaari Tower of Law was fairly modest, as planetary council meeting places went, topping the three-level marketplace beside it by only a couple of floors. Inside, they were led to a large room on the ground floor where, framed by huge tapestries covering the walls, another group of Bimms waited. Three of them stood and sang as Leia entered.

"They add their greetings to those given you at the landing area, Princess Leia," Threepio translated. "They apologize, however, for the fact that the talks will not be able to begin quite yet. It appears that their chief negotiator became ill just moments ago."

"Oh," Leia said, taken slightly aback. "Please express our sympathies, and ask if there's anything we can do to help."

"They thank you," Threepio said after another exchange of songs. "But they assure you that will not be necessary. There is no danger to him, merely inconvenience." The droid hesitated. "I really don't think you should inquire further, Your Highness," he added, a bit delicately. "The complaint appears to be of a rather personal nature."

"I understand," Leia said gravely, suppressing a smile at the prim tone of the droid's voice. "Well, in that case,

I suppose we might as well return to the *Falcon* until he feels ready to continue."

The droid translated, and one of their escort stepped forward and sang something in reply. "He offers an alternative, Your Highness: that he would be eager to conduct you on a tour of the marketplace while you wait."

Leia glanced at Han and Luke. "Any objections?"

The Bimm sang something else. "He further suggests that Master Luke and Captain Solo might find something to interest them in the Tower's upper chambers," Threepio said. "Apparently, there are relics there dating from the middle era of the Old Republic."

A quiet alarm went off in the back of Leia's mind. Were the Bimms trying to split them up? "Luke and Han might like the market, too," she said cautiously.

There was another exchange of arias. "He says they would find it excessively dull," Threepio told her. "Frankly, if it's anything like marketplaces I've seen—"

"I like marketplaces," Han cut him off brusquely, his voice dark with suspicion. "I like 'em a lot."

Leia looked at her brother. "What do you think?"

Luke's eyes swept the Bimms; measuring them, she knew, with all of his Jedi insight. "I don't see what danger they could be," he said slowly. "I don't sense any real duplicity in them. Nothing beyond that of normal politics, anyway."

Leia nodded, her tension easing a little. Normal politics—yes, that was probably all it was. The Bimm probably just wanted the chance to privately bend her ear on behalf of his particular viewpoint before the talks got started in earnest. "In that case," she said, inclining her head to the Bimm, "we accept."

———

"THE MARKETPLACE HAS been in this same spot for over two hundred years," Threepio translated as Han and Leia followed their host up the gentle ramp between the second and third levels of the open dome structure. "Though not in this exact form, of course. The Tower of Law, in fact, was built here precisely because it was already a common crossroads."

"Hasn't changed much, has it?" Han commented, pressing close to Leia to keep them from getting run down by a particularly determined batch of shoppers. He'd seen a lot of marketplaces on a lot of different planets, but seldom one so crowded.

Crowded with more than just locals, too. Scattered throughout the sea of yellow-clad Bimms—*don't they ever wear any other color?*—he could see several other humans, a pair of Baradas, an Ishi Tib, a group of Yuzzumi, and something that looked vaguely like a Paonnid.

"You can see why this place is worth getting into the New Republic," Leia murmured to him.

"I guess so," Han conceded, stepping to one of the booths and looking at the metalware displayed there. The owner/operator sang something toward him, gesturing to a set of carving knives. "No, thanks," Han told him, moving back. The Bimm continued to jabber at him, his gestures becoming sharper—"Threepio, will you have our host tell him that we're not interested?" he called to the droid.

There was no response. "Threepio?" he repeated, looking around.

Threepio was staring off into the crowd. "Hey, Gold-enrod," he snapped. "I'm talking to you."

Threepio spun back. "I'm terribly sorry, Captain Solo," he apologized. "But our host seems to have disappeared."

"What do you mean, disappeared?" Han demanded, looking around. Their particular Bimm, he remembered, had worn a set of shiny pins on his shoulders.

Pins that were nowhere to be seen. "How could he just disappear?"

Beside him, Leia gripped his hand. "I've got a bad feeling about this," she said tightly. "Let's get back to the Tower."

"Yeah," Han agreed. "Come on, Threepio. Don't get lost." Shifting his grip on Leia's hand, he turned—

And froze. A few meters away, islands in the churning sea of yellow, three aliens stood facing them. Short aliens, not much taller than the Bimms, with steel-gray skin, large dark eyes, and protruding jaws.

And, held ready in their hands, stokhli sticks.

"We've got trouble," he murmured to Leia, turning his head slowly to look around, hoping desperately that those three were all there were.

They weren't. There were at least eight more, arrayed in a rough circle ten meters across. A circle with Han, Leia, and Threepio at its center.

"Han!" Leia said urgently.

"I see them," he muttered. "We're in trouble, sweet-heart."

He sensed her glance behind them. "Who are they?" she breathed.

"I don't know—never seen anything like them before. But they're not kidding around. Those things are called stokhli sticks—shoot a spraynet mist two hundred meters, with enough shockstun juice to take down a good-sized Gundark." Abruptly, Han noticed that he and Leia had moved, instinctively backing away from the nearest part of the aliens' circle. He glanced over his shoulder—"They're herding us toward the down ramp," he told her. "Must be trying to take us without stirring up the crowd."

"We're doomed," Threepio moaned.

Leia gripped Han's hand. "What are we going to do?"

"Let's see how closely they're paying attention." Trying to watch all the aliens at once, Han casually reached his free hand toward the comlink attached to his collar.

The nearest alien lifted his stokhli stick warningly. Han froze, slowly lowered the hand again. "So much for that idea," he muttered. "I think it's time to pull in the welcome mat. Better give Luke a shout."

"He can't help us."

Han glanced down at her; at her glazed eyes and pinched face. "Why not?" he demanded, stomach tightening.

She sighed, just audibly. "They've got him, too."

CHAPTER 7

I T WAS MORE a feeling than anything approaching an actual word, but it echoed through Luke's mind as clearly
as if he'd heard it shouted.

Help!

He spun around, the ancient tapestry he'd been studying forgotten as his Jedi senses flared into combat readiness. Around him, the large top-floor Tower room was as
it had been a minute earlier: deserted except for a handful of Bimms strolling among the huge wall tapestries
and relic cases. No danger here, at least nothing immediate. *What is it?* he sent back, starting for the next room
and the staircase leading down.

He caught a quick vision from Leia's mind, a picture
of alien figures and a vivid impression of a contracting
noose. *Hang on*, he told her. *I'm coming*. All but running
now, he ducked through the doorway to the staircase
room, grabbing the jamb to help with his turn—

And braked to an abrupt halt. Standing between him

and the stairway was a loose semicircle of seven silent gray figures.

Luke froze, his hand still uselessly gripping the door-jamb, half a galaxy away from the lightsaber on his belt. He had no idea what the sticks were his assailants were pointing at him, but he had no desire to find out the hard way. Not unless he absolutely had to. "What do you want?" he asked aloud.

The alien in the center of the semicircle—the leader, Luke guessed—gestured with his stick. Luke glanced over his shoulder into the room he'd just left. "You want me to go back in there?" he asked.

The leader gestured again . . . and this time Luke saw it. The small, almost insignificant tactical error. "All right," he said, as soothingly as possible. "No problem." Keeping his eyes on the aliens and his hands away from his lightsaber, he began to back up.

They herded him steadily back across the room toward another archway and a room he hadn't gotten to before Leia's emergency call had come. "If you'd just tell me what you want, I'm sure we could come to some sort of agreement," Luke suggested as he walked. Faint scuffling sounds told him that there were still some Bimms wandering around, presumably the reason the aliens hadn't already attacked. "I would hope we could at least talk about it. There's no particular reason why any of you has to be hurt."

Reflexively, the leader's left thumb moved. Not much, but Luke was watching, and it was enough. A thumb trigger, then. "If you have some business with me, I'm willing to talk," he continued. "You don't need my friends in the marketplace for that."

He was almost to the archway now. A couple more steps to go. If they'd just hold off shooting him that long . . .

And then he was there, with the carved stone looming over him. "Now where?" he asked, forcing his muscles to relax. This was it.

Again, the leader gestured with his stick . . . and midway through the motion, for a single instant, the weapon was pointed not at Luke but at two of his own companions.

And reaching out through the Force, Luke triggered the thumb switch. There was a loud, sharp hiss as the stick bucked in its owner's hands and what looked like a fine spray shot out the end.

Luke didn't wait to see what exactly the spray did. The maneuver had bought him maybe a half second of confusion, and he couldn't afford to waste any of it. Throwing himself back and to the side, he did a flip into the room behind him, angling to get to the slight protection afforded by the wall beside the doorway.

He just barely made it. Even as he cleared the archway there was a stuttering salvo of sharp hisses, and as he flipped back to his feet he saw that the doorjamb had grown strange semisolid tendrils of some thin, translucent material. Another tendril shot through the doorway as he hastily backed farther away, sweeping in a spiral curve that seemed to turn from fine mist to liquid stream to solid cylinder even as it curved.

His lightsaber was in his hand now, igniting with a *snap-hiss* of its own. They'd be through that doorway in seconds, he knew, all efforts at subtlety abandoned. And when they came—

He clenched his teeth, a memory of his brief skiff-battle encounter with Boba Fett flashing through his mind. Wrapped in the bounty hunter's smart-rope, he'd escaped only by snapping the cable with a deflected blaster shot. But here there would be no blasters to try that trick with.

For that matter, he wasn't absolutely sure what his lightsaber could do directly against the sprays. It would be like trying to cut through a rope that was continually re-creating itself.

Or rather, like trying to cut seven such ropes.

He could hear their footsteps now, sprinting toward his room even as the spiraling tendril sweeping the doorway made sure he stayed too far back to ambush them as they came through it. A standard military technique, played out with the kind of precision that showed he wasn't dealing with amateurs.

He raised the lightsaber to en garde position, risking a quick look around. The room was decorated like all the others he'd seen on this floor, with ancient wall tapestries and other relics—no real cover anywhere. His eyes flicked across the walls, searching for the exit that by implication had to be here somewhere. But the action was so much useless reflex. Wherever the exit was, it was almost certainly too far away to do him any good.

The hiss of the spray stopped; and he turned back just in time to see the aliens charge into the room. They spotted him, spun around to bring their weapons to bear—

And reaching up with the Force, Luke ripped one of the tapestries from the wall beside him and brought it down on top of them.

It was a trick that only a Jedi could have pulled off, and it was a trick that, by all rights, ought to have worked. All seven of the aliens were in the room by the time he got the tapestry loose, and all seven were beneath it as it began its fall. But by the time it landed in a huge wrinkled pile on the floor, all seven had somehow managed to back completely out of its way.

From behind the heap came the sharp hiss of their weapons, and Luke ducked back involuntarily before he realized the webbing sprays weren't coming anywhere near him. Instead, the misty tendrils were sweeping outward, shooting around and past the downed tapestry to crisscross the walls.

His first thought was that the weapons must have gone off accidentally, jostled or bumped as the aliens tried to get out from under the falling tapestry. But a split second later he realized the truth: that they were deliberately webbing the other tapestries into place on the walls to prevent him from trying the same trick twice. Belatedly, Luke tugged at the heaped tapestry, hoping to sweep them back with it, and found that it, too, was now solidly webbed in place.

The spraying ceased, and a single dark eye poked cautiously around the tapestry mountain . . . and with a strange sort of sadness, Luke realized that he no longer had any choices left. There was, now, only one way to end this if Han and Leia were to be saved.

He locked his lightsaber on and let his mind relax, reaching out with Jedi senses toward the seven figures, forming their image in his mind's eye. The alien watching him brought his weapon around the edge of the tapestry—

And, reaching back over his left shoulder, Luke hurled his lightsaber with all his strength.

The blade scythed toward the edge of the tapestry, spinning through the air like some strange and fiery predator. The alien saw it, reflexively ducked back—

And died as the lightsaber sliced through the tapestry and cut him in half.

The others must have realized in that instant that they, too, were dead; but even then they didn't give up. Howling a strangely chilling wail, they attacked: four throwing themselves around the sides of the barrier, the other two actually leaping straight up to try to shoot over it.

It made no difference. Guided by the Force, the spinning lightsaber cut through their ranks in a twisting curve, striking each of them in turn.

A heartbeat later, it was all over.

Luke took a shuddering breath. He'd done it. Not the way he'd wanted to, but he'd done it. Now, he could only hope he'd done it in time. Calling the lightsaber back to his hand on a dead run, he sprinted past the crumpled alien bodies and stretched out again through the Force. *Leia?*

THE DECORATIVE COLUMNS flanking the downward ramp were visible just beyond the next row of booths when, beside him, Han felt Leia twitch. "He's free," she said. "He's on his way."

"Great," Han muttered. "Great. Let's hope our pals don't find out before he gets here."

The words were barely out of his mouth when, in

what looked like complete unison, the circle of aliens raised their stokhli sticks and started pushing their way through the milling crowd of Bimms. "Too late," Han gritted. "Here they come."

Leia gripped his arm. "Should I try to take their weapons away from them?"

"You'll never get all eleven," Han told her, looking around desperately for inspiration.

His eyes fell on a nearby table loaded with jewelry display boxes . . . and he had it. Maybe. "Leia—that jewelry over there? Grab some of it."

He sensed her throw a startled look up at him. "What—?"

"Just do it!" he hissed, watching the approaching aliens. "Grab it and throw it to me."

Out of the corner of his eye he saw one of the smaller display boxes stir as she strained to establish a grip on it. Then, with a sudden lurch, it leaped toward him, slapping into his hands and scattering small neckpieces to the ground before he managed to get hold of the rest.

And abruptly the raucous conversational hum of the marketplace was split by a piercing shriek. Han turned toward it, just in time to see the owner of the pilfered merchandise stabbing two fingers toward him. "Han!" he heard Leia shout over the scream.

"Get ready to duck!" he shouted back—

And was literally bowled off his feet as a yellow wave of enraged Bimms leaped atop him, knocking the accused shoplifter to the ground.

And with their bodies forming a barrier between him and the stokhli sticks, he dropped the jewelry and grabbed for his comlink. "Chewie!" he bellowed over the din.

LUKE HEARD THE shriek even from the top Tower floor; and from the sudden turmoil in Leia's mind, it was instantly clear that he would never make it to the market-place in time.

He skidded to a halt, mind racing. Across the room a large open window faced the open-domed structure; but five floors was too far for even a Jedi to safely leap. He glanced back to the room he'd just left, searching for possibilities . . . and his eye fell on the end of one of the aliens' weapons, just visible through the archway.

It was a long shot, but it was as good a chance as he was going to get. Reaching out through the Force, he called the weapon flying to his hand, studying its controls as he ran to the window. They were simple enough: spray profile and pressure, plus the thumb trigger. Setting for the narrowest spray and the highest pressure, he braced himself against the side of the window, aimed for the marketplace's partial dome covering, and fired.

The stick kicked harder against his shoulder than he'd expected it to as the spray shot out, but the results were all he could have hoped for. The front end of the arching tendril struck the roof, forming a leisurely sort of pile as more of the semisolid spray pushed forward to join it. Luke held the switch down for a count of five, then eased up, keeping a firm Force grip on the near end of the tendril to prevent it from falling away from the stick. He gave it a few seconds to harden before touching it tentatively with a finger, gave it a few seconds more to make sure it was solidly attached to the marketplace roof. Then, taking a deep breath, he grabbed his makeshift rope with both hands and jumped.

A tornado of air blew at him, tugging at his hair and clothes as he swung down and across. Below and partway across the top level he could see the mass of yellow-clad Bimms and the handful of gray figures struggling to get past them to Han and Leia. There was a flicker of light, visible even in the bright sunshine, and one of the Bimms slumped to the ground—stunned or dead, Luke couldn't tell which. The floor was rushing up at him—he braced himself to land—

And with a roar that must have rattled windows for blocks around, the *Millennium Falcon* screamed by overhead.

The shock wave threw Luke's landing off, sending him sprawling across the floor and into two of the Bimms. But even as he rolled back up to his feet, he realized that Chewbacca's arrival couldn't have been better timed. Barely ten meters away, the two alien attackers nearest him had turned their attention upward, their weapons poised to ensnare the *Falcon* when it returned. Snatching his lightsaber from his belt, Luke leaped over a half dozen bystanding Bimms, cutting both attackers down before they even knew he was there.

From overhead came another roar; but this time Chewbacca didn't simply fly the *Falcon* past the marketplace. Instead, forward maneuvering jets blasting, he brought it to a hard stop. Hovering directly over his beleaguered companions, swivel blaster extended from the ship's underside, he opened fire.

The Bimms weren't stupid. Whatever Han and Leia

had done to stir up the hornet's nest, the hornets themselves clearly had no desire to get shot at from the sky. In an instant the roiling yellow mass dissolved, the Bimms abandoning their attack and streaming away in terror from the *Falcon*. Forcing his way through the crowd, using the Bimms for visual cover as much as he could, Luke started around the attackers' circle.

Between his lightsaber and the *Falcon*'s swivel blaster, they made a very fast, very clean sweep of it.

"You," Luke said with a shake of his head, "are a mess."

"I'm sorry, Master Luke," Threepio apologized, his voice almost inaudible beneath the layers of hardened spraynet that covered much of his upper body like some bizarre sort of gift wrapping. "I seem to always be causing you trouble."

"That's not true, and you know it," Luke soothed him, considering the small collection of solvents arrayed in front of him on the *Falcon*'s lounge table. So far none of the ones he'd tried had been even marginally effective against the webbing. "You've been a great help to all of us over the years. You just have to learn when to duck."

Beside Luke, Artoo twittered something. "No, Captain Solo did *not* tell me to duck," Threepio told the squat droid stiffly. "What he said was, 'Get ready to duck.' I should think the difference would be apparent even to you."

Artoo beeped something else. Threepio ignored it. "Well, let's try this one," Luke suggested, picking up the next solvent in line. He was hunting for a clean cloth among his pile of rejects when Leia came into the lounge.

"How is he?" she asked, walking over and peering at Threepio.

"He'll be all right," Luke assured her. "He may have to stay like this until we get back to Coruscant, though. Han told me these stokhli sticks are used mostly by big-game hunters on out-of-the-way planets, and the spraynet they use is a pretty exotic mixture." He indicated the discarded solvent bottles.

"Maybe the Bimms can suggest something," Leia said, picking up one of the bottles and looking at its label. "We'll ask them when we get back down."

Luke frowned at her. "We're going back down?"

She frowned at him in turn. "We have to, Luke—you know that. This is a diplomatic mission, not a pleasure cruise. It's considered bad form to pull out right after one of your ships has just shot up a major local marketplace."

"I would think the Bimms would consider themselves lucky that none of their people got killed in the process," Luke pointed out. "Particularly when what happened was at least partly their fault."

"You can't blame a whole society for the actions of a few individuals," Leia said—rather severely, Luke thought. "Especially not when a single political maverick has simply made a bad decision."

"A bad *decision*?" Luke snorted. "Is *that* what they're calling it?"

"That's what they're calling it," Leia nodded. "Apparently, the Bimm who led us into the marketplace trap was bribed to take us there. He had no idea what was going to happen, though."

"And I suppose he had no idea what the stuff he gave the chief negotiator would do, either?"

Leia shrugged. "Actually, there's still no hard evidence that he or anyone else poisoned the negotiator," she said. "Though under the circumstances, they're willing to concede that that's a possibility."

Luke made a face. "Generous of them. What does Han have to say about us putting back down?"

"Han doesn't have any choice in the matter," Leia said firmly. "This is *my* mission, not his."

"That's right," Han agreed, stepping into the lounge. "Your mission. But *my* ship."

Leia stared at him, a look of disbelief on her face. "You didn't," she breathed.

"I sure did," he told her calmly, dropping into one of the seats across the lounge. "We made the jump to light-speed about two minutes ago. Next stop, Coruscant."

"Han!" she flared, as angry as Luke had ever seen her, "I told the Bimms we were coming right back down."

"And I told them there'd be a short delay," Han countered. "Like long enough for us to collect a squadron of X-wings or maybe a Star Cruiser to bring back with us."

"And what if you've offended them?" Leia snapped. "Do you have any *idea* how much groundwork went into this mission?"

"Yeah, as it happens, I do," Han said, his voice hardening. "I also have a pretty good idea what could happen if our late pals with the stokhli sticks brought friends with them."

For a long minute Leia stared at him, and Luke sensed the momentary anger fading from her mind. "You still shouldn't have left without consulting me first," she said.

"You're right," Han conceded. "But I didn't want to take the time. If they *did* have friends, those friends probably had a ship." He tried a tentative smile. "There wasn't time to discuss it in committee."

Leia smiled lopsidedly in return. "I am *not* a committee," she said wryly.

And with that, the brief storm passed and the tension was gone. Someday, Luke promised himself, he would get around to asking one of them just what that particular private joke of theirs referred to. "Speaking of our pals," he said, "did either of you happen to ask the Bimms who or what they were?"

"The Bimms didn't know," Leia said, shaking her head. "I've certainly never seen anything like them before."

"We can check the Imperial archives when we get back to Coruscant," Han said, feeling gingerly at one cheek where a bruise was already becoming visible. "There'll be a record of them somewhere."

"Unless," Leia said quietly, "they're something the Empire found out in the Unknown Regions."

Luke looked at her. "You think the Empire was behind this?"

"Who else could it have been?" she said. "The only question is why."

"Well, whatever the reason, they're going to be disappointed," Han told her, getting to his feet. "I'm going back to the cockpit, see if I can muddle our course a little more. No point in taking chances."

A memory flashed through Luke's mind: Han and the *Falcon*, sweeping right through the middle of that first Death Star battle to shoot Darth Vader's fighters off his back. "Hard to imagine Han Solo not wanting to take chances," he commented.

Han leveled a finger at him. "Yeah, well, before you get cocky, try to remember that the people I'm protecting are you, your sister, your niece, and your nephew. That make any difference?"

Luke smiled. "Touché," he admitted, saluting with an imaginary lightsaber.

"And speaking of that," Han added, "isn't it about time Leia had a lightsaber of her own?"

Luke shrugged. "I can make her one anytime she's ready," he said, looking at his sister. "Leia?"

Leia hesitated. "I don't know," she confessed. "I've never really felt comfortable with the things." She looked at Han. "But I suppose I ought to make the effort."

"I think you should," Luke agreed. "Your talents may lie along a different direction, but you should still learn all the basics. As far as I can tell, nearly all the Jedi of the Old Republic carried lightsabers, even those who were primarily healers or teachers."

She nodded. "All right," she said. "As soon as my work load lightens up a little."

"*Before* your work load lightens," Han insisted. "I mean that, Leia. All these wonderful diplomacy skills of yours aren't going to do you or anyone else any good if the Empire locks you away in an interrogation room somewhere."

Reluctantly, Leia nodded again. "I suppose you're right. As soon as we get back, I'll tell Mon Mothma she's just going to have to cut down on my assignments." She smiled at Luke. "I guess semester break's over, Teacher."

"I guess so," Luke said, trying to hide the sudden lump in his throat.

Leia noticed it anyway; and, for a wonder, misinterpreted it. "Oh, come on," she chided gently. "I'm not *that* bad a student. Anyway, look on it as good practice—after all, someday you'll have to teach all this to the twins, too."

"I know," Luke said softly.

"Good," Han said. "That's settled, then. I'm heading up; see you later."

" 'Bye," Leia said. "Now—" She turned to give Three-pio a critical look. "Let's see what we can do about all this goop."

Leaning back in his seat, Luke watched her tackle the hardened webbing, a familiar hollow pain in the pit of his stomach. *I took it upon myself*, Ben Kenobi had said about Darth Vader, *to train him as a Jedi. I thought that I could instruct him just as well as Yoda.*

I was wrong.

The words echoed through Luke's mind, all the way back to Coruscant.

CHAPTER 8

FOR A LONG minute Grand Admiral Thrawn sat in his chair, surrounded by his holographic works of art, and said nothing. Pellaeon kept himself at a motionless attention, watching the other's expressionless face and glowing red eyes and trying not to think about the fate couriers of bad news had often suffered at the hands of Lord Vader. "All died but the coordinator, then?" Thrawn asked at last.

"Yes, sir," Pellaeon confirmed. He glanced across the room, to where C'baoth stood studying one of the wall displays, and lowered his voice a bit. "We're still not entirely sure what went wrong."

"Instruct Central to give the coordinator a thorough debriefing," Thrawn said. "What report from Wayland?"

Pellaeon had thought they'd been talking too quietly for C'baoth to hear them. He was wrong. "Is that it, then?" C'baoth demanded, turning away from the display and striding over to tower over Thrawn's command chair. "Your Noghri have failed; so too bad, and on to more pressing business? You promised me Jedi, Grand Admiral Thrawn."

Thrawn gazed coolly up at him. "I promised you Jedi," he acknowledged. "And I will deliver them." Deliberately, he turned back to Pellaeon. "What report from Wayland?" he repeated.

Pellaeon swallowed, trying hard to remember that with ysalamiri scattered all through the command room, C'baoth had no power whatsoever. At least for the moment. "The engineering team has finished its analysis, sir," he told Thrawn. "They report that the cloaking shield schematics seem complete, but that to actually build one will take some time. It'll also be highly expensive, at least for a ship the size of the *Chimaera*."

"Fortunately, they won't have to start with anything nearly this big," Thrawn said, handing Pellaeon a data card. "Here are the specs for what we'll need at Sluis Van."

"The shipyards?" Pellaeon frowned, taking the data card. The Grand Admiral had so far been very secretive about both his goals and the strategy for that attack.

"Yes. Oh, and we're also going to need some advanced mining machines—mole miners, I believe they're informally called. Have Intelligence start a records search; we'll need a minimum of forty."

"Yes, sir." Pellaeon made a note on his data pad. "One other thing, sir." He threw a quick glance at C'baoth. "The engineers also report that nearly eighty percent of the Spaarti cylinders we'll need are functional or can be restored to working order with relative ease."

"Spaarti cylinders?" C'baoth frowned. "What are those?"

"Just that other little bit of technology I was hoping to find in the mountain," Thrawn soothed him, throwing a quick warning look in Pellaeon's direction. An unnecessary precaution; Pellaeon had already decided that discussing Spaarti cylinders with C'baoth would not be a smart thing to do. "So. Eighty percent. That's excellent, Captain. Excellent." A gleam came into those glowing eyes. "How very thoughtful of the Emperor to have left such fine equipment for us to rebuild his Empire with. What about the mountain's power and defense systems?"

"Also operational, for the most part," Pellaeon said. "Three of the four reactors have already been brought on line. Some of the more esoteric defenses seem to have decayed, but what's left should defend the storehouse more than adequately."

"Again, excellent," Thrawn nodded. The brief flicker of emotion was gone, and he was all cool business again. "Instruct them to begin bringing the cylinders to full operational status. The *Death's Head* should arrive within two or three days with the extra specialists and two hundred ysalamiri they'll need to get things started. At that point—" he smiled faintly "—we'll be ready to begin the operation in earnest. Beginning with the Sluis Van shipyards."

"Yes, sir." Pellaeon glanced at C'baoth again. "And about Skywalker and his sister?"

"We'll use Team Four next," the Grand Admiral said. "Transmit a message telling them to withdraw from their current assignment and stand ready for further orders."

"You want *me* to transmit the message, sir?" Pellaeon asked. "Not that I'm questioning the order," he added hastily. "But in the past you've usually preferred to contact them yourself."

Thrawn's eyebrows lifted slightly. "Team Eight failed me," he said softly. "Sending the message through you will let the others know how displeased I am."

"And when Team Four also fails you?" C'baoth put in. "They will, you know. Will you be merely *displeased* with them, too? Or will you admit your professional killing machines simply can't handle a Jedi?"

"They've never yet met any foe they can't handle, Master C'baoth," Thrawn said coolly. "One group or another will succeed. Until then—" He shrugged. "A few Noghri, more or less, won't seriously drain our resources."

Pellaeon winced, throwing a reflexive glance at the chamber door. Rukh, he suspected, wouldn't be nearly that phlegmatic about the casually proposed deaths of some of his people. "On the other hand, Admiral, this attempt will have put them on their guard," he pointed out.

"He's right," C'baoth said, jabbing a finger in Pellaeon's direction. "You can't fool a Jedi twice with the same trick."

"Perhaps," Thrawn said, the word polite but his tone not conceding anything. "What alternative do you suggest? That we concentrate on his sister and leave him alone?"

"That *you* concentrate on his sister, yes," C'baoth agreed loftily. "I think it best that I deal with the young Jedi myself."

Again, the eyebrows went up. "And how would you propose to do that?"

C'baoth smiled. "He is a Jedi; I am a Jedi. If I call, he will come to me."

For a long moment Thrawn looked up at him. "I need you with my fleet," he said at last. "Preparations for the assault on the Rebellion's Sluis Van space dock facilities have already begun. Some of the preliminaries to that assault will require a Jedi Master's coordination."

C'baoth drew himself up to his full height. "My assistance was promised only upon *your* promise to deliver my Jedi to me. I will have them, Grand Admiral Thrawn."

Thrawn's glowing eyes bored into C'baoth's. "Does a Jedi Master go back on his word, then? You knew that obtaining Skywalker for you might take some time."

"All the more reason for me to begin now," C'baoth shot back.

"Why can't we do both?" Pellaeon cut in.

Both looked at him. "Explain, Captain," Thrawn ordered, a hint of threat audible in his tone.

Pellaeon gritted his teeth, but it was too late to back out now. "We could begin by starting rumors of your presence somewhere, Master C'baoth," he said. "Some sparsely populated world where you might have lived for years without anyone really noticing. Rumors of that sort would be certain to make their way back to the New Rep—to the Rebellion," he corrected, glancing at Thrawn. "Particularly with the name Jorus C'baoth attached to them."

C'baoth snorted. "And you think that on the strength of an idle rumor he'll rush foolishly to find me?"

"Let him be as cautious as he likes," Thrawn said thoughtfully, the threat gone from his voice. "Let him bring half the Rebellion's forces with him, if he chooses. There will be nothing there to connect you to us."

Pellaeon nodded. "And while we find a suitable planet and start the rumors into motion, you can remain here to assist with the Sluis Van preliminaries. Hopefully, their response to our activities will keep Skywalker too busy to check out the stories until after the Sluis Van part is over."

"And if not," Thrawn added, "we'll know when he makes his move, and in plenty of time to get you there ahead of him."

"Hmm," C'baoth murmured, stroking his long beard, his gaze drifting off to infinity. Pellaeon held his breath . . . and after a minute the other abruptly nodded. "Very well," he said. "The plan is sound. I will go to my chambers now, Grand Admiral Thrawn, and choose a world from which to make my appearance." With an almost regal nod to each of them, he strode out.

"Congratulations, Captain," Thrawn said, eyeing Pellaeon coolly. "Your idea seems to have caught Master C'baoth's fancy."

Pellaeon forced himself to meet that gaze. "I apologize, Admiral, if I spoke out of turn."

Thrawn smiled faintly. "You served too long under Lord Vader, Captain," he said. "I have no qualms about accepting a useful idea merely because it wasn't my own. My position and ego are not at stake here."

Except, perhaps, when dealing with C'baoth . . . "Yes, sir," Pellaeon said aloud. "With your permission, Admiral, I'll go prepare those transmissions to the Wayland and Noghri teams."

"At your convenience, Captain. And continue to monitor the preparations for the Sluis Van operation." Thrawn's glowing eyes seemed to bore into his. "Monitor them closely, Captain. With Mount Tantiss and Sluis Van both, the long path to victory over the Rebellion will have begun. With, or even without, our Jedi Master."

IN THEORY, INNER Council meetings were supposed to be a quieter, more casual sort of encounter than the more formal Provisional Council things. In actual practice, Han had long ago found out, an Inner Council grilling could be just as rough as being raked over the fires by the larger group.

"Let me get this straight, then, Captain Solo," Borsk Fey'lya said with his usual oily politeness. "You, alone, and without consultation with anyone in official authority, made the decision to cancel the Bimmisaari mission."

"I've already said that," Han told him. He felt like suggesting to the Bothan that he pay better attention. "I've also stated my reasons for doing so."

"Which, in my opinion, were good and proper ones," Admiral Ackbar's gravelly voice interjected in Han's support. "Captain Solo's duty at that point was abundantly clear: to protect the ambassador in his charge and to return safely to alert us."

"Alert us to what?" Fey'lya countered. "Forgive me, Admiral, but I don't understand what exactly this threat is we're supposedly facing. Whoever these gray-skinned beings were, they clearly weren't considered important enough by the Old Senate to even be included in the records. I doubt a race that insignificant is likely to be capable of mounting a major offensive against us."

"We don't *know* that that's the reason they aren't in the records," Leia put in. "It could simply be an oversight or gap damage."

"Or else a deliberate erasure," Luke said.

Fey'lya's fur rippled, indicating polite disbelief. "And why would the Imperial Senate want to erase the records of an entire race's existence?"

"I didn't say it was necessarily the Senate's idea," Luke said. "Maybe the aliens themselves destroyed their records."

Fey'lya sniffed. "Farfetched. Even if it was possible, why would anyone want to do it?"

"Perhaps Councilor Organa Solo can answer that," Mon Mothma interjected calmly, looking at Leia. "You were more involved in the informational side of the Imperial Senate than I was, Leia. Would such a manipulation have been possible?"

"I really don't know," Leia said, shaking her head. "I never got all that deeply into the actual mechanics of how the Senate's records were handled. Common wisdom, though, would suggest that it's impossible to create a security system that can't be broken by someone determined enough to do it."

"That still doesn't answer the question of why these aliens of yours would be that determined," Fey'lya sniffed.

"Maybe they saw the Old Republic's coming demise," Leia told him, her voice starting to sound a little irritated. "They might have erased all references to themselves and their world in hopes the rising Empire might not notice them."

Fey'lya was fast, all right; Han had to give him that. "In that case," the Bothan smoothly switched gears, "perhaps a fear of rediscovery was all that motivated *this* attack, as well." He looked at Ackbar. "Regardless, I see no reason to make a full-fledged military operation out of this. To reduce our glorious forces to the level of a mere diplomatic entourage is an insult to their courage and their fighting spirit."

"You can dispense with the speeches, Councilor," Ackbar rumbled. "None of our 'glorious forces' are here to be impressed by them."

"I say only what I feel, Admiral," Fey'lya said, with that air of wounded pride he did so well.

Ackbar's eyes swiveled toward Fey'lya—"I wonder," Leia spoke up quickly, "if we could get back to the original subject here. I presume it hasn't escaped anyone's notice that, whatever their motivation, the aliens were ready and waiting for us when we reached Bimmisaari."

"We're going to need tighter security for these missions, obviously," Ackbar said. "At both ends—your attackers *did* suborn a local Bimm politician, after all."

"All of which will cost that much more time and effort," Fey'lya murmured, a section of his fur rippling.

"It can't be helped," Mon Mothma said firmly. "If we don't protect our negotiators, the New Republic will stagnate and wither. Accordingly—" she looked at Ackbar "—you will detail a force to accompany Councilor Organa Solo on her trip back to Bimmisaari tomorrow."

Tomorrow? Han threw a sharp look at Leia, got an

equally surprised look in return. "Excuse me," he said, raising a finger. "Tomorrow?"

Mon Mothma looked at him, an expression of mild surprise on her face. "Yes, tomorrow. The Bimms are still waiting, Captain."

"I know, but—"

"What Han is trying to say," Leia jumped in, "is that I had intended at this meeting to ask for a brief leave of absence from my diplomatic duties."

"I'm afraid that's impossible," Mon Mothma said with a slight frown. "There's far too much work to be done."

"We're not talking about a vacation here," Han told her, trying to remember his diplomatic manners. "Leia needs more time to concentrate on her Jedi training."

Mon Mothma pursed her lips, throwing glances at Ackbar and Fey'lya. "I'm sorry," she said, shaking her head. "I, of all people, recognize the need to add new Jedi to our ranks. But for now there are simply too many urgent demands on our time." She looked at Fey'lya again—almost, Han thought sourly, as if seeking his permission. "In another year—possibly sooner," she added, glancing at Leia's stomach, "we'll have enough experienced diplomats for you to devote the bulk of your time to your studies. But right now I'm afraid we need you here."

For a long, awkward moment the room was silent. Ackbar spoke first. "If you'll excuse me, I'll go and have that escort force prepared."

"Of course," Mon Mothma nodded. "Unless there's something more, we stand adjourned."

And that was that. Jaw clenched tightly, Han began collecting his data cards together. "You all right?" Leia asked quietly from beside him.

"You know, it was a lot easier back when we were just taking on the Empire," he growled. He threw a glare across the table at Fey'lya. "At least *then* we knew who our enemies were."

Leia squeezed his arm. "Come on," she said. "Let's go see if they've gotten Threepio cleaned up yet."

CHAPTER 9

THE TACTICAL OFFICER stepped up to the *Chimaera*'s bridge command station, bringing his heels smartly together. "All units signal ready, Admiral," he reported.

"Excellent," Thrawn said, his voice glacially calm. "Prepare for lightspeed."

Pellaeon threw a glance at the Grand Admiral, then returned his attention to the bank of tactical and status readouts facing him. To the readouts, and to the blackness outside that seemed to have swallowed up the rest of Pellaeon's five-ship task force. Three-thousandths of a light-year away, the Bpfassh system's sun was a mere pinprick, indistinguishable from the other stars blazing all around them. Conventional military wisdom frowned on this business of picking a spot just outside the target system as a jumping-off point—it was considered dangerously easy for one or more ships to get lost on the way to such a rendezvous, and it was difficult to make an accurate hyperspace jump over so short a distance. He and

Thrawn, in fact, had had a long and barely civilized argument over the idea the first time the Grand Admiral had included it in one of his attack plans. Now, after nearly a year of practice, the procedure had become almost routine.

Perhaps, Pellaeon thought, the *Chimaera*'s crew wasn't as inexperienced as their ignorance of proper military protocol sometimes made them seem.

"Captain? Is my flagship ready?"

Pellaeon brought his mind back to the business at hand. All ship defenses showed ready; the TIE fighters in their bays were manned and poised. "The *Chimaera* is fully at your command, Admiral," he said, the formal question and response a ghostly remembrance of the days when proper military protocol was the order of the day throughout the galaxy.

"Excellent," Thrawn said. He swiveled in his chair to face the figure seated near the rear of the bridge. "Master C'baoth," he nodded. "Are my other two task forces ready?"

"They are," C'baoth said gravely. "They await merely my command."

Pellaeon winced and threw another glance at Thrawn. But the Grand Admiral had apparently decided to let the comment pass. "Then command them," he told C'baoth, reaching up to stroke the ysalamir draped across the framework fastened to his chair. "Captain: begin the count."

"Yes, sir." Pellaeon reached to his board, touched the timer switch. Scattered around them, the other ships would be locking onto that signal, all of them counting down together . . .

The timer went to zero, and with a flare of starlines through the forward ports, the *Chimaera* jumped.

Ahead, the starlines faded into the mottling of hyperspace. "Speed, Point Three," the helmsman in the crew pit below called out, confirming the readout on the displays.

"Acknowledged," Pellaeon said, flexing his fingers once and settling his mind into combat mode as he watched the timer now counting up from zero. Seventy seconds; seventy-four, seventy-five, seventy-six—

The starlines flared again through the mottled sky, and shrank back into stars, and the *Chimaera* had arrived.

"All fighters: launch," Pellaeon called, throwing a quick look at the tactical holo floating over his display bank. They had come out of hyperspace exactly as planned, within easy striking range of the double planet of Bpfassh and its complicated system of moons. "Response?" he called to the tactical officer.

"Defending fighters launching from the third moon," the other reported. "Nothing larger visible as yet."

"Get a location on that fighter base," Thrawn ordered, "and detail the *Inexorable* to move in and destroy it."

"Yes, sir."

Pellaeon could see the fighters now, coming at them like a swarm of angry insects. Off on the *Chimaera*'s starboard flank, the Star Destroyer *Inexorable* was moving toward their base, its TIE fighter wedge sweeping ahead of it to engage the defenders. "Change course to the farther of the twin planets," he ordered the helmsman. "TIE fighters to set up an advance screen. The *Ju-*

dicator will take the other planet." He looked at Thrawn. "Any special orders, Admiral?"

Thrawn was gazing at a mid-distance scan of the twin planets. "Stay with the program for now, Captain," he said. "Our preliminary data appear to have been adequate; you may choose targets at will. Remind your gunners once again that the plan is to hurt and frighten, not obliterate."

"Relay that," Pellaeon nodded toward the communications station. "Have TIE fighters so reminded, as well."

Out of the corner of his eye, he saw Thrawn turn. "Master C'baoth?" he said. "What's the status of the attacks in the other two systems?"

"They proceed."

Frowning, Pellaeon swiveled around. It had been C'baoth's voice, but so throaty and strained as to be nearly unrecognizable.

As was, indeed, his appearance.

For a long moment Pellaeon stared at him, a cold feeling in the pit of his stomach. C'baoth sat with unnatural stiffness, his eyes closed but visibly and rapidly moving behind the lids. His hands gripped the arms of his chair, and his lips were pressed so tightly together that the veins and cords in his neck stood out. "Are you all right, Master C'baoth?" he asked.

"Save your concern, Captain," Thrawn told him coldly. "He's doing what he enjoys most: controlling people."

C'baoth made a sound somewhere between a snort and a derisive chuckle. "I told you once, Grand Admiral Thrawn, that this is not true power."

"So you've said," Thrawn said, his tone neutral. "Can you tell what sort of resistance they're facing?"

C'baoth's frowning face frowned harder. "Not precisely. But neither force is in danger. That much I can feel in their minds."

"Good. Then have the *Nemesis* break off from the rest of its group and report back to the rendezvous to await us."

Pellaeon frowned at the Grand Admiral. "Sir—?"

Thrawn turned to him, a warning gleam in his glowing eyes. "Attend to your duties, Captain," he said.

—and with a sudden flash of insight, Pellaeon realized that this multiedged attack on New Republic territory was more than simply part of the setup for the Sluis Van raid. It was, in addition, a test. A test of C'baoth's abilities, yes; but also a test of his willingness to accept orders. "Yes, Admiral," Pellaeon murmured, and turned back to his displays.

The *Chimaera* was in range now, and tiny sparks started to appear on the tactical holo as the ship's huge turbolaser batteries began firing. Communications stations flared and went black; planetside industrial targets flared, went dark, then flared again as secondary fires were ignited. A pair of old *Carrack*-class light cruisers swept in from starboard, the *Chimaera*'s TIE fighter screen breaking formation to engage them. Off in the distance, the *Stormhawk*'s batteries were blazing against an orbiting defense platform; and even as Pellaeon watched, the station flared into vapor. The battle seemed to be going well.

Remarkably well, in fact . . .

An unpleasant feeling began to stir in the pit of Pellaeon's stomach as he checked his board's real-time status readout. Thus far the Imperial forces had lost only three

TIE fighters and sustained superficial damage to the Star Destroyers, compared to eight of the enemy's line ships and eighteen of its fighters gone. Granted, the Imperials vastly outgunned the defenders. But still . . .

Slowly, reluctantly, Pellaeon reached to his board. A few weeks back he'd made up a statistical composite of the *Chimaera*'s battle profiles for the past year. He called it up, superimposed it over the current analysis.

There was no mistake. In every single category and subcategory of speed, coordination, efficiency, and accuracy, the *Chimaera* and its crew were running no less than 40 percent more effective than usual.

He turned to look at C'baoth's strained face, an icy shiver running up his back. He'd never really bought into Thrawn's theory as to how and why the Fleet had lost the Battle of Endor. Certainly he'd never *wanted* to believe it. But now, suddenly, the issue was no longer open to argument.

And with the bulk of his attention and power on the task of mentally communicating with two other task forces nearly four light-years away, C'baoth still had enough left to do all this.

Pellaeon had wondered, with a certain private contempt, just what had given the old man the right to add the word *Master* to his title. Now, he knew.

"Getting another set of transmissions," the communications officer reported. "A new group of mid-range planetary cruisers launching."

"Have the *Stormhawk* move to intercept," Thrawn ordered.

"Yes, sir. We've now also pinpointed the location of their distress transmissions, Admiral."

Shaking away his musings, Pellaeon glanced across the holo. The newly flashing circle was on the farthest of the system's moons. "Order Squadron Four to move in and destroy it," he ordered.

"Belay that," Thrawn said. "We'll be long gone before any reinforcements can arrive. We might as well let the Rebellion waste its resources rushing useless forces to the rescue. In fact—" the Grand Admiral consulted his watch "—I believe it's time for us to take our leave. Order fighters back to their ships; all ships to lightspeed as soon as their fighters are aboard."

Pellaeon tapped keys at his station, giving the *Chimaera*'s status a quick prelightspeed check. Another bit of conventional military wisdom was that Star Destroyers should play the role of mobile siege stations in this kind of full-planet engagement; that to employ them in hit-and-fade operations was both wasteful and potentially dangerous.

But then, proponents of such theories had obviously never watched someone like Grand Admiral Thrawn in action.

"Order the other two forces to break off their attacks, as well," Thrawn told C'baoth. "I presume you are in close enough contact to do that?"

"You question me too much, Grand Admiral Thrawn," C'baoth said, his voice even huskier than it had been earlier. "Far too much."

"I question all that is not yet familiar to me," Thrawn countered, swiveling back around again. "Call them back to the rendezvous point."

"As you command," the other hissed.

Pellaeon glanced back at C'baoth. Testing the other's

abilities under combat conditions was all good and proper. But there was such a thing as pushing too far.

"He must learn who's in command here," Thrawn said quietly, as if reading Pellaeon's thoughts.

"Yes, sir," Pellaeon nodded, forcing his voice to remain steady. Thrawn had proved time and again that he knew what he was doing. Still, Pellaeon couldn't help but wonder uneasily if the Grand Admiral recognized the extent of the power he'd awakened from its sleep on Wayland.

Thrawn nodded. "Good. Have there been any further leads on those mole miners I asked for?"

"Ah—no, sir." A year ago, too, he would have found a strange unreality in conversing about less than urgent matters while in the middle of a combat situation. "At least not in anything like the numbers you want. I think the Athega system's still our best bet. Or it will be if we can find a way around the problems of the sunlight intensity there."

"The problems will be minimal," Thrawn said with easy confidence. "If the jump is done with sufficient accuracy, the *Judicator* will be in direct sunlight for only a few minutes each way. Its hull can certainly handle that much. We'll simply need to take a few days first to shield the viewports and remove external sensors and communications equipment."

Pellaeon nodded, swallowing his next question. There would, of course, be none of the difficulties that would normally arise from blinding and deafening a Star Destroyer in that way. Not as long as C'baoth was with them.

"Grand Admiral Thrawn?"

Thrawn turned around. "Yes, Master C'baoth?"

"Where are my Jedi, Grand Admiral Thrawn? You promised me that your tame Noghri would bring me my Jedi."

Out of the corner of his eye, Pellaeon saw Rukh stir. "Patience, Master C'baoth," Thrawn told him. "Their preparations took time, but they're now complete. They await merely the proper time to act."

"That time had best be soon," C'baoth warned him. "I grow tired of waiting."

Thrawn threw a glance at Pellaeon, a quietly smoldering look in his glowing red eyes. "As do we all," he said quietly.

FAR AHEAD OF the freighter *Wild Karrde*, one of the Imperial Star Destroyers centered in the cockpit's forward viewport gave a flicker of pseudomotion and disappeared. "They're leaving," Mara announced.

"What, already?" Karrde said from behind her, his voice frowning.

"Already," she confirmed, keying the helm display for tactical. "One of the Star Destroyers just went to lightspeed; the others are breaking off and starting prelightspeed maneuvering."

"Interesting," Karrde murmured, coming up to look out the viewport over her shoulder. "A hit-and-fade attack—and with Star Destroyers, yet. Not something you see every day."

"I heard about something like that happening over at the Draukyze system a couple of months back," the co-pilot, a bulky man named Lachton, offered. "Same kind of hit-and-fade, except there was only one Star Destroyer on that one."

"At a guess, I'd say we're seeing Grand Admiral Thrawn's influence on Imperial strategy," Karrde said, his tone thoughtful with just a hint of concern mixed in. "Strange, though. He seems to be taking an inordinate amount of risk for the potential benefits involved. I wonder what exactly he's up to."

"Whatever it is, it'll be something complicated," Mara told him, hearing the bitterness in her voice. "Thrawn was never one to do things simply. Even back in the old days when the Empire was capable of style or subtlety, he stood out above the rest."

"You can't afford to be simple when your territory's shrinking the way the Empire's has been." Karrde paused, and Mara could feel him gazing down at her. "You seem to know something about the Grand Admiral."

"I know something about a lot of things," she countered evenly. "That's why you're grooming me to be your lieutenant, remember?"

"Touché," he said easily. "—there goes another one."

Mara looked out the viewport in time to see a third Star Destroyer go to lightspeed. One more to go.

"Shouldn't we get moving?" she asked Karrde. "That last one will be gone in a minute."

"Oh, we're scratching the delivery," he told her. "I just thought it might be instructive to watch the battle, as long as we happened to be here at the right time."

Mara frowned up at him. "What do you mean, we're scratching the delivery? They're expecting us."

"Yes, they are," he nodded. "Unfortunately, as of right now, the whole system is also expecting a small hornet's nest of New Republic ships. Hardly the sort of atmosphere one would like to fly into with a shipload of contraband materials."

"What makes you think they'll come?" Mara demanded. "They're not going to be in time to do anything."

"No, but that's not really the point of such a show," Karrde said. "The point is to score domestic political gains by bustling around, presenting a comforting display of force, and otherwise convincing the locals that something like this can never happen again."

"And promising to help clean up the wreckage," Lachton put in.

"That goes without saying," Karrde agreed dryly. "Regardless, it's not a situation we really want to fly into. We'll send a transmission from our next stop telling them we'll try to make delivery again in a week."

"I still don't like it," Mara insisted. "We promised them we'd do it. We *promised*."

There was a short pause. "It's standard procedure," Karrde told her, a touch of curiosity almost hidden beneath the usual urbane smoothness of his voice. "I'm sure they'd prefer late delivery to losing the entire shipment."

With an effort, Mara forced the black haze of memory away. Promises . . . "I suppose so," she conceded, blinking her attention back to the control board. While they'd been talking, the last Star Destroyer had apparently gone to lightspeed, leaving nothing behind but enraged and impotent defenders and mass destruction.

A mess for the New Republic's politicians and military people to clean up.

For a moment she gazed out at the distant planets. Wondering if Luke Skywalker might be among those the New Republic would send to help clean up that mess.

"Whenever you're ready, Mara."

With an effort, she shook away the thought. "Yes, sir," she said, reaching for the board. *Not yet*, she told herself silently. *Not yet. But soon. Very, very soon.*

THE REMOTE SWOOPED; hesitated; swooped again; hesitated again; swooped once more and fired. Leia, swinging her new lightsaber in an overlarge arc, was just a shade too slow. "Gah!" she grunted, taking a step backward.

"You're not giving the Force enough control," Luke told her. "You have to—Wait a minute."

Reaching out with the Force, he put the remote on pause. He remembered vividly that first practice session on the *Falcon*, when he'd had to concentrate on Ben Kenobi's instructions while at the same time keeping a wary eye on the remote. Doing both together hadn't been easy.

But perhaps that had been the whole idea. Perhaps a lesson learned under stress was learned better.

He wished he knew.

"I'm giving it all the control I can," Leia said, rubbing her arm where the remote's stinger blast had caught her. "I just don't have the proper techniques down yet." She impaled him with a look. "Or else I just wasn't cut out for this sort of fighting."

"You can learn it," Luke said firmly. "*I* learned it, and

I never had any of that self-defense training you got when you were growing up on Alderaan."

"Maybe that's the problem," Leia said. "Maybe all those old fighting reflexes are getting in my way."

"I suppose that's possible," Luke admitted, wishing he knew that, too. "In that case, the sooner you start un-learning them, the better. Now: ready—"

The door buzzed. "It's Han," Leia said, stepping away from the remote and closing down her lightsaber. "Come in," she called.

"Hi," Han said as he walked into the room, glancing in turn at Leia and Luke. He wasn't smiling. "How's the lesson going?"

"Not bad," Luke said.

"Don't ask," Leia countered, frowning at her husband. "What's wrong?"

"The Imperials," Han said sourly. "They just pulled a three-prong hit-and-fade on three systems in the Sluis sector. Some place called Bpfassh and two unpronounceable ones."

Luke whistled softly. "Three at once. Getting pretty cocky, aren't they?"

"That seems par for them these days." Leia shook her head, the skin around her eyes tight with concentration. "They're up to something, Han—I can feel it. Something big; something dangerous." She waved her hands helplessly. "But I can't for the life of me figure out what it could be."

"Yeah, Ackbar's been saying the same thing," Han nodded. "Problem is he's got nothing to back it up. Except for the style and tactics, this is all pretty much the same rear-guard harassment the Empire's been pulling for probably the last year and a half."

"I know," Leia gritted. "But don't sell Ackbar short—he's got good military instincts. No matter what certain other people say."

Han cocked an eyebrow. "Hey, sweetheart, I'm on *your* side. Remember?"

She smiled wanly. "Sorry. How bad was the damage?"

Han shrugged. "Not nearly as bad as it could have been. Especially considering that they hit each place with four Star Destroyers. But all three systems are pretty shook up."

"I can imagine," Leia sighed. "Let me guess: Mon Mothma wants me to go out there and assure them that the New Republic really *is* able and willing to protect them."

"How'd you guess?" Han growled. "Chewie's getting the *Falcon* prepped now."

"You're not going alone, are you?" Luke asked. "After Bimmisaari—"

"Oh, don't worry," Han said, throwing him a tight smile. "We're not going to be sitting ducks this time. There's a twenty-ship convoy going out to assess the damage, plus Wedge and Rogue Squadron. It'll be safe enough."

"That's what we said about Bimmisaari, too," Luke pointed out. "I'd better come along."

Han looked at Leia. "Well, actually . . . you can't."

Luke frowned at him. "Why not?"

"Because," Leia answered quietly, "the Bpfasshi don't like Jedi."

Han's lip twisted. "The story is that some of their

Jedi went bad during the Clone Wars and really mangled things before they were stopped. Or so Mon Mothma says."

"She's right," Leia nodded. "We were still getting echoes of the whole fiasco in the Imperial Senate when I was serving there. It wasn't just Bpfassh, either—some of those Dark Jedi escaped and made trouble all throughout the Sluis sector. One of them even got as far as Dagobah before he was caught."

Luke felt a jolt run through him. *Dagobah?* "When was that?" he asked as casually as possible.

"Thirty, thirty-five years ago," Leia said, her forehead creased slightly as she studied his face. "Why?"

Luke shook his head. Yoda had never mentioned a Dark Jedi ever being on Dagobah. "No reason," he murmured.

"Come on, we can discuss history later," Han put in. "The sooner we get going, the sooner we can get this over with."

"Right," Leia agreed, latching her lightsaber to her belt and heading for the door. "I'll get my travel bag and give Winter some instructions. Meet you at the ship."

Luke watched her leave; turned back to find Han eyeing him. "I don't like it," he told the other.

"Don't worry—she'll be safe," Han assured him. "Look, I know how protective you're feeling toward her these days. But she can't always have her big brother standing over her."

"Actually, we've never figured out which of us is older," Luke murmured.

"Whatever," Han waved the detail away. "The best thing you can do for her right now is what you're already doing. You make her a Jedi, and she'll be able to handle anything the Imperials can throw at her."

Luke's stomach tightened. "I suppose so."

"As long as Chewie and me are with her, that is," Han amended, heading for the door. "See you when we get back."

"Be careful," Luke called after him.

Han turned, one of those hurt/innocent expressions on his face. "Hey," he said. "It's *me*."

He left, and Luke was alone.

For a few moments he wandered around the room, fighting against the heavy weight of responsibility that seemed sometimes on the verge of smothering him. Risking his own life was one thing, but to have Leia's future in his hands was something else entirely. "I'm not a teacher," he called aloud into the empty room.

The only response was a flicker of movement from the still-paused remote. On sudden impulse, Luke kicked the device to life again, snatching his lightsaber from his belt as it moved to the attack. A dozen stinger blasts shot out in quick succession as the remote swooped like a crazed insect; effortlessly, Luke blocked each in turn, swinging the lightsaber in a flashing arc that seemed to engulf him, a strange exultation flowing through mind and body. *This* was something he could fight—not distant and shadowy like his private fears, but something solid and tangible. The remote fired again and again, each shot ricocheting harmlessly from the lightsaber blade—

With a sudden beep the remote stopped. Luke stared at it in confusion, wondering what had happened . . . and abruptly realized he was breathing heavily. Breathing heavily, and sweating. The remote had a twenty-minute time limit built in, and he'd just come to the end of it.

He closed down the lightsaber and returned it to his belt, feeling a little eerie about what had just happened. It wasn't the first time he'd lost track of time like that, but always before it had been during quiet meditation. The only times it had happened in anything like a combat situation were back on Dagobah, under Yoda's supervision.

On Dagobah . . .

Wiping the sweat out of his eyes with his sleeve, he walked over to the comm desk in the corner and punched up the spaceport. "This is Skywalker," he identified himself. "I'd like my X-wing prepped for launch in one hour."

"Yes, sir," the young maintenance officer said briskly. "We'll need you to send over your astromech unit first."

"Right," Luke nodded. He'd refused to let them wipe the X-wing's computer every few months, as per standard procedure. The inevitable result was that the computer had effectively molded itself around Artoo's unique personality, so much so that the relationship was almost up to true droid counterpart level. It made for excellent operational speed and efficiency; unfortunately, it also meant that none of the maintenance computers could talk to the X-wing anymore. "I'll have him there in a few minutes."

"Yes, sir."

Luke keyed off and straightened up, wondering vaguely why he was doing this. Surely Yoda's presence would no longer be there on Dagobah for him to talk to or ask questions of.

But then, perhaps it would.

CHAPTER 10

"As you can see," Wedge said, his voice grimly conversational as he crunched through plastic and ceramic underfoot, "the place is something of a mess."

"That's for sure," Leia agreed, feeling a little sick as she looked around at the flat-bottomed, rubble-strewn crater. A handful of other Republic representatives from her party were wandering around the area, too, holding quiet conversations with their Bpfasshi escorts and occasionally pausing to pick through the pieces of what had once been a major power plant. "How many people died in the attack?" she asked, not at all sure she wanted to hear the answer.

"In this system, a few hundred," Wedge told her, consulting a data pad. "Not too bad, really."

"No." Involuntarily, Leia glanced up at the deep bluegreen sky above them. Not bad, indeed. Especially considering that there had been no fewer than four Star

Destroyers raining destruction down on them. "A lot of damage, though."

"Yeah," Wedge nodded. "But not nearly as much as there could have been."

"I wonder why," Han muttered.

"So does everyone else," Wedge agreed. "It's been the second most popular question around here these days."

"What's the first?" Leia asked.

"Let me guess," Han put in before Wedge could answer. "The first is, why did they bother pounding on Bpfassh in the first place."

"You got it," Wedge nodded again. "It's not like they didn't have any better targets to choose from. You've got the Sluis Van shipyards about thirty light-years away, for starters—a hundred ships there at any given time, not to mention the docking facilities themselves. Then there's the Praesitlyn communications station at just under sixty, and four or five major trade centers within a hundred. An extra day of travel each way, tops, at Star Destroyer cruising speeds. So why Bpfassh?"

Leia thought it over. It *was* a good question. "Sluis Van itself is pretty heavily defended," she pointed out. "Between our Star Cruisers and the Sluissi's own permanent battle stations, any Imperial leader with a gram of sense would think twice before tackling it. And those other systems are all a lot deeper into New Republic space than Bpfassh. Maybe they didn't want to push their luck that far."

"While they tested their new transmission system under combat conditions?" Han suggested darkly.

"We don't *know* that they've got a new system,"

Wedge cautioned him. "Coordinated simultaneous attacks have been done before."

"No." Han shook his head, looking around. "No, they've got something new. Some kind of booster that lets them punch subspace transmissions through deflector shields and battle debris."

"I don't think it's a booster," Leia said, a shiver running up her back. Something was starting to tingle, way back at the edge of her mind. "No one in any of the three systems picked up any transmissions."

Han frowned down at her. "You okay?" he asked quietly.

"Yes," she murmured, shivering again. "I was just remembering that when—well, when Darth Vader was having us tortured on Bespin, Luke knew it was happening from wherever he was at the time. And there were rumors that the Emperor and Vader could do that, too."

"Yeah, but they're both dead," Han reminded her. "Luke said so."

"I know," she said. The tingling at the edge of her mind was getting stronger . . . "But what if the Imperials have found another Dark Jedi?"

Wedge had gotten ahead of them, but now he turned back. "You talking about C'baoth?"

"What?" Leia frowned.

"Joruus C'baoth," Wedge said. "I thought I heard you mention Jedi."

"I did," Leia said. "Who's Joruus C'baoth?"

"He was one of the major Jedi Masters back in pre-Empire days," Wedge said. "Supposed to have disappeared before the Clone Wars started. I heard a rumor a

STAR WARS: HEIR TO THE EMPIRE   133

couple of days ago that he's surfaced again and set up shop on some minor world named Jomark."

"Right." Han snorted. "And he was just sitting around doing nothing during the Rebellion?"

Wedge shrugged. "I just report 'em, General. I don't make 'em up."

"We can ask Luke," Leia said. "Maybe he knows something. Are we ready to move on?"

"Sure," Wedge said. "The airspeeders are over this way—"

And in a sudden rush of sensation, the tingling in Leia's mind abruptly exploded into certain knowledge. "Han, Wedge—*duck!*"

—and at the rim of the crater a handful of well-remembered gray-skinned aliens appeared.

"Cover!" Han shouted to the other Republic reps in the crater as the aliens opened up with blasters. Grabbing Leia's wrist, he dived for the limited protection of a huge but badly twisted plate of shielding metal that had somehow gotten itself dug halfway into the ground. Wedge was right behind them, slamming hard into Leia as he reached cover.

"Sorry," he panted in apology, yanking out his blaster and turning to throw a cautious look around the edge of their shelter. One look was all he got before a blaster bolt spattered metal near his face and sent him jerking back. "I'm not sure," he said, "but I think we've got trouble."

"I think you're right," Han agreed grimly. Leia turned to see him, blaster drawn, returning his comlink to his belt with his free hand. "They've learned. This time they're jamming our communications."

Leia felt cold all over. Way out here, without com-links, they were as good as helpless. Totally cut off from any possibility of help . . .

Her hand, reaching automatically for her stomach, brushed her new lightsaber instead. She pulled it free, a fresh determination pushing past the fear. Jedi or not, experienced or not, she wasn't going to give up without a fight.

"Sounds like you've run into these guys before," Wedge said, reaching around the barrier to squeeze off a couple of blind shots in the general direction of their attackers.

"We've met," Han grunted back, trying to get into position for a clear shot. "Haven't really figured out what they want, though."

Leia reached for her lightsaber's control stud, wondering if she had enough skill yet to block blaster fire . . . and paused. Over the noise of blasters and crackling metal she could hear a new sound. A very familiar sound . . . "Han!"

"I hear it," Han said. "Way to go, Chewie."

"What?" Wedge asked.

"That whine you hear is the *Falcon*," Han told him, leaning back to look over their shelter. "Probably discovered they were jamming us and put two and two together. Here he comes."

With a screaming roar the familiar shape of the *Millennium Falcon* swooped by overhead. It circled once, ignoring the ineffectual blasts ricocheting from its underside, and dropped to a bumpy landing directly between them and their attackers. Peering cautiously around their barrier, Leia saw the ramp lower toward them.

"Great," Han said, looking past her shoulder. "Okay. I'll go first and cover you from the bottom of the ramp. Leia, you're next; Wedge, you bring up the rear. Stay sharp—they may try to flank us."

"Got it," Wedge nodded. "Ready when you are."

"Okay." Han got his feet under him—

"Wait a minute," Leia said suddenly, gripping his arm. "There's something wrong."

"Right—we're getting shot at," Wedge put in.

"I'm serious," Leia snapped. "Something here's not right."

"Like what?" Han asked, frowning at her. "Come on, Leia, we can't sit here all day."

Leia gritted her teeth, trying to chase down the feeling tingling through her. It was still so nebulous . . . and then suddenly she had it. "It's Chewie," she told them. "I can't feel his presence on the ship."

"He's probably just too far away," Wedge said, a distinct note of impatience in his voice. "Come on—he's going to get the ship shot out from under him if we don't get going."

"Hang on a minute," Han growled, still frowning at Leia. "He's okay for now—all they're using is hand blasters. Anyway, if things get too hot, he can always use the—"

He broke off, a strange look on his face. A second later, Leia got it, too. "The underside swivel blaster," she said. "Why isn't he using it?"

"Good question," Han said grimly. He leaned out again, taking a hard look this time . . . and when he ducked back under cover there was a sardonic half-grin on his face. "Simple answer: that's not the *Falcon*."

"What?" Wedge asked, his jaw dropping a couple of centimeters.

"It's a fake," Han told him. "I can't believe it—these guys actually dug up another working YT-1300 freighter somewhere."

Wedge whistled softly. "Boy, they must really want you bad."

"Yeah, I'm starting to get that impression myself," Han said. "Got any good ideas?"

Wedge glanced around the edge of the barrier. "I don't suppose running for it qualifies."

"Not with them sitting out there at the edge of the crater waiting to pick us off," Leia told him.

"Yeah," Han agreed. "And as soon as they realize we're not going to just walk into their decoy, it'll probably get worse."

"Is there any way we can at least disable that ship?" Leia asked him. "Keep it from taking off and attacking us from above?"

"There are lots of ways," he grunted. "The problem is you have to be inside for most of them. The outside shielding isn't great, but it blocks hand blasters just fine."

"Will it block a lightsaber?"

He threw a suspicious frown at her. "You're not suggesting . . . ?"

"I don't think we've got any choice," she told him. "Do we?"

"I suppose not," he grimaced. "All right—but *I'll* go."

Leia shook her head. "We all go," she said. "We know they want at least one of us alive—otherwise, they'd just have flown by overhead and blasted us. If we all go together, they won't be able to fire. We'll head straight in as if we're going aboard, then split off to the sides at the last second and take cover behind the ramp. Wedge and I can fire up and inside to keep them busy while you take the lightsaber and disable them."

"I don't know," Han muttered. "I think just Wedge and me should go."

"No, it has to be all of us," Leia insisted. "That's the only way to guarantee they won't shoot."

Han looked at Wedge. "What do you think?"

"I think it's the best chance we're going to get," the other said. "But if we do it, we'd better do it fast."

"Yeah." Han took a deep breath and handed Leia his blaster. "All right. Give me the lightsaber. Okay; ready . . . go."

He ducked out from cover and charged for the ship, crouching down as he ran to avoid the blaster fire criss-crossing the crater—the other Republic reps, Leia noted as she and Wedge followed, doing a good job of keeping the rim attackers busy. Inside the ship she could see a hint of movement, and she gripped Han's blaster a little tighter. A half second in the lead, Han reached the ramp; and swerving suddenly to the side ducked under the hull.

The aliens must have realized instantly that their trap had failed. Even as Leia and Wedge skidded to a halt at opposite sides of the ramp, they were greeted by a burst of blaster fire from the open hatch. Dropping to the ground, Leia squirmed as far back as she could under the ramp, firing blindly into the hatch to discourage those inside from coming down after them. Across the ramp, Wedge was also firing; somewhere behind her, she could hear a faint scrabbling across the ground as Han got into position for whatever sabotage he was planning. A shot blazed past from above, narrowly missing her left shoulder, and she tried to back a little farther into the ramp's shadow. Behind her, clearly audible through the blaster fire, she heard a *snap-hiss* as Han ignited her lightsaber. Gritting her teeth, she braced herself, not knowing quite why—

And with a blast and shock wave that knocked her flat against the ground, the whole ship bounced a meter in the air and then slammed back down again.

Through the ringing in her ears, she heard someone give a war whoop. The firing from the hatch had abruptly stopped, and in the silence she could hear a strange hissing roar coming from above her. Cautiously, she eased away from the ramp and crawled a little ways out of concealment.

She'd been prepared to see the freighter leaking something as a result of Han's sabotage. She wasn't prepared for the huge white gaseous plume that was shooting skyward like the venting of a ruptured volcano.

"You like it?" Han asked, easing over beside her and glancing up to admire his handiwork.

"That probably depends on whether the ship's about to blow up," Leia countered. "What did you *do*?"

"Cut through the coolant lines to the main drive," he told her, retrieving his blaster and handing back her lightsaber. "That's all their pressurized korfaise gas floating away."

"I thought coolant gases were dangerous to breathe," Leia said, looking warily at the billowing cloud.

"They are," Han agreed. "But korfaise is lighter than

air, so we won't have any trouble down here. *Inside* the ship is another matter. I hope."

Abruptly, Leia became aware of the silence around them. "They've stopped shooting," she said.

Han listened. "You're right. Not just the ones inside the ship, either."

"I wonder what they're up to," Leia murmured, tightening her grip on the lightsaber.

A second later she got her answer. A violent thunderclap came from above them, flattening her to the ground with the shock wave. For a horrifying second she thought the aliens had set the ship to self-destruct; but the sound faded away, and the ramp beside her was still intact. "What was *that*?"

"That, sweetheart," Han said, pulling himself to his feet, "was the sound of an escape pod being jettisoned." He eased cautiously away from the relative protection of the ramp, scanning the sky. "Probably modified for atmospheric maneuvering. Never realized before how loud those things were."

"They usually take off in vacuum," Leia reminded him, standing up herself. "So. Now what?"

"Now—" Han pointed "—we collect our escort and get out of here."

"Our escort?" Leia frowned. "What esc—?"

Her question was cut off by the roar of engines as three X-wings shot overhead, wings in attack position and clearly primed for trouble. She looked up at the white tower of korfaise gas . . . and suddenly understood. "You did that deliberately, didn't you?"

"Well, sure," Han said, looking innocent. "Why just disable a ship when you can disable it *and* send up a distress signal at the same time?" He gazed up at the cloud. "You know," he said thoughtfully, "sometimes I still amaze myself."

"I CAN ASSURE you, Captain Solo," Admiral Ackbar's gravelly voice came over the *Falcon*'s speaker, "that we are doing everything in our power to find out how this happened."

"That's what you said four days ago," Han reminded him, trying hard to be civil. It wasn't easy. He'd long since gotten used to being shot at himself, but having Leia under the hammer with him was something else entirely. "Come on—there can't be all *that* many people who knew we were coming to Bpfassh."

"You might be surprised," Ackbar said. "Between the Council members, their staffs, the prep crews at the spaceport, and various security and support personnel, there may be up to two hundred people who had direct access to your itinerary. And that doesn't count friends and colleagues any of those two hundred might have mentioned it to. Tracking through all of them is going to take time."

Han grimaced. "That's great. May I ask what you suggest we do in the meantime?"

"You have your escort."

"We had them four days ago, too," Han countered. "It didn't do us a lot of good. Commander Antilles and Rogue Squadron are fine in a space battle, but this kind of stuff isn't exactly their area of expertise. We'd do better with Lieutenant Page and some of his commandos."

"Unfortunately, they're all out on assignment," Ackbar said. "Under the circumstances, perhaps it would be best if you simply brought Councilor Organa Solo back here where she can be properly protected."

"I'd love to," Han said. "The question is whether she'll be any safer on Coruscant than she is here."

There was a long moment of silence, and Han could imagine Ackbar's huge eyes swiveling in their sockets, "I'm not sure I appreciate the tone of that question, Captain."

"I don't much like it either, Admiral," Han told him. "But face it: if the Imperials are getting information *out* of the Palace, they might just as easily be able to get their agents *in*."

"I think that highly unlikely," Ackbar said, and there was no missing the frostiness in his tone. "The security arrangements I've set up on Coruscant are quite capable of handling anything the Imperials might try."

"I'm sure they are, Admiral," Han sighed. "I only meant—"

"We'll let you know when we have further information, Captain," Ackbar said. "Until then, do whatever you feel is necessary. Coruscant out."

The faint hum of the carrier cut off. "Right," Han muttered under his breath. "Bpfassh out, too."

For a minute he just sat there in the *Falcon*'s cockpit, thinking evil thoughts about politics in general and Ackbar in particular. In front of him the displays that normally monitored ship's status were showing views of the landing field around them, with special emphasis on the areas just outside the hatch. The underside swivel blaster was extended and ready, the deflector shields set for hair-trigger activation, despite the fact that the things weren't all that effective inside an atmosphere.

Han shook his head, a mixture of frustration and disgust in his mouth. *Who'd ever have thought*, he marveled to himself, *that the day would come when I was actually paranoid?*

From the rear of the cockpit came the sound of a soft footstep. Han turned, hand automatically dropping to his blaster—

"It's just me," Leia assured him, coming forward and glancing at the displays. She looked tired. "You finished talking with Ackbar already?"

"It wasn't much of a conversation," Han told her sourly. "I asked what they were doing to find out how our pals with the blasters knew we were coming here, he assured me they were doing everything possible to find out, I managed to step on his toes, and he signed off in a huff. Pretty much like usual with Ackbar these days."

Leia gave him a wry smile. "You *do* have a way with people, don't you?"

"This one's not my fault," Han objected. "All I did was suggest that his security people *might* not be up to keeping these guys out of the Imperial Palace. *He's* the one who overreacted."

"I know," Leia nodded, dropping wearily into the co-pilot's seat. "For all his military genius, Ackbar just doesn't have the polish to be a good politician. And with Fey'lya nipping at his heels . . ." She shrugged uncomfortably. "He just gets more and more overprotective of his territory."

"Yeah, well, if he's trying to keep Fey'lya away from

the military, he's got the wrong end of the blaster," Han growled. "Half of them are already convinced that Fey'lya's the guy to listen to."

"Unfortunately, he often is," Leia conceded. "Charisma and ambition. Dangerous combination."

Han frowned. There had been something in her voice just then . . . "What do you mean, dangerous?"

"Nothing," she said, a guilty look flicking across her face. "Sorry—talking out of turn."

"Leia, if you know something—"

"I don't *know* anything," she said, in a tone that warned him to drop it. "It's just a feeling I have. A sense that Fey'lya has his eye on more than just Ackbar's job as supreme commander. But it's just a feeling."

Like the feeling she had that the Empire was up to something big? "Okay," he said soothingly. "I understand. So. You all done here?"

"As done as I can be," she said, the tiredness back in her voice. "The rebuilding's going to take some time, but the organization for that will have to be handled from Coruscant." She leaned back in her seat and closed her eyes. "Convoys of replacement equipment, consultants and maybe extra workers—you know the sort of thing."

"Yeah," Han said. "And I suppose you're anxious to get right back and start the ball rolling."

She opened her eyes and gave him a curious look. "You sound like you're not."

Han gave the outside displays a thoughtful scan. "Well, it's what everyone's going to expect you to do," he pointed out. "So maybe we ought to do something else."

"Such as?"

"I don't know. Find somewhere no one would think to look for you, I guess."

"And then . . . ?" she asked, her voice ominous.

Unconsciously, Han braced himself. "And then hole up there for a while."

"You know I can't do that," she said, her tone just about what he'd expected. "I have commitments back on Coruscant."

"You've got commitments to yourself, too," he countered. "Not to mention to the twins."

She glared at him. "That's not fair."

"Isn't it?"

She turned away from him, an unreadable expression on her face. "I can't be out of touch, Han," she said quietly. "I just can't. There's too much happening back there for me to bury myself away."

Han gritted his teeth. They seemed to be running over this same territory a lot lately. "Well, if all you need right now is to keep in touch, how about if we go some place that has a diplomatic station? You'd at least be able to get official Coruscant news there."

"And how do we make sure the local ambassador doesn't give us away?" She shook her head. "I can't believe I'm talking like this," she muttered. "It's like we're back being the Rebellion again, not the legitimate government."

"Who says the ambassador has to know?" Han asked. "We've got a diplomatic receiver on the *Falcon*—we can tap into the transmission on our own."

"Only if we can get hold of the station's encrypt scheme," she reminded him. "And then plug it into our receiver. That may not be possible."

"We can find a way," Han insisted. "At least it would buy Ackbar some time to track down the leak."

"True." Leia considered, slowly shook her head. "I don't know. The New Republic's encrypt codes are nearly impossible to break."

Han snorted. "I hate to disillusion you, sweetheart, but there are slicers running around loose who eat government encrypt codes for breakfast. All we have to do is find one of them."

"And pay him enormous sums of money?" Leia said dryly.

"Something like that," Han agreed, thinking hard. "On the other hand, even slicers occasionally owe other people favors."

"Oh?" Leia threw him a sideways look. "I don't suppose you'd know any of them."

"As a matter of fact, I do." Han pursed his lips. "Trouble is, if the Imperials have done their homework, they probably know all about it and have someone watching him."

"Meaning . . . ?"

"Meaning we're going to have to find someone who's got his own list of slicer contacts." He reached over to the console and tapped the *Falcon*'s comm switch. "Antilles, this is Solo. You copy?"

"Right here, General," Wedge's voice came back promptly.

"We're leaving Bpfassh, Wedge," Han told him. "That's not official yet—you're in charge of telling the rest of the delegation about it once we're off the ground."

"I understand," Wedge said. "You want me to assign you an escort, or would you rather slip out quietly? I've got a couple of people I'd trust all the way to the end of the galaxy."

Han sent Leia a lopsided smile. Wedge understood, all right. "Thanks, but we wouldn't want the rest of the delegation to feel unprotected."

"Whatever you want. I can handle anything that needs doing at this end. See you back at Coruscant."

"Right." Han cut off the comm. "Eventually," he added under his breath as he keyed for intercom. "Chewie? We ready to fly?"

The Wookiee growled an affirmative. "Okay. Make sure everything's bolted down and then come on up. Better bring Threepio, too—we might have to talk to Bpfasshi Control on the way out."

"Do I get to know where we're going?" Leia asked as he started the prelaunch sequence.

"I already told you," Han said. "We need to find someone we can trust who has his own list of illegals."

A suspicious glint came into her eye. "You don't mean . . . Lando?"

"Who else?" Han said innocently. "Upstanding citizen, former war hero, honest businessman. Of *course* he'll have slicer contacts."

Leia rolled her eyes skyward. "Why," she murmured, "do I suddenly have a bad feeling about this?"

CHAPTER 11

"HANG ON, ARTOO," Luke called as the first gusts of atmospheric turbulence began to bounce the X-wing around. "We're coming in. Scanners all working okay?"

There was an affirmative twitter from the rear, the translation appearing across his computer scope. "Good," Luke said, and turned his attention back to the cloud-shrouded planet rushing up to meet them. It was odd, he thought, how it had only been on that first trip in to Dagobah that the sensors had so totally failed on approach.

Or perhaps not so odd. Perhaps that had been Yoda, deliberately suppressing his instruments so as to be able to guide him unsuspectingly to the proper landing site.

And now Yoda was gone . . .

Firmly, Luke put the thought out of his mind. Mourning the loss of a friend and teacher was both fitting and honorable, but to dwell unnecessarily on that loss was to give the past too much power over the present.

The X-wing dropped into the lower atmosphere, and within seconds was completely enveloped by thick white clouds. Luke watched the instruments, taking the approach slow and easy. The last time he'd come here, just before the Battle of Endor, he'd made the landing without incident; but just the same, he had no intention of pushing his luck. The landing sensors had Yoda's old homestead pinpointed now. "Artoo?" he called. "Find me a good level spot to set down, will you?"

In response, a red rectangle appeared on the forward scope, a ways east of the house but within walking distance of it. "Thanks," Luke told the droid, and keyed in the landing cycle. A moment later, with one last mad flurry of displaced tree branches, they were down.

Slipping off his helmet, Luke popped the canopy. The rich odors of the Dagobah swamp flooded in on him, a strange combination of sweet and decay that sent a hundred memories flashing through his mind. That slow twitch of Yoda's ears—the strange but tasty stew he'd often made—the way that wispy hair of his had tickled Luke's ears whenever he rode on Luke's back during training. The training itself: the long hours, the physical and mental fatigue, the gradually increasing sense of and confidence in the Force, the cave and its dark side images—

The cave?

Abruptly, Luke stood up in the cockpit, hand going reflexively to his lightsaber as he peered through the haze. Surely he hadn't brought his X-wing down by the cave.

He had. There, no more than fifty meters away, was

the tree that grew from just above that evil place, its huge blackened shape jutting upward through the surrounding trees. Beneath and between its tangled roots, just visible through the mists and shorter vegetation, he could see the dark entrance to the cave itself.

"Wonderful," he muttered. "Just wonderful."

From behind him came an interrogative set of beeps. "Never mind, Artoo," he called over his shoulder, dropping his helmet back onto the seat. "It's all right. Why don't you stay here, and I'll—"

The X-wing rocked, just a bit, and he looked back to find Artoo already out of his socket and working his way gingerly forward. "Or if you'd rather, you can come along," he added wryly.

Artoo beeped again—not a cheerful beep, exactly, but one that definitely sounded relieved. The little droid hated being left alone. "Hang on," Luke directed him. "I'll get down and give you a hand."

He jumped down. The ground felt a little squishy beneath his feet, but it was easily firm enough to support the X-wing's weight. Satisfied, he reached out with the Force to lift Artoo from his perch and lower the droid to the ground beside him. "There you go," he said.

From off in the distance came the long, trilling wail of one of Dagobah's birds. Luke listened as it ran down the scale, eyes searching the swamp around him and wondering why exactly he'd come here. Back on Coruscant it had seemed important—even vital—that he do so. But now that he was actually standing here it all seemed hazy. Hazy, and more than a little silly.

Beside him, Artoo beeped questioningly. With an effort, Luke shook off the uncertainties. "I thought Yoda might have left something behind that we could use," he told the droid, choosing the most easily verbalized of his reasons. "The house should be—" he glanced around to get his bearings "—that way. Let's go."

The distance wasn't great, but the trip took longer than Luke had anticipated. Partly it was the general terrain and vegetation—he'd forgotten just how difficult it was to get from one place to another through the Dagobah swamps. But there was something else, too: a low-level but persistent pressure at the back of his mind that seemed to press inward, clouding his ability to think.

But at last they arrived . . . to find the house effectively gone.

For a long minute Luke just stood there, gazing at the mass of vegetation occupying the spot where the house had been, a freshly renewed sense of loss struggling against the embarrassing realization that he'd been a fool. Growing up in the deserts of Tatooine, where an abandoned structure could last for half a century or more, it had somehow never even occurred to him to consider what would happen to that same structure after five years in a swamp.

Beside him, Artoo twittered a question. "I thought Yoda might have left some tapes or books behind," Luke explained. "Something that would tell me more about the methods of Jedi training. Not much left, though, is there?"

In response, Artoo extended his little sensor plate. "Never mind," Luke told him, starting forward. "As long as we're here, I guess we might as well take a look."

It took only a few minutes to cut a path through the bushes and vines with his lightsaber and to reach what was left of the house's outer walls. For the most part they were rubble, reaching only to his waist at their highest, and covered with a crisscrossing of tiny vines. Inside was more vegetation, pushing up against, and in some places through, the old stone hearth. Half buried in the mud were Yoda's old iron pots, covered with a strange-looking moss.

Behind him, Artoo gave a quiet whistle. "No, I don't think we're going to find anything useful," Luke agreed, squatting down to pull one of the pots out of the ground. A small lizard darted out as he did so, and disappeared into the reedy grass. "Artoo, see if you can find anything electronic around here, will you? I never saw him use anything like that, but . . ." He shrugged.

The droid obediently raised his sensor plate again. Luke watched as it tracked back and forth . . . and suddenly stopped. "Find something?" Luke asked.

Artoo twittered excitedly, his dome swiveling to look back the way they'd come. "Back that way?" Luke frowned. He looked down at the debris around him. "Not here?"

Artoo beeped again and turned around, rolling with some difficulty across the uneven surface. Pausing, he swiveled his dome back toward Luke and made a series of sounds that could only have been a question. "Okay, I'm coming," Luke sighed, forcing back the odd sense of dread that had suddenly seized him. "Lead the way."

THE SUNLIGHT FILTERING through the leafy canopy overhead had become noticeably dimmer by the time they came within sight of the X-wing. "Now where?" Luke asked Artoo. "I hope you're not going to tell me that all you were picking up was our own ship."

Artoo swiveled his dome back around, trilling a decidedly indignant denial. His sensor plate turned slightly—

To point directly at the cave.

Luke swallowed hard. "You're sure?"

The droid trilled again. "You're sure," Luke said.

For a minute he just looked across through the mists at the cave, indecision swirling through his mind. There was no genuine need for him to go in there—of that much he was certain. Whatever it was Artoo had detected, it would not be anything Yoda had left behind. Not in there.

But then what was it? Leia had referred to a Bpfasshi Dark Jedi who'd come here. Could it be something of his?

Luke gritted his teeth. "Stay here, Artoo," he instructed the droid as he started across to the cave. "I'll be back as soon as I can."

Fear and anger, Yoda had often warned him, were the slaves of the dark side. Vaguely, Luke wondered which side curiosity served.

Up close, the tree straddling the cave looked as evil as he remembered it: twisted, dark, and vaguely brooding, as if it was itself alive with the dark side of the Force. Perhaps it was. Luke couldn't tell for sure, not with the overwhelming emanations of the cave flooding his senses. It was, clearly, the source of the low-level pressure he'd felt ever since his arrival on Dagobah, and for a moment he wondered why the effect had never been this strong before.

Perhaps because Yoda had always been here before, his presence shielding Luke from the true strength of the cave's power.

But now Yoda was gone . . . and Luke was facing the cave alone.

He took a deep breath. *I am a Jedi*, he reminded himself firmly. Slipping his comlink from his belt, he thumbed it on. "Artoo? You copy?"

The comlink trilled back. "Okay. I'm starting in. Give me a signal when I get close to whatever it is you're picking up."

He got an affirmative-sounding beep. Returning the comlink to his belt, he drew his lightsaber. Taking another deep breath, he ducked under the gnarled tree roots and stepped into the cave.

This, too, was as bad as he remembered it. Dark, dank, alive with skittering insects and slimy plants, it was generally as unpleasant a place as Luke had ever been in. The footing seemed more treacherous than it had been before, and twice in the first dozen steps he nearly fell on his face as the ground gave way beneath his weight; not badly, but enough to throw him off balance. Through the mists ahead a well-remembered spot loomed, and he found himself gripping his lightsaber all the more tightly as he neared it. On this spot, once, he'd fought a nightmare battle with a shadowy, unreal Darth Vader . . .

He reached the place and stopped, fighting back the fear and memories. But this time, to his relief, nothing happened. No hissing breath came from the shadows; no Dark Lord glided forward to confront him. Nothing.

Luke licked his lips and pulled the comlink off his

belt. No; of course there would be nothing. He had already faced that crisis—had faced it and conquered it. With Vader redeemed and gone, the cave had nothing further to threaten him with except nameless and unreal fears, and those only if he allowed them to have power over him. He should have realized that from the start. "Artoo?" he called. "You still there?"

The little droid buzzed in reply. "All right," Luke said, starting forward again. "How far do I have to—?"

And right in the middle of his sentence—practically in the middle of a step—the haze of the cave abruptly coalesced around him into a flickering, surreal vision . . .

He was on a small, open-air ground vehicle, hovering low over some sort of pit. The ground itself was indistinct, but he could feel a terrible heat rising all around him from it. Something poked hard in his back, urging him forward onto a narrow board protruding horizontally from the vehicle's side—

Luke caught his breath, the scene suddenly coming clear. He was back on Jabba the Hutt's skiff, being prepared for his execution in the Great Pit of Carkoon—

Ahead, he could see the shape of Jabba's Sail Barge now, drifting a bit closer as the courtiers jostled one another for a better view of the coming spectacle. Many of the barge's details were indistinct through the dream mists, but he could see clearly the small, dome-topped figure of Artoo at the top of the ship. Awaiting Luke's signal . . .

"I'm not going to play this game," Luke called out toward the vision. "I'm not. I've faced this crisis, too, and I've defeated it."

But his words seemed dead even in his own ears . . .

and even as he spoke them, he could feel the jab of the guard's spear in his back, and could feel himself drop off the end of the plank. In midair he twisted around, grabbing the end of the board and flipping high over the guards' heads—

He landed and turned back toward the Sail Barge, hand extended for the lightsaber Artoo had just sent arcing toward him.

It never reached him. Even as he stood there waiting for it, the weapon changed direction, curving back toward the other end of the Sail Barge. Frantically, Luke reached out for it with the Force; but to no avail. The lightsaber continued its flight—

And came to rest in the hand of a slender woman standing alone at the top of the barge.

Luke stared at her, a feeling of horror surging through him. In the mists, with the sun behind her, he could see no details of her face . . . but the lightsaber she now held aloft like a prize told him all he needed to know. She had the power of the Force . . . and had just condemned him and his friends to death.

And as the spears pushed him again onto the plank he heard, clearly through the dream mists, her mocking laughter . . .

"No!" Luke shouted; and as suddenly as it had appeared, the vision vanished. He was back in the cave on Dagobah, his forehead and tunic soaked with sweat, a frantic electronic beeping coming from the comlink in his hand.

He took a shuddering breath, squeezing his lightsaber hard to reassure himself that he did indeed still have it. "It's—" He worked moisture into a dry throat and tried again. "It's okay, Artoo," he reassured the droid. "I'm all right. Uh . . ." He paused, fighting through the disorientation to try to remember what he was doing here. "Are you still picking up that electronic signal?"

Artoo beeped affirmatively. "Is it still ahead of me?"

Another affirmative beep. "Okay," Luke said. Shifting the lightsaber in his hand, he wiped more of the sweat from his forehead and started cautiously forward, trying to watch all directions at once.

But the cave had apparently done its worst. No more visions rose to challenge his way as he continued deeper in . . . and at last, Artoo signaled that he was there.

The device, once he'd finally pried it out of the mud and moss, was a distinct disappointment: a small, somewhat flattened cylinder a little longer than his hand, with five triangular, rust-encrusted keys on one side and some flowing alien script engraved on the other. "This is it?" Luke asked, not sure he liked the idea of having come all the way in here just for something so totally nondescript. "There's nothing else?"

Artoo beeped affirmatively, and gave a whistle that could only be a question. "I don't know what it is," Luke told the droid. "Maybe you'll recognize it. Hang on; I'm coming out."

The return trip was unpleasant but also uneventful, and a short time later he emerged from under the tree roots with a sigh of relief into the relatively fresh air of the swamp.

It had grown dark while he'd been inside, he noted to his mild surprise; that twisted vision of the past must have lasted longer than it had seemed. Artoo had the X-wing's landing lights on; the beams were visible as hazy cones in the air. Wading his way through the ground vegetation, Luke headed toward the X-wing.

Artoo was waiting for him, beeping quietly to himself. The beeping became a relieved whistle as Luke came into the light, the little droid rocking back and forth like a nervous child. "Relax, Artoo, I'm all right," Luke assured him, squatting down and pulling the flattened cylinder out of his side pocket. "What do you think?"

The droid chirped thoughtfully, his dome swiveling around to examine the object from a couple of different directions. Then, abruptly, the chirping exploded into an excited electronic jabbering. "What?" Luke asked, trying to read the flurry of sounds and wondering wryly why Threepio was never around when you needed him. "Slow down, Artoo. I can't—never mind," he interrupted himself, getting to his feet and glancing around in the gathering darkness. "I don't think there's any point in hanging around here anymore, anyway."

He looked back at the cave, now almost swallowed up by the deepening gloom, and shivered. No, there was no reason to stay . . . and at least one very good reason to leave. So much, he thought glumly, for finding any kind of enlightenment here. He should have known better. "Come on," he told the droid. "Let's get you back in your socket. You can tell me all about it on the way home."

ARTOO'S REPORT ON the cylinder was, it turned out, fairly short and decidedly negative. The little droid did not recognize the design, could not decipher its function from what his general-purpose scanners could pick up, and didn't even know what language the script on the side

was written in, let alone what it said. Luke was beginning to wonder what all the droid's earlier excitement
had been about . . . until the last sentence scrolled across
his computer scope.

"Lando?" Luke frowned, reading the sentence again.
"I don't remember ever seeing Lando with anything like
this."

More words scrolled across the scope. "Yes, I realize I
was busy at the time," Luke agreed, unconsciously flexing the fingers of his artificial right hand. "Getting fitted
with a new hand will do that. So did he give it to General
Madine, or was he just showing it to him?"

Another sentence appeared. "That's okay," Luke assured the droid. "I imagine you were busy, too."

He looked into his rear display, at the crescent of
Dagobah growing ever smaller behind him. He had intended to go straight back to Coruscant and wait for
Leia and Han to return from Bpfassh. But from what
he'd heard, their mission there could run a couple of
weeks or even more. And Lando had invited him more
than once to visit his new rare-ore mining operation on
the superhot planet of Nkllon.

"Change in plans, Artoo," he announced, keying in a
new course. "We're going to swing over to the Athega
system and see Lando. Maybe he can tell us what this
thing is."

And on the way, he'd have time to think about that
disturbing dream or vision or whatever it was he'd had in
the cave. And to decide whether it had been, in fact,
nothing more than a dream.

CHAPTER 12

"No, I don't have a transit permit for Nkllon," Han said patiently into the *Falcon*'s transmitter, glaring across at the modified B-wing running beside them. "I also don't have any accounts here. I'm trying to reach Lando Calrissian."

From the seat behind him came a sound that might have been a stifled laugh. "You say something?" he asked over his shoulder.

"No," Leia said innocently. "Just remembering the past."

"Right," Han growled. He remembered, too; and Bespin wasn't on his list of fond memories. "Look, just give Lando a call, will you?" he suggested to the B-wing. "Tell him that an old friend is here, and thought we might play a hand of sabacc for my choice of his stock. Lando will understand."

"We want to *what*?" Leia asked, leaning forward around his chair to give him a startled look.

Han muted the transmitter. "The Imperials might have spies here, too," he reminded her. "If they do, announcing our names to the whole Athega system wouldn't be very smart."

"Point," Leia conceded reluctantly. "That's a pretty strange message, though."

"Not to Lando," Han assured her. "He'll know it's me—provided that middle-level button pusher out there loosens up and sends it in."

Beside him, Chewbacca growled a warning: something big was approaching from aft-starboard. "Any make on it?" Han asked, craning his neck to try to get a look.

The transmitter crackled back to life before the Wookiee could answer. "Unidentified ship, General Calrissian has authorized a special transit waiver for you," the B-wing said, his tone sounding a little disappointed. He'd probably been looking forward to personally kicking the troublemakers out of his system. "Your escort is moving to intercept; hold your current position until he arrives."

"Acknowledged," Han said, not quite able to bring himself to thank the man.

"Escort?" Leia asked cautiously. "Why an escort?"

"That's what you get for going off and doing politics stuff when Lando drops by the Palace for a visit," Han admonished her, still craning his neck. There it was . . . "Nkllon's a superhot planet—way too close to its sun for any normal ship to get to without getting part of its hull peeled off. Hence—" he waved Leia's attention to the right "—the escort."

There was a sharp intake of air from behind him, and

even Han, who'd seen Lando's holos of these things, had to admit it was an impressive sight. More than anything else the shieldship resembled a monstrous flying umbrella, a curved dish fully half as big across as an Imperial Star Destroyer. The underside of the dish was ridged with tubes and fins—pumping and storage equipment for the coolant that helped keep the dish from burning up during the trip inward. Where the umbrella's handle would have been was a thick cylindrical pylon, reaching half as far back as the umbrella dish was wide, its far end bristling with huge radiator fins. In the center of the pylon, looking almost like an afterthought, was the tug ship that drove the thing.

"Good skies," Leia murmured, sounding stunned. "And it actually *flies*?"

"Yeah, but not easily," Han told her, watching with a slight trickle of apprehension as the monstrosity moved ever closer to his ship. It didn't have to move all *that* close—the *Falcon* was considerably smaller than the huge container ships the shieldships normally escorted. "Lando told me they had all sorts of trouble getting the things designed properly in the first place, and almost as much trouble teaching people how to fly them."

Leia nodded. "I believe it."

The transmitter crackled again. "Unidentified ship, this is Shieldship Nine. Ready to lock; please transmit your slave circuit code."

"Right," Han muttered under his breath, touching the transmit switch. "Shieldship Nine, we don't have a slave circuit. Just give me your course and we'll stay with you."

There was a moment of silence. "Very well, unidentified ship," the voice said at last—reluctantly, Han thought. "Set your course at two-eight-four; speed, point six sublight."

Without waiting for an acknowledgment, the huge umbrella began to drift off. "Stay with him, Chewie," Han told the copilot. Not that that would be a problem; the *Falcon* was faster and infinitely more maneuverable than anything that size. "Shieldship Nine, what's our ETA for Nkllon?"

"You in a hurry, unidentified ship?"

"How could we be in a hurry, with this wonderful view?" Han asked sarcastically, looking at the underside of the dish that filled pretty much the entire sky. "Yeah, we're in kind of a hurry."

"Sorry to hear that," the other said. "You see, if you had a slave circuit, we could do a quick hyperspace hop inward together and be at Nkllon in maybe an hour. Doing it this way—well, it'll take us about ten."

Han grimaced. "Great."

"We could probably set up a temporary slave circuit," Leia suggested. "Threepio knows the *Falcon*'s computer well enough to do that."

Chewbacca half turned toward her, growling a refusal that left no room for argument, even if Han had been inclined to argue. Which he wasn't. "Chewie's right," he told Leia firmly. "We don't slave this ship to anything. Ever. You copy that, shieldship?"

"Okay by me, unidentified ship," the other said. They all seemed to be taking a perverse pleasure in using that phrase. "I get paid by the hour anyway."

"Fine," Han said. "Let's get to it."

"Sure."

The transmission cut off, and Han poised his hands over the controls. The umbrella was still drifting, but nothing more. "Chewie, has he got his engines off standby yet?"

The Wookiee rumbled a negative.

"What's wrong?" Leia asked, leaning forward again.

"I don't know," Han said, looking around. With the umbrella in the way, there wasn't a lot to see. "I don't like it, though." He tapped the transmitter. "Shieldship Nine, what's the holdup?"

"Not to worry, unidentified ship," the voice came back soothingly. "We've got another craft coming in that also doesn't have a slave circuit, so we're going to take you both in together. No point in tying up two of us, right?"

The hairs on the back of Han's neck began to tingle. Another ship that just happened to be coming into Nkllon the same time they were. "You have an ID on that other ship?" he asked.

The other snorted. "Hey, friend, we don't even have an ID on *you*."

"You're a big help," Han said, muting the transmitter again. "Chewie, you got an approach yet on this guy?"

The Wookiee's reply was short and succinct. And disturbing. "Cute," Han growled. "Real cute."

"I missed that," Leia murmured, looking over his shoulder.

"He's coming in from the far side of the shieldship's central pylon," Han told her grimly, pointing to the inference brackets on the scanner scope. "Keeping it between him and us where we can't see him."

"Is he doing it on purpose?"

"Probably," Han nodded, hitting his restraint release. "Chewie, take over; I'm going to fire up the quads."

He ran back along the cockpit corridor to the central core and headed up the ladder. "Captain Solo," a nervous mechanical voice called after him from the direction of the lounge. "Is something wrong?"

"Probably, Threepio," Han shouted back. "Better strap in."

He got up the ladder, passed through the right-angle gravity discontinuity at the gun well, and dropped himself into the seat. The control board went on with satisfying quickness, as he keyed for power with one hand and grabbed the headset with the other. "Anything yet, Chewie?" he called into his mike.

The other growled a negative: the approaching craft was still completely hidden by the shieldship's pylon. But the inference scope was now giving a distance reading, and from that the Wookiee had been able to compute an upper size limit for the craft. It wasn't very big. "Well, that's something," Han told him, running through his mental list of starship types and trying to figure out what the Empire might be throwing at them that would be that small. Some variety of TIE fighter, maybe? "Stay sharp—this might be a decoy."

The inference scope pinged: the unknown ship was starting to come around the pylon. Han braced himself, fingers resting lightly on the fire controls . . .

And with a suddenness that surprised him, the ship burst into sight, rounding the pylon in a twisting spiral. It steadied slightly—

"It's an X-wing," Leia identified it, sounding greatly relieved. "With Republic markings—"

"Hello, strangers," Luke's voice crackled into Han's ear. "Good to see you."

"Uh . . . hi," Han said, stifling the automatic urge to greet Luke by name. Theoretically, they were on a secure frequency, but it was easy enough for anyone with sufficient motivation to get around such formalities. "What are you doing here?"

"I came to see Lando," Luke told him. "Sorry if I startled you. When they told me I'd be going in with an unidentified ship I thought it might be a trap. I wasn't completely sure it was you until a minute ago."

"Ah," Han said, watching as the other ship settled into a parallel course. It was Luke's X-wing, all right.

Or at least, it *looked* like Luke's X-wing. "So," he said casually, swiveling the laser cannons around to target the other. Situated the way it was, the X-wing would have to yaw 90 degrees around before it could fire at them. Unless, of course, it had been modified. "This just a social call, or what?"

"Not really. I found an old gadget that . . . well, I thought Lando might be able to identify it." He hesitated. "I don't think we ought to discuss it out in the open like this. How about you?"

"I don't think we should talk about that, either," Han told him, mind racing. It sounded like Luke, too; but after that near-disastrous decoy attempt on Bpfassh, he wasn't about to take anything for granted. Somehow, they needed to make a positive identification, and fast.

He tapped a switch, cutting himself out of the radio circuit. "Leia, can you tell whether or not that's really Luke out there?"

"I think so," she said slowly. "I'm almost positive it is."

"'Almost positive' won't cut it, sweetheart," he warned her.

"I know," she said. "Hang on; I've got an idea."

Han cut himself back into the radio circuit. "—said that if I had a slave circuit they could get me in a lot faster," Luke was saying. "A hyperspace jump as close to Nkllon as the gravity well will permit, and then just a few minutes of cover before I'd be in the planetary umbra and could go the rest of the way in on my own."

"Except that X-wings don't come equipped with slave circuits?" Han suggested.

"Right," Luke said, a little dryly. "Some oversight in the design phase, no doubt."

"No doubt," Han echoed, beginning to sweat a little. Whatever Leia was up to, he wished she'd get to it.

"Actually, I'm glad you don't have one," Leia spoke up. "It feels safer traveling in convoy this way. Oh, before I forget, there's someone here who wants to say hello."

"Artoo?" Threepio's prissy voice said tentatively. "Are you there?"

Han's headphone erupted with a blather of electronic beeps and twitters. "Well, I don't *know* where else you might have been," Threepio said stiffly. "From past experience, there are a considerable variety of difficulties you could have gotten yourself into. Certainly without me along to smooth things out for you."

The headphone made a noise that sounded suspiciously like an electronic snort. "Yes, well, you've *always* believed that," Threepio countered, even more stiffly. "I suppose you're entitled to your delusions."

Artoo snorted again; and, smiling tightly to himself,

Han keyed off his control board and dropped the lasers back into standby status. He'd known a lot of men, back in his smuggling days, who wouldn't have wanted a wife who could sometimes think faster than they could.

Speaking for himself, Han had long ago decided he wouldn't have it any other way.

THE SHIELDSHIP PILOT hadn't been exaggerating. It was nearly ten hours later when he finally signaled that they were on their own, made one final not-quite-impolite comment, and pulled off to the side, out of the way.

There wasn't much to see; but then, Han decided, the dark side of an undeveloped planet was seldom very scenic. A homing signal winked at him from one of the scopes, and he made a leisurely turn in the indicated direction.

From behind him came the sound of a footstep. "What's happening?" Leia asked, yawning as she sat down in the copilot's seat.

"We're in Nkllon's shadow," Han told her, nodding toward the starless mass directly ahead of them. "I've got a lock on Lando's mining operation—looks like we'll be there in ten or fifteen minutes."

"Okay." Leia looked off to the side, at the running lights of the X-wing pacing them. "Have you talked with Luke lately?"

"Not for a couple of hours. He said he was going to try and get some sleep. I think Artoo's running the ship at the moment."

"Yes, he is," Leia nodded, with that slightly absent

voice she always used when practicing her new Jedi skills. "Luke's not sleeping very well, though. Something's bothering him."

"Something's been bothering him for the past couple of months," Han reminded her. "He'll get over it."

"No, this is something different," Leia shook her head. "Something more—I don't know; more *urgent*, somehow." She turned back to face him. "Winter thought that maybe he'd be willing to talk to you about it."

"Well, he hasn't yet," Han said. "Look, don't worry. When he's ready to talk, he'll talk."

"I suppose so." She peered out of the cockpit at the edge of the planetary mass they were speeding toward. "Incredible. Do you realize you can actually see part of the solar corona from here?"

"Yeah, well, don't ask me to take you out for a closer look," Han told her. "Those shieldships aren't just for show, you know—the sunlight out there is strong enough to fry every sensor we have in a few seconds and take the *Falcon*'s hull off a couple of minutes later."

She shook her head wonderingly. "First Bespin, now Nkllon. Have you ever known Lando when he *wasn't* involved in some kind of crazy scheme?"

"Not very often," Han had to admit. "Though at Bespin, at least, he had a known technology to work with— Cloud City had been running for years before he got hold of it. This—" he nodded out the viewport "—they had to think up pretty much from scratch."

Leia leaned forward. "I think I see the city—that group of lights over there."

Han looked where she was pointing. "Too small," he said. "More likely it's an outrider group of mole miners.

Last I heard he had just over a hundred of the things digging stuff out of the surface."

"Those are, what, those asteroid ships we helped him
get from Stonehill Industries?"

"No, he's using those in the outer system for tug
work," Han corrected. "These are little two-man jobs
that look like cones with the points chopped off. They've
got a set of plasma-jet drills pointing down around the
underside hatch—you just land where you want to drill,
fire the jets for a minute or two to chop up the ground,
then go on down through the hatch and pick up the
pieces."

"Oh, right, I remember those now," Leia nodded.
"They were originally asteroid miners, too, weren't
they?"

"The style was. Lando found this particular batch
being used in a smelting complex somewhere. Instead of
just removing the plasma jets, the owners had hauled the
things up whole and wedged them into place on the line."

"I wonder how Lando got hold of them."

"We probably don't want to know."

The transmitter crackled. "Unidentified ships, this is
Nomad City Control," a crisp voice said. "You've been
cleared for landing on Platforms Five and Six. Follow the
beacon in, and watch out for the bumps."

"Got it," Han said. The *Falcon* was skimming the
ground now, the altimeter reading them as just under
fifty meters up. Ahead, a low ridge rose to meet them;
giving the controls a tap, Han nudged them over it—

And there, directly ahead, was Nomad City.

"Tell me again," he invited Leia, "about Lando and
crazy schemes?"

She shook her head wordlessly . . . and even Han, who'd more or less known what to expect, had to admit the view was stunning. Huge, humpbacked, blazing with thousands of lights in the darkside gloom, the mining complex looked like some sort of exotic monstrous living creature as it lumbered its way across the terrain, dwarfing the low ridges over which it walked. Searchlights crisscrossed the area in front of it; a handful of tiny ships buzzed like insect parasites around its back or scuttered across the ground in front of its feet.

It took Han's brain a handful of seconds to resolve the monster into its component parts: the old Dreadnaught Cruiser on top, the forty captured Imperial AT-ATs underneath carrying it across the ground, the shuttles and pilot vehicles moving around and in front of it.

Somehow, knowing what it was didn't make it the least bit less impressive.

The transmitter crackled again. "Unidentified ship," a familiar voice said, "welcome to Nomad City. What's this about playing a hand of sabacc?"

Han grinned lopsidedly. "Hello, Lando. We were just talking about you."

"I'll bet," Lando said wryly. "Probably remarking on my business skills and creativity."

"Something like that," Han told him. "Any special trick involved in landing on that thing?"

"Not really," the other assured them. "We're only going a few kilometers an hour, after all. Is that Luke in the X-wing?"

"Yes, I'm here," Luke put in before Han could answer. "This place is amazing, Lando."

"Wait till you see it from the inside. It's about time

you people came to visit, I might add. Are Leia and Chewie with you?"

"We're all here," Leia said.

"It's not exactly a social call," Han warned him. "We need a little help."

"Well, sure," Lando said, with just the slightest bit of hesitation. "Anything I can do. Look, I'm in Project Central at the moment, supervising a difficult dig. I'll have someone meet you on the landing platform and bring you down here. Don't forget there's no air here—make sure you wait for the docking tube to connect before you try popping the hatch."

"Right," Han said. "Make sure your reception committee is someone you can trust."

Another slight pause. "Oh?" Lando asked, casually. "Is there something—?"

He was cut off by a sudden electronic squeal from the transmitter. "What's that?" Leia snapped.

"Someone's jamming us," Han growled, jabbing at the transmitter cutoff. The squealing vanished, leaving an unpleasant ringing in his ears as he keyed for intercom. "Chewie, we've got trouble," he called. "Get up here."

He got an acknowledgment, turned back to the transmitter. "Get us a scan of the area," he told Leia. "See if there's anything coming in."

"Right," Leia said, already working the keys. "What are you going to do?"

"I'm going to find us a clear frequency." He pulled the *Falcon* out of its approach vector, made sure they had an open field around them, then turned the transmitter back on, keeping the volume low. There were freq-scanning and mixing tricks that he'd used in the past against this kind of jamming. The question now was whether he was going to have the time to implement them.

Abruptly, much quicker than he'd expected, the squeal dissolved into a voice. "—peating: any ships who can read me, please check in."

"Lando, it's me," Han called. "What's going on?"

"I'm not sure," Lando said, sounding distracted. "It could be just a solar flare scrambling our communications—that happens sometimes. But the pattern here doesn't seem quite right for . . ."

His voice trailed off. "What?" Han demanded.

There was a faint hiss from the speaker, the sound of someone inhaling deeply. "Imperial Star Destroyer," Lando said quietly. "Coming in fast toward the planetary shadow."

Han looked at Leia, saw her face turn to stone as she looked back at him. "They've found us," she whispered.

CHAPTER 13

"I SEE IT, ARTOO, I see it," Luke soothed. "Let me worry about the Star Destroyer; you just keep trying to find a way through that jamming."

The little droid warbled a nervous-sounding acknowledgment and got back to work. Ahead, the *Millennium Falcon* had pulled out of its landing approach and was swinging back on what looked like an intercept course for the approaching ship. Hoping Han knew what he was doing, Luke keyed the X-wing for attack status and followed. *Leia?* he called silently.

Her response contained no words; but the anger and frustration and quiet fear came through all too clearly. *Hang on, I'm with you*, he told her, putting as much reassurance and confidence into the thought as he could.

A confidence which, he had to admit, he didn't particularly feel. The Star Destroyer itself didn't worry him—if Lando's descriptions of the sunlight's intensity were right, the big ship itself was probably helpless by now, its sensors and maybe even a fair amount of its armament vaporized right off its hull.

But the TIE fighters protected in its hangars weren't so handicapped . . . and as soon as the ship reached Nkllon's shadow, those fighters would be free to launch.

Abruptly, the static cleared. "Luke?"

"I'm here," Luke confirmed. "What's the plan?"

"I was hoping *you'd* have one," the other said dryly. "Looks like we're a little outnumbered here."

"Does Lando have any fighters?"

"He's scrambling what he's got, but he's going to keep them close in to protect the complex. I get the feeling the crews aren't all that experienced."

"Looks like we're the attack front, then," Luke said. A stray memory flicked through his mind: walking into Jabba's palace on Tatooine five years ago, using the Force to befuddle the Gamorrean guards. "Let's try this," he told Han. "I'll run ahead of you, try to confuse or slow down their reflexes as much as I can. You follow right behind me and take them out."

"Sounds as good as we're going to get," Han grunted. "Stay close to the ground; with luck, we'll be able to run some of them into those low ridges."

"But don't get *too* low," Leia warned. "Remember that you're not going to be able to concentrate very much on your flying."

"I can handle both," Luke assured her, giving the instruments one last scan. His first space combat as a full Jedi. Distantly, he wondered if this was how the Jedi of the Old Republic had handled such battles. Or even if they'd fought like this at all.

"Here they come," Han announced. "Out of the hangar and on their way. Looks like . . . probably only one squadron. Overconfident."

"Maybe." Luke frowned at his tactical scope. "What are those other ships with them?"

"I don't know," Han said slowly. "They're pretty big, though. Could be troop carriers."

"Let's hope not." If this was a full-scale invasion, and not just another hit-and-fade like at Bpfassh . . . "You'd better warn Lando."

"Leia's on it. You ready?"

Luke took a deep breath. The TIE fighters had formed into three four-ship groups now, sweeping directly toward them. "I'm ready," he said.

"Okay. Let's do it."

The first group was coming in fast. Half closing his eyes, flying entirely on reflex, Luke reached out with the Force.

It was a strange sensation. Strange, and more than a little unpleasant. To touch another mind with the intent of communication was one thing; to touch that same mind with the intent of deliberately distorting its perception was something else entirely.

He'd had a similar feeling at Jabba's, with those guards, but had put it down then to nervousness about his mission to rescue Han. Now, he realized that there was more to it than that. Perhaps this sort of action—even done purely in self-defense—was dangerously close to the edge of the dark areas where Jedi were forbidden to go.

He wondered why neither Yoda nor Ben had ever told him about this. Wondered what else there was about being a Jedi that he was going to have to discover on his own.

Luke?

Dimly, he felt himself being jammed into his straps as he twitched the X-wing to one side. The voice whispering into his mind . . . "Ben?" he called aloud. It didn't sound like Ben Kenobi; but if it wasn't him, then who—?

You will come to me, Luke, the voice said again. *You must come to me. I will await you.*

Who are you? Luke asked, focusing as much of his strength on the contact as he could without risking a crash. But the other mind was too elusive to track, skittering away like a bubble in a hurricane. *Where are you?*

You will find me. Even as Luke strained, he could feel the contact slipping away. *You will find me . . . and the Jedi shall rise again. Until then, farewell.*

Wait! But the call was fading into nothingness. Clenching his teeth, Luke strained . . . and gradually began to realize that another, more familiar voice was calling his name. "Leia?" he croaked back through a mouth that was inexplicably dry.

"Luke, are you all right?" Leia asked anxiously.

"Sure," he said. His voice sounded better this time. "I'm fine. What's wrong?"

"*You're* what's wrong," Han cut in. "You planning to chase them all the way home?"

Luke blinked, looking around in surprise. The buzzing TIE fighters were gone, leaving nothing but bits of wreckage strewn across the landscape. On his scope, he could see that the Star Destroyer had left Nkllon's shadow again, driving hard away from the planet toward a point far enough out of the gravity well for a lightspeed jump. Beyond it, a pair of miniature suns were approaching: two of Lando's shieldships, belatedly arriving—now that it was too late—to assist in the fight. "It's all over?" he asked stupidly.

"It's all over," Leia assured him. "We got two of the TIE fighters before the rest disengaged and retreated."

"What about the troop carriers?"

"They went back with the fighters," Han said. "We still don't know what they were doing here—we sort of lost track of them during the fight. Didn't look like they ever went very close to the city itself, though."

Luke took a deep breath, glanced at the X-wing's chrono. In and among all of that, he'd somehow lost over half an hour. Half an hour that his internal time sense had no recollection of whatsoever. Could that strange Jedi contact really have lasted that long?

It was something he would have to look into. Very carefully.

ON THE MAIN bridge screen, showing as little more than a bright spot against Nkllon's dark backdrop, the *Judicator* made its jump to lightspeed. "They're clear, Admiral," Pellaeon announced, looking over at Thrawn.

"Good." The Grand Admiral gave the other displays an almost lazy examination, though there was little to worry about this far out in the Athega system. "So," he said, swiveling his chair around. "Master C'baoth?"

"They fulfilled their mission," C'baoth said, that strangely taut expression on his face again. "They obtained fifty-one of the mole miner machines you sent them for."

"Fifty-one," Thrawn repeated with obvious satisfaction. "Excellent. You had no problem guiding them in and out?"

C'baoth focused his eyes on Thrawn. "They fulfilled their mission," he repeated. "How many times do you intend to ask me the same question?"

"Until I'm sure I have the correct answer," Thrawn replied coolly. "For a while there your face looked as if you were having trouble."

"I had no trouble, Grand Admiral Thrawn," C'baoth said loftily. "What I had was conversation." He paused, a slight smile on his face. "With Luke Skywalker."

"What are you talking about?" Pellaeon snorted. "Current intelligence reports indicate that Skywalker is—"

He broke off at a gesture from Thrawn. "Explain," the Grand Admiral said.

C'baoth nodded toward the display. "He's there right now, Grand Admiral Thrawn. He arrived on Nkllon just ahead of the *Judicator*."

Thrawn's glowing red eyes narrowed. "Skywalker is on Nkllon?" he asked, his voice dangerously quiet.

"In the very center of the battle," C'baoth told him, very clearly enjoying the Grand Admiral's discomfiture.

"And you said nothing to me?" Thrawn demanded in that same deadly voice.

C'baoth's smile vanished. "I told you before, Grand Admiral Thrawn: you will leave Skywalker alone. *I* will deal with him—in my own time, in my own way. All I require of you is the fulfillment of your promise to take me to Jomark."

For a long moment Thrawn gazed at the Jedi Master,

his eyes glowing red slits, his face hard and totally un-readable. Pellaeon held his breath . . . "It's too soon," the Grand Admiral said at last.

C'baoth snorted. "Why? Because you find my talents too useful to give up?"

"Not at all," Thrawn said, his voice icy. "It's a simple matter of efficiency. The rumors of your presence haven't had enough time to spread. Until we can be sure Sky-walker will respond, you'll just be wasting your time there."

A strangely dreamy look seeped onto C'baoth's face. "Oh, he'll respond," he said softly. "Trust me, Grand Admiral Thrawn. He *will* respond."

"I always trust you," Thrawn said sardonically. He reached a hand up to stroke the ysalamir draped over his command chair, as if to remind the Jedi Master just how far he trusted him. "At any rate, I suppose it's your own time to waste. Captain Pellaeon, how long will it take to repair the damage to the *Judicator*?"

"Several days at the least, Admiral," Pellaeon told him. "Depending on the damage, it could take as long as three or four weeks."

"All right. We'll go to the rendezvous point, stay with them long enough to make sure repairs are properly un-derway, and then take Master C'baoth to Jomark. I trust that will be satisfactory?" he added, looking back at C'baoth.

"Yes." Carefully, C'baoth unfolded himself from his chair and stood up. "I will rest now, Grand Admiral Thrawn. Alert me if you need my assistance."

"Certainly."

Thrawn watched the other wend his way back across

the bridge; and as the doors slid solidly shut behind him, the Grand Admiral turned to Pellaeon. Pellaeon braced himself, trying not to wince. "I want a course projection, Captain," Thrawn said, his voice cold but steady. "The most direct line from Nkllon to Jomark, at the best speed a hyperdrive-equipped X-wing could take it."

"Yes, Admiral." Pellaeon signaled to the navigator, who nodded and got busy. "You think he's right about Skywalker going there?"

Thrawn shrugged fractionally. "The Jedi had ways of influencing people, Captain, even over considerable distances. It's possible that even out here he was close enough to Skywalker to plant a suggestion or compulsion. Whether those techniques will work on another Jedi—" He shrugged again. "We'll see."

"Yes, sir." The numbers were starting to track across Pellaeon's display now. "Well, even if Skywalker leaves Nkllon immediately, there won't be any problem getting C'baoth to Jomark ahead of him."

"I knew that much already, Captain," Thrawn said. "What I need is a bit more challenging. We're going to drop C'baoth off on Jomark, then backtrack to a point on Skywalker's projected course. A point at least twenty light-years away, I think."

Pellaeon frowned at him. The expression on Thrawn's face made the back of his neck tingle . . . "I don't understand, sir," he said carefully.

The glowing eyes regarded him thoughtfully. "It's quite simple, Captain. I mean to disabuse our great and glorious Jedi Master of his growing belief that he's indispensable to us."

Pellaeon got it then. "So we wait along Skywalker's projected approach to Jomark and ambush him?"

"Precisely," Thrawn nodded. "At which point we decide whether to capture him for C'baoth—" his eyes hardened "—or simply kill him."

Pellaeon stared at him, feeling his jaw drop. "You promised C'baoth he could have him."

"I'm reconsidering the deal," Thrawn told him coolly. "Skywalker has proved himself to be highly dangerous, and by all accounts has already withstood at least one attempt to turn him. C'baoth should have more success bending Skywalker's sister and her twins to his will."

Pellaeon glanced behind him at the closed doors, reminding himself firmly that there was no way for C'baoth to eavesdrop on their conversation with all the ysalamiri scattered around the *Chimaera*'s bridge. "Perhaps he's looking forward to the challenge, sir," he suggested cautiously.

"There will be many challenges for him to face before the Empire is reestablished. Let him save his talents and cunning for those." Thrawn turned back to his monitors. "At any rate, he'll likely forget all about Skywalker once he has the sister. I expect our Jedi Master's wants and desires will prove to be as erratic as his moods."

Pellaeon thought back. On the matter of Skywalker, at least, C'baoth's desire seemed to have remained remarkably steady. "I respectfully suggest, Admiral, that we still make every possible effort to take Skywalker alive." He had a flash of inspiration—"Particularly since his death might induce C'baoth to leave Jomark and return to Wayland."

Thrawn looked back at him, glowing eyes narrowed. "Interesting point, Captain," he murmured softly. "Interesting point, indeed. You're right, of course. By all means, we must keep him off Wayland. At least until the work on the Spaarti cylinders is finished and we have all the ysalamiri there we're going to need." He smiled tightly. "His reaction to what we're doing there might not be at all pleasant."

"Agreed, sir," Pellaeon said.

Thrawn's lip twitched. "Very well, Captain: I accede to your suggestion." He straightened himself in his seat. "It's time to be going. Prepare the *Chimaera* for light-speed."

Pellaeon turned back to his displays. "Yes, sir. Direct route to the rendezvous point?"

"We'll be making a short detour first. I want you to swing us around the system to the commercial out-vector near the shieldship depot and drop some probes to watch for Skywalker's departure. Near-system and farther out." He looked out the viewport in Nkllon's direction. "And who knows? Where Skywalker goes, the *Millennium Falcon* often goes, as well.

"And then we'll have them all."

CHAPTER 14

"Fifty-one," Lando Calrissian growled, throwing a glare at Han and Leia as he paced a convoluted path around the low chairs in the lounge. "Fifty-one of my best reconditioned mole miners. *Fifty-one.* That's almost half my work force. You realize that?—*half* my work force."

He dropped down into a chair, but was on his feet again almost immediately, stalking around the room, his black cloak billowing behind him like a tame storm cloud. Leia opened her mouth to offer commiseration, felt Han squeeze her hand warningly. Obviously, Han had seen Lando in this state before. Swallowing back the words, she watched as he continued his caged-animal pacing.

And without obvious warning, it was over. "I'm sorry," he said abruptly, coming to a halt in front of Leia and taking her hand. "I'm neglecting my duties as host, aren't I? Welcome to Nkllon." He raised her hand, kissed it, and waved his free hand toward the lounge window. "So. What do you think of my little enterprise?"

"Impressive," Leia said, and meant it. "How did you ever come up with the idea for this place?"

"Oh, it's been kicking around for years," he shrugged, pulling her gently to her feet and guiding her over to the window, his hand resting against the small of her back. Ever since she and Han had gotten married, Leia had noticed a resurgence of this kind of courtly behavior toward her from Lando—behavior that harkened back to their first meeting at Cloud City. She'd puzzled over that for a while, until she'd noticed that all the attention seemed to annoy Han.

Or, at least, it normally annoyed him. Right now, he didn't even seem to notice.

"I found plans for something similar once in the Cloud City files, dating back to when Lord Ecclessis Figg first built the place," Lando continued, waving a hand toward the window. The horizon rolled gently as the city walked, the motion and view reminding Leia of her handful of experiences aboard sailing ships. "Most of the metal they used came from the hot inner planet, Miser, and even with Ugnaughts doing the mining they had a devil of a time with it. Figg sketched out an idea for a rolling mining center that could stay permanently out of direct sunlight on Miser's dark side. But nothing ever came of it."

"It wasn't practical," Han said, coming up behind Leia. "Miser's terrain was too rough for something on wheels to get across easily."

Lando looked at him in surprise. "How do you know about that?"

Han shook his head distractedly, his eyes searching

the landscape and the starry sky above it. "I spent an afternoon going through the Imperial files once, back when you were trying to talk Mon Mothma into helping fund this place. Wanted to make sure someone else hadn't already tried it and found out it didn't work."

"Nice of you to go to that kind of trouble." Lando cocked an eyebrow. "So, what's going on?"

"We should probably wait until Luke gets here to talk about it," Leia suggested quietly before Han could answer.

Lando glanced past Han, as if only just noticing Luke's absence. "Where is he, anyway?"

"He wanted to catch a fast shower and change," Han told him, shifting his attention to a small ore shuttle coming in for a landing. "Those X-wings don't have much in the way of comfort."

"Especially over long trips," Lando agreed, tracing Han's gaze with his eyes. "I've always thought putting a hyperdrive on something that small was a poor idea."

"I'd better see what's keeping him," Han decided suddenly. "You have a comm in this room?"

"It's over there," Lando said, pointing toward a curved wooden bar at one end of the lounge. "Key for central; they'll track him down for you."

"Thanks," Han called over his shoulder, already halfway there.

"It's bad, isn't it?" Lando murmured to Leia, his eyes following Han across the room.

"Bad enough," she admitted. "There's a chance that that Star Destroyer came here looking for me."

For a moment, Lando was silent. "You came here for help." It wasn't a question.

"Yes."

He took a deep breath. "Well . . . I'll do what I can, of course."

"Thank you," Leia said.

"Sure," he said. But his eyes drifted from Han to the window and the activity beyond it, his expression hardening as he did so. Perhaps he was thinking of the last time Han and Leia had come to him for help.

And what giving that help had cost him.

LANDO LISTENED TO the whole story in silence, then shook his head. "No," he said positively. "If there was a leak, it didn't come from Nkllon."

"How can you be sure of that?" Leia asked.

"Because there's been no bounty offered for you," Lando told her. "We have our fair share of shady people here, but they're all out for profit. None of them would turn you over to the Empire just for the fun of it. Besides, why would the Imperials steal my mole miners if they were after you?"

"Harassment, maybe," Han suggested. "I mean, why steal mole miners anyway?"

"You got me," Lando conceded. "Maybe they're trying to put economic pressure on one of my clients, or maybe they just want to disrupt the New Republic's flow of raw materials generally. Anyway, that's beside the point. The point is that they took the mole miners, and they didn't take you."

"How do you know there's been no bounty offer?" Luke asked from his seat off to the right—a seat, Leia had already noted, where he and his lightsaber would be between his friends and the room's only door. Apparently, he didn't feel any safer here than she did.

"Because I'd have heard about it," Lando said, sounding a little miffed. "Just because I'm respectable doesn't mean I'm out of touch."

"I told you he'd have contacts," Han said with a grimly satisfied nod. "Great. So which of these contacts do you trust, Lando?"

"Well—" Lando broke off as a beep came from his wrist. "Excuse me," he said, sliding a compact comlink from the decorative wristband and flicking it on. "Yes?"

A voice said something, inaudible from where Leia was sitting. "What kind of transmitter?" Lando asked, frowning. The voice said something else. "All right, I'll take care of it. Continue scanning."

He closed down the comlink and replaced it in his wristband. "That was my communications section," he said, looking around the room. "They've picked up a short-range transmitter on a very unusual frequency . . . which appears to be sending from this lounge."

Beside her, Leia felt Han stiffen. "What kind of transmitter?" he demanded.

"This kind, probably," Luke said. Standing up, he pulled a flattened cylinder from his tunic and stepped over to Lando. "I thought you might be able to identify it for me."

Lando took the cylinder, hefted it. "Interesting," he commented, peering closely at the alien script on its surface. "I haven't seen one of these in years. Not this style, anyway. Where'd you get it?"

"It was buried in mud in the middle of a swamp. Artoo was able to pick it up from pretty far away, but he couldn't tell me what it was."

"That's our transmitter, all right," Lando nodded. "Amazing that it's still running."

"What exactly is it transmitting?" Han asked, eyeing the device as if it were a dangerous snake.

"Just a carrier signal," Lando assured him. "And the range is small—well under a planetary radius. Nobody used it to follow Luke here, if that's what you were wondering."

"Do you know what it is?" Luke asked.

"Sure," Lando said, handing it back. "It's an old beckon call. Pre-Clone Wars vintage, from the looks of it."

"A beckon call?" Luke frowned, cupping it in his hand. "You mean like a ship's remote?"

"Right," Lando nodded. "Only a lot more sophisticated. If you had a ship with a full-rig slave system you could tap in a single command on the call and the ship would come straight to you, automatically maneuvering around any obstacles along the way. Some of them would even fight their way through opposing ships, if necessary, with a reasonable degree of skill." He shook his head in memory. "Which could be extremely useful at times."

Han snorted under his breath. "Tell that to the *Katana* fleet."

"Well, of course you have to build in some safeguards," Lando countered. "But to simply decentralize important ship's functions into dozens or hundreds of droids just creates its own set of problems. The limited jump-slave circuits we use here between transports and shieldships are certainly safe enough."

"Did you use jump-slave circuits on Cloud City, too?" Luke asked. "Artoo said he saw you with one of these right after we got out of there."

"My personal ship was full-rigged," Lando said. "I wanted something I could get at a moment's warning, just in case." His lip twitched. "Vader's people must have found it and shut it down while they were waiting for you, because it sure didn't come when I called it. You say you found it in a *swamp*?"

"Yes." Luke looked at Leia. "On Dagobah."

Leia stared at him. "Dagobah?" she asked. "As in the planet that Dark Jedi from Bpfassh fled to?"

Luke nodded. "That's the place." He fingered the beckon call, an odd expression on his face. "This must have been his."

"It could just as easily have been lost some other time by someone else," Lando pointed out. "Pre-Clone Wars calls could run for a century or more on standby."

"No," Luke said, shaking his head slowly. "It was his, all right. The cave where I found it absolutely tingles with the dark side. I think it must have been the place where he died."

For a long moment they all sat in silence. Leia studied her brother closely, sensing the new tension lying just beneath the surface of his thoughts. Something else, besides the beckon call, must have happened to him on Dagobah. Something that tied in with the new sense of urgency she'd felt on the way in toward Nkllon . . .

Luke looked up sharply, as if sensing the flow of Leia's

thoughts. "We were talking about Lando's smuggler contacts," he said. The message was clear: this was not the
time to ask him about it.

"Right," Han said quickly. Apparently, he'd gotten
the hint, too. "I need to know which of your marginally
legal friends you can trust."

The other shrugged. "Depends on what you need to
trust them with."

Han looked him straight in the eye. "Leia's life."

Seated on Han's other side, Chewbacca growled
something that sounded startled. Lando's mouth fell
open, just slightly. "You're not serious."

Han nodded, his eyes still locked on Lando's face.
"You saw how close the Imperials are breathing down our
necks. We need a place to hide her until Ackbar can find
out how they're getting their information. She needs to
stay in touch with what's happening on Coruscant, which
means a diplomatic station we can quietly tap into."

"And a diplomatic station means encrypt codes,"
Lando said heavily. "And quietly tapping into encrypt
codes means finding a slicer."

"A slicer you can trust."

Lando hissed softly between his teeth and slowly
shook his head. "I'm sorry, Han, but I don't know any
slicers I trust that far."

"Do you know any smuggler groups that have one or
two on retainer?" Han persisted.

"That I trust?" Lando pondered. "Not really. The
only one who might even come close is a smuggler chief
named Talon Karrde—everyone I've talked to says he's
extremely honest in his trade dealings."

"Have you ever met him?" Luke asked.

"Once," Lando said. "He struck me as a pretty cold fish—calculating and highly mercenary."

"I've heard of Karrde," Han said. "Been trying for months to contact him, in fact. Dravis—you remember Dravis?—he told me Karrde's group was probably the biggest one around these days."

"Could be," Lando shrugged. "Unlike Jabba, Karrde doesn't go around flaunting his power and influence. I'm not even sure where his base is, let alone what his loyalties are."

"If he *has* any loyalties," Han grunted; and in his eyes Leia could see the echoes of all those fruitless contacts with smuggling groups who preferred to sit on the political fence. "A lot of them out there don't."

"It's an occupational hazard." Lando rubbed his chin, forehead wrinkled in thought. "I don't know, Han. I'd offer to put the two of you up here, but we just don't have the defenses to stop a really serious attack." He frowned into the distance. "Unless . . . we do something clever."

"Such as?"

"Such as taking a shuttle or living module and burying it underground," Lando said, a gleam coming into his eye. "We put it right by the dawn line, and within a few hours you'd be under direct sunlight. The Imperials wouldn't even be able to find you there, let alone get to you."

Han shook his head. "Too risky. If we ran into any problems, there also wouldn't be any way for anyone to get help to us." Chewbacca pawed at his arm, grunting softly, and Han turned to face the Wookiee.

"It wouldn't be as risky as it looks," Lando said, shifting his attention to Leia. "We should be able to make the capsule itself foolproof—we've done similar things with delicate survey instrument packs without damaging them."

"How long is Nkllon's rotation?" Leia asked. Chewbacca's grunting was getting insistent, but it still wasn't loud enough for her to make out what the discussion was all about.

"Just over ninety standard days," Lando told her.

"Which means we'd be completely out of touch with Coruscant for a minimum of forty-five. Unless you've got a transmitter that would operate on the sunside."

Lando shook his head. "The best we've got would be fried in minutes."

"In that case, I'm afraid—"

She broke off as, beside her, Han cleared his throat. "Chewie has a suggestion," he said, his face and voice a study in mixed feelings.

They all looked at him. "Well?" Leia prompted.

Han's lip twitched. "He says that if you want, he's willing to take you to Kashyyyk."

Leia looked past him to Chewbacca, a strange and not entirely pleasant thrill running through her. "I was under the impression," she said carefully, "that Wookiees discouraged human visitors to their world."

Chewbacca's reply was as mixed as Han's expression. Mixed, but solidly confident. "The Wookiees were friendly enough to humans before the Empire came in and started enslaving them," Han said. "Anyway, it ought to be possible to keep the visit pretty quiet: you, Chewie, the New Republic rep, and a couple of others."

"Except that we're back to the New Republic rep knowing about me," Leia pointed out.

"Yes, but he'll be a Wookiee," Lando pointed out. "If he accepts you under his personal protection, he won't betray you. Period."

Leia studied Han's face. "Sounds good. So tell me why you don't like it."

A muscle in Han's cheek twitched. "Kashyyyk isn't exactly the safest place in the galaxy," he said bluntly. "Especially for non-Wookiees. You'll be living in trees, hundreds of meters above the ground—"

"I'll be with Chewie," she reminded him firmly, suppressing a shiver. She'd heard stories about Kashyyyk's lethal ecology, too. "You've trusted your own life to him often enough."

He shrugged uncomfortably. "This is different."

"Why don't you go with them?" Luke suggested. "Then she'll be doubly protected."

"Right," Han said sourly. "I was planning to; except that Chewie thinks it'll gain us more time if Leia and I split up. He takes her to Kashyyyk; I fly around in the *Falcon*, pretending she's still with me. Somehow."

Lando nodded. "Makes sense to me."

Leia looked at Luke, the obvious suggestion coming to her lips . . . and dying there unsaid. Something in his face warned her not to ask him to come with them. "Chewie and I will be fine," she said, squeezing Han's hand. "Don't worry."

"I guess that's settled, then," Lando said. "You can use my ship, of course, Chewie. In fact—" he looked thoughtful "—if you want company, Han, maybe I'll come along with you."

Han shrugged, clearly still unhappy with the arrangement. "If you want to, sure."

"Good," Lando said. "We should probably fly out of Nkllon together—I've been planning an offworld purchasing trip for a couple of weeks now, so I've got an excuse to leave. Once we're past the shieldship depot, Chewie and Leia can take my ship and no one'll be the wiser."

"And then Han sends some messages to Coruscant pretending Leia's aboard?" Luke asked.

Lando smiled slyly. "Actually, I think we can do a little bit better than that. You still have Threepio with you?"

"He's helping Artoo run a damage check on the *Falcon*," Leia told him. "Why?"

"You'll see," Lando said, getting to his feet. "This'll take a little time, but I think it'll be worth it. Come on— let's go talk to my chief programmer."

THE CHIEF PROGRAMMER was a little man with dreamy blue eyes, a thin swath of hair arcing like a gray rainbow from just over his eyebrows to the nape of his neck, and a shiny borg implant wrapped around the back of his head. Luke listened as Lando outlined the procedure and watched long enough to make sure it was all going smoothly. Then, quietly, he slipped out, returning to the quarters Lando's people had assigned him.

He was still there an hour later, poring uselessly over what seemed to be an endless stream of star charts, when Leia found him.

"There you are," she said, coming in and glancing at the charts on his display. "We were starting to wonder where you went."

"I had some things to check on," Luke said. "You finished already?"

"My part is," Leia said, pulling a chair over to him and sitting down. "They're working on tailoring the program now. After that it'll be Threepio's turn."

Luke shook his head. "Seems to me the whole thing ought to be simpler than all that."

"Oh, the basic technique is," Leia agreed. "Apparently, the hard part is slipping it past the relevant part of Threepio's watchdog programming without changing his personality in the process." She looked again at the screen. "I was going to ask you if you'd be interested in coming to Kashyyyk with me," she said, her voice trying hard to be casual. "But it looks like you've got somewhere else to go."

Luke winced. "I'm not running out on you, Leia," he insisted, wishing he could truly believe that. "Really I'm not. This is something that in the long run could mean more for you and the twins than anything I could do on Kashyyyk."

"All right," she said, calmly accepting the statement. "Can you at least tell me where you're going?"

"I don't know yet," he confessed. "There's someone out there I have to find, but I'm not sure yet even where to start looking." He hesitated, suddenly aware of how strange and maybe even crazy this was going to sound. But he was going to have to tell them eventually. "He's another Jedi."

She stared at him. "You're not serious."

"Why not?" Luke asked, frowning at her. Her reaction seemed vaguely wrong, somehow. "It's a big galaxy, you know."

"A galaxy in which you were supposedly the last of the Jedi," she countered. "Isn't that what you said Yoda told you before he died?"

"Yes," he nodded. "But I'm beginning to think he might have been mistaken."

Her eyebrows lifted slightly. "Mistaken? A Jedi Master?"

A memory flashed through Luke's mind: a ghostly Obi-wan, in the middle of the Dagobah swamp, trying to explain his earlier statements about Darth Vader. "Jedi sometimes say things that are misleading," he told her. "And even Jedi Masters aren't omniscient."

He paused, gazing at his sister, wondering how much of this he should tell her. The Empire was far from defeated, and the mysterious Jedi's life might depend on his defense remaining a secret. Leia waited in silence, that concerned expression on her face . . .

"You'll have to keep this to yourself," Luke said at last. "I mean *really* to yourself. I don't even want you to tell Han or Lando, unless it becomes absolutely necessary. They don't have the resistance to interrogation that you do."

Leia shuddered, but her eyes stayed clear. "I understand," she said evenly.

"All right. Did it ever occur to you to wonder why Master Yoda was able to stay hidden from the Emperor and Vader all those years?"

She shrugged. "I suppose I assumed they didn't know he existed."

"Yes, but they should have," Luke pointed out. "They knew *I* existed by my effect on the Force. Why not Yoda?"

"Some kind of mental shielding?"

"Maybe. But I think it's more likely it was because of where he chose to live. Or maybe," he amended, "where events chose for him to live."

A faint smile brushed Leia's lips. "Is this where I finally get to find out where this secret training center of yours was?"

"I didn't want anyone else to know," Luke said, moved by some obscure impulse to try to justify that decision to her. "He was so perfectly hidden—and even after his death I was afraid the Empire might be able to do something—"

He broke off. "Anyway, I can't see that it matters now. Yoda's home was on Dagobah. Practically next door to the darkside cave where I found that beckon call."

Her eyes widened in surprise, a surprise that faded into understanding. "Dagobah," she murmured, nodding slowly as if a private and long-standing problem had just been resolved. "I've always wondered how that renegade Dark Jedi was finally defeated. It must have been Yoda who . . ." She grimaced.

"Who stopped him," Luke finished for her, a shiver running up his back. His own skirmishes with Darth Vader had been bad enough; a full-scale Force war between Jedi Masters would be terrifying. "And he probably didn't stop him with a lot of time to spare."

"The beckon call was already on standby," Leia remembered. "He must have been getting ready to call his ship."

Luke nodded. "All of which could explain why the cave was so heavy with the dark side. What it *doesn't* explain is why Yoda decided to stay there."

He paused, watching her closely; and a moment later,

the understanding came. "The cave shielded him," she breathed. "Just like a pair of positive and negative electric charges close enough together—to a distant observer they look almost like no charge at all."

"I think that's it," Luke nodded again. "And if that's really how Master Yoda stayed hidden, there's no reason why another Jedi couldn't have pulled the same trick."

"I'm sure another Jedi could have," Leia agreed, sounding reluctant. "But I don't think this C'baoth rumor is anywhere near solid enough to chase off after."

Luke frowned. "What C'baoth rumor?"

It was Leia's turn to frown. "The story that a Jedi Master named Jorus C'baoth has reemerged from wherever it was he's spent the past few decades." She stared at him. "You hadn't heard it?"

He shook his head. "No."

"But then, how—?"

"Someone called to me, Leia, during the battle this afternoon. In my mind. The way another Jedi would."

For a long moment they just looked at each other. "I don't believe it," Leia said. "I just don't. Where could someone with C'baoth's power and history have hidden for so long? And why?"

"The *why* I don't know," Luke admitted. "As to the *where*—" He nodded toward the display. "That's what I've been looking for. Someplace where a Dark Jedi might once have died." He looked at Leia again. "Do the rumors say where C'baoth is supposed to be?"

"It could be an Imperial trap," Leia warned, her voice abruptly harsh. "The person who called to you could just as easily be a Dark Jedi like Vader, with this C'baoth rumor dangled in front of us to lure you in. Don't forget that Yoda wasn't counting them—both Vader and the Emperor were still alive when he said you were the last Jedi."

"That's a possibility," he conceded. "It could also be just a garbled rumor. But if it's not . . ."

He let the sentence hang, unfinished, in the air between them. There were deep uncertainties in Leia's face and mind, he could see, woven through by equally deep fears for his safety. But even as he watched her he could sense her gain control over both emotions. In those aspects of her training, she was making good progress. "He's on Jomark," she said at last, her voice quiet. "At least according to the rumor Wedge quoted for us."

Luke turned to the display, called up the data on Jomark. There wasn't much there. "Not very populated," he said, glancing over the stats and the limited selection of maps. "Less than three million people, all told. Or at least back when this was compiled," he amended, searching for the publication date. "Doesn't look like anyone's taken official notice of the planet in fifteen years." He looked back at Leia. "Just the sort of place a Jedi might choose to hide from the Empire."

"You'll be leaving right away?"

He looked at her, swallowing the quick and obvious answer. "No, I'll wait until you and Chewie are ready to go," he said. "That way I can fly out with your shield-ship. Give you that much protection, at least."

"Thanks." Taking a deep breath, she stood up. "I hope you know what you're doing."

"So do I," he said frankly. "But whether I do or not, it's something I have to try. That much I know for sure."

Leia's lip twitched. "I suppose that's one of the things

I'm going to have to get used to. Letting the Force move me around."

"Don't worry about it," Luke advised her, getting to his feet and switching off the display. "It doesn't happen all at once—you get to ease into it. Come on; let's go see how they're coming with Threepio."

"AT LAST!" THREEPIO cried, waving his arms in desperate relief as Luke and Leia stepped into the room. "Master Luke! Please, *please* tell General Calrissian that what he intends is a serious violation of my primary programming."

"It'll be okay, Threepio," Luke soothed, stepping over to him. From the front the droid seemed to be just sitting there; it was only as Luke got closer that he could see the maze of wires snaking from both headpiece and dorsal junction box into the computer console behind him. "Lando and his people will be careful that nothing happens to you." He glanced at Lando, got a confirming nod in return.

"But Master Luke—"

"Actually, Threepio," Lando put in, "you could think of this as really just fulfilling your primary programming in a more complete way. I mean, isn't a translation droid supposed to speak for the person he's translating for?"

"I am primarily a protocol droid," Threepio corrected in as frosty a tone as he could probably manage. "And I say again that this is *not* the sort of thing covered by any possible stretch of protocol."

The borg looked up from the panel, nodded. "We're

ready," Lando announced, touching a switch. "Give it a second . . . all right. Say something, Threepio."

"Oh, dear," the droid said—

In a perfect imitation of Leia's voice.

Artoo, standing across the room, trilled softly. "That's it," Lando said, looking decidedly pleased with himself. "The perfect decoy—" he inclined his head to Leia "—for the perfect lady."

"This feels decidedly strange," Threepio continued— Leia's voice, this time, in a thoughtful mood.

"Sounds good," Han said, looking around at the others. "We ready to go, then?"

"Give me an hour to log some last-minute instructions," Lando said, starting toward the door. "It'll take our shieldship that long to get here, anyway."

"We'll meet you at the ship," Han called after him, stepping over to Leia and taking her arm. "Come on— we'd better get back to the *Falcon*."

She put her hand on his, smiling reassuringly up at him. "It'll be all right, Han. Chewie and the other Wookiees will take good care of me."

"They'd better," Han growled, glancing to where the borg was undoing the last of the cables connecting Threepio to the console. "Let's go, Threepio. I can hardly wait to hear what Chewie thinks of your new voice."

"Oh, dear," the droid murmured again. "Oh, *dear*."

Leia shook her head in wonder as they headed for the door. "Do I really," she asked, "sound like that?"

CHAPTER 15

HAN HAD FULLY expected that they would be attacked during the long shieldship journey out from Nkllon. For once, thankfully, his hunch was wrong. The three ships reached the shieldship depot without incident and made a short hyperspace jump together to the outer fringes of the Athega system. There, Chewbacca and Leia replaced Lando aboard his yacht-style ship, the *Lady Luck*, and started off toward Kashyyyk. Luke waited until they were safely away before securing his X-wing back from defense posture and heading off on some mysterious errand of his own.

Leaving Han alone on the *Falcon* with Lando and Threepio.

"She'll be fine," Lando assured him, punching at the nav computer from the copilot's seat. "She's as safe now as she's ever likely to be. Don't worry."

With an effort, Han turned from the viewport to face

him. There was nothing to see out there, anyway—the *Lady Luck* was long gone. "You know, that's almost exactly the same thing you said back on Boordii," he reminded Lando sourly. "That botched dolfrimia run—remember? You said, 'It'll be fine; don't worry about it.'"

Lando chuckled. "Yes, but this time I mean it."

"That's nice to know. So, what do you have planned for entertainment?"

"Well, the first thing we ought to do is have Threepio send off a message to Coruscant," Lando said. "Give the impression that Leia's aboard to any Imperials who might be listening. After that, we could move a couple of systems over and send another message. And after that—" he threw Han a sideways glance "—I thought we might like to do a little sightseeing."

"Sightseeing?" Han echoed suspiciously. Lando was practically glowing with innocence, a look he almost never used except when he was trying to sucker someone into something. "You mean as in flying all over the galaxy looking for replacement mole miners?"

"Han!" Lando protested, looking hurt now. "Are you suggesting I'd stoop so low as to try and con you into helping me run my business?"

"Forgive me," Han said, trying not to sound too sarcastic. "I forgot—you're respectable now. So what sights *are* we going to see?"

"Well . . ." Casually, Lando leaned back and laced his fingers together behind his head. "You mentioned earlier that you hadn't been able to get in touch with Talon Karrde. I thought we might take another crack at it."

Han frowned at him. "You serious?"

"Why not? You want cargo ships, and you want a good slicer. Karrde can supply both."

"I don't need a slicer anymore," Han said. "Leia's as safe now as she's ever likely to be. Remember?"

"Sure—until someone leaks the news that she's there," Lando countered. "I don't think the Wookiees would, but there are non-Wookiee traders flying in and out of Kashyyyk all the time. All it takes is one person spotting her, and you'll be right back where you were when you first got here." He cocked an eyebrow. "And Karrde might also have something on this mysterious Imperial commander who's been running you in circles lately."

The commander who was almost certainly also the man behind the attacks on Leia . . . "You know how to make contact with Karrde?"

"Not directly, but I know how to get to his people. And I thought that as long as we had Threepio and his umpteen million languages aboard anyway, we'd just go ahead and cut a new contact path."

"That'll take time."

"Not as much as you might think," Lando assured him. "Besides, a new path will cover our trail better— yours and mine both."

Han grimaced, but Lando was right. And with Leia safely hidden away, at least for now, they could afford to play it cautious. "All right," he said. "Assuming we don't wind up playing tag with a Star Destroyer or two."

"Right," Lando agreed soberly. "The last thing we want is to draw the Imperials onto Karrde's tail. We've got enough enemies out there as it is." He tapped the ship's intercom switch. "Threepio? You there?"

"Of course," Leia's voice returned.

"Come on up here," Lando told the droid. "Time for your debut performance."

THE COMMAND ROOM was filled with sculptures instead of pictures this time: over a hundred of them, lining the walls in holographic niches as well as scattered around the floor on ornate pedestals. The variety, as Pellaeon had come to expect, was astonishing, ranging from human-style chunks of simple stone and wood to others that were more like tethered living creatures than works of art. Each was illuminated by a hazy globe of light, giving sharp contrast to the darkness of the spaces between them. "Admiral?" Pellaeon called uncertainly, trying to see around the artwork and through the gloom.

"Come in, Captain," Thrawn's coolly modulated voice beckoned. Over at the command chair, just above the hazy white of the Grand Admiral's uniform, two glowing red slits appeared. "You have something?"

"Yes, sir," Pellaeon told him, walking to the console ring and handing a data card over it. "One of our probes in the outer Athega system has picked up Skywalker. *And* his companions."

"*And* his companions," Thrawn echoed thoughtfully. He took the data card, inserted it, and for a minute watched the replay in silence. "Interesting," he murmured. "Interesting, indeed. What's that third ship—the one maneuvering to link with the *Millennium Falcon*'s dorsal hatch?"

"We've tentatively identified it as the *Lady Luck*," Pellaeon said. "Administrator Lando Calrissian's personal ship. One of the other probes copied a transmission stating that Calrissian was leaving Nkllon on a purchasing trip."

"Do we know that Calrissian did, in fact, board the ship at Nkllon?"

"Ah . . . no, sir, not for certain. We can try to get that information, though."

"Unnecessary," Thrawn said. "Our enemies are clearly past the stage of such childish tricks." Thrawn pointed to the display, where the *Millennium Falcon* and the *Lady Luck* were now joined together. "Observe, Captain, their strategy. Captain Solo and his wife and probably the Wookiee Chewbacca board their ship on Nkllon, while Calrissian similarly boards his. They fly to the outer Athega system . . . and there they make a switch."

Pellaeon frowned. "But we've—"

"Shh," Thrawn cut him off sharply, holding up a finger for silence, his eyes on the display. Pellaeon watched, too, as absolutely nothing happened. After a few minutes the two ships separated, maneuvering carefully away from each other.

"Excellent," Thrawn said, freezing the frame. "Four minutes fifty-three seconds. They're in a hurry, of course, locked together so vulnerably. Which means . . ." His forehead furrowed in concentration, then cleared. "Three people," he said, a touch of satisfaction in his voice. "Three people transferred, in one direction or the other, between those two ships."

"Yes, sir," Pellaeon nodded, wondering how in the

Empire the Grand Admiral had figured *that* one out. "At any rate, we know that Leia Organa Solo remained aboard the *Millennium Falcon*."

"Do we?" Thrawn asked, lazily polite. "Do we indeed?"

"I believe we do, sir, yes," Pellaeon said, quietly insistent. The Grand Admiral hadn't seen the entire playback, after all. "Right after the *Lady Luck* and Skywalkers X-wing left, we intercepted a transmission from her that definitely originated from the *Millennium Falcon*."

Thrawn shook his head. "A recording," he said, his voice leaving no room for argument. "No; they're cleverer than that. A voiceprint-doctored droid, then— probably Skywalker's 3PO protocol droid. Leia Organa Solo, you see, was one of the two people who left with the *Lady Luck*."

Pellaeon looked at the display. "I don't understand."

"Consider the possibilities," Thrawn said, leaning back in his chair and steepling his fingertips in front of him. "Three people start out aboard the *Millennium Falcon*, one aboard the *Lady Luck*. Three people then transfer. But neither Solo nor Calrissian is the type to turn his ship over to the dubious command of a computer or droid. So each ship must end up with at least one person aboard. You follow so far?"

"Yes, sir," Pellaeon said. "That doesn't tell us who is where, though."

"Patience, Captain," Thrawn interrupted him. "Patience. As you say, the question now is that of the final makeup of the crews. Fortunately, once we know there were three transfers, there are only two possible combinations. Either Solo and Organa Solo are together aboard the *Lady Luck*, or else Organa Solo and the Wookiee are there."

"Unless one of the transfers was a droid," Pellaeon pointed out.

"Unlikely," Thrawn shook his head. "Historically, Solo has never liked droids, nor allowed them to travel aboard his ship except under highly unusual circumstances. Skywalker's droid and its astromech counterpart appear to be the sole exceptions; and thanks to your transmission data, we already know that that droid has remained on the *Millennium Falcon*."

"Yes, sir," Pellaeon said, not entirely convinced but knowing better than to argue the point. "Shall I put out an alert on the *Lady Luck*, then?"

"That won't be necessary," Thrawn said, and this time the satisfaction came through clearly. "I know exactly where Leia Organa Solo is going."

Pellaeon stared at him. "You're not serious. Sir."

"Perfectly serious, Captain," Thrawn said evenly. "Consider. Solo and Organa Solo have nothing to gain by simply transferring together to the *Lady Luck*—the *Millennium Falcon* is faster and far better defended. This exercise only makes sense if Organa Solo and the Wookiee are together." Thrawn smiled up at Pellaeon. "And given that, there is only one logical place for them to go."

Pellaeon looked at the display, feeling slightly sandbagged. But the Grand Admiral's logic tracked clean. "Kashyyyk?"

"Kashyyyk," Thrawn confirmed. "They know they can't evade our Noghri forever, and so they've decided to surround her with Wookiees. For all the good it will do them."

Pellaeon felt his lip twitch. He'd been aboard one of the ships that had been sent to Kashyyyk to capture Wookiees for the Empire's slave trade. "It may not be as easy as it sounds, Admiral," he cautioned. "Kashyyyk's ecology can best be described as a layered deathtrap. And the Wookiees themselves are extremely capable fighters."

"So are the Noghri," Thrawn countered coldly. "Now. What of Skywalker?"

"His vector away from Athega was consistent with a course toward Jomark," Pellaeon told him. "Of course, he could easily have altered it once he was out of range of our probes."

"He's going there," Thrawn said, lip twisting in a tight smile. "Our Jedi Master has said so, hasn't he?" The Grand Admiral glanced at the chrono on his display board. "We'll leave for Jomark immediately. How much lead time will we have?"

"A minimum of four days, assuming that Skywalker's X-wing hasn't been overly modified. More than that, depending on how many stopovers he has to make on the way."

"He'll make no stopovers," Thrawn said. "Jedi use a hibernation state for trips of such length. For our purposes, though, four days will be quite adequate."

He straightened in his chair and touched a switch. The command room's lights came back up, the holographic sculptures fading away. "We'll need two more ships," he told Pellaeon. "An Interdictor Cruiser to bring Skywalker out of hyperspace where we want him, and some kind of freighter. An expendable one, preferably."

Pellaeon blinked. "Expendable, sir?"

"Expendable, Captain. We're going to set up the attack as a pure accident—an opportunity that will seem to have arisen while we were investigating a suspicious freighter for Rebellion munitions." He cocked an eyebrow. "That way, you see, we retain the option of turning him over to C'baoth if we choose to do so, without even Skywalker realizing he was actually ambushed."

"Understood, sir," Pellaeon said. "With your permission, I'll get the *Chimaera* underway." He turned to go—

And paused. Halfway across the room, one of the sculptures had not disappeared with the others. Sitting all alone in its globe of light, it slowly writhed on its pedestal like a wave in some bizarre alien ocean. "Yes," Thrawn said from behind him. "That one is indeed real."

"It's . . . very interesting," Pellaeon managed. The sculpture was strangely hypnotic.

"Isn't it?" Thrawn agreed, his voice sounding almost wistful. "It was my one failure, out on the Fringes. The one time when understanding a race's art gave me no insight at all into its psyche. At least not at the time. Now, I believe I'm finally beginning to understand them."

"I'm sure that will prove useful in the future," Pellaeon offered diplomatically.

"I doubt it," Thrawn said, in that same wistful voice. "I wound up destroying their world."

Pellaeon swallowed. "Yes, sir," he said, starting again for the door. He winced only a little as he passed the sculpture.

CHAPTER 16

THERE WAS NO dreaming in the Jedi hibernation trance. No dreaming, no consciousness, virtually no awareness of the outside world. It was very much like a coma, in fact, except for one interesting anomaly: despite the absence of true consciousness, Luke's time sense still somehow managed to function. He didn't understand it, exactly, but it was something he'd learned to recognize and use.

It was that time sense, coupled with Artoo's frantic gurgling in the foggy distance, that was his first hint something was wrong.

"All right, Artoo, I'm awake," he reassured the droid as he worked his way back toward consciousness. Blinking the gummy feeling out of his eyes, he gave the instruments a quick scan. The readings confirmed what his time sense had already told him: the X-wing had come out of hyperspace nearly twenty light-years short of Jomark. The proximity indicator registered two ships practically on top of him ahead, with a third off to one side in the distance. Still blinking, he raised his head for a look.

And with a rush of adrenaline came fully awake. Directly ahead of him was what looked like a light freighter, a blazing overload in its engine section visible through crumpled and half-vaporized hull plates. Beyond it, looming like a dark cliff face, was an Imperial Star Destroyer.

Anger, fear, aggression—the dark side of the Force are they. With an effort, Luke forced down his fear. The freighter was between him and the Star Destroyer; concentrating on their larger prey, the Imperials might not even have noticed his arrival. "Let's get out of here, Artoo," he said, keying the controls back to manual and swinging the X-wing hard around. The etheric rudder whined in protest with the turn—

"Unidentified starfighter," a harsh voice boomed from the speaker. "This is the Imperial Star Destroyer *Chimaera.* Transmit your identification code and state your business."

So much for hoping he wouldn't be noticed. In the distance now, Luke could see what it was that had yanked the X-wing out of hyperspace: the third ship was an Interdictor Cruiser, the Empire's favorite tool for keeping opponents from jumping to lightspeed. Obviously, they'd been lying in wait for the freighter; it was just his bad luck that he'd run across the Interdictor's projected mass shadow and been kicked out of hyperspace along with it.

The freighter. Closing his eyes briefly with concentration, Luke reached out with the Force, trying to discover whether it was a Republic ship, a neutral, or even a pirate that the *Chimaera* had caught. But there was no hint of any life aboard. Either the crew had escaped, or else they'd already been taken prisoner.

Either way, there was nothing Luke could do for them now. "Artoo, find me the nearest edge of that Interdictor's gravity-wave cone," he ordered, throwing the X-wing into a stomach-churning downward drop that even the acceleration compensator couldn't quite handle. If he could keep the freighter directly between him and the Star Destroyer, he might be able to get out of range before they could bring a tractor beam to bear.

"Unidentified starfighter." The harsh voice was starting to get angry. "I repeat, transmit your identification code or prepare to be detained."

"Should have brought one of Han's false ID codes with me," Luke muttered to himself. "Artoo? Where's that edge estimate?"

The droid beeped, and a diagram appeared on the computer scope. "That far, huh?" Luke murmured. "Well, nothing to do but go for it. Hang on."

"Unidentified starfighter—"

The rest of the harangue was drowned out by the roar of the drive as Luke abruptly kicked the ship to full power. Almost lost in the noise was Artoo's questioning trilling. "No, I want the deflector shields down," Luke shouted back. "We need the extra speed."

He didn't add that if the Star Destroyer was really serious about vaporizing them, the presence or absence of shields wouldn't matter much at this range, anyway. But Artoo probably already knew that.

But if the Imperials didn't seem interested in vaporizing him out of hand, neither were they willing to just let him go. On the rear scope, he could see the Star Destroyer moving up and over the damaged freighter, trying to get clear of its interference.

Luke threw a quick look at the proximity indicator. He was still within tractor beam range, and at their current relative speeds would remain so for the next couple of minutes. What he needed was some way to distract or blind them . . .

"Artoo, I need a fast reprogramming on one of the proton torpedoes," he called. "I want to drop it at zero delta-v, then have it turn around and head straight aft. No sensors or homing codes, either—I want it to go out cold. Can you do that?" There was an affirmative beep. "Good. As soon as it's ready, give me a warning and then let it go."

He turned his attention back to the rear scope, gave the X-wing's course a slight readjustment. With its guidance sensors in their normal active state, the torpedo would be subject to the Star Destroyer's impressive array of jamming equipment; going out cold like this would limit the Imperials' response to trying to shoot it down with laser fire. The flip side of that, of course, was that if it wasn't aimed *very* accurately, it would shoot right past its intended target without even a twitch.

Artoo beeped; and with a slight lurch, the torpedo was away. Luke watched it go, reaching out with the Force to give it a slight realignment tap—

And a second later, with a spectacular multiple flash of sympathetic detonations, the freighter blew up.

Luke looked at the proximity indicator, mentally crossing his fingers. Almost out of range now. If the debris from the freighter could screen off the tractor beam for a few more seconds, they should make it.

Artoo warbled a warning. Luke glanced at the translation, then at the long-range scope, and felt his stomach tighten. Artoo warbled again, more insistently this time. "I see it, Artoo," Luke growled. It was, of course, the obvious tactic for the Imperials to employ. With the freighter no longer of any interest whatsoever, the Interdictor was changing position, swinging around to try to bring its huge gravity field projectors more fully to bear on the escaping X-wing. Luke watched as the cone-shaped field area angled across the scope . . .

"Hang on, Artoo," he called; and, again too abruptly for the compensators to totally negate, he swung the X-wing into a right-angle turn, blasting laterally to their original course.

From behind him came a shocked screech. "Quiet, Artoo, I know what I'm doing," he told the droid. Off to starboard now, the Star Destroyer was belatedly trying to shift its massive bulk, pivoting to track Luke's maneuver . . . and for the first time since the beginning of the encounter, flashes of laser fire began lancing out.

Luke made a quick decision. Speed alone wasn't going to save him now, and a near miss could end the contest right here and now. "Deflectors up, Artoo," he instructed the droid, giving his full attention to his best evasive maneuvering. "Give me a balance between shield power and speed."

Artoo beeped a response, and there was a slight drop in engine noise as the shields began drawing power. They were going slower, but so far the gamble seemed to be working. Caught off balance by Luke's right-angle maneuver, the Interdictor was now rotating in the wrong direction, its gravity beam sweeping across Luke's previous course instead of tracking the current one. Its commander was obviously trying to correct that mistake, but the sheer inertia of the ship's massive gravity generators was on Luke's side. If he could stay out of the Star Destroyer's range for another few seconds, he'd be out of the beam and free to escape to hyperspace. "Stand by for lightspeed," he told Artoo. "Don't worry about direction—we can do a short hop and set things up more carefully once we're clear."

Artoo acknowledged—

And without warning, Luke was slammed hard against his harness.

The Star Destroyer's tractor beam had them.

Artoo shrilled in dismay; but Luke had no time to comfort the droid now. His straight-line course had suddenly become an arc, a sort of pseudoorbit with the Star Destroyer playing the role of planet at its center. Unlike a true orbit, though, this one wasn't stable, and as soon as the Imperials got another beam focused on him, the circle would quickly degenerate into a tight inward spiral. A spiral whose end point would be inside the Star Destroyer's hangar bay.

He dropped the shields, throwing full power once again to the drive, knowing full well it was most likely a futile gesture. And he was right—for a second the beam seemed to falter, but it quickly caught back up with him. Such a relatively minor change in speed was too small to foul up the beam's tracking equipment.

But if he could find a way to arrange a more major change in speed . . .

"Unidentified starfighter." The harsh voice was back, unmistakably gloating this time. "You have no chance of escape; further efforts will merely damage your vehicle. You are ordered to power down and prepare to dock."

Luke clenched his teeth. This was going to be dangerous, but he'd run out of choices. And he *had* heard stories of this working at least once before. Somewhere. "Artoo, we're going to try something tricky," he called to the droid. "On my signal, I want you to reverse-trigger the acceleration compensator—full power, and bypass the cutoffs if you have to." Something warbled from the control panel, and he risked a quick look at the scope. His curving arc had brought him right to the edge of the Interdictor's gravity projection. "Artoo: *now*."

And with a scream of horribly stressed electronics, the X-wing came to a sudden dead stop.

There wasn't even enough time for Luke to wonder what aboard his ship could possibly have made a scream like that before he was again thrown, even harder this time, against his harness. His thumbs, ready on the firing buttons, jabbed down hard, sending a pair of proton torpedoes lancing forward; simultaneously, he pulled the X-wing upward. The Star Destroyer's tractor beam, tracking him along his path, had momentarily gotten lost by his sudden maneuver. If the computers guiding that lock would now be considerate enough to latch onto the proton torpedoes instead of him—

And suddenly the torpedoes were gone, leaving behind only a wisp of their exhaust trail to show that they'd been snatched off their original course. The gamble had succeeded; the Star Destroyer was now steadily pulling in the wrong target.

"We're free!" he snapped to Artoo, throwing full power to the drive. "Get ready for lightspeed."

The droid trilled something, but Luke had no time to look down at the computer scope for the translation. Realizing their error, and recognizing there was insufficient time to reestablish a tractor lock, the Imperials had apparently decided to go for a straight kill. All the Star Destroyer's batteries seemed to open up at once, and Luke suddenly found himself trying to dodge a virtual sandstorm of laser fire. Forcing himself to relax, he let the Force flow through him, allowing it to guide his hands on the controls the way it did his lightsaber. The ship jumped once as a shot got through; in his peripheral vision he saw the tip of his dorsal/starboard laser cannon flash and disappear into a cloud of superheated plasma. A near miss burned past overhead; another, closer, scorched a line across the transparisteel canopy.

Another warble came from the scope: they were clear of the Interdictor's gravity shadow. "Go!" Luke shouted to Artoo.

And with a second, even more nerve-wrenching electronic scream from behind him, the sky ahead abruptly turned to starlines.

They'd made it.

FOR WHAT SEEMED like a small eternity Thrawn gazed out the viewport, staring at the spot where Skywalker's X-wing had been when it had vanished. Surreptitiously,

Pellaeon watched him, wondering tautly when the inevitable explosion would come. With half an ear he listened to the damage control reports coming from the Number Four tractor beam projector, carefully not getting himself involved with the cleanup.

The destruction of one of the *Chimaera*'s ten projectors was a relatively minor loss. Skywalker's escape was not.

Thrawn stirred and turned around. Pellaeon tensed— "Come with me, Captain," the Grand Admiral said quietly, striding away down the bridge command walkway.

"Yes, sir," Pellaeon murmured, falling into step behind him, the stories of how Darth Vader had dealt with subordinates' failures running through his mind.

The bridge was uncommonly quiet as Thrawn led the way to the aft stairway and descended into the starboard crew pit. He walked past the crewers at their consoles, past the officers standing painfully erect behind them, and came to a halt at the control station for the starboard tractor beams. "Your name," he said, his voice excruciatingly calm.

"Cris Pieterson, sir," the young man seated at the console answered, his eyes wary.

"You were in charge of the tractor beam during our engagement with the starfighter." It was a statement, not a question.

"Yes, sir—but what happened wasn't my fault."

Thrawn's eyebrows arched, just a bit. "Explain."

Pieterson started to gesture to the side, changed his mind in midmotion. "The target did something with his acceleration compensator that killed his velocity vector—"

"I'm aware of the facts," Thrawn cut in. "I'm waiting to hear why his escape wasn't your fault."

"I was never properly trained for such an occurrence, sir," Pieterson said, a flicker of defiance touching his eyes. "The computer lost the lock, but seemed to pick it up again right away. There was no way for me to know it had really picked up something else until—"

"Until the proton torpedoes detonated against the projector?"

Pieterson held his gaze evenly. "Yes, sir."

For a long moment Thrawn studied him. "Who is your officer?" he asked at last.

Pieterson's eyes shifted to the right. "Ensign Colclazure, sir."

Slowly, deliberately, Thrawn turned to the tall man standing rigidly at attention with his back to the walkway. "You are in charge of this man?"

Colclazure swallowed visibly. "Yes, sir," he said.

"Was his training also your responsibility?"

"Yes, sir," Colclazure said again.

"Did you, during that training, run through any scenarios similar to what just happened?"

"I . . . don't remember, sir," the ensign admitted. "The standard training package *does* include scenarios concerning loss of lock and subsequent reestablishment confirmation."

Thrawn threw a brief glance back down at Pieterson. "Did you recruit him as well, Ensign?"

"No, sir. He was a conscript."

"Does that make him less worthy of your training time than a normal enlistee?"

"No, sir." Colclazure's eyes flicked to Pieterson. "I've always tried to treat my subordinates equally."

"I see." Thrawn considered a moment, then half turned to look past Pellaeon's shoulder. "Rukh."

Pellaeon started as Rukh brushed silently past him; he hadn't realized the Noghri had followed them down. Thrawn waited until Rukh was standing at his side, then turned back to Colclazure. "Do you know the difference between an error and a mistake, Ensign?"

The entire bridge had gone deathly still. Colclazure swallowed again, his face starting to go pale. "No, sir."

"Anyone can make an error, Ensign. But that error doesn't become a mistake until you refuse to correct it." He raised a finger—

And, almost lazily, pointed.

Pellaeon never even saw Rukh move. Pieterson certainly never had time to scream.

From farther down the crew pit came the sound of someone trying valiantly not to be sick. Thrawn glanced over Pellaeon's shoulder again and gestured, and the silence was further broken by the sound of a pair of stormtroopers coming forward. "Dispose of it," the Grand Admiral ordered them, turning away from Pieterson's crumpled body and pinning Colclazure with a stare. "The error, Ensign," he told the other softly, "has now been corrected. You may begin training a replacement."

He held Colclazure's eyes another heartbeat. Then, seemingly oblivious to the tension around him, he turned back to Pellaeon. "I want a full technical/tactical readout on the last few seconds of that encounter, Captain," he said, all calm business again. "I'm particularly interested in his lightspeed vector."

"I have it all here, sir," a lieutenant spoke up a bit hesitantly, stepping forward to offer the Grand Admiral a data pad.

"Thank you." Thrawn glanced at it briefly, handed it to Pellaeon. "We'll have him, Captain," he said, starting back down the crew pit toward the stairway. "Very soon now, we'll have him."

"Yes, sir," Pellaeon agreed cautiously, hurrying to catch up with the other. "I'm sure it's just a matter of time."

Thrawn raised an eyebrow. "You misunderstand me," he said mildly. "I mean that literally. He's out there right now, not very far away. And—" he smiled slyly at Pellaeon "—he's helpless."

Pellaeon frowned. "I don't understand, sir."

"That maneuver he used has an interesting side effect I suspect he didn't know about," the Grand Admiral explained. "Backfiring an acceleration compensator like that does severe damage to the adjoining hyperdrive. A light-year away, no farther, and it will fail completely. All we have to do is make a search along that vector, or persuade others to do our searching for us, and he'll be ours. You follow?"

"Yes, sir," Pellaeon said. "Shall I contact the rest of the fleet?"

Thrawn shook his head. "Preparing for the Sluis Van attack is the fleet's top priority at the moment. No, I think we'll subcontract this one out. I want you to send messages to all the major smuggling chiefs whose groups operate in this area—Brasck, Karrde, Par'tah, any others we have on file. Use their private frequencies and encrypt codes—a little reminder of how much we know about each of them should help ensure their cooperation. Give them Skywalker's hyperspace vector and offer a bounty of thirty thousand for his capture."

"Yes, sir." Pellaeon glanced back down the crew pit, at the activity still going on around the tractor beam station. "Sir, if you knew that Skywalker's escape was only temporary . . . ?"

"The Empire is at war, Captain," the Grand Admiral said, his voice cold. "We cannot afford the luxury of men whose minds are so limited they cannot adapt to unexpected situations."

He looked significantly at Rukh, then turned those glowing eyes back on Pellaeon. "Carry out your orders, Captain. Skywalker *will* be ours. Alive . . . or otherwise."

CHAPTER 17

I N FRONT OF Luke, the scopes and displays glowed softly as the diagnostic messages, most of them bordered in red, scrolled past. Beyond the displays, through the canopy, he could see the X-wing's nose, lit faintly by the sheen of distant starlight. Beyond that were the stars themselves, blazing all around him with cold brilliance.

And that was all. No sun, no planets, no asteroids, no cometary bodies. No warships, transports, satellites, or probes. Nothing. He and Artoo were stranded, very literally, in the middle of nowhere.

The computer's diagnostic package came to an end. "Artoo?" he called. "What've you got?"

From behind him came a distinctly mournful electronic moan, and the droid's reply appeared on the computer scope. "That bad, huh?"

Artoo moaned again, and the computer's summary was replaced by the droid's own assessment of their situation.

It wasn't good. Luke's reverse-triggering of the acceleration compensator had caused an unanticipated feedback surge into both hyperdrive motivators—not enough to fry them on the spot, but scorching them badly enough to cause sudden failure ten minutes into their escape. At the Point Four the ship had been doing at the time, that translated into approximately half a light-year of distance. Just for good measure, the same power surge had also completely crystallized the subspace radio antenna.

"In other words," Luke said, "we can't leave, we aren't likely to be found, and we can't call for help. Does that about sum it up?"

Artoo beeped an addition. "Right," Luke sighed. "And we can't stay here. Not for long, anyway."

Luke rubbed a hand across his chin, forcing back the sense of dread gnawing at him. Giving in to fear would only rob him of the ability to think, and that was the last thing he could afford to lose at this point. "All right," he said slowly. "Try this. We take the hyperdrive motivators off both engines and see if we can salvage enough components to put together a single functional one. If we can, we remount it somewhere in the middle of the aft fuselage where it can handle both engines. Maybe where the S-Foil servo actuator is now—we don't need that to get home. Possible?"

Artoo whistled thoughtfully. "I'm not asking if it'll be easy," Luke said patiently as the droid's response came up. "Just if it would be possible."

Another whistle, another pessimistic message. "Well, let's give it a try anyway," Luke told him, unstrapping his restraints and trying to wriggle around in the cramped confines of the cockpit. If he pulled off the back of the ejection seat, he would be able to get into the cargo compartment and the tools stored there.

Artoo warbled something else. "Don't worry, I'm not going to get stuck," Luke assured him, changing his mind and reaching for the in-cockpit pouches instead. The gloves and helmet seals for his flight suit were stored there; it'd be just as easy at this point to gear himself for vacuum and then get into the cargo compartment through its underside hatch. "If you want to be helpful, you might pull up the maintenance specs and find out exactly how I go about getting one of those motivators out. And cheer up, will you? You're starting to sound like Threepio."

Artoo was still jabbering indignantly over that characterization when the last of Luke's helmet seals cut off the sound. But he *did* sound less frightened.

It took nearly two hours for Luke to get past all the other cables and tubing in the way and remove the port engine hyperdrive motivator from its socket.

It took less than a minute more to discover that Artoo's earlier pessimism had been justified.

"It's riddled with cracks," Luke told the droid grimly, turning the bulky box over in his hands. "The whole shield casing. Just hairlines, really—you can barely see some of them. But they run most of the length of the sides."

Artoo gave a soft gurgle, a comment which required no translation. Luke hadn't done a lot of X-wing maintenance, but he knew enough to recognize that without an intact superconducting shield, a hyperdrive motivator was little more than a box of interconnected spare parts. "Let's not give up yet," he reminded Artoo. "If the other motivator's casing is all right we may still be in business."

Collecting his tool kit, feeling inordinately clumsy in zero-gee freefall, he made his way under the X-wing's fuselage to the starboard engine. It took only a few minutes to remove the proper access cover and tie back some of the interfering cables. Then, trying to get both his faceplate and his glow rod together in the opening without blinding himself, he peered inside.

A careful look at the motivator casing showed that there was no need to continue the operation.

For a long moment he just hung there, one knee bumping gently against the power surge vent, wondering what in the name of the Force they were going to do now. His X-wing, so sturdy and secure in even the thick of combat, seemed now to be little more than a terribly fragile thread by which his life was hanging.

He looked around him—looked at the emptiness and the distant stars—and as he did so, the vague sense of falling that always accompanied zero-gee came flooding back in on him. A memory flashed: hanging from the underside of Cloud City, weak from fear and the shock of losing his right hand, wondering how long he would have the strength to hang on. *Leia*, he called silently, putting all the power of his new Jedi skill into the effort. *Leia, hear me. Answer me.*

There was no answer except for the echoing of the call through Luke's own mind. But then, he hadn't expected one. Leia was long gone, safe on Kashyyyk by now, under the protection of Chewbacca and a whole planet of Wookiees.

He wondered if she'd ever find out what had happened to him.

For the Jedi, there is no emotion; there is peace. Luke took a deep breath, forcing back the black thoughts. No, he would not give up. And if the hyperdrive couldn't be fixed . . . well, perhaps there was something else they could try. "I'm coming in, Artoo," he announced, replacing the access panel and again collecting his tools. "While you're waiting, I want you to pull everything we've got on the subspace radio antenna."

Artoo had the data assembled by the time Luke got the cockpit canopy sealed over him again. Like the hyperdrive data, it wasn't especially encouraging. Made of ten kilometers of ultrathin superconducting wire wound tightly around a U-shaped core, a subspace radio antenna wasn't something that was supposed to be field-repairable.

But then, Luke wasn't the average X-wing pilot, either.

"All right, here's what we're going to do," he told the droid slowly. "The antenna's outer wiring is useless, but it doesn't look like the core itself was damaged. If we can find ten kilometers of superconducting wire somewhere else on the ship, we should be able to make ourselves a new one. Right?"

Artoo thought about that, gurgled an answer. "Oh, come on now," Luke admonished him. "You mean to tell me you can't do what some nonintelligent wire-wrapping machine does all day?"

The droid's beeping response sounded decidedly indignant. The translation that scrolled across the computer scope was even more so. "Well, then, there's no problem," Luke said, suppressing a smile. "I'd guess either the repulsorlift drive or else the sensor jammer will have all the wire we need. Check on that, will you?"

There was a pause, and Artoo quietly whistled something. "Yes, I know what the life support's limitations are," Luke agreed. "That's why you'll be the one doing all the wiring. I'm going to have to spend most of the time back in hibernation trance."

Another series of whistles. "Don't worry about it," Luke assured him. "As long as I come up every few days for food and water, hibernation is perfectly safe. You've seen me do it a dozen times, remember? Now get busy and run those checks."

Neither of the two components had quite the length of wiring they needed, but after poking around a little in the more esoteric sections of his technical memory, Artoo came to the conclusion that the eight kilometers available in the sensor jammer should be adequate to create at least a low-efficiency antenna. He conceded, however, that there was no way to know for sure until they actually tried it.

It was another hour's work for Luke to get the jammer and antenna out of the ship, strip the ruined wire off the core of the latter, and move everything to the upper aft fuselage where Artoo's two graspers could reach it. Jury-rigging a framework to feed the wire and protect it from snagging took another hour, and he took a half hour more to watch the operation from inside to make sure it was going smoothly.

At which point there was nothing left for him to do.

"Now, don't forget," he warned the droid as he settled himself as comfortably into the cockpit seat as possible.

"If anything goes wrong—or you even *think* something's about to go wrong—you go ahead and wake me up. Got that?"

Artoo whistled his assurances. "All right," Luke said, more to himself than to the droid. "I guess this is it, then."

He took a deep breath, letting his gaze sweep one last time across the starry sky. If this didn't work . . . But there was no point in worrying about that now. He'd done all he could for the moment. It was time now for him to draw upon inner peace, and to entrust his fate to Artoo.

To Artoo . . . and to the Force.

He took another deep breath. *Leia*, he called, uselessly, one last time. Then, turning his mind and thoughts inward, he began to slow his heart.

The last thing he remembered before the darkness took him was the odd sense that someone, somewhere, had in fact heard that final call. . . .

LEIA . . .

Leia jerked awake. "Luke?" she called, propping herself up on one elbow and peering into the dimness surrounding her. She could have sworn she'd heard his voice. His voice, or perhaps the touch of his mind.

But there was no one. Nothing but the cramped space of the *Lady Luck*'s main cabin and the pounding of her own heart and the familiar background sounds of a ship in flight. And, a dozen meters away in the cockpit, the unmistakable sense of Chewbacca's presence. And as she woke further, she remembered that Luke was hundreds of light-years away.

It must have been a dream.

With a sigh, she lay back down. But even as she did so, she heard the subtle change in sound and vibration pattern as the main sublight drive shut down and the repulsorlift kicked in. Listening closer, she could hear the faint sound of air rushing past the hull.

Slightly ahead of schedule, they were coming in to Kashyyyk.

She got out of bed and found her clothes, feeling her quiet misgivings gnawing with renewed force as she got dressed. Han and Chewbacca could make all the reassuring noises they wanted, but she'd read the diplomatic reports, and she knew full well how strong the undercurrent of resentment was that the Wookiees still harbored toward humans. Whether her status as a member of the New Republic hierarchy would make up for that was, in her view, entirely problematical.

Especially given her chronic difficulty in understanding their language.

The thought made her wince, and not for the first time since leaving Nkllon, she wished she'd had Lando use some other droid for his little voice-matching trick. Having Threepio and his seven-million-language translator along would have made this whole thing so much less awkward.

The *Lady Luck* was already deep into the atmosphere by the time she arrived in the cockpit, skimming low over a surprisingly flat layer of clouds and making smooth curves around the treetops that were occasionally visible poking through them. She remembered when she'd first come across a reference to the size of Kashyyyk's trees; she'd had a full-blown argument with the Senate librarian at the time about how the government could not afford to have its records data shot through with such clearly absurd errors. Even now, with them right in front of her, she found the things hard to believe. "Is that size typical for *wroshyr* trees?" she asked Chewbacca as she slipped into the seat beside him.

Chewbacca growled a negative: the ones visible above the clouds were probably half a kilometer taller than the average. "They're the ones you put nursery rings on, then," Leia nodded.

He looked at her, and even with her limited ability to read Wookiee faces his surprise was quite evident. "Don't look so shocked," she admonished him with a smile. "Some of us humans know a little about Wookiee culture. We aren't *all* ignorant savages, you know."

For a moment he just stared at her. Then, with an urf-urf-urf of laughter, he turned back to the controls.

Ahead and to the right, a tighter group of the extra-tall *wroshyr* trees had come into view. Chewbacca turned the *Lady Luck* toward it, and within a few minutes they were close enough for Leia to see the network of cables or thin branches linking them together just above cloud height. Chewbacca circled the ship partway around, bringing it within the perimeter; and then, with just a growl of warning, dropped sharply down into the clouds.

Leia grimaced. She'd never really liked flying blind, especially in an area crowded with obstacles the size of *wroshyr* trees. But almost before the *Lady Luck* was

completely enveloped by the thick white fog they were
clear of it again. Immediately below them was another
cloud layer. Chewbacca dropped them into that one, too,
and drove through it to clear air again—

Leia inhaled sharply. Filling the entire gap between
the group of massive trees, apparently hanging suspended in midair, was a city.

Not just a collection of primitive huts and fires like
the Ewok tree villages on Endor. This was a real, genuine
city, stretching out over a square kilometer or more of
space. Even from this distance she could see that the
buildings were large and complex, some of them two or
three stories high, and that the avenues between them
were straight and carefully laid out. The huge boles of
the trees poked up around and, in some places, through
the city, giving the illusion of giant brown columns supporting a rooftop of clouds. Surrounding the city on all
sides, strangely colored searchlight beams lanced outward.

Beside her, Chewbacca rumbled a question. "No, I've
never even seen holos of a Wookiee village," she breathed.
"My loss, obviously." They were getting closer now; close
enough for her to see that the Cloud City-type unipod
she'd expected was nowhere to be seen.

For that matter, there was no support of *any* kind visible. Was the whole city being held up by repulsorlifts?

The *Lady Luck* banked slightly to the left. Directly
ahead of them now, at one edge of the city and a little
above it, was a circular platform rimmed with landing
lights. The platform seemed to be sticking straight out
from one of the trees, and it took a few seconds for her

to realize that the whole thing was nothing more or less than the remnant of a huge limb that had been horizontally cut off near the trunk.

A not insignificant engineering feat. Dimly, she wondered how they'd disposed of the rest of the limb.

The platform didn't look nearly big enough to accommodate a ship the size of the *Lady Luck*, but a quick glance back at the city itself showed that the apparent smallness was merely a trick of the tree's deceptive scale. By the time Chewbacca put them down on the fire-blackened wood, in fact, it was clear that the platform could not only easily handle the *Lady Luck*, but probably full-sized passenger liners, as well.

Or, for that matter, Imperial Strike Cruisers. Perhaps, Leia decided, she shouldn't inquire too deeply into the circumstances of the platform's construction.

She had half expected the Wookiees to send a delegation out to meet her, and she turned out to have been half right. Two of the giant aliens were waiting beside the *Lady Luck* as Chewbacca lowered the entry ramp, indistinguishable to her untrained eye except for their slightly different heights and the noticeably different designs of the wide baldrics curving from shoulder to waist across their brown fur. The taller of the two, his baldric composed of gold-threaded tan, took a step forward as Leia headed down the ramp. She continued toward him, using all the calming Jedi techniques she knew, praying that this wouldn't be as awkward as she was very much afraid it would be. Chewbacca was hard enough for her to understand, and he'd been living out among humans for decades. A native Wookiee, speaking a native dialect, was likely to be totally incomprehensible.

The tall Wookiee bowed his head slightly and opened his mouth. Leia braced herself—

[I to you, Leiaorganasolo, bring greetings,] he roared. [I to Rwookrrorro welcome you.]

Leia felt her jaw drop in astonishment. "Ah . . . thank you," she managed. "I'm—all—honored to be here."

[As we by yourr presence arre honored,] he growled politely. [I am Ralrracheen. You may find it easierr to call me Ralrra.]

"I'm honored to meet you," Leia nodded, still feeling a little dazed by it all. Apart from the odd extended growling of his final *r* sounds, Ralrra's Wookiee speech was perfectly understandable. Listening to him, in fact, it was as if all the static she'd always had to plow through had suddenly cleared away. She could feel her face warming, and hoped her surprise didn't show.

Apparently, it did. Beside her, Chewbacca was urf-urf-urfing quietly again. "Let me guess," she suggested dryly, looking up at him. "You've had a speech impediment all these years and never thought to mention it to me?"

Chewbacca laughed even louder. [Chewbacca speaks most excellently,] Ralrra told her. [It is I who has a speech impediment. Strangely, it is the kind of trouble that humans find easierr to understand.]

"I see," Leia said, though she didn't entirely. "Were you an ambassador, then?"

Abruptly, the air around her seemed to grow chilly. [I was a slave to the Empirre,] Ralrra growled softly. [As was Chewbacca also, beforre Hansolo freed him. My captorrs found me useful, to speak with the otherr Wookiee slaves.]

Leia shivered. "I'm sorry," was all she could think of to say.

[You must not be,] he insisted. [My role gave me much information about the Empirre's forces. Information that proved useful when yourr Alliance freed us.]

Abruptly, Leia realized that Chewbacca was no longer standing at her side. To her shock, she saw that he was locked in a death grip with the other Wookiee, his bowcaster trapped uselessly against his shoulder by the other's massive arm. "Chewie!" she snapped, hand dropping to the blaster belted at her side.

She'd barely gotten hold of it, though, before Ralrra's shaggy hand landed in an iron grip on top of hers. [Do not disturb them,] the Wookiee told her firmly. [Chewbacca and Salporin have been friends since childhood, and have not seen each otherr in many yearrs. Theirr greeting must not be interrupted.]

"Sorry," Leia murmured, dropping her hand to her side and feeling like an idiot.

[Chewbacca said in his message that you requirre sanctuary,] Ralrra continued, perhaps recognizing her embarrassment. [Come. I will show you the preparations we have made.]

Leia's eyes flicked to Chewbacca and Salporin, still clinging to each other. "Perhaps we should wait for the others," she suggested, a little uncertainly.

[Therre will be no dangerr.] Ralrra drew himself up to his full height. [Leiaorganasolo, you must understand. Without you and yourr people many of us would still be slaves to the Empirre. Slaves, orr dead at theirr hand. To you and yourr Republic we owe a life debt.]

"Thank you," Leia said, feeling the last bit of residual

tension draining away. There was a great deal about Wookiee culture and psychology that was still opaque to her; but the life debt, at least, she understood very well. Ralrra had formally committed himself to her safety now, that commitment backed up by Wookiee honor, tenacity, and raw strength.

[Come,] Ralrra growled, gesturing toward what looked like an open-cage liftcar at the edge of the platform. [We will go to the village.]

"Certainly," Leia said. "That reminds me—I was going to ask how you keep the village in place. Do you use repulsorlifts?"

[Come,] Ralrra said. [I will show you.]

THE VILLAGE WAS not, in fact, being held up by repulsorlifts. Nor with unipods, tractor anchorlines, or any other clever scheme of modern technology. Which made it all the more sobering for Leia to realize that the Wookiees' method was, in its own way, more sophisticated than any of them.

The village was held up by branches.

[It was a great task, a village of this size to build,] Ralrra told her, waving a massive hand upward at the latticework above them. [Many of the branches at the level desired werre removed. Those which remained then grew strongerr and fasterr.]

"It looks almost like a giant spiderweb," Leia commented, peering from the liftcar at the underside of the village and trying not to think about the kilometers of empty space directly beneath them. "How did you mesh them together like that?"

[We did not. Through theirr own growth they arre a unity.]

Leia blinked. "Excuse me?"

[They have grown togetherr,] Ralrra explained. [When two *wroshyr* branches meet, they grow into one. Togetherr then they sprout new branches in all directions.]

He growled something under his breath, a word or phrase for which Leia had no translation. [It is a living reminderr of the unity and strength of the Wookiee people,] he added, almost to himself.

Leia nodded silently. It was also, she realized, a strong indication that all the *wroshyr* trees in this bunch were a single giant plant, with a unified or at least an intermixed root system. Did the Wookiees realize that? Or had their obvious reverence for the trees forbidden such thinking and research?

Not that curiosity would help them all that much in this case. Dropping her gaze, she peered down into the hazy dimness beneath the liftcar. Somewhere down there were the shorter *wroshyrs* and hundreds of other types of trees that made up the vast jungles of Kashyyyk. Several different arboreal ecosystems were reputed to exist in the jungle, arranged in roughly horizontal layers descending toward the ground, each layer more deadly than the one above. She didn't know whether the Wookiees had ever even made it all the way down to the surface; it was for sure that no one who had would have taken the time for leisurely botanical studies.

[They arre called *kroyies*,] Ralrra said.

Leia blinked at the odd non sequitur. But even as she

opened her mouth to ask what he was talking about, she spotted the double wedge of birds flying swiftly through the sky beneath them. "Those birds?" she asked.

[Yes. Once they werre a prize food to the Wookiee people. Now even the poorr may eat them.] He pointed toward the edge of the village above them, to the haze of light coming from the searchlights she'd seen during their approach. [*Kroyies* will come to those lights,] he explained. [Hunterrs therre await them.]

Leia nodded understanding; she'd seen visual lures of varying degrees of sophistication used to attract food animals on other worlds. "Don't all those clouds interfere with their effectiveness, though?"

[Through the clouds they work best,] Ralrra said. [The clouds spread the light. A *kroyie* will see it from great distances and come.]

As he spoke, the double wedge of birds banked sharply, climbing toward the clouds overhead and the lights playing against them. [Even so, you see. Tonight we shall perhaps dine on one of them.]

"I'd like that," she said. "I remember Chewie saying once that they were delicious."

[Then we must return to the village,] Ralrra said, touching the liftcar's control. With a creak of the cable, it started upward. [We had hoped to shelterr you in one of the morre luxurious homes,] he commented as they started upward. [But Chewbacca would not allow it.]

He gestured, and for the first time Leia noticed the homes built directly into the tree beside them. Some of them were multistoried and quite elaborate; all of them seemed to open up directly onto empty space. "Chewbacca understands my preferences," she told Ralrra, suppressing a shiver. "I was wondering why the liftcar went this far down past the village proper."

[The liftcarr is used mainly forr cargo transportation orr the ill,] Ralrra said. [Most Wookiees preferr to climb the trees naturally.]

He held out a hand to her, palm up; and as the muscles under the skin and fur flexed, a set of wickedly curved claws slid into sight from hidden fingertip sheaths.

Leia swallowed hard. "I didn't realize Wookiees had claws like those," she said. "Though I suppose I should have. You *are* arboreal, after all."

[To live among trees without them would be impossible,] Ralrra agreed. The claws retracted again, and the Wookiee waved the hand upward. [Even vine travel would be difficult without them.]

"Vines?" Leia echoed, frowning up through the liftcar's transparent roof. She hadn't noticed any vines on the trees earlier, and didn't really see any now. Her eyes fell on the cable running from the liftcar up into the leaves and branches above . . .

The dark *green* cable.

"That cable?" she asked carefully, nodding toward it. "That's a vine?"

[It a *kshyy* vine is,] he assured her. [Do not worry about its strength. It is strongerr than composite cable material, and cannot even by blasterrs be cut. Too, it is self-repairing.]

"I see," Leia said, staring at the vine and fighting hard against the sudden sense of panic. She'd flown all around the galaxy in hundreds of different types of airspeeders and spaceships without the slightest twinge of acrophobia, but this hanging out on the edge of nowhere without a solid powered cockpit around her was something else entirely. The warm sense of security she'd been feeling at being on Kashyyyk was starting to evaporate. "Have the vines ever broken?" she asked, trying to sound casual.

[In the past, it sometimes happened,] Ralrra said. [Various parasites and fungi, if unchecked, can erode them. Now, we employ safeguards which ourr ancestors did not have. Liftcarrs such as this one contain emergency repulsorlift systems.]

"Ah," Leia said, the momentary discomfort easing as she once again found herself feeling like a raw and not very bright diplomatic beginner. It was easy to forget that, despite their somewhat quaint-looking arboreal villages and their own animalistic appearance, Wookiees generally were quite at home with high technology.

The liftcar rose above the level of the village floor. Chewbacca and Salporin were standing there waiting for them, the former fingering his bowcaster and giving the little twitches that Leia had learned to associate with impatience. Ralrra brought them to a stop at the level of the wide exit ramp and opened the door, Salporin stepping forward as he did so to offer Leia his hand in assistance.

[We have made arrangements forr you and Chewbacca to stay at Salporin's home,] Ralrra said as they stepped out onto relatively solid ground again. [It is not farr. Therre arre transports available, if you wish.]

Leia looked out across the nearest parts of the village. She wanted very much to walk, to get out among the people and start getting the feel of the place. But after all the effort they'd put into sneaking her onto Kashyyyk in the first place, parading herself in front of the whole population would probably not be the smartest thing to do. "A transport would probably be best," she told Ralrra.

Chewbacca growled something as they came up to him. [She wished to see the village's structurre,] Ralrra told him. [We arre now ready to go.]

Chewbacca gave another growl of displeasure, but returned his bowcaster to his shoulder and strode off without further comment toward a repulsor sled parked at the side of the road perhaps twenty meters away. Ralrra and Leia followed, with Salporin bringing up the rear. The houses and other buildings began right at the edge of the matted branches, Leia had already noted, without anything more substantial than a few twisted *kshyy* vines between them and empty space. Ralrra had implied that the homes clinging to the trees themselves were the more prestigious ones; perhaps those here at the edge belonged to the upper middle class. Idly, she looked at the nearest of them, glancing into the windows as they passed. A face moved into view in the shadows behind one of them, catching her eye—

"Chewie!" she gasped. Even as her hand darted for her blaster the face vanished. But there was no mistaking those bulging eyes and protruding jaw and steel-gray skin.

Chewbacca was at her side in an instant, bowcaster in hand. "One of those creatures who attacked us on Bimmisaari is in there," she told him, reaching out with all the Jedi sense she could muster. Nothing. "At that window," she added, pointing with her blaster. "He was right there."

Chewbacca barked an order, sliding his massive bulk between Leia and the house and easing her slowly backwards, his bowcaster weaving back and forth across the structure in a covering pattern. Ralrra and Salporin were already at the house, each carrying a pair of wicked-looking knives they'd pulled from somewhere. They took up flanking positions beside the front door; and with a brilliant flash from his bowcaster, Chewbacca shot the door in.

From somewhere in toward the center of the village someone roared—a long, ululating Wookiee howl of anger or alarm that seemed to echo from the buildings and massive trees. Even before Ralrra and Salporin had disappeared into the house the howl was being taken up by other voices, rising in number and volume until it seemed as if half the village had joined in. Leia found herself pressing against Chewbacca's hairy back, wincing at the sheer ferocity in that call and flashing back to the Bimmisaari marketplace reacting to her jewelry theft.

Except that these weren't funny little yellow-clad Bimms. They were giant, violently strong Wookiees.

A large crowd had begun to form by the time Ralrra and Salporin emerged from the house—a crowd that Chewbacca paid no more attention to than he had the howling as he kept his eyes and bowcaster trained on the house. The other two Wookiees also ignored the crowd, disappearing around opposite sides of the house. They reappeared seconds later, their manner that of hunters who'd come up dry.

"He was there," Leia insisted as they returned to where she and Chewbacca stood. "I saw him."

[That may be true,] Ralrra said, slipping his knives

back into hidden sheaths behind his baldric. Salporin, his attention still back on the house, kept his own knives ready. [But we found no trace of anyone.]

Leia bit at her lip, eyes flicking across the area. There were no other houses near enough for the alien to have crossed to without her and Chewbacca seeing him. No cover of any sort, for that matter, on this side of the house. On the other side, there was nothing but the edge of the village.

"He went over the edge," she realized suddenly. "He must have. Either worked his way under the village with climbing gear or else met a craft hovering down below."

[That is unlikely,] Ralrra said, starting past her. [But possible. I will go down the liftcarr, to try and discoverr him.]

Chewbacca reached a hand out to stop him, growling a negative. [You arre right,] Ralrra conceded, though clearly reluctantly. [Yourr safety, Leiaorganasolo, is the most important thing at this point. We will take you to safety first, and then make inquiries about this alien.]

To safety. Leia gazed at the house, a shiver running up her back. And wondered if there would ever again be such a thing for her as safety.

CHAPTER 18

THE TRILLING CODE, coming from somewhere far behind him, startled Luke up out of his dreamless sleep. "Okay, Artoo, I'm awake," he said groggily, reaching up to rub at his eyes. His knuckles bumped into the visor of his flight helmet, and the impact did a bit to dissipate the fog still swirling through his mind. He couldn't remember exactly the circumstances under which he'd gone into hibernation, but he had the distinct feeling that Artoo had brought him out too soon. "Is anything wrong?" he asked, trying to track down exactly what it was the droid was supposed to be doing.

The trilling changed to an anxious-sounding warble. Still fighting to get his eyes properly focused, Luke searched out the computer scope for the translation. To his mild surprise, it was dark. As were all the rest of his instruments; and then it came back to him. He was trapped in deep space, with all the X-wing's systems shut down except power for Artoo and minimal life support for himself.

And Artoo was supposed to be winding a new subspace radio antenna. Twisting a slightly stiff neck, he turned halfway around to look back at the droid, wondering what the problem was—

And felt his muscles twitch with surprise. There, bearing rapidly down on them, was another ship.

He spun back around, fully awake now, hands jabbing for the bank of power switches and slapping them all on. But it was so much useless reflex. Even with shortcuts, it would still take nearly fifteen minutes to bring the X-wing's engines from a cold start to any serious possibility of flight, let alone combat. If the intruder was unfriendly . . .

Using the emergency maneuvering jets, he got the X-wing turning slowly around to face the approaching ship. The scopes and sensors were starting to come back on line again, confirming what his eyes had already told him: his visitor was a midsized, slightly dilapidated-looking Corellian bulk freighter. Not the sort of ship the Imperials usually used, and there were certainly no Imperial markings on its hull.

But under the circumstances, it was just as unlikely that it was an innocent freight handler, either. A pirate, perhaps? Luke reached out with the Force, trying to get a sense of the crew . . .

Artoo warbled, and Luke glanced down at the computer scope. "Yes, I noticed that, too," Luke told him. "But a normal bulk freighter might be able to pull that kind of deceleration if it was empty. Why don't you do a quick analysis of the sensor readings, see if you can spot any weapons emplacements."

The droid beeped an acknowledgment, and Luke gave the other instruments a quick scan. The primary laser cannon capacitors were at half charge now, with the main sublight drive about halfway through its preflight sequence.

And the flashing radio signal indicated that he was being hailed.

Bracing himself, Luke flipped on the receiver. "—need assistance?" a cool female voice said. "Repeating: unidentified starfighter, this is the freighter *Wild Karrde*. Do you need assistance?"

"*Wild Karrde*, this is New Republic X-wing AA-589," Luke identified himself. "As a matter of fact, yes, I could use some help."

"Acknowledged, X-wing," the other said. "What seems to be the problem?"

"Hyperdrive," Luke told her, watching the ship closely as it continued its approach. A minute earlier he'd rotated to face the freighter's approach; the other pilot had responded with a slight sidling drift of her own, with the result that the *Wild Karrde* was no longer in line with the X-wing's lasers. Probably just being cautious . . . but there were other possibilities. "I've lost both motivators," he continued. "Cracked shield cases, probably some other problems, too. I don't suppose you'd be carrying any spares?"

"Not for a ship that size." There was a short pause. "I'm instructed to tell you that if you'd care to come aboard, we can offer you passage to our destination system."

Luke reached out with the Force, trying to measure the sense behind the words. But if there was deceit there,

he couldn't detect it. And even if there was, he had precious little choice. "Sounds good," he said. "Any chance
you could take my ship, too?"

"I doubt you could afford our shipping rates," the
other told him dryly. "I'll check with the captain, but
don't get your hopes up. We'd have to take it in tow,
anyway—our holds are pretty full at the moment."

Luke felt his lip twitch. A fully loaded bulk freighter
couldn't possibly have managed the deceleration profile
Artoo had noted earlier. Either they were lying about
that, or else that normal-looking drive system had undergone a complete and massive upgrading.

Which made the *Wild Karrde* either a smuggler, a pirate, or a disguised warship. And the New Republic had
no disguised warships.

The other pilot was talking again. "If you'll hold your
present position, X-wing, we'll move up close enough to
throw a force cylinder out to you," she said. "Unless
you'd rather suit up and spacewalk across."

"The cylinder sounds fastest," Luke said, deciding to
try a light verbal probe. "I don't suppose either of us has
any reason to hang around this place. How did you happen to wind up out here, anyway?"

"We can handle a limited amount of baggage," the
other went on, ignoring the question. "I imagine you'll
want to bring your astromech droid along, too."

So much for the light verbal probe. "Yes, I will," he
told her.

"All right, then, stand by. Incidentally, the captain says
the transport fee will be five thousand."

"Understood," Luke said, unstrapping his restraints.
Opening the side pouches, he pulled out his gloves and

helmet seal and folded them into his flight suit's chest
pockets where he'd have quick access to them. A force
cylinder was relatively foolproof, but accidents could always happen. Besides which, if the *Wild Karrde*'s crew
was hoping to pick themselves up a free X-wing, shutting
the cylinder down halfway through the operation would
be the simplest and least messy way to dispose of him.

The crew. Luke paused, straining his senses toward
the ship moving steadily toward him. There was something wrong there; something he could feel but couldn't
quite track down.

Artoo warbled anxiously. "No, she didn't answer the
question," Luke agreed. "But I can't think of any legitimate reason for them to be out this far. Can you?"

The droid gave a soft, electronic moan. "Agreed,"
Luke nodded. "But refusing the offer doesn't buy us anything at all. We'll just have to stay alert."

Reaching into the other side pouch, he pulled out his
blaster, checked its power level, and slid it into the holster pocket built into his flight suit. His comlink went
into another pocket, though what use it would be aboard
the *Wild Karrde* he couldn't imagine, The emergency
survival pack went around his waist, awkward to fasten
in the cramped quarters. And last, he pulled out his lightsaber and fastened it to his belt.

"Okay, X-wing, we've got the cylinder established,"
the voice came. "Whenever you're ready."

The *Wild Karrde*'s small docking bay was directly
above him, its outer door gaping invitingly. Luke checked
his instruments, confirmed there was indeed a corridor
of air between the two ships, and took a deep breath.
"Here we go, Artoo," he said, and popped the canopy.

A puff of breeze brushed across his face as the air pressures equalized. Giving himself a careful push, he eased up and out, gripping the edge of the canopy to turn himself around. Artoo, he saw, had ejected from his socket and was drifting freely just above the X-wing, making distinctly unhappy noises about his situation. "I've got you, Artoo," Luke soothed, reaching out with the Force to pull the droid toward him. Getting his bearings one last time, he bent his knees and pushed off.

He reached the airlock at the back of the bay a half second ahead of Artoo, grabbed hold of the straps fastened to the walls, and brought both of them to a smooth halt. Someone was obviously watching; they were still moving when the outer lock door slid shut. Gravity came back, slowly enough for him to adjust his stance to it, and a moment later the inner door slid open.

There was a young man waiting for them, wearing a casual coverall of an unfamiliar cut. "Welcome aboard the *Wild Karrde*," he said, nodding gravely. "If you'll follow me, the captain would like to see you."

Without waiting for a reply, he turned and headed down the curving corridor. "Come on, Artoo," Luke murmured, starting after him and reaching out with the Force for a quick survey of the ship. Aside from their guide, he could sense only four others aboard, all of them in the forward sections. Behind him, in the aft sections . . .

He shook his head, trying to clear it. It didn't help: the aft sections of the ship still remained oddly dark to him. An aftereffect of the long hibernation, probably. It was for certain, though, that there were no crew members or droids back there, and that was all he needed to know for the moment.

The guide led them to a door, which slid open as he stepped to one side. "Captain Karrde will see you now," he said, waving toward the open door.

"Thank you," Luke nodded to him. With Artoo bumping against his heels, he stepped into the room.

It was an office of sorts; small, with much of its wall space taken up with what looked like highly sophisticated communications and encrypt equipment. In the center was a large desk/console combination . . . and seated behind it, watching Luke's approach, was a slender man, thin-faced, with short dark hair and pale blue eyes.

"Good evening," he said in a cool, carefully modulated voice. "I'm Talon Karrde." His eyes flicked up and down Luke, as if measuring him. "And you, I presume, are Commander Luke Skywalker."

Luke stared at him. How in the worlds . . . ? "Private citizen Skywalker," he said, striving to keep his own voice calm. "I resigned my Alliance commission nearly four years ago."

An almost-smile twitched the corners of Karrde's mouth. "I stand corrected. I must say, you've certainly found a good place to get away from it all."

The question was unstated, but no less obvious for that. "I had some help choosing it," Luke told him. "A small run-in with an Imperial Star Destroyer about half a light-year away."

"Ah," Karrde said, without any surprise that Luke could see or sense. "Yes, the Empire is still quite active in this part of the galaxy. Growing more so, too, particularly of late." He cocked his head slightly to the side, his eyes never leaving Luke's face. "Though I presume you've already noticed that. Incidentally, it looks like we'll be able to take your ship in tow, after all. I'm having the cables rigged now."

"Thank you," Luke said, feeling the skin on the back of his neck start to tingle. Whether a pirate or a smuggler, Karrde should certainly have reacted more strongly to the news that there was a Star Destroyer in the area. Unless, of course, he already had an understanding with the Imperials . . . "Allow me to thank you for the rescue, as well," he continued. "Artoo and I are lucky you happened along."

"And Artoo is—? Oh, of course—your astromech droid." The blue eyes flicked down briefly. "You must be a formidable warrior indeed, Skywalker—escaping from an Imperial Star Destroyer is no mean trick. Though I imagine a man like yourself is accustomed to giving the Imperials trouble."

"I don't see much front-line action anymore," Luke told him. "You haven't told me how you came to be out here, Captain. Or, for that matter, how you knew who I was."

Another almost-smile. "With a lightsaber attached to your belt?" he asked wryly. "Come now. You were either Luke Skywalker, Jedi, or else someone with a taste for antiques and an insufferably high opinion of his swordsmanship." Again, the blue eyes flicked up and down Luke. "You're not really what I expected, somehow. Though I suppose that's not all that surprising—the vast majority of Jedi lore has been so twisted by myth and ignorance that to get a clear picture is almost impossible."

The warning bell in the back of Luke's mind began to ring louder. "You almost sound as if you were expecting to find me here," he said, easing his body into a combat stance and letting his senses reach out. All five of the crewers were still more or less where they'd been a few minutes earlier, farther up toward the forward part of the ship. None except Karrde himself was close enough to pose any kind of immediate threat.

"As a matter of fact, we were," Karrde agreed calmly. "Though I can't actually take any of the credit for that. It was one of my associates, Mara Jade, who led us here." His head inclined slightly to his right. "She's on the bridge at the moment."

He paused, obviously waiting. It could be a setup, Luke knew; but the suggestion that someone might actually have been able to sense his presence from light-years away was too intriguing to pass up. Keeping his overall awareness clear, Luke narrowed a portion of his mind to the *Wild Karrde*'s bridge. At the helm was the young woman he'd spoken to earlier from the X-wing. Beside her, an older man was busy running a calculation through the nav computer. And sitting behind them—

The jolt of that mind shot through him like an electric current. "Yes, that's her," Karrde confirmed, almost offhandedly. "She hides it quite well, actually—though not, I suppose, from a Jedi. It took me several months of careful observation to establish that it was you, and you personally, for whom she had these feelings."

It took Luke another second to find his voice. Never before, not even from the Emperor, had he ever felt such a black and bitter hatred. "I've never met her before," he managed.

"No?" Karrde shrugged. "A pity. I was rather hoping you'd be able to tell me why she feels this way. Ah, well." He got to his feet. "I suppose, then, there's nothing more for us to talk about for the moment . . . and let me say in advance that I'm very sorry it has to be this way."

Reflexively, Luke's hand darted for his lightsaber. He'd barely begun the movement when the shock of a stun weapon coursed through him from behind.

There were Jedi methods for fighting off unconsciousness. But they all took at least a split second of preparation—a split second that Luke did not have. Dimly, he felt himself falling; heard Artoo's frantic trilling in the distance; and wondered with his last conscious thought how in the worlds Karrde had done this to him.

CHAPTER 19

HE AWOKE SLOWLY, in stages, aware of nothing but the twin facts that, one, he was lying flat on his back and, two, he felt terrible.

Slowly, gradually, the haze began to coalesce into more localized sensations. The air around him was warm but damp, a light and shifting breeze carrying several unfamiliar odors along with it. The surface beneath him had the soft/firm feel of a bed; the general sense of his skin and mouth implied he'd been asleep for probably several days.

It took another minute for the implications of that to percolate through the mental fog filling his brain. More than an hour or two was well beyond the safe capabilities of any stun weapon he'd ever heard of. Clearly, after being shot, he'd been drugged.

Inwardly, he smiled. Karrde was probably expecting him to be incapacitated for a while longer; and Karrde was in for a surprise. Forcing his mind into focus, he ran through the Jedi technique for detoxifying poisons and then waited for the haze to clear.

It took him some time to realize that nothing was, in fact, happening.

Somewhere in there he fell asleep again; and when he next awoke, his mind had cleared completely. Blinking against the sunlight streaming across his face, he opened his eyes and lifted his head.

He was lying on a bed, still in his flight suit, in a small but comfortably furnished room. Directly across from him was an open window, the source of the aroma-laden breezes he'd already noted. Through the window, too, he could see the edge of a forest fifty meters or so away, above which a yellowish-orange sun hovered—rising or setting, he didn't know which. The furnishings of the room itself didn't look much like those of a prison cell—

"Finally awake, are you?" a woman's voice said from the side.

Startled, Luke twisted his head toward the voice. His first, instantaneous thought was that he had somehow missed sensing whoever was over there; his second, following on the heels of the first, was that that was clearly ridiculous and that the voice must be coming instead from an intercom or comlink.

He finished his turn, to discover that the first thought had indeed been correct.

She was sitting in a high-backed chair, her arms draped loosely over the arms in a posture that seemed strangely familiar: a slender woman about Luke's own age, with brilliant red-gold hair and equally brilliant green eyes. Her legs were casually crossed; a compact but wicked-looking blaster lay on her lap.

A genuine, living human being . . . and yet, impossibly, he couldn't sense her.

The confusion must have shown in his face. "That's right," she said, favoring him with a smile. Not a friendly or even a polite smile, but one that seemed to be made up of equal parts bitterness and malicious amusement. "Welcome back to the world of mere mortals."

—and with a surge of adrenaline, Luke realized that the strange mental veiling wasn't limited to just her. He couldn't sense *anything*. Not people, not droids, not even the forest beyond his window.

It was like suddenly going blind.

"Don't like it, do you?" the woman mocked. "It's not easy to suddenly lose everything that once made you special, is it?"

Slowly, carefully, Luke eased his legs over the side of the bed and sat up, giving his body plenty of time to get used to moving again. The woman watched him, her right hand dropping to her lap to rest on top of the blaster. "If the purpose of all this activity is to impress me with your remarkable powers of recuperation," she offered, "you don't need to bother."

"Nothing so devious," Luke advised, breathing hard and trying not to wheeze. "The purpose of all this activity is to get me back on my feet." He looked her hard in the eye, wondering if she would flinch away from his gaze. She didn't even twitch. "Don't tell me; let me guess. You're Mara Jade."

"That doesn't impress me, either," she said coldly.

"Karrde already told me he'd mentioned my name to you."

Luke nodded. "He also told me that you were the one who found my X-wing. Thank you."

Her eyes flashed. "Save your gratitude," she bit out. "As far as I'm concerned, the only question left is whether we turn you over to the Imperials or kill you ourselves."

Abruptly she stood up, the blaster ready in her hand. "On your feet. Karrde wants to see you."

Carefully, Luke stood up, and as he did so, he noticed for the first time that Mara had attached his lightsaber to her own belt. Was she, then, a Jedi herself? Powerful enough, perhaps, to smother Luke's abilities? "I can't say that either of those options sounds appealing," he commented.

"There's one other one." She took half a step forward, moving close enough that he could have reached out and touched her. Lifting the blaster, she pointed it directly at his face. "You try to escape . . . and I kill you right here and now."

For a long moment they stood there, frozen. The bitter hatred was blazing again in those eyes . . . but even as Luke gazed back at her, he saw something else along with the anger. Something that looked like a deep and lingering pain.

He stood quietly, not moving; and almost reluctantly, she lowered the weapon. "Move. Karrde's waiting."

LUKE'S ROOM WAS at the end of a long hallway with identical doors spaced at regular intervals along its length. A barracks of sorts, he decided, as they left it and started across a grassy clearing toward a large, high-roofed building. Several other structures clustered around the latter, including another barracks building, a handful that looked like storehouses, and one that was clearly a servicing hangar. Grouped around the hangar on both sides were over a dozen starships, including at least two bulk cruisers like the *Wild Karrde* and several smaller craft, some of them hidden a ways back into the forest that pressed closely in on the compound from all sides. Tucked away behind one of the bulk cruisers, he could just see the nose of his X-wing. For a moment he considered asking Mara what had happened to Artoo, decided he'd do better to save the question for Karrde.

They reached the large central building and Mara reached past Luke to slap the sensor plate beside the door. "He's in the greatroom," Mara said as the panel slid open in response. "Straight ahead."

They walked down a long hallway, passing a pair of what seemed to be medium-sized dining and recreation rooms. Ahead, a large door at the end of the hallway slid open at their approach. Mara ushered him inside—

And into a scene straight out of ancient legend.

For a moment Luke just stood in the doorway, staring. The room was large and spacious, its high ceiling translucent and crisscrossed by a webwork of carved rafters. The walls were composed of a dark brown wood, much of it elaborately open-mesh carved, with a deep blue light glowing through the interstices. Other luxuries were scattered sparingly about: a small sculpture here, an unrecognizable alien artifact there. Chairs, couches, and large cushions were arranged in well-separated conversation circles, giving a distinctly relaxed, almost informal air to the place.

But all that was secondary, taken in peripherally or at a later time entirely. For that first astonishing moment Luke's full attention was fixed solidly on the tree growing through the center of the room.

Not a small tree, either, like the delicate saplings that lined one of the hallways in the Imperial Palace. This one was huge, a meter in diameter at the base, extending from a section of plain dirt floor through the translucent ceiling and far beyond. Thick limbs starting perhaps two meters from the ground stretched their way across the room, some of them nearly touching the walls, almost like arms reaching out to encompass everything in sight.

"Ah; Skywalker," a voice called from in front of him. With an effort, Luke shifted his gaze downward, to find Karrde sitting comfortably in a chair at the base of the tree. On either side two long-legged quadrupeds crouched, their vaguely doglike muzzles pointing stiffly in Lukes direction. "Come and join me."

Swallowing, Luke started toward him. There were stories he remembered from his childhood about fortresses with trees growing up through them. Frightening stories, some of them, full of danger and helplessness and fear.

And in every one of those stories, such fortresses were the home of evil.

"Welcome back to the land of the living," Karrde said as Luke approached. He picked up a silvery pitcher from the low table at his side, poured a reddish liquid into a pair of cups. "I must apologize for having kept you asleep all this time. But I'm sure you appreciate the special problems involved in making sure a Jedi stays where you've put him."

"Of course," Luke said, his attention on the two animals beside Karrde's chair. They were still staring at him with an uncomfortable intensity. "Though if you'd just asked nicely," he added, "you might have found me quite willing to cooperate."

A flicker of a smile touched Karrde's lips. "Perhaps. Perhaps not." He gestured to the chair across from him. "Please sit down."

Luke started forward; but as he did so, one of the animals rose up slightly on his haunches, making a strange sort of choked purr. "Easy, Sturm," Karrde admonished, looking down at the animal. "This man is our guest."

The creature ignored him, its full attention clearly on Luke. "I don't think it believes you," Luke suggested carefully. Even as he spoke, the second animal made the same sort of sound as the first had.

"Perhaps not." Karrde had a light grip on each of the animals' collars now and was glancing around the room. "Chin!" he called toward the three men lounging in one of the conversation circles. "Come and take them out, will you?"

"Sure." A middle-aged man with a Froffli-style haircut got up and trotted over. "Come on, fellows," he grunted, taking over Karrde's grip on the collars and leading the animals away. "What hai we go for a walk, hee?"

"My apologies, Skywalker," Karrde said, frowning slightly as he watched the others go. "They're usually better behaved than that with guests. Now; please sit down."

Luke did so, accepting the cup Karrde offered him. Mara stepped past him and took up position next to her chief. Her blaster, Luke noted, was now in a wrist holster on her left forearm, nearly as accessible as it would have been in her hand.

"It's just a mild stimulant," Karrde said, nodding to the cup in Luke's hand. "Something to help you wake up." He took a drink from his own cup and set it back down on the low table.

Luke took a sip. It tasted all right; and anyway, if Karrde had wanted to drug him, there was hardly any need to stoop to such a childish subterfuge. "Would you mind telling me where my droid is?"

"Oh, he's perfectly all right," Karrde assured him. "I have him in one of my equipment sheds for safekeeping."

"I'd like to see him, if I may."

"I'm sure that can be arranged. But later." Karrde leaned back in his seat, his forehead furrowing slightly. "Perhaps after we've figured out just exactly what we're going to do with you."

Luke glanced up at Mara. "Your associate mentioned the possibilities. I'd hoped I could add another to the list."

"That we send you back home?" Karrde suggested.

"With due compensation, of course," Luke assured him. "Say, double whatever the Empire would offer?"

"You're very generous with other people's money," Karrde said dryly. "The problem, unfortunately, doesn't arise from money, but from politics. Our operations, you see, extend rather deeply into both Imperial and Republic space. If the Empire discovered we'd released you back to the Republic, they would be highly displeased with us."

"And vice versa if you turned me over to the Empire," Luke pointed out.

"True," Karrde said. "Except that given the damage to your X-wing's subspace radio, the Republic presumably has no idea what happened to you. The Empire, unfortunately, does."

"And it's not what they *would* offer," Mara put in. "It's what they *have* offered. Thirty thousand."

Luke pursed his lips. "I had no idea I was so valuable," he said.

"You could be the difference between solvency and failure for any number of marginal operators," Karrde said bluntly. "There are probably dozens of ships out there right now, ignoring schedules and prior commitments to hunt for you." He smiled tightly. "Operators who haven't given even a moment of consideration to how they would hold on to a Jedi even if they caught one."

"Your method seems to work pretty well," Luke told him. "I don't suppose you'd be willing to tell me how you've managed it."

Karrde smiled again. "Secrets of that magnitude are worth a great deal of money. Have you any secrets of equal value to trade?"

"Probably not," Luke said evenly. "But, again, I'm sure the New Republic would be willing to pay market value."

Karrde sipped from his drink, eyeing Luke thoughtfully over the rim of the cup. "I'll make you a deal," he said, putting the cup back on the table beside him. "You tell me why the Empire is suddenly so interested in you, and I'll tell you why your Jedi powers aren't working."

"Why don't you ask the Imperials directly?"

Karrde smiled. "Thank you, but no. I'd just as soon not have them start wondering at my sudden interest. Particularly after we pleaded prior commitments when the request came in for us to help hunt you down."

Luke frowned at him. "You weren't hunting for me?"

"No, we weren't." Karrde's lip twisted. "One of those little ironies that make life so interesting. We were simply returning from a cargo pickup when Mara dropped us out of hyperspace on the spur of the moment to do a nav reading."

Luke studied Mara's stony expression. "How fortunate for you," he said.

"Perhaps," Karrde said. "The net result, though, was to put us in the middle of the exact situation that I'd hoped to avoid."

Luke held his hands out, palms upward. "Then let me go and pretend none of this happened. I give you my word I'll keep your part in it quiet."

"The Empire would find out anyway," Karrde shook his head. "Their new commander is extremely good at piecing bits of information together. No, I think your best hope right now is for us to find a compromise. Some way we can let you go while still giving the Imperials what they want." He cocked his head slightly. "Which leads us back to my original question."

"And from there back to my original answer," Luke said. "I really *don't* know what the Empire wants with me." He hesitated, but Leia should be well beyond Imperial reach by now. "I can tell you, though, that it's not just me. There have been two attempts on my sister Leia, too."

"Killing attempts?"

Luke thought about it. "I don't think so. The one I was present for felt more like a kidnapping."

"Interesting," Karrde murmured, his eyes defocusing slightly. "Leia Organa Solo. Who is in training to be a Jedi like her brother. That could explain . . . certain recent Imperial actions."

Luke waited, but after a moment it became clear that Karrde wasn't going to elaborate. "You spoke of a compromise," he reminded the other.

Karrde seemed to pull his thoughts back to the room. "Yes, I did," he said. "It's occurred to me that your privileged position in the New Republic might be what the Empire was interested in—that they wanted information on the inner workings of the Provisional Council. In such a case, we might have been able to work out a deal whereby you went free while your R2 droid went to the Imperials for debriefing."

Luke felt his stomach tighten. "It wouldn't do them any good," he said as casually as he could manage. The thought of Artoo being sold into Imperial slavery . . . "Artoo has never been to any of the Council meetings."

"But he does have a great deal of knowledge of you personally," Karrde pointed out. "As well as of your sister, her husband, and various other highly placed members of the New Republic." He shrugged. "It's a moot question now, of course. The fact that the focus is exclusively on the New Republic's Jedi and potential Jedi means they're not simply after information. Where did these two attacks take place?"

"The first was on Bimmisaari, the second on Bpfassh."

Karrde nodded. "We've got a contact on Bpfassh; perhaps we can get him to do some backtracking on the Imperials. Until then, I'm afraid you'll have to remain here as our guest."

It sounded like a dismissal. "Let me just point out one other thing before I go," Luke said. "No matter what happens to me—or what happens to Leia, for that matter—the Empire is still doomed. There are more planets in the New Republic now than there are under Imperial rule, and that number increases daily. We'll win eventually, if only by sheer weight of numbers."

"I understand that was the Emperor's own argument when discussing your Rebellion," Karrde countered dryly. "Still, that *is* the crux of the dilemma, isn't it? While the Empire will wreak swift retribution on me if I don't give you over to them, the New Republic looks more likely to win out in the long run."

"Only if he and his sister are there to hold Mon Mothma's hand," Mara put in contemptuously. "If they aren't—"

"If they aren't, the final time frame is somewhat less clear," Karrde agreed. "At any rate, I thank you for your time, Skywalker. I hope we can come to a decision without too much of a delay."

"Don't hurry on my account," Luke told him. "This seems a pleasant enough world to spend a few days on."

"Don't believe it for a moment," Karrde warned. "My two pet vornskrs have a large number of relatives out in the forest. Relatives who haven't had the benefits of modern domestication."

"I understand," Luke said. On the other hand, if he could get out of Karrde's encampment and clear of whatever this strange interference was they were using on him . . .

"And don't count on your Jedi skills to protect you, either," Karrde added, almost lazily. "You'll be just as helpless in the forest. Probably more so." He looked up at the tree towering above him. "There are, after all, considerably more ysalamiri out there than there are here."

"Ysalamiri?" Luke followed his gesture . . . and for the first time noticed the slender, gray-brown creature hanging on to the tree limb directly over Karrde's head. "What is it?"

"The reason you're staying where we put you," Karrde said. "They seem to have the unusual ability to push back the Force—to create bubbles, so to speak, where the Force simply doesn't exist."

"I've never heard of them," Luke said, wondering if there was any truth at all to the story. Certainly neither Yoda nor Ben had ever mentioned the possibility of such a thing.

"Not very many have," Karrde agreed. "And in the past, most of those who did had a vested interest in keeping it that way. The Jedi of the Old Republic avoided the planet, for obvious reasons, which was why a fair number of smuggling groups back then had their bases here. After the Emperor destroyed the Jedi, most of the groups pulled up roots and left, preferring to be closer to their potential markets. Now that the Jedi are rising again—" he nodded gravely to Luke "—perhaps some of them will return. Though I dare say the general populace would probably not appreciate that."

Luke glanced around the tree. Now that he knew what to look for, he could see several other ysalamiri wrapped around and across various of the limbs and branches. "What makes you think it's the ysalamiri and not something else that's responsible for this bubbling in the Force?"

"Partly local legend," Karrde said. "Mainly, the fact that you're standing here talking with me. How else could a man with a stun weapon and an extremely nervous mind have walked right up behind a Jedi without being noticed?"

Luke looked at him sharply, the last piece falling into place. "You had ysalamiri aboard the *Wild Karrde*."

"Correct," Karrde said. "Purely by chance, actually. Well—" He looked up at Mara. "Perhaps not *entirely* by chance."

Luke glanced again at the ysalamiri above Karrde's head. "How far does this bubbling extend?"

"Actually, I'm not sure anyone knows," Karrde conceded. "Legend says that individual ysalamiri have bubbles from one to ten meters in radius, but that groups of them together have considerably larger ones. Some sort of reinforcement, I gather. Perhaps you'll do us the courtesy of participating in a few experiments regarding them before you leave."

"Perhaps," Luke said. "Though that probably depends on which direction I'm headed at the time."

"It probably will," Karrde agreed. "Well. I imagine you'd like to get cleaned up—you've been living in that flight suit for several days now. Did you bring any changes of clothing with you?"

"There's a small case in the cargo compartment of my X-wing," Luke told him. "Thank you for bringing it along, incidentally."

"I try never to waste anything that may someday prove useful," Karrde said. "I'll have your things sent over as soon as my associates have determined that there are no hidden weapons or other equipment among them." He smiled slightly. "I doubt that a Jedi would bother with such things, but I believe in being thorough. Good evening, Skywalker."

Mara had her tiny blaster in hand again. "Let's go," she said, gesturing with the weapon.

Luke stood up. "Let me offer you one other option," he said to Karrde. "If you decide you'd rather pretend none of this ever happened, you could just return Artoo and me to where you found us. I'd be willing to take my chances with the other searchers."

"Including the Imperials?" Karrde asked.

"Including the Imperials," Luke nodded.

A small smile touched Karrde's lips. "You might be surprised. But I'll keep the option in mind."

THE SUN HAD disappeared behind the trees and the sky was noticeably darker as Mara escorted him back across the compound. "Did I miss dinner?" he asked as they walked down the corridor toward his room.

"Something can be brought to you," Mara said, her voice little more than a thinly veiled snarl.

"Thank you." Luke took a careful breath. "I don't know why you dislike me so much—"

"Shut up," she cut him off. "Just shut up."

Grimacing, Luke did so. They reached his room and she nudged him inside. "We don't have any lock for the window," she said, "but there's an alarm on it. You try going out, and it'll be a toss-up as to whether the vornskrs get to you before I do." She smiled, mock-sweetly. "But don't take my word for it. Try it and find out."

Luke looked at the window, then back at Mara. "I'll pass, thanks."

Without another word she left the room, closing the door behind her. There was the click of an electronic lock being engaged, and then silence.

He went to the window, peered out. There were lights showing in some of the other barracks windows, though he hadn't noticed any other lights in his own building. Which made sense, he supposed. Whether Karrde decided to turn him over to the Empire or release him back to the New Republic, there was no point in more of his associates knowing about it than absolutely necessary.

All the more so if Karrde decided to take Mara's advice and just kill him.

He turned away from the window and went back to his bed, fighting back the fear trying to rise inside him. Never since facing the Emperor had he felt so helpless.

Or, for that matter, actually *been* so helpless.

He took a deep breath. *For the Jedi, there is no emotion; there is peace.* Somehow, he knew, there had to be a way out of this prison.

All he had to do was to stay alive long enough to find it.

CHAPTER 20

"No, I ASSURE you, everything is fine," Threepio said in Leia's voice, looking just about as unhappy beneath his headset as a droid could possibly look. "Han and I decided that as long as we were out this way we might as well take a look around the Abregado system."

"I understand, Your Highness," Winter's voice came back over the *Falcon*'s speaker. To Han, she sounded tired. Tired, and more than a little tense. "May I recommend, though, that you don't stay away too much longer."

Threepio looked helplessly at Han. "We'll be back soon," Han muttered into his comlink.

"We'll be back soon," Threepio echoed into the *Falcon*'s mike.

"I just want to check out—"

"I just want to check out—"

"—the Gados's—"

"—the Gados's—"

"—manufacturing infrastructure."

"—manufacturing infrastructure."

"Yes, Your Highness," Winter said. "I'll pass that information on to the Council. I'm sure they'll be pleased to hear it." She paused, just noticeably. "I wonder if I might be permitted to speak with Captain Solo for a moment."

Across the cockpit, Lando grimaced. *She knows*, he mouthed silently.

No kidding, Han mouthed back. He caught Threepio's eye and nodded. "Of course," the droid said, sagging with obvious relief. "Han—?"

Han switched his comlink over, "I'm here, Winter. What's up?"

"I wanted to know if you had any idea yet when you and Princess Leia would be returning," she said. "Admiral Ackbar, particularly, has been asking about you."

Han frowned at the comlink. Ackbar probably hadn't spoken two words to him outside of official business since he'd resigned his general's commission a few months back. "You'll have to thank the Admiral for his interest," he told Winter, picking his words carefully. "I trust he's doing all right himself?"

"About as usual," Winter said. "He's having some problems with his family, though, now that school is in full swing."

"A little squabbling among the children?" Han suggested.

"Bedtime arguments, mainly," she said. "Problems with the little one over who's going to get to stay up and read—that sort of thing. You understand."

"Yeah," Han said. "I know the kids pretty well. How about the neighbors? He still having trouble with them?"

There was a brief pause. "I'm . . . not exactly sure," she said. "He hasn't mentioned anything about them to me. I can ask, if you'd like."

"It's no big deal," Han said. "As long as the family's doing okay—that's the important thing."

"I agree. At any rate, I think he mainly just wanted to be remembered to you."

"Thanks for passing on the message." He threw Lando a look. "Go ahead and tell him that we won't be out here too much longer. We'll go to Abregado and maybe look in on a couple of others and then head back."

"All right," Winter said. "Anything else?"

"No—yes," Han corrected himself. "What's the latest on the Bpfasshi recovery program?"

"Those three systems the Imperials hit?"

"Right." And where he and Leia had had their second brush with those gray-skinned alien kidnappers; but there was no point in dwelling on that.

"Let me call up the proper file," Winter said. ". . . It's coming along reasonably well. There were some problems with supply shipments, but the material seems to be moving well enough now."

Han frowned at the speaker. "What did Ackbar do, dig up some mothballed container ships from somewhere?"

"Actually, he made his own," Winter came back dryly. "He's taken some capital ships—Star Cruisers and Attack Frigates, mostly—cut the crews back to skeleton size and put in extra droids, and turned them into cargo ships."

Han grimaced. "I hope he's got some good escorts

along with them. Empty Star Cruisers would make great target practice for the Imperials."

"I'm sure he's thought of that," Winter assured him. "And the orbit dock and shipyards at Sluis Van are very well defended."

"I'm not sure anything's really well defended these days," Han returned sourly. "Not with the Imperials running loose like they are. Anyway. Got to go; talk to you later."

"Enjoy your trip. Your Highness? Good-bye."

Lando snapped his fingers at Threepio. "Good-bye, Winter," the droid said.

Han made a slashing motion across his throat, and Lando shut off the transmitter. "If those Star Cruisers had been built with proper slave circuits, they wouldn't have to load them with droids to make container ships out of them," he pointed out innocently.

"Yeah," Han nodded, his mind just barely registering Lando's words. "Come on—we've got to cut this short and get back." He climbed out of the cockpit seat and checked his blaster. "Something's about to burn through on Coruscant."

"You mean all that stuff about Ackbar's family?" Lando asked, standing up.

"Right," Han said, heading back toward the *Falcon*'s hatchway. "If I'm reading Winter right, it sounds like Fey'lya has started a major push toward Ackbar's territory. Come on, Threepio—you need to lock up behind us."

"Captain Solo, I must once again protest this whole arrangement," the droid said plaintively, scuttling up behind Han. "I really feel that to impersonate Princess Leia—"

"All right, all right," Han cut him off. "As soon as we get back, I'll have Lando undo the programming."

"It's over already?" Lando asked, pushing past Three-pio to join Han at the lock. "I thought you told Winter—"

"That was for the benefit of anyone tapping in," Han said. "As soon as we've worked through this contact, we're going to head back. Maybe even stop by Kashyyyk on the way and pick up Leia."

Lando whistled softly. "That bad, huh?"

"It's hard to say, exactly," Han had to admit as he slapped the release. The ramp dropped smoothly down to the dusty permcrete beneath them. "That 'staying up late to read' is the part I don't understand. I suppose it could mean some of the intelligence work that Ackbar's been doing along with the Supreme Commander position. Or worse—maybe Fey'lya's going for the whole sabacc pot."

"You and Winter should have worked out a better verbal code," Lando said as they started down the ramp.

"We should have worked out a verbal code, period," Han growled back. "I've been meaning for three years to sit down with her and Leia and set one up. Never got around to it."

"Well, if it helps, the analysis makes sense," Lando offered, glancing around the docking pit. "It fits the rumors I've heard, anyway. I take it the neighbors you referred to are the Empire?"

"Right. Winter should have heard something about it if Ackbar had had any luck plugging the security leaks."

"Won't that make it dangerous to go back, then?" Lando asked as they started toward the exit.

"Yeah," Han agreed, feeling his lip twist. "But we're going to have to risk it. Without Leia there to play peace-maker, Fey'lya might just be able to beg or bully the rest of the Council into giving him whatever it is he wants."

"Mmm." Lando paused at the bottom of the ramp leading to the docking pit exit and looked up. "Let's hope this is the last contact in the line."

"Let's hope first that the guy shows," Han countered, heading up the ramp.

The Abregado-rae Spaceport had had a terrible repu-tation among the pilots Han had flown with in his smug-gling days, ranking right down at the bottom with places like the Mos Eisley port on Tatooine. It was therefore something of a shock, though a pleasant one, to find a bright, clean cityscape waiting for them when they stepped through the landing pit door. "Well, well," Lando murmured from beside him. "Has civilization fi-nally come to Abregado?"

"Stranger things have happened," Han agreed, look-ing around. Clean and almost painfully neat, yet with that same unmistakable air that every general freight port seemed to have. That air of the not-entirely tame . . .

"Uh-oh," Lando said quietly, his eyes on something past Han's shoulder. "Looks like someone's just bought the heavy end of the hammer."

Han turned. Fifty meters down the port perimeter street, a small group of uniformed men with light-armor vests and blaster rifles had gathered at one of the other landing pit entrances. Even as Han watched, half of them slipped inside, leaving the rest on guard in the street.

"That's the hammer, all right," Han agreed, craning his neck to try and read the number above the door. Sixty-three. "Let's hope that's not our contact in there. Where are we meeting him, anyway?"

"Right over there," Lando said, pointing to a small windowless building built in the gap between two much older ones. A carved wooden plank with the single word "LoBue" hung over the door. "We're supposed to take one of the tables near the bar and the casino area and wait. He'll contact us there."

The LoBue was surprisingly large, given its modest street front, extending both back from the street and also into the older building to its left. Just inside the entrance were a group of conversation-oriented tables overlooking a small but elaborate dance floor, the latter deserted but with some annoying variety of taped music playing in the background. On the far side of the dance floor were a group of private booths, too dark for Han to see into. Off to the left, up a few steps and separated from the dance floor by a transparent etched plastic wall, was the casino area. "I think I see the bar up there," Lando murmured. "Just back of the sabacc tables to the left. That's probably where he wants us."

"You ever been here before?" Han asked over his shoulder as they skirted the conversation tables and headed up the steps.

"Not this place, no. Last time I was at Abregado-rae was years ago. It was worse than Mos Eisley, and I didn't stay long." Lando shook his head. "Whatever problems you might have with the new government here, you have to admit they've done a good job of cleaning the planet up."

"Yeah, well, whatever problems you have with the new government, let's keep them quiet, okay?" Han warned. "Just for once, I'd like to keep a low profile."

Lando chuckled. "Whatever you say."

The lighting in the bar area was lower than that in the casino proper, but not so low that seeing was difficult. Choosing a table near the gaming tables, they sat down. A holo of an attractive girl rose from the center of the table as they did so. "Good day, gentles," she said in pleasantly accented Basic. "How may I serve?"

"Do you have any Necr'ygor Omic wine?" Lando asked.

"We do, indeed: '47, '49, '50, and '52."

"We'll have a half carafe of the '49," Lando told her.

"Thank you, gentles," she said, and the holo vanished.

"Was that part of the countersign?" Han asked, letting his gaze drift around the casino. It was only the middle of the afternoon, local time, but even so over half the tables were occupied. The bar area, in contrast, was nearly empty, with only a handful of humans and aliens scattered around. Drinking, apparently, ranked much lower than gambling on the list of popular Gado vices.

"Actually, he didn't say anything about what we should order," Lando said. "But since I happen to like a good Necr'ygor Omic wine—"

"And since Coruscant will be picking up the tab for it?"

"Something like that."

The wine arrived on a tray delivered through a slide-hatch in the center of the table. "Will there be anything else, gentles?" the holo girl asked.

Lando shook his head, picking up the carafe and the two glasses that had come with it. "Not right now, thank you."

"Thank you." She and the tray disappeared.

"So," Lando said, pouring the wine. "I guess we wait."

"Well, while you're busy waiting, do a casual one-eighty," Han said. "Third sabacc table back—five men and a woman. Tell me if the guy second from the right is who I think it is."

Lifting his wine glass, Lando held it up to the light, as if studying its color. In the process he turned halfway around—"Not Fynn Torve?"

"Sure looks like him to me," Han agreed. "I figured you'd probably seen him more recently than I have."

"Not since the last Kessel run you and I did together." Lando cocked an eyebrow at Han. "Just before that *other* big sabacc table," he added dryly.

Han gave him an injured look. "You're not still sore about the *Falcon*, are you?"

"Now . . ." Lando considered. "No, probably not. No sorer than I was at losing the game to an amateur like you in the first place."

"*Amateur?*"

"—but I'll admit there were times right afterward when I lay awake at night plotting elaborate revenge. Good thing I never got around to doing any of it."

Han looked back at the sabacc table. "If it makes you feel any better . . . if you hadn't lost the *Falcon* to me, we probably wouldn't be sitting here right now. The Empire's first Death Star would have taken out Yavin and then picked the Alliance apart planet by planet. And that would have been the end of it."

Lando shrugged. "Maybe; maybe not. With people like Ackbar and Leia running things—"

"Leia would have been dead," Han cut him off. "She was already slated for execution when Luke, Chewie, and I pulled her out of the Death Star." A shiver ran through him at the memory. He'd been *that* close to losing her forever. And would never even have known what he'd missed.

And now that he knew . . . he might still lose her.

"She'll be okay, Han," Lando said quietly. "Don't worry." He shook his head. "I just wish we knew what the Imperials wanted with her."

"I know what they want," Han growled. "They want the twins."

Lando stared at him, a startled look on his face. "Are you sure?"

"As sure as I am of any of this," Han said. "Why else didn't they just use stun weapons on us in that Bpfassh ambush? Because the things have a better than fifty-fifty chance of sparking a miscarriage, that's why."

"Sounds reasonable," Lando agreed grimly. "Does Leia know?"

"I don't know. Probably."

He looked at the sabacc tables, the cheerful decadence of the whole scene suddenly grating against his mood. If Torve really was Karrde's contact man, he wished the other would quit this nonsense and get on with it. It wasn't like there were a lot of possibilities hanging around here to choose from.

His eyes drifted away from the casino, into the bar area . . . and stopped. There, sitting at a shadowy table at the far end, were three men.

There was an unmistakable air about a general freight port, a combination of sounds and smells and vibrations that every pilot who'd been in the business long enough knew instantly. There was an equally unmistakable air about planetary security officers. "Uh-oh," he muttered.

"What?" Lando asked, throwing a casual glance of his own around the room. The glance reached the far table—"Uh-oh, indeed," he agreed soberly. "Offhand, I'd say that explains why Torve's hiding at a sabacc table."

"And doing his best to ignore us," Han said, watching the security agents out of the corner of his eye and trying to gauge the focus of their attention. If they'd tumbled to this whole contact meeting there probably wasn't much he could do about it, short of hauling out his New Republic ID and trying to pull rank on them. Which might or might not work; and he could just hear the polite screaming fit Fey'lya would have over it either way.

But if they were just after Torve, maybe as part of that landing pit raid he and Lando had seen on the way in . . .

It was worth the gamble. Reaching over, he tapped the center of the table. "Attendant?"

The holo reappeared. "Yes, gentles?"

"Give me twenty sabacc chips, will you?"

"Certainly," she said, and vanished.

"Wait a minute," Lando said cautiously as Han drained his glass. "You're not going to go over there, are you?"

"You got a better idea?" Han countered, reaching down to resettle his blaster in its holster. "If he's our contact, I sure don't want to lose him now."

Lando gave a sigh of resignation. "So much for keeping a low profile. What do you want me to do?"

"Be ready to run some interference." The center of the table opened up and a neat stack of sabacc chips arrived. "So far it looks like they're just watching him—maybe we can get him out of here before their pals arrive in force."

"If not?"

Han collected the chips and got to his feet. "Then I'll try to create a diversion, and meet you back at the *Falcon*."

"Right. Good luck."

There were two seats not quite halfway across the sabacc table from Torve. Han chose one and sat down, dropping his stack of chips onto the table with a metallic *thud*. "Deal me in," he said.

The others looked up at him, their expressions varying from surprised to annoyed. Torve himself glanced up, came back for another look. Han cocked an eyebrow at him. "You the dealer, sonny? Come on, deal me in."

"Ah—no, it's not my deal," Torve said, his eyes flicking to the pudgy man on his right.

"And we've already started," the pudgy man said, his voice surly. "Wait until the next game."

"What, you haven't all even bet yet," Han countered, gesturing toward the handful of chips in the hand pot. The sabacc pot, in contrast, was pretty rich—the session must have been going for a couple of hours at least. Probably one reason the dealer didn't want fresh blood in the game who might conceivably win it all. "Come on, give me my cards," he told the other, tossing a chip into the hand pot.

Slowly, glaring the whole time, the dealer peeled the

top two cards off the deck and slid them over. "That's more like it," Han said approvingly. "Brings back memories, this does. I used to drop the heavy end of the hammer on the guys back home all the time."

Torve looked at him sharply, his expression freezing to stone. "Did you, now," he said, his voice deliberately casual. "Well, you're playing with the big boys here, not the little people. You may not find the sort of rewards you're used to."

"I'm not exactly an amateur myself," Han said airily. The locals at the spaceport had been raiding landing pit sixty-three . . . "I've won—oh, probably sixty-three games in the last month alone."

Another flicker of recognition crossed Torve's face. So it *was* his landing pit. "Lot of rewards in numbers like that," he murmured, letting one hand drop beneath the level of the table. Han tensed, but the hand came back up empty. Torve's eyes flicked around the room once, lingering for a second on the table where Lando was sitting before turning back to Han. "You willing to put your money where your mouth is?"

Han met his gaze evenly. "I'll meet anything you've got."

Torve nodded slowly. "I may just take you up on it."

"This is all very interesting, I'm sure," one of the other players spoke up. "Some of us would like to play cards, though."

Torve raised his eyebrows at Han. "The bet's at four," he invited.

Han glanced at his cards: the Mistress of Staves and the four of Coins. "Sure," he said, lifting six chips from his stack and dropping them into the hand pot. "I'll see the four, and raise you two." There was a rustle of air behind him—

"Cheater!" a deep voice bellowed in his ear.

Han jumped and spun around, reaching reflexively toward his blaster, but even as he did so a large hand shot over his shoulder to snatch the two cards from his other hand. "You are a *cheater*, sir," the voice bellowed again.

"I don't know what you're talking about," Han said, craning his neck up to get a look at his assailant.

He was almost sorry he had. Towering over him like a bushy-bearded thundercloud twice his own size, the man was glaring down at him with an expression that could only be described as enflamed with religious fervor. "You know full well what I'm talking about," the man said, biting out each word. "This card—" he waved one of Han's cards "—is a *skifter*."

Han blinked. "It is not," he protested. A crowd was rapidly gathering around the table: casino security and other employees, curious onlookers, and probably a few who were hoping to see a little blood. "It's the same card I was dealt."

"Oh, is it?" The man cupped the card in one massive hand, held it in front of Han's face, and touched the corner with a fingertip.

The Mistress of Staves abruptly became the six of Sabres. The man tapped the corner again and it became the Moderation face card. And then the eight of Flasks . . . and then the Idiot face card . . . and then the Commander of Coins . . .

"That's the card I was dealt," Han repeated, feeling sweat starting to collect under his collar. So much, indeed, for keeping a low profile. "If it's a skifter, it's not my fault."

A short man with a hard-bitten face elbowed past the bearded man. "Keep your hands on the table," he ordered Han in a voice that matched his face. "Move aside, Reverend—we'll handle this."

Reverend? Han looked up at the glowering thundercloud again, and this time he saw the black, crystal-embedded band nestled against the tufts of hair at the other's throat. "Reverend, huh?" he said with a sinking feeling. There were extreme religious groups all over the galaxy, he'd found, whose main passion in life seemed to be the elimination of all forms of gambling. And all forms of gamblers.

"Hands on the table, I said," the security man snapped, reaching over to pluck the suspect card from the Reverend's hand. He glanced at it, tried it himself, and nodded. "Cute skifter, con," he said, giving Han what was probably his best scowl.

"He must have palmed the card he was dealt," the Reverend put in. He hadn't budged from his place at Han's side. "Where is it, cheater?"

"The card I was dealt is right there in your friend's hand," Han snapped back. "I don't need a skifter to win at sabacc. If I had one, it's because it was dealt to me."

"Oh, really?" Without warning, the Reverend abruptly turned to face the pudgy sabacc dealer, still sitting at the table but almost lost in the hovering crowd. "Your cards, sir, if you don't mind," he said, holding out his hand.

The other's jaw dropped. "What are you talking about? Why would I give someone else a skifter? Anyway, it's a house deck—see?"

"Well, there's one way to be sure, isn't there?" the Reverend said, reaching over to scoop up the deck. "And then you—*and* you—" he leveled fingers at the dealer and Han "—can be scanned to see who's hiding an extra card. I dare say that would settle the issue, wouldn't you, Kampl?" he added, looking down at the scowling security man.

"Don't tell us our job, Reverend," Kampl growled. "Cyru—get that scanner over here, will you?"

The scanner was a small palm-fitting job, obviously designed for surreptitious operation. "That one first," Kampl ordered, pointing at Han.

"Right." Expertly, the other circled Han with the instrument. "Nothing."

The first touch of uncertainty cracked through Kampl's scowl. "Try it again."

The other did so. "Still nothing. He's got a blaster, comlink, and ID, and that's it."

For a long moment Kampl continued staring at Han. Then, reluctantly, he turned to the sabacc dealer. "I protest!" the dealer sputtered, pushing himself to his feet. "I'm a Class Double-A citizen—you have no right to put me through this sort of *totally* unfounded accusation."

"You do it here or down at the station," Kampl snarled. "Your choice."

The dealer threw a look at Han that was pure venom, but he stood in stiff silence while the security tech scanned him down. "He's clean, too," the other reported, a slight frown on his face.

"Scan around the floor," Kampl ordered. "See if someone ditched it."

"And count the cards still in the deck," the Reverend spoke up.

Kampl spun to face him. "For the last time—"

"Because if all we have here are the requisite seventy-six cards," the Reverend cut him off, his voice heavy with suspicion, "perhaps what we're really looking at is a fixed deck."

Kampl jerked as if he'd been stung. "We don't fix decks in here," he insisted.

"No?" the Reverend glared. "Not even when special people are sitting in on the game? People who might know to look for a special card when it comes up?"

"That's ridiculous," Kampl snarled, taking a step toward him. "The LoBue is a respectable and perfectly legal establishment. None of these players has any connection with—"

"Hey!" the pudgy dealer said suddenly. "The guy who was sitting next to me—where'd he go?"

The Reverend snorted. "So. None of them has any connection with you, do they?"

Someone swore violently and started pushing his way through the crowd—one of the three planetary security types who'd been watching the table. Kampl watched him go, took a deep breath, and turned to glare at Han. "You want to tell me your partner's name?"

"He wasn't my partner," Han said. "And I was not cheating. You want to make a formal accusation, take me down to the station and do it there. If you don't—" he got to his feet, scooping up his remaining chips in the process "—then I'm leaving."

For a long moment he thought Kampl was going to call his bluff. But the other had no real evidence, and he knew it; and apparently he had better things to do than indulge in what would be really nothing more than petty harassment. "Sure—get out of here," the other snarled. "Don't ever come back."

"Don't worry," Han told him.

The crowd was starting to dissolve, and he had no trouble making his way back to his table. Lando, not surprisingly, was long gone. What *was* surprising was that he'd settled the bill before he had left.

"That was quick," Lando greeted him from the top of the *Falcon*'s entry ramp. "I wasn't expecting them to turn you loose for at least an hour."

"They didn't have much of a case," Han said, climbing up the ramp and slapping the hatch button. "I hope Torve didn't give you the slip."

Lando shook his head. "He's waiting in the lounge." He raised his eyebrows. "And considers himself in our debt."

"That could be useful," Han agreed, heading down the curved corridor.

Torve was seated at the lounge holo board, three small data pads spread out in front of him. "Good to see you again, Torve," Han said as he stepped in.

"You, too, Solo," the other said gravely, getting to his feet and offering Han his hand. "I've thanked Calrissian already, but I wanted to thank you, too. Both for the warning and for helping me get out of there. I'm in your debt."

"No problem," Han waved the thanks away. "I take it that *is* your ship in pit sixty-three?"

"My employer's ship, yes," Torve said, grimacing. "Fortunately, there's nothing contraband in it at the moment—I've already off-loaded. They obviously suspect me, though."

"What kind of contraband were you running?" Lando asked, coming up behind Han. "If it's not a secret, that is?"

Torve cocked an eyebrow. "No secret, but you're not going to believe it. I was running food."

"You're right," Lando said. "I don't believe it."

Torve nodded vaguely off to one side. "I didn't either, at first. Seems there's a clan of people living off in the southern hills who don't find much about the new government to appreciate."

"Rebels?"

"No, and that's what's strange about it," Torve said. "They're not rebelling or making trouble or even sitting on vital resources. They're simple people, and all they want is to be left alone to continue living that way. The government's apparently decided to make an example of them, and among other things has cut off all food and medical supplies going that way until they agree to fall into step like everyone else."

"That sounds like this government," Lando agreed heavily. "Not much into regional autonomy of any kind."

"Hence, we smuggle in food," Torve concluded. "Crazy business. Anyway, it's nice to see you two again. Nice to see you're still working together, too. So many teams have broken up over the past few years, especially since Jabba bought the *really* heavy end of the hammer."

Han exchanged glances with Lando. "Well, it's actually more like we're *back* together," he corrected Torve.

"We sort of wound up on the same side during the war. Up till then . . ."

"Up till then I wanted to kill him," Lando explained helpfully. "No big deal, really."

"Sure," Torve said guardedly, looking back and forth between them. "Let me guess: the *Falcon*, right? I remember hearing rumors that you stole it."

Han looked at Lando, eyebrows raised. "*Stole* it?"

"Like I said, I was mad," Lando shrugged. "It wasn't an out-and-out theft, actually, though it came pretty close. I had a little semilegit clearinghouse for used ships at the time, and I ran short of money in a sabacc game Han and I were playing. I offered him his pick of any of my ships if he won." He threw Han a mock glare. "He was *supposed* to go for one of the flashy chrome-plate yachts that had been collecting dust in the front row, not the freighter I'd been quietly upgrading on the side for myself."

"You did a good job, too," Han said. "Though Chewie and I wound up pulling a lot of the stuff out and redoing it ourselves."

"Nice," Lando growled. "Another crack like that and I may just take it back."

"Chewie would probably take great exception to that," Han said. He fixed Torve with a hard look. "Of course, you knew all this already, didn't you."

Torve grinned. "No offense, Solo. I like to feel out my customers before we do business—get an idea of whether I can expect 'em to play straight with me. People who lie about their history usually lie about the job, too."

"I trust we passed?"

"Like babes in the tall grass," Torve nodded, still grinning. "So. What can Talon Karrde do for you?"

Han took a careful breath. Finally. Now all he had to worry about was fouling this up. "I want to offer Karrde a deal: the chance to work directly with the New Republic."

Torve nodded. "I'd heard that you were going around trying to push that scheme with other smuggling groups. The general feeling is that you're trying to set them up for Ackbar to take down."

"I'm not," Han assured him. "Ackbar's not exactly thrilled at the idea, but he's accepted it. We need to get more shipping capacity from somewhere, and smugglers are the logical supply to tap."

Torve pursed his lips. "From what I've heard it sounds like an interesting offer. 'Course, I'm not the one who makes decisions like that."

"So take us to Karrde," Lando suggested. "Let Han talk to him directly."

"Sorry, but he's at the main base at the moment," Torve said, shaking his head. "I can't take you there."

"Why not?"

"Because we don't let strangers just flit in and out," Torve said patiently. "We don't have anything like the kind of massive, overbearing security Jabba had on Tatooine, for starters."

"We're not exactly—" Lando began.

Han cut him off with a gesture. "All right, then," he said to Torve. "How are you going to get back there?"

Torve opened his mouth, then closed it again. "I guess I'll have to figure out a way to get my ship out of impoundment, won't I?"

"That'll take time," Han pointed out. "Besides which, you're known here. On the other hand, someone who showed up with the proper credentials could probably pry it loose before anyone knew what had happened."

Torve cocked an eyebrow. "You, for instance?"

Han shrugged. "I might be able to. After that thing at the LoBue I probably should lie low, too. But I'm sure I could set it up."

"I'm sure," Torve said, heavily sardonic. "And the catch . . . ?"

"No catch," Han told him. "All I want in return is for you to let us give you a lift back to your base, and then have fifteen minutes to talk with Karrde."

Torve gazed at him, his mouth tight. "I'll get in trouble if I do this. You know that."

"We're not exactly random strangers," Lando reminded him. "Karrde met me once, and both Han and I kept major military secrets for the Alliance for years. We've got a good record of people being able to trust us."

Torve looked at Lando. Looked again at Han. "I'll get in trouble," he repeated with a sigh. "But I guess I really *do* owe you. One condition, though: I do all the navigation on the way in, and set it up in a coded, erasable module. Whether you have to do the same thing on the way out will be up to Karrde."

"Good enough," Han agreed. Paranoia was a common enough ailment among smugglers. Anyway, he had no particular interest in knowing where Karrde had set up shop. "When can we leave?"

"As soon as you're ready." Torve nodded at the sabacc chips cupped in Han's hand. "Unless you want to go back to the LoBue and play those," he added.

Han had forgotten he was still holding the chips. "Forget it," he growled, dropping the stack onto the holo board. "I try not to play sabacc when there are fanatics breathing down my neck."

"Yes, the Reverend put on a good show, didn't he?" Torve agreed. "Don't know what we would have done without him."

"Wait a minute," Lando put in. "You *know* him?"

"Sure," Torve grinned. "He's my contact with the hill clan. He couldn't have made nearly so much fuss without a stranger like you there for him to pick on, though."

"Why, that rotten—" Han clamped his teeth together. "I suppose that was *his* skifter, huh?"

"Sure was." Torve looked innocently at Han. "What are you complaining about? You got what you wanted— I'm taking you to see Karrde. Right?"

Han thought about it. Torve was right, of course. But still . . . "Right," he conceded. "So much for heroics, I guess."

Torve snorted gently. "Tell me about it. Come on, let's get into your computer and start coding up a nav module."

CHAPTER 21

MARA STEPPED UP to the comm room door, wondering uneasily what this sudden summons was all about. Karrde hadn't said, but there had been something in his voice that had set her old survival instincts tingling. Checking the tiny blaster hanging upside down in its sleeve sheath, she slapped at the door release.

She'd expected to find at least two people already in the room: Karrde plus the comm room duty man plus whoever else had been called in on this. To her mild surprise, Karrde was alone. "Come in, Mara," he invited, looking up from his data pad. "Close the door behind you."

She did so. "Trouble?" she asked.

"A minor problem only," he assured her. "A bit of an awkward one, though. Fynn Torve just called to say he was on his way in . . . and he has guests. Former New Republic generals Lando Calrissian and Han Solo."

Mara felt her stomach tighten. "What do they want?"

Karrde shrugged fractionally. "Apparently, just to talk to me."

For a second, Mara's thoughts flicked to Skywalker, still locked away in his barracks room across the compound. But, no—there was no way anyone in the New Republic could possibly know he was here. Most of Karrde's own people didn't know it, including the majority of those right here on Myrkr. "Did they bring their own ship?" she asked.

"Theirs is the only one coming in, actually," Karrde nodded. "Torve's riding with them."

Mara's eyes flicked to the comm equipment behind him. "A hostage?"

Karrde shook his head. "I don't think so. He gave all the proper all-clear passwords. The *Etherway*'s still on Abregado—been impounded by the local authorities or some such. Apparently, Calrissian and Solo helped Torve avoid a similar fate."

"Then thank them, have them put Torve down, and tell them to get off the planet," she said. "You didn't invite them here."

"True," Karrde agreed, watching her closely. "On the other hand, Torve seems to think he's under a certain obligation to them."

"Then let him pay it back on his own time."

The skin around Karrde's eyes seemed to harden. "Torve is one of my associates," he said, his voice cold. "His debts are the organization's. You should know that by now."

Mara's throat tightened as a sudden, horrible thought

occurred to her. "You're not going to give Skywalker to them, are you?" she demanded.

"Alive, you mean?" Karrde countered.

For a long moment Mara just stared at him; at that small smile and those slightly heavy eyelids and the rest of that carefully constructed expression of complete disinterest in the matter. But it was all an act, and she knew it. He wanted to know why she hated Skywalker, all right—wanted it with as close to genuine passion as the man ever got.

And as far as she was concerned, he could go right on wanting it. "I don't suppose it's occurred to you," she bit out, "that Solo and Calrissian might have engineered this whole thing, including the *Etherway*'s impoundment, as a way of finding this base."

"It's occurred to me, yes," Karrde said. "I dismissed it as somewhat farfetched."

"Of course," Mara said sardonically. "The great and noble Han Solo would never do something so devious, would he? You never answered my question."

"About Skywalker? I thought I'd made it clear, Mara, that he stays here until I know why Grand Admiral Thrawn is so interested in acquiring him. At the very least, we need to know what he's worth, and to whom, before we can set a fair market price for him. I have some feelers out; with luck, we should know in a few more days."

"And meanwhile, his allies will be here in a few more minutes."

"Yes," Karrde agreed, his lips puckering slightly. "Skywalker will have to be moved somewhere a bit more out of the way—we obviously can't risk Solo and Calrissian stumbling over him. I want you to move him to the number four storage shed."

"That's where we're keeping that droid of his," Mara reminded him.

"The shed's got two rooms; put him in the other one." Karrde waved toward her waist. "And do remember to lose that before our guests arrive. I doubt they'd fail to recognize it."

Mara glanced down at Skywalker's lightsaber hanging from her belt. "Don't worry. If it's all the same to you, I'd just as soon not have much to do with them."

"I wasn't planning for you to," Karrde assured her. "I'd like you here when I greet them, and possibly to join us for dinner, as well. Other than that, you're excused from all social activities."

"So they're staying the day?"

"And possibly the night, as well." He eyed her. "Requirements of a proper host aside, can you think of a better way for us to prove to the Republic, should the need arise, that Skywalker was never here?"

It made sense. But that didn't mean she had to like it. "Are you warning the rest of the *Wild Karrde*'s crew to keep quiet?"

"I'm doing better than that," Karrde said, nodding back toward the comm equipment. "I've sent everyone who knows about Skywalker off to get the *Starry Ice* prepped. Which reminds me—after you move Skywalker, I want you to run his X-wing farther back under the trees. No more than half a kilometer—I don't want you to go through any more of the forest alone than you have to. Can you fly an X-wing?"

"I can fly anything."

"Good," he said, smiling slightly. "You'd better be off, then. The *Millennium Falcon* will be landing in less than twenty minutes."

Mara took a deep breath. "All right," she said. Turning, she left the room.

The compound was empty as she walked across it to the barracks building. By Karrde's design, undoubtedly; he must have shifted people around to inside duties to give her a clear path for taking Skywalker to the storage shed. Reaching his room, she keyed off the lock and slid open the door.

He was standing by the window, dressed in that same black tunic, pants, and high boots that he'd worn that day at Jabba's palace.

That day she'd stood silently by and watched . . . and let him destroy her life.

"Get your case and let's go," she growled, gesturing with the blaster. "It's moving day."

His eyes stayed on her as he stepped over to the bed. Not on the blaster in her hand, but on her face. "Karrde's made a decision?" he asked calmly as he picked up the case.

For a long moment she was tempted to tell him that, no, this was on her own initiative, just to see if the implications would crack that maddening Jedi serenity. But even a Jedi would probably fight if he thought he was going to his death, and they were on a tight enough schedule as it was. "You're moving to one of the storage sheds," she told him. "We've got company coming, and we don't have any formal wear your size. Come on, move."

She walked him past the central building to the number four shed, a two-room structure tucked conveniently back out of the compound's major traffic patterns. The room on the left, normally used for sensitive or dangerous equipment, was also the only one of the storage areas with a lock, undoubtedly the reason Karrde had chosen it to serve the role of impromptu prison. Keeping one eye on Skywalker, she keyed open the lock, wondering as she did so whether Karrde had had time to disable the inside mechanism. A quick look as the door slid open showed that he hadn't.

Well, that could easily be corrected. "In here," she ordered, flicking on the inside light and gesturing for him to enter.

He complied. "Looks cozy," he said, glancing around the windowless room and the piled shipping boxes that took up perhaps half the floor space to the right. "Probably quiet, too."

"Ideal for Jedi meditation," she countered, stepping over to an open box marked *Blasting Disks* and taking a look inside. No problem; it was being used for spare coveralls at the moment. She gave the rest of the box markings a quick check, confirmed that there was nothing here he could possibly use to escape. "We'll get a cot or something in for you later," she said, moving back to the door. "Food, too."

"I'm all right for now."

"Ask me if I care." The inner lock mechanism was behind a thin metal plate. Two shots from her blaster unsealed one end of the plate and curled it back; a third vaporized a selected group of wires. "Enjoy the quiet," she said, and left.

———

THE DOOR CLOSED behind her, and locked . . . and Luke was once again alone.

He looked around him. Piled boxes, no windows, a single locked door. "I've been in worse places," he muttered under his breath. "At least there's no Rancor here."

For a moment he frowned at the odd thought, wondering why the Rancor pit at Jabba's palace should suddenly have flashed to mind. But he only gave it a moment. The lack of proper preparation and facilities in his new prison strongly suggested that moving him here had been a spur-of-the-moment decision, possibly precipitated by the imminent arrival of whoever the visitors were Mara had mentioned.

And if so, there was a good possibility that somewhere in the mad scramble they might finally have made a mistake.

He went over to the door, easing the still-warm metal plate a little farther back and kneeling down to peer inside at the lock mechanism. Han had spent a few idle hours once trying to teach him the finer points of hot-wiring locks, and if Mara's shot hadn't damaged it too badly, there was a chance he might be able to persuade it to disengage.

It didn't look promising. Whether by design or accident, Mara's shot had taken out the wires to the inside control's power supply, vaporizing them all the way back into the wall conduit, where there was no chance at all of getting hold of them.

But if he could find another power supply . . .

He got to his feet again, brushed off his knees, and headed over to the neatly piled boxes. Mara had glanced at their labels, but she'd actually looked inside only one of them. Perhaps a more complete search would turn up something useful.

The search, unfortunately, took even less time than his examination of the ruined lock. Most of the boxes were sealed beyond his capability to open without tools, and the handful that weren't held such innocuous items as clothing or replacement equipment modules.

All right, then, he told himself, sitting down on the edge of one of the boxes and looking around for inspiration. *I can't use the door. There aren't any windows.* But there *was* another room in this shed—he'd seen the other door while Mara was opening this one. Perhaps there was some kind of half-height doorway or crawl space between them, hidden out of sight behind the stacked boxes.

It wasn't likely, of course, that Mara would have missed anything that obvious. But he had time, and nothing else to occupy it. Getting up from his seat, he began unstacking the boxes and moving them away from the wall.

He'd barely begun when he found it. Not a doorway, but something almost as good: a multisocket power outlet, set into the wall just above the baseboard.

Karrde and Mara had made their mistake.

The metal doorplate, already stressed by the blaster fire Mara had used to peel it back, was relatively easy to bend. Luke kept at it, bending it back and forth, until a roughly triangular piece broke off in his hand. It was too soft to be of any use against the sealed equipment boxes, but it would probably be adequate for unscrewing the cover of a common power outlet.

He returned to the outlet and lay down in the narrow gap between wall and boxes. He was just trying to wedge his makeshift screwdriver against the first screw when he heard a quiet beep.

He froze, listening. The beep came again, followed by a series of equally soft warbles. Warbles that sounded very familiar . . . "Artoo?" he called softly. "Is that you?"

For a pair of heartbeats there was silence from the other room. Then, abruptly, the wall erupted with a minor explosion of electronic jabbering. Artoo, without a doubt. "Steady, Artoo," Luke called back. "I'm going to try and get this power outlet open. There's probably one on your side, too—can you get it open?"

There was a distinctly disgusted-sounding gurgle. "No, huh? Well, just hang on, then."

The broken metal triangle wasn't the easiest thing to work with, particularly in the cramped space available. Still, it took Luke only a couple of minutes to get the cover plate off and pull the wires out of his way. Hunching forward, he could see through the hole to the back of the outlet in Artoo's room. "I don't think I can get your outlet open from here," he called to the droid. "Is your room locked?"

There was a negative beep, followed by an odd sort of whining, as if Artoo was spinning his wheels. "Restraining bolt?" Luke asked. The spinning/whine came again— "Or a restraint collar?"

An affirmative beep, with frustrated overtones. It figured, in retrospect: a restraining bolt would leave a mark, whereas a collar snugged around Artoo's lower half would do nothing but let him wear out his wheels a little. "Never mind," Luke reassured him. "If there's enough wire in here to reach to the door, I should be able to unlock it. Then we can both get out of here."

Carefully, mindful of the possibility of shock from the higher-current lines nearby, he found the low-voltage wire and started easing it gently toward him out of the conduit. There was more than he'd expected; he got nearly one and a half meters coiled on the floor by his head before it stopped coming.

More than he'd expected, but far less than he needed. The door was a good four meters away in a straight line, and he would need some slack to get it spliced into the lock mechanism. "It's going to be a few more minutes," he called to Artoo, trying to think. The low-power line had a meter and a half of slack to it, which implied the other lines probably did, as well. If he could cut that much length off two of them, he should have more than enough to reach the lock.

Which left only the problem of finding something to cut them with. And, of course, managing to not electrocute himself along the way.

"What I wouldn't give to have my lightsaber back for a minute," he muttered, examining the edge of his makeshift screwdriver. It wasn't very sharp; but then, the superconducting wires weren't very thick, either.

It was the work of a couple of minutes to pull the other wires as far out of the conduit as they would go. Standing up, he took off his tunic, wrapped one of the sleeves twice around the metal, and started sawing.

He was halfway through the first of the wires when

his hand slipped off the insulating sleeve and for a second touched the bare metal. Reflexively he jerked back, banging his hand against the wall.

And then his brain caught up with him. "Uh-oh," he murmured, staring at the half-cut wire.

There was an interrogative whistle from the other room. "I just touched one of the wires," he told the droid, "and I didn't get a shock."

Artoo whistled. "Yeah," Luke agreed. He tapped at the wire . . . touched it again . . . held his finger against it.

So Karrde and Mara hadn't made a mistake, after all. They'd already cut the power to the outlet.

For a moment he knelt there, holding the wire, wondering what he was going to do now. He still had all this wire, but no power supply for it to connect with. Conversely, there were probably any number of small power sources in the room, attached to the stored replacement modules, but they were all packed away in boxes he couldn't get into. Could he somehow use the wire to get into the boxes? Use it to slice through the outer sealant layer, perhaps?

He got a firm grip on the wire and pulled on it, trying to judge its tensile strength. His fingers slipped along the insulation; shifting his grip, he wrapped it firmly around his right hand—

And stopped, a sudden prickly feeling on the back of his neck. His right hand. His artificial right hand. His artificial, dual-power-supply right hand . . . "Artoo, you know anything about cybernetic limb replacements?" he called, levering the wrist access port open with his metal triangle.

There was a short pause, then a cautious and

ambiguous-sounding warble. "It shouldn't take too much," he reassured the droid, peering at the maze of wiring and servos inside his hand. He'd forgotten how incredibly complex the whole thing was. "All I need to do is get one of the power supplies out. Think you can walk me through the procedure?"

The pause this time was shorter, and the reply more confident. "Good," Luke said. "Let's get to it."

CHAPTER 22

H AN FINISHED HIS presentation, sat back in his chair, and waited.

"Interesting," Karrde said, that faintly amused, totally noncommittal expression of his hiding whatever it was he was really thinking. "Interesting, indeed. I presume the Provisional Council would be willing to record legal guarantees of all this."

"We'll guarantee what we can," Han told him. "Your protection, legality of operation, and so forth. Naturally, we can't guarantee particular profit margins or anything like that."

"Naturally," Karrde agreed, his gaze shifting to Lando. "You've been rather quiet, General Calrissian. How exactly do you fit into all of this?"

"Just as a friend," Lando said. "Someone who knew how to get in touch with you. And someone who can vouch for Han's integrity and honesty."

A slight smile touched Karrde's lips. "Integrity and

honesty," he repeated. "Interesting words to use in regard to a man with Captain Solo's somewhat checkered reputation."

Han grimaced, wondering which particular incident Karrde might be referring to. There were, he had to admit, a fair number to choose from. "Any checkering that existed is all in the past," he said.

"Of course," Karrde agreed. "Your proposal is, as I said, very interesting. But not, I think, for my organization."

"May I ask why not?" Han asked.

"Very simply, because it would look to certain parties as if we were taking sides," Karrde explained, sipping from the cup at his side. "Given the extent of our operations, and the regions in which those operations take place, that might not be an especially politic thing to do."

"I understand," Han nodded. "I'd like the chance to convince you that there are ways to keep your other clients from knowing about it."

Karrde smiled again. "I think you underestimate the Empire's intelligence capabilities, Captain Solo," he said. "They know far more about Republic movements than you might think."

"Tell me about it," Han grimaced, glancing at Lando. "That reminds me of something else I wanted to ask you. Lando said you might know a slicer who was good enough to crack diplomatic codes."

Karrde cocked his head slightly to the side. "Interesting request," he commented. "Particularly coming from someone who should already have access to such codes. Is intrigue beginning to form among the New Republic hierarchy, perhaps?"

That last conversation with Winter, and her veiled warnings, flashed through Han's mind. "This is purely personal," he assured Karrde. "Mostly personal, anyway."

"Ah," the other said. "As it happens, one of the best slicers in the trade will be at dinner this afternoon. You'll join us, of course?"

Han glanced at his watch in surprise. Between business and small talk, the fifteen-minute interview that Torve had promised him with Karrde had now stretched out into two hours. "We don't want to impose on your time—"

"It's no imposition at all," Karrde assured him, setting his cup down and standing. "With the press of business and all, we tend to miss the midday meal entirely and compensate by pushing the evening dinner up to late afternoon."

"I remember those wonderful smuggler schedules," Han nodded wryly, memories flashing through his mind. "You're lucky to get even two meals."

"Indeed," Karrde agreed. "If you'll follow me . . . ?"

The main building, Han had noted on the way in, seemed to be composed of three or four circular zones centering on the greatroom with the strange tree growing through it. The room Karrde took them to now was in the layer just outside the greatroom, taking perhaps a quarter of that circle. A number of round tables were set up, with several of them already occupied. "We don't stand on protocol regarding meals here," Karrde said, leading the way to a table in the center of the room. Four people were already sitting there: three men and a woman.

Karrde steered them to three vacant seats. "Good evening, all," he nodded to the others at the table. "May I present Calrissian and Solo, who'll be dining with us tonight." He gestured to each of the men in turn. "Three of my associates: Wadewarn, Chin, and Ghent. Ghent is the slicer I mentioned; possibly the best in the business." He waved to the woman. "And of course you've already met Mara Jade."

"Yes," Han agreed, nodding to her and sitting down, a small shiver running up his back. Mara had been with Karrde when he'd first welcomed them into that makeshift throne room of his. She hadn't stayed long; but for the whole of that brief time she'd glowered darkly at Lando and him with those incredible green eyes of hers.

Almost exactly the same way she was glowering at them right now.

"So you're Han Solo," the slicer, Ghent, said brightly. "I've heard a lot about you. Always wanted to meet you."

Han shifted his attention away from Mara to Ghent. He wasn't much more than a kid, really, barely out of his teens. "It's nice to be famous," Han told him. "Just remember that whatever you've heard has been hearsay. And that hearsay stories grow an extra leg every time they're told."

"You're too modest," Karrde said, signaling to the side. In response, a squat droid rolled toward them from around the room's curve, a tray of what looked like rolled leaves perched on top of it. "It would be difficult to embellish that Zygerrian slaver incident, for example."

Lando looked up from the droid's tray. "Zygerrian slavers?" he echoed. "You never told me that one."

"It wasn't anything important," Han said, warning Lando with a look to drop the subject.

Unfortunately, Ghent either missed the look or was too young to know what it meant. "He and Chewbacca attacked a Zygerrian slaver ship," the kid explained eagerly. "Just the two of them. The Zygerrians were so scared they abandoned ship."

"They were more pirates than slavers," Han said, giving up. "And they weren't afraid of me—they abandoned ship because I told them I had twenty stormtroopers with me and was coming aboard to check their shipping licenses."

Lando raised his eyebrows. "And they *bought* that?"

Han shrugged. "I was broadcasting a borrowed Imperial ID at the time."

"But then you know what he did?" Ghent put in. "He gave the ship over to the slaves they found locked up in the hold. *Gave* it to them—just like that! Including all the cargo, too."

"Why, you old softie," Lando grinned, taking a bite from one of the rolled leaves. "No wonder you never told me that one."

With an effort, Han held on to his patience. "The cargo was pirate plunder," he growled. "Some of it extremely traceable. We were off Janodral Mizar—they had a strange local law at the time that pirate or slaver victims got to split up the proceeds if the pirates were taken or killed."

"That law's still in force, as far as I know," Karrde murmured.

"Probably. Anyway, Chewie was with me . . . and you know Chewie's opinion of slavers."

"Yeah," Lando said dryly. "They'd have had a better chance with the twenty stormtroopers."

"And if I hadn't just given away the ship—" Han broke off as a quiet beep sounded.

"Excuse me," Karrde said, pulling a comlink from his belt. "—Karrde here."

Han couldn't hear what was being said . . . but abruptly Karrde's face seemed to tighten. "I'll be right there."

He got to his feet and slipped the comlink back onto his belt. "Excuse me again," he said. "A small matter needs my attention."

"Trouble?" Han asked.

"I hope not." Karrde glanced across the table, and Han turned in time to see Mara stand up. "Hopefully, this will only take a few minutes. Please enjoy your meal."

They left the table, and Han looked back at Lando. "I've got a bad feeling about this," he muttered.

Lando nodded, his eyes still following Mara and Karrde, a strange expression on his face. "I've seen her before, Han," he murmured back. "I don't know where, but I know I've seen her . . . and I don't think she was a smuggler at the time."

Han looked around the table at the others, at the wariness in their eyes and the guarded murmuring back and forth between them. Even Ghent had noticed the sudden tension and was studiously eating away at his appetizers. "Well, figure it out fast, buddy," he told Lando quietly. "We might be about to wear out our welcome."

"I'm working on it. What do we do until then?"

Another droid was trundling up, his tray laden with filled soup bowls. "Until then," Han said, "I guess we enjoy our meal."

———

"He came in from lightspeed about ten minutes ago," Aves said tightly, tapping the mark on the sensor display. "Captain Pellaeon signaled two minutes later. Asking for you personally."

Karrde rubbed a finger gently across his lower lip. "Any signs of landing craft or fighters?" he asked.

"Not yet," Aves shook his head. "But from his insertion angle, I'd guess he'll be dropping some soon—downpoint probably somewhere in this part of the forest."

Karrde nodded thoughtfully. Such propitious timing . . . for someone. "Where did we wind up putting the *Millennium Falcon*?"

"It's over on pad eight," Aves said.

Back in under the edge of the forest, then. That was good—the high metal content of Myrkr's trees would help shield it from the *Chimaera*'s sensors. "Take two men and go throw a camo net over it," he told the other. "There's no point in taking chances. And do it quietly—we don't want to alarm our guests."

"Right." Aves pulled off his headset and headed out of the room at a brisk trot.

Karrde looked at Mara. "Interesting timing, this visit."

She met his gaze without flinching. "If that's a subtle way of asking whether or not I called them, don't bother. I didn't."

He cocked his head. "Really. I'm a little surprised."

"So am I," she countered. "I should have thought of it

days ago." She nodded toward the headset. "You going to talk to him or not?"

"I don't suppose I have much choice." Mentally bracing himself, Karrde sat down in the seat Aves had just vacated and touched a switch. "Captain Pellaeon, this is Talon Karrde," he said. "My apologies for the delay. What can I do for you?"

The distant image of the *Chimaera* disappeared, but it wasn't Pellaeon's face that replaced it. This face was a nightmare image: long and lean, with pale blue skin and eyes that glittered like two bits of red-hot metal. "Good afternoon, Captain Karrde," the other said, his voice clear and smooth and very civilized. "I'm Grand Admiral Thrawn."

"Good afternoon, Admiral," Karrde nodded in greeting, taking it in stride. "This is an unexpected honor. May I ask the purpose of your call?"

"Part of it I'm sure you've already guessed," Thrawn told him. "We find ourselves in need of more ysalamiri, and would like your permission to harvest some more of them."

"Certainly," Karrde said, a funny feeling starting to tug at the back of his mind. There was something strange about Thrawn's posture . . . and the Imperials hardly needed his permission to come pull ysalamiri off their trees. "If I may say so, you seem to be running through them rather quickly. Are you having trouble keeping them alive?"

Thrawn raised an eyebrow in polite surprise. "None of them has died, Captain. We simply need more of them."

"Ah," Karrde said. "I see."

"I doubt that. But no matter. It occurred to me, Captain, that as long as we were coming here, it might be a good time for us to have a little talk."

"What sort of talk?"

"I'm sure we can find some topics of mutual interest," Thrawn said. "For example, I'm in the market for new warships."

Long practice kept any guilty reaction from leaking out through Karrde's face or voice. But it was a near thing. "Warships?" he asked carefully.

"Yes." Thrawn favored him with a thin smile. "Don't worry—I'm not expecting you to actually have any capital starships in stock. But a man with your contacts may possibly be able to acquire them."

"I doubt that my contacts are quite that extensive, Admiral," Karrde told him, trying hard to read that not-quite-human face. Did he know? Or was the question merely an exquisitely dangerous coincidence? "I don't think we'll be able to help you."

Thrawn's expression didn't change . . . but abruptly there was an edge of menace to his smile. "You'll try anyway. And then there's the matter of your refusal to help in our search for Luke Skywalker."

Some of the tightness in Karrde's chest eased. This was safer territory. "I'm sorry we were also unable to help there, Admiral. As I explained before to your representative, we were under several tight scheduling deadlines at the time. We simply couldn't spare the ships."

Thrawn's eyebrows lifted slightly. "At the time, you say? But the search is still going on, Captain."

Silently, Karrde cursed himself for the slip. "Still going on?" he echoed, frowning. "But your representative said

Skywalker was flying an Incom X-wing starfighter. If you haven't found him by now, his life support will surely have given out."

"Ah," Thrawn said, nodding. "I see the misunderstanding. Normally, yes, you'd be correct. But Skywalker is a Jedi; and among a Jedi's bag of tricks is the ability to go into a sort of comatose state." He paused, and the image on the screen flickered momentarily. "So there's still plenty of time for you to join in the hunt."

"I see," Karrde said. "Interesting. I suppose that's just one of the many things the average person never knew about Jedi."

"Perhaps we'll have time to discuss such things when I arrive on Myrkr," Thrawn said.

Karrde froze, a horrible realization shooting through him like an electric shock. That brief flickering of Thrawn's image—

A glance at the auxiliary sensor display confirmed it: three *Lambda*-class shuttles and a full TIE fighter escort had left the *Chimaera*, heading toward the surface. "I'm afraid we don't have much to entertain you with," he said between suddenly stiff lips. "Certainly not on such short notice."

"No need for entertainment," Thrawn assured him. "As I said, I'm simply coming for a talk. A *brief* talk, of course; I know how busy you are."

"I appreciate your consideration," Karrde said. "If you'll excuse me, Admiral, I need to begin the preparations to receive you."

"I look forward to our meeting," Thrawn said. His face vanished, and the display returned to its distant view of the *Chimaera*.

For a long moment Karrde just sat there, the possibilities and potential disasters flipping through his mind at top speed. "Get on the comlink to Chin," he told Mara. "Tell him we have Imperial guests coming, and he's to begin preparations to receive them properly. Then go to pad eight and have Aves move the *Millennium Falcon* farther back under cover. Go there in person—the *Chimaera* and its shuttles might be able to tap into our comlink transmissions."

"What about Solo and Calrissian?"

Karrde pursed his lips. "We'll have to get them out, of course. Move them into the forest, perhaps at or near their ship. I'd better deal with that myself."

"Why not turn them over to Thrawn?"

He looked up at her. At those burning eyes and that rigid, tightly controlled face . . . "With no offer of a bounty?" he asked. "Relying on the Grand Admiral's generosity after the fact?"

"I don't find that a compelling reason," Mara said bluntly.

"Neither do I," he countered coldly. "What I *do* find compelling is that they're our guests. They've sat at our table and eaten our food . . . and like it or not, that means they're under our protection."

Mara's lip twitched. "And do these rules of hospitality apply to Skywalker, too?" she asked sardonically.

"You know they don't," he said. "But now is not the time or the place to turn him over to the Empire, even if that's the way the decision ultimately goes. Do you understand?"

"No," she growled. "I don't."

Karrde eyed her, strongly tempted to tell her that she

didn't need to understand, only to obey. "It's a matter of relative strength," he told her instead. "Here on the ground, with an Imperial Star Destroyer orbiting overhead, we have no bargaining position at all. I wouldn't do business under such circumstances even if Thrawn was the most trustworthy client in the galaxy. Which he's not. *Now* do you understand?"

She took a deep breath, let it out. "I don't agree," she gritted. "But I'll accept your decision."

"Thank you. Perhaps after the Imperials leave, you can ask General Calrissian about the perils of making bargains while stormtroopers are strolling around your territory." Karrde looked back at the display. "So. *Falcon* moved; Solo and Calrissian moved. Skywalker and the droid should be all right where they are—the four shed has enough shielding to keep out anything but a fairly determined probe."

"And if Thrawn *is* determined?"

"Then we may have trouble," Karrde agreed calmly. "On the other hand, I doubt that Thrawn would be coming down himself if he thought there was the possibility of a firefight. The upper military ranks don't achieve that status by risking their own lives unnecessarily." He nodded at the door. "Enough talk. You have your job; I have mine. Let's get to them."

She nodded and turned to the door; and as she did so, a sudden thought struck him. "Where did you put Skywalker's lightsaber?" he asked.

"It's in my room," she said, turning back. "Why?"

"Better get it and put it somewhere else. Lightsabers aren't supposed to be highly detectable, but there's no point in taking chances. Put it in with the resonator cavities in three shed; they ought to provide adequate shielding from stray sensor probes."

"Right." She regarded him thoughtfully. "What was all that business about capital starships?"

"You heard everything that was said."

"I know. I was talking about your reaction to it."

He grimaced to himself. "I'd hoped it wasn't that obvious."

"It wasn't." She waited expectantly.

He pursed his lips. "Ask me again later. Right now, we have work to do."

For another second she studied him. Then, without a word, she nodded and left.

Taking a deep breath, Karrde got to his feet. First thing to do would be to get back to the dining room and inform his guests of the sudden change in plans. And after that, to prepare himself for a face-to-face confrontation with the most dangerous man in the Empire. With Skywalker and spare warships as two of the topics of conversation.

It was going to be a most interesting afternoon.

"OKAY, ARTOO," LUKE called as he made the last of the connections. "I think we're ready to try it. Cross your fingers."

From the next room came a complicated series of electronic jabbers. Probably, Luke decided, the droid reminding him that he didn't have any fingers to cross.

Fingers. For a moment Luke looked down at his right hand, flexing his fingers and feeling the unpleasant pins-and-needles tingling/numbness there. It had been five years since he'd really thought of the hand as being a machine attached to his arm. Now, suddenly, it was impossible to think of it as anything but that.

Artoo beeped impatiently. "Right," Luke agreed, forcing his attention away from his hand as best he could and moving the end of the wire toward what he hoped was the proper contact point. It could have been worse, he realized: the hand could have been designed with only a single power supply, in which case he wouldn't have even this much use of it. "Here goes," he said, and touched the wire.

And with no fuss or dramatics whatsoever, the door slid quietly open.

"Got it," Luke hissed. Carefully, trying not to lose the contact point, he leaned over and peered outside.

The sun was starting to sink behind the trees, throwing long shadows across the compound. From his position Luke could see only a little of the grounds, but what he could see seemed to be deserted. Setting his feet, he let go of the wire and dived for the doorway.

With the contact broken, the door slid shut again, nearly catching his left ankle as he hit the ground and rolled awkwardly into a crouch. He froze, waiting to see if the noise would spark any reaction. But the silence continued; and after a few seconds, he got to his feet and ran to the shed's other door.

Artoo had been right: there was indeed no lock on this half of the shed. Luke hit the release, threw one last glance around, and slipped inside.

The droid beeped an enthusiastic greeting, bobbing back and forth awkwardly in the restraint collar, a torus-shaped device that fit snugly around his legs and wheels.

"Quiet, Artoo," Luke warned the other, kneeling down to examine the collar. "And hold still."

He'd been worried that the collar would be locked or intertwined into Artoo's wheel system in some way, requiring special tools to disengage. But the device was much simpler than that—it merely held enough of the droid's weight off the floor so that he couldn't get any real traction. Luke released a pair of clasps and pushed the hinged halves apart, and Artoo was free. "Come on," he told the droid, and headed back to the door.

As far as he could see, the compound was still deserted. "The ship's around that way," he whispered, pointing toward the central building. "Looks like the best approach would be to circle to the left, keeping inside the trees as much as we can. Can you handle the terrain?"

Artoo raised his scanner, beeped a cautious affirmative. "Okay. Keep an eye out for anyone coming out of the buildings."

They'd made it into the woods, and were perhaps a quarter of the way around the circle, when Artoo gave a warning chirp. "Freeze," Luke whispered, stopping dead beside a large tree trunk and hoping they were enough in the shadows. His own black outfit should blend adequately into the darkening forest background, but Artoo's white and blue were another matter entirely.

Fortunately, the three men who came out of the central building never looked in their direction, but headed straight toward the edge of the forest.

Headed there at a fast, determined trot . . . and just before they disappeared into the trees, all three drew their blasters.

Artoo moaned softly. "I don't like it, either," Luke told him. "Let's hope it doesn't have anything to do with us. All clear?"

The droid beeped affirmation, and they started off again. Luke kept half an eye on the forest behind them, remembering Mara's veiled hints about large predators. It could have been a lie, of course, designed to discourage him from trying to escape. For that matter, he'd never spotted any real evidence that the window of his previous room had had an alarm on it.

Artoo beeped again. Luke twisted his attention back to the compound . . . and froze.

Mara had stepped out of the central building.

For what seemed like a long time she just stood there on the doorstep, looking distractedly up into the sky. Luke watched her, not daring even to look down to see how well concealed Artoo might be. If she turned in their direction—or if she went to the shed to see how he was doing . . .

Abruptly, she looked down again, a determined expression on her face. She turned toward the second barracks building and headed off at a brisk walk.

Luke let out a breath he hadn't realized he'd been holding. They were far from being out of danger—all Mara had to do was turn her head 90 degrees to her left and she'd be looking directly at them. But something about her posture seemed to indicate that her attention and thoughts were turned inward.

As if she'd suddenly made a hard decision . . .

She went into the barracks, and Luke made a quick decision of his own. "Come on, Artoo," he murmured. "It's getting too crowded out here. We're going to cut

farther into the forest, come up on the ships from behind."

It was, fortunately, a short distance to the mainte-
nance hangar and the group of ships parked alongside it.
They arrived after only a few minutes—to discover their
X-wing gone.

"No, I don't know where they've moved it to," Luke
gritted, looking around as best he could while still staying under cover. "Can your sensors pick it up?"

Artoo beeped a negative, adding a chirping explanation Luke couldn't even begin to follow. "Well, it doesn't
matter," he reassured the droid. "We'd have had to put
down somewhere else on the planet and find something
with a working hyperdrive, anyway. We'll just skip that
step and take one of these."

He glanced around, hoping to find a Z-95 or Y-wing
or something else he was at least marginally familiar
with. But the only ships he recognized were a Corellian
Corvette and what looked like a downsized bulk freighter.
"Got any suggestions?" he asked Artoo.

The droid beeped a prompt affirmative, his little sensor dish settling on a pair of long, lean ships about twice
the length of Luke's X-wing. Fighters, obviously, but not
like anything the Alliance had ever used. "One of those?"
he asked doubtfully.

Artoo beeped again, a distinct note of impatience to
the sound. "Right; we're a little pressed for time," Luke
agreed.

They made it across to one of the fighters without
incident. Unlike the X-wing design, the entrance was a
hinged hatchway door in the side—possibly one reason
Artoo had chosen it, Luke decided as he manhandled the

droid inside. The pilot's cockpit wasn't much roomier than an X-wing's, but directly behind it was a three-seat tech/weapons area. The seats weren't designed for astromech droids, of course, but with a little ingenuity on Luke's part and some stretch on the restraints', he managed to get Artoo wedged between two of the seats and firmly strapped in place. "Looks like everything's already on standby," he commented, glancing at the flickering lights on the control boards. "There's an outlet right there—give everything a quick check while I strap in. With a little luck, maybe we can be out of here before anyone even knows we're gone."

SHE HAD DELIVERED the open comlink message to Chin, and the quieter ones to Aves and the others at the *Millennium Falcon;* and as she stalked her way glowering across the compound toward the number three shed, Mara decided once more that she hated the universe.

She'd been the one who'd found Skywalker. She, by herself, alone. There was no question about that; no argument even possible. It should be she, not Karrde, who had the final say on his fate.

I should have left him out there, she told herself bitterly as she stomped across the beaten ground. *Should have just let him die in the cold of space.* She'd considered that, too, at the time. But if he'd died out there, all alone, she might never have known for sure that he was, in fact, dead.

And she certainly wouldn't have had the satisfaction of killing him herself.

She looked down at the lightsaber clenched in her

hand, watching the afternoon sunlight glint from the silvery metal as she hefted its weight. She could do it now, she knew. Could go in there to check on him and claim he had tried to jump her. Without the Force to call on, he would be an easy target, even for someone like her who hadn't picked up a lightsaber more than a handful of times in her life. It would be easy, clean, and very fast.

And she didn't owe Karrde anything, no matter how well his organization might have treated her. Not about something like this.

And yet . . .

She was coming up on four shed, still undecided, when she heard the faint whine of a repulsorlift.

She peered up into the sky, shading her eyes with her free hand as she tried to spot the incoming ship. But nothing was visible . . . and as the whine grew louder, she realized abruptly that it was the sound of one of their own vehicles. She spun around and looked over toward the maintenance hangar—

Just in time to see one of their two Skipray blastboats rise above the treetops.

For a pair of heartbeats she stared at the ship, wondering what in the Empire Karrde thought he was doing. Sending an escort or pilot ship for the Imperials, perhaps?

And then, abruptly, it clicked.

She twisted back and sprinted for the four shed, pulling her blaster from its forearm sheath as she ran. The lock on the room inexplicably refused to open; she tried it twice and then blasted it.

Skywalker was gone.

She swore, viciously, and ran out into the compound.

The Skipray had shifted to forward motion now, disappearing behind the trees to the west. Jamming her blaster back into its sheath, she grabbed the comlink off her belt—

And swore again. The Imperials could be here at any minute, and any mention of Skywalker's presence would land them all in very deep trouble indeed.

Which left her with exactly one option.

She reached the second Skipray at a dead run and had it in the air within two minutes. Skywalker would not—would *not*—get away now.

Kicking the drive to full power, she screamed off in pursuit.

CHAPTER 23

THEY SHOWED UP almost simultaneously on the scopes:
the other of Karrde's fighter ships pursuing him from
behind, and the Imperial Star Destroyer in orbit far overhead. "I think," Luke called back to Artoo, "that we're
in trouble."

The droid's reply was almost swallowed up in the roar
as Luke gingerly eased the drive up as high as he dared.
The strange fighter's handling wasn't even remotely like
anything he'd ever flown before; slightly reminiscent of
the snowspeeders the Alliance had used on Hoth, but
with the kind of sluggish response time that implied a
great deal of armor and engine mass. With time, he was
pretty sure he'd be able to master it.

But time was something he was rapidly running out of.

He risked a glance at the aft-vision display. The other
fighter was coming up fast, with no more than a minute
or two now separating the two ships. Obviously, the pilot
had far more experience with the craft than Luke had.

That, or else such a fierce determination to recapture Luke that it completely overrode normal common-sense caution.

Either way, it meant Mara Jade.

The fighter dipped a little too deep, scraping its ventral tail fin against the tops of the trees and drawing a sharp squeal of protest from Artoo. "Sorry," Luke called back, feeling a fresh surge of perspiration break out on his forehead as he again carefully eased the drive up a notch. Speaking of overriding common sense . . . But at the moment, sticking to the treetops was about the only option he had. The forest below, for some unknown reason, seemed to have a scattering or scrambling effect on sensor scans, both detection and navigational. Staying low forced his pursuer to stay low, too, lest she lose visual contact with him against the mottled forest backdrop, and also at least partially hid him from the orbiting Star Destroyer.

The Star Destroyer. Luke glanced at the image on his overhead scope, feeling his stomach tighten. At least he knew now who the company was Mara had mentioned. It looked like he'd gotten out just in the nick of time.

On the other hand, perhaps the move to that storage shed implied that Karrde had decided not to sell him to the Imperials after all. It might be worth asking Karrde about someday. Preferably from a great distance.

Behind him, Artoo suddenly trilled a warning. Luke jerked in his seat, eyes flickering across the scopes as he searched for the source of the trouble—

And jerked again. There, directly above his dorsal tail fin and less than a ship's length away, was the other fighter.

"Hang on!" Luke shouted at Artoo, clenching his

teeth tightly together. His one chance now was to pull a drop-kick Koiogran turn, killing his forward momentum and loop-rolling into another direction. Twisting the control stick with one hand, he jammed the throttle forward with the other—

And abruptly, the cockpit canopy exploded into a slapping tangle of tree branches, and he was thrown hard against his restraints as the fighter spun and twisted and rolled out of control.

The last thing he heard before the darkness took him was Artoo's shrill electronic scream.

THE THREE SHUTTLES came to a perfectly synchronized landing as, overhead, the TIE fighter escort shot by in equally perfect formation. "The Empire's parade-ground expertise hasn't eroded, anyway," Aves murmured.

"Quiet," Karrde murmured back, watching the shuttle ramps lower to the ground. The center one, almost certainly, would be Thrawn's.

Marching with blaster rifles held ceremonially across their chests, a line of stormtroopers filed down each of the three ramps. Behind them, emerging not from the center but from the right-most of the shuttles, came a handful of midranking officers. Following them came a short, wiry being of unknown race with dark gray skin, bulging eyes, a protruding jaw, and the look of a bodyguard. Following him came Grand Admiral Thrawn.

So much, Karrde thought, *for him doing things the obvious way*. It would be something to make a note of for future reference.

With his small reception committee beside him, he

walked toward the approaching group of Imperials, trying to ignore the stares of the stormtroopers. "Grand Admiral Thrawn," he nodded in greeting. "Welcome to our little corner of Myrkr. I'm Talon Karrde."

"Pleased to meet you, Captain," Thrawn said, inclining his head slightly. Those glowing eyes, Karrde decided, were even more impressive in person than they were on a comm display. And considerably more intimidating.

"I apologize for our somewhat less than formal greeting," Karrde continued, waving a hand at his group. "We don't often entertain people of your status here."

Thrawn cocked a blue-black eyebrow. "Really. I'd have thought a man in your position would be used to dealing with the elite. Particularly high planetary officials whose cooperation, shall we say, you find you require?"

Karrde smiled easily. "We deal with the elite from time to time. But not here. This is—was, I should say," he added, glancing significantly at the stormtroopers, "—our private operations base."

"Of course," Thrawn said. "Interesting drama a few minutes ago out there to the west. Tell me about it."

With an effort, Karrde hid a grimace. He'd hoped the sensor-scrambling effect of Myrkr's trees would have hidden the Skipray chase from Thrawn's view. Obviously, it hadn't. "Merely a small internal problem," he assured the Grand Admiral. "A former and somewhat disgruntled employee broke into one of our storage sheds, stole some merchandise, and made off with one of our ships. Another of our people is in pursuit."

"*Was* in pursuit, Captain," Thrawn corrected lazily, those eyes seeming to burn into Karrde's face. "Or didn't you know they both went down?"

Karrde stared at him, a thin needle of ice running through him. "I didn't know that, no," he said. "Our sensors—the metallic content of the trees fouls them up badly."

"We had a higher observation angle," Thrawn said. "It looked as if the first ship hit the trees, with the pursuer getting caught in the slipstream." He regarded Karrde thoughtfully. "I take it the pursuer was someone special?"

Karrde let his face harden a bit. "All my associates are special," he said, pulling out his comlink. "Please excuse me a moment; I have to get a rescue team organized."

Thrawn took a long step forward, reaching two pale blue fingers to cover the top of the comlink. "Permit me," he said smoothly. "Troop commander?"

One of the stormtroopers stepped forward. "Sir?"

"Take a detail out to the crash site," Thrawn ordered, his eyes still on Karrde. "Examine the wreckage, and bring back any survivors. And anything that looks like it wouldn't normally belong in a Skipray blastboat."

"Yes, sir." The other gestured, and one of the columns of stormtroopers turned and retraced their steps up the ramp of the left-most shuttle.

"I appreciate your assistance, Admiral," Karrde said, his mouth suddenly a little dry. "But it really isn't necessary."

"On the contrary, Captain," Thrawn said softly. "Your assistance with the ysalamiri has left us in your debt. How better for us to repay you?"

"How better, indeed?" Karrde murmured. The ramp lifted into place, and with the hum of repulsorlifts, the shuttle rose into the air. The cards were dealt, and there was nothing he could do now to alter them. He could only hope that Mara somehow had things under control.

With anyone else, he wouldn't have bet on it. With Mara . . . there was a chance.

"And now," Thrawn said, "I believe you were going to show me around?"

"Yes," Karrde nodded. "If you'll come this way, please?"

"Looks like the stormtroopers are leaving," Han said quietly, pressing the macrobinoculars a little harder against his forehead. "Some of them, anyway. Filing back into one of the shuttles."

"Let me see," Lando muttered from the other side of the tree.

Keeping his movements slow and careful, Han handed the macrobinoculars over. There was no telling what kind of equipment they had on those shuttles and TIE fighters, and he didn't especially trust all this talk about how good the trees were at sensor shielding.

"Yes, it seems to be just the one shuttle that's going," Lando agreed.

Han half turned, the serrated, grasslike plants they were lying on top of digging into his shirt with the movement. "You get Imperial visitors here often?" he demanded.

"Not here," Ghent shook his head nervously, his teeth almost chattering with tension. "They've been to the forest once or twice to pick up some ysalamiri, but they've never come to the base. At least, not while I was here."

"Ysalamiri?" Lando frowned. "What are those?"

"Little furry snakes with legs," Ghent said. "I don't know what they're good for. Look, couldn't we get back to the ship now? Karrde told me I was supposed to keep you there, where you'd be safe."

Han ignored him. "What do you think?" he asked Lando.

The other shrugged. "Got to have something to do with that Skipray that went burning out of here just as Karrde was herding us out."

"There was some kind of prisoner," Ghent offered. "Karrde and Jade had him stashed away—maybe he got out. Now, can we *please* get back to—"

"A prisoner?" Lando repeated, frowning back at the kid. "When did Karrde start dealing with prisoners?"

"Maybe when he started dealing with kidnappers," Han growled before Ghent could answer.

"We don't deal with kidnappers," Ghent protested.

"Well, you're dealing with one now." Han told him, nodding toward the group of Imperials. "That little gray guy in there?—that's one of the aliens who tried to kidnap Leia and me."

"What?" Lando peered through the macrobinoculars again. "Are you sure?"

"It's one of the species, anyway. We didn't stop at the time to get names." Han looked back at Ghent. "This prisoner—who was he?"

"I don't know," Ghent shook his head. "They brought him back on the *Wild Karrde* a few days ago and put him in the short-term barracks. I think they'd just moved him over to one of the storage sheds when we got the word that the Imperials were coming down for a visit."

"What did he look like?"

"I don't *know*!" Ghent hissed, what little was left of his composure going fast. Skulking around forests and spying on armed stormtroopers was clearly not the sort of thing an expert slicer was supposed to have to put up with. "None of us was supposed to go near him or ask any questions about him."

Lando caught Han's eye. "Could be someone they don't want the Imperials to get hold of. A defector, maybe, trying to get to the New Republic?"

Han felt his lip twist. "I'm more worried right now about them having moved him out of the barracks. That could mean the stormtroopers are planning to move in for a while."

"Karrde didn't say anything about that," Ghent objected.

"Karrde may not know it yet," Lando said dryly. "Trust me—I was on the short end of a stormtrooper bargain once." He handed the macrobinoculars back to Han. "Looks like they're going inside."

They were, indeed. Han watched as the procession set off: Karrde and the blue-skinned Imperial officer in front, their respective entourages following, the twin columns of stormtroopers flanking the whole parade. "Any idea who that guy with the red eyes is?" he asked Ghent.

"I think he's a Grand Admiral or something," the other said. "Took over Imperial operations a while back. I don't know his name."

Han looked at Lando, found the other sending the same look right back at him. "A Grand Admiral?" Lando repeated carefully.

"Yeah. Look, they're going—there's nothing else to see. Can we *please*—?"

"Let's get back to the *Falcon*," Han muttered, stowing the macrobinoculars in their belt pouch and starting a backwards elbows-and-knees crawl from their covering tree. A Grand Admiral. No wonder the New Republic had been getting the sky cut out from under them lately.

"I don't suppose you have any records on Imperial Grand Admirals back on the *Falcon*," Lando murmured, backing up alongside him.

"No," Han told him. "But they've got 'em on Coruscant."

"Great," Lando said, the words almost lost in the hissing of the sharp-bladed grass as they elbowed their way through it. "Let's hope we live long enough to get this tidbit back there."

"We will," Han assured him grimly. "We'll stick around long enough to find out what kind of game Karrde's playing, but then we're gone. Even if we have to blow out of here with that camo net still hanging off the ship."

THE STRANGEST THING about waking up this time, Luke decided dimly, was that he didn't actually hurt anywhere.

And he should have. From what he remembered of those last few seconds—and from the view of splintered trees outside the fighter's twisted canopy—he would have counted himself lucky even to be alive, let alone undamaged. Clearly, the restraints and crash balloons had been augmented by something more sophisticated—an emergency acceleration compensator, perhaps.

A shaky sort of gurgle came from behind him. "You okay, Artoo?" he called, levering himself out of his seat and climbing awkwardly across the canted floor. "Hang on, I'm coming."

The droid's information retrieval jack had been snapped off in the crash, but apart from that and a couple of minor dents, he didn't seem to have been damaged. "We'd better get moving," Luke told him, untangling him from his restraints. "That other ship could be back with a ground party anytime."

With an effort, he got Artoo aft. The hatchway door popped open without serious complaint; hopping down, he looked around.

The second fighter would not be returning with any ground parties. It was right here. In worse shape, if possible, than Luke's.

From the hatchway, Artoo whistled in squeamish-sounding awe. Luke glanced up at him, looked back at the ruined craft. Given the fighters' safety equipment, it was unlikely that Mara was seriously injured. A backup flight was inevitable—she would probably be able to hold out until then.

But then again, she might not.

"Wait here, Artoo," he told the droid. "I'm going to take a quick look."

Even though the exterior of the fighter was in worse shape than Luke's, the interior actually seemed to be a little better off. Crunching his way across the bits of debris in the weapons/tech area, he stepped into the cockpit doorway.

Only the top of the pilot's head showed over the seat back, but that shimmering red-gold hair was all he needed to see to know that his earlier guess had been correct. It was indeed Mara Jade who'd been chasing him.

For a pair of heartbeats he stayed where he was, torn between the need for haste and the need to satisfy his internal sense of ethics. He and Artoo had to get out of here with all possible speed; that much was obvious. But if he turned his back on Mara now, without even pausing to check her condition . . .

His mind flashed back to Coruscant, to the night Ben Kenobi had said his final farewells. *In other words*, he'd told Threepio later up on the roof, *a Jedi can't get so caught up in matters of galactic importance that it interferes with his concern for individual people.* And it would, after all, only take a minute. Stepping into the room, he looked around the seat back.

Directly into a pair of wide-open, perfectly conscious green eyes. Green eyes that stared at him over the barrel of a tiny blaster.

"I figured you'd come," she said, her voice grimly satisfied. "Back up. Now."

He did as ordered. "Are you hurt at all?" he asked.

"None of your business," she retorted. She climbed out of the seat, pulling a small flat case from under the chair with her free hand as she stood up. Another glitter caught his eye: she was again wearing his lightsaber on her belt. "There's a case in that compartment just over the exit hatch," she told him. "Get it."

He found the release and got the compartment open. Inside was an unfamiliarly labeled metal case with the very familiar look of a survival kit to it. "I hope we're not going to have to walk the whole way back," he commented, pulling the case out and dropping out of the hatchway.

"*I* won't," she countered. She seemed to hesitate, just

a little, before following him down to the ground. "Whether you make the trip back at all is another question."

He locked gazes with her. "Finishing what you started with this?" he asked, nodding at his wrecked ship.

She snorted. "Listen, buddy boy, it was *you* who took us down, not me. My only mistake was being stupid enough to be sitting too close to your tail when you hit the trees. Put the bag down and get that droid out of there."

Luke did as he was told. By the time Artoo was down beside him she had the survival kit's lid open and was fiddling one-handed with something inside. "Just stay right there," she told him. "And keep your hands where I can see them."

She paused, cocking her head slightly to the side as if listening. A moment later, in the distance, Luke could hear the faint sound of an approaching ship. "Sounds like our ride back is already on the way," Mara said. "I want you and the droid—"

She stopped in midsentence, her eyes going strangely unfocused, her throat tight with concentration. Luke frowned, eyes and ears searching for the problem . . .

Abruptly, she slammed the survival kit lid shut and scooped it up. "Move!" she snapped, gesturing away from the wrecked fighters. With her blaster hand she picked up the flat box she'd been carrying and wedged it under her left arm. "Into the trees—both of you. I said *move!*"

There was something in her voice—command, or urgency, or both—that stifled argument or even question. Within a handful of seconds Luke and Artoo were under cover of the nearest trees. "Farther in," she ordered. "Come on, move it."

Belatedly, it occurred to Luke that this might all be some macabre joke—that all Mara really wanted was to shoot him in the back and be able to claim afterward that he'd been running away. But she was right behind him, close enough that he could hear her breathing and occasionally feel the tip of her blaster as it brushed his back. They made it perhaps ten meters farther in—Luke leaned down to help Artoo across a particularly wide root—

"Far enough," Mara hissed in his ear. "Hide the droid and then hit dirt."

Luke got Artoo over the root and behind a tree . . . and as he dropped down beside Mara, he suddenly understood.

Hanging in midair over the wrecked fighters, rotating slowly like a hovering raptor searching for prey, was an Imperial shuttle.

A small motion caught the corner of his eye, and he turned his head to look directly into the muzzle of Mara's blaster. "Not a move," she whispered, her breath warm on his cheek. "Not a sound."

He nodded understanding and turned back to watch the shuttle. Mara slid her arm over his shoulders, pressed her blaster into the hinge of his jaw, and did the same.

The shuttle finished its circle and settled gingerly to the torn-up ground between the ruined fighters. Even before it was completely down, the ramp dropped and began disgorging stormtroopers.

Luke watched as they split up and headed off to search the two ships, the strangeness of the whole situation adding an unreal tinge to the scene. There; less than twenty meters away, was Mara's golden opportunity to turn him over to the Imperials . . . and yet, here they both lay, hiding behind a tree root and trying not to breathe too loudly. Had she suddenly changed her mind?

Or was it simply that she didn't want any witnesses nearby when she killed him?

In which case, Luke realized abruptly, his best chance might actually be to find some way of surrendering to the stormtroopers. Once away from this planet, with the Force as his ally again, he would at least have a fighting chance. If he could just find a way to distract Mara long enough to get rid of her blaster . . .

Lying pressed against his side, her arm slung across his shoulders, she must have sensed the sudden tensing of muscles. "Whatever you're thinking about trying, don't," she breathed in his ear, digging her blaster a little harder into his skin. "I can easily claim you were holding me prisoner out here and that I managed to snatch the blaster away from you."

Luke swallowed, and settled in to wait.

The wait wasn't very long. Two groups of stormtroopers disappeared into the fighters, while the rest walked around the edge of the newly created clearing, probing with eyes and portable sensors into the forest. After a few minutes those inside the fighters emerged, and what seemed to be a short meeting was held between them at the base of the shuttle ramp. At an inaudible command the outer ring of searchers came back in to join them, and the whole crowd trooped into their ship. The ramp sealed, and the shuttle disappeared once more into the sky, leaving nothing but the hum of its repulsorlifts behind. A minute later, even that was gone.

Luke got his hands under him, started to get up. "Well—"

He broke off at another jab of the blaster. "Quiet," Mara muttered. "They'll have left a sensor behind, just in case someone comes back."

Luke frowned. "How do you know?"

"Because that's standard stormtrooper procedure in a case like this," she growled. "Real quiet, now; we get up and grab some more distance. And keep the droid quiet, too."

They were completely out of sight of the wrecked fighters, and probably another fifty meters past that, before she called a halt. "What now?" Luke asked.

"We sit down," she told him.

Luke nodded and eased to the ground. "Thank you for not turning me in to the stormtroopers."

"Save it," she said shortly, sitting down carefully herself and laying her blaster on the ground beside her. "Don't worry, there wasn't anything altruistic about it. The incoming shuttles must have seen us and sent a group over to investigate. Karrde's going to have to spin them some sort of sugar story about what happened, and I can't just walk into their arms until I know what that story is." She set the small flat box on her lap and opened it.

"You could call him," Luke reminded her.

"I could also call the Imperials directly and save myself some time," she retorted. "Unless you don't think they've got the equipment to monitor anything I send. Now shut up; I've got work to do."

For a few minutes she worked at the flat box in silence, fiddling with a tiny keyboard and frowning at something Luke couldn't see from his angle. At irregular intervals she looked up, apparently to make sure he wasn't trying anything. Luke waited; and abruptly she grunted in satisfaction. "Three days," she said aloud, closing the box.

"Three days to what?" Luke asked.

"The edge of the forest," she told him, gazing at him with unblinking eyes. "Civilization. Well, Hyllyard City, anyway, which is about as close as this part of the planet gets to it."

"And how many of us will be going there?" Luke asked quietly.

"That's the question, isn't it?" she agreed, her tone icy. "Can you give me any reason why I should bother taking you along?"

"Sure." Luke inclined his head to the side. "Artoo."

"Don't be absurd." Her eyes flicked to the droid, back at Luke. "Whatever happens, the droid stays here. In pieces."

Luke stared at her. "In *pieces*?"

"What, you need it spelled out?" she retorted. "The droid knows too much. We can't leave it here for the stormtroopers to find."

"Knows too much about what?"

"You, of course. You, Karrde, me—this whole stupid mess."

Artoo moaned softly. "He won't tell them anything," Luke insisted.

"Not after it's in pieces, no," Mara agreed.

With an effort, Luke forced himself to calm down. Logic, not fervor, was the only way to change her mind. "We need him," he told her. "You told me yourself the forest was dangerous. Artoo has sensors that can spot predators before they get close enough to strike."

"Maybe; maybe not," she countered. "The vegetation here limits sensor ranges down to practically zero."

"It'll still be better than you or I could do," Luke said. "And he'll also be able to watch while we're sleeping."

She raised her eyebrows slightly. "*We?*"

"We," Luke said. "I don't think he'll be willing to protect you unless I'm along."

Mara shook her head. "No good," she said, picking up her blaster. "I can get along without him. And I certainly don't need you."

Luke felt his throat tighten. "Are you sure you're not letting your emotions get in the way of your judgment?" he asked.

He hadn't thought her eyes could get any harder than they already were. He was wrong. "Let me tell you something, Skywalker," she said in a voice almost too soft for him to hear. "I've wanted to kill you for a long time. I dreamed about your death every night for most of that first year. Dreamed it, plotted it—I must have run through a thousand scenarios, trying to find exactly the right way to do it. You can call it a cloud on my judgment if you want to; I'm used to it by now. It's the closest thing I've got to a permanent companion."

Luke looked back into those eyes, shaken right down to the core of his soul. "What did I do to you?" he whispered.

"You destroyed my life," she said bitterly. "It's only fair that I destroy yours."

"Will killing me bring your old life back?"

"You know better than that," she said, her voice trembling slightly. "But it's still something I have to do. For myself, and for—" She broke off.

"What about Karrde?" Luke asked.

"What about him?"

"I thought he still wanted me kept alive."

She snorted. "We all want things we can't have."

But for just a second, there was something in her eyes. Something else that had flickered through the hatred . . .

But whatever it was, it wasn't enough. "I almost wish I could drag it out a little more," she said, glacially calm again as she lifted the blaster. "But I don't have the time to spare."

Luke stared at the muzzle of her blaster, his mind frantically searching for inspiration . . . "Wait a minute," he said suddenly. "You said you needed to find out what Karrde had told the Imperials. What if I could get you a secure comm channel to him?"

The muzzle of the blaster wavered. "How?" she asked suspiciously.

Luke nodded toward her survival kit. "Does the communicator in there have enough range to reach back to the base? I mean, without satellite boosting or anything."

She was still looking suspicious. "There's a sonde balloon included that can take the antenna high enough to get past most of the forest damping. But it's nondirectional, which means the Imperials and anyone else in this hemisphere will be able to listen in."

"That's okay," Luke said. "I can encrypt it so that no one else will be able to get anything out of it. Or rather, Artoo can."

Mara smiled thinly. "Wonderful. Except for one minor detail: if the encrypt is that good, how is Karrde supposed to decrypt it?"

"He won't have to," Luke told her. "The computer in my X-wing will do it for him."

The thin smile vanished from Mara's face. "You're stalling," she snarled. "You can't do a counterpart encrypt between an astromech droid and a ship computer."

"Why not? Artoo's the only droid who's worked with that computer in more than five years, with close to three thousand hours of flight time. He's bound to have molded it to his own personality by now. In fact, I know he has—the ground maintenance people have to run diagnostics through him to make any sense out of them."

"I thought standard procedure was to wipe and reload droid memories every six months to keep that from happening."

"I like Artoo the way he is," Luke said. "And he and the X-wing work better together this way."

"How much better?"

Luke searched his memory. Maintenance had run that test just a few months ago. "I don't remember the exact number. It was something like thirty percent faster than a baseline astromech/X-wing interface. Maybe thirty-five."

Mara was staring hard at Artoo. "That's counterpart-level speed, all right," she agreed reluctantly. "The Imperials could still crack it, though."

"Eventually. But it would take some specialized equipment to do it. And you said yourself we'd be out of here in three days."

For a long minute she stared at him, her jaw tight with clenched teeth, her face a mirror of fiercely battling emotions. Bitterness, hatred, desire for survival . . . and something else. Something that Luke could almost believe might be a touch of loyalty. "Your ship's sitting all alone out in the forest," she growled at last. "How are you going to get the message back to Karrde?"

"Someone's bound to check on the ship eventually," he pointed out. "All we have to do is dump the message into storage and leave some kind of signal flashing that it's there. You have people who know how to pull a dump, don't you?"

"Any idiot knows how to pull a dump." Mara glared at him. "Funny, isn't it, how this scheme just *happens* to require that I keep both of you alive a while longer."

Luke remained silent, meeting that bitter gaze without flinching . . . and then, abruptly, Mara's internal battle seemed to end. "What about the droid?" she demanded. "It'll take forever to get it across this terrain."

"Artoo's made it through forests before. However . . ." Luke looked around, spotted a tree with two low branches just the right size. "I should be able to rig up a dragging frame to carry him on—a travois, or something like that." He started to get up. "If you'll give me my lightsaber for a minute I can cut a couple of those branches off."

"Sit down," she ordered, standing up. "I'll do it."

Well, it had been worth a try. "Those two," he told her, pointing. "Be careful—lightsabers are tricky to handle."

"Your concern for my welfare is touching," she said,

her voice dripping sarcasm. She drew the lightsaber and stepped over to the indicated tree, keeping an eye on Luke the whole time. She raised the weapon, ignited it—

And in a handful of quick, sure swipes trimmed, shortened, and cut the branches from the tree.

She closed down the weapon and returned it to her belt in a single smooth motion. "Help yourself," she said, moving away.

"Right," Luke said mechanically, his mind tingling with astonishment as he stumbled over to collect the branches. The way she'd done that . . . "You've used a lightsaber before."

She gazed at him coldly. "Just so you know I can handle it. In case you should feel tempted to try and make a grab for my blaster." She glanced upward at the darkening sky. "Come on—get busy with that travois. We'll need to find some kind of clearing to put the sonde balloon up, and I want to get that done before nightfall."

CHAPTER 24

"I MUST APOLOGIZE FOR chasing you out like that," Karrde said as he walked Han toward the central building. "Particularly in the middle of a meal. Not exactly the sort of hospitality we strive for here."

"No problem," Han told him, eyeing him as best he could in the gathering dusk. The light from the building ahead was casting a faint glow on Karrde's face; with luck, it would be enough to read the other's expression by. "What was that all about, anyway?"

"Nothing serious," Karrde assured him easily. "Some people with whom I've had business dealings wanted to come and look the place over."

"Ah," Han said. "So you're working directly for the Empire now?"

Karrde's expression cracked, just a little. Han expected him to make some sort of reflexive denial; instead, he stopped and turned to look at Lando and Ghent, walking behind them. "Ghent?" he asked mildly.

"I'm sorry, sir," the kid said, sounding miserable. "They insisted on coming out to see what was happening."

"I see." Karrde looked back at Han, his face calm again. "No harm done, probably. Not the wisest of risks to take, though."

"I'm used to taking risks," Han told him. "You haven't answered my question."

Karrde resumed walking. "If I'm not interested in working for the Republic, I'm certainly not interested in working for the Empire. The Imperials have been coming here for the past few weeks to collect ysalamiri—sessile creatures, like the ones hanging on to the tree in the greatroom. I offered my assistance in helping them safely remove the ysalamiri from their trees."

"What did you get in return?"

"The privilege of watching them work," Karrde said. "Giving me that much extra information to try to figure out what they wanted with the things."

"And what *did* they want with them?"

Karrde glanced at Han. "Information costs money here, Solo. Actually, to be perfectly honest, we don't know what they're up to. We're working on it, though."

"I see. But you *do* know their commander personally."

Karrde smiled faintly. "That's information again."

Han was starting to get sick of this. "Have it your way. What'll this Grand Admiral's name cost me?"

"For the moment, the name's not for sale," he told Han. "Perhaps we'll talk about it later."

"Thanks, but I don't think there's going to be a later,"

Han growled, stopping. "If you don't mind, we'll just say our good-byes here and get back to the ship."

Karrde turned to him in mild surprise. "You're not going to finish our dinner? You hardly had a chance to get started."

Han looked him straight in the eye. "I don't especially like sitting on the ground like a practice target when there are stormtroopers wandering around," he said bluntly.

Karrde's face hardened. "At the moment, sitting on the ground is preferable to drawing attention in the air," he said coldly. "The Star Destroyer hasn't left orbit yet. Lifting off now would be an open invitation for them to swat you down."

"The *Falcon*'s outrun Star Destroyers before," Han countered. But Karrde had a point . . . and the fact that he hadn't turned the two of them over to the Imperials probably meant that he could be trusted, at least for now. Probably.

On the other hand, if they *did* stay . . . "But I suppose it wouldn't hurt us to stick around a little longer," he conceded. "All right, sure, we'll finish dinner."

"Good," Karrde said. "It will just take a few minutes to get things put back together."

"You took everything apart?" Lando asked.

"Everything that might have indicated we had guests," Karrde said. "The Grand Admiral is highly observant, and I wouldn't have put it past him to know exactly how many of my associates are staying here at the moment."

"Well, while you're getting things ready," Han said, "I

want to go back to the ship and check on a couple of things."

Karrde's eyes narrowed slightly. "But you *will* be back."

Han gave him an innocent smile. "Trust me."

Karrde gazed at him a moment longer, then shrugged. "Very well. Watch yourselves, though. The local predators don't normally come this close in to our encampment, but there are exceptions."

"We'll be careful," Han promised. "Come on, Lando."

They headed back the way they'd come. "So what did we forget to do back at the *Falcon*?" Lando asked quietly as they reached the trees.

"Nothing," Han murmured back. "I just thought it'd be a good time to go check out Karrde's storage sheds. Particularly the one that was supposed to have a prisoner in it."

They went about five meters into the forest, then changed direction to circle the compound. A quarter of the way around the circle, they found a likely looking group of small buildings.

"Look for a door with a lock," Lando suggested as they came out among the sheds. "Either permanent or temporary."

"Right." Han peered through the darkness. "That one over there—the one with two doors?"

"Could be," Lando agreed. "Let's take a look."

The left-most of the two doors did indeed have a lock. Or, rather, it had *had* a lock. "It's been shot off," Lando said, poking at it with a finger. "Strange."

"Maybe the prisoner had friends," Han suggested,

STAR WARS: HEIR TO THE EMPIRE   351

glancing around. There was no one else in sight. "Let's go inside."

They slid the door open and went in, closing it behind them before turning on the light. The shed was less than half full, with most of the boxes piled against the right-hand wall. The exceptions to that rule . . .

Han stepped over for a closer look. "Well, well," he murmured, gazing at the removed power outlet plate and the wires poking through the gap. "Someone's been busy over here."

"Someone's been even busier over here," Lando commented from behind him. "Come have a look."

Lando was crouched down beside the door, peering into the inside of the door lock mechanism. Like the outside, half of its covering plate had been blasted off. "That must have been one beaut of a shot," Han frowned, coming over.

"It wasn't a single shot," Lando said, shaking his head. "The stuff in between is mostly intact." He pushed back the cover a little, poking at the electronics inside with his fingers. "Looks like our mysterious prisoner was tampering with the equipment."

"I wonder how he got it open." Han glanced back at the removed power plate. "I'm going to take a look next door," he told Lando, stepping back to the entrance and tapping the release.

The door didn't open. "Uh-oh," he muttered, trying again.

"Wait a second—I see the problem," Lando said, fiddling with something behind the plate. "There's a power supply been half spliced into the works . . ."

Abruptly, the door slid open. "Back in a second," Han told him, and slipped outside.

The shed's right-hand room wasn't much different from the other one. Except for one thing: in the center, in a space that had very obviously been cleared for the purpose, lay an open droid restraint collar.

Han frowned down at it. The collar hadn't been properly put away, or even closed again—hardly the way someone in an organization like Karrde's would be expected to take care of company equipment. Roughly in the center of the collar's open jaws were three faint marks on the floor. Skid marks, he decided, formed by the restrained droid's attempts to move or get free.

Behind him, the door whispered open. Han spun around, blaster in hand—

"You seem to have gotten lost," Karrde said calmly. His eyes flicked around the room. "And to have lost General Calrissian along the way."

Han lowered the blaster. "You need to tell your people to put their toys away when they're done," he said, nodding his head at the abandoned restraint collar. "You were holding a droid prisoner, too?"

Karrde smiled thinly. "I see Ghent was talking out of turn again. Amazing, isn't it, how so many expert slicers know everything about computers and droids and yet don't know when to keep their mouths shut."

"It's also amazing how so many expert smugglers don't know when to leave a messy deal alone," Han shot back. "So what's your Grand Admiral got you doing? Formal slaving, or just random kidnappings?"

Karrde's eyes flashed. "I don't deal in slaves, Solo. Slaves or kidnapping. Never."

"What was this one, then? An accident?"

"I didn't ask for him to come into my life," Karrde countered. "Nor did I especially want him there."

Han snorted. "You're stretching, Karrde. What'd he do, drop in out of the sky on top of you?"

"As a matter of fact, that's very nearly the way it happened," Karrde said stiffly.

"Oh, well, that's a good reason to lock someone up," Han said sardonically. "Who was he?"

"That information's not for sale."

"Maybe we don't need to buy it," Lando said from behind him.

Karrde turned. "Ah," he said as Lando stepped past him into the room. "There you are. Exploring the other half of the shed, were you?"

"Yeah, we don't stay lost very long," Han assured him. "What'd you find, Lando?"

"This." Lando held up a tiny red cylinder with a pair of wires coming out of each end. "It's a micrel power supply—the kind used for low-draw applications. Our prisoner wired it into the door lock control after the power lines had been burned away—that's how he got out." He moved it a little closer. "The manufacturer's logo is small, but readable. Recognize it?"

Han squinted at it. The script was alien, but it seemed vaguely familiar. "I've seen it before, but I don't remember where."

"You saw it during the war," Lando told him, his gaze steady on Karrde. "It's the logo of the Sibha Habadeet."

Han stared at the tiny cylinder, a strange chill running through him. The Sibha Habadeet had been one of the Alliance's major suppliers of micrel equipment. And their specialty had been—"That's a bioelectronic power supply?"

"That's right," Lando said grimly. "Just like the kind that would have been put in, say, an artificial hand."

Slowly, the muzzle of Han's blaster came up again to point at Karrde's stomach. "There was a droid in here," he told Lando. "The skid marks on the floor look just about right for an R2 unit." He raised his eyebrows. "Feel free to join the conversation anytime, Karrde."

Karrde sighed, his face a mixture of annoyance and resignation. "What do you want me to say?—that Luke Skywalker was a prisoner here? All right—consider it said."

Han felt his jaw tighten. And he and Lando had been right here. Blissfully unaware . . . "Where is he now?" he demanded.

"I thought Ghent would have told you," Karrde said darkly. "He escaped in one of my Skipray blastboats." His lips twisted. "Crashing it in the process."

"He *what*?"

"He's all right," Karrde assured him. "Or at least he was a couple of hours ago. The stormtroopers who went to investigate said that both wrecks were deserted." His eyes seemed to flatten, just for a minute. "I hope that means they're working together to make their way out."

"You don't sound sure of that," Han prompted.

The eyes flattened a little more. "Mara Jade was the one who went after him. She has a certain—well, why mince words. In point of fact, she wants very much to kill him."

Han threw a startled glance at Lando. "Why?"

Karrde shook his head. "I don't know."

For a moment the room was silent. "How did he get here?" Lando asked.

"As I said, purely by accident," Karrde said. "No—I take that back. It wasn't an accident for Mara—she led us directly to his crippled starfighter."

"How?"

"Again, I don't know." He fixed Han with a hard look. "And before you ask, we had nothing to do with the damage to his ship. He'd burned out both hyperdrive motivators tangling with one of the Empire's Star Destroyers. If we hadn't picked him up, he'd almost certainly be dead by now."

"Instead of roaming a forest with someone who still wants him that way," Han countered. "Yeah, you're a real hero."

The hard look hardened even further. "The Imperials want Skywalker, Solo. They want him very badly. If you look carefully, you'll notice that I *didn't* give him to them."

"Because he escaped first."

"He escaped because he was in this shed," Karrde retorted. "And he was in this shed because I didn't want the Imperials stumbling over him during their unannounced visit."

He paused. "You'll also notice," he added quietly, "that I didn't turn the two of *you* over to them, either."

Slowly, Han lowered the blaster. Anything said at the point of a gun was of course suspect; but the fact that Karrde had indeed not betrayed them to the Imperials was a strong argument in his favor.

Or rather, he hadn't betrayed them yet. That could always change. "I want to see Luke's X-wing," he told Karrde.

"Certainly," Karrde said. "I'd recommend not going there until tomorrow morning, though. We moved it somewhat farther into the forest than your ship; and there *will* be predators roaming around it in the darkness."

Han hesitated, then nodded. If Karrde had something subtle going here, he almost certainly would have already erased or altered the X-wing's computer log. A few more hours wouldn't make any difference. "All right. So what are we going to do about Luke?"

Karrde shook his head, his gaze not quite focused on Han. "There's nothing we can do for them tonight. Not with vornskrs roaming the forest and the Grand Admiral still in orbit. Tomorrow . . . We'll have to discuss it, see what we can come up with." His focus came back, and with it a slightly ironic smile. "In the meantime, dinner should be ready by now. If you'll follow me . . . ?"

THE DIMLY LIT holographic art gallery had changed again, this time to a collection of remarkably similar flame-shaped works that seemed to pulsate and alter in form as Pellaeon moved carefully between the pedestals. He studied them as he walked, wondering where this batch had come from. "Have you found them, Captain?" Thrawn asked as Pellaeon reached the double display circle.

He braced himself. "I'm afraid not, sir. We'd hoped that with the arrival of local nightfall we'd be able to get some results from the infrared sensors. But they don't seem able to penetrate the tree canopy, either."

Thrawn nodded. "What about that pulse transmission we picked up just after sundown?"

"We were able to confirm that it originated from the approximate location of the crash site," Pellaeon told him. "But it was too brief for a precise location check. The encrypt on it is a very strange one—Decrypt thinks it might be a type of counterpart coding. They're still working on it."

"They've tried all the known Rebellion encrypts, I presume."

"Yes, sir, as per your orders."

Thrawn nodded thoughtfully. "It looks like we're at something of a stalemate, then, Captain. At least as long as they're in the forest. Have you calculated their likely emergence points?"

"There's really only one practical choice," Pellaeon said, wondering why they were making so much of a fuss over this. "A town called Hyllyard City, on the edge of the forest and almost directly along their path. It's the only population center anywhere for more than a hundred kilometers. With only the one survival pack between them, they almost have to come out there."

"Excellent," Thrawn nodded. "I want you to detail three squads of stormtroopers to set up an observation post there. They're to assemble and depart ship immediately."

Pellaeon blinked. "Stormtroopers, sir?"

"Stormtroopers," Thrawn repeated, turning his gaze to one of the flame sculptures. "Better add half a biker scout unit, too, and three Chariot light assault vehicles."

"Yes, sir," Pellaeon said cautiously. Stormtroopers were in critically short supply these days. To waste them like this, on something so utterly unimportant as a smuggler squabble . . .

"Karrde lied to us, you see," Thrawn continued, as if reading Pellaeon's mind. "Whatever that little drama was this afternoon, it was not the common pursuit of a common thief. I'd like to know what, in fact, it was."

"I . . . don't think I follow, sir."

"It's very simple, Captain," Thrawn said, in that tone of voice he always seemed to use when explaining the obvious. "The pilot of the chase vehicle never reported in during the pursuit. Nor did anyone from Karrde's base communicate with him. We know that—we'd have intercepted any such transmissions. No progress reports; no assistance requests; nothing but complete radio silence." He looked back at Pellaeon. "Speculation, Captain?"

"Whatever it was," Pellaeon said slowly, "it was something they didn't want us knowing about. Beyond that . . ." He shook his head. "I don't know, sir. There could be any number of things they wouldn't want outsiders to know about. They *are* smugglers, after all."

"Agreed." Thrawn's eyes seemed to glitter. "But now consider the additional fact that Karrde refused our invitation to join in the search for Skywalker . . . and the fact that this afternoon he implied the search was over." He raised an eyebrow. "What does *that* suggest to you, Captain?"

Pellaeon felt his jaw drop. "You mean . . . that was *Skywalker* in that Skipray?"

"An interesting speculation, isn't it?" Thrawn agreed.

"Unlikely, I'll admit. But likely enough to be worth following up on."

"Yes, sir." Pellaeon glanced at the chrono, did a quick calculation. "Though if we stay here more than another day or two, we may have to move back the Sluis Van attack."

"We're not moving Sluis Van," Thrawn said emphatically. "Our entire victory campaign against the Rebellion begins there, and I'll not have so complex and far-reaching a schedule altered. Not for Skywalker; not for anyone else." He nodded at the flame statues surrounding them. "Sluissi art clearly indicates a biannual cyclic pattern, and I want to hit them at their most sluggish point. We'll leave for our rendezvous with the *Inexorable* and the cloaking shield test as soon as the troops and vehicles have been dropped. Three squads of stormtroopers should be adequate to handle Skywalker, if he is indeed here."

His eyes bored into Pellaeon's face. "And to handle Karrde," he added softly, "if he turns out to be a traitor."

THE LAST BITS of dark blue had faded from the tiny gaps in the canopy overhead, leaving nothing but blackness above them. Turning the survival kit's worklight to its lowest setting, Mara set it down and sank gratefully to the ground against a large tree bole. Her right ankle, twisted somehow in the Skipray crash, had started to ache again, and it felt good to get the weight off it.

Skywalker was already stretched out a couple of meters on the other side of the worklight, his head pillowed on his tunic, his loyal droid standing at his side. She wondered if he'd guessed about the ankle, dismissed the question as irrelevant. She'd had worse injuries without being slowed down by them.

"Reminds me of Endor," Skywalker said quietly as Mara arranged her glow rod and blaster in her lap where they'd be accessible. "A forest always sounds so busy at night."

"Oh, it's busy, all right," Mara grunted. "A lot of the animals here are nocturnal. Including the vornskrs."

"Strange," he murmured. "Karrde's pet vornskrs seemed wide enough awake in late afternoon."

She looked across at him, mildly surprised he'd noticed that. "Actually, even in the wild they take small naps around the clock," she said. "I call them nocturnal because they do most of their hunting at night."

Skywalker mulled that over for a moment. "Maybe we ought to travel at night, then," he suggested. "They'll be hunting us either way—at least then we'd be awake and alert while they were on the prowl."

Mara shook her head. "It'd be more trouble than it's worth. We need to be able to see the terrain as far ahead of us as possible if we're going to avoid running into dead ends. Besides, this whole forest is dotted with small clearings."

"Through which a glow rod beam would show very clearly to an orbiting ship," he conceded. "Point. You seem to know a lot about this place."

"It wouldn't take more than an observant pilot flying over the forest to see that," she growled. But he was right, she knew, as she eased back against the rough bark. *Know your territory* was the first rule that had been drilled into her . . . and the first thing she'd done after establishing herself in Karrde's organization had been to do precisely that. She'd studied the aerial maps of the forest and surrounding territory; had taken long walks, in both daylight and at night, to familiarize herself with the sights and sounds; had sought out and killed several vornskrs and other predators to learn the fastest ways of taking them down; had even talked one of Karrde's people into running bio tests on a crateload of native plants to find out which were edible and which weren't. Outside the forest, she knew something about the settlers, understood the local politics, and had stashed a small but adequate part of her earnings out where she could get hold of it.

More than anyone else in Karrde's organization, she was equipped to survive outside the confines of his encampment. So why was she trying so hard to get back there?

It wasn't for Karrde's sake—that much she was sure of. All that he'd done for her—her job, her position, her promotions—she'd more than repaid with hard work and good service. She didn't owe him anything, any more than he owed her. Whatever the story was he'd concocted this afternoon to explain the Skipray chase to Thrawn, it would have been designed to protect his own neck, not hers; and if he saw that the Grand Admiral wasn't buying it, he was at perfect liberty to pull his group off Myrkr tonight and disappear down one of the other ratholes he had scattered throughout the galaxy.

Except that he wouldn't. He would sit there, sending out search party after search party, and wait for Mara to come out of the forest. Even if she never did.

Even if by doing so he overstayed Thrawn's patience.

Mara clenched her teeth, the unpleasant image of Karrde pinned against a cell wall by an interrogation droid dancing in front of her eyes. Because she knew Thrawn—knew the Grand Admiral's tenacity and the limits of his patience both. He would wait and watch, or set someone to do it for him, and follow through on Karrde's story.

And if neither she nor Skywalker ever reappeared from the forest, he would almost certainly jump to the wrong conclusion. At which point he would take Karrde in for a professional Imperial interrogation, and eventually would find out who the escaping prisoner had been.

And then he'd have Karrde put to death.

Across from her, the droid's dome rotated a few degrees and it gave a quietly insistent gurgle. "I think Artoo's picked up something," Skywalker said, hiking himself up on his elbows.

"No kidding," Mara said. She picked up her glow rod, pointed it at the shadow she'd already seen moving stealthily toward them, and flicked it on.

A vornskr stood framed in the circle of light, its front claws dug into the ground, its whip tail pointed stiffly back and waving slowly up and down. It paid no attention to the light, but continued moving slowly toward Skywalker.

Mara let it get another two paces, then shot it neatly through the head.

The beast collapsed to the ground, its tail giving one last spasmodic twitch before doing likewise. Mara gave the rest of the area a quick sweep with the glow rod, then flicked it off. "Awfully good thing we have your droid's sensors along," she said sarcastically into the relative darkness.

"Well, *I* wouldn't have known there was any danger without him," Skywalker came back wryly, "Thank you."

"Forget it," she grunted.

There was a short silence. "Are Karrde's pet vornskrs a different species?" Skywalker asked. "Or did he have their tails removed?"

Mara peered across the gloom at him, impressed in spite of herself. Most men staring down a vornskr's gullet wouldn't have noticed a detail like that. "The latter," she told him. "They use those tails as whips—pretty painful, and there's a mild poison in them, too. At first it was just that Karrde didn't want his people walking around with whip welts all over them; we found out later that removing the tails also kills a lot of their normal hunting aggression."

"They seemed pretty domestic," he agreed. "Even friendly."

Only they hadn't been friendly to Skywalker, she remembered. And here, the vornskr had ignored her and gone directly for him. Coincidence? "They are," she said aloud. "He's thought occasionally about offering them for sale as guard animals. Never gotten around to exploring the potential market."

"Well, you can tell him I'd be glad to serve as a reference," Skywalker said dryly. "Having looked a vornskr square in the teeth, I can tell you it's not something the average intruder would like to do twice."

Her lip twisted. "Get used to it," she advised him. "It's a long way to the edge of the forest."

"I know." Skywalker lay back down again. "Fortunately, you seem to be an excellent shot."

He fell silent. Getting ready to sleep . . . and probably assuming she was going to do the same.

Wish away, she thought sardonically at him. Reaching into her pocket, she pulled out the survival kit's tube of stimpills. A steady stream of the things could ruin one's health in short order, but going to sleep five meters away from an enemy would ruin it a lot faster.

She paused, tube in hand, and frowned at Skywalker. At his closed eyes and calm, apparently totally unworried face. Which seemed strange, because if anyone had ever had reason to be worried, it was he. Stripped of all his vaunted Jedi powers by a planetful of ysalamiri, trapped in a forest on a world whose name and location he didn't even know, with her, the Imperials, and the vornskrs lining up for the privilege of killing him—he should by rights be wide-eyed with pumping adrenaline by now.

Maybe he was just faking it, hoping she would lower her guard. It was probably something she would try, under reversed circumstances.

But then, maybe there was more to him than met the eye. More than just a family name, a political position, and a bag of Jedi tricks.

Her mouth tightened, and she ran her fingers along the side of the lightsaber hanging from her belt. Yes, of course there was more there. Whatever had happened at the end—at that terrible, confused, life-destroying end—it hadn't been his Jedi tricks that had saved him. It had been something else. Something she would make sure to find out from him before his own end came.

She thumbed a stimpill from the tube and swallowed

it, a fresh determination surging through her as she did so. No, the vornskrs weren't going to get Luke Skywalker. And neither were the Imperials. When the time came, she would kill him herself. It was her right, and her privilege, and her duty.

Shifting to a more comfortable position against her tree, she settled in to wait out the night.

The nighttime sounds of the forest came faintly from the distance, mixed in with the faint sounds of civilization from the building at his back. Karrde sipped at his cup, gazing into the darkness, feeling fatigue tugging at him as he'd seldom felt it before.

In a single day, his whole life had just been turned over.

Beside him, Drang raised his head and turned it to the right. "Company?" Karrde asked him, looking in that direction. A shadowy figure, hardly visible in the starlight, was moving toward him. "Karrde?" Aves's voice called softly.

"Over here," Karrde told him. "Go get a chair and join me."

"This is okay," Aves said, coming over beside him and sitting down cross-legged on the ground. "I've got to get back to Central pretty soon, anyway."

"The mystery message?"

"Yeah. What in the worlds was Mara thinking of?"

"I don't know," Karrde admitted. "Something clever, though."

"Probably," Aves conceded. "I just hope were going to be clever enough to decrypt it."

Karrde nodded. "Did Solo and Calrissian get bedded down all right?"

"They went back to their ship," Aves said, his voice scowling. "I don't think they trust us."

"Under the circumstances, you can hardly blame them." Karrde reached down to scratch Drang's head. "Maybe pulling Skywalker's computer logs tomorrow morning will help convince them we're on their side."

"Yeah. Are we?"

Karrde pursed his lips. "We don't really have a choice anymore, Aves. They're our guests."

Aves umphed. "The Grand Admiral isn't going to be happy."

Karrde shrugged. "They're our guests," he repeated.

In the darkness, he sensed Aves shrug back. He understood, Aves did—understood the requirements and duties of a host. Unlike Mara, who'd wanted him to send the *Millennium Falcon* away.

He wished now that he'd listened to her. Wished it very much indeed.

"I'll want you to organize a search party for tomorrow morning," he told Aves. "Probably futile, all things considered, but it has to be tried."

"Right. Do we defer to the Imperials in that regard?"

Karrde grimaced to himself. "I doubt if they'll be doing any more searching. That ship that sneaked out from the Star Destroyer an hour ago looked suspiciously like a stripped-down assault shuttle. My guess is that they'll set up in Hyllyard City and wait for Mara and Skywalker to come to them."

"Sounds reasonable," Aves said. "What if we don't get to them first?"

"We'll just have to take them away from the stormtroopers, I suppose. Think you can put a team together for the purpose?"

Aves snorted gently. "Easier done than said. I've sat in on a couple of conversations since you made the announcement, and I can tell you that feelings in camp are running pretty strong. Hero of the Rebellion and all that aside, a bunch of our people figure they owe Skywalker big for getting them out of permanent hock to Jabba the Hutt."

"I know," Karrde said grimly. "And all that warm enthusiasm could be a problem. Because if we can't get Skywalker free from the Imperials . . . well, we can't let them have him alive."

There was a long silence from the shadow beside him. "I see," Aves said at last, very quietly. "It probably won't make any difference, you know, in what Thrawn suspects."

"Suspicion is better than unequivocal proof," Karrde reminded him. "And if we can't intercept them while they're still in the forest, it may be the best we're going to get."

Aves shook his head. "I don't like it."

"Neither do I. But we need to be prepared for every eventuality."

"Understood." For another moment Aves sat there in silence. Then, with a grunted sigh, he stood up. "I'd better get back, see if Ghent's made any progress on Mara's message."

"And after that you'd better hit the sack," Karrde told him. "Tomorrow's going to be a busy day."

"Right. Good night."

Aves left, and once again the soft mixture of forest sounds filled the night air. Sounds that meant a great deal to the creatures who made them but nothing at all to him.

Meaningless sounds . . .

He shook his head tiredly. What *had* Mara been trying to do with that opaque message of hers? Was it something simple—something that he or someone else here ought to be able to decrypt with ease?

Or had the lady who always played the sabacc cards close to her chest finally outsmarted herself?

In the distance, a vornskr emitted its distinctive cackle/purr. Beside his chair, Drang lifted his head. "Friend of yours?" Karrde inquired mildly, listening as another vornskr echoed the first's cry. Sturm and Drang had been wild like that once, before they'd been domesticated.

Just like Mara had been, when he'd first taken her in. He wondered if she would ever be similarly tamed.

Wondered if she would solve this whole problem by killing Skywalker first.

The cackle/purr came again, closer this time. "Come on, Drang," he told the vornskr, getting to his feet. "Time to go inside."

He paused at the door to take one last look at the forest, a shiver of melancholy and something that felt disturbingly like fear running through him. No, the Grand Admiral wasn't going to be happy about this. Wasn't going to be happy at all.

And one way or the other, Karrde knew that his life here was at an end.

CHAPTER 25

T HE ROOM WAS quiet and dark, the faint nighttime
sounds of Rwookrrorro floating in through the mesh
window with the cool night breeze. Staring at the curtains, Leia gripped her blaster with a sweaty hand, and
wondered what had awakened her.

She lay there for several minutes, heart thudding in
her chest. But there was nothing. No sounds, no movements, no threats that her limited Jedi senses could detect. Nothing but a creepy feeling in the back of her mind
that she was no longer safe here.

She took a deep breath, let it out silently as she continued to listen. It wasn't any fault of her hosts, or at
least nothing she could blame them for. The city's leaders
had been on incredibly tight alert the first couple of days,
providing her with over a dozen Wookiee bodyguards
while other volunteers combed through the city like hairy
Imperial Walkers, searching for the alien she'd spotted
that first day here. The whole thing had been carried out

with a speed, efficiency, and thoroughness that Leia had seldom seen even in the top ranks of the Rebel Alliance.

But as the days passed without anyone finding a trace of the alien, the alert had gradually softened. By the time the negative reports also began coming in from other Kashyyyk cities, the number of searchers had dwindled to a handful and the dozen bodyguards had been reduced to three.

And now even those three were gone, returning to their regular jobs and lives. Leaving her with just Chewbacca, Ralrra, and Salporin to watch over her.

It was a classic strategy. Lying alone in the dark, with the advantage of hindsight, she could see that. Sentient beings, human and Wookiee alike, simply could not maintain a continual state of vigilance when there was no visible enemy to be vigilant toward. It was a tendency they'd had to fight hard against in the Alliance.

As they'd also had to fight against the too-often lethal inertia that seduced a person into staying too long in one place.

She winced, memories of the near disaster on the ice world of Hoth coming back to haunt her. She and Chewbacca should have left Rwookrrorro days ago, she knew. Probably should have left Kashyyyk entirely, for that matter. The place had become too comfortable, too familiar—her mind no longer really *saw* everything that went on around her, but merely saw some of it and filled in the rest from memory. It was the kind of psychological weakness that a clever enemy could easily exploit, simply by finding a way to fit himself into her normal routine.

It was time for that routine to be broken.

She peered over at the bedside chrono, did a quick cal-

culation. About an hour until dawn. There was a repulsorlift sled parked just outside; if she and Chewbacca got
going now, they should be able to get the *Lady Luck* into
space a little after sunrise. Sitting halfway up, she slid
across the bed, set her blaster down on the nightstand,
and picked up her comlink.

And in the darkness, a sinewy hand reached out to
seize her wrist.

There was no time to think; but for that first half second there was no need. Even as her mind froze, stunned
by the unexpectedness of the attack, old self-defense reflexes were already swinging into action. Falling away
from her assailant, using the pull on her arm for balance,
she swiveled on her hip, tucked her right leg under her,
and kicked out with all her strength.

The edge of her foot thudded against something
unyielding—body armor of some kind. Reaching back
over her shoulder with her free hand, she grabbed the
corner of her pillow and hurled it at the shadowy outline
of his head.

Under the pillow was her lightsaber.

It was doubtful that he ever saw the blow coming. He
was still in the process of scooping the pillow away from
his face when the ignited lightsaber lit up the room. She
got just a glimpse of huge black eyes and protruding jaw
before the blazing blade sliced him almost in half.

The grip on her arm was abruptly gone. Closing down
the lightsaber, she rolled out of bed and back to her feet,
igniting the weapon again as she looked around—

And with a sudden, numbing blow to her wrist, the
lightsaber was knocked across the room. It shut down in
midflight, plunging the room again into darkness.

She dropped instantly into combat stance, but even as she did so she knew it was a useless gesture. The first alien had perhaps been lulled by the apparent helplessness of his victim; the second had obviously learned the lesson. She hadn't even turned all the way toward the attacker before her wrist was again captured and twisted around behind her. Another hand snaked around to cover her mouth, at the same time jamming her neck hard against the attacker's muzzle. One leg twined somehow around her knees, blocking any attempt she might make to kick him. She tried anyway, struggling to free at least one leg, while at the same time trying to get a clear shot at those eyes with her free hand. His breath was hot on her neck, and she could feel the shapes of needle teeth through the jaw skin pressing against her. The aliens body went abruptly rigid—

And suddenly, without any warning at all, she was free.

She spun around to face the alien, fighting to regain her balance in the sudden loss of anything solid to lean against and wondering what this new game was he was playing. Her eyes searched frantically in the dim light, trying to locate the weapon he was surely now bringing to bear on her—

But there was no weapon pointed at her. The alien just stood there, his back to the door, his empty hands splayed off to the sides as if preparing to protect himself from a backwards fall. "*Mal'ary'ush,*" he hissed, his voice soft and gravelly. Leia took a step backwards, wondering if she could get to the window before he launched his next attack.

The attack never came. Behind the alien, the door

slammed open; and with a roar, Chewbacca boiled into the room.

The attacker didn't turn. He made no move at all, in fact, as the Wookiee leaped toward him, massive hands reaching for his neck—

"Don't kill him!" Leia snapped.

The words probably startled Chewbacca almost as much as they startled her. But the Wookiee's reflexes were equal to the task. Passing up the alien's throat, he swung a hand instead to cuff him solidly across the side of the head.

The blow sent the alien flying halfway across the room and up against the wall. He slid down and remained still.

"Come on," Leia said, rolling across her bed to retrieve her lightsaber. "There may be more of them."

[Not any morre,] a Wookiee voice rumbled, and she looked up to see Ralrra leaning against the doorway. [The otherr three have been dealt with.]

"Are you sure?" Leia asked, taking a step toward him. He was still leaning against the doorjamb—

Leaning *hard* against it, she suddenly realized. "You're hurt," she exclaimed, flicking on the room light and giving him a quick examination. There were no marks she could see. "Blaster?"

[Stun weapon,] he corrected. [A quieterr weapon, but it was set too low forr Wookiees. I am only a little weak. Chewbacca it is who is wounded.]

Startled, Leia looked over at Chewbacca . . . and for the first time saw the small patch of matted brown hair midway down his torso. "Chewie!" she breathed, starting toward him.

He waved her away with an impatient growl. [He is

right,] Ralrra agreed. [We must get you away from herre, beforre the second attack comes.]

From somewhere outside a Wookiee began howling an alert. "There won't be a second attack," she told Ralrra. "They've been noticed—there'll be people converging on this house in minutes."

[Not on this house,] Ralrra rumbled, a strange grimness to his voice. [Therre is a firre fourr houses away.]

Leia stared at him, a chill running up her back. "A diversion," she murmured. "They set a house on fire to mask any alert you try to make."

Chewbacca growled an affirmative. [We must get you away from herre,] Ralrra repeated, easing himself carefully upright.

Leia glanced past him through the doorway to the darker hallway beyond, a strange dread suddenly twisting into her stomach. There had been *three* Wookiees in the house with her. "Where's Salporin?" she asked.

Ralrra hesitated, just long enough for her suspicions to become a terrible certainty. [He did not survive the attack,] the Wookiee said, almost too softly for her to hear.

Leia swallowed hard. "I'm sorry," she said, the words sounding painfully trite and meaningless in her ears.

[As arre we. But the time forr mourning is not now.]

Leia nodded, blinking back sudden tears as she turned to the window. She'd lost many friends and companions in the midst of battle through the years, and she knew that Ralrra was right. But all the logic in the universe didn't make it any easier.

There were no aliens visible outside. But they were there—that much she was sure of. Both of the previous teams she and Han had tangled with had consisted of considerably more than five members, and there was no reason to expect this one to be any different. Chances were that any attempt to escape overland would meet with a quick ambush.

Worse, as soon as the hue and cry over the burning house really got going, the aliens could likely launch a second attack with impunity, counting on the commotion down the street to cover up any noise they made in the process.

She glanced at the burning house, feeling a brief pang of guilt for the Wookiees who owned it. Resolutely, she forced the emotion out of her mind. There, too, there was nothing she could do for now. "The aliens seem to want me alive," she said, dropping the edge of the curtain and turning back to Chewbacca and Ralrra. "If we can get the sled into the sky, they probably won't try to shoot us down."

[Do you trust the sled?] Ralrra asked pointedly.

Leia stopped short, lips pressed tightly together in annoyance with herself. No, of course she didn't trust the sled—the first thing the aliens would have done would have been to disable any escape vehicle within reach. Disable it, or worse: they could have modified it to simply fly her directly into their arms.

She couldn't stay put; she couldn't go sideways; and she couldn't go up. Which left exactly one direction.

"I'll need some rope," she said, scooping up an armful of clothes and starting to get dressed. "Strong enough to hold my weight. As much as you've got."

They were fast, all right. A quick glance between

them—[You cannot be serious,] Ralrra told her. [The dangerr would be great even forr a Wookiee. Forr a human it would be suicide.]

"I don't think so," Leia shook her head, pulling on her boots. "I saw how the branches twist together, when we looked at the bottom of the city. It should be possible for me to climb along between them."

[You will neverr reach the landing platform alone,] Ralrra objected. [We will come with you.]

"You're in no shape to travel down the street, let alone underneath it," Leia countered bluntly. She picked up her blaster, holstered it, and stepped to the doorway. "Neither is Chewbacca. Get out of my way, please."

Ralrra didn't budge. [You do not fool us, Leiaorrganasolo. You believe that if we stay herre the enemy will follow you and leave us in peace.]

Leia grimaced. So much for the quiet, noble self-sacrifice. "There's a good chance they will," she insisted. "It's me they want. And they want me alive."

[Therre is no time to argue,] Ralrra said. [We will stay togetherr. Herre, orr underr the city.]

Leia took a deep breath. She didn't like it, but it was clear she wasn't going to be able to talk them out of it. "All right, you win," she sighed. The alien Chewbacca had hit was still lying unconscious, and for a moment she debated whether or not they dared take the time to tie him up. The need for haste won. "Let's find some rope and get moving."

And besides, a small voice in the back of her head reminded her, even if she went alone, the aliens might still attack the house. And might prefer leaving no witnesses behind.

———

THE FLAT, SOMEWHAT spongy material that formed the "ground" of Rwookrrorro was less than a meter thick. Leia's lightsaber cut through both it and the house's floor with ease, dropping a roughly square chunk between the braided branches to vanish into the darkness below.

[I will go first,] Ralrra said, dropping into the hole before anyone could argue the point. He was still moving a little slowly, but at least the stun-induced dizzy spells seemed to have passed.

Leia looked up as Chewbacca stepped close to her and flipped Ralrra's baldric around her shoulders. "Last chance to change your mind about this arrangement," she warned him.

His answer was short and to the point. By the time Ralrra's quiet [All clearr] floated up, they were ready.

And with Leia strapped firmly to his torso, Chewbacca eased his way through the hole.

Leia had fully expected the experience to be unpleasant. She hadn't realized that it was going to be terrifying, as well. The Wookiees didn't crawl across the tops of the plaited branches, the way she'd anticipated doing. Instead, using the climbing claws she'd seen her first day here, they hung by all fours underneath the branches to travel.

And then they *traveled*.

The side of her face pressed against Chewbacca's hairy chest, Leia clenched her teeth tightly together, partly to keep them from chattering with the bouncing, but mostly to keep moans of fear from escaping. It was like the acrophobia she'd felt in the liftcar, multiplied by a thousand.

Here, there wasn't even a relatively thick vine between her and the nothingness below—only Wookiee claws and the thin rope connecting them to another set of Wookiee claws. She wanted to say something—to plead that they stop and at least belay the end of their rope to something solid—but she was afraid to make even a sound lest it break Chewbacca's concentration. The sound of his breathing was like the roar of a waterfall in her ears, and she could feel the warm wetness of his blood seeping through the thin material of her undertunic. How badly had he been hurt? Huddled against him, listening to his heart pounding, she was afraid to ask.

Abruptly, he stopped.

She opened her eyes, unaware until that moment that she'd closed them. "What's wrong?" she asked, her voice trembling.

[The enemy has found us,] Ralrra growled softly from beside her.

Bracing herself, Leia turned her head as far as she could, searching the dark predawn gray behind them. There it was: a small patch of darker black set motionlessly against it. A repulsorlift airspeeder of some kind, staying well back out of bowcaster range. "It couldn't be a Wookiee rescue ship, I don't suppose," she offered hopefully.

Chewbacca growled the obvious flaw: the airspeeder wasn't showing even running lights. [Yet it does not approach,] Ralrra pointed out.

"They want me alive," Leia said, more to reassure herself than to remind them. "They don't want to spook us." She looked around, searching the void around them and the matted branches above them for inspiration.

And found it. "I need the rest of the rope," she told Ralrra, peering back at the hovering airspeeder. "All of it."

Steeling herself, she twisted partway around in her makeshift harness, taking the coil he gave her and tying one end securely to one of the smaller branches. Chewbacca growled an objection. "No, I'm not belaying us," she assured him. "So don't fall. I've got something else in mind. Okay, let's go."

They set off again, perhaps a shade faster than before . . . and as she bounced along against Chewbacca's torso, Leia realized with mild surprise that while she was still frightened, she was no longer terrified. Perhaps, she decided, because she was no longer simply a pawn or excess baggage, with her fate totally in the hands of Wookiees or gray-skinned aliens or the forces of gravity. *She* was now at least partially in control of what happened.

They continued on, Leia playing out the rope as they traveled. The dark airspeeder followed, still without lights, still keeping well back from them. She kept an eye on it as they bounced along, knowing that the timing and distance on this were going to be crucial. Just a little bit farther . . .

There were perhaps three meters of rope left in the coil. Quickly, she tied a firm knot and peered back at their pursuer. "Get ready," she said to Chewbacca. "Now . . . *stop.*"

Chewbacca came to a halt. Mentally crossing her fingers, Leia ignited her lightsaber beneath the Wookiee's back, locked it on, and let it drop.

And like a blazing chunk of wayward lightning, it fell away, swinging down and back on the end of the rope in a long pendulum arc. It reached bottom and swung back up the other direction—

And into the underside of the airspeeder.

There was a spectacular flash as the lightsaber blade sliced through the repulsorlift generator. An instant later the airspeeder was dropping like a stone, two separate blazes flaring from either side. The craft fell into the mists below, and for a long moment the fires were visible as first two, and then as a single diffuse spot of light. Then even that faded, leaving only the lightsaber swinging gently in the darkness.

Leia took a shuddering breath. "Let's go retrieve the lightsaber," she told Chewbacca. "After that, I think we can probably just cut our way back up. I doubt there are any of them left now."

[And then directly to yourr ship?] Ralrra asked as they headed back to the branch where she'd tied the rope.

Leia hesitated, the image of that second alien in her room coming back to mind. Standing there facing her, an unreadable emotion in face and body language, so stunned or enraptured or frightened that he didn't even notice Chewbacca's entry . . . "Back to the ship," she answered Ralrra. "But not directly."

THE ALIEN WAS sitting motionless in a low seat in the tiny police interrogation room, a small bandage on the side of his head the only external evidence of Chewbacca's blow. His hands were resting in his lap, the fingers laced intricately together. Stripped of all clothing and equipment, he'd been given a loose Wookiee robe to wear. On someone else the effect of the outsized garment might have been comical. But not on him. Neither the robe nor his inactivity did anything to hide the aura of deadly competence that he wore like a second skin. He was—probably always would be—a member of a dangerous and persistent group of trained killing machines.

And he'd asked specifically to see Leia. In person.

Towering beside her, Chewbacca growled one final objection. "I don't much like it either," Leia conceded, gazing at the monitor display and trying to screw up her courage. "But he let me go back at the house, before you came in. I want to know—I *need* to know—what that was all about."

Briefly, her conversation with Luke on the eve of the Battle of Endor flashed to mind. His quiet firmness, in the face of all her fears, that confronting Darth Vader was something he had to do. That decision had nearly killed him . . . and had ultimately brought them victory.

But Luke had felt some faint wisps of good still buried deep inside Vader. Did she feel something similar in this alien killer? Or was she driven merely by morbid curiosity?

Or perhaps by mercy?

"You can watch and listen from here," she told Chewbacca, handing him her blaster and stepping to the door. The lightsaber she left hooked onto her belt, though what use it would be in such close quarters she didn't know. "Don't come in unless I'm in trouble." Taking a deep breath, she unlocked the door and pressed the release.

The alien looked up as the door slid open, and it seemed to Leia that he sat up straighter as she stepped inside. The door slid shut behind her, and for a long moment they just eyed each other. "I'm Leia Organa Solo," she said at last. "You wanted to talk to me?"

He gazed at her for another moment. Then, slowly, he stood up and reached out a hand. "Your hand," he said, his voice gravelly and strangely accented. "May I have it?"

Leia took a step forward and offered him her hand, acutely aware that she had just committed an irrevocable act of trust. From here, if he so chose, he could pull her to him and snap her neck before anyone outside could possibly intervene.

He didn't pull her toward him. Leaning forward, holding her hand in an oddly gentle grip, he raised it to his snout and pressed it against two large nostrils half hidden beneath strands of hair.

And smelled it.

He smelled it again, and again, taking long, deep breaths. Leia found herself staring at his nostrils, noticing for the first time their size and the soft flexibility of the skin folds around them. Like those of a tracking animal, she realized. A memory flashed to mind: how, as he'd held her helpless back at the house, those same nostrils had been pressed into her neck.

And right after that was when he'd let her go . . .

Slowly, almost tenderly, the alien straightened up. "It is then true," he grated, releasing her hand and letting his own fall to his side. Those huge eyes stared at her, brimming with an emotion whose nature her Jedi skills could vaguely sense but couldn't begin to identify. "I was not mistaken before."

Abruptly, he dropped to both knees. "I seek forgiveness, Leia Organa Solo, for my actions," he said, ducking his head to the floor, his hands splayed out to the sides as they had been in that encounter back at the house. "Our orders did not identify you, but gave only your name."

"I understand," she nodded, wishing she did. "But now you know who I am?"

The alien's face dropped a couple of centimeters closer to the floor. "You are the *Mal'ary'ush*," he said. "The daughter and heir of the Lord Darth Vader.

"He who was our master."

Leia stared down at him, feeling her mouth fall open as she struggled to regain her mental balance. The right-angle turns were all coming too quickly. "Your master?" she repeated carefully.

"He who came to us in our desperate need," the alien said, his voice almost reverent. "Who lifted us from our despair, and gave us hope."

"I see," she managed. This whole thing was rapidly becoming unreal . . . but one fact already stood out. The alien prostrating himself before her was prepared to treat her as royalty.

And she knew how to behave like royalty.

"You may rise," she told him, feeling her voice and posture and manner settling into the almost-forgotten patterns of the Alderaanian court. "What is your name?"

"I am called Khabarakh by our lord," the alien said, getting to his feet. "In the language of the Noghri—" He made a long, convoluted roiling noise that Leia's vocal cords didn't have a hope of imitating.

"I'll call you Khabarakh," she said. "Your people are called the Noghri?"

"Yes." The first hint of uncertainty seemed to cross the dark eyes. "But you are the *Mal'ary'ush*," he added, with obvious question.

"My father had many secrets," she told him grimly. "You, obviously, were one of them. You said he brought you hope. Tell me how."

"He came to us," the Noghri said. "After the mighty battle. After the destruction."

"What battle?"

Khabarakh's eyes seemed to drift into memory. "Two great starships met in the space over our world," he said, his gravelly voice low. "Perhaps more than two; we never knew for certain. They fought all the day and much of the night . . . and when the battle was over, our land was devastated."

Leia winced, a pang of sympathetic ache running through her. Of ache, and of guilt. "We never hurt non-Imperial forces or worlds on purpose," she said softly. "Whatever happened, it was an accident."

The dark eyes fixed again on her. "The Lord Vader did not think so. He believed it was done on purpose, to drive fear and terror into the souls of the Emperor's enemies."

"Then the Lord Vader was mistaken," Leia said, meeting that gaze firmly. "Our battle was with the Emperor, not his subjugated servants."

Khabarakh drew himself up stiffly. "We were not the Emperor's servants," he grated. "We were a simple people, content to live our lives without concern for the dealings of others."

"You serve the Empire now," Leia pointed out.

"In return for the Emperor's help," Khabarakh said, a

hint of pride showing through his deference. "Only he came to our aid when we so desperately needed it. In his memory, we serve his designated heir—the man to whom the Lord Vader long ago entrusted us."

"I find it difficult to believe the Emperor ever really cared about you," Leia told him bluntly. "That's not the sort of man he was. All he cared about was obtaining your service against us."

"Only he came to our aid," Khabarakh repeated.

"Because we were unaware of your plight," Leia told him.

"So you say."

Leia raised her eyebrows. "Then give me a chance to prove it. Tell me where your world is."

Khabarakh jerked back. "That is impossible. You would seek us out and complete the destruction—"

"Khabarakh," Leia cut him off. "Who am I?"

The folds around the Noghri's nostrils seemed to flatten. "You are the Lady Vader. The *Mal'ary'ush*."

"Did the Lord Vader ever lie to you?"

"You said he did."

"I said he was mistaken," Leia reminded him, perspiration starting to collect beneath her collar as she recognized the knife edge she was now walking along here. Her newfound status with Khabarakh rested solely on the Noghri's reverence for Darth Vader. Somehow, she had to attack Vader's words without simultaneously damaging that respect. "Even the Lord Vader could be deceived . . . and the Emperor was a master of deception."

"The Lord Vader served the Emperor," Khabarakh insisted. "The Emperor would not have lied to him."

Leia gritted her teeth. Stalemate. "Is your new lord equally honest with you?"

Khabarakh hesitated. "I don't know."

"Yes, you do—you said yourself he didn't tell you who it was you'd been sent to capture."

A strange sort of low moan rumbled in Khabarakh's throat. "I am only a soldier, my lady. These matters are far beyond my authority and ability. My duty is to obey my orders. *All* of my orders."

Leia frowned. Something about the way he'd said that . . . and abruptly, she knew what it was. For a captured commando facing interrogation, there could be only one order left to follow. "Yet you now know something none of your people are aware of," she said quickly. "You must live, to bring this information to them."

Khabarakh had brought his palms to face each other, as if preparing to clap them together. Now he froze, staring at her. "The Lord Vader could read the souls of the Noghri," he said softly. "You are indeed his *Mal'ary'ush*."

"Your people need you, Khabarakh," she told him. "As do I. Your death now would only hurt those you seek to help."

Slowly, he lowered his hands. "How is it you need me?"

"Because I need your help if I'm to do anything for your people," she said. "You must tell me the location of your world."

"I cannot," he said firmly. "To do so could bring ultimate destruction upon my world. And upon me, if it were learned I had given you such information."

Leia pursed her lips. "Then take me there."

"I cannot!"

"Why not?"

"I . . . cannot."

She fixed him with her best regal stare. "I am the daughter—the *Mal'ary'ush*—of the Lord Darth Vader," she said firmly. "By your own admission, he was the hope of your world. Have matters improved since he delivered you to your new leader?"

He hesitated. "No. He has told us there is little more that he or anyone else can do."

"I would prefer to judge that for myself," she told him loftily. "Or would your people consider a single human to be such a threat?"

Khabarakh twitched. "You would come alone? To a people seeking your capture?"

Leia swallowed hard, a shiver running down her back. No, she hadn't meant to imply that. But then, she hadn't been sure of why she'd wanted to talk to Khabarakh in the first place. She could only hope that the Force was guiding her intuition in all this. "I trust your people to be honorable," she said quietly. "I trust them to grant me a hearing."

She turned and stepped to the door. "Consider my offer," she told him. "Discuss it with those whose counsel you value. Then, if you choose, meet me in orbit above the world of Endor in one month's time."

"You will come alone?" Khabarakh asked, apparently still not believing it.

She turned and looked him straight in that nightmare face. "I will come alone. Will you?"

He faced her stare without flinching. "If I come," he said, "I will come alone."

She held his gaze a moment longer, then nodded. "I hope to see you there. Farewell."

"Farewell . . . Lady Vader."

He was still staring at her as the door opened and she left.

THE TINY SHIP shot upward through the clouds, vanishing quickly from the Rwookrrorro air-control visual monitor. Beside Leia, Chewbacca growled angrily. "I can't say I'm really happy with it, either," she confessed. "But we can't dodge them forever. If we have even a chance of getting them out from under Imperial control . . ." She shook her head.

Chewbacca growled again. "I know," she said softly, some of his pain finding its way into her own heart. "I wasn't as close to Salporin as you were, but he was still my friend."

The Wookiee turned away from the monitors and stomped across the room. Leia watched him, wishing there was something she could do to help. But there wasn't. Caught between conflicting demands of honor, he would have to work this out in the privacy of his own mind.

Behind her, someone stirred. [It is time,] Ralrra said. [The memorial period has begun. We must join the otherrs.]

Chewbacca growled an acknowledgment and went over to join him. Leia looked at Ralrra—[This period is forr Wookiees only,] he rumbled. [Laterr, you will be permitted to join us.]

"I understand," Leia said. "If you need me, I'll be on the landing platform, getting the *Lady Luck* ready to fly."

[If you truly feel it is safe to leave,] Ralrra said, still sounding doubtful.

"It is," Leia told him. And even if it wasn't, she added silently to herself, she would still have no choice. She had a species name now—Noghri—and it was vital that she return to Coruscant and get another records search underway.

[Very well. The mourning period will begin in two hourrs.]

Leia nodded, blinking back tears. "I'll be there," she promised.

And wondered if this war would ever truly be over.

CHAPTER 26

THE MASS OF vines hung twisted around and between half a dozen trees, looking like the web of a giant spider gone berserk. Fingering Skywalker's lightsaber, Mara studied the tangle, trying to figure out the fastest way to clear the path.

Out of the corner of her eye, she saw Skywalker fidgeting. "Just keep your shirt on," she told him. "This'll only take a minute."

"You really don't have to go for finesse, you know," he offered. "It's not like the lightsaber's running low on power."

"Yes, but *we're* running low on forest," she retorted. "You have any idea how far the hum of a lightsaber can carry in woods like this?"

"Not really."

"Me, neither. I'd like to keep it that way." She shifted her blaster to her left hand, ignited the lightsaber with her right, and made three quick cuts. The tangle of vines

STAR WARS: HEIR TO THE EMPIRE

dropped to the ground as she closed the weapon down. "That wasn't so hard, now, was it?" she said, turning to face Skywalker and hooking the lightsaber back onto her belt. She started to turn away—

The droid's warning squeal came a fraction of a second before the sudden rustle of leaves. She whirled back, flipping her blaster into her right hand as the vornskr leaped toward Skywalker from a branch three trees away.

Even after two long days of travel, Skywalker's reflexes were still adequate to the task. He let go the handles of the travois and dropped to the ground just ahead of the vornskr's trajectory. Four sets of claws and a whip tail took a concerted swipe at him as the predator shot by overhead. Mara waited until it had landed, and as it spun back around toward its intended prey, she shot it.

Cautiously, Skywalker got back to his feet and looked warily around. "I wish you'd change your mind about giving me back my lightsaber," he commented as he bent down to pick up the travois handles again. "You must be getting tired of shooting vornskrs off me."

"What, you afraid I'm going to miss?" she retorted, stepping over to prod the vornskr with her foot. It was dead, all right.

"You're an excellent shot," he conceded, dragging the travois toward the tangle of vines she'd just cleared out. "But you've also gone two nights without any sleep. That's going to catch up with you eventually."

"You just worry about yourself," she snapped. "Come on, get moving—we need to find someplace clear enough to send up the sonde balloon."

Skywalker headed off, the droid strapped to the travois behind him beeping softly to itself. Mara brought up the rear, watching to make sure the travois wasn't leaving too clear a trail and scowling hard at the back of Skywalker's head.

The really irritating part was that he was right. That pass from left to right hand a minute ago—a technique she'd done a thousand times before—she'd come within a hair of missing the catch completely. Her heart thudded constantly now, not quieting down even during rest. And there were long periods during their march where her mind simply drifted, instead of focusing on the task at hand.

Once, long ago, she'd gone six days without sleep. Now, after only two, she was already starting to fall apart.

She clenched her teeth and scowled a little harder. If he was hoping to see the collapse, he was going to be sorely disappointed. If for no other reason than professional pride, she was going to see this through.

Ahead, Skywalker stumbled slightly as he crossed a patch of rough ground. The right travois handle slipped out of his grip, nearly dumping the droid off the travois and eliciting a squeal of protest from the machine. "So who's getting tired now?" Mara growled as he stooped to pick up the stick again. "That's the third time in the past hour."

"It's just my hand," he replied calmly. "It seems to be permanently numb this afternoon."

"Sure," she said. Ahead, a small patch of blue sky winked down through the tree branches. "There's our hole," she said, nodding to it. "Put the droid in the middle."

Skywalker did as he was instructed, then went and sat

down against one of the trees edging the tiny clearing.
Mara got the small sonde balloon filled and sent it aloft
on its antenna wire, running a line from the receiver into
the socket where the droid's retrieval jack had once been.
"All set," she said, glancing over at Skywalker.

Leaning back against his tree, he was sound asleep.

Mara snorted with contempt. *Jedi!* she threw the epi-
thet at him as she turned back to the droid. "Come on,
let's get going," she told it, sitting down carefully on the
ground. Her twisted ankle seemed to be largely healed,
but she knew better than to push it.

The droid beeped questioningly, its dome swiveling
around to look briefly at Skywalker. "I said let's get
going," she repeated harshly.

The droid beeped again, a resigned sort of sound. The
communicator's pulse indicator flashed once as the droid
requested a message dump from the distant X-wing's
computer; flashed again as the dump came back.

Abruptly the droid squealed in obvious excitement.
"What?" Mara demanded, snatching out her blaster and
giving the area a quick scan. Nothing seemed out of
place. "What, there's finally a message?"

The droid beeped affirmatively, its dome again turning toward Skywalker. "Well, let's have it," Mara growled.
"Come on—if there's anything in it he needs to hear, you
can play it for him later."

Assuming—she didn't add—there wasn't anything in
the message that suggested she needed to come out of
the forest alone. If there was . . .

The droid bent forward slightly, and a holographic
image appeared on the matted leaves.

But not an image of Karrde, as she'd expected. It was,

instead, an image of a golden-skinned protocol droid. "Good day, Master Luke," the protocol droid said in a remarkably prissy voice. "I bring greetings to you from Captain Karrde—and, of course, to you as well, Mistress Mara," it added, almost as an afterthought. "He and Captain Solo are most pleased to hear you are both alive and well after your accident."

Captain Solo? Mara stared at the holograph, feeling totally stunned. What in the Empire did Karrde think he was doing?—he'd actually *told* Solo and Calrissian about Skywalker?

"I trust you'll be able to decrypt this message, Artoo," the protocol prissily continued. "Captain Karrde suggested that I be used to add a bit more confusion to the counterpart encrypt. According to him, there are Imperial stormtroopers waiting in Hyllyard City for you to make your appearance."

Mara clenched her teeth, throwing a look at her sleeping prisoner. So Thrawn hadn't been fooled. He knew Skywalker was here, and was waiting to take them both.

With a vicious effort, she stifled the fatigue-fed panic rising in her throat. No. Thrawn didn't *know*—at least, not for sure. He only suspected. If he'd known for sure, there wouldn't have been anyone left back at the camp to send her this message.

"The story Captain Karrde told the Imperials was that a former employee stole valuable merchandise and tried to escape, with a current employee named Jade in pursuit. He suggests that, since he never specified Jade as being a woman, that perhaps you and Mistress Mara could switch roles when you leave the forest."

"Right," Mara muttered under her breath. If Karrde thought she was going to cheerfully hand her blaster over for Skywalker to stick in her back, he'd better try thinking again.

"At any rate," the protocol droid continued, "he says he and Captain Solo are working out a plan to try to intercept you before the stormtroopers do. If not, they will do their best to rescue you from them. I'm afraid there's nothing more I can say at the moment—Captain Karrde has put a one-minute real-time limit on this message, to prevent anyone from locating the transmission point. He wishes you good luck. Take good care of Master Luke, Artoo . . . and yourself, too."

The image vanished and the droid's projector winked out. Mara shut down the communicator, setting the antenna spool to begin winding the balloon back down.

"It's a good idea," Skywalker murmured.

She looked sharply at him. His eyes were still closed. "I *thought* you were faking," she spat, not really truthfully.

"Not faking," he corrected her sleepily. "Drifting in and out. It's still a good idea."

She snorted. "Forget it. We'll try going a couple of kilometers north instead, circling out and back to Hyllyard from the plains." She glanced at her chrono, then up through the trees. Dark clouds had moved in over the past few minutes, covering the blue sky that had been there. Not rain clouds, she decided, but they would still cut rather strongly into what was left of the available daylight. "We might as well save that for tomorrow," she said, favoring her ankle again as she got back to her feet.

"You want to get—oh, never mind," she interrupted herself. If his breathing was anything to go by, he'd drifted off again.

Which left the task of putting camp together up to her. Terrific. "Stay put," she growled to the droid. She turned back to where she'd dropped the survival kit—

The droid's electronic shriek brought her spinning back around again, hand clawing for her blaster, eyes flicking around for the danger—

And then a heavy weight slammed full onto her shoulders and back, sending hot needles of pain into her skin and throwing her face-first to the ground.

Her last thought, before the darkness took her, was to wish desperately that she'd killed Skywalker when she'd had the chance.

ARTOO'S WARBLING ALERT jerked Luke out of his doze. His eyes snapped open, just as a blur of muscle and claw launched itself through space onto Mara's back.

He bounded to his feet, sleepiness abruptly gone. The vornskr was standing over Mara, its front claws planted on her shoulders, its head turned to the side as it prepared to sink its teeth into her neck. Mara herself lay unmoving, the back of her head toward Luke—dead or merely stunned, it was impossible to tell. Artoo, clearly too far away to reach her in time, was nevertheless moving in that direction as fast as his wheels could manage, his small electric arc welder extended as if for battle.

Taking a deep breath, Luke screamed.

Not an ordinary scream; but a shivering, booming, inhuman howl that seemed to fill the entire clearing and reverberate back from the distant hills. It was the blood-freezing call of a krayt dragon, the same call Ben Kenobi had used to scare the sand people away from him all those years ago on Tatooine.

The vornskr wasn't scared away. But it was clearly startled, its prey temporarily forgotten. Shifting its weight partially off Mara's back, it turned, crouching, to stare toward the sound.

For a long moment Luke locked gazes with the creature, afraid to move lest he break the spell. If he could distract it long enough for Artoo to get there with his welder . . .

And then, still pinned to the ground, Mara twitched. Luke cupped his hands around his mouth and howled again. Again, the vornskr shifted its weight in response.

And with a sound that was half grunt and half combat yell, Mara twisted around onto her back beneath the predator, her hands snaking past the front claws to grip its throat.

It was the only opening Luke was going to get; and with a vornskr against an injured human, it wasn't going to last for long. Pushing off from the tree trunk behind him, Luke charged, aiming for the vornskr's flank.

He never got there. Even as he braced himself for the impact, the vornskr's whip tail whistled out of nowhere to catch him solidly along shoulder and face and send him sprawling sideways to the ground.

He was on his feet again in an instant, dimly aware of the line of fire burning across cheek and forehead. The vornskr hissed as he came toward it again, slashing razor-sharp claws at him to ward him back. Artoo reached the struggle and sent a spark into the predator's left front paw; almost casually, the vornskr swung at the welder, snapping it off and sending the pieces flying. Simultaneously, the tail whipped around, the impact lifting Artoo up on one set of wheels. It swung again and again, each time coming closer to knocking the droid over.

Luke gritted his teeth, mind searching furiously for a plan. Shadowboxing at the creature's head like this wasn't anything more than a delaying tactic; but the minute the distraction ceased, Mara was as good as dead. The vornskr would either slash her arms with its claws or else simply overwhelm her grip by brute force. With the loss of his welder, Artoo had no fighting capability left; and if the vornskr kept at him with that whip tail . . .

The tail. "Artoo!" Luke snapped. "Next time that tail hits you, try to grab it."

Artoo beeped a shaky acknowledgment and extended his heavy grasping arm. Luke watched out of the corner of his eye, still trying to keep the vornskr's head and front paws busy. The tail whipped around again, and with a warble of triumph, Artoo caught it.

A warble that turned quickly into a screech. Again with almost casual strength, the vornskr ripped its tail free, taking most of the grasping arm with it.

But it had been pinned out of action for a pair of heartbeats, and that was all the time Luke needed. Diving around Artoo's bulk and under the trapped whip tail, he darted his hand to Mara's side and snatched back his lightsaber.

The whip tail slashed toward him as he rolled back to his feet, but by the time it got there Luke was out of range around Artoo's side again. Igniting the lightsaber, he reached the blazing blade past the flailing claws and brushed the vornskrs nose.

The predator screamed, in anger or pain, shying back from this bizarre creature that had bit it. Luke tapped it again and again, trying to drive it away from Mara where he could safely deliver a killing blow.

Abruptly, in a single smooth motion, the vornskr leaped backwards onto solid ground, then sprang straight at Luke. Also in a single smooth motion, Luke cut it in half.

"About time," a hoarse voice croaked from beneath his feet. He looked down to see Mara push half the dead vornskr off her chest and raise herself up on one elbow. "What in blazes was that stupid game you were playing?"

"I didn't think you'd like your hands cut off if I missed," Luke told her, breathing hard. He took a step back as she sat up and offered her a helping hand.

She waved the hand away. Rolling slowly onto hands and knees, she pushed herself tiredly to her feet and turned back to face him.

With her blaster back in her hand.

"Just drop the lightsaber and move back," she panted, gesturing with the weapon for emphasis.

Luke sighed, shaking his head. "I don't believe you," he said, shutting down the lightsaber and dropping it onto the ground. The adrenaline was receding from his system now, leaving both face and shoulder aching like fury. "Or didn't you notice that Artoo and I just saved your life?"

"I noticed. Thanks." Keeping her blaster trained on him, Mara stooped to retrieve the lightsaber. "I figure that's my reward for not shooting you two days ago. Get over there and sit down."

Luke looked over at Artoo, who was moaning softly to himself. "Do you mind if I look at Artoo first?"

Mara looked down at the droid, her lips compressed into a thin line. "Sure, go ahead." Moving clear of both of them, she picked up the survival pack and trudged off to one of the trees at the edge of the clearing.

Artoo wasn't in as bad shape as Luke had feared. Both the welder and the grasping arm had broken off cleanly, leaving no trailing wires or partial components that might get caught on something else. Speaking quiet encouragement to the droid, Luke got the two compartments sealed.

"Well?" Mara asked, sitting with her back to a tree and gingerly applying salve to the oozing claw marks on her arms.

"He's okay for now," Luke told her as he went back over to his own tree and sat down. "He's been damaged worse than this before."

"I'm so glad to hear it," she said sourly. She glanced at Luke, took a longer look. "He got you good, didn't he?"

Carefully, Luke touched the welt running across his cheek and forehead. "I'll be all right."

She snorted. "Sure you will," she said, her voice laced with sarcasm as she went back to treating her gashes. "I forgot—you're a hero, too."

For a long minute Luke watched her, trying once more to understand the complexities and contradictions of this strange woman. Even from three meters away he could see that her hand was shaking as she applied the salve: with reaction, perhaps, or muscle fatigue. Almost certainly with fear—she'd escaped a bloody death by a bare handful of centimeters, and she would have to be a fool not to recognize that.

And yet, whatever she was feeling inside, she was clearly determined not to let any of it out past that rock-hard surface she'd so carefully built up around herself. As if she was afraid to let weakness of any sort show through . . .

Abruptly, as if feeling his eyes on her, Mara looked up. "I said thanks already," she growled. "What do you want, a medal?"

Luke shook his head. "I just want to know what happened to you."

For a moment those green eyes flashed again with the old hatred. But only for a moment. The vornskr attack, coming on top of two days of laborious travel and no sleep, had taken a severe toll on her emotional strength. The anger faded from her eyes, leaving only a tired coldness behind. "*You* happened to me," she told him, her voice more fatigued than embittered. "You came out of a grubby sixth-rate farm on a tenth-rate planet, and destroyed my life."

"How?"

Contempt briefly filled her face. "You don't have the faintest idea who I am, do you?"

Luke shook his head. "I'm sure I'd remember you if we'd met."

"Oh, right," she said sardonically. "The great, omniscient Jedi. See all, hear all, know all, understand all. No, we didn't actually meet; but I was there, if you'd bothered to notice me. I was a dancer at Jabba the Hutt's palace the day you came for Solo."

So that was it. She'd worked for Jabba; and when he'd killed Jabba, he'd ruined her life . . .

Luke frowned at her. No. Her slim figure, her agility and grace—those certainly could belong to a professional dancer. But her piloting skills, her expert marksmanship, her inexplicable working knowledge of lightsabers—those most certainly did not.

Mara was still waiting, daring him with her expression to figure it out. "You weren't just a dancer, though," he told her. "That was only a cover."

Her lip twisted. "Very good. That vaunted Jedi insight, no doubt. Keep going; you're doing so well. What was I really doing there?"

Luke hesitated. There were all sorts of possibilities for this one: bounty hunter, smuggler, quiet bodyguard for Jabba, spy from some rival criminal organization . . .

No. Her knowledge of lightsabers . . . and suddenly, all the pieces fell together with a rush. "You were waiting for me," he said. "Vader knew I'd go there to try and rescue Han, and he sent you to capture me."

"Vader?" She all but spat the name. "Don't make me laugh. Vader was a fool, and skating on the edge of treason along with it. My master sent me to Jabba's to kill you, not recruit you."

Luke stared at her, an icy shiver running up his back. It couldn't be . . . but even as he gazed into that tortured face, he knew with sudden certainty that it was. "And your master," he said quietly, "was the Emperor."

"Yes," she said, her voice a snake's hiss. "And you destroyed him."

Luke swallowed hard, the pounding of his own heart the only sound. He hadn't killed the Emperor—Darth

Vader had done that—but Mara didn't seem inclined to worry over such subtleties. "You're wrong, though," he said. "He *did* try to recruit me."

"Only because I failed," she ground out, her throat muscles tight. "And only when Vader had you standing right there in front of him. What, you don't think he knew Vader had offered to help you overthrow him?"

Unconsciously, Luke flexed the fingers of his numbed artificial hand. Yes, Vader had indeed suggested such an alliance during their Cloud City duel. "I don't think it was a serious offer," he murmured.

"The Emperor did," Mara said flatly. "He knew. And what he knew, I knew."

Her eyes filled with distant pain. "I was his hand, Skywalker," she said, her voice remembering. "That's how I was known to his inner court: as the Emperor's Hand. I served him all over the galaxy, doing jobs the Imperial Fleet and stormtroopers couldn't handle. That was my one great talent, you see—I could hear his call from anywhere in the Empire, and report back to him the same way. I exposed traitors for him, brought down his enemies, helped him keep the kind of control over the mindless bureaucracies that he needed. I had prestige, and power, and respect."

Slowly, her eyes came back from the past. "And you took it all away from me. If only for that, you deserve to die."

"What went wrong?" Luke forced himself to ask.

Her lip twisted. "Jabba wouldn't let me go with the execution party. That was it—pure and simple. I tried begging, cajoling, bargaining—I couldn't change his mind."

"No," Luke said soberly. "Jabba was highly resistant to the mind-controlling aspects of the Force."

But if she *had* been on the Sail Barge . . .

Luke shivered, seeing in his mind's eye that terrifying vision in the dark cave on Dagobah. The mysterious silhouetted woman standing there on the Sail Barge's upper deck, laughing at him as she held his captured lightsaber high.

The first time, years ago, the cave had spun him an image of a possible future. This time, he knew now, it had shown him a possible past. "You would have succeeded," he said quietly.

Mara looked sharply at him. "I'm not asking for understanding or sympathy," she bit out. "You wanted to know. Fine; now you know."

He let her tend her wounds in silence for a moment. "So why are you here?" he asked. "Why not with the Empire?"

"What Empire?" she countered. "It's dying—you know that as well as I do."

"But while it's still there—"

She cut him off with a withering glare. "Who would I go to?" she demanded. "They didn't know me—none of them did. Not as the Emperor's Hand, anyway. I was a shadow, working outside the normal lines of command and protocol. There were no records kept of my activities. Those few I was formally introduced to thought of me as court-hanging froth, a minor bit of mobile decoration kept around the palace to amuse the Emperor."

Her eyes went distant again with memory. "There was nowhere for me to go after Endor," she said bitterly. "No contacts, no resources—I didn't even have a real identity anymore. I was on my own."

"And so you linked up with Karrde."

"Eventually. First I spent four and a half years sloshing around the rotten underfringes of the galaxy, doing whatever I could." Her eyes were steady on him, with a trace of hatred fire back in them. "I worked hard to get where I am, Skywalker. You're not going to ruin it for me. Not this time."

"I don't want to ruin anything for you," Luke told her evenly. "All I want is to get back to the New Republic."

"And I want the old Empire back," she retorted. "We don't always get what we want, do we?"

Luke shook his head. "No. We don't."

For a moment she glared at him. Then, abruptly, she scooped up a tube of salve and tossed it at him. "Here—get that welt fixed up. And get some sleep. Tomorrow's going to be a busy day."

CHAPTER 27

THE BATTERED A-CLASS bulk freighter drifted off the *Chimaera*'s starboard side: a giant space-going box with a hyperdrive attached, its faded plating glistening dully in the glare of the Star Destroyer's floodlights. Sitting at his command station, Thrawn studied the sensor data and nodded. "It looks good, Captain," he said to Pellaeon. "Exactly the way it should. You may proceed with the test when ready."

"It'll be a few more minutes yet, sir," Pellaeon told him, studying the readouts on his console. "The technicians are still having some problems getting the cloaking shield tuned."

He held his breath, half afraid of a verbal explosion. The untested cloaking shield and the specially modified freighter it was mounted to had cost hideous amounts of money—money the Empire really didn't have to spare. For the technology to now suddenly come up finicky, particularly with the whole of the Sluis Van operation hanging squarely in the balance . . .

But the Grand Admiral merely nodded. "There's time," he said calmly. "What word from Myrkr?"

"The last regular report came in two hours ago," Pellaeon told him. "Still negative."

Thrawn nodded again. "And the latest count from Sluis Van?"

"Uh . . ." Pellaeon checked the appropriate file. "A hundred twelve transient warships in all. Sixty-five being used as cargo carriers, the others on escort duty."

"Sixty-five," Thrawn repeated with obvious satisfaction. "Excellent. It means we get to pick and choose."

Pellaeon stirred uncomfortably. "Yes, sir."

Thrawn turned away from his contemplation of the freighter to look at Pellaeon. "You have a concern, Captain?"

Pellaeon nodded at the ship. "I don't like sending them into enemy territory without any communications."

"We don't have much choice in the matter," Thrawn reminded him dryly. "That's how a cloaking shield works—nothing gets out, nothing gets in." He cocked an eyebrow. "Assuming, of course, that it works at all," he added pointedly.

"Yes, sir. But . . ."

"But what, Captain?"

Pellaeon braced himself and took the plunge. "It seems to me, Admiral, that this is the sort of operation we ought to use C'baoth on."

Thrawn's gaze hardened, just a bit. "C'baoth?"

"Yes, sir. He could give us communications with—"

"We don't need communications, Captain," Thrawn cut him off. "Careful timing will be adequate for our purposes."

"I disagree, Admiral. Under normal circumstances, yes, careful timing would get them into position. But there's no way to anticipate how long it'll take to get clearance from Sluis Control."

"On the contrary," Thrawn countered coolly. "I've studied the Sluissi very carefully. I can anticipate exactly how long it will take them to clear the freighter."

Pellaeon gritted his teeth. "If the controllers were all Sluissi, perhaps. But with the Rebellion funneling so much of their own material through the Sluis Van system, they're bound to have some of their own people in Control, as well."

"It's of no consequence," Thrawn told him. "The Sluissi will be in charge. *Their* timing will determine events."

Pellaeon exhaled and conceded defeat. "Yes, sir," he muttered.

Thrawn eyed him. "It's not a question of bravado, Captain. Or of proving that the Imperial Fleet can function without him. The simple fact of the matter is that we can't afford to use C'baoth too much or too often."

"Because we'll start depending on him," Pellaeon growled. "As if we were all borg-implanted into a combat computer."

Thrawn smiled. "That still bothers you, doesn't it? No matter. That's part of it, but only a very small part. What concerns me more is that we don't give Master C'baoth too much of a taste for this kind of power."

Pellaeon frowned at him. "He said he doesn't want power."

"Then he lies," Thrawn returned coldly. "All men want power. And the more they have, the more they want."

Pellaeon thought about that. "But if he's a threat to us . . ." He broke off, suddenly aware of the other officers and men working all around them.

The Grand Admiral had no such reticence. "Why not dispose of him?" he finished the question. "It's very simple. Because we'll soon have the ability to fill his taste for power to the fullest . . . and once we've done so, he'll be no more of a threat than any other tool."

"Leia Organa Solo and her twins?"

"Exactly," Thrawn nodded, his eyes glittering. "Once C'baoth has them in his hand, these little excursions with the Fleet will be no more to him than distracting interludes that take him away from his *real* work."

Pellaeon found himself looking away from the intensity of that gaze. The theory seemed good enough; but in actual practice . . . "That assumes, of course, that the Noghri are ever able to connect with her."

"They will." Thrawn was quietly confident. "She and her guardians will eventually run out of tricks. Certainly long before we run out of Noghri."

In front of Pellaeon, the display cleared. "They're ready, sir," he said.

Thrawn turned back to the freighter. "At your convenience, Captain."

Pellaeon took a deep breath and tapped the comm switch. "Cloaking shield: *activate*."

And outside the view window, the battered freighter—
Stayed exactly as it was.

Thrawn gazed hard at the freighter. Looked at his

command displays, back at the freighter . . . and then turned to Pellaeon, a satisfied smile on his face. "Excellent, Captain. Precisely what I wanted. I congratulate you and your technicians."

"Thank you, sir," Pellaeon said, relaxing muscles he hadn't realized were tense. "Then I take it the light is green?"

The Grand Admiral's smile remained unchanged, his face hardening around it. "The light is green, Captain," he said grimly. "Alert the task force; prepare to move to the rendezvous point.

"The Sluis Van shipyards are ours."

WEDGE ANTILLES LOOKED up from the data pad with disbelief. "You've got to be kidding," he told the dispatcher. "*Escort* duty?"

The other gave him an innocent look. "What's the big deal?" he asked. "You guys are X-wings—you do escort all the time."

"We escort *people*," Wedge retorted. "We don't watchdog cargo ships."

The dispatcher's innocent look collapsed into thinly veiled disgust, and Wedge got the sudden impression that he'd gone through this same argument a lot lately. "Look, Commander, don't dump it on me," he growled back. "It's a standard Frigate escort—what's the difference whether the Frigate's got people or a break-down reactor aboard?"

Wedge looked back at the data pad. It was a matter of professional pride, that's what the difference was. "Sluis Van's a pretty long haul for X-wings," he said instead.

"Yeah, well, the spec line says you'll be staying aboard the Frigate until you actually hit the system," the dispatcher said, reaching over his desk to tap the paging key on Wedge's data pad. "You'll just ride him in from there."

Wedge scanned the rest of the spec line. They'd then have to sit there in the shipyards and wait for the rest of the convoy to assemble before finally taking the cargo on to Bpfassh. "We're going to be a long time away from Coruscant with this," he said.

"I'd look on that as a plus if I were you, Commander," the dispatcher said, lowering his voice. "Something here's coming to a head. I think Councilor Fey'lya and his people are about to make their move."

Wedge felt a chill run through him. "You don't mean . . . a *coup*?"

The dispatcher jumped as if scalded. "*No*, of course not. What do you think Fey'lya is—?"

He broke off, his eyes going wary. "Oh, I got it. You're one of Ackbar's diehards, huh? Face it, Commander; Ackbar's lost whatever touch he ever had with the common fighting man of the Alliance. Fey'lya's the only one on the Council who really cares about our welfare." He gestured at the data pad. "Case in point. All this garbage came down from Ackbar's office."

"Yeah, well, there's still an Empire out there," Wedge muttered, uncomfortably aware that the dispatcher's verbal attack on Ackbar had neatly shifted him to the other side of his own argument. He wondered if the other had done that on purpose . . . or whether he really was one of the growing number of Fey'lya supporters in the military.

And come to think of it, a little vacation away from Coruscant might not be such a bad idea, after all. At least it would get him away from all this crazy political stuff. "When do we leave?"

"Soon as you can get your people together and aboard," the dispatcher said. "They're already loading your fighters."

"Right." Wedge turned away from the desk and headed down the corridor toward the ready rooms. Yes, a quiet little run back out to Sluis Van and Bpfassh would be just the thing right now. Give him some breathing space to try to sort out just what was happening to this New Republic he'd risked so much to help build.

And if the Imperials took a poke at them along the way . . . well, at least *that* was a threat he could fight back against.

CHAPTER 28

I T WAS JUST before noon when they began to notice the faint sounds wafting occasionally to them through the forest. It was another hour after that before they were close enough for Luke to finally identify them.

Speeder bikes.

"You're sure that's a military model?" Mara muttered as the whine/drone rose and fell twice more before fading again into the distance.

"I'm sure," Luke told her grimly. "I nearly ran one of them into a tree on Endor."

She didn't reply, and for a moment Luke wondered if the mention of Endor might not have been a good idea. But a glance at Mara's face relieved that fear. She was not brooding, but listening. "Sounds like they're off to the south, too," she said after a minute. "North . . . I don't hear anything from that direction."

Luke listened. "Neither do I," he said. "I wonder . . . Artoo, can you make up an audio map for us?"

There was an acknowledging beep. A moment later the droid's holo projector came on and a two-color map appeared, hovering a few centimeters over the matted leaves underfoot.

"I was right," Mara said, pointing. "A few units directly ahead of us, the rest off to the south. Nothing at all north."

"Which means we must have veered to the north," Luke said.

Mara frowned at him. "How do you figure that?"

"Well, they must know we'll make for Hyllyard City," he said. "They're bound to center their search on the direct approach."

Mara smiled thinly. "Such wonderful Jedi naïveté," she said. "I don't suppose you considered the fact that just because we can't hear them doesn't mean they aren't there."

Luke frowned down at the holographic map. "Well, of course they *could* have a force lying in wait there," he agreed. "But what would it gain them?"

"Oh, come on, Skywalker—it's the oldest tactical trick in the book. If the perimeter looks impossible to crack, the quarry goes to ground and waits for a better opportunity. You don't want him to do that, so you give him what looks like a possible way through." She squatted down, ran a finger through the "quiet" section on the map. "In this case, they get a bonus: if we swing north to avoid the obvious speeder bikes, it's instant proof that we've got something to hide from them."

Luke grimaced. "Not that they really need any proof."

Mara shrugged and straightened up again. "Some officers are more legal-minded than others. The question is, what do we do now?"

Luke looked back down at the map. By Mara's reckoning, they were no more than four or five kilometers from the edge of the forest—two hours, more or less. If the Imperials had this much organization already set up in front of them . . . "They're probably going to try to ring us," he said slowly. "Move units around to the north and south, and eventually behind us."

"If they haven't done so already," Mara said. "No reason we would have heard them—they don't know exactly how fast we're moving, so they'll have made it a big circle. Probably using a wide ring of Chariot assault vehicles or hoverscouts with a group of speeder bikes working around each focal point. It's the standard stormtrooper format for a web."

Luke pursed his lips. But what the Imperials *didn't* know was that one of the quarry knew exactly what they were up to. "So how do we break out?" he asked.

Mara hissed between her teeth. "We don't," she said flatly. "Not without a lot more equipment and resources than we've got."

The faint whine/drone came again from somewhere ahead of them, rising and then fading as it passed by in the distance. "In that case," Luke said, "we might as well go straight up the middle. Call to them before they see us, maybe."

Mara snorted. "Like we were casual tourists out here with nothing to hide?"

"You have a better idea?"

She glared at him. But it was a reflexive glare, without

any real argument behind it. "Not really," she conceded at last. "I suppose you're also going to want to do that role-switch thing Karrde suggested."

Luke shrugged. "We're not going to be able to blast our way through them," he reminded her. "And if you're right about that pincer movement, we're not going to sneak through them, either. All that's left is a bluff, and the better a bluff it is, the better chance we've got."

Mara's lip twisted. "I suppose so." With only a slight hesitation, she dropped the power pack from her blaster and handed it and the forearm holster to him.

Luke took them, hefted the blaster in his hand. "They may check to see if it's loaded," he pointed out mildly. "I would."

"Look, Skywalker, if you think I'm going to give you a loaded weapon—"

"And if another vornskr finds us before the Imperials do," Luke cut her off quietly, "you'll never get it reloaded fast enough."

"Maybe I don't care," she shot back.

Luke nodded. "Maybe you don't."

She glared at him again, but again, the glare lacked conviction. Teeth visibly grinding together, she slapped the power pack into his hand. "Thank you," Luke said, reloading the blaster and fastening it to his left forearm. "Now. Artoo?"

The droid understood. One of the trapezoidal sections at the top of his upper dome, indistinguishable from all the other segments, slid open to reveal a long, deep storage compartment beneath it. Turning back to Mara, Luke held out his hand.

She looked at the open hand, then at the storage compartment. "So that's how you did it," she commented sourly, unhooking his lightsaber and handing it over. "I always wondered how you smuggled that thing into Jabba's."

Luke dropped the lightsaber in, and Artoo slid the door shut behind it. "I'll call for it if I need it," he told the droid.

"Don't count on being very good with it," Mara warned. "The ysalamiri effect is supposed to extend several kilometers past the edge of the forest—none of those little attack-anticipation tricks will work anywhere near Hyllyard City."

"I understand," Luke nodded. "I guess we're ready to go, then."

"Not quite," Mara said, eyeing him. "There's still that face of yours."

Luke cocked an eyebrow. "I don't think Artoo's got anywhere to hide *that*."

"Funny. I had something else in mind." Mara glanced around, then headed off toward a stand of odd-looking bushes a few meters away. Reaching it, she pulled the end of her tunic sleeve down to cover her hand and carefully picked a few of the leaves. "Pull up your sleeve and hold out your arm," she ordered as she returned with them.

He did so, and she brushed his forearm lightly with the tip of one of the leaves. "Now. Let's see if this works."

"What exactly is it supposed to—*aah*!" The last of Luke's air came out in an explosive burst as a searing pain lanced through his forearm.

"Perfect," Mara said with grim satisfaction. "You're allergic as anything to them. Oh, relax—the pain will be gone in a few seconds."

"Oh, thanks," Luke gritted back. The pain was indeed receding. "Right. Now, what about this—mmm!— this blasted *itch*?"

"That'll hang on a little longer," she said, gesturing at his arm. "But never mind that. What do you think?"

Luke gritted his teeth. The itching was not-so-subtle torture . . . but she was right. Where she'd brushed the leaf the skin had turned dark and puffy, sprinkled with tiny pustules. "Looks disgusting," he said.

"Sure does," she agreed. "You want to do it yourself, or you want me to do it for you?"

Luke gritted his teeth. This was *not* going to be pleasant. "I can do it."

It was indeed unpleasant; but by the time he finished brushing his chin with the leaves the pain had already begun to recede from his forehead. "I hope I didn't get it too close to my eyes," he commented between clenched teeth, throwing the leaves away into the forest and fighting hard against the urge to dig into his face with both sets of fingernails. "It'd be handy to be able to see the rest of the afternoon."

"I think you'll be all right," Mara assured him, studying the result. "The rest of your face is pretty horrendous, though. You won't look anything like whatever pictures they have, that's for sure."

"Glad to hear it." Luke took a deep breath and ran through the Jedi pain suppression exercises. Without the Force they weren't all that effective, but they seemed to help a little. "How long will I look like this?"

"The puffiness should start going down in a few hours. It won't be completely gone until tomorrow."

"Good enough. We ready, then?"

"As ready as we'll ever be." Turning her back to Artoo, she took the travois handles and started walking. "Come on."

THEY MADE GOOD time, despite the lingering tenderness of Mara's ankle and the distractions inherent in a faceful of itch. To Luke's relief, the itching began to fade after about half an hour, leaving only puffy numbness behind it.

Mara's ankle was another story, however, and as he walked behind her and Artoo he could see clearly how she was having to favor it. The added burden of Artoo's travois wasn't helping, and twice he almost suggested that they give up on the role switching. But he resisted the urge. It was their best chance of getting out of this, and they both knew it.

Besides which, she had far too much pride to agree.

They'd gone perhaps another kilometer, with the whine/drone of the speeder bikes rising and falling in the distance, when suddenly they were there.

There were two of them: biker scouts in glistening white armor, swooping up to them and braking to a halt almost before Luke's ears had registered the sound of their approach. Which meant a very short ride, with target position already known.

Which meant that the entire search party must have had them located and vectored for at least the past few minutes. It was just as well, Luke reflected, that he hadn't tried switching roles with Mara.

"Halt!" one of the scouts called unnecessarily as they hovered there, both swivel blaster cannons trained and ready. "Identify yourselves, in the name of the Empire."

And it was performance time. "Boy, am I glad *you* showed up," Luke called back, putting as much relief into his voice as the puffy cheeks allowed. "You don't happen to have some sort of transport handy, do you? I'm about walked off my feet."

There was just the slightest flicker of hesitation. "Identify yourself," the scout repeated.

"My name's Jade," Luke told him. He gestured at Mara. "Got a gift here for Talon Karrde. I don't suppose *he* sent some transport, did he?"

There was a short pause. The scouts conferring privately between themselves, Luke decided, or else calling back to base for instructions. The fact that the prisoner was a woman did indeed seem to have thrown them. Whether it would be enough, of course, was another question entirely.

"You'll come with us," the scout ordered. "Our officer wants to talk to you. You—woman—put the droid down and move away from it."

"Fine with me," Luke said as the second scout maneuvered his speeder bike to a position in front of Artoo's travois. "But I want both of you to witness, for the record, that I had her fair and square before you showed up. Karrde weasels his way out of these capture fees too often; he's not going to weasel out of this one."

"You're a bounty hunter?" the scout asked, a clear note of disdain in his voice.

"That's right," Luke said, putting some professional dignity in his voice as a counter to the scout's contempt.

Not that he minded their distaste. He was, in fact, counting on it. The more firmly the Imperials had the wrong image of him set in their minds, the longer it would take them to see through the deception.

Somewhere in the back of his mind, though, he couldn't help but wonder if this was the sort of trick a Jedi should use.

The second scout had dismounted and fastened the handles of Artoo's travois to the rear of his speeder bike. Remounting, he headed off at about the speed of a brisk walk. "You two follow him," the first scout ordered, swinging around to take up the rear. "Drop your blaster on the ground first, Jade."

Luke complied, and they set off. The first scout put down just long enough to scoop up the abandoned blaster and then followed.

It took another hour to reach the edge of the forest. The two speeder bikes stayed with them the whole time; but as they traveled, the party began to grow. More speeder bikes swept in from both sides, falling into close formation on either side of Luke and Mara or else joining up with the guards to both front and rear. As they neared the forest's edge, fully armored stormtroopers began to appear, too, moving in with blaster rifles held ready across their chests to take up positions around the two prisoners. As they did so, the scouts began drifting away, ranging farther out to form a kind of moving screen.

By the time they finally stepped out from under the forest canopy, their escort numbered no fewer than ten biker scouts and twenty stormtroopers. It was an impressive display of military power . . . and more even than the

fact of the search itself, it drove home to Luke the seriousness with which the mysterious man in charge of the
Empire was treating this incident. Even at the height of
their power, the Imperials hadn't spent stormtroopers
lightly.

Three more people were waiting for them in the fifty-
meter strip of open land between the forest and the nearest structures of Hyllyard City: two more stormtroopers
and a hard-faced man wearing a major's insignia on his
dusty brown Imperial uniform. "About time," the latter
muttered under his breath as Mara and Luke were nudged
in his direction. "Who are they?"

"The male says his name is Jade," one of the stormtroopers in front reported in that slightly filtered voice
they all seemed to have. "Bounty hunter; works for
Karrde. He claims the female is his prisoner."

"*Was* his prisoner," the major corrected, looking at
Mara. "What's your name, thief?"

"Senni Kiffu," Mara said, her voice surly. "And I'm
not a thief. Talon Karrde owes me—he owes me big. I
didn't take any more than I had coming."

The major looked at Luke, and Luke shrugged.
"Karrde's other dealings aren't any of my business. He
said bring her back. I brought her back."

"And her theft, too, I see." He looked at Artoo, still
tied to his travois and dragging behind the speeder bike.
"Get that droid off your bike," he ordered the scout.
"The ground's flat enough here, and I want you on perimeter. Put it with the prisoners. Cuff them, too—
they're hardly likely to fall over tree roots out here."

"Wait a minute," Luke objected as one of the stormtroopers stepped toward him. "Me, too?"

The major raised his eyebrows slightly. "You got a problem with that, bounty hunter?" he asked, his voice challenging.

"Yeah, I got a problem with it," Luke shot back. "*She*'s the prisoner here, not me."

"For the moment you're both prisoners," the other countered. "So shut up." He frowned at Luke's face. "What in the Empire happened to you, anyway?"

So they weren't going to be able to pass the puffiness off as Luke's natural features. "Ran into some kind of bush while I was chasing her," he growled as the storm-trooper roughly cuffed his hands in front of him. "It itched like blazes for a while."

The major smiled thinly. "How very inconvenient for you," he said dryly. "How fortunate that we have a fully qualified medic back at HQ. He should be able to bring that swelling down in no time." He held Luke's gaze a moment longer, then shifted his attention to the storm-trooper leader. "You disarmed him, of course."

The stormtrooper gestured, and the first of the biker scouts swooped close to hand Mara's blaster to the major. "Interesting weapon," the major murmured, turning it over in his hands before sliding it into his belt. From overhead came a soft hum, and Luke looked up to see a repulsorlift craft settle into place overhead. A Chariot assault vehicle, just as Mara had predicted. "Ah," the major said, glancing up at it. "All right, Commander. Let's go."

In many ways, Hyllyard City reminded Luke of Mos Eisley: small houses and commercial buildings crammed fairly tightly together, with relatively narrow streets running between them. The troop headed around the perimeter, clearly aiming for one of the wider avenues that

TIMOTHY ZAHN

seemed to radiate, spokelike, from the center of town. Looking into the city as they passed by the outer buildings, Luke was able to catch occasional glimpses of what seemed to be an open area a few blocks away. The town square, possibly, or else a spacecraft landing area.

The vanguard had just reached the target street when, in perfect synchronization, the stormtroopers abruptly changed formation. Those in the inner circle pulled in closer to Luke and Mara while those in the outer circle moved farther away, the whole crowd coming to a halt and gesturing to their prisoners to do the same. A moment later, the reason for the sudden maneuver came around the corner: four scruffy-looking men walking briskly toward them with a fifth man in the center of their square, his hands chained behind him.

They had barely emerged from the street when they were intercepted by a group of four stormtroopers. A short and inaudible conversation ensued, which concluded with the strangers handing their blasters over to the stormtroopers with obvious reluctance. Escorted now by the Imperials, they continued on toward the main group . . . and as they walked, Luke finally got a clear look at the prisoner.

It was Han Solo.

The stormtroopers opened their ranks slightly to let the newcomers through. "What do you want?" the major demanded as they stopped in front of him.

"Name's Chin," one of them said. "We caught this ratch snooping around the forest—maybe looking for your prisoners there. Figured you might want to have a talk with him, hee?"

"Uncommonly generous of you," the major said sardonically, giving Han a quick, measuring glance. "You come to this conclusion all by yourself?"

Chin drew himself up. "Just because I don't live in a big flashy city doesn't mean I'm stupid," he said stiffly. "What hai—you think we don't know what it means when Imperial stormtroopers start setting up a temporary garrison?"

The major gave him a long, cool look. "You'd best just hope that the garrison *is* temporary." He glanced at the stormtrooper beside him, jerked his head toward Han. "Check him for weapons."

"We already—" Chin began. The major looked at him, and he fell silent.

The frisking took only a minute, and came up empty. "Put him in the pocket with the others," the major ordered. "All right, Chin, you and your friends can go. If he turns out to be worth anything, I'll see you get a piece of it."

"Uncommonly generous of you," Chin said with an expression that was just short of a sneer. "Can we have our guns back now?"

The major's expression hardened. "You can pick them up later at our HQ," he said. "Hyllyard Hotel, straight across the square—but I'm sure a sophisticated citizen like yourself already knows where it is."

For a moment Chin seemed inclined to argue the point. But a glance at the stormtroopers clustered around evidently changed his mind for him. Without a word he turned, and he and his three companions strode back toward the city.

"Move out," the major ordered, and they started up again.

"Well," Han muttered, falling into step beside Luke. "Together again, huh?"

"I wouldn't miss it," Luke muttered back. "Your friends there seem in a hurry to get away."

"Probably don't want to miss the party," Han told him. "A little something they threw together to celebrate my capture."

Luke threw him a sideways look. "Shame we weren't invited."

"Real shame," Han agreed with a straight face. "You never know, though."

They had turned into the avenue now, moving toward the center of town. Just visible over the heads of the stormtroopers, he could see something gray and rounded directly ahead of them. Craning his neck for a better view, he saw that the structure was in fact a freestanding archway, rising from the ground near the far end of the open village square he had noticed earlier.

A fairly impressive archway, too, especially for a city this far outside the mainstream of the galaxy. The upper part was composed of different types of fitted stone, the crown flaring outward like a cross between an umbrella and a section of sliced mushroom. The lower part curved in and downward, to end in a pair of meter-square supporting pillars on each side. The entire arch rose a good ten meters into the sky, with the distance between the pillars perhaps half that. Lying directly in front of it was the village square, a fifteen-meter expanse of empty ground.

The perfect place for an ambush.

Luke felt his stomach tighten. The perfect place for an

ambush . . . except that if it was obvious to him, it must be obvious to the stormtroopers, as well.

And it was. The vanguard of the party had reached the square now, and as the stormtroopers moved out of the confines of the narrow avenue, each lifted his blaster rifle a little higher and moved a little farther apart from his fellows. They were expecting an ambush, all right. And they were expecting it right here.

Gritting his teeth, Luke focused again on the archway. "Is Threepio here?" he muttered to Han.

He sensed Han's frown, but the other didn't waste time with unnecessary questions. "He's with Lando, yeah."

Luke nodded and glanced down to his right. Beside him, Artoo was rolling along the bumpy street, trying hard to keep up. Bracing himself, Luke took a step in that direction—

And with a squeal, Artoo tripped over Luke's outstretched foot and fell flat with a crash.

Luke was crouched beside him in an instant, leaning over him as he struggled with his manacled hands to get the little droid upright again. He sensed some of the stormtroopers moving forward to assist, but for that single moment, there was no one else close enough to hear him. "Artoo, call to Threepio," he breathed into the droid's audio receptor. "Tell him to wait until we're at the archway to attack."

The droid complied instantly, its loud warble nearly deafening Luke as he crouched there beside him. Luke's head was still ringing when rough hands grabbed him under the arms and hauled him to his feet. He regained his balance—

To find the major standing in front of him, a suspicious scowl on his face. "What was that?" the other demanded.

"He fell over," Luke told him. "I think he tripped—"

"I meant that transmission," the major cut him off harshly. "What did he say?"

"He was probably telling me off for tripping him," Luke shot back. "How should *I* know what he said?"

For a long minute the major glared at him. "Move out, Commander," he said at last to the stormtrooper at his side. "Everyone stay alert."

He turned away, and they started walking again. "I hope," Han murmured from beside him, "you know what you're doing."

Luke took a deep breath and fixed his eyes on the archway ahead. "So do I," he murmured back.

In a very few minutes, he knew, they would both find out.

CHAPTER 29

"OH, MY!" THREEPIO gasped. "General Calrissian, I have—"

"Quiet, Threepio," Lando ordered, peering carefully around the edge of the window at the minor commotion going on across the square. "Did you see what happened, Aves?"

Crouched down beneath the windowsill, Aves shook his head. "Looked like Skywalker and his droid both fell over," he said. "Couldn't tell for sure—too many storm-troopers in the way."

"General Calrissian—"

"Quiet, Threepio." Lando watched tensely as two stormtroopers pulled Luke to his feet, then righted Artoo. "Looks like they're okay."

"Yeah." Aves reached down to the floor beside him, picked up the small transmitter. "Here we go. Let's hope everyone's ready."

TIMOTHY ZAHN

"And that Chin and the others aren't still carrying their blasters," Lando added under his breath.

Aves snorted. "They aren't. Don't worry— stormtroopers are always confiscating other people's weapons."

Lando nodded, adjusting his grip on his blaster, wishing they could get this over with. Across the way, the Imperials seemed to have gotten themselves sorted out and were starting to move again. As soon as they were all inside the square, away from any possible cover . . .

"General Calrissian, I *must* speak to you," Threepio insisted. "I have a message from Master Luke."

Lando blinked at him. "From *Luke*?"

—but even as he said it he suddenly remembered that electronic wail from Artoo just after he'd fallen over. Could that have been—? "What is it?"

"Master Luke wants you to hold off the attack," Threepio said, obviously relieved that someone was finally listening to him. "He says you're to wait until the stormtroopers are at the arch before firing."

Aves twisted around. "What? That's crazy. They outnumber us three to one—we give them any chance at all at cover and they'll cut us to pieces."

Lando looked out the window, grinding his teeth together. Aves was right—he knew enough of ground tactics to realize that. But on the other hand . . . "They're awfully spread out out there," he said. "Cover or no cover, they're going to be hard to take out. Especially with those speeder bikes on their perimeter."

Aves shook his head. "It's crazy," he repeated. "I'm not going to risk my people that way."

"Luke knows what he's doing," Lando insisted. "He's a Jedi."

"He's not a Jedi now," Aves snorted. "Didn't Karrde explain about the ysalamiri?"

"Whether he has Jedi powers or not, he's still a Jedi," Lando insisted. His blaster, he realized suddenly, was pointed at Aves. But that was okay, because Aves's blaster was pointed at him, too. "Anyway, his life is more on the line here than any of yours—you can always abort and pull back."

"Oh, sure," Aves snorted, throwing a glance out the window. The Imperials were nearing the middle of the square now, Lando saw, the stormtroopers looking wary and alert as anything. "Except that if we leave any of them alive, they'll seal off the city. And what about that Chariot up there?"

"What about it?" Lando countered. "I still haven't heard how you're planning to take it out."

"Well, we sure as blazes don't want it on the ground," Aves retorted. "And that's what'll happen if we let the stormtroopers get to the arch. The Chariot'll put down right across the front of it, right between us and them. That, plus the arch itself, will give them all the cover they need to sit back and take us out at their leisure." He shook his head and shifted his grip on the transmitter. "Anyway, it's too late to clue in the others to any plan changes."

"You don't have to clue them in," Lando said, feeling sweat collecting under his collar. Luke was counting on him. "No one's supposed to do anything until you trigger the booby-trapped weapons."

Aves shook his head again. "It's too risky." He turned back to the window, raised the transmitter.

And here, Lando realized—right here—was where it all came down to the wire. Where you decided who or what it was you trusted. Tactics and abstract logic . . . or people. Lowering his blaster, he gently rested the tip of the muzzle against Aves's neck. "We wait," he said quietly.

Aves didn't move; but suddenly there was something in the way he crouched there that reminded Lando of a hunting predator. "I won't forget this, Calrissian," he said, his voice icy soft.

"I wouldn't want you to," Lando said. He looked out at the stormtroopers . . . and hoped that Luke did indeed know what he was doing.

THE VANGUARD HAD already passed the archway, and the major was only a few steps away from it, when four of the stormtroopers abruptly blew up.

Quite spectacularly, too. The simultaneous flashes of yellow-white fire lit up the landscape to almost painful intensity; the thunderclap of the multiple detonations nearly knocked Luke over.

The sound was still ringing in his ears when the blasters opened up behind them.

The stormtroopers were good, all right. There was no panic that Luke could detect; no sudden freezing in astonishment or indecision. They were moving into combat position almost before the blaster fire had begun: those already at the archway hugging close to the stone pillars to return covering fire, the rest moving quickly to join them. Above the sound of the blasters, he could hear the increased whine of the speeder bikes kicking into high speed; overhead, he caught just a glimpse of the Chariot assault vehicle swiveling around to face the unseen attackers.

And then an armored hand caught him under each armpit, and suddenly he was being hauled toward the archway. A few seconds later he was dumped unceremoniously in the narrow gap between the two pillars supporting the north side of the arch. Mara was already crouched there; a second later, two more stormtroopers tossed Han in to join them. Four of the Imperials moved into position over them, using the pillars for cover as they began returning fire. Struggling to his knees, Luke leaned out for a look.

Out in the fire zone, looking small and helpless amid the deadly horizontal hail of blaster fire, Artoo was rolling toward them as fast as his little wheels would carry him.

"I think we're in trouble," Han muttered in his ear. "Not to mention Lando and the others."

"It's not over yet," Luke told him tightly. "Just stick close. How are you at causing distractions?"

"Terrific," Han said; and to Luke's surprise, he brought his hands out from behind his back, the chain and manacles he'd been wearing hanging loosely from his left wrist. "Trick cuffs," he grunted, pulling a concealed strip of metal from the inside of the open cuff and probing at Luke's restraints. "I hope this thing—ah." The pressure on Luke's wrists was suddenly gone; the cuffs opened and dropped to the ground. "You ready for your distraction?" Han asked, taking the loose end of his chain in his free hand.

"Hang on a minute," Luke told him, looking up. Most of the speeder bikes had taken refuge under the arch, looking like some strange species of giant birds hiding from a storm as they hovered close to the stone, their laser cannon spitting toward the surrounding houses. In front of them and just below their line of fire, the Chariot had swiveled parallel to the arch and was coming down. Once it was on the ground . . .

A hand gripped Luke's arm, fingernails digging hard into the skin. "Whatever you're going to do, *do* it!" Mara hissed viciously. "If the Chariot gets down, you'll never get them out from cover."

"I know," Luke nodded. "I'm counting on it."

THE CHARIOT SETTLED smoothly to the ground directly in front of the arch, blocking the last of the attackers' firing vectors. Crouched at the window, Aves swore violently. "Well, there's your Jedi for you," he bit out. "You got any other great ideas, Calrissian?"

Lando swallowed hard. "We've just got to give him—"

He never finished the sentence. From the arch a blaster bolt glanced off the window frame, and suddenly Lando's upper arm flashed with pain. The shock sent him stumbling backward, just as a second shot blew apart that whole section of the frame, driving wooden splinters and chunks of masonry like shrapnel across his chest and arm.

He hit the floor, landing hard enough to see stars.

Blinking, gritting his teeth against the pain, he looked up—

To find Aves leaning over him.

Lando looked up into the other's face. *I won't forget this*, Aves had said, no more than three minutes ago. And from the look on his face, he wasn't anticipating any need to hold that memory for much longer. "He'll come through," Lando whispered through the pain. "He will."

But he could tell that Aves wasn't listening . . . and, down deep, Lando couldn't blame him. Lando Calrissian, the professional gambler, had gambled one last time. And he'd lost.

And the debt from that gamble—the last in a long line of such debts—had come due.

THE CHARIOT SETTLED smoothly to the ground directly in front of the arch, and Luke got his feet under him. This was it. "All right, Han," he muttered. "Go."

Han nodded and surged to his feet, coming up right in the middle of the four stormtroopers standing over them. With a bellow, he swung his former shackles full across the faceplate of the nearest guard, then threw the looped chain around the neck of the next and pulled backwards, away from the pillars. The other two reacted instantly, leaping after him and taking the whole group down in a tangle.

And for the next few seconds, Luke was free.

He stood up and leaned out to look around the pillar. Artoo was still in the middle of no-man's-land, hurrying to reach cover before he could be hit by a stray shot. He warbled plaintively as he saw Luke—

Artoo!—*now!*" Luke shouted, holding out his hand and glancing across toward the southern end of the archway. Between the stone pillars and the grounded Chariot, the stormtroopers were indeed solidly entrenched. If this didn't work, Han was right: Lando and everyone else out there were dead. Gritting his teeth, hoping fervently that his counterattack wasn't already too late, he turned back to Artoo—

Just as, with a flicker of silver metal and perfect accuracy, his lightsaber dropped neatly into his outstretched hand.

Beside him, the guards had subdued Han's crazy attack and were getting back to their feet, leaving Han on his knees between them. Luke took them all in a single sweep, the blazing green lightsaber blade slicing through the glistening stormtrooper armor with hardly a tug to mark its passing. "Get behind me," he snapped to Han and Mara, stepping back to the gap between the two northern pillars and focusing on the mass of Imperials standing and crouching between him and the southern pillars. They were suddenly aware that they had an unexpected threat on their flank, and a few were already starting to bring their blasters to bear on him.

With the Force to guide his hand, he could have held out against them indefinitely, blocking their blaster shots with the lightsaber. Mara had been right, though: the ysalamiri effect did indeed extend this far outside the forest, and the Force was still silent.

But then, he'd never had any intention of fighting the stormtroopers anyway. Turning his back on the blasters tracking toward him, he slashed the lightsaber across and upward—

Neatly slicing one of the stone pillars in half.

There was a loud *crack* as suddenly released tension sent a shiver through the structure. Another stroke cut through the second pillar—

And the noise of the battle was abruptly drowned out by the awful grinding of stone on stone as the two fractured pillars began sliding apart.

Luke swung back around, peripherally aware of Han and Mara scrambling out from under the arch to safety behind him. The stormtroopers' expressions were hidden behind their masks, but the look of sudden horror on the major's face said it for all of them. Overhead, the mass of the arch creaked warningly; setting his teeth, Luke locked the lightsaber on and hurled it across the gap toward the pillars there. It cut through one of them and nicked the other—

And with a roar, the whole thing came crashing down.

Luke, standing at the edge, barely got out from under it in time. The stormtroopers, crouched in the center, didn't.

CHAPTER 30

KARRDE WALKED AROUND the mass of stone to where the crumpled nose of the Chariot assault vehicle poked out, a sense of slightly stunned disbelief coloring his vision. "One man," he murmured.

"Well, *we* helped some," Aves reminded him. But the sarcasm of the words faded beneath the grudging respect clearly there behind it.

"And without the Force, too," Karrde said.

He sensed Aves shrug uncomfortably. "That's what Mara said. Though of course Skywalker might have lied to her about it."

"Unlikely." A motion at the edge of the square caught his eye, and Karrde looked over to see Solo and Skywalker helping a distinctly shaky-looking Lando Calrissian to one of the airspeeders parked around the perimeter. "Took a shot, did he?"

Aves grunted. "Came close to taking one of mine,

too," he said. "I thought he'd betrayed us—figured I'd make sure he didn't walk away from it."

"In retrospect, it's just as well you didn't." Karrde looked up, searching the skies. Wondering how long it would take the Imperials to respond to what had happened here today.

Aves looked up, too. "We might still be able to hunt down the other two Chariots before they get a chance to report," he suggested. "I don't think the headquarters people got any messages away before we took them out."

Karrde shook his head, feeling a deep surge of sadness rising through the sense of urgency within him. Not until now had he truly realized just how much he'd come to love this place—his base, the forest, the planet Myrkr itself. Now, when there was no choice but to abandon it. "No," he told Aves. "There's no way to cover up our part in what happened here. Not from a man like Thrawn."

"You're probably right," Aves said, his voice taking on a sense of urgency of its own. He understood the implications of that, all right. "You want me to head back and start the evacuation?"

"Yes. And take Mara with you. Make sure she keeps busy—somewhere away from the *Millennium Falcon* and Skywalker's X-wing."

He felt Aves's eyes on him. But if the other wondered, he kept his wonderings to himself. "Right. See you later."

He hurried away. The airspeeder with Calrissian aboard was lifting off now, heading back to where the *Falcon* was being prepped for flight. Solo and Skywalker were heading over toward a second airspeeder; with just a moment's hesitation, Karrde went over to intercept them.

They reached the craft at the same time, and for a moment eyed each other across its bow. "Karrde," Solo said at last. "I owe you one."

Karrde nodded. "Are you still going to get the *Etherway* out of impoundment for me?"

"I said I would," Solo told him. "Where do you want it delivered?"

"Just leave it on Abregado. Someone will pick it up." He turned his attention to Skywalker. "An interesting little trick," he commented, tilting his head back toward the mass of rubble. "Unorthodox, to say the least."

Skywalker shrugged. "It worked," he said simply.

"That it did," Karrde agreed. "Likely saving several of my people's lives in the bargain."

Skywalker looked him straight back in the eye. "Does that mean you've made your decision?"

Karrde gave him a slight smile. "I don't really see as I have much choice anymore." He looked back at Solo. "I presume you'll be leaving immediately?"

"As soon as we can get Luke's X-wing rigged for towing," Solo nodded. "Lando's doing okay, but he's going to need more specialized medical attention than the *Falcon* can handle."

"It could have been worse," Karrde said.

Solo gave him a knowing look. "A *lot* worse," he agreed, his voice hard.

"So could all of it," Karrde reminded him, putting an edge into his own voice. He could, after all, just as easily have turned the three of them over to the Imperials in the first place.

And Solo knew it. "Yeah," he conceded. "Well . . . so long."

Karrde watched as they got into the airspeeder. "One other thing," he said as they strapped in. "Obviously, we're going to have to pull out of here before the Imperials figure out what's happened. That means a lot of lifting capacity if we're going to do it quickly. You wouldn't happen to have any surplus cargo or stripped-down military ships lying around I could have, would you?"

Solo gave him a strange look. "We don't have enough cargo capacity for the New Republic's normal business," he said. "I think I might have mentioned that to you."

"Well, then, a loan, perhaps," Karrde persisted. "A stripped-down Mon Calamari Star Cruiser would do nicely."

"I'm sure it would," Solo returned with more than a hint of sarcasm. "I'll see what I can do."

The canopy dropped smoothly down over them and sealed in place. Karrde stepped back, and with a whine of repulsorlifts, the airspeeder rose into the sky. Orienting itself, it shot off toward the forest.

Karrde watched it go, wondering if that last suggestion had been too little too late. But perhaps not. Solo was the type to hold debts of honor sacred—something he'd probably picked up from his Wookiee friend somewhere along the line. If he could find a spare Star Cruiser, he'd likely send it along.

And once here, it would be easy enough to steal from whatever handlers Solo sent with it. Perhaps such a gift would help assuage Grand Admiral Thrawn's inevitable anger over what had happened here today.

But then, perhaps it wouldn't.

Karrde looked back at the ruins of the collapsed arch, a shiver running through him. No, a warship wasn't going to help. Not on this. Thrawn had lost too much here to simply shrug it off as the fortunes of war. He would be back . . . and he would be coming for blood.

And for perhaps the first time in his life, Karrde felt the unpleasant stirrings of genuine fear.

In the distance, the airspeeder disappeared over the forest canopy. Karrde turned and gave Hyllyard City one final, lingering look. One way or the other, he knew he would never see it again.

LUKE GOT LANDO settled into one of the *Falcon*'s bunks while Han and a couple of Karrde's men busied themselves outside getting a tow cable attached to the X-wing. The *Falcon*'s medical package was fairly primitive, but it was up to the task of cleaning and bandaging a blaster burn. A complete healing job would have to wait until they could get him to a bacta tank, but for the moment he seemed comfortable enough. Leaving Artoo and Threepio to watch over him—despite his protestations that he didn't need watching over and, furthermore, had had enough of Threepio—Luke returned to the cockpit just as the ship lifted off.

"Any problems with the tow cable?" he asked, sliding into the copilot's seat.

"Not so far," Han said, leaning forward and looking all around them as the *Falcon* cleared the trees. "The extra weight's not bothering us, anyway. We should be all right."

"Good. You expecting company?"

"You never know," Han said, giving the sky one last look before settling back into his seat and gunning the repulsorlifts. "Karrde said there were still a couple of Chariots and a few speeder bikes unaccounted for. One of them might have figured that a last-ditch suicide run was better than having to go back to the Grand Admiral and report."

Luke stared at him. "Grand Admiral?" he asked carefully.

Han's lip twisted. "Yeah. That's who seems to be running the show now for the Empire."

A cold chill ran up Luke's back. "I thought we'd accounted for all the Grand Admirals."

"Me, too. We must have missed one."

And abruptly, right in the middle of Han's last word, Luke felt a surge of awareness and strength fill him. As if he were waking up from a deep sleep, or stepping from a dark room into the light, or suddenly understanding the universe again.

The Force was again with him.

He took a deep breath, eyes flicking across the control board for the altimeter. Just over twelve kilometers. Karrde had been right—those ysalamiri did, indeed, reinforce one another. "I don't suppose you got a name," he murmured.

"Karrde wouldn't give it to me," Han said, throwing a curious frown in Luke's direction. "Maybe we can bargain the use of that Star Cruiser he wants for it. You okay?"

"I'm fine," Luke assured him. "I just—it's like being able to see again after having been blind."

Han snorted under his breath. "Yeah, I know how that is," he said wryly.

"I guess you would." Luke looked at him. "I didn't get

a chance to say this earlier . . . but thanks for coming after me."

Han waved it away. "No charge. And *I* didn't get a chance to say it earlier—" he glanced at Luke again "—but you look like something the proom dragged in."

"My wonderful disguise," Luke told him, touching his face gingerly. "Mara assures me it'll wear off in a few more hours."

"Yeah—Mara," Han said. "You and she seemed to be hitting it off pretty well there."

Luke grimaced. "Don't count on it," he said. "A matter of having a common enemy, that's all. First the forest, then the Imperials."

He could sense Han casting around for a way to ask the next question, decided to save him the trouble. "She wants to kill me," he told the other.

"Any idea why?"

Luke opened his mouth . . . and, to his own surprise, closed it again. There wasn't any particular reason not to tell Han what he knew about Mara's past—certainly no reason he could think of. And yet, somehow, he felt a strangely compelling reluctance to do so. "It's something personal," he said at last.

Han threw him an odd look. "Something *personal*? How personal can a death mark get?"

"It's not a death mark," Luke insisted. "It's something—well, *personal*."

Han gazed at him a moment longer, then turned back to his piloting. "Oh," he said.

The *Falcon* had cleared the atmosphere now and was gunning for deep space. From this high up, Luke decided, the forest looked rather pleasant. "You know, I never did find out what planet this was," he commented.

"It's called Myrkr," Han told him. "And *I* just found out this morning. I think Karrde must have already decided to abandon the place, even before the battle—he had real tight security around it when Lando and I first got here."

A few minutes later a light flashed on the control board: the *Falcon* was far enough out of Myrkr's gravity well for the hyperdrive to function. "Good," Han nodded at it. "Course's already programmed in; let's get out of here." He wrapped his hand around the central levers and pulled; and with a burst of starlines, they were off.

"Where are we going?" Luke asked as the starlines faded into the familiar mottled sky. "Coruscant?"

"A little side trip first," Han said. "I want to swing by the Sluis Van shipyards, see if we can get Lando and your X-wing fixed up."

Luke threw him a sideways glance. "And maybe find a Star Cruiser to borrow for Karrde?"

"Maybe," Han said, a little defensively. "I mean, Ackbar's got a bunch of stripped-down warships ferrying stuff to the Sluis sector already. No reason why we can't borrow one of them for a couple of days, is there?"

"Probably not," Luke conceded with a sigh. Suddenly, it felt really good to just sit back and do nothing. "I suppose Coruscant can do without us for a few more days."

"I hope so," Han said, his voice abruptly grim. "But something's about to happen back there. If it hasn't happened already."

And his sense was as grim as his words. "Maybe we shouldn't bother with Sluis Van, then," Luke suggested, feeling a sympathetic shiver. "Lando's hurting, but he's not in any danger."

Han shook his head. "No. I want to get him taken care of—and *you*, buddy, need some downtime, too," he added, glancing at Luke. "I just wanted you to know that when we hit Coruscant, we're going to hit it running. So enjoy Sluis Van while you can. It'll probably be the last peace and quiet you'll get for a while."

IN THE BLACKNESS of deep space, three-thousandths of a light-year out from the Sluis Van shipyards, the task force assembled for battle.

"The *Judicator* has just reported in, Captain," the communications officer told Pellaeon. "They confirm battle ready, and request order update."

"Inform Captain Brandei that there have been no changes," Pellaeon told him, standing at the starboard viewport and gazing out at the shadowy shapes gathered around the *Chimaera*, all but the closest identifiable only by the distinctive patterns of their running lights. It was an impressive task force, one worthy of the old days: five Imperial Star Destroyers, twelve *Strike*-class cruisers, twenty-two of the old *Carrack*-class light cruisers, and thirty full squadrons of TIE fighters standing ready in their hangar bays.

And riding there in the middle of all that awesome firepower, like someone's twisted idea of a joke, sat the battered old A-class bulk freighter.

The key to this whole operation.

"Status, Captain?" Thrawn's voice came quietly from behind him.

Pellaeon turned to face the Grand Admiral. "All ships are on line, sir," he reported. "The freighter's cloaking shield has been checked out and primed; all TIE fighters are prepped and manned. I think we're ready."

Thrawn nodded, his glowing eyes sweeping the field of running lights around them. "Excellent," he murmured. "What word from Myrkr?"

The question threw Pellaeon off stride—he hadn't thought about Myrkr for days. "I don't know, Admiral," he confessed, looking over Thrawn's shoulder at the communications officer. "Lieutenant—the last report from the Myrkr landing force?"

The other was already calling up the record. "It was a routine report, sir," he said. "Time log . . . fourteen hours ten minutes ago."

Thrawn turned to face him. "Fourteen hours?" he repeated, his voice suddenly very quiet and very deadly. "I left orders for them to report every twelve."

"Yes, Admiral," the comm man said, starting to look a little nervous. "I have that order logged, right here on their file. They must have . . ." He trailed off, looking helplessly at Pellaeon.

They must have forgotten to report in, was Pellaeon's first, hopeful reaction. But it died stillborn. Stormtroopers didn't forget such things. Ever. "Perhaps they're having trouble with their transmitter," he suggested hesitantly.

For a handful of heartbeats Thrawn just stood there, silent. "No," he said at last. "They've been taken. Skywalker was indeed there."

Pellaeon hesitated, shook his head. "I can't believe that, sir," he said. "Skywalker couldn't have taken all of them. Not with all those ysalamiri blocking his Jedi power."

Thrawn turned those glittering eyes back on Pellaeon. "I agree," he said coldly. "Obviously, he had help."

Pellaeon forced himself to meet that gaze. "Karrde?"

"Who, else was there?" Thrawn countered. "So much for his protestations of neutrality."

Pellaeon glanced at the status board. "Perhaps we should send someone to investigate. We could probably spare a Strike Cruiser; maybe even the *Stormhawk*."

Thrawn took a deep breath, let it out slowly. "No," he said, his voice steady and controlled again. "The Sluis Van operation is our primary concern at the moment—and battles have been lost before on the presence or absence of a single ship. Karrde and his betrayal will keep for later."

He turned back to the communications officer. "Signal the freighter," he ordered. "Have them activate the cloaking shield."

"Yes, sir."

Pellaeon turned back to the viewport. The freighter, bathed in the *Chimaera*'s lights, just sat there looking innocent. "Cloaking shield on, Admiral," the comm man reported.

Thrawn nodded. "Order them to proceed."

"Yes, sir." Moving rather sluggishly, the freighter maneuvered past the *Chimaera*, oriented itself toward the distant sun of the Sluis Van system, and with a flicker of pseudovelocity jumped to lightspeed.

"Time mark," Thrawn ordered.

"Time marked," one of the deck officers acknowledged.

Thrawn looked at Pellaeon. "Is my flagship ready,
Captain?" he asked the formal question.

"The *Chimaera* is fully at your command, Admiral,"
Pellaeon gave the formal answer.

"Good. We follow the freighter in exactly six hours
twenty minutes. I want a final check from all ships . . .
and I want you to remind them one last time that our
task is only to engage and pin down the system's defenses. There are to be no special heroics or risks taken.
Make that clearly understood, Captain. We're here to
gain ships, not lose them."

"Yes, sir." Pellaeon started toward his command station—

"And Captain . . . ?"

"Yes, Admiral?"

There was a tight smile on Thrawn's face. "Remind
them, too," he added softly, "that our final victory over
the Rebellion begins here."

CHAPTER 31

CAPTAIN AFYON OF the Escort Frigate *Larkhess* shook his head with thinly disguised contempt, glaring at Wedge from the depths of his pilot's seat. "You X-wing hotshots," he growled. "You've really got it made—you know that?"

Wedge shrugged, trying hard not to take offense. It wasn't easy; but then, he'd had lots of practice in the past few days. Afyon had started out from Coruscant with a planetary-mass chip on his shoulder, and he'd been nursing it the whole way.

And looking out the viewport at the confused mass of ships crowding the Sluis Van orbit-dock area, it wasn't hard to figure out why. "Yeah, well, we're stuck out here, too," he reminded the captain.

The other snorted. "Yeah. Big sacrifice. You lounge around my ship like overpriced trampers for a couple of days, then flit around for two hours while I try to dodge bulk freighters and get this thing into a docking station designed for scavenger pickers. And then you pull your snubbies back inside and go back to lounging again. Doesn't exactly qualify as earning your pay, in my book."

Wedge clamped his teeth firmly around his tongue and stirred his tea a little harder. It was considered bad form to mouth back at senior officers, after all—even senior officers who'd long since passed their prime. For probably the first time since he had been given command of Rogue Squadron, he regretted having passed up all the rest of the promotions he'd been offered. A higher rank would at least have entitled him to snarl back a little.

Lifting his cup for a cautious sip, he gazed out the viewport at the scene around them. No, he amended—he wasn't sorry at all that he'd stayed with his X-wing. If he hadn't, he'd probably be in exactly the same position as Afyon was right now: trying to run a 920-crew ship with just fifteen men, hauling cargo in a ship meant for war.

And, like as not, having to put up with hotshot X-wing pilots who sat around his bridge drinking tea and claiming with perfect justification that they were doing exactly what they'd been ordered to do.

He hid a smile behind his mug. Yes, in Afyon's place, he'd probably be ready to spit bulkhead shavings, too. Maybe he ought to go ahead and let the other drag him into an argument, in fact, let him drain off some of that excess nervous energy of his. Eventually—within the hour, even, if Sluis Control's latest departure estimate was anywhere close—it would finally be the *Larkhess*'s turn to get out of here and head for Bpfassh. It would be nice, when that time came, for Afyon to be calm enough to handle the ship.

Taking another sip of his tea, Wedge looked out the

viewport. A couple of refitted passenger liners were making their own break for freedom now, he saw, accompanied by four Corellian Corvettes. Beyond them, just visible in the faint light of the space-lane marker buoys, was what looked like one of the slightly ovoid transports he used to escort during the height of the war, with a pair of B-wings following.

And off to the side, moving parallel to their departure vector, an A-class bulk freighter was coming into the docking pattern.

Without any escort at all.

Wedge watched it creep toward them, his smile fading as old combat senses began to tingle. Swiveling around in his seat, he reached over to the console beside him and punched for a sensor scan.

It looked innocent enough. An older freighter, probably a knockoff of the original Corellian Action IV design, with the kind of exterior that came from either a lifetime of honest work or else a short and spectacularly unsuccessful career of piracy. Its cargo bay registered completely empty, and there were no weapons emplacements that the *Larkhess*'s sensors could pick up.

A totally empty freighter. How long had it been, he wondered uneasily, since he'd run across a totally empty freighter?

"Trouble?"

Wedge focused on the captain in mild surprise. The other's frustrated anger of a minute ago was gone, replaced by something calm, alert, and battle-ready. Perhaps, the thought strayed through Wedge's mind, Afyon wasn't past his prime after all. "That incoming freighter," he told the other, setting his cup down on the edge of the console and keying for a comm channel. "There's something about it that doesn't feel right."

The captain peered out the viewport, then at the sensor scan data Wedge had pulled up. "I don't see anything," he said.

"Me, either," Wedge had to admit. "There's just something . . . Blast."

"What?"

"Control won't let me in," Wedge told him as he keyed off. "Too much traffic on the circuits already, they say."

"Allow me." Afyon turned to his own console. The freighter was shifting course now, the kind of slow and careful maneuver that usually indicated a full load. But the cargo bay was still registering empty . . .

"There we go," Afyon said, glancing at Wedge with grim satisfaction. "I've got a tap into their records computer. Little trick you never learn flitting around in an X-wing. Let's see now . . . freighter *Nartissteu*, out of Nellac Kram. They were jumped by pirates, got their main drive damaged in the fight, and had to dump their cargo to get away. They're hoping to get some repair work done; Sluis Control's basically told them to get in line."

"I thought all this relief shipping had more or less taken over the whole place," Wedge frowned.

Afyon shrugged. "Theoretically. In practice . . . well, the Sluissi are easy enough to talk into bending that kind of rule. You just have to know how to phrase the request."

Reluctantly, Wedge nodded. It *did* all seem reasonable enough, he supposed. And a damaged, empty ship would probably handle something like an intact full one. And the freighter *was* empty—the *Larkhess*'s sensors said so.

But the tingles refused to go away.

Abruptly, he dug his comlink from his belt. "Rogue Squadron, this is Rogue Leader," he called. "Everyone to your ships."

He got acknowledgments, looked up to find Afyon's eyes steady on him. "You still think there's trouble?" the other asked quietly.

Wedge grimaced, throwing one last look out the viewport at the freighter. "Probably not. But it won't hurt to be ready. Anyway, I can't have my pilots sitting around drinking tea all day." He turned and left the bridge at a quick jog.

The other eleven members of Rogue Squadron were in their X-wings by the time he reached the *Larkhess*'s docking bay. Three minutes later, they launched.

The freighter hadn't made much headway, Wedge saw as they swung up over the *Larkhess*'s hull and pulled together into a loose patrol formation. Oddly enough, though, it had moved a considerable distance laterally, drifting away from the *Larkhess* and toward a pair of Calamari Star Cruisers orbiting together a few kilometers away. "Spread out formation," Wedge ordered his pilots, shifting to an asymptotic approach course. "Let's swing by and take a nice, casual little look."

The others acknowledged. Wedge glanced down at his nav scope, made a minor adjustment to his speed, looked back up again—

And in the space of a single heartbeat, the whole thing went straight to hell.

The freighter blew up. All at once, without any warning from sensors, without any hint from previous visual observation, it just came apart.

Reflexively, Wedge jabbed for his comm control. "Emergency!" he barked. "Ship explosion near orbit-dock V-475. Send rescue team."

For an instant, as chunks of the cargo bay flew outward, he could see into the emptiness there . . . but even as his eyes and brain registered the odd fact that he could see *into* the disintegrating cargo bay but not *beyond* it—

The bay was suddenly no longer empty.

One of the X-wing pilots gasped. A tight-packed mass of something was in there, totally filling the space where the *Larkhess*'s sensors had read nothing. A mass that was even now exploding outward like a hornet's nest behind the pieces of the bay.

A mass that in seconds had resolved itself into a boiling wave front of TIE fighters.

"Pull up!" Wedge snapped to his squadron, leaning his X-wing into a tight turn to get out of the path of that deadly surge. "Come around and re-form; S-foils in attack position."

And as they swung around in response, he knew with a sinking feeling that Captain Afyon had been wrong. Rogue Squadron was indeed going to earn its pay today.

The battle for Sluis Van had begun.

THEY'D CLEARED THE outer system defense network and the bureaucratic overload that passed for Control at Sluis Van these days, and Han was just getting a bearing on the slot they'd given him when the emergency call came through. "Luke!" he shouted back down the cockpit corridor. "Got a ship explosion. I'm going to go check it out." He glanced at the orbit-dock map to locate V-475, gave the ship a fractional turn to put them on the right vector—

And jerked in his seat as a laser bolt slapped the *Falcon* hard from behind.

He had them gunning into a full forward evasive maneuver before the second shot went sizzling past the cockpit. Over the roar of the engines he heard Luke's startled-sounding yelp; and as the third bolt went past he finally had a chance to check the aft sensors to see just what was going on.

He almost wished he hadn't. Directly behind them, batteries already engaging one of the Sluis Van perimeter battle stations, was an Imperial Star Destroyer.

He swore under his breath and kicked the engines a little harder. Beside him, Luke clawed his way forward against the not-quite-compensated acceleration and into the copilot's seat. "What's going on?" he asked.

"We just walked into an Imperial attack," Han growled, eyes flying over the readouts. "Got a Star Destroyer behind us—there's another one over to starboard—looks like some other ships with them."

"They've got the system bottled up," Luke said, his voice glacially calm. A far cry, Han thought, from the panicky kid he'd pulled off Tatooine out from under Star Destroyer fire all those years back. "I make it five Star Destroyers and something over twenty smaller ships."

Han grunted. "At least we know now why they hit Bpfassh and the others. Wanted to pull enough ships here to make an attack worth their while."

The words were barely out of his mouth when the

emergency comm channel suddenly came to life again. "Emergency! Imperial TIE fighters in orbit-dock area. All ships to battle stations."

Luke started. "That sounded like Wedge," he said, punching for transmission. "Wedge? That you?"

"Luke?" the other came back. "We got trouble here—at least forty TIE fighters and fifty truncated-cone-shaped things I've never seen before—"

He broke off as a screech from the X-wing's etheric rudder came faintly over the speaker. "I hope you've brought a couple wings of fighters with you," he said. "We're going to be a little pressed here."

Luke glanced at Han. "Afraid it's just Han and me and the *Falcon*. But we're on our way."

"Make it fast."

Luke keyed off the speaker. "Is there any way to get me into my X-wing?" he asked.

"Not fast enough," Han shook his head. "We're going to have to drop it here and go in alone."

Luke nodded, getting out of his seat. "I'd better make sure Lando and the droids are strapped in and then get up into the gun well."

"Take the top one," Han called after him. The upper deflector shields were running stronger at the moment, and Luke would have more protection there.

If there was any protection to be had from forty TIE fighters and fifty truncated flying cones.

For a moment he frowned as a strange thought suddenly struck him. But no. They couldn't possibly be Lando's missing mole miners. Even a Grand Admiral wouldn't be crazy enough to try to use something like *that* in battle.

Boosting power to the forward deflectors, he took a deep breath and headed in.

"ALL SHIPS, COMMENCE attack," Pellaeon called. "Full engagement; maintain position and status."

He got confirmations, turned to Thrawn. "All ships report engaged, sir," he said.

But the Grand Admiral didn't seem to hear him. He just stood there at the viewport, gazing outward at the New Republic ships scrambling to meet them, his hands gripped tightly behind his back. "Admiral?" Pellaeon asked cautiously.

"That was them, Captain," Thrawn said, his voice unreadable. "That ship straight ahead. That was the *Millennium Falcon*. And it was towing an X-wing starfighter behind it."

Pellaeon frowned past the other. The glow of a drive was indeed barely visible past the flashing laser bolts of the battle, already pretty well out of combat range and trying hard to be even more so. But as to the design of the craft, much less its identity . . . "Yes, sir," he said, keeping his tone neutral. "Cloak Leader reports a successful breakout, and that the command section of the freighter is making its escape to the periphery. They're encountering some resistance from escort vehicles and a squadron of X-wings, but the general response has so far been weak and diffuse."

Thrawn took a deep breath and turned away from viewport. "That will change," he told Pellaeon, back in control again. "Remind him not to push his envelope too far, or to waste excessive time in choosing his targets. Also that the spacetrooper mole miners should concentrate on Calamari Star Cruisers—they're likely to have the largest number of defenders aboard." The red eyes glittered. "And inform him that the *Millennium Falcon* is on its way in."

"Yes, sir," Pellaeon said. He glanced out the viewport again, at the distant fleeing ship. Towing an X-wing . . . ? "You don't think . . . Skywalker?"

Thrawn's face hardened. "We'll know soon," he said quietly. "And if so, Talon Karrde will have a great deal to answer for. A *great* deal."

"WATCH IT, ROGUE FIVE," Wedge warned as a flash of laser fire from somewhere behind him shot past and nicked the wing of one of the X-wings ahead. "We've picked up a tail."

"I noticed," the other came back. "Pincer?"

"On my mark," Wedge confirmed as a second bolt shot past him. Directly ahead, a Calamari Star Cruiser was pulling sluggishly away, trying to get out of the battle zone. Perfect cover for this kind of maneuver. Together, he and Rogue Five dived underneath it—

"*Now.*" Leaning hard on his etheric rudder, he peeled off hard to the right. Rogue Five did the same thing to the left. The pursuing TIE fighter hesitated between his diverging targets a split second too long; and even as he swung around to follow Wedge, Rogue Five blew him out of the sky.

"Nice shooting," Wedge said, giving the area a quick

scan. The TIE fighters still seemed to be everywhere, but for the moment, at least, none of them was close enough to give them any trouble.

Five noticed that, too. "We seem to be out of it, Rogue Leader," he commented.

"Easy enough to fix," Wedge told him. His momentum was taking him farther under the Star Cruiser they'd used for cover. Curving up and around it, he started to spiral back toward the main battle area.

He was just swinging up along the Star Cruiser's side when he noticed the small cone-shaped thing nestled up against the larger ship's hull.

He craned his neck for a better look as he shot past. It was one of the little craft that had come out with the TIE fighters, all right. Sitting pressed up against the Star Cruiser's bridge blister as if it were welded in place.

There was a battle going on nearby, a battle in which his people were fighting and very possibly dying. But something told Wedge that this was important. "Hang on a minute," he told Five. "I want to check this out."

His momentum had already taken him to the Star Cruiser's bow. He curved around in front of the ship, leaning back into a spiral again—

And suddenly his canopy lit up with laser fire, and his X-wing jolted like a startled animal beneath him.

The Star Cruiser had fired on him.

In his ear, he heard Five shout something. "Stay back," Wedge snapped, fighting against a sudden drop in power and giving his scopes a quick scan. "I'm hit, but not bad."

"They fired on you!"

"Yeah, I know," Wedge said, trying to maintain some

kind of evasive maneuvering with what little control he had left. Fortunately, the systems were starting to come back online as his R2 unit did some fast rerouting. Even more fortunately, the Star Cruiser didn't seem inclined to shoot at him again.

But why had it fired in the first place?

Unless . . .

His own R2 was too busy with rerouting chores to handle anything else at the moment. "Rogue Five, I need a fast sensor scan," he called. "Where are the rest of those cone things?"

"Hang on, I'll check," the other replied. "Scope shows . . . I don't find more than about fifteen of them. Nearest one's ten kilometers away—bearing one-one-eight mark four."

Wedge felt something hard settle into his stomach. Fifteen, out of the fifty that had been in that freighter with the TIE fighters. So where had the rest of them gone? "Let's go take a look," he said, turning into an intercept vector.

The cone thing was heading toward another Escort Frigate like the *Larkhess*, he saw, with four TIE fighters running interference for it. Not that there was much potential for interference—if the Frigate was manned anywhere near as sparsely as the *Larkhess*, it would have precious little chance of fighting back. "Let's see if we can take them before they notice us," he told Five as they closed the distance.

Abruptly, all four TIE fighters peeled off and came around. So much for surprise. "Take the two on the right, Rogue Five; I'll take the others."

"Copy."

Wedge waited until the last second before firing on the first of his targets, swinging around instantly to avoid collision with the other. It swept past beneath him, his X-wing shuddering as it took another hit. He leaned hard into the turn, catching a glimpse of the TIE fighter dropping into a pursuit slot as he did so—

And suddenly something shot past him, spitting laser fire and twisting back and around in some kind of insane variant on a drunkard's-walk evasive maneuver. The TIE fighter caught a direct hit and blew into a spectacular cloud of fiery gas. Wedge finished his turn, just as Rogue Five's second target fighter did likewise.

"All clear, Wedge," a familiar voice called into his ear. "You damaged?"

"I'm fine, Luke," Wedge assured him. "Thanks."

"Look—there it goes," Han's voice cut in. "Over by the Frigate. It's one of Lando's mole miners, all right."

"I see it," Luke said. "What's it doing out here?"

"I saw one stuck onto the Star Cruiser back there," Wedge told him, swinging back on course for the Frigate. "Looks like this one's trying to do the same thing. I don't know why."

"Whatever it's doing, let's stop it," Han said.

"Right."

It was, Wedge saw, going to be a close race; but it was quickly clear that the mole miner was going to win it. Already it had turned its base around toward the Frigate and was starting to nestle up against the hull.

And just before it closed the gap completely, he caught a glimpse of an acridly brilliant light.

"What was *that*?" Luke asked.

"I don't know," Wedge said, blinking away the after-image. "It looked too bright for laser fire."

"It was a plasma jet," Han grunted as the *Falcon* came up alongside him. "Right on top of the bridge emergency escape hatch. That's what they wanted the mole miners for. They're using them to burn through the hulls—"

He broke off; and, abruptly, he swore. "Luke—we got it backwards. They're not here to wreck the fleet.

"They're here to *steal* it."

FOR A LONG heartbeat Luke just stared at the Frigate . . . and then, like pieces clicking together in a puzzle, it all fell into place. The mole miners, the undermanned and underdefended capital ships that the New Republic had been forced to press into shipping service, the Imperial fleet out there that seemed to be making no real effort to push its way past the system's defenses—

And a New Republic Star Cruiser, mole miner planted firmly on its side, that had just fired on Wedge's X-wing.

He took a moment to scan the sky around him. Moving with deceptive slowness through the continuing starfighter battle, a number of warships were beginning to pull out. "We've got to stop them," he told the others.

"Good thinking," Han agreed. "How?"

"Is there any way we can get aboard them ourselves?" he asked. "Lando said the mole miners were two-man ships—the Imperials can't possibly have packed more than four or five stormtroopers in each one of them."

"The way those warships are manned at the moment, four stormtroopers would be plenty," Wedge pointed out.

"Yes, but I could take them," Luke said.

"On all fifty ships?" Han countered. "Besides, you blast a hatch open to vacuum and you'll have pressure bulkheads closing all over the ship. Take you forever to even get to the bridge."

Luke gritted his teeth; but Han was right. "Then we have to disable them," he said. "Knock out their engines or control systems or something. If they get out to the perimeter and those Star Destroyers, we'll never see them again."

"Oh, we'll see them again," Han growled. "Pointed straight back at us. You're right—disabling as many as we can is our best shot. We're never going to stop all fifty, though."

"We don't have fifty to stop, at least not yet," Wedge put in. "There are still twelve mole miners that haven't attached themselves to ships."

"Good—let's take them out first," Han said. "You got vectors on them?"

"Feeding your computer now."

"Okay . . . okay, here we go." The *Falcon* twisted around and headed off in a new direction. "Luke, get on the comm and tell Sluis Control what's happening," he added. "Tell them not to let any ships out of the orbit-dock area."

"Right." Luke switched channels on the comm; and as he did so, he was suddenly aware of a slight change in sense from the *Falcon*'s cockpit. "Han? You all right?"

"Huh? Sure. Why?"

"I don't know. You seemed to change."

"I had half a grip on some idea," Han said. "But it's

gone now. Come on, make that call. I want you back on
the quads when we get there."

The call to Sluis Control was over well before they
reached their target mole miner. "They thank us for the
information," Luke reported to the others, "but they say
they don't have anything to spare at the moment to help
us."

"Probably don't," Han agreed. "Okay, I see two TIE
fighters running escort. Wedge, you and Rogue Five take
them out while Luke and I hit the mole miner."

"Got it," Wedge confirmed. The two X-wings shot
past Luke's canopy, flaring apart into intercept mode as
the TIE fighters broke formation and came around to
meet the attack.

"Luke, try to blow it apart instead of disintegrating
it," Han suggested. "Let's see how many people the Imperials have got stuffed inside."

"Got it," Luke said. The mole miner was in his sights
now. Adjusting his power level down, he fired.

The truncated cone flared as the metal dead center of
the shot boiled away into glowing gas. The rest of the
craft seemed intact, though, and Luke was just lining up
for a second shot when the hatch at the top abruptly
popped open.

And through the opening, a monstrous, robotlike figure came charging out.

"What—?"

"It's a spacetrooper," Han snapped back. "A stormtrooper in zero-gee armor. Hang on."

He spun the *Falcon* around away from the
spacetrooper, but not before there was a flash from a pro-

tuberance atop the other's backpack and the hull around Luke slammed with a violent concussion. Han rolled the ship around, blocking Luke's view, as another concussion rocked them.

And then they were pulling away—pulling away, but with agonizing slowness. Luke swallowed hard, wondering what kind of damage they'd taken.

"Han, Luke—you all right?" Wedge's voice called anxiously.

"Yeah, for now," Han called back. "You get the TIE fighters?"

"Yes. I think the mole miner's still underway, though."

"Well, then, blast it," Han said. "Nothing cute; just blow it apart. But watch out for that spacetrooper—he's using miniature proton torpedoes or something. I'm trying to draw him away; I don't know if he'll fall for it."

"He's not," Wedge said grimly. "He's staying right on top of the mole miner. They're heading for a passenger liner—looks like they'll make it, too."

Han swore under his breath. "Probably got a few regular stormtrooper buddies still in there. All right, I guess we do this the hard way. Hang on, Luke—we're going to ram him."

"We're *what*?"

Luke's last word was lost in the roar from the engines as Han sent the *Falcon* flying straight out and then around in a hard turn. The mole miner and spacetrooper came back into Luke's line of sight—

Wedge had been wrong. The spacetrooper wasn't standing by the damaged mole miner; he was, in fact, sidling quickly away from it. The twin protuberances on top of his backpack began flashing again, and a couple of seconds later the *Falcon*'s hull began ringing with proton torpedo blasts. "Get ready," Han called.

Luke braced himself, trying not to think about what would happen if one of those torpedoes hit his canopy—and trying, too, not to wonder if Han could really ram the spacetrooper without also plowing into the passenger liner directly behind him. Ignoring the proton blasts, the *Falcon* continued accelerating—

And without warning, Han dropped the ship beneath the spacetrooper's line of fire. "Wedge: go!"

From beneath Luke's line of sight an X-wing flashed upward, laser cannon blazing.

And the mole miner shattered into flaming dust.

"Good shot," Han told him, a note of satisfaction in his voice as he veered underneath the liner, nearly taking the *Falcon*'s main sensor dish off in the process. "There you go, hotshot—enjoy your view of the battle."

Belatedly, the light dawned. "He was listening in on our channel," Luke said. "You just wanted to decoy him into moving away from the mole miner."

"You got it," Han said. "I figured he'd tap in—Imperials always do when they can . . ."

He trailed off. "What is it?" Luke asked.

"I don't know," Han said slowly. "There's something about this whole thing that keeps poking at me, but I can't figure out what it is. Never mind. Our hotshot spacetrooper will keep for now—let's go hit some more mole miners."

———

IT WAS JUST as well, Pellaeon thought, that they were only here to keep the enemy tied up. The Sluissi and their New Republic allies were putting up one terrific fight.

On his status board, a section of the *Chimaera*'s shield schematic went red. "Get that starboard shield back up," he ordered, giving the sky in that direction a quick scan. There were half a dozen warships out there, all of them firing like mad, with a battle station in back-stop position behind them. If their sensors showed that the *Chimaera*'s starboard shields were starting to go—

"Starboard turbolasers: focus all fire on the Assault Frigate at thirty-two mark forty," Thrawn spoke up calmly. "Concentrate on the starboard side of the ship only."

The *Chimaera* gun crews responded with a withering hail of laser fire. The Assault Frigate tried to swerve away; but even as it turned, its entire starboard side seemed to flash with vaporized metal. The weapons from that section, which had been firing nonstop, went abruptly silent.

"Excellent," Thrawn said. "Starboard tractor crews: lock on and bring it in close. Try to keep it between the damaged shields and the enemy. And be sure to keep its starboard side facing toward us; the port side may still have active weapons and a crew to use them."

Clearly against its will, the Assault Frigate began to move inward. Pellaeon watched it for a moment, then returned his attention to the overall battle. He had no doubt the tractor crew would do the job right; they'd shown a remarkable increase in efficiency and competence lately. "TIE Squadron Four, keep after that B-wing group," he instructed. "Port ion cannon: keep up the pressure on that command center." He looked at Thrawn. "Any specific orders, Admiral?"

Thrawn shook his head. "No, the battle seems to be progressing as planned." He turned his glowing eyes on Pellaeon. "What word from Cloak Leader?"

Pellaeon checked the proper display. "The TIE fighters are still engaging the various escort ships," he reported. "Forty-three of the mole miners have successfully attached to target ships. Of those, thirty-nine are secure and making for the perimeter. Four are still encountering internal resistance, though they anticipate a quick victory."

"And the other eight?"

"They've been destroyed," Pellaeon told him. "Including two of those with a spacetrooper aboard. One of those spacetroopers is failing to respond to comm, presumably killed with his craft; the other is still functional. Cloak Leader has ordered him to join the attack on the escort ships."

"Countermand that," Thrawn said. "I'm quite aware that stormtroopers have infinite confidence in themselves, but that sort of deep-space combat is not what spacetrooper suits were designed for. Have Cloak Leader detail a TIE fighter to bring him out. And also inform him that his wing is to begin pulling back to the perimeter."

Pellaeon frowned. "You mean *now*, sir?"

"Certainly, now." Thrawn nodded toward the viewport. "The first of our new ships will begin arriving within fifteen minutes. As soon as they're all with us, the task force will be withdrawing,"

"But . . ."

"The Rebel forces within the perimeter are of no further concern to us, Captain," Thrawn said with quiet satisfaction. "The captured ships are on their way. With or without TIE fighter cover, there's nothing the Rebels can do to stop them."

HAN BROUGHT THE *Falcon* as close as he could to the Frigate's engines without risking a backwash, feeling the slight multiple dips in ship's power as Luke repeatedly fired the quads. "Anything?" he asked as they came up around the other side.

"Doesn't look like it," Luke said. "There's just too much armor over the coolant-feeder lines."

Han glanced along the Frigate's course, fighting back the urge to swear. They were already uncomfortably close to the perimeter battle, and getting closer all the time. "This isn't getting us anywhere. There's got to be *some* way to take out a capital ship."

"That's what other capital ships are for," Wedge put in. "But you're right—this isn't working."

Han pursed his lips. "Artoo?—you still on line back there?" he called.

The droid's beeping came faintly up the cockpit corridor. "Go through your schematics again," Han ordered. "See if you can find us another weak point."

Artoo beeped again in acknowledgment. But it wasn't a very optimistic beep. "He's not going to find anything better, Han," Luke said, echoing Han's own private assessment. "I don't think we've got any choice left. I'm going to have to go topside and use my lightsaber on it."

"That's crazy, and you know it," Han growled. "Without a proper pressure suit—and with engine coolant spraying all over you if it works—"

"How about using one of the droids?" Wedge suggested.

"Neither of them can do it," Luke told him. "Artoo hasn't got the manipulative ability, and I wouldn't trust Threepio with a weapon. Especially not with all the high-acceleration maneuvers we're making."

"What we need is a remote manipulator arm," Han said. "Something that Luke could use inside while . . ."

He broke off. In a flash of inspiration, there it was—the thing that had been bothering him ever since they'd walked into this crazy battle. "Lando," he called into the intercom. "*Lando*! Get up here."

"I've got him strapped in," Luke reminded him.

"Well, go *un*strap him and get him up here," Han snapped. "*Now*."

Luke didn't waste time with questions. "Right," he said.

"What is it?" Wedge asked tensely.

Han clenched his teeth. "We were there on Nkllon when the Imperials stole these mole miners from Lando," he told the other. "We had to reroute our communications through some jamming."

"Okay. So?"

"So why were they jamming us?" Han asked. "To keep us from calling for help? From who? They're not jamming us *here*, you notice."

"I give up," Wedge said, starting to sound a little testy. "Why?"

"Because they had to. Because—"

"Because most of the mole miners on Nkllon were

running on radio remote," came a tired voice from behind him.

Han turned around, to see Lando easing his way carefully into the cockpit, clearly running at half speed but just as clearly determined to make it. Luke was right behind him, a steadying hand on his elbow. "You heard all that?" Han asked him.

"Every part that mattered," Lando said, dropping into the copilot's seat. "I could kick myself for not seeing it long ago."

"Me, too. You remember any of the command codes?"

"Most of them," Lando said. "What do you need?"

"We don't have time for anything fancy." Han nodded toward the Frigate, now lying below them. "The mole miners are still attached to the ships. Just start 'em all running."

Lando looked at him in surprise. "Start them *running*?" he echoed.

"You got it," Han confirmed. "All of them are going to be near a bridge or control wing—if they can burn through enough equipment and wiring, it should knock out the whole lot of them."

Lando exhaled noisily, tilting his head sideways in a familiar gesture of reluctant acceptance. "You're the boss," he said, fingers moving over the comm keyboard. "I just hope you know what you're doing. Ready?"

Han braced himself. "Do it."

Lando keyed a final section of code . . . and beneath them, the Frigate twitched.

Not a big twitch, not at first. But as the seconds passed, it became increasingly clear that something down there was wrong. The main engines flickered a few times and then died, amid short bursts from the auxiliaries. Its drive toward the perimeter fighting faltered, its etheric control surfaces kicking in and then out again, striving to change course in random directions. The big ship floundered almost to a halt.

And suddenly, the side of the hull directly opposite the mole miners position erupted in a brilliant burst of flame.

"It's cut all the way through!" Lando gasped, his tone not sure whether to be proud or dismayed by his handi-work. A TIE fighter, perhaps answering a distress call from the stormtroopers inside, swept directly into the stream of superheated plasma before it could maneuver away. It emerged from the other side, its solar panels blazing with fire, and exploded.

"It's working," Wedge called, sounding awed. "Look—it's working."

Han looked up from the Frigate. All around them— all throughout the orbit-dock area—ships that had been making for deep space were suddenly twisting around like metallic animals in the throes of death.

All of them with tongues of flame shooting from their sides.

FOR A LONG minute Thrawn sat in silence, staring down at his status boards, apparently oblivious to the battle still raging on all around them. Pellaeon held his breath, waiting for the inevitable explosion of injured pride at the unexpected reversal. Wondering what form that ex-plosion would take.

Abruptly, the Grand Admiral raised his eyes to the

viewport. "Have all the remaining Cloak Force TIE fighters returned to our ships, Captain?" he asked calmly.

"Yes, sir," Pellaeon told him, still waiting.

Thrawn nodded. "Then order the task force to begin its withdrawal."

"Ah . . . withdrawal?" Pellaeon asked cautiously. It was not exactly the order he'd been anticipating.

Thrawn looked at him, a faint smile on his face. "You were expecting, perhaps, that I'd order an all-out attack?" he asked. "That I would seek to cover our defeat in a frenzy of false and futile heroics?"

"Of course not," Pellaeon protested.

But he knew down deep that the other knew the truth. Thrawn's smile remained, but was suddenly cold. "We haven't been defeated, Captain," he said quietly. "Merely slowed down a bit. We have Wayland, and we have the treasures of the Emperor's storehouse. Sluis Van was to be merely a preliminary to the campaign, not the campaign itself. As long as we have Mount Tantiss, our ultimate victory is still assured."

He looked out the viewport, a thoughtful expression on his face. "We've lost this particular prize, Captain. But that's all we've lost. I will not waste ships and men trying to change that which cannot be changed. There will be many more opportunities to obtain the ships we need. Carry out your orders."

"Yes, Admiral," Pellaeon said, turning back to his status board, a surge of relief washing through him. So there would not be an explosion, after all . . . and with a twinge of guilt, he realized that he should have known better from the start. Thrawn was not merely a soldier, like so many others Pellaeon had served with. He was, instead, a true warrior, with his eye set on the final goal and not on his own personal glory.

Taking one last look out the viewport, Pellaeon issued the order to retreat. And wondered, once again, what the Battle of Endor would have been like if Thrawn had been in command.

CHAPTER 32

IT TOOK A while longer after the Imperial fleet pulled out for the battle to be officially over. But with the Star Destroyers gone, the outcome was never in doubt.

The regular stormtroopers were the easiest. Most of them were dead already, killed when Lando's activation of the mole miners had ruptured the airseals of their stolen ships and left them open to vacuum, and the rest were taken without much trouble. The eight remaining spacetroopers, whose zero-gee suits had allowed them to keep fighting after their ships were disabled, were another story entirely. Ignoring all calls to surrender, they fanned out through the shipyards, clearly intent on causing as much damage as they could before the inevitable. Six were hunted down and destroyed; the other two eventually self-destructed, one managing to cripple a Corvette in the process.

He left behind him a shipyard and orbit-dock facility

in an uproar . . . and a great number of severely damaged major ships.

"Not exactly what you'd call a resounding victory," Captain Afyon grunted, surveying what was left of the *Larkhess*'s bridge through a pressure bulkhead viewport as he gingerly adjusted a battle dressing that had been applied to his forehead. "Going to take a couple months' work just to rewire all the control circuits."

"Would you rather the Imperials have gotten it whole?" Han demanded from behind him, trying to ignore his own mixed feelings about this whole thing. Yes, it had worked . . . but at what cost?

"Not at all," Afyon replied calmly. "You did what you had to—and I'd say that even if my own neck hadn't been on the line. I'm just saying what others will say: that destroying all these ships in order to save them was not exactly the optimal solution."

Han threw a look at Luke. "You sound like Councilor Fey'lya," he accused Afyon.

The other nodded. "Exactly."

"Well, fortunately, Fey'lya's only one voice," Luke offered.

"Yeah, but it's a loud one," Han said sourly.

"And one that a lot of people are starting to listen to," Wedge added. "Including important military people."

"He'll find some way to parlay this incident into his own political gain," Afyon rumbled. "You just watch him."

Han's rejoinder was interrupted by a trilling from the wall intercom. Afyon stepped over and tapped the switch. "Afyon here," he said.

"Sluis Control communications," a voice replied. "We have an incoming call from Coruscant for Captain Solo. Is he with you?"

"Right here," Han called, stepping over to the speaker. "Go ahead."

There was a slight pause; and then a familiar and sorely missed voice came on. "Han? It's Leia."

"Leia!" Han said, feeling a delighted and probably slightly foolish-looking grin spread across his face. A second later, though—"Wait a minute. What are you doing back on Coruscant?"

"I think I've taken care of our other problem," she said. Her voice, he noticed for the first time, sounded tense and more than a little ragged. "At least for the moment."

Han threw a frown across the room at Luke. "You *think*?"

"Look, that's not important right now," she insisted. "What's important is that you get back here right away."

Something cold and hard settled into Han's stomach. For Leia to be this upset . . . "What's wrong?"

He heard her take a deep breath. "Admiral Ackbar has been arrested and removed from command. On charges of treason."

The room abruptly filled with a brittle silence. Han looked in turn at Luke, at Afyon, at Wedge. But there didn't seem to be anything to say. "I'll be there as soon as I can," he told Leia. "Luke's here, too—you want me to bring him?"

"Yes, if he can manage it," she said. "Ackbar's going to need all the friends he can get."

"Okay," Han said. "Call me in the *Falcon* if there's any more news. We're heading over there right now."

"I'll see you soon. I love you, Han."

"Me, too."

He broke the connection, turned back to the others. "Well," he said, to no one in particular. "There goes the hammer. You coming, Luke?"

Luke looked at Wedge. "Have your people had a chance to do anything with my X-wing yet?"

"Not yet," Wedge said, shaking his head. "But it's just been officially bumped to the top of the priority list. We'll have it ready to fly in two hours. Even if I have to take the motivators out of my own ship to do it."

Luke nodded and looked back at Han. "I'll fly into Coruscant on my own, then," he said. "Let me just come with you and get Artoo off the *Falcon*."

"Right. Come on."

"Good luck," Afyon called softly after them.

And yes, Han thought as they hurried down the corridor toward the hatchway where the *Falcon* was docked; the hammer was indeed coming down. If Fey'lya and his faction pushed too hard and too fast—and knowing Fey'lya, he would almost certainly push too hard and too fast—

"We could be on the edge of a civil war here," Luke murmured his thought back at him.

"Yeah, well, we're not going to let that happen," Han told him with confidence he didn't feel. "We haven't gone through a war and back just to watch some overambitious Bothan wreck it."

"How are we going to stop him?"

Han grimaced. "We'll think of something."

Read on for an excerpt from

STAR WARS: DARK FORCE RISING

BY TIMOTHY ZAHN

CHAPTER 1

DIRECTLY AHEAD, THE star was a marble-sized yellow-orange ball, its intensity moderated by its distance and by the viewports' automatic sunscreens. Surrounding it and the ship itself were the stars, a spattering of blazing white pinpricks in the deep blackness of space. Directly beneath the ship, in the western part of the Great Northern Forest of the planet Myrkr, dawn was approaching.

The last dawn that some in that forest would ever see.

Standing at one of the side bridge viewports of the Imperial Star Destroyer *Chimaera*, Captain Pellaeon watched as the fuzzy terminator line crept toward the target zone on the planet below. Ten minutes ago, the ground forces surrounding the target had reported themselves ready; the *Chimaera* itself had been holding blockade position for nearly an hour. All that was missing now was the order to attack.

Slowly, feeling almost furtive about it, Pellaeon turned

his head a couple of centimeters to the side. Behind him and to his right, Grand Admiral Thrawn was seated at his command station, his blue-skinned face expressionless, his glowing red eyes focused on the bank of status readouts wrapped around his chair. He hadn't spoken or moved from that position since the last of the ground forces had reported in, and Pellaeon could tell the bridge crew was beginning to get restless.

For his own part, Pellaeon had long since stopped trying to second-guess Thrawn's actions. The fact that the late Emperor had seen fit to make Thrawn one of his twelve Grand Admirals was evidence of his own confidence in the man—all the more so given Thrawn's not-entirely-human heritage and the Emperor's well-known prejudices in such matters. Moreover, in the year since Thrawn had taken command of the *Chimaera* and had begun the task of rebuilding the Imperial Fleet, Pellaeon had seen the Grand Admiral's military genius demonstrated time and again. Whatever his reason for holding off the attack, Pellaeon knew it was a good one.

As slowly as he'd turned away, he turned back to the viewport. But his movements had apparently not gone unnoticed. "A question, Captain?" Thrawn's smoothly modulated voice cut through the low hum of bridge conversation.

"No, sir," Pellaeon assured him, turning again to face his superior.

For a moment those glowing eyes studied him, and Pellaeon unconsciously braced himself for a reprimand, or worse. But Thrawn, as Pellaeon still had a tendency to forget, did not have the legendary and lethal temper that had been the hallmark of the Lord Darth Vader. "You're perhaps wondering why we haven't yet attacked?" the Grand Admiral suggested in that same courteous tone.

"Yes, sir, I was," Pellaeon admitted. "All our forces appear to be in position."

"Our military forces are, yes," Thrawn agreed. "But not the observers I sent into Hyllyard City."

Pellaeon blinked. "Hyllyard City?"

"Yes. I find it unlikely that a man of Talon Karrde's cunning would set up a base in the middle of a forest without also setting up security contacts with others outside the immediate area. Hyllyard City is too far from Karrde's base for anyone there to directly witness our attack; hence, any sudden flurries of activity in the city will imply the existence of a more subtle line of communication. From that we'll be able to identify Karrde's contacts and put them under long-term surveillance. Eventually, they'll lead us to him."

"Yes, sir," Pellaeon said, feeling a frown crease his forehead. "Then you're not expecting to take any of Karrde's own people alive."

The Grand Admiral's smile turned brittle. "On the contrary. I fully expect our forces to find an empty and abandoned base."

Pellaeon threw a glance out the viewport at the partly lit planet below. "In that case, sir . . . why are we attacking it?"

"Three reasons, Captain. First, even men like Talon Karrde occasionally make mistakes. It could well be that in the rush to evacuate his base he left some crucial bit of information behind. Second, as I've already mentioned, an attack on the base may lead us to his contacts in Hyll-yard City. And third, it provides our ground forces with some badly needed field experience."

The glowing eyes bored into Pellaeon's face. "Never forget, Captain, that our goal is no longer merely the pitiful rear-guard harassment of the past five years. With Mount Tantiss and our late Emperor's collection of Spaarti cylinders in our hands, the initiative is once again ours. Very soon now we'll begin the process of taking planets back from the Rebellion; and for that we'll need an army every bit as well trained as the officers and crew of the Fleet."

"Understood, Admiral," Pellaeon said.

"Good." Thrawn lowered his gaze to his displays. "It's time. Signal General Covell that he may begin."

"Yes, sir," Pellaeon said, leaving the viewport and returning to his station. He gave the readouts a quick check and tapped his comm switch, peripherally aware as he did so that Thrawn had likewise activated his own comm. Some private message to his spies in Hyllyard City? "This is the *Chimaera*," Pellaeon said. "Launch the attack."

"ACKNOWLEDGED, *CHIMAERA*," GENERAL Covell said into his helmet comlink, careful to keep the quiet scorn in his gut from getting through to his voice. It was typical—typical and disgustingly predictable. You scrambled around like mad hellions, got your troops and vehicles on the ground and set up . . . and then you stood around waiting for those strutting Fleet people in their spotless uniforms and nice clean ships to finish sipping their tea and finally get around to letting you loose.

Well, get yourselves comfortable, he thought sardonically in the direction of the Star Destroyer overhead. Because whether Grand Admiral Thrawn was interested in real results or just a good rousing show, he was going to get his money's worth. Reaching to the board in front of him, he keyed for local command frequency. "General Covell to all units: we've got the light. Let's go."

The acknowledgments came in; and with a shiver from the steel deck beneath him, the huge AT-AT walker was off, lumbering its deceptively awkward-looking way through the forest toward the encampment a kilometer away. Ahead of the AT-AT, occasionally visible through the armored transparisteel viewport, a pair of AT-ST scout walkers ran in twin-point formation, tracking along the AT-AT's path and watching for enemy positions or booby traps. Not that such futile gestures would do Karrde any good. Covell had directed literally hundreds of assault campaigns in his years of Imperial service, and he knew full well the awesome capabilities of the fighting machines under his command.

Beneath the viewport, the holographic tactical display was lit up like a decorative disk, the winking red, white, and green lights showing the positions of Covell's circle of AT-ATs, AT-STs, and hoverscout attack vehicles, all closing on Karrde's encampment in good order.

Good, but not perfect. The north-flank AT-AT and its support vehicles were lagging noticeably behind the rest of the armored noose. "Unit Two, bring it up," he said into his comlink.

"Trying, sir," the voice came back, tinny and distant through the strange dampening effects of Myrkr's metal-rich flora. "We're encountering some thick vine clusters that are slowing down our scout walkers."

"Is it bothering your AT-AT any?"

"No, sir, but I wanted to keep the flank together—"

"Pattern coherence is a fine goal during academy maneuvers, Major," Covell cut him off. "But not at the expense of an overall battle plan. If the AT-STs can't keep up, leave them behind."

"Yes, sir."

Covell broke the connection with a snort. The Grand Admiral was right about one thing, at least: his troops were going to need a lot more battle seasoning before they would be up to real Imperial standards. Still, the raw material was there. Even as he watched, the north flank reformed itself, with the hoverscouts spreading forward to take up the AT-STs' former point positions while the lagging AT-STs themselves fell back into rear-guard deployment.

The energy sensor beeped a proximity warning: they were coming up on the encampment. "Status?" he asked his crew.

"All weapons charged and ready," the gunner reported, his eyes on the targeting displays.

"No indications of resistance, active or passive," the driver added.

"Stay alert," Covell ordered, keying for command frequency again. "All units: move in."

And with a final crash of mangled vegetation, the AT-AT broke through into the clearing.

It was an impressive sight. From all four sides of the

open area, in nearly perfect parade-ground unison, the other three AT-ATs appeared from the forest cover in the predawn gloom, the AT-STs and hoverscouts clustered around their feet quickly fanning out on all sides to encircle the darkened buildings.

Covell gave the sensors a quick but thorough check. Two energy sources were still functioning, one in the central building, the other in one of the outer barracks-style structures. There was no evidence of operating sensors, or of weapons or energy fields. The life-form analyzer ran through its complicated algorithms and concluded that the outer buildings were devoid of life.

The large main building, on the other hand . . .

"I'm getting approximately twenty life-form readings from the main building, General," the number four AT-AT commander reported. "All in the central section."

"They don't register as human, though," Covell's driver murmured.

"Maybe they're being shielded," Covell grunted, looking out the viewport. Still no movement from the encampment. "Let's find out. Assault squads: go."

The hoverscouts popped their aft hatchways, and from each came a squad of eight soldiers, laser rifles held tautly across battle-armored chests as they dropped to the ground. Half of each squad took up backstop position, their rifles trained on the encampment from the partial cover of their hoverscout, while the other half sprinted across the open ground to the outer line of buildings and sheds. There, they assumed covering positions, allowing their comrades in the rear to similarly advance. It was a centuries-old military tactic, executed with the kind of squeamish determination that Covell would have expected of green troops. Still, the raw material was definitely there.

The soldiers continued their leap-frog approach to the main building, with small groups breaking off the main encirclement to check out each of the outer structures as they passed. The point men reached the central building—a brilliant flash lit up the forest as they blasted down the door—a slightly confused scramble as the rest of the troops piled through.

And then, silence.

For a handful of minutes the silence continued, punctuated only by occasional short commands from the troop commanders. Covell listened, watching the sensors . . . and finally the report came through. "General Covell, this is Lieutenant Barse. We've secured the target zone, sir. There's no one here."

Covell nodded. "Very good, Lieutenant. How does it look?"

"Like they pulled out in a hurry, sir," the other said. "They left a fair amount of stuff behind, but it all looks pretty much like junk."

"That'll be for the scanning crew to decide," Covell told him. "Any indication of booby traps or other unpleasant surprises?"

"None at all, sir. Oh—and those life-forms we picked up are nothing but these long furry animals living on the tree growing up through the center of the roof."

Covell nodded again. Ysalamiri, he believed they were called. Thrawn had been making a big deal about the stupid creatures for a couple of months now, though what use they could possibly be to the war effort he couldn't guess. Eventually, he supposed, the Fleet people would get around to letting him in on the big secret. "Set up a defensive honeycomb," he ordered the lieutenant. "Signal the scanning crew when you're ready. And get comfortable. The Grand Admiral wants this place taken apart, and that's exactly what we're going to do."

"VERY GOOD, GENERAL," the voice said, almost too faint to hear despite the heavy amplification and computer scrubbing. "Proceed with the dismantling."

Seated at the *Wild Karrde*'s helm, Mara Jade half turned to face the man standing behind her. "I suppose that's it, then," she said.

For a moment Talon Karrde didn't seem to hear her. He just stood there, gazing through the viewport at the distant planet, a tiny bluish-white crescent shape visible around the jagged edge of the sun-skimmer asteroid the *Wild Karrde* was snuggled up against. Mara was just about to repeat the comment when he stirred. "Yes," he said, that calm voice showing no hint of the emotion he was obviously feeling. "I suppose it is."

Mara exchanged glances with Aves, at the copilot station, then looked back up at Karrde. "Shouldn't we be going, then?" she prompted.

Karrde took a deep breath . . . and as she watched him, Mara caught in his expression a glimmer of what the Myrkr base had meant to him. More than just a base, it had been his home.

With an effort, she suppressed the thought. So Karrde had lost his home. Big deal. She'd lost far more than that in her lifetime and had survived just fine. He'd get over it. "I asked if we should get going."

"I heard you," Karrde said, the flicker of emotion vanishing again into that slightly sardonic facade of his. "I think perhaps we ought to wait a little longer. See if we left anything behind that might point in the direction of our Rishi base."

Mara looked at Aves again. "We were pretty thorough," Aves said. "I don't think there was any mention of Rishi anywhere except the main computer, and that left with the first group out."

"I agree," Karrde said. "Are you willing to stake your life on that assessment?"

Aves's lip twitched. "Not really."

"Nor am I. So we wait."

"What if they spot us?" Mara persisted. "Skulking behind asteroids is the oldest trick on the list."

"They won't spot us." Karrde was quietly positive. "Actually, I doubt the possibility will even occur to them. The average man running from the likes of Grand Admiral Thrawn is unlikely to stop running until he's a good deal farther away than this."

Are you willing to stake your life on that assessment? Mara thought sourly. But she kept the retort to herself. He was probably right; and anyway, if the *Chimaera* or any of its TIE fighters started toward *Wild Karrde*, they would have no trouble punching the engines up to power and going to lightspeed well ahead of the attack.

The logic and tactics seemed clean. But still, Mara could feel something nagging at the back of her mind. Something that didn't feel good about all this.

Gritting her teeth, she adjusted the ship's sensors to their highest sensitivity and checked once more that the engine prestart sequence was keyed in and ready. And then settled in to wait.

THE SCANNING CREW was fast, efficient, and thorough; and it took them just over thirty minutes to come up completely dry.

"Well, so much for that." Pellaeon grimaced as he watched the negative reports scroll up his display. A good practice session for the ground forces, perhaps, but otherwise the whole exercise seemed to have been pretty useless. "Unless your observers have picked up any reactions in Hyllyard City," he added, turning to face Thrawn.

The Grand Admiral's glowing red eyes were on his displays. "There was a small twitch, as a matter of fact," he said. "Cut off almost before it began, but I think the implications are clear."

Well, that was something, anyway. "Yes, sir. Shall I have Surveillance begin equipping a long-term ground team?"

"Patience, Captain," Thrawn said. "It may not be necessary, after all. Key for a midrange scan, and tell me what you see."

Pellaeon swiveled back to his command board and tapped for the appropriate readout. There was Myrkr itself, of course, and the standard TIE fighter defense cloud ranged around the *Chimaera*. The only other object anywhere within midrange distance—"You mean that little asteroid out there?"

"That's the one," Thrawn nodded. "Nothing remarkable about it, is there? No, don't do a sensor focus," he added, almost before the thought of doing one had even occurred to Pellaeon. "We wouldn't want to prematurely flush our quarry, would we?"

"Our quarry?" Pellaeon repeated, frowning at the sensor data again. The routine sensor scans that had been done of the asteroid three hours earlier had come up negative, and nothing could have sneaked up on it since then without being detected. "With all due respect, sir, I don't see any indication that anything's out there."

"I don't either," Thrawn agreed. "But it's the only sizable cover available for nearly ten million kilometers around Myrkr. There's really no other place for Karrde to watch our operation from."

Pellaeon pursed his lips. "Your permission, Admiral, but I doubt Karrde is foolish enough to just sit around waiting for us to arrive."

The glowing red eyes narrowed, just a bit. "You forget, Captain," he said softly, "that I've met the man. More important, I've seen the sort of artwork he collects." He turned back to his displays. "No; he's out there. I'm sure of it. Talon Karrde is not merely a smuggler, you see. Perhaps not even primarily a smuggler. His real love is not goods or money but information. More than anything else in the galaxy, he craves knowledge . . . and the knowledge of what we have or have not found here is too valuable a gem for him to pass up."

Pellaeon studied the Grand Admiral's profile. It was, in his opinion, a pretty tenuous leap of logic. But on the other hand, he'd seen too many similar leaps borne out not to take this one seriously. "Shall I order a TIE fighter squadron to investigate, sir?"

"As I said, Captain, patience," Thrawn said. "Even in

sensor stealth mode with all engines shut down, he'll have made sure he can power up and escape before any attack force could reach him." He smiled at Pellaeon. "Or rather, any attack force from the *Chimaera*."

A stray memory clicked: Thrawn, reaching for his comm just as Pellaeon was giving the ground forces the order to attack. "You sent a message to the rest of the fleet," he said. "Timing it against my attack order to mask the transmission."

Thrawn's blue-black eyebrows lifted a fraction. "Very good, Captain. Very good, indeed."

Pellaeon felt a touch of warmth on his cheeks. The Grand Admiral's compliments were few and far between. "Thank you, sir."

Thrawn nodded. "More precisely, my message was to a single ship, the *Constrainer*. It will arrive in approximately ten minutes. At which point"—his eyes glittered—"we'll see just how accurate my reading of Karrde has been."

OVER THE *WILD KARRDE*'s bridge speakers, the reports from the scanning crew were beginning to taper off. "Doesn't sound like they've found anything," Aves commented.

"Like you said, we were thorough," Mara reminded him, hardly hearing her own words. The nameless thing nagging at the back of her mind seemed to be getting stronger. "Can we get out of here now?" she asked, turning to look at Karrde.

He frowned down at her. "Try to relax, Mara. They can't possibly know we're here. There's been no sensor-focus probe of the asteroid, and without one there's no way for them to detect this ship."

"Unless a Star Destroyer's sensors are better than you think," Mara retorted.

"We know all about their sensors," Aves soothed. "Ease up, Mara, Karrde knows what he's doing. The *Wild Karrde* has probably the tightest sensor stealth mode this side of—"

He broke off as the bridge door opened behind them; and Mara turned just as Karrde's two pet vornskrs bounded into the room.

Dragging, very literally, their handler behind them.

"What are you doing here, Chin?" Karrde asked.

"Sorry, Capt'," Chin puffed, digging his heels into the deck and leaning back against the taut leashes. The effort was only partially successful; the predators were still pulling him slowly forward. "I couldn't stop them. I thought maybe they wanted to see you, hee?"

"What's the matter with you two, anyway?" Karrde chided the animals, squatting down in front of them. "Don't you know we're busy?"

The vornskrs didn't look at him. Didn't even seem to notice his presence, for that matter. They continued staring straight ahead as if he wasn't even there.

Staring directly at Mara.

"Hey," Karrde said, reaching over to slap one of the animals lightly across the muzzle. "I'm talking to you, Sturm. What's gotten into you, anyway?" He glanced along their unblinking line of sight—

Paused for a second and longer look. "Are you doing something, Mara?"

Mara shook her head, a cold shiver tingling up her back. She'd seen that look before, on many of the wild vornskrs she'd run into during that long three-day trek through the Myrkr forest with Luke Skywalker.

Except that those vornskr stares hadn't been directed at her. They'd been reserved instead for Skywalker. Usually just before they attacked him.

"That's Mara, Sturm," Karrde told the animal, speaking to it as he might a child. "Mara. Come on, now—you saw her all the time back home."

Slowly, almost reluctantly, Sturm stopped his forward pull and turned his attention to his master. "Mara," Karrde repeated, looking the vornskr firmly in the eye. "A friend. You hear that, Drang?" he added, reaching over to grip the other vornskr's muzzle. "She's a friend. Understand?"

Drang seemed to consider that. Then, as reluctantly as Sturm had, he lowered his head and stopped pulling. "That's better," Karrde said, scratching both vornskrs briefly behind their ears and standing up again. "Better take them back down, Chin. Maybe walk them around the main hold—give them some exercise."

"If I can find a clear track through all the stuff in there, hee?" Chin grunted, twitching back on the leashes. "Come on, littles—we go now."

With only a slight hesitation the two vornskrs allowed him to take them off the bridge. Karrde watched as the door shut behind them. "I wonder what that was all about," he said, giving Mara a thoughtful look.

"I don't know," she told him, hearing the tightness in her voice. With the temporary distraction now gone, the strange dread she'd been feeling was back again in full force. She swiveled back to her board, half expecting to see a squadron of TIE fighters bearing down on them.

But there was nothing. Only the *Chimaera*, still sitting harmlessly out there in orbit around Myrkr. No threat any of the *Wild Karrde*'s instruments could detect. But the tingling was getting stronger and stronger . . .

And suddenly she could sit still no longer. Reaching out to the control board, she keyed for engine prestart.

"Mara!" Aves yelped, jumping in his seat as if he'd been stung. "What in—?"

"They're coming," Mara snarled back, hearing the strain of a half dozen tangled emotions in her voice. The die was irrevocably cast—her activation of the *Wild Karrde*'s engines would have set sensors screaming all over the *Chimaera*. Now there was nowhere to go but out.

She looked up at Karrde, suddenly afraid of what his expression might be saying. But he was just standing there looking down at her, a slightly quizzical frown on his face. "They don't appear to be coming," he pointed out mildly.

She shook her head, feeling the pleading in her eyes. "You have to believe me," she said, uncomfortably aware that she didn't really believe it herself. "They're getting ready to attack."

"I believe you," he said soothingly. Or perhaps he, too, recognized that there weren't any other choices left. "Aves: lightspeed calculation. Take the easiest course setting that's not anywhere toward Rishi; we'll stop and reset later."

"Karrde—"

"Mara is second in command," Karrde cut him off. "As such, she has the right and the duty to make important decisions."

"Yeah, but—" Aves stopped, the last word coming out pinched as he strangled it off. "Yeah," he said between clenched teeth. Throwing a glower at Mara, he turned to the nav computer and got to work.

"You might as well get us moving, Mara," Karrde continued, stepping over to the vacant communications chair and sitting down. "Keep the asteroid between us and the *Chimaera* as long as you can."

"Yes, sir," Mara said. Her tangle of emotions was starting to dissolve now, leaving a mixture of anger and profound embarrassment in its wake. She'd done it again. Listened to her inner feelings—tried to do things she knew full well she couldn't do—and in the process had once again wound up clutching the sharp end of the bayonet.

And it was probably the last she'd hear of being Karrde's second in command, too. Command unity in front of Aves was one thing, but once they were out of here and he could get her alone there was going to be hell to pay. She'd be lucky if he didn't bounce her out of his organization altogether. Jabbing viciously at her board, she swung the *Wild Karrde* around, turning its nose away from the asteroid and starting to drive toward deep space—

And with a flicker of pseudomotion, something big shot in from lightspeed, dropping neatly into normal space not twenty kilometers away.

An Imperial Interdictor Cruiser.

Aves yelped a startled-sounding curse. "We got company," he barked.

"I see it," Karrde said. As cool as ever . . . but Mara could hear the tinge of surprise in his voice, too. "What's our time to lightspeed?"

"It'll be another minute," Aves said tautly. "There's a lot of junk in the outer system for the computer to work through."

"We have a race, then," Karrde said. "Mara?"

"Up to point seven three," she said, nursing as much power as she could out of the still-sluggish engines. He was right; it was indeed going to be a race. With their four huge gravity-wave generators capable of simulating planet-sized masses, Interdictor Cruisers were the Empire's weapon of choice for trapping an enemy ship in normal space while TIE fighters pounded it to rubble. But coming in fresh out of lightspeed itself, the Interdictor would need another minute before it could power up those generators. If she could get the *Wild Karrde* out of range by then . . .

"More visitors," Aves announced. "A couple squadrons of TIE fighters coming from the *Chimaera*."

"We're up to point eight six power," Mara reported. "We'll be ready for lightspeed as soon as the nav computer gives me a course."

"Interdictor status?"

"Grav generators are powering up," Aves said. On Mara's tactical display a ghostly cone appeared, showing the area where the lightspeed-dampening field would soon exist. She changed course slightly, aiming for the nearest edge, and risked a glance at the nav computer display. Almost ready. The hazy grav cone was rapidly becoming more substantial . . .

The computer scope pinged. Mara wrapped her hand around the three hyperspace control levers at the front of the control board and gently pulled them toward her. The *Wild Karrde* shuddered slightly, and for a second it seemed that the Interdictor had won their deadly race. Then, abruptly, the stars outside burst into starlines.

They'd made it.

Aves heaved a sigh of relief as the starlines faded into the mottled sky of hyperspace. "Talk about slicing the my-nock close to the hull. How do you suppose they tumbled that we were out there, anyway?"

"No idea," Karrde said, his voice cool. "Mara?"

"I don't know, either." Mara kept her eyes on her displays, not daring to look at either of them. "Thrawn may have just been playing a hunch. He does that sometimes."

"Lucky for us he's not the only one who gets hunches," Aves offered, his voice sounding a little strange. "Nice going, Mara. Sorry I jumped on you."

"Yes," Karrde seconded. "A very good job indeed."

"Thanks," Mara muttered, keeping her eyes on her control board and blinking back the tears that had suddenly come to her eyes. So it was back. She'd hoped fervently that her locating of Skywalker's X-wing out in deep space had been an isolated event. A fluke, more his doing than hers.

But no. It was all coming back, as it had so many times before in the past five years. The hunches and sensory flickers, the urges and the compulsions.

Which meant that, very soon now, the dreams would probably be starting again, too.

Angrily, she swiped at her eyes, and with an effort unclenched her jaw. It was a familiar enough pattern . . . but this time things were going to be different. Always before there'd been nothing she could do about the voices and urges except to suffer through the cycle. To suffer, and to be ready to break out of whatever niche she'd managed to carve for herself when she finally betrayed herself to those around her.

But she wasn't a serving girl in a Phorliss cantina this time, or a come-up flector for a swoop gang on Caprioril, or even a hyperdrive mechanic stuck in the backwater of the Ison Corridor. She was second in command to the most powerful smuggler in the galaxy, with the kind of resources and mobility she hadn't had since the death of the Emperor.

The kind of resources that would let her find Luke Skywalker again. And kill him.

Maybe then the voices would stop.

FOR A LONG MINUTE Thrawn stood at the bridge viewport, looking out at the distant asteroid and the now superfluous Interdictor Cruiser near it. It was, Pellaeon thought uneasily, almost the identical posture the Grand Admiral had assumed when Luke Skywalker had so recently escaped a similar trap. Holding his breath, Pellaeon stared at Thrawn's back, wondering if another of the *Chimaera*'s crewers was about to be executed for this failure.

Thrawn turned around. "Interesting," he said, his voice conversational. "Did you note the sequence of events, Captain?"

"Yes, sir," Pellaeon said cautiously. "The target was already powering up before the *Constrainer* arrived."

"Yes," Thrawn nodded. "And it implies one of three things. Either Karrde was about to leave anyway, or else he panicked for some reason—" The red eyes glittered. "Or else he was somehow warned off."

Pellaeon felt his back stiffen. "I hope you're not suggesting, sir, that one of our people tipped him."

"No, of course not." Thrawn's lip twitched slightly. "Loyalties of your crewers aside, no one on the *Chimaera* knew the *Constrainer* was on its way; and no one on the *Constrainer* could have sent any messages here without our detecting them." He stepped over to his command station and sat down, a thoughtful look on his face. "An interesting puzzle, Captain. One I'll have to give some thought to. In the meantime, we have more pressing matters. The task of acquiring new warships, for one. Have there been any recent responses to our invitation?"

"Nothing particularly interesting, Admiral," Pellaeon said, pulling up the comm log and giving it a quick scan to refresh his memory. "Eight of the fifteen groups I contacted have expressed interest, though none were willing to commit themselves to anything specific. We're still waiting on the others."

Thrawn nodded. "We'll give them a few weeks. If there've been no results after that time, we'll make the invitation a bit more compulsory."

"Yes, sir." Pellaeon hesitated. "There's also been another communication from Jomark."

Thrawn turned his glowing eyes on Pellaeon. "I would very much appreciate it, Captain," he said, biting off each word, "if you would try to make it clear to our exalted Jedi Master C'baoth that if he persists in these communications he's going to subvert the whole purpose of putting him on Jomark in the first place. If the Rebels get even a hint of any connection between us, he can forget about Skywalker ever showing up there."

"I *have* explained it to him, sir," Pellaeon grimaced. "Numerous times. His reply is always that Skywalker is going to show up. And then he demands to know when you're going to get around to delivering Skywalker's sister to him."

For a long moment Thrawn said nothing. "I suppose there'll be no shutting him up until he gets what he wants," he said at last. "Nor of getting any uncomplaining work out of him, either."

"Yes, he was grumbling about the attack coordination you've been having him do," Pellaeon nodded. "He's warned me several times that he can't predict exactly when Skywalker will arrive on Jomark."

"And implied that a horrible retribution would fall upon us if he's not there when that happens," Thrawn growled. "Yes, I know the routine well. And I'm getting rather tired of it." He took a deep breath, let it out slowly. "Very well, Captain. The next time C'baoth calls, you may inform him that the Taanab operation will be his last for the immediate future. Skywalker isn't likely to make it to Jomark for at least two more weeks—the little pot of political confusion we've stirred up in the Rebellion high command should occupy him at least that long. As to Organa Solo and her unborn Jedi . . . you may also inform him that from now on I'll be taking a personal hand in that matter."

Pellaeon threw a quick glance over his shoulder, to

where the Grand Admiral's bodyguard, Rukh, stood silently near the aft bridge door. "Does that mean you'll be taking the Noghri off the job, sir?" he asked quietly.

"Do you have a problem with that, Captain?"

"No, sir. May I respectfully remind the Grand Admiral, though, that the Noghri have never liked leaving a mission uncompleted."

"The Noghri are servants of the Empire," Thrawn countered coldly. "More to the point, they're loyal to me personally. They will do as they're told." He paused. "However, I'll take your concerns under advisement. At any rate, our task here at Myrkr is completed. Order General Covell to bring his force back up."

"Yes, sir," Pellaeon said, signaling the communications officer to relay the message.

"I'll want the general's report on file in three hours," Thrawn continued. "Twelve hours after that I want his recommendations as to the three best infantry troopers and two best mechanized operators in the assault. Those five men will be transferred to the Mount Tantiss operation and given immediate transport to Wayland."

"Understood," Pellaeon nodded, dutifully logging the orders in Covell's file. Such recommendations had been part of standard Imperial procedure for several weeks now, ever since the Mount Tantiss operation had begun in earnest. But Thrawn nevertheless still periodically went out of his way to mention it to his officers. Perhaps as a not-so-subtle reminder of how vitally important those recommendations were to the Grand Admiral's sweeping plan to crush the Rebellion.

Thrawn looked out the viewport again at the planet beneath them. "And while we await the general's return, you'll contact Surveillance regarding that long-term team for Hyllyard City." He smiled. "It's a very large galaxy, Captain, but even a man like Talon Karrde can run for only so long. Eventually, he'll have to come to rest."

IT WASN'T REALLY deserving of its name, the High Castle of Jomark. Not in Joruus C'baoth's estimation, anyway. Short and dirty, its stonework ill-fitting in places and as alien as the long-gone race that had built it, it squatted uneasily between two of the larger crags on what was left of an ancient volcanic cone. Still, with the rest of the rim circling around in the distance, and the brilliant blue waters of Ring Lake four hundred meters almost straight down beneath him, C'baoth could allow that the natives had at least found some good scenery to build their castle on. Their castle, or temple, or whatever. It had been a good place for a Jedi Master to move into, if only because the colonists seemed to hold the place in awe. Then too, the dark island that filled the center of the crater and gave the lake its ring shape provided a suitably hidden landing site for Thrawn's annoyingly endless stream of shuttles.

But it was neither the scenery, nor the power, nor even the Empire that held C'baoth's thoughts as he stood on the castle terrace and gazed down into Ring Lake. It was, instead, the strange flicker he'd just felt in the Force.

He'd felt it before, this flicker. Or at least he thought he had. Threads to the past were always so hard to follow, so easily lost in the mists and the hurryings of the present. Even of his own past he had only glimpses of memory, scenes as if from a history record. He rather thought he remembered someone trying to explain the reasons to him once, but the explanation was long gone in the darkness of the past.

It didn't matter anyway. Memory wasn't important; concentration wasn't important; his own past wasn't important. He could call upon the Force when he wanted to, and *that* was what was important. As long as he could do that, no one could ever hurt him or take away what he had.

Except that Grand Admiral Thrawn had already taken it away. Hadn't he?

C'baoth looked around the terrace. Yes. Yes; this wasn't the home and city and world he'd chosen to mold and command as his own. This wasn't Wayland, which he'd wrested from the Dark Jedi whom the Emperor had set to guard his Mount Tantiss storehouse. This was Jomark, where he was waiting for . . . someone.

He stroked his fingers through his long white beard, forcing himself to concentrate. He was waiting for Luke Skywalker—that was it. Luke Skywalker was going to come to him, and Luke Skywalker's sister and her as-yet-unborn twins, and he would turn all of them into his followers. Grand Admiral Thrawn had promised them to him, in return for his help to the Empire.

He winced at the thought. It was hard, this help that Grand Admiral Thrawn wanted. He had to concentrate hard to do what they wanted; to hold his thoughts and feelings closely in line, and for long periods at a time. On Wayland he hadn't had to do anything like that, not since he'd fought against the Emperor's Guardian.

He smiled. It had been a grand battle, that fight against the Guardian. But even as he tried to remember it, the details skittered away like straws in the wind. It had been too long ago.

Long ago . . . like these flickers in the Force had been.

C'baoth's fingers slipped away from his beard, to the medallion nestled against the skin of his chest. Squeezing the warm metal against his palm, he fought against the mists of the past, trying to see beyond them. Yes. Yes, he was not mistaken. These same flickers had come three times before in the past few seasons. Had come, had stayed for a time, and then once again had gone dormant. Like someone who had learned how to utilize the Force for a time, but then somehow forgotten.

He didn't understand it. But it was of no threat to him, and so wasn't important.

Above him, he could sense now the Imperial Star Destroyer entering high orbit, far above the clouds where none of the others on Jomark would see it. When night fell, the shuttle would come, and they would take him off somewhere—Taanab, he thought—to help coordinate yet another of these multiple Imperial attacks.

He wasn't looking forward to the effort and pain. But it would all be worth it when he had his Jedi. He would remake them in his own image, and they would be his servants and his followers all the days of their lives.

And then even Grand Admiral Thrawn would have to admit that he, Joruus C'baoth, had found the true meaning of power.

THE STAR WARS LEGENDS NOVELS TIMELINE

**BEFORE THE REPUBLIC
37,000–25,000 YEARS BEFORE
STAR WARS: A NEW HOPE**

c. 25,793 YEARS BEFORE *STAR WARS: A NEW HOPE*

Dawn of the Jedi: Into the Void

**OLD REPUBLIC
5,000–67 YEARS BEFORE
STAR WARS: A NEW HOPE**

Lost Tribe of the Sith: The Collected
Stories

3,954 YEARS BEFORE *STAR WARS: A NEW HOPE*

The Old Republic: Revan

3,650 YEARS BEFORE *STAR WARS: A NEW HOPE*

The Old Republic: Deceived
Red Harvest
The Old Republic: Fatal Alliance
The Old Republic: Annihilation

1,032 YEARS BEFORE *STAR WARS: A NEW HOPE*

Knight Errant
Darth Bane: Path of Destruction
Darth Bane: Rule of Two
Darth Bane: Dynasty of Evil

**RISE OF THE EMPIRE
67–0 YEARS BEFORE
STAR WARS: A NEW HOPE**

67 YEARS BEFORE *STAR WARS: A NEW HOPE*

Darth Plagueis

33 YEARS BEFORE *STAR WARS: A NEW HOPE*

Cloak of Deception
Darth Maul: Shadow Hunter
Maul: Lockdown

32 YEARS BEFORE *STAR WARS: A NEW HOPE*

**STAR WARS: EPISODE I
THE PHANTOM MENACE**

Rogue Planet
Outbound Flight
The Approaching Storm

22 YEARS BEFORE *STAR WARS: A NEW HOPE*

**STAR WARS: EPISODE II
ATTACK OF THE CLONES**

22–19 YEARS BEFORE *STAR WARS: A NEW HOPE*

**STAR WARS: THE CLONE
WARS**

The Clone Wars: Wild Space
The Clone Wars: No Prisoners

Clone Wars Gambit
Stealth
Siege

Republic Commando
Hard Contact
Triple Zero
True Colors
Order 66

Shatterpoint
The Cestus Deception
MedStar I: Battle Surgeons
MedStar II: Jedi Healer
Jedi Trial
Yoda: Dark Rendezvous
Labyrinth of Evil

19 YEARS BEFORE *STAR WARS: A NEW HOPE*

**STAR WARS: EPISODE III
REVENGE OF THE SITH**

Kenobi
Dark Lord: The Rise of Darth Vader
Imperial Commando 501st

Coruscant Nights
Jedi Twilight
Street of Shadows
Patterns of Force

The Last Jedi

10 YEARS BEFORE *STAR WARS: A NEW HOPE*

The Han Solo Trilogy
The Paradise Snare
The Hutt Gambit
Rebel Dawn

The Adventures of Lando Calrissian
The Force Unleashed
The Han Solo Adventures
Death Troopers
The Force Unleashed II

THE STAR WARS LEGENDS NOVELS TIMELINE

REBELLION
0–5 YEARS AFTER
STAR WARS: A NEW HOPE

Death Star
Shadow Games

STAR WARS: EPISODE IV
A NEW HOPE

Tales from the Mos Eisley Cantina
Tales from the Empire
Tales from the New Republic
Scoundrels
Allegiance
Choices of One
Honor Among Thieves
Galaxies: The Ruins of Dantooine
Splinter of the Mind's Eye
Razor's Edge

3 YEARS AFTER *STAR WARS: A NEW HOPE*

STAR WARS: EPISODE V
THE EMPIRE STRIKES BACK

Tales of the Bounty Hunters
Shadows of the Empire

4 YEARS AFTER *STAR WARS: A NEW HOPE*

STAR WARS: EPISODE VI
THE RETURN OF THE JEDI

Tales from Jabba's Palace

The Bounty Hunter Wars
   The Mandalorian Armor
   Slave Ship
   Hard Merchandise

The Truce at Bakura
Luke Skywalker and the Shadows of
   Mindor

NEW REPUBLIC
5–25 YEARS AFTER
STAR WARS: A NEW HOPE

X-Wing
   Rogue Squadron
   Wedge's Gamble
   The Krytos Trap
   The Bacta War
   Wraith Squadron
   Iron Fist
   Solo Command

The Courtship of Princess Leia
Tatooine Ghost

The Thrawn Trilogy
   Heir to the Empire
   Dark Force Rising
   The Last Command

X-Wing: Isard's Revenge

The Jedi Academy Trilogy
   Jedi Search
   Dark Apprentice
   Champions of the Force

I, Jedi
Children of the Jedi
Darksaber
Planet of Twilight
X-Wing: Starfighters of Adumar
The Crystal Star

The Black Fleet Crisis Trilogy
   Before the Storm
   Shield of Lies
   Tyrant's Test

The New Rebellion

The Corellian Trilogy
   Ambush at Corellia
   Assault at Selonia
   Showdown at Centerpoint

The Hand of Thrawn Duology
   Specter of the Past
   Vision of the Future

Scourge
Survivor's Quest

TIMOTHY ZAHN is the author of more than sixty novels, nearly ninety short stories and novelettes, and five short-fiction collections. In 1984, he won the Hugo Award for Best Novella. Zahn is best known for his *Star Wars* novels (*Thrawn, Thrawn: Alliances, Thrawn: Treason, Thrawn Ascendancy: Chaos Rising, Thrawn Ascendancy: Greater Good, Heir to the Empire, Dark Force Rising, The Last Command, Specter of the Past, Vision of the Future, Survivor's Quest, Outbound Flight, Allegiance, Choices of One,* and *Scoundrels*), with more than eight million copies of his books in print. Other books include *StarCraft: Evolution,* the Cobra series, the Quadrail series, and the young adult Dragonback series. Zahn has a BS in physics from Michigan State University and an MS from the University of Illinois. He lives with his family on the Oregon coast.

Facebook.com/TimothyZahn

ABOUT THE TYPE

This book was set in Sabon, a typeface designed by the well-known German typographer Jan Tschichold (1902–74). Sabon's design is based upon the original letter forms of sixteenth-century French type designer Claude Garamond and was created specifically to be used for three sources: foundry type for hand composition, Linotype, and Monotype. Tschichold named his typeface for the famous Frankfurt typefounder Jacques Sabon (c. 1520–80).

A long time ago in a galaxy far, far away. . . .

STAR WARS™

Join up! Subscribe to our newsletter at ReadStarWars.com or find us on social.

f StarWarsBooks

🐦 @DelReyStarWars

📷 @DelReyStarWars